I0778384

Vocation of a Gadfly

Book Two of the Gadfly Saga

E.A. Bucchianeri

Batalha Publishers – USA / Portugal

Hardcover, 2018
ISBN 978-989-9644-7-8

© Copyright 2018 E.A. Bucchianeri

This is a work of fiction and any resemblance between the characters in this book and real persons living or dead is unintentional.

All trademarks, company names, registered names, products, characters, mottos, logos, jingles and catchphrases used or cited in this work are the property of their respective owners and have only been mentioned and or used as cultural references to enhance the narrative and in no way were used to disparage or harm the owners and their companies. It is the author's sincerest wish the owners of the cited trademarks, company names, etc. appreciate the success they have achieved in making their products household names and appreciate the free plug.

Library of Congress Subject Headings:

Bucchianeri, E.A.
Vocation of a Gadfly
1. Artists—New York (State)—New York—Fiction. 2. Art and society—New York (State)—New York—Fiction. 3. Brooklyn (New York, N.Y.)—Fiction. 4. Exorcism—Fiction 5. FICTION / Occult and Supernatural. 6. Manhattan (New York, N.Y.)—Fiction. 7. Man-woman relationships—New York (State)—New York—Fiction. 8. New York (N.Y.)—Fiction. 9. Paranormal Fiction. 10. Paranormal Fiction—American. 11. Paranormal Romance. 12. Supernatural Fiction.

British Library Catalogue Subject Headings

Bucchianeri, E.A.
Vocation of a Gadfly
1. Art and society—New York (State)—New York—Fiction. 2. Exorcism—Fiction. 3. FICTION / Occult and Supernatural. 4. Man-woman relationships—New York (State)—New York—Fiction. 5. New York (N.Y.)—Fiction 6. Painters—Fiction. 7. Paranormal—Fiction. 8. Paranormal Romance Stories

Books by the same author:

Fiction titles:

Brushstrokes of a Gadfly

Phantom Phantasia: Poetry for the Phantom of the Opera Phan

Non-fiction titles:

A Compendium of Essays:
Purcell, Hogarth and Handel, Beethoven, Liszt, Debussy,
and Andrew Lloyd Webber

Handel's Path to Covent Garden

Faust: My Soul be Damned for the World.   2 Volumes

Lord of the Rings: Apocalyptic Prophecies

This book is dedicated
to all souls who suffer spiritual affliction.

May they receive the help they need, in God's name.

Illúmina fáciem tuam super servum tuum,
et salvum me fac in tua misericórdia:
Dómine, non confúndar, quóniam invocávi te.

(Psalm 30, 17-18)

Vocation of a Gadfly

Book Two of the Gadfly Saga

"I'm sorry, Monsignor, I know it's late, it's urgent this time. She's asking for you, she won't see anyone else."

"All right, don't worry, I'm on my way."

"Oh, God bless you! She'll be relieved to hear that."

Peter replaced the receiver, he quickly began to dress and prepare his black case. He was used to it by now, he often received emergency calls during the bleak hours of the night and early morning requesting him to administer the Last Rites, but never remembered feeling this exhausted before. Already just a few hours into Mercy Sunday and he was back on duty, he didn't get much sleep after a gruelling day balancing his parish work and corporate duties. Never mind, don't think about it, you're needed, he told himself. There was a slight tap on the door as he prepared to exit his plainly furnished room. He knew it was Fr. Mark, a bright, enthusiastic late vocation recently ordained. Despite their difference in age, Mark had been placed under his wing to learn the ropes of managing a parish. Overflowing with zeal, Mark often came to him for advice and for his confessions, and of course, he was always available to offer his help. He looked rather comical with hair dishevelled trying to pull his robe in order, tugging his belt into a knot and breaking into a gaping yawn. Peter would have laughed, were it not for the serious nature of the occasion.

"Excuse me! I heard the phone go again. Please, I'm no spring chicken, but let me go. You can't keep running at your present pace, not with all the demands placed on you lately," he whispered, not wanting to wake the rectory.

"Thank you, I appreciate it, but don't worry about me. In any case, it's a personal request, she won't see anyone else."

"But they're *always* asking for you. You've got to give yourself a break, or you'll end up requiring the Rites long before you expect them."

"On Mercy Sunday? It would be a blessed time to be called home." Peter smiled. He wouldn't mind receiving such a grace. "Speaking of which, I must go. I'll try and catch up on some shut-eye this afternoon after Mass."

"Knowing you, it will never happen." Mark sighed and shook his head. "I guess you'd better go. Is it the same hospital?"

"Yes."

Mark offered no more protestations and let him pass. He knew Peter had another important visit to attend to that morning.

If there was one consolation in this unexpected commute in the chilly dead hour of the night, it afforded him a few moments alone with the Creator enclosed within the travel pyx safely nestled in his inside breast pocket. It was an august, humbling thought that the Word would hide in something as insignificant as bread in fulfilment of His promise that He would never leave them, placing Himself in the hands and at the mercy of His own creatures so they would not be left orphans. There were certain rules: the Blessed Sacrament was not to be removed from the tabernacle lightly. Only for Communion at Mass, Benedictions, processions that were fast becoming a memory, and for sick calls. It was an exceptional grace and privilege to be this close for a time, although occupied with driving just then.

"Lord, please give me the strength to keep going."

It was more than a gruelling weekend, the past month was beginning to take its toll. Despite the passage of weeks, 'that time' was still fresh in his mind, coming home after his usual rounds, seeing Fr. Mark's face as he told him his sister had called the parish office while he was out. His brother was in a terrible accident at the main warehouse yard, it did not look like he would pull through … then to be asked to step back into the family's international shipping company until his sister could take over his brother's place. How long it would take to train her was anyone's guess. She hadn't shown much interest in the family business up to that time. His Eminence the Cardinal Archbishop had given him special permission to help for as long as he was needed, but he still had his early morning Mass and confession duties on top of emergency runs like this, and that did not count the hectic nature of Easter Week that just passed, however, tired or not, this is what he was called to do.

"Well Lord, you didn't have a place to rest Your head, at least I have that."

I know I'm needed, that I have work to do, but please, just don't let me get snared back into the world … .

It was only one of his many apprehensions, his younger brother's job used to be his, Senior Manager of International Distribution at Reinold Enterprises, and now through tragic circumstances he had been recalled to man the helm. It was difficult enough all those years ago to give up his career to follow his vocation, his father had emphatically disapproved of his decision, dismissing all the privileges of his old-money inheritance accumulated in the previous century by his forefathers to embrace the humble pastoral life prescribed by the Church. An acrimonious rupture ensued. Yet, his father had finally accepted the fact he was needed elsewhere, he eventually repaired the rift and began speaking to him again only a few months before his brother's accident. Despite the recent tragedy it felt good to be back in familiar territory with his family like old times, but he did not want to give in to this homesickness, a honeyed barb to pull him back into a very comfortable life brimming with luxury, perks and all that the world deemed enviable accoutrements associated with this executive position and family fortune.

Once a priest, always a priest.

He continued to remind himself he must be detached from these things, and more often than not, it was easy to do. Possessing all the trappings that everyone assumed would make him happy did not happen. He learned from experience the heart tired quickly of materialism, and when all was said and done, everything the world thought important, in fact, wasn't. All that is lauded and praised one day soon grows old and becomes yesterday's trash. It was a waste of time setting one's heart on the transient possessions of the world, a burden to maintain when in the end, he would not be judged on what material wealth he had accumulated, but whether or not he had remained faithful to the Truth and his duties to do good and shun evil. It was a great relief to be content with the necessities and to concentrate on the spiritual life, if only people could see and feel that! Of course he was still human, the comforts of earth always remained enticing. It was not a sin to enjoy some comforts, but there were times when he missed his luxury cars, not for their opulence and trendy brand names, but because they had heating systems that worked. Okay, a few minutes in the cold wouldn't kill him, and it was another opportunity to offer up a sacrifice to the Lord for the good of souls. That was his main concern, his true mission. Right now, souls were in need of comfort, it was time to focus.

The Last Rites, not always the 'last', but still he had to prepare to help a soul meet its Maker, not something to be taken lightly. Confession, anointing, Viaticum, and of course, console the dying person and the family members who are present. This time the lady who urgently needed to see him was one of his first spiritual children, a mother of four and a grandmother of seven who had taken a shine to him when he was newly ordained, as some of his Irish parishioners had phrased it. Despite his effort to concentrate on this night's mission, his thoughts wandered back to those first days. She often came to him for advice, distraught that despite all her efforts, her children were not as fervent as they used to be, that half the grandkids were not being taught their faith and allowed to run amok. In her words, they had become little pagans. It was not the first time he had heard this, many parishioners had come to him with similar problems and it weighed heavily on him to hear how many were turning their backs on God.

"Oh Father, if only I could get them to talk with you, they might listen," she once pleaded during those early days when he was fresh out of the seminary and on his usual rounds to bless houses.

"Of course, Irene, perhaps we can arrange something."

He could not help thinking however that if they did not listen to her, there was no telling how receptive they would be to him. He had seen it often enough, being a priest they would expect a sermon and quickly shut him out before he could open his mouth, even if he only intended to discuss the weather.

"The problem is, I cannot intrude upon their free will."

"I know that, but people *do* listen to you. You don't fluff things, you mean and live what you say, you bring things down to a level we can understand and really put into practise," she continued, before quietly noting, "and, you've got *the gift*."

He could not forget how his heart froze a beat when she said that simple phrase.

It was as he feared. Many extraordinary things had already happened to him, he assumed they were just directing him to his true vocation, and he had hoped these heavenly favours would cease once he answered the call and became a priest. Once ordained he wanted to be ordinary, hidden, obliterated if possible in his parish life despite his repeated requests to become a diocesan exorcist, but try as he might, it could not be hidden any more—he had been granted the discernment of souls—and Irene's quiet observation told him that 'it' was now beginning, that news of 'it' was spreading around Manhattan and possibly beyond. That was what he dreaded most, exaggerated reports circulating, proclaiming that a mystic dwelled in their midst. People would start seeking him out, vying for his attention, choosing him above his other brother priests. Already his confessional was drawing crowds. It would not be long before jealousy ensued, then the persecutions, the trials, the tribulations, from the clerical and secular world alike, all because of *the gift* he never asked for yet could not refuse.

Before all this happened, it was often said he had a unique perspective, that he could see things and circumstances that other people would often miss, but once anointed a priest forever, it had grown much stronger, had become … *different*. An inexplicable sensation would visit him at times, heightening his intuition, especially in the confessional, and it often went beyond his natural ability of perception. How could he describe it? Words often failed him when he tried to figure out what was happening. Not that he saw the heart of the person who came to him seeking spiritual help or the Sacrament of Penance, the heart belonged to God, but he could *feel* situations that the Almighty wished him to see, not with the senses, but with the spirit. Just as the mind did not need to use the voice in order to speak interiorly, the soul did not need eyes to see and understand what was placed before it. However, the soul, much more receptive to the Unseen than the physical senses, it did not hear and speak the same language as the body, it used sensations, images, allegories, metaphors, to try and impart to him what was happening in the physical world. He wasn't sure if this is how it happened with anyone else who had the same gift, and if it did, if they experienced the same revelations or if their souls spoke in a different way and with another set of images to make them understand. He was afraid to rely on these strange interior movements at first. Great graces did not mean sanctity of soul, that he was more highly favoured than anyone else. Christ had warned that not everyone who cried out "Lord, Lord", cast out devils or prophesied in His name would enter heaven. Christ wanted people to rely on faith, not become attached to His miracles, and he like anyone else could fall into the trap of spiritual pride by relying on these extraordinary graces as something coming from himself rather than focusing on He who granted them.

When Peter first began to tumble to this new chapter in his vocation, he needed to talk with someone who would understand, and his first thoughts went to Sister Roberta, one of the nuns who taught him at school. She had a special awareness concerning spiritual matters, for instance, the ability to discern the path in life her students should take, including him. It was time to make another visit. Of course, she was very old and bedridden after he was ordained, but he was always allowed to visit her even when others had been refused on account of her frail health. The minute he entered the room and before he could say anything … .

"Now you know how it feels." She smiled.

"Is it … ?"

"Yes, it's real," she continued. "Don't be afraid. God needs a strong shepherd in the confessional right now, especially with the missions you'll be given."

There was always that other danger, the Enemy could also give signs to confuse. How could he tell the difference? How could he keep the Enemy and his bag of illusions at bay when leading God's people?

"You will always be aware when God is present. One thing is important, stay humble," she replied. "God loves humility, and it is through humility and faith He grants these graces, but don't seek them out. You may pray for clarification and guidance, but don't assume anything to yourself. Remember that none of this is of your doing, of your own power. Humiliate yourself, mortify your natural desires and inclinations, don't get lost in what you are shown, this is God's mission, not yours. Impart what you feel, hear and see, but don't dwell on it if you can. Keep united to God, desire to do His will alone, and know that the only reason He gave this gift to you is because he could find no other person smaller and more insignificant than you to give it to."

He had suspected this may be the answer, but it was good to hear it confirmed by another more experienced in these matters than he. There was nothing for it but to accept what was happening and shoulder the cross that would accompany it. Consider it all in a day's work, that it wasn't anything unusual, just do your duty and move on to the next task as Sister suggested, he couldn't help what would be asked of him in the future.

As it turned out, he did visit Irene's children, and one by one, they went back to Mass and had their children enrolled in catechism classes. Sometimes it was difficult to see how God could work through him, until he saw the reactions. "How did you know that? I never told anyone!" was one of the most frequent responses to a simple comment or observation he would offer. Other times, he could see what was holding the soul of a reluctant penitent back, and with a few nudges, had them opening all their concealed woes before him as though he were a surgeon lancing an infected wound. He was glad to be of use to God, but it was distressing when gratitude was applied thickly on *him*, he was just the tool, the mouthpiece, he didn't want people bowing and scraping to *him*. If only his Eminence had not slapped that title of Monsignor on his head! He preferred being addressed simply as Father, already people were making him out to be more than he was. Often he wished to run from the confessional and escape to the relative sanctuary of the sacristy when he went out to face the crowded pews, but it was all for the salvation of souls, he must also accept that dealing with this unwanted, mortifying adulation was part of the penance. If only it could all be taken from him … .

Peter, what are you about? Prepare. Her soul will be called soon.

That interior, soundless Voice had spoken. All he could do was quietly apologize.

By now, he was at the hospital. Turning off the engine he sat quietly in the parking lot, the orange glow of the street lamps keeping the darkness at bay. He pressed the pyx closer to him for a few moments, cleared his mind of these useless thoughts and calmly asked the Lord to illuminate him before reaching for his case and making his way to the main entrance.

After a month of continuous visits, Peter was a familiar figure. The attendants at the front desk looked up, noticed him prepared with his purple stole and black case, and let him through. Greeting them with a silent nod, he preferred not to speak with the Blessed Sacrament present. He passed by and waited for the elevator. By this time they understood and did not intrude, he had come on Eternal business. The bell dinged, the sliding doors closed, he was gone.

"Is it his brother, do you think?"

"Oh no! At least I hope not. It's got to be one of his parishioners, I heard Deborah say there's a patient that calls for him a lot, you would think she would give him a break. He looks wrecked."

"Man, he's dedicated. You've got to give him that."

"Yeah. You know, it's a pity he's a priest. Why does God pick all the good looking ones?"

"Janet! I'm so glad he's not here right now and didn't hear that."

"Oh lighten up, I'm only kidding. You've got to admit though, it's an awful waste."

"Hmm, there's something about him. Haven't you ever felt he could see all the dirt you want kept hidden under the rug?"

"Come to think about it, sometimes it is difficult to look him in the eyes. Have you ever seen eyes like that? Do you think it's contact lenses or something?" Her colleague just shrugged. "Got to be," Janet continued. "Anyway, I bet he'll check in on his brother too. I think their mother is watching over him tonight, and his fiancée usually comes in on Sundays, so she'll be here today."

"Geeze, what a right shame. I can't get over it, and they still haven't caught the guy who smashed into him."

"It's a crying disgrace, another good-looker completely left to rot. He may never come out of that coma, and if he does, Deborah says he'll never walk again. I wonder if they've called off the wedding yet. I haven't heard anything in the papers, but I'm sure Brandis will eventually give us the first scoop."

"How can you read her trash? That column is eye rot."

"Gosh, Carla, it's just *news* … ."

"It's entertainment at someone else's expense."

"How did you become such a goody two-shoes all of a sudden," Janet noted wryly.

"It's the truth." Carla shrugged, returning to the never-ending paperwork stacked before them.

Alone in the elevator, Peter attempted to keep his thoughts collected. He may not have heard Janet, but as he passed the desk to the elevators, he could sense her disordered inclinations. All he could do was pray for her and continue on. She was not the only one, nor would she be the last. Thank God not all women were like that, there were many who would suffer the loss of life and limb to protect his vocation and his vows, his small army of fierce lionesses he affectionately dubbed them, Irene and her girls were among the pride. The elevator stopped. He turned down the hall and headed to her room. Her eldest daughter Fiona was anxiously watching for him out in the small waiting area, her eyes red from crying and lack of sleep. She immediately jumped from her seat and practically ran to meet him.

"I'm sorry it's so late, but I'm glad you're here," she whispered quietly, the tears threatening to flow.

"Please Fiona, don't apologise."

"The doctors told us earlier this evening it won't be long, maybe a day or two, they can't be sure. She had just fallen asleep, and then suddenly she bolted awake and had to see you, she wouldn't take 'no' ... oh," she stopped short, quickly crossing herself after noticing his stole and his hand over his breast pocket.

"It's all right. Is she still awake?"

"Yes, I just came out a minute ago. Please, she's waiting and won't settle down until she talks with you."

He approached the door and paused for a moment. He could easily recognize what was happening, the Enemy was the ultimate sadist. If he could not claim a soul, he and his minions usually took out their fury and evil pleasure by tormenting it with doubts about its eternal welfare now that its journey on earth was ending. He had experienced it so often before, whirling, biting irritations like a black hoard of angry flies and gnats, scruples, scruples, nagging scruples that refused to disperse and let her meet the end in peace. Thank God that's all it was, it could be a lot worse.

'*In the Name of Jesus Christ, begone tormentors. You have no place here on this day of all days.*'

His interior prayer was heard, the sensation immediately lessened. It did not fully abate, but enough to allow him do his work. It was difficult to help anyone plagued by baseless fears. Opening the door, he quietly entered the room. Poor Irene, the cancer and the equally devastating chemo and radiotherapy had reduced her to a shadow of her former self, but her mind and spirit were alert, especially with the scruples that continued to unsettle her.

"I just knew you were here," she whispered. "I feel much better now. It's all right, she's asleep," Irene assured him as he looked over at the patient sharing her room. He pulled up a chair and sat down, she held out her hands to him.

"Did Fiona tell you?"

"Yes."

"And?"

"Yes, it will be *soon*."

"Oh Father, I know I shouldn't be, but I'm afraid! I'm so afraid! I can't pray like I used to, I just feel fear."

"Are you in any pain?"

"No, not right now, but I'm not afraid of that, I keep thinking I've forgotten something … that I've not made my peace right. That's why I needed to see you, I knew you would know if I had."

He studied her for a minute. No, he did not sense that something had been left undone.

"Irene, be at peace. As your spiritual director, I can positively assure you that you are in the state of grace."

"What about all my faults and failings?"

"We all have them, they are immediately forgiven when we see God face to face, it's the mortal sins we have to confess."

"I know, but still … ."

"Ah, Purgatory. But it's Mercy Sunday. Don't you trust Our Lord and the promises He gave for this day?"

"Of course, Father, and I believe you too, but I would feel better if I could make my confession again."

"That's what I'm here for."

"Can I make a general one?"

"Of course."

Unlike most occasions when he received penitents, his spirit was unusually silent, which was a relief. At times *the gift* often felt like a punishment, being privy to the deepest, bleakest sins and fears besetting those who came to him. It felt good to hear confession like his brother priests, she was already in a state of grace, her sins were forgiven and therefore were not open to his scrutiny. Technically, he did not have to hear her confession again, but he would never refuse a request. Unfortunately, there were priests who had no time for people with nothing major on their souls, but he knew different. He quietly listened as she examined her whole life, a willing acknowledgement of everything she had done as an act of humility, which he knew would only draw down further graces for her and add to her merit in Heaven.

"Now for your penance … penance? What penance can I give you this day when all will be wiped away, penalty and all? Instead, pray five Glory Be's in thanksgiving for the great grace of mercy you will receive. Now, your Act of Contrition."

He listened quietly as she said the required prayer and then gave her absolution.

"Thank you, Father. I do feel so much better now."

"Shall we say your Glorias together?"

"Oh yes, please."

He too had reason to make prayers of thanksgiving. To be able to see a soul through, to sense that it was prepared for the journey was a reason to rejoice. Death was then just a passage, a door to the next life. It was difficult to feel sad when he could experience that cloud of peace descend, but at the same time, he was not immune to the sorrow that also enveloped him. Everyone else would feel the parting of their loved one, it was always hardest for those left behind who still had to face the snares and traps of this world. His mission of leading, aiding and comforting would never be over. He must not slack, he had been given much, therefore much was expected.

"I shall give you the Anointing of the Sick and Communion next, but I'll call Fiona in for that."

Poor Fiona, her sadness was great indeed, she could hardly answer the prayers with him, but she tried. He continued to say them calmly, including the responses until the Rite was finished, then gave Irene her last Communion. After the period of meditation was over, Irene asked if he would say the Mercy Chaplet with her, which of course he readily agreed to.

"I'm very tired now," she noted when they had finished.

"You should rest now."

"Thank you Father, for everything. You won't forget me in your prayers," she pleaded.

"Never, but it's I who should be asking you that. Soon you will be where you will have no need of mine, but I'll have need of yours."

"Don't you worry, I'll still be watching out for you, and if they ever make you change your cassock for a suit, I'll haunt them."

"Irene, you've just been to confession," he noted, trying to suppress a smile.

"Don't worry. Warning people when they've doing wrong is a good thing, or God would not be doing it so much. Therefore, my haunting intentions are charitable, and it's not a sin to be charitable."

"It's hard to argue with you there."

Even now, she was making a joke in her exact, sensible way, but she knew what he had faced, trying to hold on to the old ways, including his choice of clerical apparel, often being ridiculed for his efforts. She had helped him start up the Latin Masses, presenting his Eminence with a petition signed by her and all the other ladies who remembered the 'good old days' when worshipping the Almighty was more reverent, reflective and less clappy-happy, as she once described the new changes to the services. Thank God the present archbishop was sympathetic and did not place too many obstacles to those who wanted to practise their faith according to Tradition, pre-Vatican II. Reaching forward, he traced a blessing in the sign of the cross on her forehead.

"Remain at peace. You get some sleep now."

"Good night, Father."

Slowly retreating from her bedside, he could not help but reflect in all probability this would be the last time he would see her on this side of eternity. Fiona went with him into the hallway for a moment.

"Thank you, Monsi ... Father, this means so much to her, and to me."

"No thanks are necessary. I know that this is a difficult time, but remember, we may be separated from our loved ones, but never parted."

"It doesn't feel that way."

"I know. If you ever need to talk, you know where to find me. Now, go to her, and don't be afraid to tell her what you wanted to say. She will be very glad to hear it."

"Father! How did you know ... oh," Fiona quickly looked down and wistfully smiled. Peter sighed, it was difficult when he was given the interior command to impart an inspiration, some people began to forget he was human and gawked at him like he was an angel from above. He quickly said goodnight and proceeded to make a hasty retreat. In any case, it was time to make that second visit. He had a strange sense of urgency or elation, a rapid change of spirits from the sober atmosphere of his death-bed visit, he was not quite sure what it signified.

"Father, I've got a message for you from upstairs," one of the nurses at the station declared as he was about to pass. He stopped in his tracks.

"It's good news, isn't it."

"Why yes, your brother just woke up. How did you ... ?"

"Thank God! When?"

"About twenty or thirty minutes ago, we knew you were busy with a sick call, so we didn't want to bother you. One of the staff told your mother you're here, she wanted us to tell you. She's waiting for you right now."

"Thank you," he beamed, the exhaustion dispersing with his lifting spirits. His steps picked up a beat as he made his way to the elevators.

That's what it was. Mom may have sent him a message, but she was also calling him, perhaps sending her guardian angel to track him down and tell him to hurry up. However, while he was with a soul who needed help, he was not allowed to know this latest occurrence until now. Anyway, what a consolation for him this Mercy Sunday after all the stresses of the past month!

His mother was waiting for him out in the public area, the doctors were busy in Gerard's room.

"Peter, I'm so glad you're here, but I wish you would let someone else do the late sick calls for you, you look positively exhausted," she noted, brushing his cheek for a moment after he had given her a hug.

"So do you, but tell me, how is he?"

"He's awake, but hazy, which is understandable, and it's not easy for him to talk, he's been out cold for a month now."

"Tell me everything."

"Well, I had finally settled down in that recliner they put in there for us, and you know how you suddenly jump awake just when you fall asleep? I turned to check on him, and I could hear he was trying to talk! Of course, his heart monitor went up and caused a stampede to the room, so I had barely a few minutes to tell him he had been in an accident, but he was all right and in a hospital. The doctors asked me to wait out here, but will call me back as soon as they have checked him over. Oh Pete, I don't know how we're going to tell him … ."

"Let's not jump to that yet. We should ask the doctors how we are to handle this first."

They did not have long to wait, just then one of the doctors exited the room and came over to brief them.

"Mrs. Reinold, Father, I won't hold you in suspense. The good news is he knows his name and address, what country this is and what year it is, so it looks like he may not have amnesia, however, he's having difficulties remembering the details of his accident, which is to be expected. Another piece of good news, he has feeling in both his feet. I don't want to get your hopes up in the walking department just yet. Until his legs and pelvis heal, we won't be able verify if he can walk, and if he can, to what extent we can expect a full recovery, if any."

"He can still feel, that has to be good, but what do we tell him in the meantime? How do we ... ?"

"Mrs. Reinold, I suggest you don't tell him anything about the possibility of being even partially incapacitated until the shock of waking up in a hospital has worn off. All he knows right now is his spleen has been taken out, his legs have been badly broken and that he will have trouble moving after being comatose for a month, which is as much of the truth as he can take right now. We will have to wait and see how his recovery develops."

"Thank you Doctor. May we see him," Peter asked.

"Of course, Father. Don't be alarmed if he falls asleep again, he'll be quite drowsy for awhile until he regains his strength, especially with all the meds he's on."

"All right, thank you again."

They quickly went into the room and tried to ignore the doctors and nursing staff still present. It was difficult seeing him like this for a whole month, the lower half of his body held together, rendered prudently immobile by steel medical scaffolding pinning his bones in place. Although covered by the bedclothes, the alien shape alone was enough to suggest to the imagination the mechanical system of metal rods and screws that lay underneath, but hopefully, this disturbing contraption would soon be taken off. This early morning, there was light at the end of the tunnel, it was so good to see Gerard's eyes even if he could barely keep them open.

"Hey Gerry, you had us worried there. Ask a stupid question, eh? But how are you feeling?"

"Like ... a truck ... hit me," he replied laboriously, then smiled faintly. Gerry had a wicked sense of humour, even now when he could not move and could hardly speak. Worry then darkened his expression. "Kathy ... she wasn't ... in the car ... with me?"

"Shh, no Gerry, love. You were going to pick her up, remember," his mother prompted.

"Not ... in the ... car?"

"No, you were by yourself. She was waiting for you at the gallery. You were going to take her to see the ballet. You don't remember any of this," Peter then added slowly.

"Just ... bright lights ... flowers ... everywhere ... and crunching ... ." His mother shivered at this last statement. "So ... glad ... Kathy ... not there."

"She's fine Gerry, and she'll be very happy to hear you're awake," Peter reassured him.

"The ... key?"

"It's all right, Kathy has it. She kept it safe for you, dear," his mother soothed him, gently stroking his hair. "She has your engagement bracelet too. She's been waiting for the day to give them back to you."

"Shall we call her for you, Gerry?"

"No Peter," their mother advised, turning to him. "That poor girl is worn out, trying to run the gallery and coming here every spare moment. She needs her rest. If you say your morning Mass today, you'll see her there, and if not, she'll be coming here anyway, so she'll find out soon enough. No point waking up the Walsinghams either. I think we should wait to tell your father and sister too, everyone is exhausted, and they could use a few hours sleep."

"You're right. I want to shout from the mountaintops, but mother knows best. Is that all right with you, Gerry?"

No need to ask. He had fallen asleep again. The Sandman had spoken for them all.

"Not everyone can keep going like you can." She smiled at Peter.

"Is that a humorous retort I hear? I haven't heard one from you in quite awhile," he noted gently.

"It just feels so good to have him back." She sighed, her eyes welling up.

∛❖√

Katherine was tempted to sleep in that morning, she could make it to a later Mass that day and then head over to the hospital, but that would mean less time with her Gerry, and she had a new book ready to read to him. She paid no attention to the hospital staff who told her he could not hear, she continued to read stories she thought he would like and quietly played music in the background when permitted on the days and nights it was her turn to keep a loving vigil by his bedside. Now that she was awake, she might just as well get up. She did not like missing Peter's morning Masses, and 'Mr. R', her father-in-law to be, might show up early this morning too. She wanted to know how they were both faring.

She loved Gerry's family, a miracle considering all the horror stories she heard about couples and their cantankerous, domineering in-laws. The

Reinolds were not like that, as they got to know her they quickly accepted her into their family like one of their own. Gerry did not have such an easy time in the beginning, to be more specific, with her Pops, a quiet ultra conservative who was not sure about who she had fallen in love with. She could not blame her father considering how the Reinolds had been the subject of several smear campaigns in the media for years and nobody knew where the lies began and ended. Thank heavens several misunderstandings had been cleared up, Gerry was too likeable to be disapproved of, Pops just needed time to get to know him better. He also hailed from a conservative family, old fashioned, quite sophisticated and cultured. Pops grew to like him, maybe he did from the beginning, but was not about to show it. Sometimes it was hard to tell with him, a crusty and overprotective Papa Bear as Gerry light-heartedly referred to him. Of course, the fact her family were strict Episcopalians and the Reinolds were Roman Catholic did not help matters, especially when she had announced she did not want a mixed marriage and wanted to join their faith. This was too much, Pops could tolerate a Catholic wedding ceremony, but he did not approve of her decision, however, he did not outright oppose her either. He knew that declaring ultimatums was futile. She and her brother were old enough now to make their own decisions and possessed the stubborn will-power to put them into action come what may.

Entering St. Patrick's cathedral that Mercy Sunday morning, she made her way to her usual pew and tried to still her mind in the quiet ecclesial surroundings, which under normal circumstances would be easy to do, however, this venerable edifice was where she was received into the Church during the Easter Vigil only a week ago. The gothic surroundings fuelled her resurging thoughts. It was difficult to pray and concentrate on the present moment when she continued to relive the recent past.

As expected, her family still had doubts about her motives, that she had been pressured to convert for the sake of marrying Gerry, but that was not the case. She did not regret her decision one iota, and despite the recent tragedy resolved that she would not wait until next year to enter the Church. It was bad enough they would have to postpone the wedding until Gerry was better. To her surprise, Gramps, Mom, and Steven her brother attended the Easter ceremonies, quietly making their way up the long central aisle and joining the Reinolds in their pew, Steves giving her a thumbs up as they took their seats despite all the jokes he darted her for weeks about going all medieval on them. It felt good that they still supported her, even if they did not agree with or understand her choice. Obviously, it was still too much for Pops to accept, he was tolerant of other religions, but could not bring himself to attend this celebration when he did not approve of her decision.

When they came home to Oak Meadows that night, she peeked into the den to find him sitting in his favourite chair with the TV turned off, obviously prey to conflicting thoughts. Gramps was about to follow her, but her mother could sense she needed a moment alone with her father, and astutely led her grandfather to the breakfast room using a pretext devised on the spur of the moment.

"Pops?"

He looked up from his melancholic reverie.

"So, there's no going back I suppose. You really wanted to do this," he stated quietly.

"Yes Pops," she replied, pulling a footstool over and sitting beside him, leaned against the armrest.

"I ... *couldn't* be there."

"I understand. I never meant to hurt you, but I had to do this. I know this must come across as a rejection of some kind, but it really isn't. I love you Pops, but I just can't believe in what you believe in, well, not in the same way. That's all. Like Gramps says, I'm still Christian. I'm sorry. I know you're disappointed."

"If this is what you truly believe in, I suppose it can't be helped. For some strange reason, I'm glad it was your decision at least. I wouldn't like to think you were forced."

"No, I wasn't forced."

There was a minute of silence.

"All disappointment aside, I'm ... very proud of you."

Now there was a contradiction if ever she heard one. She must have had an odd look on her face, for the corners of his mouth twitched into a wistful smile as he continued. "Your grandfather was right. It took courage to come and tell us when you're now old enough to go off and do your own thing, so I guess I haven't failed completely when my kids can still come to me with their plans, lectures or no lectures forthcoming."

"Well, it wasn't easy." She smiled shyly up at him.

"I can imagine," he returned, placing his hand on her head. "Just look at you, you've grown into a fine, strong young woman who always stands up for what she believes in. I'm very proud to be your father."

This was too much, hearing this praise from him when he was usually so crusty and serious. All she could do was bury her face against her arms. Pops did not often show his emotional side. More often than not, he was quiet, but on the rare occasion had a deliberate yet explosive way of putting everyone in their place in an effort to get them to shape up. When she dropped the news all those months ago about her decision to convert, she was not sure what to expect. Her worst fear was he would detonate and ultimately exile her from the family. Of course, she with her outspoken activist Save the Planet stunts and the capers of her brainy younger brother, the MIT chemistry graduate, they had given him a few occasions to lose his cool over the years, but this would be the final test of parental patience. That night, Pops unexpectedly proved to be a close relative to Job. It was a special moment she would never forget. She knew he loved her, and to hear this approbation meant everything.

What a night! The ceremonies of the Easter vigil were beautiful. It was a momentous occasion, but also haunted by other sorrows for Pops was not the only loved one absent. How she wished Gerry could have been there. He was to be her spiritual sponsor and stand with her as she accepted the faith, but under the circumstances, his sister Charlotte had to step in for him. He and Peter had helped her through the preparations in the midst of all the wedding plans, and after all, it was Gerry who eventually got her to decide on her Confirmation name.

Katherine Amelia Bernadette Walsingham. How long would she have to wait before she would be addressed as Mrs. Gerard Johannes Thomas Reinold?

While she was an independent spirit, she did not consider becoming Mrs. *Gerard* Reinold a degrading assimilation that deprived her of her identity, she had never felt more complete since she had fallen in love with him. No need to worry anyway, from Day One he had insisted she keep her maiden name on the gallery and her artwork, declaring that he did not want to interfere with her career, although he thoroughly enjoyed being a part of it. Art and literature were shared passions, he and his father were avid art collectors. It was fun teaching them how to draw and paint in the evenings in the studio when time permitted. Now, no one at the gallery felt like painting these days, especially when Gerry's latest picture lay staring them in the face half finished reminding everyone of the accident.

Don't think about that! Easter was now over. A new week, a new day, new worries, and besides, you have to get ready for confession again. Mercy Sunday, Peter told her all about it and she wanted to take part. By now the pews were filling and she did not want to be the last in line for the sin bin. She looked over to the side to see Peter dressed in his white surplus and purple stole. However, he did not enter his assigned confessional. Genuflecting towards the altar, he joined her in the pew.

"Good morning, Peter. Gosh you look … ."

"I know, tired, but don't worry about me." He smiled. "I just came from the hospital not too long ago, and I've got some good news. Gerry woke up about three thirty this morning. He was asking about you."

She gasped.

"Oh Pete! Why didn't you call me!"

"I apologize, but Mom thought it was best. You've been on the go and you needed your rest. Besides, he conked out again and you would have found him asleep once you got there."

"He's not in another coma," she whispered in alarm.

"No, it's pretty much a natural sleep now. The meds are just making him dozy."

"That's good to hear. He was asking for me, oh, I wish I was there! What did he say?"

"He couldn't quite remember what happened and was afraid you were with him in the car. He was also asking about a certain key," he noted gently.

"He was asking for that?" She couldn't help smiling. God, how she loved Gerry! Thank you for letting him come back! The tears started to trickle, Peter fished around under his surplus, trying to locate his pocket for a tissue, but Katherine beat him to it, pulling one out of her purse.

At that moment Mr. Reinold arrived, and noticing the *tete a tete*, came over to see what was happening. Peter usually went straight to the confessional unless something important in the line of parish work came up and he had to speak with someone.

"Good morning you two, what's all the conflab?"

"Good news," Katherine said, impulsively jumping up and giving him a hug, "Pete just told me Gerry woke up early this morning."

"What!"

Everyone turned around to look at them.

"What?" He whispered, quickly sitting down in the pew. "Pete! Why didn't you or you mother call me? Come on, tell us what happened." Peter quickly relayed the events from that early morning, adding:

"He hasn't been told everything, if you know what I mean. The doctors say not to say anything to him for now until they know more, which may take awhile."

"He's got a good attitude towards what he does know, considering he could crack a joke after coming out of a coma," Katherine mused.

"See, Katie? What did I tell you. We Reinolds don't give in that easily," Mr. Reinold said, putting his arm around her. "He'll prove all those so-called professionals wrong and be walking in no time. I'd bet the

Morning Glory on it." Katherine knew that was a big statement, Mr. R. loved that yacht of his and wouldn't dare jinx it with any light wager.

"Dad, you are in God's house, no betting." Peter smiled. "Listen, I have to go, confessions you know."

"Oh Pete, I was going to go, but there's no way I can examine my conscience after this," Katherine admitted. Before, she was too distracted, now, she was too happy to concentrate.

"Come anyway, I'll help you through."

"Like last time?"

"No need to be as thorough," he noted with humour before squeezing her hands, genuflecting towards the altar beside the pew once more and heading towards the confessional.

'Last time' was two weeks ago. Her first confession, which happened before Easter, would not be forgotten any time soon. As with everything else that had happened recently, she was reliving that moment too and could not help but recall that humbling half hour, unable to focus on the present, especially now that she had received such wonderful news. Perhaps the mind found comfort in processing events already experienced. She remembered feeling so nervous that first time, afraid she would forget something. She was not raised Catholic, and while Peter had patiently taught her how to prepare, the prospect of engaging in this soul-baring sacrament felt so new and unfamiliar that she was terrified of drawing a memory blank and commit some sacrilege right on the eve of her entrance into the Church. Nothing for it, she decided to write everything down and bring it with her just in case, but never realized how dark it was once the doors of those old fashioned confessionals swung shut.

*Clunk, snap. S*he was encased in blackness.

Oh no! I can't read my notes!

Feeling around, the padded kneeler squeaked and wheezed as she settled down into place. Eventually her eyes adjusted to the gloom, she could make out the grate through which Peter would speak to her, but the shutter was closed. Someone else was making their confession in the adjoining booth, she could hear a faint murmur of voices on the other side. Oh, if anyone comes in while it's my turn, I hope they won't be able to hear me, this is mortifying! No, it's muffled enough. If I'm quiet, no one will hear me other than Pete. It was bad enough she would be revealing all her faults and failings, but at least she would be confessing to Peter, there was no one else she would rather confess to. Since she had decided to learn about Catholicism to see if she could agree to the conditions of a Catholic wedding, he proved to be an amazing mentor, never inflicting dogmas on her with in implacable attitude, but answered any question she put to him. She loved his absolute frankness, and she had to admit, some of his explanations of the Bible struck her silent at times. Peter had a way of surprising her, making her think in a way she never had before, even their first encounter was beyond the ordinary run of things, but she could not think of that now. Focus! You've got to remember what you wrote!

Click. Without warning, she was bathed in light. She blinked and noticed the old box had a light bulb installed. The panel behind the grate slid back to reveal Peter's face, calm and collected considering the importance of the sacrament, but displaying amusement nevertheless.

"These things have electricity now," he noted quietly, "and please note the soundproofing, no one will hear you."

How did he know her concerns? He was right however, the walls had been lined in dotted square panels used by sound studios, she had seen them on television shows. His good humour helped to break the ice too.

"Thank you Peter, I feel better in the light. Why does everyone else want to do this in the dark?"

"Usually people do not like the priest recognizing them when they confess. Remaining anonymous makes it easier to meet us in public afterwards." Well, he had had a point there. "However," he continued, "there is also important symbolism attached. Sin is darkness and death, but once confessed, the soul is freed from the darkness of the tomb and enters the light reborn in Christ." Hmm, that was good too. "Now, take a few deep breaths. Remember, I'm not going to beat you over the head."

Katherine did as he suggested, clutching her notebook. Come on, you've got to start sometime, she thought to herself, but it's so hard to say all this out loud! If only I could just hand this to him … .

"You must say it, it's an act of humility. Difficult, yes, but you'll feel better. Trust me."

She sighed resignedly and made the sign of the cross.

"Bless me Peter, er … Father, this is my first confession, but you know that … um, right," she muttered.

Smiling, he made the sign of the cross near the grate, lowered his eyes and patiently waited in a meditative pose, his left hand on his forehead as he leaned his elbow on an armrest hidden from view. She could not help but rapidly rattle off the first few things on her peccadillo list, but then, it did feel good getting all this out in the open and she found herself slowing down, letting it all gradually pour forth, everything she did wrong that plagued her, and also things she was not sure were wrong but thought she should tell. She was so relieved when she had finished, it was not bottled up any more. The one thing that was currently worrying her was her temper, she could be unpredictable when something made her angry, she had to talk it over with him.

"Oh Pete, sometimes I get so mad, and anger is not always a sin you say, but I keep feeling like I'm sinning all the time … ."

"It depends on the type of anger you feel and how you act upon it. Remember the parable of the two sons and their reactions when asked to work in the vineyard? One said 'yes', but never did what his father asked, while the other grumbled, yelled 'no', but thought better of it later. The first son was in all likelihood very happy to help, and yet went off on his own merry way, while the second was in a bad mood, he didn't feel like working, however, he didn't want to disappoint his father and eventually did what he asked. God doesn't judge us on our feelings as much as on our actions, or lack thereof."

"So basically, there's no way I'll ever be able to get rid of my temper." She sighed.

"We're all faulty, subduing our human passions is a lifelong job. Tell me, what is making you angry lately," he asked gently, looking up.

"Life! I'm so angry about what happened to Gerry, why God would allow something like this, then I get guilty because I know God really doesn't want Gerry to suffer, even if He allows it for some unknown reason. It was that idiot's fault, and then I get mad at the police because they haven't found the creep yet, then I wish I could get my hands on him so I can string him up personally for what he's done to all of us! I know you say suffering gives us power, but I'm just *so* angry right now! About everything!"

"Katherine, this is natural. God can take our angry outbursts within reason, our knee-jerk reactions if you will, and you have a right to be angry in this instance. That man did a terrible thing, you have a right to demand justice, but *vengeance*? This is where anger crosses the line. Don't let this anger turn to poison. You must forgive, it's the only way you'll find release."

"That's so much easier said than done. I don't know how to do that, and yet I know I have to try, or my confession is not complete. Right?"

"Yes. That's true."

"I don't know how to go about it. I can't forget what's happened, so how can I forgive?"

"Forgiveness is not always about forgetting, although we still have to try. In fact, you do know what to do, you just have to bring it to a higher level," he hinted.

"What? How?"

"Remember what happened to your gatecrasher after the gala opening of the gallery? You and Mr. Smith are now best friends. How did that transformation take place?"

Katherine's jaw dropped. How did he know about *Smith*? To the rest of the world he was Robert Horace, New York's vilest art critic. She was positive she had not told anyone about him, everyone was still shaking their heads wondering how they had become close acquaintances after he repeatedly trashed her gallery in his columns, but they did not know why he was acidic on paper. As far as she was aware, she was the only one to whom he had revealed why he acted the way he did, and she felt so bad afterwards when she found out it was easy to forgive his rancorous scribblings, even turn a blind eye to them.

"Pete, you're scary at times," she noted with humour, yet calmly studied him for a moment. Her friend in Paris, Justine, was right. Peter had been given a remarkable gift. "Hey, you've just reminded me, I didn't confess I had misjudged the man entirely, it's not on my list." She quickly flipped through her book. "I hope I haven't forgotten anything else."

"No," he replied quietly.

"But Pete, that was one situation, this is another. How do I bring that experience to a 'higher level' and forgive the man who obviously had every intention to murder Gerry?"

"If you attempted to see that man's situation as God sees it, you would be less inclined to pronounce judgement and seek vengeance. Right now, you can only think of him as a hardened criminal who revels in evil and therefore in your eyes does not deserve forgiveness. So, let's try a spiritual exercise. Can you bring yourself to view that man in a light that would excite your forgiveness for him?"

"Well I … maybe if he didn't have a choice somehow, like if he or his family was threatened. I really couldn't blame the man then."

"All right, that's a start. Now, let's say your scenario is true. What about those who planned this and put that man's back to the wall?"

"Gosh, I don't know. It's pretty bad when people do that to others, it would make you wonder why they would choose to live their lives as criminals." However, she then realized some people didn't know any better, one of the artists showing in her gallery had told her how he escaped a life on the streets, how bleak it could be for people who were not born into privileged circumstances. Then, if people emphatically *wanted* to live an evil life, what a terrible waste! What a terrible black existence they carved out for themselves. You couldn't help but pity them.

"It really is pathetic when you think about it. You know, if people purposely set out to become your enemies, what an awful place they must be in to be that spiteful."

"True." Peter nodded. "Think of the darkness they are in, that they're not only destroying themselves here, but are also facing a frightful eternity if they continue. Think about it: do you in your heart of hearts want to see anyone *lost*?"

"No," she said slowly, "when it comes right down to it, I don't."

"That's loving your enemies. Mercy is far better than asking for justice, even if it is your right to ask for it. Therefore, forgive them, do good to those who persecute you, even if all you can do is pray for them. You may just bring them back from the brink of total destruction."

"But what about people who really enjoy the evil they do?"

"Can you not still pity them? To think that someone has been hardened to that extent that all goodness is eradicated in them must inspire compassion, not hatred. You would only become like they are and destroy yourself if you can't let go of the bitterness they first provoke. If bad thoughts resurface, always make an interior act of forgiveness for that person and move on, do not harbour thoughts of vengeance. Leave it to God who knows best how to punish with the hope of bringing the soul back. As King David said, it was better to be placed in the hands of God to be punished rather than in the hands of men."

"Is that why God does not leave vengeance to us? We tend towards destruction of the guilty party, not aiding in reforming them," she mused.

"Precisely. God wants us to be perfect as He is, desiring salvation for all, despite the crimes committed. Sadly, not everyone can be saved, not against their free will, which is why we must pray for our enemies before it's too late for them."

"Gosh, I was angry, and now I'm just ... sad. Sad over the whole thing, sad that someone would possibly be put up to this, and all for what? I'm sorry I wanted to hurt the man. You're right, I don't want that kind of poison affecting me either. I don't know all the circumstances. He really must be in a black place to do what he did. People really don't know what they do, do they? You can't help feel sorry when you look at it like that."

"You forgive whoever has done this?"

She took a deep breath.

"Yes. I can't forget, maybe not ever, but ... I forgive him."

"Good. When you forgive, you cannot feel anger. Sorrow, yes, but suffering and certain types of sorrow are not sins in themselves, but uncontrolled anger is. Once the anger is released and you can bear the sorrow and it will lessen in time, you will feel stronger, wiser. Trust me on this one.”

“I believe you, Pete. All I really want now is to concentrate on getting Gerry better.”

“That’s it, focus on the positive. Well, you have made a very good confession, don’t forget to put these new resolutions into practise. For your penance, say five Hail Mary’s to Our Lady to help you, and as an act of charity, would you say the Sorrowful Mysteries of the Rosary for the man who injured Gerry?”

“All right.”

“Very good. Now, it’s time to say your Act of Contrition.”

Afraid she might forget the prayer in the midst of this confession ordeal, she also had that written down in her notebook. Peter resumed his meditative pose as she thumbed for the right page and completed his request. She listened intently as he gave her absolution.

“That’s it. Go in peace, Katherine. It’s all over, you’re forgiven everything.” He smiled.

Wow, it felt really good to hear that. She felt a bit shaky as she left the confessional and took her place in the pew, opening her soul and confessing her whole life’s failings was not easy the first time around, but she did feel much better … *free* was more like it. What would the next confession session be like? Would she still feel as rickety? It was only two weeks, she had not done much in the meantime and felt guilty that she might be wasting Peter’s time, but he said she could come every day if she felt she needed to. Besides, she did want to go on Mercy Sunday to obtain the promises offered on that day.

“Bless me Father, I have sinned, this is my second confession,” she began, a little distracted after the good news he had given her that morning. She still could hardly believe Gerry had woken up.

“Yes, I know that, but you don’t have to keep count, just when your last visit was. Do you want the light on,” he asked with humour.

“No thanks, I’m okay, no notebook, and it was two weeks ago.”

He was right, this time was not as thorough as she did not have to go over her whole life’s transgressions. Her only major stumbling block the past few days was Mrs. Hunt, a friend of the Reinolds and a regular visitor to her gallery. The feisty old lady’s favourite pastime was having all the staff run around unhitching the paintings so she could view them in the lobby before painstakingly making a decision on what to add to her collection. It was maddening at times, but Katherine did her best not to let it get to her. Mrs. Hunt suffered terribly from arthritis in her hips, she could not walk very well, and Katherine did want to be kind, she was a widow living alone who only wanted some attention. Peter could only suppress a chuckle when Katherine told him what Mrs. Hunt had put them through this time. He too had been obliged to humour her on many occasions and his patience had been tested more than once.

"I need to hear your confession, not Mrs. Hunt's," he noted.

"Okay, I feel so impatient at times."

"It's just a natural failing, and you were kind to her. You're doing well. How's the anger management doing?"

"You're right, Pete. Your 'spiritual exercise' works for a lot of things. If I get angry, I just forgive and get on with things, it doesn't build up. Mom's noticed I'm not as quick with my tongue."

"Good girl. Keep it up."

"But still, I can feel it bubble under the surface. I'm not always good at keeping a lid on it."

"Hmm. Let me see, do you feel the worst of your short temper as the afternoon wears on, generally speaking?"

"Umm, well, yeah, I suppose so."

"Skipping lunch as usual?"

"Oh, I'm guilty there. Well, some days. I have so much to do I can't think of eating … is that a sin," she quickly wondered in alarm.

"No, the church *does* proscribe fasting on occasion." He chuckled. "Just as long as you don't endanger your health. The point I'm trying to make is some faults are not always from the sinful part of our nature, just our weak humanity. Coupled with your toaster tart breakfasts with no substantial amount of protein, after that sugar spike you could be suffering from a drop in blood sugar when you don't eat. That can drastically affect your mood as the day wears on."

"Gosh Pete, you're right, I never thought about … hey! Does God even tell you about our Pop Tart addictions?"

"Not this time, Gerry told me." He smiled.

"Great, when we're married, I wonder if I will have any secrets left." She laughed. "Okay, so should I stop eating Pop Tarts?"

"No! Just keep everything within moderation. Keep your diet balanced, and don't skip lunch if you can help it. Now, your Act of Contrition."

After she had received absolution and her penance, only three Hail Marys this time, Katherine could not help but ask if he would be coming to the hospital again to see Gerry.

"I would like to, but I've been up all night."

"Oh Pete, another sick call? Not again! And with all the extra work you have to do now."

"Don't worry, I'll be all right."

"You always say that, but this time, when you get back to the rectory, you'd better hit the bed right away, and tell them that unless it's nothing short of the Apocalypse, you are not to be disturbed. I really mean it."

"All right, I'll try to do that." He smiled.

He gave her a second blessing through the grille and watched her leave before sliding the shutter back. He sat in the darkness and offered a heartfelt prayer for her. She was a dear soul to him, open to grace and truth, so few were like that. A deep friendship had sprung up all those months he helped her to understand their faith and prepare for the duties of marriage. Almost from the beginning, he knew they would be kindred spirits, he could sense their souls communicating like old friends whenever they met, before he knew it, they had become close confidantes. No one could understand what he went through interiorly, Katherine could not fathom it, but she simply accepted and quietly listened, never making him uncomfortable despite his unusual disclosures that sprang out at times before he could stop himself. She was a soothing presence, someone with whom he felt absolutely safe, a privilege he missed since the only one who understood him, Sr. Roberta, had passed away. Katherine did not have their gift of discernment, but she was more observant than most, watchful, reflective, receptive to graces, although unaware of them at present. Strong, forthright and very respectful of his vocation, she loved him like an older brother. He could not help having a soft spot for this special lioness and prayed that her crosses in life would not be too heavy to bear.

ଓ ❖ ଚ

After Mass, Katherine rushed to the hospital, Mr. R following close behind. Mrs. R was talking with one of the nurses outside Gerry's room. It was good to see her looking less worried.

"Did you hear the good news?"

"We sure did Sophie," Richard beamed, gathering his wife in his arms then allowing Katherine to give her a hug. "Peter told us. He would have come, but he's off to get some well-deserved shut-eye."

34

"That's good. I don't want him falling ill now that Gerry is slowly getting better. You know, I'm so relieved, I was afraid Gerry might not wake up."

"Me too," Katherine replied. "Is he awake now?"

"Not yet, we still have to be patient. No activity for a month, he'll be suffering fatigue."

"Oh, I was hoping he'd be awake by the time we came, but it's best not to go in," Katherine added. She knew it was the right thing to do, but she did not feel very patient. Pete's right, managing our quirks isn't easy she thought, but at least Gerry was doing better, and that's what mattered. She waited days, she could wait a few hours more if need be.

"Come, let's sit out here," Sophia suggested, leading them to the all too familiar waiting lounge. "Tell me, how are you Kathy? How's the family?"

"Doing okay, all considering. That reminds me, I've got to start calling people, wait until they hear what's happened," she exclaimed, jumping up, her good spirits returning.

"Would you be a dear and call Lottie for me? I was on my way, but the nurse wanted to talk."

"Sure thing, Mrs. R," she called out as she headed to the nearest payphone. The Reinolds smiled as they watched her flit off to relay the glad tidings.

"I know how she feels. Do you think we'll have to wait long, Sophie?"

"Not too long dear, the nurse says the doctors will be doing the rounds, we should be able to see him after they check in on him."

In the meantime, Katherine called her family, Lottie, and of course, Gerry's close friends, Leroy was first on that list. After promising to keep them updated on his condition and when they could drop by for a visit, she returned to see a troop of nurses and doctors enter Gerry's room.

"It's all right dear, he's going to be their pet project for awhile," Mr. R reassured her, "it's a big thing to come through a coma, don't you know."

When they completed their duties, one of the doctors came over.

"Well, a little better than early this morning. We're not only talking, but we're trying to flex our fingers. I would say a few visitors wouldn't go amiss." He smiled before wishing them a good morning.

As much as she wanted to go in, Katherine knew this was a time for his parents first and decided she would let them go in without her.

"Are you sure, Katie?"

"Yes, you have the first visit. I'll be here all day, and Mrs. R needs to get home soon."

It was painful waiting, but just a few minutes more, she could do it. She was happy just knowing he was awake, that he was communicating and trying to move. Eventually the Reinolds came out.

"It's time to get you home, my dear," Mr. R said, turning to Sophia, "you've had a long night. You can come back later for the evening visiting hours."

"I don't want to go, but you're right. I can't give Peter advice and then refuse to follow it myself. Go on in Kathy, take good care of him for us until we come back," Mrs. R added, giving her another hug.

"I will, don't worry."

Her heart skipped as she opened the door and entered the room. Approaching his bedside, she held her breath, *he was looking at her!* Of course she knew he was awake, but to see those once closed, motionless eyes now open no matter how drowsy they were and acknowledge her presence with undisguised affection was pure bliss. Instinctively, she reached for his hand and held it to her cheek. She could feel a bare movement in his fingers as he responded to her touch, her eyes welled up.

"Hey … Princess. No tears."

"Oh Gerry, we thought we had lost you."

"Looks like … I'm found again."

Even now, he had a funny quip for everything.

"How are you feeling?"

"Mouth's … working better … but I feel so … stuck."

"I know dear," she said, gently caressing his fingers, "don't worry, we'll get you moving in no time."

"I'm sorry … we missed the ballet."

"Shh, don't worry about that. I'm just glad you're alive."

"*Sleeping Beauty* … it's … ironic."

"Well, you definitely beat my narcolepsy record."

"The princess jokes." He smiled faintly. "You know … I was dreaming. … I was talking with you … then singing … with Sinatra … then I was in Alaska … but you were … always there somehow … really odd."

She pressed his hand tighter against her cheek.

He did hear her!

"Look Gerry," she said, pointing towards the CD player and the book by his bedside. "Blame me for your dream. I was reading Jack London to you, and playing our songs. I had a new book ready for you today, too."

"You can still read to me ... I'd like that."

"Of course, anything you want. Oh, I have something of yours, look." She pulled out two gold chains concealed under her blouse, each with an ordinary-looking key dangling on the end. He smiled when he saw them.

"Two hearts made one. ... You keep it safe ... they might take it away here. ... Mom says you have the bracelet too. Did they ... find the other one?" He was referring to the surprise gift he had planned to give her that night before the ballet.

"Yes, thank you so much Gerry, you spoil me rotten. Leo found it and gave it to me. It's in my purse. I haven't worn it, I wanted to wait until you could give it to me personally."

"Leo ... was there?"

"He was the first one on the scene, he stayed with you until we arrived at the hospital."

"I don't remember much ... ."

"Shh, don't think about it." That was a mercy, she could never forget the evening news, watching Gerry's totalled Jaguar being towed away from the main warehouse yard gripped in pandemonium with police and reporters everywhere. Better tell him the good side. "You should have seen all the well-wishes and support absolute strangers have sent us both. Brandis got a tear-jerker column printed, and the hospital, our houses and the gallery got bombarded with bouquets and candle vigils. We had the candy-stripers share everything out to the other patients."

"Good idea, I'm glad ... I see there's one ... bouquet still here." He smiled, his eyes diverted to the colourful red rose and sunflower spray nearby.

"It was my turn to bring you our flowers." She stroked his hair, avoiding the tender area near the hairline of his left temple where the stitches had been. The large bandage was gone by now, it was comforting to run her fingers through his dark brown natural waves.

"Oh, I like that." He smiled. "The flowers ... and your loving attention. Tell me ... I missed it all. Did you go ahead with 'Bernadette'?"

"I did Gerry, this heathen is now officially a papist."

"Funny girl. Pappa Bear ... still upset?"

"A little, but he's accepting it. Says he's proud of me anyway."

"I suppose you ... had to go ahead ... and postpone the wedding. I'm sorry ... ."

"Shh! It's not your fault. We'll just set up everything again when you're better."

"Oh no … double trouble … not your aunt's … wedding etiquette book … again." He chuckled, but started to cough, obviously finding it difficult to speak with the feeding tube inserted through his nose. How she wished she could rescue him from that uncomfortable piece of plastic. Hand-feeding would be more dignified than that. He could guess what she was thinking.

"Go on … pull it out, you know … you want to," he egged.

"Gerry! I can't! You're as bad as Leroy, although you're right, that can't be comfortable. I'm so glad you woke up because they were preparing to medically insert a more permanent one. At least this is temporary. The nurse said it will be removed as soon as we can get you started on normal food."

"You know … what I would like right now?"

"Name it, you shall have it."

"A croissant."

To anyone else this was just a buttery French pastry, but Katherine knew better. Leaning forward she gently kissed him on the lips.

"I'd like another please." He grinned at her. She happily complied, lingering for just a few seconds longer. It felt so good to kiss him after all this time. "Third helpings," he then teased.

"Gerry, you've only got one nostril, I could smother you."

"Please, smother me."

"You're hopeless!"

"Aw, just one more."

 "One more."

Third helpings were interrupted by one of the nurses who 'ahem'd!' her presence.

"Romance in the morning, not a bad start."

"Hi, Deborah." Katherine smiled sheepishly.

"The Princess has come … to help wake up Sleeping Handsome," Gerry explained.

"I can see that," Deborah noted. "I've come to give you breakfast." Katherine grimaced, that meant a shot of some very unattractive gloop through the tube. "I know it's not pretty," the nurse continued, "but it's packed full of protein and vitamins."

"I'd rather have croissants," Gerry returned.

"I bet you would, but this'll have to do, your highness."

"Oh please, can't we try him with something easy, like soup or … soup," Katherine pleaded. "Anything's got to be better than this."

"Hmm. Soup for breakfast, but I suppose we could try it, the Doc did say he wants you on regular food as soon as possible. Can you swallow for me?"

"Yeah … I think so … but the plumbing … is in the way."

"All right, then. Hang on, this will be uncomfortable." Katherine turned away as the tube was extracted. "There, I'll be back in a sec."

"Do you feel better now," Katherine asked.

"Yep … we can have another croissant, without smothering me."

"Okay."

After one last kiss, he tried to put up his hand. She lifted it once again, giving it a kiss before placing it on her cheek.

"My poor Kathy, you look as wrecked, as I feel."

"Don't worry, I may look tired, but I don't feel it, not now," she assured him. It was good to hear his voice becoming stronger, still very slow and labourous, but more articulate. All she wanted was to hear him speak, plagued with the unreasonable fear he might relapse into a state of uncontrolled slumber should the conversation stop.

"I can't imagine, what you've all gone through, while I've been, on my backside snoozing. Pater and Mater tell me, Pete and Thomas, are trying to train Lottie, to step in, while I'm here."

"That's true, the archbishop gave Peter permission to help. Lottie is still a little bewildered by it all, but I told her not to forget to see Sammy, Dan and Leo at Warehouse One if she ever felt stuck on something. So far, she says they've been immense help."

"Good thinking. Imagine Lottie, in the offices."

"She's a trooper, Gerry. Pete said she would make an excellent business woman, she just needed something to concentrate on. Up until now, she's only had her social do's and her books. However, trying to understand the complexities of your holdings is a bit over her head right now."

"I bet it is. What about you? How is everyone, at the gallery?"

"They'll be much happier knowing you're awake and talking. Oh! You won't believe the news, guess who's now working with us."

"That's right, the job interviews. Who did you hire?"

"Kevin Alcott."

"Not Kevin, from the Sirrac? How did *that*, come about?"

Katherine started to laugh, what a picture! The look of dozy surprise on his face was worth a thousand words.

"I'll try and make it quick," she promised. She did not want to tire him out and be evicted from the room.

The Sirrac Gallery, one of the elite modern art galleries in New York situated on Fifth Avenue no less, had changed hands after the original owner suffered an unfortunate mental breakdown displaying he was no longer capable of managing anything. The new owners already had their own staff, therefore Mr. Alcott the manager had been unceremoniously discharged from his post.

"I missed a lot," Gerry noted. "Poor Joe, I didn't know, he was going down, that fast. Seemed as fit, as a fiddle. And the new people, let Kevin go? They'll regret that, they've discarded, an expert." The Reinolds were noted patrons of the Sirrac until Katherine opened her gallery, but they knew everyone at the Sirrac on a first name basis.

"Their loss, our gain."

"True. How's he fitting in?"

"He's fantastic, he's quite a character. I have some new clients who've actually followed him over from the Sirrac. However, it's getting a bit competitive around there now. Esther doesn't want to be outdone in the brainy department."

"Oh, I can see sparks, all right," Gerry grinned. Kevin Alcott an Oxford graduate was a mature gentleman with a flamboyant, rainbow-hued persona. Mrs. Esther Matthews, a lady with a dry but pleasant personality, was the former librarian of the famed Belvedere Art College, Katherine's academic *alma mater*. After her retirement Esther disliked the inactivity and was happy to work for Katherine just for the company. "How is everyone else?"

By everyone else he meant Susanna Cooper, Katherine's best friend from college who was originally from Iowa, Professor Cecil Matthews, Esther's husband and Katherine's tutor who had also retired and was given the freedom of the private studio to paint, and Dennis Harrington, a Belvedere student who graduated the same year she did. Everyone often joked that the gallery had become an extension of the college. The non-Belvedere members were Andre Garneau, an award-winning French-Canadian chef who leased the restaurant facilities on the ground floor, and Olivia Conti who had taken over the gallery gift shop.

"They're all doing fine. Oh, more news! Charlie just proposed to Suzy over Easter."

"Really? Wow, guess I have, no reason to be jealous now."

"Gerry, you never had any reason to be," Katherine gently reminded him.

Charles Kraylor was a childhood friend who was now a successful lawyer in his father's illustrious firm. She always looked on him like an elder brother, and then felt compelled to keep her distance when she discovered Charlie's feelings went a little deeper than she was prepared for. The situation had become awkward after she had fallen in love with Gerry, it was a relief knowing Charlie had now fallen for Suzy.

"I know. Anyway, this is happy news. Have they, set a date?"

"Not yet, they want to enjoy the moment. It's only been a week."

"I can understand that. Tell me, anything else, happening at the gallery?"

"Not really. No one has felt like doing much, and business wise we've had nothing but curiosity-seekers visiting the museum section to see your collection, it's kind of depressing."

"*Our* collection now, remember? Hmm, I always told you, art thrives on tragedy."

"Oh Gerry, that's not funny. This is one tragedy we could have done without."

"Hey, don't worry, I plan to get better, pronto. Lottie will be able, to go back to her books, Pete to the cathedral, and you, into my loving arms. Look, I can squeeze my hands, and lift my arms a little. Not too bad, for a morning's work." He smiled, showing her his improved albeit slow-paced mobility.

The nurse eventually returned with a covered feeding cup.

"Okay, soup it is. Mind you, we can raise your bed only so much, so be careful swallowing. Here, would you like to?" She handed the cup to Katherine.

"Yes, please."

"All righty, support his head like this, that's it."

"Uck, you'd never know this was soup," he observed dryly, stopping to take a breath.

"I'll tube you again if you like," Deborah returned.

"Pass the rot-gut, please."

At that moment, the door swung open. In bounded his old friend, a dynamo in the advertising business, Leroy McFadden. A wild rake of a young Irishman with flaming red hair and a personality to match, a man noted for his flamboyant lifestyle and partying too much.

"So we're back on the drink already, brilliant!" He dropped his briefcase on a nearby chair and leaned over the bed.

"Hi Leroy," Katherine greeted, "not exactly. It's supposed to be soup."

"You're here, bright and early. How are you?" Gerry smiled.

"Now that you're awake and almost ready to get up and about, never better. We've all been lost without you, Ger. It's good to see you return to the land of the living. Since you're on the mend, tell me, what's next? What are the doctor's orders?"

"Plenty of rest. Don't you dare wear my patient out," Deborah warned.

"No trouble, I swear on my *shillelagh*."

"I mean it, mister Lucky Charms. One false move and I'll have the orderlies in before you can say 'Erin go bragh.'"

"I gather someone has kissed the Blarney stone today," Leroy teased.

By now, Leroy's appearances at the hospital were dreaded events as he turned the place upside down trying to cheer Gerry and Katherine's respective families during his visits, not to mention having a grand time flirting with the nurses, following them around and helping himself to all the amenities of the nurses' lounge.

"Leroy, be good. You don't want to be kicked out now, do you," Katherine asked, giving Gerry another sip of his sustenance.

"Hey, no sweat. See? I shall settle down and behave," he declared, pulling the chair over.

"All right, I guess it's safe to leave you then," Deborah noted, checking her charts one last time, "but I have my eye on you," she warned Leroy before leaving her patient to his visitors.

"Good, the dragon lady is gone." Leroy smiled mischievously. "Let the fun begin."

"Ah, you promised, no surprises. You know he was threatening to change one of your drips for a whisky bottle?"

"Why am I not surprised." Gerry smiled.

"Anyway, I thought you were going to work when I called," Katherine noted.

"I was, but then thought better of it," Leroy replied.

"Even so, it's not like you, to work on a Sunday," Gerry noted.

"True, but I have this client who needs to see me before he goes to San Francisco tomorrow, so I had to arrange a meeting for today, nothing that couldn't be shoved a few hours forward. Concentration would be nigh to impossible once Kathy called, I just had to see how you two were doing."

"Awake, and obviously not going anywhere, anytime soon," Gerry joked between sips. "They really have me pinned down, don't they?"

"Do you remember anything," Leroy asked gently.

"Not really," he admitted. "Just checking my files on the car seat, then *boom*, nothing. Pater and Mater won't tell me the details. Does anyone know what happened?"

"Um, well," Katherine began, not sure if she should tell him.

"Not you too, Princess? Don't keep me in suspense. If it's about the car, I figure it's a write-off, so you're not sparing me."

"Hmm, it's like this Ger," Leroy began, ruffling his thick curls. "The police are interested in this."

"Oh?"

"Blast. Better just spit it out." Leroy sighed. "They're treating this as attempted murder."

"It's true," Katherine said in answer to Gerry's stunned expression. "The driver has gone missing, and to make matters worse, it seems your company hired someone using a fake ID, well, they borrowed it from a dead person, if you could use that term."

"The detectives have examined the scene and say there was no evidence that the ice caused a problem, not with the way you guys plough, sand and salt the yards. This was deliberate," Leroy concluded.

"God, has it finally come to this," Gerry asked quietly to himself.

They knew what he was thinking. The company trucks, shipping containers and dockyards had often been used clandestinely by criminal elements, and the Reinolds had a strong crackdown policy for whenever something suspicious was uncovered or suspected, namely, to tip-off the authorities immediately and be open to all their investigations. However, evil has a long memory, the threat of retaliation was always looming, but now it had gone past veiled threats and sinister innuendos. Whoever was behind this had decided it was time that the company or its members received a payback.

"What if it doesn't stop with me," Gerry suddenly realized. "Dad's got to do something, and Lottie's now there, you've got to … ."

"Shh, it's all right, they've stepped up the security, Stonyvale is also getting a complete new system with security on the grounds just in case, and Lottie has a private bodyguard. She doesn't like it, but your Pops insisted," Katherine explained. "Pete refused to have one, says he can't do his parish work with a guard in tow. He seems to think they've sent their message and will leave it at that."

"For now maybe," Gerry noted mordantly. "But what if you were there when they came to get me? I dread to think what might have … ."

"Now Ger, don't be borrowing more trouble," Leroy interrupted. "Katie is safe and sound, you just concentrate on getting better, you hear me?"

However, Gerry was lost in thought, his expression troubled.

"Oh now we've done it Leroy, we shouldn't have said anything, at least not until he was stronger," Katherine noted with concern. "Gerry, please don't get upset. The police are doing their best, they'll catch whoever did this, I'm sure."

"Probably not for some time," Gerry surmised, "but I am glad you told me, so don't feel bad. I'd rather know the truth than be left swinging, wondering what had happened, if anyone else got hurt."

"No, no one else was injured, although Leo was pretty shook up, he saw it happen," Leroy added.

"Kathy told me. Well, whoever did this, they haven't gotten rid of me, if that's what they were aiming for. It'll take more than an articulated truck."

"That's the spirit, good on yah!" Leroy beamed, waggishly but gently tousling Gerry's hair. "You know, we should arrange a party, when you're able to attend, naturally."

"I don't know about that." Gerry smiled, looking over at Katherine.

"Yeah, one of *your* celebrations might just put him back in here, and me too for that matter," Katherine noted dryly, remembering the 'Technicolor Extravaganza' they went to last New Year's.

"Aw Ger, if you think my parties are bad, just wait until you get the bill for the hospital, that'll kill you off for sure."

Katherine did not know whether to be scandalised at Leroy's odd humour, but Gerry found it hilarious. At that moment, another visitor arrived, it was Charlotte followed by her expressionless, beefy bodyguard clad in a black suit and dark glasses.

"Gerry, Gerry, Gerry, Gerry," she exclaimed, flying to his bed, grabbing his other free hand and giving him a kiss on the cheek.

"That's my name, don't stretch it thin." He smiled.

"I'll wait outside, miss," the guard announced before exiting the room.

"Kathy told me you had a bodyguard, but did Dad have to hire 'The Hulk'?" Gerry laughed.

"Oh, I guess it's funny, but it's *so* annoying," she added. "Especially as Dad refuses a guard and makes me put up with one. I don't know how having him around is going to keep me safe, I stand out like a sore thumb now with him tagging along. But tell me, how are you feeling?"

"Groggy, but not too bad, all considering. How do you like working in the company?"

"Out of my depth at times, I don't know how you and Pete could keep it all going," she admitted shaking her head. "Pete has great faith in me, and I'm slowly getting the hang of it, but there's still so much to learn. I do like the activity, however."

"Don't worry, I'll be up and out before you know it, you won't have to battle with distribution channels too much longer."

"Hey, you can't brush me off like that now that I'm just finding my feet. I'm sure there's something I can still do when you resume your post."

"Aha, she's a career women now Ger, been bitten by the executive life, there's no going back," Leroy smiled.

The door swung open, the dragon lady had returned.

"All right, looks like we're getting a little crowded in here, I'm going to have to restrict the number of visitors," Deborah announced.

Katherine and Leroy decided it was best to let Lottie have some time alone with her brother.

"If you don't mind, I'm famished. Hunger is getting the better of me. I'm going to see if the cafeteria is still serving breakfast, nothing like a greasy fry up with streaky rashers in the morning," Leroy declared, picking up his briefcase.

"You must be hungry if you're going to the cafeteria *here*," Katherine noted, "but I didn't have breakfast myself, so I think I'll join you."

"Okay, we'll be back soon, Ger. You don't mind me running off with your fiancée?"

"Maybe you should rephrase that question," Gerry returned. Leroy simply laughed. "Yeah, off you go, it looks like Lottie and I have a lot to catch up on."

"Okay. Come with me, m'lady," Leroy bowed, offering Katherine his arm. Gerry and Charlotte watched them leave, slightly amused with the proceedings. Leroy was a flagrant playboy and a notorious flirt, but he knew Lucky Charms would not dare try anything with Kathy, while she on the other hand would not stand for such inappropriate nonsense pulled on her. If Gerry was not mistaken, it seemed Leroy was trying to show Kathy he really could be on his best behaviour. Obviously, they had become friends while he was out cold.

"What are streaky rashers," Katherine enquired as they went down the hall. She thought she had heard all of Leroy's odd expressions, and wondered if he was sarcastically referring to the unrecognisable state of hospital cuisine. He often forgot how few Americans understood his

Irishisms and explained he was referring to bacon, the long thin kind with the fat streaks running through it, hence the term 'streaky'. Apparently, there were other varieties of bacon on the Old Sod, streaky rashers were just one to choose from. She liked listening to Leroy with his Gaelic lilt, it was a wonder how English could be used differently in another country. Jell-O was jelly, jelly was jam, cookies were biscuits, biscuits were either scones, muffins or rock buns. French fries were chips, potato chips were crisps, and hamburgers could be *ham* burgers or beef burgers depending on what you wanted for the patty. The funny part was, Leroy was actually born in the United States. Curious as to why he seemed more Irish down to his brogue he explained he was a dual citizen.

"You see, if any Irish parent or grandparent holds their citizenship, you're also entitled to it," he clarified during one of his hospital visits. His father was the first generation American-born of Irish immigrants, while his mother came straight from the Emerald Isle itself. "So, I'm a'hundred percent American, and a'hundred percent Irish."

While it was a wonderful advantage, at the same time it had its downside during his childhood he wistfully admitted. He spent his early years tossed between both sides of the Atlantic after their stormy separation and custody battles.

"Didn't you like Ireland?"

"Oh sure, half my family are there, coming back *here* wasn't always so grand. Da was always too busy, career you know, took up a lot of his time. So I was boarded out to the nuns during his custody periods."

It did not take long for Katherine to fill in the blanks with this disclosure. His household was always typically Irish, down to the daily expressions used, and the faint brogue he grew up with only grew stronger with each summer visit to his mother and the rest of his relatives. She thought about his time at school, she did not know Gerry and Pete went to boarding school too. Gerry did say he went to the same private institution as Leroy.

"Pete and Gerry didn't board, they just went to the day school facilities."

"Gosh, I always had a horror of boarding schools, it sounds so much like an orphanage," Katherine admitted.

"You wouldn't be far wrong. Oh, the nuns were great, except for the few cranky biddies mind you, but even the nice ones couldn't make up for missing your parents. As you can imagine, I didn't fit in well, and with the odd custody arrangements I usually missed parts of a school year so keeping up was a problem, and, I often lost interest. Gerry and Peter were always there however, not to mention the Reinolds always made me feel welcome, I couldn't have made it without them."

"If your dad insisted he was too busy all the time, why didn't he just let you stay with your mom," Katherine wondered.

Leroy chuckled bitterly.

"Let's say I'm *his* son. He just wanted me to upset my mother. It was a matter of who has one up on who. What really got to me was when his custody months arrived, he didn't have much time for me *then*, not with the new woman in his life, but now that I've got a career in the family firm and making a name for myself in it he wants to brag and show me off as *his* progeny. I shouldn't complain, at least he got stuck for college. Harvard fees are nothing to sneeze at."

Leroy had been an impish mystery, but much of it now made sense after he had let her in on his past. No doubt he had been bullied because of his eccentricities and slipping grades, and so Gerry came to the rescue with the result they became fast friends. Poor Leroy, with no solid family life *per se* it was not difficult to see why he had trouble remaining steady, determined to make up for an almost Charles Dickens childhood by indulging his every whim for enjoyment and excitement once he had legally become an adult. She could also understand why Gerry remained friends with Leroy notwithstanding all his wild ways. As she learned more about Gerry she discovered he always stood by the underdog, and while he had few close friends, when he offered his friendship he meant it, even if in Leroy's case there were some times he might regret it. It was funny to look back now and recall Gerry's reticence in introducing Leroy to her. Despite his roving madcap ways, the rakish red head was a good friend in return as the last few weeks had proved, cheering everyone up and offering to run errands or do favours, anything to help while they were all caught up in the aftermath of the accident.

"Look Lee, they have your streaky rashers, but the eggs don't look so good," Katherine noticed, eyeing the scrambled yellow mash left stewing in the cafeteria food warmers.

"A bacon butty it is then."

"Bacon what?"

"A toasted bacon sandwich with butter."

"Oh, *now* you say 'bacon'." She smiled. "I'll try that."

"Better have a few, one alone won't keep you going," Leroy noted, piling her bacon-filled plate with extra toast and butter packets, then filled them out a few cups of coffee. "You should try a sandwich with Irish sliced pan, bread here isn't fit for ducks. In fact, you and Ger should visit Ireland with me sometime, you'd love it."

"I bet we would, but we've got a few sites in Italy to see first," she reminded him.

"Ah, of course. Don't worry love, you and Ger will be off on your honeymoon before you know it. So, what did the doctors say again," he asked as he reached for the sugar packets.

"He has feeling in his legs, but they still can't promise a full recovery."

"Well, you heard him, he's not going to let a truck stop him. If he can feel, there's hope. He'll get around again, you'll see. Like the rest of his family he has a stubborn streak."

The conversation was interrupted as they scuffled over the tab, but Katherine finally won this time around, pointing out that he had already spent too much keeping them supplied with food during their bedside vigils. With the bill paid, they resumed their conversation as they searched for a free table.

"I know, I'm discovering all about that stubborn streak, I have one myself on occasion," she admitted. "I hope his sheer will-power to get better will work a miracle. But you know, I'm more worried about something like this happening again."

"Don't fret. Pete is probably right, whoever did this sent their message, and with all the fuzz floating around, they won't try anything else. These lunatics work in the dark, they'll keep a low profile," he reassured her as they found a free seat and settled in.

"Why the Reinolds? I don't hear of other shipping companies suffering this amount of hassle. How did they make so many enemies?"

"I wish I knew the answer to that, Katie. No one sets out to make enemies, they just happen, especially to good people," he noted matter-of-factly, while buttering his toast. "Anyway, enough torture and torment, no use dementing yourself. Are you going to stay all day?"

"Yeah, he asked me to read the new book I brought, I hope the *Old Man and the Sea* isn't too depressing for him right now. Of course, I can't be a bother, he'll need some rest. That reminds me, you won't believe what he said to me earlier, he thought he was dreaming, but he knew I was there! Everything from the books and the music turned into some kind of surreal image, but he could hear me."

"See? I told you them doctors know nothin'." Leroy grinned.

"I just knew he could still hear, but when he said that, I was so surprised."

"And to think he didn't remember my bottle of whiskey, he only had ears for you. That's a sure sign the man is truly in love."

ά❖ࠪ

The world felt like a better place the following day now that Gerry was back in the land of the living as Leroy had phrased it. After attending Peter's morning service, she went straight to her gallery in Dumbo and relayed the good news to everyone. Andre brought out a platter of his best pastries and French roast coffee to celebrate as the Gallery Gang gathered around the front desk, begging Katherine for all the details.

"My, this is just wonderful," Esther beamed, leaving the newspapers aside. She could cut out the gallery reviews for their archives later.

"This is excellent news," the Professor added with a smile, pushing his gold rimmed glasses up the bridge of his nose, "it feels like we're having a second Easter Sunday."

"You can say that again, I was dreading he might never come out of the coma," Katherine replied.

"What's next," Suzy wanted to know.

"It all depends on time now. He has to wait for his legs and pelvis to knit before they can see if he's able to walk, maybe up to four months, but the physiotherapist started working with him right away yesterday afternoon, moving his arms and head. They want to get his arms strong so he can work with the crutches."

"At least they're working to get the top half of him mobile," Olivia commented quietly.

"And he's off the tube, I'm glad to say. Right now he needs help to eat, but the way he's already pushing himself, he'll be using a knife and fork before the week is out."

"Does he remember anything," Dennis wondered.

"Not much, but overall, his memory was not affected, he even remembered we have a new president the last five months and that Clinton is his name, so the concussion didn't do any permanent damage."

"This is a cause for celebration. I've certainly missed seeing him around. I'd be happy to give him my recipe for *bouillabaisse*, just to see him up and about again." Andre laughed. Gerry had a habit of sneaking into his kitchen, trying to discover the secret to one of his celebrated dishes for Lottie and Mrs. R. Chasing Gerry out of the kitchen whenever he was caught poking in the pots had become part of the daily routine of the restaurant staff in addition to their hectic scramble to present perfect dishes to their customers. The gaiety had left the premises when his furtive visits to the pantry had stopped.

"He'll be glad to hear that." Katherine smiled. "But you know if you give him an inch, he won't stop there. He told me he also wants the secret to your special beef Bourguignon."

"Ah, ha! Wouldn't he like to know. But that only gets handed down to the next generation. Some things must be kept in the family. Well, as much as I would like to talk with you all, a chef's work is never done. I shall see you later." Bowing, Andre headed off to the service area.

"Poor guy, the way he works, he'll never have the time to settle down to have that next generation," Esther observed, shaking her head.

"I'm afraid his beef Bourguignon will be lost forever," Olivia added.

"Don't say that to my Gramps, he'll have a fit." Katherine laughed. Her grandfather was a noted gourmand, always disregarding doctor's orders and indulging his palate, partaking of every dish declared anathema by all physicians throughout the land. Katherine often thought he should know better and set a good example considering he ran their family pharmaceutical manufacturing empire for many years, but since he had passed the helm on to her father and uncle, Gramps took life easy whenever he had the chance, and he made sure these chances happened on a regular basis.

"Will your Gramps be stopping by today," the Professor enquired, he and Mr. GW had hit it off from the beginning.

"I don't know, it's hard to say since Andre started slipping low-fat ingredients into his dishes."

"You mean he hasn't tumbled to it yet?" Esther chuckled.

"No, thank heavens! Gramp's got to cut back somewhere, he's hopeless. Okay, whose turn is it to paint today," Katherine enquired. Suzy and Dennis, in addition to the Professor, had full use of the private studio when their duty on the gallery floors permitted of course. Working a rota system ensured the gallery assistants, who were nearly all creative *artistes*, had equal time for their artwork during the day, in the evenings they could work as long as they liked once they were off the clock, although that rarely happened as everyone else was glad to be heading home most nights. The Professor was the only one exempt from this system as technically he was not one of the staff, but he too would bumble down from their exclusive creative space and offer his expertise in the gallery, especially the fourth floor, the special museum section where Gerry had recently housed his famous art and ancient antiquity collection. Katherine still referred to it as 'Gerry's Collection'. They were not married yet, and already he was willingly handing over the treasures of his kingdom and calling it theirs. His generosity could be positively overwhelming.

"It's yours and Suzy's turn today," Dennis noted. "I get this Thursday and Friday."

"All right, we'll be back to let you guys off for lunch."

Katherine, Suzy and the Professor made their way to the elevator and prepared for a quiet morning of meditative creativity. Katherine would rather have been beating a track to the hospital to see Gerry, but it was Mrs. R's turn today, she could see him later tonight. In any case, she did have a lot of work to catch up on. After the accident the latest painting of her Socratic Collection had been left languishing under its white cotton sheeting. It was time to try and get this compilation of preachy paintwork near the half-way point sometime. When she thought about writing out a philosophical exercise on the ideals associated with Freedom and incorporating the actual text on canvas with visual imagery, she had no idea what she was letting herself in for, a line of paintings that seemed like they would never end. Well, there was nothing for it, she never would abandon a project once she got started, and it was an intriguing concept anyway. However, she had promised to paint Peter a larger version of a miraculous statue from a picture he had given her, and she felt guilty she had not finished it yet. She had painted Gerry and Lottie their promised pictures of Rome and the Acropolis, she had also completed Mr. R's commission to capture the *Morning Glory* on canvas, and poor Pete was the last one to receive his gift. Despite her delayed Socratic project, she did not like reneging on her promises either. Of course, he said there was no rush, he wanted her to finish her new collection, describing it as very important work, and he certainly did not expect her to work on his painting after what happened to Gerry. Still, she felt bad, she should not delay a promise, especially one she made to Peter after all his kindness.

"You look like you are in a pickle," the Professor noted as he uncovered his canvas, ready and waiting for him on his favourite easel.

"Do I look that perplexed?"

"It's not like you to stare at the sheetings," Suzy observed. "Painter's Block again?"

"Oh, nothing that can't be sorted out." She smiled. "I have a lot to do with this series, but I know I should finish Peter's Madonna."

"Then there's no time like the present, just start it my dear, Socrates and Plato can wait," he observed, swinging a spattered smock over his head, letting it settle on his shoulders.

"True, and besides, I guess there's no rush to finish the collection, seeing the first three on display haven't sold yet." Katherine sighed.

"I wonder why," Suzy noted, stifling a smile.

"Oh, I guess it *is* funny. I should have expected it really, making people rethink our country's definition of freedom was not something I should have chosen for my theme if I expected to make a quick killing," she concluded, while on her way to the cabinet where the new canvases were stored.

"However, it is an interesting thesis, and quite impressive for a beginner in philosophy. I never expected it to develop into what it has, considering our first round of disputations," the Professor commented, quietly unscrewing his tubes of paint and methodically applying the glistening oil colours onto his palette. "If I recall, on our first attempt we veered off into the topic of speeding tickets."

Katherine and Suzy laughed. When she first conceived the idea of dabbling in philosophy for the sake of art, the Professor was only too glad to be of assistance, Classical history and literature were among his passions, if 'passion' could be the right word, he never seemed to get over-excited about anything, engrossed and absorbed, but never the typical fiery artist. He and Katherine, with Gramps in attendance, bantered on the correct and incorrect use of freedom as an academic exercise and came up with a few unexpected brain twisters in the process. Suzy had missed their discussion, but Katherine still had her preliminary notes and let her read them much to Suzy's amusement. Suzy was not as daring with her pictures, still experimenting with the use of optical illusions, especially after seeing Justine's collection when it arrived from Paris, a whole series of Parisian scenes constructed from floral shapes and colours. Katherine wondered if Suzy and Justine were trying to establish a new school. Come to think of it, Illusionism was not a bad 'ism', it just might catch on, it was definitely easier to pronounce than her concept of 'Philosophism'. She really needed to come up with a believable, no-nonsense, good-sounding 'ism'.

As usual, the Professor had given good advice and so Katherine set to work, carefully taping Peter's devotional card on the projecting upper half of the easel, making sure she had fixed it straight. Looking at the picture, she might need a magnifying glass to get some of the details right. If only Pete had given her a larger image to work with.

"Gosh, it's beautiful, but her face is very sad. You would think he would pick a happier picture," Suzy commented, coming over for a closer look.

"I said it to him, but he wanted this one, said it would help keep him focused on his vocation."

Curious, the Professor left his depiction of *Manhattan at Sunset* and studied her new subject.

"Looks Spanish, definitely in the Iberian Baroque style."

"Close enough, this statue is from the sixteenth century, but it's in Ecuador."

"Interesting, I assume there is a special story attached," the Professor continued.

"Peter told me the Madonna and three angels finished it, so it must be pretty special. I keep meaning to ask him if there's more to the story, but with everything else that's happened in the meantime … ."

"Say no more, no one would expect you to remember or think of everything after the last few months," Suzy noted.

"I guess not. Time to see if I can do justice to this."

Having dallied long enough, they went to work, each artist to their own easel. Katherine cast a quick glance at the other two lonely easels left covered by the interior wall, Mr. R and Gerry's contributions to the art world. She could not wait until Gerry could join them once more, her gaze momentarily strayed over to the window where the turn-of-the-century wrought iron fire escape was located, underneath was an old wickerwork love seat for two that was hauled in and out onto the metal platform depending on the weather. She and Gerry had called it their little private Eiffel Tower overlooking Dumbo and liked nothing better than to while away the hours until it was time to head home. Although he had a romantic vein and had taken her out in style on many occasions, how she missed their simple evenings together on that rickety seating arrangement, the boxes of pizza or take-out, a painting session then spending some quiet time discussing any topic that came to mind, everything was completely innocent, which only deepened their friendship as well as their love. Without her ever needing to say one word, he instinctively knew and respected her principles, never forcing her into a situation to where she felt it necessary to put her foot down. Considering how most people ended their dates, there were times she was afraid there might be trouble, but he never pushed beyond the limits. After that, she knew she could trust him with anything. Her thoughts were interrupted as someone began knocking on the door of the partition wall separating the studio stairwell from the museum below.

"Hey, how's a reporter to get a scoop when you're all locked up like a bank after hours?"

She recognised the voice, it was Robert Horace. While he was the city's meanest art critic and cultural editor, ironically, he was also the only one she could trust to write appropriate interviews.

"In a minute," Katherine called out, shaking her head and laying down her palette, just when she had the paints extracted and ready to go. It looked like she was not getting back to work any time soon. Unlocking the door, she was about to greet him, then laughed: his signature crème trench coat had been exchanged for a stylish jet-black model, making his fair blonde hair more striking.

"Hey! That wasn't the reaction I was expecting. This was supposed to be my new 'cool' look."

"I'm sorry! Oh, it's *that* all right, it's just I never expected to see you arrive in anything else but your beloved Old Faithful. What gives?"

He rakishly tweaked his collar up.

"Your cousin said I was radically overdue a makeover and it was high time to upgrade my image. I hope the change of colour will suffice. So, do you like?"

"Yeah, real snazzy. *Trè magnifique.*"

Katherine tried not to laugh again, that would be Stephanie all right, her 'hip' younger cousin who was big into fashion photography and had her own studio in Manhattan, thanks to Gramps. She and Robert had been dating for a while, and things must be serious if he was willing to retire his favourite trench coat on her suggestion.

"Collar is a bit stiff, it needs a little breaking in. I have to say the new colour has it's advantages. I was able to get past a few of the door keepers at the galleries I've been bounced from, they didn't recognise me, so I got some ripping reviews coming up, if you care to read them when they get printed."

"Okay, I promise I'll read them this time. How corrosive are they?"

"Titanium doesn't stand a chance."

"You're wicked! I guess you want an interview from me too and melt me down with the lot." She shrugged, this type of acid attack was good for her art business.

"No, not today, my visit is more on a friendly basis so to speak, but before we get into that, I've got to see what's going on up here," he rakishly interjected, skipping past her and into the studio, the one area of the gallery that he had not yet seen.

"Hey! Not him! I thought this place was off limits," Suzy cried out in alarm as she eyed the black-coated intruder approach her easel. "No wonder he got in, he's in disguise."

"Don't worry, I won't criticise your masterpiece until it comes out into public view," he promised, peering over her shoulder, giving a side glance at the Professor's easel, then taking a look at Katherine's new subject.

"Hmm, what are you up to now? Exchanging 'Philoso-ism' for 'Religio-ism'? Preparing to impose a religious tract upon us next?"

"No." She sighed.

"Well, whatever you have cooked up in that original mind of yours, be careful. You don't want to be excommunicated, you've only been with the Romans one week."

"Come on, you." She hooked him under the arm and escorted him back to the elevator. "We shall go to the office for the remainder of this visit." Laughing, he good-naturedly waved goodbye to the remaining artists as she scurried him along.

"Okay, speaking of visits, how is your grandma doing," she enquired once she had him safely away from the studio. That was still their inner sanctum, no critiquing allowed until the new works were finished.

"She's okay the last few days, no angry outbursts, and she's not giving the nurse a bad time," he replied.

"That's good." It was difficult asking how his grandma was doing, it was never an easy subject. She suffered from severe Alzheimer's, he was the main care provider as she had no other close relatives after his parents had passed away.

"Yeah, it is. She came this close to remembering who I was too." He smiled, indicating the breadth of an inch with his fingers. "Speaking of glad tidings, I heard Gerry woke up."

"Yes, but it's too early to pronounce a full recovery."

"I know, still, he's out of the coma, that's good."

"You have no idea," Katherine said, then realising he was one of the few she had not told yet. "But how did you … ? Oh, right. It's a reporter's job. Hmm, let me guess: Beatrice the Beastie found out about it too," Katherine grimaced. Her current social columns were the bane of her life, turning Gerry's tragedy and their postponed wedding into cheap pulp entertainment. Horace was editor of the cultural section of their paper, and while he tried to get her to tone down her tattle by threatening to pull her stories, Beatrice Brandis often went over his head and would secure the go-ahead for her gossipy column directly from the Editor in Chief. While Robert as 'Horace the Horrible' would write scathing art critiques, he did not believe in destroying reputations or revealing personal misinformation, he liked splashing vitriol around and stoking a few flames, but Brandis' hogwash was a little more than he could swallow at times.

"Yeah, as always, she has her snitches. There are a few gossipy nurses on duty who love to leak out details, the Beastie has quite a huge fan following, then of course, there are those who would drop a few tips for some brown envelopes under the medicine cabinet, if you catch my drift."

The elevator doors opened and they paused their conversation until they retreated to the privacy of her office under the grand staircase behind the front reception desk.

"So, are you saying that Gerry's medical details may be leaked now," she asked as they took a seat at her desk.

"Yeah, I'm afraid so," he said, not a little disgusted.

"That's so unprofessional! Mr. R. will have the hospital manager's head on a stake."

"I assume you were keeping most of the details from Gerry, right?"

"Of course, he just woke up, we couldn't tell him he may not walk, not like he used to. We don't know how he would take it, it's too soon."

"I know, the Beastie Bug is all over it now, more sob stories about his possible handicaps, and ... well, I don't want to say it," he admitted quietly.

"I guess it's better to hear it from you. What is she storming about now?"

"Oh, speculative junk on whether you will leave him now that he's more than likely going to be ..."

"*Crippled?* I don't believe this," she exclaimed. That was way below the belt. Gerry was not even awake a full two days. All Horace, or rather, Smith, could do was apologise, he was not happy about it either. As with a few of the Beastie woman's other columns, he tried to get her to tone down this latest piece of journalistic prose, but to no avail. He could try to pull her article again, but as it was, the Editor in Chief was not too happy with him at the moment.

"There's only so much I can do, and the boss is beginning to make undertones that I might be getting soft, and that if 'Horace' isn't up to the job, there are others who are."

"Are you serious?" Katherine gasped, disgusted with this latest turn of events.

"I'm afraid so, my paper is particularly interested in dog-eat-dog reporting, especially in the social and cultural columns where objectivity is a moot point, spice and biased opinions help keep our circulation numbers high."

"Of course, you did warn me about that before."

"Like I said, there are some days when I really hate my job," he replied, ruffling his hair.

"Why not switch career? You could always become C.S. Turris full time," she hinted, "he isn't doing so bad around here lately." Besides 'Horace' for his *nom de plume*, he had assumed 'Turris' as his artistic identity. He smiled wistfully at the suggestion.

"As much as I would love to, I've now created an indissoluble paradox. Would anyone have wanted Turris' paintings to begin with were it not for Horace's griping? Methinks not. Ergo, if I kill off one, I also murder the other, and doom Christopher Smith in the process."

"Oh don't say that, but I can see the difficulty," she agreed.

"Until I know Turris is a sure thing, I'll keep the day job for now. At least Turris helps keep me sane."

"And I'm sure that special 'someone' in your life has been a great help too," Katherine noted.

"Steph! Oh yeah! Only … ."

"Bruce Wane still wondering if he should tell her about Batman?"

"Something like that." Smith smiled sheepishly.

"You'll never know unless you try."

"I … think I'll wait a bit longer."

"Okay, it's your call, Mr. Wane."

So many aliases, it was hard enough trying to juggle the daily schedule of one life let alone manage two extras. It was all for a good cause despite Horace's nefarious reputation as the 'Art Hacker'. She had to take her hat off to him.

"As much as I would love to stay, I've got to run." He rose and said his goodbyes, there was an exhibition at the Brooklyn museum he wanted to liven up a bit, and not wishing to hold him up, she thanked him for the tip-off. Warning her about the breaking news reports was becoming a regular occurrence these days.

"Sure, no sweat. I just hope this all blows over."

"Me too." She sighed as she watched him leave.

It was difficult to settle down to work after that, her mind was busy wondering what she would see in the papers, and if they could keep the latest tabloidian fare from Gerry, at least for the next few weeks until their love life was not as interesting to the public.

On her way to the hospital that night, she bought a copy of the dreaded paper. Sure enough, true to form, the first of Beatrice's columns was printed in the evening edition. Katherine quickly scanned through the text. It was not as long as she expected, but those few sentences near the conclusion felt like so many daggers through the heart, " ... *according to reliable sources, Mr. Reinold may not fully recover and could be permanently confined to a wheelchair ... so far it is not confirmed if the wedding has been merely postponed or cancelled indefinitely, chances are, the latter could well be the case. Stay tuned, fellow New Yorkers as we wait to see how this love drama unfolds.*"

Good Lord, they could not let Gerry see this!

Immediately Katherine, the Reinolds and bedside visitors launched a stringent censorship watch. All papers, magazines and periodicals were diligently searched and all offending sections were promptly removed before they were allowed in. Afraid he might see something on the news, the television in his room was officially declared banjaxed, a new term learned from Leroy, when in fact the machine was merely left unplugged. They managed well enough for the first week or two as Gerry was still fatigued from the coma, but then as he gained strength, noticed the plug peeking from behind the set and asked someone to do the honours. Leroy had the foresight to swipe the batteries from the remote when he came to visit, which bought them an extra few days. Gerry then asked someone to go see if the nurses had any spare batteries. Her brother Steves offered his assistance, and disappearing for an hour, winked at Katherine upon his return as he handed Gerry the remote.

"Hey, it still doesn't work," the patient noted as he gave the machine a few slaps before thumping it off his bedside, the number refusing to switch past the weather channel no matter what button he pushed.

"That's the way it is with these things, Ger, you have no idea who used the remote before you, they could have broken it." Steves shrugged. Katherine had to leave the room using a powder room trip as a pretext, she could not let Gerry see her laugh. Knowing Steves and his wizardry with motherboards, chips and wires, he obviously doctored the gadget in accordance with their censorship program. At least he had bought them extra time.

"All right. That's it. I'm not blind you know. You all make the KGB look like the Keystone Cops." Gerry declared one evening after noticing his favourite newspaper was exceptionally thin. Afraid he might want to get wrapped up in business before he was ready, Mr. R insisted they all start taking out the financial sections too.

"Dear, you need to relax, and we were just doing what we thought was best," Mrs. R. explained.

"But at this point all I'm left with are sports, TV guides, weather reports, the latest Agony Aunt, and I'm really getting tired of the weather."

"I'm sorry Gerry," Katherine replied, "we don't want you to get stressed out over things you can't handle right now. Let us do all the worrying for you. You'll have plenty of work facing you when you're up and at 'em again."

"That's true," he conceded with a resigned sigh, "but the not-knowing is just as bad. I can't help but stew over what's happening at good old Reinold Enterprises in my absence."

"Don't you trust your brother, dear," his mother wondered.

"Pete's fine, but he'll only be allowed to help for so long. It's Lottie I'm concerned about. There is so much for her to take in, and if Pete is called back to parish work full time, at this early stage she may be left with more than she can chew, even with Thomas to back her up."

"Well, if Pete has faith in her, you should too," Katherine reminded him. "Despite the learning curve, she's really getting into keeping the distribution channels well oiled and running smoothly."

"Hmm, you mean I might actually be out of a job when I leave this place, if I ever leave this place," he noted wryly, nodding to the steel fixators pinning him down.

"Oh Gerry, don't be like that," Katherine quickly jumped in. It was only a wry joke, he still had not been told about the uncertainty regarding his recovery, but right then it sounded like a temptation darted at Fate. "Lottie will be all right. You've been unconscious for a month, stuck in bed for almost another, and your shipping empire hasn't collapsed with her inexperience."

"That doesn't say much for my experience either." He smiled. "Out for two months, and all carries on as before."

"You know what I mean. You love getting me all wound up, don't you?"

"Ah, but you're so cute when you get flustered," he teased as he gave her hand a little squeeze. "Seriously, looking at my rebar accessories, it's obvious I'm going to be stuck here for some time," he began, revealing his personal deduction. Katherine and Mrs. Reinold glanced quickly at each other. Did he guess how bad it was? They let him continue. " ... and already I am getting the first symptoms of cabin fever, laying around with nothing constructive to do. I can't expect everyone to keep me entertained when you all have things to take care of too. I know everyone means well, but shutting me off from the outside world is not helping. Basically, I need some work to keep my mind off all of this," he concluded, motioning around the room with his free hand.

His request was understandable. Although she was very familiar with the hospital rounds by now, Katherine could only imagine what he was personally going through and suffered silently with him in sympathy sickness. Gerry was already in a delicate condition with those metal rods, the nurses had to keep constant watch where the fasteners protruded from his skin making sure infection did not set in. There was also the constant threat of bed sores now that he was bolted into place, and since his spleen had been removed he would be forever susceptible to catching infections. He may not need medications to compensate for the absence of that organ, but his health would always have to be monitored. Stuck under constant surveillance without being able to move from his bed was stressful enough, but then with the added indignities of relying on strangers for intimate necessities in the matter of personal hygiene, that was the final straw, especially when one particular indignity was exposed to visitors, his catheter bag. More often than not, it would be hanging by his bedside facing the door as she walked in. Couldn't the nurses position it out of sight at least? Despite his sense of humour, she could see past his quick quips; he had an independence streak a mile wide, and this torturous convalescent period was more than he could take, but to have evidence of his private functions dangling by his side was nothing short of humiliation, at least, that was how she felt. Perhaps all these details really didn't bother him as much, but it nettled her. She had to work hard to bottle her temper, no matter how many times she requested the nurses to please be more mindful, someone would forget, leaving her to try and cover that thing discreetly with a blanket when he was asleep, hoping he did not see what she was doing. Considering all of this, she had to agree with him, he needed a challenging distraction. It was time to lift the censorship. Thankfully, it appeared that Beatrice the Beastie had grown tired of their problems and was now focusing on someone else for her columns, a fashion model and twitty socialite with a sugar daddy almost twice her age. Fine, let her take the heat for awhile.

"I'm sorry, dear. I'll speak with your father, no doubt he will come up with a solution," Mrs. R replied.

"For now, you'll just have to make do with our company." Katherine smiled.

" 'Make do' indeed. You know I look forward to your visits, all of you. I really appreciate all the care you have lavished on me. I just wish this was all over and we could get back to our Eiffel Tower rather than have one riveted on me," he noted gently, turning to Katherine.

"So do I." She gave him a kiss on the cheek.

That evening Sophia had a word or two with Richard when he returned from the offices, explaining their son's 'ancy' condition. Mr. R. finally relented and suggested he could have Pete, Lottie and Thomas make full reports to Gerry every day and perhaps start handing over the paperwork for him to go through, little by little.

"Of course, you know the doctors aren't going to be happy if we bother him with all this business," Richard reminded her.

"Talk it over with them, see what they say. He won't get better if his morale suffers, that's just as important as his physical well-being."

"You're right about that, and I know Pete won't be able to help for much longer … okay, I'll run it past them in the morning."

True to his word, the following day Mr. Reinold explained the current situation of the patient to the specialist on duty with the therapist in tow. The doctor looked sceptical until the therapist had to agree that any return to a semblance of normality might help Gerard through the tough time that lay ahead.

"It will give him a sense of purpose," the therapist explained, "he'll need something to encourage him get out of that bed when the time comes."

"All right, I'll agree to it for now, but if I see any sign that he is becoming fatigued or stressed in any way, I'll call a halt to the Bedside Executive Scheme," the doctor warned good naturedly.

"Fair enough, Doc." Richard was appreciative of any return to normality for his son, and shook the doctor's hand. It was a right hook to the gut every day to see Gerard in his semi-incapacitated state, it would be good knowing he was getting back on top of things, even if it was only the confounded paperwork. However, this sign of improvement was also a second punch to the stomach, it meant Peter would be returning to his flock, probably sooner than he would have liked. He could not help feeling a wave of paternal satisfaction to see Peter return to his job at Reinold Enterprises like the old days before he absconded to the seminary. Richard was no longer angry about it, even the disappointment had worn off. Come to think of it, he was now rather proud of him. Despite Peter's business sense, deep down something had always nagged at him that Pete was not meant for the hustle and bustle of the commercial world, but he was afraid to face it, wishing things could go as he planned, having Pete take over with Gerry. That was not to be. It was tough to see Peter go alone into a world where he would be bound by obedience to those placed in authority over him rather than remain his own master in the family firm. It was a peculiar mix of emotions, wanting Pete to stay yet knowing he had important work elsewhere. While he was not overly religious, Richard was not an unyielding secularist either, he knew that guiding souls was far more important than managing trucks, ships and air cargo. No point thinking about it, it was done now, and Pete was doing a lot of good after all, he had seen the results for himself. He had to let one son go and now he must concentrate on getting Gerry well again. It would be a great relief to see Gerry out of that damn hospital as soon as possible, the fact he nearly lost him in the accident was too harrowing for words. Whatever he wanted, then so be it, anything to speed his recovery.

That night Gerry received the evening editions of the papers intact, the TV remote was rewired back to its original condition, and he was duly inundated with all the company reports and latest cost analyses he had missed. Katherine was afraid he might be overwhelmed with the work at this early stage, but he seemed to relish it.

"Not too bad, I thought it might be worse. Looks like it's under control," he noted as he scrutinised one of the ledgers Lottie set before him. "It's no different than when I go away on our dreaded global inspections. I'll get reoriented in no time."

"You see? There was nothing to get stressed over, I haven't broken us yet." Lottie laughed. "In fact, I finally got Finley to agree to the shipping terms on his contract renewal," she continued with satisfaction, handing him another file. He raised an eyebrow in surprise as he opened it and saw Mr. Finley's scrawl on the dotted line.

"Well, I'll be a … way to go! Good work. He's been driving us all mad for well over a year, threatening to change companies. How did you get him to agree?"

"It wasn't that hard, really," she began. "If he was serious about switching, he would have done it by now, particularly if a competitor gave him a better rate, which of course, he won't find anywhere. He was letting everyone swing, hoping to get one last deal out of us."

"I knew that, but what did you do?"

"I just got a little tough with him, politely of course, and said if he wasn't satisfied with the good service Reinold Enterprises has provided him for the last five years, he may just as well go find that company that was better suited to his needs."

"You didn't."

"I did. He was never going to leave us, so I had to put a stop to his whinging once and for all, it's bad enough he never pays on time. He's not the type you can be soft with, Gerry, not for long anyway, not if he's going to be a nuisance. You and Dad have done your best to please him, and he was trying to take advantage of it. With all the negative media attention over the years, he obviously assumed we were suffering and thought we were desperate for his custom to the point of scalping ourselves to keep him. Well, that's not the case. If he ever does leave us, there are many other customers who are quite satisfied, we won't miss his business. Good word from our other clients spreads around too you know."

"That's true.," Katherine nodded. "Pops said he's not going to pay attention to the media hype anymore, he and Uncle Tim are really satisfied with how you're handling the international deliveries for Walsingham Industries, plus, the Gallery Gang have no complaints to file," she concluded with a smile, recalling the first time she had needed his services to deliver large artwork that would not fit in her gallery van.

"That's good to know." He chuckled. He could never forget that madcap day either. "Honestly Lottie, looks like you've grown a little crusty around the edges," he replied, a little intrigued with his sister's growing business acumen. "You really are getting to like the family trade."

"I must say, it is rather exciting. I feel like I'm actually accomplishing something, doing something important. Just look at the stock we ship around the world. I'd hate to think what would happen if for some crazy reason all shipping were to disappear overnight. The world economy could collapse, famines could strike, plagues too if we couldn't get important things like the Walsighams' medications around to where they're needed."

"I wonder how we're going to manage this," he mused to himself, closing the file.

"Manage what?"

"When I get better, we can't have two Senior Managers of International Distribution, and Thomas is already Acting Manager … hmm."

"I see what you mean. Like I said before, I'm sure you and Dad can find *something* for me to do."

"Of course. Let's wait and see what happens. For now, you and Pete keep up the good work."

"We will, but we'll certainly pass everything by you first. But, I'll leave it there, enough business for one evening, we can talk about the fuel depots tomorrow, I can see when three's a crowd," she smiled, looking over at Katherine. Giving them both a hug, she left them alone, the 'Hulk' leaving his post outside the door, following close behind.

"She's right, no more business. Away with Finley! May he be exiled to the file cabinet until next year!" He flung the folder with a flick of the wrist onto the bedside table. "I'm in serious need of a croissant or two."

"Not a bad idea."

☙ ❖ ❧

Peter looked out over the Manhattan scene as the evening twilight made its entrance, bathing the surrounding towers with its ethereal hues. The corporate workday was over, and like old times he took a moment to enjoy the corner office view before packing his briefcase up for the night. Gerry had not changed the décor much when he was promoted in his place, perhaps his brother still considered it 'Pete's Office'. Obviously Gerry did not want all memory of him effaced from the family business, but it was too much like days gone by. Peter knew he could get used to this once familiar routine, which he did not want to happen. He concentrated on gathering his papers, nothing out of the ordinary occurred today thank heavens, if he could count doing double duty as priest and secular executive as ordinary. However, there was one last appointment to keep. The Archbishop had invited him to dinner at his private residence, Archbishop Morrison recently promoted to the Archdiocese of Newark would be joining them. Although it was May thirteenth, Peter could tell this invitation was not a celebratory occasion for the Marian feast day. While he greatly disliked referring to the operations of the Church as business, it was how their Eminences seemed to be treating this invitation, therefore appointment seemed like the appropriate term for this polite social summons. He wondered if he was going to be recalled back to his parish work full time. No, he sensed that could not be it, Archbishop Foley had assured his father he could be spared for a month or two more if need be, and Archbishop Morrison's presence tonight suggested something more important would be the topic of discussion. Was he to be transferred to New Jersey? *Jersey* played in his mind, he had the vague understanding he was to be 'prepared'—for what, he could not be certain. His spiritual intuition was not setting off any interior alarm for major concern, but *something* was afoot.

64

Returning to the desk to shut his briefcase, he glanced at one of the framed photographs placed there, a stylish black and white snapshot of Gerry and Kathy taken at her gallery by her cousin. He was drawn to the elegant image and could not help but study it for a moment. The impression was clear, there was no mistaking it, God wished them to be together and he was glad Ger had finally found the one whom he was meant to be with. Peter could feel their happiness. That's strange … there was an interconnection. Would this appointment with their Eminences present anything that would affect Gerry and Kathy? Perhaps their postponed wedding? No, he couldn't see how Archbishop Morrsion would have anything to do with that either. Where did New Jersey come into this? It was not a strong presentiment, but still, *something* was there. He had to be cautious with these quiet inspirations, it was easy to misread their meaning. Disclosing sins that were revealed to him in the consciences of penitents was much easier to deal with, those signs were blunt, stark, straightforward. These indistinct yet present whisperings to his spirit were another matter, gentle reminders, promptings to prepare for situations and tasks, the details of which were more often than not obscured from him until they unfolded with time, sometimes gradually, now and then abruptly. However, he did sense a slow progression would occur on this occasion. That was good to know, he was one man trying to accomplish the work of two, there were only so many things he could handle right now he thought with a sigh as he replaced the photograph and shut his case.

There was a gentle knock on the open door.

It was Mrs. Clarke, the secretary.

"Sorry to bother you, but this needs to be signed and ready for the mail round in the morning."

"Of course, come in," he replied, taking the forms.

"Is there anything else you need me to do before you leave, sir?"

"No, that will be all, thank you. And please, it's Monsignor."

"Sorry, I keep forgetting … good night then."

"Good night, Mrs. Clarke."

He heard the door close behind her. During this brief exchange, he did not look up again when he signed the papers nor when handing them back. Before he became a priest, she used to be his personal assistant. He remembered her first day on the job, nervous, wanting to do everything just right, then literally becoming indispensable after she had settled in, willing to work overtime whenever called upon. The habit of addressing him as 'sir' would not be easy to break, but then it was an odd situation: former boss turned priest back in his old job in the shipping industry. On this occasion, he was relieved he could call upon the use of his full title. When used in the right context it demanded reverence and reminded people of what he was, including him. He did not like thinking back to certain times, the office surroundings brought up depressing and uncomfortable memories as well as good ones. Of course, she became Gerry's personal assistant after he resigned his post, but time did not heal all rifts and wounds. Although she was not a Catholic, he saw her attending a few of his Masses then leave hurriedly before the service had concluded. He was afraid she had not quite accepted the fact he had entered the Church, and also afraid she might rekindle feelings he had long since conquered. Grabbing his briefcase Peter quickly exited the building and made his way to the car. Better not hang around, he thought. Nevertheless, painful images of a difficult period in his life that had remained buried rose to the surface frequently these days and continued to churn, they could never be forgotten.

He knew from an early age he was not meant to live a 'normal' life, if anything could ever be called normal, but he had always sensed the Church had been his calling. Unfortunately, he did not follow the interior summons right away, giving in to a number of wavering uncertainties. The first being his total unworthiness for the office. It was one thing to be a simple believer and live the faith, it was another matter when one assumed the dignity of the priesthood. He would be representing Christ on earth, and therefore, would be called upon to set the most perfect example possible of a sanctified life. The responsibility was mighty. Saints were known to run when asked to become a priest or bishop, even St. Ambrose had to be dragged kicking and screaming to the cathedral of Milan to be appointed to that episcopal see.

When Peter had finally conquered his apprehension regarding this august reality, there was the fear of displeasing his father, hoping and waiting that the right time would come to gradually let the family know what he was being called to do. However, as with most people who wait for the perfect moment to come in an imperfect world, it never seemed to arrive. Something or other would keep him back just that bit longer, a crisis in the firm or ill timed news would be given to the family that pushed that right moment farther away. Knowing without a doubt what he wanted to do, the thought of ever having a girlfriend or musing what it might be like to be married was kept pinned to the background and hardly thought about to the point his solitary life worried his conservative family from another aspect: that he might be a silent supporter of the rainbow parades.

Then, Mrs. Clarke came. Back in those days, she was Miss Lucinda Andrews. Although she was very attractive, Peter honestly did not hire her for that reason, he needed someone, a personal aid who did not mind assuming some of the basic secretarial duties when needed, which would prove to be demanding work this high up in the managerial chain, and according to her résumé, she had the skills and experience. Job hunting was difficult at the best of times, and with all the competition out there he knew he should not trust everything set in a CV, but of all the applicants, her references were top notch. Whatever skills she did fib about he had to allow a learning curve for her to catch up. Little did he know how much he would also learn about himself in the process. From the beginning, he sensed she was attracted to him, but decided not to pay too much attention to it, quietly maintaining a respectful distance between them as befitting a boss and his employee. It did not escape him he had always been deemed highly desirable by the fair gender, and not just for his family and elite connections. On more than one occasion he was paid unwanted flirtatious attentions by some forward women who perhaps hoped to gain more than his friendship. It became an unbearable burden to him, particularly when he tried to concentrate on his plans and decide when to put them into action. Little did he suspect that the tables would be turned after all this time and discover that the repression of feelings did not mean they could ever be eradicated. He was human, not an emotionless block of stone as his first name might suggest. Lucinda was more than just attractive. Fair complexioned, conscientious, she was quite beautiful and her smile soon acquired the power to transfix him to the spot. Several months working together and late nights pouring over troublesome paperwork now and then allowed them too much time together, that stiff boundary he had set was softening as they talked about their families and gradually shared personal details in casual conversation. Nothing had ever happened between them, but eventually, Gerry innocently showed him the dangerous situation he was in.

"Come on Pete, are you ever going to do it," his younger brother blurted out unexpectedly over dinner at his apartment.

"Do what?"

"Ask her out. It's obvious you two like each other. Who cares if she is the secretary? At this point, I don't think even Pater and Mater would mind. They're afraid you might remain a confirmed bachelor, or worse. You know how they want grandkids."

"And what about you? That goes for you too you know," he tried to joke back to his younger brother who had several girlfriends over the last few years yet was still unable to find 'the perfect one'. However, Peter was no longer in the mood for jovialities, Ger made him see he might have deeper feelings for Lucinda than he was willing to admit, and he could not allow these feelings to go unchecked. He must steel his resolve. He would have to make a break soon, tell everyone what his plans were, but Ger's comment on what their parents hoped and expected of him also made it difficult, becoming a priest meant becoming a bachelor in another sense and he dreaded to drop this bombshell on them, silently berating himself for his glaring weaknesses. It was not easy being the eldest with all the hopes of the older generation placed on his shoulders, he had a strict sense of duty, but where did it lie any more? No, he knew very well. God's will had to come first over his parents, and if he truly wanted to become a priest, he had to regain his spiritual life and make the break soon, but when? He could not bring himself to set a time just yet, however, the first thing he had to do was resume his old stance between employer and employee, crush any feelings he might have for her, nor let her entertain any false hopes. From that point, he barely replied when she spoke to him, quickly gave instructions when needed, and the most difficult of all, avoided making eye contact if possible. He had read that certain saints never raised their eyes when in the presence of a woman. Although it was not her fault, he must consider her beauty at this point a dangerous snare for him, and he could not let himself be tempted again. If only he was called to the married life and all that it offered he could have followed Gerry's advice, but it was not for him.

Those few weeks he put this resolution into practise were difficult. The Church taught that God never tested anyone beyond their strength, but sometimes he could not help wondering if he might be the exception to the rule. He could sense the hurt he was causing her with his sudden change in attitude and behaviour, each polite but curt rebuff, every small deliberate snub. Yet, he could not allow himself to show remorse, all sympathy, all emotion had to be caged within him. The simple solution would be to fire her, but that would be terribly unjust, she really was an excellent worker and he would never fire anyone simply because of his own personal struggles. On the other hand, it was a wonder she did not quit, not that he intentionally set out to accomplish that either. He would be leaving soon, there was no reason she should not keep her job. The former boundary between them just needed to be re-established for the brief length of time he intended to stay. When spring arrived he would tell the family what he planned and it would all be out in the open at last … .

However, Lucinda eventually requested to see him privately in his office and simply asked what she had done to offend him: if her work was not up to par, or she had done something wrong, if he would tell her, she would try harder … . No, it wasn't that, he admitted.

"I'm sorry if I speak out of turn, but everything seems changed between us somehow, either I've given offence somewhere, or … ."

"No, it's just … *us*. It won't work, *personally*, I mean."

"Oh." She was silent for a moment. "Figures. It wouldn't be the first time. All the men I meet are unavailable for one reason or another. If you don't mind me asking, it's true then? The closet door is shut?"

He was tempted to let her believe that false assumption, but that would have been a deception and he had to admit the truth.

"There's no closet." Well, not that kind.

"Then what's happened," she asked with concern. "I was under the distinct impression we had … feelings for each other, and now, nothing?"

"I'm sorry, but … ."

"I'm not good enough, that's it. A secretary would never be accepted by your family."

He sighed. That might have been an issue if he could allow anything to develop between them. There was nothing for it. He had to nip this in the bud.

"That's not quite … listen," he continued gently, "I'd rather not go into the details, not just now, but let's say I don't plan on being here much longer … ."

"What! Oh God, you're dying, *that's* it," she exclaimed.

"No, that's not what … well, not exactly, but something close to it," he trailed, trying to find the right words. He wasn't lying, he would be dying to the world and all its pomp as the saints used to say. He certainly felt like he was dying that moment.

"'Something close to it'," she returned quizzically. "Please no riddles or games, not with something this serious. If you have anything to say, please, just tell me."

"I'm leaving the business and I'm entering the Church."

There, it was finally disclosed, not to his family first as he would have wished, but there was nothing he could do about it now. There was stunned silence. Sitting down in the chair in front of his desk, she tried to let this information sink in.

"Are you serious?"

It must have sounded like some cruel joke to her, but he returned her incredulous expression with a firm adamantine glance, impressing upon her the sincerity of his solemn intentions.

"You *are* serious. How … how long have you been considering this?"

"For quite a long time, several years in fact, but honestly, you're the first person I've ever told about this, my family doesn't know, not even my brother."

"I suppose I should take it as an honour then," she noted bitterly after another prolonged period of silence. "Like I said, unavailable men always seem to pluck my heartstrings."

"Lucinda, I'm sorry, but I cannot allow myself to get attached to anyone."

"You don't have to explain, I quite understand now," she interrupted, quickly wiping the corner of her eyes as she stood up. "You wouldn't mind if I took the next few days off?"

Peter just shook his head to signify he did not mind, her request was granted and she left his office. It was done. He knew it was the right thing to do, but why did doing the right thing have to hurt so much? He buried himself in his work while she was gone, and when she did come back, the cool professional distance that once existed between them was re-established. A week went by almost as if nothing had happened between them, time to start thinking about making arrangements Peter noted, he had put them off for far too long. To a point, he had worked out plans on putting his financial affairs in order. All his inheritance from his grandparents, both his father and mother's sides, would be given to Gerry and Lottie, that time honoured legacy belonged to the family and it was only just to give it back to the next heirs. He felt he had done nothing to earn it, and besides, he knew it would be used well. Gerry did have several benevolent projects he liked to contribute towards. Lottie needed to find her feet yet, but knew she would use it wisely too in the end. His own fortune that he earned while working for the family business would be used for his theology courses and living expenses while attending the seminary, he planned to make Gerry the executor of this area so he could be free from all monetary ties. He and Gerry were close and he knew he could trust him. After that, whatever was left would be given to the Church and the poor. As to where he fit within the Church, when he knew what would happen next, he could break the news to his family. He called the archbishop's office and was scheduled for an appointment to discuss his options. Was he inclined to be a diocesan priest, or perhaps become a member of an order? He found the last idea appealing for some reason, maybe it was his spiritual intuition telling him what to do, but at the same time, he felt a pull towards becoming an exorcist. He might have to become a diocesan priest for that ministry. However, he would discuss everything first with the ecclesial authorities to help him discern his vocation and hear their suggestions. It was a daunting prospect, heading off on a completely new path in life, leaving everything he knew behind. The next difficult duty to perform would be to tell his parents and finally settled on a night to make his announcement.

When the day arrived, he could get little work done, distracted with thoughts on how they would react, little suspecting another difficult trial was to confront him—Lucinda *would* have to have one last private word in his office.

"Fire me if you like, but I have to say it. I *know* I could make you happy," she pleaded.

"Please, don't make this any more difficult … ."

"But I know I could! Please give me a chance, give *us* a chance! I can't believe you have made up your mind, not really … ."

That strong feeling of empathy took over, he could interiorly feel what she wanted, a happy home, a happy family, and with *him*. In truth, it was a beautiful compliment to be chosen by someone and loved that deeply, but there was another path he must follow: he had already been chosen by Another who loved him even more and his true spiritual heart had been given long ago. Yes, he had made up his mind, and she could sense it. His spirit was overwhelmed with her agony that this might all be slipping away from her.

"You will be married, have the children you've always wanted, but not with me," he said gently, but firmly. "There is someone out there for you, I'm not the one."

"Please don't say that," she replied, her voice shaking, but finally she broke into sobs. They had been standing in the middle of the room. Unnerved by her outpouring of grief, he impulsively held her firmly by the shoulders in attempt to calm her, make her see reason.

"Lucinda, I must. There can be no future for us."

"Oh, you're *wrong*," she insisted desperately, and before he could pull away, she clasped his face and drew him into a prolonged kiss.

Startled in those first few split seconds, his strength gave way, how good it was to be this close to her at last. He felt his resolve crumble and succumbed to the experience. He was tired of the struggle, so tired, sinking into the beauty of that intimate contact was an unanticipated relief. Why torment yourself? Why throw everything away? Just give it up … you could stay, be happy with her … Maybe he had been wrong? Was he throwing everything away? This felt so right … .

The agony of Christ flashed across his soul.

Father, if it be possible let this cup pass! But not as I will … .

Shocked from the enticements pulling him down, Peter broke away, stunned with the waking image that came and disappeared like lightning. His left arm began to twinge with pain, he quickly clutched it with remorse. It was not the symptom of a heart attack, but it might as well have been, an old wound that no one knew about and had branded him for life. Horrified and ashamed at himself, he tore the office door open and bolted. He was hardly conscious of the fact he nearly knocked Gerry over as he was heading his way to ask for the latest updates on the shipping consignments from Brazil. He needed help, and there was only one place where he knew he would find it.

For hours he knelt in a pew at St. Patrick's. Unable to make the usual vocal prayers, he placed himself in the closest pew before the altar, silently pleading for assistance. He knew what was coming, tonight would be one of the hardest things he ever had to do, breaking the news to everyone else, but now he had to come to terms with the added complexity of having feelings for someone, reproving himself for allowing it to go on while simultaneously battling with that *other* seditious voice undermining his conscience, that tempter lurking underneath recalling to his mind and senses that unexpected, intoxicating moment. Would he be strong enough to go ahead with his vocation now that he had been burned? He had handled everything badly. If he had done something much sooner, this never would have happened … .

"Are ye all right? Peter, isn't it?"

Peter looked up, startled to see an old friendly face he had not seen since his school days, Fr. O'Conner, a spry Irishman with pale blue eyes, his auburn hair now silver with age. The last he heard of him he had been transferred to Wisconsin.

"Ah sure, I thought it was you. I never forget a face, you never missed serving my Masses at the school. It's been a long time. My, laddie, you're looking poorly. What's happened?"

An angel of mercy had been sent. All the boys at the school trusted Fr. O'Conner, he always could inspire confidence in the doubtful with his whimsical observations and easy air. Nothing was too big or too tragic that could not be overcome. As his old mentor settled his weight beside him in the pew, Peter quietly laid bare all his anxieties, guilt and failures.

"Oh laddie, buck up. Why are ye struggling against the hook? Can't you see that the Almighty has ye by the gills and is not going to let ye go? You'd better act now, and I mean *anish*."

"I know, but after what happened today … I wonder if God still wants me that badly."

"Of course He does. Yes, family life is beautiful too, but when you've been called to something else, it's better to follow the summons. I know, 'tis not easy. The Almighty never promised a calm voyage through life, only a safe harbour in the end."

"True. I'm afraid I'll regret becoming a priest now, eventhough I'm convinced I have a vocation. I'm afraid I'll fail as a priest, always wonder … what might have been if I had stayed."

"Well now, God always brings something good out of a shock'n situation. Yes, you should have cut ties much sooner, but now you know what 'tis like to be tested to the limit. Christ did not leave His Church in the hands of angels, their perfection would drive sinful yokels like us into despair. He left it to weak men for good reason. If I remember, your namesake had a pretty difficult time of things too. When you become a priest, and you will," Fr. O'Conner affirmed, "you'll never judge another weak soul that will come to you for help. You must be a very understanding sort of man when you get into them things," he said, nodding over to the confessionals. "The sores of humanity will be opened to you every day, and you must never weary of healing and forgiving. Let's say now you're better prepared to serve."

Peter reflected on this observation.

"Ah, that pretty, was she, my lad?"

"Better to have loved and lost, right Father," Peter replied quietly.

"Not lost, *sacrificed*. I know, 'tis a big thing the Lord is ask'n of you, but I'll never forget what Sr. Roberta said when you were in school, 'You will have a bride, but not one in human form. She will be much greater'," he reminded him, looking around the cathedral. "You always were meant for this, you're going to make a grand priest."

Despite the furore that happened that night when Peter broke the news at Stonyvale, Fr. O'Conner proved to be the wiser of the two and he never regretted his choice. Of course there were difficult times, his 'bride' could be pretty demanding, but he did love her deeply and he always felt completely fulfilled. However, he never expected the set of challenges now set before him, to be thrust back into the old surroundings at Reinold Enterprises, the old temptations—no, he need not fear, he was a different person, much stronger now. What happened in that office would never happen again. He should not rehash thorny memories he continued to tell himself on his way back to the rectory. What was past, was past. He had to get ready for dinner with their Eminences. A quick shower and a change of cassock after the long day would feel good right now.

He wished he didn't have to go out tonight. As he went up the rectory stairs, he could hear the voices in the common room, his fellow pastors enjoying some community time together before dinner. The door was left ajar, he could hear Fr. Mark relaying his mishap at the hospital that day to the others. He had been sent to the wrong room and frightened a patient into thinking he was being prepared to meet his Maker when he was only staying overnight for medical observation having bumped his noggin on a shelf at home. What made it worse, the patient replied if his time had come, surely it was a rabbi that should have been sent to him? The poor bloke wasn't even Christian! The room detonated with another round of laughter. Ah Mark, how you keep forgetting what I told you! Don't rely on the nurses to keep track of the *spiritual* patients, always verify who's in the bed. Peter chuckled to himself. Mark, oh Mark, so eager to serve, but forever getting into a jam. Feeling better after a quick shower, he came down just as they were heading to the dining room.

"Ah, there you are, lad," Fr. O' Conner greeted. "Not going out again are you?"

"Yes, dinner with the superiors."

"That's right," Fr. Mark remembered. "Don't look so worried, it sounds like you may be promoted again."

"If not, look at it this way, at least you won't be subjected to Fred's cooking tonight," Fr. Jenkins noted with a big grin. One of the visiting seminarians from Africa insisted on helping with the dinners, unintentionally inflicting additional penance on them all long after the Lenten season had passed. They had no idea what national dish he would introduce to them next, the smells wafting from the kitchen were not very promising.

"Shh, you know the lad means well," Fr. O' Conner reminded him, but he too was not looking forward to their evening meal. "Just offer it up. God help us, I hope we have enough antacid to tide us over 'til the morning."

"Someone better put that on the shopping list," Fr. Mark added.

"Hey, don't let us hold you up, you don't want to keep them waiting," Fr. Jenkins replied.

"See you later then."

Back in the car, Peter headed in the direction of the Archbishop's residence, hoping they would not make it an extended occasion. The housekeeper greeted him at the door and took his coat.

"Good evening, Monsignor. They're waiting for you in the front parlour. Dinner will be served shortly."

"Thank you, Clare. So, how does it fare this evening? Is this a night of breaking bread, or is the Inquisition settling in to give me a good roast?"

"Ha ha! If they don't, I've got a nice lamb roast on, which is certainly better! But seriously, it's rather starchy tonight with another archbishop present, but they're having a laugh or two, so, I'd say, so-so. It's doesn't look like you're in any hot water."

"Thanks. You're a dear." Bless her heart, Clare was always on the look out for him, afraid he might receive the ire of His Eminence with some of the odd and unexpected pastoral care he gave to his parishioners and penitents on occasion.

"Forgive me, but I've got to check on the oven, or you're all getting charcoal for supper. Look lively now! You know how he is." Clare laughed as she returned to her duties, leaving him go. He had been to the Archbishop's residence enough times to be allowed the liberty of finding his way to the designated room whenever he was invited over. Knocking on the door, he found their Eminences partaking of a libation while they waited. They stood up as he entered.

"Good evening, Pete," Archbishop Foley greeted, shaking his hand. "I'm glad you could make it, knowing how busy you are these days. Kenneth, I believe you've already met Monsignor Reinold," he noted, turning to Archbishop Morrison.

"Yes, quite a few times in Rome, and also on this side of the pond," he replied, shaking him by the hand. "It's good to see you again. How is your family, and of course, your brother?"

"They're all holding up as well as can be expected."

"Naturally, it was a terrible thing to have happened, and to the Walsinghams too for that matter, the wedding having to be put off and all."

"It's a tragedy," Peter agreed, "but hopefully next year might be better, God willing."

"Let's hope so." Archbishop Foley nodded. "Would you like a drink? Scotch perhaps?"

Peter rarely drank these days, but accepted the scotch and sat down with them, engaging in casual conversation before it was time to go to the dining room. Morrison fondly recalled his time in Rome, Peter too could enjoy the reminiscing, having studied and received his ordination there. He had always loved visiting the grand ancient metropolis on his business trips, but as a seminarian, had enjoyed the luxury of completely concentrating on the spiritual life, visiting the famous shrines, churches and the catacombs between lectures. He had met Morrison one day at the chapel of the British

College where he had received special permission to offer his first Mass on the famous altar dating from Elizabethan times, a butcher's block, a gruesome *momento mori* reminding the newly ordained English missionaries what was facing them when they returned to their blood drenched isle. He was teased by his new friends at the North American College, about how their chapel was not good enough for him, but he needed that reminder just as the English seminarians of old. The chopping block was not confined to one era, nor one form or country. There were many types of martyrdoms, spiritual as well as physical ones; visible and invisible, the block took on many forms and could be encountered anywhere, any time.

"So, James tells me you are saying the Tridentine Rite these days."

Peter's mind snapped back to the present.

"Yes, I'm grateful for his permission. His Holiness wanted more priests to say the Latin Mass."

"Of course, of course." Archbishop Morrison nodded edgily. Peter could tell his Eminence still preferred the vernacular rite and all the supposed reformations that were to bring the Church into the modern age. Observing the old ways was often a cause of disagreement among the clergy. There were many who viewed those who clung to tradition as obstinate recusants refusing to part with an 'obsolete' past eventhough the old ways continued to be lawfully permitted by the Vatican. He decided to tread carefully.

"It keeps one part of the congregation quiet. Good thing Pete's willing to do it," Archbishop Foley replied with a civil laugh, attempting to keep the conversation on an even keel. Clare knocked on the door. "I believe dinner is served. Shall we," he noted, rising from his chair.

As usual, Clare outdid herself whenever his Eminence had company, but this time went to considerable trouble having set out the best linens, china, silverware and Waterford crystal. Raised to be the perfect cultured gentleman accustomed to these opulent settings Peter nevertheless reflected on life at the old rectory with its motley assortment of dented and outdated furniture donated by parishioners over the years, the mismatched place settings and chipped tableware that would occur over an epoch of breakage and odd replacements, not to mention the faded carpets and conflicting wallpaper that had seen better days, jumbled décor that would be found in a house with a bunch of bachelors living on parish stipends who had hardly time to worry about the aesthetic coordination of their surroundings. There was peace and contentment with his brother priests, no longer did he have to live with the rigid formality associated with his past life. While he did appreciate the occasional perks that came his way, he could let them go with serene detachment. All he really needed now was a roof, a bed, and something edible once in awhile. Sometimes that last part was sketchy depending who was doing the cooking, but he was still quite content.

Dinner passed pleasantly, discussions of the latest developments and projects in their respective parishes, including the recent funerals that Peter had officiated, before musing on the latest news from Rome such as the Pope's upcoming papal visit to Denver for World Youth Day and other world events which took up most of the conversation. The dessert dishes cleared, Archbishop Foley invited his guests back to the parlour for a brandy. Talk had circled around to parish work again, and the thread was resumed as they sat back in their armchairs.

"I suppose we should get to the subject of why we're gathered here tonight," his Eminence began.

"Yes, I think so," Archbishop Morrison agreed. "I have come to ask James a special favour, which involves you, if you're willing that is."

"I see," Peter replied calmly. He was right, he had guessed something was heading in his direction. Oh Lord, not another promotion, and please, I'd much prefer parish work. *But not as I will … .*

"Don't worry Pete, this isn't what you think," the Archbishop noted with amusement. "I don't think he's forgiven me since I gave him that title," he clarified to his peer.

"Ah, no honours, is that it, son?" Morrison turned to Peter. "Don't let it bother you. From what I hear, you deserve it."

As he feared: the rumours of his discernment were spreading far, singling him out.

"I wouldn't say that."

"No false modesty now, I hear the cathedral is receiving record attendance for confessions, and I need not mention single-handedly bringing the Walsinghams' daughter into the Church. That could not have been easy, considering how her family are strict Episcopalians. My hand to you."

"I really didn't have too much to do with that," Peter replied a little discomfited, he would never force anyone. While the Church was often referred to as a ship in mystical allegory, it was not supposed to be an unscrupulous navy shanghaiing passengers and crew. It was a Kingdom with open citizenship for anyone wishing to enter. Katherine had come of her own free will, it just happened that he was the only spiritual director she knew, one to whom she could frankly ask questions about their beliefs at length without fear of offending. How he disliked the Church discussed as though it were a business with a recruitment centre, with him portrayed as top headhunter.

"I beg to differ, but of course, you will be her brother-in-law shortly, so naturally she would turn to you," Foley noted. "It certainly *would* be an accomplishment though if any of her family followed her example, fine pillars of the community I hear."

"Yes, quite so," Morrison agreed, "you do know they frequently donate to the Catholic Relief fund."

"So you told me." He nodded. "But forgive us Pete, again we've wandered from the matter at hand. To get to the point, Kenneth has asked to enlist your services as an exorcist."

"Oh?"

"Actually, nothing too involved. I just require your opinion on a case," Archbishop Morrison clarified.

"Of course. Only, I thought that Father Xavier was your diocesan exorcist," Peter reflected., "I can't help but be surprised you would need my opinion."

"Well, this is not my idea," Morrison admitted, looking a little irked. "Father Xavier has reviewed this case and is convinced it's a matter of mental disturbance, but the family of the patient refuses to stop pestering my office. They fully believe their relative is suffering from a diabolical attack. They're demanding a second opinion."

"I see. Very well. Then I assume Father Xavier did not perform the Major Rite."

"Correct, and I will not allow it to be performed until I can be certain that there is an absolute need for it. You know how these things are looked down upon, the Church is already seen as a backward relic to begin with, while a number of its ceremonies, especially exorcism, is considered a vestige of a superstitious past. We must avoid putting out that negative image as much as possible."

Peter pursed his lips and studied the contents of his glass. It was the classic impediment to discerning a true diabolical possession as opposed to mental illness. The devil and his minions were shrewd, crafty enemies. They could mimic diseases of all kinds, hide behind them undetected and torment the afflicted for years. It took someone with a keen eye and a highly developed sense of their own soul as well as the spiritual world to discern the real from bogus mental illnesses and call a halt to this malicious siege, usually because the demons would not blow their cover unless provoked with something very powerful. The Major Rite was one sure proof as the spirits would be forced to answer and give their names, but until it was ascertained there was a case of demonic activity to begin with, exorcists were not given permission to perform it, bound by the virtue of obedience to their ecclesial superiors. The demons knew this very well and took full advantage of the Church's reluctance to use that 'backward' rite. Hell was working furiously to maintain this intolerant and condescending perception of exorcism, sometimes it sounded to Peter's interior ears of the soul as if the Enemy was laughing sadistically at his frustration with this deadlock.

"All right, well, it might help if I knew what he did do, and of course, any details on the person who is suffering from these disturbances."

"Allow me," said Foley. "I left the case file in the study. No don't get up, no ceremony, I'll be back in a minute." He placed his glass down and exiting the room. Morrison took the opportunity to engage in polite conversation.

"I appreciate this, Peter. You know, it still amazes me that you chose this particular apostolate in the Church. You could have had your pick of the enviable positions, and yet James tells me you insist on exorcist work."

"No one else seemed willing to do it."

"I wonder why," the Archbishop wryly commented. "Tell me, Pete, may I call you Pete? Any interesting episodes in your chosen career since you were appointed?"

Despite the prevailing scepticism concerning exorcism, human curiosity always prevailed. Peter did have some strange experiences with house clearings, but he was not about to open a can of worms and stuck to the issue at hand.

"If you mean a serious demonic possession case with a person, no not really. Mostly people who were suffering from depression, and two major schizophrenic cases, things of that nature, people needing deliverance prayers, nothing that would require the Major Rite."

"I see, so, you would be able to confirm Fr. Xavier's assessment."

"Yes, and also if the opposite is true, if it is as the family of the victim suspects."

"Oh come now, it's all a matter of mental disturbance, pure and simple. We know exorcism is only a help for those afflicted to help them come to terms with their illness, make them believe something dark within them has been driven away so they can move on with the healing process."

"I respectfully beg to differ," Peter said guardedly. "It just happens that diagnosing a veritable possession is a rare occurrence."

"Well, as you're the man who's doing the fieldwork, I won't argue. James tells me you have spent some time with Father Amaranth. I suppose he's showed you his famous jar collection." His Eminence snickered slightly.

Yes, that famous jar collection. How eagerly Fr. Amaranth would show to anyone willing to listen to his disturbing assortment of objects disgorged by the possessed during his exorcisms over the years: innumerable nails of all shapes and sizes, shards of broken glass, handfuls of marbles and other sundry items in the hope people would wake up to the necessity of his ministry. Instead, it opened the old priest to more ridicule by the incredulous, but he refused to give up. Yes, Peter had seen those jars, but mercifully he was spared having to answer as his superior made his way back.

"Did I miss anything," Archbishop Foley enquired, manilla file in hand.

"I was just remarking that Peter had studied with the head exorcist of Rome," Archbishop Morrison recapitulated.

"That he did. Peter here is very interested in doing this. I told him if he really wanted something to challenge him that badly, he could help out with the prison ministry, but no, he says this is what he's meant to do. Here you are, it's not a pretty picture," Foley concluded, handing him the dossier before sitting down and sipping his brandy.

Peter set down his glass and opened the file. His eyes were first confronted with the dead, expressionless features of a brown haired girl in her mid twenties, her photograph clipped to the right hand corner of the general psychiatric evaluation that had been given to her family. Her lips pursed, face gaunt and blanched, dark brown eyes glowering and devoid of light; this girl, Melissa Yardley, had been through horrific traumas. He did not have time to read everything right then and quickly glanced through the first page written by her relatives relating her personal details; she ran away from home to escape an abusive stepfather and went to live with them, a maternal uncle and his wife. However, she grew rebellious, eventually ran away from home again. Her aunt and uncle reported her missing and did not know what had happened to her for several years until she had been brought in to a hospital. She had made her way to New York, fallen in with the wrong crowd, they could only assume the worst, drugs and a promiscuous lifestyle, but no one could know for sure, she was suffering from what the clinical reports described as severe psychotic delusions and hallucinations, proving to be a danger to herself and others. Multiple scars on her arms indicated she was self-harming, not to mention other signs telling of her suicidal tendencies.

These were only the physical signs, the outward appearances. Many people suffered from psychological traumas and were not possessed. However, his soul, recoiling from the mere touch of the dossier, told him more than mere printed words and a glossy photograph could. It was similar to the feeling he experienced when handling a cursed object. His spirit could feel an evil emanating from the file as though it harboured a malevolent entity. Thankfully, up to now it was a rare occasion when he felt something like this. He was instantly reminded of one extreme case concerning a house clearing when he had been drawn to an old antique table, not in appreciative attraction for the beautiful woodwork, but as though he were a soldier scouting out a field of battle and from the corner of his eye could see through the enemy's camouflage. He eyed the piece warily, then calmly made the sign of the cross with holy water. The table abruptly cracked as if exposed to intense heat and a muffled thumping resounded over his head as if something invisible was trying to fly and escape, frightening the owner of the house. Peter instantly knew what was wrong, the table had been used for séances, ouija sessions, tarot card readings and quite possibly, black spells. No longer used for these purposes, it was still a portal bringing evil to the next generation that owned it. His advice: burn the thing, then, a total clearing would be needed to ensure any vestiges of its presence in the house were dispelled. He would say the Minor Rite of deliverance, bless the house, then say Mass in the room where the table had been. The owner protested at first, but eventually did as he suggested and allowed him to carry out the necessary rites, and the dark feelings that were felt on the premises left immediately once that was done. Peter could feel this girl was suffering from a similar attack, but much blacker, a demonic Hell-chain held her in a vice grip and would torment her for the rest of her life unless she could be released, it would drag her to the abyss if possible. God help her, how did she get tangled up in such a mess? He would not be able to tell for certain until her free will had been restored to a point and she was at liberty to confide in him, or the demon be forced to answer.

How could Fr. Xavier not see what was lurking within? Of course, Peter had to remind himself that not everyone could feel situations or pierce through them with their interior eye as he could. Still, even if the majority of priests were not granted discernment this markedly, a certain level of this spiritual skill could be acquired by detachment from the world, a constant and diligent prayer life plus careful observation. The difficulty nowadays people were too busy to be aware of the importance of nourishing a spiritual life and the true existence of Hell and Heaven. Prayer life and going to

Mass on Sunday, activities with designated time slots and forgotten once completed. It was very easy for them to miss the tangible presence of Hell despite the turmoil in the world confirming its existence. Hmm, just what *did* Fr. Xavier do?

Peter looked through the papers for Fr. Xavier's assessment and found very little to go on. His ecclesial colleague saw nothing that warranted an exorcism. All he witnessed were supposed hallucinations and at other times delusions of persecution. What looked like personality changes and the victim fighting off unseen presences were only figments of a disordered mind he concluded. While he visited her, the girl did nothing of the preternatural, such as speak in an unfamiliar or ancient language, nor disclose knowledge unknown to her. Obviously, the more pronounced supernatural occurrences didn't happen at the time Peter surmised, such as levitation of the victim or objects around her. No, the demon is too smart in this case, he's not about to show his hand that quickly. He had the distinct impression this was not one of the lesser minions at work, something knowledgeable and high up in the demonic hierarchy was calling the shots here. Peter could not help but feel disappointed with Fr. Xavier, he should have known better, but then, so many priests were not properly trained for this particular ministry in the Church, even in Rome the training for exorcism was sketchy at best. If it wasn't for 'the gift' and his own careful study of the matter over the years, Peter felt he too might have been stuck out on left field. He hoped it was just a case of inexperience on Fr. Xavier's part. At least Peter could tell instantly when something was wrong, but sometimes 'the gift' was a horrific burden, he often felt weighed down by the knowledge he received.

To make matters more complicated, Peter could not tell their Eminences right there and then what he sensed, that they had a true case of possession on their hands. His spiritual premonitions were not enough to begin the Major Rite. Documented evidence with witnesses would be needed to convince them, plus a consent form signed by the possessed once permission was granted, and in any case, he dare not mention this ability to read spiritual situations. There were those in the Church who dreaded any sign of the mystical supernatural working through one of their own. If there was not outright jealousy, there was complete disbelief to the point of ridicule and persecution. Right now, he had to keep this quiet, address the situation in a round about way if he hoped to help this girl.

"So, what do you think," Archbishop Foley enquired after a minute.

"Judging from these reports, I can see why Fr. Xavier considered this was nothing more than a mental breakdown, but I would need to see her in person to make a full assessment, and it might take a few meetings, just to be absolutely certain," Peter noted.

"Of course, James says you're always thorough, which is good for me, but I wouldn't mind getting this sorted as soon as possible," Archbishop Morrison replied.

"All right, but you don't mind if I probe a little deeper into this case? That is, that I have your full permission to do what is necessary to get some answers?"

"Er, of course, you have my full permission to probe on my pastoral turf, if that's what you need to hear," Morrison noted with some amusement. He had heard Monsignor Reinold was a stickler for certain details all right, but did he need his permission for that too? Peter ignored the bantering tone, he had what he needed. He didn't mind if getting the job done right made him an annoying pain in the neck. At least he had developed a tough hide in the corporate world, it did have some advantages after all.

"Very well then. Sundays I'm basically free, after my morning parish duties of course. I could see her beginning this weekend."

"Whenever you're free to do this, I'd be grateful."

"That's settled then, we can arrange everything with the girl's family tomorrow. More brandy," Archbishop Foley offered, glad the necessary unpleasantries of the night were over. Peter declined the top up as he had to drive home.

Presently, the evening came to a close and the Archbishop apologized for keeping them up late considering they had an early morning ahead of them. Peter took the case file with him to study in his own time and slid it into his black curate case that he left in the trunk of the car before he drove back to the rectory. He had to make sure that no one else would read the file, not just because Miss Yardley's general psychiatric evaluation was included, simply an act of charity. Unless permitted to be released by the victims and their families, the names of those requiring exorcisms were to be kept confidential by the Church to ensure that once they were set free from their tormentors they did not receive torturers in human form. What would be the point in helping someone only to have everyone single them out as a freak? The victim would be a source of gossip and sin to others, nor would they ever be able to get on with their life and have any peace. That is, if a priest was allowed to help them in the first place. Prejudice against the rite of exorcism was a terrible obstacle, not to mention the distressing lack of faith with numbers of the clergy who entertained the ludicrous notion that demons and possessions were delusions of the medieval period.

It pained Peter to see that even the highest authorities in the Church remained blindly indifferent to the Gospels, that Christ cast out demons as well as healed the sick, they were separate miraculous actions and pointedly recorded as such by the Evangelists. There was an alarming unspoken mandate operating within the Church in these desperate times: you may preach about love, forgiveness, prayer to heal the sick, helping the poor, the usual happy feel-good subjects, let us be motivators, but do not mention Hell, damnation or devils please, thank you very much. That will not keep the offertory baskets filled. What a dangerous principle Peter often mused, to teach the Good News without explaining the Bad News that must be conquered. It is no different than if generals lauded the honours and medals that could be won in victorious combat without preparing their cadets how to fight or refused to teach them their enemies' tactics because war is disagreeable. That was not good enough for him, a responsible general or captain had to know his enemy and prepare the troops. Peter had no qualms about giving rousing fire and brimstone sermons when necessary considering he would one day answer to God for the souls placed in his care.

It was good to call it a night, never before did the stairs up to the bedrooms look so inviting. By now, the rectory was quiet except for the muffled sounds of the television coming from the community room, someone was still up. Peter opened the door an inch to see Fr. O'Conner fast asleep in an armchair. Obviously, he had waited up for him. He turned off the old set and gently shook the slumbering man's arm.

"Don't mind me, I was just restin' my eyes." He stretched the stiffness away. "So, how did it go? When do you get your crosier?"

"Not ever, I hope." Peter smiled. "I don't think I'd make a good bishop, not according to today's standards, or lack thereof."

"Nonsense, lad. You're a natural leader, we could use men with some backbone. Tell me, how did the evening go? They're not transferring you, are they?"

"No, I've been given a mercy mission in fact."

"Oh? On top of all the extra work you have? Care to share, or is it confidential?"

"All I can say is I've been asked to assess a mental patient in Archbishop Morrison's area and see if there is cause to begin an exorcism."

"You don't say? Sounds mighty serious, judging from your expression. You feel you have a real one on your hands this time," he noted quietly, meeting Peter's eyes directly. He didn't have to say anything, Fr. O'Conner understood much, one of the few who did without necessarily having the gift of infused discernment himself. "I know you wanted this ministry, but sorry lad, I can't say I congratulate you," he then added, "if it were me, I'd dread what I might find. Come, let's off to bed, you'll need all the forty winks you can get."

ᘓ❖ᘔ

Sunday morning arrived, and as usual Peter was first out of the rectory. His weekday Latin Masses had been designated the early bird slot in the cathedral roster, while on the Lord's Day of rest he was given the 'Crack of Dawn' time to ensure the vernacular services were rendered more convenient. Peter didn't mind, it was a sacrifice he could offer up, and the fact he was in the cathedral early gave him some extra time to pray in solitude before penitents arrived for confessions. Although it was difficult, he was glad to see many people also made the extra effort to attend his services.

However, this morning began with an added annoyance. Contrary to all experience with the old beat up run-about that guzzled more oil than gasoline, the heating was working. While Peter appreciated this turn of events, early May mornings were still chilly, it soon grew stifling hot, even with the AC switch turned to icy blue. He banged on the dashboard of the 'Old Buzzard' with one free hand, and when that universal cure-all for mechanical problems did not work, he rolled down the windows for air as he drove to the cathedral. From Siberia to the Sahara, it was either a feast or a famine. He hoped the sudden change in temperature would not cause him to get a spring cold, he couldn't fall ill now, not with his schedule. He did not have the luxury to take to a sick bed.

Despite his car woes, he made it to the cathedral and prepared as he usually did. After praying for guidance before the altar for the duties that lay ahead of him that day, he entered his designated confessional while the building was still devoid of worshippers and appeared to slumber, the soft lighting directed on the tabernacle and the flames of the candles in their stained glass stands flickering before their respective saints, sending out a comforting glow in the dim surroundings of the vaulted edifice. Peter took advantage of the last few minutes of stillness for meditation before his first penitents arrived, he enjoyed these moments of peace, they came so seldom lately. As though waking from the most beautiful dream feeling absolute

85

contentment and wishing he could sleep on, these quiet moments in the presence of God both in church and in his spirit were difficult to let go, and he grasped them with an unquenchable yearning, always wanting more. Once that unseen connection with heaven had been felt and savoured, he could fully appreciate the biblical passage of the thirsting hart panting after the stream of living water, the soul hungering for God. Considering what lay ahead of him, he needed to lean on God for strength and guidance.

Praying silently, it was not long before he could just hear through the confessional door the sound of footsteps echo in the cathedral vestibule and clip down the aisle. He did not pay much attention, as usual, there would soon be more worshippers entering, the sound of the pews filling and confessions would begin.

Without warning, his heart froze while his interior senses bristled. Rushing towards his direction was the dreaded tidal wave of malevolence so thick and tangible that if he was not inside the confessional he could reach out and touch it, hatred rendered as corporal as the wooden walls around him, growing more oppressive with each second. The footsteps quickened to an alarming pace and continued to gather momentum, the click of steps sounding more like the approach of hooves with each passing second. His soul began to shudder with the magnitude of the evil racing towards him.

Whatever was coming was neither animal nor human.

Surreal as this was, he had felt this before, mostly in night visions when the Enemy decided to pay him a visit attempting to frighten him, but to no avail. This time however was a first: he was fully awake and caught by surprise. The Enemy had never been this bold with him before, and to *attack* within a church? Although evil always skulked around, consecrated ground normally tormented the enemy and they kept clear of it most times. Peter knew what to do, but this offensive against him was happening too fast. Before he could react, the hellish intruder had reached its destination and banged with great ferocity against the confessional door, then clutched at the handle, shaking it vigorously, but was unable to open it. Although momentarily shocked, Peter was confident, deep within he was aware nothing would be allowed to happen to him. He made the sign of the cross and demanded the spirit to depart in the name of Christ. The rattling ceased, stillness was instantly restored. Taking no chances, he said a Hail Mary and the prayer to St. Michael before opening the door. There was no one in the church, only the noxious stench of sulphur permeating the air gave evidence of his unseen visitor.

"So, that's how it's going to be, is it," he said quietly under his breath. He had not even seen the afflicted person yet, and already the

Enemy was giving him fair warning not to have anything to do with the case, a shot across the bow as it were. Well, terror tactics did not work with him, he was too used to the devil's tricks. If the demon did not want him near the poor girl, it only made him more determined to help her. For an immortal seraph, even a fallen one, it was incredible how dim-witted the devil could be at times. It would have been better if he had left him alone rather than play his usual freakish games. Although unafraid, Peter decided it was best to give himself a moment to gather his senses before he returned to the confessional and sat in the nearest pew. A mere mortal like him could only take so much of the unseen. It wasn't every day the Arch Fiend came knocking on his door! He had barely said a few prayers when the stillness was ruptured by a series of metallic snapping and crackling resounding around the cathedral ceiling causing him to look up and around. It was only the halogen lights, obviously Bill the sacristan had arrived a little earlier than usual. Peter decided this was his cue and was about to resume his post when he heard footsteps once more. Looking down the aisle, he saw Katherine making her way towards him. He was grateful to see a friendly face.

"Good morning, Pete. Whew! Someone's been lighting a lot of candles lately. Honestly, did they use up all the matches or what? What a whiff," she whispered.

"Good morning, how I wish that were the case." He could not help smiling, somehow she always managed to cheer him up.

"Oh good, that's more like it. You've been looking so tired and serious lately, and my day doesn't seem to start right if I don't see you smile."

"I'm all right. How about you? You're here a little earlier than usual."

"Um, well, I need to make a quick visit," she hinted, nodding to the confessional, "and it's not easy to see you as before, more people are coming and they keep getting ahead of me before Mass starts."

"Uh huh. Come on in, make yourself at home." He held the side door open for her before entering his section of the cubicle. Poor dear, already he could sense she had very little on her conscience, it was just too tender at this early stage of her recent conversion. Everything seemed a mortal sin to her, even if she blinked at someone crossways it felt like a crime worthy of capital punishment. It would take her some time to tell the difference between faults and venial failings that did not need confessing from the bigger transgressions that did. However, he would always oblige a confession request even if the offences were faults and did not need a formal absolution, and since Katherine was still new to all of this, was willing to let things get a little talkative during the sacrament.

"Bless me, Father, it's been two weeks since I was here last. I'm afraid I nearly lost my temper again, and it wasn't from skipping my lunch."

"*Nearly* lost it? If you didn't, you're all right then," Peter said, quietly smiling to himself.

"Well, I was still fuming, and I know I should work harder on patience, but I can't believe the nerve of some people!"

"Not Mrs. Hunt again?"

"Oh, well, I have something to confess there too," Katherine admitted, "but I didn't blow my top. She sure likes to talk my ear off though when she visits the gallery, and I have so much work to do lately … ."

"But you were still kind to her, which is good. Don't forget what I keep telling you, it's how you handle your temper that counts."

"I know, I just wish I could turn it off altogether, or at least lengthen my temperamental fuse, especially since she's been so good about supporting the gallery."

"It's merely a clash of personalities, continue to be kind to her. Tell me, what was the other reason you nearly lost your resolution to be patient?"

"It was this jerk who dropped by the gallery. Sorry, I know I shouldn't call anyone a jerk, but he really was. At first I thought it was a new customer. He asked to meet the owner, which of course is yours truly, and wanted a personal tour of the place. I didn't mind that, I give tours all the time, but then he had the gall to criticise all the art, and everything else at the gallery. When he left, I found out he's the new owner of the Sirrac Gallery! Kevin was off on his lunch break when the creep arrived and he nearly had a fit when he arrived back in time to see my tourist leave. I mean, what nerve! He literally cased my place, with *me* giving him the grand tour!"

"That was a trial, I must admit."

"Sure was, but I held my breath and counted to ten whenever I felt like giving him a good verbal whipping after each of his remarks during the so-called tour, twenty seconds when I found out who he was, but I'm still fuming over it."

"The worst is over, try and move on. You're the only one other than Kevin who is still mad over it. The unwelcome visitor is not bothered at all. If your intruder was on a corporate espionage mission, don't let him unsettle you any further or he's accomplished what he set out to do. Think of something calming and constructive, like your artwork. Tell me, how are your paintings coming?"

"They're not, that's the point. Even when I've hired extra help, people like that no-good … sorry … come along and take up what little time I have for artwork and I feel so frustrated. I'm not talking about Mrs. Hunt now," Katherine clarified, "just all the really aggravating, worthless interruptions that I could live without."

"Hmm, but they are worthy to offer up. Just think, you'll have Purgatory whittled down in no time," he noted.

"I suppose so, that is, if I don't keep adding to my Purgatory."

"Is there anything else bothering you?"

"No, that's it, I think," she trailed.

"Conscience-wise, yes, but I have the distinct impression you wanted to ask me something else," he prodded with humour.

"Pete, you always seem to know! I do actually, but I don't think we have time … ."

"Don't worry, no one has entered the other side of the box yet. What's your question?"

"Well, I was going through some of my notes from our theological coffee hour debates and I found a passage that I jotted from the Old Testament I wanted explained but never got to it. You know, I miss those coffee sessions," she mused.

"Kathy, just because you're in the Church now doesn't mean you ever stop your spiritual studies. I'm still learning something new all the time, even the angels are finding out something new about God every second we speak. We can still continue our little academy." He smiled to himself. He didn't mention it, but he missed those sessions too. To see her so interested in the faith helped to reinforce his own spirits when the daily grind plus the indifference of so many others wearied him, and besides, a little scriptural discussion would help get his mind off the disturbing morning he had.

"Oh good, I'd hate to be a bother."

"You're never a bother, but before we get off onto something else, let me give you your penance first; say a Hail Mary and ask Our Lady to help you in your determination to be more patient with people. Now your Act of Contrition." After she had complied, he gave her absolution. "All right, tell me, what passage has you in a frazzle now?"

"It's one of Solomon's sayings. I know he's supposed to be the wisest king of Israel, but he must have been having some really bad days when he said some of the things he did. Sometimes I wonder how they ended up as Scripture."

"Ah, the 'vanity of vanities' diatribe where all life seems like it's heading into a meaningless downward slump?"

"Not that, but he was really depressing there too. I think the passage I'm stuck on is in the same book in the bible."

"Ecclesiastes. Okay, let's hear it."

"Um, could you turn the bulb on? I'm reluctant to paraphrase, so I brought my book."

"Sure thing. And the people in darkness have seen a great light." Peter chuckled as he flipped the switch. Once her eyes had adjusted, Katherine hunted for her trusty notebook and opened the page to the confusing passage.

"Got it, here goes: *'And I have found a woman more bitter than death, who is the hunter's snare, and her heart is a net, and her hands are bands. He that pleaseth God shall escape from her: but he that is a sinner shall be caught by her.'* Now that sounds a bit cruel, don't you think? Was Solomon a chauvinist, or what?"

"Oh no, he's not talking about *all* women," Peter clarified.

"Really? It doesn't sound like it."

"You have to read closely there, he said '*a*' woman, not '*women*', he was speaking of a particular type of person in that passage, the Jezebels that lead men to destruction. Don't forget all the beautiful passages he wrote about wise women, and how he describes Eternal Wisdom as an allegorical woman who leads souls to salvation, you can't exclude his other books. Basically, he points out there are wise women, good women, faulty women, and bad women, but he's not singling women out, Solomon also made clear distinctions between men who are wise and those who are inveterate sinners. We're in there too you know."

"That's true, I should have noticed that. Thanks Pete, that's another question cleared up."

"You're welcome. I'm always glad to help. If you have any more questions, just keep them ready for me."

"I will. Are you coming to see Gerry today?"

"Of course, I'll be bringing him the Blessed Sacrament, but I won't have time to stay for a long visit."

"I know, another mercy mission, but I hope you will be able to make it for dinner tonight."

"Me too, but that depends on how the day goes."

"Duty first, we understand."

"Yes, I'm on the run today, and possibly the next couple of Sundays. Speaking of which, would you say a prayer or two that all goes well?"

"Sure Pete. Sounds like you've been given something difficult to handle."

"You could say that." He had not told anyone what he was going to do exactly, he had to keep it private, although this time he was not successful. Katherine was growing very intuitive.

"Oh, it's a *big* mercy mission," she realized with quiet awe, she could guess what was troubling him, he was the diocesan exorcist after all. "Oh my gosh, do be careful, won't you? While I find what you do fascinating, I can't help but feel worried."

"Please don't fret, I didn't mean to upset you. Hell can only do what heaven permits. I'll be fine," he reassured her. "Well, as much as I dislike evicting you, someone has just come in to confess."

"All right, Pete. I hope it's a nice big fish, go reel 'em in." She tried to sound cheerful for his sake.

"God bless, Kathy."

He gave her an additional blessing before she closed the door behind her. Turning off the light and sliding the panel over the grate, he sat for a moment to clear his mind and prepared to receive the next penitent. Already someone had quickly come in and taken up the other side as soon as Katherine had left. This was going to be a tough day indeed, he could feel a vague oppression outside, nothing that could be seen, he knew that for sure. When still a greenhorn it had taken him several months after his ordination to diagnose the reason for this pensive invisible struggle outside the confessional when sinners arrived: they were devilish tempters, 'throttlers' he began to call them. Worse than scruple-rakers, these particular imps spiritually choked those coming to confess in order to have their sins remain stuck in their throats, preventing them from clearing their consciences from mortal sins. In effect, tempting penitents to make a sacrilegious half-revealed confession using their shame and embarrassment as a weapon against them. They never give up, these stranglers from Hell! Peter said a prayer to clear the area, and the heavy feeling lessened. Unfortunately, they would be back. Demonic spirits never sleep or take a vacation, always plotting and waiting for the next offensive.

He remained in the box for over an hour. It used to be sufficient for the few early morning attendees to his services, but now it was no longer adequate. As Katherine had observed, more people were coming every day. Reluctantly, he had to leave the confessional with penitents still waiting outside, but they understood even if they were disappointed. If only there was some solution, he did not like turning penitents away. In the aisle he still was politely stopped; knowing he had a tendency to make a quick retreat away from the public eye whenever possible, he was quietly bombarded by parishioners with the usual requests to bless religious objects and have Masses said for individual intentions before he slipped into the sacristy to prepare. Peter could not help but reflect on the truth of the passage that the harvest is great but the labourers are few, especially for the labourers who upheld all the old ways, including the Latin blessings from the Tridentine Roman Ritual. If the hierarchy did not oppress it, they tried to ignore it. Nevertheless, despite all the efforts to discourage it, there was a growing desire among the faithful for dignified reverence and majesty in opposition to this brutal modern world with its dishevelled informality and corrupting godlessness.

Eventually reaching the sacristy, he vested for Mass. Peter intently disliked the changing times and the blatant indifference shown towards the service of the altar. Naturally, St. Patrick's had no dearth of liturgical attire, but many of the old vestments had been replaced over time with new machine-produced models, and those still made according to the traditional patterns were a mere shadow of the regal articles of the pre-Vatican II era. A charitable parishioner had given him some of the older vestments that were discarded by other parishes, but they were becoming a little too worn after years of wear. He had to be careful, or by sheer age and usage they would no longer be deemed proper by the rubrics and therefore he was compelled to use the venerable brocades only on special feast days to ensure they lasted as long as possible. The rose vestments were the only ones still in a good condition since they were used just twice a year. It was only a dream right now, but one day he hoped to acquire personal vestments that were not manufactured by a soulless profit-geared corporation but hand-crafted by prayerful nuns who had not abandoned the cloistered life. He had heard of a few convents in France that still used pure silk brocades and authentic gold thread. God deserved the best. To ascend the altar properly clad with new garments sanctified by meditation and charity … how many souls had been prayed for and saved by each careful stitch? No time to think about that, we must make do with what has been provided for now, he knew well God would rather have pure hearts that loved Him above all else than all the gold and gothic cathedrals in the world. No doubt, all the rest would be provided for when the first and most important things were taken care of.

Taking off the surplice, Peter was already wearing his cassock and fascia, and so continued to the ceremonial washing of hands, then quietly reciting the various Latin prayers as he vested with the amice, the alb, the cincture, maniple, stole, and chasuble, each prayer reminding him of the dignity of his office, preparing him for the Sacrifice he would make and to Whom he would be offering It. The vesting ritual complete, he prepared the sacred vessels. Peter went to the sacristy safe and took out the personal chalice his mother, brother and sister had custom-made in Italy as an ordination gift. Not satisfied with half-hearted miserly measures, they could not bear to see him landed with any article from the common stores made according to the bare minimum required by the Church, especially after he had graciously given them back his share of the family inheritance. No cheap plain cup with only a gilt interior, they insisted he accept a chalice of gold and gems complete with sculptured ornamentation as seen on the European vessels of old. Although Peter disliked ostentation, for the service of the altar he did not protest the expense, for nothing, no matter how precious or luxurious, could ever be good enough to contain the Blood of Christ. After preparing the chalice for service, he gave a slight nod to Bill the sacristan now dressed in his cassock and surplice who proceeded before him to the sanctuary.

Latin, it was the most distinguished of the Western languages, having the honour of being one of the three languages used on the inscription on the Cross. Peter knew the Enemy hated it with a diabolical passion and was using every means possible to eradicate Latin altogether, first beginning with the ridiculous nonsense that no one could understand what was being said at Mass and that it was necessary to change to the vernacular. Before the 'improvements' came, nearly all Catholics had their own bilingual Mass booklets and knew exactly what was happening. Did the whole nation and the rest of the Catholic world for that matter suddenly become illiterate? Of course not, but the excuses were made plausible and so they stuck. It galled Peter to observe that the Enemy had craftily made that brainless observation come true, people were so used to English services now that they had no idea how to follow the Mass properly except for those exceptional few who had clung to their old missals, refusing to throw them out. Like them, Peter was determined to continue the fight to restore all that was old and venerable in Holy Mother Church now despised by those infected by the demonic smoke that had penetrated within their very walls. All Peter could do at times was cling to the one promise that the gates of Hell would never prevail.

Arranging the altar and setting out the sacred vessels, he returned with the sacristan to the bottom steps and commenced with the sign of the cross, Peter recited the preparatory prayers with the sacristan responding.

Introíbo ad altáre Dei. … .

"I will go up to the altar of God."

"To God who giveth joy to my youth."

"Judge me, O God, and distinguish my cause from the nation that is not holy: deliver me from the unjust and deceitful man … ."

The peace when he ascended the altar steps! Despite the enormity and awe-inspiring nature of the Mass, Peter always felt a profound interior calm after the strain he often felt after helping other distressed souls. He certainly felt much better after the morning's hellish visitor. Once he entered the sanctuary, he was allowed to concentrate on his sacred role as mediator in *persona Christi* for those who worshipped behind him, facing God at the High Altar he offered the Sacrifice on their behalf while they offered their prayers through him to Christ. What ignorance to say that the priest has his back to the people when he is praying fervently for them! Another lame excuse the demon had propagated to eradicate the reverence due God that unfortunately had also taken hold.

However, there was one part of the ceremony he came to dread, the time proscribed for the sermon after the scriptural readings. It was not speaking in front of people that bothered him, but the constant danger he could lead people astray. It was a woeful responsibility to preach on the Word of God. Of paramount importance, he must not preach error but truth, he also must not bore the congregation to death and make them indifferent, and how easy it was to bore people in these days of instant gratification. It was his duty to rekindle their lukewarmness into steadfast zeal, give encouragement to lagging spirits and sow hope that leading a holy life was possible in any vocation even if difficult at the best of times. Sister Roberta had warned him he must not rely on his own strength, and therefore he knew he must not presumptuously lean on any false notion of his own powers of interpretation when it came time to preach; he of himself had no power or talent, all he had came from God, and from God he must humbly seek assistance. Every time he made his way to the pulpit, Peter begged the Holy Ghost to enlighten him and ensure all that came from his mouth would be inspired from above and filled with His Divine Wisdom. Peter also knew that good seed could fall on rocky and bramble-choked ground if it was not prepared properly, and therefore the congregation needed a little help from above as well. Before his sermons, Peter would always quietly look out and above the heads of his early morning faithfuls and silently address the invisible worshippers, the guardian angels of all those sitting in the pews, asking them to ensure their wards were more attentive.

Where would he be without his Holy Helpers? There were times when Peter was permitted to feel their presence, he could tell when the massive cathedral felt oddly cramped and bustling as though double to triple the amount of people were present and were filling the space to its utmost capacity. It did not happen very often, but there was the one or two rare occasions he sensed the invisible angelic hosts that worshipped with him around the altar, a signal consolation to keep him going amidst the trials of his vocation. It was a pity that people forgot they had a powerful defender by their side in their guardian angel and never thought to pray for his help let alone thank him for his unceasing service. His petition made, he continued with the sermon; Saint James certainly gave him plenty of ammunition this morning: be doers of the word, not hearers only and deceivers of yourselves that you are holy without concrete action. It would be nigh next to impossible to preach error with this rock-strong directive.

After he had expounded upon the readings and the proscribed Gospel, he proceeded to what he had recently dubbed 'The Refresher Course'. The older generations familiar with the Latin Masses needed no reminder of how to receive Communion when the time came, but the younger members who were now coming to his Latin services, often for the first time in their lives, had no idea how to approach the altar properly. Since word about his unusual confessions had spread, he was attracting more people from other parishes that did not offer the traditional Mass. To avoid confusion in the aisles and at the rails, Peter lately found it necessary to tack on a little extra instruction before he continued.

"A quick reminder to those who have not been here before: for the Tridentine Rite, Communion must be received kneeling, and on the tongue, not in the hand. If you are unable to kneel, Communion must still be received on the tongue. If you wish to receive in the hand, then you may attend the vernacular service later."

How he wished Communion in the hand had not been approved in the New Rite! It reduced the Body of Christ to a mere symbol, a 'token' of the Last Supper, a 'meal' downplaying the Mass as the unbloody sacrifice of Christ's Sacrifice on the Cross if not causing Catholics to disbelieve in the dogma altogether. In obedience, Peter was bound to refer people to the new services if that was what they wanted, but that was it. Everything pertaining to the Tridentine Rite would be kept as before. He had a few obstinate ones who tried to force him to give in the hand on occasion, but he would stand there patiently before them until they went to their knees. Thank heavens the Latin Rite enabled him to do that. Several older members of the congregation who also disapproved of the changes highly approved his methods of dealing with the ignorant youngsters.

Having delivered this announcement, he was about to make his way back up the steps to the High Altar for the Credo, the public proclamation of faith, when his senses leapt into high alert. He could feel something behind, but this time it wasn't the 'Holy Helpers'. He couldn't fathom what, other than it felt oppressive, almost sapping the energy from him. This was a first. Something didn't feel right, but whatever it was, he had to keep going. He couldn't stop. After the Credo, he proceeded with the Canon of the Mass, then the most sacred part, the Consecration. It was at this holy time that the bread and wine became the Body and Blood of Christ. Silently proclaiming the scared words over the host as Christ taught the Apostles, genuflecting, raising the transubstantiated Host on high, then genuflecting again with the utmost reverence, repeating the same ceremony with the chalice, there were times Peter's breath was almost taken away, that he could feel his own blood tremble in his wrists.

After completing the prayers of the Canon and receiving Communion, he absolved the congregation of their venial faults following the second Confiteor, then raised the smaller host to be venerated by the faithful before they too received the Lamb of God. Giving the sacristan Communion first, he was about to proceed to the altar rails to begin distributing the Bread of Angels when he stopped short, he felt it again, that heavy oppressiveness. Suddenly, his spiritual discernment let him know what was happening. He couldn't see it, but he realised a new set of tactics was unleashed upon the congregation by the 'throttlers', those unseen devil imps that tried to choke his penitents. This time they were trying to stop anyone from going to Communion who were in a state of grace from receiving, and those that were not worthy, the throttlers were doing everything they could to get them to go up and commit a sacrilege. Peter was not permitted to know who was receiving what temptation, he could only feel the battle, sense the shadows lingering around, but it was enough. He had to do something about this.

Before he approached the altar rails he held a Host up, made the sign of the cross over the congregation, adding a silent prayer for the imps to depart.

A rumble was heard overhead.

Was that thunder? No, it was a roar!

The congregation wasn't sure, it *sounded* like thunder, but there was no forecast of a storm approaching … .

But it almost sounded like it was *inside*!

And, why did the Monsignor hold up the Host like that? That was not normal. Busy minds were trying to figure out what had just happened. The congregation began whispering amongst themselves. The regular attendees who had come to know Monsignor Reinold could tell when something unusual was about to happen, but generally around the confessional, making this strange occurrence a cause for curiosity.

Peter however felt a lessening of the oppression, the imps obviously had been sent flying. He focused once more and approached the far end of the altar area to his left. Communion was distributed without any other incident, the sacristan positioning the brass guard plate under the chin of the first communicant as Peter prayed quietly in Latin, "May the Body of Christ preserve thy soul unto life everlasting," before carefully placing each Sacred Host on their tongues.

Katherine had never seen Peter this solemn before, and he was serious enough when it came to this part in the Mass. It was almost impossible to meditate as she was supposed to, especially with the whispering around her, some people said they were not surprised, the Monsignor had a way with him, but others were saying 'something unseen' had just happened that only the Monsignor could see or understand. The murmuring spread through the pews. Mr. R was caught between astonishment and concern, not a little ruffled that many eyes were turning towards them, being the Monsignor's kin.

"Katie, have you ever seen him do that before," he asked under his breath before they went up.

"No! Only when he's in the confessional. I've heard some pretty strange stories, not to mention the few off-the-flypaper incidents I had myself. He seems to be aware of a lot of things, but this wasn't normal, not during a service, was it," she enquired, awed by the mystic rarity she had witnessed.

"I'm afraid not."

Once Communion was over, Peter returned up the steps to the altar, the concluding rites commenced as he purified the sacred vessels, read the thanksgiving prayers, the Communion verse, the Postcommunion prayer, and then turned to declare the end of the Mass.

"Ite, missa est."

"Deo grátias," the sacristan returned.

Turning once more to the altar, Peter prayed the Pláceat before facing the people and giving them the final blessing with the sign of the Cross.

"Benedícat vos omnípotens Deus, Pater, et Fílius, et Spíritus Sanctus."

"Amen," rang around the cathedral, although the service was not quite concluded. The Last Gospel was read, the first chapter from St. John, verses one through fourteen, before Peter quietly departed from the altar with Bill leading the way.

Although it was not proscribed after a High Mass of the Double Class, a considerable group of the congregation that were sticklers for all the traditional petitions began to recite the Leonine Prayers for the protection of the Church, while others, seeing that Monsignor Reinold was no longer present in the sanctuary, could not contain their astonishment after the morning's bizarre episode and the building erupted with electrified whispering that threatened to grow into chatter.

"I don't like this," Mr. R. muttered to himself.

"Why not? What does this mean," Katherine asked.

"I don't know."

"Should we go see him?"

Mr. R shook his head.

"This is way beyond us Katie. Pete must … be about his other Father's business," Mr. R noted with quiet respect, the full impact of how many were called but few were chosen hitting home, at the same time dreading what may lie ahead for his son. Whatever was happening, it was bound to rock the boat. Not wanting to distress her, he tried to brighten up, placing an arm around her shoulder. "Come, let's go see Gerry."

In the sacristy, Peter tried to stay collected as he calmly returned the vessels and vestments to their respective places, old Bill casting an awe-struck glance at him as he also divested himself of his surplice and server's cassock, now a little intimidated to speak on a casual level after what had happened. He just knew the Monsignor had experienced something otherworldy, that freakish rumble after the impromptu blessing before Communion told him as much.

"Will … you be needing anything else before you go?"

"No, that will be all Bill. I can handle the rest from here, and thank you for abandoning your warm bed to come in at this hour of the morning. I know it's utter cruelty, way above and beyond the call of duty."

"Anything for you Padre, no need to thank me," he replied followed with a smile. It was good to hear the sound of the Monsignor's cheerful voice breaking the uncharacteristic silence between them. No time to hang about, he had to go out and see to his other duties before the next Mass, leaving Peter alone.

Peter tried to fall into his usual mode of 'act normal', 'all part of a day's work', but this time found it almost impossible. He could hear the babble of the lingering congregation echoing down the vestibule to the sacristy, excitedly spreading the news to the new arrivals assembling for Fr. O' Conner's morning service with Bill reminding them all to be quiet while in the house of God. He felt a cold chill shiver through him and had to lean on the vestment chest for a moment. He certainly wasn't expecting what happened to him this morning; first the hellish attack upon his confessional … then at Communion! Would that happen again? What did this mean? Pondering the situation, he let out a deep sigh. Of course, how could he be that blind? Everything was interconnected. If his mission regarding the Rite of exorcism was about to be stepped up, then his discernment of souls and detection of demons was advancing in the process. The most experienced exorcists understood that the Sacrament of Penance was integral to their work. Confession was preventative exorcism, so to speak. The Enemy hated confession as much as he despised the Rite of Exorcism for the simple reason those who regularly confessed received great graces and therefore were in no danger of coming under outright demonic oppression or possession. Those who lived in habitual sin, and most dreadful of all, received the Blessed Sacrament unworthily were in the greatest danger of demonic attack. Heaven was now ensuring this would not happen under his watch if possible. But why today, Lord?

Seek and you shall find.

Curious, Peter flipped through the Latin Missal to find the saint of the day, who happened to be St. Ubaldo according to the old calendar, wondering what other sacred texts were proscribed for May the sixteenth.

" … shelter us under the merciful protection of Thy right hand against all the wickedness of the devil. … The Lord made with him a covenant of peace, and made him a prince; that the dignity of priesthood should be his forever. … Behold a great priest, who in his life pleased God, and was found just; when the day of retribution came, he made amends for all. Where shall we find another to keep the law of the Most High as he kept it? Therefore the Lord took an oath, that he should be the father of His people … ."

The Gospel too was enlightening, the parable of the three servants who were entrusted with the five, three and single talents: oddly enough, the fate of the slovenly servant who hid his one talent in the ground was not included in the reading for that day, only those who had multiplied their gifts were recognized by the Master.

"Well done, good and faithful servant. Because thou hast been faithful over a few things, I will place thee over many things … ."

As he often said, there was no such thing as a coincidence or accidents in God's Creation. Although intended to honour St. Ubaldo, the passages were a clear sign of the extraordinary events happening to him. Peter quickly humbled himself, he was nothing, he certainly did not want or deserve any praise, and yet, the Lord had seen fit to give him encouragement. Many souls were now returning to the faith they had abandoned, he had not used his gift in vain, and now a greater charge was given to him in return. Peter took a deep breath and prayed for strength, he must not stop striving to be a good servant and accept whatever path had been set for him, do whatever was placed before him, public or private, no matter how discomforting or difficult.

Come, there's work to do. Bill is right, no time to linger about. Gerry was waiting for him at the hospital and he did not want his brother to miss Communion now that he had finally returned to the Church. After that, he had a weighty mission to attend to, the battle was only beginning. Peter knew he had to be ready for anything now that he was undertaking his first investigation into a veritable demonic possession.

This was going to be a very long day.

∛✦√

Katherine and Mr. Reinold arrived at the hospital to find Charlie and Suzy had also come to see the patient. By this time, Gerry was allowed to have more visitors, therefore occupancy restrictions had been lifted within moderation. This morning Suzy had happy news to share, before she left that morning Martin called from Paris with the announcement the bundle of joy they were expecting had finally arrived.

"What? How wonderful," Katherine exclaimed. "How's Justine? Is it a boy or girl?"

"Justine is elated, and it's a boy. They've decided on the name Pierre. Martin said they'll send us pictures right away."

"Wow, this is good news," Mr. R smiled, glad to see the young ones in high spirits.

"What else? Oh yes, Justine thanks you both for the baby presents, and Martin also sends his appreciation for the cigars Gerry mailed in advance, the men in the family all enjoyed a good celebratory puff or two."

"Gerry, you didn't," Katherine *tsked* accompanied by Mr. R's laughter, both amused at his secret now coming to light.

"I did, and I'm glad they enjoyed them. Can't break with tradition you know."

"What a way to celebrate the arrival of a new life, kill off the proud father and the wise elders with smoke inhalation," Charlie observed.

"Gosh, I'd love to go see them, but a trip to Paris is out of the question right now," Katherine replied, "and with the new baby, I know they won't be able to come back here for quite some time."

"Well, when they can come, I hope they bring little Pierre," Suzy noted.

The visiting group of four swelled to six with the arrival of Steves and his girlfriend Jennifer.

"Hi guys, what's up? I get the feeling we've happened upon a party."

"Great tidings, Martin and Justine are the proud parents of a baby boy." Suzy related the details once more as Steves opened a large pink box brimming with an assortment of glaze encrusted, rainbow sprinkled doughnuts he and Jennifer brought.

"Now that's a cause for celebration. Here, tuck in, nothing like an unhealthy breakfast to start the day," Steves observed.

"It's a good thing your Gramps isn't here right now, or the patient wouldn't get a crumb," Charlie noted.

"Don't we know it!" Katherine laughed.

"Thanks guys, that certainly beats the hospital's choice of fare." Gerry nodded with appreciation as he was about to reach into the box until Katherine stopped him.

"Pete should be here soon," she reminded him.

"Oh, right. Well, save me one for later, or I'll still be without a crumb."

"Sure thing."

"Hey, is Leroy coming to see you today," Steves enquired. He and the red-haired rake had much in common, one item being an annoying partiality for pulling practical jokes.

"Probably not, he has to pack. He's off to California again in the morning on business. Some hopeful clients he has to impress in person," Gerry explained.

"Well son, he does have to settle down and get back to work full-time," his father noted.

"Yeah, I know. I'm guilty he spent his bonus vacation cheering us all up, although I really do appreciate it," Gerry added.

"Me too." Steves chuckled. "Boy, did he have some stories and ideas to share."

"If you dare break your resolution and try any more of his gags on me, I'm moving out," Jennifer warned.

"Oh no." Katherine groaned. She had forgotten what it was like to be the jester's victim after he moved to his own apartment. "What did my brother do now?"

"Do 'jelly' and 'loo' ring a bell?" Steves grinned. "I just had to see if it really worked."

"It does," Jennifer wryly confirmed.

"Steves, I can't believe *you* of all people didn't know that one." Gerry laughed, there was nothing like a few wild pranks to liven up a situation, and he had many of those living in the same frat house with Leroy.

It was difficult to shift Leroy from the conversation if introduced, even when out of sight, it was nigh near impossible to keep him out of mind with his unforgettable shenanigans. Suzy and Charlie wondered which commercials Leroy had worked on after hearing he had won several awards for his catchy skits and blurbs. Mr. R and Gerry started to chortle.

"What? Come on, you've got to tell," Steves egged.

"No, better not son, you might scandalize the ladies," his father replied.

"Yeah, even Lee wasn't too pleased with his first assignment, but he took it bravely."

"Aw, be a sport, Gerry, don't leave us hanging." Steves badgered until Gerry relayed the story.

"If you *must* know, excuse me for being indelicate," Gerry added, "his first project was for a haemorrhoid cream. Leroy said he would have used 'a little dab will do ya,' if that blurb hadn't already been taken."

The giggling became contagious.

"Talk about starting from the bottom up," Steves couldn't resist, the giggling exploded into laughter, Katherine then tumbled to the ads in question.

"Oh no! Not Mr. Hembegone?"

Observing them out of breath, even Mr. R could not contain what was left of his composure. The skits Leroy and his crew conjured up were unforgettable. The first commercial featured the average Joe as he is pulled over by a steel-faced motorcycle cop. As the officer approached, the scene cut to the speeder reaching inside the glove compartment and taking out a water pistol, a voiceover was heard … .

"When life deals you a pain in the rump, don't take it sitting down … ."

On cue, the man grabs a tube of the featured cream, and with a knowing smile, fills the pistol in a hurry. The cop leans over into the car and icily demands his licence and registration …

" … fight back, with Hembegone!"

Several squirts in the face later, Nasty Cop miraculously transforms into an obliging yes-man willing to offer a police escort, sirens blaring. Nameless Joe became an instant hit across the nation and was dubbed Mr. Hembegone, his stunts with his trusty water pistol and its soothing ammunition quickly extended from the tax man with his pile of W forms, to Death with his scythe, from the dreaded visit of the wife's in-laws to the world's most difficult boss. The original concept grew beyond the control of its creators when Mr. Hembegone progressed to a vast array of weaponry, from a slingshot to a medieval catapult, until finally he was pictured dressed up as Rambo wielding a bazooka in one hand and a map of Iraq in the other in honour of Operation Desert Storm. A few patriotic zealots could not see the funny side, finding the last ad distasteful and it was pulled, thus the reign of the mighty Mr. Hembegone finally came to an end, while blasting Leroy's career off like a rocket.

"Lee's boss said if he could rake in several million on that contract, he was capable of handling anything." Gerry laughed.

"Gosh, are there *that* many people who have to buy that stuff?" Suzy giggled.

"Oh it's got more than one use," Jennifer euphemistically explained, "models use it to get rid of puffy bags under their eyes. It's an old trick."

"What?" Gerry exclaimed. "That's deflating to know."

"It's true," Steves affirmed with a snicker.

"Better not tell Gramps it was Leroy who made Snepres Biotech a packet on that series," Katherine warned, trying to catch her breath.

"No quarter to the competition," everyone rang out in unison, quoting Gramp's favourite business motto.

"Hey, maybe Pops and Uncle Tim should hire Leroy for Walsingham Industries," Steves mused, a gleam in his eye.

"That'll never happen." Katherine laughed. "You know how Pops is, Lee's brand of commercials would not be considered worthy to represent the dignity and core-values of our family-run international pharmaceutical institution."

"I know, but even I, your friendly neighbourhood geek, am getting a little tired of our stuffy scientific ads with their lab-like graphics explaining how our medicines work. It's boring, no one's going to pay attention to that. The whole idea of advertising is to draw attention and stay in the public's mind, let them all know what we have out there, and 'funny' sticks."

"I've always said that absurdity prevails, but Steves, we don't want to make a joke of ourselves either."

"I agree with Kathy," Jennifer added, "leave the cheap tricks to companies who make worthless products, a few laughs is the only way they could sell their junk."

"Oh, and how would *you* know they make worthless junk? Since when have *you* ever needed the medical assistance of Hembegone," he queried with a raised eyebrow. Jennifer gave him a warning thump on the arm.

"Cool it, mister. I work in your labs now, remember? I've informed myself on all your products and read the test results, including all the tests you did on your competitors' items."

"Hmm, just how *do* you test something like that for the market," Gerry pondered with an innocent air, although thoroughly enjoying Steve's bantering. "It can't be easy to find an adequate number of lab mice in that delicate condition." The laughing erupted again.

"Gerry, you're awful! I'm sorry Mr. R, my brother is a bad influence." Katherine sighed.

"Not to worry, your Steves can't do any more damage to him than Leroy has already," Mr. R reassured her with humour.

"Speaking of brothers, where's Pete? He's not usually late," Gerry observed.

"I don't know, but you're right," Mr. R. noted with concern, "better sober up before he comes." Katherine quickly sobered up as requested and looked over at Mr. R, recalling what had happened at church that morning and wondered if his fears for Peter, whatever they may be, were already in motion. Katherine knew about busybody do-gooders who took it upon themselves to report diligently to the bishop on anything they deemed an irregularity in the parish. She remembered when Aunt Martha had embarrassed them all and called the Episcopal bishop on certain occasions. Had Peter been called in to the Archbishop's office? No, thank goodness, she was relieved to see him walk past the interior window looking in on

Gerry's room from the hallway, purple stole around his shoulders, his hand over his breast pocket.

"Here he is. Let's give Ger some space," Steves suggested.

Familiar with Peter's solemn Sunday visits, everyone pulled themselves together after their laughing fit and gave him a quick greeting or slight nod as they left the room with reddened cheeks, allowing him to attend to the spiritual needs of his brother. After thirty minutes or so chatting in the hall, Peter opened the door and motioned them to come back in.

"You won't believe what happened to Pete on his way here," Gerry began as they resettled their seats around his bed, "some idiot back ended-him, knocked out his tail lights."

"Yes, and the bumper too, they weren't watching what they were doing," Peter added.

"Oh, that's terrible," Suzy commiserated.

"I know, I'm sorry to dampen your good spirits this morning, Gerry told me about the new arrival in Paris."

"Isn't it wonderful? But you must be in an awful state," Katherine blurted, caught between the latest happenings. "Are you sure you're not hurt? Maybe you should have one of the doctors here do a check up."

"I'm fine, the Old Buzzard has borne the brunt of it all." He did not want to alarm them, having a second car accident in the family no matter how minor was all they needed right now.

"Are you sure, son? I think Katherine has the right idea."

"I'm sure Dad, I hardly felt the bump."

"Good Lord, and that car wasn't much to begin with," his father continued, "you won't be able to drive it anywhere until it's fixed."

"I know, I'd be stopped by the highway patrol, and Fr. Jenkins will be using the other parish car today. What bad timing when I must leave for Trenton this morning. I have appointments I don't want to cancel, and unfortunately I don't have time to arrange a rental."

"Why, if you're sure you're up to it, and if it's really that important, you can take my car, son."

"Thanks Dad, I appreciate that, but it would not be good for a priest to be seen driving around in a Rolls, you understand."

"Oh, right."

"Would the gallery van be okay? I'd be happy to let you use it," Katherine offered.

"Oh Kats, think about it," Steves retorted with humour, "he can't go in *that*, a man of the cloth driving your colourful artsy advertising to do his parish work. You can have 'Delores' for the day, Pete."

"A classic vintage sports car with glitzy gull-wing doors, yeah, that's just as appropriate for a man who has renounced the world," Jennifer teased Steven, the DeLorean was his pride and joy. "I would let you use mine, but I came with Steves today," she further explained, turning to Peter.

"I guess the Beemer is out," Suzy reflected, remembering she had the car all decked up with the gallery logos as well. Charlie's new Lexus was also out of the offering.

"Well Pete, you don't have any option, you'll just have to forget about how it may look and pick something," Gerry noted. However, the impasse was resolved when their sister and the 'Hulk' arrived to visit.

"Petey, take my car, I just had her checked out and she's all tuned up," Lottie informed him.

"Looks like you're stuck with Aqua Velva." Gerry chuckled, tickled with the idea. Their sister adored that old aquamarine British Mini of hers and refused to part with it no matter how many parts she had to ship in from England, especially after she had baby blue velvet seats custom made for it.

"It's better than what I'm driving right now," Peter defended.

"Not by much," Gerry returned.

"Now don't say that about my princess, and *stop* calling her Aqua Velva! She may be petite and in her golden years, but that car has never let me down. Here, Petey, she won't let you down either," Lottie said, handing him the keys. "I'll just borrow Samuel and the limo until Peter gets his own car fixed. Is that okay?"

"Sure Lottie, you don't have to ask," Gerry affirmed. "All joking aside, I really wish you would get a new car."

"Oh, doodilly nonsense! She'll have to turn to rusty dust before I'd give her up."

"You know Pete, I don't like you driving it either," Gerry noted. "I appreciate classic cars like the next man, but that thing is ridiculous. It's a wonder Lottie has kept it running this long."

Katherine was also worried about the practical matters. "Gosh Pete, you're so tall, can you even *fit* in Lottie's car? You'll be squashed up against the windscreen. You won't be able to steer the wheel. Please reconsider taking the van, artsy or not, at least it's got more space."

"Thank you Kathy, but you'll need your van for the gallery, and the bonnie blue bug will do just fine." It was decided he would leave his old battered jalopy in the hospital parking lot until arrangements could be made for someone to retrieve it.

Peter could not stay long, he had lost so much time sorting out the fender-bender and now had to step on it if he was to make his appointments with that drive ahead of him. Saying his goodbyes, he left at a clip.

"Trenton, and with all he has to do lately, why does he have a 'mercy mission' there, I wonder," Gerry mused, "especially since it's not in his diocese."

"Maybe it has to do with the dwindling number of priests, all the parishes are stretched thin with the lack of vocations lately," his father commented.

Katherine knew that was true, but on this occasion was also aware this bleak fact did not have any bearing on this particular 'mercy mission'. Only able to guess what Peter was facing, she said a quick interior prayer for him, hoping he would be all right.

◌❖◌

"Talk about Mr. Bean to the rescue. Lord, You *must* have a sense of humour."

What a morning! Would unexpected events never cease? It certainly was a tight fit in the mini blue bomb, not to mention a little disorientating changing gears left-handed since the steering wheel was on the opposite side British fashion, but Peter was grateful that Lottie providentially arrived with the 'princess' and saved the day.

Although Peter could appreciate the funny side, he must be vigilant. There was no such thing as a coincidence. That was no ordinary bumper-cruncher despite all the outward appearances of it being a normal accident. He trusted in God, but he had been given fair warning the Enemy was lurking at every corner, waiting for the next opportunity to get to him, and that thump from behind may well have been the next attempt to keep him from his duty.

Thankfully, nothing else happened on the way and he arrived just a few minutes late at the hotel where he had arranged to meet with Miss Yardley's aunt and uncle. Not being familiar with all the suburbs of the city, it was decided he would follow them to their home where they could speak

107

in private. After the usual pleasantries, offering him something to drink while settling in their sitting room before lunch, the Fletchers gave him their sincerest gratitude for coming to their assistance.

"No need to thank me. All right, I suppose it would be better to start from the beginning. Forgive me, due to the nature of a situation like this, personal details need to be discussed, but I promise, everything will be kept strictly private," Peter assured them. "I must ask, what makes you suspect your niece is suffering from possession or demonic disturbances? Please, explain how you came to this conclusion."

The Fletchers looked at each other then timidly turned to him, not knowing how or where to start.

"Maybe we should begin just before Missy came to us. After Melissa's father passed away, her mother, my sister Rebecca, met someone else, and everything seemed to go downward from there," Mr. Fletcher started tentatively.

"Not at first though, Nathan seemed like a very nice man. I mean, excellent career, he's a lawyer, always taking an active part in the community and the church do's, he seemed perfect," Mrs. Fletcher continued.

"Yeah," Mr. Fletcher agreed, "we were both happy for them since she and Missy took Ronald's death hard, and I didn't like to see them left alone like that. Then … things seemed to turn ugly about a year after the wedding." He stopped for a moment. Did this priest care, or was he like all the others who showed little or no interest about what they said or were going through?

"Please, continue. I know this is hard, but I need to hear everything so I can tell exactly what we're dealing with."

The Fletchers looked at each other again. Maybe he did care, maybe he just appeared to, in any case, it was a relief to be able to share their anxieties, the floodgates opened.

"Nathan became a different man, staying out late, coming home drunk most nights, raging, belligerent, starting fights for no reason and making their home life a train wreck, always criticising, belittling her and Missy in private, and then appear to be the good old boy in public. I'll never forget the night Becky finally came to us with Missy in tears, asking if they could stay the night, Becky's face was bruised," Mr. Fletcher explained.

"Of course, they were welcome to stay as long as they needed," Mrs. Fletcher added. "It was terrible to find out what was happening those few years, and to think we never knew it. That new husband of hers is a street angel and a house devil. The problem is, Becky loved him, she was willing to put up with anything, so she covered for him. Of course, we all liked him, and he could be so persuasive with his apologies, we kept giving him those extra chances to change, believing him every time, but it was all crocodile tears. You know how it goes.”

“Yes, I am terribly sorry to hear this.” Peter sighed. These were not mere words, tortured humanity came to him on a regular basis, broken families, ruined lives, he felt so powerless. How often he heard similar horrific misfortunes from people who came to him for help and was able to do little on most occasions other than pray and offer counselling on how to change their situations if at all possible. “Where is Rebecca now? Does she know about what has happened to her daughter?”

“Yes, the trouble is, she finally got away from Nathan, but she’s too terrified to come back to New Jersey, she had to leave the state, he made so many veiled innuendos of what he’d do to her and Missy if they ever left him,” Mr. Fletcher continued. “She begged us to take care of Missy until everything could be sorted out, she knew she would be safe with us until she could find a place for them to live and start a new life somewhere.”

“Wait Tom, we’re not telling it right,” Mrs. Fletcher reminded him, before turning to Peter. “You see, Missy ran away and came to us before Becky did, that’s how we first found out how bad it was for them. Thinking she had been punished for something and was getting even by running away, you know how kids are, we thought Missy was making it up until she actually took a tape recorder from her pocket and played back the verbal abuse Nathan had spewed at them both that night. We were aghast. Missy told us it was like that nearly all the time. She and her mother would do or say something, and it would be taken the wrong way. He would just explode and berate them with the most rotten things. Other times he would beat Becky, Missy confessed there were times she would lock herself in her closet until it was over.”

“Yes, then he came by the next morning full of apologies, and that’s how it began, Becky coming to us for help two weeks later, her eye black and her face bruised like a boxer, then we continually believing his excuses and thinking he would try and change. I should have advised her to dump him the first night Missy came to us,” Tom said with undisguised guilt.

“Mr. Fletcher, don’t reproach yourself. There is no easy way to handle an appalling situation like this, it’s in our nature to want to give people another chance. Unfortunately, there are those who will take advantage of it. Knowing when to put your foot down and say ‘enough’ is the difficult part, especially when you did not have the final say, it was Rebecca’s choice, and in any case, it is never a good idea to come between

people in a marriage. It is up to the couple if there must be a separation.
It's a shame Rebecca did not make the break sooner."

"I know Father, she loved him, feared him, and yet was afraid to
leave, nothing but emotional chains keeping her tied to him the whole
time." Mrs. Fletcher nodded.

"That's the tragedy of it," Peter agreed, and to think this was one of
a million stories, that Rebecca and Melissa were not the only ones going
through this. "All right, let me see if I understand this correctly. Melissa
came to you first, then they both came a few weeks after that."

"Yes," Mr. Fletcher, affirmed.

"After that, Melissa ran away some time later, and came to live with
you on a permanent basis, with Rebecca's permission," Peter trailed,
checking the file. The Fletchers confirmed his statement. "You don't
happen to have Melissa's recording by any chance?"

"Actually, we kept it as evidence of the ill treatment they received,
just in case Becky ever wanted to file charges. Missy did a few more in fact,
before she came to live with us."

"Would you mind if I heard one of them?"

"No, although I must warn you, it is very offensive," Mrs. Fletcher
noted grimly. Peter assured them this was important. Mr. Fletcher went
over to a drawer by the stereo system and took out the first cassette, sliding
it into the tape deck. Although prepared to hear the worst, he recoiled
interiorly as he listened to that imageless soundtrack playing back the
physiological torture of domestic abuse, the imagination forced to fill in the
pictorial gaps. On this occasion, her husband was not beating her, but the
cruel verbal attack was just as destructive. And she stuck with him for years?
The constant barrage day after day would drive anyone to the brink of
distraction. Peter literally grew nauseous from the obscenities hurled at
Melissa's mother, the degrading comments, and most disgusting of all, the
lewd, suggestive insults, all in the presence of her young daughter, who at
that time was not more than ten. After having been exposed to every type
of sin marring the souls of penitents, Peter had become especially sensitised
to the sins of depravity, those offences bore a peculiar mark, a rotting putrid
stench that churned the stomach quicker than physical rotting flesh.
Although only a recording, the mere mention of anything on that nature
brought back everything he experienced with his penitents, his spiritual
memories revived his experiences of that gut-knotting reek, and soon, Peter
felt as though he too had been assaulted.

"Do you need to hear the rest of this?"

"No, that will be all for now, thank you."

"I'm sorry, I know, it's very distressing," Mrs. Fletcher replied quietly.

"May I borrow it, and the other recordings to study in my own time? I promise they shall not leave my possession."

"Oh Father, do you really want to go through them all," Mrs. Fletcher asked, noticing how that first tape affected him.

"Yes, I need to find out if he said anything spiritually damaging, by that I mean curses, imprecations, anything that would cause an oppression or possession."

The Fletchers looked at each other. Maybe he *did* understand!

"You don't need the recordings for *that*, we can tell you he did, although there's a recording of that too. He cursed the day he met them, the day he married Becky, the usual scathing remarks, if you could call them usual," Mr. Fletcher noted bitterly.

"Okay, that's a start. Did Melissa tell you anything he said against them, or anything on the tapes that sounded more twisted than usual? Something that struck you as particularly ominous?"

They thought for a moment until Tom noticed Nathan did say one thing that struck him more than the other threats.

"Yeah, he had a way of threatening he'd *make sure* they'd end up in Hell, normally someone who'd be angry and spouting their mouth off would use the general expression, 'ah go to hell', or 'see you in hell', you know what I'm saying? I had the distinct impression he was literally trying to send one or both of them there, and was confident of having the ability to do it."

"Is this stated on one of the tapes?"

"Yes, I think so, but I'm not sure which one. I haven't gone through them in awhile, I think you can understand why."

"Of course."

At last, he had something to go on, he now had evidence of curses pronounced against Melissa, that would be one way of bringing a demon upon her. He would have to go through the tapes, it was providential to actually have it recorded. However, it would not be enough evidence. It was an unfortunate fact people angrily flung curses at each other all the time, not knowing fully what they were doing, unaware of the evil wishes they were landing upon others and the effects they brought about. He still needed substantial proof to convince the archbishop, but it was a start.

"We'll make copies of the tapes and send them to you."

"Thank you, I would appreciate that."

"Can something as simple as a curse cause a possession?" Mr. Fletcher wondered. "If that's the case, no one would be safe."

"It can happen that way, but not all the time. Sin definitely plays a part, the lack of a prayer life can also leave someone unprotected. I will need to know more about Melissa to find out if Nathan's verbal abuse could have triggered something. Did she and her mother practise their faith?"

"It's hard to say. I don't like to pry into matters like that, you know how people get all defensive when it comes to religion, but we made sure Melissa went to church when she came to live with us. She did in the beginning, until she became a rebel without a cause."

"Yes, we put our foot down, said she would be grounded if she refused to come with us. Eventually, we threatened if she did not agree with the rules of the house, she had better find somewhere else to live. It wasn't long after that she ran away. I feel so terrible! It was just a threat to make her shape up," Mrs. Fletcher said quietly.

"No, don't feel guilty. Running away because one hour of church a week was expected doesn't sound like a convincing reason to abandon a good home. I have a feeling something else made her run away," Peter reflected.

Before they continued with their story, Mrs. Fletcher suggested they eat.

"Here we are, pouring out our problems, and you must be starving! Come, lunch is ready." They proceeded to the dining room, and Peter couldn't help feeling guilty as Mrs. Fletcher busily served their meal. Although he never asked or expected it, often his visits put people to so much trouble. The women of his parish in particular always went overboard when he came to their homes to say Mass or bless their premises. They literally took Christ at His word, "whoever welcomes you, welcomes Me," and often put out a spread fit for the Son of David.

"Thank you Mrs. Fletcher, this looks wonderful, and on such short notice. I hope my visit hasn't put you out."

"Oh, don't give it a thought," she assured before joining them, "we are so happy that you could visit us, and please, call me Margie, everyone else does."

Grace said, formalities relaxed to a comfortable first name basis, they proceeded to discuss their niece's predicament as they ate.

"All right, let me get the facts straight. Melissa then came to live with you, and her mother finally left her husband." The Fletchers nodded. "Tell me about Melissa's time here with you, before she ran away."

"Well, the poor thing, she was shell-shocked, it took her awhile to realize we weren't going to scream and go ballistic on her. We took her for counselling, we don't know if it helped, the councillor couldn't get a word out of her, eventually we stopped the sessions, she was withdrawn for a long time. What frightened us the most was Nathan may have done something ... worse to her. We didn't know what to think after all the stories we heard of stepfathers, well, we still don't know, nothing may have happened but," Margie trailed, unable to conclude her thought. The possibility had also struck Peter after hearing the foul abuse Nathan hurled. That man certainly had a mind capable of thinking about such an atrocity, and therefore was only a step removed from acting upon it.

"Then came the rebellious years we mentioned," Tom continued, moving from that distressing topic, "the sweet, polite, timid girl we knew became a real passive-aggressive delinquent, however, we kind of expected that after what she had gone through. We've had our fair share of troubled kids."

"We were foster parents for a few years," Margie explained. "I couldn't have children, and after going through all the doctors and the adoption red tape, we thought we would try giving a chance to children who never had a good home."

"That was very charitable of you. God will bless you for it."

"I don't know about that, eventually we had to give it up after those last few angry teenagers that destroyed the house. Our nerves couldn't hack it. It's a good thing I'm in the furniture business, we could repair everything at cost." Tom shook his head. "Then Melissa came, having a niece is just as close as having one of your own, we were so glad to have her with us. That was another reason we had to stop foster parenting, after what she went through, we didn't want her ending up in a similar situation with uncontrollable foster siblings and their angry rages. You know what they say about helping your own first. It seems we weren't able to help her much either."

"You're not to blame, you obviously did all you could for her. Tell me, how did her rebellion display itself, other than her disinclination to go to church?"

"The usual issues with authority, hating school, never finishing her homework, playing hookey, then she started smoking, disobeying rules, wanting to stay out late with friends, getting angry when we had to lower the boom and put our foot down with some rules. We had to do some yelling then, but she would just storm out of the house. Grounding her didn't seem to accomplish anything, often she would sneak out at night."

"I see. Okay, the problem is I've heard nothing that sounds like a possession. I know, kids can get way out of hand and can have the characteristics of a demon, sometimes they have no other way to let out their hurt and anger, and as you said, you've seen it often enough as foster parents. However, there is nothing of the demonic in your narration of events." The Fletchers looked crestfallen for a moment, afraid he too would make the same conclusion as the rest, that their Missy suffered from a psychological problem. "What I need to hear is an experience of the truly abnormal, something that goes beyond the list of mental symptoms and diagnosis." The beleaguered couple looked at each other again, he hadn't dismissed their story, he was still willing to listen, but the reluctance to speak resurfaced. "Don't be afraid, anything you have to say will not sound odd or crazy to me. There are dark forces at work in this world that some people have had the misfortune to go through, including myself. I've had enough experience to know when I'm being told the truth."

"Well, we first became suspicious when she started mouthing back at us in a fit of temper and suddenly say things that she could not possibly have known," Tom began, "right down to the gritty details."

"No one knew, I mean, she brought up events that happened before Tom and I ever met, things we wished could have been kept private," Margie, noted with embarrassment.

"God, it nearly wrecked our marriage," her husband admitted, "but Margie and I are working through that, but at the same time, it seemed Melissa was *purposely* driving a wedge between my wife and I. If she wasn't raking up the past with skeletons in the closet, she became the go between, telling lies to make us suspicious of each other and split us up. I mean, why? I don't see the point! She escaped an abusive home, there was no logical reason to break up another where she finally had security after all she experienced."

"Why indeed," Peter noted grimly. The Enemy hated marriage and would destroy families whenever possible, especially Christian families practising their faith. "Yes, I agree with you, there is something here. Then I would not be wrong in saying that whatever hidden information she revealed, you had not disclosed in confession beforehand."

"At the time, no," Tom quietly admitted, "but we've taken care of it now."

"Did you mention any of this to Fr. Xavier?"

"No, he didn't seem to want to listen to our problems," Margie noted.

Peter wished he was wrong when he could discern situations, but again, he was found correct. His spiritual colleague had missed an important piece of evidence pointing to the demonic and had brushed it off. Devils could not reveal information that was absolved in confession, unless they learned about it from another source such as a witness to the sin in question, but the Fletchers were confident no one else knew whatever was on their consciences at that time. Peter reflected for a moment, they were telling the truth, he could sense that whatever guilt they were hinting at was no longer on their souls. He would not have known if they were not willing to disclose it themselves.

"If it's any consolation, I'm here and I'm listening. Anything else strike you as 'unearthly', uncanny?"

"Sure. Some nights she would have recurring nightmares, or what we *thought* were recurring nightmares. We didn't think them unusual considering the trauma she went through, until she kept telling us something 'black' was literally standing over her at night. Sometimes it did nothing but stand there, other nights she said it tried to snatch at her."

"Like Tom said, we didn't think anything odd, just the typical bad dreams, until," Margie stopped and glanced at Tom, "until, *we* started to see it. At first, I thought I was the only one, and just put it down to Missy's bad dreams having a negative effect on me, like when you go to bed after seeing a horror movie, you imagine zombies everywhere. The shape always seemed to come just when I would fall asleep. Then Tom eventually told me he saw it too, and described exactly what was lurking in our room at night."

"Yeah, I thought I was losing it until Margie and I realized we were both seeing the exact same thing on those occasions. So we knew it wasn't something we dreamed up, although anyone we told thinks we're batty. We've stopped talking about it except between ourselves."

"Could you describe it?"

"Er, well, 'he' or 'it' changed. Sometimes it looked like a faceless person dressed in a dark coat to the ankles or a cloak, some times it also wore a brimmed hat, other times, it was just a black shape but it felt like a person, even if it was more of a shadow."

"But there was one time it felt like a monster, not like a person," Margie added with a shiver. "After Missy ran away again, these ... events ... tended to calm down, but we do get the odd thing happening around the house on occasion."

"Tell me, did you ever feel a tidal wave of raw hatred or malice directed at you during these nocturnal visits?"

The Fletchers looked surprised. Oh thank God, he *does* know! Finally, someone who understands!

"At first, we could not understand what it was. We could hardly breathe. It felt like a wave coming straight at us before 'it' would appear, like emotion had been turned into something we could actually touch rather than feel. We had never experienced hatred and rage like that before! It was a warning, we called on Our Lady and St. Michael, and it would be gone."

"Father, what is happening? Could you explain it? Nothing like this ever happened to us before," Margie admitted anxiously.

"I'm afraid you've been infested by some malevolent spirits. It's a form of spiritual oppression. I know, this sounds terrible, but what you're personally experiencing is not like a full-blown possession. If they can't get you to give up your faith through fear and discouragement by their tactics, all they can do is keep you from getting a good night's sleep," he assured them. "Apart from these visitations, do you ever get the odd bump in the night and any strange scents or smells out of the ordinary?"

"Umm, not scents, but yeah, we got weird noises, plus finding things moved into strange places where we knew we never put them, but we tend to ignore that stuff now." Tom shrugged. "We can handle that, but the creature from the black lagoon is a whole different ballgame," he wryly concluded.

"I understand. I know this is easier said than done, but don't worry too much. Your shadowy visitors are here just to cause psychological torment."

"Is there any way to stop them?"

"It would help to find out how they got here in the first place, and how this ties in with Melissa," Peter observed, sitting back for a moment. "There is usually an element of truth in the old legends and wives' tales. Have you ever heard the saying a vampire cannot enter your dwelling unless invited in?"

"Um, not really, but are there such things," Margie queried with alarm. After what they had seen, anything was possible.

"No, not unless you count those extreme horror groups obsessed with the whole vampire cult to the point of having fake fangs cosmetically implanted and drinking each other's blood."

"That's revolting." Margie shuddered.

"Do kids really do that nowadays?" Tom wondered.

"Yes, and not just kids. Unfortunately, some people are so attracted to the weird and bizarre that their fascination goes to extremes."

"We had a few kids stay with us who were into ghouly things like that, werewolves and ghosts, but I don't think anything ever went that far," Margie noted with relief, "nothing beyond the peculiar hair colours and headache music."

"Sometimes all things 'ghoulish' can be used as a gateway to deeper things. Tell me, did any of them delve into the occult?"

"I can't say for sure, at least we didn't see anything like that, and we were pretty good at finding all the hiding places where kids stash stuff." Tom shrugged. "We were constantly on the look-out for drugs, so room searches had to be carried out regularly, especially when they became secretive."

"Well, the point I was making, the evil infestation you are suffering usually cannot come by itself, it must be sent or invited in, sometimes both. This is either attracted by grievous sin, or was wished on you, maybe something happened in the house that brought it in, and now that the evil has a foothold, it can come and go as it pleases. Sometimes these unwanted visitors have a specific door by which they can enter." The Fletchers looked towards the doorway. "No, in this instance I mean something they can use as a portal, it does not need to be an opening, something as simple as a household object that's been cursed or used for evil."

"Good Lord! What could we possibly have in the house that would be like that," Margie exclaimed.

"I will get to that shortly. You know, the way Nathan used to say such terrible things, he could have cursed you too," Peter reflected. "That would have been a start to the infestation, but I have a feeling there is more."

He looked around, he did not see any antiques in their home judging from the few rooms he had seen. It looked tastefully furnished from Mr. Fletcher's business, new items that would not have been around any person or group capable of cursing them, unless he had a bad worker or two on his factory floor, but no, everything seemed all right. He would have to make a tour of the house, he certainly felt something uncomfortable coming from overhead, it was starting to become oppressive.

"Tell me, what is just above us? Is it your bedroom?"

"No Father, that would be Missy's room," Margie informed him.

"Interesting. Hot spot number one. With your permission, may I make a tour of your home? I need to identify all the 'hot spots', eliminate or bind them, then clear out your home with the Minor Rite of deliverance and bless it."

"All right. Do we have time?"

"Yes, it won't take too long. I may have to come and say Mass in your home after it's cleared. It should lessen the problem."

"Sure, that would be great, but 'lessen'? Won't that get rid of it?" Tom wondered.

"It should, but there are occasions when it is necessary to repeat the process, some cases take a while to clear up. You see, I personally do believe your niece needs to be liberated, and whatever has attacked her and your home, may continue to do so until she is set free. You are bringing her help, and let's say 'downstairs' is not too happy about that," Peter concluded with a sideways nod towards the ground. "I can lessen the attacks for now. There are several measures you can take for your protection."

"Any help would be welcome at this point." Margie sighed with relief.

They finished lunch and showed Peter around. He returned to the front hallway, and with the Fletchers quietly watching, he began with an interior prayer, then moving through the house, he concentrated on certain areas that drew his attention, in particular spaces that created a peculiar, uncomfortable impression for no apparent reason. He felt drawn to a picture on the wall, a wedding photograph, but it was not of Rebecca and her first husband.

"That's Nathan, I presume."

"Yes, it's the only photo of him we left up," Margie nodded. "That was a happy day, we saw no reason to remove all the good memories."

"I understand, but Nathan is under a dark influence. I have a feeling he is under control by evil, and whatever is using him may be using his image. You don't have to remove it, place a blessed Miraculous Medal in the frame. From my own experience I find mirrors can also be used as entry points, I'd place or tape a medal on those too, and over every window and external door of the house." The Fletchers glanced at each other, they would have thought this whole thing was crazy if suggested to them before now, but they had experienced enough of the unseen to know that the supernatural did exist. "Do you still have other pictures of him?"

"Oh yes, but we put them away with the albums."

"If you do not wish to part with the photographs, you will need to place a medal where you have stored them to keep his evil influence bound."

Peter continued his quiet, reflective tour, going through the sitting room and the dining room once more, asking if they had any antique furniture. They assured him they did not, everything was new or reproduction. This time Peter was glad to be correct on something. People could understand using blessed objects, but if the deliverance Rite wasn't enough and he had to give them advice to burn a cursed object which they considered a collectable or treasured heirloom, that was when things usually become difficult for them to comprehend and probably wondered if he was not going a little soft in the grey matter. Peter was brought to Tom's home office and felt something sinister in the corner.

"Is that where the photographs of Nathan are?" He nodded to a book cabinet.

"Yes, actually."

"Hmm. I thought so, you'll need more than a medal, perhaps blessed salt. Yes, this house also needs blessed salt. Do you use holy water," Peter then queried, by this time they all had left the office and were in the kitchen.

"Sometimes," Margie admitted.

"You will need to bless yourselves and your house every morning and night, make the sign of the cross on the front door and sprinkle each room, your cars too. If you feel in need of stronger assistance, use blessed salt. Don't worry, I've brought plenty with me that you can have. I know it's not easy to get salt blessed these days. Did Nathan also leave items in your house, like gifts or things he conveniently forgot?"

"No, not really, except for the odd bottle of bourbon or so at Christmas. It's in the cupboard over there," Margie indicated.

"May I?"

"Of course."

Peter carefully took down an array of bottles, wine, gin, vodka, and bourbon, one bottle in particular Peter did not like to handle.

"This one?"

"Why yes, the very same," Tom noted, astounded.

"Then forgive me, but this must be done." Peter pulled the cork and poured the contents down the drain.

"Aww, and that was a special reserve too," Tom noted regretfully as he watched the golden stream disappear, "the only decent thing he ever gave us."

"Don't listen to him Father, please go ahead," Margie interjected. "You know you didn't feel right when you had a glass of that stuff."

"I wouldn't be surprised, evil was wished on this bottle. It's best to send the bad intention back to the sewer, it's rightful place," Peter added, turning on the faucet and rinsing the last of it down.

The kitchen inspected, Peter diligently checked every room on the ground floor, including the pantry, bathroom and coat closet, then proceeded to the stairway. First, he looked around the two guestrooms, the upstairs bath was next, the hall storage closet, then the master bedroom.

"Hmm, let me guess, your creature from the black lagoon skulks around the foot of your bed near the dresser?"

"Yeah, basically there," Tom nodded.

"Near the mirror, of course," Peter replied half to himself. On his tour, he was glad to see some religious pictures, one of the Sacred Heart he was particularly drawn to, there was another picture in the dining room with the inspirational poem 'Footprints'. Here in their bedroom he found another image, Our Lady of Grace, there was also a statue of Mary on the dresser. That was odd, Hell's attacks were usually lessened when such objects were present.

"We do have pictures up," Margie said, noticing where he was looking, "but how come that thing is still bothering us?"

"Are they blessed?"

"Oh, I don't know, the Sacred Heart downstairs is, but the others I'm not so sure, we got them as gifts, and you know how you put things off," Margie admitted sheepishly.

"I'll bless them later, and any other object that needs it." That was important, holy images and sacramentals were not effective if left unblessed.

Finally, Peter came to Melissa's room, yes, just standing outside he could tell this was Ground Zero. Opening the door, he saw that they had left it almost exactly as it was from the time their niece ran away, a typical teenage girl's sanctuary with its pink and purple décor, lacy canopy suspended over the bed, teddy bears and plush bunny rabbits, a television and stereo, ballerina and rock star posters, jewellery boxes and diaries with tiny padlocks, videotapes and a CD collection, eclectic decorative evidence of a child becoming a young adult hodgepodged around the room. At first glance, there was no sign of anything overtly evil, however, he was first drawn to the diaries on the dressing table.

"We wanted to open them, try and see if she wrote down anything that might shed light on her condition, but we could never find the keys," Margie explained. "I don't know why, we could have broken the locks, but it didn't seem right."

"Even though you would have read them if you had the keys?" Peter smiled.

"Yeah, I know, there's no accounting for it", Tom agreed. "Breaking into her books, it just felt like we would be betraying her trust somehow if we snapped the locks, and yet we searched her room without asking. Strange, isn't it?"

"Yes, but it is understandable, the locks are more a psychological deterrent and they obviously worked. In any case, if Melissa had come home and found out you read her books, her trust would have been severely shaken, and you didn't want that to happen. Then again, something else could have been keeping you from them, with good reason. However, we do need to read them now, let's see if we can avoid breaking into them. For some reason, I don't like the idea either. Do you mind if I look?"

"No, please, go ahead."

Peter calmly studied the dressing table, no, no point looking in the jewellery boxes either, an obvious place for the keys. Nothing would be in the drawers, they would have been searched, so that also eliminated the side tables and the chest. He then looked at the reproduction white iron bed with its brass knobs and elegant curling brass headboard. Peter laid his hand on one of the brass bed knobs on the footboard as he thought. Under the mattress would be out too, the bed was left made up, meaning Mrs. Fletcher would have noticed something when she last changed the sheets. Come on, hiding places, *think*! For a moment, he did not like what was coming from the closet, that was always the place of choice to hide a secret or two. He was about to check there, but felt the knob jiggle as he moved his hand.

"Hello. What's this? Ah, of course."

The Fletchers watched in amazement as he gently twisted the knob before slowly lifting it off the post to discover it was a brass cap and not a solid metal piece. Turning it over, Peter found several minuscule keys secured inside with electrical tape to prevent them falling down into the hollow bed post.

"Hey, we never thought of looking *there*," Tom remarked as Peter handed over the long-sought items. "Kids are resourceful, aren't they?"

"I think she had a little help from a movie, in this instance, *Bedknobs and Broomsticks*," Peter noted, indicating towards the stack of videotapes by the television. The Fletchers opened one of the diaries and began skimming through it as Peter quietly walked around the bed, checking the other knobs. None of the rest jiggled, it must have taken Melissa some time to loosen that one knob judging how secure the others were welded to the posts. He was about to inspect the closet next when Margie gave a gasp.

"Father, look at this."

Peter came to their side and looked at the entry, it was not long, but written in large curly letters with a heart used to dot the minuscule 'i's' and the exclamation marks, it took up the whole page:

"Me and Ashly said 'I love you' to each other for the first time!!! He loves me! He really does! I love him so much!!!!! This is the best day ever!!!"

On the page next to this exuberant declaration was glued an image, a Tarot card, 'The Lovers'. Underneath was a handwritten caption in the same exaggerated scroll:

"I ♥ Ashly 4Ever!!!".

"Who's Ashly?"

"He was the last foster kid we took in," Tom explained.

"Did you have any idea she was in love with him?"

"Not really, not like this. She was pretty upset when we decided he could no longer stay. He came home drunk a few times from secret parties his classmates held. He was one of the violent ones," Margie added. "We told her we didn't want her having anything to do with him, and thought it would blow over after the first couple of tantrums."

"Hmm. How long was he here when Melissa moved in?"

"About four months."

"Did he move out after this date," Peter enquired, indicating the entry.

"Yes, about a month afterwards."

"Do you know if they still managed to keep in contact?"

"I don't know, but maybe the diaries may tell us something," Tom noted.

"Of course. Meanwhile," Peter trailed as he flipped back to the Tarot card and ripped it out, "let's dispose of this. I wonder where she got it."

"I don't know. Maybe some of her friends at school."

"Possibly, or maybe Ashly. Where there's one, there's a deck somewhere. If she got her hands on a pack, we must dispose of it, if it's still here. Let's hope the cards are not split up and stuck in odd places like this one, it'll take longer to clear the area of evil."

The Fletchers opened the other diaries and flipped through them, but did not find any more. Peter continued over to the closet and switched on the light. Judging from the line of clothes all neatly hanging and the shoes set out in rows, Melissa did not take much when she ran away.

"We already checked all the shoes and pockets for drugs," Margie said.

"All right, let's see what's up here," Peter continued, taking down books, puzzles and board games boxes, piling them quickly on the bed. He did not like the feel of them, he had the peculiar impression he was handling containers packed with an unidentified hazard ready to detonate in his face. The closet shelves cleared, he began flipping through the books to discover the *Complete Works of Lewis Carroll* had the inside cut out, the secret cavity filled with letters. It appeared Ashly found a way to keep in contact after all.

"How on earth did they manage that," Margie wondered. "I never saw any letter from him come through the mail."

"Was he sent to another foster family here in Trenton?"

"Yes."

"Without the envelopes, it will be near impossible to say, except he could have arranged for a friend to give them to her at school, or slip them in her locker. Of course, they may have continued to meet after school as well, not to mention the times she slipped out of the house."

"There's that too," Tom agreed. "Come to think of it, she started to grow rebellious when we began to question why she was coming home too late after school, and we had to start setting curfews."

"I see. She didn't want you to find out about her trysts with Ashly. He came from a troubled home too I assume."

"Yes, first a violent family life, a terrible divorce, then his mother lost it and went on drugs," Margie confirmed. "It was a mess."

"Hmm. Despite his anger problems, I think Melissa found someone from her age group who knew from experience what she was going through regarding a broken family. When Ashly had to leave, Melissa not only lost someone who she felt understood her, but also her boyfriend, possibly her first. That's difficult to get over. What have we here," Peter wondered as he lifted the lid off a board game box. The Fletchers were shocked to discover that under the brightly coloured images and game pieces of *Snakes and Ladders* the grim alphabetical arc of the ouija board and its triangular marker lay concealed.

Margie gasped. "Where on earth did she get that?"

"I know *we* had nothing to do with it," Tom replied.

Peter continued to go though the boxes, in *Life* he found a small book on casting love spells, in *Battlehship* a pamphlet for jinxing and hexing enemies was concealed, *Monopoly* contained a charm book on how to generate good fortune and prosperity. Talk about book cataloguing, Peter mused. On the inside of the covers they discovered the answer: "*From your Ashly, with love.*" Peter's last find was the remainder of the Tarot deck shrewdly hidden in a UNO card game box.

"Good Lord, who would have known? We checked everywhere, but board games? I can't believe she cut up that book, it belonged to my mother, she gave it to me when I was little, and I passed it on to Melissa for her birthday, I thought she would treasure it as I had," Margie noted, appalled by the ominous findings.

"Don't be too hard on her, people often fall in love with the wrong person, and if good love can blind at times, misguided love blinds completely. All she could think about was Ashly and was thoughtless of those who truly cared for her. If you had a choice, would you rather have your book repaired, or see Melissa well again?"

"When you put it that way Father, of course, a person is far more important than a book."

"Do you think he got her started on all of this," Tom wondered.

"Maybe they got started together, something sparked their curiosity. You might find it in the diaries."

"Of course, but looking at all of this, perhaps you should read them first," Margie noted, indicating to the bed where they had piled the occult items, "considering you found her hiding places in under an hour when we've searched this place for ages, no doubt you will recognise situations in her entries faster than we can."

"All right, I'll go through them as soon as possible, the letters too, and return them to you, provided there isn't anything evil written that must be burnt."

"That's fine, if you discover anything, you have our full permission to dispose of them," Tom nodded. "We don't need to see them."

"Speaking of which, let us get this lot out of the house as fast as possible. Do you have a barbecue?"

"Yeah, out back."

Together they replaced the games minus their ill-omened contents back on the closet shelves. The tidying complete, Peter began picking up the offensive materials from the bed when the ouija board flipped from his hand and fell on the floor face up, the marker landing directly in the middle. Before he could blink, he heard the sharp intake of breath from the Fletchers as they watched horror-struck while the triangle rapidly spelled:

GET OUT PRIEST

The message delivered, the marker leaped off the board and flew directly at his face, then inexplicably veered in a sharp turn defying all the known laws of aeronautics and physics, sailing past his head and hitting the wall behind.

"That's a first," Peter remarked. "If all they can do is throw words and a bit of plastic, we're not doing too bad."

"Good Lord! How can you take it so calmly?" Margie's voice shook almost as much as her knees. "That barely missed you!"

"But it did. Devils are allowed only so much power in a visible form like this, mostly to frighten and threaten. They are usually not permitted to cause any injury, or I would have a black eye right now."

"They're certainly doing a good job on us with the fear tactics," Tom observed wryly.

Peter retrieved a bottle of holy water from his pocket and sprinkled the board, marker and the spell books with the sign of the cross before picking them up, he did not want a repeat performance. It was not long before Tom had the barbecue blazing in the back yard and the menacing articles were thrown in, Peter blessed the fire with holy water, not budging until the occult material was entirely consumed by the flames. Similar to holy sacramentals that brought God's blessings, the evil one also had his physical objects to send out curses, and no trace must be allowed to come back into the house, including the burnt remains. Peter advised that the ashes be thrown away in the trash can immediately after they cooled.

The physical objects removed, it was time to cast out the spiritual evil that lingered. Returning inside, he opened his case and took out his surplice and stole, and once attired for battle, he gathered together his arsenal; the Saint Benedict's crucifix, his container of holy water, blessed salt, and a sizable package of Miraculous Medals and miniature crucifixes. Peter returned to Melissa's room with the Fletchers, it was best to attack the place where evil had first entered.

"Are you wearing any medals or a crucifix?" They nodded, Margie showed him the gold medal she wore around her neck. Tom said he had a small crucifix on a chain, which was under his shirt. Peter was glad to hear these items had been blessed. "I don't want whatever is lurking in the house to attach itself to you and follow you around when I clear it," he explained.

Peter began the Minor Rite of deliverance, first reciting the invocation to St. Michael, proceeding with the commands to drive away all evil, each command followed with the sign of the cross made with St. Benedict's crucifix. This time, nothing happened except for a loud snap from Melissa's dressing table mirror, but without leaving a visible crack in the glass. To everyone's relief, it happened only once, and Peter was left undisturbed to complete the rite, sprinkling liberal amounts of holy water and blessed salt in each room of the house when the commands for the evil spirits to depart and the last prayers for protection were said. Peter carried out the additional precautions he had mentioned, taping a blessed medal or crucifix in the corners of the mirrors, also every window and the external doors of the house. He handed the Fletchers the extras, including the blessed salt, reminding them to secure the suspect photographs. Margie then gathered up the sacred pictures, statues, and a few rosaries that had been left in a drawer that needed to be blessed. It was now time to bless their cars and place a rosary, a crucifix or medal in them. One could never be too vigilant when confronting diabolical manifestations.

"Keep your rosaries with you at all times, they are powerful sacramentals, and of course, do not neglect to say your rosary each day. After the Mass, it's the one prayer Satan hates the most. Now that we have taken care of the evil, let's call down God's blessings."

Peter took out his holy water and blessed the house from top to bottom, reciting the necessary prayer from the Latin Roman Ritual.

"Will that be an end to all the disturbance," Margie wondered.

"Hopefully," Peter replied as he took off his stole and surplice, "but in case these strange occurrences try to start up again, say the Minor Rite, I'll leave you the leaflet. It was specially written for the protection of the laity when a priest is not present, perseverance in prayer is also required, including protection prayers, and don't forget to bless your house and cars everyday."

"We won't," Margie assured him, "and we'll arrange a time when you can say a Mass here, at your convenience of course."

The proceedings did not take long as Peter promised, and Margie went to prepare coffee while they continued to discuss Melissa's case in the sitting room. She had run away after a rebellious shout-a-thon, they had no idea she was gone until the next morning when she missed breakfast. They went up to check on her to find on the dresser a curt note saying she was going to live somewhere else as they suggested and not to bother looking for her. At first, they thought Melissa might try to find her mother since Rebecca had not yet provided any address, afraid Nathan would discover her whereabouts. Unfortunately, until Melissa was reported missing, no search would be carried out. Worried sick not knowing where she could be, their stress was compounded as the police appeared disinterested, passing them off with probable but unlikely excuses saying she was sulking somewhere and exacting adolescent revenge, more than likely she would come home when she had cooled off. In any case, the police informed them there was nothing they could do until the proscribed time had passed before a search could start. In the meantime, the Fletchers began to call all the parents of her friends, hoping the police might be correct, that she was hiding out with them, but each call turned up negative. Peter knew the rest, she was declared missing for over three years, and when found, had been transferred to the Trenton Psychiatric Hospital after the medical authorities in New York diagnosed her as mentally ill. Tom closed the conversation on that note, while he did not want to appear rude, he reminded them they had to leave at that point if they wanted to make their appointed visit in time. The Fletchers took their car and Peter followed them to the medical facility that was now Melissa's home.

Trenton Psychiatric, a large rambling manor-style estate with its wooded areas, abandoned buildings covered in ivy and wild unkempt vines exuded a gloomy silent desolation in eerie contrast to the bright May afternoon. The lingering relic of Victorian medical theory, Trenton was the first institution built according to the once celebrated Kirkbride plan, a unique architectural scheme that promulgated the theory that the overall design of a hospital could contribute towards the cure of mental illness if the edifice was tailored to meet the patients' needs. Arranged *en echelon*, the near endless corridors and rooms of the storied edifice branched back in an interlocking chevron pattern leading away from the main building allowing plenty of fresh air and sunlight into every room, the extensive park grounds landscaped to provide ample recreational gardens and exercise activity areas. While the plan was admirable, removing the mentally ill from the overcrowded general hospitals and inhumane jails of that era, the grandiose manor-asylums with their bat wing design proved too costly to maintain. With the progression of time and diminishing budgets they were closed down, or partially abandoned as with Trenton, a living ghost-hospital that continued to hold close to four hundred patients in the main building while the extended wings were allowed to fall into dilapidation and decay, a myriad of ruined old rooms and walkways littered with antiquated medical apparatuses left rusting in corners and corridors, all coated with crumbling plaster and paint debris falling from the ceilings and walls, accumulating with the thick dust that blew in through the cracked windows and neglected openings.

An icy chill enveloped Peter as he entered the grounds, the chill intensified as he arrived at the main area and parked next to the Fletchers who stood there tentatively waiting for him. Glancing at the recently developed Stratton Building, a contemporary brick addition dating from the sixties ungracefully butted to the once colonnaded grand administration edifice, he was not fooled by the feeble attempt at modernization, particularly when the historic parts of the original stone structure still remained, branching out and nullifying the architectural nip and tuck. Peter had not read any history concerning this place, however, he had heard many stories about the therapeutical experimentations and the dreaded electro-shock therapies of the old hospitals to guess the tortures endured, and would have been appalled to learn of Trenton's fame, or infamy, as an asylum in the nineteen-twenties under the self-serving sadistic tenure of Dr. Henry Cotton.

It was the age of bacterial discovery. Dr. Cotton was one of the fervent adherents of the theory that focal infections were the primary cause of mental illness, arguing that toxins produced by bacteria eventually travelled to the brain, therefore mental disorders could be eradicated from a patient if their focal infections could be identified and the infected source removed. While his theory was intriguing, his proposed cures were barbaric. Convinced infection was the sole cause of mental disorders, his procedures on the mentally ill ranged from pulling previously filled teeth, removing tonsils and sinuses, to drastic measures such as colon resections and hysterectomies. In four years he claimed to have operated on almost eighteen hundred patients and achieved a seventy-seven percent success rate. However, this was far from the truth, he upheld his theory despite the alarming number of casualties, which he covered up. Other members of the psychiatric profession doubted his claims as they saw little evidence that focal infection was the primary cause for mental disorders. An investigation ensued and soon it was discovered that Cotton's records were poorly written and exceedingly unprofessional. His supposed successes were often based on falsified information, namely, multiple records of one patient enduring several horrific and unnecessary operations. One appalling case surfaced of a young woman who was admitted for recurrent bouts of manic depression. Within two days of admission, her tonsils were removed, and nine days later part of her colon was also taken out. For over a month she suffered a high fever, the cause declared 'unknown'. Sixteen of her teeth were extracted, and she was injected with various vaccines for 'streptococcus mitis' and stock colon streptococcus. She was eventually discharged into the care of relatives when she displayed 'an interest in her surroundings', but was readmitted eight months later. When it was discovered she was hiding stomach pains, no doubt terrified of the next series of operations that might be inflicted on her, she was promptly subjected to further exploratory surgery shortly followed by a colostomy. She died eight days later from post-operative peritonitis. Former patients, their families and previous staff members also testified to the inhuman practises carried on by Dr. Cotton, how patients were beaten, kicked and dragged screaming to the operating room, how trolleys laden with body parts and corpses trundling down the corridors were a familiar sight. Deaths were more common than cures, and despite this testimony, Dr. Cotton continued to inflict medical butchery for another decade as the reports of his malpractice and inventive record keeping were kept hidden from the investigation committee, securing his career until his retirement.

No, Peter had no knowledge of Dr. Cotton and his procedures, but he certainly did not like the atmosphere emanating from half-abandoned Trenton. Many times he was reluctant to approach period buildings for when he set foot upon ground that harboured any bleak history, his spiritual intuition was awakened and alert. On these rare occasions, his senses became acutely receptive to the unseen: he was in the company of the restless dead. Although there had been one or two exceptions to the rule, he did not see them. Their presence felt similar to when an evil influence was near, but they were not menacing or harboured ill will, unless they happened to be damned souls. In this place it was that quiet, urgent sense of overwhelming melancholy and woe that clung to the stones and permeated the cavernous halls of Trenton Psychiatric affirming terrible atrocities had taken place, the victims of the past walked invisibly through the abandoned corridors, searching for help, yearning for release. He could feel the terror that these helpless patients experienced when they were ill and vulnerable on earth, the sense of entrapment of those still serving their purgatorial wanderings. Sitting in the car, he prayed earnestly that they would find peace, resolving to offer Mass for their release at the earliest opportunity.

How he wished he could be spared these extraordinary graces to discern the suffering souls when he was overwhelmed with his pastoral duties to the living. He had a deep devotion to the Holy Souls, right now, he had to concentrate on his current mission with all the other difficulties to face in its accomplishment. There were the doubts, contempt, and quite possibly, the hostility of the medical staff to contend with. To most if not all, he was either a misguided idiot who foolishly believed in devilish spirits that did not exist, or an opportunistic charlatan who preyed on the hopes of patients and their families as with the elixir peddlers of the Dark Ages that poisoned thousands during the plagues. He had been granted permission to visit Melissa by her legal guardians, and unless the staff perceived him to be a threat to the health of their patient, they could not stop him, Peter thought. He needed a few doubters and atheists present anyway, at least he might be able to turn this hostility and disbelief towards a good purpose. What troubled him most was his awareness that not all the patients in the hospital were ill, they too were under diabolical attack. He would be surrounded by demons wishing him death, evil, damnation and every torturous malice that no human could ever conceive. Of course, they could do him no harm, but he would have enough evil to contend with in one demoniac without being bombarded by the malfeasant negativity of others. Then, there was the sense of helplessness in having the powers to set these others free but was forbidden to use them except under special circumstances. It was a difficult situation for him to accept with Christ-like patience, held fast by ecclesial obedience on one side and the blind ignorance of people concerning demonic possession on the other. Although allowed to pray for those others who were possessed, he could not focus on them, he must concentrate on his duty and help the one soul he was sent to assist. Having visited the Fletchers' home, he knew there was no time to delay, the demons were watching, waiting, plotting to keep him at a distance, working invisibly on the hospital staff's prejudices. He would not be granted any more visiting hours than anyone else, possibly less if they were told or suspected the reason for his visit, and he needed to get to work. Black case in hand, he followed the Fletchers inside and they quietly waited until someone escorted them to Melissa's room in the ward assigned to the most advanced psychotic cases.

The security doors clanged behind them. They noted with some relief that most of the patients of that area were confined in their rooms, a few who were less afflicted were permitted the freedom of the corridor for exercise. The Fletchers nervously avoided looking at the sufferers lest they might become the object of their dazed scrutiny and disturbing attentions, quickly following the nurse who briskly led them through. Peter was not as fortunate to slip by completely unnoticed. Several of those whom they passed seemed to know not who but *what* he was, gesticulating wildly, or wailing as he came close, their overworked attendants running up and attempting to pacify them or direct them back to their rooms, wondering what had caused the ruckus. One unfortunate inmate pressed his face to the frame of the reinforced glass of his door and with not a few grimaces, called out in a muffled, guttural tone, "What do you want with us? It's not our time! Have you come to send us back too? Ha! Not if we send you there first!" Peter ignored the threat and simply made the sign of the cross towards the man, who shrieked and disappeared from sight. Silently he followed behind the Fletchers who were alarmed at the reception he was receiving yet still amazed at his calm reserve. He seemed to have drawn within himself, shutting out the bleakness of the prison surroundings and the unrefined malice directed at him, concentrating on some hidden wellspring of inner peace.

Tom then noted they had passed Melissa's room and wondered why they were being escorted to the farthest end of the ward, and the nurse was obliged to explain she had been set apart from the rest of the residents due to several violent outbursts. The Fletchers were dismayed to find she had to be heavily sedated just before they arrived, she had savagely bit one of the orderlies and kicked another in the stomach with such force that sent him backwards across the room. The nurse had to admit she had never seen anything like it in all her time there. Peter listened with interest. The fact it took five stalwart men to hold down, with considerable difficulty, one small young woman while they administered well over the normal dosage she usually received, and then struggled to place her in restraints on the bed was more evidence of the superhuman strength caused by the presence of her spiritual occupants. To Peter, this was good news, more proof he could use to convince the Archbishop, but the Fletchers were worried. Now that they finally had been sent a priest who understood their situation, Tom and Margie were afraid that in Melissa's medically incoherent state Peter would not have the opportunity to witness how wild she could become, nor hear first-hand the strange phrases and unexpected information she let escape on occasion.

"Don't worry, they may have drugged your niece, but a demon cannot be doped," he quietly reassured before they entered.

He respectfully stayed near the door while the Fletchers went up to the bed to make their visit. It was distressing for them to see her in this manacled condition and stupefied state when before she had the freedom of her room and use of the common recreational areas when permitted. It was not much, but it was better than this. The isolation rooms were certainly more dreary and forbidding, Peter could not help but reflect on the vast contrast between the princess-style bedroom he had just visited at the Fletcher's home and the worn, white sterile desolation of her clinical surroundings. Her aunt and uncle had given her everything, had treated her like their own daughter, and now she had been reduced to this, held bound and drugged in a miserable asylum cell, all dignity stripped away.

Peter opened his case once more and quietly prepared, making sure his small camcorder was working to capture any visible evidence and that it was properly secured with a blessed medal so there would be no unseen interference. After teaching Tom how to operate it, reminding him to hold it steady no matter what they may witness, he retrieved his container of holy water, the St. Benedict crucifix and a special double-length purple stole that he kissed as was the traditional mark of respect before slipping it around his neck, silently reciting the corresponding prayer. A deep, throaty gurgling issued from the patient on the bed, the Fletchers stepped back, startled by the unexpected sound. Peter was about to approach when a nurse came in to check on the patient, casting a sceptical eye at him while she busied herself.

"That's odd, after what we gave you, you should be out cold, honey."

Lifting Melissa's eyelids and checking for pupil responses with her penlight, she was surprised to see the patient *was* out cold, nor was the patient suffering from any chest infection, the sudden onslaught of rattling wheezes were inexplicable. Peter stopped the nurse before she called one of the medics in to take a look.

"This is something that your skills cannot penetrate or alleviate," he noted calmly, yet firmly. The nurse was about to question him how he became all-knowing in the medical profession when something in his piercing glance struck her to the core, and she could only glower back at him for a moment before leaving the room.

The demon was up to his old tricks, hiding behind the signs of physical and mental illness. Peter knew if it looked like he was causing her any distress, they would be thrown out, and the evil spirit would play that trump card to the hilt if given half a chance. No time for the customary protracted scouting session, waiting for the unseen intruder to let something slip. Peter had to act fast before he was stopped; he may not be permitted to say the Major Rite of Exorcism, but there was nothing forbidding him from smoking the quarry out with the Minor Rite of deliverance since he had permission to do his investigating if not to exorcise. He signalled Tom to switch on the video recorder and quickly went forward, blessing Melissa and the entire bed in the sign of the cross with the holy water, managed to sprinkled a few drops in her ears, then touched her forehead with the crucifix. The gurgling grew into a strange muffled growl that issued deep within the body, for Melissa's mouth was tightly clamped shut as if she were in *rigour mortis*, her eyes quickly closing further into a tight line and shrank a fraction into their sockets, giving the semblance of someone in deep pain and on the threshold of death, not in a medicated state. This change from unconscious stupor to a rigid, almost corpselike condition was disturbing, but Peter did not allow any unnatural alteration in physical appearance unarm him mentally or spiritually. He had seen a fair share of similar scenes in Rome and knew what he could expect, he was not hurting her, it was part of the diabolical ruse. Stepping back and holding up the St. Benedict crucifix, he remained unflinching and proceeded with the rite.

"Most glorious Prince of the Heavenly Armies, St. Michael the Archangel, defend us in our battle against principalities and powers, against the rulers of this world of darkness … ,"

The deep growling that issued from deep within yet made by no vocal cords increased in pitch as though an animal trapped inside was in agony. Peter continued, concluding the opening prayer and proceeding to the commands to depart. The growling continued, but no verbal change from Melissa came, only that strange harrowing, inhuman growl. Peter continued with the commands, then the final prayer of deliverance. The growling lessened as he neared the end, but that did not mean a complete liberation, far from it, but all he could do was pray for her at present. After blessing her again with holy water, she writhed on the bed and growled again. As eerie as the seen was, it would be better if the demon had betrayed more of its presence. Although not able to do a full exorcism then, should he dare command a name at this point? Perhaps it was the best proof he could get, and besides, he did manage to get full permission to probe.

"In the name of Jesus Christ, the Crucified Saviour, who are you?"

The growl became a snarl.

"Answer! It is Jesus Christ, not I who commands you! He whom you are bound to obey! He who has been granted all authority in Heaven and on earth!"

Peter repeated his commands.   Perhaps the poor girl was plagued by a dumb spirit after all, a lesser demon who could not answer. Still, in all possession cases, there would always be one devil that could speak, be forced to display its presence and give a name. All he needed to do was keep up the pressure, torment it into obeying. Peter placed the crucifix on her forehead and repeated his questioning command. The growling continued. Peter tried again, keeping his crucifix on her forehead, but no avail. Once more he commanded, this time evoking the authority of Christ and the powers and graces granted through His Church. There was no answer, but the growl deepened into a chilling, stuttering rumble. Afflicted, the demon was still putting up a struggle: keeping her lips clamped, it tried to prevent her body from speaking, but Peter would not give up. Perseverance was key in all spiritual matters, including a fight like this. Time for a different tactic. He motioned for Margie to step forward and asked her to raise Melissa's head gently. At first they were afraid to approach, but did not want to refuse, she did as he asked, allowing him to slip the extra length of his stole around Melissa's neck. Immediately, she began to writhe left and right as far as the restraints would allow. Peter ignored the useless thrashing.

"In the name of Jesus Christ, Whose yoke is now around you, the law you have refused and must now obey, give me your name!"

The rumbling growl ceased and became a low wail that sounded from the depths of a cavern under their feet that could not be seen but was felt, and yet simultaneously issued from somewhere inside the girl's body as her mouth and eyes were still pressed shut although her body continued to twist in an effort to shake off the stole.

"Get it off! He burns us! Chokes us! This one knows what he is about!"

" 'Us', is it? Tell me your names. Who are you?"

"No! We won't tell! We like it here!"

"What are your names?"

"Won't say! Won't tell you!"

Tom and Margie watched wide-eyed in horror at this unearthly exchange, the sense of the natural completely shaken in them as they witnessed the hidden denizens of the preternatural kingdom at work in a visible and audible form with their waking eyes. The growls had finally become a voice, if it could be called that, the uncanny lack of distinction between male and female intonation, the English words uttered by a single yet strangely inhuman vocalization forced to answer in a wailing modulation that froze the blood, all issuing from within their niece as though an internal organ was forced to act as a substitute for vocal cords. Peter's manner was equally intimidating from a contrasting aspect, his quiet reserve suddenly revealing a steeled fire that emanated a spiritual command and authority that no earthly governor or potentate could yield, it was as though Christ had come with His knotted ropes as He once did to clear out the temple. They had to remember this severity was not directed at Melissa, but what was inside her. They could not help but be awestruck at the battle between Heaven and Hell waged right before them in that peculiar battlefield, an asylum cell.

"Lucifer! Star of the morning, how low you have fallen! To think you were the highest of the angels. And you, wretched demons, to think you also fell from your exalted state to this, through pride and disobedience you gave up the glory that was once yours and will never regain!"

"Must you torment us with that too?"

"Yes, and I call upon Mary, the Immaculate Virgin, who crushed your head, she also commands. Obey her!"

"No, don't mention *her*! Besides, you know as well as us we don't have to give a name today!"

"In the names of Jesus and Mary, who are you!"

"Oh we have many, many! For many are here!"

"How many? Speak!"

"Many! Many!"

"What are your names if you are so many? The names of Jesus and Mary compel you to answer!"

"Yes, but not now! You may stab at us, but not drive us out!" There was a long wailing cry followed by a hideous, measured, gurgling laugh. "Now leave us! You torment us."

"Soon you shall be cast out."

"Perhaps, but not today. You haven't the full permission. Only to make questions. We know everything! Ha ha! All the better for us! This black robe knows much, he is well armed and scalds us in grand style, but we shall make him pay for it."

"Be silent! In the name of Jesus and by His Precious Blood, you shall not harm anyone here," Peter concluded in a commanding tone, making the sign of the cross with the crucifix over Melissa, followed by a liberal blessing in holy water. Now that he had his visible proof, unearthly as it was, he must not let the demons speak freely in their own voices again. They were notorious liars and could cause untold damage to souls by the lies they spewed through the possessed. The vocalisations shrieked again with the blessing, but then died away, leaving Melissa in her former drugged state, the gurgling ceased, allowing Peter to draw back his stole from around her neck with Mrs. Fletchers' trembling assistance. Compelled to obey his command, the 'many' were subdued for now.

Unaware of any activity around him during the interrogation, Peter eventually noted the nurse had returned with a doctor only to be rooted to the spot by the hair-raising scene defying scientific explanation. They could see that the blood-curdling conversation was not the product of Melissa's voice and therefore could not be the psychotic babbling springing from multiple personality disorder, nor did they hear the tricks of a ventriloquist; instinctively in those few minutes they understood no human could make those chilling words or sounds despite their scepticism in the unseen. Peter quietly packed up his items, with the exception of the video recorder, which he signed for Tom to leave running for the moment.

"I know, you have come to ask me to leave your patient in peace," he stated calmly to the doctor. "I am leaving, I have done all I can for her today."

"Well, er, she seems stable now, I guess there's … no harm done. You can stay," the doctor trailed, not quite sure how to handle this situation, snapping out of the horror of the moment as he headed to the bed and checked Melissa to find she was as he had left her, sedated. The nurse however was still in a state of shock.

"Would you be so kind as to testify as witnesses to what you have seen here these past moments," Peter politely asked them.

"Er, as in a written statement," the nurse quietly returned.

"Yes, or perhaps a verbal one on my video recorder, whatever is more convenient. This is simply to affirm to my superiors that I have not harmed your patient, and that what has occurred is beyond any natural and scientific explanation according to the medical and psychiatric professions."

"Oh sure, I can confirm *that*," the doctor finally replied.

"Thank you. It won't take but a minute of your time. We can do this out in the hallway."

The doctor was just finishing up, checking Melissa's heart rate with his stethoscope when she unexpectedly began to sing in her own voice in a mocking operatic tone:

"*Eh bien, docteur, que me veux-tu? Voyons, parle! Te fais-je peur?*"

The doctor straightened up in a hurry, eyeing her in her drugged state.

"Impossible, she should be unresponsive."

Curious by this unusual display of musical prowess, Peter turned to the Fletchers. "Does she speak or know any French? Especially French opera?"

"No! She used to love ballet dancing, but she doesn't speak French at all. I don't think she knows much about Classical music either, she's into all the latest pop music," Margie disclosed.

So much the better, Peter thought, it was an extra bonus to get that bit of information. The demons were acting a bit unusual at this point, usually they didn't like to be found out, but obviously they felt they had the upper hand right now since he had been granted only a partial permission to act. Perhaps now that the infernal host had been forced to reveal its presence, the spirits were not going to hide their presence as much. Despite their desire to remain concealed, there was also a braggadocio trait about the demons in that they loved to show off their knowledge of human culture through those they possessed. Confirming his thoughts, the impromptu concert suddenly resumed with a few more strains:

*"Maudit soit le bonheur, maudites la science, a prière et la foi!
Maudite sois-tu, patience!"*

When she had finished these lines followed by a contemptuous laugh, Peter suggested they go out in the hallway where he quickly recorded the names and the depositions of the two flabbergasted medical staff, including their account of what happened with the orderlies that day. When they were finished, he switched off the video reorder and slipped it into his case, grateful and relieved he was able to acquire this much evidence. The nurse's curiosity finally got the better of her and she asked if he knew what the patient was singing.

"I wasn't sure until I heard those last lines, they're from *Faust*."

With that, he wished them a good afternoon and followed the Fletchers out.

The three remained quiet until they exited the main entrance, intuitively resolving not to look back on that kingdom of Hades until they had reached the springtime sun, their minds preoccupied with all they had heard and seen. When the brightness of the afternoon had revived their spirits, Tom asked Peter what would be the next thing to expect. Peter had to admit it was unusual that he was called to consider a case not in his diocese, therefore all he could do now was to write his assessment and pass on the information he had acquired, their Eminences would then decide what was to be done next. Margie wondered if permission for an exorcism was granted, if he would be the one to officiate. Peter had to tell them that as he was stationed in New York, probably not, but if they wished, he would request that Archbishop Morrison assign someone else other than Fr. Xavier. He knew their concerns and they were correct; if his colleague could not be bothered handling Melissa's case properly from the beginning, in all likelihood he was not up to the demands of performing the full Rite. The Fletchers thanked him and wanted to offer him something for all his trouble, especially since he had to drive all the way to Trenton in addition to all the extra work they heard he had assumed, but Peter politely declined. He could not accept donations for his ministry or set a price for sacred objects, it would be considered simony, the sacrilegious trading of God's blessings and spiritual gifts for base profit. They explained they would like him to say an extra Mass for Rebecca and Melissa apart from the Mass he had planned to say in their home, and pressed him to take the donation. In this instance, he could not refuse. One of the few personal monetary offerings he could accept was a Mass stipend, the amount of the donation left to the charity of the individual. Peter often considered it a strange paradox as the Mass was the most important celebration in the Church. He would have gladly begged for alms on the street for his daily bread rather than accept a Mass stipend, but he obediently acceded to how Providence had arranged things, until he saw the exceptionally large donation Mr. Fletcher handed to him. The Mass was incalculable, but the Church did not expect more than a few dollars for a donation. The virtue of poverty must be emulated.

"You are too generous," Peter protested.

"Please take it, a price can't be put on a Mass." Margie smiled, knowing he could not refuse when she reaffirmed this well-known truth among the faithful.

"All right, if you insist, but there is enough for a month, so I will say ten for Rebecca, ten for Melissa, and ten for your personal intentions."

"Now who's being generous." Tom laughed. "One is fine."

"No, that would not be just. I shall say thirty Masses." Peter smiled as he jotted in his booklet the next consecutive free dates he could say them.

"All right, I won't argue with you, you're the boss."

After thanking them for their offering, while they once more expressed their deepest gratitude for coming to their assistance, Peter made sure they had his telephone number and they said their goodbyes. Settling into the compact Mini as best he could, he watched as the Fletchers drove off. Hmm, better check and make sure he told himself as he rummaged in his case for the camcorder. Like the other wives' tales, there was an element of truth to 'gremlins', demons could monkey around with technology when it was used to expose them. Praying that everything had been recorded, he hit rewind then the play button. He waited. Yes, thankfully his precaution with the medal had saved him, his machine was not tampered with by anything unseen. Although the sounds captured on the videotape were not the same as the live experience, it was unsettling to see himself engaged in that harrowing conflict, to hear again that extraordinary growling and the verbal exchange with Hell's denizens; short, barely lasting twenty minutes at the most, it still shook him to the core. It was not easy to stand firm in the presence of a diabolical horde and the video brought it all back, the horror felt by the soul while simultaneously remaining courageous and standing its ground, his faith in Christ's power over the spirits unshaken. Turning off the machine, he snipped off the tab of the videocassette to ensure nothing could be accidentally recorded over it and zipped it away in his case with relief. The confrontation was physically draining and he could not wait to return home. Buckling up and starting the engine, Peter said a prayer of thanksgiving as he pulled away from the dreary asylum, mission accomplished faster than he expected.

Sunday was Katherine's only day off from the gallery, she spent most of the day with Gerry after the other morning visitors had left.

"I hope I'm not a bug."

"No, of course not. I just wish we didn't have to be stuck here in this room of doom, and on a sunny day too."

"I'm not tiring you out?"

"Heck no. You're helping to keep me sane in all this medical wilderness. I can't help thinking that I'm the nuisance. Here you are, trying to cheer me up while you could be spending your time catching up on some of your paintings."

"Gerry, you're not a nuisance. Don't ever think that."

"What a pair we are, making each other feel guilty." He chuckled.

"I know, but still, you don't need me hovering over you like a mother hen. If only we were anywhere but here. I feel so bad about tonight, I don't enjoy the family dinners without you."

"Don't feel bad. You go enjoy yourself with everyone, crack out the silverware and raid the wine cellar. I'm not completely without some recreation you know, I do have the books you brought me, and there's always the good old boob tube."

"Still, no getting cosy in the library." She smiled, holding his hand, thinking back to the old-world chamber, their favourite room in the Reinold manor. They often found themselves sneaking away to the comfort of that well-worn leather sofa where they could spend some time, just the two of them. It always felt strangely comforting, surrounded by a forest of books as they shared their innermost thoughts and feelings. Those respectable old volumes were witness to many weighty discussions on life, love and new beginnings.

"No, I am sorry about that, please, try and have a good time. I don't want you miserable on my account. Tell you what, if you get a few minutes away from the folks, ask Lottie to show you the 'Musketeers' Lair'."

"What?"

"I haven't shown you everywhere in Stonyvale yet. I was prolonging the experience of giving you a tour of all its delights, but to cheer up my princess, I shall happily relinquish that honour to another," he replied with a mysteriously playful air.

" 'Musketeers' Lair?' What else does that house have I don't know about?" Katherine laughed.

"Let me see, there's the dungeon, the counterfeiting room … ."

He smiled as he watched her expression change from dismay to comprehension as the joke sunk in.

"Gerry, you're spinning another tall tale."

"Don't I know it? Seriously, there are some great nooks and corners left for you to see, I did tell you growing up there was a blast."

"Now you have me curious. I hope Pete makes it tonight, I don't like the idea of him missing the family fun, especially now that he and your Dad have made up. Pete really needs some time to relax and unwind a bit."

"I know, Pete is always on the go. I can't help feel guilty over that too. Yes, I know it's not my fault," he quickly added, pre-empting her effort to console him, "but the guilt's still there despite the logic."

"We're hitting a low again," Katherine noted shaking her head. "I'm not doing a good job cheering you up today."

"You're fine, I'm the one wrecking your good work. Hmm, speaking of grumble-bums, let's see what our friend Horace the Horrible is up to," Gerry suggested as he flipped through the Sunday edition, opening up to the critic columns. "Well, well, well. It looks like we are finally receiving some news about the place. The Sirrac Gallery is getting a makeover, a major one at that. The new manager is renaming it in addition to the redecorating plans, but the new name won't be revealed until the grand opening a few weeks from now," he relayed, scanning though the page. Katherine leaned over to examine the pictures.

"Oh, that's him all right," she confirmed. "That's the guy who tricked me into giving him a tour while casing my place! Why, *sure* the new guy is redecorating! Twerp. I'll bet a hundred to one he's going to 'borrow' some of my ideas after the stunt he pulled. And he treated Kevin outrageously too. While I'm very glad Kevin is on our team, I don't like how it all happened. What's the nincompoop's name?"

"Sir Conrad Elverton."

"Never heard of him."

"I don't know, that name *does* sound familiar … ."

"Here, read the whole thing out. Horace is bound to get all the low-down."

Gerry cleared his throat and began reading:

"Say goodbye to the Sirrac Gallery, New Yorkers. The minimalist marvel of old has become the first overseas acquisition of the Norlofton Group, the up and coming gallery chain that has taken England by storm. It appears that the Brits are planning to rebuild an empire, not by military might, but by paint and canvas. Although yours truly baulks at the thought of what supposed masterpieces will be presented to us since so few masterpieces are created these days on either side of the pond, if there must be chains and franchises in the world, we must admit that their way of economic imperium is far superior in one aspect: artistic culture clubs in lieu of the cholesterol joints our fair land of the bold and the free has introduced to the globe. And no wonder, the once-upon-a-time Sirrac shall be managed by none other than Conrad Elverton, son of George Elverton, the founder and CEO of Norlofton Group who was recently made a peer of the realm by Her majesty the Queen in honour of services rendered to their country. Elverton the Younger due to make his mark soon here on Fifth Avenue has also received honours vis a knighthood, therefore one could truly say the aristocrats are back in town and plan to teach us Yankee Doodles a thing or two about the finer things in life. We shall see if their idea of culture is truly superior to that of Gotham's residents in a few weeks when the premises currently under the decorator's sledgehammer will have its grand opening. Until then, the new look and name of the gallery shall be kept under wraps."

"Cultured? That rude, conceited, arrogant, spying no-good? Obviously, with his sneaky tactics, 'services to the country' means a tour of duty at MI 5, or 6, or whatever."

"Careful with the name-calling, or you'll have to run back to Pete's box. Again."

"Oh, you're right." Katherine took a breath and counted slowly to ten. "The way I've been running to him, he should charge me rent for taking up the confessional."

"There now, that's it, let it all out. Feel better?"

"Almost. People like that just frustrate me. Title indeed. If you are not noble in your thoughts and actions, no title awarded by any king or queen can make you so."

"Brava, well said, my dear. Don't let Sir Nincompoop upset you."

"What was that about name calling?"

"Hey, you said it first, not me," he reminded her with humour.

"Hmm, gallery chain, that's something else, isn't it? I wonder how that works. Sell a number of limited editions at participating locations?"

"Perhaps they might offer a 'drive-thru' service," he added in good fun. "No, I think they will either concentrate on selling the work of local artists in the near vicinity of each gallery, or spread a single collection across their franchise. It's the only way I can see how it would work."

"That makes sense, but it sounds so … *commercial.* I much prefer the individual gallery model, it's more personal and not so mercenary."

"I agree. Everything is getting super-sized lately, like the new hypermarkets and all the mega bookstores opening everywhere. As much as I appreciate the new business heading our way in the shipping sphere, I pity the independents. I wonder how they're going to keep up. It gripes me to think the humanities are quickly being reduced to mass-market products. Auction houses are one thing, but this?"

"It certainly is a fast-changing world. I don't like the sound of this Norlofton Group," Katherine concluded.

"You've got to admit this tells us something. Your place must be getting pretty famous on the Old Britannia side if he came to scout your establishment. He's judging what he's up against here in the Big Apple."

"I know we've made the news quite a bit, but to be judged as serious competition like that, and all the way from Europe? Wow, I guess that really is news."

"See? It's not as bad as you think. Elverton … Elverton." Gerry thought for a moment. "It's coming back. All these meds must be addling my brain. You know the friend I told you about who sends me the raspberry curds from England?"

"You mean Percy?"

"The very same, he mentioned this Conrad Elverton once and wondered if I knew him or if I had visited his gallery when I was in England. I remember him saying that Saatchi was a client of theirs. That was about four years ago, no doubt before they started this Norlofton company, I couldn't place the name," Gerry deduced. "Of course, I've lost touch with what's happening with the European art scene, I've had so much fun over here," he noted, giving her hand a quick kiss.

"That's good to know." She smiled. "And besides, if Saatchi likes what they sell, you haven't missed much."

"True." He chuckled.

Perhaps Gerry had not been keeping track of the global art trends, but Katherine learned she had better familiarise herself with most of it considering her clients at the gallery were well informed about every blurb reporting the latest cultural news and gossip. Although she refused to sell anything that resembled the products of a kindergarten class, she did offer modern art in her establishment and was expected to be well versed in the latest blotches of some unhinged plodder hailed as the latest genius to appear since Pollock gave up the ghost. To be an artist and proud gallery owner yet be clueless about the international art scene was considered a deficiency that had to be amended, no matter how ludicrous the trends tended to be. Horace and his griping columns were packed with information. The Gallery Gang were certainly a godsend, they helped keep her up to date with most of the modern 'flapdoodle' as her Gramps called it, while Martin and Justine relayed all the latest art trends from Paris. For Gerry's amusement she recounted the recent crash-course Kevin gave her on Saatchi's latest modern art acquisitions, including a work entitled *Ghost*; a plaster cast sculpture of a Victorian drawing room, the space completely reproduced as a giant square and made to look as though someone had poured plaster into the chamber from an opening in the ceiling and peeled away the walls, leaving behind a bone-white block, a fossilized remnant of architecture gone by left as an imprint on all four sides. Gerry laughed, that was one piece he had not heard about, further remarking that Cubism had been taken to a whole new level. Katherine agreed and wondered if there was anything left in that particular 'ism' for the other artists to explore. Gerry could always make her see the funny side of things, but to think she had to be 'up' on all this nonsense! Gerry commiserated, although he invested in certain modern pieces, like her, he much preferred the old masters and artefacts of antiquity.

"What a waste of brain space," she continued. "I'd rather concentrate on my own place instead of minding what's going on in someone else's."

"Yes, but this is all part of the business, you have to keep up with your competitors, stay one step ahead of them. It's obvious Sir Spy is not resting on his laurels."

"I know, you keep telling me, but nuts! Art as 'business'. Uck. It seems such a bad combination. Why can't I just promote classic styles and establish my gallery gracefully?"

"Aw, one could not accuse you of being ungraceful. All in all, I thought you were doing pretty good."

"Some of the things I'm putting up on the walls lately for the sake of modernity has me wondering. At least they're not indecent. Besides, how on earth do I keep 'one step' ahead anyway? I can't redecorate the place every year, and I already have the 'rapid-rotation' system well oiled and running, so it's not like one-time collections stay forever on the walls. So far, business is good."

"People want pizzazz. Perhaps you might want to think of holding an event at the gallery to attract some newsworthy attention. I know you've given Horace exclusive rights to your stories, but you have to stay in the public's eye with something novel, especially now with the new and improved Sirrac about to open, just to make sure the clients don't forget you."

"Well, at least I have a few old faithfuls," she replied, hugging his arm, "and I know Horace will make sure I'm not forgotten, but you're right, the curiosity alone will pull people over to the new place, not to mention all the rest of the galleries in town. I'll have to think of something, plan counter manoeuvres. What a nuisance, I want to paint and create, not go to war."

"Aren't artists supposed to thrive on the creative struggle, battling the world and expressing it through their masterpieces?"

"I don't know about 'thrive', but new challenges help us to strive, that's for sure."

"That's it, think of it as a challenge, not a hindrance. A little strategy and a few thrills now and then keeps life interesting."

"True. Hmm, maybe this competition thing will be good after all. Yeah, why not? What better way to get back at Master Nincompoop than to make the Walsingham Gallery better than his mystery place? What to do though, that's the thing. I probably won't be able to plan any counter-attack until I see Sir Spy's new establishment."

"That's it, bide your time. Plot and plan like all good generals." Gerry smiled.

Speaking of painting made her wish they were back in the studio together. Gerry obviously felt the same, he was tired of the newspapers and instinctively reached for the pen and notebook on his adjustable table, sketching a few aimless but artful squiggles, wanting more activity in a creative sense. He was glad to be kept in the loop of Reinold Enterprises, but now found he needed something else other than business for activity, particularly on Sundays since he promised Pete no unnecessary servile toil unless it was an emergency. Katherine watched as he made some elegant curves. Although it was only an abstract meandering, he was already a master with the pen and pencil. Her eye travelled past his sketching and observed the rolling table. It was not one of their large studio worktables, but it would do.

"I've got an idea. I won't be too long."

"Oh? What's up?"

"Nope, won't tell you. I shall keep you in suspense."

"Aha, my princess has a surprise in store, and when that happens, odds are I may expect a life-changing experience. Better skip the suspense and tell me what's going on in that scheming mind of yours." Katherine laughed, one of her faults was her unpredictable impetuosity that often turned everyone's life inside out and upside down.

"That's not fair to ask since you are notorious for planning surprises."

"Touché my dear, but may I not have one little hint?"

"Don't worry, it's nothing spectacular this time, nothing that will cause danger to life or limb, at least, I don't think so, not permanent damage anyway. It should help cheer you up, me too for that matter. Toodle-oo." With that, she gave him a kiss on the cheek, grabbed her purse and was out the door in a flash.

Gerry shook his head with a smile and continued his sketching, flipping to a clean page and commencing a landscape. He would find out soon enough what she was going to propose next. Perhaps sneak in a contraband lunch from outside the hospital confines while the nurses weren't looking, that would be a welcome surprise. There were days he questioned if the fare dished up to him by his white-clad minders was intended to nourish. Often the bland, carefully measured portions seemed as though they were served only to give the innards something to work on. However, any solid rations were better than having a hose shoved though his nasal passage. He had better not complain lest one of the dragon ladies on duty would afflict him with that uncomfortable alternative.

When Gerry had finally finished a few sketches, he noticed it was close to two hours since she had left. He must have been lost in the creative moment. He was about to start worrying when Katherine appeared in the doorway toting a distinguished rose-coloured mahogany art case with brass period-style latches.

"There you are."

"Sorry about that, I had a long drive, but I think this will be worth it," she explained, setting down the case and opening it up. Inside she had stashed the smuggled lunch he had hoped for, double-decker bacon burgers, king sized fries, chocolate and vanilla milkshakes, plus a few packaged pastries. "Lunch for two, all good and greasy. I know it's better hot, and the milkshakes have probably melted into ice cream soup, but this should be a real treat compared with the daily menu served here."

"This is great." He playfully rubbed his hands in anticipation. "To think you went all the way to the gallery just to get the case to hide it in. You didn't have to do that, I'm sure you could have smuggled it in without having to go through that hassle."

"I didn't fetch this just for lunch, I've got more in there, but we'll get to that after we appease our grumbling tums. Here, tuck in," she said, laying everything out and plonking a napkin across his chest.

"Thanks love, but you know we had better eat this quick before one of the guards gets wind of our picnic."

"Right, the downside is I'm not doing you a favour with this clandestine meal. You'll have to eat the lunch they serve you too in case they think you've lost your appetite. They could put you under medical observation to find out the cause, and you'd be up a creek then."

"Ugh. Looks like I shall not be spared their intestinal filler after all."

"What do you think this stuff is? I've replaced your tasteless meal by something equally dubious."

"Quick, down the hatch. It's not getting any hotter."

Messy but tasty, watching the doorway while they ate in case they were caught, they felt like a couple of kids who had stolen the cookie jar. For Gerry, eating while propped up in bed was not easy, especially as the top half of their burgers slid with each bite. Despite Katherine's precaution with the napkin, he ended up with a ketchup splotch down his front, which he tried to mop up without too much success.

"Swell. I hope they don't think I'm bleeding. God knows what they'd do to me then," he joked. "We may have to 'fess up to spare me from their undivided medical attention."

"Oh, I should have put the smock on you, it's in the case."

"Smock? What else have you … uh oh," he stopped, "darling, we're busted."

"I'll say you're busted," Nurse Gracie said as she led in the lunch cart delivery, one hand on her hip, her patient charts in the other. "Miss Walsingham, I'm surprised at you. First, your brother with the doughnuts this morning, now this pipe-clogger of a meal. Here we are, worrying ourselves, trying to keep him healthy, and you have just burst our bubble, not to mention he'll have to be changed into a clean top."

"I'm sorry, but I couldn't help it, he was longing for something different, and I wouldn't advise changing his top yet, he'll probably look a lot more colourful before the day is over."

"Just what do you mean by that," the nurse wondered as she eyed Katherine rummaging in the mahogany case. Gerry leaned over to get a better look, watching with interest as she cleared the rolling table of their fast food wrappings and pulled out the smock, a jar, a set of brushes, a table-top easel, small canvases and a box of petite paint tubes.

"I thought you could do with some artistic recreation and decided now was a good time as any to start you on your first lesson in watercolours," she explained, turning to him. "Watercolour paintings are not as difficult to clean up after like oils, and everything can be kept in the case by the bedside table when you're not working on them."

"I'd like that." He smiled, the remainder of her surprise now finally revealed. "I was wondering when I would get my hands on a paint brush again." Since she had taught him how to draw and work with oils, he found his new artistic hobby quite fulfilling. Before the accident, focusing on colours, curves, and strokes in the quiet atmosphere of her studio helped to calm his busy mind after a hectic day at work and to forget all the stresses. The ability to make anything beautiful was cathartically satisfying, but above all, it was an enjoyable pastime he could indulge in with Katherine. There is nothing like a shared interest to draw people together.

"I guess that will be all right," the nurse noted, "but I assume Picasso's lunch is ruined. Hey, did you do this?" She set her files down and picked up his notebook while the lunch tray was taken away untouched.

"Yeah, it's not great. My gorgeous fiancée is the real master here."

"Don't knock yourself. This isn't bad, it's great, you've got talent," Gracie declared.

"He does, doesn't he? I keep telling him, but he won't listen, and he won't let me display the few pictures he finished. Says he's not gallery material yet."

"Which is true, but for any talent that is showing through right now, you have to thank her," he affirmed, sliding his arm around Katherine as she prepped him for art class with the smock, "she's my teacher and a top notch one too, no professor could teach better."

"Professor Matthews might argue with you, but my first student deserves a prize for that nice bit of flattery," she replied, giving him a kiss on the forehead.

"What? No croissant or hot fudge cake? That compliment deserves a nice big slice right here, pronto," he said, indicting his lips.

"No croissants or cake for you today, not after that lump of grease you just consumed," Nurse Gracie warned. Gerry and Katherine cast each other a humorous glance trying not to laugh, he meant something completely different.

"So you taught him? Wow. Do you have other students," the nurse wondered, turning back to the sketches.

"Just his dad, Mr. R. I'm not really offering classes … ."

"Oh what a shame, you would get loads of students, I'm sure. Well, no time to dawdle, I must attend to duty, I'm off. Have fun you two, and please, no more crashing his calorie count, okay?"

"No, Kathy, don't speak. You can't keep a promise you haven't made," Gerry pleaded.

"You're incorrigible." Gracie sighed as she checked his files and other medical equipment around the bed. When they were finally alone, Katherine could commence the tutorial.

Similar to her other introductory lessons, she let him try a few pictures by himself without any instruction to see what she was dealing with. As with all first endeavours, the first attempts at making a depiction in the new medium were not successful. Gerry 'hmmed' as he watched the wet colours dribble from his landscapes and coalesce into dark murky puddles, blending into dismal hues he did not know existed. Katherine smiled, it reminded her of his first drawing lesson and the oddity that he produced on paper.

"It's not as easy as I thought," he conceded. "Okay, it's obvious I'm missing something."

"Or you've got too much of something."

"Paint."

"Right. You're putting too much in one small section, watercolours are like markers, so the more you paint over an area, the colour grows darker, and, you have to allow drying time in between, or you end up with a soggy mess."

"That's an understatement. I've recreated a swamp in all its saturated glory. Back to the drawing board."

Already familiar with the basics of blending and applying oils, Gerry needed few lessons and did not take long to get the feel of the new medium after his first sopping mishaps. Finishing a few alpine scenes, Katherine suggested he should try an experiment in tinting the sketches he had completed in her absence. She watched with quiet fascination as he applied the colours within the dark ink lines, turning his already striking landscapes into miniature gems that had the captivating quality of stained glass windows. It reminded her of the otherworldly and entrancing illustrations seen in the fairy-tale and fantasy books printed in the turn of the century stored in his rare book collection. Gerry always had an eye for all things captivating and mysterious.

"These are gorgeous. I'm tempted to frame them and put them up in the gallery."

"Please don't. Horace is notoriously cruel to up-and-coming artists. I don't think I could handle the rejection." He chuckled.

"Stop being silly," she replied, giving him a playful tap on the arm.

"Ow. Okay, don't beat up the patient. To be honest, I'm not really an artist, it doesn't feel right to hang my stuff up with the pros."

"Nonsense, if you have the talent and can create, what's stopping you? You're the same creative person whether or not you have a degree in art. I personally declare you a capable *artiste* ready to take on the world. You just may be my next great discovery after the mysterious 'D.S'."

"Even so, I'd like you to keep them," he said gently, "if you like them that much, I don't want anyone else having them."

"Ah, a private little gift just for me? Spoiling me again, are you?"

"Naturally."

"But please, you will consider letting me show something of yours in the gallery? It doesn't have to be anything for sale, just something we could place on exhibition. Your talent shouldn't go unnoticed."

"Hmm, let me devise something that I might be tempted to call a masterpiece, then we shall see."

"I'm taking that as a 'yes', so no copping out."

"We shall see."

"I thought *I* was a perfectionist. You have to learn to recognize when you have reached perfection in a picture."

"That's a hoot! You're never satisfied with any of your paintings, you always dab at them until the bristles are worn down to the nub."

"True, but I do learn to let them go, eventually. *Please* Gerry, let me show one of yours. The nurses won't be happy, but I can bring in oil paints and some fresh canvases tomorrow, you can start that new magnum opus right here."

"We shall see."

Katherine sighed, he was stubborn to the quick. One day, she hoped she might be able to convince him to brave a public viewing. For the present, she continued to quietly observe as he drew a new ink sketch and tinted in the lines with cool aqueous tones, waiting to see what shades he would chose next. Admiring a creative soul at work is almost as satisfying as making your own paintings. It was as calming as watching a sunset and wondering what colours would be displayed before the stars appeared. So many hues in nature and yet nothing remained the same, every day, every season a work of genius, a free gift from the Artist of artists.

She could not help but think of Peter when her mind wandered into subjects like this, especially when she considered the stars. The explanation he gave on the symbolic importance of those celestial lights had proved enlightening at a time when she was struggling with her own soul-searching. Although now close as any brother or sister could be, she still looked on him with a deep respect that bordered on awe, he certainly was not like anyone she had ever met before. That morning's events continued to puzzle her, and she wondered how he was faring with his 'mercy mission', which she knew could only be one thing for an exorcist. When Gerry was not in the need of her instructions, she offered a few more silent prayers for Peter who was facing only God knew what.

The afternoon passed quickly with the new artistic activity, it was when her father arrived with a few new books for the patient that they realised how the time had flown.

"Hi Pops Number Two. Hey thanks, I appreciate the thought, but you didn't have to bring anything," Gerry reminded.

"It's nothing, I thought I'd bring you these to keep you occupied, but obviously someone has beat me to it." Harold smiled, noticing he had interrupted the artists discussing the merits of the latest drawing.

"Hi Pops." Katherine jumped up, giving him a hug and a kiss on the cheek. "I guess I have. How do you like Gerry's first watercolours? I figured he needed something fun to do."

"They're something else, aren't they," Harold noted, leaning over for a closer look. "Well son, ready to brave the life of an artist yet? It looks like you're well on your way to creating your first collection."

"Not yet, Pops. I and my scribbles shall remain hidden for now."

Katherine smiled, it was good to hear the final blocks of ice between them thaw these last few weeks with the familiar address of 'son' and 'Pops'. A crusty and overprotective father, she was afraid he would never accept her fiancé, a fear she could now lay aside.

"Pops, I can't get him to listen to me, you think they're good for the gallery, right?"

"I'm not an expert, but I'm sure any serious collector would certainly consider these worth hanging on their walls."

"There Gerry, another person who thinks you have talent. Now you will *have* to paint me that masterpiece."

"We shall see, my dear."

"You're impossible!" She laughed, shaking her head. "So, Pops, any news? How was the club today?"

Unfortunately, there was no time for the country club. Sunday or not, he had to check in the Jersey City offices with Uncle Tim to see how the latest research in the cosmetic branch of their company was doing, then rush off to the Williamsburg plant for another job since there were other matters to attend to during the week and he had to see these few places right away. However, he had to admit he was pleased how Steves' girlfriend was pulling her weight in the bio labs, just a few weeks and she was one of the team. It was not often that a newly fledged graduate was given such a coveted spot in one of their top research and development departments. Dr. Stirling, head of that branch, was pleasantly satisfied with her and how quickly she got along with the staff. Katherine reminded him that Steves assured Jennifer was a 'grade A' researcher, further commenting that she heard her say in so many words that very morning the products from Walsingham Industries were far superior in quality than those of Snepres Biotech and that she hoped they would never stoop to the level of their competitors just to make a quick profit. Gerry confirmed Jennifer said as much.

"I suppose that's something," Harold conceded, loyalty to the family and the firm were foremost in his and Gramp's set of principles.

"I really think she's proud to be working for us Pops," Katherine added, hinting that the girl in Steve's life may not be the opportunist they all thought at first, glad things were working out in the workplace at least. She hoped this improvement might extend to the private domain. Although Katherine generally kept quiet on the subject, there was no escaping the tense nature of the situation. Steves and Jennifer were still in the doghouse for living together with no sight or sound of wedding bells any time soon, and the elders of the conservative Walsingham clan, especially Aunt Martha, were not about to let the cohabiters get away with their present common law arrangement without dishing out some discomfort in the hopes they might nudge them into doing the proper thing.

Soon a few more visitors arrived, her mother, Gramps and Aunt Martha. Like Harold, they decided to drop by and see how the patient was faring and brought a few gifts before they drove to Long Island for dinner with the Reinolds.

"Well, looky here, the studio has gone mobile," Gramps noted, surveying the artists as he delivered a fresh bag of goodies.

"I guess you could say that," Katherine agreed as she helped Gerry tidy up the paints before giving everyone a kiss and a hug. Gerry opened the bag and raised an eyebrow; Gramps had discovered one of his weaknesses, chocolate peanut butter cups.

"Thanks Gramps, I think I can stomach the hospital's dinner tonight with this as a consolation," the patient beamed.

"I thought you might like that, so would I if I was faced with their plates. Great minds really do think alike," his benefactor replied.

"That was good guesswork. How did you make the right guess?"

"Some on-the-spot sleuthing, m'boy. Remember the time when Tim and I discussed that new shipping contract with you? Instead of a jelly bean jar on your desk, I noticed you had Reese's Pieces. It wasn't rocket science to put two and two together. I have an eye for these things."

"Gregory, you are not doing him any good," Aunt Martha warned, but to no avail. Gramps watched with satisfaction as Gerry opened a package and proceeded to ruin his dinner nonetheless. Katherine thought she had a chocolate problem until she saw Gramps and Gerry absorbed with the hoard of peanut butter cups.

"It's not really the chocolate as much as the peanut butter," he clarified. "I wish I knew how they get it as powdery as they do. Here, everyone dive in," Gerry offered, passing around the bag.

"No thanks son, I can't eat chocolate, upsets my stomach for some reason," Pops replied, holding up his hand. He also had to avoid peanut butter for the sake of his cholesterol count. Aunt Martha and Katherine would have loved one, but did not want to fill up. Mom Number Two also refused.

"Maybe *you* want to wreck your evening repast, but we must politely decline. How would your mother feel if she knew you just about ruined her efforts," Helen queried.

"True, my Mom would not be pleased. At least let Gramps have one, I know you're itching to grab one of these," he said turning to him.

"Thankee kindly son, but no thankee," Gramps declined, dejectedly eyeing the bag. Everyone looked at him with incredulity. Since when did he ever refuse to cheat on his diet when the opportunity had been so readily handed to him? Only one time they knew of—a looming doctor's appointment.

"Let me guess, Dr. Hendricks, 8.30 A.M. tomorrow sharp," Katherine *tsked*.

"Nailed again," Gramps admitted. "I skipped the last few check-ups, so he cornered me at the club yesterday and set up an appointment, 'No refusals or cancellations', he tells me. Hrumph! There's medical tyranny for you."

"Oh Gramps, I keep telling you, one day's diet is not enough to fool the doctor and his scales." Katherine sighed. "You have to stop cheating."

"Gregory, you should show a little self control," Aunt Martha huffed. "What kind of example are you setting for the young ones here?"

"One they don't have to follow if they don't want to, right kiddos?" Katherine and Gerry cast a guilty glance at each other, thinking about their unwholesome lunch that afternoon and how they had whole-heartedly emulated his erring ways. "Honestly," Gramps continued, "I thought I was being pretty good right now, that peanut butter smells very inviting. Gerry's darn lucky I handed over the booty," he finished with a chuckle, bringing his gleaming ebony cane down with a good-natured thump.

"Well, unlike *some* people I know, at least I thought to bring something sensible," Aunt Martha added, opening up the large bag by her side and pulling out a sizable feather pillow with a royal blue satin cover with embroidered flowers on the border. "Sit up Gerry, that's it, let's make you more comfortable. There now! All better? I could not bear it any longer, I just *had* to rectify your woeful sleeping arrangements. I simply cannot abide these synthetic public head-cushions, nothing but lumpy miseries of mesh! They are the epitome of stinginess. One cannot expect anyone to recuperate properly without the proper comforts of a well-attended sick bed, and there's nothing like a feather pillow for convalescing in style. I cannot tolerate a restorative period without a decent feather pillow, several in fact. You do like blue, don't you? Katherine did say you liked blue, or perhaps it was red? I was absolutely positive she told me it was blue … ."

Eventually, Gerry could get a word in and confirm blue was one of his favourite colours after she had plumped up the new gift and shoved it behind him, ordering him to lie back and report on how it felt and if she had positioned it correctly, giving the stately sleeping accessory a prod here and a jab there around his shoulders.

"Well, m' boy," Gramps said with a wry smile and a twinkle in his eye, "what a regal picture you present in your blue satin and pink roses. You'll be the envy of the hospital, and who knows? Maybe the start of a whole new trend on the men's floor."

"Exactly! And I want you to know, I embroidered the pink rose bouquet myself, and added the pink bow to complete the effect."

"Gee, however can I thank you, Aunt Martha, for going to such trouble for me. I didn't think ladies still embroidered for a hobby." Gerry could hardly keep a straight face, he tried to cover by lowing his head and adjusting the blankets around him. Katherine didn't know whether to laugh or be mortified for him.

"Oh, Aunt Martha, don't you think it's a little over the top, and a little … on the feminine side?"

"Nonsense! There's never enough of the Nightingale touch to soothe a man suffering in his affliction."

"Martha, you have quite outdone yourself this time. I can just imagine how Gerry feels right now, his gratitude to you and for all this work. Come now, it's fine, don't frisk him so, you're always fussing," her sister intervened. "Here, help me get rid of some of these drooping blooms, I know Katherine always brings you your favourite flowers Gerry, but I couldn't resist these," Helen noted, placing the peach coloured bouquet she had brought next to the familiar red rose and bright sunflowers on a nearby table, removing some old posies other visitors had given that had since wilted, handing them to Aunt Martha for disposal. Better to keep her busy with something lest she maim her future son-in-law any further with her well-meaning attentions. Martha gladly helped, the shrivelling posies were doing nothing to enhance the recuperative ambience she had created with her elegant cushion. Unable to find a large enough trash can in the room, she left to deposit the old bouquets in the receptacle down the hallway.

"I'm sorry son, but you know she means well," Harold replied when the coast was clear, the corner of his mouth twitching into a smile, betraying his amusement.

"I know. I shall have to keep it now, I can't just lose it somewhere, it would offend her."

"You'll just have to grin and bear it," Gramps nodded sympathetically, although he too found the sight of Gerry propped up by the blue and pink hues of the 'Nightingale touch' very funny.

"Now, it's not that bad," Helen interceded, Martha was her sister after all. "It *does* look more comfortable than what the hospital had provided."

"True, I must say it is a major improvement," Gerry diplomatically replied.

"Oh, it's my fault," Katherine piped up. "I mean all the pink roses, it has to be."

"Dare to share," Gerry wheedled.

"Well, on top of telling her you liked blue, during the wedding plans she was complaining non-stop about the pink coloured theme, how *tré ordianaire* it was, I was so tired and couldn't take her criticism another bit that day. I let it slip about how you would like to see your bride arriving down the aisle surrounded by pink roses. If you liked the scheme, that was that. The decision was final. What I said obviously stuck because she never said another word about the colour, and you have just ended up with all that glowing embroidery.”

“Mystery solved.” Gerry concluded. “Aw, I shall have to keep it now, won’t I?”

“I know, the bride not the groom should be stuck with all those flowers.” Katherine smiled. “We’ll have to think of a solution.”

“For now, just remember to be discreet when mentioning your likes and dislikes around her, or you’ll never know what to expect next.” Gramps chuckled.

At that moment, Nurse Gracie was passing by the door. Noticing the large group of visitors she decided to check in on the patient and found him propped up with the non-standard issue bed apparel and reaching into a bag laden with contraband chocolate.

“All right, that’s it. I’m calling a halt to this party. Of all things, whose bright idea was it to bring a *feather* pillow into my ward,” she noted, poking inside the satin cover. “This germ-trap has to go, only hypo-allergenic items are allowed.” Aunt Martha returned just in time to hear this lecture and watched in dismay as her thoughtful gift was pulled out from behind Gerry’s back, replaced by the uncomfortable medically approved mesh-wad and exiled in disgrace to the nearby wardrobe. “And I see my warning about calorie counts went unheeded,” Nurse Gracie continued, yanking the bag of peanut butter cups away from the patient. “I’m keeping these in a safe place, I promise to let you have a few at a time. Agreed?”

“All right, you’re the boss.” Gerry nodded reluctantly although amused with the reprimand, glad she had provided an iron-clad pretext to remove the embroidery display. At least he managed to snatch one last packet before she confiscated the booty as Gramps had called his offering. Nurse Gracie continued to hustle around, monitoring the various machines.

“I suppose that’s our cue,” Harold noted, eyeing the officious nurse as she made it obvious there were too many people crowding her patient. “I don’t want to be a spoil-sport, but we’ll have to hop to it if we intend to arrive on time at your parents’ home.”

“Sure, no problem. Say ‘hi’ for me, tell them I hope they enjoy themselves and not to worry. While I wish I was going with you, I’m fine and have plenty of things on hand to keep me busy, thanks to all your kind attentions.”

"We will. Try and get some rest too," Helen advised before they said their goodbyes. Katherine lingered for a moment after they left, she and Gerry could just hear Aunt Martha complaining as they made their way to the elevators about the inflexible rules of the hospital that had banished her pillow to the obscurity of the wardrobe. Nurse Gracie finally exited the room, giving them a minute alone to kiss each other goodnight before Katherine reluctantly left the patient to his bedside amusements.

ଊ❖ଌ

It was an uneventful drive as the Walsingham motorcade made its way to Long Island, Katherine checking her rear-view mirror, waving every now and again to Pops and Gramps who were following behind while her mother and Aunt Martha tagged along third in the row. To be more precise, the drive was *almost* uneventful. Steves and Jennifer increased the three vehicle train to four, bombing up in 'Delores' and passing them all out leap-frog fashion with a friendly honk or two as he whizzed by, no doubt making up for the lost time he suffered while caught in city traffic. Steves may be a fully-fledged masters graduate of MIT plus the youngest and newest member of the board at Walsingham Industries, but he had yet to outgrow the need for speed. Eventually the motorcade caught up with him outside the large wrought iron gates of Stonyvale Manor and it looked like he was not budging soon. Katherine wondered if the security was stepped-up, usually they could get through without much bother. After a few minutes Steves was allowed to pass and the gates swung shut. Heck, what's going on? How she missed the days when the iron portals were always left open, no cameras, no security key-code box standing like a merciless robot sentry borrowed from the set of a science fiction movie. Next in line, Katherine pulled up and was interrogated by a crackling metallic voice.

"Name please."

"Oh, come on, you know it's me," Katherine replied to the mechanical box. The CCTV camera swivelled for a better view.

"Sorry Miss, we have a new guy on tonight," came the explanation through the speaker while the gates slowly opened once more.

"That's okay, just don't close up the slammer yet, my family are in the cars behind."

"No problem."

The cortège made its way along the tree-sheltered driveway leading to the rambling manor situated on a rise overlooking the coast, surrounded by a large estate park on one side and sweeping views of the sea on the other. It was odd to observe the once sleepy historic edifice detailed with security men patrolling in shifts or keeping a watchful eye from the balconies and cupolas. For the last month, there was a fully operational battery of monitors in a room designated as the new security control area in the service quarters, not to mention the West Wing was still in the process of being fitted with the latest alarm system. After the refurbishment of her gallery, Katherine could imagine the headaches the Reinolds were suffering, their privacy invaded as the troop of workmen tramped in and out during the weekdays with their grubby machines and equipment, drilling holes for new camera lines and electric wires. Hopefully all these necessary invasive proceedings currently rendering the estate nothing short of a public museum would be over soon.

Notwithstanding the upheavals, Richard and Sophia cheerfully greeted the arrivals at the front door while Victor the butler and his staff took their guests' coats and brought their cases up to their rooms. The Reinolds had insisted many months ago that whenever the Walsinghams came for dinner they might as well stay the night considering the long trip they would have back to Englewood. Richard suggested they could save themselves the hassle of all the driving back and forth, further pointing out with a touch of humour that they had ample room for them all at Stonyvale. While the mention of 'ample room' was the understatement of the decade, no one wanted to impose, but Richard and Sophia were so glad to have company to liven up the place that they could not refuse their offer. The open invitation was gladly extended to the Reinolds whenever it was their turn to visit Oak Meadows. During the various stages of Gerry and Katherine's wedding plans, overnight and weekend sleepovers became a very practical arrangement, especially for the ladies. Soon it became a running joke that nobody knew where his or her permanent place of residence was any more.

"Good evening one and all. I'm sorry about the hold-up, we have a new fellow on the gates tonight," Richard explained, "even I got barred from my own house this afternoon."

"No apologies, we know how it is. I keep forgetting our new codes," Harold assured him. The Walsinghams also had their own security system, although not as elaborate as the Reinolds' current upgrade.

Steven did the honours of introducing Jennifer to their hosts, grateful they would extend their sleep-over invitation knowing how old fashioned they were, although Aunt Martha was not looking too thrilled at the moment; not only did she strongly disapprove of their forbidden affair, he knew from experience she was not appreciative of his wild driving skills. Under different circumstances he would be at the receiving end of a reprimand were it not for the fact they were all guests and must be on their best behaviour. One of Aunt Martha's guiding principles was to keep up appearances at all costs, and the obligation of putting their best foot forward had mercifully clamped down her present desire to promptly lower him a peg or two.

"My, you have a beautiful home Mr. and Mrs. Reinold," Jennifer complimented.

"Thank you, we just manage the place. I'm sure the girls will be happy to give you the grand tour. Speaking of which, where is Lottie," Richard wondered.

"I don't know, but she should be here soon. Which reminds me, poor Mrs Hunt won't be joining us tonight, she is feeling a little under the weather."

"That's terrible, I was hoping she might come," Helen commiserated.

"Oh, I'm sorry to hear that," Katherine replied. She meant it too, despite the myriad of times the feisty lady made her run to confession these days. Mrs. Hunt had no family living close by and was now puttering around with her arthritic hips in that big mansion of hers down the road. The Reinolds, close friends of her late husband, were practically the only close family acquaintances she had, and they always included her in their gatherings, including Sunday dinners usually reserved for relatives.

"I know, but these spells sometimes pass quickly, she'll soon be up and about."

"I'll have to give her a call in the morning," Katherine resolved.

"Very good dear, she'll appreciate that. Come, let us all go into the Rose Room. Dinner should be ready in half an hour," Sophia announced. "We're having a buffet spread tonight, something informal so we can all relax a bit, not to mention it's easier to keep the food warm, by the time it all comes up from the kitchens … ."

"Forgive me for interrupting you, Sophie dear, but is the coast clear," Helen asked as they left the entrance hall, afraid one member of the family might be making a speedy entrance: their mischievous African Grey parrot. Permitted the freedom of the main living areas, he had the disquieting habit of swooping through the air and landing on the first shoulder in sight, checking out every guest that came through the front door as thoroughly as the new security detail.

"Yes, Sinbad is locked up in the brig, and he's not coming out for some time I might add," Sophia noted.

"What? What did the rascal do," Gramps wondered, disappointed he was not greeted by the boisterous feather ball.

"One of the guards left the door to the West Wing open and he flew over to one of the 'No Go' areas," Richard informed him. "By the time we figured out he was not in the his usual haunts, he had eaten a hole in a loveseat in the Violet Room and was pulling out the stuffing, jabbering away to himself and having the time of his life."

"He waits for every opportunity to sneak off where we never think to look for him so he can demolish the place in peace," Sophia continued, "as if we didn't have enough to contend with at the moment."

"Oh! Not one of your antiques?" Martha commiserated while Helen gasped in disbelief, Helen's pride and joy was the period furnishings gracing the formal parlours of Oak Meadows after several extravagant spending sprees at the choicest auction houses.

"I'm afraid so, and it's not the first time. He wasn't named *Sin-bad* for nothing," Richard affirmed while Steven stifled a smile. Richard continued, "he's nipped corners off my picture frames too, nearly gnawed his way down to the canvas of my favourite Turner. I'd keel-haul him if it wasn't for the fact I'm too attached to the old barnacle," Richard finished with a nod. This time Katherine gasped.

"He didn't! I'm surprised you still let him out." Well, that explained why some of the old frames looked a little worse for wear than one might expect to see with a famous art collection.

The party continued into the Rose Room, discussing the adventures of Sinbad, Sophia adding that they did not have the heart to keep him confined since he came with a pair of wings, although she had to admit there were times the antique restorers were making a decent living from their magnanimity towards that bird.

Cocktails were served and everyone settled down, those who had just come from the hospital were eager to assure the Reinolds that they had left Gerry in good spirits and passed on his message when Victor politely intruded with the announcement that Master Peter had just arrived.

"There's some good news," Mr. R beamed, getting up from his chair, everyone else following suit to greet Peter as he entered the room.

"Good evening everyone," Peter tried to say while his father gave him a quick embrace with a hearty backslap or two before allowing him give his mother a hug, then the usual round of handshakes.

"I'm so glad you could make it dear," Sophia said as they once more took their seats.

"Me too. My assignment finished earlier than I expected, someone must have been sending a few prayers my way," he replied with an appreciative glance at Katherine.

His father asked what he would like to drink, but Peter just shook his head. Nothing for him right now, thank you, but Mr. R insisted Victor fix him something, especially as he looked like he could use a drink to revive him. To please him Peter chose a small glass of red wine and then wondered where Lottie was.

"I don't know, it's not like her to be late," Sophia replied, but their question was answered as she popped her head around the door.

"I'm sorry! I bumped into Thomas this afternoon and that one cup of coffee soon became a few more, we just stayed talking for hours. In fact, I brought him with me, I hope that is all right," she asked tentatively as she entered the room, knowing Sunday occasions were usually reserved for family, "I couldn't let the man go without any dinner."

"I apologize Richard, I normally wouldn't come unless you were expecting me, but Charlotte was insistent, and one should not refuse the Big Boss, nor his daughter," Thomas joked quietly as he followed her in. "I hope you will forgive my intrusion."

"Hello there! Intrusion? Why, not at all, not at all," Mr. R smiled, shaking hands with the latest arrival.

"Please don't be so formal Thomas, it's been ages since you came for a visit. I do believe you know everyone," Sophia continued as everyone stood up once more to greet the newcomers.

"Oh yes. Please, don't get up, I'll come to you," Thomas politely replied, quickly making the rounds from sofa to chair to sofa to armchair, shaking hands with each one. He too had made a few visits to the hospital to see Gerry during which he was provided the opportunities to meet all their guests.

Another long-time friend of the family, Thomas Winthorne was always welcome, the last of the great dependables as Mr. R. described him. Although she had only recently met Thomas after Gerry had asked him to be one of his groomsmen, Katherine could understand Mr. R's description of him. Generally reserved, she could tell he never felt comfortable in taking liberties no matter how long the welcome mat was, even if it was hand-edged in gold thread and rolled a hundred feet before him. There was something she liked about the dark blond gentleman. Perhaps older than Peter, she could not be sure, he gave her the impression he was a more mature version of her younger cousin William who possessed that enviable if somewhat frustrating gift of remaining calm in any situation. There were times Steves had threatened to set a firecracker under the hopeless daydreamer of their family to get him motivated about something, *anything*. However, unlike William, Katherine did not think Thomas' character flaws included the lack of ambition. Gerry did affirm he was a motivated worker, joking that he was grateful for nepotism in the family firm and could count on retaining his post as manager of international distribution despite the rampant but good-natured competition between them on the executive level.

Perchance Thomas' family misfortune had caused him to be so quiet and reflective. During one of their painting dates in the studio, Gerry had disclosed the Winthorne family history to her. An only child, Thomas had no immediate family to speak of, his mother had left them years ago and moved to London after she become jaded with her marriage. She wanted a fresh start with a younger man, which devastated Thomas and his father. Then, Mr. Winthorne Senior received an unexpected phone call relaying the horrific tidings that his ex-wife had been brutally murdered during a house robbery, she had the misfortune of arriving home early, surprising a thief rifling her belongings in a frenzied hunt for money. The authorities concluded he was an addict desperate to feed his drug habit. It was left to Mr. Winthorne to arrange her funeral and the repatriation of her body back to the States, the shock of which rendered him incapable of thinking clearly. He followed the bad investment advice of an unscrupulous business partner, the financial advisement company their family had founded went belly-up, and their private fortune was sacrificed to pay the residual debts with the result their whole legacy was all but wiped out. The Reinolds had offered their help but Mr. Winthorne refused. He died after suffering a major stroke, no doubt caused by the emotional upheavals he endured. Gerry then explained things continued to deteriorate for Thomas. He tried to resume a career in finance, but was politely informed he was over qualified for the post currently being considered. Unable to find work in that sector, he accepted the position offered to him at Reinold Enterprises.

It was a dreadful story, Katherine wondered how Thomas could function at all after these life-shattering events that would leave weaker minds utterly crippled, but perhaps that was why he was so motivated. Similar to Gerry who needed some challenges to block out the hospital environment in which he found himself currently imprisoned, work helped Thomas to deaden his personal tragedy to some extent, he welcomed the daily non-stop bustle managing the ins and outs of global shipping at the Reinold office. Looking at him now joining the lively clan gathering, politely accepting a glass of brandy while sitting with a smile next to Lottie as directed by her with a friendly pat on the neighbouring chair, it would never be known or guessed the severe trials he had suffered, nor Lottie for that matter. Her fiancé had passed away, stripping from her all sense of purpose in life until Gerry's accident yanked her from her aimless limbo and provided her with a new profession in the family firm, just like Thomas.

No, no, no! Katherine did not want to think despondent thoughts tonight, but all the same, dwelling on their sorrows reminded her Gerry was not there to enjoy the evening with them. For his and everyone else's sake, she had better try to look cheerful. She thought that might be difficult until Aunt Martha wanted the Reinolds to know how she had been dreadfully insulted by the hospital after her thoughtful gift had been declared contraband. Everyone commiserated with Aunt Martha, although it was plain to all with the exception of the gift-giver that there was something comical about Gerry propped up by a puffy royal blue satin cushion with its superfluity of pink roses.

"It certainly was a thing of splendour, no Sultan received so opulent a gift," Gramps affirmed in a solemn tone, only making the urge to laugh among the company more contagious.

"Why, thank you Gregory," Aunt Martha beamed, happy with the seeming rare compliment from the old coot. "Since you like it so much, I'll make one for you too. Like I say, you simply haven't lived if you haven't slept in a bed filled with feather pillows."

"You know, red is his favourite colour," Steves piped up.

"Yes, that's right. Hmm, I think daisies would work nice on a red background. That's it then! I shall start work on it first thing tomorrow."

"Don't forget some buttercups," Katherine could not resist adding.

"How artistic of you Kathy, thank you," her Aunt nodded in appreciation.

"I can't wait," Gramps rumbled, simultaneously disgruntled and amused, trapped in his own joke by the young whippersnappers. No point complaining, it was a waste of energy. Besides, if it kept her busy and unable to pester Gerry for the next few weeks, and all of them for that matter, he was willing to be a victim for that worthy cause.

Victor arrived to announce dinner would be served and they all proceeded with their glasses to the dining room. Although Mrs. R said she had planned something informal, her idea of informal had blossomed into the close cousin of a state dinner. The best linens, crystal and china was set out amidst the floral displays, not to mention the silverware, which tonight included a variety of salads arranged in ornate platters on one sideboard and a long line of glistening domed food warmers gracing another.

"I know, 'informal' eluded me," Sophia replied at the profusion of compliments, "but it's still buffet, so everyone may choose what they like and help themselves."

"Sounds good to me," Gramps agreed whole-heartedly.

After grace was said around the table with Peter officiating, everyone picked up their dishes and began helping themselves, ladies first. Katherine prayed Aunt Martha would not start in tonight, telling everyone why she could not eat this herb or that ingredient; her polite euphemisms rarely left anything to the imagination when it came to the various side effects they induced in her system. Oh yes, she just *had* to disclose to all on this friendly occasion that too much pepper, onions or sage gave her the zephyrs. Thank God the Reinolds knew her well enough by now and did not pay too much attention, even Mrs. Reinold was kind enough to point out which dishes were specially prepared without any offending condiments, but the mortification of her aunt's dietary annotations was worth offering up as a penance. Katherine tried to tune her out and focused on Gramps following up behind the ladies whom she could not resist giving a friendly grilling about him visibly skirting the salads as soon as possible and making his way to the main courses swimming in cream or butter sauces, especially when he had a doctor's appointment facing him.

"Hey, who keeps telling me one day's diet won't fool the scales the next morning? I'm taking you up on your observation, and besides," he continued under his breath, out of earshot from Martha, "with the thought of that flowery 'artwork' your aunt is going to beleaguer me with, I need some instant consolation."

Instant gratification was more like it, but Katherine decided to leave him in peace and went about filling her plate. Encouraged to select their own seats by Mrs. R, the elders gravitated towards the head of the table while the younger members tended to group together after them. Notwithstanding the ornate surroundings, the atmosphere was always relaxed and light. The dreaded tension of the two families meeting and getting to know each other had long since passed over the months. The ladies had become inseparable, Gramps and Mr. R got along fine from day one, but now even reserved observant Pops was more agreeable and had much to discuss with the shipping magnate. The only one who seemed shy tonight was Jennifer, but this was her first time here. Katherine asked Lottie if she wouldn't mind giving a tour after dessert since her parents had suggested the idea. Jennifer was delighted.

"I don't mean to be nosey, but this house is simply amazing, I'd love to see it," she affirmed.

"And besides, I'd love to see the 'Musketeer's Lair' myself," Katherine added with a smile, "Gerry left that honour to you."

"Oh! He did, did he?" Lottie laughed. "Of course, I'd be glad to show you guys around."

"Musketeer's Lair? Now this I have to see," Steves agreed.

"We had fun believing it was that when the three of us were kids."

"What fun, a mystery," Jennifer noted with curiosity. "Honestly, this place would make a great set for a movie."

"Now that you mention it, the Reinolds did get a request to use it for a *Great Gatsby* remake," Thomas informed.

"True, but Mom refused. She was afraid the film crews would upset the place too much," Lottie continued.

"That's a shame, studios usually restore any damage they might cause," Steves noted, "your house could have been on the big screen."

"Still, who wants anything 'restored'? I think Mrs. Reinold was right," Jennifer disagreed. Katherine seconded her.

"I would have liked the idea of it being in a movie, but then again, you never know. Damage is one thing, but there's also theft to consider, you can't trust anyone these days."

"Or the systems that were meant to protect," Thomas noted loudly as the latest advancement in burglar detection blared around them, causing all to start or wince.

"All hands on deck," Mr. R. called out with good humour, although slightly vexed. "Another false alarm, that's the third time today."

"Honestly, I don't think my heart can take it," Sophia sighed as the noise stopped abruptly. "Can't they lower the pitch at least? It's a wonder it hasn't shattered the crystal."

"Better hope they fix it soon, or no one will know when a real emergency happens," Harold observed.

"That's true. Did you hire a good company, Dad?" Peter enquired.

"Sure, the same one that rigged up Katie's gallery."

"Yeah, I recommended them," Steves informed.

"That's why the volume sounds familiar. Oh, I can vouch for it, it's a good system all right. Don't worry, it needs some fine tuning after they set it up, but they'll have it sorted out." Katherine affirmed, holding her ears, just in case the siren tripped again. After she had her own system installed, she was afraid to walk too hard or fast on the gallery floors lest her movements triggered the sensitive tripwires and summon the squad cars to come and catch a non-existent art thief.

Thankfully, the alarm remained silent after that, allowing everyone to enjoy dessert in peace after which the men decided to head off to the Red Room for a brandy and a cigar for the smokers, the matriarchs headed back to the Rose Room for a gossip session accompanied with coffee or tea, while Lottie took the younger guests on the promised tour. The house was an Aladdin's cave brimming with antiques and curiosities collected by the family over the generations. Katherine had seen a substantial part of it already, but she had fun tagging along, eagerly awaiting the time when the few chambers and passages she had not yet visited were shown to her at last. Although the Reinolds already considered her one of the family and let her come and go as she pleased, she never liked venturing beyond the main living areas uninvited despite her curiosity. She knew from experience why people were careful about who entered their homes, there was nothing more invasive than to find someone walking through your domestic sanctuary, taking the phrase 'make yourself at home' beyond its limits. She never forgot one particular night years ago when her mother threw a huge benefit in aid of one of her charities as was her custom. Running upstairs for something or other, Katherine discovered one of the lady guests had made their way to the master bedroom and was poking around the closets checking labels, helping herself to liberal spurts of her mother's expensive perfume and was about to enter the private *en suite* until she stopped their guest dead in their tracks:

"Want to know where the safe is too?"

How that woman huffed a lame answer and made a hasty retreat, begging her not to tell her parents. No harm was done, this will be our little secret, okay sweetie? Yeah, right. Once her mother was informed about the self-conducted tours occurring within Oak Meadows, all Walsingham-hosted charity events were held in public venues. Looking back, Katherine recalled how indignant she was and what guts she had too, only five years old and already she had a mouth on her! Did she ever tell Gerry that story? After all the time they spent together there was always something she had not shared with him yet, so much they would share together. While she admired the rambling manor, she knew it was one of those places where the family made the house, without them, it was just a glorious shell. She wished one member was among them tonight, how she longed to be in the library right now with Gerry and wondered if he was thinking the same thing at that moment.

Her mind was busy with these and similar thoughts, wondering what could be the 'Lair' until Lottie finally opened a set of doors, she could not help but gasp with surprise with Steves and Jennifer. Along the wainscoted walls were gleaming suits of armour and an imposing array of period weaponry; muskets, halberds, pikes, fencing swords and exotic rarities of the martial arts from the Far East displayed in smart rows.

"Cool, a *real* Samurai sword," Steves observed with delight, gesturing if he may be permitted to hold it. Lottie nodded and he carefully took it off its brackets, unsheathed the lethal blade that once upon a time had seen active duty in honour of the Japanese Emperor, and artfully chopped the air mock karate style.

"Careful! Those things can cut through lead," Jennifer cried out.

"Exaggeration, exaggeration, you're so melodramatic," he returned, swinging the blade in an arc.

"*I'm* the melodramatic one, that's a prize," Jennifer replied as they watched him battle with an invisible foe and despatch him swiftly with a thrust to the heart, relieved when he finally returned the blade to its scabbard.

"He's got the idea," Lottie noted. "We liked the French and Spanish fencing foils, they were great for putting on our own goofy renditions of Shakespeare's plays for the folks. C'mon. Let me show you the rest of the Lair."

"You mean there's more," Katherine wondered. Ohh! Right! Katherine brightened up as she watched Lottie push a square in the wainscoting. A hidden door, a place like this had secret halls and stairways for the servants to come and go. Lottie led the way, switching the lights on in the semi-disused passage, giving them a tour of the not often seen parts of the manor, up and down the narrow twisting cobwebby halls and staircases, entering a few rooms from completely different access points, the hidden passage to the library was the most entertaining as they appeared from behind a swinging bookcase, the door completely hidden from view on the other side.

"I can't believe Gerry didn't show me all of this," Katherine noted, pleased nonetheless.

"I suppose after your initial reaction to the Blue Room, he was not sure how you'd take a room full of stabbing implements." Lottie laughed.

"Hmm, you have a point, but this is different. I'm rather getting in to this swashbuckling adventure," Katherine admitted. She hated to admit it, but there was a part of her that still remained a child at a time like this, so did the others. As they returned to the dark passages, Lottie decided to 'raid' the Red Room next, it had been years since she, Petey, and Gerry and surprised her father with one of their Muskateer adventures. Katherine had to admit it was rather priceless, watching the patriarchs' stunned expressions as they came through the inconspicuous servant's doorway, demanding where the prisoner in the iron mask was being kept and that he be released immediately, or else.

"Ho! Raiding the Bastille are we? We surrender! This brings back some memories, I haven't held command of the Bastille in years." Mr. R. laughed. "So the Terrible Threesome rides again, hmm, make that Foursome."

"Where are you hoodlums going," Gramps asked next.

"To the Musaketeers' other hideout," Lottie explained, leading her troop back through the door and into to the cellars.

"What do you mean by 'other hide out'," Jennifer eventually wondered as they wended their way through a large corridor in the cellar area.

"Hold it! Turn around, nice and slow," a gruff voice resounded from behind.

"Wow, now things *are* getting exciting," Steves whispered under his breath. Startled, they turned to see one of the new security detail aiming his automatic pistol at them, then cuss under his breath and lower his weapon.

"Oh for … never mind, false alarm, it's just the kids, sorry about that," the guard continued into his walkie-talkie.

" 'Kids', humph," Steves mumbled.

A fuzzy voice crackled back through the walkie-talkie line, Katherine wasn't sure what was said, but the guard seemed to. "All right, I'm going back on my rounds," he replied before turning to the adventurers. "Sorry about that."

"No problem, just please, mind where you point that thing!" Lottie then lead the troop away.

"Wow! He could have shot us," Steves noted when out of earshot from the guard, "and, we've been marauding through the whole house for ages before he found us. Doesn't say much for their patrolling methods, does it? We could have been burglars and have the whole place stripped before we were caught."

"Doesn't say much for you either," Katherine wryly observed, "you recommended them."

"Hey! I thought you liked the team you have at the gallery?"

"Of course I do. They're great. You just can't take a teasing, can you?"

"But he has made a good observation," Lottie mused, "they may be a great company for businesses and galleries, maybe not for domestic arrangements. You know, if they are that pointless to have, perhaps I could talk Dad into firing them all, including the Hulk, then we might have our privacy back."

"Or have double the men put on to make up for the shortfall, which might not be a bad idea," Katherine observed.

"Oh no! We don't have enough privacy as it is! Better not say anything. Come on, we're almost there."

"Where?" Katherine wondered. What could be so important in the basement?

"Why, the most fun part of the 'Muskateers' Lair'," Lottie replied, answering her thought. They did not have long to wait to discover what that could be, Lottie opened a door and turned on the lights and flipped several switches. Steves whistled with admiration.

"Holy smokes, I thought we had a games den, but this is something else."

Katherine was amazed to see a ingenious cellar conversion that blared a colourful mixture of 70s décor with a gleaming bowling lane at one end of the cavernous hall and a myriad of tabletop games on the other; ping-pong, pool, classic pin ball machines, a shuffle board and table hockey, not to mention several blast-from-the past arcade games zinging and bleeping. Seating comfort was supplied with overstuffed sofas, chairs and large puffed beanbags.

"And you guys left home?" Jennifer laughed.

"Yeah, I know. The folks figured it was better to have all the games we wanted here and invite our friends over rather than have us frequenting the rough places in town for the arcade games."

"I think that was smart, actually," Katherine agreed, although she half smiled to herself, thinking about the times Gerry disclosed some of his youthful memories when keeping parties close to home still did not help to keep things under control, especially when Leroy was invited.

"Who's up for a game of bowling," Jennifer announced, disrupting her reverie.

Steves was in, so was Lottie who suggested they get some music going first and put a vinyl on the stereo system.

"Okay, I'm in too, but I have no idea how to play," Katherine admitted loudly over *You Ain't Nothing but a Hound Dog*.

"Easy Kats, just roll the ball and knock over the white things at the other end, the more that tumble the better, it's not rocket science," Steves instructed.

"Duh. I mean the *other* basics, someone would have to teach me how to keep score."

Lottie promised to show her, although they had better change shoes first, playing bowling in heels would have been quite a handicap. However, Lottie was puzzled on finding quite a few of their extra bowling shoes were missing, perhaps Victor the butler disposed of any unsightly old pairs, or maybe the extra complimentary pairs provided for guests were filched over the years. Lottie did the best with what she could find. Jennifer was provided with a good if slightly tight fit, but Katherine caught a case of the giggles when the only pair that was small enough for her was still excessively big.

"Great, clown feet. I'm flopping around in them, I'll be tripping up the alley instead of the ball." Katherine next tried to pick up one of the balls. "Gosh, you mean we're supposed to pick *these* things up and fling them along the floor? They weigh a ton," she exclaimed, lunging one up as if she were selecting watermelons at the supermarket. "I'll never get this to go straight let alone to the end!"

True to her prediction, every time her turn came to bowl, the ball lamely veered to the side and into the annoying gully, that was when Steves gave her a chance to roll the thing without any peevish distractions to throw her off her game. Eventually he relented his joking and tried to give her a few tips.

"It's not that hard really. Look, you're afraid to damage the floor. Don't be, let that thing fly, this floor was designed to take a beating."

Katherine tried to follow his advice, but sent it into a semi-arc, the ball making a whumping thud. It rolled for a bit before its run met a premature end in the gully. Being good sports, Steven and Jennifer gave her another go, but witnessed a similar result. Everyone laughed, it was more fun watching Katherine in her flipper shoes make a mess of things than actually playing the game right. They decided it was best to forget the team competition for the moment and just try to get her to roll it right for once.

"Whoops! Glad we paused the game Lottie, our team was going to bite the dust."

"That's okay, just remember it's bowling and not basketball we're playing." She chuckled.

She tried again.

"Of all the bad luck! You finally hit a few and end up with a seven–ten split," Steves chortled. "We're going to be here all night before you knock those down."

Before Katherine could answer, Peter and Thomas came through the door.

"All and sundry are wondering what could be causing all the racket beneath their feet, so the mothers have asked us to check up on you. Having a good time," Peter enquired, glad to see them enjoying themselves.

"Absolutely. Kats has been providing most of the entertainment so far," Steves informed them.

"I see," Peter noted, eyeing her oversized shoes with amusement while Lottie explained she couldn't find her anything better since all the shoes were missing, concluding with the query if they would join them in a game or two.

"Sure thing, it's been ages though," Thomas noted, flexing his arm. "Shall I be on your team?"

"Yes, Petey can join Stevie and Jenny."

"No, please count me out," Katherine pleaded as she sat down and pulled her feet from the required footwear. "I think I've had enough of the flippers."

"I'll pass too," Peter noted, "You go ahead and play, don't let the tired ones stop the fun."

"Aw no, Petey! Come on! I want to see you knock down that seven-ten," Lottie wheedled, pulling him by the arm. "You were good at that."

"Hmm, okay, just this once."

He selected his 'old faithful' from the selection of pin tumblers, made his way to the alley, took careful aim and rolled. Everyone watched with bated breath as it sped down and hit the far right pin, sending the tricky obstacle in a direct line to the other pin, but just managed to graze it. The second pin wobbled … then stubbornly resumed its standing position.

"Ow! Almost." Peter chuckled. "It's been awhile. It's a wonder I skimmed it at all." It was an excellent try everyone agreed. He waited for his ball to be returned and then hit the last pin straight and neat. "At least I haven't completely lost my touch."

Aha, Lottie beamed. Since that was the case, he might just as well join them in a match. Just one. Oh, why not? It was good to see everyone having fun, and it *was* satisfying, letting that ball thunder down the lane like old times. After the day he had, he could do with some amusing activity, a playoff might be just the ticket to help reconnect him with a sense of normality in the human sphere of things. Just being in the zipping and blipping games room brought back many good memories. Good thing that after dinner cup of java had woken him up, he needed to be on the top of his game, Lottie wasn't a bad shot as he recalled. Once he got up and running, things could get pretty close. However, they couldn't have an odd-numbered team in their midst, so Lottie cajoled until Katherine gave in and agreed to try again, this time minus the shoes, bare feet were better than duck feet. She might do better without them, even if she was handicapped as a beginner. Eventually she figured out how to roll the heavy projectile to the end of the lane and proved she was not a complete klutz to her team, however, she didn't help them win either. One game soon led to another as the losers demanded a rematch, but were vanquished a second time. Lottie was about to suggest another round, but by then Katherine figured she had jinxed her team enough while Peter decided that no matter how much he was enjoying himself, it was best to call it a night, he had an early day ahead of him. Katherine also had the gallery to check on and planned to get up early too. They wished everyone a good game and closed the door, leaving the other players to continue.

Peter wondered how she liked the 'Muskateers' Lair', to which Katherine responded with a laugh.

"Oh, that's something else. Gerry said growing up in this house was an adventure, and I can see why. I hope we didn't upset anyone with our raid."

"No, but it certainly livened things up a bit, we heard about your run-in with the guard."

"How embarrassing! We didn't mean to cause a panic."

"I know, and I can't preach to you guys either, I too am guilty of a few ambushes by sword and musket point in my youth with the 'Muskateers' before books became more interesting. Then, we got bit by the acting bug one year and set up the 'after-dinner theatre' hours, those were something. What a toss-up we used to make of old *Hamlet*! Gerry and Leroy used to put the scripts together, he had the folks suffocating with laughter they had tears steaming down their cheeks."

"Aw, he never told me! I wished I had seen one of your productions."

"Maybe he saved some of the old scripts."

"Oh, I'll have to ask him now. I hope he did. I'd bug him now about it if I could."

"If you could wrangle them from him, he's probably mortified over his youthful malcreations." Peter laughed.

"Like school photos?"

"You could say that."

"I'm curious, since Gerry and I love the old library, do you have a favourite room here?"

"Sure, I like the library too, but when I needed some space, one of my favourite hide-aways was up in the 'Planetarium'. It sounds spectacular but it's nothing fancy, it's only the large cupola tower where I could set up my telescopes and star charts."

"Of course, the perfect place for a stargazer."

"Yes. Out here we don't get any light pollution, which makes for some great viewing on clear nights. Unfortunately, I don't have as much time to gaze as I used to," he noted.

"I suppose not. I don't know how you're keeping up with everything. I hope you don't mind me asking, how did ... *today* ... go," she asked, lowering her voice.

"Better than I expected, all I can say is the soul who I was sent to assist may get the help they need faster than I anticipated."

"You won't have to handle it all personally?"

"No, I don't think so."

"That's good news," Katherine noted with relief. "I'd be terrified if I had to do it. Which reminds me, you don't mind if I ask about the *other* thing that happened today? In church, I mean. I'm sorry, I know I'm terribly curious, but your Pops says he's never seen anything like that before."

"You mean at Communion? That was a first for me too," Peter admitted candidly.

"You won't get into trouble, will you? Some people started talking, and I know what people in a parish can do when they get a bee in their bonnet, my aunt is a perfect example."

Peter laughed.

"Honestly Kathy, I have no idea what to expect at times, I just have to accept everything as God's will."

"Do you think it will continue?"

"Probably, I really can't say."

"Gosh! This is just ... fascinating! I know it's none of my business, but just how do you ... *see*," she wondered tentatively. Justine had told her about specially gifted vocations that were granted extraordinary perceptions concerning souls, but this was all so new to her.

"I wish I could put it into words for you. It's as though someone turns on a lamp and something that was hidden or darkened from view is suddenly illuminated, but it's not seen with the eyes of the body, but the interior eyes.   It usually only happens in confession, but today was a different matter, something different. Hmm, maybe it was a left turn I was supposed to make? Just joking," he smiled as he opened a door for her.

"I wouldn't be surprised if you got lost, even though you grew up here. Do you ever miss the old place?"

"I do get a bit nostalgic, you never forget your childhood home, but I know it will be left in good hands, and I also know I will always be a welcome visitor," he finished gently. Thanks to Katherine, the rupture in the Reinold household caused by his vocation was healed for which he was deeply grateful. "Come, let's take a short cut," he continued, "and besides, I have to see what Sinbad did this time."

Showing her into the Violet Room and switching on the lights, he noticed the disembowelled Louis XIV seat, the wadding peaking out in tufts from the various holes the wayward parrot had gnawed into the delicate fabric that afternoon.

"So, that's what caused the ruckus. Forth piece of furniture he's chewed up too."

"No!" Katherine gasped.

"Oh yes, he's a sneaky one," Peter affirmed. "When I was still in grade school, he bore holes in my history book when I had left the room for something. The teacher didn't believe me when I explained the parrot ate it. Sinbad has a thing for furniture and paper."

"You guys should have given him your homework more often," Katherine noted.

"I think Gerry tried, quite a number of times."

With that, they decided they had better say their goodnights before it grew too late and would get no sleep at all. By then, the men had joined the ladies for a nightcap in the Rose Room, giving them the opportunity to wish everyone pleasant dreams. Noticing the time, everyone agreed they should hit the hay too. On their way up to the bedrooms, they were followed by the bowlers who had decided to call it quits before they were tempted to begin another game and there was a merry traffic jam as everyone headed to their assigned quarters. To Helen and Aunt Martha's approval, not to mention Harold and Gramps' satisfaction, Mrs. R began to escort Jennifer way over to the opposite end of the hallway, she obviously had selected a bedroom as far away from Steven's as possible, much to his chagrin. Katherine wondered if that was going to do any good, it would not be beyond him to sneak out and rendezvous with Jennifer while the rest of them were travelling to the land of Nod. However, she suppressed the urge to laugh when she saw the exact room Jennifer was assigned, right where one of the squeaky floor boards lay hidden, which Gerry had once pointed out to her on one occasion, explaining it was a challenge for him and his siblings to skip out to play pirates by the beach at night with all the trip-boards the place contained. One false move and the light-sleepers of the house would know someone was up and about. One by one, they wished each other a last good night and 'pleasant dreams', entered their rooms and closed their doors, the cavernous upper hall left still and silent once more.

Taking a quick glance around his old room, Peter noted it certainly did feel good to be home, a consolation for the roller coaster of a day he had. Undressing for the night, he noticed two new garment bags hanging on the bathroom door, next to it lay a small travelling case. Pulling on his PJs and throwing on a robe, he opened the case and found all was as he suspected. Mothers never stop being mothers, even when their children were at his age. Nestled inside were rows of new black cotton socks neatly folded inside out into rolls, his name monogrammed on minuscule labels to prevent them getting lost among the washing in the community laundry room at the rectory. Underneath were new sets of underwear and pyjamas, and of course, two pairs of black slippers, all bearing his name and title on petite labels, 'Mon. P. Reinold.' To top it off, he discovered a few cans of his favourite shaving cream underneath and other personal toiletries. He appreciated the thought, but this was getting embarrassing! He wondered what was waiting for him in the garment bags and gently undid the zippers. Inside were four new cassocks, two for everyday wear in one bag and in the other, two for formal dress complete with a half cape to the shoulders, one cassock more magnificent than the rest with the front seam and the cape edge ribbed in a thin band of fuchsia complete with the same deep coloured sash, a privilege for monsignors who continued to wear a cassock. All were custom made to his measurements of course, his mother never spared the best, especially when it came to her children. Hearing a few taps on the door, he knew who it was.

"Come in."

"I hope you like your surprise, Peter dear," his mother greeted.

"I do, thank you very much, but you shouldn't worry about me."

"I can't help it, I know what you're like, always giving away your Mass stipends to the first needy person you see and keeping hardly enough for yourself. If I don't stock you with the necessities, who will?"

"Thanks again Mom, but there are more than just the necessities here, you didn't have to get anything formal."

"Yes I did. You never know what may come up, especially with the Pope's visit coming up, the Archbishop could invite you to an important function, and you had nothing decent to wear. I noticed your other cassocks were starting to get a little thin around the elbows. I know you want to imitate the holy poverty of the saints, but do you have to look like them in their holey robes? Promise me you won't follow the Curé of Ars to the letter and let your clothes go green with mould."

"I promise I shall not make a disgrace of myself," he assured her with humour.

"Good. In any case, you're also in the corporate world again for the time being, and you have to look good for that once more too. Here, let's see how it fits," she continued, taking the regal cassock off its hanger and handing it to him. Wishing to please her, he slipped into the *en suite* to change. It certainly was a formal transformation, the satisfaction on her face when he emerged in his new attire a few minutes later said it all. Thank Heavens the dress code of matching fuchsia socks was done away with years ago! Not to mention he was thankful he was only a Monsignor of the Third Class, or it might be a full purple cassock he would be donning right now. After trying not to stick out *too* much, that would have been a right penance to offer up!

"It's perfect on you, and with your height! However, it's more loose around the middle than I expected … are they feeding you right at the rectory? You *are* getting enough to eat aren't you," she queried as she tidied the half cape around his arms, setting the folds in order before turning her attentions to the sash.

"Yes, I'm not starving, although I do worry what the visiting seminarians intend to serve us on the nights they get the wild idea to treat us to a native dinner."

"That doesn't sound very encouraging, no wonder you're getting thin, I might skip eating under those circumstances too. Or, maybe you're fasting again. Peter dear, please don't overdo it! You are such a worry at times! When you were out in the world you seemed to take better care of yourself, which reminds me, I have a few bags of groceries all ready for you and the fellows, Victor will put them in the car before you leave. Of all things, I wish you would borrow something better than Lottie's rattletrap, I'm terrified when she drives the thing, and I don't like you driving it either. There now, come, take a look in the mirror," she finished gently turning him towards his dresser before he had a chance to say anything about her stocking the rectory larder again. "Yes, it suits you, dear. What do you think?"

"Ah, with this pampering, I shall never be able to stay a humble man," he joked with a playful air of elegiac wistfulness.

"*You* vain and prideful? Hardly. I worry about your brother more than you in that department."

"I've got my own share of faults to conquer you know. However, a new set of clothes *was* greatly needed and is deeply appreciated. Thank you for the cassocks, they're perfect."

"You're very welcome. I know dear, you don't like people accusing you of not giving up the old life, but I still like to see you impeccably dressed. Just because you've embraced the Church doesn't mean you have to let yourself go raggy now, do you?"

All he could do was smile at her maternal logic. Despite his zeal to take on a life of simple living, especially after his affluent upbringing, he had not the heart to argue with her. She had the well-meaning solicitous tenacity of his lady parishioners who wanted to mother him up and wrap him in cotton wool at every chance they got, and of course, being his mother, she above all of them had the right to worry about his welfare. He could put a foot down with the other lionesses when necessary, but the Matriarch had the final word in many areas if acquiescing to her wishes helped to allay her worry about him. She certainly had suffered enough these past few months with one of her sons in the hospital.

"As much as I would like you to try on the other ones, the fashion show must come to a premature end and let you get some rest, I know you have a gruelling schedule."

"All right. In case I don't see you in the morning considering my Mass times, I suppose this is goodnight, goodbye, and God bless. You know, Mom, you could stop by the office someday this week and have lunch with Dad, Lottie and I if you like. It's been awhile since you did that, I'll have something special arranged."

"That would be wonderful, dear. I'd like that very much. Goodnight, take care, and try not to tire yourself out. Drive carefully, after this morning's news I wasn't able to think straight! Imagine a fender bender! Don't forget, with Gerry handling some of the paperwork, Thomas can take over for a day or two if you need it. Please consider taking the afternoon off tomorrow."

"Okay, I'll think about it. Sweet dreams Mom, and thank you again for everything."

Alone once more, he took off the cassock, hung it in the garment case, said his night prayers, set the alarm and finally made it to bed. Bless her, she did spoil him at times, when he would be able to wear the two formal ones was anyone's guess, even if the Pope was coming. It was highly unlikely he would be invited to a private audience while his Holiness was there anyway since he would be conducting the Youth Day in Denver, and as it was, just the everyday cassocks were considered a bit much outside of Rome if you were not a member of an order, even if you wished to dress in the traditional garb befitting the priesthood.

An order, could it be? Maybe this was a sign from Divine Providence? His thoughts wandered to his pet pipe dream, if he could use that expression. He had long mused about the idea of founding an order with the sole mission of supporting the charitable ministry of exorcism and the binding of spiritual evil by prayer and penance. There was so much good an order like that could do, he loved to think about it. This would not be just for men, but for women as well. While a nun could not be an exorcist, nuns could offer their spiritual ammunition of prayer and fasting in support of the priests, no doubt make the procedure of exorcism go much more speedily and with greater success, quite possibly reduce the repetitive process of exorcisms and liberate an afflicted person much faster. There would be more to the order's mission than just exorcism of course, it would have a fundamental role in raising awareness among the laity on how demons and their minions worked in the world, and how everyday people could best combat them. It was all a beautiful idea, thinking about the Rule of life to be followed that would be appropriate for such an order, and of course, the habit that they would wear. It was regrettable the world found the myriad of dress codes within the Church a source of ribald amusement; it refused to see that the habit was a blessed sacramental, a special mark of separation from the world. He had often wondered how to keep it simple and dignified, until the image of what it should be continued to resurface in his dreams.

It was a curious situation, the Church taught that one should not pay attention to dreams, and yet the Bible gave several examples that the Lord could choose this means if He so wished. From his own experience he had quickly learned how to distinguish the nonsensical subconscious meanderings of a tired mind after a hard day's work and separate them from the life-like unveilings made directly to his soul while the body lay in slumber. Why God chose this way with him, he did not know, when it occurred, he could not forget each experience. A few minutes sleep felt like hours, the dream so detailed, rich in visual and sensory sensations in those few moments that it took longer to describe than the dream itself took to unfold. The intriguing part was these particular dreams continued to offer new clarification, even when he was awake and the event had happened months or years in the past. It was as though a parcel of concentrated information had plummeted on him and required the gradual process of time and quiet reflection in the waking world for the full significance of the message to be teased open and properly understood. The number of journals he used to record them for his own personal enlightenment concerning them showed the richness of the details and symbolic significance when put on paper despite the fact they happened fast and with film-like rapidity.

He never told anyone about them except his spiritual director and to Katherine, and then, disclosed only one dream to her, the one that vividly displayed his true vocation in life. There were many others, they started to come on a more frequent basis after he had entered the seminary in Rome, and they had not stopped after he had been ordained. One that continued to strike him to the core was the dream in which he was first shown the habit he assumed could only be 'the sign' that the foundation of this new Order would one day become a reality. He could still remember the details as clearly as if it happened yesterday.

He recalled he was in a parking garage, a multi-storied concrete block of grey colourless slabs and florescent lighting no different than any other city lot, although he could not tell what building he was in except it felt like one of the exclusive upmarket areas of the city. He had the impression he was with his mother and aunt, although their figures were indistinct. They were heading to the shopping mall attached to the parking lot for a day's outing and he obviously had decided to join them. Why, he did not know, he wasn't one for tagging along window shopping and mall browsing, perhaps he came to humour them. They must have already left the car and went on ahead, he had the impression he was to join them in a few minutes, maybe he had lingered behind to lock up the car. When he went to follow them they had already disappeared, obviously they were already in the mall and had commenced their browsing without him. If he hurried, he could catch up, the elevator was not far away.

The dream quickly assumed a distinct sharpness, a clarity of colour and surroundings when before the scene had been hazy and indistinct. Entering the elevator he was struck by the contrast of the interior with the ashen concrete bleakness he had left behind; it was bright, luxurious and spacious, the walls were panelled in honey coloured woods and gold tinted mirrors, complete with brass rails and buttons, the floor carpeted in a green hand woven Turkish rug. A palace hotel could not have provided a better conveyance for its guests, and to find this in a parking garage? He noticed he did not have to push any of the buttons, it began to move down of its own accord, perhaps it was a computerized apparatus. It did not matter, the sooner the thing stopped and let him off the better. The surreal change of environment was unnatural, he felt an urgency to leave the thing as soon as possible. For some reason, he instinctively knew he must not let the glittering surroundings attract too much of his attention, a difficult thing to do when he admired anything that was beautifully crafted. He kept his eyes fixed to the floor, it was then he noticed his apparel, a black cassock with half-cape to the elbows, a St. Benedict's pectoral cross hanging on his chest and a long black cloak covering all. Yes, a cloak, a detail just as important as the cassock and cross, in the dream he could feel the comforting weight of the material and received the distinct impression the mantel symbolised heavenly protection and the authority granted to him as a priest similar to the cassock. In fact, the multi-layers seemed to suggest he had been granted a double defence. The strange part was his hair seemed much thicker, he did not know what this meant until he remembered the history of Samson and how the judge of old had lowered his guard and allowed his virtues to be sheared away by Delilah. He then understood he must not allow anything to cut his spiritual strength. Despite the sense of security these signs gave him, it made him wonder what was going to happen next considering the importance of their symbolism.

The elevator seemed to go down for a long time before gliding to a stop, the chime serenely dinging as the doors slid open to reveal a large mutedly lit cellar with walkways branching off to other rooms, it appeared as though several of the walls had been broken through to another basement in order to expand the area. The walls were old red brick, the floor of dusty beige wood, the wide floorboards left plain and unvarnished, the space divided up by brick and stone pillars with low arches supporting the building above him, the architecture suggested the place had been built in the 1800s. He obviously arrived on the wrong floor, but how could this antiquated, vaulted, gloomy place be the basement of the shopping mall? Still cautious about paying too much attention as with the elevator he cast a quick glance without looking at everything directly. He could discern many objects placed in storage down here and were gathering a few cobwebs although all was very well organized; antique cars, old phonograph players, Victorian era telephones, printing presses and other similar dated machines from the turn of the century. No, this was no ordinary basement, in a second he realized this was not the shopping mall any more, at least, not one from *this* world. The items he thought were in storage were in fact exhibits, dusty curiosities in a collector's eccentric museum carefully placed on display along the edge of the walls or by the pillars, each exhibit sectioned off with a low cylinder-style brass railing. Looking behind him, the elevator had disappeared, a brick wall left in its place. However, he instinctively knew he was down in the fifth cellar of this surreal environment and that there was a way out via a set of stairs, but he had to cross the exhibit space in order to get to them. He did not like this area, a sense of malevolence lingered in the air and he wanted to leave as quickly as possible.

He had hardly gone two brisk paces when he was abruptly stopped. Around the corner on his right came a tall gaunt figure with silver grey hair just reaching the shoulders, sharp black eyes, a leering smile, long spider-like fingers slowly rubbing together in anticipation of this visit. He too was dressed all in black, a stylish evening ensemble and a long cloak; it was none other than Satan himself. However, he did not feel alarmed or threatened, this unearthly meeting was markedly different from his usual encounters with the Prince of Darkness. For one thing, that invisible yet tangible tidal wave of evil was not directed against him on this occasion. No sabre rattling and spook shows this time, the devil was not coming to terrorize. Perhaps he wanted to sway him with his diabolical wit and charm, he certainly was doing his best to play the cultured gentleman. Well, he could forget it. However, he could not move forward with the demon standing in his way. He was about to send him packing with a deliverance prayer as would usually be the case, but quickly received an interior inspiration not to do so despite his urgency to leave. The enemy seemed almost glad of his presence, in fact, he appeared eager to share the significance of this place with him. Of course, Heaven must have given the enemy permission to detain him for the present; it was clear he must witness the strange spectacle about to unfold. Holding the cloak close to him, he looked the Evil One straight in the face. Might as well see what the devil wanted.

"Please, feel free to look around," his host greeted succinctly with a leer, gallantly indicating towards the left before bowing slightly, then turning to the right and exiting the scene as swiftly as he had entered. With a sense of foreboding he suddenly understood what this place was—Satan's Trophy Room—each sin and method used to capture souls allegorically displayed as a visible exhibit. No, he did not want to look, but the prompting of his interior guide whom he assumed was his guardian angel pressed him to draw closer and observe the item the enemy had indicated.

It was the first and most prominent display situated before the disappearing elevator, although he had barely noticed the exhibit in his eagerness to get out of the place. He could not avoid it now as he reluctantly stepped forward as directed. It looked like a waxwork piece similar to the famed handiwork housed at Madame Tussauds. In this instance, the figures were a three-dimensional recreation of Joseph Wright's eerie painting *Experiment with an Airpump*. As he recalled, the original artwork on canvas was macabre enough, the wild features of a scientist in eighteenth-century dress illuminated by a single flame in a dark room, his arm outstretched over his curious machine as he is about to conduct his experiment on a living specimen; to create an airless vacuum within a glass sphere in which a small bird is held captive. The shadowy features of the spectators huddled around him stand transfixed with morbid curiosity and horror as they wait to see what happens to the unsuspecting creature as its supply of air is withheld. It was a brutal painting portraying the dawn of the Industrial Revolution and the cruelty committed in the name of scientific advancement. Although the three dimensional wax display in the devil's museum recreating the scene was simplified and contained no spectators as in Wright's painting, the 'artistic concept' in Satan's borrowing was far more appalling. In place of the bird, the scientist is shown performing a vivisection on a live human being, the specimen's arms outstretched and bound down, his chest cavity opened wide and exposed to view. The horrifying part was the male victim depicted in agony looked exactly like Christ stretched out ready to be nailed to the cross. There were no nails, cross or crown of thorns, but the likeness was unmistakable. He was not left wondering about the meaning of this exhibit as it was quickly revealed to his soul: the cruelty imposed on the Christ figure signified humanity's lack of love for God and neighbour, concisely, every sin against the virtue of Christian charity. He was reminded of what Christ had said about those who failed to perform the works of Mercy, which were also the works of love: "Whatever you do to the least of My brethren, you do to Me." How many sins of indifference and the omission to do good ripped out the heart of Christ each and every day?

He was curious why the devil did not depict pride, the cause of his own downfall, or the other manifold vices for that matter, but of course, the greatest commandment was to love God with all your mind heart and strength, and your neighbour as yourself. If one loved God and neighbour, they would not break the commandments, and certainly it could be said that Satan would never have committed the sin of pride and had fallen if he had loved God above all. This diabolical hatred against the Creator and His plan had brought the rest of the evils, even Saint Paul had said without true charity every other spiritual gift and good work is brought to nothing. For this reason this visible display of hatred was the devil's most prized exhibit and placed here in the deepest level of the museum with the other trophies that had wrecked the most havoc on the world and caused the greatest loss of souls. The less important or dangerous exhibits lay on the upper floors, the degree of sinfulness associated with them lessened as one ascended the various levels.

Peter then understood that the elevator had its own symbolism, the craving for luxury and the love of ease, two faults that could be allowed to grow into serous sin, which then rapidly conveyed a soul to the lowest levels of depravity. However he could sense there was still hope as long as there was life, it was possible to get out of this place, although it would not be as easy as when the soul was bought down. It would take hard work and a long ascent back to a life of virtue as symbolised by the stairs. Of course, how could he think there was no special exhibit for the sin of pride? That vice was certainly not missing here, he reflected. He always knew the devil was a braggart, and this 'trophy room' was just another confirmation of this fact. He felt a heaviness about him as he realised the entire building, all five floors and everything in it, notwithstanding their individual symbolism, was one great monument to self-importance, arrogance, vanity and conceit. He did not want to hang around, the wax display was distressing and he had seen enough down here despite his brief look-about. Satan may no longer be visible, but he could still feel his black presence lingering.

He crossed the floor quickly, scarcely noticing the other objects. It did not take long to find the stairs, he received a very brief impression of the fourth cellar as he passed the entry to it on his way up. It was similar to the fifth, filled with old machines. The stairs continued upward, so obviously he was not obliged to stay here and could figure out the full significance of these lower floors later. He continued to ascend and found himself on the third floor. The staircase ended at this point, he received the impression that there was another set of stairs at the other end of the exhibit space. Too bad he could not skip by this section, but since the exit lay at the other end, it was evident he must observe the items on this level. Thankfully, the atmosphere was not as heavy and foreboding, the entrapments symbolised here were obviously not as sinister and easier to escape from, but they were worldly traps all the same. While he did not feel the urgency to rush as before, he still did not like where he was. When would he ever find the way out?

Crossing the floor, he was no longer in an area that looked like a basement but more like the expansive upmarket department store he had originally expected to see earlier in the dream; high ceilings, crème coloured carpeting, gleaming parquet walkways, elegant cream-toned wood displays, all brightly lit and nothing antique. However, he was certain he was still in the trophy rooms, this level had a similar ambiance to that of the golden-hued elevator, there were no windows at all in the place, and he continued to feel like he was trapped in an infernal maze. He heard a woman's voice and stopped for a moment to look around, it was one of the department attendants. She did not seem to notice him as she busied about the latest glassware, silverware, porcelain and china that had just arrived. There was no packing material in sight, the items intended for sale were now all carefully arranged. "No, not quite ready yet, it *must* be set out just *perfect,*" she continued to tell herself, accomplishing the finishing touches with a tone of determination as she eyed the displays along one of the walls. He understood this was not the desire to be perfect for the sake of seeing a job well done, the good pride that God allowed. Instead he could sense her over solicitous, single-minded resolve to impress according to the dictates of the fashionable elite and all those who kept up with the Joneses. It was easy to see this section symbolised the hunger for riches, fine possessions and the fruitless pursuit of living up to the world's expectations. However, he understood these items would not entrap a soul if a person remained detached from them, if they lived *in* the world and not *of* the world as the old saying went. He felt the items in the lower floors also had the same significance, but much worse. He would have to think about their distinctions later. In any case, it was a relief that he did not see or hear his mother or aunt in this place, a good sign they were not entrapped by their wealth as others were. Best to be moving on.

He spied a gleaming parquet floor walkway making a more direct path through the organized displays, but it led off to the gilded elevator. Did that machine only go one way? Down? It might go up, but if it didn't, would it disappear in the fifth cellar again? While he was curious to see what would happen if he did try it, he knew better than to tempt fate. As a spiritual director, he had seen how certain souls who fell again into the same errors after their liberation were brought down to a worse condition than they were in before as their sins became habitual. Of course, there was always mercy and hope, but the spiritual struggle was made much harder. It was possible that the sad state of a sin-mired soul might be represented here too by the reappearance of the elevator, perhaps he might never find his way out of this confounded building if he gave in to his inquisitiveness in this instance. Maybe this also represented occasions of sin entered into by an unguarded curiosity. He wisely ignored the contraption and pressed on. Eventually he found the stairs again, he was allowed to skip the second floor, which was similar to the third, another department store floor filled with earthly paraphernalia.

At last, he made it up to the first floor, the least oppressive of them all. It was a curious area, it gave him the impression of an old English setting. Straight ahead was a forest green carpeted walkway that lead to the exit. Finally! He could not see a door, only a great vertical rectangle of white light. On closer inspection, he noticed that the walkway had an intersection that lead to other areas to the left and right, he could sense the elevator lay on the right-hand path, but the way out was unmistakeable. However, the walkway was not a hallway per se, on each side were what appeared to be restaurant areas separated by windowed partitions made with Victorian style glass and slender window panes, the repetition of the white squares relieved by elegant potted ferns. The various restaurants could be easily accessed by opening the doors to them, which were also made of full-length windows with white wooden panes. He thought it would be safer to stay outside with the exit in clear view and simply look in to observe one of the restaurants. He was struck by the amount of people eating, enjoying themselves, having a sing-along, living the good life to the full, yet completely oblivious they were caught in the devil's rooms. Of course, enjoying a day out, a meal here and there was not the problem; he understood it was sensual gratification with no thought of control that was symbolised here. Innocent pleasures could soon be turned into more grievous faults through excess, gluttony and lust would not be far behind. Corporeal gratifications, how little they seem in the beginning, they were the devil's 'invisible' snares, one of the first steps to lead down the path to a life of sin. "Let us eat and drink, for tomorrow we die." The sad part was this place was the easiest to escape from, the exit lay only a few paces away and the doors to the restaurants were not locked. Indeed, if they were, the glass doors could be easily broken open, but no one wanted to leave this place that was filled with sensual indulgence. People did not want to do a little penance or live a moderate life any more, self-control was becoming a thing of the past. "Where is wisdom to be found, and where is the place of understanding? Man knoweth not the price thereof, *neither is it found in the land of them that live in delights,*" his interior guide whispered to him. He had seen enough. Leaving the spiritually blind merrymakers behind, he headed down the walkway and entered into the light.

Peter remembered how difficult it was to wake from that dream, the images lingered for days ensuring they would be forever etched in his memory. He wondered why the two basement floors, the fourth and fifth, were more ominous and foreboding than the rest, Satan's presence felt particularly strong there. Wait, wasn't he told the exhibits there were among those the devil prized the most? Why though? The answer eventually came to him when he realized the antique nature of the objects and the old Victorian surroundings of those floors were part of the allegorical clue. Everything he saw was a prototype of all the modern conveniences and inventions that separated the twentieth-century from all other centuries: in those two floors he was shown a slice of time and history.

Yes, it finally made sense now, Peter mused as he lay staring up at the dark ceiling. One of his favourite mystics who had been granted numerous revelations disclosed that the age when Satan would be let loose on earth 'for a little time' as related in the Apocalypse would occur fifty or sixty years before the year two thousand, but she had warned that the devil would spend 'a time, and a time before that' to prepare the world for his release from the abyss. Did that time of demonic preparation begin with the Industrial Revolution and the mass-market culture that came to be? The 'time and time before' the twentieth century? The fact that the devil had modelled his horrific exhibit of the vivisected Christ on Wright's painting and deemed it his favourite of the whole lot seemed to confirm this. Peter recalled digging through one of Gerry's art history books in which he had discovered one of Wright's patrons was Richard Arkwright of Preston. The artist had also painted a picture of Arkwright's austere manufacturing mill, and Peter did not believe in coincidences. Arkwright was the inventor of the spinning frame, a hallmark invention in 1770 that signalled the beginning of industrial mass production in England. There was always sorrow and hardship on earth, but an unprecedented distress of society and destruction of the natural environment began when man began to mechanise everything not just for the sake of progress but for the advancement of greed and capital gain. Perhaps he also saw the rise of corrupted capitalism too in his dream of the satanic trophy rooms, half the floors did resemble an elite shopping centre after all. He could not help but recall the prophetic destruction of Babylon representing the devil's kingdom in the Apocalypse and the litany of earthy delights that would be destroyed with it, the gold, jewels, fine wine, costly materials and spices, the long passage of weeping merchants distraught that all this was now no more, the end of all tradable goods, the final days of musicians, harpers, grinding mills, it sounded eerily like the destruction of all democratic market economies as they now existed. Of course, humanity needed the things of the earth to live, but as he saw in his dream it was Mammon, the lust for money, pleasure and earthly delights that destroyed souls. In the end, the Creator would step in, and all the gifts of creation that had been misused would be destroyed in turn before the new heaven and the new earth appeared.

How could he tell people any of this? He often worried for his family considering their circumstances and hoped they could maintain a healthy detachment. It was a burden to be shown these important disclosures for he had to remain discreet in what he could share. His own personal revelations and intuitions about them were not dogmas, and as a priest, he could only say so much, especially when it came to the Book of the Apocalypse. Although everything he saw and concluded upon did not seem out of synch with the teachings of the Church, he did not want to preach error just in case he had misread anything. Still, he had been shown something terribly important, the dangers that ensnared a soul, confirmation of the period in which the devil was unleashed on the earth ... how long would *that* era last? Yes, yes, of course, he couldn't forget that Pope Leo XIII overheard Satan challenging Christ's promise that the gates of Hell would not prevail, bragging that he could destroy His Church if he was only granted a little time and freedom on earth. Taking up the challenge Christ asked how long did he think it would take to accomplish this? The devil said seventy-five to one hundred years, and the time was granted to him for the test. Leo was so horrified at what he had seen and heard that he composed the prayers to St. Michael and the Minor Rite of deliverance for the laity to use for their protection. Up to one hundred years? The way things were going, Peter dreaded to think what would be facing the world when the year two thousand arrived with fifty more years of Hell's free reign to endure. Certainly, the need for exorcists was going to be much greater, the Church would be glad to have an order specifically to combat this problem and clean up the aftermath when the infernal century closed? Perhaps it was time to think about approaching the archbishop with the idea? No, he must suppress his own will, no matter how holy and practical his desire seemed, God's will must come first. As he tried to convince himself, the Church now had the International Association of Exorcists, so he must assume this is what God wanted, at least for the present. However, it was strange that now he was presented with his first half-caped cassocks like the one he saw, but then again, he did not believe in coincidences. Perhaps the time *was* coming for the foundation of a dedicated exorcist order ... his mind began to drift, he could not muse any longer, he had fallen fast asleep.

Dawn, rise and shine, a new day, duties to accomplish. Peter woke just before the sun glimmered, showered, dressed and out on the road before the house began to stir. He had just enough time to get to the cathedral and attend to his penitents before his service, if he didn't hit a string of red lights along the way, but he was pushing it, especially in 'Aqua Velva'. Perhaps he should have skipped the big dinner on Long Island this time around, but he never knew what lay ahead of him, how many opportunities he would have for family visits considering his schedule, not to mention staying in a particular parish was never a sure thing, the Church could and would move its priests wherever they were needed, transfers were more common these days. He had to admit it, he liked being stationed close to his family, he could have been assigned anywhere in the state but was brought back directly from Rome after his ordination and placed smack dab in New York under the Archbishop's wing. Then, he was thrown through a loop yesterday at the altar rails, sensing the demon 'throttlers' at work. He wouldn't have minded, but the congregation suspected something had happened, and he dreaded public displays where his abilities were concerned. Peter wondered if what happened yesterday morning would continue. Maybe it was a once-off? He hoped it would be, but that inner voice that always knew better reminded him otherwise, the Lord had a way of keeping the waves coming, precisely because the Church needed to be shaken up from its complacency. Didn't Fr. O' Conner once tell him as much? A completely calm passage on earth was never promised, only a safe eternal harbour. The crux of the whole thing, superiors don't like waves, transfers were quite convenient then. He knew he should leave everything in the hands of Providence, worrying was a waste of time and energy, plus he also had to practise detachment from all those he held dear no matter how difficult and be prepared to move if it came for whatever reason. Still, he was human. At least being assigned the diocesan exorcist assured him to a point he could count on staying put for awhile. Thankfully, confession and Mass went quietly this morning, there were no strange occurrences, at least not today.

After his morning service at the cathedral Peter checked in on the parish office to reconfirm his first appointment with the secretary and to see if any one else had booked him, yes, and for the next few mornings as well. He jotted down the new engagements in his agenda, hmm, the parish workweek was getting busier than usual, but then again, afternoons were now off limits for his priestly duties while he was helping his family so of course the early hours would be slightly jammed up. It was either a good sign or a bad sign when people sought out *his* services, he wasn't quite sure which.

He greeted everyone he bumped into as he made his way to his assigned quarters, however, he did not always receive polite smiles and a cheerful 'Hi there,' and a friendly repartee in return. Sometimes he was met with an odd or frightened glance, other times he could see amusement. Once he had been assigned this unique position, he either evoked curiosity or unintentionally made some people feel uneasy. At least it wasn't as bad as when he first started this particular ministry, maybe they were getting used to the idea of having an exorcist on the premises. Of course, it was a rather droll if but strange set-up. His office and the adjoining waiting area were situated down in the dregs of the building, the once neglected, semi-forgotten rooms in the basement formerly used by the janitor. The maintenance man had long been given a better place to work in and these rooms had been reused as storage space until he was temporarily assigned them. Although he would have preferred the consecrated sacristy of a church, he rejected the comfortable office he was offered, he needed something uniquely secure and private as what could happen in the course of his ministry might prove very disturbing to everyone in the building. When beginning this singular path, the archbishop found his request for a place of this nature rather odd until Peter explained the possessed often became physically difficult to restrain and tight quarters could be a help, while he was in Rome he had seen an escape attempt made by a possessed man via a window, and thought it was better to be prepared for every eventuality. No matter how strange the location, the archbishop quickly conceded. Properly consecrated ground would be discussed when he had a definite case that required the full exorcism Rite, his Eminence decided. For now, Peter gladly occupied the neglected storage rooms by the old furnace area with the narrow cellar windows and shabby patina, they would do quite nicely as a matter of fact. After receiving a fresh scrubbing and a coat of paint, the waiting area was duly prepared with some basic seating arrangements and furniture to make it more comfortable, while the 'work room' was kept to Spartan practical austerity with a few chairs and a locked cabinet to contain the blessed items he needed. Naturally, every wall had several devotional pictures hanging on them specially blessed to ward off evil. Once he was set up, it came as a surprise to the clergy, workers and volunteers in the parish building how many 'clients' actually booked appointments to see him, it had become more like a veritable doctor's practise. One of the secretaries dubbed the Monsignor's basement precincts the 'Operating Room' and it stuck.

"Very funny, Nurse Mabel," he returned with good humour, "just don't call it that to my parishioners, or you might frighten them half to death."

"Okay, although 'office', just doesn't seem to fit the bill," she noted.

At least someone could find a funny side, but oddly enough, Mabel really wasn't that far from the truth back then he thought as he unlocked the door and switched on the lights. Before he was ordained, he had no idea how much the exorcist ministry would become a spiritual clinic, he felt no different than a doctor with a medical practise diagnosing a myriad of problems and attempting to find the right remedies for each situation. He put down his corporate briefcase and checked his ecclesial one. Nope, nothing tampered with. He had to make sure: with the unseen, he could never let down his guard. Those impish devils often acted like a pesky virus and could cause nothing but hold-ups and waste his time. Good thing he had thrown enough blessed salt everywhere, that was a good preventative cleansing measure against an infestation.

There was a knock on the waiting room door. Right on time, new clients to see him, a young couple had something about strange activity in their apartment to relate and they had exhausted all the possibilities of 'it' being caused by something they could naturally explain. Peter welcomed them in and motioned towards his 'office', offering them to take a seat on a set of old scratched up metal chairs upholstered with imitation leather padding that had seen better days. The couple looked around at this small cupboard of florescent-lit space far removed from the other bustling sections of the parish building, a little unsure and wondered why he was stuck down in this section. Peter tried to make the young couple feel more at ease and listened to their story with interest despite the off-putting, drab, almost clinical surroundings. He personally knew how humiliating it felt when a subject regarding the supernatural needed to be addressed but was received with condescending scepticism as though you had gone off your rocker. Come, don't be shy, he told his newcomers. What has been troubling you? Strange sounds? Scents? Screams and bumps in the night? Odd shadows following you around? None of that, hmm, just strange blasts of cold air and objects disappearing with no explanation. Have you had any problems with nightmares, sleep paralysis or seeing a therapist for any reason? Any history of mental disturbances or illnesses? No? Okay. The natural explanations also had to be considered, if only to be ruled out he explained. Neither were there any heating or air conditioning systems on when they felt those strange wafts of air for that matter. That was odd he agreed, and the detail of the missing objects was curious. They were positive they had not mislaid the items or that they were robbed, they had left things in question at conspicuous places and they simply vanished without a trace minutes later. All right, it sounded like they needed spiritual help. Peter promised he'd take a look and bless their new home, they could choose a morning slot on his agenda convenient for them for the following week before it got filled with appointments. Next week was good, they decided, and the sooner the better. The couple thanked him for his help, they didn't know who to turn to until his name had been mentioned and they looked him up. Although their place was starting to creep them out big time, they didn't want to move so soon after they had finally found the perfect apartment. Relieved to find someone who would listen to them, the young man cracked a joke as he shook hands and said goodbye: if the place was haunted as they suspected, no wonder the rent was so low for that location! With a laugh, Peter promised to get to the root of their little problem and wished them a good day.

One of his regulars was next, Mrs. Martinez. He caught a glimpse of her waiting patiently but pensively in the waiting room as his new clients left. He needed a moment of recollection and didn't show her in right away. Oh yes, he could feel it, there was a heavy grey cloud of negativity being forced upon her again. Her case was a chronic problem: ill will and jealousy had been deliberately directed against her and everyone she cared about to the point of spiritual suffocation. It first began manifesting itself through bouts of inexplicable ill health that medicines failed to alleviate properly although the doctors found no cause for this strange inefficiency, plus there was a noticeable paralysis in her family's life and prosperity. Although God often tested through hardships, there were times when the forces of evil attempted to load a person's daily crosses with additional dead-weights, and this was one of those occasions. It was a prolific problem these days and Mrs. Martinez was languishing under it, one of those curious preternatural clouds of malaise that no matter what that family did they barely ticked over, money dwindled to break-even status regardless of how hard they saved, and the successes that anyone could expect after dedicated hard work just fizzled away where they were concerned. Her children couldn't hold or maintain a job for long despite all their dedication. Never falling completely behind, but never being allowed to have those bright moments that could keep a person motivated in the midst of daily cares and prevent them from losing hope, that was the kicker. The zest of life was completely reduced to ashes in the mouth so to speak. Peter's unique intuition told him raw jealously had been sealed against her by some kind of spell from someone close enough to her who was envious of everything she had. He often observed with regret there were certain cultures attracted to spiritualism and the eeriness of the 'otherworld' more than others. To add a bit of spice to their lives many thought it nothing to play with the Tarots or fooled around with the Ouija board despite their profession of the Faith. They were not above casting a spell on those they disliked and be the first in the church pew the next day mouthing prayers as though butter wouldn't melt in their mouths. The devil did not need to work at all when people were so willing to do his dirty work for him. The sad part in a case like this, it took time and energy to break a spell, and when he did manage to break or disperse evil of this nature with a barrage of deliverance prayers, there was nothing beyond a miracle conversion from stopping the envious perpetrator from re-offending.

"Hello, Mrs. Martinez. Let me guess, things are starting to slip again," he noted as he opened the door.

"I'm afraid so," she admitted, taking a seat with him. "Nothing is going right, everything I touch seems to fall apart, it's back again."

"Just for certainty's sake, did anything out of the ordinary happen to tip you off?"

"Oh yes," she nodded. "I got a blackened egg on Saturday, and I just got that carton on Friday, the day before, it was well before the expiry date, so I *know* it was absolutely fresh. The curse is back, I tell you."

"I see."

Anyone else would have brushed this observation aside in disdain, but Peter was not anyone else. His exorcist tutor in Rome had warned him that various cultures had different ways of spotting evil at work, it always had to present itself eventually, even in the most bizarre forms. Fr. Amaranth was personally convinced that each country had its specific demons as well as its heavenly assigned angels and that these demons manifested their works in accordance with the spiritual intuition of that nation. He advised Peter not to reject anything no matter how odd it sounded until he had seen it for himself and could prove the validity of those claims. Although he had to be careful not to give credence to everything or yield to superstition, there were distinct signs Peter quickly learned about. From the Mexicans he discovered that even if there may be a scientific explanation for it, a blackened yolk cracked open from a raw egg while all the others were perfectly fresh was a sure sign someone had it in for you.

Peter dutifully went through the customary questions with her. Did she let her prayer life slacken in any way? How about her children? Still saying the prayers of deliverance every day? So far, they were still keeping up with his spiritual protection program and were practising their faith, even if the kids complied grudgingly in the beginning just to keep her quiet. It must be working for things had improved after he had helped her, the kids were sorting their lives out, but 'it' was only affecting her now. Time to try something else. Peter suggested if she suspected who was causing her the problems, she must step up her prayers for them, and if needs be, cut off all contact or minimize it as much as possible with that person or persons. He had also learned that just like certain physical illnesses that could be aggravated by location and climate, spiritual problems could also be affected by 'environment', that is, by those whom people kept close to or associated with. In this case, direct contact could be keeping the lines open for trouble he told Mrs. Martinez, especially with issues concerning malice, and advised the best tactic was to keep a low profile, out of sight out of mind. Distance could encourage loss of interest in her to a point, and she might be able to slip free from under the evil influence. If she should have to cross paths with the person or people in question, he warned her never to talk about her personal business or family life, and to keep everything very general so they wouldn't know if what they wished on her was working or not …

" … and if you *are* having a bad time, never, ever, look as though they were getting the best of you," he continued. "Always be cheerful. Be peaceful in your heart and give God the victory over your troubles. If your ne're-do-well wishers feel you are not suffering because of them, they may also grow annoyed thinking they are wasting their time, and will eventually leave you alone. In fact, when you're feeling particularly low, declare that 'Victory Day' for heaven, dress in your best and celebrate that special 'holiday' as if you were going to a wedding. God is pleased you trust in Him. This should help disperse the black clouds."

"You mean, just dress up? Go out for a … a dinner or something," she wondered with curiosity.

"Yes, by all means. Do whatever you feel equals a real celebration. God knows we all need cheering up on occasion. Just don't go overboard and turn it into one of those wild hen nights that will send you to my confessional."

"Don't worry, I know what you mean." She laughed. "You know, a celebration is a great idea, it's been awhile since all the family got together for something other than problems to discuss."

"Now you've got it. Have a reunion, but no problems are to be brought up. You're all going to have a happy day, and that's that. Don't let anything going on in your lives depress you."

Of course, these 'jealousy vibes' would take time to break. Faith and perseverance he reminded her, and to get her started on the right track, he would pray the deliverance prayer for her once more, for which she was very grateful. Standing up, he vested in his stole, took up his crucifix, and he held it over her head, praying quietly under his breath. The various commands for evil to depart, even in Latin, could unnerve a person at times and it was best to keep things on a calming level, especially when the evil influence inflicted was not the patient's fault. He had hardly started into the fourth sentence when there was a loud knocking on the door followed by a despairing male voice that made both of them jump.

"Monsignor! Let me in! You've got to cast them out!"

What the … ? Not again!

"I'm sorry Mrs. Martinez, I'll be back in a minute." Peter sighed.

Sure enough, there was frantic, paranoid Joel peering in at him as he opened the door, his gaunt figure clad in a baggy T-shirt and jeans, his eyes panicked, his short brown hair nervously rubbed around into a poky frazzle. At least there wasn't anyone else in the waiting room right then, Joel tended to give his other spiritual patients the jitters, but he was actually harmless even if a bit emotionally unpredictable. Peter closed the door behind him and patiently attempted to talk some sense to this unfortunate soul.

"Hi, Joel. Have you gone off your meds again?"

Joel looked down at his tennis shoes and shuffled his feet.

"Come, come. Don't hold back on me, you know I can't help you when you do."

Eventually, Joel looked up and admitted he had indeed skipped his meds, several days in fact.

"They make my head feel off. I don't like them, and I know *they* are still there, even when I take them. I *know* it."

"Joel, they're not real."

They happened to be the voices he kept hearing, in short, various hallucinations. Joel was a real schizophrenic case, but several of his extended family members had convinced him the doctors were idiots and that he wasn't sick but possessed with the result he sought Peter out on a continual basis to get rid of his 'demons', often showing up unexpected with no appointment.

"You've got to do an exorcism on me!"

"Now, you know you don't need one. This really is all in your head."

"But I do! They're not in my head," Joel insisted petulantly. "I don't need a shrink!"

"I can't do an exorcism, but I'll say the healing prayer over you, just like the last time. Will that help?"

"Anything," Joel consented, "just make 'em stop!"

Resigned to these emergency visits, Peter motioned him to sit on the sofa that furnished the waiting room. Taking his crucifix, he held it over Joel's head and quietly whispered the longed-for words over him as he rocked on the edge of his seat. Eventually Peter finished his almost silent intonation with the sign of the cross over him, and asked Joel if he felt any better.

"Oh yeah! Thanks, much! I think they'll leave me alone now."

"Good, and don't forget to take your meds, even the Bible says we have to pay attention to doctors and take our medicines, so be good and do what the Bible says."

The last bit of advice had to be called out after him for Joel had quickly bolted out the door. Poor fellow! All Peter could do was shake his head at times. If praying over him made him feel better, so be it.

He could not forget when Joel first came to him a year ago. At the time, he thought he had his first real case of possession, except his interior senses did not feel anything preternatural was present. However, Peter knew he had to assess the situation further and quietly said the deliverance prayers over Joel to see if there would be any reaction. Nothing. He tried it again, but Joel said he felt the same, and 'they' weren't budging. The final test, Peter checked to see how Joel would respond with his next suggestion … .

"Now, I'll try one powerful prayer for them to depart. This never fails, so you should feel something happening this time for sure … don't be afraid, just let whatever's going to happen, happen. Okay?"

Joel eagerly agreed to have this extra special prayer said over him. This time Peter spoke several phrases loudly and imperiously in Latin, Joel soon began to twitch and groan, holding his head, then began to writhe in the chair.

"Oh! It's working, they're not happy, they want you to stop."

Peter immediately ceased his intonation.

"You're not possessed, you need to seek some medical help."

"I don't need those doctors. They don't *know*! But you said this would *work*! It *was* working!"

"I apologise for deceiving you, but the supposed 'prayer' I was saying over you right now is nothing more than some old gibberish I cobbled together from an ancient Latin treatise on garden plants."

Peter was correct. Joel was mentally unstable and psychologically open to autosuggestion. If he truly was in need of his help as an exorcist, he would have reacted in some way to the real prayers and been impassive with the old spice book. Joel was angry, but calmed down when Peter offered to say a healing prayer over him instead.

"Hmm, all right, just make sure it's a real one."

"I promise," Peter smiled, placing his hands on Joel's head and fulfilling that promise in English so he could understand what was said.

Well, even if a trick was played on him in the beginning, at least he wasn't sneered at or rudely shoved out of the way, which tended to happen often. This priest treated him okay in the end, and he *did* feel good with that last prayer … .

Ever since then, Joel came for a healing prayer since he felt much better after Peter said it, but continued to wheedle for the full kit-and-caboodle exorcism in the hopes that the Monsignor would eventually relent despite his continual refusals.

Peter returned to Mrs. Martinez who smiled at him in commiseration.

"I know. We'll be seeing him again soon. Let's try again, shall we?"

He raised up his crucifix once more. After the prayer was concluded, she thanked him and wished him a good day. Okay, who was next?

The few people who now lined up had come to see him for a more routine reason, they had tried several times to go to him for confession before his morning services, but others had beaten them to it and they often missed their chance. Of course, Peter didn't mind. The 'Operating Room' was open to all the aspects of his ministry, not just the deliverance and possible exorcism cases, he was pleased to schedule confessions and spiritual guidance sessions too. However, one of his usual penitents, a smartly-dressed lady with an over-active tongue still couldn't see how she was sinning so much by gossiping about others when Peter gave her a gentle reprimand about that glaring fault. Of course, he was still a 'young one' to some of his older parishioners, why he was no older than their eldest son, and just like their sons, he had not been through all the trials of life *they* had, or so they figured. Surely they had earned the right by seniority and survival in a world of hard knocks not to let him push them around, even when he was going about God's business.

"I can't see what's wrong about a good chat now and then," she politely but matter-of-factly pointed-out. "Oh, I know we shouldn't tell lies about people, but it can't be all that bad when you're telling the God's honest truth about a person, now can it?"

"Oh? That's what you think. It's possible to commit murder over a cup of coffee you know, even with the truth."

"*Murder?* Oh, really Monsignor! It's not as bad as all that?"

"It may well slip past a fault to a venial sin, then on to something just as equally bad," he noted.

"I don't mean to argue, I still don't see how I'm doing any harm," she said, "but … I'm sorry if it's wrong. There. Umm, yes. That's all I can think of," she finished quickly, having come to the end of her sins, waiting for him to pronounce the absolution so she could go. She was sure she hadn't missed or forgotten anything.

The problem was, she wasn't entirely sorry, just apologetic she had trouble following a known teaching concerning Christian charity, but not grasping how thin the line she was treading. For the sake of being social, people didn't realize how nasty they could let things get. Those chit-chat sessions seemed like so much innocent social conversation … .

Peter waited a minute in the customary meditative pose he assumed when hearing confessions, elbow resting on the chair arm with his hand to his forehead, eyes closed. She hoped he wouldn't sit around like this for long and quickly checked her watch, she had a morning get-together with the girls to attend, which she was looking forward to. Just sitting there in silence, a minute felt like an age when she had things to do! At last, he spoke:

"All right, before I give you your penance, I'm ordering you as your confessor to do a spiritual exercise for me first."

"Er, okay … if you say so," she noted, eyeing him curiously. That sounded like he meant business.

"You are to go outside this building right now, gather a fistful of the first dandelion heads you find that have gone to seed, then come right back here with your posy."

"I'm to … *what?*"

"You heard me," he continued with a slight smile, opening his eyes and looking his penitent straight into the eyes and through the soul, "a decent sized fist-full, mind you. Chip chop! You have a manicure session you want to attend if I'm not mistaken? I think you had better hurry if you want to make it on time, for I've only given you part of your exercise."

Hey! She didn't tell him where she was going! How did he know? No, no, maybe she did say something … .

"Right now," she questioned, motioning towards the door.

"Yes, yes. Off you go, like a good girl. Don't be naughty now."

Heaving a huffing sigh, she grabbed her purse and left the office, passing by the others in the waiting room, muttering something about 'what ridiculous nonsense this all was', indignant with the patronising tone he suddenly assumed and treating her like a child, yet knowing better than to go against the Monsignor, especially when given a direct order in confession.   To be disobedient under those circumstances would be downright sacrilege, and she wasn't about to go that far, seniority or no seniority in life-experience. But dandelions? Now, *really*!

Peter calmly motioned for the next person in line to come in and commenced hearing their confession, oblivious to the pantomime his little spiritual exercise was causing upstairs. Mabel paused in the midst of attending a phone call after seeing the strangest sight from the corner of her eye out the main window and motioned Ethel to come over and take a gander. For a moment they thought the parish had another nut job on the loose when they saw the well-dressed woman with the fancy purse who came for a soul-scrubbing now hunting around the trees, flower beds and sidewalk cracks, plucking fuzzy spheres of fluff, making wild hand gestures into the air and muttering to herself, apparently angry with all and sundry that was wrong with the world. Mabel and Ethel were even more amazed when they saw the same lady come back in, march down the hall towards the basement stairs with her generous batch of fuzz, only to return a few minutes later, still muttering something, exit the main entrance and blow the handful of dandelion seeds into the air. Having dispatched every ball of feathery down to the bare stalks, she dropped the wilting remains, brushed off her hands, stormed inside, and made a beeline back down to the Operating Room. They thought they had seen the last of these strange antics until 'Mrs. Gucci handbag' came out one last time, looking entirely bewildered and searched along the ground, apparently having trouble finding what she was looking for. At last, she threw her hands up, came back in, and returned to the basement precincts.

"Hmm, I tell you Ethel, I hear a lot of peculiar stories about the Monsignor and the strange way he deals with some of his sheep, but I'd never thought I'd see one happen myself," Mabel said with a nod.

"If he ever gets a real exorcism case, I think we should find another job!" Ethel laughed. "I'd hate to think what we might see then. I wonder what *that* was all about?"

"I don't know, and we may never find out," Mabel concluded as she returned to her work.

Downstairs, Peter serenely asked his now fuming penitent to sit outside in the waiting room and mediate on what she had just done while he finished up another confession. Meditate! Meditate on what? On what a ridiculous fool she looked like out there? If his first order wasn't bad enough, wasting her time egg-hunting for those stupid seeding dandelion heads, she had to go back and puff them away! Then— *he wanted her to find every bit of fluff she had dispersed!* Impossible! What kind of training in the seminaries were they getting theses days? A lot of poppycock, if you ask me. Why couldn't he just give a few Hail Mary's as a penance and be done with it? However, she decided to bottle her impatience in case he changed his mind about finishing her confession, withhold absolution and boot her out. There had better be a good explanation for all of this, or the Archbishop might hear from her how his diocese was actually running.

"Come in, sit down," he motioned as the last penitent said good-bye and left them alone. "Now, have we learned anything today?"

Shoot, she hadn't really thought about what he was getting at when he wanted her to 'meditate', except perhaps give her time to vent her complaints to herself and cool off, now she wasn't sure what she was supposed to have learned.

"Umm, well, to be honest, not really," she finally admitted. Better to tell the truth and shame the devil.

"Aw, it's not that difficult, give a guess," he prompted with a chuckle, "think of it as a parable."

Taking a resigned breath, she shook her head as she looked up to the ceiling, then shrugged her shoulders, exhaling defeat.

"I don't know. I give up. I was never good at these types of puzzles."

"Why, it's very simple," he declared, then proceeded to elucidate the mystery of the dandelions. Children often find it great fun to gather up the small feathery spheres and blow them to smithereens, watching the seeds blow in the breeze like a string of soap bubbles. Little yellow flowers, how beautiful! So pretty! And the fluff seems as pure as snow. However, unlike soap bubbles that will pop in a few seconds and disappear, dandelion seeds were another matter. The children may laugh as they watch the white down fly away, but are oblivious to the fact they have helped spread an intrusive weed far and wide ... who knows where a new crop of weeds will spring up, and the next generation of weeds from them? Perhaps in a lawn a gardener had meticulously kept moss and weed free, or then again, a lady's beautiful flowerbed will soon become choked with the unwanted plants stealing the good nutrients form the soil from the deserving flowers. Then, what about the scrubby plants that stick out of cracks in the pavement? They could trip someone up and cause a serious injury ... to think something so innocent and pretty as yellow dandelions and their fluff could cause such work and hardship, waste so much time and resources ... .

At first, this sounded like baloney. Did children actually *sin* by blowing dandelion fuzz around? Then, she realized the Monsignor was talking about her seemingly harmless gossip.

"Ah, I think the light is dawning," he said, as he saw her expression change to understanding, then to embarrassment. "There are times when even telling the truth can be uncharitable, and above all, we must be charitable. What if the people you are talking about are trying to amend their life, but your tattle-telling prevents others from seeing the best in them and their efforts to change? Soon, one bit of gossip spreads somewhere else like the dandelion seeds and destroys fertile ground elsewhere, not to mention the exaggerations that get tacked on from place to place. You have no idea how far and wide one coffee-session can spread those seeds of malice in the ears of others, and yet like immature children, you chatter away and do untold mischief. Don't you want to be given those merciful second chances when you've done something wrong? Then do not murder a person's reputation further than they have already wounded themselves. We're not supposed to disclose our neighbours' faults and failings without cause, or we've committed the sin of detraction, which also comes under the sin of bearing false witness, for it can finish off a reputation just as quickly."

"I see what you mean now," she admitted, "but, surely if we see someone who might get into trouble if we don't *warn* them about a person … ."

"That's a different case," he jumped in. "I said *without cause*. If you have good cause, it's one of the rare times you may say something, but only if you feel the person you wish to warn may fall into real danger. Just like dandelion leaves that can be eaten, the truth becomes medicinal then so to speak, and must be dished out like a bitter herb, in the correct dosage and at the right time."

"Huh. Just one more question, why did you have me go out again and try to gather the seed fuzz I blew away?"

"To show how impossible it is to take back anything we have said. Be careful and think twice before you speak. Try to change the subject if something that may be hurtful comes up in the conversation. However, I must remind you you're still required to repair any damage already done, so the next time you hear something mentioned, try turning the discussion to something more positive about the person and don't harp on their faults."

"In other words, do a little weeding and keep them from spreading."

"Now you've got it."

Another soul helped and with no more people to see, Peter took the opportunity to lock the door when his penitent had left and laid out on the waiting room couch for a few minutes, he didn't get enough sleep and on top of it was feeling rather drained that moment. He often felt that way when grappling with curses, but it wasn't Mrs. Martinez's fault. Joel now, at least he had a real medical issue, it was a pity he really couldn't do more to help him, at least, not until he accepted he had health issues. Denial was also a huge stumbling block for the healing ministry of a priest. Better have Mabel call his brother and let him know he was off his medications again, Joel had a tendency to ramble away and get lost.

Talk about calls, what was he thinking? He didn't have time to lay around right now, he had almost forgotten the Old Buzzard needed to be towed from the hospital parking lot, plus he had a bunch of groceries in the back of his temporary means of transportation that had to be dropped off at the rectory, and he'd better make it fast. His mother could have stuck some items among the bags that needed refrigeration as she often did, and the way things were warming up that May, he might end up with a pre-stewed mess before he made it back in time, not to mention he had a corporate afternoon at the Reinold offices ahead of him.

Mabel clucked in disbelief when she received the request to call the towing company, again.

"Uh oh, figures. We saw your sister's car in your spot and wondered what happened. Did the exhaust pipe bite the dust?"

"No, I had a fender-bender yesterday."

"What? You weren't hurt, were you," Ethel exclaimed.

"No, I'm fine, but the Old Buzzard lost its tail all right."

"Well, good riddance! It's time to retire that thing. Maybe the diocese will spring for a better car now, it's a disgrace you got landed with that to begin with," Mabel *tsked*, as she hunted for the number in the phonebook, "and yes, we saw your unexpected visitor. I've already called Joel's brother and told him he'd better come look for him before he scares half the neighbourhood," she continued.

"Thanks Nurse Mabel, I don't know how I would manage without you."

"Nah, I'm sure you'd figure out how to work the phone," Mabel joked. Despite being a tough cookie, she had a soft spot for Monsignor Reinold. He was a good soul and very wise for someone his age. He always had a kind word to say and never slacked in his duty.

"I hope you don't mind, but I have to ask, just what *was* going on down there today," Ethel piped up. "It looked like one of your visitors had entered her second childhood."

"Ah ah, curiosity killed the cat. I can't break the seal of the confessional you know." Peter laughed, wagging his finger at Ethel. "Sorry ladies, as much as I'd love to chew the fat, I'm on the run, I've got to get back to the rectory. You two have a good afternoon."

"You too, see you tomorrow," Ethel called after him as he waved and left the building.

So far, so good, all in a normal day's parish work. Before getting into the car, he checked the trunk: yep, there were some veggies beginning to sweat in the heat, but at least this time the meat was put in a picnic icebox. There were a couple of other bags too, but no time to check what could be in them, he would find out at the rectory. Pedal to the metal, he was getting hungry. Hmm, Mom, what am I going to do with you, he thought as he parked the car and unloaded the back, first hanging up the garment bags in his closet before filling up the kitchen cupboards. It felt like he was back in college, she was always sending supplies to Lottie and him in those days, not to mention Gerry and Leroy's frat house on a regular basis via the Reinold Enterprises efficient package delivery service just to make sure her children got a decent supply of food now and again when they had left the parental roof. However, her shopping list now included some treats for the 'Holy Bachelors Club' as the clerics of the rectory sometimes called themselves. She always included bags of imported French roast coffee for him, custard Danishes were Fr. Jenkin's breakfast poison, then she found out Fr. O'Conner loved Irish tea and boxes of traditional English mustard that came in powdered form. Everyone would laugh as he gleefully mixed the yellow paste to the thick consistency of lava and heaped it on his ham sandwiches, causing tears to pour from his eyes and sneezing himself into a dither with every bite, yet insisting all the while he was grand and as happy as a pig in muck. Plus, she never forgot to include some convenient canned items like beef stew, there were also cans of soup, and of course, there they were, Peter chuckled as he put the last items away — spaghetti rings for Fr. Mark. Although Mark was now a widower-turned-priest, his kids when they were young had taught him one faddy eating habit he could never break, dipping a spoon in and downing the stuff straight from the can, no pre-heating.

"Uck, that's disgusting." Jenkins grimaced the first time he caught Mark in the act of opening a can and diving in despite having a developed number of odd tastes himself thanks to all those years as an army base chaplain.

"When you've got growing boys in Little League, they need fuel fast. They nearly eat us out of house and home. How they used to love this stuff! Had to keep a ton around, it's not bad actually," Mark admitted.

"At least heat it first, nuke all the preservatives," Peter joked.

"Nah, tastes good this way," he insisted, adding chunks of cold hotdogs to the mix and stirring them in.

Mark was still a kid himself in so many ways Peter mused, he would certainly be pleased to see his pasta mash of choice restocked. Come again, the canned items also came in handy when one of them was on the run and they had to heat and eat something fast when dining at the regular times with the rest of the bachelors was not an option. Looked like no one else was coming back for lunch today; everyone was out and about somewhere. Emergency rations it is then. Peter opened a can of soup and poured the pre-made contents into a bowl for the microwave then set it to heat while he made a sandwich. Nothing fancy was just the ticket, a convenient lunch would give him some extra time to say his required prayers, check his mail, and get some rest before he headed back out into the world, thirty minutes of shut-eye was all he needed. Heading up to his room, he unbuttoned his cassock and wearily lay down, sitting up to set the alarm before settling back again.

The bed felt so good, he groaned when he heard the beeping. Why in heaven's name did a half-hour's snooze feel like a few seconds? The cruelty of it! To feel a night's sleep in a matter of minutes, while a day awake never seemed to end. Still, the nap was good. He stretched, went to the bathroom to splash some water on his face and give himself a quick re-shave before redressing. At least the cold water woke him up a bit. He combed his hair back into shape, returned to the kitchen for a cup of coffee, grabbed his two cases and headed back out to face the world, this time as a hard-boiled executive.

Arriving at the Manhattan offices, he barely said 'hello' when he was informed by Mrs. Clarke there was a problem with one of their clients in England. This morning they received a call from Flora World Wholesalers, their regional manager at the Dutch flower market exchange was livid: their exotic flower shipments had been left on runways in South Africa and Kenya, and were arriving at their distribution centres half dead. This was not the only call they had about the African routes, either. Great, nothing but problems these days! If it's not about untimely food deliveries, it's the flower shipments not reaching their destination in Holland on time and disintegrating into withered bouquets of slime. There was nothing for it, profuse apologies would have to be made, funds returned, insurance claims made depending on the setback, offer a three month discount as additional compensation to prevent losing them as a customer, the aggravation of it! Sometimes he would rather battle a demon from Hell than grapple with the bureaucracy of man. Naturally, this was the downside of running a mega international shipping and distribution industry. It was particularly time-sensitive and relied on delegating tasks to hundreds of managers, not to mention thousands of other workers across the globe. A gear was bound to slip and snag up the works when there were so many variables involved, it was impossible to keep on top of everything one-hundred percent of the time. Don't lose your cool, you've handled this before, he told himself, take a big breath and dive in. The thought of tackling the job was worse than dong it. First, better find out what damage control had been put into motion without him.

Peter greeted the Hulk who was stationed out side Thomas' door and received a stony-faced nod from the bodyguard in return, his immense presence suggested Lottie must be inside. Setting down a case and knocking on the door, Thomas opened and motioned him to come in with his finger to his lips, pointing to Lottie sitting at his desk—obviously she had called the Dutch regional manager of Flora World and was making the crucial apologies with Thomas overseeing her efforts.

"Yes, we are terribly sorry for the condition of your shipments, we shall get to the bottom of it immediately. Please be assured you will receive a complete refund for those deliveries that were ruined, plus we shall offer a further discount off your contract price in compensation for the inconvenience you have … yes, I understand you are … yes, we are terribly sorry for … yes, we shall, thank you for … oh flip it! He hung up. Oh God, I hope I haven't lost our contract with them." Lottie moaned as she sank back in the chair. "Dad will kill me!"

"No he won't, don't get upset, and no, I don't think you have. In fact, it sounds like you were handling it perfectly," Peter reassured her. "I'm proud of you, and you too Thomas, you're certainly bringing my sister up to speed."

"Thanks Petey, I appreciate that. It's hard to deal with someone when they're yelling at you like that and won't listen to your solutions or the compensation being offered," Lottie replied dejectedly.

"They *are* losing hundreds of thousands of dollars of profit per spoiled delivery," Thomas noted, "you can't expect them to stay calm. Heated calls are to be expected. Besides, they're already aware of our compensation policies, etcetera, it's in their contract, this was just a courtesy call to let them know we are on top of it."

"I know, but still … ,"

"Look my dear, did they say they were cancelling their contract," Peter asked.

"Well, no … ,"

"Then they're willing to give us time to sort it out," Peter concluded.

"We'd better get on it immediately," Thomas nodded.

"Agreed. Did anyone call Gerry to keep him in the loop?"

"Oh no Petey, surely we don't have to tell him about the stressful stuff like this," Lottie wondered.

"I wish we didn't, but you know how he doesn't like to be kept in the dark, especially with his clients. He did land us the Flora World contract after all."

"That's true, but should we come to a decision on what to do before we tell him," Thomas mused. "He does have to rest too, we can't put all the work on his back yet. He was just supposed to sign off on some of the papers."

"I think we've got too many chiefs and not enough Indians," Peter observed.

"Too many family members in the family business, the siblings are scrambling up the chain of command." Lottie smiled.

"All joking aside, we've got to get on this," Thomas pointed out.

"Okay, I think we should call Gerry," Lottie replied, picking up the phone and dialling the hospital. As soon as she reached him, she switched it to speakerphone.

"Hi everyone. What's up?"

"Umm, I hate to break the news Gerry, but Flora World is up in arms," Lottie began. Their brother certainly didn't like the sound of that and wondered what had happened. Peter filled him in on the details as the others listened. Gerry quietly swore under his breath on the other end of the line.

"I know," Thomas interjected.

"I think you know what that means," Peter continued.

"Yes, another globe trot," Gerry replied impatiently, "and of all times!"

In other words, an on-the-spot international inspection the leading executives of the company were obliged to do every so often to ensure the business was running in tip-top shape. Mr. Reinold preferred family to look in on these matters since no one else but family would care as much for their business that was established by their forebears almost two centuries ago.

Peter cast a glance at Thomas, they could quickly see the myriad of difficulties Gerry was alluding to and had the same concerns: if the latest problems with the flower shipments were just a matter of human incompetence or something as stupid as the refrigerated trucks not being serviced properly and crooked mechanics pocketing the extra, they had the experience and the mettle to sort it out, but Gerry couldn't go for obvious reasons, neither could Peter who also had to stay close to home with his parish to attend. What made it worse, Mr. Reinold Senior had already completed an inspection in Africa not that long ago and would be fuming when he heard the news. Of course, he could do this globe run naturally, but in addition to all that was facing him the next few days they knew the Captain wouldn't want to leave the main offices with Gerry still recuperating and Peter only able to help part-time, while Lottie was very new to all of this even with Thomas' expertise to back her up. While their father might agree to let their sister go for the sake of gaining experience, would she be able to handle something as involved as their global inspections this early in her training as an executive? If she could have started out with the European run with Thomas helping her, maybe, but *Africa*? Unravelling the red tape of that continent was murder to begin with. It was one of the unpleasant facts of their business that almost all of the hot countries along or bordering the equator were beleaguered with one drawback or another; poor infrastructure, social unrest, corrupt officials wanting paybacks along the routes, or simply the laid-back nature of certain cultures could gum everything up. Business down south tended to slide into one big easy-going groove that boded ill for shipping. Then, there was the unfortunate and undeniable fact that the world was a man's world after all despite the growing number of women in the workplace. CEO's daughter or not, would their dear Charlotte be taken seriously despite the authority invested in her to act on behalf of the company? Notwithstanding her determination, the corporate sphere could be a pitiless battlefield, it seemed too soon to throw her out into the fray just yet when it felt like they had armed her with a peashooter. She may be catching on, but she had been there for only a couple of months, she had so much to learn, and these were just some of their concerns.

"I think we'd better notify Dad," Gerry continued, "we've got to settle this fast."

However, there was a knock on the door, Mr. Reinold had heard the news and had arrived to hear their deliberations. Yes, he was boiling mad, but relieved to hear Flora World had not threatened to cancel their contract. Still, it did not look good. Damage to their customers shipments on this level was outrageous to him, it reflected badly not just on their company but also on the family name, and to think he had just been in Africa and had not discovered anything amiss, he was indeed fuming. He agreed that if they could not find the source of the trouble over the airwaves in the next few days, an emergency inspection was facing them.

"What do you think, Dad," Peter enquired. "You know the inspector elect has to get ready just in case, and since Gerry is out and I certainly can't go, it leaves it to you or Charlotte."

"True, and I would go, but I've got the AGM and some meetings with the Teamsters union to prepare for," Richard grumbled. "I suppose the inspection could wait until I take care of that and then jet over there."

"I know I'm not the most prepared for the job yet, but why not send me," Lottie interjected. "You say you have great faith in me Petey. How about now?"

"True my dear, you have come along in leaps and bounds, but you've barely scratched the surface of our domestic holdings, the international rat-race is another animal entirely," Peter noted gently.

"Brutal at times," Gerry agreed, his voice sounding from the speakerphone on the desk. "Forgive me for stating the obvious, but you'd be dealing with unfamiliar cultures over there, and it may come as quite a shock. Yes, you've been on vacation to Europe, but this trip wouldn't be anything like what you've experienced. Many countries conduct business differently than we do," he tried to explain. Thank God it wasn't Japan they were facing! That was Gerry's most dreaded country of inspection.

However, the idea of sending Lottie off to South Africa when it had barely emerged from the apartheid days and currently entering an unpredictable time of change seemed just as dangerous. It was a nightmare re-establishing their shipping channels and air freight routes there when the trade sanctions were lifted, hang-ups were bound to happen along the way, but with her inexperience could she sort out this latest mess in an economically developing country seething with racial tension? Then, if it was not the practical business matters they had to consider, it was the trouble they seemed to find themselves in during some of the inspections, that was the most alarming aspect. The family had the misfortune of uncovering criminal organisations using their shipping containers for illegal smuggling operations in the past, and after the suspicious circumstances of Gerry's accident, sending Lottie overseas at this point in time was out of the question. Why, she needed a bodyguard on her own home turf!

Thomas cleared his throat.

"Forgive me for interrupting, but considering our current circumstances, I propose you send me, I am a willing and able candidate."

"Of course, Thomas," Mr. Reinold agreed. If they could not have a family member go, the next best thing was to send a trusted friend. "You are the Acting Manager after all. I suppose there's nothing for it. I'm sorry for this short notice."

"Don't mention it, all part of the job. I shall start making arrangements."

"Wait a minute, I don't see why you couldn't send me along with Thomas," Lottie piped up, "I've got to learn sometime, and since I've been thrown into this crash course, you can't just flunk me out now. Even if you don't want me to act in an official capacity just yet, I should at least see what one of these inspection tours are like."

"Yes, you should, but not this one," her father affirmed, "this is an emergency, not one of the routine runs, and we have enough trouble as it is with those. What will your mother think if I send you off as inexperienced as a shanghaied sailor? She'd have me swinging from a yard arm."

"But I won't be alone, Thomas would be there, and if it would make you feel more secure, you can tack on a few more bodyguards to keep the Hulk company too."

"No, I'm not having you go, and that's that."

"Dad, I know you hate to hear this, but I'm not a little girl any more," she replied, standing up from her seat and planting her palms firmly on the desk. "If you truly want me to take on my share of responsibility in the family company as one of the executives, you have to start treating me that way. You expect your other workers to pull their weight and earn their pay and bonuses, so allow me to grow up and pull my weight too. Mom knows I'm entering the business world, she may not like what I'll have to face any more than I do, but she'll understand, or she will eventually, I'm sure. No one will take me seriously around here unless you do."

Whew! Lottie standing up to the Captain and putting her foot down! Respectfully of course, but resolutely and not ready to budge an inch, she really had grown up. Gerry was speechless, so was Thomas, they had never heard or seen her this assertive. Peter chuckled, he knew she had the makings of a great businesswoman and was now finding the courage to develop and defend those once hidden talents. Still, for some reason he wished she wouldn't go on this trip, not *this* one.

"Lottie, be good and don't push too hard, there will be other inspections," Peter tried to reason with her.

"Honestly! You say I'm doing great, yet it's like everyone wants me to go back home and learn to cook," she noted impatiently, folding her arms.

"All right, all right," Richard jumped in, "we don't have time for any more squalls, and I hate to admit it, but you're right, my dear. I can't expect you to become a fledged executive member here by withholding the experience necessary for you to advance. How I'm going to face your mother about this, I don't know."

"Don't you worry Dad, tell her I twisted your arm," Lottie beamed.

"Not quite, but close enough, you sassy thing." Richard smiled. True, he hated to see her grow up, but was proud to see her tackling the business alongside her brothers. It certainly was a different world these days. "Okay, you can go, but mind you, Thomas is in charge this trip, you just watch and observe. And furthermore, you're getting two more bodyguards. Agreed?"

"Done. May I make enlightened suggestions during the course of our travels, if I have any," she wheedled.

"Urrm," he grumbled, "yes, just don't be a nuisance! You're going to see how it's done. That's it."

"Charlotte's never a nuisance, I shall thoroughly consider any observations and suggestions she offers." Thomas smiled.

"I guess that's settled," Richard stated before continuing, "and Pete, I've left an important matter for you to attend to on your desk."

"Oh?"

"Yes, something that can't be delayed."

There was a knock on the door, it was Mrs. Clarke. "There's an overseas call for … someone on line four, it's our airfreight manager in Kenya," Mrs. Clarke explained. It was difficult to know who to direct the call to with all the Top Brass of the company present.

"Thank you. Lottie, you take it, we'll oversee," Peter decided.

"Okay guys, I've got to go," Gerry's voice sounded over the speaker, "the nurses are prodding at me and pulling the phone away. Keep me updated, will you?"

"Sure thing, Gerry, love you," Lottie replied as he hung up. Time to grapple with Kenya, she looked a little unnerved but quickly resumed her professional demeanour as she punched in line four and turned up the speakerphone again. Poor Lottie was certainly getting a crash course in the family business, but as she adamantly pointed out, she had to learn somehow.

"Hello, yes this is Charlotte Reinold speaking."

They listened quietly to the conversation, the exchange soon warmed up: obviously, the manager was trying to smooth-talk his way out of a situation he should have been handling. All the Top Brass present had to fight the urge to assist her until Charlotte finished with the authoritative announcement that apologies were not good enough and that their regional office had better be prepared to receive a delegation representing the head offices from New York, for she would be accompanying their Acting Manager of International Distribution to personally investigate the matter within … Thomas scribbled a number and held up it:

" … within forty-eight hours or so. Yes, I'm sure you will. Good day," she concluded briskly, hitting the button and terminating the call.

"Well done, Miss Reinold," Thomas remarked with approval, "that's telling him. Looks like we'd better get packing."

"The Hulk and his friends too." Lottie sighed. "But I need to make some calls first."

"I'll have Mrs. Clarke start making the arrangements," Peter replied, heading towards the door.

"First, go check your desk," Richard added.

"Bye Petey, don't worry, we'll manage everything just beautifully," Lottie reassured him as he waved, grabbed his cases and went to his former office.

What was so important that needed attending before Lottie's trip? Peter was surprised to find the company chequebook with a note in his father's handwriting: a personal directive from the CEO to proceed immediately to the car dealership of his choice and pick out a few vehicles he considered suitable for the parish courtesy of Reinold Enterprises.

"What's all this?" Peter smiled, holding up the note as his father passed by the open door. Richard slipped in for a moment.

"I know it's a bit late son, but I hope you like your ordination present. No thanks now! Just take the afternoon off, go get what you and the fellows need. Will four be enough?"

"*Four?*"

"Yes, you heard me! Of course, if the others don't want one, I'm sure the archbishop will dish out the other three to someone more appreciative."

"Oh, they'll appreciate this I'm sure, but such generosity and no thanks whatsoever? This certainly deserves some display of gratitude," Peter noted.

"Belay that! Present or no present, you've done quite enough here stretching yourself thin to earn them, and besides, your old man isn't so great, this gives us a tax break you know. Now go on, *get*, you know how I hate dawdling, and mind, I said get four, no less will do," he concluded with a deep chortle before heading off down the hallway.

"All right Captain, I hear and obey."

Peter chuckled, his father knew that he was grateful, the skipper just hated overly-sentimental displays, even when it came to receiving his share of thanks when it was rightly due. No time to waste, before Peter could sort out the cars he had to see Mrs. Clarke and get the ball rolling about Africa. She was ready and waiting with her agenda and contact books in hand as he exited the office while the Hulk lingered nearby to hear the latest orders. After several years with the company Mrs. Clarke knew the drill; no commercial flights when it was an emergency, she had taken the liberty of notifying the captain of the corporate jet to prepare for an international run.

"Thank you, just confirm the details with Thomas and Charlotte for how long they will be staying for each inspection and book them the appropriate accommodations. They'll also need proper transport arranged … ."

"Yes, secure hotel locations and vetted drivers, I understand," Mrs. Clarke nodded.

"I'll take care of the drivers," the Hulk assured him, "all part of the service."

"Very good, looks like you and a couple of your colleagues are going abroad for awhile. Hope you like visiting exotic countries," Peter joked, turning towards the Hulk. The strapping bodyguard made a slight nod. Obviously their security company offered great service, but without the smile.

"Thank you, Mrs Clarke. You will have to arrange anything else that comes up with our globetrotting inspectors in my absence."

"You're leaving?"

"Yes, I'm taking the afternoon off, I'm under orders."

"Oh, all right. See you tomorrow then."

"See you tomorrow, good bye."

Lucinda felt relieved. He was only fulfilling an order, and it was just for the afternoon. The Captain didn't tell her everything at times. She wondered what he was being sent off for. Still, to see him leave so soon! It was as though a part of her withered inside as she watched him walk away towards the elevators. It was like that every evening, she felt weary until she would see him arrive and make his way to his former office each day, her spirits reviving just to catch a glimpse of him for those brief moments and to hear his polite 'good day' to all and sundry as he passed. She dreaded the time when he would return to his parish, and then it would mean back to the daily grind of Reinold Enterprises of which he would no longer be a part.

Don't torture yourself, get back to work. There was a lot to do at this short notice, Africa of all places to send his sister! Was she ready for that yet? Lucinda forced herself on, she went through the motions as personal aide, making calls, pulling up files and getting them ready, checking if vaccine shots were necessary, visas, photocopying more paperwork, but it was almost impossible not to think of *him*. It felt good to have him near these last few months, even if she didn't see him most of the time and spoke to him but for a minute on a professional level as she put a call through, had appointments to confirm or forms that needed signing off.

She could not help it—she was still not over him. How could she be? There would never be a place for anyone but him in her world. How she tried to forget it all, but found it impossible to wipe out all remembrance of him, especially of that one, last, desperate time; to finally break through in that moment of rapture that she had dared to snatch for them only to be thrust away as though she had poisoned him! She never thought he would go ahead with that mad plan to leave his family and the company until then, the way he bolted that day from her never to return could not be erased from her mind. When he left for Rome her world was shattered. She was bitterly hurt, angry, dazed, questioned for many weeks if he had any feelings at all. Her first thoughts were about quitting Reinold Enterprises, make a clean break just like he did, but she just couldn't bring herself to leave … *he* used to work here … *he* once used that office … she would imagine him in the various places she used to see him throughout the day doing his tasks, consulting with his brother, various executives or with her and her colleagues on the main floor when something needed to be discussed. The bitterness gradually abated as she recalled the time they shared before that heart-breaking day; their relationship was short, nothing that anyone would call flaming or compromising, but oh, growing in warmth, the fire was never given a chance to blaze, that's all, she just *knew* he cared for her. Over time she gathered a few cherished mementoes as though they were relics and kept them in a secret place; photos from business magazines in which he was interviewed during his executive days, some pens he had on his desk, an old form that she pulled from the file archives with his signature, copies of a few tapes on which he had dictated several business letters via voice recorder to be typed up, she couldn't help herself. It was an agony yet paradoxically comforting to still be in the building that would have been his, that *still* belonged to his family. In fact, why leave at all she concluded? If this was as close as she could ever be to him, then she was willing to settle for that. Continuing her work at Reinold Enterprises would be one sure way of remaining near, the only way she could hear personal news about him directly once he left the corporate spotlight. With this concession set in her mind, she pulled herself together, picked up the shattered pieces and continued to function, at least to the world at large. She could efficiently go through the motions and competently do her job, she was still close to *his* family, *his* memory still lingered among these walls. In fact, to feel that her life still had purpose as long as she remained here helped to spur her on. Remaining indispensable and fostering the confidence placed in her as a valued top member of staff felt very satisfying, consoling. She liked to think that she was keeping things going on his behalf while he was gone, *for his sake alone*, tending the vigil lamps, in memoriam.

He was everything to her. Lucinda often thought about him, especially in that early period after he left and wondered if he ever thought of her. Every now and then she asked her new boss Mr. Gerard how his brother was doing, innocent questions, the kind any one trusted enough would be permitted to ask and not be regarded as an intrusive imposition. So far, little news from Rome other than his studies were going well and was expected to be ordained by the Pope himself, however, they dared not speak about Peter in front of their father after his sudden departure. It *was* a shock after all, and not just to her, from the head office down to the airfreight centres, trucking depots and dockyards buzzed with it for months. She often wondered aloud how he could give up such a wonderful life, his caring family, their legacy, the penthouse, his beloved yacht, *everything*, an observation to which Mr. Gerard replied it was also a mystery to him, yet remarked at the same time that was Peter. Pete seemed to belong to another world, not one that ordinary mortals like them could understand he would try to joke. Despite Mr. Gerard's attempt at humour and taking care of business as though all was normal, she could see that he was missing him terribly. The whole family were. She certainly was.

Lucinda often reflected upon the diamond of truth in Mr. Gerard's remark. There was something strangely alluring about Peter, she could not put her finger on it. Of course, there were the usual descriptions one could certainly ascribe to him, refined, cultured, educated, polite, generous, so many attractive qualities she wondered if he had any vices at all. He certainly was Old School, in fact, the whole family was. She might have been tempted to become romantically inclined towards Gerard as an extraordinary consolation prize, especially as it meant becoming closer attached to their family, but he still was not Peter, no one would ever be like Peter, not even him. In any case, her new boss was going out with someone then, a beautiful but rather brash individual, she wondered what Mr. Gerard saw in her at times until she overheard one telephone conversation and realized he was trying to make a break from her for a long time, she just wasn't getting the hint. Thank God he finally was able to get through to that clingy slut and make the split, Peter would have been pleased. Gerard finally found someone more worthy of him in Miss Walsingham, he seemed head over heels about her, and they had certainly made a splash in the papers with their wildly romantic engagement. He was so preoccupied arranging dates and costly surprises it was a wonder they got any work done. While she was happy for her boss, the word 'engagement' circulating the building made her heart sink. If only they were talking about *her* and another member of the Reinold family ... .

On the days when she actually was mercifully distracted by work and wasn't brooding over what might have been, a sharpened dart would come from some unexpected place and stir her melancholic imagination. The last few years the alluring melody of 'La Isla Bonita' and its catchy rhythm playing over the stations drove her into a painful yet pleasant state of fixation and compelled her to buy the album. She was not a Madonna fan, but she could not help but listen intently to the lyrics that mirrored her illusive hopes and futile desires ... *I fell in love with San Pedro* ... . If only there was some tropical paradise for them where nature was wild and free, where love was not bound by cruel, relentless rules! *Warm wind carried on the sea, he called to me, te dijo te amo* ... .

Yes, she had fallen for that man who was striving so hard to reach the pinnacle of human perfection in accordance with all he held sacred. Sometimes she questioned why his faith demanded such a high price to serve, ministers in her congregation got married, had a family. Of course, maybe this celibacy craze would not be permanent, this could have been one of those drastic life-crises she heard about, perhaps one day he might wake up from this idealistic daydream he was living in and realize he had made a terrible mistake. There were so many priests leaving his church these days, anything was possible. When she heard he had been stationed at St. Patrick's cathedral after his return from Rome, she went to his services a few times to see what had attracted him to the priesthood and if that appeal had in any way dimmed. She prayed she might see a fish out of water, a man-of-the-world inept at the ecclesial pulpit, anything to prove to him his mistake and keep her last thread of hope from fraying, but instead was struck with a sense of awe. His quiet yet compelling aura of *gravitas* had not diminished but had somehow increased. The august nature of the ancient ceremonies she witnessed, his simple but compelling wisdom when he spoke and the deep respect elicited by the congregation only added to that sense of wonder, and also defeat. Her hopes faded—face it, he's gone—there was nothing left but to return to the vigil lamps and appease the inner ghosts haunting a future that could never be.

People often fell in love again after heartbreak. She tried to move on, after all, he did say she might find happiness eventually. It was possible to love someone else, wasn't it? That someone else became Edward Clarke, an intelligent, clever accountant at Birkin and Bernstein Associates. He seemed so much like … no, best not to think of *him*, but yet he was almost as tall, hair just a shade lighter but close, eyes not quite that startling violet blue, but captivating enough to hold her interest, had she fallen for someone again? He was kind and caring, was devoted to her, they seemed happy enough together, it must be the right thing to do … she accepted his proposal. The romantic summer honeymoon in sunny July on the tropical island of her dreams, the perfect newly-weds, life appeared normal, everything was as everyone expected it to be, but *something* was missing, there was still this vague emptiness … .

Then, a miracle! The old Captain reconciled with Peter! The offices buzzed again with this turn of events, then rocked again by the accident several months later. Mr. Gerard badly injured, possibly damaged for life, the resulting shock, the office thrown into a turmoil, *he* was coming back to fill in … . When she saw him come through the elevator doors once more as though he had never left, she froze, pinned to the spot. She knew what was wrong: Edward could never be Peter.

Almost breathless, Lucinda did not know how her voice sounded after seeing him, that enigmatic figure now swathed to the ground in black. She remembered saying the usual commiserations expected at such tragic times, and yes, she received the formal, expected 'thank you for your concern' in return, but to hear his voice once more! Then, to ask about *her*! How was she? He had heard about her marriage and hoped she was happy. How was Mr. Clarke? She answered the general replies of course, she was fine, Edward had received a promotion, they were doing well. He said he was happy for her, then politely excused himself and went to the office, there was much work to catch up on, especially as he had been away for so long.

Oh, to speak with him just those few moments! She felt terrible, but no, as much as she liked Gerard she wasn't all *that* sorry about him despite his horrific accident, not if it meant Peter was back, and no, she had lied, things were *not* doing well, she was *not* happy. Not now, not after she realized she could never love another. Everything up to then was a pretence, she had married a delusion, a fantasy, a passable look-alike, not the one she had truly set her heart on. Life with Edward paled after that, but she continued the charade, she was married now, she had made her bed, she had to lie in it, right? At least her husband almost looked like … it made the pretence easier. The similarity was one of the few reasons keeping them together, and yet, the thought of having anyone else's child now felt grotesque. It was a relief she could persuade Edward into not having children right away using their respective careers as a pretext. Unless it was Peter's flesh and blood, anything else conceived might as well be a parasite leeching at her entrails. If only he had never left!

Yet, with all that was happening lately, was the universe conspiring on her behalf to make her desires come true? To be reconciled with his family, then his brother's accident, perhaps this was the sign she was waiting for? It had to be, something drastic was the only way to bring Peter back, show him he should never have left … maybe he would finally see his mistake, see how much they needed him, discover that he had wrongfully abandoned his rightful place, eventually grow tired of the church … but even after these two months he continued to keep his respectful distance, that infuriating yet admirable code of formality was never dropped for a second! Perhaps it was a show of defence, yes, the cinders she had lit *must* still be alive within, awaiting to be fanned. No man could remain that indifferent for long. Yes, that *must* be it, he simply refused to accept what he truly wanted, had built an emotional wall to keep the embers from blazing forth. He was not cold-hearted, all those years ago there was that one fleeting moment he almost could not resist her, there *was* passion lying within! She heard in his church the priesthood was final, but surely he could not be truly happy? What a lonely existence he was carving out for himself, perhaps he was pretending as much as she was. Could it be he was just living through the motions of his decision now that he had made it? She reminded herself again how many were leaving. Despite their Dark Age rules, the church could not hold him to it if he did not want to stay. Her thoughts continued to weave a twisted, spiralling thread; if he could leave the church, why she could just as easily get a divorce, much easier in fact. Was it that simple? Things were happening all by themselves so far, all she had to do was wait, wait for the next sign, the final breakthrough would come and she must be ready to seize the moment. It would be so easy to file the papers the minute there was a glimmer of recognition from him. Peter just might come to his senses, realize he was meant for *her*. There was hope after all.

Peter was relieved to leave the office that afternoon, and not because his workday was cut short. His intuition continued to quietly tug at him, he must not stay too much longer at the Reinold offices, it was not an ideal situation for him. Of course he knew that from day one of his return, but what could he do at the present time? He would be needed now more than ever to help keep an eye on things after Thomas and Lottie left, and there was no telling how long their inspection might take. They may need only a couple of weeks or perhaps a whole month. Despite his inability to change his current situation the constant quiet urge needling him to remain detached was growing a little more insistent to the point it was becoming more uncomfortable. No doubt it was a warning: be alert, be vigilant, nothing and nobody must be allowed to jeopardize his vocation.

So far, he was managing pretty well he thought. The old career was not enticing him back, in truth, it was becoming a nuisance, plus he was keeping all relationships at a professional level on the executive floor, family and close friends excepted, naturally. The fact Lucinda was now married helped in that department. He had moved on, obviously so had she. Still, he felt something disordered was present, something was not quite right, she was not at peace within herself despite her assertions in the few casual conversations they had that she and her husband were doing fine. He could tell when someone was not being entirely honest with him, perhaps not as strikingly clear as when a soul opened up in the confessional, but his senses were tuned in enough. Marital problems possibly, he had counselled so many couples to know that despite the feelings they had for each other matrimony was still not a walk in the park even at the best of times. Aggravations were bound to surface. On occasion he could feel the resulting tension emanating from people. That had to be it. He hoped it was not anything Lucinda and Mr. Clarke could not get over, he certainly did not want to see her unhappy.

However, there could be more to these incessant promptings to be careful, he had to keep his distance. Strange, he would not get a persistent digging like this unless there was more to it. He then began to question if she had truly moved on. If not, he knew with their past he could become an occasion of sin to her. It was simply part of the human condition that when two people were in constant contact they could find themselves drawn together despite all social boundaries and taboos, in fact, it might even make the whole idea more attractive, forbidden fruit so to speak. Yes, be careful, even a casual acquaintance could be dangerous for her, the mutual attraction they once shared was fanned once before simply by being in close proximity. At least he was now confident about his own position, it was over between them, but for her sake he was unrelenting with the curt professional attitude. If *she* was wavering, she had to understand there was no chance of igniting any old flames with him. He was happily married to the church and she had to find her happiness in her husband. He had to be cold to be kind, that was the most difficult part. Despite his flaws, he was not by nature a vindictive man. If only he could actually return to his 'bride', he mused! Apart from the emotional dangers, this worldly career was becoming a weary burden. He was growing impatient to get back to his parish work full-time, so many people needed him, and so few were willing to do the exorcism apostolate for which he had been particularly chosen.

Still, there would always be things of the world to handle, it was wise to pay heed to the warning for other obvious reasons: it seemed like a lifetime ago since he had shopped for a car, and to think he was allowed the freedom to choose not one but four spanking brand new vehicles! What a temptation. His tastes hadn't changed, that was the penance he mused while waiting for the lights to change. How he would love to drive straight to something on the order of a Bentley dealer right now, but at the same time he could laugh at the prospect and calmly brushed the thought aside. Not a practical choice, costly, certainly would not do for a pastor trying to live a humble life, especially as the only mode of transportation Christ ever used besides a boat was a donkey. All he and the fellows at the rectory needed was a machine that worked and could take them from A to B in one piece and in relative comfort if not in luxury. Just the fact he could have something *new* again and not second-hand was a delicious extravagance. Naturally, it really wouldn't be his, not as a donation to the parish, but still this little outing was something to enjoy. Wouldn't it be funny though if he really took a leaf out of the Bible and turned up at the rectory with a pack of donkeys instead? Talk about jumping to extremes. However, all joking aside, time to think of practicalities. Peter decided with the recession still snapping at them, there was no time like the present to support his own country, a simple but nice-looking four-door, middle of the road type of deal would be the ticket, a good American-made car, down to earth, rock solid, something with stability. Let's take a look and see what's on the lot, just try to keep away from the Lincolns he chided himself with a grin, that pull could also be mighty.

By now he had become used to Lottie's blue bug he had forgotten how comical the situation was with him driving it. The face of the neatly suited salesman as he got out on the opposite side of the old Mini reminded him instantly.

"You see why I have to be here," he joked, nodding down to the car as he straightened out his cassock. His robed six-foot-something figure could be daunting at times, especially as non-Catholics had no idea what his garb represented until they noticed the white collar. The man looked even more surprised when after the priest sat in one of the sedans he asked for four more like it, and with no quibbling or haggling for a deal, either black or white cars, silver if they were short on those.

"You want *four* of these?"

"Yes please, and I was wondering," he added, settling into the driver's seat and surveying the interior features, "do any of these come with rocket launchers? An ejector seat might also be quite useful. If not, I would like some installed." Of course, this was funnier years ago when he and Gerry played this on the Aston Martin dealer when it came time for his brother to pick out his first car, but it was worth a try here too. The man looked bewildered, he knew never to question a customer, anything to make a sale, but … . After a few seconds, Peter dropped his serious air and cracked a smile. The salesman suddenly caught on.

"I hate to disappoint you Father, but unfortunately an agent by the name of Bond just bought our last rocket-launching model. It was shipped to Monte Carlo yesterday. So, four it is, without the rocket launchers. To be honest, I'm not sure what kind of trade in offer I can make with that," the man noted, nodding towards Aqua Velva, "but as a classic model, she should fetch something tidy."

"Don't you dare take that. It's my sister's pride and joy, she'll never forgive me if I trade it in."

"Ah, sentimental value."

"Yes, her first. Refuses to make the upgrade."

"That's understandable. You never forget your first."

"True. And what is it about the smell of a new car?"

The salesman laughed.

"I know. Want to take a test drive of this before you decide?"

"Sure, why not?"

A few cruising circles around the neighbourhood and it was time to close the deal. Too bad it didn't take as long to choose the cars as it did to muddle through the paperwork. The owner of the dealership came out personally and thanked him for his custom, assuring him it was no trouble at all holding them until they could be collected. At last, he could scrap the Old Buzzard, not to mention his days in Aqua Velva were numbered. Wait until the boys hear about this. Peter smiled to himself as he drove off.

What a day! Perhaps now he could have a rest before he started dinner, it was his turn at KP duty tonight. However, he heard rummaging coming from the kitchen area, a can opener grinding around … he went to check.

"Hey Pete! You're home early," Mark greeted as he prepped his favourite can of spaghetti sludge and chopped up some hot dogs.

"Yes, you too."

"Yeah, I got finished early today, took the bus home. I see your mom's been thinking about us again. Please thank her for me, she's simply marvellous."

"Will do. You know, you're going to wreck your dinner. She's spoiled us royally by giving us some prime top sirloin, I was planning a meat and potatoes night for us. After the bouts of charred fare presented by our guest seminarians, I think it's time we get something edible."

"Great! Don't you worry, there'll be plenty of room for your grub too," Mark assured him with a grin while stirring the hotdog chunks into the can. "You're certainly one mean cook. I wouldn't miss your night in the galley, though I can't be too unkind with our guests. Our clunker of an oven is cranky anyway, it seems you're the only one who can make it come to heel. So, any news?"

"Yes, actually. How would you like a new car? Minus the rocket launchers of course. That model was shipped to Monte Carlo yesterday."

"What?"

Mark was all ears as Peter explained. That certainly *was* good news, it was tough asking for a ride from everyone and relying on public transport all the time when it wasn't his turn to have one of the two cars assigned to their rectory. However, Mark grew concerned when Peter told him about his sister having to go to Africa, he was already spreading himself too thin as it was at the offices. Peter understood his worry, but there was nothing he could do, and since he had been given permission by the Archbishop to help for a few more months anyway, it looked like he was stuck. Mark noted he couldn't keep going like this, especially the late night shifts, and insisted that he at least let the other boys fill in on the sick calls and emergency jaunts to the hospital. He was looking tired, and obviously needed to get a few nights sleep. As much as Peter disliked slackening up on his share of the load, he decided to take him up on it. He was getting rather beat.

"Good, and that starts tonight. Let us worry about the night runs for a while. The last job you have to do is slap up that dinner, with my help of course. More hands make light work."

"Okay, in that case, *you* get to peel the potatoes."

"Sure thing, it's one of the few culinary skills I possess." Mark laughed as he recalled how his wife Mary, God rest her, was always ribbing how he was going to kill off the kids when he fixed them a snack.

"I wonder why she thought that," Peter replied looking over at the can of hot dogs and Os as he washed the lettuce and chopped tomatoes. He then glanced at Mark's progress with the spuds, judging by the way he was scalping most of the insides away with the skins, his peeling skills could be considered non-existent.

"Be sure you leave us some to boil, will you," Peter joked. He always tried to avoid waste, but Mark was so happy to help with his scalping, it was best to let him at it.

"Aw, don't go naggy on me now. I'll just do a few extra to make up the shortfall."

"I hope we have enough."

"Sure we do. If not, we can always chuck in some instant to spread it out. Just add a bit of hot water to the mess and, shazam! A whole pot of smash."

"Get thee behind me, you dodgy chef. Not in *my* dinner! No wonder Mary thought you were going to poison your progeny." He laughed, there were only so many articles of pre-prepared food items he could take in a day.

By the time O'Conner, Jenkins and the seminarians had arrived, the rectory was filled with the delightful aroma of grilled steak, which was served with bread rolls and butter, a tossed salad and mashed potatoes with raw spring onions mixed in, no instant smash was required, although Peter noted they had better add more spuds to that week's shopping list. A simple store-bought dessert of apple pie and ice cream was waiting to top their meal off. The bachelors said grace and sat around the table very appreciative of this simple but tasty fare, especially after the busy day they had hearing the first confessions of the last batch of Catholic grade-schoolers in their parish who had yet to make their First Communion that week.

"Aw, the poor mites," O'Conner chuckled, "always so petrified. You'd think we were conducting the Last Judgement."

"I know, and after all the consternation, the stuff they tell is priceless," Jenkins added as he passed the salad bowl around. "If only adults had such petty things on their consciences."

Of course, they couldn't say 'what' or 'who', but Peter knew what they meant after his yearly confession duty with the new crops of First Communicants; the horror of cheating on a spelling test, or a few stolen candy bars, staying up late with a flashlight to read when they were told to go to sleep, or the angry tantrums against a brother or sister to where some valuable item they owned was smashed against the wall or flushed down the toilet in retaliation. It was amazing how many times kids resorted to using the toilet to unleash their temper, not to mention how often the poor Fidos throughout the city were clandestinely fed broccoli and liver under the table while Mommy wasn't looking. Of course, there were the few lies told in order to evade getting in trouble with Daddy too; sins, yes, but it was so easy to forgive children.

"Still, I'm worried about what I'm hearing lately," Mark noted with incredulity as he eagerly cut into his steak. "What's wrong with parents these days? Kids are learning about stuff far sooner then they should have to. Heck, some of the things they know now at the age of eight or ten I didn't find out until I was married for goodness' sake."

"It's a shock'n scandal," O'Conner agreed. "It's no longer just a case of kids slipping into things through weakness, now we have a culture in which it's a badge of honour to have a tumble before you're married. Why, the thought of saving yourself before the nuptials is gone almost entirely. Ye're 'diseased' if you do."

"Then, if it's not that, some parents think nothing of telling their kids about the facts of life as soon as they can talk," Jenkins noted further. "And the movies, and shows! Even the ads are getting worse each day, kids are losing their innocence too fast."

"Isn't that the truth," Mark agreed, "nobody seems to think anything of it, and we're not even counting the sickos."

The table fell silent. The confessionals were privy to some very dark revelations as well. They all knew that these were just a few of the basic problems they were facing these days without going into the other extreme regarding the revolting perversions infecting the world; distorted desires surreptitiously but freely indulged in a myriad of revolting ways by people in all strata of society. Things were indeed getting worse and spiralling way out of control. Peter never said a word to anyone, but on more than one occasion he had been publicly cussed out and even spat upon by total strangers passing him on the street, shattered individuals who had obviously been victimized by only God knew who. When it did happen, Peter silently took the abuse and prayed for their healing as he went his way, miserable he could not undo the desolation caused to that soul. The other fellows did not say anything either, but he could tell they had experienced something equally depressing in the course of their ministry. How often the innocent received undeserved paybacks on account of a handful of evil individuals.

"Come, let's not get too glum," Peter quickly noted, not allowing them to dwell on what they could not change. Although it was a good sign people still came to confession, the confessionals could drive a priest into a sense of hopelessness if allowed. "There is still a lot of good out there. At least we can make sure the souls who come to us will know better by the time we've finished with them. Example is always the best teacher."

"A truer word was never spoken," O'Conner agreed. "You know what surprises me though, how many are neglecting to prepare their kids for Confirmation. How can any of the youth expect to stay strong when they aren't given the graces to help them?"

"You're right there. I'm constantly reminding my congregation about that," Jenkins agreed, "speaking of which, I hope the kids this year know their catechism," he continued with a chuckle. "I'll never forget when my time came. I got all the Commandments mixed up through nerves. I felt like an idiot at the examination and wondered if I was going to get kicked out until the next year."

"You're not the only one," Fred the seminarian piped up in his rhythmic African accent, "my mind went blank. I wondered how I could ever stand up for the faith like the early Christians when I couldn't even get my mouth to work, and I wasn't facing martyrdom like they did."

"You too? My bishop looked like a grumpy lion with a sore paw, which didn't help, not at all," Kwame, his fellow seminarian added.

"I've got a question for you lot," Mark beamed. "What did you all get? Tap or slap? Confess."

"Ah sure, a bare brush on the cheek was more like it," O'Conner recalled as he sipped his beer. "Bishop Gilligan was a gentle sort of man, wouldn't hurt a fly let alone strike a person."

"Yeah, I just got a tap," Jenkins declared, reaching for another bread roll while the seminarians shook their heads, they did not receive the old traditional slap as that had been removed from the ritual by their time.

"That's right, they don't do it any more. What about you, Pete," Mark prodded.

"Me? The funny part was I was so curious about the anointing and what the chrism could possibly look like that I completely forgot about what was coming next."

"You got it, didn't you."

"BAM!" Peter laughed, making a hard side swipe with his hand. "They could hear the smack a few pews back. I might as well have been hit with a two-by-four for all the shock it caused."

"That'll learn yhahs tah keep the faith," Jenkins humorously drawled. The table erupted with a few chortles. "And you Mark? Since you were so eager to know."

"Pow! Right in the kisser. Umm, not quite, but close enough."

"Slapped," they replied in unison.

"Yep."

"When did that get added to the ceremony," Kuwame wondered.

"I don't know, lad." O'Conner shrugged. "Beats me. It definitely wasn't part of the early days because you don't hear anythin' of the apostles slapping each other about after Pentecost."

"Medieval," Peter mused half to himself.

"Right, it is in a way," Jenkins noted.

"No, well, yes." Peter chuckled. "I mean, it was first meant to be a gentle touch on the cheek as a sign of peace. I think it was St. Cyril of Jerusalem who introduced the custom, but the interpretation of the gesture as a slap must have been added long after then," he explained. "I remember reading in Renaissance texts about the significance of striking someone during a moment of importance, a shock tactic if you will to wake them up and forever remind them of whatever they had said or seen."

"Ah, right lad, when knights took their oaths, they used to do that," O'Conner recalled.

"Oh yes, that's it, the *accolade*. The earliest form of the dubbing ceremony was a gauntlet to the face or a box on the ear so they would never forget the solemn promises made. The blow was later replaced with a sword tapped on each shoulder."

"Still, makes sense now, adding it to Confirmation," Fred mused. "If you're supposed to become a solider for Christ, no wonder you get the gauntlet like a knight."

"Yes, toughen you up for battle," Jenkins commented.

"Ow, it was supposed to be symbolic." Mark sighed, rubbing his cheek. "I can feel the sting now just thinking about that day."

"Pow, right in the kisser." Jenkins chuckled again. "You big wuss."

Over dessert, which was washed down with Pete's superb coffee, the seminarians regaled the older fathers about how different Catholicism was practised in the various African countries, the lively ethnic music and dancing at Mass depending on the traditions and tribes in each area, how people would walk for miles to attend one service. It certainly sounded colourful all right they had to agree. To think people of all ages would walk an eternity not to miss Mass, while in the Western countries they couldn't get people out of bed on a Sunday morning and drive a few blocks! At least Peter did not have that problem these days, even with his early service schedules, but he chose not to comment on that, it could arouse a spark of jealously among the fellows. However, he did have a problem with Superbowl Sunday, half the churches are empty when that comes on he sighed, shaking his head. The seminarians commiserated, plus, they couldn't see the excitement in America over their version of football since soccer and rugby seemed to move much faster for them. No disrespect intended Fred commented, but it *did* look rather odd, a bunch of padded players suited up from top to toe as if they were preparing for an invasion and they barely got the ball from one end of the field to the other. Everyone laughed and agreed it must seem funny to the rest of the world, which preferred football British fashion. Kuwame noted that on the other hand they liked one American sport, baseball, and while it could be slow waiting for the batter to get settled at the plate and hit anything, they could understand the skill of it and actually enjoyed watching a few games on TV now that the season was underway. Peter agreed, he didn't have time to watch much sports, but still loved to follow the Yankees and Mets when he could, although he didn't think the Mets were going to win the World Series this year. Dang, Jenkins shrugged, Peter was seldom wrong, including his baseball hunches. 'World' series? Kuwame tried not to laugh, it sounded funny when the only other country he knew that played professional baseball was Japan. America was one curious place!

"Ah, if it's a curious, furious, fast-paced game you're itching for," O'Conner jumped in, "you lads should see a game of Irish hurling, something like field hockey. A three-thousand year old sport played by the ancient Celtic warriors of old," he added, swinging his arms as though he was holding a hurly stick and nearly knocking over his beer. "Players sometimes got their teeth knocked out by the clash-of-the-ash, only in these modern days players are finally wearing helmets," he concluded with a nod. His father, God rest him, played in the All-Ireland for County Kerry as a matter of fact, one of his nephews still had the medals he merited.

Oh, talk about wanting excitement! Mark eagerly announced Peter had some good news for them. Peter laughed, how could he forget? He had so much on his mind these days ... how did new transportation arrangements suit them? Minus the ejector seats, unfortunately the dealership was all out of those models. There was a round of 'wows' when Peter eventually told them the story. Jenkins was pleased indeed, his car 'Rattling Ramona' was past her prime and he was dreading nickel and dime-ing her to death, she might end up as bad as the Buzzard. However, while O'Conner was very grateful to Mr. Reinold for his generosity, he wondered if they wouldn't mind donating one of the cars to the Sisters of Charity, they were badly in need of a new one. Although the Manhattan archdiocese was certainly well off, the parish budget allocated to them couldn't stretch that far this year for certain emergencies, not with all the costs spiralling at their various schools, community projects, plus all the other repair jobs that seemed to swallow everything up. Peter had no problems with that and would be happy to ensure the sisters would receive one.

"Okay, they can get the white car, I hope I get a black," Mark eagerly called out.

"I don't care about the colour as long as it's new. Well, that's up in the air now, Pete can't do without a car, especially as it's his family's company that's donating them, so the rest of us lot will have to draw straws for the last two," Jenkins noted.

"Ah, no need for that," O'Conner said with a wave of his hand, "you and Mark take them. I'm getting a bit dottering to sit behind a wheel now, especially with the traffic nowadays. It does me head in. M'licence has been expired for a few months now, and there's no way I can study for all them new regulations. I hope you don't mind this old cadger still bumming a ride of you younger fellas?"

"You aren't 'dottering', not yet, and no, we don't mind," Jenkins replied. "In fact, I know what you mean, the traffic just keeps getting worse, the city cracks my skull at the end of the day. I really feel for the people that have to do it for a living."

"Yes, it's rough at times," Peter agreed, "so are the cross country long hauls."

"That's right lad, you used to do that once upon a time," O'Conner recalled.

"Yep, in the big rigs too. On the go, practically non-stop; had to reach your state, make your delivery and pick up your next load before a certain deadline. However, I enjoyed my few turns of duty on the cargo ships. My father wanted us to know the business inside and out, so we did a bit of everything," he explained to the seminarians who looked surprised at this piece of news. Refined, sophisticated Monsignor Peter from an elite family spent time as a *trucker*? "Oh yeah, and I mean everything; forklifts, vans, parcel deliveries, and the big wheelers. Here's my licence to prove it," he added, digging in his pocket for his wallet. He took out his trucker's license, which was eagerly passed around with some amusement. It looked odd to see a younger Peter in a civilian shirt! "Of course, Dad wanted us to know how hard life actually was in the working man's world," he continued, "it was good training too, and I certainly got a lot of time to myself on the road to think. It was the closest thing you could come to being a hermit in the desert, especially when you drove through the desert. There are some very lonely highways along the routes."

"I bet it wasn't all lonely trails. Don't tell me you didn't have some sport on the CB airwaves and outrunning the smokies," Jenkins egged.

"Oh yeah! CB code! Do you remember any of it," Mark wondered.

"Sure do," Peter nodded and proceed to give a sample of the jargon used over the radios. The 'zipper' was the dotted line on the road, a 'super slab' was a multi-lane highway, while a 'driving award' was the exact opposite it's name suggested—a speeding ticket. Someone who was lost or seeking directions was known as an 'Alice in Wonderland', and flattened road kill was dubbed 'road pizza'. A 'blinkin winkin' or 'cheese wagon' indicated a school bus, while livestock trucks were called 'bull racks', and a 'chicken choker' was a poultry truck. Each company was also recognised by a code name, Reinold Shipping vehicles were called 'R-Bolts' after their logo with its iconic 'R' and lightning bolt. A 'buster brown' was a UPS truck, which also had other unfortunate slang names such as 'United Package Smashers' and 'United Pot Smokers' since they were their competitors after all. In fact, anything that was related to the road or hauling industry had a name, it was a wonder they could remember it all. One jot of the jingo was used to distinguish the various officers of the law, their vehicles and what they might be doing when encountered on the road. A 'Tijuana Taxi' was a marked police car, a 'Blue Light Special' meant a cop had stopped someone and had their blue lights still flashing, an 'Evil Knievel' was a cop on a motorbike, the 'Boy Scouts' were the State Police, while the cops in Ohio had their own unique code, 'Flying the Salesman', and so did the New York State Police which were dubbed the 'Sunoco Special'. Places and destinations also had their own humorous jargon, New Jersey was called 'Armpit', 'Bean Town' was Boston, 'Chocolate Town' was Hershey, Pennsylvania. Chicago and Cleveland Ohio had the misfortune to be labelled 'Mistake on the Lake', Phoenix Arizona was called the 'Sticker Patch' on account of the local cacti specimens, while Las Vegas was known as 'Lost Wages'.

"Why, it's almost as unintelligible as old London Cockney!" O'Conner laughed.

"I know, it's a miracle I remembered how to speak English after the summers," Peter concluded.

"Hey, speaking of CB radios, I'd give anything to know your radio handle," Mark remarked with a grin. The others began to prod too.

"Come on, let's have it! Your code name must have been something biblical-sounding, knowing you," O'Conner badgered. "Let me guess, 'Avenging Angel'." Peter shook his head. "Demon Slayer." Peter shook his head again. " 'God's Hammer.' No? 'Heaven's Mover', 'Doomsday Deliverer' … ."

Again, wrong guesses. Peter started to laugh.

"All 'no', but good ones. Now I'm sorry I didn't think of those back then."

"Am I close?"

"Sort of. It is a bit biblical, but not so much on the order of 'heavy metal'. Think 'classical'."

"Hmm, you *would* pick something with a bit of class, but I'm afraid you've got me," Mark admitted. "Come on, you've got to tell us."

"I'll never live this down." Peter sighed.

"Sure right you won't!" O'Conner laughed again, giving Peter a hearty slap on the back. "Let's have it lad, we're all ears."

He quickly covered his forehead, elbow on the table as though he were hearing confessions.

"Oh, all right," he groaned. "If you *must* know. It was 'Ben Hur'."

They all looked around at each other until it sunk in.

"The chariots! Ha ha! Ben Hur! I like that," Mark chortled.

"Yeah, the chariot race," Peter confirmed. "I had a bad habit of stopping a little too long on my break time when I reached the high desserts, you've never seen such clear skies on a summer night as in the Sierras. Of course, I did everything I could to make up the time, had to outrun everything and everyone with a vengeance like they were Messala with the razor-bladed chariot."

"So, you *did* outrun the smokey bears." Mark gasped. "Shame on you. I hope you confessed that. Did you ever get a 'driving award'?"

"Nope."

"They couldn't catch him, he was on a mission from God." Jenkins laughed.

"Talking about the code names, I'm curious to know what Gerry's was," O'Conner queried.

"Something just as classical: Sparticus."

The table erupted with laughter.

"Did you and your fellow charioteer ever do a cannonball run," Jenkins had to ask.

"Sort of, Gerry and I each got a delivery for Shaky Town, er, LA one summer and we tried to beat each other cross country in the big rigs. No star gazing then."

"Oh, I can just imagine it now! Ben Hur and Sparticus racing across the nation like a couple of hellions," O'Conner commented with amusement.

"I know, but still, I can't see *you* doing that Pete." Mark laughed, a little incredulous.

"I admit, I was heavy footed on the pedal a number of occasions. The things you do when you're younger! It didn't help that Gerry double-dared me, in addition he offered to switch our last of the summer jobs if I won."

"Oh? How did that wager work?" Mark wanted to know.

"I had the livestock warehouses to muck out in the Depot Yard Two before heading back out on the road, and Gerry got the home-city deliveries for the rest of the summer, which was certainly a better job than I was facing. So, the bet was on. You should have seen us two tear out of the yard that time! The Big Bosses' two sons ripping up the asphalt like the Dukes of Hazzard? Of course, the news travelled fast on what we were up to, how could it not? The guys in all the yards took bets on who they thought would make it, and our other R-Bolts already on the road kept up a live-wire commentary to our main stops on the radios. It got so competitive that even our competitors in the moving business were keeping an ear on it."

"So, who won," Fred wondered.

"We both tied, got to the front entrance of the LA yard at the same time, although we beat all our company drivers' time records that summer. Only two guys in the New York yard suspected we'd do that and made off with the pot. However, all the guys got a ratting out from Sammy our depot manager that if the Big Boss's boys can do times like that, they had better pick up the slack! We felt a bit guilty then and told him not to be too hard on the guys, admitting we had raced each other on that run, but Sammy said he knew that: it was one great opportunity he could use to keep the rest of the drivers up to speed, what a slave driver he is. However, he does keep everything going, and he's not all whip and lash. The guys like him a lot, we all do."

"Wait, if there was a tie, what did you do about the animal warehouses," Jenkins wondered.

"Gerry did the decent thing and helped me clean out the place. He also split the home-city delivery stint and the last of my long hauls. It was a tie after all."

"That was good of him. Hmm, I hate to cut the fun short, but speaking of races, we'd better hurry up or we'll miss the news," Mark noted, eyeing the wall clock.

On that note, they quickly began gathering the dishes, with everyone helping it didn't take long to get the kitchen cleaned up and settle in front the TV for the evening. Peter stayed long enough to hear the segments he was interested in then wished them all a good night, he had some work to catch up on and then he was going to bed.

"Sleep well, Judah Ben Hur," Mark replied, which was followed by a few laughs.

Peter sighed, he knew he would forever regret letting his CB handle out of the bag.

Closing his bedroom door behind him, he ignored the tempting sight of his bed and went immediately to his desk. There was a pile of papers and cards waiting for him, mostly letters from people he had met in the course of his ministry sending their latest news, or requests from his spiritual children who needed advice on personal matters of the soul. The number on his contact list had grown quite a bit, it was getting a little overwhelming. The day was fast approaching when he might have to give over and start typing his personal letters to keep up. It looked like he may even have to resort to this new fad in e-mailing. After the nuns at his old school had drilled into the minds of the pupils the value of the personal touch in writing and the importance of neat penmanship, it was going to be difficult to do, but there it was. Time waits for no man, or a penned letter these days.

Even so, his correspondence would have to wait just a little longer, Peter had one pressing matter to review that could not be delayed: piecing together the events leading to the possession of Melissa Yardley. The thought of the report he was requested to write brought back all the horrific experiences of yesterday, the demonic attack upon his confessional, the tragic tale of Melissa and her mother, the threat directed at from the ouija board, the harrowing visit at Trenton Psychiatric, this was indeed a very rare and serious case. Perhaps the best thing to do was to start straight off with the tapes Melissa had recorded of her belligerent stepfather and tackle that end of the matter first.

It was a draining hour or so as he listened to the domestic abuse Melissa and her mother Rebecca had received, everything from cutting remarks to threats of molestation, however, the tapes proved to be valuable as the Fletchers were correct, there were ominous curses levied against Rebecca and Melissa that were contextually out of character for a human tirade. Several times, he uttered deliberate threats he *planned* to send them to Hell or assure them they would die horrible deaths to where they would end up rotting like 'that traitor Judas'. From his past research Peter noted devils sometimes used that way of speaking during exorcisms and noted these remarks down to include in his report while attempting to ignore the revulsion that once more surfaced when listening to the depravity Melissa's stepfather spewed forth.

When he could think clearly after hearing that nauseating abuse, Peter examined the young girl's diaries next. Filled mostly with glossy magazine pictures, photos, stickers and odds bits of newspaper cuttings, the journals were used more for scrap-booking her favourite photos and interests as written entries were few and far between, but she did manage to jot down a few events in her life that helped him figure out how she ended up in the sad state she was now in. Melissa had included a paragraph explaining how her fascination with the occult had started when she revealed to her boyfriend Ashly some bleak events from her life, namely, that in her old home with her stepfather there were times she wished she could escape from all that she had experienced and even rubbed the bedknob as a childish consolation when he was in one of his usual foul moods, wishing to be anywhere but there despite the knowledge the movie was fantasy and that her wishful thinking would never work. Ashly then remarked to her that the magic bedknob may be an invention, but perhaps the other spells might be true. He noticed that when the characters in *Bedknobs and Broomsticks* went in search of the magical talisman to complete a spell, it looked very similar to the magical signs that people used in the real world. He noted fiction was often based on truth after all. From that moment on, she and Ashly decided to make a project of his observation and discover for themselves the elements of truth behind the fantasy.

Peter had already guessed as much, his suspicions regarding that movie were correct in more ways than one, observations that he had not voiced to the Fletchers who were already distressed enough with the information he had given them. The demon's traps lay hidden in the most innocent places: the Star of Astoroth in the movie was none other than the pentagram, while the name of 'Astoroth' was taken from Astaroth, or Astarte, pagan god of the Philistines often equated with a demon in earlier times by theologians and poets. However, the most dangerous trap was not only the fanciful storyline of the movie concerning white magic but the power of suggestion contained therein, that one could become a witch and use spells for good purposes. That was the problem with youth Peter reflected, the young and impressionable often crave for the fantastic to become real and endeavour to put their desires into practise. Unbridled curiosity leads many a soul on a broad path to Hell. The sad part was the scriptwriters in all likelihood had no idea what damage they would cause when creating their movie Peter mused, but if they *did* ... God help us! It was difficult to warn people to be on their guard when the points of entry for the enemy were astutely camouflaged by something so innocent and entertaining as a children's movie.

He continued to read the dairy. Melissa and Ashly's fascination with the occult grew when they began playing silly spell-games they learned from others at school, such as repeating a certain chant into the mirror with the lights out to see what appeared in the reflective glass. To their surprise, it worked. Strange shapes began to appear, most often it was an indistinct blurred face. After the initial fright had worn off they realised they were actually tapping into some mysterious energy and tried modifying the chant to see what happened. If they chanted for money, they would find lost dollar bills on the street. If they chanted against someone who bullied them at school, that tormentor was paid back with an injury at football practise or an unfortunate embarrassing incident that made them the laughing stock of the student population. When Melissa and Ashly discovered they were practising real magic, they then began to progress to the books, the cards, the ouija board. After Ashly had to leave her uncle and aunt's home, he managed to sneak these ominous items to her at school as Peter had suspected. After that, it was a downward spiral he noted, as was usually the case. The two teenagers became wrapped up in their uncanny skills, unaware they were letting the Enemy who truly wielded the power gain a foothold over them spell by spell. As Peter explained to the Fletchers, once evil is invited in, tremendous effort is required to show it to the door and kick its cloven hoof off the threshold. He was well aware that if Melissa's stepfather had cursed her, her willingness to dabble with the occult knowing it was wrong had not only extended the invitation, it left her wide open to the demons' influence. Her curiosity now piqued by the occult, the evil minions knew they could easily snare it elsewhere. Temptations would no longer be viewed as temptations but intriguing suggestions that should be immediately satisfied, everything suggested to her mind would be tried and tested with no willpower or desire to resist. At that point the concept of 'wrong' would be excused away, sin would be added to sin willingly and with full knowledge allowing more demons to grab hold as her will became one with theirs. Arriving at the last page of the final journal Peter discovered the reason for his and the Fletcher's reluctance to break open the books: Melissa admitted in the last entry she had put a spell on her journals, hexing anyone who would dare break them open. No wonder he was inspired to look for the keys, technically that would not be *breaking* the journals and unleashing God only knows what. Someone from above was protecting them. Nevertheless, he would have to burn the innocent-looking tomes as a precaution after he photocopied the significant passages. The books had been hexed, not their contents.

Time to make his report. Despite his knowledge and personal experience, Peter could not write everything he sensed, he had to report solely on the physical data he had gathered. Nevertheless, he was confident that their Eminences would understand the seriousness of the situation, curses and practising the occult were actions universally recognized by the Church as the widest and surest paths to possession, therefore a lengthy explanation for the suspected cause of her predicament was not required. However, he was blessed to have the videotape of his visit to Trenton, there could be no mistaking a possession with that solid piece of evidence. Peter watched the video again, continuing to jot down notes as the scene played out once more. If only he could have wrangled a name out of them, he might know more about whom they were dealing with and could suggest to the exorcist who would be appointed on the best counter-attack he should employ. For some odd reason, the demons seemed to lose ground when forced to give up their names or give a clue to their identity. The alarming part was the use of the plural form 'we' and 'many' by the possessing force when pressed to identify itself: it appeared there was more than one demon in this case. Still, even if he did not have the full authority to force a name from them at the time, the devilish conversation was enough.

Mercifully, it did not take him as long as he thought it would to write his report. Reading through everything one last time, he finished up the conclusion. However, he could not seal anything up just yet, he still had to photocopy the important passages from the journal and include them. He could finish that first thing at the parish office tomorrow. For now, Peter placed the report with the videotape and all pertinent materials in a large envelope and left it unsealed, blessing it with holy water to prevent any unseen tampering before he could deliver it personally to the archbishop.

That would have to be done tomorrow too, the sooner he could get this matter attended to the better. Thank God that was done, he was glad to get undressed and hit the bed. It had been awhile since he had used trucker lingo until that night, but could definitely say at that moment he was 'checking his eyelids for pinholes', that is, declare he was officially exhausted beyond belief.

Turning out the light, he could hear the faint muffle of voices down below, obviously the guys were enjoying a television program after the news. Peter was drifting off to sleep by the quiet murmur when he was jolted awake by the alarm clock. What? He had it preset for several hours ahead, and he certainly didn't reset it to ring ten minutes later. Or did he upset the controls? No, he was sure he did not hit the wrong button, but then again, digital clocks were a bit fiddly. No big deal, just reset the thing and go back to sleep, another early morning would soon be upon him.

The shock of that abrupt awakening had just subsided allowing him to grow drowsy and fall asleep once more when the clock bleeping jarred through his slumber. Great! Not again! Maybe he was hitting something wrong and not aware of it, he was groggy to the point of confusion. He checked out the numbers three times before settling back down, only to be pestered again. All right, this time he was positive he didn't mess up the timing. The clock was breaking down, that had to be it. Well, it was getting a bit old, and he *had* knocked it off the side table more than once when fumbling around for it in the dark. However, by now his patience was starting to fray. Irritably he took the wire, yanked the plug from the wall, and plonked the clock down on the floor. Still, he needed a timepiece to wake him up the next day. The good news was he had an old thing that wound up. The bad news was he had to get out of bed and hunt for it in his desk. The spring and cog machine also had an annoying *tictaktictaktictak* sound, which was why he got the digital clock in the first place, but it would have to do. Fantastic. He was going to be wide awake and unable to settle down fast by the time he found the old wind-up. Don't loose your cool, just retrieve the thing and get to sleep. At last, the old clock was set up, off with the lamp, mould the pillow into a comfy shape, ignore the ticking … he began to nod off as he thought of his old days on the road and his one trip on the cargo vessel, he certainly had seen some beautiful views on those trips. For a brief moment he thought he was back in one of the trucks just going through a majestic mountain pass when he was bolted awake by a clock going off—and it was not the old wind-up. The electronic clock was bleeping angrily away on the floor where he had left it unplugged.

Now completely alert, he quickly turned on the light and studied the bleeping cube that now seemed to have a life of its own. The digital screen flashed a strange array of numbers before it finally settled down to the expected black screen, the bleeping stopping as well. Peter's patience was completely restored, he knew who or what was up to their old tricks. Devils could be so trivial, but of course, the Almighty had their powers curtailed and so they could only vent their fury in stupid ways most of the time. Right now all they could do was try to deprive him of his sleep and keep him unnerved. At least he wasn't intimidated, their silly little pranks didn't phase him, but his 'gremlins' might succeed in keeping him up if he didn't try to dispel them. He made the sign of the cross over the clock. No reaction happened. He was about to turn off the light when the other clock began to ring, and like the other, not at the time he had set it. He blessed that clock too, and it stopped its annoying ring. This was insane! Still, he was not shaken, he decided to place a blessed exorcism medal on each clock and hope he would wake up on time the next day. Perhaps he should say a rosary now that he was up, it might also stop whatever was happening. Taking his beads and making the sign of the cross, he was about to start when the phone on his desk began to ring. He had promised not to take any night calls and let it ring. He could hear Mark answer the phone downstairs in the hall, but then heard him hang it up somewhat disgruntled, muttering about a silent caller. Crank call obviously. Peter began his devotion again, and was disturbed by the phone ringing again. Mark answered the summons a second time to find he was the victim of a repetitive prank caller. Or was he? Curious, Peter waited for the prankster to plague them again and at last answered on the next bout of ringing:

"Hello? St. John's rectory … who is this?"

All he could hear was crackling on the line. Peter was about to hang up until a malevolent genderless voice sounded over the line:

"*Do you like what I did to your clocks? Swear not to send your report, and we'll leave you alone.*"

Peter quickly put down the receiver. He knew better than to enter any parley with a demon, even to make a rebuke. Devils craved worship, and if they couldn't get it, they would do with receiving attention through human reactions to their antics, including irritated negative attention. Calmly ignoring them was often the best tactic. The only thing was, how long would they keep this up? The phone rang again, but if they wanted *him*, he had better not answer. This time he heard Jenkins answer downstairs, and this time he angrily put down the phone before returning to the TV room. Peter would take the phone off the hook were it not for the fact a real person might be trying to get through and needed the Last Rites. Should he go down and tell the others what was happening? Then again, would they believe him? Despite the fact that belief in the unseen as well as the seen was part and parcel of the Faith, it was amazing that there was a huge and almost inexplicable 'disconnect' between the faithful and the supernatural realms when it came to the existence of the Unseen. It all seemed like some distant, airy-fairy concept that God, the angels and the demons were *beings* and not intangible 'forces' nor symbols representing the abstract idea of good versus evil. These beings were not as distant as people imagined. Of course, the problem was the whole nature of the Unseen, humans relied too much on their physical eyes, and since the overwhelming majority of people never saw or felt the things he did nearly every day, they could not fully grasp the existence of the supernatural. If he told Mark and Jenkins they had just answered a call from hellish denizen, they would not completely credit it despite their belief in them. Still, he couldn't let this go on for the whole night, so there was nothing for it. Ignoring the pesky gremlins was not going to work this time. Pulling on his robe and getting his slippers, he made his way to the TV room.

"Aw, I'm sorry Pete, we don't mean to keep you up, but we've got a crank caller. I'd take the phone off the hook but you know how it is," Mark replied apologetically.

"I know, but this crank is after me, he won't say anything until I answer."

"Really? Who would be bugging you? Do you know who it is," Jenkins wondered.

"Yes, I've got a devil on my back tonight."

"No kidding! I hate prank calls," Mark replied.

"I mean *for real*. I'll try and put a stop to it if I can, but somehow, I think it's best that I don't answer for the rest of the night, so just be prepared if it rings again."

The seminarians just looked at each other, too polite to interrupt the proceedings, while Mark and Jenkins were about to laugh until they noticed that unflinching look from Peter that usually told everyone he was on 'higher business'. They composed themselves knowing this may be serious, yet the urge to find his comment droll didn't fully dissipate. The more they tried to remain serious, the harder it was not to laugh. Well, Peter's explanation did seem a bit out of the 'Twilight Zone' for them. O'Conner was the only one who sat up and blanched a bit, and asked what he meant by 'be prepared'.

"If the prankster calls back, just say a prayer over the line, that might do the trick. The Our Father, the Hail Mary, or St. Michael's prayer should do it. Choose whatever you are inspired to say. That's it then, I'm off to bed. Good night."

Peter was halfway up the stairs when the phone rang once more, he could just make out a quiet commotion in the TV room … .

"You go answer it."

"No way … you go answer it."

"Uh uh, I did last time."

"What if it's not … ?"

"Would *somebody* just go? I'm missing the film!"

"Oh, all right … ."

By this time Peter was in his room saying the deliverance prayer when Mark came out to answer.

"Hel … hello?"

No voice on the other end. Mark did as he was instructed and began a Hail Mary … he heard an almost human-like muttering say something unintelligible before 'it' abruptly stopped the call. He replaced the receiver and went back to the community room a little perplexed.

"Well," Jenkins enquired.

"Odd. I did as Pete said, but I got a lot of gibberish at the other end."

"Sounds just like a human prankster to me," Jenkins replied.

"Maybe, maybe not, but whoever it was, I wouldn't want to be caught alone with them in a dark street at night. Their voice gave me the jitters."

The rectory eventually got some peace as 'whoever' was trying to reach out and haunt someone got the hint their tricks would not get them anywhere this night. Peter tried to finish his rosary next, but drowsiness overcame him, a decade of beads was as far as his devotions went, forty winks quickly replaced the remaining beads.

Mr. R was correct, Sophia was not happy to hear about her daughter's emergency jaunt to the Dark Continent, but was stoically resigned to the fact Lottie would end up facing these situations anyway now that she had joined the family business, just as Lottie had surmised. Katherine could not believe the news either when Lottie called her, she could only imagine what Lottie would be facing after her own experiences with Gerry and his 'globe trots'. Poor Lottie! Like everyone else, Katherine wondered if she was ready, knowing she would certainly feel out of her depth if placed in that situation. However it was a relief Thomas was going with her and would be handling the bulk of the corporate crud for now. Katherine did not think she would see Lottie before her flight Tuesday night but she was mistaken, Lottie was up early that morning and waiting for her outside the gallery in Gerry's limo.

"What are you doing here? You should be getting ready for your trip!"

"Oh, that's pretty much done, it didn't take me long to pack. I'm not bringing an awful lot, and Mrs. Clarke is an excellent assistant, it's pretty much all set up. Good thing my passport is current. There are only a few things I need to do and get, plus I just want to run around and say goodbye while I still have some time. I knew it was your turn to open up the gallery today, so I was wondering, can I have a quick coffee with you?"

"Gee, you don't need to ask," Katherine affirmed as she unlocked the door. "Hi Samuel, how are you?"

"I'm fine ma'am," the chauffeur greeted. "It's good to see you again."

"It's good to see you too. It's been awhile." Katherine hadn't been out on a date with Gerry in the limo since his accident. "Would you like a coffee? I'm sure you would. How about a muffin?"

Samuel thanked her, but politely declined and said he would wait for Miss Charlotte. Lottie said she couldn't stay long and assured him she would be out soon. Nevertheless, Katherine promised she would still send a cup of coffee out to him. The Hulk had to go wherever Lottie went, so he came in for his portion of java but his charge promptly ordered him to bring the chauffeur his cup.

"Good, that gives me a minute alone with you, Kathy," Lottie announced as they sat at the Gallery Gang's favourite table in the restaurant. "I've got to say it, I'm so stressed out! I know Tom will be handling everything for the most part, but I've got to represent the family company in appearance at least, and I know what they're thinking; 'the family flake that can't settle on anything and get her life on track is now taking up a leading position, she's going to fall flat on her face.'."

"It can't be as bad as all that. Pete trusts you, that much I know," Katherine tried to reassure her. "So far you haven't fallen on your face. They're just worried that this type of assignment is too soon."

"I know, and on top of it, I came out with this thumping speech and *forced* Dad to let me go because I do have to learn, but now that this is upon me, I'm a mess! You always seem to pull me together in an emergency. Do you have any words of wisdom you can impart?"

For a moment, Katherine was at a loss, people always seemed to trust her with deep revelations or came to her for sage advice when she felt inadequate to the task. She certainly didn't know much about the business of shipping except she always liked to get her own orders delivered in one piece and in a timely fashion.

"I don't know what to say, Pete always seems to have those words of wisdom ready and waiting at a moment's notice."

"True, but you also have this go-get-'em approach to everything and I could use a little of that now."

"Gosh, if that's what you need, then just treat the whole thing like an adventure, like the explorers of old that braved the jungles," Katherine replied. "That should do the trick. In your case, you have a mystery that needs to be solved; shipments are not getting to where they need to be, you have to figure out why, maybe do a little yelling, chop some heads off in the process, and if needs be, find yourself some new chiefs who can handle the job better over there. It means being tough, but if you can back down Mr. R like you told me, I think you could face a tribe of Zulus on the warpath single-handed and come out on top. Besides, if it all flops over there and they do fire you at Reinold Enterprises, I'm sure we can find a job for you here at the gallery with the rest of us creative flakes."

Lottie laughed.

"Oh *you're* not a flake, but you're right, Kathy, thanks for the pep-rally. I knew this already, but maybe all I needed was some cheering up to augment my courage."

"Good! Glad I could help. Just remember, courage is not the absence of fear, it's the ability to forge ahead in spite of it."

"And you say Pete is the only one with words of wisdom."

"Well, I'm on a roll now, and besides, you put me on the spot! I had to say *something* good."

"But it's true. Thanks Kathy. You know, I'm glad Tom is going, I think … oh baloney! The 'Thing' is coming back," Lottie interrupted herself as she heard the back door to the parking lot open. "I can't have a private conversation these days! On top of it, I have to take a few more of those lugs with me too."

Katherine tried to look sympathetic for Lottie's sake, but was glad to hear that she would have a small army looking out for her.

"Just come home safe, okay?"

"I promise. Keep an eye on the family for me, will you?"

"Again, no need to ask. You know I will."

Lottie finished off the last few sips of her coffee in a hurry, she was meeting her parents and Pete for lunch, but then had to pick up a few cans of bug repellent and had to fit in a vaccine or booster shot of some kind, something she was not looking forward to she muttered before giving her a quick goodbye hug. Katherine could feel sympathetic then, she detested syringes and medical jabs. The Reinolds never had a dull life she mused as she watched Lottie leave with the Hulk.

Katherine was not left on her own for long, Andre had started opening the restaurant for gourmet breakfasts two weeks ago and had quickly acquired a loyal customer base for his special omelettes and crepes, including 'breakfasts on the go', the popular favourite was his special coffee with a selection of pastries packaged for commuter travel. Katherine switched on the lights on the other floors and settled at the front desk of the gallery for the day, enjoying the last of her chocolate muffin. She had run out of the house so fast that morning she had no time to fix her usual fare of toaster tarts. Life seemed to be all of a rush these days, at least when it came to getting to where she needed to be. The gallery certainly was an early bird business, especially now with Andre opening in the mornings, but then drifted calmly for the rest of the day in time with the slow pace of the visitors browsing around. Sometimes it became a bit lively when a school booked a field trip, or when Mrs. Hunt decided to make a disorderly visit and have all the pictures unhitched, but for the most part, it was the restaurant that stayed busy, at least where the turn-around of people was concerned. Not that she lacked customers, business was doing pretty good, but gallery visitors pretty much liked to be left alone to take a quiet look at things and needed little assistance unless the staff were politely asked for it. Ho hum, another quiet spell. She wished she could be with Gerry, but she now had a business to run. Business. Art as business. That always seemed such a contradiction. On top of it, there was nothing major to tackle at that time, all she had to do was wait until Suzy arrived with the morning papers to scan for the various art reviews. She would rather be painting, she was way behind on that too and Gerry insisted she catch up on it, but it was her turn to mind the fort that morning. The Professor had finally taken Esther on that Mediterranean cruise he had been promising for years, Kevin was out enjoying his day off, while Dennis and Suzy had their turn that morning in the studio. She would just have to wait until the afternoon. True, she could easily have one of the security guards man the desk for awhile, but since the gallery was her baby after all, it was good to stay active in all aspects of its management and that included the babysitting.

Might as well use the lull to her advantage, she needed some time to think out the pictorial subject matter in the next batch of her 'Socratic Series', she could still be creative. Where should she paint Socrates and Plato next? It would be somewhat funny if she put them seated across from each other on the sofas in the Oval Office continuing their academic dispute on freedom as the President witnessed the proceedings from behind his desk. Hmm, that might not be a bad idea. Hang on, *which* president could she put? Wow, what about Kennedy? Maybe even Lincoln? He would certainly fit the bill. Was the Oval Office constructed after his time? Who cares? The creative arts were not bound by historical accuracy when it came to allegorical depictions. She would have to see what section of her philosophical text she was currently at, but she had a hunch it would work splendidly ... oh nuts! Maybe not. She had already placed her third picture over the section of text attempting to define the horrors of slavery, so Lincoln was out. What came up next? Surely she could stick the Oval Office somewhere? She grabbed her notebook where she had recorded her dialogue on the nature of freedom and traced her finger along, looking for the next paragraphs that needed a scene. Maybe she would have to come up with a few more pictures until she could fit this presidential tableau in the perfect spot. Never mind. She also had to finish the last touches of Peter's painting, which was nearing the completion point. Although she was happy with the overall result, it looked too much like a copy of the images he had given her. She would like to add a few artistic nuances of her own if possible, but how to do that without altering the original too much? Maybe add some extra ornamentation?

Her creative roll was put on hold as she received an early morning visit from Gramps and Jasper.

"Hey kiddo, I knew I'd find you here." He smiled as he settled into the swivelling leather chair beside her while Jasper placed his furry nose in her lap and eagerly waited for a rub behind the ear. "We've been missing you at home lately with all your early mornings and late nights. Thought I'd drop by and celebrate with you."

"Hey Gramps! Celebrate? What are we celebrating?"

"My diet! It worked!"

"I wonder what diet *that* could be," she teased.

"Now, don't give your poor old Gramps any lip. You missed the good news with all this burning of the midnight oil. Yesterday Dr. Hendricks proclaimed I've lost just about three and a quarter pounds!"

"What an astounding success," she noted, her voice dripping with amused sarcasm. "You do know it's been three years since your last check-up?"

"Yeah, so?"

"You've only lost a pound a year, give a bit. I'd say we're going to have a very small party. Are you sure you put both your feet on the scales?"

"Very funny for someone who says you can't fool the scales, and yes I did. Oh all right, laugh all you want, but I did what he said, I *have* lost some weight."

"I think he expected a bit more."

"Mere trifles! A technicality of numbers. He said 'lose some weight' and so he got what he asked. It seems your idea to walk Jasper around has done the trick, and so I'm marking the occasion with a little breakfast visit with you. How're the pastries these days?"

"Good as always, and might I add? You're hopeless!"

"Hey, like I keep saying, you can't celebrate on a diet."

"What a way to celebrate, putting on the few pounds you got off."

"My weight loss, my celebration. Care to join me?"

What could she do but have one of the waiters bring their orders out to the reception desk? She had a simple coffee refill while he tucked into a deluxe shrimp and Camembert cheese omelette followed by a chocolate crepe plate with a hint of custard, throwing a few scraps Jasper's way via the doggie bowl every now and then.

Since she had come home very late yesterday after work, she hadn't told her family about the latest uproar in Reinold Enterprises and that Lottie was being shipped off to Africa with Thomas. Gramps was all ears with this piece of news and wondered how the Reinolds were managing considering their present circumstances. Katherine had to say Gerry was a bit quiet when she visited him last night, adding he seldom opened up when he worried about a situation dropped in front of him and felt driven to find a solution on his own. He had a bad habit of bottling things up instead of getting them off his chest and seeking advice when he was in one of those button-up moods. She was pretty sure he was upset that he couldn't go and handle that problem himself instead of sending Lottie into the unknown. Gramps agreed it must be tough for him and wondered when the confounded doctors would finally get his future grandson-in-law out of that steel trap. Katherine had no idea, they probably did not want to make their patient any more impatient than he already was by giving him a tentative removal date that might be too far off to give him constructive encouragement. Of course, his injuries were severe, all she knew was that the medical team were waiting to make sure his pelvis had knit enough to bear his weight again, and that sounded like it would take time. In fact, everyone was still walking on eggshells and did not want to say much in case they gave him unwarranted hope that all would be well when they were still unsure about a full recovery. At least he had his painting to help keep him distracted. Later that night she would see how he was faring when she went for her usual visit. Hopefully he would be out of his 'button-up' mood.

It didn't take long for Gramps to finish off his crepe plate, which seemed to be 'lacking something' according to him, and he couldn't help wondering how Andre was pulling such a crowd with his breakfast menu, still unaware of the non-butter items Andre substituted in his dishes for his benefit alone. She made a mental note she had better thank Andre again since he may be the one responsible for helping the hopeless gourmand lose those three pounds. Downing his coffee, Gramps said goodbye and announced he and Jasper were off to bug her father and uncle next, not to mention see how the youngest executive of the family was doing. No doubt it was still a novelty for him to see Steves confidently trooping around the offices, dishing out memos and orders before heading off to the labs when it seemed like yesterday her little brother was being pushed around in his baby buggy. She could understand the feeling, Steve's recent promotion in the family business had not fully sunk in her head either. Where did the years fly? It seemed like they were all in grade school only a few seconds ago.

Katherine was about to return to her creative musing on her various paintings when Olivia rushed in to open the gift shop, followed by Suzy and Dennis.

"Whoops! Almost late," Olivia gasped as she hurried past, opened her doors and flipped the lights on in her section of the floor. However, once her business was officially opened, she took her usual place beside Katherine at the front desk and hunted for her bottle of nail polish in her purse. Olivia could easily see the interior of the shop through the glass partition in addition to keeping on eye on the security monitors at the reception desk and could tell if a customer needed her or not. Right now, it was 'not' at that early hour, so she eagerly launched into their customary Gallery Gang chit-chat session while Suzy handed Katherine the morning papers to search for any art reviews pertaining to the gallery and its featured artists.

"Any news," Suzy wondered before she and Dennis went to the studio for the rest of that morning.

"Gramps lost a few pounds and is doing his utmost to put them back on." Katherine laughed. "You guys just missed him. Lottie was here too, she wanted to say 'goodbye' before she headed off to Africa."

"Africa! Is she going on a safari?" Olivia was dying to know. "Now that would be exciting. Frank was always promising to take me on one of those exotic adventure tours, but as usual, he gave me the typical balloon ride, a load of hot air." Olivia had come through a bitter divorce and was not about to let up on her ex for a minute, spraying him and his memory with verbal vitriol whenever possible.

"Oh no, you weren't here yesterday when she called. Lottie has an emergency to handle with the company," Katherine explained, then filled her in on the details.

"Even for business, that's still going to be one heck of a trip," Suzy had to admit while Olivia nodded as she carefully applied a coat of bright red varnish to each fingernail. "Speaking of which, I wonder how the Professor and Esther are enjoying their getaway. I'd love to go on a cruise just to try the food you hear everyone raving about," Suzy concluded.

"I don't know, this is the first real day for them since they had to fly to get to their ship, but I bet the Professor is going to spend most of his time sketching the scenery rather than noticing Esther." Dennis laughed.

Dennis had a point. While Esther was very patient and understanding about her husband's tunnel vision when it came to his art, on this occasion she just might hide his paintbrushes as she had been threatening to do, or go a step further, declare mutiny and throw them overboard altogether.

"Hmm, maybe they might send us a postcard and let us know how they're doing, let's pray there's no war in the cruise cabin," Katherine thought aloud as she glanced through the art columns before stopping for a moment to hoosh off the two artists. "Hey, what are you two doing? Don't waste your morning Muse, studio time's a'burn'n. I need a few more canvases to fill in the south partition you know. Give me some masterpieces. Don't worry, if I find any reviews, I'll give you a shout."

"Okay, we hear and obey." Suzy laughed as she and Dennis made their way to the elevator.

Olivia kept her company and gave Katherine the latest news on her children as she continued to browse the papers. So far her son George was doing great in his new position with his PR firm in LA. Rose the NBC reporter was off on assignment covering the Mississippi flood, but Olivia was not sure which state at this point, she would have to wait until Rose called back or she saw the evening news to find out. Her youngest daughter, Francis, continued to be a worry with all this nonsense of hitting it big with the 'the Great American Novel' she was about to give to the world but was becoming a great procrastinator instead.

"Honestly, I don't care if she ever writes the 'Great American Novel' or the latest pulp drivel at this point, just as long as *something* gets into a finished draft form, or *any* project of hers for that matter," Olivia sighed, carefully finishing off her last nail. "Even that Dame … what's her name? Cartland? Yes, Barbara Cartland, in England can dictate books faster than a jackpot slot machine in Atlanta spits out quarters."

Katherine did not know how to console her other than say Francis would find her 'groove' eventually.

"I hope so Kathy, but instead of a groove, maybe it's a trench she needs to stay focused. At least she's off that film-making tangent! There she was, out in the woods with a bunch of kooks and a rented camera for a whole year and no picture to show for it. One of these days she's going to regret she dropped out of college."

"College isn't for everyone either," Katherine noted, recalling how a number of her family found the university had hampered rather than progressed their talents but they ended up sticking it out until they could get their qualifications to practise whatever they had chosen in life. "Francis just needs to find her real passion. What about business? She doesn't need to be a rocket scientist with a degree in calculus for that."

"True, and she has a certain amount of ambition all right, but Francis just doesn't have staying power, you know? She might have a great idea, but either doesn't know the full extent of the work involved in such a project and end up tossing it aside, or get bored to death after she got it off the ground. It can go either way with her, she has these funny moods every now and again."

Katherine didn't know what advice she could give in that instance and continued her paper browsing, stopping every now and again to read aloud some other articles of interest. So far so good, she thought as she breathed a sigh of relief, the Beastie woman was not mentioning anything about her and Gerry these days in the gossip columns. She still kept an eye out for those narkish articles just in case she needed to be prepared to handle a backlash of some kind.

"Oh, I forgot, something for you was stuck in with my mail yesterday, but you were gone before I realized it. I meant to put it on the desk, *before* I started this," Olivia noted, looking down at her wet nails and giving them a few puffs. "Can't get it now, it's in my bag at the pocket side. It's all right, go ahead and rummage for it."

Katherine carefully looked inside Olivia's handbag and pulled out an elegant envelope with no return address. Hmm, looked like something important, she could tell by the printed gold lettering and the quality of the paper. This was no cheap greeting card. A wedding invitation? She opened the envelope. She was half right, it was an invitation, but not to a nuptial event:

You and your guest are cordially invited to the private
Grand Opening of the new Elverton Gallery on Fifth Avenue,
June 26, 1993, at 8 PM …

She did not know what to make of this and was about to toss the card onto the desk. Olivia asked if she might look, Katherine did not mind and gingerly handed it to her lest she swipe off the newly applied nail polish.

"Would you imagine that? That takes some guts, having the new competition on the block send you an invite to their affair."

"I know, I would consider it just a business thing since everyone in the arts tend to support each other despite the competition, but the way that Elverton idiot cased my place! He's got some nerve."

To make it worse, this impudent rival had selected what was to be her and Gerry's wedding date for their private gala before the new gallery opened the next day. Of course, it could not possibly be intentional, but seeing such an insolent challenger open on what should have been a very special day for her and Gerry, and be invited to the event no less, felt as though a wound in her heart had been rubbed afresh with a fistful of salt. Needless to say she would not give two thoughts on attending their opening and wondered what Gerry would think of this as she returned to her papers.

"Hmm, speak of the devil," Olivia intoned under her breath, giving Katherine a nudge followed by a quick nod over to the restaurant area. She glanced up from her papers to see a smartly dressed Sir Conrad Elverton leaving *Chez Garneu* with breakfast to go, and heading straight for them at the reception desk.

Katherine bristled inside as the brown-haired, hazel-eyed ferret sauntered through her place. Come all the way to Brooklyn for breakfast? Yeah right. Pretext for more snooping no doubt. How dare this no good, low down … *nope, nope, nope!* She was not going to think unkind thoughts, especially as she was getting better at handling her temper. Count to ten, keep calm, can't throw the creep out anyway, not without due cause to call security, and you just can't arrest a guy for buying a bag of pastries, Andre did have rent to pay. Although still bristling, her curiosity did get the better of her, might as well play it ice cool and see what he wants. Sir Nincompoop had already cased her place, he couldn't do any worse than that, and if he did try anything, she was better prepared for him this time around.

"I think I'll leave you to it," Olivia announced, getting up and heading to the gift shop after he had placed his breakfast on the counter and wished them a good morning.

"Good morning," Katherine replied trying hard to be polite, a knot beginning to tighten in her stomach. "May I help you with something?"

"Yes, actually, there are two, no, make it four pieces I'd like to see again with your assistance, if I may."

"Oh really? And why is that, pray tell? Come to steal my artists right out from under my nose now that you've scouted the competition?"

"My my, I can see everything is straight out and above board with you." He smiled as he languidly leaned on the desk. "Not too happy with my tour of your gallery I assume, but that was just business, nothing personal."

"I see. And is this new 'tour' business as well? Fool me twice you know."

"Let's say I'm here as a customer, I have a private collection, and I would like to add to it."

"A likely story."

"No, really, and besides, I already have my own artists lined up for the gala. It's a good thing too because so far yours are quite loyal, which is a rare thing, they refused to supply me with a few paintings for my opening despite the allure of Fifth Avenue." He smiled, before looking down. "I see my invitation was delivered. I do hope you're coming."

"Sorry, bad timing. I won't be able to make it." She stood up and shoved the card in a pigeon-hole out of sight.

"Ah, that's a pity. Everyone who is anyone is going to be there, with the exception of your lovely presence," he replied as he straightened up and tidied his cuff links. "You'll miss a good showing too. Speaking of which, may I still see those paintings? I *am* serious about that private collection. In fact, you should come see it, a tour in return for the one you gave me."

"Oh, I don't think so."

"I insist. How about after my gala opening?"

"I have a full schedule."

"Schedules can be changed. I'll fit mine around yours, do say 'yes'," he returned.

His cute, over polite, unrelenting way in an attempt to win her over was getting a little annoying and would not mend fences, especially as he seemed to think attempting to shanghai her artists with no qualms in telling her was simply droll.

"Er, excuse me, I hardly know you, in fact, I don't know you at all, except through the news media."

"Ah yes, we have not been formally introduced. I'm … " he began, ready to hold out his hand, but she stopped him from proceeding.

"Yes, I know. You're Sir Conrad Elverton, and you know I'm Katherine Walsingham. I'm afraid you've already blown your opportunity for polite introductions some time ago."

"All right, I do apologize for casing your establishment and tempting your artists, but like I said, nothing personal. Since I cannot make amends with a tour, may I take you out for lunch sometime?"

"If it was just business, there is no need to make amends. Lunch is not necessary."

"I suppose there is logic in that. Then, let me take you out, just because."

"I don't think so."

"Dinner then."

"You don't give up, do you?"

"Never."

"I am engaged you know, and I'm not talking business. I'm not at liberty to date, not now, not ever."

"Then let's make dinner business. There's nothing wrong with a business-only dinner."

That depended on what he meant by business. This guy had some nerve! Obviously one of those relentless pests who assumed when a woman said 'no' she meant 'yes'.

"No thank you, I don't think we have any 'business' to discuss."

"Then how about those four paintings? I am seriously considering investing in those optical illusion works you have. They're quite charming I have to say. That would be classified as legitimate business I believe?"

Oh no, she knew he meant either Suzy or Justine's paintings. If it were not for the fact they could use the money, Justine with a new baby and

Suzy with a wedding to plan plus make a home, she would turn this overconfident creep right out on his ear. She called down Kyle the security guard from the museum upstairs to watch the desk as she politely but frostily led the way to the stairs. Something told her she did not want to be confined alone in the elevator with this idiot and felt more secure with the relative openness of the stairway. Arriving on the second floor, it was as she suspected, he had cast his eye on two of Justine's pictures, one of Martin's, and Suzy's latest piece. Katherine did as duty required for the sake of her friends and affirmed she would place a reserve on them, politely inquiring from the flirtatious knight where and when he would like them delivered as they returned downstairs.

"Perhaps the first week of July at your convenience, just have them dropped off at the gallery, I believe you know where it is," he said, also insisting on paying a generous down payment in cash.

"Yes, I know. All right, business is accomplished. For the sake of my artists, thank you for your custom. Now, that should conclude our business, I believe."

"Can't blame a man for trying." He laughed, tapping his reserve receipt twice on the counter in a devil-may-care attitude before picking up his breakfast and bidding her a good day. Olivia scurried out to hear the news once he had left.

"He tried to chat me up and ask me out, and there's not a person left in the art world who doesn't know I'm engaged to Gerry. He's one arrogant, conceited individual. Something about him just gets right under my skin to where I feel the need to scratch or take a shower, can't figure out which."

"Still, he's a handsome one at that. Did you get a load of his accent? Dishy! That Shakespeare troop are missing out on a good thing there. Gerry better keep you close."

"Olivia! Honestly!"

"Oh, not that I think *you* would ever waver dear, but seriously, an engagement ring to a would-be home wrecker is not a deterrent but a challenge to overcome, so is a wedding ring for that matter. I should know, look at the silicone bimbo my Frank got cosy with. Just keep an eye out. That's all I'm saying."

Bolted down in the hospital room, Gerry stared at the ceiling for a minute to clear his head after the paperwork he just ploughed through in addition to yesterday's news. How he was getting tired of that view. He had studied every little hole in the panels above his head a thousand times by now and had even discovered a few 'constellations' among them. Usually finding odd patterns helped, but today his mind continued to pick out shapes that resembled a huge land mass. He rubbed his eyes. Africa, he only did it once and hated that route almost as bad as their inspections in Japan, but he would rather be going instead of sending Lottie. There was nothing he could do and hoped Thomas would take good care of her. He felt so useless tied down like this. He had the paperwork, which helped keep him focused on something constructive all that morning, but there was only so much of that he could take. He needed a break. He had buried himself in it for a few hours trying not to think about Thomas and Lottie. If it were not for the accident, he would be handling this right now. True, none of this was his fault, but in his current debilitated state it felt as though he was shirking his duty, letting his load fall on other shoulders, and he always pulled his weight no matter what. However, it was no good stressing out with an irrational self-blame game, better force himself to relax. Maybe someone might stop by for an early visit before the lunch cart came around, that would help cheer him up and distract his mind to somewhere else.

Sure enough, Lottie rushed in to say a last goodbye and give him a final hug before her trip. She couldn't stay for long, a few more necessary errands had come up unexpectedly and she was feeling the pinch where time was concerned. Also, Peter had managed to arrange on the hop a special catered lunch with the Captain and their mother, something he already wanted to do but pushed it ahead as a nice surprise to see her off and so she had to rush to meet them on time. However, she was sure they wouldn't leave him all by his lonesome and was positive their parents would come by later to see him. So much to do, and her flight was leaving that night, time was ticking.

"Take a breath Sis, or you'll pass out. That was good of Pete to arrange lunch, say 'hi' to everyone for me?"

"Of course, and oh, I saw Kathy this morning and told her to keep an eye on you all. I'm going to miss you terribly, but it's my turn to handle the globe trot this time, you just concentrate on getting better."

"Will do, Sis. Love you, and take care."

One last hug and she was out the door. It was difficult watching her leave this time. That visit he was looking forward to had just reminded him of how useless he was feeling, and he hated falling right back into a stewing period as everyone called them just when he thought he was getting over the frustration of yesterday and had accepted the current situation. Although he did have a temper like almost everyone else, he rarely indulged blowing his stack. He had been through enough of his father's outbursts over the years to know that it was not a pleasant experience to be caught dead-centre in a verbal pyroclastic blast. It was true verbal bomb raids could produce results, but often caused a lot of collateral damage in the process. People were oblivious to the fact that sound was also a physical force despite its invisibility. If spoken sharp enough, words had the power to strike as hard and deadly as sticks and stones. It was an experience he never wished to inflict on anyone else. Not to mention it was a terrible waste of time and energy losing one's temper. Surely finding a solution to whatever problem was facing you was better than hollering about it and upsetting everyone to the point of alienating them. As a consequence, he went to another extreme and grew introverted upon occasion in his effort not to bother people with his worries, compelled to mull them over to a pulp until he had found some answer. Once he had found an adequate solution in his thought mill he was usually back to his bright, chipper self. This time there was nothing he could do. In fact, sending Thomas off with Lottie as she refused to stay home was the only way out anyway, and since that had been decided there was no point worrying. He would just have to trust Tom. It was a good thing he was someone reliable. Don't stew, relax. Think about something nice for a change. You can't run the whole Reinold shipping empire on your own.

His eyes were a little too tired to read, but not to work on some of his drawings. That's it, do some artwork. That certainly had a way of calming him, the simple activity of focusing on lines and colours had the merciful effect of submerging the daily barrages of a hectic world, and he certainly needed to bring the frenetic pace of his thoughts down a few gears. He reached for the large sketchpad by his bedside and flipped through the pages for a clean sheet. He needed a new idea for his next painting, working with watercolours was interesting, but what he truly appreciated was the glistening vibrant quality of an oil canvas. Unfortunately, he was in a cumbersome predicament to set up for oil work, but at least the watercolours would help tint in any ideas he had until he was finally out of the hospital. What to paint though? Kathy was nudging him to do a masterpiece for a gallery showing, but despite her encouragement, he was not comfortable with the idea. He and his family, not to mention hers, were already too much in the public eye when it came to the media, and while his art would probably be a positive way of redirecting the public's attention, this was one of those things he wanted to keep private and not make available to the oogling crowd. His artistic expression was something very personal to him and there were only a few close individuals he felt comfortable baring his soul to. Yes, that was what it felt like. Art reveals the inner psyche of the artist. It takes a certain type of hardiness for a creative person to share their works to the public. He had to admire Katherine for doing it. Perhaps it was stupid to continue producing pictures when they would be hidden away somewhere, Katherine admitted to him she had to overcome that herself, but for now just creating satisfied him. However, he didn't mind if she wanted to hang a few up in the apartment just for the two of them whenever she got around to decorating it, she really enjoyed his work, and naturally Kathy was one of the rare few he could open up to about his feelings, except when he fell prey to his bouts of bottling up and did not want to worry her.

A masterpiece she wants for the gallery, eh? Something like that would mean choosing a very personal subject to make it unique enough to be deemed a magnum opus, and he didn't want anything like that hanging up just yet. Maybe he was too self-conscious. He was also a bit pessimistic and questioned if he was good enough for a gallery since he had rather refined ideas about what he liked in art and was worthy to hang on display despite the modern pieces he bought. Perhaps he could get away with another landscape? They seemed to be turning out okay. No, nice try, that won't do. Katherine was too wise for that decoy to work, and he didn't want them out in the public's eye yet either. Wait a minute, there was only one subject matter that he truly deemed worthy to be called a masterpiece and would also get him out of this scrape of a public viewing. Yes, that would definitely be one painting he would love to do, and it would certainly be kept well away from the gallery spotlight he mused. In fact, this would be fun, it was just like the time when they caught each other out with that silly 'Truth or Dare' wager during those awkward first dates when she was timid beyond belief and he terrified of blowing his chances with her. All right then, if he was going to be caught with a compromising penalty of being put on public display, he could also compromise the penalty. Time again to tap dance.

He chuckled to himself as he began to sketch with enthusiasm, she was so fun to wind up at times, there was something so fascinating about her when her dander was up, not angry, just flustered into a corner because she had finally met her match. To be honest, he had met his match too. He could not wait to see her reaction this time around. Ah Katherine, what would I do without you? You make everything in life worthwhile. The humbling thing was he knew she felt the same about him. Love, what a rare, inexplicable state of being as well as feeling. There were so many things he loved about her, well bred and refined, she could rise to any occasion and come out dressed to impress for their formal evenings out, yet had no qualms jumping into an R-Bolt with him and the guys on a delivery round. She was sophisticated, cultured, drop dead gorgeous, and yet was so darn irresistible when she was on a grunge day in the studio in her track suit covered in paint, involuntarily rubbing a smudgy rainbow all over her nose when it tickled, her long brown hair rustled up into a make-shift bun and speared out of the way with an old paintbrush handle, a few loose strands attempting to make a wavy escape. He loved to watch her when they were together working on their art projects, glancing away when she would look up in case she caught him admiring her. He noticed her doing the same every now and then too, the corners of her mouth twitching into a smile when she was caught. Obviously, she found him and all his little mannerisms just as fascinating, and these were a few of the million little things. When she looked at him a certain way, his heart wanted to seize up or it did the complete opposite and thundered away like mad. God forbid, if anything happened to her, his life might as well be over. He never felt like this about anyone else before.

He looked up as the door opened, thinking it was time for the lunch cart, but found he had unexpected visitors. Caught off guard, he quickly flipped the notebook shut and slid it away under a stack of magazines beside the bed. Hell, it was Sherry 'The Burr', the last girl-fiend he had whom he was unable to shake off for almost a year. His old college friend Harry was with her, both were in jovial spirits.

"Hey Ger, how are you doing?" He handed him a get well card.

"Hey, thanks." He read it and placed it on the table. "Not too bad. How have you been? It's been an age, I haven't seen you since Leroy's New Year bash."

"I know, sorry I haven't been able to see you before now, we both haven't for good reasons, look," Harry beamed, holding up Sherry's left hand.

"Whew, that's some rock. I guess congratulations are in order." Gerry smiled, a little relived he was now completely off the hook for good.

"Isn't it though? Harry took us on a long getaway to Tahiti and a tour of the Caribbean to celebrate." Sherry giggled before Harry sobered up a bit, looking apologetic.

"Oh God, that was real swift of us, maybe we shouldn't've … ."

"Geeze, yeah. I'm so sorry Ger," Sherry added.

"Sorry for what," Gerry asked, a little perplexed.

"Er, having to call off the wedding and all because of ... well, you know," Harry blurted in confusion.

"Hold your horses, this is the first I've heard of *that*," Gerry noticed, trying to sit up a notch. "Nothing's been called off. Just delayed a bit, that's all."

"Oh, whew! Man," Harry noted, giving a quick swipe across his forehead and brightening up again. "Thought we had done it that time. For a while the papers were full of talk about you guys cancelling the whole thing, so we thought ... never mind what we thought. We were gone, so what do we know, and what do those gossip columnists know? Diddly-squat! Right?" He nestled against Sherry and pulled her towards him for a kiss.

"That's right, baby," she cooed before returning the smooch.

"So, when do we get to meet the lucky girl," Harry eventually asked.

"Whenever you plan not to spike the punch when she's around."

Gerry had brought Katherine to the New Year's 'bash' just mentioned, but she had succumbed to the intoxicating effects of the refreshments before she could be introduced to everyone in his old group. Katherine had an odd quirk, she was one of those few who could not handle her libations and tended to doze off wherever she happened to be if given one glass too much.

"Oh! Geeze! The party? The snoring dame was *her*?" Harry laughed. "Ti many Martoonies, eh? Sorry about that, but honestly, I didn't improve Lee's punch that time, it was definitely Colin. I saw him empty two bottles of vodka and something else I didn't recognize into the bowl before you guys showed up."

"It's true." Sherry nodded, wrinkling up the corner of her mouth in affirmation.

"Blast it! Colin! So he was the one that did it! I should've guessed."

Gerry had warned Leroy he was bringing a teetotaller to the party, but the rest of the former fratsters had not yet outgrown their stupid phase enough and nearly killed off Katherine thinking it was funny to replay some of their old pranks. Well, maybe they wouldn't have *killed* her, but he nearly didn't get her home that night, she was pretty ill. No wonder he had shifted away from most of his college mates over the years, having quickly outgrown the frat house days. He could always forgive that big-hearted scamp Leroy who never left him down in the end, he never meant any real harm to anyone, but Colin was a shifty ... never mind. That was months ago, and it was unlikely that Katherine would ever be a victim of his spiked punch a second time. When it came time to send out the wedding invitations when the date was reset, he might consider striking one name off his guest list just to make sure.

"So, no wonder we didn't hit it off." Sherry laughed. "You really do like a girl who can give you a quiet life."

"I suppose I do," Gerry replied, a little amused. There *were* some out of the ordinary occasions when Katherine never gave him a dull moment. "Anyway, when's the date for you two? Come on Harry, give us the news. How and when did this all come about?"

They happily revealed to him things really took off that night after the party, Harry proposed on Valentine's Day with tickets to the Caribbean, and that was that. In fact, they only got back a couple of days ago, but they didn't plan to wait around long and were going to get married that July, for the honeymoon they were going to a super luxury beach resort in Bali. They promised to send him and his fiancée an invite, providing he was up to coming by then, naturally. After they had told him their gossip, they were off, had a million things to plan, but would drop by again when they could.

A quick whirlwind of a visit, and they were gone. Oh well. Gerry took out his sketchpad again, mulling their news over. Hmm, no wonder the family had been hiding the papers from him at that time, those stupid reporters and their damned rumours! Cancelling the wedding date didn't mean it was called off entirely. Where in blazes did they get that idea? Misinformation no doubt, much like misspelling people's names. That had to be it. He could not figure out why his or Kathy's family were afraid he might be upset by that though, the papers always printed erroneous trash about them before. Odd. Of course, they didn't want him stressed out by anything, so everyone just went a little over the top. That had to be it, everyone was strung out with the accident as it was.

He sketched a bit more until the lunch cart finally arrived, and as usual, there was not much to look forward to, literally. Too bad those peanut butter cups were kept well out of reach, he needed something to augment the dietician-approved portions. Maybe he might be able to wheedle one from the nurse when she came in. No luck, he was promised one after dinner though. Oh well, better later than none at all. No one else came in for a lunchtime visit, so Gerry resumed his sketching, eager to see how it looked now that he had been distracted for a bit and could view his work with fresh eyes. Yes, that's it! Perfect. He wondered how it would turn out with a few shades of colour added … . Now *this* he could truly call a magnum opus. He couldn't wait until he could render it into a proper oil painting.

Not unexpectedly, his mind drifted as he applied the first tints. Poor Harry, he hoped he would be happy. Glad now that Sherry was finally spoken for, at the same time, Gerry didn't know whether or not he should warn him that the 'Burr' might be marrying him for his connections, wealth, or both. No, Harry was a different guy, he liked the girls who were fashionably hot in all the current, shallow ways. Warning him would probably do no good. Maybe it would work out for them, those two were very much alike. Blast, despite being off the hook, he still wished she hadn't stopped by, she had brought up quite a number of unpleasant memories. Sure, Sherry was drop dead gorgeous in her own way, he wouldn't have been attracted to her himself if she hadn't been, but that was where things fell apart, it was just chemistry, there was no real meeting of the minds let alone the heart. Gerry didn't notice it at first, their bedroom romance was certainly too distracting in the beginning, but then their differences began to tell. He liked some rock and pop all right, but he really loved the old jazz clubs, both the smoky laid back atmospheric kind and the more elegant establishments with the big bands that you could really dance to. He enjoyed collecting rare books, the art scene, going to the Broadway shows, theatre occasionally, and yes, he listened to classical music, including opera. So he was old-fashioned and strangely nostalgic for an idealised golden age he wished he had grown up in, so what? Sherry on the other hand was addicted to the rave clubs and the head-splitting discos, but at least he could take that every now and again and didn't make her feel like an outcast for her preferences as she tended to do. There was that irritating way she would crinkle her nose with that slight look of disdain when he tried to share a passion of his with her, notwithstanding he often did things with her without much complaint, that is, until she really let him in on her wild side. That did not include a hiking adventure that he indulged in every now and again. Okay, he could hack the fact people were different and enjoyed diverse recreations, but things really got hairy when she started introducing him to the dark underbelly of the New York fad scene. When the raves and discos were exhausted, she would take him somewhere but refused to tell him where at first in an effort to surprise him, laughingly informing him that there was a whole different world out there and he needed to try a few new things. There was one neon-lighted place were the guys licked exotic honey off the diet-skimmed bodies of their dates in full view of everyone at five-thousand dollar a jar, then there was that sadist dominatrix joint with all the leather, whips and chains situated in a grim remodelled cellar … what the hell? Maybe he was liberal on the concept of saving yourself before marriage back then, but there was a limit to trying 'new things', thank you very much. He simply turned around at the door and walked out when he found himself in this type of predicament. No wonder devious Sherry wouldn't tell him at first, he would have flatly refused if he knew what was on her mind and where they were going. In addition to her blatantly kinky side, she also had the typical superficiality of letting him know in certain ways she liked expensive gifts and expected them on a regular basis if he wanted peace and be spared a tissy fit. Okay, he could never be accused of being a cheapskate, but soon it become evident that his bank account and how she wanted it spent was all she really cared about.

Of course, he didn't want to accept it at first, chemistry was also difficult to make a break from, until he was presented with the final proof of their incompatibility when he took her home to Stonyvale for the first time: his mother brought out the porcelain salt and pepper shakers. Everyone in the house knew this was a subconscious clue to her adamant disapproval, but the real sign of doom was the fact the condiment containers were left almost empty. That was certainly a first in the history of all the guests ever brought to dinner! However, the final straw came when Sherry opened her mouth as she usually did in her tactless way. Crinkling her nose as he took her on a tour of the interior of the manor, she wondered what he planned to do once he inherited it.

"Move in eventually, it is our family legacy after all."

"What? This old mothball? Why would you want to be shackled to this antique? I thought you were a city man."

"To a point. True, the old place is something to maintain I have to admit, but … ."

"It must be worth something though. Ever have it appraised?"

"For insurances purposes naturally," he evasively answered. "Don't you like big houses?"

"That depends. Fashionable, yes. Medievally morbid, no. You know me, I'm a modern girl myself."

Medievally morbid. So that's what she really thought of him. The dollar value of his inheritance alone gave him a more acceptable pallor: almighty greenbacks.

"So, you don't like tradition? Family? What about kids?"

"Eww!" She grimaced, then tittered. "Not for a while anyway. There will be time enough for that. Life is for living. Oh, Ger, don't let yourself get buried alive here, letting your family shift their old burdens onto your back. Break free, get rid of this old graveyard if you have to. You've got to make your own life."

Something inside just snapped. Sure, he may have needed to get his own place after college, anything to prove to himself that he could get out there in the world and not feel like everything was handed to him, but his heart always lay with home and family. Now that Pete had relinquished the Reinold reins to him, he may not be able to have the satisfaction of going out and building up something of his own from scratch, but had come to realize that assuming the legacy of his forefathers and ensuring it would continue for the benefit of the next generation would also be a satisfying challenge to assume as well as a duty. Instead of a burden, it finally struck him it truly was a blessing to have a successful empire entrusted to you. All he had to do was ensure he would not become that dreaded descendant that ended up losing it all, which was a very palpable anxiety. No matter how diligent he was, no one could predict what the future would bring, or how world events might shape their destiny. *Continual* success was not a sure thing, no matter how good you were at business. One had to adapt, be ready for anything … hell! That's all he needed to hear from Sherry with this one dread hanging over him, how quickly she wanted to flog everything off, family history and legacy be damned. Yes, these were only temporal possessions, there were many other important things in life, but where he and his family were concerned there was a certain dignity to uphold. She obviously would never be able to rise to that occasion, and he was tired of being dragged down to her vulgar level. This was just not going to work. What *was* he thinking? The two of them were a definite mismatch and a marriage could not be built on chemistry alone. Just look at the stuff she was 'in' to! God knows what was happening behind his back! Did she even remain loyal to him while they were dating? He had his doubts now, but still, even if she were, she definitely would not be a suitable role model for children, if she ever deigned to have any that is. What made it worse was the realization of how much she was actually trying to change him, mould him into what she wanted him to be, not try and help him to become better for his sake but have him hop to her every little beck and call when she wouldn't even bother to meet him half way in the small things. She never understood him or even bothered to try. Her idea of 'making a life for himself' would destroy him in the end, and there was no way he would ever be able to influence her for the better. One thing was certain, she would never darken the door of Stonyvale again.

The time came to call it off, sit her down and say this was not going to work. That was a pleasure to do, but getting her to accept it was the difficult part. It took an age before he finally got her to move out of his penthouse, she coming up with a million excuses why she couldn't find her own place yet, in addition to the tears, the sobs, and the 'maybe we should just take a break and then try again' routine. Garbage, she was not bad off, her father was the East Coast distributor of two Italian sports car manufacturers for heaven's sake! She had plenty of her own cash, there was no reason she couldn't find somewhere to stay and rent storage space if she needed to. He was sick of the drama, it was time the circus left town! He was way too patient as it was. Two months after he had broken it off, she dragging her feet, he finally took her belongings, left them in the hall and had the locks changed, leaving instructions with the doormen she was only allowed to claim her things, the welcome mat was to be pulled from then on. The suitcases and clutter eventually disappeared when he was out at work one day, and that was that, or so he thought. She made a nuisance of herself, 'bumping' into him in his usual coffee haunts or restaurants, plaguing him on the phone, and more embarrassingly, sitting right down with him when he had taken another girl out on their first date, the 'Burr' making a right mess of it and chasing the new lady off before they ever had a chance. Not that he was afraid Sherry would do anything worse, she just wasn't going to give up on him, or rather his inheritance, that much was certain. Maybe she thought he was a pushover because of his generosity and expected he would cave in eventually, especially as he did believe in giving people second chances. This time, however, he was not going to allow his kindness to be abused. In a disagreeable relationship with no future, things were never going to work anyway, so it was best to cut his losses. The problem was, how to get rid of the 'Burr' before things really turned ugly? Maybe he had to get nasty this time. No, all he needed was something to shake her up and back her off.

One day he bumped into one of the old gang who asked how he was doing, he admitted things were not going well with him and Sherry, in fact, he might have to get a restraining order. As he had hoped, the rumour spread fast and did the trick without him having to actually involve the law and create a public scandal, the family had enough problems with the press as it was. At last, he could breathe again, but the experience made him look over his shoulder for a spell, not to mention put him off making an attempt to meet someone new, he had the habit of being attracted to the wrong person. What was he doing wrong? Maybe he should take a break before he tried again.

One day when he decided to brave the dating scene, he thought it best to humble it out and ask a woman what to do and sought advice from Lottie.

"Of course, I could be in this 'pattern cycle', I keep getting mixed up with the wrong people, I mean, they're from High Society and Forbes top 500 lists all right, people our parents would think are not beneath us, I hoped I might find someone cultured, someone with finesse *there*, still … ."

"But Gerry, 'High Society' doesn't guarantee that. Hmm, you're a gentleman all right and do things with style, but I think it's time to take a step back in time. Come with me, I've got an idea."

Curious, he went with her to see what she had in mind and was further baffled when she took him to a men's luxury shop that specialized in classic vintage apparel. It was one of those puzzling facts of life that women either celebrated a happy event or solved their problems with a shopping spree. Better not argue and go with it for the moment.

"Try this," she said, handing him a black viscount wool coat with half cape to the shoulders. Okay, he had a closet full of tailored wools from London and a vicuna no less, but … ?

"Seriously?"

"Yes! If you want to attract a real accomplished *lady* and not a shallow fluff ball you've got to look like a gentleman who abides comfortably by old-fashioned values. Opposites don't always attract, like and like can meet up too you know. Go on." The shop attendant slipped it over his shoulders. "Oh, I wish men would dress up more. That looks heavenly."

"You don't think it's a bit much, Sis? *Too* dressed up and people might think, you know … I'm on the fruity side," he whispered in her ear.

"Oh Gerry! Not you. You're one of the few straight guys who can actually pull it off. That really suits you. Come, take a look." She took him by the shoulders and facing him towards the mirror.

Hmm, it *did* feel good, very stylish as a matter of fact. Those Victorians probably knew what they were doing.

"I guess the opera season *is* nearly upon us … ."

"That's the spirit! Don't be afraid to show who you really are and what you like. Just be sure when you take a date out, make a mental note of her reaction, you might get a clue how she thinks, especially if she's the type with the same old-fashioned sensibilities."

Looking back, Lottie had something there. The way Katherine paused and gazed at him those few seconds the night when he first wore it, and she, a vision of loveliness herself. Not one to play coy games, she often revealed her thoughts and feelings through her eyes, she was guileless and couldn't help it. What a difference from the 'Burr'! Night and day had more in common with each other. Katherine was definitely a play-it-safe girl with traditional values, almost to the point of being a shut-in that rarely left the house. He hoped he hadn't jumped to extremes and had fallen madly in love with a prude! No, having been sheltered quite a bit, she couldn't be *that* bad, she was just overly sensitive about certain things. She hinted she had a few bad run-ins during her school years, something about crude jock idiots that made her shy away from meeting anyone despite her love for classic romance novels. It was hard to believe it, but no, she really hadn't dated anyone. In fact, he was her first and only love, it was a pleasant shock to find that out. It was almost too good to be true. He was anxious about scaring her off after that and took extreme care not to show any indecorous intention in a supreme effort to earn her trust. He knew she was the girl who not only wanted to do things 'just right' for perfection's sake, but also because she didn't want to live a life of regret. Without her having to say a word, he knew that's the way things had to be, nothing was going to happen until the honeymoon. Well, he did want to find a woman with traditional values, right? Now, don't blow it! However, Katherine was so shy and awkward in the beginning, no doubt she was too engrossed on getting her gallery together and afraid to let any kind of feelings mess with her head let alone her heart, would he ever be able to win her? Those early days were filled with trepidation! Women were such a mystery to begin with and Katherine was one of the biggest enigmas he had ever come across.

Finally, he took the next step and asked his mother for her opinion and for any advice to ensure he didn't mess things up before they ever had a chance to start. He found her one afternoon in her garden clothes, having an earthy day in the great conservatory busy rearranging her latest creation, her Firepearl Glory roses, just before the winter settled in. How she loved her flowers. Despite the fact she was in her work clothes and making a right mess pruning everything and littering potting soil about, there still was something lovely about her in her gardening gear surrounded by the lush foliage and colours, the graceful white ironwork of the glasshouse arching high above.

"Ah, so you have finally met someone." She smiled, levelling out the rich earth. "Come, pot a plant with me and talk. There's something satisfying about getting your hands in the soil."

Smiling, he rolled up his sleeves and began teasing out roots from a pot bound rose plant.

"I have, I really have found someone. I've barely been with her a few times, but still, I now know why it never could nor would work with anyone else. Yet, she's, um, how do I put it? Almost too perfect," he trailed. Sophia looked up at her son quizzically. "Oh sure, she's modern in that she's outspoken on many things and has just opened up her own gallery, but she's not a bash-it-in-your-face feminist either. She's so traditional in other respects she's an outright paradox. I mean, she still lives with her family to whom she's very loyal, but she keeps herself at a distance despite going out with me, she's never been with anyone, even at her age, I think you know what I mean. How do I romance a girl like that? I mean, romance I can *do*, but sometimes I wish I knew what woman wanted and why. I've never been accused of not being a gentleman, and I'm doing my best, but … what does she *want*?"

"Oh, she's like that is she? That old fashioned? You sure she isn't Amish or thinking about a convent?"

"Mom, don't joke. It's true."

"I see." Sophia nodded, all joking aside. She paused for a moment. "You mean the Walsinghams' daughter?"

"Yes, how did you … ?"

"Lottie told me. She really has made an impression on you. When do we get to meet her?"

"If I can ever chip away at that ice block wall. Oh, she's not really cold, I thought it was the hard-to-get routine at first, but she's not like that either."

His mother took off her gloves, pulled over one of the wicker chairs and sat down.

"Well, if she is really that conservative, from my point of view it's like this: yes, a girl likes to be romanced, it does feel good to be pampered once in awhile." She smiled, before continuing. "But romance is not just to get her attention, although it's a start. Your traditional woman is settled and happy where she's at, that's the thing. You will have to show her that there can be more, that having you love her and getting her to love you can be a wonderful thing. You know this already, but I'll remind you, falling in love also carries great responsibilities with it. Stepping out into the unknown is a frightening prospect. Think about it. Why would a girl wish to leave the security of her family if it is a happy one to start a new home with a complete stranger? A woman has fears too you know."

"Fears? She wouldn't want for anything … ."

"I know that dear. Hmm, let me put this another way and ask you a question. As a man, what is it you fear most about women? What can they do to you that would instil a deep fear into you?"

Gerry thought for a moment.

"I suppose, betrayal, being humiliated, being used … ."

"Honest, valid fears. True, no one likes to be used or valued just for their monetary assets. Women have the exact same fears, which are made worse by some pre-conceived notions, that men have only 'one thing on their minds' and because of that are incapable of remaining faithful. Women in general fear becoming property and being used, and then in the end, being abandoned or find they have to leave the relationship if they've made the wrong choice after they risk giving their heart, which is a pretty painful process."

"Okay, I hear you," Gerry noted slowly, "but to be honest, from my latest experience, the 'Burr' doesn't seem to fit here."

"Of course, and I can't box all women in this category, the tables can be switched on men too, but you now know how it feels. At least you were not in a life-long commitment then, which is getting back to my point. If you're serious about this young lady, there will come a time when the relationship will need to move past the allure of attraction and romance. Yes, romance will continue to sparkle now and then, it's important to keep that alive, but you will have to rely on something much deeper. Everything must be built on the bedrock of trust. It could be that the young lady is reticent because she is aware of the risks of getting hurt and is simply afraid. Don't hide your personality and be someone you're not just to get her attention, because getting to know the real you is part of the trust-building process. If she feels you've been acting in any way just to please her, your going to start on shaky ground."

"I am trying, although I do have to try hard to get her attention. I definitely feel she has trust issues, and you're right about her being afraid to leave the security of her family … ."

"Then once you have her attention, earn her trust, and she'll have earned yours too. Let her get to know the real you, no pretences. Also, the woman you have set your heart on needs to be shown that she's respected, that she's one of the most important people in your life, that you can give her exactly what she had, and I'm not talking just about financial security. She needs to feel truly wanted but *not* something to be used, because let's face it, the hidden burdens of running a home and raising a family falls mainly on the wife. The husband may be the breadwinner, but the stresses of family life doesn't seem to affect a man as much, even in these days where the husband shares more in the home-making duties. Now in addition to managing a career, a wife has to ensure her husband is happy, her children are happy and secure, clothed and fed, also, that their home is a safe and loving place, her own needs are often sacrificed to where she comes last if at all in quite a number of things, and still, she cannot shield everyone from life's hard knocks no matter what she tries, which makes it more difficult."

"But we are very well off to say the least, doesn't that help?"

"Yes, financial security cushions the sharp corners, but the emotional and physiological stresses will always remain. What I'm trying to say is this, a woman can endure almost anything if she knows that the man she loves is honest with her and feels the same way about her, that she'll be the only one in his life and that he loves his children as much as she does. It's a serious step, expecting her to leave the security she knows for a life she doesn't yet. She needs to know she can trust you not to hurt or betray her and that you are serious about a *faithful* lifelong relationship. It's a big thing giving your heart to someone."

"A leap of faith, don't I know it. You've certainly given me a lot to think about."

"A sombre chat, but I'm glad we've had it. She must be one very impressive young lady. It's not often you come to ask advice like this from your mother." She smiled again.

"Oh, you know, we men think we can handle everything on our own, manly image to maintain and all that." He smiled back, smoothing out the soil. "The roses were looking very good this year. It's a pity winter is upon us."

"They were, weren't they? Don't worry, we'll get a few more blooms yet in here. So, when do we get to meet this charming damsel of yours?"

"Like I said, I've got to get through the ice first. I think I've got a glacier on my hands." He laughed.

"You'll get through eventually, just be your warm, charming self, but let her come to you at her pace. You want a gentle springtime thaw followed by flowers, not a heat wave followed by a flood then a mudslide."

"Point well taken. Hmm, what if you don't like her after all my wooing?"

"We won't know until you can get her to come out here for dinner, will we," she returned, leaving her seat to trim another rose.

How come Mom was seldom wrong if ever? Although he did go overboard to get Katherine's attention at first, once he had it, he let things go at her pace, and what results! It was all working out. He and everyone else in the house were mad about her, the old manor hadn't felt this happy in ages, in fact, he was certain she had something to do with bringing Pete and the old Captain back together, but how, he didn't know. Best not to question a miracle. Then, to have this blasted accident! The universe was truly testing his patience. No matter. Just a few more months or so before he and Kathy would start a new life together, he could wait.

By now he had finished his sketching along with his ruminating. Closing the pad, he slipped it away and reached for his earphones, a little music would be good right now. In a few minutes he had dozed off to the sound of a light jazz track, only to be awakened by the staff bringing in the evening meal. He turned off the CD and forced himself to eat the crud dished up to him, reminding the nurse of the promised peanut butter cups, which she eventually relinquished with a sigh and a shake of her head. He was tempted to open the pack and leave his tray when true to Lottie's word, his parents stopped by for a visit and told him their news, which mostly featured Lottie. In a few moments, Thomas and his sister would be jetting across the Atlantic, and they hoped everything would go all right. Soon they were joined by Katherine who had just left the gallery a little earlier than usual.

"Hey, Princess. I trust you got some painting done at last."

"Hello Mr. and Mrs. R. Hi Gerry. Yes I did, this afternoon, but I'd rather be here with you. How are you feeling," she asked, giving him a hug over the bed railing.

"All right, I'm just finishing dinner, if you could call it that. I think they consider us patients no more than living garbage disposal units."

"Gerry! It can't be that bad," Sophia *tsked*. "Do you want us to speak with the dietician?"

"Mom, I'm only joking."

"Sometimes there's an element of truth in a smidgeon of sarcasm." His father chuckled as he eyed the remains of the dinner tray, "but I guess it's time to go and leave you two lovebirds have some space. Goodnight and pleasant dreams."

"Wait, here're the files from yesterday you wanted me to go over for the union guys, all done," Gerry announced, leaning over and picking them off the side table.

"Thanks son. Now, enough with work! Goodnight you two, and don't stay up late either."

"All right Mr. R, good night," Katherine replied, giving them both a hug, "see you tomorrow."

"Ah, time for a croissant," Gerry smiled as she leaned over to give him his kiss once his parents had left. "Tell me, what news do you bring today?"

"You won't believe it," she began, launching into a flustered tirade about Sir Snoop profaning her gallery the second time with his presence, and had the audacity to get flirty with her too. "If it wasn't for the fact Justine and Suzy could use the extra sales right now, I would have had the guards show him to the door."

"This guy has some gall," Gerry noted, his bright mood dampening. "Are you all right?"

"Yeah, I'm fine. What a jerk! Oh, he sent me this too, I just got it today. I'm not sure if I should show it to you, but I thought you'd be interested to know what's going on since it's related to the art world and all," she noted, taking out the invitation to the new gallery gala. He read the card, then noticed the date for the grand opening.

"What bad timing, to get that handed to you," he commiserated, his expression softening then darkening once more.

"Maybe I shouldn't have shown it, I don't want to upset you, but we said we could share anything."

"Yes we did," he noted, giving her hands a reassuring squeeze before brightening up. "Hey, at least we now know what his gallery is called. Come to think of it, this is a good opportunity to return the gesture and send a few spies over."

"What?"

"I know you're not going to go, and frankly, if he's that forward with you, I wouldn't like the idea of you going over there anyway, but why not have someone scout the place? You do need to know what's going on over there regardless. Business strategy, and all that."

"Plan and plot like all good generals, huh? You are terrible." She laughed. "But it is an open invitation after all. Maybe Charlie and Suzy would like to go, see what's happening. I can trust Suzy to give a detailed report. Hmm, wait a minute. What if this gives Sir Creep the idea to keep returning counter-attacks though, tit for tat type of thing? It could turn into something worse than creative competition. He's pushy enough to begin with."

"True. Rivalry or no rivalry, it's probably best to leave it alone. News of the place will filter over eventually, we can certainly trust Horace for that."

"Yeah. Let's forget about Sir Spy for now, although I'll give Suzy the invite anyway, she and Charlie need a night out. So, do you have any news?"

"Not before you finish all yours. Surely some good things happened today?"

Katherine told about Gramps and Lottie stopping by. Gerry laughed when he heard about the 'weight loss celebration', wishing he could have joined him for that luxurious breakfast, then thanked Katherine for cheering up Lottie and giving her that extra boost of confidence. He next enquired how her painting projects were progressing. She noted so far so good, she worked on some of the finishing touches of Pete's picture and was trying to find some inspiration for the next image in her Socratic Series. Gerry was amused by her Oval Office idea, she seemed to be doing pretty good so far.

"I see you've been busy too," Katherine turned, observing the paint set by the bedside in addition to some new watercolour spots on the smock she left him.

"Ah yes, I believe I have finally found the perfect subject for my first real masterpiece," he affirmed, growing a little mysterious. "I've been busy with the preliminary sketch. Would you care to see?"

"Really?" Katherine was excited with this news. "How wonderful! Of course I'd love to see it."

"Naturally, you'd have to wait until it's rendered into a magnificent oil painting worthy of your fine establishment, but I think you will be surprised, pleasantly I hope," he continued, reaching for the sketchbook and handing it over with slow chivalric deliberation as though he had just relinquished the fabled Excalibur to her, his eyes twinkling. Carefully opening the sketchpad, Katherine wondered what could have him in this playful but curious mood, which seemed quite familiar … .

She was indeed surprised to see herself descending the large staircase of Oak Meadows in her formal royal blue evening dress. He had captured to perfection the night he arrived to take her to the opera. Once she recovered from the surprise of seeing her portrait, she was amazed at his attention to detail. Gerry was not only talented, he possessed the gift of a photographic memory. The entrance hall and the staircase was an exact match of her home. Admiring his technique, it quickly dawned on her that she was seeing herself through his eyes on that occasion, recalling how she in turn had held her breath when she saw him in that elegant caped coat. How she wished that night had lasted, it was a night of wonderful surprises, and now he had captured that night in time. If only he was in it too, but her heart would never forget what he looked like that evening.

"Oh, Gerry. It is stunning. You really want to do an oil," she stammered, not knowing what to say. It sounded like she was complimenting herself in an odd way!

"Yes, just like that big canvas that Rhett Butler has of Scarlet in her blue dress over the mantelpiece," he continued softly, that same look of admiration in his eyes.

"You have a real gift for detail, Gerry, I don't know why you keep putting yourself down, it's just so strange to be looking at myself like this but … ." Suddenly she sobered up a bit. "Hey! I'm not putting a picture of myself in the gallery! Especially that night, it's *too* special! How embarrassing! You knew I wouldn't too, didn't you?"

Gerry grew playful again.

"Ah my love, now you know what it's like not wanting to be put on exhibit."

"You cheeky thing! At least you cured me of a phobia. Why won't you let me do the same for you and your remarkable talent?"

"Touché my dear, maybe one day, but not today. However, this really is a masterpiece to me, I can't wait to do that on a real canvas," he affirmed gently. "I want to keep that picture of you forever."

"Gerry, your sketch is beautiful, I can't argue with that, even though it's strange to see myself like this," she admitted shyly, putting the sketchbook down.

"*You're* beautiful," he complimented quietly, taking her hands in his.

"But I'm *not* going up in the gallery. What a pair we are! The penalty has been compromised, we're tap dancing again, aren't we?"

"Quite! You are so adorable when we do that."

 number

June arrived, and at last, the doctors finally had some good news. They felt it was time to remove the external steel fixators and begin the next phase of Gerry's recuperation process, announcing they had scheduled the surgical procedure for the fifteenth. However, this meant filling Gerry in on the remainder of what he might be facing could no longer be avoided and everyone dreaded how he might take it. The specialist wanted to see him alone first, but Gerry did not mind if his parents wished to attend the consultation, they too had a right to know what was happening. With that settled, the doctor gradually laid out one morning what they could all expect next.

First, he reminded him he would have to be extra vigilant in looking after his health as his spleen had been removed. He would be more susceptible to infections and would always need to keep antibiotics on hand, just in case. This would mean being overcautious if he ever had chills, sore throats, fevers, colds, and to make sure his vaccinations were kept up to date. In other words, he would need check-ups on a regular basis. Gerry understood that, so it meant from this day forward he had to be a perpetual hypochondriac he quipped before asking what was next in the recuperation process he was not yet made aware of. The doctor continued; naturally, there was the matter of regaining his bladder control after being bedridden for so long, but the most difficult phase would be to get him mobile again, which would require much patience. This could take a few months and he would need special nursing care and regular sessions of physiotherapy. This could not be rushed, he was going to need help even in the daily necessary tasks such as dressing and bathing. If all went well, and they could see he was able to use crutches comfortably, he could be discharged from the hospital and continue recuperating in a convalescent centre, or even his home for that matter, as long as he understood he would need professional help for the rest of his recuperation.

Heck, crutches, nurses, months of limited mobility, that didn't sound great, but of course he would need to learn how to walk again. Gerry mulled that over a minute, then shrugged. The doctors had hinted a few times already the last few days while on their rounds that he was facing a long recovery, and judging by the amount of steel attached to him, he had pretty much figured out that it was not going to be an easy process, arduous in fact. Okay, just grin and bear it. He could do this. In any case, it would be an improvement to get out of the hospital and he tried to find the funny side.

"Just be sure when you guys go in with your scalpels this time you don't miss any nuts and bolts or I'll never be able to fly commercially again, I'd never pass the metal detectors." So far, he was in good spirits, but saw from the doctor's expression that there was more to come and sobered up a bit to hear the rest.

"There is no easy way to say this," the doctor trailed, his parents growing more tense as he finally came to the crux of their worry. "You may not be able to walk as you once did. Your injuries are pretty extensive. You have a slight length discrepancy in your left leg here," the doctor began, holding up an x-ray. It looked appalling, seeing all the internal pins and strips holding his bones in place.

"Discrepancy," Gerry repeated, unsure of the term.

"Your leg has mended slightly shorter than its natural length, and there is a malunion here," he pointed out on the x-ray image somewhere near the right hip. "The pelvis hasn't knit quite as clean as we had hoped here and here," he pointed out twice more on the x-rays, which looked like grey alien moonscapes to Gerry, "but there is nothing more we can safely do. We could attempt additional corrective surgery, but there is a high risk we may cause further damage. The pelvis is one dangerous area to work with. It's a miracle your back wasn't broken in that accident, that the internal bleeding didn't kill you, and that you came through the surgery at all."

"So, what are you trying to get at," Gerry slowly questioned.

"The thing is Mr. Reinold, we don't know yet if you will be able to progress *to* the crutches, but until we try, we cannot ascertain how serious your case truly is."

"You mean … I won't be able to walk?"

"Until we get those fixators off, it's too soon to say, but still, that is a very real possibility."

"But … I have feeling in my legs, and I can move my feet a bit, I'm not paralysed," he stammered. "How could I not be able to walk?"

"If you can, it may be with extreme difficulty, and if the worst occurs, you might have to rely on a wheelchair for the more difficult times. It's like this," the doctor continued as he closed his folder, drew a chair close and sat down, "with your injuries in addition to a discrepancy and a malunion, I and my colleagues fear you may be among the rare ten percent of cases that display nerve damage. In addition to that, as you get older rheumatism may settle in the break areas. You may be facing a future of brutal chronic pain, son. Right now you can't feel anything like that since we've got you on enough drugs to souse an ox, but we will develop a daily program of pain relief and chronic pain management classes during the rehabilitation process so you can live life as normally as possible. Hopefully, it will not be as bad as we fear, but you had better be warned and be prepared for the worse."

"God, is there anything more," Sophia wondered in dismay.

"Unfortunately, yes. My colleagues have recently had another look at the charts and have brought up another unpleasant possibility. If there is severe nerve damage, there could be dysfunction as well. Gerry, you may have some difficulty having children, if at all. Of course, we will need to do a test to find out for sure, but despite the issue of virility, you still may have some challenges in, well, you understand," he finished euphemistically, "but there are ways to manage that, there are treatments available."

The room grew quiet, faces blanched. This last disclosure was a bitter blow, even his parents who looked forward to grandchildren in the near future had not been previously informed the injuries extended that far, let alone him. However, Mr. Reinold Senior took a breath and regained some composure.

"But, this is still one big 'if,'" his father slowly observed, "this is a rare ten percent probability, you say."

"Yes, all the variables of your son's future recovery are unknown, but you still will have pain and mobility issues, Gerry," the doctor replied, turning back to him, "so be prepared for that."

Be prepared for that.

How could anyone be prepared for that?

"Listen, a brick load has just been dropped on you right now, so I've already taken the liberty of notifying our councillors and they will schedule a therapist to drop by."

"I don't mean to be rude, Doc, but I don't need a shrink," Gerry informed him flatly.

"That's what everyone says at first," the doctor continued, "you will need to talk, and we have some excellent people who can help see you through this."

Gerry involuntarily half tuned out this section of the conversation. Shrinks. See me through this, yeah right. How could they help him? Take notes and yak his condition away? How could they even grasp what he was going through this minute? He had formed his own opinions on shrink-work long ago and could instantly see at a time like this all they could do was have him analyse his situation over and over in an effort to come to some form of acceptance about it, and *that* he could do very well on his own. In fact, what was there to analyse? Excruciating pain, the inability to walk upright, his plans of starting a family with Katherine looking bleak, he didn't need some stranger who would have no idea what he was going through tinker around with his innermost thoughts and feelings, playing some stalemate Pollyanna game with no possible answer in sight. If the worst did come to the worst, they would have no solution for him, no magic wand to make it all go away, it would still be up to him to live through it day by day. All this he could see in a flash now that the grim realities facing him were finally disclosed, however … .

If. If. If! *If* this all happened! I, F, — he had to hang on to those two little letters, just one tiny two letter word. If. So much hope and dread hung in the balance on those two little blips in the alphabet! A chasm in fact! He just had to hold on to that hope. After all, a ten percent chance of serious nerve damage was still slim. He had to look on the possible bright side of being the lucky one in the ninety percent bracket. Ninety out of a hundred were pretty good odds. Come to think of it, the medics weren't all-knowing, even when the docs kept telling everyone he couldn't hear them while in the coma he still did to a point. Mobility. Pain. Okay. It was going to be tough going, but maybe he would not be facing a chronic situation after all, maybe he would feel all that only during the re-learning process, and besides, they didn't know that ingrained Reinold determination of his. He'd get himself moving again, just wait and see.

Gerry tuned back in as the doctor announced he would leave him alone with his parents for a moment, seeing they had a lot to process.

"At least the scaffold will be coming off," he noted, trying to sound confident.

"Oh Gerry, we know the road ahead will be difficult, come home to Stonyvale while you get back on your feet, we can set up a nice bedroom for you downstairs in the Morning Room, it's so cheery and ... ," his mother began, her eyes welling up.

"Now, don't cry Mom, I'll be fine, this is not going to lick me. Thank you for your offer, but I was thinking I'd like to get back to the penthouse as soon as possible, with nursing staff of course. I'd need to be close to the city to help out with the offices if I can."

"There's no need to worry about that, I don't want you stressing about work," his father huffed quietly, still ashen in the face from the news they had just received. "It would be good for you to come out to the manor, fresh sea air and all of that. The perfect place to concentrate on getting better. It is home after all."

"True, I'll think about it. There's one thing you both must promise me," Gerry added, growing serious.

"Anything, son."

"Please, whatever you tell Katherine, don't tell her about ... you know. Not until we see how everything goes. I don't know how she will take that, and there's no point worrying her if everything turns out all right."

"But Kathy still has a right to know, doesn't she," his mother queried.

"Yes, but she's so traditional, if she thinks we can't start a family, that might put paid to the engagement, and I'd hate to frighten her with that possibility if there's nothing to worry about in the end. There is so much up in the air right now. In fact, don't tell anyone right now, it could get back to her."

"Son, you don't know if she'd think like that, don't shut the girl out," Richard tried to reason.

"No Dad, please. I'm not shutting her out, just delaying some details for now. I need to handle this in my own way. Promise me, *promise*," he insisted gravely.

Not wishing to upset him further, they both assured they would leave the timing up to him.

It was a distracting morning, Katherine tried to blank out her restless mind with a bout of painting, knowing that today the specialist would be telling Gerry he may be physically challenged for the rest of his life and dreaded how he was going to receive the news. Mrs. R had promised to drop by as soon as she could to let her know how it went over, and Katherine kept eyeing the clock almost as much as her canvas. Eventually, she calmed down and settled in to her work. It was a good thing too she decided to hide out for the morning in the studio for some peace, that idiot Sir Nincompoop was making a habit of slithering in for a morning pastry these last few days, and if he spotted her at all, she was bound to get cornered. She was getting seriously annoyed with his small talk and brazen attempts to make polite let's-get-to-know-each-other conversations when she had serious matters to worry about in addition to things she had to take care of. Not that she couldn't handle him and brush him off royally, but she just could not face that, not today. At least she felt safe up in her creative sanctuary.

Lunchtime rolled around and true to her promise, Sophia came to relay the news. Katherine invited her over to their table in the restaurant and sat down with trepidation, waiting for her to begin, food the last thing on her mind. Sophia related everything she could without breaking her other promise to Gerry and not giving all the details, although it was difficult.

"We had no idea how extensive his injuries were, or that there would be problems during the healing process," she gravely concluded, "at least he's trying to be positive about it, no doubt to cheer us up."

"But, there is a chance the doctors could be wrong," Katherine pointed out. She too found herself instinctively holding on to that little word 'if'. Gerry may have trouble walking, but surely, he would not be facing a life of excruciating agony!

"A chance, but we have to be ready, come what may. In any case, when he's discharged, he said he wanted to go straight back to the penthouse, but I've asked him to consider coming back to Stonyvale for the rest of his convalescence. It would be peaceful there."

"True, but if he insists on the penthouse, I could move into his place to be with him, the guest room of course, but he should be surrounded by family too, so maybe Stonyvale is best," Katherine agreed. "Besides, his place is pretty bare since he had all his art moved here, not to mention my stuff is still in boxes everywhere. He was patient with my mess while we had the wedding plans going on, but how's he going to recuperate in all of that?"

Sophia smiled, the penthouse was a little chaotic while Katherine was trying to sort herself out, especially as she had not planned to move in or decorate until after the honeymoon and was now caught between two residences.

"Well, he may try, I have a feeling he's afraid we'll smother him too much at Stonyvale. However, would you be willing to do that? Move in?"

"Yes, if it would help him. Oh, I'll still be in the guest room, don't worry. Besides, I'm halfway moved in there anyway." She smiled. Gerry had already given her a set of keys and she stayed overnight when it was too late to go home after work or after her late night hospital visits she explained. "I know, Mrs. R, to think I told him flat out I was not the type of girlfriend that moved right on in with the boyfriend, but if he insists on going back to his place, I don't think he should do this on his own."

"That's the point, with that stubborn streak of his, he's going to try regardless."

"Hmm, I hear you. The thing is, we'll have to get *something* settled soon, because we're going to have to set some place up, prep bathrooms with handlebars and things like that," Katherine mused. After Gramps had his hip replaced a few years ago, she had an idea what may be facing her. "Wait a minute, that's all going to have to be done anyway, right? While he's still in the recuperating phase, I can get that ready for him, and while I'm at it, why not start some of the decorating? He's going to have to go through this rehabilitation program for at least a couple of months or so, and since it's going to take a while to get the wedding arrangements set up again, why not do something that he will look forward to? Of course, I shouldn't be thinking about something as frivolous as decorating at a time like this … ."

"Frivolous? On the contrary, getting your future home put together is not frivolous, plus, that might cheer him up, you too for that matter. Positive activity is just the thing needed right now, and moving ahead with your plans might be just the thing to keep him motivated. Did you have some decorating ideas ready?"

"I do actually," Katherine revealed, "but if we can get him to Stonyvale, I can have quite a bit done by the time he's ready to move back in, I hope so anyway."

"All right, dear, I think that is a wonderful idea. When you see him tonight, tell him about it, that should help get his mind off what he just heard this morning. So, what improvements do you have in mind?"

"How does 'palazzo' sound?"

"Oh, you two do get on well. He's going to love that, very much," Sophia confirmed as she finally opened the menu.

A brick load had been dropped on him all right, and since there was nothing he could do about it for the time being, Gerry found himself stewing over that morning's consultation, or rather, wishing to heat up the metaphorical smelting pot to render down his thoughts, but was prevented from doing so. The therapist did not waste time and arrived not long after his parents had left, attempting to strike while the iron was hot and pry open a channel of communication. However, that was what irritated Gerry, he needed time to think everything over first, but found himself getting prodded by a stranger with badly veiled attempts to gain his trust, which he didn't want to face right now. He was in no mood for pleasantries, although he remained polite while she said her little piece and laid out the various stages of loss he would feel similar to a bereavement; denial, grief, anger, bargaining, depression, acceptance, blah, blah, blah. Surely, his life as he once knew it would not be dead and gone? He certainly did not want to buy into that. Already expecting the 'you-can't-hide-from-your-situation' spiel, he eventually tuned her out. She's a nice lady only trying to do her job, but please, *just go away*, he thought. I need some time to think this out for myself without badgering! His reaction was not unexpected, the 'First Contact' with a patient was always the most challenging. The therapist knew not to push her luck, reminding him before she left she would check in on him again in a few days, adding as she gave him her card that if he needed her she was always available.

Good, she's gone, he thought with relief putting her card on the side table and began to sift through his mental brick load of lead. However, despite the prognosis laid out before him, the seething mass of problems continued to reduce itself down to those two little letters, i.f. There was no way of knowing what still lay ahead of him. None of this was certain yet. However, one little, niggling 'if' continued to unsettle him: if he could have children or not. That too was an unknown variable now, but until he knew for sure, there was one other matter pressing down on him, Kathy wanted a church wedding with Peter doing the honours, and so did he. The problem was the Church stressed that a marriage wasn't valid if the couple didn't want children, being open to having children at all times was one of the conditions, so he didn't know where he currently stood if for some biological or accidental reason this was made impossible. He dreaded he might lose Katherine because of it. He needed to find out and wished he could see Pete. If he ever needed to talk to anyone, it was his brother right now. If he didn't come someday that week, he would certainly stop by that Sunday. Would he be able to wait that long? Hearing a knock, he was relieved to see his brother open the door.

"Hi, Ger. Dad told me yesterday the doctors were coming to see you, and I had a hunch I had better drop by as soon as I could. How are you feeling," he asked as he pulled up a chair.

"Your intuition is dead-on as always," Gerry noted, "and I'm awfully glad to see you. Honestly, I don't know how I'm really feeling yet. I need to talk to you about something very serious."

"Lay it on me."

Gerry started from the beginning, relating all the details he had been given. Peter quietly listened, biting his lip when he heard the extent of the pain that could be facing his little brother.

"Don't worry Pete, all that's still not certain, but there's something more. I might not be able to have kids. I need to know where I stand with this. I mean, would a Church wedding still be valid? I need to know before I break the news to Kathy."

"Ger, is it that bad?"

"That's just it, they don't know! It's still one, big, fat 'if'. Nothing is known for sure, but as circumstances currently are, where do I stand with a Church wedding? If there's still a question, it won't be forbidden, will it?"

"Thankfully, no. Don't worry Gerry, if your condition is still uncertain and there's even a slight possibility you can have children naturally, then there's no impediment, but I do have to remind you, there are only two lawful ways permitted by the Church for you to take a fertility test should there be a need for it, so don't be tempted to take the easy way. No manual forcing of a sample, if you catch my meaning."

"Now we're getting into the gory details, but I understand. So, what are the lawful means," Gerry wondered, raising an eyebrow.

"You still have to be open to the gift of life at all times, so even when assessing your medical condition, a test sample can be collected only after the marital act has taken place." Somehow, despite Church approval, that sounded appalling.

"That's so clinical, and in Katherine's case, invasive and undignified. She would never go for that! How can I even bring this up with her? She's too private a person, she gives the term blushing bride a whole new meaning. If I even mention 'honeymoon' she goes a little red in the face. It's a wonder she hasn't run away from the thought of marriage at all. Let's face it, you can't tell me you haven't at least once considered sheltering her away in a convent." Peter smiled with this last statement.

"True, I have to say I did think about it, but convent life is not her calling. She has so much love to give you, and the love between a man and wife is sanctified before God too. About these tests, I also have to admit I personally wouldn't want to put Katherine through that, so you do have the second option."

"Good. What is it?"

"The second is, a sample can be taken from you from a perforated prophylactic."

"But only after we … ?"

"Yes, you still must be open to life at all times."

"I suppose it would be better than submitting Katherine to anything invasive, but it's still so crude. Definitely kills the romance, doesn't it?"

"At least you won't have to kill the romance right away, just wait and see if everything sorts itself out naturally before you have to resort to testing," Peter advised.

Well, he may have been given the gory details, but at least this was not an issue that would separate him and Katherine.

"Still, this is a very touchy thing to bring up with her, maybe I should wait until after the wedding? We won't know for sure until afterwards anyway," Gerry mused aloud.

"Obviously my pre-marriage counselling sessions on trust have fallen short somewhere," Peter noted with a shake of his head. "Have you forgotten what I told you about being open with your spouse? That goes for before the wedding too."

"Yeah, I know Pete, but you also know how she is, her principles are set on such a lofty plane she won't even allow any nudes into the gallery no matter how popular an artist is. She thinks it's vulgar, high art or no high art. If she'd have her way, all of Michelangelo's masterpieces would have a cloth or a pair of shorts tacked onto them. Surely she told you how she got through her sketching courses in Belvedere," Gerry queried with an amused smile.

"Actually no, she didn't," Pete admitted. Heavens, that was right, sketching and painting live human models clad and unclad was a core component in every classical art curriculum. How *did* she manage to get through that compromising situation?

"And you're her confessor," Gerry chuckled.

"That doesn't mean I know everything. How did you find out? Did she tell you?"

"No, she didn't tell me either. The Professor gladly clued me in one evening during our painting sessions when she was called away for some reason or another," Gerry explained.

"We're getting off topic, but now that you've opened the can of beans, you had better spill them. What happened?"

As the story went, Katherine first refused to attend anything morally questionable on the tutorial roster, however, the Professor was eventually obliged to call her in for a meeting to discuss the reason for her singular successive absences from that one class on the art of sketching the nude form. She politely but firmly gave him an earful; perhaps it was fine for the Classical and Renaissance artists, but she was not one of them, this was the twentieth century after all. She already knew she would never paint that kind of art, and so there was no need to oblige her to take a class that was not going to be of any practical use to her in the future. The Professor tried to reason with her. Since she loved the French Neo-Classic and Romantic artists, surely she would want to appreciate their technique with practical experience? Even the Neo-Classic artist Jacque Louis David used to draw his figures nude before clothing them to ensure the material draped perfectly on the figures. Katherine counter argued she had no problems drawing figures with their clothes on the first time around, so why do double the work by drawing them on afterwards? And besides, it offended her sensibilities to be forced to draw people's jiggly bits. If her opinion was asked, the Romantics, and many other artists for that matter, were simply using High Art as an excuse to legitimise voyeurism, she even had an art example ready to defend her argument, *The Painter's Studio* by the Realist painter, Gustave Courbet. Courbet did not want to spend one drop of paint on something that he deemed was an untruth, whether it be about art or the injustice and hypocrisy of society, and if he held fast to his principles like he said, according to her interpretation Courbet obviously displayed in his painting how the crowd used art as a pretext to look at a naked nude, even a child was allowed in to view the scene! If it's for art, it cannot be immoral, can it? Courbet was obviously debunking that universal perception. The Professor calmly pointed out the subject matter was only an allegory of the artist's life and possibly not his real studio, but Katherine noted allegories had many other truths hidden in them too. Be that as it may, her tutor returned, she still was obliged to attend the last three classes if she intended to pass the sketching course at all that semester, he could not alter the college syllabus for her benefit, despite her ethical opposition to the time-honoured tradition of drawing people's 'jiggly bits'.

"So what did she do," Peter wondered.

"Wait for it, she attended all right, but took the Professor at his word and drew what did *not* offend her sensibilities. He did say she just had to *attend* after all."

As it happened, she turned her easel completely around and painted the other side of the classroom. In the next tutorial she was obliged to face the model, but she quickly picked up her easel and plopped it behind the subject, so all she could see in front of her was the back view of their shoulders and head, jiggly bits not included. The final challenge came when in the last class she was herded into a full frontal view—she quickly retrieved a pair of blacked-out sunglasses from her case and put them on, painting only what she could see from the peripheral, so the top and the middle of her canvas was a black wall of paint, and the remainder around the bottom edges of her canvas was a quaint painting of the floor, her feet, and the feet of her neighbouring students.

When Peter finally stopped chuckling, he wondered how she passed at all, but Gerry explained the Professor had not the heart to fail her and gave her extra credit for being resourceful, which allowed her to squeak through that course. He had to think of something anyway since it was relayed to him from the dean it would not do to flunk the CEO's daughter of Walsingham Industries after their generous donation to the college the previous year. Of course, Katherine was never told, but nevertheless, she still had to make up the dismal pass with some extra coursework for the credits and she managed it.

"Ah, that explains the extra medieval art classes she took," Peter mused. "So she ended up doing double the work after all, and then some, bless her. She certainly stands up for her principles. No wonder the Professor thinks highly of her."

"I know, it was brave of her to do that in front of her classmates too."

"Speaking of which, you should borrow her book on courage," Peter noted, returning to the matter at hand. "Personally, I don't think keeping the news from Kathy is the best thing to do, she has a right to know what's facing both of you."

"I won't keep it from her, I just need to wait for the right time to … ."

"Gerard, for once, get out of your 'stewing habit' and break the news to her as soon as possible. You have spent so much love and time building up her trust with all the pleasantries of life, your hobbies and evenings out, it's time now to trust each other in the serious issues, which is what marriage is all about. Don't hold back, talk to her, you have to learn to face life together as a team."

"Okay, just, don't say anything to her. I've already made Mom and Dad promise to keep quiet. I'll tell her, soon."

"All right, it's your duty as her future husband to tell her anyway. So, I'll keep quiet for now. Just don't wait around too long, she needs time to process this news too."

That *was* the problem! He did not know how she was going to process everything and it worried him. However, everything Pete said was true, he knew he would have to tell her soon.

With the serious side of his condition addressed, Gerry tried to get his mind off that morning's events and asked how he was doing with his parish work. So far, Pete had many house clearings that week, so it got him out of the basement of the parish office for a while. Gerry was glad to hear that, he thought it was awful that of all the offices the parish could have given him, he chose the furnace cellar for his ministry. As it was, he could not understand Pete's interest in exorcist work, sometimes his brother was just as big a mystery as Katherine. He then asked how Tom and Lottie were doing on their African globe trot and if there were any updates. Pete was pleased to report that not all of the wilting flower deliveries were due to their company's negligence. Some of the flower farms had botched certain shipments and loaded the trucks with consignments that were from cancelled orders from other wholesalers in the area with the result old stock that should have been sent to the garbage dumps were sent to Holland instead.

"A simple mix up," Peter concluded, "although I'm sorry Reinold Shipping got blamed and Flora World bore the brunt of it. I've already alerted Flora World about some of the snags we've found, it will be up to them if they want to stay with those suppliers now. In fact, the suppliers tried to pin it on our drivers picking up the wrong thing, they even tried to cover it up by sticking on false shipment bar codes on some of the boxes, but Tom says Lottie grilled them until they admitted to mixing up the batches. It sounds like our two are handling things well."

"Sounds just like that tomato fiasco we had a while back. Well, kudos to Lottie. Since it was the suppliers' fault, we will not have to give a refund for those incidents, at least that's another worry, or a partial worry, off our backs," Gerry said, relieved something was working out somewhere.

"True, now Tom and Lottie just have to figure out what's happening in South Africa, maybe it's the same thing. Hopefully, our two travellers will have everything cleared up in the next couple of weeks, and then they'll be home."

At least things were still ticking over at the company despite all the recent upheavals. Gerry then noted the time and reminded Peter he had better vamoose if he wanted to get to the office in time to help keep it ticking that way.

"You're right, I've got to go. Do keep in mind what I've told you."

"I will Pete, and thanks for dropping by."

"No problem, Ger. You know I'm here for you, we all are, and when you see Kathy tonight, whatever you do, don't stew!"

Gerry promised he'd try. It was not easy breaking an old habit.

Alone once more with his thoughts, he mulled everything down to pulp for the umpteenth time, the day seemed to drag with this horrific 'not knowing', whether he could regain any semblance of a normal life or not, or if he would have to face a drastic situation at all. If, if, if! It seemed such a terrible burden to lay on Katherine right now not to mention terribly embarrassing for him when there was no way of knowing, it was tempting just to leave it alone until they knew more for certain, but they also had to face this situation together. Pete was right, he couldn't hide it from Katherine in the end anyway. Best to get this over with tonight.

As much as he looked forward to her visits, for the first time he dreaded to see her arrive that evening and deliberated how he could possibly broach the sensitive issue now set before them. At last she did come, there was no escaping her worried expression despite her efforts to sound calm. As for her, she could tell he had ground down quite enough in his mind-mill already and wondered how he was faring but was reticent to ask. She knew not to ask stupid questions at a serious time like this, although he did need to talk about it. She sat down beside him, taking his hand in hers.

"I know Gerry, you were given some terrible news today. Care to share a bowl of stew with me?"

"Oh, I don't think you'd like it, there are a few bitter ingredients in the mix," he returned quietly.

"Even so, there are some good ones too, at least the ironwork will be coming off. That's something to look forward to."

"True, I was afraid if they left this on much longer I might start attracting all the refrigerator magnets in the city." He smiled, then grew pensive again. No time for jokes, she'll have to be told anyway, stop stalling. "Kathy, there are some things you don't know yet, and I … ." Geeze, this was difficult! Why can't you just spit it out?

"Gerry, to be honest, we've already heard quite a bit before you woke up from the coma, not the full details of your injuries, but enough, so don't be afraid to tell me whatever it is, I can handle it."

He took a slow breath.

"The doctors think it could be worse than just the issue of walking," he started tentatively, waiting for that to sink in. Katherine looked at him puzzled. What could be worse than the threat of facing a wheelchair for the rest of his life? She waited for him to continue. "If there's nerve damage, and if it's worse than they think, we might have trouble having children, maybe we may not be able to have any at all."

Hearing himself say the words to her made him cringe interiorly. He knew none of this was his fault, nevertheless, even the threat of physical incapacity to this extent pervaded him with a mortifying sense of inadequacy. At least he said it, he did not bottle it up and hide it from her despite the feeling of vulnerability he felt for being candid. He quietly awaited her reaction.

Katherine remained silent for a moment, however, despite the knot forming in her stomach at hearing this news, she was not completely shocked either. Maybe deep down she already knew without knowing, strange as that seemed. One thing she quickly grasped was he needed support. She knew Gerry too well already. She had noticed that like most men, he could not deal with emotional displays at a time like this, and who could blame him? There were times when drama should be kept at the theatre. True, she could not help looking worried, but any sign of pity would bring a crippling blow to the dignity he had left in his current state. Best to address the situation as calmly and rationally as she could.

"But they don't know for sure," she returned slowly.

"No, that's uncertain too."

"How rotten! To drop a load of maybes and could be's on you when there may be nothing to worry about at all." Suddenly, it struck her this could be an issue where a church ceremony was concerned. It was hard to stay calm then, maybe that's why he looked so dejected. "Gerry, if it is as bad as they say, what about the wedding? You know how the Church is about children, we may have to talk to Pete."

"Don't worry, he was here today, I asked him all the pertinent questions," Gerry quickly reassured her before saying there would be no impediment to the wedding.

"Thank goodness!" She sighed, brightening up a bit. "If that's the case, what are we worrying about? We said we'd face anything together, no matter what it was. It still is a 'maybe' like everything else."

"We did, but there could be some embarrassing things to address if … ."

"Then dear, let's not talk about them now, we can't cross a bridge until we get to it, and a person can only cross one at a time. As long as nothing keeps us from bridge number one, getting married, I'll quite happily go along on a need to know basis from there," she replied.

"Are you sure," he asked hesitantly, "don't you want to know it all? I did ask Pete everything we would need to do if … ."

"Then you know what we need to do when and if it's needed," she replied matter-of-factly. "You can tell me then. We'll just take one step at a time, we won't jump the whole staircase at once. Let's concentrate on getting you back on your feet. Agreed?"

"Okay. Agreed."

Gerry couldn't help smiling. His spirits quickly recovered. After all that 'stewing' he need not have worried at all. She had done it again! His princess was quite the master of deflection. Obviously, talking about anything more intimate than the word 'honeymoon' was still off limits with her for now, but at least the romance need not be killed off before its time. Sometimes he did not know what to make of her, but right now, he was greatly appreciative of her reserve, not to mention her ability to understand how difficult this was for him too. Okay Katherine, we'll take things at your speed, it's worked for us so far.

"Good! There's that handsome smile of yours, and now that you're in a more cheerful frame of mind, I've got something to run past you," she informed him.

"Oh? What's that?"

"Let's say we may have to take a detour via an overpass before we get to Matrimony Bridge."

"Overpass? Your highness has another riddle up her sleeve I take it."

She laughed.

"Not really, it's just that now with the wedding put off, why not move ahead with the decorating while you get better? I talked it over with your Mom today and we thought it might cheer you up. Of course, you'd have to go to Stonyvale for your recuperation program in the meantime if I did that, but wouldn't it be something to look forward to?"

"It would indeed, anything to make you happy."

"I'm trying to make *you* happy."

"*Us* happy," he finished with a smile. "All right dear, I already gave you *carte blanche* to rip the apartment apart whenever you were ready, but I'll say it again, do whatever you want with the place. If it's even a jot as beautiful as your gallery, I'll be pleased no end, which reminds me," he noted, reaching over for his briefcase, "I've got the papers here to open our joint account. I've put in a bit to get us started. Just sign them, take the lot to the bank, and deplete it to your heart's content, spare no expense. I can always add more."

Katherine froze when she saw 'the bit' he had placed at her disposal in a mere current account.

"Gerry, I'd have to buy out the Louvre to deplete that. Okay, I'm exaggerating, but you are way too generous, it's obscene!"

"Then you won't have to worry about going over budget, will you? Just don't spend it all in once place, you'll have to buy out the Metropolitan too," he joked.

"And, we're not even married yet! Why are you so good to me?"

"Because you love me as I love you, beyond reason, and I want to spoil you rotten because you can never be spoiled nor will you ever become rotten."

"Now who's talking in riddles? You *are* nuts, you are spoiling me. However, I insist on paying my share, you know I'm going to contribute to our household anyway so … ."

"No way. You have fun with this, no bickering. Besides, I'm well able to provide for us, so no wrangling over 'contributing to the household' and all of that. You know how I am about women putting their hands in their pockets."

"You're terrible! Of course, I appreciate you wanting to assume your duties as man of the house, ready to and willing to support the family and all of that, but let me provide a slush fund, or something for us."

"Save us from independent women! We'll discuss it later. For now, have a ball, have two, throw in a parade while you're at it."

"Now who's being silly? Here, let me show you what I've got in mind to date, you certainly deserve to hear my decorating ideas after handing over an account like this," she said, searching in her purse for her trusty notebook.

"No my dear, surprise me."

"What? As the primary financial contributor to our future home, don't you even want a peek?"

"Nope. I trust your artistic judgement, and besides it will really give me something to look forward to if I don't know. Keep me in suspense."

"You're bonkers. You really don't want to hear what I've got in mind?"

"It's not that," he replied gently, "of *course* I do, I just don't want you to feel uncomfortable, or afraid you might do something wrong, like it's not your home too, if that makes any sense. I want you to feel absolutely free to do anything you want, and this way you don't have to keep running for permission or approval like it wasn't your place. To be honest, I may have fine taste in art and all that, but I'm a terrible decorator. I know what I like all right, but I can't seem to put it all together, hence my dependence on interior designers up to now."

"Surely, you'd want to share some ideas *you* might have?"

"Trust me, you don't want my input in this department because I can't envision decorating plans until they're finished. I'd stick stripes and paisley blots together and not see the problem until it's too late, well, maybe not that bad, but you get what I mean, and I really *do* want to be surprised. You'll just have to wait for compliments and praise when you're done."

"Okay." She smiled. "If that's the way you want it. I hope you like it in the end so *you* don't end up uncomfortable in your own home. Just so you know, I won't be touching your library-dash-office for now, and it's probably best until I have your personal supervision anyway, I'd be afraid of damaging your book collection. I won't be doing the bedrooms yet either, and I may not touch the kitchen at all, I like what was done there so there's no point ripping it out for the sake of change."

"The cook will certainly be happy to hear about that. What rooms *will* you be doing?"

"For now, I'm just going to concentrate on the parlour and dining room, and maybe the entertainment den if that's all right. I'll consider the bedrooms and the rest afterwards when I see how these turn out. Just, be sure to give me a list of your favourite pieces of furniture so I don't toss them into the dumpster, I'll see if I can work them in somewhere."

"Fair enough, that's settled then. For now, *in lieu* of seeing the details of your plans I shall settle for a croissant, maybe two," he hinted.

She smiled. "That can be arranged. You're easy to please."

⚜

Finally, the day arrived for Gerry's surgery, everyone wanted to wait at the hospital with Sophia until he came out of the recovery room, but of course it was impossible considering all their various work schedules and the limited number of visitors allowed at any one time. They would have to make a visit when they could. Katherine however could not bear waiting anymore and not long after opening, she left the gallery in the capable hands of the Gallery Gang on duty that day. Gramps had pointed out long ago that having the workers do your work for you was one of the beauties in owning the business and so she decided now was a good time to take advantage of that. She arrived only a few minutes after Gerry had been wheeled back to his room fast asleep. He had conked out again, no doubt one of the after-effects of the anaesthetic and the other medications he was on. Nevertheless, he looked much better without the bevy of weird contraptions that used to be concealed under the bedclothes. In their place, he was given a very puffy-looking mattress and more pillows, which certainly were a big improvement, especially with the latest arrivals of get-well bouquets and cards surrounding him. That should cheer him when he woke up she thought as she added her own large sunflower and red rose bouquet to the motley assortments. Sophia was relieved to tell her that according to the surgeons, they had no trouble removing the fixators, all went smoothly. Now, the remainder of his recuperation would be a matter of time.

Eagerly, Katherine began making the much anticipated telephone calls, conveying the glad tidings of his successful surgery to everyone before she returned to her loving watch by his bedside with Mrs. R. This vigil was so different from the last time he was brought out of surgery right after the accident, a sleepless night wandering the hospital hallways, wondering if he would pull through and fearing the worst. True, they had some trepidation ahead of them yet, but nothing life threatening like that night all those months ago, they certainly were thankful for that. In the meantime, Katherine and Mrs. R. quietly discussed how their current projects were faring. Mrs. R just had a new tub and shower installed at Stonyvale in the main downstairs bathroom not far from the Morning Room that had now been transformed into a bedroom, while Katherine was just getting into her role as the 'moonlight interior decorator' at the penthouse since she would have to make do with what free time she had at night, explaining she only had a few days out of the week after business hours plus the times she came for hospital visits. However, she had decided that she had better finish some projects before she spread herself too thin and was happy to announce she had at last completed Peter's painting.

"That's wonderful dear. I know he'll love it. However, in case there's no one at the rectory during the day, you might want to consider sending it to the parish office or his Manhattan office instead."

"All right, I'll do that," Katherine agreed, "as soon as the framers are finished with it."

A quiet rustle of bed sheets just then interrupted their conversation. They quickly looked up to see Gerry slowly opening his eyes.

"School day, just five more minutes, wish … Saturday," he drowsily mumbled, closing his eyes again.

"How often did I hear that? Looks like someone is not ready to get up." Sophia chuckled.

"Not to mention regressed a few years," Katherine noted.

However, Gerry opened his eyes again, looking at the ceiling slightly dazed as though trying to figure out where he was, then recognition of his surroundings began to sink in through the drug induced drowsiness.

"Hospital, still, here, flip," he mumbled to himself, "geeze, I, feel, seasick, only, no boat."

Deborah the nurse came in just in time to hear the last utterance and reassured the two concerned visitors that this was perfectly natural.

"Don't worry ladies, it's the after-affects of the anaesthetic. He's going to feel pretty nauseous for a few hours. Looks like our hung-over patient won't be in the mood for any peanut butter cups today. Good morning, Mr. Gerard. Shall I get you a bowl or a towel?"

"Urgh," he replied, slowly shaking his head 'no'. "Are they gone?"

"Who?"

"The nuts, and bolts," he clarified lethargically, meaning 'what', not 'who'.

"Yeah, you're stripped. No more lightning rods," Deborah declared as she checked his drips, "look who's come to see you." Gerry turned his head and smiled faintly.

"Hi."

"Hey there, handsome." Katherine took his hand.

"Ugh, don't feel handsome, you two look beautiful though. Have you been waiting long?"

"No dear," his mother replied, "not long at all. The doctors say it all went well. We just wanted to be here when you woke up, but it looks like you need more rest now."

"You don't mind," he asked apologetically, "I'm sorry to send you away, but it's like I had all of Leroy's parties rolled in to one, and I'm afraid I'm going to need that bucket after all."

"Uh oh, don't worry dear, we'll leave you in peace, we'll try again when the bilge pumps are not on high alert," his mother nodded as the nurse quickly gave him the desired receptacle. Although wanting to take care of her child herself, Sophia knew he was a grown man now who was mortified to have her and his fiancée see him in this wretched state and she rose to leave. Katherine understood and followed suit. Poor Gerry, Katherine knew from experience Leroy's bashes were not for the feint of stomach, even for the seasoned drinkers, and she went outside with Mrs. R to give him some privacy.

The next few days went better after Gerry's stomach settled and he started on his first physiotherapy sessions. He was not allowed to leave the bed yet, but the therapists were gently working his legs, the first step in slowly building up his muscle tone. Gerry felt like he was held captive by some alien force in not being able to move his legs by his own volition, but he had been stuck in a stationary position for months after all. It was mind over matter right now. So far, he did not feel any pain, but of course, he was still soused on plenty of painkillers as the specialist put it. However, the fact he looked more like a human being than a cyborg put Gerry and everyone else in good spirits even if he was still bed ridden. The best part was, he could now turn ever so slightly on his side and the bed railing could be lowered a tad, which meant he could give a decent hug to his loved ones, especially his princess.

"I'm sorry dear, I wish I could visit more often, but now with the decorating, plus I've some plasterers coming tomorrow evening," Katherine began.

"No sweat, you're busy with our little nest. I hope you're having fun despite the workload."

"I am, I just wish I could tell you what I'm up to, but in accordance with your instructions, I shall keep you guessing."

"Good, although if you do want to know, my curiosity *is* getting the better of me," he wheedled.

"Nope, not going to tell you, no matter how difficult it is for you and for me. I shall stick to your original order to the letter. Besides, if I don't obey you now when you make things easy, how will I be able to after we say 'I do'?"

Gerry laughed.

"I didn't think of it like that. So you're really taking this 'obey your husband' thing to heart."

"Yes, 'to heart'. You're so lovable, it's easy."

"That's good to know." He smiled. "I shall add to my order then, don't get too overtired. If you find it a bit much, take some time off. I don't want you ending up in here as their latest patient due to exhaustion. Okay?"

"Okay, deal, if I get exhausted that is. So far, I'm holding up pretty good, although everyone at home is missing me a bit. I'm staying in the apartment so much now, I've practically left Oak Meadows except for weekend visits. Poor Mom is having a hard time, that dreaded day of seeing my wings spread has come too soon. Pops has gone quiet, even poor Gramps has gone a bit glum."

"I'm sorry about that, but you are happy, right?"

"Oh yes, it's just, weird, this moving away from home thing, but I *am* moving home too, you know?"

"I get you. So, you've finally moved in, huh? To think the boyfriend has actually gotten you to that step," he joked, the words out of his mouth before he realised it. Katherine blushed a bit and smiled bashfully.

"Guest room," she clarified.

"Of course." He did not say any more than that. It was enough knowing that the honeymoon was still on their agendas. "You don't mind being on your own? Go ahead and invite someone over for a few nights if you like, maybe you and Suzy could have a girls night in, or how about your cousin?"

"Suzy is a bit busy right now, she and Charlie are starting to get into their wedding plans in earnest, and cousin Stephie is really busy with her photography, she likes to develop her photos at night unless she has an event to cover, so a girl's night in will have to wait. I'm okay though, and there are times I need the peace and quiet, wait until you hear the latest doings at Oak Meadows," she continued.

Last Saturday night she had arrived for dinner in the old neighbourhood to find a few loading vans parked down the road, apparently someone had finally bought the house around the corner and was in the process of moving in. Aunt Martha, who had stopped by for lunch with Helen, was all a flurry once she spotted the new happenings and tried all afternoon to see what was going on down the way from the dining room window, seeing if she would catch a glimpse of the new people and wondering if they would prove to be suitable neighbours considering their fine exclusive address. She eventually cajoled Mrs. Gonzales to see if Steves left behind his old telescope in aid of her neighbourly snooping efforts. Katherine found out because Aunt Martha had stayed for dinner and told her all about the latest arrivals, while Mrs. Gonzales admitted about hunting for the telescope.

"There was nothing I could do, Miss Kathy." The housekeeper sighed as she took her aside for a moment. "Anything to keep peace in the fort. You know how it is."

Unfortunately, since the Oak Meadows neighbourhood was a grand cul-de-sac of sizeable mansion estates, the grounds were just that bit too expansive to allow a decent view, especially as the mature greenery of the gardens got in the way and Aunt Martha had a time of it trying to figure out how to focus the lens properly on the telescope. Of course, Gramps had to add his two-cents worth when he came home from the country club, reminding Martha she could have made it easier on herself if she simply went over to borrow a cup of sugar, helpful advice that she did not quite appreciate.

"Don't be absurd, it's too soon for that. Why, you have to give them time to get groceries first," Martha replied, squinting through the spyglass. Pops just shook his head and continued with his dinner. Silence was always a safe refuge.

Katherine laughed then continued her story, saying the two of them had also caught it that evening from her aunt, hearing needling comments on how it was a pity she and Gerry didn't think about moving in the house instead to guarantee any 'unknown element' would be unable to take up residence within the foreseeable future. Now, there was no knowing 'who' or 'what' had moved in.

"Swell. I'm nagged *in absentia*. So what did you tell her?"

"There's not much you can do to pacify Aunt Martha when she's in one of her tizzies. I just apologised that our plans to live in Manhattan were not conducive to saving the neighbourhood. It will have to manage on its own." Katherine shrugged.

"I assume the apology was not accepted."

"No, especially as she's having a hard time watching us kids leave home. She's as bad as Mom, she just wants to keep us all together."

"Are you sorry though, not getting the place down the block?" He did ask her a long time ago if she wanted to start out with a traditional home complete with lawns and gardens.

"Oh no, why would I? I love the apartment, this city living is all new to me. I'm looking on it like an adventure, and besides, it's much closer to the gallery. I'm finding the shorter commute a big plus, not to mention that house in Oak Meadows would be a long commute for you too, so no regrets about our plans. Like you said before, we're only a hop, skip, and a jump away from all our family, it's not like we're going to Siberia."

"True." He smiled.

"The thing is now, Aunt Martha is already pressuring Mom to invite the new neighbours over for dinner once they get settled. She's anxious that the Fitzgeralds will beat them to it, and she wants our family to be the first to welcome them to the area.

"More like suss out the blow-ins first," Gerry noted.

"You said it! Gosh, and she doesn't even live at Oak Meadows! But now she's hovering around and keeping an eye out to see when that first sign of 'settled in' has arrived, which reminds me, she actually made Gramps that big, red, satin pillow covered in daisies and buttercups like she promised. Now if he wants a quiet life he has to take it out of hiding and place it on his favourite recliner before she arrives, which is practically every day now since the new people down the block came."

Gerry laughed, he knew how Mr. GW felt. Whenever Aunt Martha dropped by the hospital, the first thing she did was rescue the blue flowery pillow that she gave him from its exile in the wardrobe and plump it up behind his head when the nurse on duty left the room, despite the fact the nurse would simply chuck it away again once the over-solicitous visitor had departed. He noted to Katherine she might have to add that blue satin pillow to her decorating ideas at the penthouse if they planned to keep the peace on their domestic patch as well. Katherine gasped, she had not thought of that! No matter, one pillow was no big deal when compared with the plaster job facing her first. The good part was, after her extensive scouting campaigns during her renovation of the gallery, she knew exactly what was available and where to go for any type of bolt, nut, light fixture, fabric, or piece of furniture, which made the process of designing their domestic patch that much easier. Now, if only she had more time for everything, especially sleep, the complaint of every human being living the modern metropolitan life. Gerry reminded her not to burn out. Empires were not built in a day, nor homes in an hour.

"Speaking of homes, Bret must have come back in the last few days, I hear things moving about, and there's a dog barking too. Oh, not loud to be annoying, but I can still hear it," Katherine informed.

The apartment below belonged to an oil exploration and pipeline magnate, Bret Corbet, and it was usually left vacant for long stretches. Gerry had explained to Katherine that Bret was always busy and on the move due to the nature of his company, much like the Reinolds were with their global tours, only worse. In addition to meeting clients around the world, Bret often had to make extended inspections on various oil rigs, and since their summer was the optimum time for travel out to remote oil and gas platforms in the frigid seas of the northern hemisphere, Gerry did not think he would be back at this time of the year. Even when he did return to the mainland, Gerry rarely ever saw his neighbour below, except for the odd times they bumped into each other in the main hall downstairs or shared the elevator. Perhaps Bret bought the condo just for investment purposes and the odd vacation in New York.

"That's news. Back from Alaska already?"

"I don't know, I wouldn't know him if I saw him anyway, since we've never had the chance to meet."

"You could ask the doorman or the concierge, you know." Gerry laughed, no doubt she was still a bit shy to ask. "Never mind, at this point I probably wouldn't recognize him either, he's been gone for ages. I've practically forgotten what he looks like."

"Well, he's got a dog now, sounds like something small, it yaps a lot," Katherine noted. "Maybe he's settled down or retired, you can't have a dog if you're planning to be on the go, internationally speaking."

"That's true, or perhaps he's rented or leased out the place, great. That could prove troublesome." Gerry frowned. Despite the elite address next to Central Park, there was always the possibility of things going askew. It might be great to live in a city, but residential buildings no matter what their address or architectural eminence also had their drawbacks. He had heard horror stories about the condo rented out on the seventh floor; since the tenants were not the owners, they were less than respectful of their furnished surroundings and left a huge repair job for the Wilcoxes, not to mention a few valuables were taken. Who knows what might be facing them now? Gerry hoped that if Bret did decide to lease out his place, the new crowd below were not a bunch that threw loud parties, there might be trouble. Katherine wondered what he meant by 'trouble', did he mean lots of hoodlums? Drugs?

"No. Petitions."

There was the Residents Association they had to contend with on occasion, a handful of the building's retired occupants that had been reluctantly recruited by a well-meaning but loopy and somewhat obnoxious lady that lived on the tenth floor, Mrs. Beechworz, who continually pestered everyone about coming to regular meetings if they were truly interested in the welfare of their building. As official chairperson, she plagued every resident with constant reminders on paying their condominium fees on time including him, despite the fact he was never late, and on one occasion she even started a petition to have all the elevators, both service and residential shafts, locked down at eleven at night to stop the constant cable 'noise' at a reasonable hour. What a batty idea! No one else heard or complained about the elevators before she arrived, and he certainly never heard them to the point of annoyance eventhough he was in a top floor penthouse and closer to the machinery. Despite his life-long phobia concerning that vertical manner of transportation indispensable to a skyscraper, he was not going to slog up and down all those flights of stairs after a late night at work or an evening out just to ensure her beauty sleep remained undisturbed. She was a nutty resident, but then, almost every apartment block in New York had at least one of them.

Katherine was amused by this, she had not yet run up against the intrigues of Mrs. Beechworz and her committee, especially with her remodelling just getting underway. She wondered how she had escaped so far until Gerry admitted he and the neighbours had deftly kept her sheltered up to now. There was a certain understanding among the residents, it was possible to keep things quiet and not let much news flow too far to where it filtered to the tenth floor. The secret was to live and let live, plus ask those living closest to them to keep hush-hush if possible about any projects going on, which they were glad to do as they did not want to become enmeshed with the pro-active badgering of the committee, or rather, their chairperson. In fact, when he had the art collection moved out to the gallery he had already notified the residents on the two floors below personally and by letter about the future redecorating that would occur in his apartment, so they were already used to the idea she might make a racket now and then once she got started.

"Ah, that explains it, I thought I might get a few angry complaints, but everyone has been very understanding."

"Good, that means you'll be clear of Mrs. Beechworz for awhile. You don't want her getting her nose in, she'll start one of those blasted petitions to have engineers come inspect the remodelling every second day to ensure it is in keeping with all the latest building codes and safety regulations, you get the picture. Your aunt is a pushover compared to that sourpuss."

"Good thing the building has service elevators, or there's no way I'd be able to sneak the workmen past this Mrs. Beechwart."

"Beech*worz*, but close enough," Gerry noted, the corner of his mouth twitching into a smile. "Problem is, I'm stuck in here now for the foreseeable future, so I hope you can handle her if for some reason she decides to pay you a visit."

"Don't worry, she can't possibly hear any hammering all the way down on her floor. That reminds me, I'll have to let the neighbours below know what's happening since they're new to the place and may not have been told why there's a ruckus above their heads."

"I'm sure the concierge has already done that for you, maybe even one of the doorman, they also help keep things on an even keel."

"Still, it would be the polite thing to do, I shouldn't leave it to the doormen, plus it would be a chance to welcome our new neighbour, I'll do that first thing tonight."

"Don't forget to ask for that cup of sugar," Gerry joked. Katherine playfully rapped him on the arm.

"Don't' go cheeky on me now."

Driving back to the apartment building that evening, she couldn't help wondering who had taken up occupancy down below them. She hoped she wasn't being nosy like Aunt Martha despite her curiosity. They might have very nice people living there, but after what Gerry had said about the Wilcoxes, they did have a legitimate concern. Suppose they ended up with an 'all-nighter' who insisted on supporting the local wildlife by throwing abundant parties as Gerry thought? There would be no living at all. Just how do you handle that in a calm, neighbourly way? Living in a residential complex was certainly a new experience.

Parking in her usual spot in their allocated parking spaces in the private garage, she quickly learned how one resident handled things. Katherine had hardly turned off the ignition, picked up her purse and opened the door when she came face to face with a buxom, beefy lady dressed in something that was more fashionable during the last World War, her only ornaments consisting of a wide choker of pearls around the neck and a pair of large matching pearl studs embedded in her ear lobes. Her salt and pepper hair was thickly braided and wrapped around the back of her head in a basket-like bun, her dark eyes resolute as though challenging her to a no-blinking match made all that more difficult to engage in by the bulbous wart hunkered down by her left nostril. Katherine suddenly realized this must be the dreaded Mrs. Beechwart … Beech*worz*!

"Excuse Miss, you no park here, you go to service bay," the lady in black declared in a thick Eastern European accent, pointing over to the loading zones set aside for deliveries near the service elevators. For a split second, Katherine could not understand why she was being redirected until she realized she did not look like a resident, especially as they had not met before. She had grown so used to driving her snazzy little gallery van around the place she could easily forget it was not a conventional 'people vehicle'.

"Oh, I'm sorry, but I'm not here for deliveries. I live here, and this is my means of transport for the time being. My name's Katherine, Katherine Walsingham." She smiled, trying to be polite. She would have offered her hand for a handshake if she was not still pinned close to the van. The lady frowned, accentuating her wrinkly brow.

"Where you live? Who you live with," she darted, skipping the custom of introducing herself in turn, her inquisitor tone revealing she had assumed the worst of this 'residency'.

"I'm Mr. Reinold's fiancée. You know, top floor?"

Oh dear, Katherine thought, this first introduction with Mrs. Beechwart, (Beechworz!), was not starting out well. Surely, she had heard of Mr. Reinold's fiancée? Her name was emblazoned on the van after all, not to mention she was in one of his parking spaces. Obviously the residents were good at keeping things hush-hush from the busybody as Gerry hinted. Nevermind, perhaps it was time to finally meet her and get this out of the way, she wouldn't be able to avoid her forever.

"So *you* fiancée," the grim lady noted with satisfaction, finally placing her in her mental notebook for future facial recognition. "Live here now, suppose no other place for van. Overlook for time being."

"Thank you," Katherine replied, eventually unpinning herself and locking the van, but the following escape to the elevators was not an easy manoeuvre as Mrs. Beechworz tagged along right beside her, or rather dragged her down to a speed a notch above a slug's pace since it would be rude to try and dash off when still being spoken to. She had the feeling a large ball and chain in human form had somehow materialized by her side.

"How Mr. Reinold? Better? Home now?"

"Yes. Much better, thank you, although it may be some time before he comes home."

"Good news, but still bad, need new member for Resident's Committee. Must ask someone else. Maybe you think to join. You live here now, must care about building like everyone too."

Uh oh, this did not sound good. Not that she did not care about being a good neighbour, but something told her she did not need nor want to be roped into this semi-totalitarian residential organization right now. Judging by Gerry's tone that evening she knew that those who were unlucky to be recruited, often joined just to be civil, did not escape so easily as though it was some fanatical sect that demanded a soul-binding oath. It would explain why Mrs. Beechworz was avoided like the plague. Katherine wisely declined the invitation thrust upon her, explaining as she toiled towards the elevator that there was no way she could reliably fulfil all the duties and responsibilities expected of a member on the Resident's Committee at the present time, not with running her gallery business during the day and visiting her fiancé in the hospital during the evenings.

"All right, understand, too busy. Think about it, we have big pot-looky after meeting. I make good borscht, goulash too. Always room for new members."

"Okay, I'll think about it, good night," Katherine replied politely as she managed to slip away into the elevator at last. Thank goodness she did not follow her up and pry an invitation into the penthouse, not in its current predicament. Maybe there was someone else from the building she planned to pounce on when they came home that evening, God help them.

Arriving at the penthouse, she laid the keys and purse down, glad to have escaped unwanted company. Before she made herself too comfortable she decided she had better see if the neighbour below was home and apologize for any upcoming home improvement noise as she had promised. Calling the apartment below via the concierge, there was no answer, obviously no one was home yet. She could call again later tonight, but maybe meeting one new neighbour from the building was enough for now. Tomorrow was another day.

CB ❖ BO

Katherine jumped out of bed and began her usual mad dash of getting ready for work, which didn't begin very well that morning after waking up disorientated, thinking she was in her bedroom at Oak Meadows and ended up heading in the direction of the closet instead of the bathroom. Once she realised she was in the city and could actually get herself ready, she then remembered she must notify the neighbour about the plasterers arriving that night, but the early hours of morning were not a proper time to make introductions. The best thing to do would be to call at a more reasonable hour from the gallery, plus cover all bases by leaving a note with the concierge just in case no one was home when she called. Finishing her coffee while writing in a hurry, she slipped her note into an envelope addressed 'To the New Neighbour Below — An Apology for the Noise' and headed out the door. She was grateful to have a busy schedule, she did not want to be reminded that this was supposed to be her and Gerry's wedding day. Just pretend you've decided on a longer engagement she continued to tell herself, sometimes that worked too.

Settling into the studio, her creative bout with Suzy and the Professor was soon interrupted by a telephone call from the framers, the latest paintings were ready to be picked up for the gallery. Good, she thought, it was about time. Despite the number of paintings she sent to them, they never used to take this long. However, the owner of the frame shop had called her personally and asked if she didn't mind, she might want to come herself to inspect one particular painting, they had something very unusual happen and they didn't know what to make of it. Curious, she agreed to come over. She would have been upset by the summons pulling her away from her neglected artwork were it not for the fact this sounded very odd indeed. Capping her paint tubes, she left her Oval Office canvas and drove straight to their shop a few blocks away.

"I'm sorry to trouble you, Miss Walsingham, but I thought it better you take a look. I'm afraid one of your items was damaged and we had to do some repair work," Mr. Hanks disclosed, looking very rueful.

"Damaged? How? What kind of damage?"

"Urm, maybe you should come back and see for yourself, make sure we did a good job repairing it. Of course, no charge for the framing or repairs."

Mr. Hanks led her away from the bright showroom with its myriad of frame displays and matting board samplers lining the walls back into the sawdust scented work area, bringing her directly in front of Peter's painting.

Oh no! Not *that* one! What happened? After all the time she spent working on it! Wait a minute, it did not *look* damaged. In fact, from where she was standing there did not seem to be anything wrong with it at all, the ornate image of the Madonna of Quito looked positively gorgeous in its golden Baroque Rococo frame. She quickly approached the canvas to inspect it and then noticed several differences; the wood frame supporting the canvas seemed bigger, obviously they had reset it with a completely new support, and there were extra fissures in the paint. Thankfully they were not too noticeable unless she was literally nose-to-nose with the canvas, but there were definitely minute hairline breaks visible, small faults that were not there when she brought it in. Did that happen when they reset that canvas, and *why* did they reset the canvas?

"Yes, we had to re-back your painting, and I apologize for that. In fact, I don't know what to make of it," Mr. Hanks answered, "I hate to say this, but there's more damage you haven't seen."

Taking the picture from off its hook, he turned it around and showed her that the canvas had been slit vertically down the left side near where the original wood backing had been. Flabbergasted, Katherine angrily demanded to know what had happened as she looked closely at the repair job, the cut mark carefully knit together with professional patching. She turned the painting back to try and locate the damage on the image, but it had been carefully repaired, the long slit was skilfully concealed.

"I'm sorry Miss, but I wish I had an answer for that," Mr. Hanks replied. "I've never seen anything like it. When we opened up for work a little over a week ago, we found your canvas crumpled in the corner of the workroom over there," he began, nodding over to a wall opposite them, "the backing was completely splintered into smithereens and left in a neat little pile right next to it, along with the staples. It was weird, I mean, not your typical wilful destruction. The edges of the work weren't torn, so the staples must have been taken out one by one," he continued, retrieving a plastic bag from a shelf next to them and handing it to her. Inside was the wooden backing, or what was left of it, hacked down into bits, only one or two decent sized pieces were left to show it was indeed the original frame. "When I unfolded the canvas it was split down the side as you can see from the binding behind. There was nothing for it, but to try and reset it and repair the damage, we do restoration work on split canvases," he concluded.

Well, that would explain the fine cracks, but the cut down the side? Who would do something like that? Just walk right up, slit the thing with a blade, but then decide to take it out of its frame and carefully unstaple it off the wood backing just to crumple it up and throw it into a corner? That would be a rather painstaking job to accomplish. A thief would have finished the knife slit all around and stolen the picture straight from the frame if they wanted to make a quick getaway, but for the thief to change their mind, morph into slow-motion destructive mode and then make toothpicks out of the support yet not run off with the artwork?

"That's just outlandish! Did you have any idea who did this," she demanded as she ran her finger around in the bag to see what else remained, which was nothing but rough sawdust and with the original staples mixed in.

"No, at first I thought it was a burglar, but that didn't make sense. There was no sign of a break-in either. My office wasn't even rifled. Then I thought that someone was trying to settle a score, but who? It's possible one of our new workers might have done it, but I can't believe they'd do something like this, even though nothing like this has ever happened before they came. Of course, I have no proof either, it's a wild accusation to make against them, and they were on their day off before it happened, so it's most likely not them, and I don't have time to get in trouble with the labour commission on charges of unfair dismissal. Makes me wish I had some security cameras back here, then we could figure out what happened."

"Me too, but at least it wasn't destroyed entirely," Katherine replied, returning once more to survey the canvas. She then realized that whoever did the work had painted over the cut ever so astutely, they cloned her colours and brush strokes to perfection. Still, if she had known, Katherine would have preferred to do that part of the repair work herself, but decided not to make a bad situation worse with her temper and interiorly started to count to ten. Pete might be disappointed if she broke her resolution to practise the virtue of patience over his picture no matter what had happened to it.

"I hope you're not dissatisfied with the repair work," Mr. Hanks asked tentatively. He had taken a big liberty in going ahead with the repairs.

"No, whoever did it they did an excellent job. In fact, I can't see the slit. I probably wouldn't have seen it if you didn't show me. However, I wished you had told me so I could have touched it up myself, but since you saved me the time, I'll overlook it."

"Thank you," Mr Hanks replied, looking very relieved.

"So, how much for the work? All of it, including the fix-it job."

"Like I said, no charge Miss, this happened on our floor, we'll bear the brunt of it."

"No way, that gilded frame isn't cheap, and your restorer deserves to be paid."

Mr. Hanks looked at her slightly stunned, but she insisted he tell the price, so he gave it to her, with her usual discount considering the volume of artwork she sent to him on a regular basis.

"Honestly, you shouldn't have to pay at all," he tried to say, but she stopped him.

"Look, you shouldn't have to pay for someone else's maliciousness either. I know this couldn't have been done on purpose by anyone here, it wouldn't make sense to risk losing a customer that gives you consistent framing orders."

"It's relief that you are so understanding, but I promise, I'll try and get to the bottom of what happened," Mr. Hanks assured her, "although I can't think of who might be carrying a grudge against me or the business."

"Or with me either … uh oh, I may have to take that back," she suddenly realized, she had experienced a vicious art attack before at the hands of a schizo. Had lightning struck again?"

"We heard about what happened," Mr. Hanks recalled, "but I certainly don't think this is related. The nut case would have gone for all the works intended for your gallery, not just this one. Maybe they have a grudge against religion?"

"I don't know, but that whacko we had was a weird fanatic all right. Geeze, not again!"

"Do you want me to get the cops in on this? Maybe we should check it out, make sure that nut's not out loose and trying to cause you trouble."

"Gosh no! No more cops," she said shaking her head. "At least this was damage on a minimal scale, if I could call it that, and no spray paint or acid was involved. Besides, the idiot that attacked the gallery has a habit of going for stuff in full public view, it seems she was aiming for the notoriety. This is different, it happened behind closed doors and in private, so can't be the same motive or the same person," Katherine mused as she looked through the sawdust again, just then noticing how perfect the staples seemed to be as though they had never been pulled out, or had left the staple gun for that matter. How odd!

"Maybe, but we'll do our best to find out what happened."

"Okay, we'll keep it quiet, no need to make a news headline about it, it wouldn't do your business any good either," Katherine decided as she dropped the sawdust bag into a trash can. Hopefully the culprit would be caught by the time she had to bring in her next assignment of paintings to be framed. She did not want to have to change her frame supplier now with so many other things on her mind and little time to take care of them. She helped Mr. Hanks box the picture, borrowing a black marker for a moment to write on the front in large letters 'Peter's Madonna' so she could tell it apart from the rest of the boxed art consignment.

Disgruntled, she returned to the gallery with the latest collection ready to be displayed. Before the Gallery Gang began the repetitive process of hauling the new works from the van through the boiler house storeroom to the elevator and on to the various floors and back again, Suzy and Kevin were dying to know what had happened that Mr. Hanks insisted she go to his place personally that morning, and were shocked when Katherine dropped the bombshell.

"Oh Miss Kathy, not one of *your* paintings, and of all things, it *had* to be that exquisite gem!" Kevin gasped, hand over his heart as though someone dear had passed away. "I hope it is not completely ruined, what a tragedy!"

"What?! Who did it," Suzy jumped in next.

"That's just it, nobody knows, and it doesn't look like a robbery, more like another case of vandalism, but thankfully they repaired it."

Suzy shook her head, they had experienced an attack before, but this was strange she had to agree, and they repeatedly asked Katherine to relay the details as they tried to fathom this terrible destruction. The Professor soon appeared from the elevator on his way for another cup of coffee from Andre's place, Olivia came out from the shop when she heard the commotion, and they too heard the news.

"My, that is rather peculiar," the Professor agreed. "Esther will not believe it when I tell her tonight," he said. Dennis was also missing as it too was his day off. He would also hear about it soon enough.

"At least it could be repaired in record time, and the damage is practically invisible. If Mr. Hanks didn't show me, I wouldn't have noticed anything was wrong," Katherine admitted.

"My, that is good news," Olivia sighed in relief before asking if they may see it. Katherine nodded, went to the van where she had left it ready for delivery and brought it in for them to survey. They all gathered around as she placed it against the desk counter and lifted it out of its box, which the Professor carefully held in place for her.

"True, this is not as bad as the last time, I can't believe we had to send that tapestry to Florence to have it repaired," Katherine said, shaking her head. Kevin still grew white with the thought: a rare tapestry from Flanders to have been desecrated in that manner? Nothing short of sacrilege! Even the Professor also looked rueful as that wanton act of destruction was brought once more to mind. "At least this is certainly not as bad as that," Katherine continued, "It's just that I feel like I'm giving Pete damaged goods now no matter how beautiful it is, like it's second hand now," she sighed.

"Aren't nearly all famous paintings 'second hand'," the Professor sagely pointed out.

"Not to mention many renowned and priceless works end up going through some kind of restoration process as they age, it would have happened eventually," Kevin added, trying to find the bright side.

"Hey, maybe it's a sign your painting will become wildly famous before its time," Suzy observed.

"You mean while the artist is still alive to enjoy the acclaim," Katherine quipped despite the tragedy of it all. "I didn't think of it that way, but still … ."

"Yeah, I know, but don't worry, he will love it all the same," Suzy noted.

"Take heart, Miss Kathy," Kevin encouraged, "where Monsignor Reinold is concerned, I do believe the image itself is more important to him than the prestige of owning it as a collector. The spiritual and sentimental value will be beyond priceless."

"You know, that's Pete exactly. I can't help but feel bad about it though."

"It's not your fault, and he will understand that," Olivia reminded her, "at least it could be fixed, and the extra hairline cracks actually give it a very classy antique look, like you did it on purpose for effect."

"I wish I did, then it would be all right. Never mind, there's nothing I can do about it now unless I repaint the whole thing from scratch on a new canvas, but I don't think I'd ever paint it this good a second time around, and Pete's waited long enough. What a shame, if I try to touch up the cracks, I could make it worse. Anyway, let's get the new pieces on display, we can't sell what we don't have on the walls," she continued, trying to take her mind off the problem. "Kevin, will you continue to man the front desk?"

"Certainly Miss Kathy, right away," he replied, straightening up to attention and resuming his position. The Professor rambled off to get his coffee and give his creative Muse a helpful caffeine jolt after he helped Katherine re-box the painting, while Olivia resumed her dusting in the gift shop, a job she hated, but there was a colony of dust bunnies growing quite prolific among the display units that needed to be exterminated before the day was done.

"So, are you and Charlie all geared up for the Elverton opening," Katherine asked Suzy as they began unloading the van.

"Oh yeah! Thanks for giving the invitation to us. I'll be sure to notice every little change and take notes on what he's got in there, like a good scout," Suzy promised.

"Good, we need to know what we're up against."

"True, and to think he tried to entice me over and play traitor on my best friend. Fifth Avenue may be a temptation, but Sir Tempter-Shmempter will have to do better than that, even if he did buy my work," Suzy declared.

"Thanks, Suzy."

"You know, once we get these up, you should go right away and deliver Peter's painting, no point having it sit here, plus, it would give you some time to see Gerry. You go take the afternoon off, it's quiet today, we can handle the rest."

"Are you sure? I did take the morning off already."

"To pick up paintings for here? I think that counts as a good morning's work. Besides, with the plasterers coming tonight at your place, you won't get to see Gerry unless you play truant this afternoon. Go on, get out of here while you can! You're the one who said we have to part from our paint brushes and get a life once in a while, as I keep reminding you."

"Okay, thanks Suzy. I really appreciate it. Go ahead and clock out early tonight, give yourself some time to get ready for the big opening. Kevin is well able to lock up the place."

"Great, will do, and we both know Kevin will be delighted you have entrusted him with the momentous duty of securing the place for the night," Suzy noted.

"I know, he takes everything so seriously, with an exuberant dash of sophistication."

After discussing where the new artwork should be situated, Katherine left the arrangement details in Suzy's capable hands and drove straight to Manhattan with Peter's picture tightly secured in the back of the van. Suzy was right, better not to have it hang around and invite more disaster upon it. He had waited for his gift long enough already despite his assurances she need not rush and to take her time. She just hoped it would not be an imposition to drop of it off at the Reinold offices, but since Mrs. R first suggested the idea, this impromptu delivery should be all right.

On her way to their building, her mind rambled over a hundred and one things, most of all, wistful musings on how this was supposed to be one of the happiest days of her life, which was now put off to another time. Once again she imagined what should have happened, seeing herself slowly stepping down the aisle of St. Patrick's in that beautiful gown, her father soberly yet proudly escorting her to meet a nervous but smiling Gerry waiting for her in the foremost pew, Pete at the altar dressed in white vestments waiting to do the honours of saying their nuptial Mass. She could picture everyone in formal dress, the ladies in their various hats and floral colours, the men in their crisp suits and ties, or at least how she thought the scene would look. Gramps would certainly look quite dandy. No doubt Aunt Martha might be weeping along with her mother at how fast she had grown up, Uncle Tim and Aunt Barbara would also be as proud, and she could just picture Steves and Leroy doing their best trying not to pull a practical joke during the proceedings but coming close to breaking their resolve with Mr. R doing his best to keep them in line, while cousin Jon might miss most of the reception trying to find cousin William a girlfriend, anything to get his little brother's life moving somewhere! Oh yes, jean-and-shirt Stephie would probably resemble a grumpy porcupine having to be stuck in a lacy satin dress all day, but rising to the occasion with camera in tow.

Come on get a grip, it *will* happen, just not today. Katherine knew she shouldn't be doing this to herself, so she tried to think of something more positive. Instead, no matter how hard she tried to think happy thoughts, the bizarre incident at the framers would take the place of her wedding imaginings, or annoying bugs in the brain would eat at her, calling to mind the coincidence that Sir Snoop had the audacity to open his gallery on this day of all days and have the gall to make an attempt to steal her artists plus send her an invitation to boot. In fact, she had recently discovered the presumptuous knight had also sent invitations to her family, the Reinolds, almost all of their friends, including Mrs. Hunt and the Professor and Esther, but they were not about to go at a time like this. Charlie wouldn't have gone either, except for the fact she and Suzy insisted that they needed some spies, so he decided might as well give the new gallery a once-over and promised to give his two-cents worth on what he thought of the place. The only other people who were making an appearance that Katherine knew were Robert Horace as art critic and cousin Stephie as freelance photographer, both loved making dates of working nights, or working nights out of dates, she wasn't sure which came first with them. With a smile, she wondered what deliberately belligerent tirade Horace would print, and was glad Stephie was going so she might see some pictures of the place, including private additional snapshots that may not make it into the paper. Okay, despite the aggravating actions of Sir Snoop, she was still curious about his new base of operations, and her ruminating on what it might be like didn't help to curb her inquisitiveness. Hmm, she may not be going to the gala, but it wouldn't hurt just to drive past the place and see if anything was happening yet now, would it? Fifth Avenue was not far off her course, all she needed was a fly-by to get a gist ... . It wasn't the first time she or anyone else at the gallery had done it.

Of course she soon realised that making a quick cruise through the heart of New York City just before lunch hour on a Saturday was not the brightest idea. If the traffic wasn't enough to contend with, she hit a wave of red lights that made her forward progress appear like regression, especially with all the jaywalking pedestrians taking advantage of the hold-up. Still, the impeding lights snarling up the traffic did her a favour when she made it outside the location she intended to scout, the pesky signals giving her plenty of time to survey the building when she finally snailed past it. The annoying part was—she couldn't see anything. The entire front façade was concealed behind great swathes of royal red material, the sweeping folds hanging not unlike an expansive theatre curtain. There were a few workmen outside arranging a red carpet to the front door. Drat! For the last month there was nothing to be seen except scaffolding and protective construction netting as thick as military grade camouflage, and now to see this pop up without a hint of what was lurking behind. It was literally going to be a surprise unveiling! To think she got stuck in traffic and chugged away time and gas to see nothing but a towering wall of vermilion swags. Well, now that she was there, she took a glance at the men about their work while another man emerged from under the titanic draping folds, untangling himself, then wheeling out a podium, followed by Sir Snoop, who obviously came out to oversee the last of the outdoor preparations. Hmm, it looked like the opening was going to happen smack dab out here in the avenue, obviously some big-wig dignitary would be pulling a rope and down would come the veil first before the drinks and nibbles were served inside. Darn it! Why didn't she think of that? Well, she couldn't have done it with her place anyway, a whole semi-detached former factory conversion featuring three external walls, she would have had to buy out an entire fabric factory to do the honours. Still, it was what was on the inside that counted, and who knows? Perhaps Snoop's gallery was nothing but fancy wrapping on the outside and would have precious little else to show once the packaging came off. As she was watching the proceedings, Sir Snoop turned towards the street. Uh oh, she didn't want to be seen cruising by and quickly slunk down in the seat, hoping he didn't see her. She then realized if he didn't spot her behind the wheel, he would certainly perceive 'Walsingham Gallery' brightly painted down the side in larger-than-life Classical Roman letters on the van. Nope, this was not the brightest idea. Come on lights, go green! Go green! *Stupid, stupid, stupid!*

Eventually, the traffic signals become more obliging and she arrived later than she had originally planned at the Reinold Tower, an historic Art

Deco skyscraper famed for its sleek outline and stair-stepped levels tapering near the summit adding its own contribution to the distinctive Manhattan skyline, the outer corners of the topmost floors near the pinnacle ornamented by elegant Grecian style figureheads in polished bronze, their understated features smiling down on the miniscule crowds below bustling in and out the revolving doorway on their way to business, the arch over the entryway featuring the company's iconic 'R' and lightning bolt surrounded by a stylish geometric representation of 1930s steam ships and propeller planes in a polished bronze *bas relief.* Katherine had often driven past the building before, but had never stopped for a visit since she did not want to bother anyone while they were at work, in fact, she rarely went to the Walsingham building unless there was a big public family occasion hosted on the premises or there was an emergency of some kind.

Parking in the nearest loading zone, she made her way through the great revolving doors into the main lobby with her sizable package. She would have been tempted to take an extra minute to admire the pristine Art Deco marble surroundings with giant bas-relief bronze murals continuing the artistic theme of the doorways were it not for an abrupt and unexpected introduction to a security checkpoint barring the way. All bags, briefcases and packages had to be x-rayed or searched, plus everyone had to be screened through metal detectors as they entered, the exceptions being well-known employees and the higher ranked executives that had a special pass that allowed them through immediately. For a moment, she felt as though she was checking into the headquarters of the FBI. Was this always the case, or did the Reinolds have to crank up the security to this extent? Waiting her turn to be screened, she was finally allowed to pass after her cumbersome box was x-rayed and she approached the main reception desk, requesting her package to be delivered to Monsignor Reinold. Thanking the receptionist, she turned to leave but was politely stopped by a smartly dressed woman who was on her way to the elevators with a slender leather attaché case hanging from her shoulder.

"Excuse me, did I hear you say you are Miss Walsingham?"

Katherine replied in the affirmative.

"It's a pleasure to meet you at last. I'm Mrs. Clarke, Mr. Gerard's personal assistant, well, his brother's assistant for the time being, plus, whenever the 'Captain' adds a few commands or two." She smiled, shaking hands.

"Pleased to meet you, I thought you sounded familiar." That sounded dumb, but it was true, Katherine had left some funny messages for Gerry in the past and recognised the voice that had answered the phone.

"The Bosses should be back from lunch in about five minutes if they're not here already. Would you like to come on up?"

"Oh no, I didn't mean to bother anyone, I just came to make a delivery. It's for Peter," Katherine explained, nodding over to the large box leaning against the reception desk.

"By the looks of it, a piece of artwork?"

Katherine nodded. A mail room assistant was just about to take it away when Mrs. Clarke flagged him down and retrieved it.

"Just in time. New person on the desk, probably not aware that if the family are not here to collect them, all art deliveries to this building are to pass through me or Mr. Kells, Mr. Richard's personal aide. The Captain doesn't like anyone from the mail room handling them in case they get dinged on the carts," she explained. "Are you sure you wouldn't like to stay and deliver it personally?"

"I would, but I'd hate to be a nuisance, and I can't stay parked long in the loading zone."

"Don't mind the loading zone, it's ours anyway. Stay as long as you like," a voice happily boomed from behind and above the lobby bustle. Of course, she instantly knew it was Mr. R. "You're a sight for sore eyes in this burly town! What brings you here, Katie," he asked as he gave her a bear hug. She attempted to indicate down to the box.

"Peter's long overdue present. I just wanted to drop it off."

"Now that you're here, come on up and have some coffee with me. Pete will be close behind I'm sure," he said, giving a quick nod to the elevators.

"I won't hold you up, or anything?"

"Not at all! I could use a longer break today. Mrs Clarke, have Kells hold my calls for the next half hour or so, no, make it an hour at least, and could you kindly have him get some coffee and maybe rustle up some of those flaky rolls? They were a hit with the board this morning."

"Certainly, sir," Mrs. Clarke affirmed, "again it was nice meeting you, Miss Walsingham," she added before quickly making her way to the elevators to carry out her new orders from the Captain.

"So Katie, this is your first time here, and it's about time, too. What do you think?"

"It's beautiful. There's nothing like working in style."

"You said it. Wish I could claim the credit, but this is all the forebears' handiwork. I'm surprised Ger didn't invite you here before now, but I think he was having too much fun in your gallery. Beautiful or not, this place reminds him of work. Come to think of it, why didn't I invite you over? Must be getting rather numb up here in my old age," he joked, tapping his temple. "We'll have to arrange a tour for you, just the interesting bits of course, I'm sure you wouldn't find the file cabinets and the copy rooms very exciting. Here, let me take that," he offered, sweeping up her box and proceeding towards the elevators, the crowd of executives and curious office assistants parting respectfully as the Big Boss and his guest approached, leaving an elevator free for them.

"Thank you, Mr. R, but I won't have time for a tour. I hoped to swing by the hospital after I said 'hello' to Pete."

"No need to explain that, especially today," he noted gently. "Could you hit the button? My arms are full at the moment. That's it. Now, how are *you* holding up?"

"All right, I suppose. I'm trying to keep active," she replied as the elevator doors closed and the car began its upward journey.

"Hmm," he nodded. "I know, it's a hard course set right through the doldrums, all this waiting, everything coming to a standstill. Funny enough, reminds me of the time Ger and I got stuck in this for a spell." He gave a quick nod around the elevator car.

"Really? He told me he got stuck in an elevator with you, but I didn't know it was this. It happened during the Great Blackout, right?"

"Exactly so. Ger was not more than a sprout then. How he came to be with me during a late night at the office I can't quite recall, but there we were, bang! Stopped near the top, no lights, waiting ages for someone to figure out where we were, then, to find we were dangling between floors with only a gap to escape through when the doors were finally pried open. We had to be pulled out, and then the electricity came on only a minute after. Poor Ger, keelhauling couldn't be much worse than that, he can't stand an elevator since, although he uses them anyway."

"I know, he admitted getting pulled through to the next floor above is what freaked him out the most."

"Can't blame him, I'd hate to think … ," Mr R, commented, shaking his head, but leaving the remainder of his thought stay silent. "Come, no need to dwell on that. Good to see you're not stuck and that you've gone on with things. How's your decorating coming?"

"It's just started really. Tonight I've got a crew coming to do some ceiling work and a few of the walls, it was the only time I could get them for this one small job. They're too busy trying to get a hotel finished somewhere. I'm fortunate they squeezed me in."

"I know what you mean, unless you're building from scratch or a roof blows off, these workers today don't want the work! I hope Ger likes what you have in mind."

"I hope so, he says he likes my decorating style in the gallery anyway. I know he's itching to figure out what I'm doing, but he did say to keep it secret."

"You don't say? Looks like he's painted himself into a corner." Mr. R. chuckled.

A minute later, the car came to stop at the elite executive level of the building, the doors opening to reveal another reception area with spacious passages leading to the left and right, the gleaming wood and golden-hue décor more modern than the lobby, yet not clashing with the original architecture. An officious young man with agenda in hand quickly met them as they entered.

"Hello, Kells. Pete here yet?"

"No, not yet, sir."

"All right, just let him know he's got a visitor, that's if Clarke doesn't tell him first."

"Yes sir, will do, and all calls will be held as requested."

"Good. Oh! Where's my manners? Kells, meet Miss Katherine Walsingham, Gerard's fiancée. Kathy, this is George Kells, my personal assistant, and tip top man at that."

"Pleased to meet you."

"It's nice to meet you at last," the young man replied, looking quite pleasantly surprised as he shook her hand, "we've heard so much about you, but wondered when we might hope for a visit."

"She's here now, so as you can already guess, she's to be treated like a VIP around here from this day forward," Mr. R declared.

"Yes sir," Kells nodded, "red carpet treatment. We'll notify the guards downstairs to have a pass issued to you so you can skip the security line the next time you come."

"That's right. I hope they didn't frisk you about Katie. You don't need to go through that, you're family now."

Katherine smiled shyly, bashful with all the exuberant attention, explaining she wouldn't be bothering them the whole time to the point of needing a pass.

"Nonsense," Mr. R. retorted cheerfully. "Bother us all you like. It's high time you get to see your future hubby's place of work, the desk-end of it anyway. Come, come! This way, private offices hard to starboard," Mr. R. directed, "you can meet the crew on the port side later."

"Aye aye, sir," Katherine found herself saying.

Kells gave her an understanding smile as she was steered to the right, all parleys cut short as they went on about their business. Obviously, the crew were used to the Captain's brisk but good-natured way of getting on with things. She waved a little 'goodbye, see you later' to Kells as she went where she was directed down the passageway with Mr. R following, still insisting on carrying the box. It was impossible to curb her curiosity as she quickly glanced at several paintings adorning the walls illuminated with muted lighting, works that depicted the various decades of the company's evolution through its shipping vessels from tall ships and Victorian ocean steamers to the great container carriers and tankers of the modern age. Their ever-changing fleet of ships, land vehicles and aircraft was also represented in specially commissioned works depicting every make and model; horse-drawn delivery wagons, trains, cargo planes and articulated trucks, even the various progressive stages of their famous R-bolt logo was recorded for posterity, the font and lines gradually varying in shape and depth according to the aesthetic tastes of the times.

Mr. R eventually indicated a set of double doors that opened into his office: considering his love for the sea, Katherine was not surprised to see a nautical theme incorporated into the surroundings and was delighted to find that his choice of decorating included a few of his famed art collection in the form of a blustery Turner, a hazy seascape by Monet, and two choppy seas with bobbing ships painted by an artist whose style she couldn't recall off hand until Mr. R disclosed they were by Simon de Vlieger, a contemporary with Rembrandt who specialised in nautical images.

"However, don't get too excited," he advised as she took a closer look while he placed the box down and carefully leaned it against the nearest chair, "all these beauties are the handiwork of a few forgers."

"What? Oh, Mr R! It's bad enough Gerry buys knock-offs now and then, but *you?*"

"Don't worry, I have the originals secured away. Not everything I get is for the private collection, these were investments made in the company's name, so it's safer to keep the real ones tucked down in the hold and place a few copies around as decoys considering all the people that come and go around here. Can't have our assets walking out of here and ending up on the black art market now, can we?"

"No, I suppose not." She smiled. "Your secret is safe with me."

"Good, this only works if everyone thinks they're real. Very few know, so mum's the word."

"Gotcha," she whispered back as Kells entered with the requested refreshments and inquired if there would be anything else.

"No, that will be all for now," Mr R affirmed, "except let us know when Pete gets here, or send him in, will you?"

"Of course, sir." After he left, they discussed all things artistic as they made themselves comfortable. Katherine could not help but be impressed with the rest of the surroundings, especially the magnificent view of the colossal bronze figurehead outside just visible above the corner windows. From the ground it appeared delicate and minute, but here on the top floor it was seen in its full proportions, a great giant standing guard quietly observing the busy ant race scurrying around below. Mr. R explained the figures were allegories of the four winds, while the fellows on the floor below represented the four cardinal directions of north, south, east and west.

"A pain they are too," he noted as he poured the coffee, "the architect insisted on doing something classical in bronze, which means unless they're kept up and maintained, they're always turning bright green like a bunch of seasick landlubbers! We just had them polished up again, but that won't last for long. So, I suppose I don't get to see your latest masterpiece before Pete comes."

"Nope, you'll just have to be patient."

"Sassy thing. Well, while we wait, there's something I'd like to go over with you. It's been on my mind for awhile. I know you're up to your neck in it lately, but would you be interested in squeezing in another commission between your other canvasses?"

"Really? Oh yeah, sure. What do you have in mind?"

"It's high time we had a new family portrait done. Something for Sophie you understand, something positive for her to think on, like your decorating. I'm sure she would rather have a picture suitable to hang in the manor along with the other portraits, so I'm leaning towards an oil. The only thing is, I don't know if I can get Pete in on this, he hates his photograph taken, so we might have some arm-twisting to do."

"Plus, we'd have to wait for Gerry to feel up to it and Lottie to come home, but I'd love to do it for you," Katherine beamed. "I'll talk to Pete, I'm sure he won't mind. Do you want it done before a specific date?"

"Not really. Whenever you can get to it, and, you're to be in it too, you know," Mr. R finished, taking a sip from his coffee.

"What? Oh no! You're as bad as Gerry."

"Why? What's he done now," Mr. R. quizzed.

"Oh, nothing, he just wants me to be the subject of his first oil painting. It's mortifying!"

"Why, it's a compliment, isn't it?"

"Yes, of course, but not when I wanted to hang his first masterpiece in the gallery."

"I see. If it's any consolation, this will just be for us, won't go past the manor."

"Er, okay. I guess I can't say 'no', even if I am including my first ever self-portrait. You really want me in it? Don't you want just yourselves?"

"Wouldn't think of it," he returned as he helped himself to a flaky roll after Katherine had selected one, "a new chapter has begun in our family, and aren't you right at the top of the page?"

"Well, when you put it like *that*," she conceded. "Okay, but I'm not taking a fee this time, I don't charge family. In fact, I shouldn't have taken anything for your first commission on the *Morning Glory* as it is."

"Now, don't feel bad about that. You weren't family yet when I asked for that painting, even then you didn't ask much for it," he observed, brushing off some crumbs from his lap. "Honest work has it's payment due. You've done enough presents for everyone, so no 'buts'."

"One 'but', I'm not exactly a starving artist," she pointed out.

"Yes you are, you're starved for time, so don't be giving it away for free, unless it's for a do-gooder charity case. Are we a charity case?"

"Er, no, … not unless you consider the real meaning of the word 'charity', which is 'love', and since we're all family now as you say, and I do love you all to bits, then you *have* to accept this portrait as a gift. You can't put a price on love."

"I'll be jiggered!" He chuckled, amused at her answer. "I'm paying for time and effort, not for love."

"But art is also a labour of love, not just a business; I therefore decree as the artist I reserve the right to take on a commission for love or money as I see fit. I shall do this for love alone, or not at all."

"I must say this is a rarity, having to talk someone into taking my ready money, and failing at it too! Let's see … a gift. That's the way it's going to be, huh? All right, since a financial transaction is so disagreeable to you, we'll have to come to some other arrangement. It's common practise for gifts to be exchanged, so how about a gift for a gift? You can't argue against *that*, loved ones do that all the time so I hear," he noted before taking another sip from his cup.

This time she was stumped. So this is where Gerry got his stubborn streak. Katherine smiled to herself.

"Oh all right. You win this time, Captain Insistence."

"That's it then. Mind you, it must be something you truly want, and better find something decent. I don't want you settling on any old ho-hum trinket just to keep me quiet."

"Gee, there's nothing I want, I'd have to think about it, to tell the truth."

"Then, keep your options open. You can tell me what you want later after you've had a good think," he concluded as a knock on the door interrupted the proceedings. "Come in!"

"Hi Dad, and hello Kathy! So you're my unexpected VIP visitor." It was Peter.

"Hey son, about time! We were wondering when you'd come. Pull up a chair and have a cup of brew, good stuff this is, no ordinary swill water. Hold on, let me get Kells, we need another cup, and a fresh pot at that."

"Hi Pete. The rolls are good too," Katherine added as Mr. R. went to his desk to make the necessary call.

"Sounds good to me," Peter agreed as he settled into a seat. "How are you today, my dear?"

"Oh, you know how it is, stiff upper lip, but I'm not going to let the postponement bog me or anyone else down. So, enough about me, and open your present!" He turned his attention to the box leaning against the chair beside him.

"Is this what I think it is?"

"Yes, it's ready at last. I'm sorry it took so long."

"No apologies. Wow, thank you Kathy, I feel like a kid at Christmas."

"Um, I do have a confession to make." She sighed as he began opening the top.

"Oh?"

"Not the ones you're used to," she continued sheepishly, dreading to give the news about the damage.

"Hey! Not without me! She insisted on waiting for you, and I'm not about to miss the grand unveiling," Mr R called over from his desk.

"Looks like your confession will have to wait a minute," Peter replied, pausing while the extra coffee was ordered.

"Okay, go ahead," Mr. R prompted as he returned to his seat.

Carefully Peter pulled out the work, unwrapping the frame from its protective packing and quietly looked in amazement as the colours of the glistening oil colours were gradually revealed. Standing up, he held out the painting at arm's length for a moment to study it before following his father's suggestion he lean it up on the leather couch behind them so they could get a better look from a distance. Better yet, Mr R jumped from his seat again, grabbed one of the counterfeit Vliegers off the wall and motioned for Peter to hang the bejewelled Madonna in its place under the light.

"Magnificent." Mr R nodded in approval.

"Indeed! Thank you so much Kathy, you certainly outdid yourself this time. She looks more splendid here than in the original cards I gave you."

Pleased to see he was happy with it, Katherine explained she wanted to do more than just copy the little devotional cards, and since it was impossible to discern the fine details on them, had decided to make some changes on the Madonna's dress, adding more lace and jewels where possible without altering the overall Spanish style too much. Peter thought that was what was different and complimented her on her artistic additions, a myriad of regal touches befitting a picture depicting the Queen of Heaven. However, when Peter noted he had the strange feeling that the completion of this work entailed more difficulty than was expected, Katherine was afraid the time had come she had better get the bad news over with and 'fess up'.

"It's funny you should say that," she began, but was stopped as Kells buzzed through, apologizing for the interruption and said it was urgent.

"Now what," Mr R grumbled to find that the bane of the company, the troublesome Mr. Finley, had arrived unannounced without a scheduled appointment and was insisting on talking to someone about his shipping contract, again. "Of all the … ! I've got half a mind to cut the anchor on this fellow and let him float off! I'm sick of this!"

"We can't be rude either, customer service and all that pleasant marketing stuff," Peter reminded. "I'll handle it."

"Nonsense. Katie came to see you, I'll go parley with him," Mr R. reluctantly decided, setting down the bogus Vleiger he still had in his hand. "Oh, might as well run past Pete our new art project while I'm gone and see if he wouldn't mind coming aboard. Now that I've seen this, I know you're the right artist for the job," he hinted to Katherine before heading off to deal with the intrusive scallywag, passing by Kells as he brought in the coffee.

"New project? Sounds intriguing, but first thing's first though. You were saying you had a confession to get off your chest," Peter continued once the refreshments were delivered and they had the office to themselves.

"I hate to spill the beans now since you love the picture, because after I tell you what happened, you're eyes will always be drawn to the flaws," she ruefully began.

"Let me guess, someone tried to destroy it."

"Yes actually." Katherine was surprised. 'Destroy' just about summed it up! His uncanny sense of perception still threw her through a loop at times. For some reason it was easier to tell him now what happened after he had laid bare the problem and she immediately launched into a detailed account of her trip to the framers that morning. While she was still flabbergasted about the whole thing, Peter remained calm, but was reflective with the news.

"I'm not surprised at all. Instead of 'someone' I should say some 'thing' is gnashing its teeth and wishes this picture would disappear," he quietly observed. She was about to ask 'what', then realised what he meant.

"No way. Seriously?"

Okay, that was creepy.

"I'm afraid so. Don't worry Kathy, the spite was directed at me, and at the Madonna of course," he concluded, giving a respectful little bow towards the painting. He said nothing to Katherine just then, but it wasn't the first time something sacred he owned was tampered with, prayer books, medals and rosary beads occasionally became the brunt of the evil spirits' psychological games. Sometimes these objects went missing yet would mysteriously turn up again, or if playing 'hide and seek' wasn't enough, they suffered some degree of inexplicable damage that could only have happened by unseen means. One set of beads that a parishioner had brought him from their pilgrimage to the Holy Land that he cherished were brutally dismembered one night while he slept, the beads crushed and left in a little pile in a corner of his room while the links that had held them together were found scattered everywhere on the floor and got stuck in the carpet. The obvious conclusion was the prayers said on those little beads were saving too many souls and 'downstairs' didn't like it one bit! Now, to have something attacked before it was even presented to him was a new experience, but then he was not at all astonished. The devil was forever in a venomous rage against the Mother of God, the fiend even admitted once in a vision to a mystic that it was because of Her that he fell, disclosing in a fit of temper that She had always defeated him while She replied sadly, "not without wear and tear".

"But can you actually see the damage?" Katherine pulled his thoughts back to the present.

"Not from here," he admitted, before moving closer to the canvas, "I can't ... oh, along there, is it? Why, it's hardly noticeable. It's so near the border edge, you'd really have to search for it."

Katherine agreed that was true, the framers did an excellent repair job, she couldn't find fault with their work, and neither could Peter.

"Still, you'll always notice the weak spot now," she continued with regret.

"Not really, your rendering of our Holy Mother is so beautiful that what happened to the canvas itself just fades into the background, you can't take your eyes off Her, which is how it should be." He smiled. "Thank you so much, my dear. I really appreciate the effort and time you put into this."

"Aw, it's nothing, really," she replied bashfully. "I'm just glad you still like it. I was tempted to start the whole thing over on a new canvas when I saw what had happened, but you'd have to wait all over again, and then I wasn't sure about the face, I know I'd never do it justice a second time. Faces are the hardest to get right, especially expressions. As a devotional picture, it really had to be perfect, more so than with other pictures. I mean, how can anyone pray to someone when they're cross-eyed?"

Peter laughed. That was true, he agreed. Quite apart from the great masterpieces of the world, there were so many amateurish devotional artworks out there that defied all taste and proportion. He especially disliked those that were overly sweet or too fluffy in a sentimental way, or were given exaggerated melodramatic rolling eyes that suggested insanity rather than spiritual ecstasy, which was quite a sobering experience if anyone was privileged to witness it in real life. How often sanctity was depicted as sappiness! On the contrary, saints were quite down to earth and looked one directly in the face, however, it was understood most devotional items were slapped together just for the pilgrim markets. His parishioners often gave him gifts of pictures and little statues, but some had chosen a few that fell short of eternal perfection somewhere along the production line, yet had managed to sneak past the inspectors and out onto the shop shelves. He knew the gift-givers meant well, what the images represented was more important, but that did not make it any easier to pray in a collected manner before them. One lady had given him a small resin statue of St. Peter she bought during her tour of Rome, but despite the Apostle's patriarchal bearing, he found it near impossible to look upon it without some amusement. The eyebrows were painted in broad strokes so close together they could practically be counted as one. Katherine laughed and offered to try and fix the statue's unruly unibrow for him if he wanted. Peter thanked her but declined, the scowling' saint's brow may be difficult to pray with, but it was a good if but comical reminder to keep his own short fuse in check. At least he wasn't as bad as Fr. Mark's little plastic statue of St. Jude, which on top of its assembly-line appearance had suffered a tumble. Mark had accidentally knocked it off his dresser, leaving poor St. Jude with one gaping doll's eye and an empty socket, a woebegone condition that seemed strangely apropos for the patron saint of hopeless cases.

"I should ask St. Anthony to find the other eye so we can try to fix it, but it's long gone in some vacuum bag by now."

"Oh Pete, that's awful." Katherine chuckled. "Speaking of faces, I should tell you about the new commission your Dad has just given me."

Curious to hear what this could be about, they sat back down as she disclosed the new project, Peter assuming a slightly pained expression over his coffee when she told him.

"I know, your Dad said you hate to have your picture taken," she continued, taking another flaky roll, "and I can commiserate with you, he wants me in it too. On top of having to paint my own portrait, Gerry has gotten the bright idea of doing a painting of me, so at least you're not as bad off. I'm getting the portrait-treatment in spades, so in my estimation, you'll be getting off lightly."

"I suppose I am. Well, it was only a matter of time before Dad got the notion to have one done and stick us with all the other old portraits in the house. Of course, if this might give Mom something to look forward to, I'll go for it. However, a photo is one thing, but a painting is an entirely new ball game. The only problem is knowing when if ever I will be free long enough for a proper sitting."

"No sweat, everybody doesn't have to be together at one time, I can do separate sketches plus photos and build up the painting from there, gone are the days a subject has to sit for days on end."

"Okay, in that case, batter up to the plate. I'm in."

"Great! One thing I can definitely promise you, artistic licence has its many perks. I'll make triple sure you won't look like your school, passport, or driving licence photos."

"That's a relief, though it would be a good chunk of humble pie if I did." He laughed. "I'll be quite content if you just draw me as I am."

They chatted for a good half hour afterwards until Peter wondered if anyone had given her a decent tour of the place now that she was here, remembering this was her first visit.

"Gosh Pete! Look at the time! I won't right now, maybe another day, if that's all right. I was planning to visit Gerry after I dropped off your present and didn't intend to stay this long."

"You'd better vamoose then. I won't hold you up any longer, but your visit was most welcome, and thank you again for your present. It is sublime, I feel utterly spoiled. I should at least contribute something towards the frame."

"Oh no you don't! Your Dad and I had a hard enough time talking each other in and out of paying or not paying for his new commission, and I'm not about to start again on this one too! A gift is a gift, and the frame goes with it. Period."

"All right, but I'll say a special Mass for you, how about that?"

"You just offered me something I can't refuse, didn't you? You're just as insistent as your Dad, but thank you very much. I do appreciate it."

"I know, and you're welcome." Peter smiled, happy to mark in a space for her in his Mass booklet before insisting he see her to the elevators.

On the way back, he could hear a slightly heated conversation coming from behind his office door, obviously the Captain and Finley were going over the small print in the contract in there. Best to work from his father's office until their conflab was concluded and he informed Mrs. Clarke of the temporary relocation, instructing that his calls be put through the Captain's quarters instead, also asking if she wouldn't mind fetching the third quarter projections as he looked over the messages she had collected for him. Sure enough, Lottie had sent him a quick communication that read like a telegram: '*All is well, inspection almost completed, taking some time to do a little sight-seeing, food good if you know where to go, Africa is so exotic* (!!!)'

"She insisted I include the exclamation marks," Mrs. Clarke explained. She was about to close the door, he motioned for her to leave it open.

"That's Lottie all right," Peter nodded as he sat down behind the desk, relieved there wasn't a calamity waiting for him to tackle as he glanced through the other slips of paper. By the looks of it, just some usual calls to return and no surprises turned up at the board meeting that morning according to a transcript of the minutes, all looked within the ordinary run of things.

As he carried out his telephonic duties, his eyes were continually drawn over to the wall. Naturally, the new picture in the room attracted his attention, which reminded him he should bless it right away. Oh, right, his case was in his office, which was still occupied thanks to the unexpected arrival of the contract haggler. No problem, before he received another call he could go ahead with a simple vernacular blessing and do the formal ritual later when he could get to his bottle of holy water and book of Latin ceremonies. Once he had that completed for now, he grew thoughtful as he contemplated the unusual view. Below the golden Madonna sat the seascape by Vlieger where his father had left it, propped up on its side as though laid at Her feet like a votive offering. This sea scene also happened to be one of his favourite pictures in the collection too. The tableaux was curiously in keeping with the Madonna's other title of 'Star of the Sea', the beneficent Mother guiding Her children through the perilous voyage of Life to the Eternal heavenly port. The symbolism instantly recalled to mind Fr. O'Conner's wise words of comfort way back when he was facing momentous decisions at one of the biggest crossroads in his life; that God never promised a calm voyage to those who followed Him, but a safe harbour at the end. However, the now vertical horizon of Vlieger's nautical image oddly suggested the scene of a sinking ship as it sat in a disorientating perspective, the bow of the vessel pointing downwards to the floor. That can't be right! Our Lady was supposed to help keep the boat afloat, not watch it flounder. Hmm, that only happens when people allow themselves to drift beyond Her help he reflected. Uh oh, thank you Holy Mother for the warning, I get the message. Wasn't he currently caught in rocky waters with all this business of helping out in the office? He certainly was trying to manage two vastly different ships at once, the 'USS Secular World' and the 'HMS Religious Life', which was not an easy feat. How he longed to get back to his regular parish duties full time, the executive life was certainly putting a considerable strain on his spiritual one. As a priest he was supposed to be guiding a 'boat' filled with souls, not shipping containers! He sighed as he returned to the desk, of course he must always accept whatever happens as part of The Plan, God's unfathomable Will. No doubt this was a test. Well, come what may, he did not intend to fail and resolved that as long as he was temporarily stepping in to help at Reinold Enterprises, he would be extra vigilant.

A few minutes later his father returned mumbling after his tour of duty with that insufferable Finley, but brightened up when Peter informed him that he was signed up and all in for the family portrait as he re-boxed the Madonna and put the ship back in its place.

"Good! That's settled then, we'll figure out the details later, we have to discuss it all with Katie anyway. Now off you go sailor, time to hoist the sails, there's work to be done."

"Yes, sir."

In a few minutes he was back in his own space in the other corner office and placed the box on the sofa with the intention of leaving the picture safely packed until he could hang it in his waiting room at the parish basement. On one hand, it seemed a shame that it was not going to be displayed in a church, but he had always wanted a very powerful image to help spread consolation and grace in that rather dismal reception area. His working quarters desperately needed some extra brightening up despite his various improvements on the spiritual level as well as the decorating, and was very glad he had chosen the Madonna of Quito to be painted as his present. Katherine's rendering of her was certainly magnificent, as his father had noted. However, on second thought, after the little loving warning the Madonna had given him with the topsy-turvy ship, perhaps it was best if She stay here for a while, just to keep an eye on him. In fact, that was a very good idea. How could he drift off course when he beheld the plaintive gaze of his heavenly Mother? As it was, Gerry had left a bare place or two on the walls where a few of his paintings had hung before he shipped off everything in his private art collection to Kathy's gallery. Peter unboxed the painting once more and hung it up near the desk. Yes, that's perfect. It was as if the place had been prepared for Her on purpose, but of course, Divine Providence always had a way of arranging things in the most natural and timely way. As he believed, there was no such thing as a coincidence. Heaven's ways do not always display themselves in a spectacular science-defying manner.

Before he forgot, he had better bless Kathy's painting properly and retrieved the necessary items from his ecclesial case. Just as he finished making the final sign of the cross with the holy water there was a knock, it was Mrs. Clarke waiting at the open door with the third quarter projections he had requested.

"I'm sorry, I didn't mean to interrupt anything," she apologised as she placed them on the desk.

"No, you're not, I've finished, and I did say 'come in'," he replied, putting his book and bottle away. "Thank you, I needed these," he continued, taking the folder and glancing through the papers.

"I'm sorry, may I?"

"Hmm? Oh yes, go ahead," he replied when he noticed she wished to take a closer look at the new art delivery.

"I couldn't help but wonder what was in the box, it's very beautiful. Mr. Gerard said Miss Walsingham was very talented."

"Yes, she is quite an artist. Her style is a little unusual in her other works, ground-breaking in a quasi-Classical way," he continued, sitting down with the reports.

"Your brother did say she was not your typical modern artist. Well … I'd better get back to work. Will there be anything else?"

"No … oh yes, could you take that please and keep it some place where it won't get thrown out," he asked, nodding to the box on the sofa, "I'll need it to repack the painting later."

"Yes sir, I'll keep it in the filing room. Will there be anything else?"

"No, that'll be all for now, thank you."

Taking her cue, she stored the box as requested and returned to the myriad of tasks awaiting her, a little annoyed, but not with her secretarial duties. Still always so cool and aloof! After all this time back with the family and his former career, he hadn't thawed one iota! In fact, he seemed even a little more distant just then, more so than usual if that could be possible, she couldn't be imagining it. In the 'good old days' before the priesthood he used to engage her in a friendly chat about something interesting that happened during work hours, the art collected by his family used to be one of those subjects, but this time … short, polite, almost standoffish. Certainly not what she was hoping for or expecting! When she came across Mr. Gerard's fiancée in the lobby with that box, her heart gave a little flip, knowing this could be one of those ice-breaking moments that might melt the barrier between them, if only by a slight degree or two. Instead, the chilling opposite had happened. Maybe he was just stuck into work right now she thought as she printed out a few business letters. Hmm, no, it wasn't that either, she couldn't help but notice it was a warm, cheerful Peter who escorted Miss Walsingham to the elevators, he was obviously delighted with *her* visit. She would have been struck with a blinding fit of jealously were it not for the fact she knew there was nothing going on between them, Mr. Gerard had told her that his brother and Katherine were very good friends, that it was through him that he met her in the first place. No, Miss Walsingham had no designs on Peter and was just an accepted member of the family. Miss Charlotte was constantly singing her praises and it was apparent the Captain thought highly of her too, which was a rare thing. It was not an easy thing to impress the Big Boss, he was usually so tetchy and sceptical of people until they were tried, tested, and proved true to their word.

No need to be jealous? Perhaps not, but there was another strain of envy that she could very well catch right now, the regret-filled kind that manifested itself with the recollection of how she had dismissed the chance of settling for second best in Mr. Gerard long ago, thanks to her single-mindedness with the fact he wasn't Peter. Now, she wished she hadn't been so inflexible after witnessing the reception Miss Walsingham received, it made her realise how much closer she could have been to Peter on a personal level as his sister-in-law, if there was any 'second-best settling' in life she had to accept. She certainly would be treated much better by him right now, not to mention get to see him more often and for longer periods of time than she did as his personal aide, and even *that* would come to an end when he returned to his pastoral work full-time. How she dreaded that approaching day!

That evening she was one of the few employees in the building after hours, there were one or two things she had to get done before she clocked off that had taken more time than she had planned. Peter too was staying a bit late she noted with curiosity, not that she didn't appreciate having him around a little longer! She wondered what he could be up to and was glad she could invent a valid pretext to knock on his open door. Invited to enter, she found the scene strangely atmospheric as the evening twilight descended, Peter seated quite stately under the noble gaze of the new picture, busy at work as though he were writing down a royal decree dictated to him by the image of the crowned Queen. Approaching the desk, she enquired if it was necessary to bring such and such a report to Mr. Gerard on Monday, or would he like to handle this himself? As Peter thumbed through the papers she had brought in, she quickly glanced down at what currently absorbed his thoughts. She was not far from the mark. On the desk lay a small pocket Bible and a type of prayer book. He was working on something theological judging from what he had written as a heading on a yellow legal pad, 'Fourth Sunday After Pentecost'. It was difficult to decipher it upside down from where she was standing, but it looked like his sermon for tomorrow.

"Yes, Gerard might want to tackle these personally," Peter broke in.

"All right, I'll drop them off to him on Monday."

"Thank you, Mrs. Clarke. Have a pleasant evening," he returned, already back to his writing without hardly looking up.

"Good night."

Only a minute or two, that was all. How she lived for those minutes!

Eventually wrapping up work, her thoughts were still fixated on the events of that afternoon and Peter's unrelenting reserve. It was difficult to believe, despite being surrounded by all the familiar comforts of his former life these past months, he showed no signs of wishing to return to the company or a secular life. She was in danger of losing him again! Maybe she should just get over it? No, it was too soon yet! She just had to give it time, he couldn't remain indifferent to everything here, especially her …yet, it was staring her in the face. Peter's affections lay elsewhere despite her various little attempts to attract him, she had to admit his heart was not *here* where it should be!

Peter had already left by the time she was packing up to go home, she didn't see him leave. She paused for a moment, then found herself opening the door to his office and switching on the wall lights, the lustrous oil colours of the Madonna came into view, the painting commanding her gaze. Situated close to the desk, the regal Lady seemed to extend a quiet authority over the room, it felt as though a living person had taken up residence within the office and planned to stay for some time. Strange, since she knew Peter would be taking the picture with him, especially after he had requested her to store its box. If only he hadn't! That simple cardboard container was now another reminder of his inevitable departure, that he would one day pack up the little he had brought with him and take it all away forever. Face it! He's not going to stay. To top it off, she was duty bound to guard this latest harbinger of rejection and ensure it didn't get tossed away with the rest of the trash! Every time she went into the filing room she saw it, 'Peter's Madonna' was written on the front in black permanent marker, *La Isla Bonita* continued to replay in her head every time she read those words that afternoon … *I fell in love with San Pedro.*

Unexpectedly, it dawned on Lucinda that she *was* jealous, not on account of Miss Katherine, but because she did indeed have a rival, there *was* another Woman in the way. This Church of his, he considered it his 'Bride' as well as his 'Mother', why, he even wore a gold band on his wedding finger! These Catholics had a strange way of thinking about religion. Earlier she thought she had a good chance to win Peter back with the offer of a real life when it seemed he had his affections tangled with an ethereal idealism that would prove tiresome and unfulfilling, but now she realised that despite all this mystical nonsense, she was indeed dealing with a Woman standing in the way of her bliss just like any other adversary. So, it really was to be spirit against flesh, is that it? Huh. Even God said it wasn't good for Man to be left alone, Peter had to crumble eventually despite his high set of principles. She drew closer to read again the ornate inscription painted within a curling scroll near the bottom: *Our Lady of Good Success, Quito Ecuador.* 'Good Success', what a title!

"So, you think you can hold onto him, don't you," Lucinda thought, eyes steadily fixed on the painting, "we'll see. There still is time.

May the best woman win," she declared silently as she left the room, turning out the lights.

ᚼᚼ❖ᚼᚼ

Unable to wait for Suzy and Charlie to get in contact and furnish her with all the dirt about Sir Snoop's official arrival on Fifth Avenue, Katherine ignored the mess left by the plasterers the night before and went out to buy a copy of nearly every Sunday periodical that printed any semblance of a cultural column before she went to church. Sure enough, there were big colour-page splashes of the new gallery's façade as the red curtain came down, the senator having the honour of pulling the cord with Sir Snoop and the mayor politely applauding. The disappointing part was, that after all the secrecy there was no surprise about the latest name of the place thanks to the invitations, 'The Elverton Gallery', positioned vertically down the front of the building in trendy gold metal letters that were lit from behind with blue-hued lights, not too bright or tacky to resemble the neon blare of a Las Vegas casino, but just jazzy and elegant enough to be worthy of the Big Apple accustomed to the vibrancy of Times Square, not to mention the sophisticated glitz of the artistic scene.

Hmm, it was hard to get an actual gist of the place when the photographs mostly featured all the dignitaries and big wigs that showed up, generally posing with their arms around someone's shoulders or with glasses of bubbly fizzing away. In addition to the Senator and the Mayor, there were the usual assorted pillars of society, some notable actors from Broadway, several pop stars, and a few sports legends had been invited too. Of course, there was the expected photos of the artists present to see their works on display. Katherine did not see a shot of Suzy or Charlie among the guests, and was disappointed Suzy didn't make it in the first papers she viewed as a visiting artist, even if her work wasn't on show, but she could soon see the reason why as there were some surprises basking in the limelight at the Elverton Gallery such as Lemnen, the latest and rising star of the current 'Neo-Pop-Futuristic' trend currently catching everyone's eye—and *gasp*! Sir Snoop managed to entice the city's most notorious art-recluse out from under his rock, Kroger, who rarely showed his work in public and yet demanded outrageous prices, which nobody seemed to mind and were very happy to pay. She thought she had an issue about letting non-Gallery

Gang members into her studio to view all the works in progress, but Kroger was known to go ballistic if a prospective investor dared to criticise him after he deigned to let them into his secretive studio apartment for a viewing. It was common knowledge one patron got doused with a jar of indigo coloured spirit-rinse together with the soaking brushes and a fistful of paint tubes quickly following when they had made the unfortunate remark the proportions in his latest masterpiece were slightly eschewed. From what she had seen of Kroger's scrubby work on display in the Museum of Modern Art, Katherine believed she had figured out what caused that colourful uproar: she observed no proportion to his style at all, but woe betide anyone who dared question his visionary genius! Oh well, no time to read the columns in the papers. First she had to go to church, then it was off to the hospital to see Gerry. She could wait and read Horace's narky witticisms with him later, hopefully they might have a good laugh over it because right now the photographs were a bit telling. It looked like she might have more than a serious competitor on her hands, especially if Kroger became a regular at the Elverton. Gosh, what on earth did Horace have to say about last night's event? I wonder if cousin Stephie got some better photos? There was no time to find out now, she would have to wait until after church.

Running a bit behind, she made it in time to find a seat near the back as by now they were nearly all filled up despite the size of the cathedral. Maybe she should have waited until afterwards to get the newspapers. It was a challenge to focus on the spiritual world when 'art-as-business' continued to intrude upon her thoughts. It was only human to mull things over, but come on, get a grip! This was supposed to be the holy day of rest after all. If the new gallery wasn't intruding upon her thoughts, the hushed bustle of the parishioners arriving proved a bit distracting, however, she was happy to see Mr. and Mrs. R join her in the pew before it filled up, giving them a quick hug.

"My, it is getting crowded, even at this hour, and for a Latin service too. Looks like we're stuck in the trunk today," Mrs. R. whispered.

"Yeah, I know," Katherine softly replied, but was unable to finish her sentence as the bell rang, announcing the celebrant was about to enter. Everyone stood to attention, while a few latecomers hunted around in the back for the last of the seats. From the corner of her eye, Katherine thought she saw someone familiar enter with the stragglers and take one of the few remaining spaces, it looked like Mrs. Clarke … oh yes, it was. Maybe she was Catholic too.

It was almost effortless to become collected once Peter entered the sanctuary following his faithful altar server, even if she could barely see him from that distance. The worshippers dutifully kneeled as he commenced the preparatory prayers. Katherine couldn't explain why, but it cheered her up when she saw him even as a speck on the horizon, it was as though he had given her some wise words of encouragement to get through the day without having said anything. Always dignified and reverential, he unconsciously generated a numinous peace that made her wish she could figure out how to attain the same inner serenity. Some days that sense of grace surrounding him was more palpable than others, and this was one of those mornings. It was such a contrast, remembering him at his family's office the day before and seeing him now in the cathedral. Although he always radiated that inner harmony wherever he happened to be, it was obvious he had left the pecuniary bustle of the business world and was much happier here.

After the various opening prayers, there were the readings; first a rambling passage from St. Paul to the Romans, no doubt the ancient way of expressing things was not easy to translate into modern English, then an excerpt from St. Luke. Considering Pete's enthusiastic interest in sailing, not to mention his vocation, Katherine couldn't help but smile to herself as he read the Gospel passage for the day—Jesus teaching the crowds around the shore of Lake Genesareth from Simon-Peter's boat, then astonishing him by the miraculous draught of fish after which the dumbfounded fisherman babbled for the Lord to depart from him, yet was told that henceforth he would become a fisher of men. With the reading concluded, the echoing noises in the cathedral increased for a minute or two as everyone settled back down to hear the sermon. After the stillness returned, Peter calmly looked ahead for a moment as was his custom before launching out into the deep:

"I assume St. Paul has just about confused everyone this morning, am I right?"

A few chuckles issued from the congregation, including a nod or two.

"Very well, it looks like I shall have to tackle his epistle first. Essentially, the Apostle is reminding us of the struggle between the flesh and the spirit, the desire to follow God's Will and the war we still have to fight in order to follow It if we truly desire salvation. Since the moment Original Sin was committed, the combat against temptation is hard and incessant for our fallen humanity leads us downward and away from what we know God wishes us to do, jarring with our spiritual aspirations to do what is right.

All of creation feels the vanity of the world, *every* creature and not just us: everything 'groans' with all the struggles associated with the instability of this life filled with turmoil and the suffering rightly due to our sins. What St. Paul is trying to say is we and all of creation await that time of ultimate deliverance, when the battle is finally accomplished and we may enjoy the spiritual fruits of eternal life forever as the victorious children of God in the new heaven and the new earth. Despite all the sacrifices and persecutions we undergo for the sake of God, they are passing and cannot be compared with the everlasting joys of Heaven. Okay, I haven't lost anyone, have I?"

The congregation chuckled again, a few shook their heads.

"Good. Now that we've straightened out St. Paul's letter, you're probably wondering what all that has to do with the Gospel for today, so bear with me, we have a puzzle to connect. In the same chapter of St. Paul's epistle, we find a few connecting pieces, for instance, his encouraging battle cry, 'If God be for us, who is against us?', and also, 'Who then shall separate us from the love of Christ? Shall tribulation? Or distress? Or famine? Or nakedness? Or danger? Or persecution' Or the sword?' True, we have a tough battle ahead of us as we follow the Will of God, defying everything that would try to knock us off His path, 'groaning along' with all of creation as St. Paul expressed it, but as long as we have God on our side and do everything to remain in God's sanctifying grace, who can be against us? Why be afraid of the battle and life's hardships when we have God and will possess Him for Eternity? Doesn't that sound very similar to the Introit in today's Mass? 'The Lord is my light and my salvation, whom shall I fear?'— and this is one of many lessons we learn in today's Gospel, even if it is not apparent at first. So, now it's time to put together the final pieces of our puzzle.

The Lord has just commenced His ministry around the Lake of Galilee and announces that the Kingdom of God is at hand. In this way does the Light of the World begin the great work of Salvation, fulfilling the prophecy of Isaiah concerning the despised land of Galilee: 'Galilee of the Gentiles: The people that sat in darkness have seen a great light: and to them that sat in the region of the shadow of death, light is sprung up.' Christ begins to call His disciples, shortly after to be known as His Apostles who in turn will become bright lamps reflecting His Light as they announce the gospel. St. Luke's narrative of Simon's call is particularly enlightening because it not only shows his future role as the head of the Apostles, but how he comes to recognise and accept the Lord as the promised Light.

After preaching to the crowd from Simon's boat, Jesus tells him to sail out and cast his net. Of course, we know what Simon says; 'Master, we have laboured all the night and have taken nothing: but at thy word I will let down the net.' There! We first see the holy virtue of *obedience*. Simon hears, and despite all logic contrary to his experience of how fishing 'should be done', not to mention the exhaustion of having worked all night with no results, he hears the voice of the Master and obeys nevertheless. Lo and behold, what do we have? The net rapidly fills up with such abundance to the point it breaks. Isn't it interesting that the Hebrew name 'Simon' means 'he has heard'? Some say it also means 'obedience', and seeing Simon's actions just here, I am inclined to agree with both. Therefore, blessed are they who hear the Word of God and keep it, their efforts shall bear much fruit, or in Simon's case, a lot of fish.

Next, we have the virtue of *humility*, which is part and parcel with obedience, for one must be humble to obey. We also see this virtue in action when Simon calls over James and John to help as they cannot take all the fish in on their own. We must be humble and know we cannot do anything without God, nor forget to ask for assistance when necessary from those whom He sends to our aid. Simon then realises he has witnessed a sign, a miracle in fact, and caught up in the revelation of that moment, knows he is in the presence of 'Someone' great. Of course, we know from St. John's gospel Simon has been told by his brother Andrew that they have found the Messiah, but here we see that Simon is just beginning to grasp that truth. In the presence of that Great Light that has just sprung up in Galilee, the darkness obscuring Simon's spiritual life is lifted and the poor fellow falls on his knees and begs the Lord to depart, realising that he is a sinful man not worthy to be in Christ's presence. Here we not only have humility, but a *confession*: Simon acknowledges the truth of what he is and accepts the consequence of his actions, which he immediately understands is a deserved separation from his Lord. It takes a good dollop of humility to open up like that, as most of you know from your visits over there." Peter smiled and pointed to a confessional. "Without repentance and a humble confession, we cannot be restored into God's grace. From that angle, of course we see the *fear of God* enter the picture, which is in fact a great gift from the Holy Spirit as a holy, righteous fear of the Eternal is a good preventative measure from falling again. We all dread the punishments reserved for sin, and certainly, no one wants to go to Hell! May I remind you where the confessionals are again?"

The congregation stifled a few chortles.

"Now we see poor Simon in that 'groaning struggle' St. Paul mentions, the desire to do good contending with the downward tug of his fallen human nature. Simon knows he is not worthy to be in the presence of the Lord, yet he cannot bear to leave Him. Unable to move from the spot, in his anguish he tells the Lord to go away instead. However, God does not want us paralysed in the wrong type of fear, afraid to draw near Him when we are repentant, for Jesus also said He came to heal the sick. In his inability to move, we can almost sense a holy *hope* in Simon, a silent prayer begging he be not separated from His Lord although he knows he deserves no better. Is that not *love* and *desire* for God? No doubt the Lord recognises Simon's repentance in that impulsive remark, and also his love and desire to do good despite his fallen nature. Much is forgiven for they who love much. Like Mary who sat at His feet, Simon is on his knees before the Lord and desires the best part, and it shall not be taken from him. Jesus tells Simon not to be afraid, he does not send him away or leave him, but remains with him, and what is more astounding, gives him a great mission in His Kingdom: the vocation to help save souls. True to his name 'Simon' with an open ear and the desire to obey leaves everything to follow the call. Family, business, worldly security. He launches out into the unknown to become a fisher of men, no longer afraid having understood that the Eternal Light is with him, that Love and Mercy itself is with him. He could endure anything knowing that one, eternally consoling thought. Of course, he does get knocked off course every now and again. Doubt and false misplaced fears are terrible cripplers to the soul, but the important thing is he repents and rises up renewed, knowing the Light does not wish to leave him. 'The Lord is my Light and my salvation, whom shall I fear?'

May I remind everyone that this is true for any vocation in life, not just the religious one, everyone has his or her own soul to save be they married or single, and hopefully, inspire others through their good example. The world cannot comprehend those who wish to live according to God's precepts and persecutes those who try, but the struggle is worth it as St. Paul reminds us today. Eternity is the prize! So let us keep in mind the lessons we have learned today and 'groan along'. When the way gets difficult and we seem to lose our course in this vast ocean of the world when times grow dark, let us also remember we have been given a guiding light in our Holy Mother, the 'Star of the Sea'. Have recourse to Our Lady's intercession, She will ensure spiritual success in all our undertakings. Ever desirous that we should find our way back to Her Divine Son, She will not leave us helpless or defenceless."

The homily concluded, the congregation rose to begin praying the Credo. Sophie gave her husband a little squeeze on the hand as they stood up, Katherine commiserated with them. Pete's sermon today was a tough one to take, but Richard just gave his wife a little reassuring gesture in return. He had accepted his son's new path in life, it was just difficult to be reminded that he would be leaving Reinold Enterprises a second time. Katherine knew it must have been hard for Peter to say as well. She couldn't help but feel awed and a little proud of him for doing what he knew he had to do without any apparent flicker of trepidation. Just as everyone began reciting the profession of faith, Katherine couldn't help but notice from the corner of her eye that someone was leaving, it was Mrs. Clarke who in her opinion looked a bit miffed. For a moment, Katherine wondered what that was all about, but not suspecting that his sermon had provoked a very different response from that of the Reinolds, her attention was quickly drawn back to the prayer.

The service continued with quiet reverence as would be expected, until it came time to receive Communion. The air became almost electric with undisguised curiosity, for the unexpected was happening again. Peter suddenly stopped and looked out into the congregation, it was as though he could sense something. He then made the sign of the cross. This time a loud *snap snap* was heard and it was not from a creaking pew. It was hard to tell where it came from. Was it wood splitting? Glass cracking? The congregation looked around. They couldn't see anything, but the sound and the Monsignor's solemn gesture must be related. He had been doing this for awhile now, not at every Mass, but enough at this point to draw additional attention and greater numbers of worshippers waiting to hear anything unusual with the expectation that one day they might actually be witness to something more spectacular. A sound always occurred when he gave that extra solemn blessing. One time it was a short loud burst of hissing like a steam pipe had been opened and was immediately clamped shut, another morning it was a strange cry, yet nobody knew if it was a baby or a cat in the congregation or not. Natural, yet ... not. This time seated at the back with some tall people in front of her, Katherine couldn't tell if he had made that gesture, but a few people situated two rows ahead were sure they had seen him do it. Today they certainly heard the strange snap! It sure was odd. Nobody knew what to make of it, other than something *unseen* must be going on. One day maybe the mystery would be unravelled.

After the service, Katherine followed the Reinolds back to the sacristy.

"Good morning everyone," Peter greeted.

"Hey son, we were just wondering, can you spare some time and have breakfast with us before you head out on your duties?" The question sounded wistful as Mr. R asked it, no doubt the gospel for the day still weighed upon him.

"As a matter of fact, I've got an hour or so free, and a colossal hankering for bacon."

"What? No eggs to go with it," his mother wondered.

"I thought that was a given!" Peter smiled as he picked up his black case. "I'm famished! I know I shouldn't be exacting or ungrateful about what's placed before me, but it was Mark's turn to cook last night, so let's say I didn't dare eat too much." His mother gave him a knowing smile.

"Come on then! Let's get you unfamished," his father announced.

Knowing Peter didn't have too much time, they selected a restaurant close by. While everyone else wanted the traditional eggs and bacon, Katherine was torn between the choice of hot fudge waffles or strawberry pancakes, then decided on the latter. At least it had some fruit going with it, so it couldn't be too bad, right? At least it was an attempt to break her morning chocolate toaster-tart addiction.

"I hear you visited the offices yesterday, Kathy," Sophia noted once their orders were placed.

"Yes, I had a very important delivery, and was given the VIP treatment."

"Richard says your picture for Peter is a sight to behold. I hope I get to see it, dear."

"Of course you will, I'm keeping it at the office for now. Drop by whenever you wish, Mom. It is very beautiful, you have a very fine touch, Kathy."

"Aw nuts, all this praise! I'm not good at taking compliments," she admitted, especially when they came from someone who knew all her faults!

"You'd better take them. Like a chip off the old block, Peter only gives them to someone who deserves them," Mr R nodded. "That reminds me, I think it's time we tell Sophie about our latest artistic enterprise," he hinted.

"Oh? What artistic enterprise could that be?" Sophia was indeed surprised when her husband told her about the family portrait he had commissioned. They just had to tell Lottie next. "That is a splendid idea," she agreed, "but Richard, you shouldn't have loaded Kathy with that right now, not with everything that's happening, not to mention Peter's doing two jobs at once … ."

"Don't worry Mrs. R, this is something I can fit in between projects," Katherine reassured her.

"And I've been assured we don't need to sit for months," Peter added.

"The funny part is, I get to do a portrait of Gerry now. He looked quite perplexed when I told him yesterday! Serves him right, a masterpiece for a masterpiece!" Katherine laughed.

Sophia wondered what she meant until Katherine disclosed her son's latest art project, namely her.

"I see," Sophia noted with amusement.

"I know, he's impossible. Well, now that were discussing it, there's one detail I wanted to run past you before we get into the practical details about the overall scene. Since this is a family project, would it be okay if I included Sinbad? It just wouldn't be the same if I left the feathered member out."

"Ho, I hadn't thought of that, but why not?" Mr. R was chuffed with the suggestion.

After saying grace, they discussed the latest doings in the city as they enjoyed their breakfast, the opening of Sir Elverton's gallery dominating the conversation. Mr. R. wondered if anyone had read the papers yet. Peter and Sophia said they hadn't, while Katherine informed she had only enough time that morning to skim through the photos and a few of the captions, adding she was dying to know what Horace had thought of the place and see what Stephie caught on camera. Mr. R called over one of the waiters and asked if they had a copy of the infamous critic's paper anywhere, maybe one left behind by one of their customers. The waiter was not sure but said he would look. After a few minutes of enquiring around the establishment, he didn't find the requested cultural editorial, but found another paper instead. Never mind, they could wait and read it when they went to visit Gerry. For now, they made do with whatever critical commentary they could find in the journal offered to them.

"Ho, look at this—Kroger! Can't believe it," Mr. R. huffed as he held up the paper, forgetting the column as he eyed the photographs, "for months I've been trying to get a hold of him for a viewing, but he just blew me off like a pile of flotsam. We're not good enough for the likes of him, yet here he is, peddling his wares with that scallywag."

"Try not to take it personally, dear," Sophia consoled.

"Do you actually *like* his work," Katherine wondered.

"No, it's as ugly as sin, but has profitable investment potential."

"Thus is the state of the world today," Peter noted, casting a humorous glance as he buttered a piece of toast.

"In case you ever *do* get to meet Kroger, don't either of you tell him that! You just might get belted over the head with an easel," Katherine interjected.

"Come Richard dear, forget Kroger and read the column, we're all ears. What does it say?"

He cleared his throat and read out the review, a glowing report of the lavish red curtain unveiling with a superstar listing of all the dignitaries that had attended, combined with a paean to the artists on display that included praise of the colourful and innovative method of interior design setting off the artworks in their best light, not to mention a flattering account of the spanking new five star restaurant located on the top floor that was given the glorious description of being a paradise abounding with epicurean delights. In all, it was one of those wow-the-critic articles that Katherine was dreading.

"And here I was hoping his big opening night might lay an egg. Yeah I know, you'll be hearing that it my next confession," Katherine continued as she observed the corner of Peter's mouth twitch into a smile. "Nuts! It's hard to stay charitable when Sir Snoop is involved. I can't help it."

"I don't think that's a mortal sin where that pirate is involved, so you're forgiven," Mr. R returned, equally annoyed with Elverton's underhanded efforts.

"Hey, who's supposed to be the confessor around here?" Peter laughed. "Anyway, what about all those diligently prepared sermons I've been giving about blessing your enemies, and so on and so forth," he humorously intoned.

"You're right, son. May the brigand be blessed according to his actions."

Katherine stifled a laugh into her napkin while Sophia just *tsked* at her husband, amused nonetheless.

After breakfast the next port of call was the hospital, except for Peter who had a house blessing to run to and two spiritual direction sessions booked for the afternoon. He asked everyone to say 'hi' to Gerry and tell him he would drop by later that evening. Fair enough, they said their goodbyes to him and continued on their way, reluctant to see him go. It was good they could spend the morning together considering he was in such high demand. Hopping into the van, Katherine was tempted to read Horace's column before she drove off since the papers were laying next to her on the passenger's seat, but no, she would wait until she could pour over them with Gerry, better get moving.

As it turned out, she must have had a heavy foot on the pedal this morning, for she arrived first before the Reinolds. In addition to the reams of newspapers draped over her arm, he smiled when he saw her enter with a bag of cinnamon custard Danishes.

"Good morning, dear. I had the waiter bag up a few of these for you, I don't think the nurses will be too upset," Katherine explained as she handed over the goods.

"Morning Princess, thanks! You're my saviour. You have no idea what they served me this morning, and come to think of it, neither do I. However, a croissant first, then your Danishes."

"How are you feeling today," she asked once the desired 'croissant' was delivered.

"Not too bad, not a hint of an ache. Of course, they just came around with their little cart full of pills, talk about giving a new meaning to drug pushers, I'm well juiced up for the morning."

"I suppose that's a good thing, as long as you're not tripping to Neptune."

"*Fly me to the moon and let me play among the stars, let me see what spring is like on Jupiter and Mars … .*"

"We're doing Frank Sinatra impersonations again," she beamed. She loved hearing him sing, he had a captivating voice well suited to swinging jazz tunes.

"Yep, don't know what was in that little paper cup, but I'm in a rather happy place right now," he joked. "Seriously, my mind is functioning coherently enough, I'm not too fuzzy, so they didn't get their prescriptions mixed up. Enough about me, how are you?"

"I'm fine, your parents were at Mass today and should be along in a minute, Pete says 'hello', and to tell you that he will come by later this evening."

"That's good. How was the service this morning?"

"Packed! You know, I used to hate going to church, but not with Pete. To think I actually look forward to a sermon now. The Bible makes much more sense when he explains it."

"Care to preach to me?"

"It was all about Simon-Peter leaving his boat and following the Lord." Gerry smiled, how appropriate! "I know, he can preach first hand on that. It was really touching, I could never repeat what he said exactly, I'll just jumble it all up. I wish he would compile all his sermons in a book. Listen, you'll never guess who I saw there today … ."

"Who?"

"Your secretary, she left early. I didn't know she was Catholic."

"Clarke? No, she's not. Huh."

"Maybe she had something urgent she wanted to see Pete about after the service, but realised it was not a good time. Maybe she couldn't wait around, she looked a bit impatient before she left."

"That could be it," Gerry agreed, however, his thoughts were piecing together a different picture.

"Have you read the papers yet? It's a disaster! A beautiful, successful, disaster!"

"No, the candy-stripers haven't delivered the papers yet, I'm guessing last night's event at Fifth Avenue is the cause of our lamentation," he replied, her paradoxical muddle drawing his thoughts back to the present.

"You don't know the half of it! Truthfully, me neither. I've only read one column with your parents over breakfast, and it wasn't Horace's, I can't wait another minute. I said I'd hold off until we could read his mutterings together."

"In that case, let's see what we've got here," he proposed, laying down his pastry and licking a sticky crumb off his finger before thumbing through the papers. "Where are you, big mouth Horace? Ha ha, here you are … ."

Gerry was about to read the review when his parents arrived with some hot coffee to go with the pastries.

"Good morning son, here's a little something to help wash that down," his father greeted, placing the styrocup on the table and pulling over a couple of extra chairs. "How are you feeling?"

"Not too shabby, I'm all voiced up and raring for Radio City Hall."

"He's doing Sinatra again," Katherine explained.

"Sounds like we're starting the morning on a good note." His mother smiled.

"For now anyway, until we see what Horace has to say about the 'beautiful, successful disaster' on Fifth Avenue," Gerry replied, casting a comical glance at Katherine.

"Huh? Oh, the new gallery I assume. Go on son, lay it on us," his father prodded. Gerry cleared his throat and obliged his listeners:

"The Fifth Avenue Carnival"

"At long last, the big event all art enthusiasts have been waiting for has come and gone: the grand unveiling of

that bright red circus called the 'Elverton Gallery' that had us dangling for months. The secrecy behind the name was a fizzler if you ask this critic, not the big surprise we were all led to believe it would be, but did that put a dampener on the occasion? Of course not. The star-studded bash continued to shine into the night as the rich and famous rubbed shoulders with the artistic comets of our day—talk about sending in the clowns: Lemnen, Holden, Hanley, Van Daard, Stilling to name just a few, and yes, this critic is rather surprised to see that highly sought-after irritable recluse come out from under his rock and put a few of his paint scrapings up for display in the Big Ring. Yes, you guessed it if you haven't already heard: the one and only fuming Kroger. He was almost on his best behaviour as he made his appearance at the Elverton on this grand occasion, only one unfortunate incident occurred when he overhead Stilling remark to a guest that his latest oeuvre, 'Study in Red Number 14', should have been named 'Study in Purple' or perhaps 'Orange' since there was no red anywhere to be seen on the mauled canvas. This critic is inclined to agree with Stilling, but was prudent enough to keep all opinions for the paper knowing Kroger was prowling about on the premises. Where's the lion-tamer when you need him? According to a few witnesses, which includes yours truly, Kroger growled 'You've missed the point, you witless specimen of an artist,' before taking off his gloves and giving Stilling a one-two whapping slap with them on either cheek, then exiting the building in high dudgeon. As it happens, Kroger's 'Study in Red' was one of the first to be put on reserve that night priced at a whopping $450,000.

In reference to the gallery, what words may one describe this conception of arty modernity? Something on the order of 'carnivalesque' this reviewer would venture, the bumper cars of Coney Island come to mind combined with a revival of the old time freak show with regards to the new artwork on offer, only the freaks are riding around in the cars, which is an interesting approach we must admit. In plain English, the Elverton Gallery has incorporated mobile partition wall units of assorted tints into their interior design, allowing them to open each floor up as large as they want like a Big Top tent, or make intimate colour co-ordinated viewing spaces, whatever is needed with each collection, each partition display can be separated into blocks or hitched along in any pattern like train cars. Novel concept? Not exactly, the prototype of mobile wall units was already introduced at the Walsingham Gallery now already well ensconced in the creative scene in Dumbo, but as they say, you don't have to come up with anything original as long as you know who to copy. You could say the Elverton has almost everything, except a flying trapeze. What I mean by 'everything' is the new restaurant on the top floor called the Pinceau catering to the palates of the patrons. My, what tantalizing delights that melt in the mouth! They are nothing to sneeze at for more than one reason—you just might blow away what little you get. I suppose a dish can no longer be counted as five star cuisine if the entire main course cannot fit inside a tumbler considering all the side dishes were neatly piled up on top of each other like an acrobatic game of Jenga balanced on a tight wire, but never mind, it was a true mouth-watering enchantment, worth trying despite being ethereal as the cotton candy spun at the State Fair. For my final verdict, I will leave you with the proverbial cliché: the circus has come to town."

"Ouch, Horace leaves nothing unscathed." Gerry chuckled. "And, you got a plug into the bargain, my dear."

"Yeah, that's good of him to make sure I'm not forgotten, although I don't know if I like being associated with Sir Snoop's circus," Katherine noted, not sure whether to be irked or amused. It was a good thing she knew Horace in real life wasn't as narky as he sounded on paper.

"At least we now know what idea that brigand borrowed from you, those rolly-pollies you designed," Mr R. observed. "Just what do these 'bumper cars' of his look like? Here son, let's take a look." Gerry handed over the paper, which his father spread out on the bed so everyone could see. "Can't quite tell from the pictures, they look like ordinary walls to me."

"Except for the colours, they are a bit bold, aren't they," Sophia observed.

Katherine had to agree, they appeared quite stationary and somewhat ordinary despite the striking colours, it was difficult to see what the fuss was about just from the photos, however, she smiled when she noticed two bystanders in the background of one shot and pointed them out: Charlie and Suzy were standing in front of Kroger's other latest master mutilation, '*Study in Red #8*'. Her cousin Stephie had obviously snapped a photo of them while they weren't looking, and judging from the way Charlie was standing with his hand on his chin with Suzy's turning her head slightly sideways at that moment, they were no doubt questioning the mental state let alone the fashionable tastes of the artistic world. Horace as editorial head of the cultural section of his paper must have included the photo knowing it would give her and the other members of the Gallery Gang a good laugh or two.

"I can't wait to hear what news they have, although I'm not sure when I'll get to see them. Maybe Suzy will be at the apartment when I go visit my folks later, but it's hard to say, she could be spending all of today with Charlie if he's free," Katherine noted.

With a wedding coming up sometime in the future, they had much to plan and discuss. Already Suzy asked her if it was okay if she take off on a long weekend with Charlie sometime before the summer was over as they were trying to co-ordinate a trip to Iowa together where he could visit with her parents, especially as her father was a school principal and would be more available in the off-school time. No problem, Suzy had more than earned that little bit of visitation period she requested. It was a good thing they already met Charlie, it would be nice for them to get together. The last major hurdle facing the newly engaged couple was the dreaded meeting of the parents for they had not met each other yet. Katherine wondered how that was going to turn out when it happened, Charlie's mother could be a bit uppity where her only son was concerned.

"I know this Sir Elverton has been a right arrogant nuisance, but I have to admit, I'm getting curious about the place now," Gerry admitted, bringing Katherine's thoughts back.

"Gerry," Katherine *tsked*, but she knew how he felt, the curiosity bug was gnawing at her too, that was the problem with Horace's column. The notorious Art Hacker of the Big Apple never had a good word to say about anything with the result his faithful albeit annoyed readers wanted to see for themselves what he was bellyaching about. "What I want to know is, how did Snoop get someone like Kroger anyway," she wondered. "As much as I like gaining a reputation for supporting new artists, how do you attract someone as fashionable as him to a gallery? I'm already offering some of the most competitive commission rates around, and I don't see Hanley, Lemnen or Stilling breaking down my door."

"So, you're finally willing to show those epitomes of modern baloney on your sacred walls," Gerry playfully teased.

"Unfortunately, yes, I've got a gallery to run. Art as 'business', yuck," she returned, not thrilled with this admission.

"Ho, I'm afraid that's the nature of business. You eventually get the art of compromise knocked into you," Mr. R. observed. "Might I suggest you start upping your prices on your best-selling artists? If they are getting popular, it's time you up the ante, it helps make them more desirable and famous in the process. I think you're selling yourself short, artists like Kroger don't like to be sold off cheap. It's not good for their creative image, no matter how uncreative their products look."

"I don't like to gouge my customers either," Katherine replied.

"It's not about gouging them, it's all about investment, most of the time anyway," Mr. R continued. "Don't worry, those who invest in the arts have the means to do so. Your prices set the value rate, much like an IPO. Would you invest thousands let alone millions in something you thought would gain no more value let alone retain it like something that you could find in a crafts fair?"

"No, I suppose not. But what about the *beauty* of something? Surely you collect something for its beauty?"

"We do that too my dear, but when it comes to investment pieces, collectors also want to be part of history in the making, hoping they get the next undiscovered Salvador Dali before they're famous and the prices really sky rocket," Gerry interjected. "As long as it looks original and different from anything that's being done, that's what goes. Just think of your gallery as a trendsetter, upping your prices is not a bad idea. In fact, look at the pieces I've bought from your friends that you have included in your museum section. Why not plug them as artists included in the famous Reinold private collection? Just watch the collectors come who don't want to miss out. Even Sir Snoop picked up a few of them, and he's also got a reputation as a serious collector. You could get an extra ten-thousand per new canvas just by a little strategic status publicity using 'Reinold' as a draw, maybe more, not to mention attract the famous artists," Gerry concluded.

"What?" Katherine gasped. "It sounds so … like opportunistic usury, that's what it is. I can't do that! I'm not marrying you for that."

Gerry laughed.

"Yes you can dear, it takes quite a while to build up a name brand, you know. 'Reinold' will be your name too, so go ahead and use it for all its worth. We do all the time," Mr. R. declared.

"Umm, okay, if you don't mind, but I'm *not* going to harp on Snoop for publicity, that's dead certain."

"Richard dear, why not see if a few of the artists you know would be interested in showing their next collection at Kathy's place, like that fellow from Moscow who depresses everyone? Can't remember his name, but he's always a sell out," Sophia suggested.

"Stansislov? Yeah, Yoris! Good old Yoris might be willing," Gerry agreed, "that is, if Kathy doesn't mind us helping out by sending a gloomy weirdo or two her way."

"Oh no, that would be marvellous, I *think*." She laughed. "Thank you, any help is appreciated. The gallery does need to acquire new artists, and as long as the work is not vulgar rot, I'll put it up, although how such diddly nonsense can even make it as investment pieces is beyond me. In art these days, absurdity always prevails."

"Very well then, I'll get in contact with Yoris plus a few other absurd fellows and see if we can't arrange something," Mr. R concluded.

"Oh my, another thing we've just dropped on you Kathy, with everything else," Sophia noted.

"That's okay, it's all part of an artist's life."

Gerry continued to tuck into the Danish box as everyone chatted. Since their families were not getting together for dinner this Sunday, everyone shared the plans they had for the evening. His parents decided a quiet night at home was just the ticket for them, while Katherine was going home to her family and would stay overnight at Oak Meadows, leaving the plasterer's mess in the apartment for Monday. The workmen would be back anyway to continue their messing, no point cleaning up anything when they were just going to get white dust everywhere again. Gerry noted with humour it was a good thing she was staying away for a night, just in case she got pinned by Mrs. Beechworz a second time. In fact, not seeing that busybody made his confinement in the hospital tolerable, it kept him out of range from the pesky lady's recruitment campaigns for her Resident's Association. However, he couldn't escape forever, it was only a matter of time before he got snared into one of her dreaded meetings, although he had to confess he was curious to know what her supposedly famous goulash tasted like at the customary bring-your-own smorgasbords. Katherine shook her head, she hoped she wouldn't get cornered, she would have to bring something, which was not a good idea since she was still a hopeless cook. Unless she asked Andre to whip up a gourmet delight to go for her, she might make the whole get-together more unbearable for the roped-in Association members. Plus, no matter how tasty the buffet promised to be, she would keep well clear of any committees for the present, which sounded no different than something managed by the government, a load of waffling and wrangling with nothing getting done and what did get done annoyed half the nation. Mr. R laughed, that reminded him of a few 'bored' meetings he suffered through on occasion, and agreed she was being wise.

"Don't get guilt-tripped into volunteering for a load of pester-your-neighbour societal activities that works more against the communal happiness of the building than for it," he concluded.

Speaking of meeting the neighbours, Sophia wondered if there were any developments concerning the new arrivals at Oak Meadows. Katherine wasn't sure, but had a hunch she would probably be told the minute she arrived through the door since Aunt Martha was still on the neighbourhood watch with her brother's old telescope, trying to figure out what was going on down the block. One thing was for sure, the new arrivals had plenty of deliveries still coming to their new house in the way of furniture and other mysterious shaped items in boxes and crates that she was dying to get to the bottom of. Until Aunt Martha found out, there would be no peace on the home front for awhile. Flustered by his sister in-law's running commentary on the proceedings combined with all her rhetorical questions, Pops was taking a bit more ulcer medication these days —'Look! I think a huge sofa was brought in … no it was a sideboard. I wonder if it's an antique? Are they a young family do you think? Do you suppose they have delinquent teenagers? I hope they keep the garden up to our standards, we can suggest they hire your gardeners, I can't abide an overgrown lawn … .' Helen simply left her at it, while Pops just headed up to his private office upstairs when he came home with extra work as a pretext until Martha got tired and went home. Even Gramps was making himself scarce and enjoying a few extra card games in the afternoons with his old friends at the Country Club, this time putting on some decent bets now that Martha was out of eyesight and too engrossed with her new victims to nag him about the corrupting vice of gambling. However, Sunday night was family night, so no escaping anywhere this time. At least, Gramps was getting a few extra hundred bucks out of the whole thing Gerry thought, and although he felt sorry for Pops Number 2, he couldn't help but find Katherine's predicament amusing, escaping Beechworz's 'pot-lookie' for the night yet ending up in her aunt's frying pan instead.

Eventually the 'mush carts' were set loose in the hospital and lunch was served, if it could be called that Gerry wryly joked. Nevertheless, he ate what was placed before him to please his mother. He felt guilty eating in front of anyone without having anything to offer them, which was quite literal he noted with humour as he eyed his plate, but they were still too full after the generous breakfast they had that morning and told him to go ahead, as if they wanted what he had been served!

"Thanks, how very thoughtful of you," Gerry replied with an audible note of sarcasm, slowly trying to lift a forkful of overly shrivelled peas to his mouth.

"You should've saved a Danish," Katherine couldn't help point out.

When the lunch ordeal was past, the nurses came in to accomplish their afternoon duties, giving the cue it was time for all visitors to leave their patient in peace, especially as he needed space for his next physiotherapy session. Saying their goodbyes and promising to drop by tomorrow, they reluctantly left Gerry to the hospital staff. While out in the hall, Mr. R asked the doctor how his son was progressing. It was early days yet, the physiotherapists were continuing to gently work on his legs while he was still in bed, they weren't ready to risk putting any weight on his hips yet, and were keeping him well dosed with pain-killers. However, they planned to begin tapering off the dosage soon in order to determine the extent of his pain threshold. Katherine knew the Reinolds' just got a knot in their stomachs, for hers just tightened when she heard that. The withdrawal from the medications would be the ultimate test to see how difficult the road ahead threatened to be, and she couldn't bear the thought of Gerry suffering pain of any kind. Having received the latest progress report, they said goodbye to each other and went their separate ways, hoping all would work out in the end.

The physiotherapists worked on Gerry's legs, taking each one at a time, gently moving them back and forth in a pedal motion for several minutes. It was a good thing he wasn't actually going on a bike, he would topple over at this speed he thought. It seemed like ages they had him on this slow-mo 'air bike' routine, but it *was* barely a couple of weeks since those iron bars came off, it would take time before he could build up his muscle tone again, his legs had been out of commission for months. It felt so odd not being able to move them on his own, not even to crook up a knee without his ankle giving way from weakness, he could barely manage a small sideways slump of his feet under the covers. It was sinking in that he really would need to learn how to walk all over again from square one and would just have to give it time. At least he wasn't feeling any pain, but that was all due to the meds for now.

When the therapists had finished their leg-o-robics and he was left alone, he decided to while away the afternoon with a book before the next round of prodding, needles, and whatever else the nursing staff planned to do to him. After awhile, his eyes got tired, so he took a break from reading and watched some TV. Blast, when at work he wished he had more free time, and now that he got it, it seemed to drag. Well, being stuck in hospital was not exactly the most comfortable extended vacation he would have wished for anyway, so it was naturally going to be a drag. Good thing Peter would be dropping by to ensure he kept up with his spiritual duties and bring him Communion, afterwards he was bound to stay for a visit, which he looked forward to. However, Kathy's news about Mrs. Clarke at the service that morning gave him food for thought, and he couldn't help but wonder what was happening in the offices in his absence. Maybe nothing at all, but knowing that *something* between her and Pete had transpired before, he was hoping everything was all right and considered whether he should bring anything up lest he let suspicions run riot with his imagination.

Finally, the afternoon wore on into evening, the last rounds of prodding for the night were over by the time Pete came by as promised, stole over his shoulders as customary when brining his Sacred Guest. Once the sober time of reflection had passed, Gerry asked how his day went.

"Not too bad, a house blessing, and a few people needing spiritual counselling, although I'm a bit beat, clearing a mountain of scruples from an over-anxious soul is painstaking," he replied, putting away his stole and pulling up a chair.

"I bet it is. So … how were things at the office this week," Gerry inquired tentatively.

"Missed the board meeting on Saturday, but of course it was in the morning and out of my time range, but nothing significant to report, which reminds me, Mrs. Clarke will be dropping some things by tomorrow for you to look over."

"Okay, will handle it. Um, speaking of Mrs. Clarke, is there anything else I should know about?"

"Not that I can think of right now, everything is running smoothly, considering all that's happened."

"Yeah, I know, and even Dad is right cheerful these days. He's glad you're back, even if it's temporary. But, that's not what I was getting at, or maybe it was … have you ever regretted leaving Pete? The family business I mean."

"Regret? No, I'm very happy with the path I've taken. There were some memorable times though, weren't there, Sparticus?"

"That's for sure, O mighty Judah Ben Hur!" Gerry laughed. "After coming back to where you once were and all of that, I just wondered."

"No, well, I do have one, not properly giving anyone advance warning of what I was planning, not just Dad, but especially you. That was not how I wanted things to go. I know you were left to pick up the slack. I'm sorry for putting the kibosh on your own projects."

Peter was one of the few who knew that Gerry as an enthusiastic art collector was seriously considering going into a partnership with a college buddy and starting their own international rare art and antiquities auction house.

"Hey, I got a promotion out of it all," Gerry cheerily reminded him, "I didn't expect to become Senior Manager of International Distribution until you became CEO, and then, who was I kidding? Everything else would have been shoved aside anyway, there's no way I could have kept up with running another global business, not full time. I wouldn't have been able to give it the attention it deserves, and I'd probably end up dissatisfied as a sleeping partner. So, I've accepted the fact the family flame is getting passed to me, and Lottie of course. She's really getting into it, isn't she?"

"She is, even at the crash course level." Peter chuckled. "I just hope I've taught her enough by the time I have to return to my spiritual pastures."

"At least this time your departure won't be as dramatic," Gerry drolly noted.

"No, I suppose not!"

"I certainly didn't suspect what you were planning, even though you always were the devout one, except for Mom maybe. The thing is, I've got something personal to ask, which is why I've brought this all up. If it's none of my business you can tell me to button my mouth, but back then I was full sure you and Clarke had a thing going, which is why I was wondering how you were doing … I hope my being stuck in here doesn't open any old wounds."

"Why? Has something been said?"

"No, only Kathy saw Mrs. Clarke at your service this morning and that she huffed out after your sermon. Kathy just thinks she wanted to see you over some emergency in the office and couldn't wait for Monday, and I've let her think that. After that day you nearly knocked me over on my feet when you ran off to Rome, Clarke seemed pretty upset and requested some time off. I don't think anyone put two and two together except me, so when Kathy told me about this morning, I couldn't help but wonder if everything was all right."

"I see," Peter noted quietly. "It wouldn't be the first time she's showed up at my Mass. I'm afraid she's not able to let go of the past."

"Uh oh, this isn't good, take it from one who's had super glue for an old girlfriend, but *whoa*, something *did* go on back then! What happened," Gerry impulsively blurted out as he tried to sit up, fascinated his brother actually might have had a love life at one time. Peter knew he would get no peace until Gerry knew the truth and so he told him everything, remarking that only his confessor was aware of what he had just heard, other than Clarke of course, and if he wouldn't mind promising to keep this revelation to himself since people could always jump to the wrong conclusions.

"Sure thing, but a first kiss is not the end of the world, and you weren't even ordained yet," Gerry replied, somewhat amused his brother was still so innocent, then growing a bit sad for him. "So you *almost* had a love life, but Pete, that must have been the hardest thing to do, giving up Clarke. You *were* falling in love you know."

"At the time, yes, but then, one can be tempted by the wrong love too."

"True, I should talk. I fell into it a few times all right, but you already know that." Gerry wryly smiled. "So you actually did make a clean break before things got really serious, but do you still care for her?"

"Of course, I want her to be happy, but I don't feel the same way any more, not *that* way, you understand. Oh sure, the first year at the seminary was rough, not only leaving you all behind abruptly with hardly a proper good-bye, but also getting to know what it might be like to have a beautiful woman in your life and sacrificing that too, but in the midst of it all, I realised my heart already belonged to someone else long before I met Lucinda, it was already betrothed to the Church. After a long period of reflection I knew that if I had actually stayed home and married her, I would have regretted it, and then come to resent her and myself. The resentment would almost certainly have festered into a soul corroding bitterness. It would have been a doomed marriage that would have destroyed us both. Once I had accepted that, there was no looking back."

"I can see that now," Gerry nodded. "You certainly are where you're supposed to be, there's no denying it. At least you can still visit *us*, but Clarke! What a sacrifice! I can't imagine giving up my Katherine," he noted quietly.

"Because you're not meant to give her up," Peter sagely pointed out, "you two were meant to be together, just like me and the Church. She really is your better half you know."

"Don't I know it! The thing is, I'm glad you told me everything, and I'm relieved you've moved on okay, but what about Clarke? She's stuck in the past. Showing up at your services, you can't tell me she hasn't tried to restart whatever little you had going on back then."

"Let's say she's been doing her best to get noticed," Peter reflected, "but I've kept everything strictly above board and all business. She won't get the wrong impression from *me* in any case. In fact, I think I can guess why she left in a huff, she knows how I stand in no uncertain terms," he said, picking up his briefcase and searching for a copy of his sermon, which he handed to him.

"Hmm, there's some mighty fine preaching in here, bro." Gerry smiled after he finished, passing him back his copy. "Good. However, if she is getting fixated like 'The Burr' was with me, you can't stay for long at the office no matter what. Some women can't take a hint. I don't know if I should say this, but you haven't met Mr. Clarke, have you?"

"No, I haven't."

"I have, and I couldn't help but notice he bears a strong resemblance to a certain big brother of mine," Gerry continued in a knowing tone. Peter pursed his lips.

"For her sake, I'm sorry to hear that. I hope she didn't enter the marriage for that reason alone, it will prove a very weak foundation to build a life on."

"I know, like butter, the copy is never as good as the original. Sorry, I had to say it," Gerry replied sheepishly as his brother looked at him askance. "Well, just look at the original! You certainly had a heap of a lot going for you when you were an eligible bachelor, and now that you're unavailable, you may be even more appealing because you're off limits. Listen, just to avoid any more difficult situations, maybe we should give Clarke her vacation time a bit early. Perhaps declare a sabbatical or something?" Peter shook his head at the suggestion.

"No, it may sound like a good idea, but her sudden departure might create a scandal where there is none. Nothing has happened, and I'm not about to let it."

"Still, it's not a good situation."

"I know, but I don't fear for myself as much as I do for her. From what you just told me, it's more than a fixation with her, it's become an obsession, maybe to the point of sickness. She may crack and do something rash she will regret, and I certainly don't want to be the cause of any situation that could lead to a break-up of her marriage."

"But it's not your fault, it sounds like she's the one with the problem. Blast it! I wish I was out of here, you wouldn't be in this spot right now," Gerry grumbled apologetically.

"Hey Ger, don't get upset. None of this is your fault either, and you take all the time you need to heal," Peter replied, giving him a gentle brotherly fist-bump on the arm. "The best we can do for now is not stir up the waters any further and hope they settle down. She must learn to deal with this and find her own inner peace.”

“I guess since we can’t send her off on vacation, we’ll just have to pile her with extra work, she’ll be so busy, she won’t be able to think,” Gerry suggested.

“That’s almost slavery. We could be charged with mistreatment of employees.”

“Darn it! I’m trying to help here,” Gerry replied, somewhat flustered but amused.

“I know, but she’s been kept pretty busy as it is,” Peter finished with a note of guilt albeit with some humour.

“In that case, I guess we can’t pile any more on her. We certainly can’t fire her either, that much is certain.”

“Unfair dismissal.”

“Yep. However, we *could* threaten it, it was the only way I could get rid of my ‘Burr’, I let it slip I might get a restraining order.”

“Did you intend to go through with it,” Peter wondered, this was news to him.

“Nah, it would’ve been a hassle, plus it might have ended up getting us dragged into the media again. It was just a threat, and it worked, the hint finally got through. Bye bye, Burr.”

“Still Ger, let’s not resort to something drastic as threats or fear tactics. She hasn’t actually done anything ostensibly improper anyway, she knows she’s risking her job if she does, that’s what I’m guessing.”

“Okay, plus I’d regret it if we had to let her go, she’s one hell of a personal assistant. I’d never be able to replace her, even if keeping her around knowing her obsession with you will be a bit awkward. This *is* a problem. Why not just go and make up a few inspection tours to get out of the office, at least until Thomas and Lottie come back and you have ‘safety in numbers’ around you?”

“I’ve actually been doing that,” Peter admitted, “which reminds me, Sammy says ‘hi’, so do all the guys in the yards.”

“Aw, that’s swell of them. Tell them the next time you see them, I’ll be up and about before they know it and surprise them with a visit. Hmph, well, about Clarke, I guess we’ve covered all the bases,” Gerry concluded, shaking his head. “I can’t think of anything else you can do other than have you run away again without any warning. Just skip off back to the rectory.”

“So much for the less dramatic leave-taking,” Peter observed. Gerry laughed.

"Okay, so we can't have you disappear into the blue again, and I'm plumb out of ideas, so the 'Icicle Treatment' it is. We'll have to stick to your plan since you seem to know what you're doing."

"I must confess, we were warned in the college to expect something like this to happen and to be on our guard."

"Really? Do tell," Gerry grinned, more than a bit inquisitive to know about what went on in a seminary. He listened with interest as Peter told how on one of the few afternoons they had free, he and a couple of new friends he had made went out for a well deserved espresso after attending a long lecture on the theology of St. Thomas Aquinas. In the midst of their conversation they were abruptly but good naturedly interrupted by a curious little wiry old priest dressed in an ordinary cassock who spoke Italian in a thick French accent, but then switched to English when he learned they were from the American College.

"Zo, I hope to zee you at my special talk then? You may have need of it."

"Er, which one," Peter asked.

"Oh, a good one! *'Avoiding the Beguiling Snares of Madame Georgette' .*"

Peter remembered looking at his cassocked comrades in surprise, they too were stunned. They had seen the special seminar announced on the main bulletin board for several weeks and thought they would go out of curiosity, just to see what on earth that could be all about, especially as the guest speaker would be the Cardinal Archbishop of Paris. There was a moment of exuberant confusion as they all rose to their feet and attempted to make room for the unexpected guest at their table and offered to buy him an espresso, or whatever he liked. He could only stay for a few minutes, but eagerly sipped his steaming *café latte* while they introduced themselves and offered him a little about their family backgrounds. Of course, his new friends were all waiting to see what his Eminence's reaction would be like when it came Peter's turn to introduce himself, discovering this was the same Peter Reinold who ditched his executive career and famed inheritance for the priesthood. Peter looked up to heaven with this admission, which amused Gerry, although he was not surprised to find his brother had become somewhat of a legend among the seminarians after the bold renunciation of his privileged life. However, Peter recalled his Eminence didn't register any surprise, he chatted on as before and sharing a few funny stories as though he expected nothing less of anyone who had a true vocation. He was truly 'old school'.

"So, who is this 'Georgette' you were going to be warned about," Gerry asked, his curiosity getting the better of him.

Peter chuckled as he remembered the scene. Turning up at the appointed lecture hall with his friends and classmates a few days later, the Archbishop entered dressed in his formal cassock and golden pectoral cross. Although they had expected him to discuss a very serious subject, which he did, the Archbishop still cut a droll figure as he laid out the dangers of 'Madame Georgette' while walking around the lecturer's stage, talking Italian style with his hands despite being French, nodding his head every now and then, which still sported a thick mass of white curly hair that encircled his scarlet zucchetto like a silver laurel crown, his dark eyes at times shinning with merriment or flashing with lightning depending on what struck him at the moment:

"Now zat you're on zee path to zee priesthood and the sacrifices it entails, it is a noble life, but as you know, it will be beezet with many snares and pitfalls to lead you into temptation and away from zee sacrifices you are about to make. And one of zee most dangerous besides ze usual znares of ambition, and fame, and a comfortable life—yes! That is a problem too! A vocation is not to be a luxurious *career*! But zat is another matter. What I am zaying is, zee most dangerous znare for young men, and older men too, is zee beauty of an attractive woman. Oh ho, my young *garçons*, beware of Madame or Mademoiselle Georgette! Oh, she will put on her pretty make-up, flutter her long eyelashes at you, wear her tiny dresses, do everything to entice you to leave, my young fellows. And oh! She is zo beautiful! And zo kind! Soon it may be a dinner, maybe an innocent coffee, but zee threads are getting spun to trap you! Then zer are zee more daring Georgettes, zee Georgettes who think notheen of making advances and uttering disgraceful suggestions to you using zee veil of zee confessional to get to you unzeen by others! Some Georgettes will purposely come to Mass and Communion with their necks uncovered down to zee point of grave sacrilegious immodesty to stir up zee passion in you! Ohhh, you must ever beware of zee Georgettes waiting to pounze like a tiger!"

At this point, one disgruntled modernist seminarian interrupted the Archbishop with a forceful question: wasn't this radical intolerance against women who were already marginalized by the Church as it was? Every woman was not a Jezebel!

"No, no, *no*! Of course not! You are not listeneeng! I'm *not* talkeen about all zee good and pious young mademoiselles and madames who respect zer parish priests and would never dream of doing such a thing. Many women are good, but there are always a few bad ones lurking around zee corner, it will only take one of zose 'Georgettes' to make you fall. *Oui,* zome are not really bad, just weak, there are women who will be attracted to you because zey see someone trying to live a very spiritual life in a world gone crazee. Many loze hope of finding zomeone, many men are bad and cruel too, zo they will be attracted by your discipline, spirituality and chaste life. You cannot help but pity them, but you must always keep your distance. Zey may open up your own human weaknesses and you may not be able to help yourself. Even if notheen happens, even if you are innocent, zey could black-mark zee rest of your vocation if it gets to zee point suspicion becomes a public scandal and you are withdrawn from your ministry while your case is put under investigation. Then, zere are thoze black Georgettes that will purposely try to get you to fall, a real conquest of ze flesh for hell! Zey went to tempt you zo bad you cannot help yourself, and will be officially defrocked! Zey are zee devil's own servants in zat case! All theze 'Georgettes', thoze humanly weak or with ze black heart of demon, you must always forever be *en garde*! To loze one priestly vocation is to loze the hundreds if not thouzands of zouls he could have zaved."

"Wow, that's serious stuff," Gerry remarked. "I wonder how the question and answer session went after that."

"Well, there was more to the seminar, the Archbishop went on about how we would be able to tell who might be a 'Georgette' and pose a threat from those who were just good pious ladies who loved helping out at a church and couldn't help but bug the priest about everything concerning the running of the parish. There are also the types who loved being the priest's pets, hogging his attention and feeling important over it. His Eminence suggested we try and keep our distance from that too if we could, just for the sake of our sanity."

Gerry laughed, he could just imagine all the pesky things his brother could be pelted with from all the busybodies. They didn't exist in church alone!

Peter continued. "However, in charity, we must make time for everybody, for you never know when a soul truly needs help, but to always be on 'en garde' for anyone who might pose a spiritual setback to us, his Eminence concluded. His advice was if we suspected we might have a problem, to never be on our own with a 'Georgette' if we could help it, and to keep a healthy distance."

"Good advice, which you're following. He sounds like quite a character."

"He is, but down to earth. It was an honour meeting him, we saw each other a few times afterwards."

"Hey! Talk about knowing someone in high places! You know, I was a little irked at how things happened all of a sudden back then, but I must admit I was also slightly envious, you getting to spend all that time in Rome while I got an 'advance promotion' with all the work going with it," Gerry noted wryly with good humour, "but I forgive you! I never really asked how it was, or get to talk to you about what you did while you where there."

"Hmm, where do I start? As you know, this was not your ordinary vacation to Italy."

"Okay, tell me about it from a seminarian's perspective then. Italy is still Italy you know, I'm all ears."

Peter laughed, they not only had the love of art and baseball in common, but also were keen Italophiles. He began by telling him how he had prepared for the new change of life, pep-talking himself on the plane he'd better get used to the idea of the austerity that would be expected in the priesthood to find the living quarters assigned to the Americans at the Casa Santa Maria a tad opulent. He certainly didn't expect to be given the privilege of eating with the ordained priests in a frescoed dining hall with waiters in white jackets and ties serving them their meals and afternoon *biscotti*. No wonder the Archbishop had warned them about getting too comfortable! He thought he was leaving that sort of life behind. After only a few meals that he choked down due to guilt, he joined the rest of his fellow seminarians to the plainer dining hall after that. Gerry laughed, they were probably letting the 'rich' Yank student accustomed to a life of convenience down gently, knowing that penny-pinching would eventually get knocked into him at his future parish rectory. Peter chuckled, maybe his little brother had a point. It was surprising the number of Europeans who had the false impression that ninety-five percent of the American population were borderline billionaires, or were at least a million times better off then those living in the 'Old Countries'. Their family just happened to be one of the few who actually were. Life could be so unpredictable simply because of people's misconceptions or their charitable intentions.

Peter then had to confess the Casa's dining hall was not the only place his past life opened some privileged doors and provided him with some wonderful experiences during the summer months. Considering their family was a generous patron of the Vatican Museums he was given private tours of the galleries, libraries, the antiquities treasuries, and especially some compelling hidden nooks that included instant access to the Secret Library to view some of the rarest historical documents on earth, not to mention the ancient Necropolis of the Dead on which the Vatican was built. It was awe-inspiring to visit the grave of his name-saint, St. Peter himself, Prince of the Apostles. Gerry 'ohhed' his good-natured envy, although he had been to the Vatican museums on his various travels, Pete really got the red carpet treatment.

"When I get out of here, and Kathy and I go on our honeymoon, I'm bringing you with us, we need a decent tour guide with all the pull," he joked. The funny part was, he knew Katherine wouldn't mind, she would love to have Pete tag along and meet up with them and see some of those rare sights.

Gerry then wondered if he had visited any of the catacombs where the early Christians were compelled to practise their faith during the great persecutions, something he didn't have the chance to do on his other trips. Naturally, Peter had, disclosing they were very gripping on so many different levels, and that also was literally speaking. Like his brother, he had seen some pictures all right, but had no idea what to expect until he descended into one of the major catacomb networks outside the city. The first thing that struck him was the dim lighting, imparting an even more sombre ambience. The guide explained that they wished visitors to see what it was like in the first days of the Church when all that the Christians had to light their way in these hidden vaults were small hand-held oil lamps that hardly gave a glimmer to dispel the darkness. Although there were spacious galleries and underground chapels, the real chilling part came when he was taken to the later catacombs that broke from the earlier ordered grid pattern and branched out into a confusing maze of narrow tunnels and chambers, the soft stone walls of each tunnel hollowed out with hundreds, perhaps thousands of burial recesses where the dead were laid to rest and then sealed with a stone covering. The shadowy chambers lined with row upon row of now empty niches in that underground honeycombed labyrinth left a deep impression as he was guided along a twisting confusing path. How the guide could keep his sense of direction was a marvel, and this was only the first hundred yards of the first level, there were many other levels lying underneath. Quite a few times an opening suddenly appeared on one side or the other, curling the path away in the opposite direction, or a black unlit tunnel abruptly yawned below him at an unexpected multi-level intersection that seemed to want to draw him down to the deeper levels while the guide beckoned to another turn and kept him focused on the well-tread passages. In fact, it was estimated there were twelve miles of tunnels in this one catacomb system alone, and many of the other levels had not yet been explored or excavated, there were many stone-sealed niches still left untouched, so many saints and martyrs in the darkness yet to be discovered and honoured. At the beginning of the tour he was told to stay close and not wander off, he could get lost and they might not be able to find him for a long, long, long time. Peter thought it was a sinister joke played on the visitors, but when he saw for himself, the guide may have been telling the truth.

Peter then had one funny albeit grisly story to tell. It was well known that it was forbidden on the pain of excommunication to remove any first class relics from the bodies of the martyrs at the catacombs without permission from the Church. However, one of the seminarians didn't think a handful of sand taken from the ground in one of the tunnels as a memento of his visit would pose a problem, that is until he got back to the Casa Santa Maria and showed his prize to his friends only to find a tooth grinning back at him in the midst of the dust! More horror stricken with the thought of excommunication than with finding the tooth, the poor guy tore out of the place, jumped on the first bus straight back to the catacombs, returned the dirt exactly where he got it, then immediately came back and banged on the door of his confessor to reveal his crime. Since it was an innocent accident with no relic-theft intended, naturally the sentence of doom was lifted immediately, much to the hilarity of everyone who heard the story.

During the school months, he and his fellow seminarians actually didn't have too much time for sight-seeing, there were many classes in addition to the daily Mass and devotions to attend, not to mention the hours of study they needed to pour over the tomes of canon law. He was blessed he had followed the inspiration years ago to keep up his Latin learned at school and to study the doctors of the Church on his own time. He had covered quite a bit of material on his own when he arrived at the seminary. It was one of the reasons he got his own apartment while attending Harvard when they were younger and didn't stay at the elite fraternity house all their forefathers had gone to. He needed the quiet to get both his college work and private studies nailed down. Of course, for him there was more to not joining a fraternity: he was not about to be conditioned by a secretive organisation with hidden codes and strange handshakes that was too much like a grooming session for some other dubious Fraternity, but didn't say that to Gerry just then. The wild life was certainly enough of a good reason for him to stay away, which he knew his brother could understand.

"Besides, with all the trouble Leroy and that pack of hooligans got you into, it's a good thing I kept myself busy," Peter wryly concluded while Gerry laughed.

It made sense now. Gerry could see why Pete stayed on his own, even if Dad was a bit disappointed at the time, however, he was happy enough his sons attended Harvard according to family tradition, so in one of his rare concessive moods, he didn't push him into the frat house if he didn't want to go.

"Yeah, you escaped all the hazing and the practical jokes. I don't think it was as wild during Dad's student days, it's a wonder we didn't maim each other, and managed to get our caps and gowns," Gerry replied, telling him how he got back at Leroy for that time he 'Jellied' up the 'loo' with another equally stupid prank. While Lee was out during one bitterly cold day in the midst of winter, he enlisted the help of the frat house guys and together they took the mattress from Lee's bed, laid it out in the snow, wet it down and waited for it to freeze solid before sticking it back in his bed with the sheets all made up. Leroy got one very cold reception when he hit the hay that night! Gerry could still hear the boisterous guffawing of everyone in the house who stayed up to await the results that erupted when Lee began hollering like an Irish lunatic. Peter couldn't help but laugh over that story, however, there must have been quite a sopping mess to clean up afterwards he noted. Gerry made a grimace then chuckled. They had to try and thaw out the stupid thing in the bathtub, then lean it up against a wall somewhere for it to dry out completely because they sure as heck couldn't keep it outside in the freezing conditions. Leroy had to bunk on one of the sofas with his legs nearly three feet in the air until that got sorted out.

"Honestly, it was a madhouse at the frat house. Speaking of frat houses, how are all the Holy Bachelors doing at the rectory?"

"Let's say we've survived last night's dinner, barely," Peter trailed.

"Uh oh, it was Fr. Mark's turn to cook," Gerry guessed.

"You don't know the half of it."

When he arrived back from the office yesterday he was met by a grey haze wafting through the hallway accompanied by an unusual aroma suggesting something was getting scorched, plus an anxious Jenkins and O'Conner who quickly took him aside into the TV room with looks of consternation on their faces. Peter wondered what was up until O'Conner said they came home to find 'this' on the dinner table and handed him a large hardbound book: *Recipes for One Hundred.*

"Honestly, laddie, at first I wondered if we were expecting company, God help us, and them poor souls!"

"Then we saw the table set for four, so that wasn't it," Fr. Jenkins added. "We asked Mark what this was all about, and he said he'd tell us over dinner, he didn't have time to explain right then. We offered to help in the kitchen, but he insists he's got it covered tonight and to put our feet up and relax."

"Although there hasn't been much relaxing with the right riddle he's set before us, and here I thought our stomachs might get a rest now that our visiting African friends have gone home," O'Conner admitted.

Peter noted they would just have to wait until dinner was served to see what Mark was about to drop on them. After a few bangs and clatters issuing from the kitchen area, it wasn't long before Mark eagerly called them to the table and set out their night's fare, running back to the kitchen when he realized he forgot the bread. They looked down at their plates and didn't know whether to laugh or cry. Mark had decided on pork chops, but put them on way too soon in the oven on high grill so that the 'Quake n' Bake' instant coating had hardened, morphing the meat into something resembling a sliced asteroid that hit the ground somewhere in Arizona. The real mashed potatoes he had painfully peeled were left warming in the pot past their prime and had crusted into a brown-black cement on the bottom, while the string beans had lost their bright verdant colour and looked like sludgy matter dredged up from a pond. To top it off, Mark had told them he got a nice bottle of Italian wine as a treat, but obviously had no idea what he had picked up, a big bottle of fizzy Lambrusco. Jenkins turned to Peter Ben Hur:

"We keep you alive to serve this ship. Row well and live."

They could barely keep a straight face when Mark came back with the bread, looking quite pleased with himself at managing to cook the dinner without using hardly any pre-processed ready-made ingredients.

"I'm sorry about the potatoes, they browned a bit, but I served from the top of the pot, so we should be okay," he continued sitting down and rubbing his hands. "All righty! Who wants to say grace?"

Peter obliged.

"Bless us oh Lord, and these Thy gifts … ."

O'Conner and Jenkins nearly lost their composure. If these were the 'gifts' the Lord gave to his friends, no wonder He didn't have many.

" … which we are about to receive from Thy bounty … "

'Lord, if You are so bountiful, how come we got stuck with this,' O'Conner thought but didn't say aloud, a shared glance said it all.

" … through Christ, Our Lord. Amen," Peter concluded, although not quite sure how to approach his meal, the knife and fork didn't seem to want to stab through the chops.

"Sorry about that, they're a little well done. Better luck next time," Mark said as he dug in.

"So, what's up with the new cookbook," Peter enquired as he continued to wrestle with his share of the moon rock.

"Oh that! Well, I said Mass for the Little Sisters of the Poor as I usually do, then decided since I had an hour or two I'd help them out with their apostolate. The dears are so overworked, I had no idea. So, I thought whenever I had time to spare, I thought I'd help out in their soup kitchen for the needy … ,"

The struggling diners looked at each other around the table.

" … so on my way home, I stopped at a book store and found this in the half price stalls. What a bargain! I've got loads of ideas to share with the Sisters to help them out. Hey, I've forgotten the gravy! Anyone want some gravy?"

"Yes please," the three replied in unison, anything to help get the desiccated cuisine down their gullets.

"Okay, don't get up. I'll be back in a jiff," Mark said, jumping up and rushing off again to the kitchen, filled with enthusiasm over everything since he had a new mercy mission in mind.

"Mother of God! Of all places!" O'Conner gasped quickly as he blessed himself. "We can't have Mark mucking around in the soup kitchen!"

"Those poor nuns! They live a penitential life as it as without him 'helping' out," Jenkins blurted under his breath.

"And the homeless people? Their lives are hard enough. We can't have Mark inflicting his culinary skills on them, or lack thereof," Peter observed.

"What can we do? We can't tell him 'no', it'll upset him no end, he's so eager to help people, he can't see the muddle he gets himself into," O'Conner continued.

They quickly sobered up as best they could when Mark came back in bearing another pot filled with instant lumpy gravy. It had gone a bit thick, but it was wet at least.

"So, I was looking up some great recipes for the nuns, I didn't know you could do so much stuff with ground beef," Mark continued as he went around the table, glooping liberal globfuls of brown-hued substance on their plates.

"Now, are ye sure y'really want to do this," O'Conner tentatively enquired, "it would take a lot of energy you know. It could interfere with your own apostolate work … ."

Everyone waited for an answer.

"Nope, I don't think so, it would only be for the lunch hour anyway. We should all help out when we can, it wouldn't take much to get lunch out for the poor. Now, I know you're busy Pete, so you might not be able to do it at the moment, but I know the nuns would appreciate any little helping hand coming their way, just thought maybe I'd run it past you guys," Mark continued as he sat down and took a sip of wine, "hmm, didn't know this was bubbly, not too bad. Oh, if anyone wants seconds, go ahead, there's more grub to be had out there."

Obviously, Mark was not going to change his mind about volunteering for his new 'mission', plus everybody else for that matter!

At that moment, the phone rang, Peter got up and answered it to the envy of everyone crunching on their supper. It was Ron, Fr. Mark's eldest son.

"Hi Ron, thank you for calling, and I mean that, your father has just served us a rather unique meal, which I needed to take a break from."

"Tell him to stick to spaghetti rings, you might all live," Ron advised at the other end of the line.

Peter chatted with Ron for awhile, he was a pleasant young man now married with two little boys. He asked Ron how on earth he survived when his father took over the cooking.

"We didn't. Neither did the dog. All the crud we stuffed that poor hound with! It was a good thing our sister took over the cooking as soon as she could, we would never have made it. Dad means well though, how he can eat his own cooking baffled us. He can't taste anything wrong with it and thinks everyone else can eat it too."

"No kidding!" Peter laughed. "It's great to talk to you, I'll go get him."

Peter reluctantly went back to his supper, such as it was. When Mark went to take his call, there was an impromptu council held as to what they could do to minimise the damage their eager soup kitchen volunteer might mete out on the nuns and their charitable institution. O'Conner pointed out one of them might just have to volunteer with Mark in the end, if only to keep an eye on him. Jenkins agreed, they could help redirect him away from the cooking galley area to something less dangerous, like the veggie preparation. He would have to be barred from the potatoes Peter added, Mark's scalping skills would leave the poor with very little food in the way of spuds. The nuns had to get the most from their donations don't you know, losing half of each potato was not an option. He was good at shredding stuff, O'Conner chuckled. Perhaps what the nuns would lose in the potatoes Mark might make up in coleslaw. They *could* get him to simply dish out the chow after the nuns had cooked it Jenkins suggested, what could go wrong *there*? O'Conner finally agreed he'd go to supervise

Mark, although not without a little whinging, "Lads, I'm gettin' too old for this malarkey!"

Gerry had to catch his breath from laughing when Peter finished his story.

"Ah Pete, you really should take up Mom's offer of getting you guys a housekeeper that can cook, you really need one."

"Thanks, but at the same time, we 'holy bachelors' need our privacy. Housekeepers get too inquisitive about how we live and are always snooping around our closets, or checking out our beds to see what kind of blankets and sheets we use. The last housekeeper we tried drove O'Conner up the wall. I don't know where they get this idea that we stopped being human after we get our collars, we live quite ordinary lives as everyone else and have cotton sheets and pyjamas, just like they do."

"I can see the problem. Okay, so how do you guys manage it? Running that place with all your schedules?"

"It's not easy, but we get there. As with the cooking, we also take turns doing the cleaning."

"That must be a sight, seeing you in work gear and rubber gloves scrubbing out the shower." Gerry chuckled, then noted Peter's expression. "So you *do* have rubber gloves and scrub out the shower. I might have to get you a frilly apron to go with your lovely ensemble," he teased, amused yet touched Peter really was taking his humble life to heart, imagining his brother dutifully doing his part cleaning out the tub and toilet. "You know Pete, if you or the guys need anything, don't hesitate to ask me, okay? To be honest, I haven't done much with your share of the inheritance, the part you gave back to me I mean. I still don't feel like I have the right to spend it."

"You mean you've left *all* that untouched?"

"Pretty much, it's accumulating interest in a separate account. I did help a few charities all right, but it still feels like it's yours, you know? I don't think Lottie used much of her part either."

"Aw Ger, you go ahead and use it with a clear conscience, all I ask is don't do something stupid with it, and to consider a few more worthy charities to give to."

"Like that soup kitchen, I could hire real help, give the sisters a break and keep Mark out of there for you guys."

"Nope, can't take away the sisters' apostolate from them either, send food and cash, they'll appreciate that. We'll figure out what to do with Mark, eventually."

Gerry still wanted to make sure Peter wasn't in need or want, and insisted he see him if there was anything at all that he could help out with.

"For instance Pete, what about that order you always wanted to set up? Do you still have plans for that?"

"Oh, that." Peter sighed. "So far, it's just an idea, a magnificent dream that may never come to fruition."

"One can always dream. Tell me about it."

Peter explained his concept of an order devoted solely to the active ministry of exorcism, people of prayer were needed in that particular ministry in addition to exorcists, and it would be wonderful to have brothers and an order of sisters take religious vows of chastity, poverty and obedience just for that purpose. With an army of prayer warriors behind them, exorcists would find that their exorcisms would be even more powerful, individual cases of deliverances from evil might be accomplished faster and with less gruelling effort. The existence of such an order would help the world understand that this was not some spooky joke or farce, but was a very serious ministry indeed. Naturally, it would be a 'slow-grow', it was difficult enough trying to get bishops to appoint enough exorcists let alone approach them about this idea, not to mention find people ready to dedicate their lives for this singular vocation.

"Not only that, but don't the different orders have to find a way to support themselves," Gerry recalled. "If I remember, the Franciscans and the Carmelites grow their own food."

"True, but the Franciscans for instance often rely on the charity of the community too, this new order of exorcists could do the same."

"You're going to starve. I think you should make beer, just like the monks in Europe. You'd be sure to have a steady income."

"So the spirit-chasers end up brewing spirits for funding. A bit ironic, don't you think?" Peter laughed.

"Hey, it is a time-honoured Church tradition, right? I'm all for it," Gerry jovially returned. "But honestly, if your dream ever gets off the ground, you're going to need funding just to set up, get you a regular monastery building or something with your own chapel, and all of that. The money would be put to good use then."

"Aw Ger, I really appreciate that, but I didn't give you back everything just to take it away again."

"Look Pete, I certainly don't have need of it, my own share of everything plus my private earnings and investments have me and Kathy set up for several lifetimes, we certainly have plenty to live on, so just keep your dream running on the back burner knowing there's the financial backing to get it going, when and if you get the go ahead. Do we have a deal?"

"Ger, I really appreciate it, thank you, you truly are one generous soul, but I won't hold you to it. Nothing may ever come of this order, and besides, what about you? You still can start your art auction house after all, or help invest in one with your friend, I couldn't take your dream away from you a second time. That would be heartless."

"Oh, if I still wanted to do *that*, I have enough of my own capital, but I've gotten past that like I said earlier. Running an auction house doesn't seem appealing any more, I'd rather just attend the auctions. I think it was one of those bright ideas that sound tantalizing in the beginning when they first strike you, but you find out later they're not anything like you thought they were going to be in the end. Since I've met Katherine I've come to realize what I really was missing was being a part of something creative, and I don't need to conquer the world to do it. The simple things are enough. I've enjoyed watching her get that gallery on its feet and helping out with it, not to mention all her art lessons, I've found a peace and contentment that I haven't felt for a long time."

"It shows." Peter smiled.

"Nah, that's the meds right now, but seriously, I am crazy about Kathy, and I want to help you do whatever you're meant to do. I wish I had given you more support back you-know-when, so I hope you don't mind if it's better late than never."

"Thank you, I don't mind at all, but I'd prefer prayers first above anything else, and you have been a great help already. I love the chalice and paten you, Mom and Lottie got for me, they're exquisite."

"We knew you'd like them, however, if you need anything else, don't be shy, okay? For instance, Kathy told me the other day she wished she could see you with some new vestments, the ones you've been using look like they should be buried, and from what I've seen, I agree. Doesn't the cathedral have any better stock than that?"

"Yes, but the modern kind, I'm afraid. The vestments for the Latin Mass are different, and since no one's been saying that rite much except for me, the old patterns don't get replaced."

"Ah ha! *Now* I know what to get you for your birthday. Honestly, we have no idea what to give you since you were ordained, I mean, what to get a priest who's given up everything? You'd have to pick out the ones you want though, I wouldn't know what to get or where to get them, and don't be stingy."

"That would mean a trip either to Italy or France, and I don't know when I could ever plan that, but I really *do* need something fitting for the altar … could I take a rain check?"

"Of course. Italy you say, eh? Looks like you may be coming with us on our honeymoon after all! The nice part is these custom vestments would be your own private stock, no one else will wreck them on you, and don't forget to get those cool cloak-like things too, you know, the ones for processions? Maybe this is the beginning of outfitting you for your future order."

"What a promise! But I won't crash your honeymoon." Peter laughed. "Thank you Gerry, this means a lot to me, you have no idea."

"No need to thank me. Besides, you've already saved up for it in advance when you think of it, just consider me your personal banker," Gerry concluded with a smile.

Peter then wondered how Gerry's artwork was progressing and he showed him his most complete watercolour sketch of Katherine and eagerly discussed his plans for an oil. Peter was impressed, this was very different from his fruit bowl paintings Katherine started him off on. It had the hallmarks of something wrought by a master.

"But this scene, it was the *second* night you took her out you say, not the first date? Since you're so crazy about her, what about first impressions?"

"Oh, let's say the second time was much better, it was a first kiss thing, you understand."

"Ah."

It was ages since they had a deep conversation like this, it was gratifying to reconnect on this level, reminding them of those times when as kids they used to sneak out to the beach in the middle of the night while the manor was still, talking about anything and everything, lying on the sand looking up at the stars as they listened to the sound of the surf rolling upon the shore. However, their conversation was interrupted by a knock on the door, one of the nurses came to remind Peter visiting hours were ending soon. They said their goodbyes for the night, glad they had relieved so much off theirs chests and had a laugh or two. Before he left, Gerry asked his brother who was cooking tonight at the rectory, it was Fr. O'Conner. Apparently, he found Mark's new cookbook interesting and was going to try shrinking one of the chicken recipes for 'one hundred' down to four. Gerry hoped for their sakes he would be successful, or they were going to end up with a lot of leftovers. Maybe the nuns might get one day free from cooking after all, Peter added with a laugh as he closed the door behind him.

Alone with his thoughts, Gerry couldn't help but grow a little anxious for Peter and wondered if he shouldn't drop a polite but acidic hint to Clarke when she came in the next morning to back off and leave Pete alone, but thought better of it. It was like one of those small but annoying cuts that gave a person the urge to scratch it against all common sense that it should be left to heal. Clarke was a volatile situation that if prodded with any good intentions to keep it in check, it could evolve into something worse if not left alone. Better to let that wound heal itself if it could, Pete seemed to know what he was doing, at least, Gerry hoped so.

⋄

Monday morning the artistic colony at the gallery were busy combing the papers to find out more about the grand opening of their latest rival in Fifth Avenue despite having spent nearly all Sunday going over the weekend editions, without Suzy that is, who was running a bit late. Katherine still hadn't seen her at Oak Meadows that Sunday, so she must have stayed in town with Charlie. She hoped she would come soon, the suspense of what the Elverton place was really like from someone who had seen it personally was eating her up no end. Rehashing the papers would have to do for now.

"Huh, 'Elverton Gallery', after all the secretive hubbub, not very original. Horace was right about that," Dennis noted, "all that hype over a new name, and duh! It's the owner's. Big fat deal."

"That's what Sir Snoop did, make a big deal out of it," Katherine commented.

"Smart though, you have to admit." Esther shrugged. "It incited curiosity and created publicity."

"True, and what is worse, good publicity is everything when there is substance! It is rather disappointing! Just how did he get Kroger to grace the floor with his presence," Kevin wanted to know.

"Um, let's see," Katherine replied, running her finger through the column she was currently reading. "Doesn't say. Of course Elverton won't reveal his business secrets, but I bet he blackmailed him, or something."

"I noticed they have a number of Belvedere graduates too, it seems Sir Elverton is trying to copy you in every department Kathy, those names

361

are very familiar," the Professor observed, "ah yes, that one was one of the anti-Ingres philistines, didn't last long in my class I must admit."

Esther looked closer to see the name.

"Oh, him? If I remember correctly, ripped jeans, ear and nose rings, he was voted by his peers to become the most avant-garde artist and make his first million before the Millennium," she recalled.

"How do you remember him just by the name, my dear," the Professor wondered. "You had so many students pass through the library over the years."

"Why, I familiarised myself with all the yearbooks. Not to mention I could easily single him out as the student who was always overdue in returning books and had the most accumulated fines of his class. He failed to return quite a few as I recall. Makes him difficult to forget."

"Whoa. Glad I never turned in anything late," Dennis interjected.

"No, you were quite the dutiful library patron. I believe you had a partiality for the colour plate collections on Miró and Duchamp."

Goodness! No wonder Esther could complete the daily crossword puzzle in ink—no pencil, no eraser, gifted with a hawk-like memory for facts just like Professor 'Get-Your Details-Right' Adams at Belvedere. Of course, one of her favourite hobbies was looking up new words in the dictionary too.

"The worst part about it all is Horace made a mean link between Eleverton's 'circus parade' and us here in Dumbo, that's below the belt," Dennis continued, scanning through the grouchy column once more. "So our artworks are 'freaks' riding around in bumper cars too? What a jerk!"

Katherine cracked a smile, she knew first hand it was difficult for artistic temperaments to have their colourful 'children' criticised in public, but Horace actually did them all a favour she noticed as a few prospective art patrons entered and began browsing through the 'bumper-car' rolly-pollies. It would be nice to begin Monday morning with a sale.

"Sorrysorrysorry! I'm so sorry," Suzy blurted as she came scurrying through the back door. "I know, I'm horribly late ... no excuse, slept in, then traffic, I'm so sorry! And Charlie never woke me up! Just went off to work," she declared breathlessly, dunking her purse out of sight under the front desk.

"He knew you needed to rest and that I'd forgive you, so you're forgiven, well, sort of! We're dying to hear news," Katherine exclaimed.

"Wait, let's order another round of coffee first, then the news," the Professor suggested.

As they enjoyed their second libations of caffeine, the Gang were all ears as Suzy described the innovative decorating of the Elverton in detail. The main design of the interior with regards to the four walls of the building were pretty much left as they were when it was formerly the Sirrac Gallery, all in white, but there were no stationary display walls inside at all, they had been taken out, except for the support pillars of the building, naturally. The colour was added with the various 'rolling' walls of different heights that could be wheeled in any direction and placed in a multitude of different angles, which meant the floor could be given a new look whenever they wanted. The cool part was the walls didn't seem to have any wheels as they were concealed inside and out of sight. Suzy then noted the former Sirrac had black floors, but not like this: spanking new jet-ebony granite was laid on every level, it simply glistened as the millions of quartz flecks embedded in the rock were revealed by the spotlights. Katherine then had a question, how could they move the walls around and light them up so well? If the display lighting was stationary, wouldn't the placement of the rolling walls be limited?

"Oh, that's one of the cool bits," Suzy admitted, "the whole ceiling is like a magnetised metal sheeting mesh thingy in black, and they can just take the track lights off and put them on wherever they want to, even on top of the rolling walls so they can act as over head lamps from there too, and oh, the lamp necks are telescopic like desk lamps, so they can be twisted wherever they need light.

"But what about wires? If they can magnetise the lamps on top of the rolling walls, how do they power the walls and keep them mobile at the same time? Electricity needs wires," Katherine pointed out.

"That's the *really* cool part, there is a black wire coming out of the top of each wall that keeps in contact with the ceiling where the power is, so as long as they stay touching each other, the walls are powered, and they can move them too! Horace got his description right, Sir Snoop gave a little demonstration and showed that they stayed lit even when being rolled around, sometimes they even give off sparks like bumper cars."

"What will they think up next?" The Professor nodded.

"Holy smokes, that is rather ingenious," Dennis conceded.

"Even so, poor Mr Sirrac would be in bits if he knew his beloved gallery was now converted into something nothing short of a fair ground!" Kevin moaned, still lamenting the tragic demise of his former employer, Mr. Sirrac.

"Yeah, just hope no one touches the ceiling, or they might get a free perm and curl job. So, did you try the restaurant? What's it like," Olivia prodded, oblivious to Kevin's grief.

"That really was a bit futuristic, huge plates with abstract designs on them, and little dainty servings. It tasted gorgeous all right, but I'd rather have more food and less graphics on my plate," Suzy shrugged. "I mean really! Look at Andre now, he gives gourmet fare at just the right amount without losing any artistic style."

"Thank goodness for that," a jovial voice issued from the side door, it was Gramps with Jasper trotting along beside him.

"Hi Gramps! What brings you to our neck of the woods?"

"Why, Andre's regal breakfasts of course. I'm gong to give him another go, maybe his skills have come up in the meantime."

"Now why would I ever think you would come to visit little old me," Katherine returned. "Give me a hug, or you don't get any breakfast."

"Just kidding pet, of course I dropped by for a visit, see how you all were doing, although a fancy pancake or three would be mighty appreciated too," Gramps said as he gave the requested hug while Jasper got rubs behind his furry ears from everyone else. "Not to mention it's 'Monday Madness', you know no one can rest in that house when the cleaners arrive. I couldn't take that after a few days of your aunt on her guard patrol, stomping back and forth glaring out the windows, so thought I'd make myself scarce as usual. Any spare chairs around here?"

"Certainly, Mr. Walsingham," Kevin declared, jumping up from his comfortable leather chair and wheeling it around, "shall I order you your favourite coffee?"

"Thank 'ee, much obliged," Gramps replied, which sent Kevin off at a clip to the restaurant area and order the desired refreshment while Gramps settled in next to the artistic community. "So, what's the verdict from our assembled jury? Sounds like you have tough competition on the other side of the metropolis."

"Your honour, the jury is hung. I wish the Elverton had never opened, but the place sounds so darn interesting despite its modernity I can't help but respect my adversary," Katherine grumbled, folding her arms. Gramps chuckled with this concession.

"Golly, I didn't get to the party part yet, there was a live swing band and everything," Suzy continued, giving a detail by detail account of who showed up, at least the famous people she could recognise, she didn't bother keeping track of the politicians as much beyond the senator and the mayor whom she and Charlie couldn't miss. The funny albeit somewhat underhanded part was she went in well armed with Walsingham Gallery business cards that they stealthily gave to all and sundry, so the evening had its uses.

"Suzy! You're an angel! I didn't think of that! Gerry says I have to plot and plan like all good generals, and you're the best military strategist of them all."

"Talk about going to the mattresses," Gramps remarked.

"Exactly! I'm putting you in my war cabinet, Suzy. Serves Sir Snoop right for crashing *our* joint!" Katherine was delighted with her friend's quick thinking. How come she never remembered to bring enough business cards with her anywhere? Art a business, and business a war—yuck!

"So, what about the artists? Get to meet any of them," Dennis wondered, still intrigued with all the famous modern contemporaries who were either on show or invited to the event.

"A few. Lemnen was a nice guy, I can't believe what Kroger did to him! However, Charlie and I missed it because Hanley wanted to talk, he was in another section showing off his latest sculptures, but the news flew around the floor I can tell you that," Suzy affirmed.

"What? You guys gabbed with Hanley?" Katherine couldn't believe it.

"Oh yeah, just a few minutes, he heard that we had one of his pieces on permanent display and he wondered which one. I told him it was his sculpture called *Serenity*, and he said we were lucky, it was one of his favourites and was almost sorry he let it go."

"You're not serious," Katherine replied, amused no end. Suzy could share in her reaction. If only he knew what they thought of the shapeless mass tucked away in the front corner they had dubbed the 'orphan', an opinion they dare not share in front of Gramps who helped secure that donation. Dennis however was impressed, she and Charlie got to meet so many creative stars who succeeded in making names and fortunes for themselves.

"Yeah, but that doesn't mean my work will get any extra publicity. I just pray the business cards work for us all," Suzy pointed out.

"Amen to that! Dear God, all I ask is a chance to prove that overnight success won't go to my head." Dennis sighed. It was difficult not to get nipped by a little beginner's anxiety since the younger members of the Gallery Gang were still recently graduated rookie professionals trying to astound the world after fledging from the art school nest.

"Oh! Speaking of famous artists, you won't believe what good news I have, I hope something comes of it," Katherine announced, telling them of Mr. R's promise to approach some absurd fellows among his artistic contacts and see if they would consider showing their next collections with them. When Katherine mentioned the name Stansislov, a few jaws dropped.

"Why, that would be just spiffy," Suzy exclaimed with a gasp.

"I thought you were generally an anti-abstractionist like me," Katherine noted, raising an eyebrow.

"I am, but Mr R. and Gerry have the right idea. We need to start pushing the nouveau-elite image if we're to compete with the likes of the Elverton and Saatchi," Suzy explained. Kevin, Esther and Dennis nodded in agreement.

"I dunno Kathy, so much for your lofty principles. That means a lot of added flapdoodle on your walls," Gramps ribbed. "Will it work here in your fancy shin-dig I wonder? It looks too much like old France to pull it off."

"I'm afraid Mr. Walsingham has a point," Kevin politely interjected. "Artists like Stansislov only wish to show their art in a place they consider displays it in its best light and in its proper setting. Now, don't take this the wrong way, personally, I *love* your new rendition of the Louvre, Miss Kathy, but for the *modernistes*, they prefer a more ... a more," Kevin trailed, searching for the right word.

"More of nothing," Esther interjected in her deadpan tone while the Professor could only look on.

"Well, I wouldn't have expressed it with such brusqueness," Kevin continued, "but yes, something on the order of archetypal starkness, the tantalizing, mesmerising quality of asceticism, something with a minimalist edge, a viewing space with an urban 'bite', if I were to make a suggestion, that is."

"I think that's four," Esther observed.

"In that case, it's a pity you spent so much loot giving this old factory a facelift Katie, you could have saved a fortune leaving it as it was. You just can't give people nice things these days," Gramps noted with a 'hrumph'!

"The sad part is, I think you may be right," Katherine returned, folding her arms again. "After all my efforts trying to pull the art world out of the nonsense it has gotten itself into, and now I'll have to play along just to stay *in* the art world."

"Let the games begin," Olivia added, "business is business after all."

"True. Rarely do the high ideals of art live beyond an artist's canvas," the Professor observed, pushing his glasses up from the tip of his nose.

"I suppose I'll just have to be content keeping my high ideals confined to my own artwork then, but what to do about the gallery though," Katherine continued. Unlike Elverton's sparky new innovations whizzing around his glossy stone floors, she couldn't move her silk-panelled European-style walls upstairs, they were all stationary, especially with the numberless security trip-wires. Even her rolly-pollies on the ground floor didn't have a mobile lighting mechanism like his, and they too were finished in classic silk-panelling like her walls yet edged in gigantic voluted frames. How to 'starken up' her place to reflect urban modernity was a new challenge she certainly wasn't expecting nor wanted. She wasn't changing her classic European interior, that was that.

"You could always open up the old boiler house out back, that seems bleak enough." Suzy suggested with a shrug. Katherine laughed.

"Good idea, but no, we can't have people going in and out of our storeroom and packing areas, not to mention where the heating system is, though it does have good wall space on the upper gangways in there. Nuts! I'll have to think about what to do."

"In the meantime, we can hope that Mr. Stansislov will consider a showing in your elegant environment," Kevin continued, "he can be an obliging fellow at times, despite his gloomy qualities."

"Well, that's good. Now to find a few more odd fellows," Katherine concluded.

"If I may Miss Kathy, are you really interested in showing exceptional specimens of modernity?"

"Yes Kevin, just as long as they're not in to 'tutti nudies'. I need additional established artists to get us all noticed, the abstractionists, the minimalists, and all the neo-'ists' I can find. If I have to go to the mattresses, I'm sure as heck going to pull out all the springs and foam."

"Splendid! In that case, may I make a few enquiries for you?" Kevin put his hand in his suit jacket and retrieved a little black book from his pocket. "I have an exclusive list of anyone and everyone who ever had a showing at the Sirrac."

"What! You mean you've been holding back all the goods on me?" Katherine laughed. "Were you ever going to tell me of that little black book of yours?"

"Er, it didn't seem like you wanted to show much of anything resembling the former Sirrac's emblematic offerings," he calmly explained, "but as you have been so kind, more than most people were to me when in my darkest hour, I am willing to share my valuable connections."

"In that case, you get a raise, and so does everyone else, as soon as those specimens of modernity start coming in," Katherine declared. If she had more profits rolling in by the way of top-dollar artists, she could certainly give them all a well-deserved pay hike. "Who have you got in there by the way?"

Everyone eyed his little book with curiosity as he began reciting names in his 'A' section since all his artists were neatly listed in alphabetical order. However, Dennis noticed the first 'A-list' artists were mostly painters.

"What about more sculptors? This place could use some 3-D pieces, if you don't mind me saying, boss," Dennis concluded.

"Nope, all suggestions are welcome, it might be interesting to stick a few statues among the walkways," Katherine nodded.

Kevin flipped ahead in his book and ran his finger down a page, stopping at a certain spot.

"Ah! Now here's a thought! How about someone you two ladies have already met? John Fielding?"

Katherine and Suzy gave a puzzled look at each other until they recalled the night Suzy had a special showing at the Sirrac.

"Oh heck! The fellow who spouts poetry? Yeah! Why not? He doesn't do nudes, right?"

"On occasion, so we would have to verify what he is working on, but it is a rarity for him. He is more into abstract objects, plus, he is more inclined to show an entire collection at once. I don't believe he would go for your 'rotation' method," Kevin gingerly pointed out.

"That's okay if he'd rather plonk a whole collection on our floors, we certainly have the space. I guess I'll let you get the ball rolling since you're a natural at this."

"Why, thank you Miss Kathy, I shall begin immediately," he announced with flair.

Obviously that was the cue coffee time was over and to give the artistic executives their space. Everyone headed off to their various pursuits, be it the gift shop, the upper floors, or the studio, except for Esther whose duty for the day was behind the front desk, and also Gramps, who was curious to see how this new arty telemarketing project would fare, so they sat and witnessed the proceedings as Kevin made himself comfortable in one of the vacated leather chairs. Before he started, Kevin wondered if Katherine wanted him to contact Stansislov first, but she decided not right now, Mr. R might get disappointed if they jumped the gun on him after he promised his assistance.

"Of course Miss Kathy, what was I thinking? All right then, shall we try skipping from A to F and reach out to Fielding?"

"By all means, skip away."

Kevin dialled the desired number, their anticipation increased as they waited for someone to answer, and hopefully, a fruitful call to unfold. They waited … .

"Hellooooo, J.F.! It's Alcott … yes … how are you darrrrling? It has been awhile, hasn't it? I'm splendiferous. I survived the Sirrac's untimely demise … yes … yes, oh reeeally, you don't say! Well, I hope I haven't caught you in a creative moment … no? That's wonderful! I have some news for you, that is, if you are not already obliged to a showing anywhere … ? How judicious! Listen to this: my new place of employment is on the lookout for a master sculptor to grace its floors … You haven't heard? I'm at the Walsingham … no, they want true modern substance this time, real art of the here and now. … Yes, I know, but would you consider it? … Oh? What's that? … Bless my stars, you don't say? A totally new medium? Why, you've broken through to another plane, how marvellous! We would be de-light-ed to set up an exhibition, but you would have to see the space available? Of course we understand. So what new medium have you been up to, you seraph of sculptors? Iron and steel? My, that is a change from sandstone … ."

At that point Kevin clapped his hand over the receiver, and shrugged his shoulders slightly at Katherine, who understood what he was asking. Was iron and steel okay for her? She paused a moment, quickly looked to heaven, then shrugged back and rolled her hand signalling to 'go ahead'. Iron and steel couldn't be any worse than his former bulbous abstract creations as she recalled them, right? She did say she wanted to pull out all the mattress springs. At least Fielding had a fiercely loyal following for whatever he made, might as well be the first gallery to display the latest phase of his sculptural career. His new metallic method of poetically expressing himself was bound to sell like hotcakes. However, she whispered to Kevin not to forget one important question, which he put to the touchy artist as delicately as he could.

"Uh hum? Listen, my delightful new employer has only oooone little stipulation about any work placed on exhibit: what manner of figures does your new collection contain? Any human representations? Yes? What kind may I ask … ? 'Something on the order of stylised sticks', that sounds very fascinating …um, will they be displaying any … prominent anatomical features? … They're 'more or less androgynous', uh huh! Very well, we should be very interested in your latest masterpieces then," Kevin noted, brightening up once more, it appeared detailed nudes would not be featured in this year's offering, much to Katherine's relief. She may have to compromise on some of her artistic principals, but she was sticking to her guns in this area, that was it. "So, when might we hope to see your creative presence," Kevin continued. "Maybe today? How marvellous! Yes, certainly Miss Walsingham will be here, she is most interested in your latest work. Excellent darling, bye bye now, don't disappoint us … ." Kevin then laughed. "Oh stop, that's priceless! See you later, ta ta!"

At last, he hung up the phone—success! Fielding was interested and would be dropping by later this afternoon.

"Wow, you got him interested, great! Well done," Katherine congratulated.

"Thank you my dear, but it was nothing really. The secret is you must give the temperamentals the BS treatment," Kevin disclosed, then noticed their faces. "What?" he returned, spreading his hands, "I mean the *'Big Smile'*! Happiness gets you everywhere."

"I could have sworn he meant the *other* kind," Esther noted under her breath to Gramps.

"So kiddo, now that you have the 'seraph of sculptors' coming by, who else is next," he wondered, his cheeks turning red trying not to chortle through their business dealings.

"My, my, my," Kevin declared as he flipped back to some skipped letters in his exclusive directory, "I haven't heard about a new collection from Denninger in a while. Shall I put out some feelers, Miss Kathy? See if he has anything in the works?"

"What? You have him too? Oh yes," she nodded eagerly. "Please do."

"Er, who's this Denninger?" Gramps was curious to know, seeing Katherine's sudden interest.

"Why, only the greatest modern impressionist of our time—the 'Palette Knife Prince' no less," Kevin imperially announced.

"Who's also a reclusive nut case. Good luck with that one," Esther dryly added.

"Now now now, nothing ventured, nothing gained," Kevin stoically returned as he dialled.

Once more Gramps and Esther were provided with some entertainment as Kevin assumed a completely different approach when he put out some feelers to the royal nut job, assuring the flighty Denninger over and over that this was indeed Alcott calling, that he had not been abducted by aliens, had all his own internal organs still intact and was now gainfully employed at the Walsingham Gallery. Yes, the phone line was indeed secure and not bugged by the FBI or the CIA, it was well swiped and cleared of all strange chips and wires he also assured. No, the new gallery was quite safe, it was in the heart of historic Brooklyn … there were no hidden laboratories … no, no, no, he was absolutely positive the Walsingham Pharmaceutical company did not do secret experiments for the government … no hallucinogens or mind-control experiments … and besides, the gallery was no longer part of that company, it was just the family name … .

Katherine had no idea that Denninger was this paranoid as she listened to Kevin trying to earn the painter's confidence, maybe she was inviting more trouble than she bargained for. She was about to whisper to Kevin to forget it and end the 'negotiations', when it appeared he had actually acquired Denninger for a showing, it was too late to say no.

"Oh, brother," Esther said, deciding to concentrate on something logical and pulled out the latest crossword from her favourite paper.

"Why, isn't this just exciting," Kevin declared as he hung up, diplomatically ignoring Esther's comment. "He is considering the gallery's location and might go for it, the man has had not one but *two* collections languishing in his studio for three and a half years, but didn't feel there was an exhibition space he could trust them with, especially since the Sirrac closed. He was approached by Elverton all right, but thinks he's untrustworthy, so we are fortunate indeed! You see, there are only a few places in this city where the Zenarks of Planet Gej cannot penetrate with their advanced technology, it seems they have stolen quite a few of his paintings in the past with their invisible tractor beams," Kevin disclosed, twirling his finger around the side of his temple, indicating what he thought of Denninger's information despite the good news at the possibility of securing his latest masterpieces before anyone else.

"You don't say? What a hoot!" Gramps hadn't heard the like!

"I'm afraid so, the man's quite *woo hoo*," Kevin intoned in falsetto, shaking his head and twirling his finger in the air this time, "however, his art is quite the thing I can tell you," he assured them in his usual tone of voice. "We will have collectors flocking from all over the minute his show is announced. For instance, he has some avid admirers in Los Angeles, Dubai and Belgium."

"No way." Katherine gasped.

"Yes way, from every which way," he assured her. "Who shall I look up next?"

"You sure you want another one? From the sound of things, they could be an axe-murderer," Gramps joked, "but if this Denninger does come, how are you going to handle him? Sounds like he needs medical supervision, and lots of it."

"Oh don't worry," Kevin replied with an accompanying hand-flutter. "He's quite harmless, once you get to know him, although while he's around I would keep very quiet about Area 51, NASA, Roswell, the KGB, the Kennedy assassination, you get the picture. However, I always keep some sedatives on hand, just in case."

"Swell, I can't wait," Esther commented, not looking up from her paper as she filled in another word.

Gramps would have stayed a bit longer to see who else they dug up from Kevin's book, but his hunger was getting the better of him, not to mention Jasper who was turning his nose towards the restaurant with a whine, then putting a friendly paw on his master's knee.

"You're right boy, time to get some vitals. Looks like it'll have to be lunch now," he noted, checking his watch. "Darn, I was looking forward to some pancakes."

"Mind if I join your grandfather," Esther asked Katherine, who nodded her approval.

"Go ahead, please do, Kevin and I have quite a few things to go over, then we can work out the rest of the lunch shifts."

"Great! Come Esther, I'm sure your hubby will join us in a moment," Gramps said as he heaved himself out of the chair with the aid of his cane.

"I don't think so, art first before everything. I swear the man can't feel hunger," she replied.

"We'll buzz him in a few minutes," Katherine promised. Professor Matthews was liable to get absorbed in a project and waste away without realising it.

"Thank you dear," Esther smiled before she and Gramps took their leave and went over to check the day's lunch specials, which a waiter had just put out on display, while Katherine and Kevin got into the nitty gritty of the gallery business.

Now that they had secured, or were eighty percent sure they had secured two celebrity artists, Katherine wondered what was the best thing to do next and didn't mind asking Kevin's opinion since he had more experience. In his estimation, it was best to check up on a few more creative people, see if and when they would like a showing and if they preferred to do whole collections at once since the première of a new series had to be carefully planned depending on when one set began to sell out or attract less attention. However, he would try and pitch her rotation method after that to see if any of them wouldn't mind keeping the gallery stocked with a never-ending supply of individual pieces. Well, since they first needed a few more artists to keep whole collections 'spaced and placed', she wondered who else he could suggest, but no axe murderers please if he could help it. Actually, Kevin had a lady vegetarian in mind. Katherine gave the signal to go ahead, that sounded good to her. The call didn't take too long, the vegetarian was interested, especially when she heard about the gallery's reasonable commission rates. One more artist might do it, he called one fellow whose abstract shapes were very popular, but he was not ready to show anything at the moment, not until next spring perhaps, but would be delighted to reserve his collection for the Walsingham Gallery for then. Still, that was great news, it gave them an opportunity to plan the schedules of the other collections, if they nabbed them.

"I must say we've had a very productive morning!" Kevin smiled, gleefully clapping his hands after he replaced the receiver.

"I'll say. Kevin, you're marvellous. Now, the next thing we should do is follow more of Mr. R's advice and see if we can't start using the other family name around here. I'm thinking we should print new title cards for the paintings of our artists who are included in the private Reinold collection upstairs. Mr. R and Gerry says everyone wants to be a part of what they collect and that we shouldn't let such publicity go to waste. Not to mention we could now consider adding to the prices if we do that."

"Why, that is a capital idea, Miss Kathy," he announced, turning to the computer, then stopping to think for a moment. "Hmm, what to say? How to be stylish and not too obvious? Must not be tactless you know, even if we do have to go to the mattresses. This is tricky tricky tricky. Of course, I have it! We could write, 'Featured artist in the private Reinold Collection' next to their credentials; simple, truthful, yet not too *gauche*."

"That sounds good. We'll beat this Elverton yet, just you wait."

"To the trenches!" Kevin tapped away with zeal, then stopped again. "How much are we increasing the prices?"

"I'm not sure. Do you think my prices are too low?"

"Positively Miss Kathy, I'm amazed you haven't given them a nudge upward already. Your artists, including your new discoveries, are now proving quite popular. It's time to up the larger pictures by another grand or two at least, can't rush it in case we come across as greedy as well as *gauche*, if you forgive me for saying."

"You're forgiven, caution is best, mustn't kill the golden goose as Gramps keeps reminding us all. You have a feel for the popular artists around here, so I'll let you determine which get the new prices, just run the cards past me before we put them up."

"Of course, and I know just who we should grace with an improved mark-up. Oh, I have a thought!" He suddenly stopped, his eyes widening with inspiration. "Mr. Gerard's collection is to all intents and purposes a private collection open freely to the public, yes?"

"Yes, that's true."

"Well, why not notify the travel guide publishers? I'm sure they would be glad to consider including a mention of the gallery. We could have art lovers from all over the world come flocking to your door during their holidays, on and off season!"

After all the book-worming she did through her travel books in scouting out the best galleries in Paris awhile back, the idea never struck her.

"You are a godsend Kevin! How do we go about that?"

"A little investigation is in order, we could get a copy of all the popular guidebooks and see who publishes them."

"Okay, we'll have to make a day of it then, but there's no rush to notify anyone just yet since the latest editions are already out for this year. As for the new title cards, I'll leave you to it."

Kevin seemed to know what he was doing, sales certainly increased since he came to their establishment, he had a very genial persona that seemed to resonate with art collectors, not to mention many of his clientèle followed him from the Sirrac when the word began to spread about where he had relocated. Katherine left him to his printing job while she decided to take a jaunt around the old boiler house out back, just in case she had to consider that as an option for the new minimal-minded artists. She opened the door to the service hallway and was surprised to see Andre all decked out as usual in his chef's gear, pacing up and down and muttering under his breath and wiping his brow with his apron, followed by Jasper with cocked ears as though he was wondering why the kind human that gave him so much good food seemed this perturbed. Startled, Katherine asked what was wrong.

"It's a catastrophe! Don Highland, the city's most astute food critic is on my floor, and the new waitress didn't know who he was, and therefore *I* didn't know he was here!"

"Oh, nerves is it," Katherine replied, a little relieved. "I thought you were hoping he'd come? You've been on the lookout for a visit from him for ages."

"I know, but his plate is a disaster!"

"Aw, how could it be? Your food is beyond excellent and the critics have always been kind, not to mention you're constantly winning awards and shiny new plaques for the door. What's to worry about?"

"Everything! You don't know what's just happened—he ordered the same dish as your grandfather and the waitress mixed them up … ."

"You mean the critic got the … ?"

"The *diet dish* jammed with just about every calorie-reduced article in my larder! There goes *Chez Garneau.* I'll be ruined!"

Katherine was stunned. After Andre was doing his best to get cheeky Gramps straightened out on his diet and was now sweating bricks for his efforts.

"Now don't jump to conclusions, you're not ruined yet! We've got to think," Katherine stammered.

"We can't do anything now! At least Highland got the right appetiser, and hopefully he might order one of my speciality desserts, it would cut the damage down to a third, but the main dish is what's important! Of all the food critics, he never tells a chef when he's coming or makes a reservation, he just drops by unannounced, obviously to see how the food is on any given day, and for *this* to happen!"

"There's nothing for it, we could try telling him what happened somehow, the truth might save the day."

"But how? I can't just approach him out there like this, it would look bad, and your Gramps will find out what we've been doing to him, in a spectacular fashion I might add," Andre replied, resuming his pacing once more with Jasper looking utterly confused. Katherine felt like pacing with him, but was struck with an idea:

"Look, you can tell the truth and be discreet. Just slip him a very nice letter explaining you have a customer with a medical condition with special dietary requirements, that he got their plate by mistake, say lunch is on the house, and offer him another free complimentary meal for two, or whatever number you like as compensation for the mix-up. It can't be any worse than what just happened, you can't leave things as they are hoping he didn't notice."

Andre stopped pacing.

"That's true. Thanks for the damage control idea Kathy, I couldn't think when I found out!"

"Off you go, quick! Before he thinks twice about getting dessert."

Andre was off like a shot to his office section in the pantry to hunt for some letter paper and a business card. Now that her own project was completely gone out of her head with that panic-stricken commotion, she followed Andre and asked him which of his diners was Don Highland after he had written and sealed his letter.

"The thin, pepper and salt haired guy in the brown suit with the black-rimmed glasses, he's at table seven," Andre replied, before motioning the culpable waitress to come over. "Is he interested in dessert?"

"Yes, he's looking over the dessert menu now, he almost passed on it, but then changed his mind," she replied contritely.

"Good! There's hope yet! When he orders, bring this to him with his coffee and say it's a message from the chef with his sincerest apologies."

"And if he doesn't order any coffee?"

"Just hand it to him anyway!" Andre was beyond frustration, exacerbated by this mortifying yet necessary act of humility before the mighty food critic. "No common sense! No wonder the order got botched," he complained through gritted teeth to Katherine followed by a few oaths in French once the waitress had left.

"Aw, don't get angry at her, these things happen. Just count to ten. That's working for me a lot these days," she consoled.

"One. The other numbers will have to wait. I've got orders to fill, but how *they're* going to turn out after this is anyone's guess," he muttered.

"Just peachy as usual. Go stir a sauce. I'll hop around out front and have my lunch now, see what happens, then give you a report."

"Thanks Kathy, I hope your idea softens things." Andre sighed, before rushing off to the pots and grills, simultaneously dishing out a few heated orders to the *sou chefs*.

Katherine returned the way she came through the service hallway and out into the gallery lobby with Jasper following. She gave a quick check-in with Kevin to see how he was getting on. He was happy as a clam with his latest project, now printing the first batch of cards and carefully cutting them out. He wondered if she wanted a card for her Socratic series on display too, she *did* have one picture in the Reinold Collection after all, that magnificent political parody of Napoleon's imperial coronation. No, better not, that might be pushing it she decided. Everyone knew her connection to the Reinolds, and since she already owned the gallery with her name plastered on the outside, let's not go overboard! She then asked if he didn't mind if she had lunch first, explaining what had happened. Kevin gasped: the Don of Delectables was here! He read his columns religiously.

He didn't see him come in, he was so busy calling artists, and to think he was given a fat-reduced dish when the worst kept secret to French cooking was cream and butter, and oodles of the two. However, he praised Miss Kathy for her quick thinking: by all means, go munch on lunch and see what's transpiring! While they were on the subject, Kevin went ahead and buzzed the Professor, he indeed had forgotten the hour and needed to be reminded he could not last without nourishment of some kind. Thanking her astute art agent and manager, she ordered Jasper who was barred from the restaurant to stay with him while she joined Gramps and Esther at their usual table.

"Hello kiddo. Glad you could join us, sit yourself down," Gramps beamed.

"How fares your head hunting," Esther wondered.

"Not bad. The last artist we called is interested, we should have quite a few shows lined up soon," she replied, yet keeping a diligent eye on table seven just behind them. Mr. Highland, with a little notebook laid open at his right hand, had assumed a critical mien over his plate as he meticulously scraped up the last delicate traces of vanilla crème and raspberry sauce with a few luscious cake crumbs. She watched as he placed his fork down with decorum, then scribble a quick note or two into his book. It was hard to tell if he was pleased, annoyed, or still mulling over whether he liked what he had eaten and if it met his exalted expectations.

"You should order what I got Katie, it was mighty fine today, and here I thought Andre was losing it. I misjudged the fellow," Gramps commented as he took a sip of his coffee. If only he knew.

By now the Professor had finally joined the group, and Katherine tried to act normal as she chatted away and ordered the usual while stealthy monitoring the activity at table seven. Mr. Highland had ordered his cup of coffee for after dessert it seemed, for the waitress came out with a solitary cup, then handed him the crucial envelope with the chef's personal message. With a curt 'thank you' and a slightly quizzical look, he slowly opened the envelope, unfolded the letter, readjusted his glasses, the end of his nose giving a twitch before duly reading the communication. She hoped the sourpuss critic wouldn't make a scene, or Gramps would find out the hard way why Andre had been losing it for quite some time. She almost held her breath as she observed the Don of Delectables give a slight sniff, folded the letter without hardly a facial flicker, then put it back in its envelop and slipped it inside his breast pocket. He jotted one more note or two, closed his notebook with a resolute *fwippt*, slipped it away in the same place with the letter, then patted his mouth one last time, laid his napkin down and got up from his table, straightening his jacket before leaving *Chez Garneau* without further ado since there was no tab to be paid. Katherine felt dejected for Andre, it looked like her letter idea didn't work: no request to see the chef, or any attempt to send an understanding reply back to the kitchen for that matter. They would continue to sweat bricks until they read The Don's final verdict in the paper tomorrow. Maybe she should let Andre know about Kevin's emergency supply of Valium, just in case.

"Hey Katie, you've gone a bit quiet. What's up," Gramps enquired.

"Nothing, and yet everything."

"Hrumph! I have a hunch that part of 'everything' was sitting behind us, you've been peeking over my shoulder as if the Grim Reaper was on my heels."

"Oh! It certainly wasn't that. Andre told me the city's most illustrious food critic stopped by unexpected and he was sitting there. That man makes and breaks eating establishments, Andre's a bundle of nerves, I hope it goes all right."

"Food critic, eh? Not to worry! Judging from what I got today, Andre will come off with flying colours," Gramps assured.

"You mean he was right next to us?" The Professor perked up with the novelty of the idea.

"Darn, didn't know what he looked like, or I would have paid more attention. I wonder what he ordered," Esther mused.

"I think the same as Gramps … ," Katherine replied.

"Aw, it's a shoe-in then! Andre will have another five-star rating for his wall, just you see," Gramps nodded. Considering the paradoxical situation, Katherine doubted it, but could not say a word.

At that moment, Charlie came in and pulled up a chair next to Esther.

"Hi everyone."

"Hey Charlie! I wondered when we might get a visit from you. Suzy should be down soon," Katherine informed him, "however, come on! How was Saturday? I'd love to hear your take on my adversary's HQ."

"Really? I was full sure everyone had beaten me to the punch by now." He grinned.

"True, but go ahead, I'm all ears. How was it?"

"It was an experience," he noted, he wasn't much of an art admirer where modernistic minimalism was concerned, so he didn't have too many compliments for the art nor the overrated prices, although he did have to admit the sparking walls were something to be seen. Too bad he missed Kroger's fiery outburst, it provided some merriment among the guests for the evening. However, he made a few more business contacts, handing out his card "Kraylor and Kraylor, Attorneys at Law" in addition to Suzy's "Walsingham Gallery" card campaign. Obviously grand openings were more about networking and hobnobbing, the collectors would have their day once the hubbub was over. Oh, and the food was great, just not enough of it.

"So, how have you been today," he asked, once he had delivered his promised report.

"Very productive, although judging from your attitude about garbage for art and the ensuing prices, I'm afraid you will not be impressed."

"Oh? That's a surprise. I thought you would agree with me. What about your vehemence against all disjointed spatters vended off as high art?" He couldn't help but remind her.

"Looks like I've got to put some of that splatter up too it seems." She sighed, resigned to his inevitable amusement as she recounted the Reinolds' explanation of the art world and her talent hunt that morning with Kevin, which reminded her she should go check out the boiler house like she originally planned and then let everyone else off for lunch.

"Fair enough kiddo, we won't hold you up," Gramps replied, "which reminds me, it's high time I go bug your father and brother at the offices, see how things are doing."

"Okay Gramps, see you later," Katherine replied giving him a goodbye hug, "say 'hi' to everyone for me."

"Will do, bye pet."

Everyone went their separate ways, the Professor went back to the studio, Esther took her station by the front desk leaving Kevin free, while Suzy met up with Charlie for lunch and was glad for the break; she had her ear talked off by a few people as they were asking about the artwork, curious to know more about the personal lives of the artists, especially hers, which she considered was none of their business. Perhaps being a reclusive artist like Kroger had its advantages! Dennis was still up in the studio, no doubt he was eating his lunch there while caught in the creative moment, not wanting to leave his canvas. As promised, Katherine delivered the paltry results of her scouting on the grim-faced food critic to Andre out back who simply bit his bottom lip and shrugged, what could he do? Nothing but wait it out and see what happened. The waitress noted that even if lunch was on the house the guy didn't bother to leave a tip, but then, she did mix up the order after all. She couldn't expect anything from him after that.

Her report delivered to the disappointed chef, Katherine at last surveyed the guts of her elegant operations, the old brick service area that housed the elaborate heating and air conditioning systems and other work areas. It contained a secure storage place for the gift shop and its back inventory, and was spacious to allow for packing up the artworks to be delivered to their new owners, however, quite a swipe of the area was now taken up with the various containers and crates that were used to store or ship Gerry's collection before he permanently sent it here in addition to all the wrapping and boxes needed when a work on the floor eventually sold. Well, Suzy did have a good idea, the place was an open plan multi-storey edifice with vintage iron walkways circling the walls at various levels that would have made it a strangely attractive space for the modern artists. All it needed was suitable lighting, but there were a few major hic-ups: it was accessed from a service hallway that also led to the bathrooms as well as the kitchen, it felt like a make-do solution, shoving such fashionable artists out there like a motley crew of superfluous curios. The ambience may be perfect, but the situation might be viewed as insulting, they may not go for it at all. Plus, Olivia might not be impressed having the public near her storage room no matter how secure it was, Olivia imported quite a number of expensive collector's limited editions from all over the world and wouldn't want to risk a break-in despite the security guards on the premises. Then, where would she stick all of Gerry's crates? She could send them to one of his warehouses all right, or wherever he stored them before, but she didn't want to bother him or the Reinolds with additional problems at this critical time. Perhaps he was now using the space he previously had and she didn't want to hold up their commercial storage premises when it was costing neither of them nothing at the moment to keep them out back. Furthermore, if the boiler house was tied up with exhibitions, they wouldn't have anywhere to pack the art that had sold unless in the studio, what a logistical mess! Things were better left as they were right now. She would just have to wait and see if the new artists would settle for old time elegance out front.

Katherine decided to go to the studio and do some artwork while she waited for the first artist on their waiting list to arrive. She wondered if Fielding had changed much since she and Suzy briefly met him almost two years ago now, it was just a few months before she opened the gallery as she recalled, he probably did not remember them. It was a polite introduction at a special showing at the Sirrac, and then he was kept busy by many of his avid admirers. She was a little nervous meeting him now on a business rather than on a social level and wondered how this second rendezvous was going to turn out. He seemed like a rather dreamy individual who liked his ego boosted a bit. Uck, she hated playing the diplomatic pump-up-your-ego game. At least Kevin was there, he seemed to know the rules and could play along quite nicely. Well, don't fuss and get nervous, get busy on some work.

Uncovering her canvas, she smiled with satisfaction. At last, her 'Oval Office' had dried, now all that was needed for its completion was the next series of sentences from her philosophical dialogue that were to lace the scene. As she began writing the desired section on strengthened tracing paper to be cut out as a form for the letters, Dennis complimented her detailed work, but wondered why she decided not to have the current or a past historic president sit behind the iconic Resolute Desk and have them discuss her weighty musing with Plato and Socrates. She replied she had thought about it, but the more she considered the scene, the more she realised it seemed symbolically apropos to leave the Presidential chair empty: in her opinion, not many presidents would agree with all her ideals, and those who might have considered them were brutally assassinated. The Professor raised an eyebrow in amusement as he overheard this conversation but said nothing as he carefully brushed at his latest cityscape. An hour later she had finished the last of the tracing and cutting when she received the call that Fielding had arrived. Dennis was impressed he actually showed up and wondered if he could meet him as soon as their business dealings were concluded. Katherine promised to introduce him as she pulled off her smock and tidied herself before getting into the elevator. Let's hope this goes well!

Arriving at the lobby, she found Fielding chatting pleasantly with Kevin, Esther and Suzy, a black portfolio case tucked under his arm. He had not changed much at all. Still dressed in an ebony three quarter length Victorian style jacket, which was his signature fashion statement, he continued to present quite the notable figure. The only difference was his long blonde hair wasn't tied back into a partial pony tail with the rest of his mane half tousled to resemble an antiquated powdered wig like the last time. Now, his golden tresses were combed sleek with hints of a curl and a wave: 'Amadeus' had become 'Soul Man' akin to Michael Bolton.

"Ah! Here she is," Kevin announced. "I do believe you have met before?"

"Yes, I recall it exactly, you were with your friend here during my last collection entitled 'Mellifluous Minds'," he greeted, shaking her hand.

"Yes, that was it. Nice to see you again," Katherine replied, "thank you for coming today, I hear you have an innovative collection that is breaking new ground."

"In a way, where my past style is concerned, so yes, a new theme if you will."

"J.F. has been very secretive I must say, he wouldn't give us even the slightest peek until you arrived," Kevin divulged. "Come! Please don't leave us hanging any longer, darling! We are dying to see the new works!"

"All right Kev, but I must warn you, this new series is a little darker and somewhat more gruesome than my last two," he disclosed as he carefully unzipped his portfolio case.

Katherine looked at Suzy, Esther and Kevin, from their expressions it was obvious this bit of information did not fail to pique their inquisitiveness. Fielding cautiously extracted a folder of photographs of his latest sculptures and laid them out on the desk, gently spreading them out to be viewed. The sculptures hardly resembled anything like they had seen of his previous work, which figured abstract yet peculiarly satisfying shapes in golden coloured globules poetically representing starry bees morphing moonbeams into honey. Here, the photographs revealed disturbing forms that were nothing short of the end of the world depicted in steel and iron as he had described, the new sculptures featuring a host of semi-globular humanoids distantly related to Henry Moore's faceless reclining figures but committing a myriad of destructive acts against unfortunate victimized stick people, while other humanoid blobs were cast in poses of despair set amid pessimistic allegorical scenes representing the horrors of the current century. Unlike his last collection, these dystopian pieces were not so abstract. There was one figure with its head down on its knees and its arms blanketing its head, imprisoned in a cell made of bits of twisted iron resembling a bombed out city. In another piece there was a stainless steel crib with an iron ballistic missile wrapped in undulating copper blankets with a stick like mother-figure tucking it in. Another scene was rather tragic featuring what looked like a host of portly people-globs smartly walking up and down a bronze city sidewalk with their bags and briefcases, oblivious to a very thin silvery humanoid sitting on the ground amidst a cluttered trash heap of rusted tin and battered aluminium with an outstretched hand seeking help and receiving none. Other scenes were witty in a twisted way: a mass of little shiny stick people were attempting to outrun a gigantic black iron tank-like vehicle, dashing about with their arms held up in panic while in its wake the war machine left behind a trail of flattened unfortunates with bright polished copper drops splattered everywhere for blood, an eerie aftermath that suggested Dali's famous image of clocks melting over blocks and branches. The *piece de resistance* of the collection centred upon one genderless iron humanoid reclining on its side, which Fielding explained was intended to be a symbolical opposite of an ornate Baroque altar carving that he once saw in Europe representing the Tree of Jesse with the roots springing straight from the patriarch's loins and forming a magnificent tree on which the persons of Christ's genealogy were seated. Fielding's contrasting 'Tree of Annihilation' did not show an unseemly picture but was nonetheless biologically vivid. Similar to his description of the Baroque carving, his modernistic figure had an atomic mushroom cloud springing upward from its side, the billowing plumes having various missiles, grenades, guns and knives dangling from bizarre tendril-like formations. Curiously, the figure also seemed to allegorically depict an outlandish birth, a gruesome nativity delivering these various inventions of destruction in addition to revealing its maleficent tree-like genealogy.

"Well! These are rather unique," Kevin first commented. "I had no idea you were delving this deep into the tortured psyche of humanity for your new theme. You are not depressed I hope? I know an excellent therapist who will do you wonders in no time. I have her number right here if you want it."

Fielding laughed.

"Thank you, but no, I'm not depressed, at least not any more. Far from it. The work may be dark, but it was rather cathartic."

"Um, you don't mind me asking, since you're usually inspired by poetry or stories, whatever gave you the idea for this new period in your creativity," Katherine politely enquired.

"Oh, miss Kathy, J.F. never reveals that until the premier of his showings," Kevin politely interjected, trying to fill her in on the eccentric artist's superstitious customs and hoping Fielding would excuse the innocent *faux pas*. Fielding was in fact, quite obliging.

"I think on this one occasion I shall bravely make an exception. After my last show, I was studying Henry Moore's work again while pondering Frost's *Fire and Ice*."

"Ah! Now I see! A marriage of shapes with that magnificent verse," Kevin beamed, delighted to witness a rare break from poetic custom for Fielding. Esther could only look askance at Suzy and Katherine.

"Yes, particularly the phrases '*I hold with those who favour fire*' and '*ice is great and would suffice*', but they weren't the only sources of my inspiration. I have to thank you for that, my dear," Fielding concluded, turning to Katherine with a little nod of grateful recognition.

"Me?   Are you serious?   Wow, I don't know what to say."
Katherine was truly flummoxed, this should be taken as a compliment, but
after seeing how his once honey-hued shapes had now evolved into metallic
harbingers of terror and mayhem, she wasn't quite sure. "How did I inspire
you with such …dread?"

Fielding gave a little chuckle before explaining.

"It was something you said, or reportedly said, that got me thinking,
for days in fact. In the middle of my ruminations, the makings of a poem
just formed in my head out of the blue, or out of the black you might say in
this case, so the majority of my latest collection is based on this original
inspiration."

"You mean to say, dear chap, you've composed an *original* poem
this time?" Kevin gasped. "Why, J.F., this *is* a surprising day! A one-of-a-
kind collection indeed! To think we've been privileged to be the first to see
this, and Miss Kathy to have inspired it!" Kevin was just over the moon.
They might have to rifle his stash and slip him a Xanax in his coffee to keep
him grounded Esther mumbled to Suzy.

"Um, what exactly did I say, or reportedly said," Katherine prodded
further, unable to recall what she had conversed about when they met. It
was only a brief chat that barely went beyond a 'good evening'.

"I think you might recall when you read the poem itself," he
continued, taking out a sheet from his case and handing it to her. Kevin and
Suzy waited with baited breath for her to read aloud the poem, but Fielding
shook his head.

"Ah ah! For Miss Walsingham's eyes only, for the present. I cannot
break with my time-honoured custom completely. You must wait until the
première. I do trust you will keep this confidential for now?"

"Of course, you have my word," she promised.

"Awww," Suzy moaned, a feeling that was shared by Kevin.

They watched eagerly as Katherine read the page, her expression
displaying some rather startlingly lines, or so they assumed. How they
wished they could take a peek!

"Wow, that's intense," she commented at last, now smiling when
she recognised the source of his inspiration, which Fielding confirmed.

"Of course, I'm not a professional poet, but it was a refreshing
change to create a collection based on something that's my own, or almost
my own, I did add a line or two for which you deserve full credit, Miss
Walsingham. As you can see, I read the art reviews and the critique of your
new gallery that included your alleged vehement comments on modern
progress."

Katherine was a bit mortified, that heated comment about the nuclear age she fired out at the critics at the gala opening of her gallery was not dying any time soon, now forever immortalized in bombastic canto, and in a succession of ground-breaking Fielding sculptures no less! However, it was a bit flattering, even if it was embarrassing. Nuts! Good thing she promised to keep the poem itself concealed for the moment.

"I have to admit those comments were authentic, an unfortunate series of explosives provoked by the nerves of the moment, and by one particular aggravating critic," she confessed.

"Say no more, I think I know who you mean," he replied wryly before continuing, "but no apologies! Art should be about Truth, right?"

"Where have I heard that before," Suzy egged Katherine under her breath followed by a giggle, while Kevin applauded J.F. for his philosophical reply with Esther casting an incredulous glance to Heaven as though seeking deliverance.

"Yes, I couldn't agree more," Katherine replied to Fielding. "Come, let me give you a tour of the gallery."

Contrary to her presumptions, Fielding seemed pleased with the surroundings as they sauntered through the walkways on the first floor and thought the new collection would make quite a splash here. Katherine was relieved and expressed her doubts, she had assumed he would not like the venue because the décor was completely opposite to the style of his art. Fielding cocked his head to one side and pursed his lips for a moment, he had to admit when he read the critiques about the place he wasn't sure his art would be considered and had some reservations if any of it would look good here, but now that he had seen the place, there was something to be said about sticking two completely opposite styles together for effect, especially with his latest collection.

"When you think of it, it's like contrasting the world with how it was and to what we as a species have done to it now. Sure, the world has always had its troubles, but has our culture ever been as globally destructive as this? Yes, I can see these sculptures set all around here now. I think it's a fascinating concept, the collection might make an even bigger impact here than I first thought, clashing two chronological styles together, your glory days of Europe with my dour atomic epoch," he observed, turning slowly in a full circle, holding out his hands at arm's length as though he was a director visualising a screen shot. "Of course, I had to see the art palace my current muse built, there couldn't be a more appropriate venue." He smiled before turning to look at the paintings they were walking past. "Hmm, these are interesting, oh, they're yours. I see I am in the company of a fellow artist who is also inspired by words."

"Yes, it's an imaginary dialogue between Socrates and Plato about what they might think of our democratic society. It's not finished yet, it's a collection in progress," she explained as he looked closer at the first painting in the series.

"You wrote this? That's impressive," he nodded, slowly making out the text, "certainly puts my little doggerel to shame."

"Oh, it's not doggerel, and it's certainly not 'little', anything that packs a punch like that cannot be considered little by any means. I like it, it's very good, and while I have issues accepting certain modern styles, there's something very striking about your latest work, very compelling."

"Why, thank you."

"You know, I didn't think anyone would agree with my 'gadfly' comments let alone write verses and craft art about them. It seems you've become a gadfly too."

"Gadfly? I suppose that's what you could call this new creative phase. It's good to get a few social injustices off your chest, isn't it?"

Katherine couldn't agree more. Now, if only their art could get people to change instead of simply think and then do nothing she commented. Fielding shook his head, that was the challenge of the ages, however, 'Gadflyism' was an intriguing concept for a new art period, that just might take off, if only it sounded a bit better, it didn't quite roll off the tongue. Maybe not, but that would be an interesting nomenclature for the style of all the disgruntled artists in the world!

Continuing their tour and chatting a little more, Katherine couldn't help but like him, he seemed real down to earth when not before an audience where he usually let the odd artistic flair loose. Eventually, they got down to business after visiting the museum section. He still had two statues that needed to be properly polished up, and another needed a few cogs or two, but once that was done, the collection would be ready for delivery in about a month's time. There were the practical things to review, such as how much did each piece weigh? They had to consider how much her floors could take, she didn't want anything unexpectedly crashing through and crushing anyone below, that would be taking the apocalyptic theme too far! Fielding noted several were large and free standing, however, he did have a number of smaller items and required pedestals, so they couldn't be too heavy. Good thing the place was a factory conversion and had once supported an extensive amount of heavy machinery, the collective weight of his series might have become a serious issue. However, the photographs only gave a very limited idea of what the collection was like, perhaps it would be best if she dropped by his new studio he suggested, which was currently in the neighbourhood. Katherine was surprised, she didn't know he was close by to which he explained he needed a bigger place with smithy facilities for his latest works, so one of the old unconverted factories in Dumbo was available for lease at a good price and he decided to take it. That made sense, she would be happy to drop by whenever it was convenient. The last details they needed to discuss were the prices and her commission for showing, which she decided they should review with Kevin since he was more familiar with the current market value of his art.

On that note, they collected Kevin at the desk, who was only too happy to join them for refreshments at Andre's while some price estimates were hashed out. Over a round of white coffees Kevin agreed a studio visit would be necessary in this case considering the new metallic medium, he would need to see everything before they made such an important final decision. Metalwork was expensive he understood, they would need to crunch the numbers and find out how much each sculpture roughly cost, the artist needed to be compensated for the time and outlay that went into them as well as figure out an acceptable profit. Fielding in turn was satisfied with their commission rate, in fact, he was surprised, they were quite reasonable. The old Sirrac grabbed practically half of everything an artist earned.

"Nothing personal," Fielding then noted to Kevin who simply shrugged, nothing personal was assumed, it was Mr. Sirrac who had decided on that high rate.

Fielding also observed the Elverton was no better, at least here at her place they were only taking just a third from the final price. Well, Katherine wasn't like Mr. Sirrac or Sir Elverton, she didn't believe in scalping the artists, she was one too and wouldn't like to be treated that way, a little of the 'Golden Rule' goes a long way she figured. Fielding was also pleased to hear she never sat around when a piece sold, all her artists could expect a cheque as soon as the sale went through. Again a little of the 'Golden Rule' she pointed out, it was not a nice thing to do to delay payment to someone, everyone needed to eat and pay their bills. Of course, she did not say it then, but she could never forget what Peter taught her about the importance of paying decent living wages one time during her catechism lessons: defrauding a labourer of his pay or delaying payment beyond a reasonable time, especially to the less well off, was one of four dreaded 'vengeance' sins that cried to Heaven for retribution. That was one thing she didn't want to bring down on her head! Kevin then wondered if he had any odd pieces currently without a home, giving Katherine a polite wink and a nod as he asked the question.

"Yes, I do, five in fact, a few ideas I wanted to bring to life for the heck of it."

"Would you be interested in bringing them here? We also show single pieces if an artist would like to display them, we call it a 'rotation method', keeping a piece or two by our artists on display even when they don't have full collections."

"That's not a bad idea. Honestly I would like a few out when assembling a series," Fielding mused. "Sure, you can have those five too, only, I'd wait until after the new collection gets a showing first in case they get wrongly associated with the dystopian theme. They're one of my positive products, so to speak."

"No problem. That's good news, we'll be glad to show them. Er, I hope there aren't any nudes," Katherine tentatively asked.

"No, just some semi-abstractions. What is it about you and nudes," Fielding then wondered, amusement lacing his voice. "An artist who can't stomach them? How did you ever get through art college?"

"I survived," she replied with a raised eyebrow, vacillating on whether or not she should enlighten him about her passive aggressive protest against the unabashed striptease tradition imposed on students under the glorious name of high art.

"I see. Isn't the human form the most beautiful form of art? A temple to be admired?"

"Yes, which is given its full due of respect through the sacred veil of clothing, which I see you so passionately display by attiring your 'temple' in Victorian-style regalia."

"Ha ha! Right back at me. So, if you had your way, you would have all nudes covered, even paintings. You can't sell art if all of it is covered with fig leaves or sheeting," he prodded with good humour.

"In art, it seems anyone can do anything these days."

Fielding laughed.

"Okay then, each to his or her own. I promise anything I offer here will not be without its sacred veil be it suitable attire or genderless nothings."

"Fair enough then, we will be happy to show those," Katherine confirmed.

As they finished their coffee, they speculated about a working première date. Since he said the last works would be ready in a month, maybe the first week of August would be good to plan the première.

Fielding agreed, then added with a wry smile it was a pity he couldn't work faster, he would have liked to have had it ready much sooner for a showing on 'Atheists' Day'.

"What? I didn't know there was one," Katherine wondered.

"Yes, April the first," Fielding confirmed as he finished off his frothy brew.

Katherine laughed when the joke sunk in.

"August will have to do, even a month is still a tight pinch, but if we stick to a schedule we would have time to send the invitations," Kevin mused aloud.

"Invitations?"

"Why yes, Miss Kathy, for the private showing among our special customers and art admirers, then the collection would be open to the public in the following days. Many collectors like to have first dibs when possible, plus, a little publicity needs to be created with a showing and around a showing, you know," Kevin concluded.

"I suppose that's when everyone gets to hear your thumping verses." She smiled at Fielding.

"Exactly, according to my time-honoured tradition at an opening."

"I say, that gives me an idea dear chap. What would you say if we have cards printed with your magnificent poem with a picture of your collection? You could sign them as a memento of the evening. It would certainly make for a fascinating souvenir of the occasion," Kevin observed.

"Trying to get the poem early, eh? Kevin, you sly devil you."

Kevin looked a bit sheepish, but shrugged. It was worth a try.

"Honestly, that's not a bad idea, you always come up with some good ones, Kev. All right, I shall do the unprecedented. When we get closer to the première date, I'll allow Miss Walsingham to release it to you. Fair enough?"

"Splendid!

"But nothing past the staff, no one outside of here must read or hear of it before the première. I don't want this jinxed."

"Mum's the word, old boy, mum's the word," Kevin assured him gravely before brightening up again. "So, what's this collection entitled?"

"You know, that's the one thing I'm hung up on. I have a few ideas, none of which really grab me."

"Why not 'April One'." Katherine smiled, darting a joke back, but Fielding brightened up with the idea.

"Hey, not shabby, not shabby at all. *April One*, I like that. I was going to go with the title of the poem itself, but Latin sounded a bit archaic despite its majestic appeal. *April One*, yes, that's it! Modern and snappy with a pointed connection going straight to the poem's theme. Again, I am indebted to you."

"Aw shucks, it just jumped out," Katherine bashfully admitted. For someone who wasn't overjoyed about modern art, she seemed to be pretty good at it!

"Then what an inspired exclamation it is, Miss Kathy," Kevin affirmed with enthusiasm, thrilled to be part of this collective brainstorming session eventhough he didn't have a clue what the original poem was about.

Since the showing was tentatively to be in August, they concluded their meeting with the decision they visit his studio as soon as possible to get the ball rolling and settled on July first for a formal visit. Before Fielding left, she kept her promise and had Esther buzz the two artists upstairs to come down and meet him. Dennis was certainly eager and asked for his autograph as he shook hands with the 'seraph of sculptors', talking a little about his art and excited to hear Fielding was going to have a showing right here.

"What's your theme this year," the Professor enquired, always a little curious to see how the next generation were expressing themselves these days. Fielding simply smiled and replied all he was telling was April One. The Professor took off his specs and gave them a rub on his arm, rebalanced them on the bridge of his nose, then quietly pondered what the enigmatic clue could mean. "Why Kathy, I do believe I am stumped on this one, other than I can see from your photos that you are lambasting the 'foolishness' of mankind."

"Very good Professor, but I'm afraid you'll have to wait for the original poem until later."

"Man, that's a bit rough," Dennis commented. "I can't handle the suspense, and I'm not one for poetry."

"I shall give you another clue then: let us say just because we have entered the Age of Science and Reason it doesn't mean we should reject the wisdom garnered from the experience of our ancestors recorded in ancient texts, including the sacred ones."

Katherine could have sworn she saw the Professor looking a little chuffed upon discovering that the modernist Fielding had classical views hidden in the personal closet and valued principles akin to his own philosophy of life.

Fielding chatted a little more before he said his goodbyes. He had another meeting that afternoon with a metal worker who had promised to deliver a few more copper panels plus a bag full of gears and bits that were imperative to finishing off the last few pieces. They were sorry he couldn't stay longer, it looked like he was going to get along very well here with the gang. One thing was sure, considering the interesting day she had, she certainly had news for Gerry tonight.

 CB ❖ BO

June was drawing to a close on a high note with Fielding's visit, the Gallery Gang now had some real planning to do with a première in the works. Andre also had some interesting results from the unexpected arrival of the 'Don' to his gourmet restaurant. Katherine and the Gang missed the first set of events as the fussy critic actually came back the very night of the mixed lunch mishap to claim his free meal and ordered the exact same plate, only with a different starter and dessert. On this occasion he received the correct dish, and when he was finished, requested to see Andre. The stressed out chef thought that there would be a scene this time over what had happened earlier in the day, but to his surprise, The Don asked if he was always prepared to make alterations to his dishes for diners with medical conditions? Andre was a bit flustered and replied with a truth-bending answer, he did it all the time, (he just didn't let him know it was for only one customer). Andre didn't know why he said it, maybe to fill in the awkward gap in the conversation as The Don wrote down something in his book, but rambled he was actually considering launching a specialized menu for those who had to watch their health. He didn't know if The Don was impressed or sceptical about the 'diet plan'. He simply continued to scribble something in his little book, said 'goodnight' then exited the premises much as he did earlier that day. The surprise happened the next morning when the Gang read The Don's column: the critic told the story of what had happened in minute detail about the plates getting mixed up, however, he gave a glowing report of each dish and lauded Andre's plan to add a 'healthy options' section to his gourmet menus, finishing off his column with the final observations:

" ... *If the one swapped dish is anything to go by, Master Chef Garneau will have another mouth watering hit on his*

391

"Geeze, you mean my cuisine tastes like diet fare? I don't know whether to be insulted, or relieved he didn't spot the difference."

However, the Gang were happy that Andre was out of hot water and was not closing down any time soon. The only problem now was he had to come up with a decent health menu, which included some starters and desserts too, or his bluff might be called out as The Don would be on the lookout for the new offerings! The funny part was, Gramps was still in the dark up to this point.

"You know, Katie, I really should try and get my diet together. Maybe when the new vittals are sorted out, I'll give them a go since this critic fellow thinks they're so darn good," he declared after he read the thumbs-up report for himself. "In fact, if Andre has offered this for customers already, I'll see if he'll fix me a plate, starting today."

"You do that Gramps." Katherine couldn't help but feel a bit sheepish as he mulled over his slimming fare. No doubt he was recalling the delight he had yesterday and was mentally comparing it to today's doctored lunch. She watched as his expression changed from curiosity, to puzzled uncertainty, and finally to 'Shucky darn, I think I've been had'.

"Hmm … mixed plates he says, so if he ordered the same as me yesterday … thundering tarnations! I was the coot with the 'medical condition', eh? You bunch of scheming scallywags! You've been pulling the wool over my eyes for yonkers, and all this time I thought Andre was slipping. How could you do this to your poor old grandpa?"

"Sorry Gramps, it was Andre's idea. He was afraid this place wasn't doing you any good. You are supposed to watch it, doctor's orders, 'medical tyranny', and all of that annoying advice the experts give. We do want to keep you alive and healthy, you know."

However, Gramps wasn't too pushed out of shape, he found it a bit funny to have had his taste buds deprived of Andre's authentic cooking for ages and to find out about it the way he did.

"Hrumph! 'Can't tell the difference' indeed! A grub lord that can't detect a swap between 'I-Can-Definitely-Believe-I'm-Not-Eating-Butter' and the real McCoy from the cow? Why, I should be writing that foody article."

"Hey, maybe you should become a critic, umm, maybe not, we're trying to keep you on a diet. Forget I said that."

"What's been heard cannot be unheard. That's a mighty fine idea. Critics get all the best chow in town, so they say."

"Be good now, or we're going to have to ground you."

"At my age? What a thought!"

"Well, second childhood, and all of that," Katherine teased.

"Aw, no respect for elders these days."

"Of course I respect my elders. I admire a man who carries a lot of weight."

"There we go, poor old Gramps getting more big lip," he returned, yet chuckling all the while. He loved getting a good-natured roasting from the grandkids. "So then, I shall lose your respect if I become half the man that I am today, eh?"

"Now you're being silly Gramps. Aside from the jokes, forget being a critic, there's too many of them in the world. How about volunteering your expertise on Andre's behalf and help him with some of his dishes? Since you can spot the difference between the diet ingredients, maybe you could give him some suggestions about how to mask them a bit better? You could save him a lot of time, which he hasn't got."

"I dunno Katie, I have an inkling a skilled master chef like Andre doesn't like old fogies like me meddling in his pots."

"You could offer at least. I'm guessing he'll be happy to know there aren't any hard feelings about the switch-a-roo he's being doing to you."

"Oh, okay. I am a bit to blame for this diet menu mishap anyway, and if he *has* to use some non-cow products, I can certainly list some better tasting plastic goos for him to play around with. Gotta keep up the gourmet end as best we can under the circumstances."

"That's the spirit. Just look at all the dishes you'll get to taste test if he agrees."

"Not a bad idea, but it's a shame it's going to be all slim fare the rest of the summer."

"Winter too, and next spring. No goofing around with your health this time, I mean it."

"Uncle! Uncle! I give in, you Diet Dictator," he replied, holding his hands up in submission. "Okay, let's go talk to Andre, you never know, I just might discover the secret to his beef Bourguignon."

"Fat chance of that happening," Katherine assured him.

Toodling around to the kitchen, they pulled the master chef aside. Contrary to what Gramps assumed, Andre was indeed appreciative of any suggestions he could give, it was good to have someone else do a little testing, especially someone who was as familiar with his menu as him. Katherine left the two of them alone to discuss the particulars of ingredient experimenting and wondered what 'non-cow' surprises they might concoct.

Once Andre's culinary dilemma was getting itself sorted out, Katherine concentrated on the next pressing set of business uppermost on her mind, Fielding's première. While the date was tentatively set for August, there was quite a bit they needed to do right now, already Kevin was drawing up an impressive list of preferential collectors that were either admirers of the artist or had frequented the Sirrac, and had already drafted a suitable message for the invitations to be printed as soon as the official date was decided. Katherine couldn't help but be impressed with Kevin's contact list, which was diligently kept in a second book apart from his artists that he was also pleased to share with her.

"Don't forget the 'Art Hacker', he gets all the news exclusives," she reminded.

"Miss Kathy, are you sure you want only him? I know some glowing critics who would be happy to write a few good words."

"Thanks Kevin, but it's a lot of bad ones we really need, especially his."

Kevin sighed but soldiered on, adding Robert Horace to the list: to think this riff-raff art-ripper was to be granted preferential treatment the same as their honoured art-loving VIPs! This was one time Esther agreed with Kevin.

"I know, but a promise is a promise, and I owe him big time," she explained. "Don't worry, he may have a poison pen, but it always comes up gold in the end."

"If you say so, Miss Kathy," Kevin acquiesced.

Now that she was thinking of him, it might be a good idea to give Horace a call, let him know what was happening, he might love to get the first announcements out in his paper. Although Kevin loathed the idea of their venerable artists receiving the Hacker's sharp criticisms, starting the publicity train along its track was quite the savvy thing to do he agreed. Katherine decided to go into the office to make the call. She hoped he wasn't out on location covering a cultural do, considering the art scene in the city, it wasn't always easy to get a hold of him.

"Hello, you have reached New York's most loved-to-be-hated art critic."

"Hey Horace, you're in! It's Kathy. How're you doing?"

"Hi there, not too bad. I've just finished ripping up the new exhibition at the MOMA in my latest column, just shredded it to ribbons."

"All in a day's work, I guess."

"Unfortunately, yes. Nasty work, but it has to be done. So, what's up with you?"

"I've got one for you, want our latest scoop?"

"Latest scoop? That means a news exclusive. Great! I'm listening."

"How would you like to attend a John Fielding première sometime in August?"

"Hey, Fielding you say? Now there's some news, he's been under the radar since his honey droppings a few years back. Has he really got a new collection?"

"Yep, and it's totally off the flypaper, completely different from his last creative period. He's gone into heavy metal, and he wants to show it here at the Walsingham."

"You don't say? In that case, I would love to bash your party. Well, whatever he's done, I'd bash it anyway. You've got to tell me more, I never thought you might give a showing to something he'd create."

Katherine laughed before giving him some of the details, although deciding not to tell she happened to be one of Fielding's latest sources of inspiration, some things had to be kept for the première.

"Wow, this makes for a great column, but I won't tell it all at once, I shall save the full kit and caboodle for after the grand showing, we shall tease the public until then. I can't wait to hear what piece of poetry inspired him this time. Speaking of artwork, 'Turris' has a few more paintings to bring in, if that's okay."

"Sure! I could put them up right away as soon as they're framed, or I won't put them up until Fielding's grand night, that way Turris gets a grand showing with all the city's elite present. What do you say?"

" 'Turris' says the second option is very agreeable," Horace was pleased to announce. "Just for that, this critic might do the unthinkable and write a radiant report of your next social splash."

"Oh no he won't! If Horace goes soft now, the whole thing might flop!"

"Ha ha! Okay, boiling acid it is then."

"Listen, how have you been lately? I haven't seen you in a while."

"Busy, plus I've been spending some extra time with grandma, she's not been too well this last month."

"Gosh, I'm sorry to hear that. How are you holding up?"

"Burning the candle at both ends, to tell you the truth."

Grandma had lately come down with a stubborn chest infection and it was difficult getting her to take her medications due to her state of dementia. She had the tendency to panic often as she continually failed to recognise the private nurse taking care of her while he was at work, so getting her healthy again was a challenge as she refused to take anything that the 'stranger' was handing her. Not that when he was home things were any better, she only recognised him some of the time as she usually mistook him for a workman of some kind if not another member of the family. One day she assumed he was the garbage man, another day the cable guy, but most days it was the plumber; she often wondered why he was around a lot, remarking she had no idea the pipes were that bad and was afraid to get the estimate for the work. Other than that, he was okay, it was just hard seeing grandma becoming more forgetful and always fearful due to her inability to recognise people. Katherine was terribly sorry for him, it was one of those gut-wrenching situations with no positive solution ahead. Despite all the care he ensured his grandmother received, she knew he was facing the inevitable in the end. She hoped for his sake things were working out between him and Stephie, he needed someone close in his life right now. She was about to ask how he and her cousin were getting along, but he beat her to the punch and asked how she was first.

"Heck, listen to me, when you've got problems of your own. How's Gerry doing? I haven't dropped by the hospital for a visit in awhile, but I promise to amend that."

"Great, you might cheer him up. Right now, it's slow going, the bars are off and they are just getting his legs in shape. However, he's going to need months to recover."

"But he's going to be able to walk? To be honest, from the old gossip I heard going around, it doesn't sound good."

"The news is grim all right, of course, please keep this to yourself, I wouldn't want Brandis to overhear and stick this in a column."

"Sure. I know when to zip my mouth and cap my pens."

"The specialists still don't know everything, yet they say he could be facing a future of chronic pain, and even if he can walk a bit, he may still need a wheelchair."

"Geeze. I wish I could do something. Does he know yet?"

"Yes, he's been told, but he's in denial, I think we all are to a point. We're hoping it won't be as bad as the doctors think it could be, we won't know until they try to get him up and about." For now, she explained they were all trying to get on with life as positively as possible, moving ahead with their future plans such as her decorating the penthouse and getting the last of her stuff moved over. It would help to keep Gerry motivated. Christopher agreed that seemed the best thing to do under the circumstances.

"So, talking about staying positive, how are you and Stephie getting along," Katherine continued. "I think you two make a nice couple."

"Really? I think so too. You know, we have a chance of going beyond steady, I'm really stuck on her. I can't help but get that unshakable feeling she could be 'The One'... ."

"What? Oh, that's fabulous! Does she know it yet? That's important you know."

"Um, well ... ."

"So, 'Smith' is not out in the open yet, huh?"

"You know how it is! Taking things to the next level means opening certain doors a little wider, and I'm not sure how she's going to take all of that. It could ruin everything."

"How? Look, she's had a few lousy boyfriends in the past, so she just might appreciate the honesty."

"This time, honesty could be a killer."

"Since when?"

"Since this whole thing started. I don't think you get the full enormity of my situation, as they say, it's complicated. However, I can't really talk about it over the phone, especially at work. If I drop by with the paintings later this afternoon, can we talk then?"

Katherine agreed, sounds like he needed a willing ear at the moment, and as usual, she always ended up being that trustworthy ear for whomever needed a serious chat but didn't know who to turn to. Why, she didn't know. Maybe she radiated some mysterious wave of infallible assurance to others that she knew all the answers to life's riddles, which was a bit ironic considering she always felt like she was winging things herself and making quite a muddle of it.

That afternoon 'Horace' came by as arranged clad in his old faithful crème trench coat once again, obviously the new black one Stephie insisted he get was too stark for the summer. He quickly slipped his portfolio cases in her office while Kevin and Esther were both busy on the upper floors, good thing two tours were booked in for the day. The identity of 'C.S. Turris' was still a big secret in the New York art scene, and he needed it to be kept that way, even Esther was not aware of his real name nor his artistic alter ego. While she was dying with curiosity to see the new paintings, she could admire them all she wanted later for it was obvious Christopher Smith needed to put 'Horace' aside and have that chat first to get whatever it was off his chest. Katherine ordered a round of refreshments while he took off his coat and swung it around the back of one of the swivelling leather chairs which he then occupied, languidly turning himself right and left for a minute as was his habit when he settled in for a visit.

"Like I say, this is the life." He smiled as coffee was delivered from the restaurant.

"So, while we're on our lonesome, what's the big dilemma weighing you down and keeping you from your bliss?"

"Oh well, it's this whole double-triple identity thing," he began quietly, stopping his swivelling now that she had launched straight into serious territory. "It's worked for me up to now, but this is the first time it could wreck something wonderful, so I'm caught at an important crossroads. Do I tell Steph everything? Should I? Maybe I shouldn't? Big decision, and I mean, big."

"Okay, Bruce Wayne wants to come out despite the need to keep Batman a secret, but Stephie is not dumb. I'm pretty sure she would keep 'Horace' under wraps for you. Are you afraid if things don't work out and you break up, there's a lose cannon who could let the secret slip?"

"There's that, but if she is the 'One', then that won't happen. The real thing is, I wish I really was Bruce Wayne, or even Clark Kent, then it wouldn't be so much of a problem," he noted. Katherine was still a little puzzled until he humbly began to let her in on what was truly nagging him. "Look, you are one of the few who know why I'm Robert Horace in print, but behind the scenes I'm just plain boring Chris … ."

"You think she will lose interest if she thinks you're boring and not as pointed as your alter ego." Katherine could understand that, he had created a curiously magnetic persona as 'Robert Horace', the spiteful highbrow critic. Under his pen name he had garnered a huge following and acquired some fame in his own right despite the fact everyone thought his witty criticisms were searingly obnoxious.

"Oh, okay, that too, but that's not just it. Despite the cushy pay, it doesn't stay cushy for long, not with all the medical bills. The health care world has no qualms landing a man with quite a hefty load of 'payment due' notices. Sorry, nothing personal," he then added, remembering her family was in the global pharmaceutical trade.

"Nothing personal taken," she reassured him, she understood how he felt.

During her student protest days when she thought joining the colourful clan at Greenpeace was to be her future calling, she often gave an ethical grilling to Gramps and Pops about the prices some of their specialised prescription medicines boasted. True, millions of dollars went into research, but once the costs had been recouped, why keep the prices high? Just to please the investors? A just profit was one thing, but gouging the sick on their life-saving prescriptions? That was despicable! She wanted to make a point, but there was only so far she could go in roasting the elders without appearing disrespectful and drawing down their ire instead of their attention to this serious issue. Eventually she thought of a silent protest— plastering a poignant reminder over the entire door of Pop's home office one night via a few empty Walsingham pill cartons with the following message: "Healing the sick was once considered a sacred gift bestowed on mortals by the gods. Let the investors find their recompense in the good they have done and not in monetary returns alone." She wondered what the reply would be if any, which she received one morning taped to her bedroom door in a formal response typed on the company's official letter paper no less:

"Dear Anonymous Protester,

Thank you for your message of concern. The CEO of Walsingham Industries has received your notice and has taken it into consideration. If the disgruntled activist has a viable plan to present to the board on how to run an international enterprise of this magnitude on donations alone, he would gladly consider readjusting the retail costs of our pharmaceutical products to reflect these admirable philanthropic ideals."

If that wasn't enough, her father signed it! For awhile, Katherine thought he was really serious and tried to come up with a solution for this daunting project. Trying to get volunteers to go out with collecting buckets was one idea, but they would need legions of self-sacrificing volunteers willing to go collecting every day be it sun, rain or snow. In the end, the only thing she could think of was something along the line of those charitable sponsorship programs that the good-hearted percentage of the public gave to on a monthly basis, like World Vision for the developing nations or for the children at St. Jude's Hospital who couldn't afford the chemotherapy they needed. It sounded like a great idea and she actually wrote down this suggestion for the board and slipped it under Pop's door, but when she discovered a hefty envelope accompanied by boxes and boxes of several bulky ring binders at the threshold of her bedroom door a few days later with the cost analysis of just one of the latest ground-breaking drugs starting from the basics beginning with water and electricity rates and progressing to every nut and bolt of all the equipment in the labs, including the numbers of surgical lab gloves, test tubes, the chemicals *ad infinitum*, on up to the salaries of each researcher and the legal costs of the safety checks involved, then the production overheads when it went to market, it was obvious Walsingham Industries was not going to make it on charity alone. There were a few humorous glances cast around the breakfast table that morning not to mention a few droll jokes from her brother when she entered the dining room admitting defeat, flopping the armful of reports on the table as she sat down with a disgruntled sigh. At least she gave it her best shot, Gramps consoled with a rumbling chuckle.

"What I'm trying to say is," Christopher continued, pulling her thoughts back, "what have I got to offer to someone like Steph? She doesn't know my full circumstances, and even if I didn't have all these bills on my back, I'm not in the same financial league with her, nor her social standing, not by a long shot."

"Gosh, is that what's troubling you? I'm guessing she wouldn't mind, she wouldn't be going out with you in the first place if she was hung up on things like that."

"True, but since I'm in the bill-mill with these debts, what if she thinks I'm an opportunist? This is where being honest about who I am and why could backfire."

"Chris, are you really in a bad strait? Are you okay?"

"Aw geeze, that's not why I was bringing this up," he replied mortified, ruffling the hair on the back of his head. "But since you've asked, I'm okay, I'm making payments just fine. I have you to thank for that, with the paintings 'Turris' is selling here, Smith can begin to see the light at the end of the tunnel."

"Well, I'm glad I could help somewhere. You know, if you need anything … ."

"Gosh no, thanks for the offer, but a man's got to dig his own way out, and besides, if Steph knew how much you've helped me already, even if it is art related business, that's another reason for her to get the wrong impression, 'gold digger', you know what I mean? The one good thing about her photography is that I've been able to offer her a few freelance gigs for the paper plus a few shoots at some magazines. Anything to show I'm not taking advantage."

Katherine could see the problem from his viewpoint. This was difficult, how could she give him advice in a situation like this?

"You know," he continued, "it might help me to make a decision on whether to come clean about 'Horace' if I could get a better feel about things from someone who knows her. She hasn't said anything about us, has she? I know, it's personal to pry, but any hint that she may have similar feelings of us going somewhere and Batman might just come out of his cave."

"You could just ask her, you know."

"Urmph," Smith returned, a little uncomfortable with the thought, "everything would really come out then in one big, hesitant, disordered, sappy gush. Not the best way to make a revelation."

"I don't know, you're doing pretty good talking to me right now."

"You're different! I don't know why, but you are." He sat back in the chair, amused and flustered. "You know everything already, and you seem to get things. Steph's a bit volatile at times, I don't know how to approach her with this."

"And I'm not volatile? You forget our first encounters. Kaboom!"

"Ha ha! True, but still, this is different. I just don't want to blow my chances with her."

"Well, I haven't seen her much, I haven't had a really good conversation with her lately, so about her feelings for you, you're going to have to investigate for yourself there," Christopher groaned slightly with this news, "but I *do* have some observations that might help. You actually have a few things in your favour, Stephie doesn't like to be bought. If she likes you, she *really* likes you, which means she's in it for who you are, not just what you have. If your relationship goes farther, she's not going to go for the traditional role of being kept at home with an allowance to run the house. She's a full-blooded modern woman, if the relationship feels right to her, she'll go with it no matter the financial circumstances. That's what I get from her anyway."

"Aha, so there's hope," he replied enthusiastically, sitting up a bit. "Still, I can't help but think the man of the house should be the main breadwinner and take care of the basics, you know? It's stuck in the blood. I'm conditioned."

Katherine smiled, she had heard that somewhere before.

"You'll have to decide which is more important, having Stephie in your life and getting your multi-personality crisis sorted out, or upholding the manly custom of bread-winning to the point of remaining Batman, the mighty mysterious bachelor moping in his cave."

"Self esteem be stifled, is it? The agony!"

"The 'One' is supposed to be worth it, right?" She chuckled.

"I know, but it's going to be agony either way."

"Love does that to a person. So, you really love her if you're even thinking of getting close to taking 'the plunge'."

"Yeah, it's a big step to consider. I never imagined myself tying the knot until now, it always felt like that was something people did all right, but it's weird when it finally hits *you*, you know? Oh, that's right, you do. As you can probably guess, I'm becoming a basket case." He smiled sheepishly. "I can't think clearly when she's around, or when she's not around for that matter, I can't get her out of my head. Nothing's the same when we're not together to the point I can't imagine life without her any more."

"Oh, you're definitely in love, as I've finally found out from experience," Katherine agreed, swirling around the dregs of foam in her cup.

She had seen that flighty yet somewhat distracted, hope-filled look several times before; twice with Charlie when he had fallen in love with her then later with Suzy, and of course with Gerry before they became engaged. Poor 'Lancelot'! She now realised how she had unconsciously left Gerry in a sort of lingering limbo during that discomfiting period when she just couldn't come to grips with her own emotions simply because she was fearful of the inevitable life-changing consequences.

"It's obvious you've just decided what to do. It's time for Batman to brave the daylight." Christopher looked a bit pained. "I know it's difficult, sharing your feelings leaves you in a vulnerable state, but you've got to tell her how you care about her. Maybe you don't have to go so far as proposing just yet, not until you find out where her heart's at, but you've got to make a start if you want to find out if there's any chance of taking things to the next level."

"I know, maybe I just needed to hear myself say all this to realise it."

"No problem, glad I could help untangle the heartstrings. The awkward thing is I know what your future hopes are before Stephie does!"

"I'm sorry, it's a tight spot to put you in, but you can certainly keep a secret."

"Yeah, don't worry. I've got this."

It was true she had successfully kept his numerous personas to herself, however, he didn't know she had once again become the Cosmic Secret Keeper to an important milestone in a friend's life. The funny thing was this was the second time she was privy to a marriage proposal before the longed-for fiancée knew, so by now she had considerable practise in keeping weighty secrets under wraps!

"The thing is," Christopher continued looking troubled again, "How can I have a family of my own when I have Grandma who needs me? Would it be fair to Steph considering the responsibilities I have now?"

Katherine really felt for him, if only she had a solution to his predicament.

"The thing is, if you keep going out with Stephie all this will have to come out eventually. She's going to want to hear more about your family, your history and all of that, and if you keep shutting her out and stringing her along as 'Horace', it will end badly."

"So, what are my options?"

"Option one, you don't tell her, and things deteriorate because you continue to keep secrets until you reach the point of a very painful break-up with no logical explanation to give her, which will leave her very angry and perhaps eternally bitter towards you, which would make you another one of 'those guys' in her bad books, and you don't want to be one of them. Option Two," Katherine went on, counting down the probabilities on her fingers, "you tell her everything, which will give you two scenarios in my opinion. She may arrive at the conclusion that things won't work out between you, but she will leave the relationship with a sense of closure about why it may not have worked, or, she may be willing to see how things go despite the challenging circumstances you are in."

"When you put it like that, I guess it would be better to tell her everything. If things don't work out, I'd rather we could part amicably over it. Thanks for putting up with me and playing therapist for the afternoon, you've been a great help."

"You're welcome. Want another cup of coffee?"

"I would actually, but I've got to run. Sounds like your tour groups are coming back," he noticed as he got up from the chair with a quick upward nod to the floors overhead. He was right, from the sound of the footfalls, one of the two groups was on its way back down the stairs.

"About your pictures, same type of frames as last time?"

"Sure Kathy, you know the ones. I'd better go, or someone else will find out about 'Turris'," he said as he swung on his coat. "Thanks again."

"You're welcome, I hope it all works out."

"Me too."

Horace just made it out the back door before the tours returned, ensuring his real identity remained incognito for another while. While the two tour guides were saying their final farewells to their visitors, Katherine ducked into the office to see what new beauties 'Turris' had brought for her walls. As usual, he had painted very compelling night scenes of the city plus one rare canvas featuring an afternoon setting of the skyscrapers. Maybe he loved the night like the enigmatic Batman, but then, with his day-job as an art reporter and cultural editor, when else did he have time to paint? For the present, his Muse obviously could only come out when the sun withdrew its light, just like the Caped Crusader.

Katherine opened the office door once most of the visitors had gone or had wended their way over to the gift shop to have a look and were keeping Olivia hopping. Good, the cost was clear, she couldn't have the public catch a peek of Turris' new works just yet. Esther and Kevin were both surprised to see the new art deliveries and wondered when Turris had come in, they would have loved to meet him, but all Katherine could say was he arrived the same time as Horace so they had missed them both. It was the truth, albeit it was a stretch. She silently hoped to herself that one day the Higher Powers of the Universe would find someone else to designate as the 'Secret Keeper', this was getting a bit too much!

03 ❖ 80

Like all things in life, planning was necessary to ensure everything got done considering the projects were now mounting. Katherine figured they could easily take Turris' pictures in to be framed the day she and Kevin were going to drop by Fielding's new studio. Come to think of it, she could also get another task accomplished then too—delivering Sir Snoop's art purchases. He did say bring them any time the first week of July, so the first day of the month would have to do. The sooner they were delivered, the sooner she, Suzy and Justine could get the rest of their commissions. She also had to admit she was gnawed by curiosity to see Snoop's modern marvel of a gallery, although another part of her wished she didn't have to go for some odd reason and was glad Kevin would be coming with her, just thinking about Snoop irritated her. At least his gallery was keeping him busy, she hadn't seen him prowling around for his usual pastries the last few days.

"I quite agree with you Miss Kathy, considering Mr. Gerard is indisposed and unable to accompany you, I shall gladly be your chaperone,"

Kevin chivalrously returned when Katherine voiced her disapproval of the gallery-crasher.

"I don't know about a chaperone, but the company would be good." She smiled back, a bit amused by this impulsive gallant turn of events.

"I'm serious Miss Kathy, there is something not quite right about that chap, and I'm not just harping on the old Oxford-Cambridge boat race rivalry," Kevin quietly replied, his voice assuming that distinctive air of English sobriety when matters of propriety and decorum were brought up. No doubt the flirtatious Sir Snoop had gone beyond the acceptable somewhere along the line in the unspoken gentlemanly code observed by the upper and educated classes of the British Isles in Kevin's estimation and would ensure he would not be allowed to do so again, even if Snoop outranked him with a knighthood. Not that she couldn't take care of herself, but Gerry said he didn't want her going to the Elverton Gallery alone, and since she wouldn't like to do anything that might upset him, she guessed it was good thing Kevin was willing to assume the duty of chaperone on his behalf.

Their projects planned out for the day, Katherine and Kevin went their rounds in the van, dropping off Turris' pictures early in the morning at the framers then heading straight to Fielding's current creative haunt. At first, they weren't sure they had reached the correct address, the large dilapidated factory with its galvanised roofing and dust-enshrouded windows hunkered in its dusty, weedy plot of urban decay appeared as though it hadn't been operating for years, but when they heard a few hammer blows ringing upon an old blacksmith's anvil from within, they knew they had come to the right place. Approaching the woebegone premises and peeking inside the great metal doors, they found a sooty Fielding who had not expected them yet clad in a pair of overalls and sweating over a glowing fire, taking out bits of red hot metal and pounding them into the desired shapes like the ancient god of yore crafting weapons for the warriors of Mount Olympus. Just like Hephaestus, Fielding was limping a bit as he put down his heavy implements and came over to greet them.

"I'm sorry, forgive my appearance," he began, "I'd shake hands, but considering my present condition, I'm afraid that's out of the question. I hope you don't mind, I'll be showered and presentable in a few minutes. Please, there's some refreshments over there in the fridge, or you can get the coffee pot going if you like. I've got some fresh blueberry muffins too," he concluded, indicating a tidy area with some chairs, a comfy sofa, a coffee table with a large bouquet of summer flowers, and some cupboards. There were also plenty of bookshelves brimming with books.

"Thank you, but please, finish what you're doing first. What happened to your leg," Katherine noticed. "You're hobbling!"

"Oh that," Fielding grimaced as he wiped the sweat from his forehead with a towel, "a fire iron slipped out of my hands two days ago, got a nasty burn. It'll heal, but it's still sore. Never mind, they say an artist must suffer if the work is to turn out half-way genius."

"I don't think the proverb was meant to be taken that literal, my dear fellow," Kevin commiserated. "Are you all right? Should you be on your feet?"

"Don't worry, I'll be fine, but I think you'll agree I must have that shower, 'Old Decapitated' can wait," Fielding laughed, nodding to the faceless humanoid head glowing in the fire. "Bloody piece fell over and dented his brainpan just when I had finished polishing him. Must have been a weak area in the neck section, so back to the flames he goes. Excuse me, just make yourself at home."

While the injured artist limped off to a private area closed off by an aluminium door to make himself more presentable to his guests, Katherine and Kevin tried to do as he suggested in the industrial surroundings. The heat from the blackened foundry division was making things a little hot to put it mildly, so they left the eerie sight of 'Old Decapitated' roasting on the coals like a lost soul weltering in Dante's *Inferno* and decided to take a stroll among the sculptures posing around the floor or peeking from nooks and corners. The semi-abandoned ambiance of the old building did not make the scene any lighter. Somehow, it felt like they hadn't progressed far from the fiery circle of the abyss and just managed to make it to Purgatory as they wandered along Fielding's renditions of angst-ridden humanity. The tortured shapes seemed to call for succour from their dusty niches in the towering and aged factory with its cobweb curtains dangling in tatters from the steel ceiling girders, the dull glow of daylight barely filtering down in partial rays from the sandy windows and skylights above. Every now and then, a pigeon would flutter overhead like an unseen ghost, its whirring wings startling them for a second while the feathery tenant found a new place to roost.

"To think I helped inspire this. I must be Miss Congeniality's evil twin."

"Nonsense Miss Kathy, never mind the surroundings, I'm sure they will all look much better in the gallery. You stirred Fielding with the desire to make a real difference with art and not merely create art for art's sake, that's quite an honour."

While it was true Kevin was a born flatterer, it was nice he could actually uncover a positive cause for all this metallic doom and gloom. He did make one good point, the dark brooding environment wasn't showing the sculptures in their best light, the photos they were shown were brighter but still, pictures could never do justice to a three dimensional work, they were impressive once you got used to them. Certainly the 'Atomic Patriarch' with the genealogical mushroom cloud of armaments malignantly springing from its side and festering into an arborescent growth was strangely mesmerising, and quite grandiose. She was going to need a brigade of Gerry's tip-top movers to get it hauled!

Fielding soon returned freshened up and suitably attired in a crisp white shirt and black slacks, all ready for business. He invited them over to his seating area and offered them something cold with the muffins since the place was somewhat hot for coffee, an uncomfortable factor that had to be put up with while the smithy work was still underway. Katherine glanced around, first to the beautiful floral display helping to alleviate the harsh surroundings, then to his books featuring every topic from art, novels and poetry, to astrology, astronomy and atomic physics, also Hinduism and Buddhism to Islam and Judeo-Christianity. Obviously, Fielding liked to explore every topic available within the realm of faith and knowledge. When she complimented him on his bouquet and commented about his varied interests, not to mention the amount of books, he calmly explained:

"How can you be inspired if you do not surround yourself with the things that inspire you?"

Kevin of course could not help but exclaim his approval on that pithy observation.

After a pleasant chat, he wanted to show her the pieces not on display in the foundry, so they went to an area sectioned off by another metallic sliding panel that he rolled back, revealing another sight of shiny humanoids waiting to be viewed. He turned on the lighting, which wasn't much of an improvement as the florescent white rods flickered a disturbing glare over the scene. Despite the gloominess, the polished shapes were artistically captivating, even if his style had taken a somewhat macabre turn. Macabre indeed! It then struck her how the gathered forms seemed like a silent group of cattle destined for the abattoir, or worse yet, captives before a slave auction. Maybe she just wasn't used to this yet, viewing sculptures for display when up to now she had dealt mainly in paintings. She couldn't help but wonder if he liked to surround himself with things that inspired him, how could he remain passively indifferent to the strange shift of style displayed in his latest collection? Fielding provided a riddling answer: Truth and Wisdom are always attractive and beautiful even when they are not attractive and beautiful, or mankind would not be seeking them so much despite the harsh reality they portrayed at times.

"Didn't you ever read in the Bible how Wisdom describes herself? '*I am black but beautiful.*'"

She probably did, but couldn't remember at that moment, the Bible was one lengthy collection of books. Curious, she would have to ask Peter about that passage some time and what he thought it meant.

Katherine and Kevin went back with Fielding to the seating area set up for visitors and they got down to the nitty gritty of business, which certainly began to feel like those vile auctions of humanity that once took place in the 'Gracious South' as they hammered out prices for the latest masterpieces. Art as business, heavenly artistic inspiration reduced to dollars and cents—it was the vulgar necessity of running a gallery. Talk about beauty and unpleasant reality closely intertwined. It seemed so irreconcilable that something theoretically priceless as artistic expression and philosophical thought was bought and sold like sheep and sacks of turnips. However, unless an artist was God Himself, they could not live without hard currency or a generous patron. Although the idealistic Fielding presented the air of someone absolutely laid back without a shred of business acumen, he surprised her by handing them a folder containing a detailed itemised listing of the current collection in which he had carefully laid out the cost of each statue to date and approximately how much he hoped to make for each piece considering the materials, the size and time he worked on them. Kevin, who was used to doing business with Fielding just went over the file with his employer not surprised to see this hidden business acumen come to the fore. They made a second tour of the forms, this time with Fielding's list, familiarising themselves with the various titles of the pieces. The prices seemed reasonable when the various factors of artistry and work were considered. Of course, how much Katherine expected was another issue.

Fielding and Kevin politely waited and chatted a bit while she figured out this part of the negotiations with her calculator, jotting down numbers in her trusty notebook. She hoped her commission wouldn't mess up the numbers too much, even if the well-to-do were gaga about his artwork, the very shape of certain figures could turn buyers off for some reason, it was a bizarre psychological tick in people she proved just this past week. There was one beautiful painting that she had a hard time selling in the gallery, which was originally set at $4,775. Obviously, the artwork was not at fault, it was catching. The price seemed very reasonable for work of that calibre, but still it was not budging off her wall. She thought maybe it was overpriced and nobody wanted to pay that high, until out of inquisitiveness she decided to experiment and changed the number to $4,995. It sold within two days. She realised if the number was too low, people received the wrong impression that the art was 'cheap' or of 'inferior' worth! Gramps always said don't be too greedy, but Mr. R said not to sell herself short either, and now she grasped what he was trying to tell her. However, considering the work currently set before her, she wouldn't know if the numbers would look right until she began adding her commission.

Hmm, she silently mused. Although she was still new to the gallery business, she had quickly figured out a basic ratio to work from to ensure the artists got what they asked for after the commission deduction. It generally worked out okay if she took one half of their asking price and added it to their sum, however, the numbers could be off, meaning she still had to manually work out each price as though it were a puzzle. So if he wants ten thousand for this bronze piece, and I have a thirty-three percent commission rate, he'd only make $6,666 instead of the ten he wants, that's not a very good number anyway, so lets bump this up with the ratio and round off numbers until we get the right retail price …$15,000? That would mean $4,950 for the gallery … yep, that works, and the number looked good too, people seemed to like the shape of fives. However, it didn't always round out so easily on the first try, in some cases she had to keep on scribbling out each figure with each of his pieces until she hit the magic number. Negotiating the prices this way always reminded her of those ridiculous math assignments in school that began with if 'Jack had thirty melons, and Jill had twenty oranges, and Bill bought five melons from Jack and two oranges from Jill and gave ninety-seven bananas to Will, how many apples were left for Bob before Lill ate all the kumquats going for half price special?' One thing those types of problems taught her—it was a good thing she was not interested in selling fruit for a career. Of course, basic math would always be needed, she was grateful the grass roots level of the business world rarely required anything past adding, subtraction, multiplication and division most of the time, other than weights, measurements and geometry, naturally. The rocket scientists can keep their calculus.

Once the prices were set and met with the artists' approval, Fielding signed the contract. He had no problems with her stipulation that artists who agreed to show their pieces in her gallery as the official agent were required to leave them for a minimum of three months before they could collect them should they happen not to sell right away. After a few run-ins, she learned from experience that some rule of order had to be established if things were to operate in a professional manner. It was quite a chaotic learning curve in the beginning when some of the artists had second thoughts about showing one or two of their paintings and wanted to whip them off her walls just when they were delivered. They couldn't have art appearing and disappearing willy-nilly from the place just as the word got out among collectors a new canvas was up on offer! It would be nearly impossible to keep the gallery stocked and make record-keeping a joke.

When the paperwork was finished, Fielding said they could lighten up a little and call him John, J.F., or even 'Jiff' if they liked.

"Jiff?" Katherine smiled.

"Yeah, just smash 'J.F.' together, it's easier to pronounce," he explained with humour. "Everyone at school called me 'Jiff', I was meticulous in keeping my tools spic and span back then. Now I've got too many ideas to work on to worry about keeping everything looking like it was straight out of the store. As long as the machinery is maintained, the majority of the muck is scraped off, and the artwork is polished, you're doing well I figure. Which reminds me, we forgot about the other loose pieces you wanted to see. Come, I've got them over here," he explained nodding over to a steel door. Curious, they followed him to a special secured room. "I had to lock them away. Everything else is a bit heavy and would be difficult to lift, but these ones despite their small size cost a bit to put together, and considering the neighbourhood, I didn't want these to disappear. It wouldn't be too hard to break into an old place like this undetected," he explained as he unlocked the door and turned on the lights.

It was a bare, windowless, white painted room with a few work tables cluttered with polishing and engraving machines lined against the cement block walls, a nondescript place lit by florescent lighting as expected in an old factory, but the surroundings were swiftly ignored as the eye was quickly attracted to the bright shapes taking up residence on a table. There were five in all, each a flawlessly round sphere of various colours sitting like miniature worlds upon gleaming slender columns resembling silver candle stands. At first, the five spheres, which were not much bigger than a grapefruit, appeared to be the epitome of modernistic simplicity, that is until Katherine and Kevin drew closer to examine the fine details: there were intricate designs and shapes visible on the globes. To her surprise, they were stunning petite mosaics, the crust of each tiny world was minutely decorated in perfectly cut and polished pieces of semi-precious stones and marble seamlessly fitted together into decorative patterns, except for one, which was more detailed as it was a miniature replica of the Earth exactly as seen from space. The others featured a myriad of hues, the predominate shades ranged from white and blue for the first globe, blue and green for the second, green and rose the third, then red and mottled stone pieces for the last. The colour schemes reminded Katherine of the four seasons, and she was correct. Each sphere depicted a season in universal symbolic shapes. The first was covered in intricate mother of pearl snowflakes embedded upon a brilliant royal blue background of lapis lazuli, the second displayed tiny blue lapis and turquoise rain drops and water splashes falling upon a green malachite and jade stone field representing the grass, the third featured pink marble and red carnelian roses with a few mother of pearl arum lilies upon another emerald green malachite and jade background although the stones were cut to resemble a leafy bush, while the last featured red carnelian maple leaves in amid other species of multicoloured tree leaves shaped from agate and sardonyx.

"Wow, these are exquisite," Katherine complimented. "I had no idea you could do such intricate work like this."

"Thank you, I studied in Italy for awhile and spent some time learning how to do mosaics, and not just the bathroom tile kind!" He laughed.

"Yes Miss Kathy, you should see the series he did years ago, a reinvention of Art Deco yet fused with the ancient classics styles of Rome, they were magnificent," Kevin affirmed. "Mr. Gerard tried to secure them, but was outbid by another art lover."

"Really?" Katherine wondered. Well, if Fielding did works like this, no wonder! Gerry loved anything Italianate, and judging from the calibre of the intricate mosaic globes before her that had all the appeal of Fabergé eggs, modernity without the usual absurdity, she could see why he wanted those last mosaic pieces so badly. "These are very beautiful. If I may, what piece of poetry inspired you this time?"

"Oh, a multitude of little things really, letting a thought suggest one thing and then letting it lead to another, a muse-chain if you will. The first inspiration came from William Blake's verses, his mystic line about seeing the world in a grain of sand. It reminded me of my time in Italy in the workshop learning the craft and selling some of my resulting wares to help get me through art school, small replicas of *David*, the *Pietá*, things like that, and also mosaics. I made a lot of these," he said, reaching into the desk and opening a drawer from which he took out several colourful pieces that looked like jewellery, which in fact they were; small round brooches and pendants featuring decorative designs in tiny brightly coloured minuscule mosaic patterns in gold plated settings. "I have a few left over, the tourists in Italy loved them. They sell all the stuff the art students produce and reproduce in the shops," he said as he handed them to his guests to examine. Unlike the globes, the tiny stones in the fashion accessories were more visible and surprisingly tactile as their floral patterns possessed a satisfying three-dimensional texture resembling Braille.

"These are really pretty," Katherine complimented.

"Thanks. They weren't high art of course, but I enjoyed working on them too. It was like I was making miniature worlds with tiny grains of sand, and that memory combined with Blake's line gave me the idea to make an actual globe of the Earth, just to see if I could do it, but in a polished form like the altarpieces at the Vatican, one would never know those scenes were mosaics unless one looked very closely, the tessellation is suburb on those. Of course, I wanted the best stone, hence the semi-precious material. It took some work getting it right. Once I was done, I waxed a little philosophical as one is bound to do when they hold the world in their hands and I thought about the book of Genesis. Forget religion for a moment and just imagine the immense artistry of the scene! An unfathomable God looking down on the perfect world He just created and making His last and best creation, Mankind, male and female, all starting with a pinch of dust into which an immortal soul was breathed. What was the first human compared with the Creator? Or any human for that matter? A grain of sand, that is all! Yet, a whole world within a world once an immortal soul was infused within."

"Very true," Katherine nodded. It reminded her of a story Peter told her about a mystic who was pondering the vastness of creation and was visited by Christ who wanted to show her something. The mystic noticed the Lord held a small orb that seemed no bigger than a marble that just fit in the hollow of the hand. When she asked what it was He calmly replied, "This? It is the Universe."

"Splendid sources of inspiration, my dear fellow," Kevin complimented. "So how did the four seasons come about?"

"Well, like poor Adam who appeared a little lonely, it didn't seem right to leave the Earth by itself. I was thinking of doing the solar system, but then looking at the globe, that famous line jumped into my head, 'To give your soul for the entire world, but for Wales?'... ."

"*A Man for All Seasons,*" Katherine recalled.

"Exactly. The idea was perfect, the theme just breathes forth Italy, you know? Everything from Vivaldi's *Four Seasons* to five star Roman hotels and the world's most popular pizza topping," Jiff concluded with a laugh.

"I love the Renaissance period, but what is it about all you guys and Italy," Katherine playfully joked.

"Oh, it's a religious experience, and I'm not just referring to the Vatican," Jiff returned with an air of comical solemnity. "A man has not fully lived until he experiences that gentle balmy clime of ancient empires, the land of lemon trees and the genius of Michelangelo."

"Quite so," Kevin nodded back. "The time-honoured Grand Tour. No cultured education is complete without it."

"I suppose so, but I can't help loving Paris," Katherine noted.

"Don't feel bad, France is the only other western country of culture worth visiting after one has seen Italy," Jiff sagely consoled.

"Britain has some respectable qualities too," Kevin replied with humour, "however, I too am drawn to the elegance of Versailles, so you are forgiven old chap."

"You said these were 'loose' pieces," Katherine noted, returning to the artwork at hand, "yet they seem to go together as a set. Did you actually plan to sell them separately?"

"Well, I did, but then like you noticed, they do seem to be inseparable, but together that would make 'one' piece, and therefore one 'loose' work that stood apart and was not part of a normal collection or series, if you understand me."

"I see. These are really something else. You know, they would look gorgeous on a flat polished stone surface, maybe something dark? Black marble or granite? It would be like they were in outer space, like real planets. The solar system idea wouldn't be entirely scrapped."

"Hey! Now there's a brainstorm, such a simple solution too. I was wondering how to sign these pieces without wrecking them, but I could just engrave my name on the side of the stone base," Jiff remarked, pleased with the suggestion. "Yes, a nice oval shape would work wonders. Again, I owe you, what a muse you're turning out to be! Here, take a good look, don't be shy, you can hold them," he continued, plucking the rosy sphere of Summer from its stand and handing it to her, then giving Kevin a look at the splashy images of Spring.

Katherine found the globe heavier than it looked, yet beautifully smooth and cool, like the billiard balls she used to play with in the den at home when she was little, only these were slightly larger. In fact, she found the five spheres incredibly charming as she gently rolled Summer around, admiring the roses and bright green designs. She could immediately tell this was something Gerry would absolutely love for a variety of reasons. Pondering on them for a moment, it all seemed so perfect: the theme of the little geocentric mosaic display of the seasons revolving around the earth and the Italianate sources of Fielding's inspiration, especially one of Gerry's most favourite pieces of classical music and the play *A Man for All Seasons* dramatising the life of Sir Thomas Moore, who of all things, was Gerry's Confirmation name-saint. The more she thought about it, the more she realised it would make the ideal surprise gift that was also in complete agreement with her 'palazzo' decorating plan. However, apart from everything else going in the penthouse, this was going to be completely on her. Yes, she couldn't resist this piece, she had to have it. After all the times Gerry had ruined her royally with his lavish surprises, it was time he got a little spoiling in return. He deserved the world!

"Forget about putting this in the gallery, I'm not letting anyone else get near it. How much do you want for it? The whole thing," she enquired.

"You want it?"

"Yes, a surprise for Gerry. I don't know what you did the last time, but if he liked your work then, he'll definitely go ape when he sees this, especially when I tell him about your inspirations."

"Why Miss Kathy, what a generous gift! Mr. Gerard will be absolutely thrilled with it," Kevin affirmed, clapping his hands together. "I would have loved it myself, but before we even know what the price is, I can safely guess it will be well beyond my means."

"Well, speaking of prices, I'm not quite sure what to ask for now as I need to add the base you suggested," Jiff mused, "on top of it, you just gave me another idea with your mention of 'outer space' and 'galaxy', but it would add to the price a bit, work time basically."

"Oh? What did I suggest to your muse now?"

"Since you noticed I don't have to scrap the solar system, what about another matching mosaic with stars, galaxies, planets and nebulas in precious stone set in the black? I could recreate a Hubble telescope image on the base to set off the globes just handsomely. Although they were painstaking work, I was sorry when the last ball was finished. This idea just gave me a good excuse to work on it some more, not to mention help use up some of the left over stone bits. With this idea, not all of it will go to scrap now, that was really bothering me, I hate waste."

"Me too, especially semiprecious material like this," Katherine agreed.

"I thought I might have to make a few more of those pins and brooches just to use it up, but it might add to the overall cost," he trailed.

"Yes, but what a fantastic idea! How much would the original five globes have gone for?"

"Well, some were more expensive than others, but about ten thousand, considering the time and semi-precious stones that went in to them, not to mention the stands are Stirling silver."

"Steep, but not. Considering your fame, I was expecting an even higher price. I definitely want it," Katherine noted. Collecting designer art would be beyond most people, but that was well within her means thanks to Gramp's trust fund, getting something like this was a wonderful possibility since she was saving the growing profits from the gallery for a rainy day. It had been awhile since she had bought anything substantial with the exception of the gallery refurbishments, and since her brainy brother Steves helped to recoup nearly all her construction spending in a short space of time on the stock market, she could certainly afford to splurge a bit now. Besides, she would rather get this for Gerry and support an artist than spend the money on something else she didn't need or want.

"The thing is, I don't know about making an estimate for the base, it depends on the design, how detailed it's going to be and if I need to order more stones depending on the colours. I won't have a clue until I design a pattern, which might give me an idea on the stones. The good thing is working on a flat surface should be quicker work, it won't be as difficult to set as the spheres were, cutting everything with the correct degree of curvature was a nightmare."

"I can imagine," Katherine replied, examining Summer once again with its roses, admiring the brilliantly smooth surface concealing the intricate labour that was spent on the interlocking jigsaw of coloured semiprecious gemstone particles. "I like the idea. Go ahead and finish it, and I'll be happy to pay the extra for the base. Gerry's going to just love it."

"Okay, like I said, with the extra leftover stone I have, it'll mostly be for the time. The base won't be as high priced as the spheres, not since I've pretty much already factored in the stone I had to cut away. Would you like me to do a few designs for you to see first, since there is an opportunity to choose what you would like?"

"No, I don't want to tie you to anything, and I'm sure you won't want a fussy patron looking over your shoulder. You won't do your best unless your creative fire is allowed to burn free. Do whatever it is you're inspired to do. If the base turns out to be anything like this work here, I know it will look quite stunning."

"Much appreciated! Okay then, I shall get started on it right away, as soon as the last pieces of *April One* are finished. Speaking of which, I'd better check in on 'Old Decapitated' before he melts away, excuse me," he jumped, quickly running out the door.

Katherine and Kevin admired the orbs for a few more minutes before gently putting them back on their silver stands. Talking about the black stone base reminded her of another place they had to go today, a place that had shiny black floors and sparking walls.

"Well, I'm sorry we have to go, but we have a delivery to make," Katherine announced as they went back out to the smithy area. "Is 'Decapitated' all right?"

"Yeah, nothing I can't fix. We've got plenty of time, everything will be ready for the première in August, provided I don't knock another one over," Jiff reassured her with a chuckle. "It was a pleasure doing business with you."

"Likewise." She shook his hand.

"As always," Kevin replied, also making the polite parting gesture.

"Feel free to stop by any time, you can check the base in progress."

"All right. Oh! I forgot! You'll need a reserve plus a down payment put on it to get you started, and to hold the rest for me, but I didn't bring anything, not that much anyway."

"Don't worry about it."

"I don't know when I can drop by again, can I leave it for you at the gallery?"

"Sure, I'll run by later."

"Okay, and just give us a call when *April One* is ready to be crated and delivered, but please make sure you give us enough days to set them up, with your supervision of course. I'd hate to think of the panic that would ensue if we left arranging such heavy pieces to the last minute before the première!"

"All right, will do. Take care," Jiff waved as he saw them off, then headed back to work.

Naturally, the two art dealers couldn't help but discuss that morning's events as they drove to their next destination. Setting up Fielding's première was an exciting project, which was definitely something to look forward to. Kevin had to agree the new statues were very impressive in person. Considering J.F.'s divergent style for this series contra to his accustomed mode of expression, the public were in for one unanticipated treat! Katherine also mused to herself that was good, if Jiff happened to be a sell-out, that would keep the bills paid for quite some time. She was hoping she wouldn't ever have to dip into her trust fund to keep her business operational for the times when sales were slow, and so far, she didn't have to do that. Of course, Kevin was still all agog about the *Four Seasons*, it was fortunate for Mr. Gerard's sake that J.F. hadn't shown them to anyone else, or that piece would have been snapped up and long gone before they came. Katherine was also thrilled, it was one of the few modern pieces she had seen that she really liked to the point of buying it, her first real foray into the art world as a collector. Everything else up to now was either gifts or donations to the museum section of the gallery, and now she could personally give something to her prince in shining amour that she knew he would really appreciate. Kevin broke into her thoughts once more, it was a pity Jiff didn't do more work like that, wouldn't that be something to show? It certainly would, Katherine nodded. Maybe they could get him to do some more of his flat surfaced mosaics since he loved working on them so much. That would be something unique. Kevin noted they could suggest it to him when he came around later that day to pick up his reserve.

The time seemed to fly as they discussed that morning's events, she had pulled up outside the Elverton Gallery virtually on autopilot before they knew it. Despite their curiosity about the place, it was an anticlimax having to do business with Sir Nincompoop Snoop after all the positive activity of the morning. At least this visitation would result in a 'full payment received' for her friends and then she would have done with him. Let's get this over with! They each took a painting from the back of the van and made their way inside, albeit a little awkwardly considering the long, narrow boxed parcels. The darkly tinted glass doors softly shut behind them, cocooning them in the purposefully stylised atmosphere created by the art and its modish urban surroundings. The blatant starkness of the famed gleaming floors struck them as soon as they entered, the polished darkness under their feet immediately pulling their vision upward and outward onto the spotlighted and brightly coloured movable walls placed at strategically yet jauntily stylish angles, the eye drawn in further still by the larger-than-life canvases bedecked with mighty two-tone streaks and rippled splotches: they were in the august presence of Kroger's enigmatic *Study in Red*. Naturally, no ultra modern New York setting was complete without a whirling harmonic muddle of futuristic music attempting to sound like Jazz quietly playing in the background led by a soprano saxophone, the improvised note patterns harmonizing at sporadic intervals with the electronic keyboard, bass guitar, 'cello and snare drum accompaniment.

Moving closer, she took her attention off the grandiose neo-minimalist painting and examined the track of halogen lights sitting on top of the first wall in front of them, their little telescope necks arching downwards illuminating the great tidal wave of colour. Could one really pluck that off and stick it on the ceiling? Too bad the wall was a bit too high for her, plus there was a security camera with its shiny glass eye quietly blinking in the corner observing all that went on. She might have tried if she could have gotten away with it unnoticed! Katherine then espied the stiff thick wire poking out of the top corner of the wall. That must be it, the semi-wireless circuit that kept the lights powered even while the walls were in transit. She examined the charcoal grey futuristic expansive panelling overhead; she could just make out the fine electrical meshwork powering the quirky no-cords displays dotted throughout the expansive space. Did the walls really spark? The urge to move just a little closer and tip the wall oh-ever-so-slightly with the edge of the box she was holding just to see for herself was growing by the second.

She didn't know if she actually did or not, but Katherine found herself quickly jumping back slightly with a guilt-ridden conscience when Sir Snoop unexpectedly came around the wall, Kevin nowhere in sight. Her chaperone must have gone exploring for the reception desk while she was busy battling her impish temptations. Well, the fact Snoop was in his gallery *wasn't* unexpected, but being this close to the displays while suppressing the tantalizing pull to ignore the old rule of look but don't touch, and sensing like she was caught doing something mischievous by *him* no less, certainly made things a bit awkward. To make it worse, he seemed to have guessed what she was up to.

"Go on, you can give it a shove," he grinned, the typical polite greetings now forgone by the droll scene he interrupted.

"Er, no thanks, I was just getting a closer look at Kroger's disaster-pieces, that's all."

"I see. Here, let me give you a demonstration," he continued, gently rolling the wall. True to the various reports, the partition continued to stay lit while the wire sent out a glittery display, but perhaps the descriptions were a bit over hyped. It reminded her of the sparklers used on top of birthday cakes, although the bumper car analogy was not misplaced either. Maybe the walls sparked brighter the faster they were rolled, but she was not about to ask and give him the satisfaction of showing off any more than he already was. She tried not to look interested as he continued his demonstration, plucking off the lights and pushing them straight on to the ceiling, the bulbs dimming before going dark then brightening up again as they were pulled from their power source and magnetised onto their new location overhead.

"Neat. Well, as you can probably guess, your paintings have arrived. Where would you like them delivered?"

"What? All business and no play? You *must* have a private tour of the place first since you missed the grand opening, followed by the best gourmet experience you will ever have. Lunch is on me."

"I don't think so," she continued.

"I insist," he continued.

"But I shall not desist on 'no'," she replied. "I'm here on business, that is all."

"As I've mentioned before, business lunches happen all the time, work can be fun too," he continued, approaching a little too close for her liking.

Geeze, he was getting a bit fresh again! She hated being made uncomfortable, 'no' meant 'no'. Time to throw the discomfort back at him, see how he would like it.

"Lunch is on you, you say? All right. Oh Kevin?"

"Yes Miss Kathy?" Kevin quickly materialised by her side from wherever he had skipped off to.

"Sir Elverton has kindly offered us a tour, and lunch. Isn't that kind of him?"

"Oh, is that so? It is indeed, how spiffing of you," Kevin replied, suddenly understanding from her polite but edged tone of voice what was happening.

"Not at all, it would be my pleasure."

It seemed to work. Sir Snoop cooled a bit when Kevin appeared wielding his box, the unexpected male guest had put a dampener on his flirty frame of mind. To Sir Elverton's chagrin, the prospect of being alone with this gorgeous specimen of flowering womanhood in Katherine had evaporated, but he quickly straightened up and was polite according to time-honoured decorum, playing the perfect host and shaking hands with Mr. Alcott.

"However, I'm afraid we won't be able to stay. Isn't that correct," Katherine continued.

"Yes it is, I'm afraid business must be attended to. I'm sure you understand," Kevin added.

"Of course, I won't hold you up," Snoop replied, letting them off the hook and not insisting any further. Good thing too, she didn't know how she could have eaten anything under the sticky circumstances, every morsel would certainly have lodged itself in her craw. "Here, let me take that," he continued as he retrieved the box from Katherine. "The main reception desk is back here."

He led them though the floor, but the direct path he took at a faster pace barely gave them a chance to take in the rest of the space or glance at the other canvases on display. Apart from the rolling walls, the only other notable feature she could discover in the revamped gallery was the escalator system placed nearer the back offering to lift guests to the upper floors. Unlike most models that hid the workings of their insides with steel or aluminium plating, this rendition was a see-through custom made item, the operations quietly churning away yet completely exposed to view behind a thick transparent PVC glass casing and illuminated by a variety of soft fibre optic lights. It reminded her of the steel modules of the Lloyd's Building in London and the funky coloured pipes of the Pompidou Centre in Paris, buildings that appeared as if they were completely turned inside out. Well, the escalator was definitely in keeping with the innovative theme of the art gallery. Modernity! She could never understand the new rules of aesthetics, giving a peep show of all the clunky electrics and plumbing in buildings was now the thing to do. Come to think of it, Snoop the Nincompoop probably had a glass elevator too somewhere, ah yes, over by the right side wall. Nothing was left to the imagination there either, all the cogs, cables and wheels where visible behind the glass car. Good thing Gerry had no real desire to visit the Elverton Gallery, he wouldn't have liked that contraption one bit! Considering the transparent condition of the escalator, he might not have been overjoyed with that as an alternative either.

At the quick clip they were going, they didn't waste time getting to the desk which was nearly in the back. Katherine wondered why the reception desk was placed here, but then the answer came to her almost immediately: this was a smart move, which she wished she had made. People tended to get put off when a desk is the first thing they come across. She had experienced it herself at her own gallery, new visitors would be happily browsing around the rolly-pollies on the ground floor, but then grow timid when they approached the stairs or the elevator as the reception desk was right close by. Did they have to ask for permission to go up? Was the rest of the building closed to the public? Somehow, the desk suggested a barrier that needed the right clearance permissions okayed by the management just like a security point. Of course, once the gallery had been set up she couldn't fix the floor plan when she discovered this anomaly occurring, but did her best to overcome this impasse by painting a welcoming vintage style sign with a Victorian index hand inviting them to go upstairs followed by a list of what was available on the other floors with a comical note underneath in parentheses reminding them they may take the elevator too. Once she had it framed and placed on an ornate period display easel by the stairs, new visitors were more confident about meandering upstairs on their own or searching for the elevator. A few petite signs on the rolly-pollies declaring there were more artworks to discover above on the upper floors also did wonders.

Snoop asked if they would like a coffee or anything while they conducted their business. They both shook their heads and politely declined. Setting down his box against the desk, Kevin returned to the van to bring in the remainder of the delivery while Katherine concluded the financial transaction. However, Snoop suddenly declared he would still like a coffee and had the receptionist hop off to fetch him a cup. Once more alone with her, Snoop quickly regained some of his flirty warmth and dropped the suggestion she come back another time for lunch, maybe even an afternoon drink … this time growing more familiar than usual, casually placing a hand on her arm. She firmly pulled her arm away as she said a polite nothing and left him dangling as usual. He was getting right annoying, the 'Ice Queen' treatment that Gerry used to tease her about wasn't phasing him one bit! Well, it obviously didn't phase Gerry either, but that was beside the point. At least she was not engaged when she met Gerry, he who would be the love of her life, but now that she was, everyone else should just back off. She was engaged, off limits, unavailable— no comma, full stop, period. Under those circumstances, flirting was no longer a tolerable if impish way to get to know someone and she was incensed with this jerk for trying, especially as she absolutely detested a man who had 'Russian' hands and 'Roman' fingers. Gerry in his semi-desperate persistence to get noticed never annoyed her, but Snoop did and didn't care if he did, or it seemed like he didn't. What was his game? Never mind, she was not going to stick around to get handed a rule book. Good thing she wasn't alone for long, once more Kevin played 'Ice Maker' as he dropped off the last box just as Snoop handed her the cheque while she gave him his receipt. They said their 'thank you's' and 'good byes' and left the premises.

"Whew! That's that," she said as they climbed back into the van.

"Thank goodness! Despite the innovations which one cannot help but envy, it's just not the same old place without Mr. Sirrac," Kevin grieved, shaking his head as he buckled himself in.

"Come let's get a bite to eat, lunch is on me," Katherine replied as she started the engine.

"Oh no, allow me! Let this be my treat, Miss Kathy."

"Now isn't this something? Another guy who won't let a lady pay for anything? Every girl complains chivalry is dead, but I'm surrounded by a bunch of Knights of the Round Table." She laughed. "Kevin, you've been gallant enough and have done your duty well. You certainly helped to cool down Snoop quite nicely I must say. Come now, since we have done quite a bit of work this morning, I believe I can bend the rules a bit and take lunch off my tax returns as a business expense. You deserve a good meal as a reward for your faithful service."

"Oh, very well then, this chivalric chaperone shall go off the clock and take you up your offer courtesy of Uncle Sam's deduction scheme. I am positively wilting from hunger."

"It's a good thing we escaped Snoop's lunch offer. If the reports about his restaurant's fare are true, even after a seven course meal you'd be left wilting."

After a delectable lunch, which Kevin assured her it was, Katherine asked him if he wouldn't mind if they stopped at the hospital to visit Gerry. He didn't mind at all and was delighted with the suggestion, he would be happy to do so. Of course, she had the bistro box up a lovely gourmet sandwich and dessert to go for the patient. They both received a surprise when Katherine opened the door and did not see him in the bed as they expected, but sitting beside it in a special chair, albeit he remained attached to a drip, but that didn't matter. Seeing him sitting and dressed nicely in his formal robe for visitors after all that time stuck in bed was a remarkable sight!

"Gerry! You're out!"

"Not quite, I'm still confined to the hospital," he observed, but clearly pleased to elicit this happy reaction.

"Even so, I must say, this is wonderful to see you have progressed this far," Kevin greeted, shaking his free hand, for Katherine had already rushed to his side and was not letting go of the other after she had dropped off his 'doggie box' and had given him a kiss on the cheek followed by a hug.

"Yes," she jumped in. "When was this new phase in your physiotherapy planned?"

Gerry explained the physiotherapists wanted to try the first experiments of getting him into a sitting position out of bed that morning, but considering her schedule running about town for that day, he had a hunch she might drop by earlier than usual and so talked them into making the attempt a little closer to lunchtime to surprise her.

"You guys certainly did that! How do you feel? Are you in any pain?"

"Not with what they put in there," he said, nodding to the drip, "I'm fuzzy, but fine. Although I wish I could have stood up, but they had to use that thing to get me out, they didn't want me to put any strain on my hips yet."

Katherine then looked over and noticed the crane-like machine at the other side of the room, which from Gerry's comments she now understood was a hoist.

"Still, this is another step, one that gets you closer to getting out of here," she reminded.

"True. So, how fares the art world," he asked as he tucked into the treat they had provided. It felt good, sitting upright again in a chair, properly seated! Eating in bed was overrated.

"Swimmingly," Kevin announced. "Fielding's new collection will be one for the history books."

"I wish I was there with you, I enjoy making studio visits," Gerry admitted, "to be invited see a collection before the rest of the world, there's nothing like it."

"I'll say." Katherine chuckled, telling him about the tour of J.F.'s 'Inferno' and poor 'Old Decapitated' frying on the fire. She couldn't resist: she hadn't told him during her last visits at the hospital, but today she let him in on Jiff's latest source of inspiration, Frost's 'Fire and Ice' combined with her explosive one liner … .

"I mean really! He literally wrote a poem around it, and what a doozie it is too," she laughed. "I've got some philosophical competition."

"Jiff?"

"Yeah, he said we could call him that, J and F smashed into a nickname that he acquired in art school."

"It seems like you got on quite well today."

"But that's not all … ," Kevin hinted.

"Shhh! Don't spoil the surprise!" Katherine hastily jumped in, afraid her eager art administrator might just spill the beans.

"I wasn't," Kevin returned, shaking his head.

"What surprise?"

"Nope, I'm not going to tell you, it's suppose to be a surprise after all," she returned.

"Another one? I'm regretting I insisted you keep your decorating plans a secret, now this! Just a hint, please?"

"Oh, okay, a hint mind you! … I got you a present today."

"A present? It's not my birthday, and we're nowhere near Christmas. What's the occasion?"

"For being your loving, charming, adorable self."

"I guess that's a good enough reason," Gerry nodded. "I'm guessing you found something unique during your studio visit," he then noted, his interest completely hooked.

"Bingo! Jiff showed us a new work that I know you would love, but that's all the information I'm giving you."

"What? *You* of all people purchase a modern Fielding piece, and then to withhold the details? The suspense is going to kill me if the food here doesn't," Gerry piped up as he made a disgruntled gesture to the half-touched lunch tray beside him waiting to be collected.

"You've survived the medical mush so far, so you should survive the suspense," she replied with humour.

"Ah, you're cruel," he moaned, but enjoying every bit of teasing. "Come on Kevin, at least you give me another hint."

"Hmm, let's say the world shall be your oyster, Mr Gerard," he grinned with a wink and nod to Katherine, enjoying every minute of being privy to the surprise.

"Is that all? I'm dying here!" Gerry laughed. "I can safely guess it is a sculpture of some kind. Can you at least tell me the medium he used?"

"Oh okay; it's a sculpture *and* a mosaic, inspired by Italy. Now, that's it! No more clues." Katherine shook her finger at him.

"Uh oh, the suspense is growing. Those clues have just made it worse. No more badgering, but I can't think what in the world he could have sculpted, with mosaics too. Hmm, Italy," Gerry mused, pondering the riddle yet not realising he had come close to the answer as he took another bite out of his sandwich.

"It's not actually finished yet, it seems I gave him another idea, and he wants to work on it some more to polish it off nicely, so, you could say I've also commissioned a bit of it," Katherine continued.

"Really? *You?* Commission a modern piece?"

"Well, just the finishing touch."

"Still, there's another precedent broken. I'm afraid to look outside in case the sky is upside down. The suspense! But you're not going to tell me what it is, huh."

"Right. Surprise, surprise!"

"But, it's probably *looks* like something old or 'classic', or you wouldn't go for it," Gerry continued to ruminate, trying to figure out the riddle.

"No more badgering," she reminded.

"All right! I promise." He smiled, looked like no more clues were forthcoming. He would just have to wait.

Katherine was just about to launch into an account of their quick trip to Sir Snoop's zingy place of operation when the nurses returned, and not too pleased to see the 'doggie box' sending their patient's calorie count askew, however, they were used to it by now and decided to go easy on them today.

"Okay, time to get you back into bed, Prince Handsome, too much of a good thing you know. We don't want to tire you out," Deborah announced.

"To the swinging crane already, there goes the shred of dignity I regained today," Gerry sighed in good humour. "When will you praetorian guards ever let me stand up?"

"All in good time," Deborah replied. "Contrary to the old proverb, you'll have to fly this time before you can walk. Be grateful we permitted you to be enthroned to receive your sweetheart."

"Shall we leave," Kevin wondered.

"Please, at least while they have me swinging in the air, you can come back when the test flight is over," Gerry declared. Despite the inglorious method of moving him around, it still was an encouraging sign of progress as evidenced by his sense of humour.

"You and your stubborn Reinold pride." Katherine smiled, giving him another quick kiss on the cheek before she and Kevin left him in the care of the air traffic controllers, that is, the nurses.

ल❖ॐ

Progress! The month of July was teeming with promise. Gerry was getting closer to moving about on his own two feet, her gallery was getting some tip top new artists, and the decorating at the penthouse was shaping up quite nicely, once the messy side of the plastering and all the dust was cleared. Everything had the invigorating feel that all was on the move and definitely for the better. However, that meant Katherine was left with hardly a moment's rest, one thing after another was always calling upon her attention. Progress also meant unceasing activity. Then, there were a few unexpected challenges that came with the forward march of progress. Stansislov was one of them. Mr. R was true to his word and didn't sit around, calling up the gloomy artist as he promised. He came slumping through the door one day as Katherine, Suzy, Kevin and Esther were going over the costs of Fielding's upcoming première to date, his grey hair semi-combed into grudging respectability, his wrinkled shirt unbuttoned with no tie of course. True to the temperamental contradiction that often manifested itself in his dour personality, Stansislov did not stand on dress-code ceremony since he considered himself a representative of the common man resistant to the etiquette expected by the elite of both society and the art world, despite his hatred for Communism that failed to alleviate the working classes after seeing first hand how it had reduced Mother Russia to a shadow of her former glory. Gerry told Katherine at one time that the touchy artist would give anything to have the Imperial Days of grandeur without the Tsar if that was at all possible; a gilded, romanticised Russia yet stripped of all impotent, effeminate idealism of a monarchical past long since dead. Stansislov was living in an impossible paradox of envisioning a Golden Age without all the golden touches that made a golden age luxurious, but Gerry found him strangely interesting nonetheless. There wasn't a person yet born on this earth that didn't want to see the world shaped to their own vision, no matter how fractured that vision was. Katherine noticed there was some truth in Gerry's observation. However, judging by what she had seen of Stansislov's canvases a few years ago, his ideas of 'Golden Magnificence' had fallen short somewhere and noted that it was probably a good thing the artist's sphere of activity did not go beyond the paintbrushes. There were too many nut cases in history that attempted to make their daydreams a reality, and not a few ended with some disastrous or ludicrous consequences. Now, things had taken a humorous turn as the artist longing for the renaissance of a non-gilded Golden Age in the land of his birth was looming before her and looking around at her shining tribute to Old Europe with a sceptical eye.

"Yoris old boy! How magnificent to see you," Kevin enthusiastically greeted.

"Likewise," he grunted back in a thick Russian accent, shaking hands.

"Miss Katherine was hoping for a visit, and here you are!"

"Obviously," Stansislov returned, "a ghost does not have flesh and bones."

"You are priceless! I believe you have met Miss Katherine Walsingham and Miss Susanna Cooper," Kevin continued, not flustered by the artist's blunt rationale.

"Yes, the Sirrac I recall," he nodded, shaking hands again, then was introduced to Esther. "Forgive my directness Miss Walsingham," he then continued, getting down to business, "I'm here as a courtesy to Mr. Reinold as I am greatly indebted to him, but to save us all from an afternoon of futile pleasantries, I should state here and now that from what I can see, I'm afraid this venue will not suit my latest collection."

"Come, come! You must give it a good look," Kevin continued, jumping to the fore, "not all the floors are decorated quite the same."

"Yes, now that you're here, let us give you a tour at least," Katherine offered.

Stansislov gave a slight bow of agreement and followed them to the elevator. Unfortunately, Stansislov may be crustily polite, but was not very obliging as Kevin had once hoped he might be, insisting everything was still a little too 'old world' and 'French' for his next collection, including the less colourful third floor. Although Katherine still had plenty of artists to choose from in Kevin's book should this fall through, it seemed a shame that such a popular if somewhat dismal artist slipped through their fingers. It looked like he might take up Elverton on his offer to show there if things continued to slide downhill during this tour like they were. Katherine was beginning to grow a little anxious, and then thought of Fielding's upcoming première. Maybe the elegant surroundings might be hardened with those sculptures of woe? Stansislov had co-premiered a collection with Fielding before, perhaps he might be open to the suggestion? Stansislov seemed interested when he heard of Fielding's latest offerings, but even Katherine and Kevin's vivid descriptions of Jiff's despondent oddities weren't enough to win him over. He wanted grittier surroundings, the walls were just too colourful and would jar with his latest theme, and although he was tempted, her reasonable commission rates were not attractive enough. Katherine nearly suggested the boiler house at that point, but refrained from descending to the ridiculous. There was nothing for it but to thank him for coming and hope he had a pleasant afternoon. Katherine sighed as she saw him leave, well, they couldn't win them all. At least they gave it their best shot, but it was so disheartening when your best shot wasn't good enough.

Five minutes barely passed when something unexpected occurred—Stansislov was back at the desk and placed before them the following proposal for a venue: what about next door?

"Next door," Katherine quizzically repeated.

"Yes, the empty place. Could we set up something there?"

"The old factory?" Kevin wondered. Curious, they followed the tetchy artist outside to where he pointed up at the old building next to the gallery, a semi-detached edifice and now left vacant, a shadow of what her gallery used to be like when it too was an old manufacturing workhorse producing everything from cardboard boxes to powders and pills, not to mention quality cotton undergarments.

"Er, I suppose we could look into it," Katherine replied, caught a little off guard.

"Maybe the owners would consider a short temporary rental," Suzy tentatively suggested as they rubbed a view hole on the dusty front windows and attempted to peer inside.

"We'd have to view the place properly," Katherine noted, "but I bet it would need some clean-up, it certainly is not professionally fitted out for an art exhibition, not in this condition. Are you sure about this Mr. Stansislov?"

"I'd like to take a look, and please, call me Yoris," he continued, trying the door. Of course it was locked.

"Wait, there's a '*For Lease or Sale*' sign, we could call the agent," Esther suggested, fixating the number in her memory. Returning to the gallery, she called the real estate office listed and made the enquiries about a viewing. The agent would be pleased to drop by in an hour, if that was all right. Yoris said that would be very agreeable, and so Katherine invited him over for lunch with her and Kevin while they waited.

It was a sombre meal as they hardly got more than two words out of Yoris while they ate, but Kevin helped to keep the conversation going while Katherine was busy figuring out to herself what this unexpected development thrust upon her would mean while trying to remain attentive to the discussion. Just how much would it cost to rent that place? A few months for a commercial place of that size just might wipe out whatever profit the showing would make, and then some. She would have to put more than one artist on, which meant another digging expedition in Kevin's book if he didn't mind. Then of course, the brick building would need some improvements for an exhibition of a professional calibre, and hopefully it would be safe to let the public in there. Thankfully, the factory hadn't been shut up for long, it closed just a few months before she started the refurbishment on her own place, so it still had to be in good shape. It wasn't exactly dilapidated, even if certain features were now tired and looked like they belonged in the fifties or sixties, such as the old front door and the sign overhead advertising the now defunct "Boomer's Bottling Plant, Est.

1957." At least anything from that era had a 'classic' quality about it thanks to America's nostalgia for its own golden age of Elvis, Rock n' Roll and pink tail-finned Cadillacs.

The agent arrived a few minutes late thanks to the gruelling lunch hour traffic, but once the introductions were made, they proceeded directly to the building. As the key was turning, Katherine dreaded what she might find. She could never forget the former condition she had to improve upon when she set up her own gallery. Sure enough, being a semi-detached edifice, how could she expect anything different when this side of the building was practically a mirror image of the other? Once they passed the old reception front, they entered into a mighty space once dedicated to capitalist industry. The agent flipped on the switches and a battery of florescent light rods flickered into action, illuminating the sleeping bottling dragons taking up residence between the support pillars of the old nineteenth-century wooden beam factory. Katherine suppressed the urge to groan for the ground floor was home to never-ending conveyance apparatuses that once whisked teems of vintage-style sarsaparilla and lemonade bottles from one floor to another and from the front to the back in a quick-fire production process, starting from empty to full then packed for shipment to their various wholesale outlets. Of course, the place possessed an old boiler house exactly like hers on the other side, but instead of underwear, it was packed with empty glass bottles that were never used or had been returned, waiting to be washed and refilled but never made it before the plant closed and now lay lustreless under a blanket of fine dust. There were stacks upon stacks of brown coloured nineteenth-century reproduction bottles with distinctive Wild West designs featuring cowboys and lassos pressed into the glass for the sarsaparilla brand, and white 1950s style bottles with lemon patterns for the lemonade all lined up like soldiers in their 'Boomer's Pop' plastic crates. Katherine didn't know what she could do with them, or if the owner had a stipulation that they stay here in storage. Since she was facing a rental arrangement, it was to be expected she wouldn't be allowed to change much in the building. How could she ever work with this? She dreaded to see what else lay in wait!

While Katherine was trying to control the rising wave of panic, Yoris and Kevin seemed to be in their element with the modern grunge look of the industrial equipment.

"This is it," Yoris nodded with approval. "Perfect. I would be satisfied with this."

"Why, it *is* perfect! It does possess a distinct urban 'edge'," Kevin agreed.

Once the agent picked up on what they were actually looking for, he changed tactics and began drawing their attention to the other spacious features rather than the manufacturing facilities. The inside wall to the left could be used to display paintings or murals, and there was something stylish in the way the engineers had cut away some of the floors above to make room for the vats and other bottling works, allowing the viewer to see right up through to the upper levels, giving the place a hanging garden or mezzanine effect. Katherine had to agree it was interesting, but she had to concentrate on the practicalities. What about floor space? There was plenty around the machines all right, the place wasn't that cramped at all, and she was told there were even more walking areas in the upper levels where there was less machinery, which was mostly located on the ground floor level, but would anyone be enticed to visit and view *art* here? Modernity equalled starkness she conceded, but the lighting was terrible, it definitely needed a paint job at least, and she dreaded to see what the old public bathrooms were like! Trying to ignore the agent's babble, Katherine knew she would have another old brick box on her hands that needed some improvements and was taking a bold new step if she was to seriously consider renting this place.

However, should she? That was the question. For just a few showings, was it worth going to all that trouble? She wisely decided no matter how enthusiastic Kevin and Yoris were, art for art's sake had to come down to earth. She would not allow herself to be talked into making a costly decision. Business was not only a type of warfare, but it was also a gambler's den at times, and if she had to take any risks, she wanted to have those risks all calculated down to the microscopic level if possible. Unlike Gramps and Pops, she was not a great Poker player and was a miserable bluffer, she had a feeling this was not something she should wing her way through. Tread carefully, she told herself. For now, Katherine decided she might as well let the agent show them around since he had come all this way, there was no harm in looking to get a feel about the situation and see if her instincts had any input.

Although she was wary of hastily jumping into anything she remained reflective as they made their way upstairs via the clunky industrial freight elevator in the back. Kevin was positively elated with the possibilities before them, and she wondered how much was bluff to please Yoris or was authentic enthusiasm, but continued to listen for a bit. True, she had already come to the realisation that modern was 'in' and here to stay, she needed to work that theme into the gallery somehow, but darn it! That was not *her* style! Just thinking about it was similar to hearing nails dragged at an excruciatingly deliberate pace across a dry chalkboard. Well, forget next door for a moment. She had her Old France, and it was not like she was going to have to rip it out. Tune out from what you would *like* to do and think about what you *need* to do, maybe then you might be able to accept what it may entail. Okay, now look around. Think like someone who loves modern art: what would *they* do? What would *they* find attractive?

Attempting to immerse herself in the stylised romanticised contemporary ambiance of 'New York', 'industrial', and 'film noire', there was something rather cool about the place, it began to grow on her, or perhaps it was the aromatic scent of sarsaparilla still lingering in the air? Never mind. The upper storeys were certainly fascinating as she looked through the various sections cut away in the floors and encircled by security railings matching the antique period stairs, preventing anyone falling to their demise below. Just being able to peek up and see what may be above or peer below at the other levels was a captivating feature, it was literally a ready-made curiosity magnet. She would have no trouble drawing people up and encouraging them to mosey around the place to have a look, even the machines were an appealing rarity; if they were spruced up a bit, just polished and left as they were, she would have another feature to draw people in, she might be able to hang art on them, who knows? Maybe Snoop was on to something about his glass escalators, people were always curious to see how things worked. There was a fascination to all that lay hidden from public view, nearly everyone yearned to peer behind the veil and see how objects were manufactured and were no different to a child taking apart a watch to see where the ticking came from. Yes, she could see it alright, the factory did give the stark ambience that would captivate the modernists. In fact, that was the strange and paradoxical beauty of it all she noted as Gramp's quip suddenly came to mind about not being able to give people nice things theses days—she did not have to spend a huge fortune fixing up a place like this since desolation is what the art world wanted. After all, factory-galleries with the old workings left intact were becoming the latest rage in urban art exhibition centres in all the major cities, or so she heard. She never thought she would hear herself say this: but the place had possibilities.

"Well, Mr. Stanisislov ... Yoris, I might consider it, but as you can see, it's not properly set up with lighting, not to mention this place probably has only the most basic of security features, maybe a few cameras if we're lucky, not anything like what is wired up in the gallery next door. Would you feel comfortable bringing your art here under those circumstances?"

"Doesn't matter." He shrugged. "Stolen paintings create publicity that cannot be bought, and we do not need to rush a show. If you would be willing to set up an exhibition here, we can make do. The less done, the better, too many improvements could wreck everything."

Okay, no pressure, right?

Nevertheless, whatever potential the old bottler of a building might possess, she had to get all the facts and details first. "Just as long as we don't bring the public in to a death trap. When was this place last brought up to code, and all of that," Katherine asked the agent as she looked around, so far, the wiring looked okay, just open to view as expected in a factory, running along the ceiling or tacked discreetly into edges and corners.

"Not too long ago, '88 according to the owner. The air conditioning and heating system was also replaced in '88. The fire safety systems were done just before the factory closed, and while we're discussing upgrades, the roof was redone three years ago, so you don't have to worry about that," he assured her as he checked his folder.

That was good news, many of the safety aspects were taken care of in the last five years, and she didn't see any sign of ghastly watermarks dripping down walls or from corners meaning the roofing job was done properly. She checked the wood pillars, they appeared okay, no rot or woodworm, and the floors were sturdy enough for the engineers had added steel pillars and supports in the vulnerable places where the floors in the early nineteenth-century building were sectioned away to make room for the machines. The one disappointment was the bathrooms looked a bit tired, old white tile fittings, sixties sinks—and drat! There they stood like a gaggle of drunken oafs, rickety pull chain toilets with the tanks up in the air sporting the old black upside down U-shaped seats with the gap in the front showing off a peep of their grimy rust-stained rims, those seats were the pits! Of course, the stalls, perfect specimens of kitschy bawdiness. No matter how far the modernists wanted to descend into the 'grunge', she was not putting up with the graffiti blush-inducers scratch-a-doodled into the metal partitions—out, out, out! They would have to go! Okay, so the bathrooms might need an upgrade, however, she need not go overboard and make them as luxurious as her marble and mosaic water closets next door. Considering she was actually viewing the place because it *was* an old plant, the bathroom fixtures had a 'retro' feel that worked here, even the black gappy toilet seats … all she needed to do was see if the bathroom suppliers had abandoned back-stock of these things lying around, or replace them with reproduction models, maybe find period tiles to match, and she already knew where to go thanks to all her previous work next door. This couldn't be too expensive, right? First, she needed to sleep on it though. If Yoris said she need not rush, she was going to take him up on that.

Katherine was about to suggest they return to the gallery so she could discuss particulars with the agent when she heard a voice holler up to them from the ground floor:

"Yo! Anyone in here?"

She along with Kevin poked their heads over the railing of the nearest cut-way through the floor to find cousin Stephie peering up from below.

"So there you are! Esther said I'd find you in here."

"Hang on, I'm coming down," Katherine called back, "just give me a sec. This is a nice surprise. I thought you were busy with a photo shoot."

"I was, but it finished sooner than I expected, so here I am. Thought I might as well drop these off while I'm free," she explained, holding up a large manilla envelope, it was the latest batch of photos she had developed of the newly framed artworks on display. Good timing too! When Stephie heard from Suzy and Esther why nearly half the Gang was next door, she had to see for herself that the impossible had actually happened.

"As I live and breathe, you're coming off your high horse at last." Her cousin teased as Katherine exited the whining elevator and gave her a hug before handing over the envelope.

"Just one stirrup," Katherine corrected with mortified amusement. "I'm forced into a compromise for the sake of art."

"So I hear! Stansislov is in the building! Geeze, I'd love to meet him."

"You will in a minute. I'm hoping he'll agree to a showing, but of all things, he prefers this place."

"I can see why," Stephie nodded, viewing the building with an approving nod, right hand on her hip. "It's awesome! I'd love to set up a shoot here. Cleaned up a bit, this would make a really cool gallery space."

"I know. Thinking like a modern, it has possibilities. If I can, I might lease it for a few showings, see how it goes. It needs only a slight make-over, clean it up, but the lights? These flickering sticks are an eyesore." Katherine grimaced as she glanced up at the florescent fixtures humming a buzzing drone overhead.

"Aw, that's easy to fix," Stephie declared with a wave of her hand. "I know where you can rent studio lighting."

"Studio lights? You mean like in Hollywood? With the flaps on the sides?"

"Yeah! Theatre lights and things like that, they would really go in a place like this, you can stand, hang or clamp them anywhere, not to mention you can use photographer's equipment and dot soft lighting where you need it."

"Oh! Those soft bulbs behind the umbrella thingys," Katherine blurted out, excited with the suggestion.

"Exactamundo. It wouldn't take much to make this place down-and-out cool."

"I thought so. Thanks Stephie! If I can fix the lighting, we just might have a winner here, but I still have to do some thinking … ."

"Man, I can't get over it." Her cousin laughed again, shaking her head. "I've got half a mind to run next door and fetch my camera, I want to capture this priceless moment as proof that you are actually considering this for an expansion. You know, if you were going this route, you could have just left the other place as it was."

"Oh, don't start Stephie, Gramps has already beaten you to the jokes."

"Aw, you know I'm just pulling your leg. All joking aside, this is neat. Can I look around?"

"Sure, I don't see why not."

Katherine accompanied Stephie, introducing her to Yoris when they bumped into him and Kevin. Sensing Katherine needed a moment or two alone, Kevin enquired if it would be all right if he took their guests back to the gallery for a *latte* with a dash of cocoa and cinnamon.

"Please do, I hope you don't mind, but I would like to consider this," Katherine nodded.

"No problem, take all the time you need." The agent smiled, knowing when to leave a prospective client alone to inspect the merchandise at their leisure.

"Unfortunately, I can't stay," Yoris announced, "I must be off, but if you find this arrangement agreeable, you may give me a call." The agent courteously supplied him with a slip of notepaper from the folder and his pen for a moment to jot down his particulars, which he handed to Katherine.

"Thank you, I'll probably need a few days, if you don't mind."

"Not at all. Good day, Miss Katherine. No ceremony, I can see my way out."

After shaking hands firmly but politely with everyone, he slumped off to wherever he had to be. The agent decided even if the artist didn't want one, he could use a coffee if that was all right, and so he joined Kevin at the elevator.

Now that they were alone, Katherine wondered what her cousin thought of the idea. She had two thumbs-up from Kevin and Yoris, but forget them for the moment: as much as she would like to secure his collection, she didn't want one artist alone to be the deciding factor, and she couldn't really place all her confidence in Kevin to help her come to a decision simply because she never knew when he was truly serious or was carried away by a fit of emotion that clouded his judgement. Either he loved all styles of art, or was giving her the 'Big Smile' treatment, it was hard to tell. All in all, for the 'neo-trendy' artists, would it be worth it to lease the premises, maybe for a year or so? Stephie thought it was worth the experiment. If she was in her shoes, she might be tempted to give it a go, a year's lease wouldn't exactly break the bank, especially if she has some successful shows. If she didn't make a profit, she would certainly brake even and wouldn't suffer a huge loss. However, there was no harm in asking her other artists for their opinions, see what they thought, do her homework and all that boring stuff, but the place was so neat! Just a lick or two of paint, maybe wax a bit of the dust off the old wooden pillars and flooring, but leave the scuff marks, the scars added character Stephie declared. Hmm, Katherine mused, give all the walls a new coat of matt paint ... the iron railings around the place could be painted too, maybe in gloss, plus the steel accordion-gate freight elevator: keep everything old, but just clean it up with the studio lighting concept ... yeah, she could envision it. What to do with the ground section was a bit of a puzzle. The floor was nothing but smooth dark charcoal grey concrete streaked with a rainbow of various coloured direction lines and arrows showing the former bottling workers where to wheel shipments for loading, the closest fire exits, the manager's office ... Katherine was stumped. Stephie however noted she wouldn't change that at all, the lines were trendy and they added some colour to the place. Why not just have it cleaned, then paint on a thick clear floor varnish to gloss it up? It wouldn't look worn at all then, it might even give the industrial look a touch of elegance, and such a simple way to do it too.

"Stephie, that's not a bad idea! The lines are rather colourful, aren't they?"

"Yeah, and this way you'd keep the history of the place alive. You don't want to wipe out all the elements that make it a factory, or you won't have a factory gallery. Who knows? You might even want to get the machines working again, make a few bottles of soda to show the public all the workings, just for fun."

"Oh no! Even if Gramps and Steves might get a kick out of it, I don't know if I want to go into the sarsaparilla business too." Katherine laughed. "I think I'll stick to running a gallery for the time being."

Katherine, however, noticed a few glitches with the idea, she might need more wall space for paintings than the place had. The upper levels had *space*, but not enough walls because of all the windows. She wouldn't be showing statues or sculptures all the time. Stephie agreed, but then, the huge expanse was also part of the attraction, not to mention it would be a waste to lay out the extra cash just to block in some walls if she was only going to lease the thing for a short time. Maybe she could steal back her own idea and put in more rolly-pollies? She could always wheel them back and use them in her own gallery. Katherine thought about it, but then, she didn't want to appear like she was copying Sir Nincompoop, even if he did borrow her idea in the first place.

"Oh! You could hang the paintings from the ceiling, simple chains or semi-invisible steel wiring! They would look like they were suspended in the air. You wouldn't have to worry about walls at all, the whole space could be your wall. Now that would look awesome!"

"Geeze, I can't have artwork hanging around like that! It would be worse than that scene from *Coma* with all the patients dangling around like half-dead string puppets." Katherine groaned.

"Aw, no it won't," Stephie *tsked*. "I'm surprised at you. For an artist, you're not seeing the big picture. That would be way out cool. Not just modern, futuristic in fact."

"But I *am* seeing the big picture. You'd have everyone dying to touch them, or perhaps knock into them and set them swinging," Katherine observed, guiltily recalling her wayward temptation to set Nincompoop's walls a-rolling just to see them spark. "I don't think the artists would appreciate that."

"Somehow, I don't think that will happen too much."

However, Katherine knew that 'much' could indeed happen.

"What if the air currents from the conditioning and heating system gets them going? That would look stupid, not awesome, everyone would get dizzy trying to view them," she then noted.

"Maybe," Stephie snickered a bit, "but at least you'd have one way of securing the pictures if they're chained or wired to the place."

"True, there's that to consider," Katherine reflected. Perhaps Yoris didn't mind if a few pictures went missing, but she did, and certainly would not like an art heist on her hands.

"Or look," Stephie continued, her left hand on her hip, gesturing around to the wooden support pillars with her right, "you could do a curtain thingamajig on adjustable rods between these, or something like that."

"Curtain rods?"

"Yeah, they could be adjustable, just have them sit on rack brackets like those barriers for equestrian show jumping. You could make 'curtain walls' as high or as low as you want, and if you place the brackets equally on all four sides of the pillars you could switch the rods around and hang your 'walls' just about anywhere since all the pillars look about the same distance apart. You could make movable mazes."

Now there's an idea. Katherine brightened up with the suggestion: that would be one cost-effective way to introduce display walls without doing any major cosmetic changes to the structure of the building. The owner might be happy to lease under those circumstances. The good thing about that was, she could make the 'walls' different heights all over the place, it would not be unlike the silk panelled walls she had blocked in next door, only these 'curtains' would not be stationary. The great part was the 'maze-like' theme would be carried through, meaning the new style might be made to compliment the old world fashion next door despite the gritty urban look. Plus, the rough backside of the canvases wouldn't be exposed to view if she hung them from the rods with a curtain discreetly covering the workings. Despite the modernist craze to let everything hang out, she wanted some niceties to be maintained. Plus, the material might soften up the hard look just a tad, and she could pick any colour or patterns for the curtain walls, keep them plain or liven them up a bit—an instant make-over whenever she needed. Yes, this really could work!

"But you'll have to do something about the bathrooms, they really reek," Stephie concluded.

"Heaven help me." Katherine moaned then laughed. "It's history repeating itself. New gallery, fresh refurbishments."

"But at least you don't have to do much, not like the other place."

"That's the beauty of it. I still have to do my homework, but thanks Stephie for all the ideas, you've been a big help."

"No problem, but I don't know why I'm helping you, I'm mad at you actually," she suddenly pronounced, folding her arms.

"Me? What did I do," Katherine returned, slightly puzzled. What bug was up her nose now?

"It's what you *didn't* do. Does 'Smith' ring any bells?"

Uh oh. Batman had finally flown the coop.

"Why didn't you tell me?"

"It wasn't for me to tell, I was sworn to secrecy," Katherine returned.

"Still, we're practically sisters, you could have told me."

"Oh Steph, think about it! Chris' real identity might ruin him if it gets out, and he just didn't know how to break the news to you, not to mention he was afraid of what you might think of him," she tried to reason with her.

Stephie cooled a bit when she heard this pointed out to her again from her cousin. She was miffed all right, but not *really* angry at Kathy, while Katherine knew she just needed to storm the situation out with her in her blustery way.

"But how come he told you first?"

"Because I knew him first before you did, duh. We're not exactly enemies any more, you know."

"Oh, yeah," Stephanie realised. "But still! I wish I had known sooner!"

"Why? So you could have dumped him sooner if you knew he was faced with the responsibilities he has?"

"I dunno," she replied, shuffling her right toe a bit, "I like him, I really do, but he's certainly tied down, you know? He not only told me everything, but came straight out and took me to meet his grandmother over the weekend. She is a sweet old lady, but needs a lot of care. She needs him constantly, I'm not sure how this could work."

Hmm, it appeared Stephie didn't mind about Christopher's *financial* circumstances, so she was right about her cousin not being the type to suffer a complex for having more affluence than the boyfriend. As long as the guy she was seeing had a respectable enough career, worked hard and wasn't a loaf-about loser who cheated on her behind her back, there was hope, and Chris definitely had that going for him. It was the extended family issue. No doubt Stephie wanted him all to herself. That was understandable, it was wonderful to be alone with the one you loved, but family was family, and you can't expect the man in your life to ditch all their responsibilities to their own flesh and blood, and *vice versa*. Both Christopher and Stephie had busy schedules as it was, so that could also be an issue, but Katherine knew that love would always find a way no matter what. Although she didn't expect Batman to toss his wings this soon, Katherine was already well armed and had some points handy to dish out for her cousin to ponder just in case she did the unexpected and come running to her for advice.

"Look, you said you were sick and tired of all the dead-beats and creeps you used to get stuck with, right?"

"Yeah, I did say that."

"Is Chris anything like those jerks?"

"Gosh no," Stephie returned, almost surprised at the suggestion.

"Good. Has he failed to make time for you?"

"No, even when we had to call off a night out over work or something, despite his schedule, I can't accuse him of that either, even with all his extra painting on the side," she noted with a sly smile, "which you hid from me too."

"I know, but let's not get off topic here," Katherine continued, pulling her back to this much needed priority check.

"Okay, back on topic. We do have dating time, and enough of it. There, you happy now Miss Forty Questions?"

"The question is, are *you*," Katherine returned. "How does he make you feel, and then you have to think, how do you make *him* feel? Do you make him happy, and do you *want* to? When you find a really good person and you care for them, you care enough to where you'll want to be with them no matter what the difficulties are."

"I suppose so … ."

"Well, I know for one he's really stuck on you Stephie, big time."

"Really?"

"Yes really! And you have to hand it to him. He is one decent guy to take care of his grandmother practically single-handed despite the costs and the hardship. If he treats her like that, how do you think he will treat the special woman in his life? Pretty much the same I think, not to mention he's trusted you with his trade secrets so to speak, which is no small thing. So here's my concluding thought, and then I'll forever hold my peace. Remember those black and white shots you took of Gerry and I?"

"Yeah, of course," Stephie returned quizzically.

"Remember what you said when you gave them to me? 'I wish I had someone who looked at me like that.' I think you've found him, or he has found you, so don't blow it."

Stephie looked like she was about to say something, stopped, was thoughtful for a moment, then shook her head with that same 'shucky darn' expression just like Gramps when one of his own wisdom-laden quips was directed back at him.

"Geeze, you're right. How come I didn't see that before?"

"Probably because you were just about to friend-zone him."

"Huh, I take it this comes from someone with experience." Stephie then grinned back, recalling Katherine's once snail-paced love life.

"You could say that. Come on, I've got a yancy art manager and an eager agent to deal with next door, while you have some thinking to do. I assume you declared you wanted some space to think all this out and left him wallowing in anguish?"

"Yeah, I kinda did."

"Then think about it, but not too long, and go make up! Give him a chance at least. Oh, and here's one last piece of your own advice I'm flinging back at you: considering all the creeps in this world, when you find someone decent, hang on to him."

"Okay, are you done now, Miss Preachy? I get the message," Stephie pouted, but glad for the pep talk. "Thanks, Cos."

"Any time."

Stephie dashed off, no doubt to find Robert Christopher Horace Smith wherever he was wallowing, while Katherine joined Kevin and the agent to ask the pertinent questions about the building and get a much-needed coffee. Naturally, the first enquiry was how much would it cost per month for a one-year lease?

"*What?*", she thought to herself while trying not to betray her surprise. Come on, easy does it, pull yourself together, make whatever expressionless Poker face you can. Drat! She could almost buy a house with that rental! The price just for a lease was a whopping thump, but this was commercial property after all, and quite a huge chunk of it too—half of a Brooklyn city block to be precise. To charge that much considering the recession was pushing it too, but maybe the owner knew what he had.

Slowly, the inevitable 'gentrification' metamorphosis was gradually stealing in to humble Dumbo formerly left to its moribund devises under the bridge. Old factories and warehouses dating from the last century onward that were once the passé embarrassment of the glistening towers soaring across the river in Manhattan were now attracting attention as the latest trend in development possibilities thanks to the artists and other creative enterprises that had moved in to the tired neighbourhood with its cheap or abandoned buildings due to economic necessity. The irony of course, she had helped to bring about this gradual upgrade and renewed interest in this now charming locale with her lavish improvements to her place, and the surrounding brick buildings with their rows of period windows set in old Belgian block cobbled streets were certainly attractive in their own way. Already in these few short years a few buildings had been gutted and remodelled into comfortable studio apartments, new shops were opening up, an independent publisher had taken up residence around the corner and was selling books, coffee shops and niche pastry bakeries were competing with André's culinary delights, even her local framer had power-hosed and pointed the bricks of their building, and spruced up their windows and doors with a new coat of paint. Yes, it was slow, but the roughness was fading in patches, pride of ownership was starting to show in the once weary area, Dumbo was on the verge of blossoming into the art hub she hoped it would. The next step, to have it zoned as a historical preservation area, and then watch the prices soar! Not to mention the building codes and preservations orders, no one would be able to touch or fix a square inch of property without some stupid historical committee giving the go-ahead on every nail and screw put into the place.

Just when she was getting used to the idea of what the lease might cost for a year and trying to figure out if she could make art pay, the agent dropped an unexpected monkey-wrench into an already daunting prospect: the owner had received a few offers from developers wanting to either turn the old place into conversion apartments or knock the whole side out and build up something new from scratch, he wasn't sure if the owner was now willing to lease since he was currently considering the offers. Great! There goes her whole prospect of picking up a quirky urban space! Well, if she lost Yoris and his latest gloomy collection, she couldn't help it, however, it seemed such a shame to have the place slip through her fingers now that the idea was beginning to grow on her. She apologised to the agent for bringing him out and taking up his afternoon, since she was only thinking of a temporary lease, but for the sake of curiosity, what was the asking price for the soda pop plant?

What?!

Poker face, poker face, poker face … .

If she thought the lease was bad, the price was certainly a bombshell. Humph, it was half a city block not far from Manhattan after all. Katherine thanked the agent for his time and asked if he wouldn't mind checking in with the owner to see if he would still considering a lease, it didn't hurt to try anyway.

So much for concentrating on her own pictures for the rest of the day, this unexpected project now had Katherine's mind in a whirl with a million and one thoughts in addition to the plans she had to make for Fielding's new showing. Suzy was dying to know what had transpired with the agent, but Katherine said it was too soon to say yet, especially as it showed every sign of falling through.

"It was a good idea though," Suzy shrugged, "really neat, for an urban setting. So, he wants to sell, huh?"

"It's looking that way." Katherine sighed settling back in the desk chair, slowly swivelling from side to side for a bit, Kevin quietly wondering what his boss would decide.

"The price is nothing to sneeze at," Esther nodded.

"True, but neither is the rent money, if we *can* lease," Katherine continued, mulling over all the pros and cons. Maybe that's why most of the galleries in the major cities charged the whopping commissions they did.

"Yes, it is a frightful outlay, dead money so they say," Kevin agreed.

"I know, that's the one thing about this whole lease idea, it seems like such a waste," Katherine continued.

Leasing would be like someone was getting a chunk of flesh out of her and all the other artists' work without doing anything to put the exhibitions together, someone reaping where they didn't sow. Still, she had to give the owner his due too, if he hadn't put in all the costly machinery, it might not be as 'urban' and 'cool' as it looked, which is what she needed. He expected to get something back on his investments too. However, there were a few drawbacks with the idea of just using the space as it was. For one thing, there was no convenient access between the two buildings other than going out the front door of one place and in through the other, and it had been hard enough trying to encourage people to explore upstairs without a little nudge from her welcoming posters let alone try and notify them there was more to see in another building—just go back down, go outside, turn left and left again, there you are! Nope, it would be like herding a gathering of curious but independent cats that were resistant to the idea of being told where or when to mosey around. Convenience was the catchword she had learned, people's inquisitiveness was not always enough. This new plan might not work, but then it was only an experiment and one year would be enough to test the waters, or the soda pop so to speak, if 'Mr. Boomer's Bottles' was willing to draw up a lease that is.

The problem was, she couldn't move ahead until she found out what the owner wanted, yet she couldn't turn off her thoughts once set on their whirling course. She had to look at the figures, see if this was viable and worth the effort. Excusing herself from the Gang at the desk, Katherine sequestered herself in the office and began pouring over the books with her ever-ready calculator. Hmm, it could do more than break even if she had enough showings with the right artists at the right prices, even with her reasonable commissions. She need not become a fashionable gouger like the Elverton. Still, despite her calculations she would like to get some of the artists' opinions like Stephie suggested, see if they might like the new venue, nevertheless, they might want to view the place first and she couldn't keep calling the estate agent back and forth just to open everything up for their assessments. Katherine had a feeling this was going to be one of those semi-blind business gambles. The best thing to do when faced with a business gamble was to talk to some serious players, and she had two families full of them, time to bother everyone and get their valuable opinions. First Gerry at the hospital after work, then Pops and Gramps she decided, they could help with the business end, while Mom had valuable experience organizing large events. Katherine could easily guess she might worry about her taking on too much, yet would not hesitate to offer words of wisdom from another angle. Not to mention, a night home at the homestead in Oak Meadows would be welcome too.

Excited by the prospects laid before her that day, she opened the door to Gerry's room but quickly stopped short, the main lights were off with only the bed lamp overhead casting its dim glow, he was sound asleep and she didn't want to wake him. Setting aside her news and quietly sitting down by the bed, she smiled as she resisted the urge to gently stroke his cheek and steal a kiss. The nurses may have taken him up on his jokes and called him Prince Charming and Sleeping Handsome, but there was great truth to the witticisms making his new titles more endearing. Her heart certainly melted with every little look he gave, and now when he lay still and peaceful, giving her a chance to wordlessly admire him. She was caught in her moment of reflection when he opened his eyes and returned her appreciative smile.

"Behold, graceful Serene gazing upon her beloved Endymion."

"Who?"

"The Greek goddess of the moon who fell in love with a handsome fellow and cast him into a deep sleep so she could have him all to herself," Gerry explained dozily.

"Aw, that's sweet. I'm sorry, I didn't mean to wake you, love." She stroked his cheek as she wished. He took her hand and gave it a kiss on the palm.

"How long have you been here, Princess? I hope I didn't keep you waiting."

"Not too long, and yet not long enough, 'Endymion'," she shyly admitted.

"Basking in my good looks, are we?"

"Yes silly, which is not doing your ego any good either. But I'm glad you're awake, the sad part is I can't stay too long. The moon is driving to Oak Meadows for the night."

"Oh? Sudden plans for dinner? Feeling homesick are we? Is it an emergency? I hope everything is okay," he wondered, the last traces of drowsiness dissipating with this thought.

"More of a business meeting," she reassured him, "I had something dropped on me today I wasn't expecting and I'm in need of some expert advice. I was going to ask you before I drove out, but didn't want to disturb you. It can wait until tomorrow."

"I'm awake now. Disturb me," he pleaded with good-humoured curiosity, wondering what this 'business meeting' was all about.

Katherine filled Gerry in on the Russian's sudden arrival and what he had in mind for an art venue.

"The old bottling joint next door? What an idea! Forget leasing and buy the thing," he replied. "If it falls through, you can always make the best root beer floats in town. Gotta keep your options open, you know."

"Gerry, this is serious," she *tsked*.

"I know." He gave her palm another kiss. "All joking aside, you've got a wonderful expansion opportunity, I'm surprised you didn't make a bid for the building before now."

"Really?"

"Yeah. You'd have the whole thing then, not just half of it, plus you can tidy up that dilapidated part, it was making your place look like Jekyll and Hyde. You know surroundings can add to or decrease the value of your own property, and that empty half wasn't helping yours much. You could spruce the place up and not have it drag down your gallery."

Katherine had to admit Gerry was right, the bottling plant looked almost the same as the former Walsingham pill factory before she had her way with it. The disparity between the two sides always bothered her, Boomer's old plant with its weedy parking lot out back made her fine establishment look like it was forever frozen between a set of 'before' and 'after' photographs, but she was so busy with art, life, love, and trying to get her business off the ground once the refurbishments were done that she just turned a blind eye to that mess, never considered an expansion until now. Was it too much too soon? So much had happened in the last few years! Expanding just for the sake of cosmetic concerns wasn't enough, she reminded Gerry. True, but he then hit upon a few points she had already considered that day: investment opportunity. The area was picking up, prices were going to rise, and if she snapped up the building now before the historical basket-cases get around to preserving the area, she could do whatever was needed to the place, in fact, she could solve that problem of having no access between the two by breaking a few interior walls in and make some doorways between the floors, something she couldn't do if she just leased, which was dead money out the window. Why not put the capital into something she could own? She might eliminate the element of the unknown from happening since there was a question about what the other developers making offers planned to do with it, and the beauty was—she didn't have to do much if she was going 'modern'.

"That's the great part, being able to leave it pretty much *au naturel*, but nuts! I was trying to fill up my side of the place by getting new artists, and now they have me expanding and needing more artists, again," she noted with a sigh.

"That's capitalism, my dear. Aw, I'm sorry, we were hoping Yoris would be a help, not add more trouble on your back," Gerry apologised. "Dad and I had the best intentions."

"Oh, I know." She smiled, giving his hand a squeeze. "Don't get me wrong, I definitely see the possibilities, and I never thought of breaking archways through the walls through. That would solve the cat-herding challenge for sure. Now you're really making me *want* the place, for keeps."

"Good! You've finally seen something you wanted, now I know what to get you for a wedding gift," Gerry teased.

"Don't be silly, this is business, and I've got to see my way through this," she noted resolutely.

"Hey, I'm not really joking this time, you are the most difficult person to get a gift for since you never ask for anything. Spare your trust fund and let me splurge on you."

"Uh uh, no way, not again, and besides, I'm not jumping into this, I need to look over everything carefully, and I want everyone's input, so I'm off to Oak Meadows, and then I'm going to bug your Dad tomorrow. I want all their input as fast as possible."

"Okay, get everyone's advice then. You've heard mine, and it's good too, they will all probably agree with me."

"Maybe, but this is a huge thing, and on top of everything else I have to do! I'm stuck mid-way in decorating the penthouse, I've got a show coming up, possibly another to plan right after that, a portrait commission, and now an *expansion*? Am I going crazy?"

"I know, I'm a great one for pushing this when I told you not to get exhausted, but at the same time, I'd hate to see you lose this chance. A great prospect has just opened, and with nearly all good things in life, it has come at a time when you least expected it. Sometimes we can make our own opportunities, sometimes we can see them coming, but more often than not they are like pop quizzes, they are sprung on you like a challenge to test your skills, almost like a dare to see if you can take that leap of faith to make whatever it is a success. Wait too long, and an excellent opportunity might slip away. Besides, buying the building next door is not a terribly reckless thing, considering you are in a good position of not needing a bank loan, it's just an added option. You might be kicking yourself if you let this go."

Opportunity a dare? Uh oh, she never refused a dare … .

"Hmm, I see what you mean, but it's such a huge expense, but an investment too. Calculated risk, right?"

"Yep, but go see what all the paters have to say, and speaking of paters, don't forget to ask Pete too. He may be a saint in the making, but there's also an astute businessman under that robe of his."

"Okay, I'll do that."

"You'd better vamoose, or you'll miss dinner, it's one of the best times to get advice. Everyone is in such a good mood when they've eaten well."

"Is that so? And how come you've given such good advice tonight when the food here isn't fit for convicts?"

"Because I'm living on love, my dear," he smiled back.

"I bet Leroy probably dropped by with some grub."

"That too," Gerry confessed. "Now off you go, my bright, beautiful Selene, before you miss your dinner. Give everyone my regards."

"I will. Good night, Endymion, pleasant dreams, see you tomorrow," she returned, giving him his favourite dessert, their customary 'croissant'.

Forget leasing and buy the thing … .

Gerry's exuberant words gave her much to think about during the drive home. Leasing was a huge project, but to outright purchase the place? No, it wasn't a bad idea, not by a long shot, but that new prospect also opened up another huge can of worms she wasn't exactly prepared for. Still, that's exactly what a golden opportunity usually did to a person as Gerry reminded her, catch them by surprise. Now, should she reach out and grab the tempting item while it dangled before her?

Although it was exciting making future plans with Gerry and putting their own home together, it was comforting to walk through the front door of her familiar childhood romping grounds, Jasper running up barking his greeting while she could hear the TV jabbering in the den knowing everyone was there. Pops and Gramps no doubt were enjoying a well-earned glass of wine or beer with Mom before dinner. However, Aunt Martha was still on the prowl as Katherine quickly discovered, for she popped her head out from the dining room doorway the minute Jasper's barking had announced her arrival.

"Good! You're here Kathy, it's a relief to see you haven't forgotten us entirely," she greeted, still getting used to the idea her niece was not moving into the house down the block with Gerry. "Come here and see what they're up to now!"

"Gee, do I have to," Katherine intoned, not really enthused about playing neighbourhood watch with her inquisitive aunt. Yes she did. In lieu of a verbal answer, she was eagerly tugged in by the arm and directed to the telescope still strategically positioned by the window. Maybe a quick peek would keep her aunt happy for the rest of the evening. It was hard to tell with the greenery, but after adjusting the focus, she could catch bright glimpses of a hefty yellow machine digging a big hole in the back garden of the house targeted by her aunt's sting operation. Maybe they were doing some major landscaping, it was the only reason she could think of as she watched the huge article tearing the ground up. Well the less grass they had, the better, or they would be catching it from Aunt Martha if it grew an inch above the acceptable green carpet level.

"That's not all," her Aunt happily announced, "they're coming over for dinner this Sunday, and you must be here, no skipping off and staying overnight in the city."

"Er, okay, I'll be here," Katherine replied, "are the Reinolds invited?"

"No, of course not, we don't want to overload the new neighbours, let them get to know who's in the community first before they meet all the extended almost-married-in members," Aunt Martha explained. "I've already called Steven and told him he is not to miss this event, and don't you miss it either. All the family are to be here, just like old times."

"Sure thing. Whatever you say."

Sometimes Katherine didn't know what to make of her. Her aunt nearly drove her crazy for years trying to get her introduced in society, then date and wed the first acceptable boyfriend that came along, and now acted like she wanted to turn back the clock and prevent her and her brother from growing up and adding to the family circle. Well, maybe Aunt Martha still hadn't fully accepted her new religion and held the Reinolds to account, and Katherine couldn't help but notice there was no mention of Jennifer coming to this dinner either, so Steve's girlfriend was still in the hot seat for lowering the dignity of the female gender by accepting a co-habiting arrangement.

Katherine was permitted to leave once she had peered through the scope as requested, her aunt immediately resuming the watch as she left for the den.

"Hi everyone! Anything interesting on the news?"

"Hey kiddo! Not as good as seeing you, come here and put up your feet with us," Gramps greeted.

Katherine went around, kissing and giving hugs before settling down in her favourite end of the sofa.

"I was ever so glad you called and said you were coming to dinner, I've missed you," Mom confessed, "plus, I was hoping you might distract your aunt, but I see she's not budging from her spying."

"Sorry about that, she actually made me join her local CIA appreciation society."

"Hmm, so anything new transpiring beyond the hedge?" Pops smiled.

"Just a big digger mucking things up, they could be putting in a new pool, who knows? I hear they're coming over to dinner this weekend, and Steves and I have been summoned to attend on pain of death, no excuses accepted."

"Now, don't be so dramatic," her mother *tsked*, but chuckled all the same.

"Gosh, she didn't say who they are, or what their name is. Did she tell you?"

"Yes, an Italian family from Jersey City, it seems they own a lot of restaurants. Benino, I think," Pops noted.

"Yes, she said Benino, or something like that," Gramps nodded.

"Italian, huh? I guess we're getting pasta this weekend." Katherine laughed.

"I hope so! May there be lots of it," Gramps replied. "All diets are off when guests are present you know."

"Speaking of dinners, I take it there is more to this visit than a visit," Mom guessed.

"Oh, you know I love to come home, but I have to 'fess, there are business matters attached to this visit, but that can wait until dinner when we can all have a nice chat."

"Hmm, sounds serious. What's up?" Gramps wondered.

"Well, an opportunity has just been presented to me, and I don't know if it's a real opportunity or a very tantalizing temptation. I wanted to discuss everything with you, and anyone else with entrepreneur experience, just to sound the depths before I decide on anything."

"Sounds like you're starting off the right way," Pops observed, "I'm glad you're seeking advice. Since we don't know too much about the art world, I'm guessing it's an investment opportunity of some kind if you're asking us."

"Yes, property actually, but we can discuss it later."

"Property, eh? Now you've jabbed my curiosity, but okay, we'll wait until chow time. You shall have our undivided attention then," Gramps replied.

"Provided Martha hasn't seen anything new to report about down the lane," Helen reminded them.

"True," Gramps agreed.

They didn't have to wait long for dinner, which was diet pickings as the household was still adhering to a healthy menu for Gramp's sake and to make things easier for Mrs. Gonzales. However, Katherine was too busy telling everyone the latest doings from that afternoon to worry about what she ate, and even her news distracted Gramps from the grilled chicken fillet and steamed butterless broccoli affair as he listened to her eagerly jumping from her account of Yoris' visit, to the old plant, and all the pros and cons of why she should or shouldn't go for placing an offer on the building, and jumbling up all the details due to a mixture of nerves, anxiety, and excitement. However, everyone got the gist when they made her slow down and repeat a few things and in the right order.

"So, you just want to leave the place as it is, eh," Gramps checked, once the narrative was unscrambled.

"Yeah, pretty much. It's like what you said the other day. If people want old factories as they are, it was a shame I spent so much on the refurbishment."

"I was just yanking your chain, Katie." Gramps chuckled before continuing. "Sounds like you've pretty much nailed the main points already, and fast too."

"Gerry agreed with a few things I noticed, and he says I should just outright buy the place."

"Even so, it's still a big step," Pops noted, "and Gerry is correct in saying that it's not imperative you get into debt to do this, you have your fund, and you can always come to us if you like."

"Thanks Pops, but I've got to make this business work and pay for itself. But it's true, it's a pity to drain my fund just when it's topped up again. It would take a while to get back up with a purchase this size."

"Yep, it's easier to spend dough than to make it, that's for sure," Gramps nodded, "but it is an investment, not money down the tube, and we would be happy to help you with it. I know, we old fogies aren't stupid, you want to be independent and all that stuff, keep things business-like, so I won't push anything, but I'll give you something to think about, an open offer. We'd be willing to give you a loan, maybe enough to keep you for draining everything, and you just pay it back in dribs and drabs when you like, no interest, no time restrictions."

"Agreed," Pops nodded, "like I said, we'd be happy to help out."

"Aw, I'm not asking for a loans, that's not why I came tonight. I've already refused Gerry, he wanted to get it for me as a wedding present, the generous goof ball!"

"I know, but we'd rather you do it that way than be tempted to go to the bank for the sake of independence. At least a loan is still business, save you from having to put up collateral too, which would mean the gallery itself most likely, sometimes cash collateral isn't enough to satisfy them," Pops pointed out.

Drat. She had forgotten about collateral. A mortgage might have been a good option to keep her lump sum intact, but was not enthused about the idea of putting the gallery in hock.

"Look Katie, you have enough stress on your back now without those crooks having something to hang over your head, threatening to take your fancy shin-dig now that you've shined it up so nicely," Gramps continued, "especially as it was the cradle of our elixir empire. Gotta keep things in the family when we can, not let these shysters have an excuse to get their hooks in. I don't want to see you paying any of them interest, and all that tripe."

"True," Pops added. "I am in agreement here, in fact, you're still going to need some of your gallery profits or some of your fund to clean up the other half, even if you want to leave the structure for the most part untouched. You said something about breaking archways through to connect the buildings? That'll mean hiring engineers again, not to mention you'll need to pave the back lot, things like that. That'll take some working capital too. I'll supply the other half of the asking price along with your grandfather."

"I dunno," Katherine replied, "Gramps has already given me the gallery, that almost sounds like I'm getting greedy."

"Honestly Kathy, I don't know why you would go ahead with it, they shouldn't be egging you into this," Aunt Martha sniffed, "you have so much to do already, why do you want to put more work on your back? I'm sure you can find plenty of other artists who would feel quite privileged to be granted the opportunity to show in your elegant gallery. Tell this Boris Yugoslav he can go swing. Imagine, dictating to you and making such demands, the shamefaced Commie!"

"Um, it's Yoris Stansislov, and he's not exactly a Communist."

"Whatever," her Aunt returned. "Don't let him push you into anything just to secure his wretched daubings."

"Now Martha, don't be so negative. If Kathy thinks she can do this, it's up to her, although I am worried you might be overextending yourself, my dear," her mother warned. "The only thing keeping me from suggesting you not consider this expansion is I'm relieved to see you moving ahead and you're excited over something progressive. You're not letting past disappointments hold you back, and if Gerry thinks it's all right, and if you think you can handle everything, then do consider it."

"Yes, please do consider the loan offer, it is a sound investment opportunity after all," Pops added. "As much as I would like to be cautious for your sake and advise you not to move too fast, I think leasing is a waste of money for this type of project. It would be worth adding to the gallery permanently and consolidating those two buildings into one, even at this early stage."

"You know, it would be terrible if after fixing the older side the owner decides not to renew the lease for whatever unforeseen reason, or the developers come in and do only God knows what. The construction works might disrupt your own business too, while your plans to leave things pretty much the same wouldn't disturb anything too much, I don't think," Mom observed.

"Yep, and what a way to compete with your arch rival, Nincompoop," Gramps rumbled with a 'hrumph!'. "You will have elegance *and* modernity. The best of both worlds, and you still have the best restaurant to boot."

"Plus the gift shop." Katherine smiled.

"That's the spirit," Gramps replied, finishing off the last of his chicken fillet plate and wishing there was more to come other than a fruit salad cup with a critical cream deficiency in both the whipped and iced varieties.

Over their healthy dessert, her mother's expertise in arranging large charity events came to the fore as she wondered if Katherine had thought about what leasing or purchasing the building might mean for her upcoming art première in August—she was facing another gala opening, and that meant festivities of some kind, lining up more artists, getting Andre prepared to cater the affairs, it was a tall order. Would she be ready in time to include Fielding's premiere, or would the gala opening be a totally separate event? Considering Fielding was introducing a new style of art of which she was the principal muse, it might be wise and a very courteous thing to do if she could arrange the two showings as one event.

Plan a new gala, another *opening* gala, Katherine hadn't thought things out that far yet! Mom was right as usual, hosting Fielding's première as a separate event before an opening gala of the modern section was missing an opportunity as all of Fielding's admiring fans would be present if she co-ordinated the two, but would Yoris be pleased if Fielding got the first showing in the new modern section before he did especially after he suggested the idea? He was touchy after all. Plus, Jiff's showing was happening in just a month, it wasn't leaving her much time to plan his exhibition as it was. The best thing to do was to ask Jiff what he wanted, especially as it might mean a co-showing with Yoris. Well, if he wanted to go solo, so what? It would mean planning two separate events, but think of all that publicity! Extending into the building next door and doubling the size of her gallery was certainly a new development that would put her up one on Sir Snoop. Time to get down to business, starting tomorrow. Plot and plan like all good generals. One thing for sure, she was going to be kept very, very busy.

☘❖☙

Katherine devoted the following day to research all the pros and cons of this future investment. She would have tried to consult Pete first thing in the confessional, but that would mean getting up before cock-crow to get there first knowing how fast the pews would fill up. On second thought, discussing business in confession didn't seem quite right, so she decided to kill two birds with one stone and make an appointment to meet Pete and the Captain that afternoon at the Reinold building when her morning duties were accomplished and she got the gallery opened for the day. She could still bother her brother for his two-cents worth that morning, but she had to call around until she could run him down. Finally, she located his whereabouts at their labs in Jersey.

"Hi Kats! Howya doing?"

"Great! I'm seeking some business advice, if you could spare a minute, or two."

"Business? You've called the right person. What's up?"

She had the chance overnight to get over all the excitement of yesterday, so she was more collected when relaying everything to Steves, who was thoroughly amused by the whole project.

"So, it looks like the gallery is getting some added sugar with artificial colours and flavourings," he joked.

"Ha ha, very funny."

"Seriously, I think it's a cool idea, plus it would make for a perfect expansion. I agree with all the advice you've received up to now. Considering what you plan to do with the place, which is practically nothing, it wouldn't take you long to get it ready, but if you can get it done in time for your show is another matter. You'll be knotted up in red tape getting the other place legally annexed to your own to make it one building, that sort of thing, so until that's done you'll be paying two sets of taxes, and electric bills, and all that fun stuff. How convenient to have our lawyer friend, Charlie, to help speed up the paperwork for you. You also need a licence to operate it as a gallery, whether you buy the building or lease it. All that red tape, you know."

"Aw heck! I never thought about that. Looks like I'll have to call Charlie to get him to look into all the particulars, not to mention all the other pending legalities, but it's cutting it tight, he and Suzy are heading out to Iowa this weekend to see her folks. No pressure, right?"

"Ah yes, the joys of free enterprise, which is never free of anything be it taxes, bills, or stress."

"Touché." Katherine laughed. "One more thing bothering me, I'm not sure about accepting Pops and Gramp's loan offer, I know they mean well, but would it be all right for me to take them up on their offer?"

"I know what you mean, but the idea of paying interest to the bank is a gut-thumper."

"But you went for a mortgage for your apartment," she pointed out.

"Yeah, but I got the mortgage for that because it was a different type of property deal. With a mortgage I can off-load the place quicker if and when I want to, but the soda factory, now that's a different matter. This would be a permanent addition to your gallery, and I don't think you have any plans to retire any time soon? So it'll be like an heirloom, part of the family business. The patriarchs just want to help with that, and besides, you'd be paying them back, so it's still strictly business, not a hand out. Heck, I'll throw in a sum, I like your idea."

"Really? You'd do that?"

"Sure! I can just picture the place now, it'll be just like Harvey Dent when he was transformed into Two-Face."

"That's just great." Katherine groaned into the phone.

"Honestly! That's the cool part of it all! Elegance with the dark side peeking through. It's so arty in an industrialised Goth way, you'll be an even bigger hit than you are now."

"Hmm, I guess that's what I'm aiming for," she mused.

"Listen, if you do go for the place Kats, what in Gotham are you going to do with all those empty bottles?"

"Oh my gosh! I forgot that! I haven't a clue. Send them to a recycling plant I guess. At least I'd get a few cents back on each one. Consider it a discount off the original price of the building."

"Ha ha! I don't know how much of a discount you'd make. You know, if the bottles are antique style, people like to collect them. Maybe you could stick them in the gift shop for a buck each?"

"Are you kidding? I'd give Olivia a stroke, she nearly had a cow with the mere suggestion of offering T-shirts."

"Okay, scratch that one. Maybe an artist or two might want to make a sculpture out of them. Hey presto! A hundred thousand bucks of profit with little effort other than using a trendy name," Steves snickered.

"You know, I wouldn't put it past some of them," Katherine noted. Quite a few of her creative 'suppliers' happily lived up to Andy Warhol's motto—art is what you can get away with—and tested that motto to its outermost limits. Maybe someone could make some weird art out of those bottles, but trying to sell it off was another matter. Somehow, it didn't seem right to do that, it felt like cheating the public, but it was also a matter of taste, and she couldn't help what people wanted and demanded to spend their money on. Never mind, it wasn't like she really needed the space in that other boiler house, so finding a new home or practical purpose for the soda receptacles wasn't the most imperative thing on her 'to do' list. They could wait.

"So, all geared up for this weekend?"

"You mean Aunt Martha's 'Come-Or-Die' dinner?" Steves laughed. "I keep saying this, but we seriously need to be put on Amnesty International's protection list since we're now too old to seek help from Child Protective Services."

"I hear Jennifer's not been invited."

"No, but I'm kinda glad. She'll be escaping a night of starched shirts welcoming people she doesn't have to live next to and may never see again on top of Aunt M's preachy darts and Pop's crusty glances. I'm used to it, but Aunt Sergeant Major is rough on Jen as it is without the added stress of that kind of event."

"True. You know, you *could* do the right thing and make an honest woman of her ... ."

"Argh! Not you too!" Steves groaned into the line. "I'm hanging up. See you this Sunday, only, there better not be any preaching!"

"Okay okay! No preaching. I'll be too busy trying to be on my best behaviour for the guests to bother pestering you into a life of virtue."

"You 'trying' to be good? Understatement of the year. Now *me* on the other hand, the effort is mighty and the temptation is great. I just might add a few ingredients to the pans to provide us with some light entertainment for the evening ... ."

"Don't you dare!" Katherine gasped, fully conscious of what her jokester brother could cook up at times since she was a veteran victim of his for years.

"Ha ha! Just kidding. Or, maybe not. Bye Kats!"

With that, the phone went dead, leaving her hanging in trepidation wondering what stunt or gag he might pull on Aunt Martha's formal supper. Just great! She had better keep a sharp eye on Steves that night, or the new neighbours were going to be welcomed to Oak Meadows with a bang. Better be safe and call Mrs. Gonzales, warn her that 'Little Bandito Bro' was threatening to fall off the jokey wagon and have the cavalry prepared.

Her warning duly issued, Katherine wondered what had to be handled before she drove to the Reinold building. Perhaps call Jiff and ask what he wanted to do: go ahead with his première in her 'Old Elegance', or wait until she made more inquires about acquiring 'Harvey Dent'? Fielding was intrigued by the idea, considering his three dimensional rant about the modern industrial world, the old plant might be perfect for his new sculptures, in fact, why not place his statues in both sides? It would be an interesting mix, that's if she could get the building ready in time, it would be a stretch. No sweat, he wouldn't hold her to it and would be happy to go with whatever she could arrange. Maybe he was just being nice, but she guessed she had now raised his hopes about a showing in an industrial neo-Goth venue.

No pressure, no pressure, no pressure!

Thanking Jiff for his reassurance, she promised she would let him know how things turned out. For the moment, she better continue to investigate all the pros and cons. Hmm, would it be worth bothering Mr. R and Pete since everyone seemed to think buying it was a good idea, including Gerry who was an avid art collector? Well, the Captain was an art collector too, it would be good to have the opinion of two arty experts, and Gerry said not to forgo seeking Peter's advice, so she decided that since she had made the appointment to meet with them, she had better go and get their input.

Driving to Manhattan, Katherine felt chuffed having her own VIP pass granting her free access to the Reinold building, not to mention the parking spaces reserved for the executives and special guests. Exiting the elevator, she had just greeted Kells at the front desk when Mr. R and Peter approached from the executive area, looking very pleased to see her.

"Right on time, Kathy. 180 degrees, hard to port and right back out we go, my dear. I've booked us in for a late lunch, we're having a treat on me. I bet you haven't eaten anything," the Captain noted, a correct assumption Katherine had to admit as she was promptly redirected back toward the elevators. "I'd have taken us to the 'C'est la Vie', but the place isn't as good as it used to be since *someone* managed to nab their best chef." He winked.

"So, where are we off to?"

"Where else when there's business to discuss?" Peter chuckled.

Katherine could easily guess: the 21 Club famous for its quirky exclusive décor and favoured by the executive moguls as *the* place to close a deal while enjoying their elegant fare. Funny, their choice of venue seemed apropos for her advice-seeking session considering the Club was where she decided to take over the original family pill factory for her gallery in the first place. While being seated to their table in the colourful Bar Room with its prolific collection of memorabilia and chequered tablecloths, the Captain wondered what was so important that she felt the need to make an *appointment.*

"You're family, you don't need an appointment," he reminded as he scanned the menu.

"I know, but I needed to get advice as soon as possible, and I didn't want to drop in unannounced, I have a lot of stuff to go over."

"Huh. Well then, better get started, the sooner you tell us, the sooner we can advise."

While they figured out what they wanted to eat, Katherine launched into the latest opportunity placed before her, wondering whether she should lease, or take up everyone on their advice and buy the place outright. The Captain thought the second suggestion was the way to go.

"Why, buy it lock stock and barrel. Or in your case, bottles. I'm surprised you didn't up to now. Opportunities are like fish on a hook, haul them in when you get the chance before they slip away. You'll always be kicking yourself if you let the Big One go."

"That's what Gerry says, sort of. So, what do you think, Pete? Gerry says I'm also to ask you, since you're an astute business man."

"Did he now? Putting me on the hot seat, is he," Peter noted with amusement. "Okay, from a business point of view, it's always been my personal opinion that it's better to be the landlord than the renter. However, would going that route put you in financial hardship or under a serious debt load?"

"Not really," Katherine said, shaking her head, explaining her financial situation and her family's helpful loan offer.

"That's very generous," Peter nodded. "Good, because it's actually a sin to get into serious unnecessary debt."

"Really?"

"Yes, banking up loads of credit card debt you can't pay, enabling you to live beyond your means, that sort of thing. Now don't panic," Peter smiled, noticing Katherine's expression, "that doesn't apply here. Business requires a certain amount of calculated risk with regard to capital for expansion, and it seems the risk is cut down quite a notch or two in your case. Will you be able to pay off your family with the profits from your expanded art shows?"

"I think so, provided I can keep the famous artists coming. The thing is, I feel bad taking Pops and Gramps up on their offer, I mean everyone has been so very generous helping me up to this point."

"They just want to help some more, and besides, you'll be paying them back. It's not exactly a freebie. They're giving in to your need for independence," the Captain noted with humour.

"I'm not being greedy though, am I? The gallery is big enough as it is, it's just that Yoris and everyone else thinks its cool and would prefer to show in the old plant."

"I'm sorry, did we get you walked into this?" Mr. R. wondered. "We were only trying to help, roping in the grumpy Muscovite. His doom and gloom sells after all."

"I know, but don't worry, Yoris has proven to be the catalyst into getting me to do something about my picky moderns who want an urban setting."

"There's no denying it, that's what the younger yuppies want," Mr. R conceded. They paused as they placed their orders, then continued.

"Look at it this way, if getting that plant is something you have to do to keep your business successful, then it's not an unnecessary or greedy risk."

"True." Pete nodded. "There's a difference between a blessed increase and greedy over-solicitous hoarding."

"How can you tell the difference," Katherine wondered.

"You mean you want a sermon? Wow, it's not even Sunday."

"We have all lunch time son, so better clear her conscience and let her know it's not a mortal sin to run a successful business," Mr. R prodded.

"That depends on how you go about running a business," Peter returned with a chuckle.

"That's what I want to know, so preach away, I'm in need of some good, hard truths right now," Katherine piped up eagerly, while Mr. R waited to see what Peter had to say, his curiosity getting the better of him.

"I must say, this is unusual, a sermon on demand! Are you not afraid I shall prove insufferable?"

"Oh, *you're* not insufferable, at least, I don't think so. Come on, lay it on me."

"But keep it short if you can," the Captain added.

"Okay then." Peter smiled. "To start with, greed steps in when you are never satisfied and always want more far beyond your own needs or that of your business or what your state in life requires. Greed is a sickness, and nothing will ever be enough when you've caught that virus. However, I don't think greed is the issue here, in your case my dear, what you need to consider is the grace of *detachment*, wealth is also a gift when used correctly, *everything* is to be used as a tool to help us in our spiritual advancement, we should not make anything of this earth into chains to tie us down. In fact, this reminds me of a parable once given by a saint, which I think you will appreciate. Wealth and earthly goods are like all the variety of medicines and potential poisons filling a pharmacist's shop. A detached person is like a pharmacist who uses only what he needs when he needs it to cure the ailments of his customers, and can leave all his potions and pills behind him without a second thought when he locks up his shop each night. In contrast, a greedy person would be like a pharmacist who becomes addicted to his own substances, makes himself sicker with each dose and hungers after them when he goes home at night. He sinks even further and grumbles when a customer comes, needing the ingredients for a medicine that he uses to feed his own cravings. His addiction takes over until it eventually destroys him."

"Huh. That's a good analogy. So, why are certain increases considered a blessing and not greed," Katherine wondered as their salads were served.

"Well, in Genesis God blessed all His creatures, saying 'increase and multiply', those words were not merely a command. Life would not continue to exist if it didn't multiply, and that's the same for business profits to a certain extent. The cost of living constantly increases, it doubles about every ten years or thereabouts, so it's prudent to make a profit for your needs and put some away for a rainy day, but most of all, do good with the monetary rewards you have earned from your hard work. Even Christ used examples of successful trading to explain the Kingdom of Heaven and how we are expected to work and increase upon the spiritual and temporal gifts He gives us, giving his workers talents in different amounts and rewarding those who doubled them."

"So, doubling the size of the gallery is not a bad thing then."

"It depends. Do you really need it?"

"If I'm to attract the latest artists and remain commercially competitive, I'm afraid so … not to mention everyone I've asked so far seems to think it's a good idea."

"Then, you are not being greedy. You treat your workers well, pay everyone on time, give to Caesar what belongs to Caesar … ."

The Captain began to cough a bit, something going down the wrong way on that reminder.

"Hey, you alright?" Pete turned.

"Yeah, fine son, proceed."

"Let me take this opportunity to detour for a moment and say if Caesar graciously grants any exemptions, deductions, credits and so forth to the plebs, it is not wrong to take advantage of them, so you may use any legal means to avoid taxes."

"That's good to know. I wish Cesar would grant a few more of them," the Captain added.

"Okay, what else? Of course, don't forget to contribute to charities without grudging, remain detached knowing the gallery is a gift that has been given into your keeping and may one day be passed on to someone else, I think you'll be fine," Peter continued. "Of course, you have already embarked on an important vocation, which also must be maintained."

"Me? What? How," Katherine blurted, dropping a tomato slice off her fork.

"As an artist, my dear! Vocations are not just for priests, we all have to help each other up that narrow road." Peter smiled. "If I remember correctly, you have embarked on a mission to tell a few hard truths through your work, which the world needs to see. Art is not just about revealing beauty, it can also be used to reveal truth."

"If that's the case, just wait until you see Fielding's new pieces. I think he's got that cornered." She laughed.

"Fielding? I hope I'm getting an invite to that opening, Katie," the Captain nudged.

"Of course you are, everybody is," Katherine promised, "and what a show that promises to be, but still, me with a 'vocation'?"

"Yes, just like me, a duty to direct mankind back on the right path to heaven, you have answered the call to do the same, by different means. Not only have you used your talent to address serious issues, but you have taken it upon yourself to reclaim art from the atrocities committed against it, for instance, refusing obscenity in your gallery. Not many would dare take a stand like that today, especially when success in the art world nowadays seems to demand you give in to such outrages against taste, talent and subject matter. You are very brave to fight the tide."

"Oh shucks, I don't know about bravery, although Gramps has dubbed me the gadfly of the nation after all."

"Did he now? That's funny, but so apropos," the Captain mused.

"But Pete, I feel like a stupid hypocrite now too," she admitted, "I mean, I *hate* modern art! You know, the senseless and the obscene stuff. To think I have to go weirdo somewhere to keep the gallery *chic*. If Raphael lived today, he'd starve on the streets," she sighed, poking at a cucumber slice.

"Aw, I'm pretty sure he would have found a sympathetic patron *somewhere*. I wonder who?" Mr R smiled, giving her a wink.

"Yeah, I guess he would," she agreed.

"Still, this is where I think this curious addition to your premises might do some good," Peter nodded reflectively. "If you need to attract new collectors using the latest modern conventions, fine, but they will also see your artworks too and you will attract much attention to your work, which certain members of the public might not see otherwise. Even Christ said we had to be as wise as serpents."

"You mean 'Harvey Dent' has a gadfly purpose? I never thought of that, but you're right."

"The way culture is going, we need all the help we can get," the Captain noted as their salad plates were cleared and the main course was served.

"I agree. As long as you refuse to sell obscenities, crude nudes, and anything that's blasphemous, I think you'll be all right," Peter assured her, although he raised an eyebrow a little. She wondered why until … . *Oh, it was just one picture*, Katherine thought, looking a little sheepish, remembering a certain nativity scene she had painted in an attempt to alert mankind to the commercial destruction of traditional Christmas values. At least blasphemy was not intended! He seemed to return a kindly look that said: *I know, just don't cross the line from message to insult.* Pete seemed to know so much, it was scary, yet in an awesome sort of way.

"So, it looks like you'll still be censoring the nudes, eh? How did you ever make it through art school," Mr R. enquired, unaware of the message imparted by a glance.

"Oh! It's a long story." Katherine laughed.

"I can imagine," Peter returned, his eyes twinkling with amusement as he took a sip of wine.

03 ❖ 80

More input! For the next few days, those were the foremost buzzwords spurring her on. After everyone had pointed out the advantages of buying the new plant instead of leasing it, she realised she needed a lot more detailed information and could sympathise with the robot Johnny Five in *Short Circuit* and his insatiable thirst for facts. Uncle Tim thought getting the old factory was a good idea. The Gallery Gang were all for it, even Charlie said he would be happy to look into the paperwork once she had made her final decision and if the owner accepted her offer, coming out of his usually reserved shell for a moment to tease her on compromising her high art principles just a tad. Still, he warned her not to rush in to things, take her time, Yoris could wait, and she might secure more artists for a grand opening event in the meantime. Obviously, the makeover would take a lot of planning, even if major structural alterations would be minimal. There were the safety inspections that needed to be considered, the security and the alarms would have to be upgraded on that side, and the insurance details would have to be updated, but that would be no problem, she was not new to this now. Charlie could see her idea of a chic modern décor would be less expensive, but just as involved. Take your time to figure out the details he advised, this project could not be realised within a month.

Katherine knew Charlie was right, despite her minimalist ideas, it would still be a major refurbishment project that needed to be planned carefully. The good thing was, as he pointed out, she knew what to expect. The one shock was the asking price, one huge outlay. Buying the other half of the building outright would be her first true big business risk as a gallery owner, but she felt odd about accepting her family's loan offer. Gramps guessed it during lunchtime the following day when she seemed more interested in her notebook than taking a break and trying his latest 'non-cow' diet experiment he cooked up with Andre.

"Look kiddo, as you know, I keep telling everyone to keep one third of their assets liquid, you can't eat bricks or cement blocks in a recession, and recessions always circle back around, no matter how good the good times are. If you don't like the idea of accepting our loan, at least consider taking half of it. You wouldn't fork out all your own funds at once, you'd have enough to play around with, not to mention whatever you make off the art you will still be selling on this side of the gallery."

"I know buying the bottler sounds good, but I still have to think about it," Katherine replied, tallying up her latest round of figures. "Doubling the size of this place means my expenses will in all likelihood double as well, I have to factor this in … ."

"True, but double the artwork should mean double the profits, right?"

"That's if and when a piece sells, sometimes it takes awhile to get an artwork moved off the walls."

"I thought that's what your whacko telethon recruiting campaign was for in the first place." Gramps chuckled. "Maybe I was wrong, but I gathered their modern masterpieces were hotter than our SinuBreeze nasal squirts during the flu season."

"Er, they are," Katherine agreed, finally cracking a smile as she laid her pen down for a moment, "but nothing in the art world is as guaranteed as the flu season. Fashion and status is time sensitive depending on the artist too. I know I have a good chance with Fielding, and Yoris if I can keep him interested, but statues are still new territory for me."

"If it's any consolation, you now have loyal customers and have made your artistic presence known in the city, you won't be starting out with a blank page, not like the first time with this side of things," Gramps nodded around. "Think some more if you have to, but not too long. If offers have been made already, you have to get yours in too, or else the whole project will be dead and buried if another developer gets the property first."

Of course, there was that to consider. All her input hunting would come to nothing if she lost the building in the end. When it came right down to it, there were more advantages in buying the building than leasing it, even all the executives in the family were more in favour of that idea than taking out a lease. Still, she felt so indecisive despite having all the odds stacked in her favour! Gramps returned to his lunch and left the matter rest, although his old experienced noggin was set working. Katherine was looking down from the edge of the high dive and just needed a little push, metaphorically speaking,

The next morning she received an unexpected visit only a few minutes after she opened up. A quiet, well groomed man in his sixties now balding a bit introduced himself and asked if he could have a word with her. It was none other than Mr. 'Boomer', or rather, Mr. 'Boomer' Junior. He explained his real name was Norman Barnes, but his father had acquired the nickname and it stuck, literally everywhere, including the family bottling trade. It certainly made for an interesting business card, he added. Surprised and curious, Katherine invited him over to the Gallery Gang's table in the restaurant to hear what he had to say.

"I hear you're thinking about investing in the old place next door," he began as he poured some milk into his coffee.

"Yes, that is correct," Katherine affirmed. "For additional art space, it's perfect for the urban art scene." Gee, she hadn't even called the estate agent yet, and was sure she only mentioned leasing when she first saw the place … .

"I hear you're also thinking of keeping the factory practically as is, including the machines, cleaned up of course," he continued, a tone of enquiry lacing his voice.

"Yes, perhaps I'd take out some of the office cubicles on the top floor to make more space, plus knock some openings through the interior wall on each floor by the stairs for access points into the gallery. I'm also thinking of adding the same coloured awnings out front, just some minor cosmetic changes to make it match this side, but that's about it. The machines add to the urban charm so I've been told, which means if I decide to place an offer, I'd be keeping them."

"You know, I'm mighty pleased to hear that." He smiled. "The other points are just moot. It needed a sprucing up anyway, but I'm tickled about you keeping the machines and that everything would be left almost intact. You see, my father got the place years ago, it's where we first started out, so I'm attached to the patch."

Katherine smiled, that sounded familiar. Gramps also had a sentimental twang when it came to the former pill factory turned gallery. It then dawned on her where Mr. Boomer Junior received his latest information … .

"Forgive me for interrupting, but did my grandfather get in contact with you recently?"

"Yes, I must admit Gregory called me yesterday and leaked your plans. He's a mighty fine man, your grandfather."

"That he is. So, your father started the bottling business."

"Yep, sarsaparilla and lemon pop. I have some very fond memories of the place. I became the most popular kid in my class when I could sneak out to my friends all the soda they wanted."

"I bet you did! What then?"

"Oh, we came up with the bright idea of opening our own soda pop stand on a busy corner and made quite a few bucks. Why wouldn't we when we were selling the stuff for half of what you could buy it at a store or bar? Of course, I got caught and Dad didn't know how to address the situation, so I got praised for my business sense, but my rear end whopped for stealing."

"Talk about sending mixed messages!"

"Yeah, still, those were great times. Then time came for me to take over the business, then the need to expand with those new fandangled plastic bottles and all, not to mention add some colas and those clear pops to the list when they become more popular. So, aware of the changing tastes along with the changing times, we got new premises and all of that, but I hung onto the original plant and tried to make it pay as best I could, for old time's sake. I did find a few niche markets out west and other places where the original glass bottles were popular, you know, the old wild west tourist towns, but now that the kids are all grown up and have pretty much taken over the business, they're all progressive these days. They say it's not worth keeping it, they're not interested, so I thought it was time to let someone else have it."

"Still, it must be tough deciding to let it go."

"True, I know we shouldn't be sentimental in business, but there are some things where that rule shouldn't apply."

"Well, Mr. Barns,"

"Please, call me Norm, it makes me feel normal." He smiled.

"Okay Norm, I've only just started to consider investing in this expansion project, but if you don't mind me asking, have you received any other offers?"

"Oh boy, have I, and what offers. Some worse than the others."

Uh oh, that didn't sound good. Was he now starting to set her up for a high asking price?

"Trying to get the place for nothing, huh?"

"Sure, I had a few opportunists flocking, but it's not the price I'm talking about: it's what they want to *do* to it. The kids may not care who it goes to, so I thought I would dispose of it as respectfully and painlessly as possible. Apartment complexes are one thing, but that would mean a total gutting of the factory, and that just hit me the wrong way. Then, one guy wanted to put in a night club, another wanted to open a strip tease place. I held out for a bit, then I thought if it's time to let go, the apartment idea was the least offensive and I was about to accept the offer for it until I got a call from your grandfather. When I heard you wanted it pretty much as is and were going to leave it in museum condition, that just hit the spot. I do hope you'll consider it. In fact, I'll help sweeten the deal."

Oh dear, if she didn't take it, that would mean months of obstruction and noise pollution from construction works, or worse yet, *vice bars*! She couldn't allow that next door! It would ruin the growing upmarket atmosphere her gallery was attracting to the area. However, she was curious to know what he was going to offer.

"What kind of sweetener did you have in mind?"

"If you are really serious about keeping the old machines in place, how about I knock five hundred g's off the asking price?"

"That's a lot of added sweetener," Katherine replied, somewhat taken aback.

"Everyone has a sweet tooth. If they say they don't, they have to be lying. You just have to find the right candy."

"But a deal like that just for sentiment's sake? You'll be the one suffering a cavity."

"A filling made of modern art can't be all that bad. I'm willing to go for it if you are." He grinned. "It would be nice to know someone who's interested in the history of the place will be taking care of it."

"Well, if it would make you happier than the other offers. You know, I wasn't quite prepared for your deal. Would you mind if I think it over the next few days and then get back to you?"

"No, not at all. I promise not to consider other offers until you do. Here's my card," he said slipping it out of his jacket pocket and handing it to her.

"All right, thank you. I won't keep you waiting too long."

"Fair enough."

Katherine gave Norm a tour of the gallery when they had finished their coffee, explaining what she had in mind in more detail and showing him where she was thinking of breaking doorways through the walls, if she decided to accept his offer. Despite the fact she would not be refurbishing his factory in the same style, Norm was impressed and a little amused to think his bottling plant might become all the rage with the cultured set. He returned the tour offer and they made an inspection of the old plant next door. Norm even set the machines running for a few minutes to show how they worked, albeit the few bottles that zipped by were capped empty since there was no soda in the vats. He wondered what she had planned to keep or tear out, and when her first item was the bathrooms, he agreed they did need some serious help. Other than that, he liked her minimalist plans, including Stephie's idea of studio lighting and movable 'curtain walls' without damaging or altering the original structure.

"You got all those ideas just from seeing the place once? Those are some nifty concepts, simple, but simple always works out the best. Tell you what, I'll show you how to work the security system and where the lights are, and I'll let you have the keys for a few days, just so you can get a better feel for the place."

"You mean you trust me with the keys? Are you sure?"

"Sure I'm sure! I know I can trust Gregory's kin, and besides, you look like an honest person. Anyway, if you did want to filtch something, what could you take out of here but a bunch of bottles, and you're welcome to those."

"When you put it that way," Katherine laughed. "Thank you, I know a few of my artists might want a look out of curiosity, and it would be great to get their feedback … ."

"All righty then, I'll show you how to put the machines on safety lock, just so if anyone gets the urge to set them going, they can't. You don't want an accident on your hands, these machines can whip an arm off if you're not careful."

That sounded ominous, so she paid close attention to his instructions when he showed her the control switches. Good thing they could be locked down with a key, once locked, nothing would work. Plus, the electrical mains to the bottlers could be switched off and locked, so they could be rendered completely safe. That was good to know! After he had showed her the lights and security systems, they called it an afternoon, Mr. Boomer handing her his set of keys after he locked up the door and heartily shook her hand again.

As she watched him walk around the corner of the building and out of sight, the weight of the keys gave her a feeling that was hard to describe. The building already felt like it was hers, everything seemed to be set in motion, all that was left was to close the deal. Things were falling into a nice groove, but was it all just *too* easy? Hmm, there was usually one explanation when that happened … .

"Gramps," she *tsked* and looked up to heaven, not only did he leak her plans, he must have offered Norm a lump sum to cover the machines to lower the price, just to make the idea more tempting. Darn it, it was working! However, if her over-helpful Gramps was the cause of Norm's 'sweetened deal', she couldn't have him fork out the extra, that would have to be paid back immediately, or, consider that part of his loan offer and pay him back accordingly, *if* she went though with it. 'If'— it was one of the most paralysing words in the English language. Decisions, decisions!

The Gallery Gang were curious to know what transpired with Mr. Boomer when she sat behind the reception desk, wondering if she had made an offer, but there was no news to tell just yet, she had some thinking to do. Perhaps when the weekend was over she might finally make her mind up after she had one last advice-seeking session from the folks, not to mention survive Aunt Martha's dinner for the new neighbours, that hurdle had yet to be faced.

☙ ❖ ❧

"There you are! Come on! Step lively! Help us set the table, they'll be here soon," Aunt Martha commanded without a 'hello' after beating Jasper to the door, all elated yet in anxious jitters over the whole affair.

"Okay, but I just got here. Let me put away my case first," Katherine replied as she went up the stairs, pretty sure her Aunt wouldn't want their guests to trip over it as they entered the front door.

"Go on up dear, I'll try and keep her calm," her mother assured with an amused smile, although she too was already in her dinner dress and slightly keyed up with all the last minute preparations still looming before them.

Safe in her bedroom with Jasper who followed her up, the few minutes she needed to unpack her toiletries and hang up her outfit for work the next day gave her some pep-time to brace herself for the night of starchy formalities. She appreciated elegance, but this night felt over the top. The fact they didn't know much about their guests was a little unnerving, Katherine always found first introductions stiff when made under ceremonial conditions such as candlelight and silverware dinners, especially when Aunt Martha planned them. Unless it was a wedding, a charity benefit, or a dinner out at an elite jacket and tie restaurant, hardly anyone they knew gave dinners with that level of ceremony any more besides the Reinolds, but Aunt Martha refused to lessen her dignity with the modern times and insisted her nieces and nephews learn the decorum and time-honoured traditions expected in a family of their social standing. Every plate, side dish, crystal glass, eating utensil for each course, plus the artfully folded linen napkins, were to be placed 'just so' at the appropriate intervals that would make the white-gloved butlery setting forth the state banquets for the Queen of England jade green with envy. Woe betide anyone whom she espied eating a shrimp cocktail with the salad fork, or using the fish knife to butter their bread roll! She would not say anything while guests were present, but if they were ignorant in the elegant niceties of the dinner table, the family would never hear the end of it the rest of the night once their visitors left, for the guests would catch it behind their backs. It was a mercy they wouldn't hear the not-so-nice commentary they accidentally elicited by their *faux pas* during the meal. Katherine hoped nothing like that would happen tonight! It reminded her of when she was allowed to sit at the 'grown-up' table for the first time all those years ago and stressed stiff she might make a mistake in case Aunt Martha spotted something amiss. No worries now of course, age and experience now made such matters second nature.

Katherine sighed as she thought of the bustle awaiting her downstairs. She'd better hurry up or she could expect a summons from below resounding up the stairs ordering her not to dawdle. She may be an adult with a fiancé, but Aunt Martha still treated her like she was six a good portion of the time. Changing into a dinner dress and tidying herself up with a fresh coat of make-up and a nice hair-do, her tresses appropriately swept up and arranged with a beaded clip featuring floral ornaments, Katherine took one last look in the mirror and gave a quick nod of approval, she was presentable. Time to brave the dining room. She impulsively gave a quick rub behind Jasper's ear, it was hard to resist that winsome sappy-eyed expression when he wanted a pat, but then realised she had to wash her hands again. Delays, delays. At last, she was ready to go down, the faithful pooch simply wagged his tail and followed her as usual, also dressed up in his doggie Dickey bow that Gramps got him for these grand occasions.

"You look lovely," her mother complimented.

"Thanks. You do too as always. What's the latest news? All excitement?"

"To put it mildly. Your aunt is busy checking out the first course and driving Mrs. Gonzales and Juanita up the wall. The men are all hunkered down in the relative safety of the den. I've got the silverware covered, you'd better start on the napkins before she comes back, or you might get your ear bent before the guests come."

"No problem. We aim to help. Oops! Not again! Jasp! Stop licking me! And you're not supposed to be in the dining room, out like a good boy."

Katherine went quickly to wash her hands thanks to Jasper who insisted on a few more ear rubs before obediently joining his master in the den. Prepared for duty, she returned to the task at hand and retrieved the desired number of linen cloths.

"All set. What shape?"

"Considering this is a 'let us be elegant or die' affair, I think you'd better go all out and do the curly fan shaped ones. The fancier the better, for all our sakes."

"Right, you got it."

This was one of those rare times when her once seemingly useless fascination with *origami* had its advantages. Deftly she folded the crisp cloths into elaborate rings with fan-shaped embellishments while her mother spaced out the cutlery and checked the crystal ware for the umpteeth time, ensuring there were no water spots marring their brilliant lustre. It was true Aunt Martha had her issues concerning a dinner table, but they were both just as bad when it came to watermarks. Sure enough, Mom caught a spot on one of the knives and gave it a quick, vigorous rub with a buff cloth. If cleanliness was closer to godliness, then shininess equalled cleanliness and displayed their household was completely attentive to kitchen hygiene. Katherine could understand that paranoia, even if the articles were clean, placing a spoon or a glass with ghostly drizzle traces from rinse water before a guest felt no different than setting out grimy used items that had seen the inside of someone's mouth and not the dishwasher before being put back in the drawer.

Finishing up with the last piece of napkin art, Katherine wondered if they needed her for anything else. Mom shook her head, Aunt Martha had pretty much taken care of it herself this time. True to her Biblical namesake, her aunt had a fault of being over attentive about any event she planned herself.

"Go say 'hello' to your brother and the patriarchs, and tell them it's almost time, our guests should be arriving soon."

"Okay."

Suddenly, it struck her she had forgotten her brother's threat to unleash his practical joking upon the company that night. With all the latest doings at the gallery, it had completely slipped her mind.

"Mom! Steves alert! Did you remember to … ?"

"Oh yes. We've swept the place three times a day for the last two days. So far, we haven't found anything, not even the tiniest Whoopee cushion," her mother reported with a sigh as she examined another glass. "Your father has given him some sharp warnings and we're still on high alert in case he tries to set up anything, which is another reason why I'm not about to leave this room, but that doesn't mean we're in the clear just yet. You know how we've missed catching him in the act before. Honestly! We don't need this right now!"

"I guess I'd better go and keep on eye on him, preventative measures, you know."

Mom had spoken the truth, they certainly didn't need the added tension of wondering when the next gag would suddenly reveal itself and dreading what form it could possibly take. Steves never failed to amaze as well as annoy, but with the unknown element of new guests as the victims, this was a bit unnerving! The worst thing about the threatened trickery for this particular night was he had plenty of scope to cook up something truly wicked since a *dinner party* was involved, food was an easy target and the kitchen the most vulnerable location to infiltrate, in addition to the fact he had access to something that few if any pranksters did—industrial grade laboratories chock full with a staggering number of dyes, scents, chemicals, gases, bugs, bacteria and viruses.

Katherine took a quick detour to the kitchen to say 'hi' to Mrs. Gonzales and Juanita and see how they were faring. Sure enough, they were on point duty near the pots, the stove, the oven and the main refrigerator. So far, they had found nothing and had ordered Mr. Steven on pain of life and limb to stay out of the kitchen area, Mrs. Gonzales shaking her head when she further reported her aunt was busy in the pantry at the extra refrigerator checking out the desserts. While Mrs. Gonzales was a spot-on cook, Aunt Martha prided herself on her cakes and other sugary delectables and would provide the desserts for special occasions, and this dinner would certainly not be an exception. Katherine could imagine Aunt Martha carefully poking each item with a toothpick to ensure they were the authentic version and had been left inviolate. One birthday party Steves had managed to swap her famous 'Paradise Cake' with an ingenious clone dexterously crafted from synthetic car wash sponges and frosted exactly like her own fruity wonder complete with birthday candles stuck in exactly the right spots. The bafflement was mighty as Pops tried to cut the cake to find the knife wouldn't budge through the interior, the confectionary bouncing back into shape with each brave attempt yet sending the frosting and filling sliding all over the place.

Steves rarely played the same joke twice, but 'rare' was enough to keep everyone checking just the same. Considering this night was going to be an all-out Italian dinner, certain ingredients were checked five times over such as the black olives intended for the *antipasti* course. Years ago Steves had once laced Mrs. Gonzales' Mediterranean salad with black rubber faucet washers that were easily mistaken for additional olive slices. It was a good thing Gramps was the first to take a bite and noticed the salad was a bit chewy then caught on to the trick, preventing anyone else from swallowing a mouthful and suffering a night of indigestion, although Gramps wasn't so sure if a loose 'olive slice' had escaped him or not. In a panic, Mom called Dr. Hendricks and reported the latest family medical emergency, but the good doctor told her not to worry. Having treated a numberless gaggle of kids over the years who had swallowed everything from broken glass to pennies and beads, a rubber ring was nothing to panic over and couldn't help but see the funny side of Steve's prank despite it having gone farther south than anticipated. The Doc simply instructed Mom to have the patient eat some dry bread, within twenty-four hours or so, the Sanitation Department could expect an extra gift from their household in the form of a free faucet washer. Talk about jokes going too far! Katherine decided she had better go see what Steves was up to and perhaps nip this in the bud if it all possible.

"Hi everyone. My, don't you all look just dandy," she greeted, giving Pops and Gramps a hug and a kiss, but glaring at Steves who looked the picture of innocence as though ice wouldn't melt in his presence.

"Hello dear you look lovely too," Pops replied, putting his paper down as he received his hug and kiss.

"Thanks Pops, I believe I am passable for this grand night."

"Hi pet. You're more than passable I must say. Come, you can play guard duty with us." Gramps smiled raising an eyebrow with a quick nod to her brother.

"Thanks Gramps. Oh yes, as for *you* and guard duty," she said turning to Steves, her voice assuming the tone necessary when reprimanding a naughty child. "What have you done? Better reveal it now and let's not have any high jinks tonight, especially when Mom and Aunt Martha are a bundle of nerves as it is."

"What? *Moi?* Seriously, I haven't done anything," Steves protested, hands held out.

"Yeah sure, and I'm the Loch Ness monster. 'Fess up."

"But there's nothing to 'fess to," he replied, looking more amused than irritated that his word of honour was being questioned.

"Right. The last time we heard that, Mrs. Gonzales discovered all the eggs in the house were super-glued into the cartons, and when she finally *did* get to make those devilled eggs, you swapped the yolks with yellow frosting before they got served."

"Save your breath, Katie. The rascal isn't going to rat out his trick, even if he has to fib to do it," Gramps advised.

"The age old Jokester's Code of Honour, it's as sacrosanct as a magician's," Pops sighed as he shook his head, he then turned to Steves, "I just pray you haven't decided to target one of our guests tonight, or you really will be in the soup, and I mean it."

Although Pops was being serious, his choice of words didn't help. Gramps and Steves couldn't help but guffaw a bit on that one, no doubt the word 'soup' reminded them of the time the family prankster had slipped a few bouillon cubes into Katherine's shower head the night they were all getting ready for one of Mom's swanky charitable evening fund raisers. Katherine was struck with dazed dismay when warm beefy broth began to spout overhead instead of water, then grew livid upon discovering the simple trick. She had to use the guest bathroom until the mess was cleaned up and her shower declared fit for purpose again. Little brothers could be so annoying!

"There had better *not* be any more soup! I'm keeping an eye on you," Katherine warned.

"Whatever, but there's nothing to worry about," Steves assured them, although the corner of his mouth was twitching as he said it.

Katherine tested the cushion before she sat down with Gramps on the sofa, just in case, then shot her little Bro another suspecting glance.

Hmm, perhaps Mom was right, there may not be any extra 'cushions' hiding anywhere, but tonight she could not be sure.

For the next few minutes, Katherine tried to have a chat with the patriarchs and approach Gramps about his meeting with Mr. Boomer Jr, although the second Steves attempted to leave his seat, she ordered him to sit and stay put, distracting her each time. Steves meekly obliged until he said he had to go to the bathroom. Surely, he had permission to leave her despotic detention for *that*? No problem, only much to the patriarchs' amusement she made him march upstairs and use his own *en suite* rather than risk him doing something crazy to the main bathroom downstairs and shock the guests should they need to use it.

"Geeze, it's like having the Gestapo on my heels," he noted before closing the door while she stood as sentry outside his bedroom in the hallway. The curious thing was he was still all grins and taking this double guard duty in good form, making Big Sister even more suspicious. Just *what* had he planned that they hadn't found yet? She was tempted to lock him in his bedroom for the night to keep their company safe, but that wouldn't work, he could always pick the lock or escape out the window *via* the drain pipe and garden trellis, which he often used to do during high school when there was a party in the offering and had not obtained official parental permission to attend. Besides, she couldn't have him miss the dinner.

They were both on their way down the stairs when the gate buzzer went off, signalling a car was on its way, sending Aunt Martha scurrying out of the kitchen and beating Jasper to the front door, calling out their guests had arrived. However, there was a flustered detour as she suddenly remembered the telescope was still in the dining room. Wondering where to hide the evidence of her snooping patrols with only seconds to find a solution, she bolted from the dining room in a hurry and jammed the contraption in the coat closet under the stairs, slamming the door shut.

"Hey! Careful with that! You break it, you bought it," Steves piped up as they reached the bottom step, although enjoying the little pantomime.

"Now don't be difficult," Aunt Martha returned, tidying herself quickly. "You're to be on your best behaviour tonight, understand?"

"Understood," he returned, looking every second like a close relative to the Cheshire cat as the bell rang again.

By now, the rest of the family were in the front hallway ready to meet their new neighbours as their car pulled up, including Jasper who stayed close to Gramps, wagging his tail, knowing something big was happening.

"Here goes," Helen said under her breath to Pops and Gramps as Martha opened the door.

"Hello! Welcome! Do come in," Aunt Martha greeted. "We're so glad you could come, especially after moving in so soon."

"Not at all! Swell of yous to invite us, thanks! Very much appreciated, and I do mean that. Honestly, we were told this was a nice family sort of 'burb, but seemed pretty iced up, antisocial like and all, not until we got the invite. No *bienvenuto* until now, what do yah think of that? Wow, something smells pretty good, just like my *nonna's* cooking," the gentleman replied in a thick Jersey accent.

"We thought you and your family would appreciate something Italian, Mr. Benino," Aunt Martha replied.

"Becchino, but s'alright, easy to mix up, no harm done," he smiled as he let his wife and teenage son enter in ahead of him.

For a split second, the atmosphere went still while Martha was still chirpy as usual, blissfully ignorant of whom she had invited into their home. Katherine knew she had seen the man somewhere before but couldn't place him, that is, not until the name was jovially corrected. He was often in the papers, but not in those sections usually associated with the members of New York's or even Jersey City's High Society, and they certainly weren't respected members of the business community: the Becchinos were one of the most notorious mob families in the state and ran a lot more than a chain of clubs, restaurants and delis, which were no doubt a front for their many more lucrative if but seedy hidden operations. No wonder the welcome wagons weren't forthcoming! For the world's Master Hedge Sleuth, how come Aunt Martha didn't have a clue? Then again, she had a sieve for a head when it came to certain names and placing faces, including infamous ones.

Mr. Ludovico Becchino didn't seem to notice anything amiss in the reception by the family, vigorously shaking hands while he genially introducing his wife Carla who insisted everyone call her 'Cee', and their second son Giovanni, but 'Gio' was fine. He would have introduced his eldest son, Paulo, but he was away on family business in Chicago, but there was always another time. In any case, Mr. Becchino said all his friends called him 'Vic' or 'Vico', so no fuss with formalities. He then handed Pops several bottles of what he assured were the best Sicilian Nero D'Avola and Moscato wines, plus a generous sized box packed with deluxe spicy sausages from their speciality delicatessen import business christened 'Papa Vico's', the box emblazoned with a caricature logo of an apron clad deli-man holding up a Parma ham, while Cee offered her hosts a large tray decorated with embroidered cloths and lined with her famous homemade *cannoli*.

"I wasn't sure what ta bring, but I figyah'd everyone loves *cannolis*, yah can't go wrong with them, right," Cee reasoned.

"No, they look positively delightful. Why thank you, Mr. and Mrs. Becchino, you didn't have to bring anything," Helen replied.

"Please, just Vico, Cee and Gio."

"Of course. Please, let me introduce you to everyone, this is my husband, Harold … ."

Recovering quickly lest anything should look amiss, Helen continued the introductions while simultaneously passing on the other gifts to anyone standing close, snapping everyone out of their astonishment, although her politeness was tinged with a smidgeon of apprehension.

"Steven, Katherine, would you please take these in to Mrs. Gonzales and have her put them in the fridge?"

"Sure Mom, be back in a sec," Steves replied as he retrieved the sausages from Gramps, who was amused and chuffed with the offerings despite the initial surprise at the identities of their guests, while Katherine was given the *cannoli*. She could understand Mom's jitteriness, Katherine had the sneaking suspicion that they had better not do anything that might be mistaken as a token of disrespect lest they ended up on their new neighbours' bad books! The scene was a bit surreal as Aunt Martha, still unaware of the reputation of their guests, happily suggested they all go to the front parlour for a drink before dinner, promising them a tour of the house later while Helen asked to be excused for a moment so she could put the wine in the dining room.

"Er, do we have other guests," Pops wondered, noticing the two men still in the car outside.

"Nah. Just my driver, and some protection, yah never can be too safe, yah know. They'll be just fine," Vico explained.

"Um, if you say so," Aunt Martha replied as she closed the door. Now she was curious, but still not getting the full picture, despite the sight of Cee in her jungle print ensemble. Auntie then looked young Gio up and down since he decided to come in a pair of jeans and a leather jacket, but quickly moved on, resigned that she could do nothing with the rebellious dress codes of the youth. Katherine and Steves needed to get away for a moment and quickly retreated to the kitchen for a breather in case they let some sort of involuntary reaction escape them. Mrs. Gonzales and Juanita were busy preparing the *antipasti* when they entered.

"What on earth is *that*," the occupied cook wondered as she observed Steves putting away the box in the meat drawer.

"Half the sausages of Palermo. You won't believe who's just arrived for dinner."

Forgetting he was not supposed to be anywhere near the kitchen let alone the fridge that night, Mrs. Gonzales' brown eyes widened as Steves quickly filled her in while Katherine stored the *cannoli* in the spare fridge in the pantry and overheard the reaction.

"*Mio Dios*! I've cooked an *Italian* dinner too! If only … I would have cooked southern … tomato sauces, different pasta … certainly *not* Fettuccini Alfredo! Your aunt has really done it this time," she exclaimed with a few oaths in Spanish, her sentences fragmented with the shock.

"Oh, you know how she is, always mixing up names and faces. I'm sure she didn't mean to invite America's Most Wanted," Katherine noted from the pantry, "but what's wrong with fettuccini? I thought Sicily was part of Italy? Don't they like that? They invented it after all, er, after the Chinese did."

"The historians and geographers may have combined Sicily with Italy, but the peninsular Italians and the islander Sicilians think differently, their pasta sauces display their region as much a Scotsman's kilt displays his clan," Mrs. Gonzales tried to explain while arranging the artichoke hearts, her explanation eliciting a burst of laughter from the youngsters. Mrs. G had learned quite a thing or two about the various regional tensions after a cousin somehow managed to marry into an Italian family that prided itself on being Tuscan.

"Oh yeah, Tuscans consider themselves the cream of the mainland, the Romans are just tolerated, the people from Milan are considered too northern, too close to the Swiss-Germans, while anyone from Naples are considered of questionable heritage, while everyone else feels just the same about the Tuscans," Juanita added. Obviously, their cousin had a load to tell.

"Hello Machiavelli! It seems the old squabbles of the Renaissance refuse to die," Steves commented.

"Gosh that's right! When you think about it, Italy was once a mash of mini-kingdoms and micro-republics, I guess they still think along those lines. France is still a bit like that too," Katherine mused aloud, her friend Justine explained all the various regions in France still considered themselves 'little countries' to a certain degree attached to the greater 'whole'. French-Canadian Andre prided himself on his family originating from Burgundy while paying respectful tribute to his old world heritage. It was certainly different from the US that had constructed its own territory from the time of the colonists and pioneers, gradually expanding into one united country from sea to shining sea. True, each state was a little country to itself, but still, America was America, everyone pulled together and was 'American' no matter what state they were born in.

"Okay you two, enough of the history lesson. You'd better get back out there, or they'll wondered where you've disappeared to, maybe *literally*," Mrs. Gonzales prompted, "and I hope Master Steven you haven't done anything jokey to one of my dishes, it's now a menu-planning disaster as it is, and I'm in no mood to be fitted for a pair of custom made cement shoes and take a stroll down the river!"

"Relax! I didn't touch a dish," he reassured her, although his eyes widened with the thought, whether from shock or amusement, Katherine couldn't quite tell. She gave him a quick dressing down as they went through he hallway back to the parlour.

"Considering who's just come to dinner, you'd better 'fess up and now and call off whatever you've got planned," she whispered fast, "or the whole family could have their own pairs of cement shoes before daybreak."

"Aren't you the paranoid one," he smiled.

"Yes, I am actually, and with good reason too! The paranoid survive they say."

"Aw, Don't worry, I bet they have a great sense of humour. How much do you want to wager?"

"Steves! Dad's going to kill you if the Becchinos don't," she returned, but couldn't say any more, they were already at the parlour. Did they walk that fast? Or, maybe Steves had started them on a fast pace now curious to see what was transpiring with their guests? She was a bit flustered, but composed herself before they entered the room.

It was certainly an interesting scene, the family trying to make their new neighbours feel welcome and at home while yet feeling oddly constrained as they began thawing the ice. Their guests seemed not to notice anything amiss, much like Aunt Martha who was still ignorant of the situation, chatting away with the usual pleasantries, the conversations eventually breaking away between the men and woman as they addressed topics of interest to them.

"Yous got one beautiful home here, Helen," Cee complimented looking around, her sending her golden ear-hoops swinging. It was a marvel they didn't get caught in that voluptuous mass of wavy brown hair Katherine thought, wondering how Cee could feel comfortable in her tight, low cut dress complete with a matching big-cat leopard print spotted shoulder bag and high heels. "You *must* tell me where you find such classy things, I certainly haven't seen anythin' as nice as this, trying to get ideas for the new house, yah know. Just some odd bits, but no new furniture yet."

"Thank you. Well, in this room, they're mostly English manor antiques, plus a few French pieces. Have you thought about trying Sothebys, or perhaps Christies," Helen suggested, trying to make pleasant conversation.

"No, but I'll do that, I always wanted to see what those places were like, maybe next week, that's if they get finished mucking up the ground for the new pool out back. Can't leave the place unattended with workmen around, yah know how that is."

"Yes, that is true, you don't know who you could be inviting into your home these days," Martha nodded in agreement, innocently oblivious to the fleeting incredulous glance cast in her direction by her sister accompanied by a frosty look from Pops, who managed to overhear that bit despite Vico's animated conversation complete with the indispensable hand gestures. At that point Vico, was in the midst of proudly telling Harold, Gramps and Steves that 'Gio here' had just finished high school and was going to university this fall, giving his younger son a few proud thumping pats on the shoulder. However, it seems Gio was not too enthused about this prospect as he continued to chew his gum and looked up to the ceiling somewhat irked.

"Pa, I keep tellin' yah, I *ain't* goin' to Uni!"

"Yeah ya are, your brother went and got his degree, and if you know what's good for yah, yah're goin' too," Vico returned flatly.

"Aww! I *told* you I wanna go straight inta business, you don't need fancy degrees for that, waste of time, I'm tell'n yah," Gio insisted petulantly.

"Geeooh … wha'did I say about mind'n your manners? We're guests here," Cee, then broke in quietly, but forcefully. "Don't mouth off to your old man, we can talk about this later."

Gio sullenly complied, chewing his gum with eyes fixed to the floor, arms folded in resignation to this reminder on putting his best foot forward for the remainder of the evening while he listened to his proud father laying out the promising academic future awaiting him before this polite gathering. To Katherine it was plainly obvious a career that brought in cold hard cash the quick and dodgy way was what appealed most to young Gio and he would rather jump off a cliff in Capri than take the long bookish haul towards scholastic respectability before making his way in the world.

"Don't worry, just a few years and it will all be over." Steves smiled, he knew what it was like to have to go to college, but for a different reason. He had the genius and the know-how to head straight into the family labs were it not for the fact he needed the official credentials. "Have you any ideas about what you want to study," he politely enquired.

"I dunno, maybe you should ask *him*," Gio replied still chewing languidly, making a sideways cynical head bob in Vico's direction that amused Steves but shocked Katherine. It appeared 'The Fonz' had no qualms about airing his various domestic disagreements with his folks in public. Despite giving Gramps a comical roasting now and then, which was different, she couldn't conceive how anyone could be so backmouthy towards their parents and think nothing of it. However, it was a good thing Gio's parents were once more engrossed in their various conversations with her folks and didn't catch his sarcastic gesture, she had a sneaking suspicion Papa Vico would not be above reasserting his authority and head-whap a little respect into him there and then *ala* the Three Stooges since none of them seemed to care too much about letting anything hang out.

At that moment, Juanita came to announce dinner was ready, which was Helen's cue to invite them all into the dining room, with Martha busily conducting everyone to their places. Harold helped his wife with her chair as he always did, Steven also doing the honour for Katherine on this formal night. Cee quickly caught Vico by the sleeve and tugged him into imitating his hosts.

"Oh, there yah go," he replied, shoving her into the table with enthusiasm, his helpful gesture proving more of a hindrance as she manoeuvred her chair back into a more comfortable distance while he swaggerly lumbered to his own seat, oblivious to the clumsy mishap, though neither of them seemed put out by it all and continued with Cee jabbering on about the beautifully set dinner table, while Gio coolly meandered to his seat, hands in his pockets and still wearing his leather jacket, finally drawing them out as he settled in to the table with the rest of the men, following their lead since all the ladies were now seated. Mrs. Gonzales brought out the *antipasti* with her niece's assistance.

"Aw, this looks really good Mrs. W, yous went all out, I'm impressed," Vico beamed. So far, the Italian menu wasn't phasing the Sicilians. Good food was still good food no matter where it came from, north, south, east or west.

"Harold dear, will you say grace," Helen prompted her husband, eventually getting a word in after Cee's numerous compliments while feeling the edge of the table linens and wondering where she found such lovely china, asking where it was made while upturning her bread plate to see the trademark stamp, then peering closely at a knife to see 'Stirling silver' was indeed etched into the blade before resuming a reflective pose with everyone else. However, Mama Cee quickly looked up for she had to keep on top of Gio about his etiquette issues:

"Geeeooh, wha'da I keep saying?" She spread her hands and raised her eyebrows a little.

"Oh yeah, sorry." He took out his gum and stuck it to the side of his salad plate.

Cee seemed satisfied with that and resumed her reflected pose. Somewhat aghast as evidenced by a minute twitch of an eyebrow, Harold mustered his dignified composure and said the blessing while everyone listened respectfully then responded with 'amen' group-fashion before the conversations started up again. However, Katherine had a feeling that was not the end of it. Sure enough, Gio grabbed the wrong eating implement, so did Vico who started using the dinner knife on his artichokes, while Cee was busy breaking open her bread roll with her fingers. She seemed to be making the most innocent mistake of them all, which some people among the various bread purists of society would not consider a mistake, that is, proposing it was more proper to break bread, but their household sided with the bread knife partisans who maintained neatly cutting the roll was the more polite way, therefore this uncouth ripping did not escape Aunt Martha —the blinders were finally lifting with those few telling displays. Well, if there was a bright side to it all, at least Gio didn't stick his gum wad under the table, Katherine thought

However, she realised that she had forgotten about 'guard duty' over her brother and her stomach froze as she wondered what might happen. The anticipated prank could strike at any minute. It was difficult trying to eat and join in the conversation, looking around casually, trying to see where exactly the practical joke would pounce from, perhaps the floral display, or in a sauce server. Mom, Pops and Gramps suddenly remembered too, and they also were somewhat on edge as they gingerly took a bite of their appetizers, then looked relived that nothing tasted amiss and proceeded ahead, one hurdle having been passed and no joke manifesting itself, yet. Katherine could have sworn she saw the corner of Steve's mouth twitch again as they gingerly tasted everything before continuing the conversations while politely overlooking the tableware foibles of their guests—that was the least of their worries!

Enjoying the hospitality, Vico praised the food again, and then wondered if they wouldn't mind giving him some helpful advice seeing they manufactured a good portion of the world's medications.

"I dread the fall and winter comin' with all the change of weather, yah know? It's my back, sciatica, one cloud comes in, and it hurts like hell! Do yous make anything for that?"

"Why sure," Gramps returned, "in fact, I've got an extra bottle of my own stash you can have, I've got a hip replacement and a cranky knee you understand, so that should fix you up."

"Hey, thanks! That's swell of yah. Can I just get it over the counter like if I need any more?"

"Um well, it's only available by prescription," Gramps then continued.

"Oh well, I'll get the doc to write me one then, heck, I'll get me a new doctor, I trust yah, and if he's been holding out on me and prescribing the cheap pills, he's gonna get it from me. Yah know, your meds are the best, your BronchioClear does the trick for my brother Freddy, bad tubes. Never had a good chest, always spittin' up stuff during the winter, nothin' else seem to work as good as yours. Just one dose, and he's made in the shade, he can breathe easy after that, I tell yah. Real good drain-o for the lungs, I tell you that."

"Glad to hear it," Harold returned, although feeling a bit sickened at that last mental picture, even if their cough syrup brand was receiving public approval. He felt his stomach ulcers could go on the blink any second. At the best of times, it didn't take much to start it going when hit with a queasy image, and that was quite apart from the stress he was feeling that night. Gramps however didn't want the unknown doctor to get into any trouble, which could range from a simple 'you're fired', to literally being shot and thrown into a back alley dumpster considering who was sitting at the table with them that night.

"You know, your doc probably didn't want to give these particular pills because they are pretty heavy," Gramps continued.

"No kiddin? No operatin' heavy machinery, that type of thing huh?"

"Right. One every eight hours, so careful on them, but no need for a prescription, just let me know when you need another bottle."

"Swell! Thanks," Vico beamed, while the quick look Harold shot his father betokened disbelief that he had just made that offer: handing out free pills to the new mob boss in their vicinity? Was he insane or something? However, Harold retained his composure, no doubt praying dinner would end soon so no more surprises could be sprung on them that he could not deflect.

At the other end of the table, Katherine and Steves tried to draw Gio out of his leather-clad shell, it was obvious he was compelled to come to this dinner to be polite, so the least they could do was try to make it less painful for him. At last Steves sparked some interest when he struck up a conversation on cars, it was one topic Gio seemed happy about. He wanted a Lamborghini, but was impressed none the less when he heard Steves had a Porsche sitting in the garage.

"Nice, and here I thought yous was a douche bag with that drip can n'all," Geo nodded, voicing his disapproval over the DeLorean parked out front while showing his approval at the unseen Porsche, "no trouble getting a couple'a nice look'n chicks with that. No problem if I got me a Lambo either, I wanted one for my graduation present, but my old man won't get me one unless I go to Uni too."

Although she wondered how Steves took to being misjudged by his favourite nerdy car, Katherine decided this little 'oil, gears and chicks' chat left her out and was glad they were all too busy at the other end of the table to hear Gio's glowing choice of vocabulary and topic of conversation. Leaving this section of the table to the guys, she turned her attention to the other just as the main course was served to see what had developed in that direction, (although she couldn't miss Gio's request for ketchup and then watch incredulously from the corner of her eye as he dolloped several blobfuls over everything, including the spinach, then smeared the processed sauce over his veal Piccatta). Since they were new to the neighbourhood, Vico and Cee were enquiring at the other end about what people did around here to leave off some steam.

"Anywhere to go fish'n'? Do you like fish'n," Vico asked, diving into his Fettuccini Alfredo, spearing the long pasta, then deftly twirling the fork around and polishing the payload off, chin ducking over the dish.

"Er, no. Well, I used to, not in a long while," Gramps clarified, "I'm more of a card man myself now, used to play more golf at the country club until my hip got at me. Harold here still plays a few mean rounds, when he has time of course."

"Oh, you have a club here! Great! I bet it's a real fancy place. Haven't taken my clubs out in awhile. Maybe it's time to dust them off. I'm also a Bridge and Poker man, cards are in the blood. I'll have to drop by sometime, could use a little relaxation myself now and then."

Harold shot another quick look at his father, Helen and Martha, who also looked a bit sceptical, full membership to the country club was open only to a special few who passed the stringent criteria of the governing board, not everyone was allowed in. How that visit would fare they could only imagine.

"Oh!" Cee piped up. "Sounds like fun. Do you ladies go there often?"

"Why, yes," Helen snapped back to attention, "it's nice to get out of the house, and of course, we hold several of our charity events there."

"Really! You know, that's not a bad idea, no more PTA for me now, not with little Geewoh going to college," she nodded thoughtfully as she ground her knife into her veal, while Gio looked mortified at being called 'little' as though he was still two and sucking his thumb, and in baby-talk no less. "It'd be nice to do something good too, when I'm finished getting settled of course. What charities do yous do?"

Martha reluctantly listed their current favourite charitable organisations, the Heart Foundation, the Wheelchair Association, for a time they helped with the World Vision drives during the famines in Ethiopia.

"Hmm, they are good causes … sure! I'll help out. Whenever yous need a hand, just give me a call."

"Er, okay, thank you," Helen replied, not quite sure how to show her appreciation.

"You know, that's good, real good. I like them education things too. Just look at Cousin Benny now," Vico jumped in, pausing his eating and pointing his fork at Cee for emphasis before continuing his Fettuccini twirling.

"Oh yeah! That's right! Cousin Benny has a year left to do, says he'd go stark crazy in the slammer if he didn't have that educational group keep'n him occupied, you know, the kind that teaches art and all that stuff? He's nearly got his law degree too, he'll be able to defend himself, probably better than all those no-good suits he's been hiring." The way Aunt Martha's eyes widened Katherine knew the blinkers were finally off all the way as it dawned on her at last who she had invited over, but Cee continued with her lively chatter and Aunt Martha was left to stew. "Great program that! We should help them. What's it called again? The 'Renfold Learning Indicative?', or was it 'Wyneold'," she trailed, trying to recall the name.

"Um, you mean the 'Reinold Education Initiative'," Katherine tentatively ventured.

"Bingo! That's the one!" Vico nodded, shaking his fork again enthusiastically, sending a few droplets of cream sauce her way.

"Yeah! That's it! You know about it?" Cee wondered.

"Yes, I do actually," Katherine replied, hoping they wouldn't go any further, but of course, there was no avoiding it now.

"Oh right, of course, numbskull," Cee noted, tapping her head. "I just didn't connect. You know, it really is a good program, you can tell him from me. How is your fiancé? It's a heartbreak, that's what it is," she continued, answering before Katherine could get in a word.

"Yeah, heard it all over the news, hit and run, and then nothin' lately," Vico continued. "so, they don't have a clue who dunnit yet, do they?"

"No, unfortunately they don't, not yet," Katherine confirmed, "the case is still ongoing."

"That's a shame. Hmm, if I recall, he experienced some problems in Chinkyland not too far back, right? What a bad rap! Lousy rat-eating Chinks an' cross-eyed Japs coming over here and buying up everything these days! Tell yah what, I know some people, who knows some people who knows other people, yah know what I mean? I could put the word out, see if they can dig up something for yah if yah like."

"Er, thank you for your offer, but for now I think it's best if we leave the detectives carry on their investigations," Harold returned, looking cool amidst this glaring racial slur to the Asian races, while Katherine guessed her father's interior 'alarm meter' was blinging off the charts where his ulcers were concerned.

"No problem, but whenever you get sick of the cops lettin' the 'all above board' end slide, just give me the word. There's ways of getting news, and there's ways of gettin' news, yah know?"

It wasn't long before Vico was asking for seconds, Mrs. Gonzales would certainly be relieved to hear that Katherine concluded, considering her apprehensions over the menu earlier that evening. In confirmation of her thought, another full hot plate quickly issued from the kitchen, plus one for Gio who too had now asked for seconds, (which he drowned in ketchup again), while Cee said she would save room for the next course, the salad, as Mrs Gonzales had prepared everything Italian, including the formal order in which the courses were served. Gramps eyed the black olive slices carefully as did all the family and ventured the first bite, chewing slowly, then gave a little nod to everyone sending them the 'all clear', letting them know their salad was free of black rubbery additives.

As they continued their meal, the conversation inevitably led to Katherine's artwork and the gallery now that Gerry's art program had been mentioned, and of course, the artists who were about to have special exhibitions in the next month or so. Cee seemed very impressed and would love to make a visit to her gallery, she had already been to a few in Chelsea and picked up some nice knickknacks for her sitting room, then insisted they all come over and see them one day, when they were unpacked of course, the new house wasn't quite set up just yet. Helen thanked her for her invitation, no doubt hoping along with the rest of them that tidying the new habitation would take quite some time. Katherine then realised that since return invitations were being exchanged already, she may have to do the polite thing and issue some to her grand events at the Walsingham Gallery along with her other neighbours, especially as Cee seemed interested: if the Becchinos found out everyone else in the Oakwood Meadows vicinity had been invited and they weren't, she could only imagine the consequences. When Katherine said she was 'going to the mattresses' to ensure her gallery remained successful, she never expected life to take her this seriously!

At long last, dessert was served, and no, Aunt Martha's special sponge cake was not swapped for anything synthetically bouncy. Although the cake had been duly checked in the pantry, they never knew when the family jokester would make the actual swap-o-roo, and a renewed yet subtle wave of relief went around the table as another classic gag of Steve's went unpranked. Naturally, Mrs Gonzales brought out Cee's embroidery-shrouded platter of *cannolis* for everyone to try since it would be very rude not to offer them. Katherine wondered where all this food was going, she was running out of space big time, but helped herself to one and laid it next to her piece of cake. Showing kindness to the Becchinos may in fact be a matter of life and death, even down to showing their appreciation for a cream roll. Well, it wasn't hard to be nice there, the *cannolis* were rather good, Gramps and Steves helped themselves to more than one. After coffee, Harold took the opportunity to end the pleasantries with an apology, stating he had an early day ahead of him and hoped they wouldn't mind if he excused himself from their company. Martha quickly took him up on his cue. The faster they could cut this night short, the better.

"Why yes, that's right Harold, and after your heart attack, you need to get some rest, doesn't he Helen?"

However, Helen didn't get to respond as Vico broke in.

"Whoa, heart attack huh? That's a bum rap too, we wont be keeping yous all up late then, gotta get up myself, early morning ahead too," he replied, wiping his mouth, then with a loud honking snort, blew his nose into the white linen napkin before plonking it next to his plate, shoving his chair back and lumbering up. Slowly, the host family rose from the table, a few eyebrows raised in silent dismay.

"This was real nice of yous, I'm stuffed! We haven't had a spread like this since Tia Zia's Christmas party. It's our turn next time," Cee declared.

"Oh yeah! You'll have to come over, or maybe, we'll plan something special out somewhere, our turn, our treat," Vico nodded eagerly.

"How nice of you, but there's no need to rush, whenever you're fully settled in," Helen returned, hoping to defer the promised treat for as long as possible.

As Mrs. Gonzales came to collect some of the plates, Gramps asked her to bring the extra bottle of painkillers he promised their guest, which Vico accepted with appreciation.

"Yous remembered. Thanks again! I like that, a man who can keep his promises," Vico said, shaking his hand as they meandered out to the front hall, Jasper getting some much wanted attention after being exiled to the hallway during the dinner.

"Oh, I'm sorry, we can't give you the promised tour," Helen jumped in, realising that this expected act of hospitality hadn't been completed yet, despite their earnest desire have this evening draw to a close as soon as possible.

"Maybe next time, we won't hold yah up, it is getting late, and we ladies need out beauty sleep yah know," Cee chipped in with a snorting giggle, much to Helen's relief. "Thank yous so much, we've had a real good time tonight, haven't we," she then prompted, prodding Gio in the elbow.

"Oh yeah, real nice. Thanks Mrs. W, real good chow, a bit too much cream sauce for me, but good."

"You're welcome, we're so glad you enjoyed it," Martha replied, looking put out, wondering when they would finally get to the front door.

At last, they made it, and with one final round of 'thank yous', their guests crossed the threshold and went to their car, the menacing bodyguard opening the door for them.

Harold slowly and deliberately closed the front door, the family waiting just a few minutes until they were certain the car was on its way down the drive. Once they heard it was at a safe distance, everyone immediately let out a breath as the tension rapidly deflated, while Harold sat in the nearest chair, clutching his stomach, the ulcers now refusing to be ignored.

"Somebody please get me my … oh thank you dear." He smiled weakly at Mrs. Gonzales who had already foreseen the summons and came running with a glass of water and the much needed medication.

"Pops, are you okay," Katherine exclaimed.

"I'm fine, just have to give this time to work," he said shaking out a pill.

"Here, I think I might need one, thank heavens that's over," Martha sighed as she grabbed the bottle from him and gulped down two without the aid of any liquid.

"I'm not sorry for *you*, you deserve it this time, Martha! Imagine inviting those people over, into our *home*," Helen noted as she sank down on the stairs, giving in to the shock and the clashing sense of relief they had survived the unexpected surprise regarding their guests' disreputable identity.

"How was *I* supposed to know who they were? I certainly don't spend my time reading about the criminal elements of the state, let alone ingratiating myself with them, and besides, I was *positive* they had said their name was 'Benino'," Aunt Martha wailed.

"The way they accepted your invitation should have told you something was strange, I knew I shouldn't have left you handle this on your own," Helen returned, "a bodyguard not letting you in, then to receive a phone call to confirm attendance, no personal 'how do you do, come on in … '."

Well, Katherine had to agree with her mother it was a bit odd, but obviously Aunt Martha was so insistent on being the first in the area to welcome them and beating the Fitzgeralds and the Williamsons to the punch she didn't pay attention to the strange way her dinner invitation was received with a bodyguard as the go-between and no face-to-face polite introduction.

"Unfortunately, the damage is done now," Pops replied, still clutching his stomach, "and now, we're caught in the predicament of actually having to do some ingratiating!"

"Aw son, it shouldn't be too bad, we just don't interfere with their 'business' and they will keep out of ours, that's how it usually works, right?" Gramps shrugged.

"Not quite," Harold returned, still clutching his stomach, "just to keep things on an even keel, we may have to play nice' with favours all the time, which means if they insist on joining the country club, and no one will recommend them to the board, you can be sure of that, we may end up having to just to stay in their good books and out of trouble! Oh God, this could have serious repercussions I can't even fathom yet. I can see it in the papers now, 'Walsingham Industries connected with the New Jersey mafia.'"

Helen and Martha gasped, they still hadn't got past the image of the Becchinos at the club—that was never going to work!

"That's not all, I don't think Gerry will be impressed when he hears that Carla Becchino wants to get involved with his education program just to keep herself busy now that her PTA meetings have come to an end," Katherine observed, wondering how on earth she was going to relate all of this to him.

"Geeze, aren't you guys blowing this out of all proportion? They may have only said all of that to be nice," Steves observed, shrugging his shoulders, only to get nagged at by Martha.

"No we are not young man, you do not understand the gravity of the situation and the magnitude of this nefarious encounter! And you Gregory, I'm surprised at you," she fired, turning to Gramps.

"Me? *Now* what did I do?"

"Why, to think you offered them free prescriptions! We'll never be able to keep them off our doorstep now," she cried.

"Hrumph! That's funny coming from the obliging neighbour who invited them in the first place," he returned, leaning back on his cane. "Besides, if I can keep him well doped up, he'll be out of commission and perhaps too looped to bother us. Our opiates may actually bring down this Napoleon of crime. We might even got a commendation from the Police Commissioner and medal from the Mayor, who knows?"

"Really," Aunt Martha returned, nonplussed.

"Seriously, we might as well make the best of it, be nice and we'll get all the free garlic sausages we could want, just as long as they don't make us one of those 'offers' we can't refuse. It's a good thing we don't own any prize-winning horses, isn't it," he continued, enjoying the opportunity of winding her up, especially after the night she put them through. Gramps seemed to be taking it pretty good trying to crack a joke, even if the rest of them were limp from the shock after the starchy night they endured for politeness' sake, which reminded Katherine … .

"You know, I'm glad you came to your senses and didn't play that prank of yours," she gratefully observed, turning to Steves, who was still quiet after all the hubbub, but smiling nonetheless.

"But I keep telling you, there *was no joke planned.*"

They all looked at him.

"Come on that's not like you," Katherine said, voicing their scepticism.

"Honestly! I didn't! Your idea to do 'nothing' with your gallery expansion gave me the idea do nothing myself, and boy, the results were funnier than if I had."

"So, you scamp! After all these years pulling stuff on us, you tried the 'cry wolf' routine, only backwards," Gramps began to chortle, now enjoying the funny side of the evening from Steve's point of view.

"Exactly. I truly didn't have to do anything, and then to find out who *actually* got invited for dinner, *that* I wasn't expecting. You should have seen yourselves tonight, it was priceless. I had a front row seat to an exceptional showing of the 'Eggshell Ballet En Pointe'."

"Steves! I'm gonna *kill* you," Katherine returned.

"Oh yeah? And guess what, I'm going to call you 'Nessie' from now on."

"Huh? What are you on about now?"

"You said earlier tonight that if I was lying, you must be the Lock Ness monster. I'm *sooo* going to enjoy holding you to that."

Katherine pucked him on the arm.

⚜

"KathyKathyKathy! It's so good to be back! I missed you!"

Katherine looked up from her paperwork at the front desk, startled by the exuberant greeting. Of course, she quickly recognised the voice. Lottie and Thomas had just arrived from Africa the day before, but didn't expect her to drop by this early in the morning before the arrival of the Gallery Gang. It was a comical sight as she saw Lottie make her way through the door toting a peculiar humanoid sculpture in polished black wood under one arm, a goatskin drum in another, while sporting a bushy native African headdress together with a brightly coloured beaded choker collar necklace. She was followed by the dark-suited Hulk in his gleaming sunshades who was commandeered as porter to the expedition evidenced by the large warrior's shield he carried fashioned from a hide and painted with simplistic geometric designs, the ensemble complete with the addition of a long, menacing spear.

"Hi Lottie, what on earth is that?"

"Oh, just a few gifts I brought back for you and Gerry. I didn't know what to get, so I thought these would make an interesting addition to your world-culture arts-and-bits section in your museum," she explained, setting down the sculpture and drum on the desk and scurrying around to give her a hug, still beaded up, the motley headdress perched on her head. "I forget what tribes these all come from, I've written it down somewhere, but never mind! Tell me all the news! What have I missed," she exclaimed

489

as she finally removed the native accessories and laid them next to the mawkish statue.

"The things is, I should be asking you! How did the trip go? You tell me first."

"Well," Lottie began, settling behind the desk. Apart from the business knots, which they untangled admirably according to her father the Captain, they had a marvellous time sightseeing, the safari was something else. There was a tense moment when a heard of elephants blocked the road and seemed to initiate a face-off with their jeep caravan, but then they turned away and calmly went on through the bush leaving the visitors record the close encounter with their cameras. They saw a pride of lions and a bunch of baboons too, the giraffes were just adorable, but something else happened she was dying to talk over with Katherine, and so sent the Hulk away to get them more coffee from the restaurant after he had laid down his primitive weaponry with the rest of the colourful offerings.

"You won't believe it, but Tom says he loves me, and … I think I'm really falling for him too," she admitted breathlessly.

"What? Wow, a safari romance? Just what *did* happen over there?"

Bubbling over with a sundry range of conflicting emotions from excitement to bashfulness, Lottie told how it all came about, that after escorting her to her room after an exciting day and an elegant dinner out, Thomas couldn't help himself and gave her a parting kiss goodnight, then feeling aghast he had let the moment take hold of him, said a rueful apology assuring her it would never happen again and was about to make a shamefaced retreat when she found herself holding him back by the arm.

"I mean, it didn't feel like it was because of too much wine, or anything like that. I could tell this was something his heart was breaking to do for some time, that was a kiss that cared, deeply," Lottie noted, almost losing herself in that moment for a second before continuing. "All I could ask was 'How long have you felt this way?' and he said, 'A long time, beyond counting the days.'"

"That is so romantic!"

"I know, isn't it," Lottie squealed, but then hushed up when the Hulk came out with the coffee. Katherine grabbed the tray then nodded for Lottie to follow her into her private office. Lottie was grateful for the cue and ordered the Hulk to stay outside and guard her colourful contributions to the gallery.

"Now, where were you?" Katherine was all eager to hear the next bit as they settled next to her desk, adding sugar and milk to their cups. "Oh yes, the unexpected kiss. Please go on."

"Honestly, I know we've always considered him part of the family, but I had no idea how he felt for *me* until then. There was this silence that seemed to last forever, but was really only a few seconds, then he didn't know how to explain himself and babbled on in this really sweet way about knowing he wasn't good enough for me and perhaps even a bit too old, then he knew how heartbroken I was over Alex and perhaps not thinking about getting involved with anyone at that time, maybe not ever again, he understood, but then wondered that if there was any hope at all … ."

"What did you say?"

"I don't remember exactly, but I *felt* something. Surprise, yes, but nothing uncomfortable or even awkward. You know how there's a part of you that just realises things without needing words? I suddenly knew that there could be *something* there, and I wanted to see if there was, I couldn't help but return the kiss, this time it really felt right."

"Lottie, you didn't … ?"

"Oh no! Don't get the wrong idea, it stopped right there, but I confess I was tempted," she trailed guiltily. "It's just that I realised that while I always cared for Tom, there were feelings lying deep underneath I didn't expect. However, I ended the moment first, and Tom agreed too we had better leave it there in case we really did something we might really regret and mess up everything now that I had given him some hope! Let's face it, it was happening a bit too fast, discovering all of this, it really was a surprise for both of us. I asked if he didn't mind if we started at square one and go at a slower pace. He didn't mind at all, well, of course not, but oh, I don't know what, I didn't think I could feel for anyone again, not after Alex, but there *is* something there … ."

"Then, give it a chance," Katherine advised, surprised herself that she was once again made a trusted confidant of a momentous epiphany in a friend's love-life. "So, what then?"

"Not anything *too* exciting anyway after that, other than a few hours to get away by ourselves, a dinner here, a long walk there, we did nothing but talk when we had a chance to be alone after the daily grind of business was taken care of, but it wasn't easy, not with an extra bunch of goons following me around."

"I suppose you did manage an extra kiss or two, I imagine." Katherine smiled as she sipped her morning brew.

"That too," Lottie nodded gleefully, before continuing with her heart's confession. "Tom is really a gentle soul, you know? He's so kind and attentive, more so now since … I don't know why I didn't notice before how he felt, not *that* way anyway. When I and Alex became engaged, Tom admitted it was a torment, but of course, he didn't say anything and hoped I would be happy."

"The poor man, I can imagine. To finally find out how you feel, it certainly looks like he's being cured of his misery now, right in the ICU ward."

"I know!" Lottie laughed. "I've never seen him look this happy before! But still, we're taking this slowly, as I said."

"I wonder why he just didn't say anything before you met Alex? Maybe he couldn't pluck up the courage?"

"Definitely. In addition to not knowing if I'd reject him or not, there are a few things that are ticked against a relationship from the get-go."

"Oh? How so? Your whole family loves him, the 'last of the great dependables' as the Captain calls him," Katherine pointed out. "Even Gerry said having the affection and the esteem of the in-laws is half the battle won, and he's right you know. I really like Tom too, he seems a real honourable guy, and if he's really stuck on you big time, he will always do his best to make you happy. What's not to like about him?"

"True, but you're not getting a few things," Lottie sighed, her mind now prey to the worries she had just addressed. The first issue was Tom had already pointed out he might be considered a little too old for her, not much to make a difference now, but maybe later the differences might create some strain, he even told her she deserved someone closer to her age.

"You don't think he's too old for me, do you?"

Katherine didn't know how to respond to that at first, but then realised what difference did age make if you were loved to that extent? Lottie nodded eagerly, what she said was true, but having a family might be made difficult, could he handle the demands of toddlers in the house?

"So, even taking things slowly, you're already thinking about the next step," Katherine smiled, Lottie's heart was always set on having a large boisterous family with the sound of little feet pattering everywhere.

"Yeah! He said he always wanted a family, but couldn't bring himself to start one with someone else if I didn't feel anything for him," Lottie revealed.

"Then there's hope for you guys, and age shouldn't keep you apart. It might just be an advantage. By now he's well settled and ready to have the family you both have wanted, and besides, it's not like he's rest-home material you know, he's not exactly dottering around! And for goodness sake, he's not *that* old to be considered your father, the man is just well matured, like a good bottle of Cabernet Sauvignon," Katherine pointed out. Lottie laughed.

"Oh, he's that all right! Mature and wise with experience," she agreed, "As much as I loved Alex, he was a bit of a hot-head. I was always unsure if he was really ready to have a family, it was like he was burning for danger. If you suggested strapping on a rocket suit and jumping off the Brooklyn Bridge, he might just try it. The thing is," Lottie continued, growing pensive again, "Tom is worried about the Captain, how he's going to react to this. Oh yes, Dad likes him *now*, but that doesn't really mean anything."

Katherine wondered what she meant by that. How could you like and trust someone that much, then not approve of the match despite Tom's more mature age?

"Well, you haven't seen Dad when he loses his temper, and I mean, he can be Mount St. Helens a thousand times over," Lottie explained, "he suddenly takes things the wrong way and BOOM! Run for your life! He can't help it at times, he just explodes, then the damage is done, almost beyond repair at times. Once when we were little, he frightened Gerry so much he wouldn't speak to him for a month. It took him a long time to get over it."

"My father can get explosive too at times, but I still don't see how … ."

"Hmm, how can I … ? Take what happened to Petey for example," Lottie continued, "before he went off into the priesthood, Dad was always dutiful to the Church, oh, not overly saintly or anything like that, but he always supported Mater Ecclesiae and was faithful to his obligations, that is, until Pete decided to do what he wanted to do, and then torpedoes away! Dad just lost it entirely. He dug into Petey something awful, us too for supporting his decision, then he stopped going to church after that, donations stopped, *everything* went, he wouldn't speak to the Archbishop after being such good friends for years. It was tough. I think it might be the same way with Tom. Dad thinks the world of him *now*, but he might find something in Tom's attentions that gets his bile boiling and … ."

"Oh. You and Tom are afraid he might be seen as an opportunist, considering his unfortunate family history and all of that."

Lottie nodded.

"He's never been able to shake the reputation pinned to him because his family business failed, and it was mostly his dad's mistakes thanks to some dishonest so-called friends, the demise of their business wasn't Tom's fault. But you know? Tom is not as bad off as he was way back when. He's never lost his knack for investments and trading, he's been busy building up his nest egg all this time. Oh, he probably won't start up his financial enterprise again, but he has enough to be considered extremely wealthy and not beneath me now, he told me so himself," she revealed. "He has assets all over the place! Still, I wonder if that would be enough to convince the Captain?"

"Oh dear, I don't know, but you can't run from this, you'll just have to brave him, when you both feel the time is right."

"I know, another reason why we want to take this slowly. We may not be engaged, but we both know a serious relationship will end there eventually, especially as we already want a family of our own. Poor Tomsy! I just hope when Dad finds out, he won't be at the receiving end of a cannon blast, me too for that matter." She sighed as she finished the end of her now lukewarm coffee. "Oh listen to me rattling on, what have you been up to? How's Gerry? I haven't seen him yet. How's the decorating coming?"

Katherine didn't know where to start, so much had happened since she and Tom left for Africa. First, she gave Lottie the latest progress report on Gerry's recuperation. This past week they had managed to get him away from the confines of the bed with the aid of crutches, even if it was for only a few paces forward. Lottie thought that was very hopeful, especially as they were all afraid at one point he might not be able to use the crutches at all, but Katherine admitted it was still rough going, he could barely manage with the nurse and physiotherapist hanging on to him and holding him steady. The thing is, they were only now going to start taking him off the pain medication, and not knowing the extent of his pain threshold yet, they still didn't know if his legs would work properly on their own, he might only manage a bare shuffle. The shrink came by a few times to see if he wanted to talk, but Gerry kept shooing her away. Lottie was devastated, but Katherine consoled her with the thought Gerry was still in good spirits and still cracking a few jokes, telling everyone this wasn't so bad despite the clumsy tottering and that he would be up and running in the New York Marathon in no time. Despite the uncertainty, he could still come out on top, his recuperation had only just begun. By now the Morning Room at Stonyvale was all set up and ready to welcome him home as soon as he was declared fit to leave the hospital, while she in the meantime was busy getting draperies made and some custom made furniture ordered for the penthouse. Lottie said she was dying to see it, but Katherine disclosed the best was yet to come, there was still one major thing to do, and would probably be the most time-consuming part of her 'Palazzo Project'—painting a Baroque style ceiling. She hoped Gerry would like it. Lottie gasped with excitement.

"You mean you're going to paint the ceiling too?"

"Yep, oh, nothing *too* fancy, I'd never get it done. I don't have the luxury of time to recreate the Sistine Chapel, but if I do a bit each night, the design I have should be complete when Gerry's ready to plan this wedding of ours again. I really don't know how I'm fitting this all in, especially as the Captain has commissioned a family portrait."

"So I hear."

Lottie wasn't sure if she was happy about that, she was as bad as Petey when it came to having her picture taken, and now she would be expected to sit really long for a painting! At least that project wouldn't be going ahead for awhile yet Katherine assured Lottie as something else had come up:

"I've bought the old factory next door, this place is undergoing an urban expansion."

"What? Are you serious? Tell me the news!"

Katherine had just decided that week to buy the factory after she talked to Gramps about his 'sweetened deal' with Mr. Norm 'Boomer' and her deal to pay him back, (she was correct, Gramps had offered Norm an extra sum so he would take it off the asking price), but Lottie hadn't heard about the factory project at all, so had to start from the beginning. When she was finished and had explained her minimal but *chic* factory look she had envisioned, Lottie thought the expansion was a great idea, but wasn't she taking on just a bit too much?

"Maybe, but I'm not going to push too much for an early Grand Opening, so I'll just take my time if I can. I've decided my new artists will just have to make do with the elegant side of 'Harvey Dent'."

"Okay, only you can decide if you're putting too much on your plate and when to stop putting more on. Just promise me one thing."

"Anything Lottie."

"Whatever you do, cease and desist calling this place 'Harvey Dent', or it just might stick." She smiled.

"Too late. Everyone's calling that side 'Harvey' now, but that's not the worst of it," she trailed before explaining she may have to invite New Jersey's foremost mob family to her opening and other gala events. Lottie's eyes widened as Katherine relayed to her the proceedings of last Sunday's dinner.

"Wow, I've missed a lot in the last week alone. Anything else I should know about?"

"Isn't that enough?"

"Definitely. But really! What is your family going to do? You can't get all chumsy whumsy with those people," Lottie exclaimed.

"That too may already be too late. Cee showed up at the Club yesterday and wanted to get charitable with my Mom's Bridge and fund raising group. She brought *cannolis* for everyone, and a ton of pastrami."

Lottie groaned in sympathy when she heard that last report, then caught a glimpse of her watch. "Oh flip! I've got to run."

"I guess that goes for me too, back to work," Katherine replied, only to see a comical sight from the security monitors: the Gang had arrived, but had not taken up their posts behind the front desk yet and were warily standing back a few paces. Apparently, the formidable mass of the Hulk standing to attention while guarding the office door from behind the desk, holding the war-lord shield and spear no less, with all the other colourful trappings laid out before him had deterred them from approaching any closer. Obviously, the unwieldy primitive armaments wouldn't fit on the desk with the other items, and rather than leave them in a precarious leaning position somewhere, the Hulk had no option but to arm himself while on guard duty. "We'd better go rescue them," Katherine observed as they stood up, while Lottie began to giggle.

"Dr. Livingstone, I presume," Esther drolly quipped as they finally emerged from the office.

"We come in peace," Suzy smiled.

"Have we been ambushed?" Dennis laughed.

"It appears the natives are restless today," Kevin replied.

"Hey, what's going on over there," Olivia wondered, popping her head out from the gift shop doorway. "I didn't know Kwanzaa is early this year."

"Don't worry, just some new additions for our Ethnic and World Cultures Collection upstairs have arrived, thanks to Lottie and Thomas, plus one over-dutiful body guard, which is not included," Katherine clarified before quietly advising Lottie, "Bye, have a good day, and remember, just take things one step at a time."

"Thanks Kathy, see you later. Hi, everyone, bye everyone one! Sorry to hold you up. Okay, Shaka Zulu, you may now trail me again," she then turned to the Hulk, taking the shield and spear and handing them to Katherine, still irked with the added security fuss in her life before heading out the door.

"Hmm, I suppose we should find a new home for these first before we tackle the rest of the day's challenges," Katherine decided.

"Are you sure? You might get a better estimate for the new access ways if Mr. Harding sees you brandishing weapons at him," Suzy laughed, aware Katherine had already called the contractor to overlook 'Harvey Dent' next door and expected him that day.

"You have a point, er, or maybe *I* do," Katherine returned, looking up at the spearhead and seeing the funny side. However, it was only a few new archways in the walls, it wasn't a major job to begin with, she could lay her spear and shield aside. A good thing too, she didn't want to frighten off her prospective customers. Already their first visitors were entering and beginning to browse around. Kevin was pleased to be given the task of assigning the tools of the warrior's trade to their new quarters along with the rest of the new acquisitions in the appropriate cabinet in the museum collection while everyone assumed their posts for the morning, it promised to be a productive day.

ଔ❖ଓ

It was one of the rare times that Peter looked forward to coming in to the family offices, knowing Tom and Lottie would be back at work that day. For awhile, he had a feeling something was wrong, that they could even be in some sort of peril if he wasn't mistaking the feelings imparted by the interior nudging he kept getting, and not knowing what could be wrong when everything sounded okay on the phone during their daily calls, decided that the only recourse available to him was to pray. Whenever he had a moment during the day, he turned his thoughts On High, doubling his efforts during the calm of the night. Then, the wary feeling dissipated the last week or so, replaced by an interior peace indicating that everything was going the way it should and he could relax his watchful vigil.

Peter was the first in after the lunch hour, even beating the ever-punctual Mrs. Clarke to the building. Walking into the office, a strange figure met him on the desk, a statue of the Madonna carved in black wood that was tribal in origin, a gift brought back from the wanderers no doubt. He couldn't help but smile at the strange elongated form supposedly representing the Queen of Heaven with its angular facial features and clasped pointy hands that looked ready to execute a karate chop rather than represent an attitude of prayer. Never mind, it was the thought that counted. He began to unpack his case and was interrupted by someone else who also arrived early. Of course it was Tom knocking on his door, toting several files pertaining to his recent trip, ready to give a personal report of the 'globe trot', but also to say 'hello, long time, no-see', hoping Peter had come early.

"Welcome back, Mr. Quartermain," Peter cheerfully greeted, shaking his hand, amused to see that the pale indoor-loving office executive had bronzed a shade or two in the African sun while tracking down container trucks and sidetracked flower consignments.

"Hey Pete, as you can see we've returned victorious from our quest," Tom reported, glad the trip was successful in more ways than one. "Oh, Lottie picked this out for you, she wanted you to have it right away and so left it for you for this morning."

"Thank you, I know you helped to pick it out, or rather, patiently suffered through it all while she tried to make up her mind which one to get." Peter smiled. "Forget the files, tell me how everything went."

Tom laughed, Peter had his sister down pat! However, before Tom got a few words out, suddenly the interior nudging Peter had received awhile back made perfect sense, the veil of the Unseen lifting for a brief moment as Tom started with their travels in Kenya first. Peter politely listened as Tom continued on, but it was what Tom *wasn't* telling him that he was interested in. When the business end of the reports had been delivered, he couldn't help but ask:

"So, when are you going to pop the question to Lottie?"

"Er ... I ... we ... we're just taking things one step at a time ... how did you ... did Lottie ... ?" Tom stammered.

"No, and relax, I just do, and, it's about time too. You shouldn't have bottled up your feelings like that for so long. Timid love never won fair lady."

Tom was still in shock and could only just sit there for a moment, but then found his voice.

"Er, you're not against it, me falling for your sister? I'm not exactly a spring chicken any more."

"You're not a winter rooster either," Peter returned, "and of course I'm not against it. I'm very happy for both of you, plus your resolutions to keep things balanced. I trust you can continue to wait to bring things to another level until *after* the wedding."

"Er, yes, of course," Tom agreed, knowing what he meant, stunned once more Peter knew about their close brush with temptation too. True, it would be difficult to keep things on that balance after waiting for so long without any hope, now that he knew Charlotte was on the brink of falling in love with him, but somehow he also knew that he would never be able to look Peter in the face again if he didn't keep things on an honourable footing with his sister. As strange as it seemed, disappointing Peter would be far worse than provoking the Captain's wrath. Although Peter was a few years younger, Tom deeply respected him, he had this inexplicable quality of paternal authority and wisdom that elicited respect and confidence, admiration even. Often he found himself talking to Peter as if he was his own father despite the age difference, it was comforting in a way.

"I'm glad I've earned big brother's approval."

"You'll have Gerry's too, and our mother's. About Dad, I understand, there's uncertainty there, but I know he wants to see Lottie happy, and isn't it about time you were officially made a member of the family?"

Tom smiled.

"I can already guess she wants a church ceremony, so I know the conditions," Tom informed him as he wasn't Catholic. "If it means locking up all our future kids in a Jesuit monastery, so be it. Anything for Lottie."

Peter laughed.

"Nothing need be that drastic. Just as long as you don't mind having them raised in the faith, you have my blessing, and a church wedding."

"That's good to know. Now, if only I had the Captain's blessing," Tom wistfully mused aloud, glad he could finally get this final worry out in the open.

"That I cannot tell how it will go, but you don't have to tell him just yet, you and Lottie need to spend some time together, enjoy that first."

"Will do," Tom beamed. "Funny, I thought priests were dead against romance."

"Only the unbalanced kind."

"Okay, okay! I get the picture."

They were interrupted by Lottie who immediately rushed in and gave her brother a hug.

"Can I have one too," Tom enquired to her surprise. "Don't worry, he knows, don't ask me how, but he does," he continued, answering her startled look questioning how he could leave their promising relationship out of the bag so early.

"What? Really?" She gasped, looking up at Peter. "Oh! Does the Captain … ?" Lottie gasped again in alarm although grinning bashfully, now that the secret was out.

"No, not yet, and you'd better give Tom that hug before someone else comes in." Peter smiled. "And thank you for the statue, it's … very unique."

"I know, isn't it? I though you might like it, but oh! I couldn't help but tell Kathy this morning, is that all right," she asked Tom, switching the topic in a confused muddle once the hug had been delivered.

"Sure, why not? We really shouldn't have to hide you know," he observed. "Dating is not a crime, not the last time I checked."

"No, but the Captain may have a different law book," she returned, unable to forget the grilling her deceased fiancé had received on various occasions.

"Don't worry, you will have quite a few advocates that will come to your defence," Peter assured them, with a nod, "in addition to yours truly, I know Mom and Gerry will be happy for you both."

"Might as well tell them the next time we see them," Lottie decided, "they might be irked that they're practically the last to know, other than the Captain. Oh, maybe we should just get it over with and make the announcement to him we're seeing each other." She then sighed resignedly.

"Er, perhaps doing the formal thing might smooth things over. I could go and ask your father's permission to court you, we just won't let him know I've already started," Tom suggested in a quiet, yet slightly comical tone.

"Oh yes, that's the way to go!" Lottie beamed. "But if you're going to do it, you'd better do it right, drop by the manor to see him personally, not during work type of thing."

"You will be in my prayers," Peter added.

"Thanks, Pete." Tom laughed. "So, since we're going to do this properly, we shall see each other properly. May I pick you up for dinner, let's say eight," he enquired, turning to the object of his affections.

"That sounds like a winner," Lottie agreed.

By now, the floor was beginning to bustle as the staff members that had left were returning after the lunch shift. Taking the commotion as their cue to get back to work, Tom and Lottie promised as they left to drop off the new estimates drawn up by the Acquisitions Department later, which Tom was still going over with Lottie in the process of showing her the ropes. Nothing but a file of reports that were delivered that morning concerning the new replacement delivery vans currently under consideration for the routes in Jersey City, they just wanted his opinion once the tutorial was finished.

"No problem, I'll tell you what I think, then bring them to Gerry after work."

"Great, see you later," Lottie replied.

Well, well, well!

Peter stopped to muse for a moment. Another romance was on the wings in the family, and he was truly happy for his sister. Everyone wondered if she would ever be able to move on after Alex, feeling guilty she was betraying his memory somehow if she began seeing anyone else, but no doubt with Tom, it didn't feel that way to her. Perhaps it was due to the advantage they were already good friends, not to mention Tom had also weathered many sorrows in his life, their mutual need to experience love and happiness again were drawing them together, and Peter couldn't see why they shouldn't see if they could find that happiness with each other. Age compatibility didn't necessarily guarantee a successful marriage, nor did age disparity promise a miserable one either.

Hmm, time for him to get back to work too. Not many messages left for him that morning as he thumbed through the slips of paper, therefore, not many extra things for him to handle. Just as well, he already had a meeting that afternoon with a Canadian textile firm interested in leasing warehouse units in Toronto not to mention enquiring more about their competitive shipping and distribution rates to the US. The Captain would certainly be proud if he could land that contract for them. Things were looking good with their end in Canada, he might suggest they consider expanding in that market, warehousing would be a good investment, demand for storage space was always at a premium in their distribution hubs, and if things continued to pick up State side ... no doubt Gerry was thinking along those lines as well, he had a knack when it came to surging trends and envisioning when expansion projects were needed.

There was a knock at the open door, Mrs. Clarke had returned from her lunch break, bringing him his favourite French roast blend in a to-go cup, plus another thoughtful item he wasn't expecting, a small package of walnut nutmeg loaf, his favourite, all sliced and ready to eat from a boutique bakery that had just opened up. She had heard some of the secretaries and aides raving about their new muffin blends with the crazy frosting artwork that was too pretty to eat and had to give it a try.

"Everyone's recommending the place, thought you might like to try some of this," she said, laying the offerings on his desk, inadvertently giving a quick quizzical look to the new statue.

"Thank you, Mrs. Clarke, but as always, you shouldn't have, and yes, you can see my sister has brought back a memento."

"If you don't mind me saying, she has a strange taste in souvenirs."

"Can't be helped, I'm afraid."

"Or exchanged."

Peter couldn't help flicker a smile on that one. It was true, Lottie liked to bring back something national or ethnic that reflected the countries she visited, one time everyone got cuckoo clocks after that skiing trip to Switzerland with her friends, another time they all ended up wearing berets for a day when she arrived back from one of her jaunts to France.

"So, anything important come up this morning," Peter continued.

"Nothing out of the way, it's all right there on your desk, oh, except Mr. Linacre from Pinelake Limited wanted to know if it would be possible to push back your meeting from three to four."

"Okay, that's not a problem."

"Shall I call to confirm?"

"Yes, please."

"Will do."

Peter was left to prepare his notes for the meeting once Mrs. Clarke had made the call and informed him the new time was a go. Hmm, this looked exciting, landing a contract like Pinelake would be a multi-million feather in their cap, Gerry would either be impressed or grow impishly competitive and attempt to beat that with something better in the hunt for new clients. If things were really like the old times, he and Gerry would be neck and neck right now. A little good natured sibling rivalry always kept things interesting, getting one over on each other then laugh about it come the end of the day.

Reaching over for a second file without really looking while he read the one already in hand, he was startled by a sudden movement from the black Madonna. It wobbled then fell right in his direction, knocking over the tall cup and sending a rapid java flow over the desk. In that split second between tumble and overflow, Peter foresaw what was coming from the corner of his eye and jumped up, but was not quick enough to escape the inevitable, some of the coffee had hit his chest, creating a small cascade running down his front. Did he tip it while reaching for the file? Annoyed with himself for his clumsy inattention, he grabbed for the box of tissues situated behind him on another table and began to mop up the desk before the brown wave spread further and made its way to the computer equipment, cornering the last of the spill as best he could with his limited supply of tissues, wet tacky spots lingered in puddles on the desk. In addition to some of his documents, the cake was a soggy casualty of the brown tsunami and had to be discarded. He gave the Madonna another quick wipe, removing the ring under the base that had formed from a few coffee traces he had missed. No, how could he have tipped it? He certainly didn't feel he had bumped into anything as he reached for the second file. The strange part, the statue was unusually heavy for its size, so even if he did brush against it with the folder, how could a bare tip send it toppling around like a kid's punching dummy? Odd.

Putting the statue down, he next worked on dabbing his front. Wearing black had its advantages, but on this occasion he would not be able to hide the accident as the tissues quickly crumbled into white sludgy particles that imbedded themselves into the material as he rubbed, plus he was bound to smell like old French roast and stale hot milk as the afternoon wore on. Great, this cassock was dry-clean only too, no way he could do a quick clean up in the executive washroom, he would have to make a run for it and change at the rectory. The worst part was the whole desk was now sticky from the mishap, nothing for it but to have Clarke call maintenance and send someone up to clean everything properly before the wood was destroyed. Served him right for not starting work with a prayer he reflected as he tried to wipe his hands off before summoning Clarke. Good thing the meeting was pushed back. Divine Providence, it had to be.

He reached for the phone, then stopped for a moment, studying the statue again. Hmm, no such thing as a coincidence, maybe there was a message there, things were getting just too comfortable, the little black figure that looked more like it belonged with a troop of bush hunters than a convent had given a reminder that he should not let himself get too cosy in the comfortable groove of the executive life again. He also remembered he needed to bless the statue too.

"Okay, I guess I deserved that." He smiled. "I get the message, thank you, but did it *have* to come through baptism by *café au lait*?" Well, coffee was supposed to wake a person up after all!

All humour aside, he knew this double-life between office and rectory just couldn't go on. A priest had no business being in the worldly sphere of business. How long more, he wondered, glancing up at the painting quietly gazing down on the scene. Best to leave things in Her hands, she seemed to be handling things pretty well.

Once he had blessed the statue, Peter called in Clarke and gave the next set of directions: to please call maintenance, and also if she wouldn't mind making more copies of the reports that had been drenched and made illegible by the spill.

"Of course, but let's try and get you cleaned up, hand soap might …
"

"I'm afraid that won't work on this, I'll have to take an hour off. If Tom brings the latest acquisition estimates before I come back, tell him I'll get to them when I can."

"All right. I will."

"Thank you."

Grabbing his two cases, he quickly left to do some damage control to his wardrobe, bumping into the Captain on the way out.

"Ho son! Where's the fire?"

"No fire, unexpected coffee shower, must go and change out of this. I'll be back as soon as I can."

"You didn't get burned did you?"

"No, wasn't that hot, but I'm drenched."

"Okay, you have permission to leave the ship." Mr. R chuckled over his shoulder as he watched Peter exit the premises, his expression resembling a disgruntled cat that had been rudely dropped into a water trough without warning.

Peter arrived at the rectory to be greeted by the wafting aroma of over browned bread and burning cheese. By the smell of it, Mark must have come home for lunch. It was a wonder the smoke detector wasn't blaring all the time with him! Maybe he had better check the batteries in that thing … later though. He had enough to do right now. Hmm, that's odd, wasn't Mark supposed to be helping out the sisters in the soup kitchen? Never mind. Better get changed. The thing was, he had finally ditched some of his older cassocks that had gone a little threadbare, which left him with a change of two daily ones and the rest of the formal items his mother had thoughtfully given him. No way he wanted to break those in yet, and besides, they were a little too formal, even for his important business meeting. That meant he would have to wear the other daily cassock, which was currently hanging in the laundry room waiting to go to the cleaners. He had only brought it down there that morning, planning to take it with him tomorrow after he had a chance to ask the other fellows if they had some black suits that needed to go too. For now, it was far more presentable than what he currently had on, so it would have to do for the afternoon. Rushing down the hall, he was curiously surprised when he heard a rattling and bustling coming from the laundry area to discover Mark was indeed home and making himself useful.

"Hey Pete! Whatcha doing here so early?"

"Needed to change, then I've got to head back. What are you doing?"

"I'm planting daffodils," Mark teased.

"Ask a stupid question. Of *course* I know what you're doing, which is much appreciated." Peter laughed, it was his turn this week, whenever he could get to it. "What I mean is, what happened to your soup-kitchen ministry? Did they rapid-fire the food out to everyone and throw out the dishes? I'd thought you would still be out helping with the clean-up."

"They said I wasn't needed today, they had a few more volunteers come that they weren't expecting, so that was that. Thought I'd help us catch up on a few things here, then go hear confessions," he explained with a shrug as he dragged a load of towels from the drier and began to fold them.

Peter smiled to himself as he began to help with the towels, no doubt the nuns did some fast recruiting to keep the Dodgy Chef from entering their kitchen. Peter suddenly realised they didn't have grey towels before today, they were supposed to be light blue, and they were crispy to the touch.

"Um, Mark did you set the temperature to 'high' on the drier?"

"Yep, dries everything much faster that way. Oh, and I found this," he replied, sounding pleased with himself as he took a bottle down from the shelf. "'*Removes tough stubborn stains and household grime*,'. Those pre-wash stain removers aren't any good, so I thought I'd add this. Odd, this brand doesn't say how much you should put in."

Of all things, Mark had dashed heavy-duty chlorine bleach into the wash. That explained it. However, Peter realised that the washing machine was still churning with a second load of 'something' sloshing around, and then quickly looked behind the door where he and the fellows usually hung their black items destined for the cleaners. With dismay he observed the hook was bare.

Mark, you didn't … .

"No, I'm not *that* dense, duh," the industrious towel-folder replied, reading Peter's expression. "Bleach and black don't go together, everyone knows *that*. Hmm, now I find out not so well with blue either … ."

Well, maybe bleach wasn't put in this particular wash, but Mark was still semi-hopeless with the fine art of knowing what should get put in the machine. Peter lifted the lid, stopping the churning mid cycle to survey the damage. Sure enough, he had dumped the Holy Bachelors' black shirts and pants plus his cassock together with all their underwear, turning the once white privies into a sickly shade of motley grey that strangely matched the crispy towels. If there was a bright side to this, at least they wouldn't be seen. Unfortunately, Peter was now bereft of a less formal cassock for the afternoon as it was completely drenched.

"You do know that it says 'dry clean only' on the label," Peter intoned as he dropped the cassock back into the machine, it was too wet to drip dry at that point.

"Er, does it? Dang it, I'm sorry, but it looks like it washes out well. Since you need it, are you sure you just don't want to pop it in … ?"

"*No!*" No way did he want to end up with toast for apparel! Even so, setting the temperature to 'blast furnace' on the drier wouldn't get it ready in time. "Listen, I'm sorry I can't help you finish this up, but just promise me you'll hang the cassock to drip, and turn the drier down on the other items? I don't think the other bachelors like their shirts well done, medium rare will do."

"Sure thing, Pete."

Hmm, using a cooking analogy to get through to Mark was probably not the smartest thing in the world to do, but he couldn't think of anything else less dangerous on the hop as he had to change and rush off. However, his choice of wardrobe was now restricted even further. Nothing for it, he thought as he went to his room, half cloak it is.

"May the Force be with you," Kells greeted with humour as the elevator doors slid open.

"And also with you."

Peter could only join in the humour as no one in the offices had seen him in a caped cassock yet, he was bound to get a few curiosity-induced reactions.

"Pulling out all the stops are we? You're only having a meeting, not convening Vatican III," his father noted, bumping into him on the way. Clarke looked up from her desk as she heard them approach.

"This? Wait until you see me in my blazing buttons," Peter returned as they walked along.

"Ho there! Reverse all engines! Since when did you make archbishop?"

"Never I pray! But I'm allowed coloured trim now, only a touch mind you. One of the perks of being a Monsignor, Third Class."

"No say? But of course, new rank, new stripes. Seriously though, you look all business, no messing about, which reminds me," the Captain then added, going a little quiet, "the chancellery office called not long after you left. Could we step in for a moment?"

"Of course."

Peter followed his father into his office and closed the door. The Captain didn't wait for them to sit down.

"I know you've got a lot on your mind with that meeting, but better spit this out now. This wasn't just a call to check up on you. Foley called me personally."

"I see, that means … ."

His father nodded, a resigned, acceptance-laden glance saying it all. This was the day the Captain had been dreading: the summons had come calling his son to return to his pastoral duties.

"However, you don't have to rush back tomorrow," his father continued, quickly resuming his matter-of-fact comportment, "you have until the end of this month. Foley needs you to get back before he has to join the pope for this Youth Day convention, or whatever it is in Denver. He's giving us these few weeks to wrap things up here as best we can."

"Still, it's going to be a push to try and get Lottie up to scratch as quickly as possible, and Gerry certainly won't be able to take up all the responsibilities of his post by then, we can't rush his recovery."

"I know. Thank the stars for Tom, he's been pulling double-duty everywhere. He's earned his bonus this year, I can tell you that. Oh, which reminds me, he asked if he could come out to the manor to speak with me privately. What could be so important he just couldn't see me here about it? Have you an idea? I'm in the deep briny blue without a chart on that one."

"Maybe he needs to discuss something as a family friend," Peter continued trying to keep the reason for Tom's urgent request for a visit under wraps, however, his reply was cut short by a knock on the door.

"Seems you've got a point there, can't have a private conversation with my own son these days. In a minute," the Captain bellowed at the door before resuming his conversational tone. "Talking about private meetings, Foley also wondered if you could drop by his place tonight for dinner at the usual time."

"Tonight? Sure, I think so, provided the meeting with Mr. Linacre from Pinelake doesn't take too long."

"Don't worry about that, I'll have Tom cut in if needs be, how's that?"

"You're the boss."

They were interrupted again.

"Stop that infernal knocking, or I swear, I'll keel-haul you!"

The handle turned, a timid Lottie poked her head in.

"Oh, of all the … get in here, girl! Why didn't you say it was you," The Captain then retorted grumpily, albeit with the blustery part of the tempest taken out of his sails.

"Um, has anyone taken a look at these van estimates yet," she ventured hesitantly, not yet daring to cross the threshold further than a foot or two. Peter calmly beckoned her in.

"No, but you can give me the file now. I have some time yet before the meeting."

Poor thing. It wasn't her fault the Captain was in a hollering mood, she just happened to be the hapless brunt of their father's melancholic aggravation now that the inevitable summons had struck, ultimately setting a deadline for his full-time departure back to the cathedral. She also knew her father enough to guess something was eating at him and cast a quick glance at Peter, who knew her own anxiety: Tom didn't approach the Captain already about their seeing each other? Is that why he's upset? Peter quickly gave a little shake of his head, a wave of relief dispelling her nervous expression. Of all times for the Archbishop to call, Peter hoped that Tom didn't plan to go to the manor that night, there was no telling how the wind would be blowing across the Captain's sails then, fair or foul. Peter excused himself and headed back to his own office, Lottie deciding to go with him, the Captain needed to cool off!

"What was that all about," she wondered. "Are we getting audited, or what?"

"No, but he probably wishes it was the IRS. The Archbishop called earlier."

"Oh! That means … when are you heading back?"

"Two weeks. At least it's not like I'm leaving everyone in the lurch this time," he consoled as he opened his office door and let her enter.

"That explains it. He's gone all Black Beard! But I know how he feels, we're going to miss you so much Petey, not seeing you around here I mean, but I suppose it was time, you couldn't stay to help out forever … ."

The door closed, leaving a shaken Clarke to silently mull the overheard news.

"Maybe I should have said this was an *informal* gathering." Archbishop Foley smiled when Clare showed Peter in that evening, somewhat amused by his new caped cassock.

"It's a long story."

"I bet. Come, you've arrived just in time, dinner is ready. So, I take it your father has told you we need you back full time," as they went to the dining room, the table set for two.

"Yes, starting the first of next month. Everyone is grateful you allowed me to help out for as long as you have, it is an unorthodox situation."

"We do preach upon charity, and charity should be practised close to home first, right? Your father tells me Gerry is just beginning to get back on his feet. That certainly is good news."

"It is, but he can't walk yet, not without help, and he's not off his medications, but it's a start."

"Thank God. I'll offer my Mass for him tomorrow. So, are you ready to tackle your parish work full time?"

Peter knew why he was asking, to be pulled back into the sphere of the world he had left behind would normally be a huge temptation for someone else, but his vocation had not diminished, he had no desire to leave the priesthood. He was ready to return, and reassured Foley on that point.

"That's good, because you're certainly needed. The Pope comes for only three days and you think it was a conclave that was happening! Not to mention we have the Feast of the Assumption to prepare for."

Foley continued chatting with Peter about the various logistic upheavals the Youth Day event was causing as dinner was served, it was wonderful to see all the young attend, flying in from all over and overflowing with zeal when about ninety-five percent of them would probably never get to see His Holiness up close anyway. However, another problem had come up: the chaplain assigned to chaperone the local youth group along with a few of the parents who were going had to back out two days ago, and the archbishop wondered who he might suggest could fill his place, they were going to need priests at the event to hear confessions considering the amount of people they expected to attend. Peter noticed he wasn't asked to go, so no doubt he would be filling in at the chancellery or other services in the cathedral, something like that. He wondered whom he could suggest, everyone he knew was already over strung in their own parish work, but what about … ? Yes, Mark was perfect, the only one who hadn't quite found his niche in the run of things. This would be a great experience for him, in any case, he was great with kids having raised a few of his own, and since travelling as a chaplain on this type of pilgrimage did not require cooking or laundry to be done, the kids would survive.

Foley thought Fr. Mark was an excellent candidate and asked Peter if he wouldn't mind informing Mark to get together with the group as soon as possible. If this worked out, he might consider assigning him to one of the local youth ministries.

With that one challenge solved, the usual topics came up as dinner progressed then ended with coffee served in the sitting room. Yet, despite the polite and jovial conversation, Peter knew from experience that unless his family were invited, these private dinners were rarely for social reasons, they were convenient pretexts to discus more pressing or urgent official issues in private. Asking for suggestions on who could be assigned as chaplain to the bereft youth group was something that could have been handled over the phone, so that was not the reason he was invited tonight. He hoped to be proven wrong, but eventually the small talk led around to the purpose of this unofficial summons:

"Speaking of which, Pete, there's something I have to discuss with you." The Archbishop hesitated for a moment before continuing, "I have to ask, what has been going on at the altar rails not to mention your confession times? Barring revealing any sins, I've been getting some odd reports, and I'd like to hear your side of things. Is it true you once booted a whole group from the confession line?"

It had begun.

Peter wondered when that would be brought up, in fact, he was surprised he wasn't called to task much sooner, normally the boom would be lowered fast and heavy if it was any other priest, but since the Archbishop was close with his family, he was going to receive every benefit of the doubt. While he did not want special treatment, Peter nevertheless was appreciative of the delay. He was not one to lack confidence, but on the matters of his spiritual gifts in the confessional he felt awkward and strangely exposed when they manifested themselves, and even more so when asked to talk about them. Now the awkward and inevitable situation to explain his seemingly peculiar actions could no longer be avoided. True, he had prepared for this, but still, there was no escaping that humbling yet necessary sting of interior spiritual mortification. Now he finally had to reveal to his superior his gift of discernment and leave the outcome in the hands of Divine Providence.

"The simple truth is, I can see the condition of a sinner."

"Now Peter, you know what the church teaches about judging others. You just can't … ." He was about to continue, but then realized that wasn't it. Peter was never one to jump to quick judgements. The archbishop shifted a little in his seat and cleared his throat. "Seriously? Are you saying you have the discernment of souls?"

Peter nodded.

"Have you always had it?"

"No, not right away. I think the first time it happened was about six months after my ordination. At first, it generally happened when hearing confessions, on some rare occasions I'm permitted to see a soul's condition outside those times, usually if it's a spiritual emergency."

"So, you saw something in the souls of that group you turned away, something really serious."

"Yes, beyond lacking purpose of amendment. Pure malice. True, I must admit what I saw actually got my temper up, I could have been kinder in my reaction."

Yes, in fact he yelled them right out of the church! But, maybe a sharp jolt is what they needed. One man came back a few months later, admitted to him he had been absolutely right, could see exactly where he and his friends were heading before they even opened their mouths, and apologised for coming to test him. That rebuke had helped him change his life for the better.

Foley sat back, pondering this for a moment. At first, he had thought all the whisperings about Peter were a bunch of maudlin figments of the imagination dreamed up by the lonely biddies and eccentrics of the congregation desperate to add a little supernatural animation into their lives, hoping to be those chosen few privileged enough to be the first followers of the next Padre Pio before anyone else discovered him. But *here*? This was something that happened in other parishes, but right under his own nose in his own cathedral, and with someone who was once a man of the world? Peter Reinold! Then again, these charisims were sometimes given to those who appeared to be the most unlikeliest of candidates, even wealthy Lazarus was a close friend of Christ! He certainly would never forget the day Peter first approached him about his desire to enter the priesthood, it was one for the record books. The archbishop had to indulge his curiosity.

"It only happens at confession, for the most part you say. So, you can't just flip it on or off yourself?"

"No, it's not something I can control, only use properly when 'it' happens, so to speak. And I can't describe 'it'. It's like standing in front of a stage with a closed curtain. Someone unseen draws it back, you find there's a scene behind that you never knew was set up and you stop to take a look. Sometimes the curtain is drawn slowly, sometimes in a sweeping rush, then closed again."

It was a poor analogy for the Unseen, but it was the best he could come up with.

"And you as the stage prompter helps when something goes amiss," Foley concluded.

"I suppose you could say that, yes," Peter agreed.

"And now, what about the incidents before Communion? What are the extra blessings for? I've been hearing that you're performing an exorcism right on the spot!"

Peter looked up. Either gossip had gone out of control, or someone wanted to cause him serious trouble, but he wasn't worried. It was to be expected, knowing the human condition.

"Not exactly. I can sense when people are getting choked by 'something' before confession, trying to keep them from revealing everything, now, this 'sense' is happening before Communion. That 'something' is trying to keep people from going, or, tempting those who are unworthy to go up. I say a quiet prayer invoking St. Michael and then bless the congregation again. It seems to help lessen the problem, and that 'something' makes itself heard as its confronted with the blessing, but I'm certainly not performing a full exorcism in the explicit use of the term."

"I must admit, this certainly is an unexpected turn of events. Has anything else happened at your Masses that I should be aware of?"

"No."

Good thing he only asked about his Masses! There were a few other *private* things, strangely prophetic dreams and the odd visit from the dead a few years ago, not counting the bizarre occurrences that sometimes happened when he went to spiritually clear a house during his exorcism ministry, but that's not what the Archbishop was really asking about. As long as other *public* manifestations weren't occurring such as a second Lourdes or the visible materialization of the stigmata, then his superior just didn't want to know.

Contrary to what many thought, the authorities of the Church dreaded the littlest whisper of a new public apparition or miracle. Unless they were pushing forward the canonisation of someone already enjoying their heavenly reward, any sign of supernatural favour to the living meant years of interrogations and investigations into the matter to ensure that the case was spiritually authentic and not a fake, not to mention the annoying arrival of curious hordes, both sceptics and faithful alike, that would come to witness the heavenly miracles if they could no matter what was pronounced, be it canonical approval or formal denunciation. Few in the hierarchy wanted to deal with that be the outcome good or bad, it was a massive pain in the neck that just threw a monkey wrench in the daily run of things and made a parish look like another candidate for 'Ripley's Believe it or Not'.

Peter could already see it in the way Archbishop Foley couldn't completely disguise his relief before he lightened up the conversation a notch or two, then drew the evening to a close not too long after that with the usual goodnight pleasantries, stating his understanding of how they both had a busy day tomorrow and they needed their night's rest and wouldn't keep them up any later now that the matter had been explained. Well, all was now said and out in the open. Peter shook hands and wished him a good evening, leaving the archbishop alone with his thoughts—and mull things over he certainly did.

Unorthodox situations, here was another one for the books. He often received complaints from parishioners all over the archdiocese with the usual gripings from the laity who decided to skip going to their own local bishops and come to him directly: a priest said something that wasn't exactly what Christ taught having gone a little enthusiastic while preaching off the cuff or had decided to leave out a reading, or did something not by the books during the consecration, or choir members in a parish church were in a tiff with the parish priest over who should be directing, or Fr. So and So had been harsh in saying Mrs. So and So was making a mess of the altar linens, or there were complaints about priests who were a bit strict and came down a little heavy in their dealings with the lay members, and this was a tiny number in the growing list of the less serious aggravations. Yes, the petty things could go on, but never expected to deal with anything on the order of the mystically mysterious, (or hoped he wouldn't have to!) especially with Peter.

Of all times! Considering Peter's extensive experience in the global business world in addition to his theological erudition, he had long before come to the conclusion that he could prove quite an asset concerning administrative matters on a large scale, and was about to put forward his recommendation to His Holiness that he be promoted to auxiliary bishop in one of the larger dioceses of New York, a mere grooming for better things to come. Without being aware of it, Peter bore a compelling stamp of authority about him, and considering his excellent background, the choice of promoting him with the hope he would one day make Archbishop of New York seemed the most natural one to make. Of course, the archbishop knew that despite his family history and privileged social status in society, Peter didn't want all these fine promotions, which was blaringly obvious after he left all that behind to enter the priesthood. A position bearing that magnitude or influence was not what he wanted, but Foley also knew that out of obedience this spiritual son would assume the new duties placed before him. He had planned to put in a word or two for him, letting his

Holiness know how suited Peter was and how they might have to do a little persuading for him to accept the mitre and crosier, but now to his chagrin something unexpected put paid to all these plans: he had the gift of discernment, but rather than stay hidden in the confessional as was usually the case with these things, it had leapt out into the open and was making a public scene. The stories and reports over the years were coming in too fast and furious to be a lie, and Peter was always forthright in everything, he wouldn't make up something like this. Still, they couldn't have a bishop, auxiliary or otherwise causing this kind of stir. True, Peter's Masses were receiving record attendances, but now he wondered was it all from theatrics? He certainly didn't want his cathedral turning into a fairground. It was bad enough this spiritual son was so persistent on becoming an exorcist, at least Peter wasn't levitating into the air like the mystics of yore!

Now, what to do. Making him a bishop was out of the question, for the time being anyway. Perhaps these displays would stop of their own accord, there was no way of telling. The problem was, he didn't want to whip him out and hide him in some obscure parish in the boondocks until it did, he was needed here, and it just wouldn't look good to send him away from the archdiocese cathedral. While transfers were common in the Church, the tongues of the ultra-traditionalists could get set wagging that Peter was either being unfairly suppressed by a pro-progress superior, or the usual gossips might assume he had been moved on for some horrifying transgression, and he certainly didn't want Peter or himself placed in an untruthful compromising situation like that. He had enough real cases of vocations going south to try and smooth over as it was. Not to mention he didn't want to rub Richard Reinold the wrong way now that there had been a miraculous reconciliation between father and son. He had a hunch that certain over-generous anonymous donations to the maintenance fund that reappeared after their paternal-filial reunion would dry up should anything that even bordered on a demotion or a reprimand happen to Peter. Foley was at a loss what to do, until he realised a localised transfer wouldn't be too bad, he could place him close enough to keep an eye on him and clear the circus from his own cathedral at the same time, after he attended the World Youth Day that is. There was so much to handle. Where to place him though? That was the question.

03 ❖ 80

"Hi Bossy Boy, I hate to call you, but I've got something you need to see, it's urgent."

"What? What's wrong, Sammy?"

"Sorry, I can't tell yah, not on the phone, you'll have to see for yourself," Sammy replied, his Jimmy Durante accent overshadowed with an apologetic tone that sounded as though all belonged to him had contracted the black plague.

Wow. Peter wondered what on earth the urgent matter could be, he had barely walked into the building on his last day at Reinold Enterprises, and already he had some emergency to deal with at Yard One. Sammy rarely called him like this, and to catch him right at the front desk in the lobby no less, it *had* to be urgent. Did a warehouse collapse, or something flammable in their hazardous material shipment unit go up in smoke? Peter left the usual instructions with the staff at the desk to tell everyone upstairs where to find him, then quickly turned around and headed straight back to the elevators not a little concerned about the unspecified emergency facing him. Did it have to end with a headache, Lord? It would have been nice to tie things up neatly before he had to say farewell.

Pulling up rather fast in his old parking space at Warehouse One in Williamsburg, he wondered what was wrong, everything seemed to be running okay, the same non-stop chugging of rigs and forklifts in and out seemed normal, and he didn't see any smoke billowing from anywhere! Bolting into the industrial building through the back door, he was met by an apologetic Sammy dressed in his customary hard hat and reflective jacket gear.

"Okay, where's the fire? What's happened?"

"Urm, I hate tah yell yah, but nothin'. Not an emergency anyway."

Peter was puzzled until Sammy explained he wasn't supposed to say anything but try and keep him busy for a few hours. The Big Boss had a surprise farewell party getting set up, and couldn't think of a better way on the hop to keep him away from the city building.

"Honestly, I didn't know what tah do, I couldn't make up an emergency, and since I've got permission tah do whatever I have tah do tah keep yah busy, it isn't often I get a few hours tah bum around the middle of the day in the depot yard, so I thought, hey? A few of the guys around here might like tah say farewell too. So, we have a fine lunch waiting in the cafeteria, if that's okay."

Surprised, that sounded fine by him. Dan and Leo were among the well wishers, plus a few familiar faces who were now retired but had trained him back in the day how to drive the trucks and forklifts were also present.

Sammy, or perhaps Dan and Leo must have contacted them. It was nice they wanted to come and say their goodbyes. They also didn't want him to leave empty handed. Peter didn't expect presents, but they didn't want Ben Hur to leave without some mementos to help remember them by. The first souvenir was a black T-shirt with the following caption printed across the front: '*You don't scare me, I was taught by nuns.*' He then received a bumper sticker that read: '*You can't catch me, I'm on a mission from God*', a quip that was a bit old by now thanks to Fr. Jenkins, but still funny. He then received a huge coffee mug with a cartoon of a priest sitting in a confessional booth holding a mug with the following caption: "*Let me recaffeinate, then tell me your sins.*" They certainly had a sense of humour.

When it was deemed it was time to let him go, they said their farewells. "And please, don't let the Big Boss know I told yah about the party," Sammy implored.

"I'll try not to, but you're asking me to, well, lie!"

"I know, Heaven forgive me!"

"Bye Sammy, and thanks. I'll think of something. You take care now."

"Okay, you too! Bye bye, Bossy Bo … um … Monsignor! Say a prayer for us, will yah?"

"You know I will."

Driving back into the heart of Manhattan, Peter wondered how he could keep from letting them know he was on to their surprise without lying, but it wasn't hard to actually be shocked when he was greeted by a thundering 'SURPRISE!' followed by cheers and a lively tone-deaf choral rendition of 'For He's a Jolly Good Fellow' despite having a musical ensemble present. The Captain had certainly gone all out, he was expecting maybe something small up in the boardroom and he wondered how they could set up this elegant catered event in the grand Art Deco lobby complete with tables and floral arrangements in the few hours he was 'kept busy'. Of course, they had to keep the dress code semi-informal as only a few fortunate guests had time to change into something appropriate for the surprise part cocktail, part buffet party. Some attendees were just getting off work to join them and had to come in their executive wear, in fact, a few were still arriving, but odd timing didn't matter. It was touching to see so many wanted to come and help make his last official day there something to remember. Not only were his family and all the executive staff present, many other surprise guests were there, including Katherine, and of course Leroy who came on Gerry's behalf. The Captain came forward, gave him a thumping slap on the back, while someone who had brought a camera to record the event was blinding him with the flash.

"Hey! What's all *this*?"

"You didn't think we'd leave you off into the briny blue without so much as a 'fare thee well', did you," his father replied before drawing closer to him for a moment, continuing quietly, "it's not often someone gets a second chance to do things right, so here's the send-off party you never got."

All Peter could do was return a heartfelt smile and grip him firmly on the arm. Although not one for parties, coming from him this meant so much. He next gave his mother and sister a quick hug, the Hulk impassively looking on as he continued to guard Lottie from a moderate distance. After a champagne toast, the social mingling began, the musical ensemble complete with xylophone now setting a genteel tone for the party after the man of the evening was duly welcomed.

I'm so glad you're here," Peter greeted, finally making his way to them after so many wanted to stop and say 'hello', shake hands and wish him well.

"It's a shame Gerry couldn't be here too."

"Oh, but he is! He said he didn't want to be left out for a moment, he's on a cell phone," Katherine explained, looking around, wondering where the specially designated phone was currently at, it shouldn't be that difficult to find: someone had thought of sticking a picture of Gerry on the back. After two seconds, Leroy found it with Tom.

"May I cut in? Thank you!" He jumped in, whisking it away from Tom's ear and darting off to Peter. There was nothing for it, Tom tagged along and joined their merry gathering.

"Hey! Ben Hur! Or should I now say, Young Arius of Rome? How are you enjoying the party," Gerry enquired, the volume turned up so they could hear him.

"Very much, I wasn't expecting anything like this," Peter chuckled.

"Ach! Gerry! It's nothin' short of a tomb here! Good thing I'm around to liven it up," Leroy called over Peter's shoulder.

"Don't listen to him, I for one am having a good time," Peter reassured his brother, while Katherine intoned to the red-haired imp;

"Easy Lee, none of your 'Technicolor Extravaganzas'."

"No one has a sense of humour. Besides, can't arrange a Hawaiian indoor-outdoor beach party in a pinch anyway. Instead, what about a thumpin' tequila arm wrestling match? Or whisky musical chairs? We have the perfect floor for it, I think I can find us some wheelie articles, just to make things more interesting," Leroy mused aloud, running the sole of his shoe on the potential playground area, checking its gleaming slickness.

"Be good now," Lottie commanded, "or you'll make us regret we invited you."

"Perhaps another time," Tom further prompted.

"All right, I'm just joking. I don't think anyone here would appreciate it anyway. Speaking of 'another time', that reminds me, I know Gerry will be lepin' and kicking his heels by New Year's, so you're all invited to me next big boozy bash."

"Er, aren't you a little ahead of schedule? The last day of July and we're thinking about December thirty-first," Katherine heard Gerry observe over the line.

"Sure, everyone should have something to look forward to, right?" Leroy reasoned.

"Gee, and I get upset when stores start putting up Christmas baubles in November," Katherine noted, "but now that we're on this topic, I'm going to brace myself. What *exactly* will be your party theme this year, Lee?"

"I haven't set m'heart on anythin' yet, but the mention of wheelie whiskies and tequila wrestling just gave me a brilliant idea, what about a cowboy rodeo? Everyone can come in fancy dress as cowboys and indians. We can have a right shoot 'em up! Yeah, and I could get one of them clockwork buckin' bull things. Smashing!" Leroy's eyes brightened with this sudden light bulb moment.

"Mechanical bull? Oh no *way*, Wyatt Earp. You aren't getting me on one of those," Lottie declined with a laugh.

"And I bet the thing would fling you off in a second," Katherine added.

"Rubbish, I have practical experience, I'll have you know," he replied with flair.

"Since when," Lottie wondered.

"When I was little I used to ride me grandad's cows around the farm in Galway. Great *craic* it was."

"Somehow, riding Bessie the dairy cow and getting up on a bucking bull, be it ever so mechanical, isn't the same thing," Peter replied drolly.

The conversation was jovially interrupted when Peter noticed an unexpected but familiar face show up, Fr. O'Conner. Apparently, someone wanted to add more to the surprise for him that evening by inviting the Holy Bachelors.

"Hello Pete m'boy, you've got one nice party! Mark would have come, but Saturday night he has the youth group Mass and of course, ye know he can't cancel. He'll try and make it afterwards if he can. Sure, he's happier than a leprechaun in a shoe shop since he got that new ministry. He says 'hello', and so does Jenkins, you know he's stuck too, has a wedding rehearsal tonight. Hello ladies, and as I live and breathe, if it isn't Leroy McFadden, you divil you! After all these years! Where have you been, laddie," he finally ended, giving him a friendly handshake.

"Hey Father! Oh, here and there. I believe you haven't met Thomas," Leroy replied, obviously glad to see another friendly face from his school days, yet, was on the sheepish side judging by the quick deflection in making introductions. Peter could easily guess why. Like all the boys from school, he had a soft spot for his former sport-loving, wise-owl mentor and would do anything to make him proud, but in Leroy's case these days that 'anything' did not include going to confession! Peter had kept O'Conner in the loop about his and Gerry's friends who had kept in contact over the years, but Lee in particular was always on O'Conner's mind as well as his own. When would he ever settle down? Leroy was a right worry, he was! All those school Mass sermons on sticking to the straight path, giving up ye'r sins, and aiming for the pearly gates now going to waste! Even so, O'Conner had an unquenchable sense of humour almost as bad as Lee's.

" 'Here and there', eh? Between the two, I hope you haven't made any further contributions to the local stars and stripes since that fateful day," O'Conner commented, merriment twinkling in his eyes.

"No, but I must confess Father, that was my finest moment," Leroy quipped.

Gerry could be heard laughing over the phone, while Peter just shook his head, but couldn't maintain a serious face. Lottie was threatening to get a case of the giggles as she quietly explained to Katherine and Tom that Leroy once snuck in to the convent during lunchtime, rifled Mother Bridget's bloomer drawer and ran a fine navy blue specimen right up the school flag pole that night. The student population had a whale of a time at assembly the next morning when no one could sing the national anthem without bursting into hysterics and it had to be called off, the first time ever in the history of the academy. It was a wonder he wasn't expelled!

"You *didn't*." Katherine turned in surprise.

"I sure did! They were still wearing the old habits then, even the granny knickers down to the knees. What a glorious decoration on the pole that was, I tell ya!"

Katherine couldn't keep a straight face after that. Of all people, Leroy could get away with murder.

"I hear they still talk about it at the school." O'Conner continued to chuckle.

"What did I say? My finest hour, worth every bit of detention."

"Oh, I don't know, there were a few other glowing moments too," Peter noted with an eyebrow lowered followed by a wry smile, looking as though he were caught between wanting to have a good laugh and itching to throw Leroy into a confessional box if it were close.

"Ah, mum's the word! If ye tell any more, Tom here will judge all of us Paddies by this yokel standing next to me," O'Conner pleaded with good humour, nodding over to Leroy.

"Don't worry, I know there's no one else quite like Mr. McFadden," Tom assured him.

"Okay, just what else did he do?" Katherine was curious to know.

"Let's say, the school was never the same before nor since he graced its hallowed halls," O'Conner poetically implied.

"Let's see, there was the time *someone* locked Sister Agnes in the teachers' bathroom, and blocked all the toilets before hand," Gerry began, while Lottie continued, "then we had the winter of stink bombs hidden in the heating system, but I have to say your most scheming act was sabotaging the Christmas pageant," Lottie finished, looking a bit disgusted with him.

"Yes, I did it, but it's no use *you* gettin' all high and mighty, Miss Milky Moo! I saw ya laugh ye're head off that night. I gave you ye're sweet revenge too," Leroy pointed out to Lottie in a 'you should be thanking me' tone of voice.

Katherine, Tom, Peter and the padre wondered what that was all about, including Gerry who hadn't heard this detail before and listened with interest as Leroy finally gave them the dirt on *why* he became the Grinchy mastermind behind the dastardly deed one Christmas oh so long ago. When in the bitty years of grade school they performed the same old play in the pageant without any innovative alterations, the same people were cast in the same parts, but what made it worse was that Sr. Ursula, the Master of the Seasonal Ceremonies, insisted on holding auditions every year and putting everyone through their paces. After suffering through the hope-filled angst of wondering what part you might get in the Nativity scene, everyone's expectations were ruthlessly dashed: she had her favourites for certain roles and was not about to tweak a thing if she could help it. The first year was fine, you made it into the play after all, plus in the second year you already knew your lines should you be graced to have a speaking part, but after two more years a nine year old Leroy was fed up of the sham, he was always stuck in the back end of that hot old smelly donkey gear and wanted to be promoted, at least to a shepherd just once before he became too old and was shoved ahead to next year's choir with no acting roles. T'was no use, Sr. Ursula cast him as the jackass once again. Then, poor Lottie for her first time in the play was cast as the dumb ox stuck in another hot pongy outfit, and Leroy wasn't too impressed with that either since smarmy little Laura Snyden who stole from everyone's desks during recess (and could never be brought to justice as it was her word against theirs) was always cast as Mary. If anyone deserved to be the cow, it was that thieving little git Leroy figured, so he got the brilliant idea of giving the baby doll playing the new arrival a hearty feed of sticky cola before the show. When Mary tried to follow the stage direction of wrapping the 'poor craytur' in swaddling clothes and laying it in the manger … .

"It was a gas, I tell ya," Leroy ended.

Katherine gasped, wondering how he could be so wicked to do that, even Steves with all his pranking had his limits, barely. Yet, that was not all to the story: the Three Kings got more than they expected when they arrived from the far East for the snowflake machine was stealthily laced with gag itching powder.

"So that's what it was all about! If ye wanted a change to the original script, ye certainly got it," O'Conner observed. "We wondered what had happened. It looked like ye were all struck with St. Vitus' Dance. For a moment, we thought Sr. Ursula had done the unthinkable and snuck in a boogie-woogie number. I know I shouldn't have, but I never laughed so much in all me life!"

"Ah, but Sr. Ursula figured out who dunnit. I was forever banished from the stage, even from the choir. There went m'acting career," Leroy returned in a tone of mock regret.

"Well, what did yah expect," O'Conner replied.

"You may have lost your future Tony Award, but you both got your sweet revenge," Tom noted.

"Everyone paid the price though, itching for a week," Peter recalled.

"Hey, at least you were no longer Joseph and were safely warbling in the choir number afterwards, but what about *me*? I was the Moor King and painted up with brown grease paint, the stupid powder got plastered all over my face and I couldn't rub it off during the show," Gerry retorted over the line.

"You suffered bravely. Comrade, I salute you," Leroy teased his old friend.

"One for all and all for one," Lottie couldn't help adding. "On top of it, Laura was so shocked with the dowsing she got from the doll, she jumped out of the stable and right under the snow shaker, she got a doubly whammy. I couldn't stop laughing, she really deserved to be taught a lesson."

"Hey Lee, you said her last name was Snyder, that's not," Tom trailed.

"Congresswoman Snyder, the very same," Leroy confirmed with a nod before taking a sip from his glass.

Katherine couldn't help but laugh at that last detail.

Eventually, they were politely interrupted by members of the social gathering, each wanting to introduce them to someone they just had to meet and pulling them aside, or offering if they could get them a refreshment between the introductions, meaning the time for mingling was periodically interrupted by trips to the bar. Tom and Lottie made sure Leroy didn't get out of hand as they carried Gerry around via the cell phone, while Fr. Conner got chatting with the Reinolds, Peter making sure Katherine met everyone else now that she was semi-officially a member of the family. The rest of the board members were delighted to be introduced to her at last. There were so many new faces, she wondered if she would remember them all, at least the names were familiar thanks to the guest list Gerry had helped her to make for her upcoming art events. Then of course, there were those she had already met while visiting the office, Kells and his new girlfriend stopped to chat, Mrs. Clarke also attempted to make polite conversation with them for a few minutes, answering Pete's enquiry if Mr. Clarke was coming to which she replied he wasn't due to some snarl-up at his office before being pulled off by someone else into another group. Everyone wanted to meet and greet, and ask all the expected questions. Naturally, they had all heard about the new expansion for her gallery, and wondered how it was coming along. Katherine politely gave her latest 'public' news since they had already been sent invitations to John Fielding's showing set for the last Friday in August: the grand opening for the newest section of the gallery was going to happen the end of September featuring Stansislov's newest canvases. They could expect the next set of invitations soon.

At last, it was time for the buffet. Once they had filled their plates, Peter and Katherine sat down at the head table and waited for his parents and those assigned to their table to arrive. Alone for the moment, Peter finally had a chance to ask how things were going and how she was holding up considering all that she was handling.

"I'm fine, even if stretched for time. Jiff was kind enough to offer to have his showing before the Grand Opening, which gives me some space to get ready for the next event, but it's cutting it tight! Gramps must be pulling some strings along with Charlie because the legal work went fast enough getting the other side of the building annexed to my half. Oh, there's a million things to do yet, or so it seems. Thank goodness my decorating is *chic*-minimalism, it's keeping things simple."

"I often wondered if it wasn't a stroke of calculated genius among the minimalist artists, making the style fashionable so they could earn a handsome living painting as little as they could," Peter noted.

"I often wondered that myself," she smiled, "but don't get the wrong idea! It's turning out better than I expected, the *chic* element is showing more than the minimalism. One thing is for sure, it's saving me time with a minimal amount of effort."

"All joking aside, are *you* okay," he asked again, a little more quietly. He had the instinctive feeling something was worrying her.

"Oh yeah, I'm just tired, that's all. I'm still working on painting the penthouse ceiling during the evenings when I can in between the decorating. I'm glad I asked Mrs. Moritz if she wouldn't mind doing dinners again, she's saved me more time by not having to go out. Gerry found a wonderful cook. She's a dear, even if she always looks a bit grouchy."

"Mrs. M. has had a long paid vacation since mid-March, she's probably glad to be getting back to managing the kitchen."

"True, although she's worse than our own Mrs. Gonzales. She doesn't want me messing in her drawers or pots. I'm glad I didn't change the kitchen."

"That means you've gotten off to a good start," Peter observed. From what he had heard from Gerry and from the few times he met her, Mrs. Moritz didn't like change, she had a system that worked to a T, thank you very much. He recalled Gerry laughing two weeks after he had hired her, saying that with raising five kids and a worthless husband when it came to household tasks, she didn't want a spoiled bachelor like him telling her how to fry the bacon, stock a pantry or stack a dishwasher. So, he left her to it and wasn't disappointed. There was the rare time he hired caterers on holidays and the like when he had invited someone to his humble abode during her days off much to her chagrin, but she overlooked the trespassers in 'her' kitchen since he was a generous and easy to please boss, plus kept things tidy when he did feel like raiding the fridge at night.

"I'm glad about that, but Pete, here I am jabbering about my stuff, when it's you this party is about," Katherine noted. "I know everyone wants you to have a good time, but this must be tough too, having to say 'goodbye' again. How are *you* holding up?"

Deflecting to daily hassles, then asking about him, it looked like she was not ready to talk about her own personal problems. However, he knew she would come for advice when she needed it and decided not to push.

"Never better, really," he answered. "Certainly not like the first time around, it's a grace to have a send-off like this," he noted, looking over to see his father laughing with one of the board members before joining them at their table.

"Hello you two. All by your lonesome? Where's the rest of the crew?"

"Probably caught up with someone," Peter noted, looking around. Sure enough, one of the ladies invited to the event was chatting with his mother. Eventually she broke away and joined them as well. Tom and Lottie were still meandering down the buffet line, Tom trying to have a conversation with Gerry, holding the cell phone in place against his shoulder with no hands as he attempted to fill his plate, Lottie also adding to the conversation, interjecting a phrase or two towards his ear acting as a phone holder as they went along. Sophia smiled at the sight, since the last week she was now in the loop and glad to see another romance was flourishing in the family. Sadly she reflected, the Captain was the last to know. Since Peter had been given the summons to return to his parish duties, Tom wisely had found a pretext to avoid coming to the manor as he requested, leaving the Captain in the lurch since it would not be prudent to bring forward another drastic change in their family circumstances so soon. At least Mr. R. decided not to press into the matter, for which Tom was grateful. Even if he was helping to keep him in check, Fr. O'Conner in the meantime was having a grand time with Leroy, which Peter was glad to see. They were obviously catching up on old times, judging from the jovial exchange of expressions, head nods and the odd burst of laughter. If anything, they helped to break the ice, people were a bit stiff in the beginning of the evening despite the fact most of them were work colleagues during the day, but had mellowed with those two gadding about, introducing themselves or being introduced, making themselves quite at home. At last, they made their way to the table.

Since the buffet supper party was semi-informal, people had already started nibbling standing around or seated at the tables, going back for seconds, each to their own, so no ceremony. Everybody tucked in with

Peter and Fr. O'Conner quietly saying grace under their breaths first. Tom and Lottie finally joined them, laying the cell phone down on the table, speaker option switched on, thereby including the walkie-talkie member of the event.

"So, love birds, when are you going to stop sneaking about and tell the Old Captain," Mr. R dropped unexpectedly as he jabbed at a piece of lettuce that continued to elude the tines of his fork.

Everybody stopped eating and looked at him.

"What? You think I can't see things too? I'm not blind you know, those two have been as thick as barnacles since they came home," he continued, looking up for a minute and giving Tom and Lottie a nod before retuning to his plate. "I had my hunches, but when you wanted to see me then quickly declined, the game was up."

"Er, sir," Tom stammered, completely caught off guard, trying to ascertain if the Captain was mad, pleased, or simply awaiting his reply so he could detonate afterwards. Lottie also looked apprehensive, obviously thinking the same thing. After all their attempts to keep things hush hush! Only Leroy and Fr. O'Conner didn't feel the same heightened sense of silent panic, wondering what this was all about. Curious as ever, they waited for events to unfold.

" 'Er sir' nothing," Mr. R. continued, liberally peppering his fare a second time while everyone remained suspended between a state of disbelief and trepidation. "If anyone has been blind for a long time, it's our Lottie. Sorry my dear, but the man has been pining over you, it's about time you figured it out."

"Dad?" Lottie was shocked at this revelation. True, in the past month or so she at last realised how much Tom had cared for her, but to think her father knew it long before then! And, to sound as though *he approved*! "You're ... you're not mad we're together?"

"Why? Should I be?"

"Er, I ... ," she stammered.

"Not you too! Don't be gaping at me like a codfish. You couldn't do better than Tom here, I'm glad to see you've finally come to your senses. You're young. You can't live chained to a dead man's memory forever. Pardon me for saying, but I don't know what you ever saw in that other no-good, God rest his soul. Since there was nothing I could do to get you to drop him back then, all I could do was to put the fear of Davy Jones' locker into him so he'd shape up and treat you properly, but now, things have finally worked out the way they should have."

"Whoa, if *this* isn't news," Gerry finally broke through the line with astonishment. "Hey Pete, did *you* see this coming?"

"Nope, this is a revelation to me too," Peter admitted, quite pleased as well as surprised to have witnessed this unexpected paternal approval. Despite having an interior sixth sense so to speak, that didn't mean he knew *everything*!

Astonishment gave way to sentiments of joy and the instant desire to wish the couple well that further added to the already festive atmosphere. Liberated from the heavy weight caused by their now apparently groundless fear, the relief at the realisation they no longer had to conceal their feelings was irresistible. Lottie and Tom instinctively reached for each other's hand with undisguised affection amidst the well-wishers. Katherine recognised the warm fixation they shared, yet, they were sharing more than a glance as she also knew very well. A life-changing moment had swiftly opened their eyes and became a force propelling them onward that they had no power or will to resist: that inexplicable, electrifying bolt from the blue announcing that this was The One, the person you were meant to love and be with for the rest of you life. In Lottie and Tom's case, they had already known each other for years, no need to enter a conventional courtship to discern if they wanted to be together. He had already set his heart on her, while now in addition to loving him as a friend she was in love in all the romantic significance of the word. They had always wanted to start a family of their own, the years of waiting, hoping, silent torments, wondering if it would ever happen was now at an end, since they knew it would inevitably end up becoming something serious, why delay any further?

"Charlotte, will you ma … ?"

"Yes, Tom," she replied simply, before he could finish.

"Blimey! Did what I think I saw happen just happen?" Leroy beamed.

Their kiss in sight of the company confirmed the proposal had indeed been made and accepted, she not minding in the least that he had been taken unawares and had no ring with him while seizing that serendipitous moment.

"Hey, what's going on," Gerry inquired through the line.

"Someone is enjoying a big croissant and hot fudge cake," Katherine explained. Happy for Lottie and Tom, the scene also made her heart give a little pang for Gerry at that moment, wishing her own Lancelot was near.

"Okay, belay that, it's hard enough seeing her grow up," the Captain retorted to Tom and Lottie as he buttered his roll, while Sophie was quietly wiping the corners of her eyes, this happy event such an unexpected surprise. Tom and Lottie drew apart with a satisfactory smile to each other, not regretting that public display of affection one bit. "I guess you won't mind dropping by the manor like you originally planned. Come tomorrow, we have a lot to discuss," he continued quietly to Tom.

"Since the match has been approved and the proposal accepted, shall we go ahead and make the announcement," Peter inquired.

"But Pete, wouldn't that trump your own party? This is your night, it wouldn't be right," Tom pointed out.

"Nonsense. Let it be trumped. This is a reason to celebrate."

"Yes, let's announce. Why, everyone's here! We've even got Gerry on the line," Lottie agreed eagerly, caught up in the elation of it all. "Dad? Petey? Who wants to do the honours?"

"You go ahead son, it may be my prerogative to do the announcing, but it's your party after all, and your idea. Go make your sister happy, that's an order!"

"Yes sir, Captain sir." Peter stood up, clinking his wine glass, bringing everything to a momentary standstill, a field of curious faces turning in his direction.

"I know it's a little early for all the speeches that everyone had planned to make tonight, but I have an announcement that must come first. Come you two, stand up … my dear sister, Charlotte, and our good friend, Thomas Winthorne, are as of this moment engaged. Would you please all rise as we toast their future happiness."

There was a sound of delighted gasps and 'oh's!" among the guests as the news was broken followed by the rasping of chairs as glasses were hastily topped up and raised. Peter turned to his father, remarking he was not going to usurp *all* his prerogatives, leaving the honours of the toast to him.

"Right, then," he agreed, clearing his throat. "To your new life: as you embark on this new voyage and navigate your future course together, may your days be calm and clear with few squalls, may the nights be bright with friendly stars to guide you, may there be plenty of joy and good cheer on deck, and may you be blessed with many healthy, happy future additions to the crew. Bottoms up!"

The lobby resounded with calls of "Hear! Hear!" and hearty good-natured laughs at the nautical references that the Captain could not refrain from using. It may not have been Shakespearean, but the newly engaged couple were very content with the toast considering that only a few moments ago they were fully convinced he would have fired a few warning shots across the bow at the prospect of them even seeing each other. Now with the news formally broken to the guests, Tom, Lottie and the rest of the family at the table were besieged by people coming up and wishing them well, shaking hands and generally keeping them from getting to eat anything past a morsel every few minutes, but nobody minded. Peter was certainly pleased with this meteoric twist to the event, turning what was to be a semi-melancholic yet enjoyable goodbye gathering for him into a real family celebration at the company. It felt good to be leaving Reinold Enterprises on this high note.

Of course, when it was assumed everyone had enough to eat, the Captain began to clink his glass, brining everything to a standstill once more. It was time for the goodbye gift planned for Peter.

"As you all know," the Captain began, "Peter here has moved on to other pastures, and we wish him all the best. I'm not one for long-winded rambles, but it only seems fair, son, that you get the credit due you for being a valued member of the company. We and the members of the board wish to give you a token of our esteem for all your dedicated years of service, for which we thank you," he continued, turning to Peter and beckoning Kells who snapped to it, bringing a small sleek case to the Captain who handed it to its intended recipient.

Peter opened it to find himself presented with the traditional gold watch and complimentary collector's limited edition fountain pen custom made for such occasions. Most of the senior members of the executive staff dreaded the inevitable when they would be given that little black box officially announcing they were being put out to pasture, but tonight in his atypical situation the irony of it tickled him—pasture was right. He erupted with laughter, his tenor-baritone voice ringing out, making his mirth quite infectious among the crowd.

"Why, thank you, one and all. So, I'm up for early retirement, eh?"

"Complete with full redundancy package," his father continued amidst a few chortles, "you can blame your brother for this one. Ger thought this would be the most appropriate gift."

"We're going to miss you around here, Pete." Tom smiled, amused with the scene.

Before Peter could utter a syllable of the 'thank you for coming' speech he had interiorly practised, the Captain announced in his typical abrupt way that everyone return 'as they were', cutting off any opportunity for maudlin speeches, obviously trying his best to avoid having any nostalgic melancholic bilge water dampen down the spirit of the event now that this had evolved into a happier night than they anticipated. About to sit down,

Peter looked up to see Fr. Mark making his way through the arrangement of tables, another happy face among the well-wishers.

"Look who's here! Glad you could join us," Peter greeted.

"Hey! What a send off you're getting. Did I miss anything?"

O'Conner noted he had indeed, another wedding was in the works he relayed as everyone shook hands with Mark. It was a bit late, but Sophia ensured he got a plate from the buffet before it was cleared, while Katherine was suddenly distracted by a soft beeping from the table warning they were about to lose the Walkie-Talkie member of the event on account of a drained battery that needed immediate recharging. With only a minute left, Katherine dashed off with the phone to the lobby desk where the cord was plugged and waiting, while Leroy took that as his cue to go a-mingling, getting up from the table with an 'excuse me, ladies, gentlemen'. He couldn't help but feel that having too many collar-clad ministers around was a sign he was being ganged up on from Above, and didn't want to do anything about it quite yet. He still had quite a few wild oats to spare! Spotting a lovely looking number across the way who seemed to be returning his attentions with a 'come hither' glance or two, it was time to get acquainted. It had been a long month since he asked a lady out for a night on the town, the nurses in Gerry's hospital were just too nanny-like. After a flighty chorus girl from 'The Strip' and a nagging nurse, it was worth a shot venturing into the universe of single dishy office aides again. It wasn't long before he came back to the head table to say goodnight to everyone, remarking it was a grand party before jauntily making his way back to the latest object of his attentions who went arm in arm with him out the door. Sophia, who practically raised him along with her own children, just sighed and shook her head, he was off again! True, she was hoping he would one day find someone and settle down, leaving his prodigal ways behind, but considering his track record, she doubted this was the day. O'Conner noting her reaction commiserated with her, trying to give the both of them some hope with the observation that Lee there was not a bad lad, just a weak one with a good heart, which would see him through in the end. Sophia noted euphemistically it was the roving detours until then that troubled her, but she was told not to worry, the Almighty would have His way with that good heart, at least, he prayed so.

The evening waning, other guests who also felt they had sufficiently made their appearances began to come forward intermittently to personally convey their congratulations to the happy couple and also to wish Peter well one last time, saying their goodbyes and calling it a night. The family graciously thanked them for coming, chatting a moment before wishing them a pleasant evening, or a 'see you Monday'. It wasn't long before the crowd had thinned out to a few lingering couples, the catering staff and the band taking that as their cue to begin packing up.

However, the good thing about the surprise party was it had saved Peter from the sad one-to-one goodbyes at the office itself, but now he was afraid that the Captain in his best efforts to keep things on a pleasant footing by dismissing the requisite for Memory Lane speeches, had made things somewhat more awkward, even painful, for one valued member of staff. Peter had hoped that during his now abandoned speech he could have kept things on the level of a public statement, which would have allowed him to thank one certain individual for all their dedicated hard work and say farewell at a professional distance, but that was now impossible as Mrs. Clarke too came forward to wish them all a goodnight, him in particular.

No, he hadn't deliberately avoided her during the evening, he did try and make pleasant conversation with her earlier after all, but he truly had been kept busy with the other guests who had pulled him here and there in the desire to meet someone, or catch up with each other's news, elaborate upon a funny story they had heard from so-and-so, or have a good reminisce about the days when he was still a member of the secular world and at the company full time. He had thought perhaps it was a good thing he didn't step forward earlier and seek her out to be polite, and now was convinced of it as she approached, that calm yet apologetic expression betraying her sadness at the recognition that this was indeed one of the last goodbyes. Oh yes, they may briefly see each other in the future, a passing 'hello' and so forth in the street, or perhaps if he had to call the office for some reason, but this truly was the visible defining moment marking the parting of the ways. He was leaving for good this time, and it was improbable that he would ever be back at Reinold Enterprises in this manner again. It was all there in her professional yet emotive expression when for the first time in ages he actually shook hands with her, thanking her again for her hard work over the years, especially tonight in helping to arrange this surprise. He knew as usual she was the hidden mover and shaker behind the scenes helping to make things run smoothly. He wished her well and truly meant it. Having said her goodbyes, she retreated to the elevator, she had some things to collect at her desk before she went home.

The lobby now practically empty except for the cleaners and the change of security staff, the Captain declared they had done their duty, staying on deck and seeing their guests off down to the last man so to speak, it was time to call it a night. Katherine had finally let Gerry get some rest after the talkative evening he had and shut off the phone, it was getting late and was time to go to her half decorated lodgings. Giving everyone a hug, she disappeared into another elevator, while Tom offered to drive Lottie (and the Hulk) home. Lottie laughed quietly into his ear as she gave him another quick kiss on the cheek, noting that once they were married and he was there full-time to protect her, maybe she could *finally* get rid of the Not-So Secret Service once and for all, maybe even sooner. Wishing the Reinolds a good evening after Lottie gave her parents a hug, Tom departed contentedly escorting his lady betrothed with his arm around her, the bodyguard following a few paces behind. Taking up his 'retirement' gift, Peter noted that he had better go and pack up his things in the office, he had planned to do it earlier, but the surprise party had waylaid those plans. The Captain and Sophia decided to come with him, his father suggesting that he have one last drink in his office for old time's sake. Peter thought that was a good idea. He might not be able to have that last drink since he had to drive home, but he could enjoy a few private moments with them.

Getting out of the elevator, he decided he had better take care of first things first before he could relax, promising to join them in the 'Captain's Lounge' when he was done. Peter didn't have too much to pack up, he had brought very little with him, and what was there already mostly consisted of Gerry's photos and desktop paraphernalia. However, he was surprised when he found a rather silly looking flat box with a gift tag reading 'From Sparticus to Ben Hur'. He took off the colourful polkadot paper and flamboyant ribbon, and once the lid was gone, carefully lifted the tissue inside to discover a frilly apron, rubber gloves a few scrubbing pads and a toilet brush accompanied by a large bottle of something marked "*Soul Scrubber! Wash your Sins Away!*" Leave it up to little Bro to find some way to razz him! Reading the soap label he didn't know what to make of it: '*A soothing shower gel made from frankincense and myrrh extracts*', to find that the liquid soap was authentic and could be used, opening the cap and squeezing out a bit onto his fingers to investigate the nature of the purple liquid. Did he actually expect him to use this? Where the heck did he find it? And, it actually had frankincense in there. It sure smelt exotic. Oh, it *was* funny. If only the road to Heaven could be that easy—exfoliation instead of expiation!

That wasn't all, Peter noticed the box was still a tad heavy and lifted the apron to see Gerry wasn't all that clownish in his souvenirs. Under his new household maintenance ensemble for his turn at the housecleaning at the rectory was a stylish photo album filled with snaps of all their years together in the company. Obviously he had help rustling up pictures of him when he was a younger Bossy Boy, unforgettable days of running his first delivery jobs, plus his few tours of duty on the cargo ships, followed by snapshots of the time Gerry eventually joined him in the workplace, great memories! Wow, he remembered that, giving Gerry a double-thumbs up after getting his hauling license, a second shot showing the two of them in a R-bolt cab on Gerry's first long haul before Peter went back to his own trucking route that summer. There was one he himself had taken of a disgruntled Gerry helping him to muck out the livestock trucks. It was an age ago now, but seemed like only a few minutes when looking at all of these. Sure enough, the days in the offices were also included, Peter was surprised to see Ger had dug up a rare photo taken when he was showing him the ropes in the Acquisitions Department. He remembered at the time they were investing in a new fleet of big rigs for the northwestern routes and were considering their options, the trucking fleet they had over there was experiencing too many oil leaks and other frustrating repair issues. As with all vehicle investments they needed something solid in the line of heavy haulers: a road-safe, easy maintenance, reliable brand that gave good mileage to the gallon and could boast of having the least amount of lemons, part recalls and other sundry breakdowns, and of course, had a good trade-in value.

"Pete, you sound like a housewife picking out a station wagon," Gerry joked. "What about speed? Horsepower! We are a shipping company after all, things need to get where they need to and fast. Forget about those and lets get a fleet of *these*," he enthusiastically suggested, turning the pages of the haulage magazine showcasing the latest models to hit the market.

"Ferrari rigs? Are you insane?"

"Since genius borders on insanity, maybe."

Peter remembered launching into a 'please-see-reason' monologue, patiently trying to explain it was impractical on so many levels, it was uneconomical to spend that much when the health plans and the pensions of the workers had to be considered, not to mention the scholarship programs they had set up, plus it would look too ostentatious and send the wrong message to their clients, giving the impression they were being overcharged if the company could splash out on such flashy models when they were already getting the best haulage deals, we need workhorses, not show horses, … etcetera … etcetera, until Gerry broke into a grin and told him to lighten up, he was only joking! He wasn't completely stupid! Although it was nice to dream, if they *could* get them, the guys on the routes would thank them forever. Plus, he had to admit, flash or no flash, their R-bolt logo *would* look rather fine down the side of a truck like that, excuse the pun Gerry concluded. That year the closest Gerry got to having a Ferrari big rig with an R-bolt down the side was a collectors model Peter had specially ordered for his birthday as a joke, which Gerry continued to keep in his home office on his desk next to his family photos. Ever a good sport, Gerry got right back at him that Christmas by giving him a cheesy die cast 70s station wagon with the wood panelling print down the sides, which he still kept, having parked it on his writing desk.

Peter would have to thank Gerry for finding the pictures. Whoops, time to get packing. After locating the box for the painting in the copy room, it certainly felt strange selecting an empty copier paper box and neatly putting his few bits and pieces in it to take away. Hmm, on that note he couldn't resist helping himself one last time to Ger's inviting jar of peanut butter bits that sat temptingly on the corner of the desk. Yes, leaving quietly like this was a big improvement from the last time, but it really felt like the end of a chapter in his life. Still, he was relieved, relieved and eager to be getting back to his spiritual duties. Thinking of which, Peter wondered if he should leave the wooden Black Madonna for Gerry since once it and his painting were gone, his brother didn't have any devotional reminders in that executive den of hassle and worldly profit to keep him on the spiritual track. No, better not, Lottie might get the wrong impression he didn't want her gift and it was best not to upset her. He could always send something to Gerry later, a nice memento he could keep there without being too preachy about it. Oh … that's it, he had the perfect solution. He could always give him his 'Unibrow Apostle'. Peter smiled to himself. Despite the fact the little grumpy statue would prove a constant reminder that Big Brother was still his keeper, Ger wouldn't have the heart to refuse it for that exact reason.

"Two pennies for them, dear," Sophia enquired as she came to see how he was doing.

"I think I've hit upon the most appropriate gift to repay Gerry for my retirement present, which I think you will approve," he admitted with a chuckle, letting her in on his idea as they left to have that last night cap with his father.

Unbeknown to them, Clarke was secretly eavesdropping as they chatted on the way. Only a few minutes earlier she was about to head back to the elevators after picking up her purse and valise, plus ensure everything looked set for the next morning before she went home, but hearing the elevator chime echoing around the almost deserted executive floor, she instinctively knew it was Peter coming back up, he still had to get his things together after all. It wouldn't be wrong to say one last farewell. Or rather, this could be the last chance she had to make him see reason. Why she held on to the thought let alone hope for a breakthrough she didn't know, it certainly didn't work the first time around when she stole that fleeting intimate moment before he bolted off to Italy. 'Peter the Rock', boy, was that right. He was so stubborn. Still, she couldn't give up without one last effort, a rock could be cracked after all. Hell! He's not alone ... who is ... ? Oh. His parents are with him, she knew their voices. Well, there went *that* chance. It would be only one last generic farewell after all, a brief nod and a goodnight to them, and that would be it. No! She needed to be close! Just a few minutes with him nearby. That's all! This would be the last time he would be here! She didn't want to go. Wait, why should she? *They have no idea you're still here. For all they know, you've already gone home ... .*

For a split second, she tried to ignore the compulsion, but it won out over reason. She darted into the boardroom and closed the door before they had turned in her direction, hoping she hadn't been spotted, her heart pounding both from the shock of her audacity and the sheer thrill of having got away with it, for now. You idiot! What are you doing this to yourself? Not to mention she may have embarrassed herself in front of the security camera in the corridor, that is if the guards were on the ball at this hour of the night and had seen her acting weird just then. Oh, who cared? It felt good to hear him, to see him through the crack she opened slightly in the double doors as soon as they passed, turning the knob ever so careful so it couldn't be heard.

From her obstructed viewpoint it was hard to make out what was happening and had to rely mostly on what she could hear, judging from what doors were opening and closing and guessing where the footsteps where heading. Okay, they've gone to the Captain's office, no ... the First Lady's out again ... asking where to find the coffee grounds ... hmm, someone is not having a drink ... Peter's out too ...gone off to the copy room ... boxes, right, of course he'd need those. She was tempted to come from her hiding place, pretend she was there late to finish up some stuff just so she could ask if she could help him one last time, it might be the last opportunity to be alone with him. Should I, or shouldn't I? Great! She had lost those precious minutes in her indecision, his mother was coming back to check up on him. She watched as they went back to the Captain's quarters ... what were they talking about? Something funny about Mr. Gerard and a unibrow, they were joking about it. That's odd. Peter's brother didn't have one, or if he did at one point, he was careful to keep *that* fact about his facial features well hidden and shaved from view.

Lucinda waited for what seemed like ages, wondering when they would come out of the Captain's office. As the time ticked by, her heart stopped thumping as wildly as it did when she hid away to play the lovesick spy. Eventually she grew more confident, leaving the door open to a bare slit and languidly pulled out the chair at the head of the boardroom table. Might as well make herself comfortable, they're going to be stuck in there for awhile, having one last family chat before they called it a night. Alone with her thoughts … waiting … waiting … she pondered on the past month, wondering where she had gone wrong. She had tried everything she knew, digging ever so softly to uncover where his feelings for her had been buried, reanimate them without being too alluringly obvious, but he had warily set that invisible boundary between them. Perhaps she was too cautious, was that it? No, his defences would not only have gone up, they would be bolted with reinforced steel so to speak. Cautious was the only way to go, but still, despite all her efforts to chip away at his resolve, nothing worked. All those little attentions, treats, thoughtful errands anticipating his every need or request gone to waste. Or, maybe she *had* hit upon something, why else would he be so aloof and defensive otherwise? She just *didn't know!* He was such a mystery, and it made her heartsick even more. If only he would love her, there wasn't anything she wouldn't do for him! Then, come to think of it, how could she *possibly* succeed in getting him to see that a full and happy life with her was here for the taking when he was constantly sought out, not for his official signature or expert executive opinion, *but for absolution!*

It began with one of the interns, shyly approaching him when he arrived for work after the lunch hour, an annoying motor mouth carroty head named Christie who never stopped yakkiting about the most trivial details several tones above normal speaking pitch and in a speed that reminded one of a hamster stuck in its go-nowhere circular treadmill.

"CanIseeyouforaminute?   Iknowyou'rebusy, butIhaven'tbeenabletogettothe churchlatelywithworkandeverything … ."

Peter being Peter, he showed her into his office since there was no urgent business on hand right then. Christie emerged a few minutes later, a little red-eyed and sniffing, but very grateful, thanking Peter for his time. Always quiet and reserved, it was assumed by most that he just didn't like to be around people, but it soon spread how understanding and approachable the Boss actually was. It wasn't long before one or two more penitents were waiting outside his office door, also hoping to catch him after lunch.

Lucinda next heard something else whispered around the place that piqued her curiosity: he *knew* things, things no one else could possibly have known about, with one glance it was like he had simply opened them up like a box. She found herself coming back after lunch early just to sit and watch the proceedings from her desk, allowing her to kill two birds with the one stone; to satisfy her curiosity and to catch up on work, the latter being the one she was having to do quite often these days. Was it just her, or did it seem like he was keeping her pretty busy of late with research hunting, calls, runs to the various depots and managers, loading her with odd jobs and other sundry issues? It was annoying not being able to stay close to him at his office all the time! Still, she had quite an eyeful to take in. It was peculiar to watch the amount of visitors who seemed like different people as they emerged, leaving either teary-eyed or thunderstruck with astonishment. Eventually even the non-Catholics were coming to seek out some spiritual and other help in their personal lives if not confession, the line after lunch hour growing into a considerable gaggle to the point she heard the Captain getting a bit grumbly about the disruption in the workplace, muttering under his breath. True, he'd put up with a lot for Peter's sake, but *odds bodkins*! The workers could get absolution on their own time! At last, to keep the peace between God the Father and his father on earth, Peter finally had to stick a note outside on his door saying he would be available for pastoral counselling after hours, or to please make an appointment with him at his parish office. That seemed to keep an even keel on things. She hoped having to set boundaries might get him to concentrate on *this* place more, but her hopes always seemed to be crushed to the point there wasn't much to hang on to. When not busy with penitents, she spotted Peter as he was going somewhere through the building, silently running his black beads through his fingers as he passed, trying to fit in his personal devotions during the busy day when he could. Once when she needed him over another contract issue, she couldn't find him in the usual places, and after looking everywhere else, was told they had seen him in the elevator and had pushed the top button. Kells confirmed where he was going. Of course, the observation deck where sure enough he was quietly walking around at a leisurely pace just before the sun set with his prayer book in hand, snatching some spiritual time alone while the light lasted and as close as he could get to the heavens before he left for the night. It was testing for her, yet observing him in his eyrie-like element was strangely captivating. If he was so all-seeing as they all said, why couldn't he see how she felt? Didn't he see she needed him? That she would do anything for him? *I fell in love with San Pedro … .*

And now? This was his last night here, and he seemed *happy* about it, even finding that poignant retirement gift presented to him an object of mirth. She couldn't help but observe his reactions, hoping for a sign that he regretted he was now going, but no, he was ready, and having his other priest friends there just made things worse in her opinion, a last reminder his place was with *them*. The hard part was, the Captain had asked her to invite them to the party, thinking Peter would like that. She didn't know why she kept tormenting herself, but she wanted to know more about his life in the rectory. Making polite conversation with the Big Boss about Peter's acquaintances there, she discovered Fr. Mark had been married and had entered the priesthood after his wife's death. It was a painful bit of information to hear. Yes, she knew a widower could become a priest, but at least he had the chance to know what it was like to have a wife and had a couple of kids to show for it. If only that had been her and Peter! Why couldn't his church let them have the best of both worlds? It just sounded so stupid and cruel to her. Either he would have to leave the priesthood for her, or she would just have to let him go, and it was becoming more obvious that he wasn't about to surrender, not yet anyway. Then, on top of it all, on Peter's last night here, the party that she had helped to put together just for him had morphed into a merciless travesty—an *engagement party*— it was unbearable! That's all she would hear about for weeks, months in fact. Another wedding in the Reinold family, but again, not the wedding *she* fantasized about, another heartbreak to endure as she tended the vigil flames. She breathed a weary sigh, sitting alone in the dark boardroom wasn't going to do any good, but still, she couldn't help herself. One last look at him, maybe she could have that one last word with him after all if his parents decided to leave first ... *I fell in love with San Pedro ... .*

Wait, what are you doing? You're really pushing it you know! Suppose Kells comes back, having forgotten something like he usually does every so often, and catches you here? Then, how do you explain yourself to them all? You just won't get that one last chance with Peter, face it! And you certainly don't want to make the attempt to speak to him with his family present. What a scene that would turn out to be. If there was that one last chance in the offing, it was something she had to face with Peter alone, but not with the whole family there. You could lose your job over this! And if you lose your place here, you've lost all connection with him. Just *go!*

Reason was slowly regaining the upper hand. She was just getting up when she heard someone coming quickly ... yes ... it *was* Kells. Too late! Her heart raced again at the thought of being caught with no logical excuse or plausible lie to cover up the reason for her to be there in that particular room at that time of night. If only she had thought to bring in a file or something! She could have looked officious and might have gotten away with a lame 'I had to stay late' fib. The old lost-an-earring-on-the-floor gag was a flimsy excuse to be sure. There was nowhere to hide in here! Was the table wide enough? If she slipped under, would she be spotted? He just might come in to see why the door was open but not think to look near the floor … that would *really* look stupid if he thought to look! You'd have to use the earring ruse then. Idiot! The adrenaline was surging now, panic freezing her to the spot, preventing her from ducking under for cover.

Snap!

The door was drawn shut.

Lucinda exhaled with relief. Kells was in too much of a hurry to bother about checking anything. She nearly had a heart attack over nothing. Well, this wasn't exactly *nothing*, she wasn't out of the woods yet. Better not open the door again, if it was seen ajar a second time that would look suspicious, it would be a stupid thing to do. Don't risk it. Great! Not only would she not see anything, now her ability to hear anything outside was hampered considerably. Wait, she could hear the Captain, she couldn't make out anything, but could guess he was greeting Kells, wondering what he was still doing there at that hour. She heard conversation, Kells talking, a woman's voice, no doubt the First Lady, and then Peter saying something … the voices grew louder … her heart pounded again … they were heading back her way. Of all the luck! They were all going together. Peter wasn't staying behind. No doubt Kell's untimely appearance reminded them how late it was getting and they decided to call it a night. She heard them pass the door, how she wanted to open it! However, her near miss just a few minutes ago made her more cautious. Heart still racing, she waited until they had gone down a safe distance before peeking through the door again, catching a bare glimpse of them as they walked out of view, the Captain and Kells helping Peter out with his boxes, Sophia chatting pleasantly with them. One quick back swish of Peter's cassock and he was gone, a bare murmur of his voice, and then that too was silenced as the elevator closed. They were gone. Peter was gone.

Lucinda left the boardroom behind and found herself making her way back to his now vacated office. The emptiness was palpable. Oh yes, the office was full of *things*, there were Mr. Gerard's belongings as would be expected, but Peter's presence was already fading, which was made all the more apparent by the conspicuous gaping hole where the painting once hung. He had made his choice, he had taken her rival with him. She had lost the fight. Defeat, she had to face it, but it was always a bitter blow to the chin. Would there ever be a chance at a rematch? With a game, there was always that possibility, but with the matters of the heart, things were different. All that was left to her now was an office that used to be his, plus an empty chair and a bare wall. She decided to sit in that chair for a moment as she pondered upon this, his last night there, tormenting herself all over again. Same agony, different room. She looked at Mr. Gerard's photos, images she had seen a hundred times over, family photos, he was definitely a family man. Why couldn't his brother be that way? Of course, Peter was in a few of them, her eyes were drawn to Peter. She was suddenly seized with the longing to have them. Up until then she had only kept the occasional pictures she found of him published in the various business and financial magazines. His last night here ... she hungered for some new mementos ... something that she could take with her. After helping Mr. Gerard round up all those old snaps for Peter's farewell album, she had taken the opportunity to make herself some copies from those that the employees gave her while she was compiling it, and nobody was the wiser. Still, it wasn't enough. She had an opportunity now ... no one was there, no one would be looking ... .

Her heart pounding again, she opened the few frames that held his picture, one when he and Mr. Gerard were kids, another with him at one of their birthday parties ... she could always cut out the other figures. Taking her trophies, she ran off a few copies on the colour machine, quickly putting the original photos back into their places when she was done. She was pleased with herself, but the hunger for more grew, reason was losing the upper hand again as she became more daring and decided to snatch one more trophy, for there was one picture displayed in the Captain's office that she prized and was not yet part of her little collection: Peter sailing his yacht the 'Pillar of Ivory' the year before he sold it and left for Rome. He looked so striking in his yachting jacket manfully hauling up a sail with the radiant golden hues of a morning sky filled with billowing clouds joined with the deep blues of the sea behind him. It was a dramatic image fit for a professional photography journal, and she longed to have it. The door wasn't locked, she made her way to the desk and found what she was looking for. This was too easy! She should have done this ages ago! One last trip to the copy room, trophy secured, she retuned the original without getting caught. No one would ever know. Too bad the photocopier couldn't give it a glossy finish like the original, not to mention the other pics, maybe the laminator would do the trick? Lucinda plugged it in and set to work. Not bad she thought as she examined the colour copies with their added sheen. She would have to be happy with these. She'd rather have Peter, but for now the hunger was assuaged a bit, it felt so satisfying to have snatched them unawares. As for winning Peter back, who knows? There was a time she thought she would never see him back here again, and how she was proven wrong! One day there could be that rematch after all. Stranger things have happened. Good things always come to those who wait. *I fell in love with San Pedro … .*

☙ ❖ ❧

Go on, hit the snooze button, five more minutes won't make a difference. Famous last words, don't listen to that temptation! Come on, up up up! Turning off the alarm, he stretched away the drowsiness and prepared for a new day. It certainly began with a comical start when he opened his bedroom door to find that while he slept one of the Holy Bachelors had pinned up a cartoon caricature of him larger than life driving a chariot yoked up to some daft looking devils that were yelping in pain and galloping at a clip, for he was whipping them on with a large rosary, his caped cassock billowing in the wind. Underneath a caption ran, '*Welcome Back, Ben Hur! Go get 'em!*' Peter chuckled as he took down the picture. Jenkins, it had to be Jenkins. He had a knack for scribbling this kind of thing. Still, jokes or no jokes about his particular apostolate, it was good to be getting back to it full time.

As to be expected, his confessional was kept busy up until the last minute he could squeeze in before Mass, and yet there were more people to be seen than ever before. The hopeful crowds eagerly waiting for him even at this early hour were now proving to be overwhelming. He would have to pray about it, maybe Heaven would inspire him with a solution to where he wouldn't have to disappoint so many. Communion time came, and as was now becoming the norm, there was that stifling sense of 'throttlers' sifting through the congregation. He said his customary prayer and gave the blessing, weakening their hold. This time, the annoyance of the imps was manifested by an unexpected blast from the organ, a quick wail of a discordant tritone. Startled, the congregation quickly looked back. Was someone tinkering around with the instrument? They couldn't see anybody!

540

However, a few in the congregation knowledgeable about the music of spheres finally made the connection, those two notes giving away what the Monsignor was constantly dispelling … .

Once Mass was concluded, Peter was met once again with a sizeable crowd of people waiting for him as he left the church, asking for a blessing, or trying to book a Mass intention or make an appointment with him there right on the street. Peter tried to accommodate them as best he could, but then had to make his excuses, reminding them to please call the parish office to make appointments! Now, he even had to turn down some Mass requests, his book was overflowing and it was not a good idea to fill it up too much in advance as he learned from experience. When a fellow priest died, their unsaid Masses had to be given to another priest so the requests were fulfilled, and once he stepped in to do the honours, but the deceased's Mass requests were considerably overbooked in addition to the requests he already had, it was quite awhile before he could accept Masses again. One never knew when God would decide to take someone Home, and in this case when his own number would finally come, Peter didn't want to overburden the priest that would volunteer or be asked to fulfil his obligations. In addition to the Mass requests, now those who thought they understood his unusual extra blessings before Communion wanted to hear him finally confirm it. Was he really *seeing* anything? He quickly made his getaway with an evasive answer – he only saw that an extra blessing never hurt anyone – then slipped away to the parish office as fast as he could!

Nodding good morning to the 'nurses' while managing his case and his curious-looking box, they had to ask what was inside.

"This?" He smiled. "A new treasure to adorn the waiting room."

"Really? Can't wait to see it. Oh, this was just dropped off for you," Mabel continued, holding up a formal-looking envelope along with the rest of the bulky pile of letters that awaited him.

Hmm, what now? Looked official. He laid down everything to open it, the ladies watching as he read the contents of the enclosed missive printed with the letterhead bearing the archbishop's crest, scanning through it at first, then slowing down.

"I hope it's nothing serious," Ethel ventured, curiosity growing into concern.

"No, nothing serious. I'm being transferred."

Their expressions changed to one of surprise mixed with dismay.

"You're not being sent far I hope," Mabel wondered.

"Actually, I get to keep my office here for my ministry, but as for my parish duties it seems I will be of more use uptown."

Ethel couldn't help wondering where, to which Mabel guessed off the bat, "St. Peter's. I'll be dog-gonned if you haven't been sent to St. Peter's."

"Good call. Right you are."

"Rather apropos," Ethel smiled, relived he wasn't being sent to some far-flung country parish upstate to where they might not get to see him again for a long time. "When do you start there?"

"Says after His Excellency returns from Youth Day, so I have two weeks to make arrangements for a smooth transition."

"I don't know how *that's* going to go. St. Peter's is in for one big tidal wave of souls," Mabel wittily observed, to which he couldn't help but laugh.

"Speaking of which," he trailed, indicating towards the direction of the basement door with his thumb.

"Yep, you have quite a line up down there already, including Joel," she confirmed.

"Oh no, off his meds again, poor guy. All right, thanks for the warning, I'd better vamoose before he spooks my other patients. See you later."

Gathering up his things, he mused for a moment as he 'vamoosed'. A transfer, he wondered when it was coming. It was to be expected, especially after his latest dinner meeting with His Excellency. Mabel got tidal wave right. He was making too many waves, and so they were going to be directed elsewhere, for the time being. At least he was not moving far. No time to dwell on his new appointment, the next wave of the morning was sitting on the chairs and a few discarded pew benches he rustled up and had set along the wall in the hallway outside his waiting room, which was no longer large enough to handle all the people that came to him. Nodding a good morning to everyone, he looked into the waiting room to see Joel the only one pacing around in there. No wonder the hall was more crowded than normal.

"This one's an emergency, I'll be out in a moment," he assured everyone, laying down everything inside the door and closing it behind him. Those who were his regulars were used to his system and knew the drill. Anything the Monsignor declared an emergency received precedence on the spot, which meant even booked sessions could be held up. Next came the appointments, as long as an emergency case didn't appear out of the blue, and if there were few of either of those, then he would see anyone who had just dropped by without an appointment and did not have an urgent matter that needed attending. Of course, it was annoying at times, to wait and then to have someone suddenly getting ER priority! However, they realised the Monsignor must have known what they were thinking, for one day not too long ago his visitors discovered a new notice hung up in the hallway along with the other devotional posters and pictures: '*You may not be feeling virtuous right now, but please be patient.*' Everyone would smile at the sign, it certainly helped to lighten the mood for they never knew if they were ever sitting next to someone who actually needed an *exorcism* … .

There were a few startled looks shared when a raised voice was heard behind the closed door that didn't sound too happy. Something about 'I hate those meds' … the Monsignor had his hands full today. There was a strange moaning, then the door suddenly opened, and a disgruntled Joel came bursting out burbling gibberish.

"Okay, give me ten minutes everyone, then we may proceed." Peter smiled as he looked out into the hall, trying to cheer up the startled company. He didn't want the room to be left without its new treasure. He unwrapped it fast and hung it on the main wall facing the door out into the hallway, he wanted it to be the first thing everyone saw as they entered. What a grace to have something so beautiful. True, he had added a few touches to the place in the last month, some decent looking table lamps so he didn't have to have the fluorescent lighting on in here at least, plus a new mahogany bookshelf on which to place appropriate reading material, but the waiting room definitely assumed a new welcoming ambiance the moment the painting was in its designated place.

Peter whisked the wrappings and box away into the 'OR', took one last look around to see if everything in the waiting room was all right, yes, there were plenty of prayer cards laying around for people to take if they needed them, the Minor Exorcism, St. Michael's Prayers, catechetical leaflets, other devotional pocket pictures … hmm, they were running low. He went to his store cabinet in the operating room to bring out some more, blessed and restocked them, then examined the bookcase. Yep, looks like some of the booklets were taken, that's all right, as long as they were being read. He didn't mind if they were taken then. It was one of his many little spiritual charities he liked to do. He looked through his business briefcase that was now assigned the new task of carrying his prayer card and leaflet stock, he kept extra booklets too, but was out of them. He'd have to make a quick trip to the bookstore and fill that up later this week. Nothing else needed, okay, he was ready to begin.

"Here we go, Holy Mother." He smiled at the picture. "The rush begins. Please intercede to your Son for me, may everything today be done according to His Will."

He opened the door, and indeed the rush began, the first wave filled the waiting couch and armchairs with approving and admiring 'oh's!' at the new arrival greeting them as they came in. For a moment, their own troubles were forgotten as they eagerly asked about the picture, where he got it and what the story was concerning that particular Madonna that was so beautiful, yet so sad. He happily gave them several leaflets he had printed on the growing fame of the once little-known Marian apparitions of Ecuador. It looked like he had another doctor on hand, the Mother of the Sick and Comforter of the Afflicted.

However, not all were appreciative of the painting: one of his patients seemed to take a sudden dislike to it, a man in his fifties who was accompanying his wife.

"Are you here for confession," Peter asked.

"No, my wife is," he retorted with a slightly disgruntled sneer. *Him* go to confession? The thought of it!

"You're all right. Be at peace," Peter consoled her before turning to her husband, "it's *you* that's in need of healing."

"Me? I'm not … ."

"Oh, your mouth says one thing, but your wavering will says another, and right now, it's screaming to be informed. Come, in you go," Peter interjected with dignified authority, opening the door to the operating room much to the chagrin of the man, the elated bafflement of his wife, and the surprise of the other visitors who were there to witness this unexpected switch.

Of all the … ! Looking Peter up and down trying to intimidate him, it didn't work, he found he couldn't look the Monsignor in the eyes. Even that picture looked tragically at him. He suddenly felt transparent like glass, glass that was once radiant and glistening, but was marred with a grotesque accumulation of filth, an interior truth that was now inexplicably laid bare to him. *What was happening?*

"I don't bite, you'll feel better when we've had a talk," Peter encouraged kindly.

Why did it feel like his feet were so heavy? At first, all he could do was just stand there, but then did as the Monsignor instructed. He was not sure what to expect … .

It was a long twenty minutes for the patients waiting for their turn outside, especially for the poor woman who had originally wanted to see Peter, not knowing what was happening inside and feeling like some odd specimen undergoing their scrutiny herself since everyone probably wondered what 'that' was all about! Everyone perked up with curiosity when the door finally opened, inquisitive to see if they could guess what had happened in there, but not much was given away other than the emerging patent's remarkable change in manner: gone was the arrogant 'I don't need anybody, especially you' look. He now bore the aspect of a regretful man who had been given a lot to think about and needed some quiet time alone, but was more at peace with himself than before.

Peter called out the next appointment, so many waiting for him. Mostly confessions, a few people who had some odd things to tell all right, asking if they were in need of his exorcist expertise, and indeed, there was one case that got him wondering … .

"Monsignor, I can't stop saying or thinking awful, blasphemous things, but I don't want to! I find myself repeating other prayers and sentences to calm myself, even counting numbers as a 'safe' distraction, then, all of a sudden, I can't stop bad words wanting to spurt up out of nowhere, especially when I pray! I'm terrified of making a bad Communion! It's then when it gets worse … ," the young girl admitted, ashamed and with tears threatening to flow.

That did sound terrible, but that was not possession either. It could be a special kind of attack that felt very similar—spiritual obsession. Someone could be afflicted by a demon tempting them with these incessant, intrusive and disquieting mental onslaughts. In fact, it was sometimes a rare form of purification for the soul, for it was not unknown for those specially befriended by God to suffer these exceptional attacks to where they were unable to stop themselves from spouting forth blasphemies contrary to their will, or had no control over what they could do, again, contrary to their will. Why God worked this way, Peter wished he knew, other than he understood it was an extreme form of instilling humility in these befriended souls.

This poor young girl could be suffering from a spiritual oppression, however, he decided to play it safe first by saying the Minor Exorcism. When it was over, Peter asked if she felt anything: just the usual bad thoughts trying to get her to say swear words, but she clamped down on it and concentrated on something spiritual. In fact, she was afraid she might say or do something awful and make a scene. Okay, not a possession, but this *could* be spiritual obsession, but there was also the medical bevy of obsessive compulsive disorders that had to be considered. Peter personally wondered that since the cross borne by the victims of both the spiritual and the medical obsessions were very similar if there actually *was* any difference between the two, still, he had to follow church teachings and attempt to distinguish illness from real spiritual issues.

Peter asked the pertinent questions, and when he heard that she and another member of the family were diagnosed with impulsive disorders, decided to approach the case as if it was an illness for now, namely, advising her on how to combat the addictiveness of these involuntary, impulsive thoughts with spiritual means in conjunction with the advice given by her therapist. It was difficult to help a tender conscience like this, it was a specific excruciating kind of scrupulosity, they always felt so guilty as if they had committed mortal sins every day, but since their will was impaired, mortal sin did not enter here.

"If you were truly possessed, you'd be unable to control yourself at all, something would have manifested itself, and since you were trying your best to combat the obsessive thoughts, it's clear your will is not in them. So be at peace, you're not in mortal sin. Since you've been diagnosed with compulsive issues, you do realise it's an illness? You are not an evil person you know."

She looked up, hoping he had an answer for all of this. She certainly *felt* so bad!

"It should be a comfort knowing what you are dealing with: you do not have some horrific malicious desire to sin and sin and sin. It's not the same situation as with the habitual sinners we preach about, those who have no desire to reform their lives or can't see anything wrong in what they do and who *want* to live that way. If you did not have a good will, not wanting to be good and not doing what God wants, you would not be here talking to me."

"Then why does it feel … ?"

"Hmm, it's similar to a repetitive temptation. Have you felt tempted to do something over and over and over again to where it seems like it will never end?"

She nodded dejectedly, she had a problem with that too. Peter looked at her for a moment, that also could be a spiritual obsessive attack.

"Sometimes that *feels* like a sin, but it's not," he continued gently. "Just because it keeps coming doesn't mean you have sinned. It's when you truly *want* to do the evil action that makes it a sin. You have no desire to do anything evil, my dear. Don't let you or the devil disturb your inner peace and your trust in God's mercy."

"But sometimes I get so *angry* and upset at myself that I keep failing too, in the stuff that *is* venial, I want to stop, but I seem to keep confessing the same things all the time. Will I ever overcome them I wonder?"

Uh oh. This soul was truly beating herself up. She would never be able to advance forward in the spiritual life caught in a turmoil like this.

Maybe she did suffer from a spiritual obsession after all, even so, his advice would be the same either way.

"What you are feeling in that instance is not true repentance. It may feel like it, but it's actually a form of pride stirred up by the devil."

She looked up in alarm.

"Don't worry, you didn't realise what you were doing, but I will tell you how that cunning enemy works so you can be aware. He is trying to whip up an anger in you over not being perfect, a self-detestation of being 'inferior'. We don't like being shown we're so faulty and weak, which is why this interior agitation and frustration is related to pride. On the contrary, when God works in our hearts and brings us to repentance, He does it peacefully and with gentleness. God makes us feel a calm sorrow, a peaceful humility in knowing we are not perfect, we must realise we are sinners, yet remain confident in Him and His mercy. Since scripture declares we must love and be charitable to others the same *as* ourselves, it shows we too have to be charitable *to* ourselves, even when we fall. Jesus is the Prince of Peace, you should still feel a spirit of peace within you despite all your sins and faults, even in grievous sin. Then you know you have a repentance inspired by grace. He wants to heal us, not drive us insane. Driving someone to insanity is the devil's work."

"I never though of it like that, but it's not *accepting* the sin, is it? Making excuses for it and trying to sluff over it? We're not to presume on God's mercy either."

"True. You keep a very careful watch over your conscience, don't you?" He smiled. "But no, it's not presumption. Presumption is when you go on sinning with the notion that 'Oh, God loves me as I am, He'll forgive me, I just have to ask,' without any true effort to improve. This is lacking the purpose of amendment and is no real sorrow for sin. A true peaceful repentance means we know what is wrong, we are sorry for it, we will try to do better, but we don't let it torment us, especially to the point it keeps us from trying again no mater how many times we fall or leaves us dejected that we think we will never reach heaven. We must be confident and try, try, try again. As to your obsessive thoughts, God understands what you're going through, He knows you intend no sacrilege. If you feel you need to confess, do if it makes you feel better and helps retain your inner peace, it's good to even confess the temptations too, but don't stop praying or going to Communion, okay? That's exactly what the devil wants. He wants to break all personal union between you and God. Your will is not in those disturbing thoughts and words that just keep tormenting you, therefore, you are not in mortal sin. Your confessor is aware of your situation?"

"Well … yes … ,"

"And he tells you to go to Communion?"

"Yes … ."

"Continue to go! Your obedience pleases God very much. It's only when you're in mortal sin or if you have broken the fast before Communion without a valid reason like a medical condition that should keep you from going. When these thoughts come back, just don't panic over them, your anxiety could be fuelling the problem. When you're anxious or stressed, it gets worse doesn't it?"

"Umm, yes … it kinda gets faster, heavier, something like that."

"Then take a deep breath, slow your mind down, apologise to God or the saint you are praying to, they understand, then continue with your prayers, and keep going to Mass. Don't let something that's not in your control destroy your inner peace. Okay?"

"Okay." She smiled.

The fact he was so kind and was willing to hear her confession helped a lot, not to mention he wanted to give her a special blessing, tracing a cross on her forehead with his thumb like on Ash Wednesday, which made her feel better prepared now. They said he could see souls, and if he didn't see anything on her conscience, then, these intrusive compulsions really were a condition, a special temptation that needed to be managed, that's all! He was right, knowing she was not willing this made it easier to deal with. She didn't feel so fearful and frustrated now, and with the anxiety lessened, she really could be at peace as he recommended.

"Oh, and another thing, you can tell your sister she shouldn't poke fun when you pray, mocking is catching. In fact, if you can convince her, she should make an appointment to see me, that is, if she really wants to discover Truth. I'll give it to her straight between the eyes."

She gasped. She didn't tell him that, she wanted to, but was feeling guilty she had already taken up too much of his time. She had worried about her Tom-boyish elder sister making fun of her devotions and the little devotional statues she rescued from second hand shops and gave as gifts to everyone. Then, to hear that expression! Her sister used it frequently, 'If so and so says anything to me again, I'll knock them into tomorrow, straight between the eyes.' It was true, he really did know things. Now, she really did feel better! Oh, if only she could get her sister to see him … .

A very relieved and happy 'thank you' and 'goodbye' followed, and the OR was ready for the next penitent patient.

Yes, the waves did keep coming, there were more confessions, more advice sessions asking about exorcisms, mostly appointments made for house assessments to see if they were inhabited by the restless dead, or people asking if someone in their family could be possessed, he got a lot of those. However, he also did some marriage counselling too, but today's case was a little taxing: it *would* be a couple whose only problem was 'he' kept leaving the toilet seat up, left the empty roll unchanged, and tracked muck through the house when 'he' knew she wanted him to take his shoes off when he came home. Okay, some venial unthinking sins were committed, but these were basically household issues! Nevertheless, Peter patiently listened since the little things could escalate into worse situations that would eventually drive a wedge between them. At the end of the wife spilling out all her woes, 'he' gave a little look as if to say, 'you see what I'm putting up with', thinking the Monsignor being a man and all would side with him, but was 'he' in for a surprise. Peter with his years of hearing women's confessions possessed an exceptional understanding of the differences in their spiritual and emotional makeup, and was quite sympathetic. Peter calmly asked would it actually kill him to place the seat down, replace the toilet roll and to put on some house loafers when he came home? Isn't having a happy wife and happy home more important? Not to mention you'd be upset too if someone undid your work and you had to make it up, double the effort. It's only a little thing, and you'd save you and your wife a lot of agro.

Now, he had to give the wife a few words too together with the husband, since she suddenly assumed an 'hmph, there you are' smugness that would soon grow intolerable: true, she worked hard to keep a lovely home for them both, but it was for them *both*. A bit of mud, an empty paper dispenser and a lifted toilet lid once in awhile is not adultery or the end of the world. Don't become a nagging tyrant of mundane details to where your husband dreads to come home, at least he *wants* to come home. Think of all the marriages falling apart lately. You two fell in love once, remember? Where did it go? Are these little things worth destroying what you feel for each other? When something goes wrong, or you get those irksome splinters of life, even when caused by each other, they are worthy sacrifices to offer up. Face it, you would feel all the same little aggravations from the other loved ones in your life, your brothers, your sisters, your parents, your cousins if you were all living together, and living with the love of your life would not be any different. You were never promised a fairytale existence on earth, nor is marriage supposed to be a one-on-one battle of who gets one up on who. You were meant to be in a loving partnership to help each other through life. Converse with each other more. Forgive, attempt to please each other in the little things including the household chores that you know the other appreciates even if you don't understand why they like things like that, then move on, okay?

The wife had to reflect on that, the Monsignor was right, she would rather have a messy bathroom than to have a husband that didn't come home or came home late raving drunk, and the husband also had a good 'think': his wife really wasn't asking much of him … . The troubled couple were troubled no longer, they stole a shy smile at each other as if to say, 'what a bunch of idiots we are', then thanked the Monsignor for his time.

At last, he was alone for a while, that being his last appointment before lunch. He'd better run before someone else dropped by. He couldn't help but look up at the picture before he left to get something to eat.

"Holy Mother, they're now coming to me over empty toilet rolls." He groaned, then started to chuckle. That was a first. Never mind. If the good Lord had to talk about the 'privy' to His creatures, he should expect nothing different in his own ministry.

He checked his watch, it was well after the lunch hour. Never mind, at least he cleared the morning rush. Bounding up the steps to the main floor, he let his nurses know he was off to get some needed fuel, then would be back promptly. A Reuben sandwich sounded good, he hadn't had one in awhile, he needed something with a good jot of meat to it, then back to his spiritual clinic. He decided to have it packed to go. He didn't get very far with it, a homeless man asked him for change, and since Peter felt guilty only having two quarters and a nickel left in his pocket, gave his lunch along with it to make up for the meagre offering. The man looked like he needed it more than he did. Besides, a little extra fasting wouldn't kill him. Back to the OR, maybe the nurses had some coffee left in the pot. That would keep him going.

Since it was his first full day back, he didn't schedule anything for the afternoon, he wanted to give himself some space to adjust back into the rhythm of things and so had left the rest of the time open to anyone who might drop by. First come, first serve, emergency cases excepted, naturally. He glanced up and down the empty basement hall. That was strange, no one yet, and he didn't hear anyone wandering around lost or looking out of curiosity, which also happened from time to time. Getting to explore areas that were usually off limits was enticing, it was like wanting to peek behind a door that said 'employees only'. Of course, no wonder it was dead, he hadn't been in here on a Sunday afternoon in ages, the word probably hadn't gotten around he was now available. He should use this time well and say his daily devotions.

Closing the door and settling into the armchair that gave him the best view of the Madonna, he started his rosary, the Glorious Mysteries for Sunday. It was certainly restful down here in the quiet. There were people walking on the upper floor all right, he could hear the footsteps overhead, but it wasn't intrusive. For a moment he closed his eyes while he said the third mystery, he began to feel heavy. No, he didn't want to get sleepy now! C'mon coffee, do your thing! Maybe the fact he was up with the dawn chorus was the cause, then, the rosary with its calm repetition didn't help at times. He blinked his eyes and sat up, he tried to focus on the painting as he finished the fourth and started the fifth mystery, Our Lady's coronation. It certainly was the perfect image to look upon for the final decade of beads and the closing prayer hailing her as the Queen of Heaven.

" … to Thee do we cry, poor banished children of Eve, to Thee do we send up our sighs, mourning and weeping in this valley of tears. Turn then, O gracious Advocate, thine eyes of mercy towards us, and after this our exile … ."

He closed his eyes for a moment after finishing, he was feeling unbelievably heavy that moment.

Rap, rap rap! Three knocks at the door, then it swung open, announcing the arrival of someone with its characteristic squeaky hinge. He was about to get up, but his latest visitor swiftly entered before he could rise, the door closing of its own accord, which was odd.

"No, no, sit. You are very tired," the young man insisted with a smile, holding his hand up.

Peter could have sworn he had seen this pleasant young fellow before, but he couldn't place him just then. Dressed in a crisp shirt and slacks, rather exceptionally well groomed for a kid who looked like he was in high school considering they all would rather die these days if they dressed in nothing but their T-shirt fashions, ripped jeans and tennis shoes. A Jehovah's Witness out on a mission? Why would he come *here*? The young man's smile broadened with absolute delight.

"No, not that kind, but you are close."

Wait, he hadn't spoken a word.

"You don't recognise me? I was there when you were given that wound," his visitor continued, indicating with an open palm towards Peter's left arm, "I've always been with you."

With a shock Peter now recognised who was visiting, he wanted to get on his knees and fast, but the youth stopped him again, holding his hand up. "No! We are both servants, you don't kneel to me." The youth then withdrew his hand and turned to look up at the picture. "Our Queen, she is so beautiful. She surpasses all of us. It has pleased the Eternal that it should be so," he declared with a profound bow, "and your office is even higher than that of us messengers, the highest office," he then continued, turning to Peter with another respectful bow.

He didn't know what to say, although he felt completely humbled with this acknowledgement. "My friend, what brings you here," Peter finally asked, finding his voice and wanting to ask him so many questions but could only sit there stunned and amazed. The youth smiled again.

"I come with a message from Our King and Queen, and also a gift. You were tested these past months and came through as silver is purified from dross. When tempted you turned to Her and did not falter, nor regretted ever entering the Master's service. They are well pleased. As you have not wasted the gifts given to you, they shall be increased. What was first given was entrusted to a good steward, and therefore shall you be given more, that is the gift. Close your eyes."

Peter could only obey, wondering what was about to happen. He felt something warm slowly and gently brushed over his eyelids by a fingertip. Was it oil? It felt like a liquid was placed on them, but it didn't run or drip, and the fragrance was unbelievable, he felt restored by the invigorating scent that filled the room. He continued to keep his eyes closed, waiting for whatever would come next.

"The gifts you have been given have now been increased, and the more you give, the more you shall receive. But, I also come with a message of warning: be prepared. Great gifts require great sacrifice. The days are coming when you will be tried as gold in a furnace, as a diamond that is under the cutter's blades, but take heart! Our Lord and Our Queen will never abandon you. They wish to increase your eternal merits as well as your gifts as you labour to save souls, which are so dear to them and for which they Themselves suffered so much. You will receive consolations as well as sorrows. I also am always with you. Be at peace."

For a minute there was silence. There was another knock on the door, slightly louder this time that made him sit up and open his eyes. His young visitor was gone, nowhere to be seen, but of course, *he* would not need to leave by any door. Peter was sorry this encounter was so brief, he would have given anything to talk longer with him, although now he was met with something altogether remarkable: there were new sources of light in the room, and they had nothing in common with the electric light from the table lamps. His latest decorative accessories on the few tables had once given the room a warm nice touch but now were meagre glimmers in comparison. It was another strange shock, but not frightening, the various points and sources of light were gentle, glowing yet oh so captivating, it gave a wonderful sense of peace just to look at them, but it was all so new to take in, he felt bewildered. They were coming from *objects*, and he wasn't quite sure what he was seeing or what it meant. The pictures were glowing a golden tone ringed in colours matching the robes of the saints depicted in them, in particular, the Madonna was very bright, the very jewels in the painting assuming a life of their own and seemed to glitter. The floor was slightly glowing too with a soft white light, but in patches resembling a light snowdrift, he wasn't sure what that meant, then he couldn't help but make a quick intake of breath when he saw his rosary, the beads and crucifix were shimmering like a string of fiery gems with a sky blue light, which intermittently changed colours for a split second before returning to their blue tone. Then he noticed the gold wedding band on his left ring finger he received at his ordination, a fantastic circle of red and blue flames danced around it, but without emitting any searing heat. There were so many different points of light emanating different glows and hues, and while they outshined the electric lamps, they were soft and didn't blaze out the room. He could still observe his environment with his normal human vision too, it simply was inexplicable. Attempting to take this all in just a few seconds, he still wasn't sure what it meant yet, and caught in the quiet rapture over this new sight given him, had forgotten there was someone outside waiting until he heard the knock again, yet still transfixed in a state of wonderment, he couldn't get to his feet.

The door opened with its soft squeak, it was Mabel and Ethel who had come to ask if they could see the painting now that they were off from office duty, and smiled as they looked down at the Monsignor.

"Oops, sorry, did we wake you," Ethel enquired apologetically. They knew he would sometimes catch a few winks there when it was quiet. He certainly had been run off his feet these last few months.

"Er, no, or, maybe I was … ? Never mind," he mumbled.

Had he fallen asleep? With his eyes closed and the heaviness he had felt earlier, it was hard to tell. Was it all a dream? If it was, it was without a doubt one of the 'other kind', for this was not a hallucination, he blinked his eyes for a second … no, the light was still there!

"What smells so lovely? If it's a new air freshener, pah-*leeze* you've got to tell me what it is. I'm getting drunk on the scent … oh, you have something on your eyes," Mabel noticed. Did he have allergies, or something?

He carefully placed a finger near the corner of his right eyelid, he could feel traces of the unknown substance still there. Without saying a word, he went to the other room and quickly took a white linen finger towel from his store of altar linens in the cupboard that he kept just in case he needed them. He always liked to be prepared, but never expected he might need a cloth dedicated to the service of the altar for something like this, but then reflected this special liquid should not be mopped up with anything less. He carefully wiped the traces off and examined the cloth. There was a golden hued essence visible, he gingerly lifted it to take in the scent, yes, still there, it had not dissipated, and indeed, the substance was *glowing*. It certainly felt invigorating, restorative. My, the floor in the operating room had the same lustrous snowdrift effect, and so did the pictures in here ... it was breathtaking. He was distracted by this new vision granted to him. No, he hadn't been given a new sacrament, that would be impossible, but it was definitely some great blessing that he had to figure out. An 'increase' of his gifts, isn't that what his friend said? Had it enhanced the spiritual gifts received at his Confirmation? Was it possible? Maybe, for it didn't seem *impossible* ... . Then, he was struck with a new realisation: if it was a magnification of previously bestowed gifts, had he been sent chrism from Paradise? What a grace!

"Monsignor, are you okay? Are your eyes hurting or something?" Ethel then came to check, standing at the doorway into the operating room.

"No, no, I'm fine," he reassured her, folding the cloth very carefully. Wow! The cloth and liquid were emitting golden and red flames, something like his ring. He was about to open his special ecclesial case and noticed that too was gleaming with a red glow. He opened it gingerly to see all the sacred objects of his ministry were literally bathed in similar flames. The chalice and paten were emitting golden and red flames, the travel crucifix for Mass too, in fact, everything was either glowing, shimmering, or giving off flames. Some objects had different colours, or variations of the same colour, the Miraculous Medal he had pinned inside the lining of his case was giving off white and blue flames, while his special exorcist crucifix was bathed in a purple glow surrounded by red tongues of fire. His case had become a treasure chest of heavenly light!

Ah. *Now it made sense.*

He could see in a glance everything that was blessed or contained a blessed article, and the light distinguished the type of blessing or object that was blessed, and what ministry it was blessed for. Hmm, this would take some time to become familiar with, what the various colours, glows and flames meant, but now he knew what had been given him. The incandescent 'snowdrift' was the most puzzling part, then he realised that was the blessed salt he had sprinkled everywhere, the glass jar of holy salt in his cupboard was softly pulsating with the same radiant glow. How beautiful! He hadn't felt happy like this in a long time, it was a joy that just wanted to bubble forth. He just couldn't stop smiling. He carefully placed the sacred cloth next to the flaming travel paten and chalice, then came out to see Mabel, still caught in that distracted but blissful state of revelation and spiritual joy.

"My, looks like someone took their happy pill," she remarked, amused and somewhat puzzled by his preoccupied state. He was looking around like a blind man who had his sight miraculously restored and was drinking in the colours of the world for the first time.

"Um, yes," he replied quietly, he didn't want this to get out! How could he keep something like this quiet? Oh no, he just wanted to hide away, but this was a gift not meant for him alone, it was to help others too. Just act normal and don't make too much of a deal about it, just go on as usual, he advised himself. "So nurses, what do you think of the Madonna?"

"She's beautiful, it's such a shame she's stuck down here in the basement, it belongs in a church," Ethel commented.

"Christ was born in a stable, we can't get too exacting about our operating room," he reminded, but the place no longer seemed drab to him, not when he could see heavenly light dancing all around. *Everything* on earth seemed pale in comparison now. If these were only a few blessed objects, *what did Heaven look like?* The reflection struck him straight to the core, it was a great grace, but now he began to feel the flipside he was warned about. Great mystic graces come with a price.

Ah, the joy—*and the pain!*

They could not be separated from each other, just like true love and suffering could not be divided. He felt a sudden homesickness that was acute, a deep longing for his true Eternal Home. His heart literally began to feel a constricting ache in his chest. He had felt it before, not feeling exactly tied to the earth anymore despite looking back fondly on occasion at the memories of his childhood home and being with his family, but oh, this was so pronounced, he was beginning to understand the full significance of the words 'poor banished children of Eve', 'valley of tears' and 'exile'. The human race belonged to an Eternal Royal House, they were sons and daughters of A Royal God, A Thrice Holy God, and here, *here* was a bitter place of expiation: exile, exile, *exile!* He could feel the separation, yet knew he was not out of God's favour, a hope, a consolation, for the sense of this spiritual homesickness also signalled a deep desire for the union with God.

"Are you all right? You must have had a rough morning, you should take the rest of the afternoon off," Ethel suggested, noticing his curious reactions.

"No, I'm all right," he assured them, glancing up and observing the light again. The painting was scintillating in a way that no earthly illumination could. Just, look at the jewels sparkle! True, earthly gemstones sparkled when held up to light, but their display was a dead, spiritless patina compared to this—this brilliance was truly *alive*! It was a *living* light! He couldn't say anything to them of course. If he was still trying to fathom it all, they certainly wouldn't understand.

"Look, if you don't mind me doing the preaching for once, you need some time for yourself too you know." Mabel nodded matter of factly. "The doctor can't cure anyone if he's in more need of R and R than the patients are."

Peter couldn't argue with that either, but since that blessed unction occurred and filled the room with fragrance, he didn't feel tired anymore, still, he did need time alone to observe and study this new development, but he couldn't say that either.

"Maybe you're right, I need some time."

Packing up his other case and shutting off the earthly lights, he took a quick double take: the waiting room was still glowing from the various blessed objects notwithstanding the darkness, he could walk around the room unaided by electric light if he wanted to, it was something to behold. It was even difficult to take his eyes off his ring and ecclesial case. This was a serious state of affairs, but the child in him couldn't help but notice this was *way* better than Christmas twinkles. The ladies waited in the hall not a little curious as they saw him look around again for a moment, then lock the door. He was certainly in a strange mood today, like a yancy excitable kid quite driven to distraction. He wasn't like that when he came in that morning … but oddly enough, he was still the same Monsignor, politely making conversation with them as they went down the hallway, despite glancing up and around every ten seconds or so, they didn't quite know what to make of it. Regardless of looking like he was in pain only ten minutes back, he was also quite cheerful, in fact, it was infectious. It was peculiar and a bit funny, they found they couldn't stop smiling.

Walking along, almost coming to the stairs he abruptly stopped, they stopped with him.

"Mabel, may I see your medal?"

"Sure, here you go," she nodded, holding up the slender chain around her neck on which the medal was hung, an oval pendant of the

Sacred Heart surrounded by detailed scroll work. "Lovely, isn't it? My sister gave it to me for my birthday."

"What a beautiful and thoughtful gift," a comment that was true, but he was not interested in its provenance or *human* artistry. He usually had a feeling when religious articles were blessed or not, but was never quite sure of his hidden intuition on these things, until now.

Curious, they watched as he took out his little blessing book and bottle of holy water and did the honours. His expression changed into one of joyful satisfaction once the rite was accomplished. He couldn't take his eyes off the medal, was about to continue, but stopped again.

"Hmm, let me give this an extra blessing," he announced, taking the medal up again. They watched inquisitively as he said something under his breath followed by the sign of the cross over the medal, not sure what he was saying, but he seemed amazed when he was finished, almost like a 'Eureka' moment as if he had discovered something he hadn't known or witnessed before. Without any explanation, he then just picked up his two cases again and politely motioned the ladies to go up the stairs first, his joyful mood still quite contagious.

Progressing on to the main entrance, he talked as before with them, again, taking a quick look at certain religious pictures as they passed and the statues that were there or dotted around on their office desks and out in the reception area. He tried to act normal, but felt he wasn't succeeding very well. Eventually, he was able to say a 'see you tomorrow' and get to the car. He glanced around, the rosary hanging off the rear view mirror was also gleaming a mystic blue glow that made the sky look under the weather in comparison. How could he do his work when he was this distracted? He said a quick prayer, wondering if it was okay to ask for the lights to 'dim' so to speak. The light faded at this request, he had normal vision again. Oh no, maybe he should have waited a bit, as soon as it faded he longed to see it again, but there would have been no way he could have driven home this unfocused. Is that what the Apostles and disciples felt like when You ascended and disappeared from their view by a cloud? He hoped the gift hadn't been taken away permanently because he asked for it to go … could he just see the light for one more second? There! It flamed back! Elated, he realised he was given the grace to see or not to see the luminous presence when he willed, obviously Heaven knew there would be times he would need to concentrate, and had actually provided the proverbial 'off' switch. Gifts had to be used wisely too. Then, it was probably best not to get *too* used to that blessed consolation, he might stare at everything and pine for

Eternity, and let's not get into the matter he would look anything but normal when caught unawares in that state.

He once more willed the light to fade and it obeyed. Ah, the earth looked so lacklustre in comparison, he felt the pang for Heaven again. His emotions were in a beautiful but agonizing state of flux. He definitely needed some time to get used to this, maybe he would adjust quickly. Perhaps it may not be that different from when the gift of discernment revealed itself, he had to get used to that too, now that just felt normal for him. Hmm, that wasn't such a good thing either, he didn't want to take what he had been given for granted. Heavens! Thanksgiving! He was so caught up in the revelation of it all, he hadn't made a proper thanksgiving for the graces! God forgive me! With the Luminescence still 'switched off', he wasn't sure how to term this new condition, he went straight to the cathedral. He just had to give thanks.

The place was now a little more quiet than usual as the morning services were over. He would have used the side entrance, but couldn't refrain his curiosity, he hoped the Almighty wouldn't mind if he took a look, this was all so new. Standing in front of the cathedral, he gazed upon the neo-gothic carvings of the triple doorway and its archways and up at the pinnacles. Bracing himself so as to control all reaction to what he might see, he willed the luminescence to return, and was transfixed to the spot. The building was bathed in a seraphic spectrum of colour that would make the sign of God's covenant with Noah envious, if a rainbow was animate and could be tempted to commit the sin of envy. The delight felt at such magnificence was sheer ecstasy, soul wrenching even, but of course, he would expect nothing less of a building consecrated to the service of the Creator. Taking in the sight, he wasn't sure if he could withstand the treasures waiting within. Willing off the Luminescence, he slowly went inside, blessed himself with the holy water provided at the font, selected the last pew in the back, genuflected, kneeled for a moment, then, asked for the Light. No, no *no!* It was too exquisite! He didn't know if he could handle it, he started to shake with the shock and the joy. Each saint, each nook, each corner, had a light a colour, a flame or glow of its own, the very stone of the pillars came alive with vibrant hues, it was too beautiful to bear. The most frightening was the tabernacle, which literally shimmered and blazed like a furnace raised to the intensity of the whitest heat and ready to liquefy the chapel. He was afraid the whole place might catch on fire, yet the knowledge that this was no ordinary flame and would never cause that manner of destruction helped to dispel the dread a little, this was the Fire of

Love Itself clamouring to save souls. He felt completely unworthy to look upon it.

Please, could it fade only a fraction?

The light did as he silently asked, the building dimming to a gentle translucence. He could look around without feeling terrified out of his wits, but the shock had set in, he was still unnerved. He couldn't kneel anymore, he had to sit. No wonder God kept the Unseen veiled from the human race, only so much of the supernatural on that level could be taken in by a meagre mortal that had not yet entered Eternity. Clearly, he would have to learn how to adjust the 'toner'! Yet, he had a feeling that glorious burst was still only the tip of the iceberg. If he actually saw the full Divine Light of Heaven in the full measure of Its Glory, his imperfect human nature would melt into nothing. He slowly willed it off and attempted to make his thanksgiving. What thanks could his poor fallen humanity give for this most recent display of God's love? If only he had brought his prayer book with him, the jubilant canticle of the Three Children in the Fiery Furnace seemed rather apropos for this occasion, but perhaps in his current condition he may not have been able to hold the book open let alone read it. For the present, all he could say was a trembling and heartfelt 'thank you' again and again, further praying for guidance begging that he would use this new gift wisely and in complete accordance with His Will.

Trying to concentrate, he finally calmed down to where his knees could function again, he realised someone was standing behind him, patiently waiting, but not wanting to disturb him.

"Can I help you?"

"Yes, please Father, that's if you're not too busy. Are you hearing confessions?"

He looked at his watch, yes, he had some time. With a smile, he motioned over to the confessional closest to him near the back, not his usual one. Obviously, this penitent was not a local and didn't know him, and so decided to try and stay incognito for the moment if he could. If he got flooded, there would be no going home until midnight, and it was his turn to cook dinner.

This soul was a pretty well kept one, no mortal sins to wipe clean, it was what he could describe as a fairly routine session that required no major exercise of his interior discernment, with one exception, he had been given a new gift and no doubt it must be used for the benefit of others right away. After giving his visitor their penance, he asked if she had any religious objects with her that she wanted or needed to be blessed. She wasn't expecting that, usually it was up to the person to come to the priest and ask for it, but was happy to receive the offer.

"Umm, well, I have my rosary on me of course, and a few medals … ."

She held them up to him at the grate. He was about to will the Luminescence into action, but then the thought struck him, was it possible to direct this new sense of sight only onto specific objects? He didn't want to get distracted by the other blessed articles in there, not to mention the confession box itself might start shining again. It would be helpful if he could … my! It was not only possible to adjust the 'toner', but he could direct his focus if needs be and turn up the intensity on single objects to see what was already there … yes, the rosary was blessed, it was glowing that entrancing sky blue hue, but no additional colours showed. Interesting. It was like his other rosary in the car, sky blue must mean an object associated with the Mother of God, but the different colours that had manifested on his personal rosary no doubt signified the rare graces attached by having touched it to first and second class relics of the saints when he came across them and had the honour of venerating them.

Okay, he was learning. He already conducted his first 'experiment' on Mabel's medal and found after giving it the official Latin blessing that anything with the Sacred Heart was given a particular royal red glow with a single flame. Then, was there more he could do? He had always wondered if a special blessing that was spiritually inspired and pronounced on the spot held any unique authority since it was not one of the 'official' blessings approved by the Church, and wishing to discover the truth, added an extra blessing with which he was inspired to pronounce over her medal that would please the Lord and be spiritually useful to the wearer. When he took Mabel's medal a second time, he prayed that it would not only be blessed, but would draw grace upon grace for the salvation of the wearer's soul and those she prayed for, and be a veritable terror to the demons. Surprised, he saw the red flame burst into additional flames tipped with royal purple tongues of fire, enhancing the original blessing.

So, it was true, it was exactly as Irene, God rest her soul, used to tell him: a priest had to be extra vigilant with what he wished on people or things. He represented Christ and was granted the privilege of ministering in His Name and with the selfsame powers of healing, forgiving, but could also punish and chastise. At the time, he wondered if she was being superstitious, but now knew otherwise. She even remarked a priest had to be careful what he even said in jest or in casual conversation, for it could come to pass … even in odd ways that was not expected, but his words *would* come to pass. He remembered asking her what she meant by that, and she told him a story of a young priest who had a habit of making light about everything, and not just an innocent joke, he was always flippant and unguarded about what he said. One Saturday someone heard him remark with a sarcastic laugh he hoped the car would go on strike so he didn't have to come in early in the morning and get a rest. That evening he loaned the car out to a friend who on the way home tried to avoid hitting a dog and swerved right into the front wall of the church and destroyed both car and church gates. The priest couldn't get to morning Mass the next day until later, fulfilling what he wished upon himself and the car: it did go 'on strike', it struck the church and temporarily prevented him from fulfilling the morning duties he had sinned in complaining about.

Now, he began to see the wisdom in her observations. Oh yes, he always knew that if he pronounced a blessing, it would be held, if he withheld forgiveness, it was withheld, but now saw that if he was ever tempted and rashly flung a curse, it could also strike a person. What a thought! Of *course*, he would never, ever fling a *curse*, unthinkable! Nor would he ever withhold absolution unless the dire conditions were there, but it was clear he would have to be extra cautious in what he said or spoke about. Hmm, looked like he was not finished with this rosary either he noted. The one advantage with this heavenly light given to him was that the details of the article under scrutiny could be perfectly seen in the earthly dark. He noticed there was a St. Benedict's medal at the principal join holding the decade beads and the introductory beads with their crucifix, but it seemed to be lacking the distinctive purple flame his exorcist articles and the Sacred Heart medal possessed after blessing it to be a terror to demons. He prayed the same blessing on the rosary and the blue glow became intense and shot little flames, however, the purple glow around the Benedictine medal was only a faint purple, but he knew why, those medals required a particular blessing, and he needed his prayer book for that. What to do ... he didn't want to leave this confessional and get spotted in the building at this hour if he could help it, he would definitely get waylaid, and he didn't have time for any more confessions. He wondered if the little books stashed in this confessional might have it, but he wasn't sure ... wait a minute, one booklet began to glow. He picked it up and flipped through the pages, he could read the words in the dark, and one page was brighter than the rest, he flipped back to it ... there! This was something else!

He apologised to his penitent for the slight delay, but explained her rosary was lacking all the necessary blessings and continued on. Ah, there's that purple flame. Hmm, he still wasn't satisfied, something still 'tugged' within, prompting him not to let the rosary go just yet. Of course, there was actually a special blessing just for crucifixes too, but even he forgot to do it at times, usually the rosary alone received a blessing and that used to be sufficient, but now he knew he must do more: much was given, much must be shared. He thumbed for the proper blessing and fulfilled that duty, the little crucifix broke out into red flames. He then noticed her medals, blessed all right, but not with his unique blessing for additional graces and the request for them to become 'demon repellents'. Ah! Better! Their unique glows representing the saints they were stamped with broke out into little tongues of fire tinged with purple. For a moment he couldn't help be distracted by the St. Philomena medal, it flamed a beautiful shade of rosy pink edged in purple. It looked like everything was taken care of, he told her to guard her special 'treasures' as they were especially blessed. Don't lose them he advised, and to go in peace before he closed the shutter.

That was weird she thought, she had never heard about objects getting *that* many blessings before, or had ever seen a priest read in near pitch darkness for that matter!

Willing off the Luminescence, he said one last prayer of thanksgiving, then decided he had better go if he was to get dinner started for the Holy Bachelors. That sounded and felt so … lame. It was difficult now to think of the mundane tasks of the earth after seeing what he had today! That definitely had to be part of the sacrifice he had to feel. Never mind. Didn't St. Theresa say one had to learn to look for God amidst the pots and pans? If Christ could leave the magnificence of Heaven and take up the humble work of a carpenter for a time, Peter noted he could very well roast a chicken or two.

φ✿υ

Two weeks. With the new development in his spiritual gifts, he had almost forgotten about his new appointment at St. Peters. It seemed like a respectable amount of time to get used to the idea of being sent to minister at another church, but at the same time, Peter knew it was going to speed right on by. Better start getting everyone else used to the idea too. He didn't waste time and broke the news that night over dinner. After the surprise subsided, the Bachelors were happy to hear he wasn't been sent to a new rectory closer to his new parish church, the place wouldn't be the same without him, but also worried what it would do to him in the long run. St. Peter's was all the way in the financial district next to the World Trade Center, and already he was stretched thin and had a lot of work lately with all the people coming to him, the crowds showed no signs of abating, and his 'fan mail' and other correspondence was growing into an unbelievable pile. Then, they had to reflect that Fr. Mark was also kept on the run with the kiddos under his care in his new ministry, not to mention he would be gone the few days to the Youth Day, and he was bound to be kept hopping after that. There were so many after school activities that needed supervising in the Youth Centre. Fr. Jenkins was now given another hospital in his rounds, and Fr. Conner had to admit he was getting a bit winded after his own duties every day. Like them, he wasn't getting any younger, so how were they going to keep up with the rectory? Trying to manage dinner and the basic household humdrums was slipping beyond them. There was nothing for it. Peter suggested they try hiring a housekeeper again.

"Agh! No! Has it come to that at last," O'Conner entreated good naturedly, but not thrilled with the idea.

"I'm afraid so," Jenkins replied sympathetically. "We just can't manage everything, not any more, not with all our crazy schedules, and isn't it about time you got to relax a bit in your old age," he continued, ribbing O'Conner a bit.

"Relax? Now there's a thought! With a woman fussin' and poking into all our privy drawers and corners, will I be able to? There'll be no peace here, I can tell ye that!"

"Oh, don't get so worked up. We'll just make our bedrooms off limits, how's that? I'm pretty sure we can manage to take care of those ourselves," Mark shrugged.

"As long as you don't pour bleach into the wash when we're doing our laundry, Fr. Clorox," Jenkins grinned.

"Ha ha, very funny, just laaaaaugh it up," Mark returned. He hadn't heard the end of his washing mishap from the Bachelors who were not too enthused with his crispy towels either.

"You know, it would be swell if this new housekeeper can also cook. That would give us an extra break, not to mention give the smoke alarm a rest," Jenkins had to add. Since Peter had changed the old batteries in the thing, it felt like they were living at a fire house, not a rectory! The last occasion for alarm happened when Mark set the thing blaring when he left the roast beef smoulder slightly beyond well-done. However, they weren't too hard on him with the jokes that time, at least he got the broccoli up at just the right colour green for once!

Whatever about their housing arrangement, it was one thing telling the guys about his transfer, but it was another thing with his faithful parishioners from that area of the city who made the supreme effort to drag themselves out of bed to come to his early Latin Masses. He would have to break the news to them too, and decided the best time would be right away on Monday morning after his service. There were bound to be some rather disappointed people, it was hard for everyone in a parish when their spiritual guide was moved to another place after they had gotten to know him and *vice versa*, but it was a sacrifice that a congregation had to accept and offer up.

As to his other 'situation', he quickly decided he had better not get used or complacent with his Luminescent ability and resolved from that day on he would will it off until he absolutely needed it for his ministry. However, he also discovered the Lord wanted him to witness certain wonders when it pleased Him and that there would be no hiding from it.

Preparing for Mass the next morning, he had everything 'switched off', even resisting the pull to look at the jewelled chalice his family had given him with his increased vision, offering it up as a sacrificial mortification of his curiosity, yet making his way to the altar in his customary composed manner with Bill the sacristan in attendance, he couldn't help but stop short the moment his foot crossed the sanctuary boundary, the Luminescence flared up and was something to behold! It was different from yesterday where the altar shimmered with a myriad of different colours. Today the high altar was bathed in a gentle yet diamond white radiance, his vestments also radiating the same glow. The tabernacle was also flaming, but gently, nothing as glorious as when he thought the altar would melt, but the whole effect was so entrancing to look upon! The rest of the church was left as it was, only the area of the sanctuary was pulsing with white light. It wasn't difficult to figure out what was happening, the sanctuary was illuminated with the liturgical colour associated with the day, white for the feast day of St. Alphonsus de Ligouri. The chalice and paten were the only differences, they were gently flaming gold, white and red, the jewels transforming into living globules of light, but nothing awe-frightening like yesterday that would prevent him from doing his sacerdotal duty. He quickly realised he was being watched by the voluminous crowd and proceeded as normal, acting as if nothing had happened.

He was successful to a point, he didn't hesitate that much in the beginning, so he hoped it might be assumed he just stumbled or forgot something before coming out and had 'realised' everything was okay before proceeding. He thought he had managed pretty well acting as normal as possible, it helped having his back to the congregation, that is, until he came to the Consecration. He had no sooner pronounced those august words when the round wafer of bread shimmered into the most brilliant white light resembling the flames he saw yesterday in the tabernacle. It was a miracle he didn't drop the Host! Making the first genuflection, he couldn't get up, the moment was too profound, that sense of abject unworthiness took over. The congregation began to whisper a bit, but an extra moment of adoration wasn't unusual from the Monsignor at times … . Peter knew he couldn't stay this way and had to complete the Elevation, lifting the Host up.

How long he stayed like that, he didn't know, it felt so short, but now the congregation began to murmur. It was the longest he had held It up before, and it was now clear something was the matter, but they weren't sure what. Bill, who had the closest view of them all as altar server and who was surprised at the ecstatic expression of the Monsignor a moment ago, was now witness to silent tears, tears of both sheer bliss and bitter agony as the Host was elevated. Bill was almost on the verge of tears himself, he had never witnessed anything like it. Finally, Peter laid down the Host, made the second genuflection, this time much longer than the first, the tears stopping for a moment allowing him to proceed to the Consecration of the wine. Again, Bill was witness to a repeat of the extraordinary sight of Peter transfixed at the first genuflection, then the Elevation of the chalice accompanied by that distressing adoration, and concluded with a profound genuflection giving him time to compose himself for the rest of the service, using the maniple hanging from his arm to quickly clear away the tears. It had been an age since anyone had seen a maniple used according to its original purpose, to wipe away the sweat of penitential sorrow and humble service, and, tears of unworthiness and pure love.

Now, it was clear something had happened. Bill was positive the Monsignor had seen something, but wasn't sure what, while the congregation could only guess there was an unusual event happening and began murmuring again. Something's wrong, is he all right? What could it be? The server isn't looking so good either … . The people in the front pews weren't sure what to think until the *Domine Non Sum Dignus* when Peter tuned around and presented the Living God to them, but even then, they were more perplexed than before: his expression was completely transfixed with awe at the Host and the Chalice, but his face displaying he had indeed been weeping only a few moments ago. The murmuring grew again. People looked over one another's heads to get a better view before he turned around ... . Time for Communion came and it appeared the Monsignor was back to his usual self, no additional blessing today, the exception being his awestruck gaze fixed on each Host. Eventually Mass came to a conclusion, and they were surprised the Monsignor had an announcement to make before he left the altar—in two weeks he was being transferred.

As Peter had expected, not a few gasps and stifled reactions of disappointment were heard in the cathedral. The congregation was sad about the news, especially his faithful altar server. How apropos, but how tragic! The parishioners at St. Peter's were getting their treasure! It felt like he was taken from them. Was that why he was upset? This was a very sad day for all of them, that had to be it. Yes, they could still go to other services at the cathedral, or their own churches closer to them, but it was not like going to their saintly Monsignor. For quite a few of them, it was hard enough to get to his Masses in the early mornings, it was quite a sacrifice, but to travel to the financial district? For many that would mean extra commute time. Would they be able to keep that up they wondered? The more seasoned long-time regulars realised that at least he wasn't being sent all the way to Brooklyn like the last time he was transferred, but still, it was a bitter blow. Judging from the display of emotion at the altar it sounded like the transfer would be permanent. There was the one bit of good news that he was still going to be available at his underground office, but the thought of him saying Mass and hearing confessions elsewhere! They were so used to him at St. Patrick's, now they wished they hadn't taken him for granted and had bothered to go to more of his services. There were now a few additional tears flowing in the pews.

Once the announcement was given, Peter and Bill went to the sacristy as usual and began putting everything away. Bill was the only one who still suspected the Monsignor saw something and couldn't help ask what had happened. A flicker of quiet consternation passed Peter's expression, he had been observed, but there was nothing he could do about it. He pursed his lips then lowered his eyes, what could he say? How can you tell someone you saw the Heart of Christ beating as a living flame in your very hands?

The next two weeks were certainly one of profound adjustment when Peter entered the sanctuary to say Mass, the area would light up according to the feast day and the miraculous event of the Transubstantiation was continually open to his sight. This was one thing he would not be allowed to will off for the sake of appearing normal, it was difficult not to appear caught in a rapture, and in his effort to be as ordinary as possible, his manner became more august at that most sacred time, a profound, slow, deliberate, exacting reverence. The first few days were still very emotional, but he prayed for the grace not to break down at the altar again and it was answered. Nevertheless, his expression filled eyes gave him away the few times the faithful saw his face at the Latin service, his demeanour of transfixed, solemn bliss could not help but deeply impress the faithful. The days ticked down ... soon he would be leaving. As could be expected, the 'lionesses' did not want him to go without a proper goodbye gathering, so he together with his fellow priests was duly invited for a modest party at the community hall with his long-time regulars the afternoon of his last Mass at St. Patrick's on the Sunday before he left, giving everyone a chance to attend. Of course, he could not refuse, and so kept his appointment book free for the afternoon, passing the invitation on to anyone whom he thought would like to come, his parents plus Lottie and Tom. He also invited Leroy, but the scamp found some way to politely wriggle out of it, any hint of a church gathering with a load of 'Holy Marys' still made him feel like he was being ganged up on from Above!

Peter of course invited Katherine but found out that he was beaten to the punch there, she being his future sister in-law had already been approached by the other lionesses after service one weekday morning before she skipped off to work and was delighted to be asked if she could contribute in some way. It was hard to hear he was moving, she was so used to seeing him there, but Katherine wanted to help make this goodbye event as nice as possible. She wasn't a great cook, but food should still be easy enough to do. Since she was used to these kinds of community after-service get-togethers in her former Protestant parish, she figured the Catholic ones couldn't be all that different. This called for lots of doughnuts and finger dainties, and other buffet nibbles that could be eaten off a picnic plate with relative ease, not to mention an array of plug-in tanks filled with coffee, plus fruit juices and punch for the kids, all of which she ordered from Andre who was only too pleased to fulfil the catering request and arrange for the goodies to be delivered on the day. Thank goodness it was arranged for a Sunday, which gave her some time to help set it up with the ladies, who were surprised to see some people arrive early, including the main guest, and began to make them feel welcome, pressuring them to grab something to eat or drink.

"Hello Kathy, I'm glad to see you have met some more of the congregation." Peter smiled, giving her a quick hug and appreciative handshake to the other lionesses. "Wow, this looks really nice. Thank you so much."

"Honestly, we didn't get to do much this time, all thanks to your brother's smashing fianceé here. Kathy had her chef friend whip all this up for us." Fiona smiled.

"Ah, I thought I recognised those éclairs, and no wonder the coffee smells so good," Peter nodded to Katherine. "Leave it to Andre to figure out how to make French roast stay aromatic in the coffee dispensers."

Peter then asked if he could be politely excused for a minute before helping himself to the fare and brought Fiona aside for a quick chat: it was only four months since her mother Irene had died and he had offered her funeral Mass. How was she and the family coping? He had been terribly occupied and unable to check up on them as often as he would like, and Fiona was unable to see him considering her crazy schedule, running with the kids. Fiona went a little teary, but held it in, assuring him it was certainly a beautiful funeral and everyone kept talking about it, it had been ages since anyone else in the family had attended a Latin Mass until then, it seemed like a novelty to them. To tell the truth though, these months had been tough, both her parents were gone now, and the kids were missing their Nan a lot, but her littlest one, Deirdre, seemed not too upset. Perhaps she was too young to understand and it would sink in later. She simply nodded when she was told her Nan was now in heaven with Grandad, and pretty much left it at that. Perhaps it was a good thing, they say kids have a way of coping with sorrow and loss a lot easier than adults. Peter did his best to offer some comfort on the spot and told her he hadn't forgotten them in his prayers, adding that hopefully he might be able to drop by for a visit to see how they were doing as he was no longer stuck in the business world, if that was all right with her.

"Sure, Monsignor, any time. You're always welcome, the house could do with another dousing of holy water, especially after all the roarin' and threatenin' I have to do with my boys to keep them in line. They're becoming right terrors and driving me mental, but I love 'em," she replied with a sigh and a chuckle, looking to heaven before quickly turning in the direction of the outer vestibule where there could be heard a few merry screeches and a holler. "Oops! Looks like 'tag' is getting a bit noisy. Let me go check on the *childers*, I'll be back in a minute, excuse me ... go grab something to eat! You must be starving," she called over her shoulder as she hurried out, saying a quick 'hello' to other early arrivals just coming in.

"Hello, we're back together again!" O'Conner smiled, shaking hands with the Reinolds who had come early like them and had joined the picnic line.

"Yes, it seems like our Peter is giving us quite a few reasons to celebrate lately," Mr R observed.

"I wish it wasn't all departures," Peter returned, "but at least you all know I'm not going far."

"True, and I feel a little pleased you are closer to us at the Long Island side," Sophia noticed with a smile, while Katherine observed,

"It's odd, I can't help but wonder why you're being moved to the other part of town when you have quite a set of responsibilities and a whole herd of faithful parishioners here already at St. Patrick's."

"Actually, it's quite a feather in his cap to be sent there, you of all people might appreciate the history of the place," O'Conner was quick to point out with a knowing humorous nod, explaining St. Peter's was one of their most beloved churches, being the oldest Catholic parish in New York State, and having the honoured distinction of being the site where North America's first saint, who originally was Episcopalian, was converted.

"Really? Gosh, I've never been there," Katherine mused. Of course, she didn't have a reason to go before her own conversion, now, it looked like she was going to be visiting there a lot!

Fr. O'Conner was a wealth of information. He noted that in the early 1800s St. Peter's parish was also the site of a historical spiritual and political battle waged in the defence of the sacrosanct right of secrecy between priest and penitent in the confessional in accordance with the right to practise freedom of religion. Even to Peter, this was a new bit of information.

"Go on, you have our full attention," he prodded as he sipped his coffee, even the lionesses had their ears pricked up waiting to overhear the details.

"Let's see now, if me memory serves," he began, rocking his weight back and forth on his heels in an attitude of reflection, gently rolling out the nineteenth-century tale of stolen goods, jewellery to be precise, that was reported to the police by one of the parishioners. However, the complainant soon withdrew his report and wished to drop the matter as the goods had been returned to him. "You see, things got into a right twisht when the peelers didn't want to let the case go, a theft had been reported, and they were determined to catch their man, but sure, the *real* thing that got their goat was the thief had come forward in confession to the rector, who became a charitable go-between for the thief and the injured party, and ensured the stolen property was returned without revealing the identity of the forgiven sinner. The good rector refused to give up the name of the thief and was threatened with jail.”

Katherine couldn't figure out what the hubbub was about, especially as the injured party dropped the case, but O'Conner pointed out that back then the Irish Catholic minority often had a tough time with the Protestant majority who were in control of everything. So, it was a way to harass a priest and his flock. Yet, to his credit, a Protestant actually came to the rescue and declared that the priest had a right to freely practice his religion, which was one of the founding principles of their new nation, and if his religion had set forth that he could not reveal the identity of a criminal if they came to confession, even in a case of law, it should be respected and protected. It was the first time the case of freedom of religion was brought up in an American court, and henceforth, protected the secrecy of the confessional.

“Not to mention, this case helped to ensure that everyone got the right to practise what they believed without harassment or hindrance,” Fr. O'Conner concluded with a satisfactory nod. “Did ye also know that we can all thank St. Patrick for bringin’ about the right to a private confession?”

“Is that so? How come?” Katherine wanted to find out, but Fr. O'Conner lost his attentive audience when the impromptu history seminar was cut short by more arrivals to Peter's farewell do.

It quickly became a noisy, cheerful gathering as the parishioners came up to shake hands with Peter, including Fr. Jenkins and Bill the sacristan, then broke out into other little groups with cups of punch or coffee in hand, their plates filled with food. There were quite a few mothers with buggies plus a number of toddlers and even a few teenagers. To all their amusement, one little girl who looked no more than six quickly ran up to Peter yelling “Fawther Petey!” and couldn't help but remind him of her opinion that despite all he said, ‘it’ still looked like a ‘dwess’ to her, aka, his cassock!

“Hey Kathy, I assume you've already met our Deirdre here.” He laughed before adding, “she has independent views on my attire that I still have trouble amending.”

“I see that! We did meet, she was helping me to set up all the treats, or actually helping to eat them, right?”

"They're weally weally good too! I like dem way better dan Twinkies," Deirdre was only too happy to compliment, however, her mother had caught what she said to Peter about his 'dress'.

"Deirdre! That's not a nice thing to say to Father!" Fiona gasped, running up. "Say you're sorry right now!"

"It's all right, she's forgiven, she'll figure it out when she's older." He laughed. He loved the guileless innocence of children, their sense of absolute fairness and leaving nothing overlooked, even if the observations offered were quite mortifyingly entertaining, which was one of those occasions.

"If you *have* to have a dwess, why bwack? Why can't you have a diffwent col-or?"

"Well, it's the rules."

"*Everywon* don't follow wules," she noted, eyeing her brothers warily.

"But I have to. Who else doesn't follow the rules?"

"I think he don't, he gets to werar red. You shood have red dwess, hats and ribbons, like him," she noted, pointing to the picture of the cardinal archbishop on the wall.

"Ho son! Out of the mouth of babes," Mr. R. chuckled along with Sophia.

"You know, I do have a nice dress with purple buttons, and a purple shash, how about I wear it for you when I come for a visit?"

"Weally? Oh, that would be nice, but wat about that pwetty one, that's nice-wer," Deirdre cried out eagerly, pointing to the picture of the Pope.

Everyone laughed, especially as the picture was the popular shot of His Holiness, John Paul II, caught on camera giving off an impish grin to the press, but Deirdre didn't know what was so funny, she was being serious both to Peter's amusement and mortification!

"Honey, you want Father Petey to be pope?" Her mother had to know, giving a quick comical glance Peter and his parents.

"Suwar! Wasn't the first 'ope called Petey? He get's to be king over aaaaalll the Church. I think Fawther Petey would be a very good king," she explained with glee, holding out her arms again.

Who could argue with that logic? The gathering erupted with laughter again.

"I'm afraid the pint-sized oracle has spoken," Fr. Jenkins added, ribbing his friend.

"Hmm, so how old are you now? Five?" Peter finally was able to redirect.

The pint-sized one indeed held up five fingers, before adding with emphasis: "And a quarter!"

Katherine smiled. "My, you're a big girl, aren't you?"

"I sewar am! I can tie my shoolaces all by myself now, do my buttons, *and* bwush my teeth, but I don't like that, I like shoolaces bettor," Deirdre admitted.

"Oh gee, that's something to yell about," her older brother Sean noted sarcastically before turning to Peter, "hey *Mon*, how's it going?" giving him a cool-man fist bump and a cooler shortened title, which was repeated by another boy, obviously his brother.

"Pretty good, but you know, you shouldn't knock your sister's accomplishments, tying shoelaces is a pretty big thing, it takes a while to learn that stuff," he noted, giving Deirdre a little appreciative nod. "I guess you must be eleven now, right Sean?"

"Not yet, almost! Next month. Catch any demons yet?"

"No, but I'm still chasing them."

"Far out! Let us know when you do, me an' Finn here are dying to hear all about it. So, when are you coming to see us? It's been awhile you know, you promised to teach us Chess," Sean reminded him.

"Yeah I know, I haven't forgotten you guys."

"Chess? Wat's dat? Is that weally fun? I want to play," Deirdre piped up eagerly.

"Hmm, I think I might have to start you on Checkers first," he noted.

"Good! They showed me, but I don't think theywar doing it wight," she noted with another annoyed glance at them, while the two brothers snickered. Indeed, they had a habit of making up so many non-existent harebrained rules when she played it was fun watching her get wound up when she found it impossible to win and she suspected something was amiss, but didn't quite know why.

"Now kids, don't be putting pressure on Fr. Peter, he promised to come soon," Fiona reminded, "go off and play, don't be a bug."

"Nah, they're fine," he assured her, then looked down at Deirdre who was now tugging at the skirts of his cassock.

"Fawther Petey?"

"Yes, dear?"

"Is it twue we can tell you seecwets, and you won't tell anywon, not if we say 'no'?"

"Yes, that's true."

"Cross your heart an' hope to die?"

"Cross my heart and hope to die, stick a needle in my eye, well, I hope I don't have to do *that*, but I promise," he returned with a chuckle, crossing his heart and holding up his fingers to declared his solemn pledge. Looking around at the big grown-ups and then her brothers who apparently often teased her a lot, she timidly asked:

"Can I wishper?"

"I guess so. You want to make a confession, huh?"

Little Deirdre nodded her head, bouncing her ringlets.

"Hmm, must be a big thing you want to tell me," he deduced, crouching down so he could hear her, pretending to look serious, but giving a quick look of amusement up at everyone before giving her his full attention again. "Let's have it then," he noted, pointing to his ear, allowing her to cup her hand around it and leave him in on her little secret. Stopping at one point he turned to her with a seemingly surprised expression, "You don't say? Really?" She nodded, then beckoned him to turn his ear again. At some points, her breathy 'wishper' directed nearly smack-dab against his ear for most of the session was difficult to understand, so he asked her to repeat some of her words a couple of times. Everyone glanced at each other, wondering what on earth she was in a gab about and just had to tell 'Fawther Petey'.

"Bless us, there's confidentiality in action for ye," O'Conner chuckled. "Looks like the child has kissed the Blarney stone."

Indeed, the session went on for a little longer than anyone might have guessed it would for some silly tale she wanted to tell. Surely, the child didn't have that many *sins* to tell, or what could be so important? Peter turning at one point and whispering something back, to which she eventually nodded her head and said 'Okay! I'll see what she says. Now, you pwomised, no telling anywon. It's our seecwet."

"I certainly did promise, and I won't tell a single person, not until you say so," he reaffirmed, the whispering now having come to a satisfactory conclusion.

"Okay, run along now!" Her mother scooted her and her brothers off to go play something with the other kids and give the adults a chance to talk. A lively game of hide-and-seek ensued, the hiding place of choice being under the buffet tables that were covered in cloths down to the floor and offered excellent shelter. Lottie and Tom arrived, the Hulk nowhere in site this time as his sister persuaded the Captain not to let him come.

Imagine having a bodyguard at a church hall! She didn't want to freak out Peter's congregation.

"Hi! You just missed the most adorable thing, ever." Katherine commenced, recapping everything that just happened.

It was a boisterous gathering, the noise in the hall rising several notches with all the conversations, meeting and greeting, plus Fr. O'Conner had the *figari* to start up a game of soccer with the kiddies in one corner in an effort to keep them occupied after they got bored with Hide-and-Seek, kicking a beach ball around that he discovered in one of the store cupboards. He was having a grand time, it reminded him of his days as chaplain to the Academy when he got all the lads together for sports after school hours, although he got winded quickly and ended up sitting down talking with a few of the men in a corner. Having to blow up the huge multicoloured sphere beforehand the old fashioned way resuscitation style didn't help matters, not to mention he wasn't filled full of Vim and vinegar like he used to be. Peter rustled up another cup of coffee for him, then spent time with everyone, giving and hearing the news, introducing Katherine, Lottie and Tom, sitting down for a moment with someone who needed a quick opinion on a matter, or listened to a good yarn or two from the men. He didn't want anyone to feel they had been neglected or left out on this his last parish get-together. It was a shame Fr. Mark was missing, but he was no doubt having a great time with his group on this the last day of the Youth convention despite the weather, which was also a topic of conversation. Everyone had heard or seen the TV footage from the Catholic channels or the national news: the heavens had opened, but didn't dampen the spirit of the event, His Holiness as usual was greeted with ecstatic cheers from the crowds who had travelled for this special pilgrim experience. However, it was also a hot topic of conversation when everyone couldn't help but bring up the latest 'brouhaha' over the mime troupe acting out the Stations of the Cross at the event, and to top it off, had the audacity to cast a woman in the place of Christ. Everyone wanted to know what Peter thought of that, and of course without hesitation declared it blasphemous. Once he gave his opinion, he decided not to dwell on the subject for long, they all already knew his stance anyway on matters such as these, this could develop into a hot debating session rather than a goodbye gathering, so he changed the subject although he couldn't help but dwell on the incident. He had seen a replay of the televised programme, and also the scathing review and denunciation of the mime representation given by the foundress of the nation's most watched Catholic television network. He agreed with her statement heartily, hoping she would indeed be able to keep her resolution to return her cloister to the traditional Poor Claire habit and ensure the channel continued to promote authentic teaching. God help her, he knew the uphill battle she would be facing from that time onward and sensed he would be facing something similar himself.

Nevertheless, he decided to enjoy the present, tomorrow was another day. The hard thing for him, Katherine and the rest of his family was that Gerry couldn't be here too, his little brother was missing out on all the family events, but it wasn't anyone's fault and couldn't be helped. Peter made sure to give him a call before the event wrapped up, a few of the congregation who knew Gerry also chatted with him for a bit, trying to stay cheerful, but they all admitted they were going to miss their brother at St. Patrick's. At last, Peter gave a goodbye speech, short, but to the point, reminding them it was not really a 'goodbye', that they knew where to find him, and then gave them a final group blessing.

It was talk like this when people started to say their goodbyes to Peter for the evening before they left that the kids who remained with the last of the lionesses who stayed to help clean up started looking a little glum, especially the pint-sized one who didn't understand why Peter was going away: for how long, and was it verwy verwy verwy fawar? Would they ever see him again?

"Of course you will, I'm just going to another church in the city, that's all," he tried to comfort, the tears starting to well up in her eyes as she looked up at him.

"Gosh, Deirdre! He said he's coming to see us soon," her brother Finn tried to point out to her, exasperated how she just couldn't grasp a whole lot of things yet.

"Okay, jus don't foget to see us," she reminded, feeling better, "and don't foget yoar pwomise."

"How could I ever?" He smiled, giving her and her brothers an extra special blessing on the forehead, making the sign of the cross with his thumb. "And you two be good now, don't tease your little sister, and we'll see about teaching you Chess."

"Right on," Sean smiled, giving him another fist-bump.

Once the ladies had helped to wash up Andre's dishes and pack them into Katherine's gallery van, they said their goodbyes, Fiona deciding to pull Peter over for a moment.

"About that 'confession' Deirdre made, I know your lips are sealed like the book of the Last Judgement, but just to ease my mind, is there anything I should be worrying about?"

"No, it's nothing that constitutes a danger to life or limb," he reassured, much to her relief.

"Some odd rubbish then," Fiona concluded, shaking her head. "She has a wild imagination, that one. You know, she has an invisible friend named 'Flippy'! Okay, I'd better run, goodbye Monsignor, call me and we'll schedule a time when you can drop by," she said as she rushed after her 'childers', trying to stop the latest game of tag and herd them out to the car.

"Will do," he called after them. Although he couldn't say anything about what was confided to him, Peter had a suspicion little half-pint didn't have such a wild imagination on this occasion, but he wouldn't know for sure until he made his visit as 'pwomised'. Deirdre had whispered to him a curious tale indeed he reflected, waving to them as they left.

By now, it was just the Reinolds, Tom and Katherine who were left outside, the hall locked up for the night.

"I guess we must be off too," Sophia noted.

"I know I shouldn't wish you 'luck' in your new parish work, but you know what I mean," Mr. R added.

"I do, and thank you all for coming, I really appreciate it."

"Hey, now that I'm here, and you're all here, I have to ask, what do we do about the portrait commission?" Katherine wondered. "I mean, we have another addition to the family to consider," she reminded them.

"Aw, you don't have to put me in," Tom tried to interject, but Mr. R wouldn't have any of it.

"Ho! You're right Katie, and yes, you've got to be in it too. It's a good thing it wasn't started yet."

"True. Hmm, I haven't quite decided on the setting yet, I certainly don't want to line us all up in one of those awful army drill formation type things," Katherine thought aloud, "and I probably wont be able to start on the actual canvas anyway, not until after Fielding's big showing, maybe not until the Grand opening in September is over."

"You just have a good think on it, just let us know when you have something to suggest," Mr. R nodded. "No stress. Just fit us in when you can."

"Well, there's a lot more than just thinking up the scheme, I have to think about scheduling in the preliminary sketches of you all so I have the first drawings to work from. That won't take too much time, I hope."

"Would you like us all together, or separately," Peter rechecked.

"Separately I think, because I'll be 'building' up this picture, it won't be a group sitting."

"Okay, who's first," Lottie wondered.

"Better do Peter," Sophia suggested.

He agreed, there was no time like the present to nail down one or two of his free hours in his appointment book while he still had them, there was no telling what his future appointment at St. Peter's would throw at him until he settled in. Still, it would have to be after Fielding's showing at the end of the month Katherine realised, looking through her own book, she had a ton and a half of organising details to take care of the next twelve days. For Peter, that would be fine, he had to see Fiona and her family too, so he could probably schedule in a day before then with them. How about the Saturday after the show? The 28th? Katherine nodded, that was 'do-able'. Would she be able to make it to his OR, or did she want him to come to her studio? Katherine didn't want to put him out, he might be needed in the parish, so she would come to him. In any case, she was doubly curious to see where he worked as an exorcist, especially after he let slip the term 'OR'. With a laugh, the details were settled and they called it a night. They all had an early day ahead of them.

Despite the adage that a change was as good as a rest, something uprooting as a transfer promised that the experience may prove good in the end, yet would feel anything but tranquil in the beginning. Changes were never easy, but that was the point. It was only through challenge could a soul truly progress, and Peter was already warned that he could expect nothing but trials. Nevertheless, the plough must move forward, and he wasted no time reporting in to his new superior after he had received the notification of transfer, Monsignor Inigo Hernandez, an individual who looked like he was used to getting his way and nothing was going to interfere with how he managed his parish. He was of course quite polite and welcomed Peter, introducing him to the other priests, the staff in the parish office plus other members of the parish council, and to his relief assured him he would be allotted a special time to say the Extraordinary Rite as the Archbishop had expressly informed him. However, if Peter thought that the reception of his request to uphold Tradition was granted too easily, he was right.

The first rude awakening he received on his first morning in his new parish was the high altar wasn't set up for him, but the modern altar facing the congregation was: the deacon explained to Peter he was actually slotted in for the first vernacular service of the day. To his disappointment, a separate time had not been designated to him for the Latin Mass as he had been assured, a state of affairs he didn't think he would find himself considering his new superior had said otherwise. After all, the Archbishop had sent notification several weeks in advance stating that he was to be allowed the special privilege of saying the Latin Mass for the weekdays as well as on Sundays. Of course, Peter would never be disobedient, but it wrenched his heart to be compelled back to the vernacular rite that had more in common with the Protestant celebration instituted by the Anglicans as a defiant mark of their separation from Rome. Still, if Rome declared the New Form was now acceptable to fulfil the obligation of offering the daily sacrifice, there was nothing he could do about it, and so Peter was obedient to the letter of the law for that morning. At least he could see the Light still shining about the altar, but was it him, or did it seem dimmer than usual?

If that wasn't enough, the few worshippers that did show up that morning were impatient. As he was now facing the congregation while offering the vernacular form, he couldn't help but notice quite a few attendees checking their watches not once, but a few times. That was not a good sign concerning the spiritual state of things. Yes, he did like to make sure everything was reverent, but he seldom went over the usual time it took, and this was not one of those rare mornings. He had never seen such impatience like this. Then, to give out Communion in the hand, a grossly liberal privilege which led to too many abuses, over-familiarity with the Sacred had often led to outright sacrilege! He was forced to do it because it was accepted within the New Rite, a real heartbreak. Looks like he had his work cut out for him here.

First things first. That afternoon he sought out Monsignor Hernandez and respectfully enquired what had happened to his promised timeslot for the traditional service.

"I apologise you weren't notified, it wasn't possible to make out a new roster yet, you see, things are run a bit different around here," Hernandez began. The congregation from this part of the city was accustomed to their set schedules, and it wasn't convenient to change them at the moment. Being in the financial district, things had to run like clockwork so people could fit Mass into their frenetic-paced life. Masses therefore were often timed down to the minute. "You of all people should know the markets stop for no man," Hernandez joked. "Most of our members here are under pressure to get to their trading desks on time and don't have time for novelties, but I'll see about your request as soon as I can. For now, you'll have to say the form everyone knows."

The form everyone knows.

That was another disconcerting thing to hear. It wasn't that long ago everyone in the Church was attending the Latin service, now only a few decades later, it was viewed as curiosity from the Jurassic Period. The truly ironic part was he was implicitly accused of seeking after novelties, when the Latin Rite was centuries old! If anything was a novelty, it was the changes inflicted on the faithful after the strange misapplications of Vatican II. Still, there were worse things he could be accused of than being a holier-than-thou eccentric, but what worried him was how Mass was being made to fit around the time-dictates of the world. True, people had to earn a living, the Church was always considerate of a person's duties in that regard, but when Mater Ecclesiae began conforming to the pace of the day traders and Wall Street, that did not bode well. Peter could not help but reflect upon the mystics of old who warned that when the Church and the Mammonian world became one, the End of Days was snapping at their heels.

'Market Masses', that was another bitter irony he reflected the next morning as he stopped for a moment on the steps of his new parish headquarters, taking in the sight. Located at 22 Barclay Street on the corner of Church Street with the Twin Towers of the World Trade Center towering nearby, the stocky nineteenth-century Greek Revival building with steps leading up to a portico entrance supported by ionic pillars and nestled amongst the contemporary high rises looked more like a banking institution than a place of worship. However, there was something to be said about the granite edifice notwithstanding its blocky stature, it gave the unmistakable impression of cornerstone stability when contrasted with the glitzy modern structures encircling it. The church truly felt like a rock, and wasn't that apropos? Perhaps he should not be too critical that the exterior seemed so bankish. After all, the Lord had compared Heaven to the ultimate safety deposit box where no thief could steal, no moth could consume, no rust could destroy. Perhaps this is why the Lord allowed him to be transferred here, to remind everyone in this borough where they should *really* be banking, that 'Petrus, Providence and Prudential' provided the best interest paying accounts of all.

Okay, there was nothing he could do about the vernacular service for now. Peter knew God would be pleased with his obedience, suppressing his desire to offer the more beautiful Latin form of the Sacrifice as a form of personal sacrifice. It was a grievance to him though, but he was warned sorrows would come, just accept all in conformity to the Holy Will. Another source of regret was there was little time allotted for confessions at St. Peter's, half an hour, maybe forty-five minutes at the most. He could not help read into this curt schedule that few people came for that sacrament, most likely because they did not see how important it was to unburden and purify their souls. For now, the short time wouldn't be a problem yet as few of the parishioners here knew about his abilities and his old parishioners at St. Patrick's hadn't figured out when his services were or when he was in the confessional, but when the news would eventually begin to spread, half an hour just wouldn't cut it! To make things more difficult, he was only assigned two days a week to hear confession at St. Peter's. Again, why God would suddenly restrict everything on him when He had granted him these extraordinary gifts was a mystery, but then, that was exactly how He worked, often against the very mission given to a soul to test its obedience and perseverance, and to show in the end that the mission was truly given from Above. For the moment, he could only do the job set before him, pray, work, don't worry and wait, the solution might present itself.

Indeed, St. Peter's was a beautiful sanctuary of spiritual calm in the midst of the bustling district. The doors closing behind him, he took a seat in the back and entered into the presence of the Lord, calming his mind and saying his preparatory prayers before Mass. In the past, he liked to pray here when he had a chance to drop by, and now that this was his parish, that would be every morning. True, the Neo-Gothic splendour of St. Patrick's was a majestic setting befitting the house of God, but here the white marble surroundings modelled after the classical Greek fashion reminded him of the churches in Rome and his first days as a priest on so many different levels. No, he didn't indulge in his newly bestowed gift of Light as he prayed in his new ecclesial headquarters, he was determined to keep his resolution not to turn on the Luminosity as another sacrifice he could offer up. In any case, he already had plenty of subjects to meditate upon, for although the church was mostly in white, including the statues of the saints all carved in marble, the sanctuary was adorned with two distinctive masterpieces in colours reminiscent of the Renaissance masters: St. Peter overhead suffering his unorthodox execution head to the ground, while Our Lord underneath was raised up to the world on the High Altar. Rarely did a church have a double crucifixion scene like this, and Peter could not help but think of the warning he had received. God needed his gifts here, and since much was given, much would be expected. When the goldsmith's furnace would be lit and the cutter's blades be sharpened, he did not know. Pray and wait like Our

Lord in Gethsemane, that's all he could do, but at least Christ knew the hour, he did not. That would be one of the quiet agonies too, waiting for the metaphorical executioners to come, not knowing when the hour would strike and from what quarter they would appear.

The first few days were difficult at the altar, continuing to say the new Mass as reverently as possible while breaking in his new congregation so to speak, trying to instil a sense of the sacred, many were still checking their watches, and these little trials were in addition to trying to look normal while facing the people since he could still see the Luminosity at the time of the Consecration. However, the times he needed to give an extra blessing to chase away the 'throttlers' seemed to have helped, the odd manifestations that occurred with his blessing seemed to have alerted the congregation that something serious was indeed happening. Also, the short time allotted to him to hear confessions was put to good use. In addition to a few regulars of St. Peter's, he had a couple of people who hadn't been in to see a confessor in several years and felt drawn there not knowing the reason why they felt this mysterious attraction to drop in for a visit. Were they in for a shock when not one thing both mortal and trifling was left marring the souls by the time he was done with them! The word rapidly spread among the regulars that the new priest wasn't like any of the others, and then the excitement began to fly when they discovered he was the same one that had caused a stir at St. Patrick's. Not everyone knew what was going on in the other churches of the city down to the last detail, but his story was certainly making the rounds. Tales of what happened 'over there' were often dismissed as rumour or gossip by those who hadn't seen for themselves what was going on. Now, several of the stories were confirmed when the Monsignor's old faithfuls from the cathedral began filtering over to his new parish by the end of the week to attend his Masses, the word having reached them when his services were being held. Barely a few spiders attending on that first Monday became packed pews by the following Friday to where there was no standing room at the back to the surprise (and annoyance!) of the parishioners at St. Peter's church, which was smaller than St. Patrick's.

As to be expected, Peter was politely accosted by a few disappointed die-hard faithfuls from his former congregation after Mass the Friday morning of his first week as he made his way to the confessional. Why on earth was he saying the New Rite? They didn't expect him of all people to go back to it! They were so looking forward to his Latin service as it wasn't being offered at St. Patrick's since he left, the vernacular had been put back on there too, even in the early morning hour. Peter was sorry to hear this, but he explained the situation concerning the roster at St. Peter's and was hoping that he would be able to have his customary Latin service scheduled in soon.

They didn't say it to his face, but a few of the seasoned old-timers guessed there was no 'mix up' in the roster. It was a sad fact that there were a huge majority in the Church both clerical and laity that were opposed to everything that was once held sacred, jettisoning out everything ancient in favour of the untried and untested experimental forms of modernity. Quite a number of priests who attempted to maintain the old ways were blocked at every possible turn from celebrating or practising the old rites either by outright ridicule, or by the spread of misinformation that the former rites were abolished since Vatican II, which was an outright lie. However, the most insidious stoppage came in a variety of nicey passive aggressive blockades making it nearly impossible to practise Tradition without looking like a disobedient troublemaker. Many parishioners had seen it before, permission had to be obtained to say the Latin rite, and when it was given to an old priest and he had finally secured a time to say it in a church, it was made frustratingly difficult for everyone, the time being changed around so often that no one could attend his services on a regular basis as people naturally had to rely on dependable schedules. In the end, they stopped going due to the inconvenience, and then permission would be withdrawn from the priest as there was no one showing up! In other cases, the priest would be continually fobbed off with plausible sounding reasons why he couldn't offer the Latin rite, usually because it just wasn't convenient for the parish at the time, or again, the same old excuse that there weren't enough people interested in having the old rites to make it worth while scheduling them. 'But you do understand don't you? Perhaps some other time, we'll look into it,' was the typical diplomatic string-along offered with a smile.

No, his old faithfuls didn't say it to him, but Peter could guess what they were thinking without having to peer into their souls for he was not ignorant of the quiet relentless tide he was up against. He had experienced it before. In the past, Peter had to struggle against those hushed, diplomatic, glass wall blockades, but he did not say a word to his die-hards. Despite the difficulties, he would never, ever, give bad example and speak or murmur against his superiors. Rather than jump to judgemental conclusions without enough proof or evidence of a passive aggressive stand-off against him, he decided it would be prudent to wait it out and see if he would actually be given a time on the roster as promised. For now, like a good son, he would have to place all his faith in the virtue of obedience. It was the anchor of the religious life. Still, he could not help but reflect it was another painful irony. One of the signs that marked out the True Church was that it was the one most persecuted by the world because it resisted it, but the fact that the Church itself was trying to modernize in harmony *with* the world and was challenging everything once held sacred in its own Catholic Tradition that contradicted the world was indeed ominously telling.

In addition to his duties at his new church, he did not forget to call Fiona and arrange a time to bless her home. It was good to connect with his parishioners on a day-to-day level and see how they were doing. The funny part was when Deirdre heard her mother talking to him on the phone, she requested the receiver:

"Sorry Father, she won't give me any peace until she talks to you," Fiona sighed.

"Let's give you some peace then," he chuckled, "put her on."

"Fawther! You didn't foget us!"

"Of course not, I promised. And how could I forget you guys?"

"Will you werar yore nice dwess wit the colors too?"

She didn't forget a thing either, did she?

"I sure will, if you promise to be good, say your prayers, remember your guardian angel, and maybe stick me somewhere in your prayers?"

"I pwomise!"

Saturday afternoon was decided upon, and word spread among the family he was coming, so it was a lively gathering as Fiona's sister Ciara was there with her two little girls, Mary and Aisling, plus Fiona's younger brother, Joseph, and his wife, Heather, who both had a day off and brought their one year old, Aoife. Of course, it wasn't expected, but Peter didn't like visiting empty-handed, especially as he knew what visiting an Irish family was like: leaving a guest, especially a priest, go away hungry was unthinkable. He'd end up with a huge late-lunch instead of an afternoon coffee and might end up waddling back to the rectory. So, this time he was not going to a dinner without something for the kids at least and stopped by his favourite Catholic book store, he picked up a few colouring books with tasteful illustrations of the Scriptures, not cartoony things that made the gospels look ridiculous. He was a firm believer that respect for the sacred must be inculcated at an early age.

However, he was not a dogmatic spoil-sport either. If there was no joy, there was no true faith present. With this in mind, Peter picked up a few 'sweeties'. Giving candies was not considered inappropriate by an Irish family, even if the kids didn't get their dinner first. They didn't believe in denying life's little pleasures to the innocent all the time, and having a visitor was always a cause of celebration of sorts, meaning everyone was allowed to indulge in some treats. Sure, didn't Heaven belong to children? He was glad Gerry had lately insisted on seeing he had some kind of income coming in for which he was grateful, it helped with giving out the niceties like this during his ministry when his Mass stipends ran short due to his other charitable and catechetical projects.

Fiona's house was abuzz with anticipation the whole morning, having Peter drop by was definitely a cause for a mini-celebration with her family. They missed his regular visits they were used to receiving during the first years after his ordination, and now that his spiritual abilities in the confessional were made manifest, it certainly felt like a special privilege to be among his initial parochial acquaintances before the crowds had descended upon him. To have him alone to themselves again for an afternoon was just lovely! Yes, they were taken aback he brought anything, it was enough he was taking the time to see them and to bless the house, but the children were certainly thrilled, it was almost like Christmas had come early. Of course, Deirdre was all smiles he had come 'dwessed' for the occasion as he had promised, coloured sash included.

First things first though, before he engaged in anything social, he blessed every room in the apartment, and with his new luminous gifts, checked to ensure everything sacred in the place from a picture to the tiniest medal was thoroughly attended to as well. The other members of her family were probably not that observant, but Fiona like her mother had a keen eye and didn't miss a thing. She couldn't help but notice how Peter was much more thorough then he had ever been, gave a glance to everything and yet skipped a couple of items, in particular the blue lapis lazuli stone rosary hanging on the bedstead that her mother had given her, when at the same time he was so diligent about other things eventhough she was sure they had been blessed already. She couldn't help but wonder.

The sacred purpose of his visit now dutifully attended, it was time to relax, and Peter was right: Fiona and her sister had fixed enough food befitting a causal but festive indoor picnic party. It was all buffet style, everyone help themselves from pots, pans and platters in the kitchen before sitting to the carefully decorated table, and so Fiona wouldn't let him sit down until he had adequately filled his plate, 'self-service' didn't mean he was to be stingy with himself. If it looked like he hadn't taken enough of something, she quickly grabbed an extra spoonful and dropped it on top of the portion she deemed was too meagre. Good thing it wasn't Lent and he was trying to keep a fast! Then, there was dessert swimming in thick cream poured on top instead of the whipped variety along with a serving of ice cream, and of course, there was plenty of coffee or Irish tea to go with it all, whatever he wished, but it ended up to be a lot of tea since Fiona insisted he try the package of special Gold Blend they shipped straight from the old country thanks to her cousin, which Peter had to admit was pretty good actually. The funny part was, the Irish had been stuck under the stereotype they drank way too much alcohol, but they were certainly just as liberal with the tea, which didn't seem to stop flowing from the teapot to his cup.

In addition to eating lunch, Peter learned holding a conversation in an Irish household, especially Irene's family, God rest her soul, was quite an experience as everyone dreaded on missing out on something someone else was saying. Several running topics happened simultaneously between the various members. Usually if people broke into different groups they didn't expect anyone to keep with the others, but here they did. It was like playing a doubles tennis tournament with lightning bolts for team players with a special rule saying the players had to change the side of the net they were on every few minutes, considering how fast the topics jumped. It certainly was a cerebral and auricular exercise with everyone striking off conversations with each other, all having to keep tabs on who was saying what to who, because the attention of any exchange could suddenly be lobbed back into your own side of the court. Peter had to be quick on the uptake, especially as he also had to give his attention to the little ones who wanted to talk to him, running back and forth from the table showing him things from their toys, or bringing him a picture they just coloured for him while they picked at their plates, not wanting much of the healthier food and just waiting for the jelly and custard trifle, plus the cream and ice cream to be served, while all the time he had to be careful not to lose one jot of the multiple dialogues flipping back and forth between the adults.

"Would you like more trifle? Ah, go on, of course you do," Fiona asked, dropping another liberal spoonful of the unique blend of Jello-O and sponge cake into his bowl, then pouring extra thick custard on it along with the other creamy additions before he could protest her generosity. Frankly, he didn't know where he was putting all of this. Heather, the sister-in-law, shot him an understanding look. She had married into this Irishness and could see the funny side in Peter's predicament, getting thrown into the deep end of it all, be it having your ear gabbed off or filling your gob.

"We usually don't eat this much." Joseph then chuckled. "But since it's a special visit and all … ."

When lunch was over, the children were glad to hear the mothers order Joseph to go make himself useful by burping the baby and changing the diaper, but tell Father they wouldn't dream of having him help with the washing up. That meant they had him to themselves! Kids just gravitated towards him, he drew them like a magnet. Maybe because they actually liked the authority he projected, the silent, strong but secure type of clout that wasn't annoying, and the fact he was outright honest. Then he also had a great sense of humour when he was willing to show it, which was often with kids around, and he didn't think it beneath him to be interested in all the things that they found was the most important thing in the world like most dull adults tended to do. He never brushed them out of the way, demanding that they be quiet, telling them to 'stop bugging everyone, and go play now'. No, Peter never did any of that, (except at Mass when they understood it was a time to be quiet anyway).

Peter went along with the kids who eagerly tugged him into the sitting room so they could show off their other treasures. Right now Deirdre and her cousins, Mary and Aisling, were happy with their glittery plastic pegasus collection with wings that could be flapped, while Sean and Finn were really into anything Ninja. Whatever will the toy creators think up next he mused as the boys told him how the the semi-human creatures in the half-shell he was now holding had come to be, thanks to some mutagenic sludge called Agent X.

"And the turtles' martial arts master is a human *rat*?" Peter couldn't help but grimace at that bizarre addition to the story. Although they were God's creation, he hated rats. The kids laughed at his reaction.

"Yeah, but it wasn't his fault, he was in the sewer, got messed up with the Agent X, and 'cause he was around all those rats, he became the animal he was around the most, sooooo," Finn trailed, with a shrug.

"He's still a good guy though!" Sean jumped in.

"Are they looking for a cure to turn him human again?"

"Umm, I haven't heard that yet in the story, but maybe they might … I'm sure he doesn't want to end up in the sewers for the rest of his life, 'cause that's what's gonna happen if they don't," Finn concluded.

"Hey *Mon*, have you ever played Nintendo?" Sean hoped he was up for a game of *Super Mario Brothers Three*.

"Nooooo," Deidre cried out, "What about Chess? Or Chekors? Fawther Petey pwomised to teach me that first!"

Uncle Joe came in with baby Aoife to see what they were up to since it had gone a bit quiet, but saw all was well as the children were huddled around the game board on the coffee table, watching Peter lay out the pieces. As Peter and Deirdre played, Finn and Sean sat on the sidelines, letting him in on some of the special rules they had a habit of inventing just for their little sister's sake.

"Um, don't you remember that if you get back to the other end of the board, you get third piece on top, then you get to move on any square any way yah want?" Sean prompted, winking at him and Finn, then snickering as Deirdre glanced up at Fawther Petey to see if this was indeed twue.

"Oh, we're playing the 'Professional Rascals' version today," he observed, giving a quick glance to Joe, who also found his nephews' rendition an amusement.

Deirdre gasped when she saw Fawther's expression, she knew she had been had.

"So, it's not twue! You made that up," she retorted to her brothers, who were also laughing. Eventually, Peter straightened out the game for her, much to her satisfaction. Of course, there was no fair match between them, so Peter let Deirdre win a few games after which they were all summoned in again for another round of refreshments, coffee and cookies, before it was time to call it an afternoon. Again, he wondered where he was going to put another cup of anything after the non-stop meal he just had, but some coffee did sound good.

"Fawther, down't you wan t'know wat you wanted to know," Deirdre then wondered, holding him back.

Ah, he wondered if she would bring that up. He didn't want to push the subject until she brought it up herself.

"Of course I do, we just haven't had any time to ourselves yet, have we?"

Deirdre shook her head.

"No, an dis is still owar seecwet," she noted, looking up at Uncle Joe who was waiting for them to follow.

Okay, it seemed she was not going to tell the rest of her secrets until they were alone.

"We'll be with you in a minute, it seems half-pint here needs to make another confession, right?"

She nodded happily, glad that he caught on.

"Okay, you know where the coffee is." Joe laughed, bringing the baby along and leaving the sitting room to themselves. Deirdre ran to the door, scouted the hallway, saw and heard everyone else busy fussing and fuming in the kitchen, then closed the door.

"Guess what," she began gleefully, skipping to the couch and sitting next to him. "Nan wanned me to say that she said to you she would haun' anyone if dey told you you couldn' werar yowar dwesses no more, but she used a big word, the one Mummy used, caswock."

"Cassock?"

She nodded.

"Nan said she said that, but now she knows it is much, much better to pway for them. Jus like you, she says I must never, ever, *ever* stop pwaying."

"Very good advice," Peter nodded back, surprised, yet not surprised at all. Rather, he felt a stir of delighted astonishment that comes from receiving a hoped-for confirmation. He had guessed something special was indeed going on with the child and wasn't disappointed: the child was seeing her grandmother from beyond the grave. She couldn't have made that up, the last conversation Irene had with him on her death bed, saying she would 'haunt anyone' if they ordered him to stop wearing his traditional attire. He asked her if Nan told her anything else, and Deirdre said she had, to always listen to Mummy and Daddy, to be good and say her prayers, to pray for everyone, and to never forget him in her prayers either. Peter asked if Nan was in need of prayers herself, but Deirde shook her head. Nan told her the 'Mercy Day' had secured a quick entrance in to Heaven.

"Nan says it's sooo beyootaful! We must be verwy verwy good to go there."

Deirdre then had some additional interesting information: she was going to have a new sister soon, but not to say to anyone but Fawther Petey. He would 'know what to do'. Peter was again surprised, and a bit puzzled on that one. He waited to see what would unfold.

"Well, won't it be nice to have a sister?"

"Oh yes, things were not fair awound heewar," Deirdre nodded, obviously glad to have someone coming to help round out the sibling numbers. Too many boys, it seemed, and her cousins couldn't come to play all the time.

"Do you know what Nan meant when she wanted you to 'tell me first'?"

"Not weally," Deirdre noted, looking a bit puzzled herself. "She says dat she knows, she's aware of what goes on, she's wit us all the time, and dat you wud know wat to do."

"Okay. Anything else?"

"Umm … oh yes! She said I must weally, weally, pway for you, and dat she is pwaying for you too. She said you have a big job to do, it's coming. You have ta be weally, weally strong."

They didn't get much further in the conversation as Fiona called out from the kitchen to Deirdre, telling her to hurry up and let Father get his coffee.

"Okay, dat's all I have to say, for now anyway," Deirdre noted as she skipped out for her share of the cookies before her brothers and cousins gobbled them all, Peter following along behind, mulling over the riddle set before him by little half-pint.

After they had chin wagged lightning-fashion some more, Ciara noted it was time she get home with the kids. Joe and Heather agreed, time to get baby Aoife home too. After they thanked him again for his gifts, the parents prodding the little ones to remember their manners and also show their appreciation, they said their goodbyes, leaving Father with Fiona and her lively threesome.

Fiona was glad to have him to herself for a few minutes before he too would have to leave, hooshing the kids out to play their video games, making sure they stayed out by bribing them with the package of cookies, which they happily took with them. Okay, the childers were getting overdosed on sugar and be up half the night, but she needed to talk with him alone. It had been rather difficult lately with her husband Nevin having to travel long distances and stay away stretches at a time, since he was an architectural engineer and worked with a firm that sent him to inspect their various projects throughout the state, sometimes they sent him on international inspections. She didn't say it, but she had her worries. It wasn't in managing the kids by herself when he was gone, she could hack that, but that deep-seated worry a wife has when a husband is gone too long and afraid of the temptations that brings upon him. She wished she could tell Father her concerns, but Nevin was a good man, she would just have to trust him. What she did tell Peter was how hard it was these past months without her mother now, she used to be so busy helping out with the kids, there was a big hole in their lives and Fiona missed her terribly.

"The saddest part is," Fiona began, the tears welling up, "there's another one on the way. I just found out. I know, this should be a happy time, and I should be telling Nevin first, but it's just that I miss Mum so much. I can't help but think she will never get to see or hold her new grandchild. If I say all this to Nevin, I just might depress him, I know he doesn't like seeing me as sad as I am to begin with."

Depressing Nevin was another worry, she didn't want to drive him away into the temptations she dreaded.

"Wait, before you continue, I think there's something you need to hear, but I have to get permission first," Peter interrupted politely. "Excuse me for a moment."

Fiona watched with undisguised curiosity as he left the table. Within a few seconds he had brought back little half-pint with him after making a very special request in the hallway first.

"We just had an important conversation out there," he began, smiling to a confused Fiona wondering what was going on.

"Uh huh," Deirdre nodded.

"We've just come to an agreement that it's time for the secret to come out, since I'm 'supposed to know what to do', right?"

"Yep."

Deirdre nodded again, finally agreeing to come clean since Peter thought that was the best thing to do, and if Nan said Fawther would know what to do, and he said it was time to tell, well, it was time to tell.

Still confused at first, thinking the child was going on about her usual gibberish, Fiona was stunned as she revealed Nan was in Heaven and knew she was going to have a sister, and that not to worry, she was watching over them all. Fiona had not told anyone except Father right now she was expecting, and it was certainly too soon to know if the baby was to be a girl or boy, but how did she … ?

"You mean, she's … she's been *really* seeing Mum all this time?"

"Yes, she told me something that only I and your mother could have known, so yes, she is."

Fiona burst into tears at this, grabbing a handful of napkins from the table.

"Mummy, don't be sad! Did we just make her sad? I thought you knew wat ta do," Deirdre returned with alarm, a little miffed at Peter!

"Oh no! No! I'm not sad, I'm just very surprised, and so happy."

"Weally? You don' look like it," Deirdre returned, afraid she had done the wrong thing in telling.

"Grown-ups cry when they're very happy too, we're weird." Peter smiled as he tried to explain the complexities of adult emotions to half-pint. Fiona laughed at that through her tears, nodding to Deirdre that was true, then pulled herself together.

"Sorry about that," she sniffed, drying her face.

"Nothing to be sorry about, there are times when tears are good. Now that you know she's telling the truth, I've asked Deirdre if she doesn't mind sitting for as long as it takes for her to tell you everything, from the time she first started seeing Nan, what she looked like, plus everything she said, and you are to write it down before half-pint here starts forgetting all the details."

"I won't foget!" Deirde piped up, "I remembers evwything."

"I'm sure you do. Well, when you get older, you will have a lot more things to remember, and just in case Nan keeps coming, you might mix up some details with all the new stuff you will learn. It's like trying to remember a very, very long story, and Mommy hasn't heard it all yet. I want you and Mommy to write a book about it all, just for yourselves."

"Oh, okay."

That made sense. Deirdre liked books, they had wonderful things in them, if only she could get people to read to her more often, but this would be just for her and Mummy, and that felt really, really nice.

Peter then turned to Fiona. "This will prove a great consolation for you, especially as you don't know for how long your mother will be granted this grace to visit. Start tonight by recording everything so far, and then note down each visit after that."

"Oh I will, you can be sure of that," Fiona nodded, still amazed at what she had just heard. "Honey, can we start right now?"

"Suwar! Can I have more cookies?"

"Of course you can, pet."

"I guess I will leave you to it then," he noted, riddle solved, or at least one of them. While Fiona had received a great consolation, he wondered what the big job facing him was going to be. He would have to be prepared for anything.

ό❦ȣ

If Peter had a flicker of a hope things would be resolved concerning his morning services by the start of the week, it was quenched with the same old resistance that Sunday. Again, the knife of disappointment. He was not given any indication the provisions had been made for the Latin rite, and the new altar was set up as before, indicating that 'this' is where they wanted him blatantly contrary to the Archbishop's permission. If he hadn't learned to keep a lid on his temper for the most part long ago, he might have been fuming. Instead, he felt a keen sorrow and a looming sense of foreboding, not for himself, but for those who would dare to defy a simple order contrary to the virtue of obedience, especially when it came to the service of the altar. It wasn't like he was making an outrageous change to the parish. All that was needed was a public announcement, a notice up on the boards and the parish newsletter, and just leave him to it, there would be no disruption at all, apart from the crowds, (they would be coming anyway!) The sad part was it wasn't *him* they were resisting in the end, but God Almighty Whom they had sworn to serve. Unless he was illicitly ordered to defy the sacrosanct immutable teachings of the Church, Peter would never pay disobedience with disobedience, but with a heavy heart said the new rite again. God was willing this trial for the time being, he could only leave everything in His hands. It was a consolation seeing the Luminescence had not left him.

Still, he couldn't help feeling spiritually troubled as he made his way to the parish office after service. This uncomfortable situation stuck him between a terrible rock and a hard place. Should he eventually push back quietly by saying the Latin rite regardless since he did have permission? That could create more tensions and disturb the peace further, and one must not cause strife and division. Then on the other hand, if the hushed vehemence against the Archbishop's orders continued, he certainly did not want to be an occasion of sin for his new superior by becoming a handy pretext for resistance against Tradition. The thought of being a source of division was a sharp interior agonising dart. Peter realised he might have to consider requesting a transfer to another parish in the end, for now he was not sure if this could be resolved amicably without stirring up resentment in either case.

Then, *was that what God wanted?* There were times when He expected a soul to stand its ground for His glory like David against Goliath, and other times when it was good to submit to certain situations for the sake of peace and stay where one is placed, take the punches, then let God take care of the battle and come to the defence like a zealous parent for a defenceless child. Of course, it was better to be persecuted and humbly accept humiliations as Christ did, but He too took knotted cords and drove the merchants from the Temple in His righteous zeal and called people vipers when the occasion arose. Which was it to be *now?* To arm himself with sword of spiritual battle or remain the meek dove of peace? What to do? This certainly couldn't be resolved overnight. Serious matters, especially those involving God, should never be decided upon without invoking God. He would have to pray about it first and not lose his tranquillity and peace of soul despite the interior cross he was feeling. Worrying never presents solutions but only fuels anxiety. Just pray and wait. He had a lot of work to do in the meantime.

As usual, there was the morning line up waiting for him in the basement seeking his spiritual assistance, but in addition to the mix of familiar faces he was greeted by Tom and Margaret Fletcher from Trenton whom he wasn't expecting, a heavy sense of surrender weighing them down.

"I'm sorry, I know we don't have an appointment, but we had to come see you," Mrs. Fletcher began, but Peter nodded it was okay as he shook hands. He unlocked the door and allowed everyone into the waiting room, then checked his agenda and did a head count, all present were here with booked appointments except for the Fletchers. He would have declared them an ER priority right then and there were it not for the fact he needed considerable time alone to hear their news without the pressure of knowing people were waiting. Once he had attended the confession seekers, he informed his 'nurses' upstairs in the office he was not seeing anyone else for the morning. Now, the Fletchers had his undivided attention.

"Forgive me for jumping straight into the heart of the matter," he began as he closed the waiting room door and pulled over one of the armchairs, "but I assume help was not forthcoming for Melissa."

"Actually, Fr. Xavier did start the exorcism, or rather, the first of a few, but he didn't get very far," Tom wryly noted, but in a tone of alarm.

"Melissa broke free from the orderlies spouting the most awful profanities I've ever heard, also things I never heard, and attacked him, nearly broke his arm," Margie continued, the trauma of the scene obviously haunting her still.

That was not good, not good at all. Rarely did anyone get hurt during an exorcism, including the victims, and if they did, it was because it was handled badly or the priest was not prepared properly, or if he was prepared, got outsmarted. Peter almost dreaded to hear the details.

"I can see much has passed since the last time we met."

That happened to be near the end of that past June when he said Mass in their home as promised. He apologised he hadn't kept in touch after that.

"No, we knew you were incredibly busy, and it's our fault, we should have given you an update sooner, but here we are," Tom replied.

"Yes, that's the important thing, let's pick up the threads. Tell me what happened."

After they had seen him the first time when he came to bless their home and assess the situation in May, they were contacted by Fr. Xavier who after being given permission by the bishop insisted on a consent form before he started the ritual. Peter nodded and explained that was part of the procedure, a necessary legality. Tom noted the problem was rarely did Melissa come out of her strange state, which was compounded by the drugs she was now given at times to keep her sedated. When they heard about the necessary form, they were afraid she might never be lucid enough to ask her if she knew what was happening and if she was willing to sign it for a last-ditch-effort to help her.

Then, that's when the remarkable happened: the day he came to say Mass in their home, she inexplicably snapped out of her strange rages and had a period of calmness she hadn't experienced in weeks.

"It's true. One of the nurses said she kept asking where the 'man in black was', and they thought it was one of her 'hallucinations'," Margie explained, "but when they asked her if it was the 'demons' she kept seeing since she saw those too in black, she insisted it wasn't, 'he' wasn't terrifying, and was holding up a white disc, almost like a small bright sun. Well! When we figured out the time this happened, it was when you were saying Mass at our house."

Despite the wonder of the Fletchers, Peter wasn't surprised, but waited for them to finish.

"Not only that," Tom continued, "she stayed lucid and calm for the next few days, almost like her old self, enough that two of her doctors deemed her competent to sign the form. When we told her about your visit, she wasn't aware of what happened, other than she remembered the vague impression of a man looking very much like the one holding up the 'white disk', he was the only one who had really frightened the 'thing'. She wasn't going to sign the form until she put these two events together."

"So, does she remember anything of her dark fits when the demon displays its presence?"

"No, she's basically unaware of everything she does when she's 'out', except that she's in a place of 'darkness' internally, and hears awful voices tormenting her. Sometimes they leave her alone and she 'comes to', the fastest was when she saw you saying Mass. That's why eventhough she was reluctant to receive spiritual help and didn't want to sign the form at first, she knows something is wrong beyond a medical diagnosis, she's willing to do anything to stop the blackouts." Tom sighed with relief, glad to have this breakthrough.

"Even Dr. Fareed admitted to us that from everything he has seen and heard, this definitely was not a case of mental illness, especially after your visit, and that perhaps it was time the spiritual experts took a look," Margie added.

"Good. Are the doctors still in agreement there? They haven't changed their opinion?"

"No, especially after the exorcism started. Let's say a few things came out that they weren't expecting," Margie trailed.

"Hmm, I understand. Where did the exorcism take place? At the hospital?"

"Yes, the doctors didn't think it wise to discharge her, even under our care at home," Tom answered. "So, it was done in her room, the one you saw her in. Honestly, I thought it would only need to be done once, but Fr. Xavier said it might take more than once."

"Yes, that's true. Did he explain why?"

"Not really, other than it takes awhile to get rid of evil, like you mentioned to us before. He said it was just like an illness that requires a long course of medication to effect a cure."

"He's not wrong there, that's true, but there's a reason for the lengthy, repetitive process in an exorcism case. Contrary to what people think, possession is not a sin of and by itself, but sin can be an invitation for the devil to enter. Sin doesn't always lead to possession, but when God permits it to happen, it's for the good of the soul, usually to secure their final, unwavering conversion and to allow them gain more eternal merits. God never allows evil to happen without a purpose, greater good will be brought out of it if we are willing to follow His Will. There have been saints that were possessed as a trial to purify their souls further."

"That's a bit extreme," Margie commented quietly.

"Yes, but possession of this nature is actually rare, so rarely does God go to extremes," Peter reassured her, "however in this instance, not all is Melissa's fault. Since she was cursed first, she is innocent of opening the initial pathway to possession, but from what I recall of Melissa's history, her willingness to dabble in the occult later just opened the gateway wider. God is dong the extreme to wake her up to what she has done wrong, including whatever life she may have led when she ran away, and in the process of bringing her back it will prove to those who witness it, that the next life is not a fable dreamed up by fanatics, but that the supernatural does exist."

"It's made a semi-convert of Dr. Fareed and a couple of the nurses, that's for sure," Tom couldn't help but add. "They're not quite as sceptical as they used to be."

"What happened next?"

"Fr. Xavier came once a week, starting the first week of July. He'd say the whole rite, and I can't tell you the reaction she gave! It wasn't normal, the third week, things started flying across the room—by themselves. Even Fr. Xavier got a shock and walked out. He nearly didn't want to come back the fourth time, but he did, and that's when she was unable to be controlled and practically attacked him. He's walked off the job, said he wasn't up for this, and promised he'd have someone else sent.

As far as I know, he's asked the bishop to assign someone, but so far no one is ready to fill the post, so to speak," Tom concluded with a shake of his head.

This was bad. Not only were Melissa and the Fletchers left high and dry, but their diocese was without an exorcist for a month, and no one was trained, experienced, or confident enough to assume the apostolate. It explained why his professional advice to assign a different exorcist to the case wasn't followed from the start.

"The strange part was, the … thing … inside her said he wouldn't be able to do it. It sounded like a threat that 'it' was going to frighten off the priest."

"Which unfortunately happened," Peter replied.

"Yes, but it was more than that, a few times it said things like 'he wasn't the one chosen', " Margie revealed.

That was interesting.

"So you came to me."

"Er, it must have been you it meant, because when Fr. Xavier asked the question 'who' was supposed to be the 'chosen one', it said things like 'the black robe who is to banish us is elsewhere', and he is 'the one who scalded us'. 'He didn't have permission then, and we'll make sure he never gets it'. That's what was said," Margie explained, giving a few chilling quotes.

"I see."

He sat silent for a moment. There were singular occasions when not any exorcist would do, but the one chosen by God for the specific case. It was rare, but not unheard of for devils to name the priest predestined to cast them out. It certainly explained Fr. Xavier's lack of success. To be singled out like this was weighty indeed. The King of kings had selected a champion, it was up to him now to accept the gauntlet thrown down by the demons or to refuse. He and only he would be given the authority to dispel them. He was their last and only hope.

Although not attuned to all the complexities of this theological world, the Fletchers could grasp that this was a make or break moment. They waited with baited breath.

"I must admit, your niece being stuck in a hospital in another diocese will pose a difficulty, but since you have a consent form already, not to mention the support of some of the medical staff, it might work out quicker if I can get permission to come to you."

Relief showed instantly.

"You'll do it," Margie tentatively asked, just to make sure.

"Of course, as soon as I can get permission to work in your diocese and parish, but I'm not sure how long that will take. Also, to see if we can get her out of that hospital, preferably onto consecrated grounds with some privacy, although that's going to be a tough one. It will depend if Melissa will stay in a normal state long enough to be discharged into your care, but we have to leave that up to Divine Providence. It means being patient for a little longer."

That was okay, as long as he was not turning them away!

"Oh thank you," Margie replied, grateful beyond belief.

Naturally, he returned her gratitude with 'you're welcome', but they needn't thank him, this was his mission, a fact confirmed by the demons themselves who were compelled under the previous exorcism to reveal the one chosen to finally cast them out.

So, it begins.

He was born to do this.

It was a semi-distracted drive to the hospital that afternoon to visit Gerry, trying to remain spiritually collected with the Blessed Sacrament present while reflecting upon the grave matter that was now entrusted to him. Not that he was afraid, but he had already been warned from the next world that the job would be a trial. Of course, exorcisms always were, but he obviously was going to be up against something more disquieting that even he would not expect despite all his preparation and study into the subject, which included having witnessed a few exorcisms in Rome. He knew this task was assigned to him, for even if the demons *did* lie during Fr. Xavier's exorcism in naming him, Peter knew little Deirdre didn't. The child had a keen sense of right and wrong, abhorred her brothers lying to her, and after his little test into the matter, knew she certainly didn't make up the message sent to him by her grandmother from beyond the grave. The next task was to inform the archbishop of the latest developments in Melissa's case to get the ball rolling, but he could see to that later. For the present, he had a brother who needed him, he could feel something was not right as he searched for a parking space … .

Sure enough, Gerry had guilt hanging over him and looked troubled, distressed even, the mental stew churning within set on a steady but intense heat.

"I see we need to talk, or confess something," Peter kindly prompted, pulling up a chair.

"Both, I guess." The patient sighed, self-reproach etched in his face, his voice mordant with something weighing on him.

Peter began the with the sign of the cross, and immediately knew what was wrong before his brother had the chance to say a thing, but as required for the sacrament, let him go ahead and heave the guilt off.

"I lost my temper this morning, but of all people, I lost it with Katherine."

No wonder he looked like the world had ended. Best to finish confession and Communion first, then they could talk it out. When the appointed time for silence had passed, Peter gently got the conversation started before Gerry felt tempted to bottle up again.

"You do know losing your temper wasn't mortal this time," he reminded him. "The other things you had to tell me were more culpable than this."

"Really? It doesn't feel like it," Gerry returned crestfallen. "You know me! I never blow my top. And now when I do? It's at the one person who certainly didn't deserve it."

Gerry laid out the whole scene. The doctors decided they were moving on to the next phase of his recovery by tapering off the medications further, and had that morning scheduled in a physiotherapy session at the bars to see if he could manage to bear his own weight and attempt a few paces, no crutches. Using those props was awkward before, especially as he was growing more aware of the throbbing aches without the full dose of meds when limping along, but that morning he certainly wasn't expecting the level of pain that hit him. It was quite a shock, and unfortunately, was confirming the doctors' worst fears about a rare case of nerve damage. It was a sickening disappointment, he thought he would be slightly more mobile than he was by now, he was missing out on so much being stuck in here. The realisation of the pain facing him wouldn't have been so bad if it was just the doctors attending, but he had another visit from the shrink that morning before he was brought to the bars in the physio gym, trying to lay a guilt trip on him for not wanting to seek her professional help, or it sure seemed that way. He didn't like the woman, and he sure didn't like opening up to people he didn't like! He was irked after that. Then, Katherine had showed up early and wanted to encourage him as she had a few times when he was on the crutches. Already it was hard having her see him in his tottering state, but today it was just a bit much. As he was painfully not even limping along hunched over the bars, more like an agonising shuffle without being completely off the meds, it suddenly hit that he was in fact truly crippled, this might be the best he could expect from this day forward.

At this sudden lurch into that loathsome feeling of vulnerability, her encouraging words cheerfully spurring him on to his next step when he was so miserable did the opposite of what they intended and felt more like tormenting goads. He didn't want an audience! Clutching the bars trying to battle the pain, he snapped.

"Good God Katherine! *Do you always have to be here?!*"

"N … no, dear I'll just go outside if you like … ."

As he watched her pick up her bag and leave quickly, the remorse pummelled him worse than the searing jolts stabbing his hips.

It was the first time he blew at her. After all this time together, they never had what he would call a fight. Just occasional disagreements about some little insignificant thing or another, but nothing that got either of them that upset let alone fuming at each other. Most of the time they ended up laughing, but never really *angry*.

"It's wasn't deliberate, Gerry," Peter consoled again. "I'm sure Katherine understands that too. She knows this isn't easy for you."

"I know, I know," his brother groaned. "My wounded pride too had a lot to do with it, but you get that already."

The excruciating pain, the fact he was agonising at every shuffling footstep, he was not in the best condition, it was mortifying to have her see him like this. He just couldn't help recalling every second of the incident, the quick shock then her hurt expression and the way she left the room, and after all these years when he swore he would never be like his stack-blowing father. He *had* hurt her no matter how unintentional or understandable his momentary eruption of temper was, and sincerely apologising wasn't enough when she eventually came back in. He could tell she had been crying. At last, she smiled when he remembered the 'truce' they had decided upon should anything go wrong between them and apologetically held up the key hanging around his neck, jingling it on its gold chain.

"Stop beating yourself up. Forgive yourself too. Frankly, she's seen you in a far worse condition when you were flat out comatose hitched up to so many machines practically dead to the world. She, and all of us I might add, are grateful to see you alive and attempting to make those painful steps."

Only, Peter wished they weren't excruciatingly painful. He and everyone they knew had prayed that the doctors might be proven wrong, the same prayer and hope everyone was living on for the last few months, but now he like Gerry could see things were going to be very rough indeed.

"She loves you," Peter then continued, seeing Gerry wasn't quite coming out of his self-destructive remorse. "This won't be the first time you'll get short either, you're bound to get on each other's nerves now and then. It's inevitable. Loving someone to the threshold of marriage doesn't mean the difficulties of life are suddenly going to disappear. You're both going to do a lot of forgiving and overlooking each other's faults over the years if you truly want a happy marriage. Look at our own family for instance. Despite the ups, the downs, Dad's explosions and other crosses, it still has been a happy marriage for our parents over all, and us kids didn't fare out so bad. Why? Patience and forgiveness is the key as well as love, although love does make it easier."

Gerry had to ponder on that as he slowly caressed the key in his fingers. Peter was right. Maybe his brother meant something more metaphorical, but he couldn't help think about the key and what it meant to him and Kathy.

"This isn't going to be easy, is it? Everything I mean."

"No Ger, but when was anything in life really worth having ever easy?"

03 ❖ 80

That week a heavy cloud hung over everyone in the Reinold and Walsingham households while Gerry's condition was reassessed as he continued to shuffle painfully along on the bars. It was now blatantly obvious to the medical experts that severe nerve damage was present, and that he would need to carefully monitor a steady course of painkillers, probably for the rest of his life. Yet, there was some good news: since he was able to get into a wheelchair, manage a few steps, and make it to the bathroom with some help, he was getting closer to being sent home and continue his convalescence with the aid of private nursing care. It was something to look forward to, and perhaps the walking part would improve if he was on medications. It was hard to tell. At least everyone could continue to hope, but again, it was wait and see.

There was nothing they could do but worry for Gerry as they went through the motions. Life has a cruel way of reminding one and all it stops for no one and simply marches on, dragging everyone with it. There were things that had to be done and couldn't be put on hold. Duty needed attending. Peter had promptly hunted down Fr. Xavier's number and verified the Fletchers' report, if it was true what was said about there being

600

another priest who was meant to finish the exorcism. Fr. Xavier affirmed what he had been told, and when he heard Peter explain that he might possibly be the one indicated, Xavier quickly offered to put in a good word with his own bishop and suggest that he be granted permission to come. Good. That's what Peter wanted to hear. Next, he scheduled a private meeting with Archbishop Foley and explained the situation. At first, His Eminence was reluctant to let him take on a case in another diocese, except Peter assured him he need not be transferred there on a full-time basis, he could travel to do the exorcisms needed and come back to fulfil his other parish duties. Contrary to what was generally thought, a full time, day in day out exclusive exorcism session wasn't the norm, once or twice a week would do, three at the most. In fact, to push it any further than a couple of days a week would be to tire the victim needlessly and perhaps even harm her. He didn't want to have a disastrous repeat of one notorious case that occurred years ago that ended in tragedy with the death of the victim because she was forced past her physical limitations.

"All right, I'll have a word with Morrison, see if we can't accommodate something," Foley nodded.

Peter wasn't sure how long he would have to wait. Back to parish life it was until he heard something. That included getting used to Gertrude, the new housekeeper recruited to tackle the domestic complexities of the rectory. She was welcomed kindly, but he and Fr. O'Conner left strict instructions their rooms weren't to be entered let alone touched, and she stuck to that rule as far as they could tell, until O'Conner saw when he came home Friday evening that his bed had been 'woman-handled'. Unlike Peter, he didn't bother to lock his door when he was out for the day.

"I knew it! Rummagin' in me sheets! She just couldn't keep away, could she," he groaned.

"Aw, she just changed the thing and made it up, and a lot better than you do I might add, Mr. Lumpy Corners. It's obvious you were never in the Army the way you tuck in your bed," Fr. Jenkins returned with a laugh.

"I've never seen the place look this slick. Sorry Pete, nothing personal. I know you're fastidious, but she's outright killing herself off trying to shape this place up to it's former glory, if it ever had a former glory," Fr. Mark added.

"Don't I know it? I believe she's managed it, in a week no less. I'm getting intoxicated on the detergent and polish vapours," Peter replied as he jogged up the stairs to his room.

It *was* getting a bit whiffy, but in the nicest possible way via waxes, polish, bleach and soap. Already she had washed the patina off the walls and had most of the odd improvement jobs done that he wished he could have finished off when it was up to them to keep things spic and span. All the old wood furniture with its dings and dents were repaired with scratch remover and shined up to a respectable sheen. Of course, the old kitchen was still in a dated state and Gertie did her best to whip it into line, but her cooking wasn't bad either considering what she had to work with. Since Gerry insisted he take his redundancy package from Reinold Enterprises, Peter reflected perhaps it was high time he did something about the place and upgraded those rickety appliances, the gas stove and oven didn't look all that safe. One thing was for certain, they were all eternally grateful that in addition to the time she freed up for them, O'Conner and Jenkins were particularly grateful they were now liberated from the cruddy wonders that Mark, the enthusiastic but useless chef, dished up for their sustenance.

Tonight, however, he was not staying in. Peter had been invited to the new art showing at Katherine's gallery, and while he was not one for high society hobnobbing any more, especially after all the events he had been to lately, this was a big night for her and he wasn't about to disappoint. It was sad enough Gerry couldn't attend, and he did promise his brother he would go and give Kathy additional support. Once again, he retrieved his best cassock and dressed for the grand occasion.

"I see we're back in our fancy frock," O'Conner noted with a laugh.

"Yes, with all the trimmings," Peter returned as he straightened out his collar before the hall mirror, brushed a piece of lint off the half-cloak, smoothed the sash and grabbed his car keys. If he was willing to dress up for little half-pint for a house visit, he was certainly not going to do anything less for family. In fact, after hearing Katherine's description of Fielding's pieces, he was curious to see the sculptures of *April One* for himself, but more important, he had a strange inkling he *had* to go … he must not miss tonight.

Showing his invitation to the guard at the door, he was glad to see for Katherine's sake that the night promised to be a glittering success judging by the crowd. Horace's latest columns enigmatically hinting at without saying anything about the latest subject matter that inspired the sculptor ensured that gossip and rumours ran high concerning this latest ground-breaking work, and therefore everyone who received an invitation was there and would not have missed the showing for the world.

Kathy certainly went all out for this. Not only did she arrange for live music, there were waiters in tails serving champagne to the guests and other edible delights in addition to Andre's magnificent buffet set up in the restaurant area. He was hardly in the door when a waiter dutifully held a tray before him. One glass of champagne was all right. Normally he would have first politely greeted the host or hostess when making an appearance at a gathering like this, but the polished metal artwork glinting in the soft glow of the lights and capturing the reflections of all the wandering guests caught his attention, in particular, the enormous reclining statue taking pride of place in the center of the floor, a strange tree-like future sprouting from its side and towering over the guests and the groups of statues. Despite the ultramodern shapes that barely resembled anything along the lines of the Roman and Greek Classical period that inspired the Renaissance, their shining forms were strangely captivating. Indeed, they were far removed from Fielding's earlier work, a leap ahead in fact, but as they were so aptly described, they were eerily grim. The dark side of humanity represented in polished, understated futuristic sophistication.

"Peter! I'm glad you made it," Katherine greeted, detaching herself from a couple of Fielding's biggest fans. "So, what do you think?"

"It's mighty … apocalyptic, I must say," he observed with some humour, taking another glance around at the other statues depicting the barbarity of humanity in the Twentieth Century before looking up at the armament tree again.

"I know, it's something else. You can't say they won't spark a few conversations. Come! Your parents are waiting for you, Tom and Lottie just arrived five minutes ago, my own folks are somewhere around on the upper floors, and … yes he's here," Katherine then called out with a cheerful wave of the hand to his mother who had just noticed them among the throng. "Leroy was one of the few who couldn't make it tonight, and of course, the only way Gerry's not going to miss a thing is by telephone, we've got the whole thing set up."

"Hey son, all cloaked up for the occasion I see," his father greeted. "You look mighty fine. An admiral with all his braid and stripes couldn't look any finer."

"Why, thank you."

Yes, it was definitely a crowded affair. In addition to family, friends and the Gallery Gang, anyone and everyone that Katherine and Kevin could think of inviting thanks to his carefully kept notebooks were nearly all present and accounted for. Peter nodded a greeting to the guests he knew. The Gang were certainly excited, a few dignitaries were meandering around, and of all things, two sheiks with connections to the Saudi Royal Family were there and very interested in acquiring a few of the larger pieces for the private royal collection. Katherine couldn't help but whisper to Peter and the Captain that it looked like Reinold Shipping was going to have a very good night too.

"The important thing is that you have a good night," Peter noted. "Enjoying it so far?"

"Frankly, I'm living on excitement and nerves. I probably won't eat a thing as usual, I've got to make sure everyone else is enjoying it. Wait, here's the man of the evening." Katherine smiled, catching a sight of Jiff in his three quarter black evening coat, and signalling him to come over. She would have introduced them, but it was obvious they had met before.

"It's been awhile, John. How have you been?"

"Quite fine, and very productive as you can see," he greeted, shaking Peter's hand. "Nice buttons."

"Thanks. So tell me, when are we going to hear your latest source of inspiration for these extravagant creations? As I recall, you never leave a showing without giving a poetry recital."

"True, but the timing is up to our lovely hostess," he pointed out, nodding to Katherine.

"Since everyone on the guest list that promised to come is almost here, I guess that would be just about now, I can't help it if people are late," she replied. "Excuse me."

Drat! She hated making speeches, but she would have to spout one eventually, perhaps a few more before the night was over.

"As someone once advised me, take a deep breath and think of the Oscars." Suzy smiled as she handed over the microphone to the PA system.

"Don't worry, you'll live. You're getting good at this," Charlie added.

Katherine motioned the ensemble to stop playing for a moment took that much needed breath as the music came to a halt. Short and sweet, this wasn't supposed to be the Gettysburg Address, that was Jiff's job! Getting everyone's attention and waiting for a few minutes for those meandering around upstairs to come down, she welcomed them to the Walsingham Gallery and announced what a privilege it was to present John Fielding's latest collection, *April One*, which no doubt they could all agree was a surprising break from his past styles. By the time she had thanked all those who helped to make the evening possible, the resulting applause between each mention stretching the time a little further, all the guests were gathered and waiting with eager anticipation for the artist's customary poetic offering.

"But I will not leave you in suspense any longer. Mr. Fielding shall now present to you a poem of his own creation, which in turn inspired his latest collection. Maestro?"

Heads turned and applause thundered as he stepped forward, took the microphone and turned to face his adoring public with debonair poise. The artist paused, letting the moment weave its spell. A hush descended, the expectant stillness adding to the suspense. At last, he spoke:

"Thank you, Miss Walsingham. Ladies and gentlemen, I must warn you, this evening what I shall recite is unlike anything you have heard at my previous showings. I give you *Dixit Insipiens*."

Peter was one of the few present who was familiar with the Latin phrase. This should be interesting he decided as the artist-poet paused, mustering his oratorical powers, then broke forth into verse:

Only a fool says in his heart
There is no Creator, no King of kings,
Only mules would dare to bray
These lethal mutterings.
Over darkened minds as these
The Darkness bears full sway,
Fruitless, yet, bearing fruit,
In their fell, destructive way.
Sterile, though proliferate,
A filthy progeny sees the day,
When Evil, Thought and Action mate:
Breeding sin, rebels and decay.
The blackest deeds and foul ideals,
Multiply throughout the earth,
Through deadened, lifeless, braying souls,
The Darkness labours and gives birth.
Taking the Lord's abundant gifts
And rotting them to the core,
They dress their dish and serve it out
Foul seeds to infect thousands more.
'The Tree of Life is dead!' they cry,
'And that of Knowledge not enough,
Let us glut on the ashen apples
Of Sodom and Gomorrha.'

Have pity on Thy children, Lord,
Left sorrowing on this earth,
While fools and all their kindred
Cast shadows with their murk,
And to the dwindling wise,
They toss their heads and wryly smirk.
The world daily grinds to dust
Virtue's fair unicorns,
Rather, it would now beget
Vice's mutant manticores.
Wisdom crushed, our joy is gone,
Buried under anxious fears
For lost rights and freedoms,
We shed many bitter tears.
Death is life, Life is no more,
Humanity buried in a tomb,
In a fatal prenatal world
Where tiny flowers
Are ripped from the womb,
Discarded, thrown away,
Inconvenient lives
That barely bloomed.
Our elders fare no better,
Their wisdom unwanted by and by,
Boarded out to end their days,
And forsaken are left to die.
Only the youthful and the useful,
In this capital age prosper and fly.
Yet, they too are quickly strangled,
Before their future plans are met,
Professions legally pre-enslaved
Held bound by mounting student debt.
Our leaders all harangue for peace
Yet perpetrate the horror,
Of economic greed shored up
Through manufactured war.
Our armies now welter
In foreign civilian gore.
How many of our kin are slain

For hollow martial honour?
As if we could forget, ignore,
The scourge of nuclear power,
Alas, victors are rarely tried
For their woeful crimes of war.
Hope and pray we never see
A repeat of Hirsoshima.

No more!
Crimes are legion,
The deeds of devil-spawn!
What has happened to the souls
Your Divine Image was minted on?
They are now recast:
Crooked coins of Caesar and
The Whore of Babylon.
How often mankind shuts its ears
To Your music celestial,
Mankind would rather march
To the anthems of Hell.
If humanity cannot be reclaimed
By Your Mercy and great Love
Deservedly we should be struck
By Vengeance from above.
Many dread the Final Day,
And the Crack of Doom
For others the Apocalypse
Will never come too soon.
'Lift up your heads, be glad',
Fools shall bray no more
For at last the Master comes
To thresh His threshing floor.

Silence iced the atmosphere as the audience listened intently to each censorious word decrying the cruelty of modern civilization. It was a stark, bold, cutting, desolate judgement on the state of the nation as well as the world. When in due course the poetic artist concluded his terrible diatribe, the silence was not yet broken, the austere change in his style having indeed been unprecedented. Were they in shock? Kevin, who was quite astute in these matters, seized the moment and ventured the initial energetic claps. If *he* didn't mind that diatribe, then, maybe Fielding was just being his electric, moody, dramatic self trying to shock with his new collection? Everyone then joined in, the room resounding with applause followed by the babble of excited commentary, those in front wanting to be the first to congratulate Fielding on such a daring presentation even if they did feel offended in places. A few guests looked ruffled to be sure, some even walked out, but much to Katherine's relief, the reception appeared to be a triumph albeit a controversial one.

"Thank you Mr. Fielding. May I remind everyone our mysterious night time artist, C.S. Turris, has some new artwork on display on the next floor. Also, there is a special souvenir for everyone, and hope you all enjoy the evening," Katherine concluded, glad to be shot of the speech-giving for another while. The Gang began to hand out the special memento cards they had printed featuring the scalding poem together with a picture of Fielding and a sample photos of his collection taken at the gallery, which were accepted by the guests. Peter thanked Suzy as she handed him his card and then examined the poem. Here he thought his sermons could be blunt at times. As he was still reading, he was approached by the author who finally broke free from the autograph requests.

"So, what do you think?"

"Strange to see something like this coming from one who claims they embrace all philosophies. Do I detect a closet covert?"

"I'm still exploring … ."

Peter nodded thoughtfully with a smile. If this new poem was anything to judge by, the explorer's compass seemed to be pointing in a steady direction at last, which was good to see. He could never forget the night when he was asked by the Captain to escort his mother and make an appearance at one of Fielding's shows years ago when he was unable to make it himself, and to pick out something to add to their collection if he found something worth investing in. Gerry was usually the one designated for these tasks, but since he was on one of their global inspections, couldn't do it that time. Peter doubted if his taste in art could be considered investment-worthy, but for the sake of his parents he went as requested and enjoyed the evening more than he expected. One interesting thing about artists, they liked to think deep, and it was refreshing to talk to someone who didn't mind discussing the topics that most people tended to shun or shy away from. Apparently, Fielding thought him interesting too, for he invited him over for a studio tour the next day, suggesting he might find something for his collection not presented yet to the public. As it turned out, the Captain was glad of this and insisted he take the day off work to see what the dreamy artist might have hidden in his workshop. Peter remembered that for the whole day they basically ended up sitting back with their feet up, Rachmaninov playing over the stereo while discussing more philosophy than anything else. A very refreshing conversation in fact, there was hardly anyone in those pre-ordination days with whom he could amicably converse theology or mysticism without occasioning annoyance, boredom or unintentional heated debates. As they talked, it was obvious Fielding was a man who was earnest but lost at the time, reading everything and anything from the manifestos of Communistic Atheism to the stringent morality sermons of the Puritans, and every other belief system from the Orient to the Amazon, whatever felt poetically moving or artistically inspiring at the time, but too hazy to build a strong foundation on which to anchor the conduct of his life. At least he eventually rejected atheism, he could believe in a Creator-Being, but just not quite sure what direction to find Him.

"You know, I admire your principles," Fielding turned to him.

"Oh?"

"You are so certain of what to live by."

"More important, I am certain of what to die by."

"Come again?"

"A lasting happiness cannot be attained by seeking temporary happiness," Peter continued, "I desire for what's Eternal, and the faith I believe in and try to follow is the only one I know for certain that promises me that."

"I see. I cannot help but envy your certainty."

Apparently, Fielding must have given much thought to their conversation since then judging from his poem, although need he jump to extremes?

"So, what's with the destructive streak," Peter ventured to ask, returning to the present.

"Dark period. Couldn't get out of it, but at least I got some art out of it," the artist joked.

"Out of it now, I hope?"

"Yes, we're on to sunnier climes, or rather, interstellar ones."

"Good. I'd hate to think your final thoughts on the Bible were nothing but doom and destruction."

"On the contrary. Why does an artist destroy when they do destroy? To start afresh and end with perfection. The Apocalypse ends with a beautiful Golden City in a new world free from pain and sorrow. As someone who desires Eternity once told me, the end of this world leads to a better one, if we prove worthy of it."

"Touché."

It was good to see that there was light at the end of the desolation. Hopefully the artist would at last find that certainty he desperately was seeking and take the steps necessary to enter that Golden City.

"Since you're out of your world-crushing Judgement Day Period, what exactly did you mean by 'interstellar'?"

"It's a piece of art I'm working on, but you'd have to ask your almost sister-in-law about that, I've been sworn to secrecy." Fielding smiled as he autographed his souvenir memento.

That's right, Gerry told him Katherine had sort of 'half commissioned' a piece as a surprise, but no one knew much about it. Like her decorating, she wasn't giving away many hints. He would have to wait along with Gerry and everyone else.

Not wanting to be remiss in the social pleasantries, Peter left his empty glass with a server and excused himself to greet Katherine's parents, remarking upon the apparent success the night was before being pulled this way and that into conversations by others he knew, or whom wanted to introduce him to someone, everyone asking him if he had had something to drink yet, or would he like another. Why everyone felt they had to keep plying him with booze was beyond him, as if his desire to keep within moderation was somehow a silent lecture meant to dampen their own enjoyment. True, one must give good example but he wasn't a spoil sport! Even Christ's first public miracle entailed making wine, and quite a few gallons of it too.

At last, he helped himself to a plate in the buffet line before deciding to take a tour around the upper floors to see what other depictions of metallic woe Fielding was offering, not to mention the new pieces on display by Turris. The line at the elevator was considerable, so he decided to take the first flight of stairs to the next floor, meeting and greeting as he went, including Gramps who was wondering where Jasper had wandered off to.

"Hey Padre, you haven't seen my furry shadow anywhere, have you?"

"No, I haven't seen him at all, but I'll keep an eye out."

"Thanks. I have to make sure Mrs. Hunt doesn't spot him, or there'll be war you know."

"I do indeed." Peter smiled, recalling the petite feisty lady's fear of 'hounds', although Jasper could hardly be described as dangerous. "So, how are things?"

"Apart from all this odkins bodkins flapdoodle I *had* to come see," he began indicating the latest artwork with some humour, "let's say things've gotten interesting since the new neighbours moved in. Wait, I think you'll get my point just about now, this is going to create quite a stir." He leaned on his cane, nodding down the stairwell with a chuckle and a gleam in his eye. Just above the chatter and music, Peter caught the loud conversation of someone arriving to the gathering below who was greeted by Katherine.

"I'm sorry we're late. Wow! Yous got one swell party here!"

"Thank you, Mr. Becchino. Er, you didn't have to bring anything."

"Vico! Call me Vico! Aw, this is nothin', just some of the best *mortadella* you've ever had in your life, even the stuff in the Old Country can't beat this."

"And I brought some more *canollis* since yous all liked them so much," a woman's voice nasally declared.

"I don't know how Andre is going to take the additions to his buffet line, but I for one wouldn't mind having more of those *canollis*," Gramps confided with a wink to Peter.

"I assume this the dreaded local Mafia family I've been hearing so much about."

"Bingo, but we can't be rude and all that, so for the sake of harmony we're being neighbourly to a fault. Still, I'd better go and see if Kathy's all right, Har's still blowing a gasket over the whole affair."

"Okay, I'd better let you go. If you need some backup, let me know." Despite their life choice in career opportunities and were wobbly on the practise of living what the Good Book proscribed, on the whole the Italian Mob showed respect for Mother Church and the men of the cloth that served Her, if only to keep a foot in with Upstairs.
Gramps laughed.

"Will do."

Resuming his art tour, Peter scanned the passageways at knee-level now and then to see if he caught a wisp of golden fur or a wagging tail. Katherine often joked Jasper was all heart and no brains, but tonight it looked like he was using his head. At least on the upper floors it was quieter and the wandering canine wouldn't get his paws stepped on. He would probably reappear when the evening was almost over and the hoards of gargantuan shoe-clad feet had diminished.

Gradually taking in a few of the new pieces on display and examining the new night scenes by 'Turris' as he leisurely walked around, he was politely interrupted by a few more acquaintances, members from the Reinold board or from Walsingham industries, and then, he bumped into Reverend Dobbson, Katherine's former Episcopal minister before she embraced her new faith. Peter was polite, he got on well with the Reverend when they first met, which happened to be at the same place during another gala event and practically on the very same spot, this time right in front of the latest instalment of her colourful Socratic series in progress of all things, but now, he couldn't help getting the feeling he was being treated like a respected yet tolerated adversary since the Reverend had lost one of his prized lambs. It was one thing to be friendly for the sake of ecumenical peace between Christian brethren, but now, poaching their believers was obviously a different ballgame with him. Looked like he was still getting all the blame for Katherine's conversion! Never mind, it was to be expected, even her father was still looking at him coolly from a distance tonight despite having accepted the fact this still all boiled down to her free choice.

Eventually, the conversation was interrupted by one careless guest that wasn't paying attention as she rounded a corner while talking over her shoulder and bumped into a gentleman scrutinizing one of the sculptures, spilling what was left in her glass on his back. There was a flurry and a turning of heads as everyone reacted to the shock event, the nearest waiter jumping to attention and trying to help slop up the mess while the lady gave profuse apologies to the man whose suit she just wrecked, offering to pay for the cleaning while he refused the offer and just enquired where he might find the restroom please.

It provided a welcome distraction, and the Reverend wandered off. One conversation ended, Peter was soon met by another acquaintance from the Reinold executive board, but had to excuse himself when catching sight of the sought-for pooch coming down the stairs, a few 'aws' uttered by those guests who weren't expecting a dog in a white collar and bow tie to be attending the event. Jasper didn't continue on down to the next floor, but decided to sit at the bottom of the steps and looked straight at him, causing a novel obstruction among the guests.

"Excuse me, Larry. I was asked to return yonder wandering Fido to his master if I should see him, so please forgive me for dropping you like this."

"No problem. It seems you get to play St. Francis for the evening."

"I guess so." Making his way over, Jasper began wagging his tail. "Hey boy, watcha doin' here, huh?" Peter smiled, crouching down and giving him a rub behind the ear. Jasper put up his paw. "Shake hands, okay, then shall we go find Mr. G?" Once Peter had shaken his paw, Jasper gave a few more friendly pats on Peter's knee, and then cocked his head upwards and to the side.

"Uuf," he returned, not exactly a bark, but obviously some playful articulation.

"Yes, yes, nice to see you again too, but we've got to find your master now."

"Uuf, errr, oof!"

"So, it seems you can talk to animals after all." Larry wandered over to witness the exchange.

"No, I'm no Dr. Doolittle." Peter laughed as he stood up. He was about to take Jasper gently by the collar until he started pawing more briskly at his knee and then cocked his head upward again.

"What is it, boy? Something humming in the sound system?"

Jasper sneezed, shook his head, flapping his ears, then pointed his nose up. Peter looked in the same direction, but then felt Jasper nipping the hem of his cassock with a tug, pulling him forward.

"I know dogs get frisky about mail men and police uniforms, but this is a new one," Larry couldn't help noticing.

"Tell me about it! Hey fella, I'm not a rawhide bone you know," Peter declared, freeing his cassock from the insistent hound's snout, but then realised Jasper wanted him to come upstairs. As the human got the hint, the canine friskily bounded up a few steps, then stopped and turned to see if he was following.

"Looks like I gotta go."

"Sure, maybe he's got a confession to make. See you later." Larry chuckled, letting Peter go figure out what the pooch wanted.

Beyond the appreciation showed when receiving a scratch behind the ear, Jasper usually didn't display this much excitement unless he was helping someone answer a door. But why him? Wouldn't he go get Mr. Walsingham or Kathy's attention first for whatever was eating him?

"Okay, okay, I'm coming, give me a chance," he called up, his guide not stopping at the third floor, but bounding on up. "Are you sure you don't want to take the elevator?"

"Urf!"

"I guess that's a 'no'," Peter assumed as he passed some of the amused guests on his way with a polite nod, continuing to the museum floor where Gerry's private collection of art and ancient antiquities was now permanently housed. However, no sign of Jasper.

"He went thatta way," Tyler indicated, one of the private security guards on duty for the evening. He had seen their jaunt up the stairs via the security monitors at his desk.

"Thanks."

Peter rounded the corner and found the pooch standing in the middle of the walkway, his trek apparently at an end. Jasper growled.

"Hmm, what's up with you?" He was about to give him another rub behind the ear, but then stopped.

For a moment, Peter stood calmly in the direction Jasper was staring. He folded his arms and took in the scene. This floor was unusually quiet, yes, strange for a gala night like this. Maybe everyone they knew who was invited had seen Gerry's collection by now and didn't want to miss all the excitement on the lower floors, but he couldn't help notice the area of the exhibits they were at, the ancient Babylonian and Egyptian sections. A strange chill permeated this area of the museum floor.

"So, he's doing it to you too," Tyler quietly interrupted as he joined them, breaking into Peter's thoughts.

"Oh? This is not new?"

"No, well, sorta. He's been acting squirrelly the last few weeks, or thereabouts," Tyler began quietly, almost under his breath. "When Mr. G drops by, Jasper just comes up and sits there, or over there, gives a growl every so often. Gives us the jitters, I'm not too eager to be on night duty after that, yah catch my drift?"

There was a pause.

"So, do you or the other guards feel odd here? Maybe like you're not alone, that sort of thing," Peter enquired, not moving an inch.

"Uh hmm. And don't get me going into the cracks and thumps we hear sometimes. Not to mention footsteps, real weird footsteps. We haven't said anything to Miss Kathy, don't want to freak her out, or nothin'. Who'd believe us anyway? Maybe you of course."

"Seen anything?"

"Not yet, thank my lucky stars."

Jasper began to growl low.

"And this only began a few weeks ago?"

"Yeah, but this corner always felt weird after these things were moved in, ya know?" Tyler motioned around, indicating the sizable stone statues lining the walls.

"Hmm."

"If I didn't think I might wreck the pieces, I had the notion to take the bottle of Lourdes water my grandmother brought me and splash this place with it. I was raised right ya know," Tyler proffered with a smile.

"Glad to hear it, but I think you'd better leave this one to me."

"A case for the pros, huh?"

Peter gave a slight nod.

"Say no more, I'll leave you to it," the guard concluded, shaking his head sidewise putting his hand up as he returned to his beat.

Peter continued his silent probing, arms crossed, letting the area tell him what was wrong, although Jasper was already doing a good job as interpreter. It was said animals could see things humans did not, dogs, cats, birds, and horses in particular. Yes, it was here, that uneasy sense of 'something' making its presence felt. The usually friendly canine was taking a particular dislike to one stone statue situated against the wall. Jasper began to whine and back up, then growled again.

"What are you hiding, Anubis," Peter intoned under his breath.

Something evil was attached to the statue, and perhaps quite a few more objects dotted around here. He had always felt troubled about Gerry collecting things from the pagan past. There were certain things the desert sands should have been left to swallow up. Yet, he wished he didn't have to guess with his spiritual intuition. Usually he was right, but there were times it might prove helpful if he could see what was in front of him. If only … .

Then will it, though be prepared! Seeing the Darkness will be far different than seeing the Light.

Peter's senses were startled with the unexpected response. His wish wasn't exactly a prayer, and even then, what he thought was too daring to ask for, but he had been heard and answered immediately. The interior voice was unmistakable. It reminded him of the Youth that came to visit him, but fast and in a metaphorical bolt dropped on his soul that only the ears of the soul could hear. It resonated without making one palpable vibration, a true inner locution.

Just 'will' it? If the message was telling what he *thought* it was … .

He took a deep breath and braced himself.

The walls and carpeted section of the wood floor walkway seemed to sicken in hue, growing pale and ailing as the though the life was haemorrhaging out of the surroundings. The unearthly change in vision filled him with a strange foreboding that froze his senses as that terrible, palpable tidal wave he could always feel coming but never see was finally revealed to his human eyes. A billowing narrow trail of jet black mist emanated from the statue, circling it in a serpentine coil then billowed towards him ready to strike. Before it moved any faster, he made the sign of the cross and the ebony fog stalled a few feet away as though it had hit a glass wall shielding him from its onslaught. Safe for now, he still felt the terror that the darkness instilled, it was almost paralysing. He had nearly been enveloped by the thick mass, it was a miracle he had the ability to move at all. Jasper whined.

He thought that was the last of that strange apparition's tricks until he was startled by a grotesque sight, a small misshapen simian-like creature with protruding yellow eyes, contorted minuscule goat horns and a long rat tail that materialised in the midst of the stream, making jeering faces at him, rolling out its forked tongue and gesticulating obscenely. Jasper growled.

"Begone, you imp of Hell," Peter commanded, making another sign of the cross.

The bulging eyes and fanged mouth immediately widened into a piercing but *noiseless* scream as the thing fled backwards into the statue without turning around, the dark effluent trail disappearing in reverse with the misshapen brute as though he were witnessing an outlandish flash rewind of the scene.

However, the thing wasn't gone yet, just trapped for now. The statue, which normally was a sandstone hue, was now a wan grey and oddly shadowed, the darker shades making the statue appear as though it were moving, the eyes looking in his direction, observing him. Peter made another sign of the cross. The shadows weakened, the eyes of the statue returned to their lifeless stony state, but the thing was obviously still there for the colours still looked sickly around the passageway.

It was a brutal shock. If seeing the Light filled him with a joy and wonder despite the sorrow from being earth-bound and separated from Heaven, this was a shattering experience. The sight of the evil he could only sense before now added to the sensation, it filled the soul with terror, making it recoil with horror as the sight of true malice rapidly drained it of joy and peace. One felt paralysed, yet yearning desperately to flee, to escape. The one thing he could still feel was hope, confidence in God, the knowledge he was not damned, that alone gave him the ability to keep moving and tackle the misshapen spirit with the sign of the cross. Otherwise, he might have been glued stiff through fear. And that was only one of the minor demons! It was a good thing knowing this too was only a small indication he was seeing of the Underworld at work, or he might have dropped dead from the shock. Taking a deep breath and calming himself for a moment, he processed what he had just witnessed.

Of course, the statue was not just a possessed object, but a *portal*. It would explain why the presence of the imp wasn't felt all the time, only the last few weeks. So, Jasper was good at patrolling more than one type of doorway! The four-legged guard began wagging his tail as he looked up at him, but whined a little. Things were not yet right.

"I know boy, the non-natives are still restless."

Now that the demon using the statue was barred for the moment, Peter wondered what else would be shown him. There was going to be another learning curve, and now for *this* to happen while he was still figuring out how to read all the nuances of the Light! The Darkness was going to take quite some getting used to, if ever. Since he could choose what to see or not when using the other gift, logic told him something similar would also happen here. First, were there any other doorways allowing the evil ones to come and go? He slowly glanced around at the exhibits, which were mostly smaller artefacts protected in professional grade glass cases that out of necessity were nestled together due to the amount of items and the manner in which the passageways were designed to resemble a petite part-French, part-Victorian labyrinth. Despite the modern conveniences of sound systems and electric light, this storey had the air of an older antiquities museum combined with an eccentric collector's mansion. Okay, nothing seemed to manifest itself in the organized clutter, wait, to the left, an inky miasma exuded from one of the jewelled scarab beetles in the case. Making the sign of the cross, he commanded the doorway to be sealed. The mist dissipated in a miniature tornado, the petite insect regained a brighter colour. Just a small portal then, easy to close.

That was interesting.

Now, were there any *cursed* ones? If anything here was used for some sinister pagan ritual in ancient days then he might have a problem on his hands. A second time he braced himself and expected the worst.

To his horror, he could feel the evil more strongly as soon as he willed his vision to change: a few items had black flames spring around them, but dead flames, an outlandish fire that did not give off light, but seemed to suck away the brightness surrounding it. If this unnatural sight wasn't alarming enough and chilled his bones to the marrow, several objects all around him turned black, but they did not appear solid. They had become black holes gaping into Nothingness, yet without losing their form. The large statue of Anubis was one of the yawning apertures. He had never felt such maliciousness before, it was so thick, he could almost grasp it, taste it. He wanted to run, yet was strangely compelled to come slightly closer to the statue, to see what lay beyond, to stare into that Void ... but *NO*. Too dangerous. This was not a time to indulge his curiosity.

Immediately, Peter willed off the vision. The passageway and the artefacts resumed their natural colours, the sensations of evil also dissipated, returning him to the world of human vision. Just when he thought he had returned to the land of the living, something shot out from around the corner of the archway ahead of him, leaped into the glass case next to him, screeched at the scarab, then turned and leaped into the statue of Anubis and disappeared. Jasper barked, then growled once more. Peter wasn't sure what he had seen, something like a misshapen mole, but with three heads and six claw-like legs. It happened in a flash, just restrained enough to see its movements, but too fast to get much of a good look at it. Another imp or demonic entity prowling around, his blessing over the scarab had closed that spirit's usual means of entry. However, the thing found another. While he knew the small creep was a bodiless spirit, it was still unnerving to have seen the thing leaping and passing through glass and stone objects as though they were made from thin air. With this new development in his vision, he understood that the statue was a bigger, stronger doorway than he thought, he was going to have to do something about it. What was more disconcerting, Peter realised that even when he 'willed off' the ability to see the evil, he would still be shown things nevertheless whether he wanted to or not, similar to entering the sanctuary of a church to say Mass and seeing the Light. To his dismay, he could now be witness to anything, any time.

He made another sign of the cross over the problem portal and commanded it to close. He could feel the evil lessen. It still may not be enough, but he dared not will to see the Void again to check. This would call for extra measures. For now, he needed to see what other mischief was hiding up here. What else did Gerry unwittingly add to his art collection? What other stowaways were lurking unseen?

Strange, he did not see any more black flames or coal-cloudy mists suggesting doorways or other cursed objects, but he noticed a peculiar grey haze clouding a few of the paintings, blurring the pictures as though he was looking at the scenes through a fog, but without that icy dart of fear projecting from them. Okay, this new second sight was puzzling, he was stumped.

What? You who preach on assisting the souls in Purgatory do not know what you are seeing?

Although not forceful, the Voice sounded surprised, patiently reproachful as though chiding a little brother. Peter interiorly apologised for his ignorance, but all these visions were new to him. He reflected for a moment. Purgatory ... Purgatory ... of course. Souls who once owned these objects were in need of help. Perhaps the haze signalled they were too attached to the things of the earth and were expiating these and other faults. He stopped before one painting by Van Gogh, one of the few relatively modern pieces that were incongruously out of place amongst the ancient antiquities section. The haze seemed rather dreary and ashen here, more dense than with the other masterpieces in the exhibition space that were displaying the same distorted symptoms of distress, he could hardly see the figures portrayed on the canvas. He took his beads from his pocket and began to pray. He tried to meditate as he let the beads slip through his fingers, keeping his gaze on the painting, hoping his spiritual experiment would result with a marked difference. It was difficult enough, getting distracted while praying during the normal run of things, but after what he had just seen, it was a wonder he could keep his thoughts together at all. Hmm, must be too unfocused, it didn't seem like he was shifting the fog, maybe ... no, the haze was getting lighter, the grey less dead, but the figures were still greatly blurred, indistinct. He continued to pray, whoever was calling for his attention was in need of incessant help. A heavy sentence must be laid upon the soul, or perhaps souls. There could be more than one, which would account for the relative imperviousness of the haze. Come on, focus. Prayer was a lifting of the heart, and he didn't want to merely repeat a formula. He closed his eyes to concentrate better. Peace, he must retain his inner peace.

"If this isn't a sight! I must admit my donation to the museum is highly prized, but this is the first time it has ever evoked idolatrous *devotion* ... ."

"Aunt Martha! Shush! Don't be rude!"

"Rude? I'm being honest. Praying to peasant potato farmers? I never!"

"I'm sure he's not praying *to* it ... ."

Intensely focused on the other world, Peter was almost completely detached from the human realm, unaware that Katherine and her voluble aunt were standing behind him, observing his very peculiar attitude. He only barely heard let alone paid attention to their voices. He might have stayed that way longer if Katherine hadn't come up next to him.

"Pete, are you okay," she gently interrupted.

"Hmm? Oh yes."

He was nudged back to the land of the living. He took one last look at the painting, it lightened for a moment, then went murky again. Much prayer was needed here.

"Er, Pete, are you *sure* you're okay?"

He nodded with a reassuring smile, putting away his beads and willing his vision back to normal. How could he explain what had happened right then, especially in front of her aunt? A few other guests had by then come up to the museum area and were wandering the corridors. Peter realised he might have been seen, it was mortifying. Yet, he had a hunch there would be many unpredictable incidents coming his way. He'd better get used to it.

"Come, you're missing the party."

"Okay, here I come, wait, hang on. Where's … ? Oh, there you are," Peter concluded as Jasper appeared from around a corner, wagging his tail. "Come on boy, let's find Mr. G." Jasper whined and pawed his knee again. "Yeah, I know, later," he nodded, but the pooch sat down, not budging.

"Well, you stay and chat if you like, I'm heading downstairs. *Someone* has to stop your grandfather from making a display of himself at the buffet," Aunt Martha announced, heading for the elevator.

"There she goes again!" Katherine sighed. "At least we can talk now. What's up? Esther couldn't help but bring my attention to the security monitors."

He forgot about the security cameras.

"What did you see?"

"Um, let's say I wasn't sure if you had gone loopy along with Jasper or not."

"No, not yet." He smiled before growing serious again. "I understand you have to return to your guests, but is there somewhere we can talk?"

"There's the studio, it's unoccupied right now, or at least I think so. You never know when the Professor might get the urge to work on a canvas, gala or no gala."

Elevator occupied, they decided to take the flight of stairs, he trying to figure out how to break the news to her, how to tread a delicate balance between deciding what to disclose and how much to disclose. He didn't want to frighten her, but it was important he not let slide what he saw tonight.

"Nope, no Professor, so we've got the place to ourselves," she quickly deduced from the lights not on. As they blinked on one after the other, she gave Jasper another pat, as she invited him to take a seat, which he refused, he didn't expect to keep her too long. "Okay then, spill the beans Pete, I'm so curious I could burst."

"How do I say this," he began, bringing his palms together almost in an attitude of prayer. "There's something otherworldly attached to objects in the antiquities section, and they need to be cleared."

"Uh oh. *Seriously?*" Of course Peter was being serious, but she couldn't help blurt it out. In reply, he simply nodded. That simple nod gave her chills. "Oh, you were exorcising the place," she continued, almost in a whisper. That would explain the strange scene she had witnessed from the monitors. "So ... so ... what now? Weren't you clearing the place already?"

"Yes, but more needs to be done, as soon as possible, and when there will be the least amount of people around."

"Er, why?"

"First of all, I don't know what may happen when I clear the area, and second, privacy is best for this." Plus, he didn't want whatever was attached to the objects he cleared to find a new home in a *person*, but he left that bit to himself.

"Okay, but with the restaurant and all, the only time you'd have this place *almost* to yourself is after the party tonight, Andre won't be open after that. The rest of the week it's back to normal with diners coming late into the evenings.

"I figured as much. With your permission, may I stay tonight and take care of it?"

"Of course, but if you don't mind me asking, you've been here so many times and didn't notice anything before. Why now?"

"From what I can tell, the trouble here has only started recently."

"Ohhh, that explains a lot," she then trailed, growing reflective. "There's been some odd things happening. One of the potted ferns in that section keeps falling over, and we haven't a clue why. The Gang thought it was the visitors just knocking it over, but we haven't seen anyone do anything, but Dennis said he saw it once topple over by itself ... ."

"Hmm."

"Oh Pete, this is scary."

"Don't be afraid. God won't permit evil entities to go past a certain boundary. Mostly their powers are curtailed to mischief and tomfoolery like your plant."

"It's still creepy. Now I'm *really* glad I told Gerry to get rid of the Canopic jar, who knows what that thing had other than some pharaoh's innards, which was bad enough. Gosh! Maybe I should just go ahead and have that part of the collection taken out? Just sweep out the whole Mess-o-potamia section?"

"No, there may be no need to resort to that yet," Peter assured her, "and in any case, I don't think Gerry would understand it all. I'm sorry you had to learn like this and now of all times, but don't let it wreck your evening. I'm here and I'll keep watch, but please don't say anything, I'll handle it."

"Well, if you think it's manageable, I'll try and not let it bother me. You're the boss. I guess we'd better head back downstairs then, or they're going to wonder where we've disappeared to."

"Yes, but would you mind if I stay up here a minute?"

"Not all Pete. Just flip the lights off when you're ready."

"Okay, I'll be down soon," he affirmed with a nod as she led Jasper to the elevator.

Alone with his thoughts, he couldn't help but find her manner of describing things at times amusing, but she was right. It was a good thing indeed she persuaded Gerry to get rid of that jar. It was one less thing he needed to handle!

Okay, time to focus. Mulling over the unearthly scenes, he folded his arms and examined the cavernous open plan room with his human vision, the only storey in the building left practically in its former factory condition with vintage wood floor and brick interior left untouched, apart from the odd paint drops and splatters the artists accidentally flipped around when in the midst of a creative session. It had little in the way of furniture, a wicker seating suite in one corner with a battered coffee table for a companion, plus a gathering of work tables, easels, carts filled with paint tubes and brushes, a countertop with work sink and store cupboards along the interior wall, not to mention the lines of paintings leaning up against the wooden support pillars of the building, drying at the far side of the room.

He unhurriedly strolled around, arms still folded, thinking about what he had to do. If he had known this was coming, he might have been better prepared. To tackle an evil portal of this magnitude penance would be required, he would have at least fasted for the day. Along with penance, he needed to be clear headed, he certainly wouldn't have had that glass of champagne earlier. No more food or drink tonight. Hmm, was there any *good* manifesting itself here? He did bless the gallery the night it opened after all. He willed to see the Light if it was present, no holding back. The walls and ceiling assumed a comforting white glow, something like the snowdrift effect with his blessed salt. Okay, good. However, he wished the glow were stronger. No matter, he could do something about that.

Swiftly, an idea struck him: was it possible to see *both* sides of the Otherworld at work? Was that question an inspiration, or his own thoughts? Maybe a spiritual hint imparted by his Friend although he 'heard' no locution this time. It was worth another spiritual experiment. Better not go to full intensity, he told himself, he was still not over his run-in with the devilish imps. Carefully, he willed to see both the Light and the Darkness. The white glow gently pulsating from the walls and the ceiling high overhead remained, but only a few yards away from him, a narrow black column of smoke was rising from the floor. It was as if a wall had been pulled away, showing him what had been concealed from him. He realised the eerie plume was originating where the ancient portal was located on the floor below. The smoke was not quite like the serpentine trail that followed the simian imp, but it was definitely related. He watched with a disorientating fusion of dread and curiosity as the narrow column of smoke rose straight and precise, then branched out as though it had left the top opening of an invisible stove pipe, wafting in all directions, yet not advancing far. It changed shape, looking as if it had hit a glass barrier transforming the escaping mist into an ominous horizontal black sheet of menace. It flowed to all sides at waist height, but it veered away as it came near, leaving a perfect circle cut around him. He saw the flames of his rosary shining through his pocket along with the other medals he had concealed on his person. They were shielding him. Peter also noticed the smoke shrank back the instant it reached the pulsating walls, the white light forcing the blackness in and down through the middle of the narrow shaft as though it was being made to devour itself. The blessing on the ceiling probably explained the sheet effect, keeping the evil from advancing upward and overcoming the place.

Curious, he slowly took his rosary from his pocket and holding it above the billowing sheet just two feet ahead of him, he dipped the flaming crucifix into the fray. The black pool of smoke sprang back as though it had been burned, retreating in a hurry, leaving another perfectly cut disk of clear space where the beads were allowed to dangle. The rapid retreat was like watching a cleansing drop of dispersant parting a section of filth on a tar polluted pond. Why he didn't see the plume rising to the studio when he was on the floor below he wasn't sure, maybe because at the time he hadn't willed to see the two Powers in combat. What a sight! It was fearsome, yet strangely awe inspiring to see the Light combating the Darkness, sending it back to the Abyss he could assume. He was told his gifts would increase, but to this extent? He had seen enough, and willed off the sight lest he grow overwhelmed by this unexpected increase in his awareness. It was a consolation to observe a blessing at work, but he knew there was still a battle ahead of him tonight. For now, the current challenge was return to the human world, pretend nothing had happened. How could anyone return to 'normal' after that?

He switched off the lights as he waited for the elevator, which returned unoccupied. As the doors slid shut behind him he realised with a shock he was staring at his prophetic dream right in the face. The freight lift now converted into a conveyance fit for a palace hotel with its soft lighting, gilded gold-backed mirrors and brass fittings along with the entire five floor gallery with its maze-like corridors and walkways was almost a clone of his phantasmal escape from Hell's Trophy Room. He was even wearing a cloaked cassock! Of course, the layout of his past dream and the real surroundings tonight weren't the same, the clothing in his dream wasn't ribbed and sashed in purple, and the floors of the gallery weren't laid out exactly like that trophy room, but Peter understood heaven-sent dreams did not need to be exact in every detail when a prophetic event was imparted in combination with a symbolic message, details would be shown slightly altered in the dream to suit many eventualities and occasions in the waking world.

Besides, he did not believe in mere coincidence, there were too many other elements fitting right in with his dream that ensured this was indeed no accident. Five floors, just like before, only here the most drab and untouched of the spaces if he could describe it as that was the studio on the top floor, not the 'cellar' underground he had seen years ago, things in his dream seemed to be switched the other way around here, but one aspect that was chillingly on the mark was the new artwork on show tonight. On the first three floors from the ground up was statuary displaying every monstrous barbarity the Age of Modernism had unleashed upon humanity, and which humankind in its greed, avarice and absolute lack of charity had unleashed upon itself. All the pieces here in the art show and the allegorical trophy room seemed to point to the cause and effect of the last two hundred years or so. The exhibits may not be the same, but they were related nonetheless.

Reaching the ground floor, he was struck with how close the symbolic connection was when he again caught sight of the huge tendrils of Fielding's cataclysmic travesty of a Jesse Tree branching out and overshadowing the guests in the lobby. It didn't look the same at all, but the links were there, it obviously was the *piece de resistance* of the whole collection and to his interior senses felt just as grotesque as the disturbing statue of the vivisectionist cutting open the chest of Christ, the principal trophy in that diabolical prize room. In his dream, the image looked as if Christ was stretched on the cross albeit horizontally, and here, the horizontal figure of 'Atomic Jesse' was also alike, the tree which was supposed to represent the genealogical life-line to Christ and also the Tree of Life of the Cross, was now strangely mutilated into a symbol of Death, just like the huge statue he dreamed of in the Trophy Room. He had thought that statue and the other exhibits in the lower levels of Satan's cellar represented the Industrial Revolution ushering in a dark period of autonomy granted to the Evil One, and now to see Fielding's statue of weaponry displayed in a converted factory was also too close for comfort. Unfortunately, even the festivity of the top floor in his dream was here represented on the ground floor of the art show, everyone caught in the trappings of the world.

The one consolation was in his dream he didn't see his family caught up and enticed by it all, and after Katherine's inquiry into if it would be a good thing for her or not to expand her gallery again, on the spiritual side as well as the financial, he knew she wasn't too attached to things either. She just loved the creative activity. The gallery kept her occupied, gave her artists a living, but she knew it wasn't the end-all and be-all of life, and the fact she was very selective on what was shown was also a good sign! He could be at peace about her knowing that. Another interesting observation was despite the scenes tonight, he was convinced Kathy was doing good work through her art. Peter was of the opinion that the creative impulse present in mankind was a minute spark of the great desire of God to create the Universe, and anyone who was of good will towards the Creator was subconsciously open to His inspirations in the progress of their own work. Yes, didn't He just use Fielding? It certainly looked like it. Still wandering but not malicious of heart, God found a way to direct the eccentric artist's ingenuity to produce a three dimensional warning: the guests tonight were viewing Satan's Trophy Room and could save themselves from it, if only they would pay attention to the poem they heard tonight. Judging from the shocked reactions tonight, the message was bitter to say the least. Sadly, how often did mankind heed a warning? Gadflies are often swatted unmercifully.

As he had expected, it was difficult to return to the world he once knew, which was far different from getting together with his parishioners. The realm of social, polite, diplomatic meeting and greeting at galas or premières in an effort to caress and advance one's social status for the sake of business was not where he was supposed to be. Not that he was ever rude, but now it all seemed so distant notwithstanding he was right in the midst of the crowd engaged in conversations and trying to do his best to appear he was completely tuned in. Yes, at his ordination he had been set apart from the world, and now, after seeing the things he did, he felt more removed than before. Not that it was a bad feeling, to yearn for that necessary solitude, but he was not caught up in a smug sense of being 'above' everyone either. Far from it. He had been introduced into a different spiritual plane and getting bound up in what was considered 'worldly enjoyments' seemed such a waste when he had such a great mission entrusted to him with only a small, paltry human life-span allotted to him on earth to accomplish it. He didn't know how to compare this sensation, perhaps the closest was a seasoned adventurer or war veteran who has travelled far from home and witnessed some truly life-changing sights on a global scale only to come home and find they can no longer fit into the society they once knew after their experiences, the battlefields of any war changes a person forever. The one thing that was different was he was not suffering any debilitating trauma, thank God.

Yes, now he could fully appreciate the feeling in his dream of his urgent need to get away from the trophy room, it represented the necessity of escaping the dangerous dead-weights holding the soul to the earth. He could sense the chasm between the world as God had intended it to be and what mankind had done with it during its stewardship. It was time to progress farther into spiritual climes, and paradoxically that meant becoming more down to earth than before and focusing on what truly mattered. True, he wanted Kathy's show to be a success, and in fact, if he hadn't come tonight he might never have found out what was wrong here in the building or have the time nor privacy to clear it. Still, he would be much more comfortable when the party was over and he could get down to the work he was called to do.

His quiet tour among the art pieces was interrupted by Cee, who *had* to have a word. Was he *really* the Monsignor the whole town was buzzing about?

"Urrm … ."

"Oh, you *are*! Hey! Vico! C'mere! I wanna introduce you! Oh, I'm Carla, but you can call me Cee, and this is my hubby, Vico." She tugged her hubby over by the arm.

"Yes, the new neighbours that moved next to the Walsinghams. Pleased to meet you, and, you make some mean *cannolis*, Mrs. Becchino."

"Aw, thanks!"

"Hey! Yous know us, but of course, you're gonna be Kathy's brother-in-law, and all that. Swell!" Vico was impressed. He then continued *sotto voce*, "yah know, would yah mind puttin' in a good word?"

"Er, with … who?"

"The Big Guy *upstairs*, you know! It wouldn't hurt to have someone like yous putting in a good reference or two … yah get my drift?" Vico gave a quick look upwards.

Ah. Peter smiled. The Mob trying to sit both sides of the fence as usual, a life of crime while hoping to slide-glide into Heaven on a wing and a prayer.

"How about I say a Mass Novena?" (From what he heard in the papers, they could use all the prayers they could get.)

"Really? Say, that's real swell of yous! Here," Vico eagerly pulled out his wallet to give a donation and continued to count … .

"Now wait a minute, that's way too much."

"Go ahead and take it. Here Vico, give some more." Cee flexed her fingers in a lemme-see-some-more attitude until she was happy with the count, her hubby not appearing to mind since it was for the Monsignor and all. "There, that's for your brother too, we like his do-gooder things he's got going at the slammer. Real classy. Cousin Benny just thinks it's great," Cee jumped in.

"Oh yeah! He thinks a lot of that. So do we, we're gonna have our own suit in the family thanks to that educational program."

"Er, thank you, and I thank you for Gerry, too." Peter didn't want to be rude, and graciously accepted the generous donation. He knew Gerry definitely wouldn't accept it, so it looked like the Little Sisters of the Poor and their soup kitchen were making out like bandits tonight.

"Ah, think nothing of it. How's your brother doin', by the way? Would love to meet him. We heard what happened, hit an' run type of deal," Cee disclosed.

"Yes, but he's doing better. Thank you for asking."

"That's good, but real bad rap. Still didn't catch the guy, huh," Vico wondered.

"No, the investigation has hit a dead end, I'm afraid."

"No kid'n? If it were my brother and I got the shmuck who did this … lousy Chinks to do that! They're takin up the whole town. Hey! Where do yah live? It's a while off yet, but I promise I'll have the boys send you a turkey for Thanksgiving." Peter tried to stop the overflowing donations, (the Mob liked to try to bribe their way to Heaven too), but Vico insisted he get a turkey. There was nothing for it but give the address of the rectory.

When it seemed like a good time to escape the crowd again for awhile, he politely made his excuses then wended back to the second floor to examine Turris' paintings, it was something he could do to appear part of the event to where he didn't have to talk all the time. He needed some space, too much sensory and spiritual overloads tonight, although he couldn't help but overhear the interview Katherine was giving Horace the Art Hacker over the works on display.

"Forgive me for asking then, what on earth would possess you to display such mediocre works by this semi-anonymous 'C.S. Turris', of whom we know very little if next to nothing about? Some describe this work as amateurish delusions of artistic greatness scraped together into observable form."

"I wouldn't say *that*, he's work is proving quite desirable with our discerning collectors … ."

"And as for the main artist on display, you have to admit, Miss Walsingham, you have some rather *explosive* pieces on display tonight. One might almost say you had a hand in making Fielding's hoard of shiny disasters yourself, considering your strong views on atomic weaponry which you voiced during your last gala event … ."

"No comment."

Peter could only smile and shake his head before he moved on to the next set of paintings.

Eventually the crowd began to thin as the guests gradually slipped away into the night, the band giving a few last encores as the attendees dwindled to family and some close friends, which thankfully did not include their new mobster neighbours, Vico and the wife had to leave earlier than expected, much to their relief. The gallery Gang were still present, naturally, plus Fielding, the man of the evening, but not entirely. 'Turris' unknown to most was busy checking his tape recorder while Stephie peered over his shoulder after she capped her lens and put away her camera, giving 'Horace' a razzing for being utterly barbaric to the artists on display that night, then surprised Chris with a playful kiss, which he appreciated no end. There was some clattering as the restaurant staff were not yet off the clock, the waiters commencing their wearisome hunt for plates and glasses abandoned in the most unlikely places, while Andre and the kitchen crew were busy taking away what was left of the buffet fare all the while dividing out the leftovers after they asked Katherine if she didn't mind. Of course not, she abhorred wasting food, not to mention what was left of Andre's nibbles was too good to leave behind, even Gramps had no qualms asking the house chef for one of his deluxe doggie bags for the road, and was willing to suffer Aunt Martha's running commentaries for it.

"I'd say that went pretty well, my dear, it looked like everyone had a good time," Helen congratulated Katherine, pleased to see her eldest had learned quite a bit from watching her manage large charity events through the years.

"Yes indeed," Harold nodded, giving a quick glance over to Gramps gleefully collecting his share of the food loot, then another to the young couple at the front desk not caring if everyone knew they were now an item. Katherine was also happy to see them together, Stephie having decided to give the role of Batgirl a chance, helping the really nice guy but semi-anonymous artist and cantankerous art columnist keep his triple identity a secret. They actually did make a cute couple. She also couldn't help notice Charlie doing his best to spend some quality time with Suzy during the evening, although she was kept pretty busy with an avid collector or two making enquiries on the gallery's reservation terms.

"I certainly had a good time, this was one of the most enjoyable shows I've ever had. Well, I guess this is goodnight. It's been a pleasure meeting you all," Fielding affirmed as he shook hands with everyone.

"Thanks Jiff, I'll call you Monday," Katherine promised before he left.

"He's one very eccentric fellow," Aunt Barbara commented, watching him leave.

"Yes, he is that, to be sure," Kevin nodded, before clasping his hands together, "but wait until you meet our *next* artists! Oh what fun!"

"I bet," Horace the Hacker grinned as he and Stephie came over to join them, "I can't wait."

Kevin's effervescent enthusiasm dissipated for a second as he gave the vile Art Hacker the once-over with an air of aristocratic disdain before becoming his usually bubbly self, which amused Katherine and Stephie.

"I dunno, Stansislov is not someone whom I would describe as 'fun', or the 'Palette Knife Prince' for that matter," Esther commented, observations Olivia agreed upon with a nod to the Professor's amusement.

"Whoa, you got *Denninger* to agree to a showing? When were you going to give me the scoop on *that*," Horace was eager to find out and looked like he was ready to snatch out his recorder for an interview right on the spot.

"He's right, *there's* some news! I wouldn't mind adding a few of his pieces to our collection," the Captain admitted, "and I know Ger was also itching to get something of his at one time, isn't that right, Ger?" Oh, right." Gerry was no longer on the phone, the nurses had decided the patient had had enough excitement and had cut the party short on him.

"Yes, I think he did mention he was interested, as an art investment basically," Sophia jumped in.

"Oh, is he someone important?" Aunt Martha was curious to find out.

"That depends on how often you can get him out of his studio, he's as bad as Kroger, and a hundred times more schizoid," Esther informed her.

"I'm afraid that's true," Kevin nodding apologetically, "but displaying his art is well worth the outburst or two."

"Just *who* are you mixing with Katherine!" Aunt Martha turned to her aghast.

"Apparently, the greatest artistic minds in the world," Steves had to interject.

"If it's any consolation, I'm going to have a lady vegetarian artist after all the nut jobs," Katherine dryly commented.

Lottie agreed that didn't sound so bad, unless she made them all eat tofu Jennifer pointed out.

On that note, it was decided it was time to head home. Katherine let the Gang off the clock, they had done a good night's work.

"Well done everyone, we had a terrific event. You're all off the hook, we can worry about the aftermath of your apocalyptic show tomorrow. Go home and put your feet up."

"Maybe you guys can go home, but a reporter's work is never done, or a photographer's, right," Stephie noted, nudging Horace.

"Yeah, I have to write this night up for the morning edition, and Steph's snaps need to be developed. Er, you don't mind if I catch up with you at the studio," he asked Steph before turning to Katherine, "I need to have a quick word with the owner of this fine establishment."

"Sure thing, no problem, see you later," she replied, giving him a quick kiss before picking up her stuff. "I gotta run, it was great getting together again," she called, giving a quick wave as she ran to the door, yanking the slipping strap of her camera case back into position.

"Looks like I need to do one last interview, if that's okay with everyone. In any case, I have to stay and finish up some other things here tonight," Katherine added.

Suzy wondered if she could help, but Katherine told them she could handle it.

"All right dear, I guess this is goodnight, and do try to get some sleep," her mother advised.

"Good advice, I'm beat," Gramps noted.

There were a few last minute chats in the parking lot before Charlie took Suzy home, the Reinold and Walsingham clans afterwards buckling up and driving away, while Peter checked to make sure Mrs. Hunt was able to get into her limo with her chauffeur's help, she was suffering terribly with her arthritis these days. Having said their goodbyes, no one had noticed that Peter didn't get into his car. Once the place was clear, he opened the trunk and retrieved his ecclesiastic case. Everyone else could call it a night, except for the art reporters and him. Time to seal up some infernal portholes.

⁍ ✦ ⁎

"Hello Katherine, it's nice to see you again," Mabel greeted, having already met her when she signed up for her wedding date.

"Hi! I guess you know who I'm here to see."

"Yep, the Doctor is in, just down thatta way, and down the stairs to the bottom. There'll be signs pointing out where to go after that."

"Okay, thanks."

Down? That was odd. Reaching the end of the stairs as directed, she followed the signs pointing out 'Monsignor Reinold' and discovered the greyish corridor lined with a pew and chairs along with some devotional pictures and Bible quotes on the walls to try and liven it up, plus a few motivational sayings of the saints. She quickly scanned the florescent lit area before knocking on his door. It was funny to hear Pete referred to as someone in the medical profession with his own OR, but down here in the *basement*? If she didn't know better, she might have thought she was being directed to a morgue.

"Come in."

The door gave a little squeak.

"Hi Pete. So this is where you're stationed," she began, but stopped when she saw the painting she had given him facing her. "Oh! So this is where you wanted it. It's a good thing too. Just why are you stuck down here of all places? Does your mother know you're down here in this … this … dismalosity?"

Peter, who had been sitting at the coffee table trying to catch up on some of his letters while waiting, rose to meet her, but couldn't help laughing at her reaction to the place.

"No, she doesn't, and don't you go telling her either. I have reasons for being in the dregs of this fine edifice."

"*You* picked here? Oh, okay, if you say so." It looked like he tried to make the place as nice as he could, but it just didn't seem right that in the whole building he got stuck in the closest thing to a modern dungeon. However, her curiosity took over. "So, this is where 'it' happens, the big 'clearing outs'?"

"Yes, but in *there* is where I do my real work," he indicated, giving the Grand Tour of his little space. "Don't get too excited, it's smaller and more drab than this, bit at least it has a window to the street above, even if it is a small one."

She took a quick look around the diminutive OR and shook her head before sitting down with him in the waiting room.

"Well, if you say you need the place, it's not for me to judge the location. Say, have you had to 'do' anything like 'that' … in there?"

"Not really, just check-ups, but speaking of which, you'll be happy to know I've cleared up your problem in the gallery."

In her bafflement on being directed to the basement, she had forgotten to ask Peter how last night went.

"That's good to know, thank you so much Pete. Was it really bad?"

"Umm, so-so." He didn't want to say too much in case it frightened her, Anubis put up quite a resistance, but it was enough that job was done and there was nothing to worry about now.

"You said you wanted privacy, and since I had Horace with me, it was best he didn't see what was gong on, so I turned off the security monitors while you where there, even the guards upstairs didn't get to see it from their desk," she explained.

"Good. As much as I would like the world to know what an exorcist does, it might be good to make an exception in this case, as you know publicity can turn negative. I wouldn't want to hurt business on you."

"Don't worry, I don't think our house reporter would have seen much anyway, he wasn't there long enough, and all I saw you doing when the monitors were back on was a load of blessings, nothing out of the ordinary.

"Basically that, and a lot of praying." He smiled. "Still, you don't want it to get out you had me exorcising the place, it could be taken the wrong way. Hope the interview went okay."

"Actually, Horace had some news to give me." Her expression changed to one of peeved disgust.

"That bad? What's up?"

"I found out why Sir Nincompoop was skulking around the neighbourhood. No wonder he was always in for pastries. Talk about casing the place! He *really* was casing the place! The whole block in fact, several blocks in fact!" She threw up her hands as if to say 'what next'.

"What? Setting up shop in your area? That's fast. He just opened up the other place in Manhattan."

"Yeah! He, or his big swanky British art company, whatever, is buying a building down the road from me, and not that far down either. I start blazing a gallery trail in the Dumbo area, and he comes in now that I've done the ground work in bringing art publicity to the block. Real slick! Just when I'm expanding my place, his own development could just overshadow my whole project. Why couldn't he just stay happy on Fifth Avenue instead of hustle in on my patch?"

"He's just taking the saying work smarter not harder up a notch, but it's nothing personal, business is business."

"I know, I know, it's just so annoying," she intoned, nettled with this turn of events that was beyond her control. "Oh, enough of Sir Slithery, just thinking of him I could spit bullets. I hope you don't mind I left last night without saying goodbye, but you said you needed to be alone, and you did look rather busy … ."

"No apologies. I didn't expect anyone to stay and wait. I hope you got a good night's rest. This reminds me, I meant to tell you I checked and blessed next door too. Since it's yours now, thought I might as well do the job while I was there, right? The guards were very helpful and opened the place up for me."

"Now there's thinking ahead. I never thought about the new section, of course that would need to be done. With that creep in the neighbourhood, I could use every blessing you can send my way. Thank you again, Pete. You must be wiped out after all that."

"Nah, I'm fine. So tell me, how's the Sistine Chapel coming along?"

"Backbreaking." She laughed as she opened her cases and scanned their interiors for the art implements needed for the day before her expression changed to sheepish regret. "I've had to come to the tough decision I may have to cheat a little."

"Oh?"

"Yeah," she replied with a shrug. "Who was I kidding? At the rate I'm going, it would take me a year to get the ceiling done, which isn't an option. I've got only weeks! Even Michelangelo would have to be the archangel himself to pull that off."

Curious, he wondered what she could possibly be sticking on the ceiling that it was so laborious to be tempted to add a minor deception or two. Was she actually executing a copy of Rome's most famous chapel?

"No, but it sure feels like it," she joked. "I'm going to break my silence and let you know what the design is, since you're a master of secret-keeping, literally tell-me-your-sins level of secrecy, I know I can trust you."

"True. I'm all ears."

She sharpened a few pencils as she revealed to him her great decorating *piece d'resistance*. To ensure the room wasn't overwhelmed, she decided on nothing too elaborate but still required classical precision: a heavenly scene with just the right amount of pudgy cherubs playing with flowing garlands amid billowing cloud formations often seen in the great paintings of Italy.

"Wow, sounds glorious."

"It does, but glory comes with a cost, time in this instance, and you cannot rush the brush. The first stages are looking good too. Puffy clouds and flowers are not difficult, but if I want to do *all* the cherubs and not leave any out of my grand design to get it done on schedule, I need to hurry things up a bit."

"So how do you plan to 'cheat'?"

"Well, I figured that since this is a decorating thing as well as an artistic project, if I wasn't painting, it might be wallpaper I was slapping about, and since that's just paper stuck on the wall and nobody minds if you didn't design the pattern yourself, I figured decals stuck up on the ceiling aren't that much different. I may have to resort to half painting and sticky-wicky cherubs if I want that main room done. Still, I'm an artist! A fresco idea should be all hand painted. I hate myself for even thinking it."

Peter chuckled after hearing this confession.

"With little Bro's interest in 'con art' the ruse of sticky angels seems rather apt."

"Oh! That's funny, but you're right. I'm always teasing him about that. Now I don't feel quite so guilty. Okay, all set. Pencils sharpened, let's get you posed."

"Ready to go. How does this work?"

"I'm going to sketch you in a few different positions, sitting, standing, views from profile, facial close ups, things like that until I have enough material to work from since the final design for the painting is up in the air yet. It means I have to scrutinize you a bit, hope you don't mind being stared at. Just relax and be yourself, we'll do all the sitting stuff first."

"Is it okay to talk?"

"Sure, just no sudden movements when I've got you situated," she replied, while examining the lighting in the room. The table lamps gave a nice glow, but not bright enough for her taste. She flipped on the overhead switch and gave a slight grimace. Ick! Florescent rod trapped in a pathetic plastic excuse for a shade. Her expression didn't escape him.

"I know, it can't be helped. I did my best with the place." They both laughed. "We can go to another room here, or how about outside? The natural light will be better to work with."

She couldn't have agreed more.

"The only thing is Pete, I hope you don't mind inevitable bystanders, it happens when artists work in the great outdoors."

As he helped her gather everything up, he apologised in that he didn't warn her about the lighting before she arrived.

"Don't worry about it. I just hope I do a good job. I'm only a few years out of art college, and poof! Your Dad entrusts me with a portrait commission when he could have hired anyone he wanted. Painting his boat was one thing, but people are another. He has great faith in me, that's for sure."

"Just have faith in yourself. The good thing is if something doesn't look right, you can scrape us all off the canvas and, splat, start again."

"True, but that's probably not a good reminder to give a perfectionist," she revealed with some humour, "your mother may never get her painting."

Observing she couldn't sketch him sitting if he didn't have something to sit on, Peter collected a chair from the visitor's area before they ventured out the main entrance. The sketching party quickly generating some curiosity among passers-by as Katherine scouted out a suitable location and directed him in the chair, trying different seating positions, then moving on to standing with her subject. Eventually she progressed to photo taking for the finer details when those bystanders who decided not to keep going started to test her serenity by quietly yet awkwardly loitering around to watch over her shoulder, one or two braving to interrupt the work in progress and asking all sorts of well-meaning questions that didn't help her to concentrate. Time to hurry this up a bit.

"I hope I don't blink," he noted. It was true, he never felt comfortable in front of a camera.

"Don't worry, Stephie just taught me how to get around that. Okay, stand there, yeah! That's great, now, close your eyes, and when I say 'three', you open them."

Maybe there was something to this reverse physiology trick. He couldn't help smiling as he patiently waited for the countdown eyes closed then opening them as directed. The smile was even bigger when he could see what was happening.

"Aha! Success! I won't know until I develop the roll, but I'm positive that snap will beat anything produced at the DMV. A few more nice mug poses like that, and I think we can call it a wrap."

"Er, speaking of which, you just may have to do that again."

"Why?"

"You left the lens cap on."

"Ah, flibberdygibbet!"

"Plus, we may have to wrap this up fast," he trailed, glancing behind her.

Pacing behind her was a new addition to the bystanders, poor Joel who had appeared from behind a corner. The 'voices' were definitely at him again. Talking to himself in a disturbing sort of way, he quickly cleared the area of most of the gawkers.

"Um, is he one of … um … one of … well, you know," Katherine asked quietly.

"Nah, he's harmless."

The appearance and unsettling mannerisms of the recent, and now practically the only bystander could have fooled her, but if Peter insisted he wasn't among the possessed she could trust him. However, she noted he obviously had a few more unscheduled emergency cases as a few of the gawkers were growing again, this time by the door of the building and patiently waiting for them to finish. He had kept his book clear that morning, but he warned her this could happen.

"I guess this means we'll have to have lunch another time."

"Sorry Kathy, duty calls."

"No problem, just hang on." She whipped the cap off and fired a few shots before Peter had a chance to blink or think and managed to catch a few natural poses before he could register the scene of a giant eye-like lens staring at him. "There! All done. Now, off you go Doc, and relieve the afflicted."

They gave each other a hug, although Katherine was disappointed she couldn't spend more time with him. There were other things she wanted to tell him when they were alone, but that chance was now gone for the present. She wanted to spill out her worries concerning Gerry knowing they both shared them eventhough she didn't want to burden him, but Pete was such a kind soul who was a comforting listener. Oh yes, she was over Gerry's uncharacteristic outburst at the hospital, it was just a shock that day, he didn't mean what he said, and of course his sudden snap was not wholly unexpected considering the pain and the challenges facing him. Heck, she was used to growing up with a crotchety father plagued with a serious ulcer problem exacerbated by an executive world brimming with a thousand and one daily hassles and who therefore could fly off the handle when his stomach went on the blink and wouldn't give him any respite despite the number of pills he was taking. Gerry was facing something just as bad if not far worse than that. She completely understood. It just would have been a consolation to talk to Peter about it because there was something else that worried her about the incident and didn't know who else to tell it to. When the initial shock of his first ever curt words to her had passed, a look of hesitation had crept in, the realisation his limits were not on a high bar like he expected, but had been dropped down several notches. It was a self-questioning glance that said '*my God, is this as good as it gets?*' Gerry was a persistent, unconquerable, stubborn, confident spirit that was rarely pessimistic despite his slightly sarcastic sense of humour, and to catch that flicker of defeatism in his eyes signalling an internal battle for his morale sent a chill through her heart worse than his outburst. It worried her, and she prayed it was only a temporary fear, that he wouldn't let the demon of self-doubt about his future crush his optimism despite whatever challenges may be facing him. While all this flashed in her mind, Peter, who also was sorry their morning together was cut short, sensed her anxiety without hearing the words.

"He loves you, and he knows you love him. That will help him live through anything."

"Thank you, Pete. I just needed to hear it."

☙ ❖ ❧

The hectic days of Fielding's art show now past, it was time to focus on the gallery expansion, and Katherine had her hands full between that, the penthouse decorating, the portrait sketches and the hospital visits, in addition to finding some way to avoid having to go to the family dinners whenever that involved including their new neighbours, the Becchinos. She had enough on her plate right now without worrying about upsetting the Jersey mob! The family agreed with her there and were relieved for once about all the work she had to attend as it gave her a pretext to extract herself from that. The good thing in the midst of all this bustling was the specialists at the hospital finally gave Gerry the all clear to be discharged from their care into the excellent hands of the private nurse and physiotherapist waiting for him at Stonyvale. That helped to brighten Gerry's spirits as well as everyone else's. It was a step in a positive direction, to be finally free of the clinical surroundings and back at the family homestead, even if he was 'moving back in with the parents', which Leroy had fun ribbing him about. The Morning Room had been set up with a comfortable bed, the live-in nurse and physiotherapist also had their own rooms and would be ensconced full time until it was deemed he no longer needed their help.

However, Gerry indeed had been shown his limits no thanks to the constant pain he would have to endure. His pain management included direct injections into his hips that were not in the least bit pleasant but the effect was most welcome when the procedure was over. He could just manage on the crutches after a dose, but when the searing pain began to jab again after awhile, was confined to a wheelchair when not in bed. At least he was mobile then, but it was certainly a shock to the system to realise mobility hinged on these additional apparatuses. Still, he once more began to hope that his back and left leg would straighten up as time went on, that he was just trying to rush a laborious healing process in an impatient fit to just get it all over with so that he could move on and actually *live* life again. He had a fiancée whom he loved and longed to take to Italy, eager to fulfil their romantic plan of having a whole month to themselves in the land of *la dolce vita*. What more beautiful way could there be to begin their life together?

Yes, things were looking slightly better, and Katherine also ploughed on, working on her decorating on the nights she wasn't visiting at Stonyvale with Gerry and his family, still refusing to divulge many details other than a few tantalising hints on her project no matter how much Gerry playfully wheedled her. His bantering became worse when he wondered why she looked sheepish and delightfully guilty every time he prodded for information about the famous ceiling, aware he wouldn't be given an answer just yet. Then, just when it looked like he had worn her down and she was about to divulge her plans, he turned about face and jokingly went inflexible with an 'aw, you don't want to tell me, that's okay' spiel, she had sworn them both to secrecy and he would wait, refusing to let her get a word in about it. It was roughish fun to have this innocent joke continually running between them, him knowing next to nothing about his former bachelor pad and she keeping everything as secret as possible, then to fluster her up a bit because she looked so adorable when he did. Good thing she knew he was only having a laugh, but he really did want to know what was going on.

Eager, tantalising curiosity was getting the better of him, thinking about her there happily if exhaustingly busy shaping their future newlywed home every spare minute she could carve away from her other projects. He would have to get better fast if only to see what she was up to without spoiling the surprise. Making it worse was knowing she had bought a Fielding piece to grace the place, and she wasn't giving away any hints about that either!

For now Katherine let him in on the news circulating the tower in that the residents finally found out who had moved into the apartment below them, Chloe Donerdale, daughter of the founder and CEO of the hair and beauty salon franchise bearing the same name. It was the doorman who told her first, and according to him their new neighbour was starting college at NYU, while the concierge observed she had a dog that reminded him of a yipping chair cushion with ears.

"Uh oh, this is going to make things interesting," Gerry noted. "Beechwarz isn't going to let this one rest."

He was right. The following week everyone received a flyer in their mailboxes that someone from the Resident's Committee would be coming around to have them sign a new petition to make the building a 'No Pets' residential complex to those who were renting. Everyone decided to be very, very busy the next week after that. In agreement with Gerry, Katherine though the whole idea was bonkers. Sure, she heard the dog barking every now and again, but it wasn't that bad, and nobody else was complaining about it as many of them had pets, except for that one singular member of the Resident's Committee who wielded the gavel. Then, things promised to heat up when the new tenant asked the concierge to put the following leaflet into the mailboxes:

"Dear President of the Resident's Committee,

I have just invited the whole building to my first party, which means they have received formal warning of the noise. I have received no complaints, except from you. No complaints from anyone else equals no majority vote against my party. Either join the fun or leave us the hell alone. And leave my dog alone too. Have a nice day."

Gerry chuckled when Katherine showed him the leaflets along with the invitation printed in colour complete with sparkles glued around

'PARTY!' It appeared the new neighbour was well able for the bully of the building.

"Are you going?"

"I thought about it, but nah. Anyone who goes is going to be caught right in the firing line of the Resident´s Committee, and right now I'm too busy to get jammed in a clash between the new tenant and Mrs. Beechwarts. As the former newest tenant of the building, I've luckily avoided that gathering's radar and will continue to do so thanks to Miss Party Hardy in the apartment below. I'm going to take advantage of that, declare neutrality so to speak and lay low for awhile." Especially as the party-thrower didn't mind cussing out the committee President in her snarky reply. Things could get ugly!

"The joys of apartment block living, you're learning fast."

What Katherine didn't expect was an unexpected visitor the night of the party, Leroy, who just happened to be in the neighbourhood.

"Hey Lee, come on in."

"Can't love, I'm off to the partaaaay! Thought I'd see if you'd like to come," he beamed, nodding down to a crate of beer and other sundry bottles of liquor brought as an offering for the promising event. Obviously, Leroy caught wind of what was going on through Gerry.

"No thanks, you scoundrel. Aren't you getting a bit too old for college girls? It's a fresher's party, you're not in college any more, and, you don't even live here."

"*She* doesn't know that, and since she's invited the whole building, it's one huge free pass for crashers! So it's not going to be only college girls. And, she's certainly not going to check every eejit like me who swings in under those circumstances, I know from experience. Besides, if I'm asked, I'll just say I'm staying up here with you."

"You're awful. When I eventually meet her, she'll think it's *you* I'm engaged to!"

"That disagreeable am I? Ach! The rejection! Seriously, you should come. You've been all knots with workin' and stressin', you could do with a little foot loosin' and fancy freein'."

"Thanks, but no, I'm beat. I'm going to bed in a few minutes, providing the entertainment issuing from the underworld allows me," alluding to the thumping rave music throbbing through the soles of her slippers. "You go ahead and continue to misspend what's left of your youth."

"With pleasure. Good night Katie, sweet dreams. Until we meet again," he jovially called. Katherine shook her head as he left the front door heaving up his libations and looking every bit as though he was about to give a cheery leap with a kick of the heels if he could have managed it with his armload of toodledee.

Katherine received a rude awakening at four in the morning when the doorbell rang announcing the return of the prodigal party crasher now three sheets in the breeze, unfit to sit behind a wheel and too sick to stick in a taxi.

"Heluuu Katie luuuv, grand evenin' for a sleep over. Ooh sakes, I'm dyin' … I'm not long for this worlld," he slurred, more than a little wobbly on his feet.

"Oh no, I don't believe this. Um, okay, get in here. Just this once! Maybe Gerry didn't mind pulling you out of scrapes and letting you snooze off the booze, but I won't put up with much of this nonsense in the future. Got it?"

"Brillnant," he agreed with a dopey nod as she attempted to guide him. She had planned to get him into the other guest room but he headed in the opposite direction she tried to steer him and never made it past the sofa that had just arrived two days ago from Italy still swaddled in its industrial clear plastic film wrappings. Great! Not there of all places! He had better be able to hold his liquor she warned him.

"Don't worry pet, I see we're weeel covered here," he noticed poking at the plastic. Despite the drunken fog, he had a point. At least the thing was more than adequately covered for any unpleasant event such as that. She ran for a bucket anyway. Of all the … ! So is this what their college days together were like? When she returned she couldn't help but smile despite her annoyance when she saw him laid out with his arms outstretched with a silly grin stretched over his face as he took in the new ceiling.

"Heaven! It must be! I didn't think I'd evrrrr make it, I see angels comin' for me!"

She didn't have all the baby cherubs on the ceiling yet, but obviously enough to make an impression. Leroy then grew slightly serious in the face and then heaved himself over to hazily scan the floor. She darted for the bucket assuming the worst, but that wasn't it, he was searching the ground for something else.

"What *are* you looking for?"

"Just wonderin' if the toast was true. Yep! Made it through the pearly doors, an' don't see any little divils looking for me. I must be dead half an hour then, 'cause they never had a clue." He then pulled himself back up on the couch and slurred something else before he finally dropped off. She fetched a blanket and draped it over him. Nuts! She wanted Gerry to be the first to see the room with all its elegant new trimmings yet this drunken oaf beat him to it, not to mention this wasn't how she planned to spend the early hours of the morning. Still, it was an odd way to receive a compliment in that the place was looking quite heavenly to be mistaken for the real thing.

After a few hours of sleep and a strong mug of coffee, she made him swear not to tell Gerry what the place looked like.

"Don't worry Katie, I'm going ta love joinin' in the fun tormentin' him with the fact I got to see it first an' not be allowed tell him anythin'. He's in for a treat, that's for sure. Why, you've done wonders with the place."

"I must have, you thought you were in the Afterlife last night and had reached the pearly gates."

"I must have been totally langer'd. Thanks for taking me in."

"You're welcome. Just try and stay on the sober path for a while, okay?"

"Ah love, I promise not to promise anything."

"You're awful."

Yes, he was roguishly awful, but so darn likeable despite his faults. True to his word, during his next visit at Stonyvale he had fun tormenting his friend about the decorations without telling him anything, much to Gerry's amusement.

"Aw, now I'm dying to see the place."

"You'll think you're in Paradise. I did."

While Gerry was slowly on the mend, there were others making their heavenly plans, Tom certainly looked like a man who had shed several years off his frame now that Lottie had finally gone past simply noticing him, while she was certainly very happy to discover love was like lightning and could strike twice – and to think Tom was right there the whole time! It was certainly a switch to be thrust from this romantic epiphany straight into considering wedding arrangements, however, it didn't seem right to upstage Gerry and Kathy's wedding currently on standby. Tom agreed with Lottie, it felt like they would be rubbing their own good fortune in right now, tying the knot before they did. They didn't say anything to anyone, but decided that depending on how Gerry progressed, the best thing for now was to wait and quietly continue as though they had just started dating each other and enjoy the romantic epiphany a little longer.

CS ❖ ♌

Everyone seemed caught in a holding pattern, except for Peter. Life quickly became fast paced when he received some news he wasn't expecting, yet wasn't surprised either: notification of another transfer, and this to hit the day when he had at last been granted permission to proceed with the Major Rite of exorcism. Nothing like adding some extra challenges! The funny part, he was just one notch away from being returned back to his former patch at St. Patrick's, but not the cathedral this time. He was to pull up stakes from St. Peter's and to settle into "Old" St. Patrick's, the former principal church before the other cathedral was built. He hadn't said anything to the archbishop about his taxing experience, never a murmur, but it was obvious that he had ruffled enough feathers with his traditional-conservative presence in the financial district to be whipped out in a hurry and placed in a curiously strategic place. Old St. Patrick's was close enough to his old parish to keep his former parishioners happy, and yet would ensure he would be kept out from underfoot regarding his unusual public displays when they did happen. Peter wasn't stupid, he could see he was now in the paradoxical state of 'demotion promotion', but that didn't matter. The sticky situation of St. Peter's was taken out of his hands without him having to make things more unpleasant. He had the 'Early Bird' slot assigned him for his Latin services and was glad to have it. This time he hoped when he arrived at his new place of service there would be no passive aggressive arrangements preventing him from proceeding. He would have to wait and see.

Despite this piece of good news, he had been thrown into a whirlwind with only one week before moving day in addition to preparing for the exorcism, not that he was unprepared for the task itself, but he had another twist added for good measure; he got landed with a new assistant. Since Fr. Xavier had relinquished his mission as exorcist in the Trenton area the call was put out to find a willing replacement, and while a few priests had declined the dubious honour of this assignment an unexpected volunteer came forward to assume the task, a Fr. Greg Simmons. The downside was the new volunteer had no experience whatsoever in the practical side of casting out demons. As this was new to him, Fr. Simmons had requested if he could take part in what Peter was about to do to acquire that much needed experience before he began his own exorcist work full time. As much as Peter understood the situation, on-the-job observation with an

643

experienced priest was the only sure way of gaining any proficiency in the exorcism ministry, on this grave occasion he was going to need his full concentration both mental and spiritual in addition to a healthy dose of stamina, and this was not the best time to be handed a fledgling apprentice. If his upcoming patient wasn't an extreme case he wouldn't have minded, but there was no telling what was going to happen, and he didn't need the compounded stress of hoping his appointed help would have a clue what to do, or worse yet, have no clue at all and threaten to make the process more arduous than he already suspected it would be. Still, this was also an act of fraternal charity, helping a brother priest in their never-ending vocation to save souls. Nevertheless, charity or not, having a greenhorn jump in unprepared would not be the brightest idea. Simmons was in need of a crash course on their ministry starting now, and therefore Peter decided if it was possible that he join him in New York for the week before participating in the exorcism to observe how he ran his OR. Fr. Simmons agreed right away with the plan and managed to rearrange his parish schedule accordingly.

If Peter entertained any prospects that his new assistant was not as green as he suspected, when the doorbell rang on the appointed day of introductions their first encounter on that warm September afternoon dented all previous attempts at nursing his wishful thinking of the volunteer. Who should he meet at the door but a tanned shorts-clad individual shod in flip-flops with sunglasses perched on the top of his sun-bleached mane, his wardrobe rendered complete with a T-shirt sporting a cartoon image of Yosemite Sam brandishing a couple of six shooters with a speech bubble that read: '*Say yer prayers, yah flea bitten varmint!*' and looking every inch like a tourist who had the intention of going to Coney Island but took a wrong turn somewhere along the line.

"Hiyah! I'm Fr. Greg. You must be my new boss." The young recruit smiled widely as they shook hands. "Don't worry, I've got my blacks in the case."

Obviously, the greenhorn could also see where he stood after taking a glance at the cassock.

"Welcome to St. John's rectory, or as Fr. Jenkins dubbed it, the Holy Bachelors Club. Let's get you settled in. Sorry you won't get to meet the guys until later tonight, there's three more of us, they're all out on duty of course," Peter returned as he helped him in and up the stairs with his few travel bags. "Thing is, you're now the junior around here if only for a week or so, hope you don't mind rattling around with us oldies."

"Piece of cake. I used to do volunteer work at a retirement home." Another grin revealed Fr. Greg looked like he would fit in just fine in the humour department. "Actually, it'll be nice to have some company. I'm in that type of parish that assigns a pastor a 'burb house straight out of a '50s sit-com with the 70s smashed in, if you know what I mean."

"Say no more, although you won't find the décor here much of an improvement. Here you are, this is your room, it's not the Ritz but it's comfortable enough. Bathroom is down the hall, best try and get in there at night, everyone else wants a morning shower slot, you can imagine the pandemonium. Oh, here's the key to your door." Just in case he didn't want his domain and personal belongings fussed over by the new housekeeper he explained.

"Housekeeper? And you say this isn't the Ritz? I'm in heaven."

"O'Conner would beg to differ with you. Okay, I'm heading to the kitchen for a cup of coffee. Once you're all set up, get changed into your clerics and come down and meet me, we'll have a chat before we head out. I'll give you a tour of the rest of the place tonight."

"We're starting today?"

"Yes, in fact one week is hardly enough, nothing for it but to throw you right in."

"Cool! I always like jumping into the deep end. I'll be down in a jiffy."

"Great, and don't forget your exorcism case, I'll need to take a look at it."

"Sure thing."

At least the new recruit was enthused. Peter went and made himself that much needed cup of coffee. Fifteen minutes later the new arrival looked more like an exorcist's apprentice, shoe-shod, dressed in his black suit and collar with the requested case in hand, although still sporting the sun glasses on top of his shock of hair.

"Take a seat. Coffee? Or perhaps you haven't eaten anything yet today?"

"Not yet," he returned, carefully setting the case down.

"That won't do, you may not be getting much for the rest of the week, but I'm not going to starve you on the first day," Peter noted as he got up and rummaged through the fridge.

"Um, you mean I'm going to starve the rest of the week," Greg tested, now slightly alarmed.

"To a point. After this week we're heading into a very rough situation, and we're going to need to do all the fasting we can stomach."

Peter glanced over. "You know the Gospel, there are certain kinds of spirits that can only be cast out by prayer and fasting."

"Oh, right. Lesson one: starve."

Greg relaxed while Peter also cracked a smile. Poor kid. He really was green at this.

"It won't be that bad. Sunday will be like during Lent, no starvation."

"Got it, but if you're doing the Rite and all, why do I need to go hungry? Just curious."

"The prayers of others can help a case get resolved faster. If they are willing to fast too, so much the better."

"Ohhh, okay. Kinda like backup."

"Exactly so. Again, don't get anxious. If you intend to continue with this ministry you'll find not all cases require fasting. You'll learn to tailor your approach according to each spiritual patient."

"Huh. Okay. How will I know?"

"You'll know. Hmm, we've got sandwich stuff, ham, cheese, salami, Jenkin's not-so appetising hunk of liverwurst, how about soup to go with it? Sorry we don't have the home made variety on hand," Peter offered apologetically, opening the cupboard and scanning the contents.

"Thanks, but it's a little hot for soup, this will do though," Greg decided, jumping up and helping himself to a can of spaghetti rings and a glass of orange soda.

"Okay, if you insist. Let me get you a pot, or do you prefer it nuked?"

"Neither, thanks. Where're the spoons," he enquired as the can ground around the electric opener.

"Uck! Not you too? I can see you and Fr. Mark are going to hit it off." Peter grimaced as Greg discovered the utensil drawer and settling into a place at the table, chomping on the tomatoey sludge straight from the can.

Of course, this quickie lunch break gave them a chance to have that chat. Peter learned quite a lot just by the mention Greg was assigned on his own with an older tract house for a rectory, it meant he was in a moderate parish just managing to make ends meet, probably blue collar area. Sure enough, Greg said he came from a line of welders and construction crews, and so he was assigned an appropriate parish.

"I'm curious. How did you hear 'The Call'? To become a priest I mean."

"Oh, it's just that I wanted to do something where I could help people. I really liked the priest in our parish, Fr. Erckhart, he was great. He was always doing stuff, setting up and working at food banks, helping people find a new place if they got kicked out, things like that. I thought 'that's something I could do with my life'. I mean, something really dedicated. Isn't that what being a priest is all about? Helping people? That's what I thought, and that's what I wanted to do. Something meaningful. So, how about you," Greg ventured once he had given a brief glimpse into his life. "Any family connection to the Reinold trucks we see around?"

"Funny you should ask that." Peter tried to hide his amusement as he took another sip.

"Really? And I was just joking. That's neat. Distant cousins maybe?"

"Not that distant. My father is CEO," Peter disclosed with a slight shrug. Too bad his former life couldn't stay incognito forever.

"Get outta here! Uh uh! No way. That's something. What made *you* decide to become a priest?"

"The short version is I knew from an early age, it wasn't like I had actually had to *decide*. The bad part was I delayed following upon this knowledge. I'm glad to see you didn't."

"No, but my dad wasn't happy about it. He wanted to send us all to college and see we had a career, ya know, being the first kids in the family able to go and all, but he figured if this is what I wanted, he couldn't stop me. He didn't kick me out or anything, but he's still upset."

"It's hard to believe, but just because he's disappointed doesn't mean he no longer cares about you."

"Yeah, I know. I'm just glad I'm not an only kid. I've got an older brother and two younger sisters, so it's not like I left them all alone. How about your family? Did they give you any trouble? I bet they must have."

"My father wouldn't speak to me for years."

Greg stopped scraping around the innards of the can.

"Whoa. That's rough, man. Is it all good with you now?"

"Yes, it's all good."

"I'm glad for yah. You'd think we'd decided to become drug dealers, or something," Greg noted as he continued his scraping, determined not to leave a bit of sauce behind.

"You can have another can. There's plenty where that came from."

"Nah, one's fine. Thanks."

"So, what made you want to volunteer for the exorcism ministry?"

"His Reverence put out the word, saying there was a need for exorcists in our diocese, and I thought, why not? It's not like the Church does that much of it any more, it's just a type of spiritual healing. Right?"

"Yes, it is." Oh boy. "So, have you studied up on what an exorcism entails?"

"I've got the book of prayers, and we can't go ahead unless we're sure it's an authentic case and we get a consent form signed. The bishop told me that much."

"I take it then you haven't read up on past cases at all, no personal study into the matter?"

"Only the movie, and some camp fire stories I heard when I was little," Greg candidly admitted. "I've never seen a real exorcism before."

The kid really was green, and it was glaringly obvious the seminary he went to was just as loose in imparting the weighty matter of the sacerdotal let alone the exorcist vocation. Did this kid have a lot to learn! Nothing like the present.

"Okay. Let's start the first tutorial. Let's see your case."

Greg eagerly lifted it up from the chair beside them and slid it over. His new mentor's expression changed into what he could only describe as 'Major Pro Mode'. Neat! He was itching to get started and into the serious stuff. If he thought he was going to be declared a natural right away, he was instantly mistaken. Strange, but it felt like he was already marked down a few points before the thing was even opened, and when it was, he got the vague inkling his new boss was eyeing the contents with a solemnity as if they were duelling pistols seen in the old movies and that the quality of the arms meant all the difference between life and death.

"Hmm. No blessed salt, no baptismal oil, and the blessing on your holy water wasn't sealed with the Sign of the Cross. Your St. Benedict medals don't have the full blessing on them either, and this crucifix won't do at all, you'll need another. We'll have to fix that."

Whoa. It was one thing to find fault with one item, but *how* could he know *all* those details? He was alone when he blessed the water and the medals, and what was wrong with the crucifix? Wasn't he supposed to have one? Greg asked about that, but he didn't get an answer right away. Peter turned over the cross. Made in China.

"Left the label on, eh?" Peter smiled before returning to mentor mode, pausing to see if the rookie might spot the problem by himself.

"Um, sorry, didn't know that made a difference. Er, too cheap, or something?"

"It's not that. The dollar value isn't the issue. See the left hand? Since when did the Lord bless anyone with His *left* hand?"

"Oh, right. Duh. Though I didn't have much of a choice with this one, I got it as a present."

"Fair enough, but that's not the only detail fuddled. See how the feet are nailed flat beside each other and not right over left? It will suffice for private prayer, it still is a blessed image, but during an exorcism devils will ridicule a crucifix that's not exact in authentic detail, and we don't want to give them any pretext for mockery. Not having the sacramentals just right makes the job longer and harder."

"Whoa. I didn't know that about the other bit about the feet. I mean … ."

"Relax. You haven't studied up yet, and you haven't been through an exorcism, but you've just learned something new, so better keep it lodged for future reference." Peter tapped the side of his head.

"Gotcha. But I didn't bring another one."

"I've got one you can use for now, if you need it before your week here is out of course."

"Wow. Do you think I will? I mean for, er … the heavy stuff?"

"In this line of the Lord's work, you never know."

"Whoa."

Rookie was right. Literally thrown onto the Big League batting plate. He definitely needed guidance, not to mention binge-study on his new apostolate. At least he was eager to get started. Zeal was good. Peter asked his new student to wait while he collected some basic necessities to properly stock his case and get him some reading material for later that night, which he was instructed to diligently study. Greg quickly flipped through the slender booklet.

"*Begone, Satan.* Huh. Title says it all, doesn't it? So, is that all I have to read?"

"Consider that *See Spot Run* to get you started. There's more to read after that. Come, we've got some work to do today."

"All *right!* Can't wait."

Yes, Greg was raring to go, but had a few surprises he wasn't expecting. Once they arrived at the place of operation he was nonplussed to find they were stuck in the basement. Then, instead of anyone coming in for an exorcism there was nothing but a long line for confession that afternoon, it looked that way anyway, and it was plain as day those patiently waiting to have their souls cleansed didn't want anyone else but the Monsignor. He could sense it when Peter first introduced him to everyone before unlocking the waiting room, telling them that he was sending a number of them on to his new protégé in another room around the corner. They were happy to meet the budding new exorcist all right and all said 'hello, hi there, nice to meet you!' accompanied with a friendly smile, wave or handshake, but when more than half the group heard they were getting him for confession instead, they quietly sighed or slumped with undisguised deflation. Sure he was a young priest not long out of the seminary, but *that* had never happened before. Was he a balloon-popper, or what? Greg wasn't upset, it was a bit funny, and they did make appointments to see his boss after all, not him. The next odd thing was even having been allotted a slew of penitents, Greg finished first and was left sitting outside waiting with the rest and growing just as introspective. Judging from how long these few were still sitting around waiting the Monsignor really must be doing things slowly. Wow. Thinking about it, was he going too fast, or not treating the whole thing serious enough? Nah, he didn't *think* so. Then, it struck him how the penitents were selected. Peter didn't simply split them up quicker into a two groups kind of method before they started, he glanced at each person there before making selective choices of who would see him … you, you, no you go over there, you too, yes, also you, not you … . Odd. Greg didn't know what to make of it as he wondered about this vetting procedure. His self examination was politely interrupted by the elderly man sitting next to him.

"So, you staying long with the Monsignor?"

"Hmm? Oh, not long, just a week. Then I'll be assisting him later."

"You don't say? You're blessed. Learn as much as you can from him, young Father." The man smiled and offered his hand. "Hi, I'm Paulie."

"Hi, Fr. Simmons, as you know already, but you can call me Fr. Greg if you like. Do you mind me asking, why did he split everyone up the way he did, and then not equally? It was sorta unusual … ."

"The Monsignor has his ways. You get used to them, and then come to think of it, sometimes he throws you through a loop. One thing's for sure, he's a saint."

"Huh. I haven't known him long, we've only met a few hours ago, but he seems kinda down to earth to me, even if he is dressed old fashioned."

"Oh he's that, but just you wait. It's how he does things, the ordinary made extraordinary as the saying goes. It's also the *way* he has about him, what you used to hear called a cradle vocation. Not unlike yourself, am I right?"

Greg laughed. "I've heard the expression, but I thought he didn't join the priesthood right away."

"Technically you're correct there, the description wouldn't fit under those circumstances, but there're those who even when they waited were touched from above. Monsignor Reinold would walk without shoes with blood-blistered feet for a thousand miles if it meant he could save a soul."

Those overhearing involuntarily nodded their heads.

"And then, there are the 'God Strikes', as I like to call 'em," Paulie continued, with a hushed reverence.

" 'God Strikes' ?"

"Yeah. God Strikes. Struck from Above. You really don't know that much about him?"

"Nope, except he's from the trucking company."

Everyone smiled at each other.

"Sonny, erm, Father, are you in for a treat. You mean to say nothing beyond the run of things has happened, even in the short time you've been together?"

Greg thought for a moment. Come to think of it, he *did* seem to have some unusual talent for detection when it came to his sacramental case earlier that afternoon ... he couldn't help but wonder.

"Uh huh, I know that look."

"I dunno really. Does ... stuff ... happen all the time?"

"Oh yes," the lady next to Paulie replied in an awestruck tone.

"Exorcisms, like?"

"Well, I wouldn't know too much about *that*," the lady noted, shrugging a little.

"Yeah, I don't know if he's done a lot of *those*, if he has, he's kept that kind of thing to himself, but just attend a Mass or go to confession with him. Better yet, do both." Paulie winked.

The group jovially chuckled or nodded again, having the secretive pleasure of insider knowledge concerning all the parish excitement involving the Monsignor. Frankly, he was more interested in seeing an exorcism, but then Father Greg had a light bulb moment.

"Hold on a sec, is he the one I've heard about who can see people's souls?"

"Ding, ding, ding, ding! We have a winner folks!" Good natured chuckles erupted among the group.

"Dude! No way? Really? Whoa. That's intense."

"You're telling *me*," a man up the line sheepishly replied. "It's my turn next in there you know."

The door opened, the merriment hushed up fast, eyes averted quickly to the floor or the wall as a red-eyed penitent with a fist of tissues shyly nodded 'bye' and quickly made an exit. Wow. Then the whisper rush took off when 'my turn next' went inside and closed the door. Man, it felt like they were a bunch of high school students sitting outside the principal's office waiting to get reprimanded, yet acting all cool among themselves while sharing the juicy gossip going on in school. At least this was all harmless talk. Hmm, they weren't *that* innocent either, they were supposed to be examining their consciences before they went in and Greg knew he shouldn't be distracting them, but still, this was some pretty cool stuff, and they sure were eager to tell him whatever they knew or heard about the Monsignor.

By the time the last one was in to be shriven, his head was spinning from the most freaky awesome stories he had ever heard. Now out on his lonesome in the basement hallway, he decided to walk up and down to stretch his legs and think a bit. If he thought learning about exorcisms was going to be interesting, spending a whole week with the next possible cause for beatification who was yet living was nothing short of mind-blowing. Were they all having him on, or what?

Eventually the door opened, Paulie nodded goodbye to Fr. Greg as he left, leaving the two priests alone. Peter at last had a chance to show him his base of operation, but noticed his apprentice had gone silent and was eyeing him curiously.

"Unfortunately, I can't do anything about the exaggerations. You're going to have to figure out which are the tall tales."

Greg stiffened a bit.

"And no, I can't read your thoughts, only God can do that, but it's easy to guess them at times. I can imagine you got an earful out there."

This time the novice exorcist smiled.

"I bet you have some questions."

"Um, yeah. Just curious. How come I got most of the people for confession? If you've got the discernment thing, why give most to me? They really came to you because of … what you do."

"True, but I had spiritual and practical reasons. We might've been here all afternoon if I didn't, and we've got a house clearing to do later, so I had to pick those who truly needed a deep confession. That's the practical side. On the spiritual end, I sent those over to you who were starting to lean too much on me."

"I don't get you."

"You see, once someone's been to confession with me, especially my regulars that are over scrupulous, they tend to lean on my discernment as a crutch instead of trusting their own judgement and practising confidence when examining their consciences, which they need to do for the times when they can't see me. Today I took those who were truly in paralysing doubt or struggling over something and in need of spiritual guidance.”

“Ohhhh, I get you. Instead of a crutch, you're supposed to be a set of training wheels.”

Peter laughed.

“I guess you could say that.”

“And, what's with the basement?”

“Ah, safe space for privacy, plus, somewhere low to where the possessed can't escape. In Rome I saw a woman nearly throw herself to her death out a window. They would find that rather difficult to do here. Come on, let's grab a cup of coffee or something before we get dropped with an unexpected emergency. We have another job ahead of us.”

During their break and afterwards during the drive to their next appointment, Greg was curious to know what their next job was, for exactly what did he mean by 'house clearing'? Peter began gradually letting Greg know he would be called upon to clean a property of any evil, how to spot it and what he could expect during their scrutiny. Greg tried to soak up as much as the Monsignor was telling him about what to be on the lookout for. Man, to think they were real life Ghost Busters. Pretty much, anyway. He wasn't expecting that. He couldn't help saying it to Peter, who for his own part had a hunch that next week there would be a lot of things Greg wasn't expecting, but no point going into it now. The kid was new to this and could only take in so much in a day he thought as Greg started to sing:

“*There's something strange, in the neigh-bour-hood. Whoya gonna call … .*”

'Saint Michael' Peter was about to respond, but let Greg continue with the original lyrics while he searched for a parking space. “Okay, this is the place. How's your Latin?”

“Umm,” Greg drew out sheepishly.

“Never mind, we'll do it in English, but come the time of the exorcism I'm going to need you to be able to respond to the Latin part of the prayers, so that will be on your reading assignment as well. You'll have to practise up.”

“Okay. I'll do my best. Er, can't that be done in English too?”

“Yes, but not the first time around. Satan hates Latin, we torment him by using it. Come, let's see what we can do here.”

They were graciously welcomed by a couple who showed them around their apartment, there was something odd about the place, rumbling, and once in awhile the place seemed liked it *moved.*

While they were walking around, Greg didn't notice anything like that, but when they returned to the living room area he stood quietly by as Peter remained silent, arms folded, eyes to the floor. There didn't seem to be … yes, *there!* He could feel it, a slight shaking, a noticeable vibration, some china began to clink on a shelf. Boy, that *was* odd. The couple looked worried, but just as they were about to say something, Peter held his finger to his lips then folded his arms again, waiting. Waited. Another vibration began. This time it seemed to come from the opposite direction, rattled slightly, then stopped. He still continued to wait. It was getting eerie, this waiting, waiting, waiting, Greg could feel the hairs beginning to stand on the back of his neck. Another vibration came, and Peter checked his watch this time.

"It seems your ghost is the subway."

"What?"

"The vibrations are at regular intervals, and this place is not that far from a major connection hub. If I'm not mistaken, another train should be passing right about … now."

The vibrations commenced, confirming his observations.

"Oh Monsignor, I'm so sorry to have troubled you," the lady replied after an embarrassment induced gasp escaped her, upset to have brought them all the way over for nothing, yet visibly relieved the underworldly activity was nothing more than the underground transport system.

"No trouble at all, it's obvious you're new to New York! I'm glad to put your mind at rest. And, giving blessings is our job, it's never a waste of time."

Even so, Day One, no exorcisms, no ghosts. Bit of a bummer Greg mused as they drove back to the rectory once the blessing was concluded. The first day on the job may not have seemed all that spectacular, other than meeting the Monsignor whom everyone was talking about, and yes, he really was down to earth. In fact, Greg was beginning to doubt what he had heard about him regarding the spectacular, other than he did the blessings rather solemnly than he had seen done before. True, it seemed the Monsignor was very watchful even after discovering the natural cause for the vibrations, checking walls, eyeing the floors, and very serious about it too. Greg wondered what he was looking for, or rather, *at*, but maybe he was just being thorough.

Disappointment aside, the day wasn't a total bummer when he finally got to meet the other fellows of the Holy Bachelor's Club. Yes, he was the youngest one among them next to Peter, but they seemed just as pleased to have him there too, and they had a load of stories about their various ministries to share as they lounged in the TV room while Jenkins prepared dinner since it was the housekeeper's night off. Mark seemed to think Jenkins doing the cooking was entertaining for some reason, but didn't pay too much attention as he listened to Fr. O'Conner tell about the time he once was chaplain in Peter's old school while he had a minute to speak about it, Peter deciding to have a shower before dinner.

"You're not serious."

"Sure thing, I practically watched him grow up. I was chuffed no end when he finally decided to get the collar, but not surprised, still the best altar server I ever had."

"So you're the master of my master?"

"I guess you could say that, lad," O'Conner agreed, followed by a laugh. "Although I must admit this master has become the student now."

Mark sitting in the chair beside them made an involuntary nod.

"So, what was he like back then?"

"Hasn't changed much at all to be honest! Honour roll, disciplined, quiet lad, pretty much liked his own company. If you wondered where he had disappeared to, you could always find him in the chapel or the library, in that order too, but he was never standoffish either. Made a couple of friends and still keeps in contact, not to mention always kept an eye out for his brother and sister when they started attending the Academy. He's got a great sense of humour too, if only a person could poke it out of him, you just have to know how. He's devoted to St. Philip Neri and St. Benedict, which explains a lot there," O'Conner concluded. Greg looked like he couldn't make the connection so O'Conner obliged, "Neri, the joke-loving man with music in his soul, lanced through the heart by an angel and ravished with the love of God, contrasted with rock-steady Benedict, patron of exorcists, builder of monasteries, saviour of Western civilisation and foe to making too light of anything lest reverence for the Almighty is diminished and the profane over lauded."

Mark nodded. "That's him all right."

The conversation was interrupted as Jenkins summoned everyone to the dining room.

"Oh, the *dining* room is it? We're definitely getting the posh treatment tonight," O'Conner noted with glee as he heftily got to his feet.

"Yeah, Jenkins said he wanted to do something special for your first night, he's gone all out," Mark added.

"Really?"

"I'm afraid so," Peter replied almost apologetically as he met them in the hallway, "I couldn't dissuade him from making his dinner plans."

"Aw, he didn't have to do anything fancy, I'll eat anything," Greg informed them as they sat down. However, Jenkins was prepared to test that universal polite response when the dish of the evening was 'something' that looked like wrinkled wood chips drowning in a thick gooey white sauce served on crispy toast.

"Um … looks good. What is it?"

" '*What is it?*' Er, since we're in polite society, I can't tell you, but it's good chow that." Jenkins beamed. "Try it, you'll like it."

Greg hesitantly picked up his fork. They all laughed.

"Relax kid, you've been pranked! I didn't really expect you to eat it. It's only beef jerky in cream. Give it over," Jenkins declared as he eagerly picked up his plate. "I've got super special burgers right off the grill for you bunch. Me on the other hand, I've been hankering for this for weeks, and I haven't been able to persuade Gertie to cook it."

"You like that stuff?"

"Oh yeah, got a taste for it at the base."

"Jenkins was an army chaplain," Peter explained.

"I dunno how you can 'be the best that you can be' when they fed you with that," Mark drolly observed, eyeing the mess.

"That's rich, coming from you." Jenkins laughed. "Dirt is easier on the digestion compared with *your* cooking."

"Verrry funny."

Greg had to admit the next plates certainly looked better, open faced burgers made with a dash of beer in the gravy served with mashed pototoes, bacon bit green beans and an interesting salad with nearly everything thrown in, including some sliced apple with an herbed oil and vinegar dressing. Greg wondered how apples and onions would fare together, but found the combo quite surprising.

"Hey, this is good, I could pick up some tips from you."

"Glad you like it! If you want seconds, don't be shy, there's more on the grill."

◕❖◖

Whatever about an easy first day, that rest of his stay turned out to be pretty jammed-packed. Peter had the last of his Masses to celebrate in the financial district, so Greg was assigned to concelebrate with Fr. O'Conner at the cathedral for the week, then meet up with the Monsignor afterwards. Confessions, emergency drops-ins, spiritual counselling, house blessings, he discovered his boss was continually in demand, and this time, there were some pretty scary occurrences, some real, others not so real. A guy named Joel freaked the living daylights out of him, but Greg soon realized he was just mentally deranged, while during a house clearing what he originally assumed was the noise made by a creaky old building turned out to be a hidden entity making life miserable for the occupants. The Monsignor went into action with the Minor Rite, and then, seemed to *see* what was happening during the prayers as he literally hunted his quarry out over tables and under chairs, chasing 'it' down with crucifix in hand as though it were some sizeable vermin trying to scurry away. Okay. That was freaky. Greg couldn't see anything, and to watch this was nothing short of mind-blowing. He would have thought the Monsignor had lost it until the hunt ended almost as fast as it had commenced.

"Uh oh. Into that wall, and there's something *in* that wall. A physical object. Excuse me, do you own the place, or are you renting?"

"Um, we've got a mortgage. So, I guess it's ours," the man of the house replied. "Why?"

"We're going to have to break through and see what's in there. I think it's a box, but I'm not sure."

"You mean, like n ... now?"

"Well, I could leave it up to you, but if that thing contains anything cursed, which I think it does, you're not going to be able to handle it on your own."

"Urm, okay you're the expert here. If only I had my tool box, but maybe there's something we could ... ."

"Will this do," the man's wife asked, having run to the kitchen and handing over the stainless steel meat pounder.

A hole and several clumps of plaster later revealed Peter was right. They discovered a rusty memento box that looked like it hadn't seen daylight in decades, and the contents were not pretty: a palm-sized antique book of spells in a leather bound casing, black candle stubs, locks of hair, a rooster and a chicken claw, several minuscule animal skulls, crystals, several pentagram amulets of various shapes, one featuring a goat head with a lolling tongue, but the most gruesome object was something not often seen: a genuine contract with the 'forces of nature' that was handwritten in a dark stain. Astonished at the find, Greg glanced at the letters and was about to enquire if the thing was truly written in the sanguine ink necessary for such a compact, but Peter crumpled it up, tossed it back into the box and slammed the lid, making them all flinch.

"*NO! Don't read the text!* It's the portal! Everything else has been cursed or used to cast them. This whole thing has to be disposed of *immediately.*"

Peter gave another quick look in the hole to see if he had missed anything, but no, this was the source of the problem. He quickly set to work, requesting some matches or a lighter, and anything inflammable in which to burn the contract and the book, something that they didn't mind having to throw out as well. A stainless steel mixing bowl had to do. Going to the rooftop of the building and placing the articles in the bowl, he set fire to them first, next blessed the articles with holy oil and salt, then diligently waited. Strange, it seemed to take ages to catch fire, even with the few drops of oil. At last, the flames licked up rapidly and enveloped the items, but without doing any apparent harm to the contents. The crumpled up ball that was the devilish contract writhed with a life of its own and refused to lay down and die. The stench was terrible, first due to the burning hair, before assuming the odour of scorched but *rotting* flesh. Finally, the cursed pile speedily reduced to ashes in a sizzle like a movie had been set into fast forward. It didn't seem normal. Greg quietly asked why not the candles too, but Peter just shook his head.

"I'll explain later," he noted, slowly emptying the ashes into the box and carefully wiping any other traces out of the bowl with holy water. "Okay, now we must take the whole lot away, but we'll be back later to finish the blessing. Unfortunately, that might be much later, but this cannot be left undone," Peter announced to the frightened couple.

"Er, okay, sure, come back whenever."

"And I'm sorry about your wall ... ."

"Don't worry Monsignor, I'd rather have the hole right now than that thing here," the lady noted emphatically, nodding to the box.

As they returned to the car, stoles still around their necks, Peter turned to him.

"Do you have a license?"

"Er, yeah."

"You're driving."

"Okay, but I don't know my way around New York all that well."

"I'll point the way, but I have to concentrate on this so we get to our destination in one piece."

"Which is ... ?"

"The dockyards. Now, interrupt only when absolutely necessary, I'm going to have my hands full."

Greg obeyed without question, trying to keep on eye on what the Monsignor was doing while steering through manic traffic that only the Big Apple could throw at them in the afternoon. Keeping the bowl and box pinned down on his knees with his left hand Peter continued to hold his St. Benedict's Crucifix over them with his right, quietly praying in Latin, once in a while stopping only to say which way to turn or to go straight ahead. At one point the rusty object lurched unexpectedly, causing both it and the bowl to slip from his grasp. Peter quickly pulled the box back onto his lap with his left hand, yet in that split second Greg *knew* he didn't hit a bump or pothole. While trying to keep his eyes on the road, he glanced over in time to see Peter give the box a deliberate commanding *thwack* with the base of the Cross, which was still grasped in his right hand before he continued with his prayers. Eventually they came to the docks and searched for a quiet section where they could park the car and remain undisturbed. Searching among a pile of abandoned construction rubble, Peter put the objects down for a moment to select a piece of concrete and test its weight. Adding it to the contents, he latched the thing shut, he flung box and bowl as far as he could out upon the water and proceeded to give the car another blessing.

"Whew, that was some ride, but we were protected, thank God," Peter concluded, relieved but exhausted as though he had come through a wrestling match.

Greg, who had been doing his proscribed reading through the week and now thought he knew a thing or two wondered why they just didn't bury the thing somewhere since the box couldn't be burnt, and speaking of burning, why couldn't the candles be gotten rid of the same way like the paper goods?

"We're in the city, there's no place handy to bury it where it wouldn't be found again, and I certainly wouldn't trust using an empty lot, that stuff could one day get cemented into a new foundation, we'd only end up with another haunted building with no way to completely extract the problem then. If you cannot bury or burn cursed items into oblivion, the next best element is salt. The remains of Sodom and Gomorrah are submerged under the Dead Sea you know, but getting as close as we can to the Atlantic will have to do. I just hope that stuff won't get dredged up."

As for the candles, they aren't the same as the other objects, they had some imprecation cast over them, so to burn them would be to risk releasing the unholy power of an anti-sacramental intended for occult rituals

Peter explained. Greg was dumbfounded. It was simple, but there were so many little details that kept escaping him, which he admitted to Peter.

"As they say, the devil is in the details, but you are getting crash-coursed after all. However, I too must admit I have an added advantage for spotting things I can't explain, but I'll teach what I can. Did you feel anything while we were there at the apartment? No interior warning, or 'hunch' something was not right with the place?"

"Er, no. I thought it a matter of clanky pipes."

"Don't feel bad. You'll have to do things the hard way, by prudent trial and error."

Peter had explained the basics to him: eliminate all possible natural causes of reported disturbances, and then work at a place spiritually bit by bit, blessings, the Minor Rite, then Mass said on the premises if need be. Perhaps more than once. Masses for the departed that may be needing help who once lived in a place, or, to break any curses or evil hold that may be there. He would then have to keep it up until the owners feel the place is cleared.

Greg nodded, then wondered aloud since they had found the evil objects that afternoon, why go back to finish the blessing? Wasn't the evil gone now?

"The evil is routed, but Good needs to be invited back in to reclaim the home. Let's hope that no grave sin is committed there again to call the evil back."

Yes, it was an interesting week, but if it wasn't for that creepy chase through the city, he thought there would be far more to see. Most of the time in the Monsignor's OR was spent with people who thought they had curses or evil wished on them, some were weird cases all right, others only false alarms, but no real demonic possessions yet. It seemed like most of the time was spent trying to suss out mental problems, but now that the week was drawing to a close, he was somewhat excited with the idea he would be assisting at a real exorcism.

His one regret was it was time to move back to his lonesome in his own parish in Trenton, he was going to miss the company. The older guys in the rectory were kinda cool and had some great stories to tell: Mark with his chaotic family once upon a time raising a herd of kids on his own and the life lessons thrown at you, such as how simultaneously brave and stupid it was to walk around the house in the dark in your bare feet. Other than building blocks, there was nothing worse than squelching into an unidentified squelchy object at 3 AM, on top of the house looking like a preschool got burgled with all the toys strewn everywhere, and speaking of toys, he never had wanted to strangle anybody before until Uncle Phil thought that a toy trumpet was the perfect birthday gift he could give to a four year old. On that note, O'Conner had his share telling about his days trying to keep all the kids at the Academy on the straight and narrow and out of mischief, thereby helping to keep the nuns' sanity intact, and Jenkins' days as a chaplain to soldiers, rising with the morning bugle, offering Mass in camouflage-patterned vestments, photographs of which were a novelty to see. Of course, they all had stories about 'Ben Hur', amusing ones yes, all the pranks they played when he first arrived, like the air horn under his bed, a story which amused Mark no end as he got that welcome prank treatment too, but they also let him in on Peter's serious side. They had to admit he certainly had grown more solemn of late. It had to be the approaching exorcism they agreed.

Peter was no doubt preparing for the event in addition to taking the time out each evening to teach Greg everything he knew with the little time they had together, and all this was in addition to his parish work. Greg observed that while he didn't come down too hard on him and left it up to himself, Peter stuck to the Old Lenten style fast for the whole week. Two small collations and one main meal, no snacking in between, which he followed as well, but in the last few days Peter went more austere into a semi-black fast: no butter on the bit of brown toast he did take for breakfast, no meat for his meals, fish or veggies only for dinner, his coffee at meals left black as well, no wine or any other alcoholic drink. No desserts after dinner either. Only water in between meals if he did need something to drink, which was seldom as far as he could tell without becoming an outright spy. Greg was grateful the boss didn't expect that full rigorous regimen from him, it was rather humbling though, thinking how such a wimp he was in comparison, wondering how he could ever survive without a scrambled egg or two for breakfast and a pat of butter to go with it.

Yes, the Monsignor was intense in his preparations, even spending the last three nights up in their little oratory in the rectory doing an extra Holy Hour at 1 AM despite the fact he had early morning Mass to offer. He also went to confession to Fr. O'Conner, and spent quite a considerable time with him. A *general* full-life confession? It had to be, but for someone who definitely was already in the state of grace? That was intense. Of course, the Monsignor advised him to go too, he need not go to *him* if he wanted, but a clean conscience was an absolute necessary if he didn't want to be embarrassed during the exorcism, and he would be assured of being completely in the clear after a session with him. Greg declined for the present, he was positive he was in the state of grace and didn't think he needed to right now. Peter didn't press him, he would never force anyone against their will, but everything was very grave with him, that was for sure.

In fact, his mentor was pulling out of all social engagements that did not have any relation to his duties. Greg couldn't help overhear him on the phone to his brother's fiancée regrettably having to say he couldn't attend her Grand Opening of the new section of her gallery, there was no way he could fit it all in. Greg felt guilty about that, he wondered if he was the cause the Monsignor couldn't be with his family at an important event like this with the extra lessons he was giving, and had to admit to Peter he overheard his cancellation to the event and felt the need to apologise.

"No, no, don't get upset. Katherine and everyone else understands my ministry has to come first now, which includes you too! Total spiritual concentration is necessary for what's coming. Speaking of which, no tutorials tonight. Pray as much as you can, then get some sleep. You're going to need your strength. Tomorrow is The Day you know."

Pray, of course, but get to sleep? Good chance that. There was a strange thrill about the thing. In case he didn't see all of the guys tomorrow due to their schedules, he said his good-byes to the Holy Bachelors then settled in to bed, wondering what the day ahead would bring. Greg could hardly wait.

ϣ ❖ Ϣ

Restlessness was transformed into mind-numbing drowsiness when the alarm went, having finally knocked off to sleep only two and half hours before the buzzer. Just great, it would start to pour today too. *Tink, tenk, plitter, plink, patter, pinkpink, tenk.* Greg hated the rain, and it looked like the sunny days of summer were making way for the autumn chill. Packing up his belongings in a daze, he brought his bags down to the front hall and hoped he had time to grab a coffee before Mass with Fr. O'Conner, then Peter was picking him up and driving them to Trenton. Yep, just ten minutes, then he was off. Now, he'd better not fall asleep during the sermon!

"Are yeh all right laddie," O'Conner enquired after they put away their vestments.

"Yeah, I'm just tired. How does he do it? Only a few hours of sleep, and the Monsignor just keeps on trucking."

"Ye've said it! Pete has had a lot of practise during his trucking days, goin'n the roads at night, existin' with as little sleep as possible, getting them loads of his delivered on time."

"Duh. That makes sense. Uh, where is he, by the way?"

"Probably waiting out in the car. If he's spotted by this place at all, he'll get mobbed with blessin's, an' confessions, and let's not get into all the biddies just waitin' to lep at him and corner him for a chin-wag. Ye'd never get out of here, and you've got some job ahead of ye. Speaking of which, ye'd better head off! Here, yeh can't manage all them cases on your own."

"Oh no, I've got 'em," Greg tried to insist, but the feisty old priest said his arthritis hadn't crippled him yet and wouldn't hear of it. Together they searched for the car while sheltering under O'Conner's umbrella, a grand specimen of a brolly, but then, the Irish were used to rain and knew how to prepare. Peter popped the trunk and helped pack up.

"I guess this means goodbye again, thanks for having me." Greg shook hands with Fr. O'Conner.

"Ye're welcome laddie, and you know ye're always welcome. Drop in for a visit any time." One last handshake, and it was time to go.

"So, I guess we're off to do battle," Greg noted as he buckled in, his drowsiness lifting with the resurge of anticipation.

"Yes, and speaking of which, we have some stops to make."

"Oh?"

The first stop in Trenton turned out to be Greg's own rectory house in the 'burbs. Peter insisted he take a look before they did anything. Not that he minded, but Greg wondered why until after a tour of his humble abode he saw the stole and surplus appear along with the book of blessings and the various phials of blessed water, salt, oil, and blessed medals for every window, door, nook and cranny.

"What? You mean this place needs a *clearing*? Like we did for everybody the whole week?" Was the house infested or haunted?

"No, that's what I'm here to prevent. We're digging our trenches and fortifying our bases so to speak. I'm placing a shield of protection over your residence. You've read the books, you know what can happen to an exorcist."

Whoa. Living alone, that reminder spooked him. Greg didn't say any more and put on his stole and responded to the prayers. Afterwards, Peter told him to get any extra clerical suits if he had them, then they went to Greg's parish church to pick up additional supplies, more surpluses, holy water, then at long last it was time to enter the battlefield.

So, this was it. Trenton Psychiatric. Greg took in the view as they drove through the expansive grounds, the wipers mechanically *screep-screep, screep-screeped* across the windscreen, the drizzle blurring the view before it was swiped away with each measured arc. Gosh. Eerily desolate, unsettling, the half abandoned edifice was an embodiment of a quasi purgatorial limbo-hell, the unfortunate inhabitants undergoing a battery of analytical probings and who knew what else. He had never been there before, he had heard plenty of stories though, and the look of the place was equal to its urban legend reputation. There was no denying it. It *felt* psycho. His last remaining thrill of macabre fascination morphed into a chilling sense of foreboding.

"We're got a few minutes, but we should wait for Mrs. Fletcher. Are you ready?"

"Um, I suppose as I'll ever be. That last book you gave me … is it really going to be like that?"

"I can't say, every case has its singularities."

"Man, and on top of it, this place is freaksome, it gives me the creeps. You know what they say about it here? Shock treatments and stuff, weird operations gone bad … *experiments* … ."

"This is a tall order, but try not to let it get to you. Observe everything, and whatever happens today, do *exactly* as I tell you. You may ask questions later. Here she is."

At the main entrance Peter introduced them, and it was clear to Greg the lady was very glad to see them.

"Nice to meet you Fr. Simmons. I'm so relieved there will be two of you."

"Well, I'm just here to learn," Greg explained followed by a smile, but he must have said something wrong for Mrs. Fletcher's expression fell.

"Don't worry," Peter reassured her, "he's new, but he's also going to be my assistant. However, we should first meet with the staff. There are a few important points that need to be gone through before we set up. After you," he replied, letting her lead the way to the reception area and announce Dr. Fareed was expecting them.

Greg politely waved 'hi' to the receptionist as they waited to be received, anything to put himself at ease in this place filled with crazy people, but the cold sceptical stare he gave them as they were asked to please wait and take a seat didn't help matters. Greg could have sworn by that look the guy had just officially numbered them among the mad and was determined to find a vacant padded cell to put them in. It was only a few minutes, but felt like forever. He was glad when the doctor arrived and shook hands with everyone. This guy seemed a little more agreeable than the receptionist, that was for sure.

"We've set aside a room next to hers as you requested."

"Thank you, but would it be all right to meet everyone who will be assisting in another place? Somewhere private if possible?"

"Er, of course. Will my office do?"

"Perfect."

"All right then, come this way."

So far, this part of the hospital didn't seem too bad, of course, it was the public administrative area, so a few recreation and sitting rooms, maybe a therapy room or two, nothing creepy yet, but it still gave Greg the goosebumps. A few more minutes and the staff were there, two large orderlies and a couple of nurses, however, the director of the hospital also showed up. He didn't look too welcoming, he reminded him of the receptionist.

"Good afternoon, I'm Mr. Lieberman. Let's skip the small talk and get straight down to it. I think what you're about to do is absolute nonsense, especially after what happened the last time with the other priest, but as the family is insistent on this, I've had several members of the staff, including Dr. Fareed, whose opinion is greatly respected among the board, suggest that since the patient seems to have mentioned you a few times this might be the only way to get a positive response that could lead to a breakthrough, no doubt due to the suggestive effect of your spirit ceremonies. For this reason I've agreed to give your hocus pocus a second chance."

Mrs. Fletcher was insulted not to mention alarmed at how the Monsignor was spoken to, but Peter remained calm.

"Thank you, Mr. Lieberman. Although I can assure you, it's not hocus pocus."

"Maybe, maybe not, but I want to be absolutely clear: the well-being of the patient is our main concern. If we see she is being harmed in any way, I will put a stop to this immediately and I will press charges against your diocese. Do I make myself clear?"

"Absolutely. Which is why we also make videos, proof that no injury or maltreatment is inflicted. Do you plan to stay for the proceedings?"

"I wish, if only to prove to myself this is all a ruse for the gullible, but I've got business to attend to, and I'm running late as it is. I also have another condition: that the hospital is given a copy of the videos you make of the proceedings."

"Fair enough. I'll ask permission from the bishop. I can't promise how long that will take, but I'm sure you'll be allowed to have them, just as long as they are not publicly broadcast."

"You can be sure *that* won't happen. In addition to protecting our patient's privacy, we have no intention of having our establishment associated with the idiotic practises of a backward age. Very well, that's settled. I shall leave you in Dr. Fareed's hands. Good afternoon." With that, he left.

Whoa. Greg was stunned. Peter had warned him about the hostility they might experience, but honestly, he expected most of it to come from the devils, if they did happen to show themselves!

"I apologise, please don't take offence, Mr. Lieberman is … a man of science you understand," the doctor diplomatically hinted.

"That's all right, none taken," Peter reassured him. "Well, I suppose it's time to get down to *our* 'business' of the day. Are any of you Catholic," he then enquired, turning to the assisting staff. He had requested from the hospital that Catholics should attend if possible, but knew he might have to do with whomever they deigned to let work with them. He was correct, only one nurse timidly raised her hand. "All right, before we begin, I suggest you come to confession first, I'll explain in a minute. May I ask what faith the rest of you belong to or believe?"

"I'm Muslim, if you haven't guessed," Dr. Fareed returned. The orderlies said they were God fearing, Bible believing Christians; one Baptist, the other Episcopalian, while the other nurse professed she was atheist.

"All right, the reason I've asked is not to question your beliefs, but I'm required to warn what may happen. For those of you who don't believe in demons or Hell, you are in for a shock. The devil and his cohorts will do anything it takes to stop you from assisting, they might even bring up the darkest sins and secrets of your past to humiliate you. He cannot see any sin that has been confessed, so if you would like to take the opportunity now to have everything wiped clean off your conscience, I strongly advise you do so before we begin. Unfortunately, I can only hear confessions of those who belong to our Church, so the best next thing is that the rest of you make the most heartfelt act of contrition to God for your past sins that you can make."

The atheist couldn't help smirk at this.

"Laugh now if you like, but I will not tolerate any flippancy in the room once the rite begins. The devil is a mocker, and is also the most cunning liar and psychological trickster you will ever come up against. He will even take something that's innocent, even a virtue, and twist it to make it sound like the biggest mortal transgression or something you have a reason to be ashamed of, again, to humiliate you in front of your colleagues. He knows we have a fallen nature than tends to fixate on the worst in everyone first and not the good. He also likes to destroy consciences if he can, to the point a person can no longer tell what is good or evil. Be prepared."

"Um, I went to confession already last week, do I really need to go again," the other nurse asked.

"I won't press you, but it's a good idea."

It seemed to Greg that the Monsignor threw him an extra glance, but took his attention away when the nurse and Mrs. Fletcher decided to take him up on his suggestion. The doctor said they may use his office.

"Thank you. Before we do, there's one other thing I must warn you about. Do *not* pay attention to what may come out of the patient, it may not be her speaking at all. He will make idle threats, do not listen to them. The devil will also try and get you into a conversation, and you don't know where that will lead. Like a poison pill hidden in the most delectable food he can bury a mote of falsehood within a huge quantity of truth, and that poisoned mote could prove your downfall. Do not answer or speak to 'It'! I cannot stress that enough. If there has to be any talking done, I must handle it. Agreed?" Everyone nodded their heads. "Very well then. Let's start. Could someone please help Fr. Simmons unpack our things while I see to these ladies?"

As Mrs. Fletcher went for confession, the orderlies offered their assistance and went with Greg to the car. It was raining pretty heavy now. There was a scramble as they relayed the items from the trunk to the entrance area in an effort to get it all in fast and as dry as possible.

"If you don't mind me asking, why so many choir boy outfits," one of the guys quipped as he looked at the number of extra cassocks and surpluses brought in. "Are we expected to dress up too?"

"No, just the exorcist, and me, the apprentice."

"I'm just kidding, but why so many outfits?"

Greg chuckled, glad for the light relief.

"Because from what I know, this is going to be a dirty business on every level, and we have to be prepared."

"He's very serious about this, isn't he?"

"The Monsignor? Yeah, this is pretty big. It's not often this happens, in the States anyway. There are more exorcisms done in Rome, so he tells me."

"Huh. But I can understand what he meant about weird things being said," the other man hinted. "That girl is not your normal kind of mental."

"You mean there's a 'normal' kind?"

The orderlies laughed nervously.

"Um, yeah. We've never seen something like this, which is why we're willing to help. It was a volunteer only thing."

"Really? Er, thanks for volunteering."

"No sweat. But honestly, I'm helping out of curiosity," the other orderly admitted. "I just hope we won't regret this later. Shall we bring this all up now?"

"Maybe just to the doctor's office I guess and wait for orders," Greg decided as he took care of their cases containing the blessed objects of their ministry. Thunder rumbled overhead. "Wow, listen to that."

"Yeah, looks like we're in for a pounder."

Peter wasn't finished hearing the nurse's confession yet, so they carefully laid their armfuls on the few chairs in the hallway outside the door and patiently stood around, Greg deciding he should join Mrs. Fletcher who was asking the doctor how Melissa was that morning. She was talking normally and was completely coherent earlier that day, even cheerful with the thought she might get well and be allowed out soon, but then went into a rigid state before noon and yelled as though there were several individuals fighting each other: 'He's coming, he's coming!', then next said something like 'Why did we say who would release her? Because we were forced to, that's why!' There wasn't another thing said by her since.

With that the door opened, confession was over. It was time. Doctor Fareed led the way to the high security isolation ward. To Greg who had not been there before, even passing through the low and medium security areas with their mesh gates was an eye-opening trek into the realm of the bizarre and unpredictable as he found himself besieged by a few of the patients, demented, gesturing nonsense. However, it appeared the Monsignor was receiving the most of their attentions and tried to keep him from passing through, and when they couldn't, hurled abuse. One particular patient in the maximum security isolation ward uttered a chilling, maniacal drawl of a laugh that could be heard down the hall from behind the reinforced glass pane of the door locking him in his chamber before shouting:

"So, you're back, black robed puss sack? You won't be able to do anything, the Master will make sure of that!"

Peter made the sign of the cross in his direction, which quickly caused his verbal abuser to duck out of sight, while the frantic scratching of fingernails was heard at the door. At this point, Greg questioned if deciding to become a diocesan exorcist was such a bright idea.

At last they came to their destination, the patient's cell at the farthest end of the ward. As requested, a room next to it was left for their use where they could vest and lay out the extra clothing and cases safely away from the main area of work. Once they were properly attired, the cell door was opened. Greg had been instructed to work quietly and quickly. While Peter laid out what he needed from his case at a convenient distance, Greg had to force himself to stay focused and not scrutinize the patient out of curiosity as he arranged the tripod at the foot of the bed and flipped on the camcorder, testing for the optimum angle. Rigid was an understatement. It was hard to act normal when the patient was anything but normal herself, oblivious to the attentions of her aunt, laying there stiffly in a semi-reclined posture, staring blankly into nowhere as though frozen in a macabre suspended animation, never blinking, then, dart her gaze at him through the camera while remaining motionless, her eyes dead glassy apertures like those of the lifeless figures resting in a morgue and whose eyelids had not been closed, her body barely appearing to draw breath as she visually pinned him down.

"Okay, that's good there, Fr. Simmons, now could you ... Fr. Simmons? *Greg* ... bring in the pictures next please," Peter gently but firmly commanded, snapping him out of that paralysing moment and rescuing him from that chilling stare. He quickly did as requested, slightly embarrassed he got caught in that unprofessional stance. When he looked back at her, she was in her former state, eyes dead and fixated off into the distance at the ceiling. Better not look into her eyes again, he thought to himself, that was just like looking into ... *nothing*.

After setting up blessed images of Christ, the Virgin Mother and St. Michael within eyeshot of the patient on the side table, Peter announced the date and time for the video recording to pick up. With the sign of the cross over the bed, then himself and those present, followed by a liberal sprinkling of holy water over them and the room, the exorcism had begun.

"Ow! What a sting! It's been awhile since we got hit with *proper* slime!"

Greg was startled not only by the snarling, male-sounding voice, but to see the patient instantly spring out of her torpor and sit up, writhing and flapping frantically as if brushing off something that was burning her.

"Go *AWAY*! And take those with you," she screamed next, springing onto the bed in a crouching position, gesticulating wildly with obscene hand and other crude bodily gestures at Peter and the blessed images on the table, along with a mouthful of curses the like of which was revolting to hear.

Greg was rooted to the spot while Peter quickly looked away and motioned for the orderlies to handle the patient. The nurses also jumped in and tried to hold her down. The doctor motioned for them to use the padded manacles. Once she was restrained and unable to repeat any offensive moves, Peter signalled for Greg to hold open the book of Rites. Greg wished they didn't have to stand so close. He tried to stay collected and answered the responses as best he could, the old languages were still a bit strange to him as they commenced with the triple invocation of the Kyrie in Greek followed by the Litany of the Saints in Latin. She began to froth at the mouth. Mrs. Fletcher and the nurses did their best to clean her face amidst the struggling. She shook her manacles, rattling them against the bed rails like a trapped rabid animal.

"*No, no, no, no, no!* Don't call those pigs, those useless pieces of filth here! We won't go! But we'll get rid of *you*! We can start with *him*."

She stopped writhing and stared Greg down with dark venom in her lifeless glare, her eyes now sunken into their sockets.

"Like the last one, but younger, weak. Juicy. Easy meat. We'll have *fun* with *him*."

"In the name of Jesus, I command you, be silent!"

Peter's voice thundered around the room. A screech later, she, or rather, they, grudgingly obeyed, shutting her eyes tight, resuming her animalistic contortions in a futile attempt to escape accompanied by a cacophony of wails, grunts and growls that seemed to come from her abdomen, not her mouth or throat.

There was no denying it, Greg was shaken. His arms trembled, his legs didn't want to hold him up, but Peter continued undaunted. As he followed through with the invocation, she began to appear more human, calming down for a moment, her normal voice returned.

"Please, please don't, it's hurting me." She sounded like she was in terrible pain. One of the nurses attempted to intervene, but Peter put his arm out.

"It's a sympathy trick. Don't listen."

"Please, *please*, he's hurting me!"

Peter sprinkled more holy water, first on the nurse to show it was not burning the patient, then forcefully onto the possessed. She screeched.

"Ow! Too smart he is, *that* priesty one, still, was worth a try," they snarled, the guttural masculine-like voice returning, this time followed by a cackling laugh. The doctor motioned for the nurse to stand back.

Peter continued with the prayers of the Litany imploring for deliverance against all misfortune and points of attack. She continued to squirm, then, lay completely still, her eyes shut and sunken into their sockets, her breathing and rattling as if labouring to draw in air. The most disturbing aspect was the sudden ageing she seemed to undergo, her face changing as if she were a wizened ninety year old withered beyond recognition, stretched skin over a bony structure, eyes encircled with dark rings making her look like a rasping corpse. This sickly posture continued for a while, no further reaction. The only sounds were Peter praying with authority accompanied by a periodic rumble of thunder, the lights flickering overhead from the storm's interference with the power grid. He then approached close to the bed, pronouncing the first of the formal commands for the demon to depart, gently laying the crucifix on her head. She sprang back to life if it could be called that, piercing the air with a ghoulish howl, shaking her bonds with frenzied rage in attempt to bite him and the crucifix, causing Greg to drop the book and jump back a few paces eventhough he knew she was tied down. Peter motioned him to come back. At first his knees didn't want to work. Peter motioned again, but Greg stood there, staring at the victim while feeling as though he was becoming a cornered victim himself. 'He' or 'they' laughed a mocking guffaw, apparently pleased with the reaction.

"*Fr. Simmons*, pick up the book."

Peter's encouraging yet firm voice of authority bolstered him, shook him out of that paralysing fear 'it' was able to induce from deep within. He did as ordered and turned to the correct page to complete the healing prayer with Peter laying his hand on her head with difficulty as she refused to lie still, then continuing to the next section of the Rite featuring readings from the Gospels.

"Dóminus vobíscum."

"Et cum spíritu tuo." Greg tried not to quaver.

"Inítium sancti Evangélii secúndum Joánnem."

"Glória tibi, Dómine."

Peter next signed himself on the forehead, the lips and over his heart with three small signs of the cross, Greg followed suit, then watched as Peter approached to do the same to the patient before he began the reading.

"*Get your hands off us you filthy … .*"

Greg flinched at the insults hurled. How could the Monsignor stay so resolute through all of this?

"In princípio erat Verbum, et Verbum erat apud Deum, et Deus erat Verbum … Hoc errat in principio apud deum … ."

"NO! Shut UP! WE are mighty! We are greater! No no no, we won't listen, we won't go!" Suddenly, the voice calmed down and turned to face Peter. "Speaking of *Joánnem*, how is your brother doing? Had a nasty big bump, didn't he? We were there, we know all about it."

Peter stopped only to command silence then continued. They didn't stay silent for long, this time trying a new avenue of verbal attack.

"Yes, this one is hard to break. He's managed to keep his virginity too! The priest scum! He's a tricky one, he's well protected, how we hate him! He's always thwarting us, destroying our work. Curses on him! Vir-*gin*, vir-*gin* vir-*gin*," throwing the words at him in a taunting sing-song similar to an insult before adding, "we got to take a good bite out of him nevertheless! Ha ha!"

For a split second Peter flexed his left arm together with a quick intake of breath, like he had experienced a sharp pain of some kind, but quickly resumed. The patient changed tactic when taunting tactics didn't phase him, they turned their malice on Greg again.

"Oh, and *you*, we know what *your* little vice is. Have an eye for the pretties, eh?"

So this is what the Monsignor meant by mind-twisting moments. He could feel his stomach knot with mortification. It was a temptation that was not going to die soon. The way they were dressing these days, surgical enhancements in every way possible with hardly any skin covered, slits in clothes that left nothing to the imagination, it was almost impossible during the summers to keep one's sight averted … but he had never purposely stared to the point of sin, or at least, he didn't think so … and the devils made it sound like he had not only looked but went farther … . Greg was about to shout a defence … .

"No! Don't answer! They want to provoke!"

Then Peter commanded silence again from 'them' before finishing the first Gospel with the blessing of the patient and a liberal flinging of holy water that made her scream, then sent his apprentice an encouraging glance to keep trucking with him and ignore the demons' prattle, which he greatly appreciated in this oppressive psychotic hell-hole.

Oppressive, that's what it was. The air had grown sultry, stifling. The change that occurred took a few minutes and was imperceptible at first as the body tried to adapt, but now it was unbearable, the sweat was running off him and everyone else. Three more Gospel readings, but Greg couldn't help be distracted and bleary headed with the swelter. He heard Mrs. Fletcher whisper to the nurse if the heat had been turned on? Could it be turned down? The heat wasn't on at all! Holding the book and trying to concentrate, Greg couldn't turn around to see what was going on, but could hear someone open the door, obviously to let air in, but there was no change in air current whatsoever, it was thick with the heat. One of the nurses went over, he could see that much from the corner of his eye. Then some whispering, the doctor and nurse seemed confused if not disturbed by something before they came back into the room.

Peter stopped and requested they close the door.

"Sorry to interrupt, but I think you might want to check this out. This is highly unusual," Doctor Fareed noted with puzzlement, wiping the sweat from his brow with his sleeve.

Peter held up his hand to Greg signalling a pause, then briskly went to the door to see what the problem was.

"Typical, pay no attention. You'll find there will be incidents like this."

"But it's freezing out there, and boiling in here, yet no draft … ?"

"Yes, and this might not be the last thing you'll witness. Now please, close the door."

Peter asked for some towels, and they all grabbed one. Greg was glad to take a moment to clean up with a quick wipe, then they went back to work, finishing the last Gospel and continuing to the more precarious section of the proceedings: the full list of commands to depart. Peter took the double length of his purple stole and laid it on her neck with his right hand on her head.

"Ecce Crucem Dómini, fúgite partes, adversae."

A torrent of yolkish vomit flecked with dark green was the result.

It hit the corner of the book and splashed Greg's hand, he recoiled with disgust and dropped the text, instinctively reaching for the towel again. Peter, however, got the brunt of the frontal attack. He too went for his towel, wiped his face and the front of his surplice, and with a resigned sigh signalled for another towel to clean the thick yellowish mass pooling down onto the purple stole like a surreal alien lava, then dropped the towels to the floor. Greg got another and tried to wipe up the back of the book.

"Did you like that? That's what we think of your *crucem*."

The rasping voice gleeful spat, then sent more of the disgusting flood in Peter's direction. He ducked just in time, the motley spew splashing all over the floor. Greg waited, wondering if the Monsignor intended to continue after he finished wiping the bottom half of his surplice. The place was now a stinking, putrid mess on top of the heat problem. Everyone looked like they wanted to be sick themselves, but forced themselves to stay. Mrs. Fletcher and the nurses too sprung into action, grabbing more cloths to mop up the bed clothes and checked to see if the patient was all right.

"She didn't eat anything like that today, and *definitely* not that much," the atheist stammered. "Only a ham and cheese sandwich."

"I think we're going to need a cleaning crew," Doctor Fareed whispered, shocked at what he had seen. He also realising that such a *voluminous* amount could not have possibly come out of the girl under natural circumstances.

"Yes, not a bad idea Doctor, but we must keep going no matter what. Fr. Simmons you'll have to position the book now as I explained."

Oh no. He was afraid of this. Greg readied himself again, this time holding it like a shield in case there were more upchucking episodes, and unfortunately, there were: as Peter forcefully demanded the demons to obey the various commands of departure each followed by the sign of the cross, a pustular green cascade was emitted that made the stomach lurch. It hit the cover of the book, and splashed down, Greg was bewildered by the force, almost like a jet stream. The shield trick helped, but not much. He could feel the moist slime hit his hands at occasions. Revolting, but he had to hold the book still. He tried to block out the sensation by focusing on the text, try to ignore the nurses, the orderlies, and now the startled maintenance attendants who thought they had seen the end product of every disgusting bodily function in this hospital at last shocked beyond belief, running for towels and mopping up around them. Peter however couldn't be completely shielded as the first set of commands required he trace the sign of the cross on the brow of the afflicted. Greg did his best, holding the book responding to the prayers when necessary, but it was an impossible situation. He was about to lose his lunch now too.

Suddenly the vomiting stopped. It was almost as eerie as when it started, this instant cessation when they had just become conditioned to the frantic scramble battling the noxious flow. Everyone exhaled with relief except for Peter who had not stopped his prayers. The staff quickly set about cleaning up while he carried on, this time the Rite required that he trace three crosses on her breast above her heart to strengthen her will to fight against the Evil One … .

Before he had a chance to approach, the tormented girl emitted a long, drawn out retching sound different from before. The doctor sprang forward. Was she choking? Peter halted as everyone gasped: slowly she let out a clear viscous phlegm that drooled thickly down her chin—there was no mistaking it, she had disgorged a razor blade.

"My God … ." Mrs. Fletcher uttered.

"What the … ? How did she swallow … ," a nurse wondered aloud.

"She didn't," Peter tried to clarify.

The retching was followed by another, then another … .

Peter was not deterred by the grisly sight, quickly making the required crosses on the victim's chest as soon as the nurse cleaned up between the manifestations.

"Quick, get something to put these in," the doctor whispered.

While the prayers continued, Mrs. Fletcher and the staff were horrified to see the bowl slowly filling with razor blades.

"Here we go again, that makes eleven … twelve … thirteen … geeze, now there's five, no, six at once … ."

"And no blood? No cuts *anywhere* in her mouth?"

"As far as I can tell without getting bitten, no."

"I can't take this, I can't take this," the atheist stammered, holding the sides of her head.

"Hang in there, this will be over soon," the other nurse consoled, although she too was terribly disturbed.

Peter continued the prayers of command and deliverance, tracing the crosses when necessary on the victim's brow or breast after the grisly objects were cleared, and then a sign of the cross over the witnesses for protection. Surely she couldn't go on like this Greg wondered. There was another set of commands for the demons to depart, this time the Monsignor didn't need to approach and touch her, only make signs of the cross, for which Greg was grateful, which meant he didn't have to get that close either. There were more readings, this time requiring responses, the first of which provoked another reaction: the retching stopped, and the howling returned, this time sounding like a pack of animals coming from deep within her before the guttural voices uttered more curses at their tormentors. As bad as the putridness surrounding them was compounded with the heat, there was something abhorrently grotesque to hear that young girl spout obscenities that would make the ears burn and the stomach heave in a different manner.

Never before did he have mere *words* make him sick! It was too much. He felt drained … drained like every ounce of energy was being sucked right out of him. He hoped he could hold out until the end, they had a way to go yet. Even Peter, despite his resoluteness, was looking just like he felt, as though he had come through the worst of all the trench wars ever dug out on earth, stained with everything spewed at him and wringing with sweat.

Peter blessed the room with holy water and motioned for Greg to get the incense prepared. Normally this part was reserved for a home if that is where the exorcism was being performed, but what 'home' could use a blessing more than this horrid place of mental darkness? Peter incensed the room, and it provoked another display of rage.

"No, no no, we won't worship! *Our* kingdom is greater! Get out of here with your stinking gas!"

Peter continued, raising his voice over the refusals to submit:

"Omnes de Saba vénient!"

"Aurum et thus deferérentes … ," Greg answered, tongue tripping over the last syllables. The heat was getting to him, it felt like the walls were closing in, the incense adding to the heady mixture of fear, putrid upchuck, sweat and humid stickiness accompanied by the cacophony of inhuman howls and distant thunder.

It was a relief when after the Athanasian Creed and a few psalms that the Monsignor finally declared it was time they stopped for a break. Shutting off the camcorder and taking out the tape, Greg was glad to get away for a breather, the apprentice exorcist was stunned when he went through the door. He could understand what the hubbub was about earlier: it was literally freezing in the hallway compared to the oven they had just come out of. Still, the sudden bracing change helped him to wake up from the sweltering torpor. Several nurses of the ward not in attendance at the proceedings were loitering in the distance, they had heard the horrific commotion and stopped the clean up crew for gossip of what was going on in there, curious to catch a glimpse of those allowed in for the procedure only to be surprised at the state of them as they exited the room. Fareed called out for someone to get drinking water and fresh apparel for the staff. The loitering nurses quickly scurried off to the business they should be doing while someone decided to go and fetch the items requested. As if being with the tormented girl wasn't bad enough, the other patient locked in the room down the hall could be heard flinging abuse and laughing manically. Peter just quietly made the sign of the cross in the hall towards the other troubled patient before he and Greg made their way to the room provided for them next door. They quickly tugged off their soiled surpluses and changed into a fresh set of cassocks. What a mess. Peter was ready for this and got out a couple of garbage bags he had handy in one of the cases, something they could tie up and close off the reek, and then wearily sat down.

The doctor knocked on the door.

"Come in."

"Here, you guys look like you could use this, I'd call for coffee, but after that heat … that was not like anything I've every seen," Fareed admitted, the nurses following with the jug of water to which they all helped themselves. Eventually everyone joined them and grabbed a chair or leaned against a wall, those against a wall eventually sliding down to a sitting position. Greg was shook, they all were, they could hardly keep their paper cups still except for Peter, who just appeared exhausted. How was he holding up? Man, he seemed unphased, like he was *used* to seeing this stuff everyday.

Finally the doctor broke the silence.

"You're not over yet, are you, Monsignor?"

"No, that was just the trial run. We've not even begun to fight."

"Er, how long does this usually go on for?"

"It could be one day, a month, six months. Maybe years, but we shall see. We'll keep at it, for as long as it takes. Speaking of which, this is an extreme case, it will be punishing. If any of you feel you cannot continue with us, you will not be forced to stay," Peter continued, turning to the others.

The staff looked at each other. Surely it couldn't get any worse? Besides, they weren't about to give up just yet.

"Very well then, but if at any time you feel you must leave, you won't be thought less of, we are dealing with powers and principalities, not anything human. If it's all right, may I have a private moment with Fr. Simmons please?"

"Sure, come on people, I could do with that coffee now," the doctor announced.

"Half an hour should do it. Then, back to the grindstone," Peter hinted.

"Coffee. Huh. If we weren't on duty I could use something stiffer than that," one of the orderlies admitted while closing the door, leaving the two priests alone.

"Are you okay?"

"Er, yeah, I'm feeling better. That was rough."

"Yes, thing is, they know you lack confidence. Have faith! Don't doubt the authority granted to you to command at a time like this. They will do their best to instil fear, but don't be afraid, they can't do anything that is not permitted by God, that includes the gross stuff. We have to suffer the penance in order to help heal her."

"So, barf it is." Greg grimaced. "Uck. Um, I hope none of that wasn't my fault, I mean, 'it' knows I don't know the language … I don't feel like I'm meaning what I'm saying … ."

"I know, but I needed to hit them with the Latin first time around. Don't worry, we'll be saying it in English the rest of this session, for the most part anyway."

"I'm sorry I didn't listen to you before, and um, it's probably not the right time now, but … will you hear my confession?"

"Of course."

To be honest with himself, he didn't go to the Monsignor because he dreaded what might come up. He knew it was a grace to be able to go to someone who had complete spiritual discernment, and yet, he was afraid, not that he ever *hid* a sin that he was aware of, but was stuck fast by that nagging feeling he had completely messed up examining his conscience at every single occasion, that he didn't know how to navigate the grey areas, and to see that jumbled intangible angst of mind and soul all laid bare and showing how far he might have messed up was a mortifying proposition. However, after that first brush with the devil's psy-op strategies, the thought of the evil one publicly dragging up whatever worried him more, and he humbly admitted it all to Peter.

Poor kid, he got hit with one of the sneaky imps that mess with one's mind and scramble it up with crippling scruples, then, strangling him, tempting him not to unburden his doubts. Those ghouls sure could do enough to knot a person up even without causing them to sin. Peter gently untangled the lines, then went deeper. He couldn't see any sins that weren't already absolved, but invited Greg to unburden himself again, anything that was still troubling him in soul, weighing him down with leaden guilt for things already forgiven, then, gently moved on to the temptations he felt, things that need not be confessed, but now was the time to be absolutely thorough, he didn't want to leave anything to chance, which he explained to Greg. It would give him extra grace and strength, not to mention he had to keep firmly fixed in his mind the difference between temptations and transgressions, so that when the tempter tried to mock him again, he would not succeed in scrambling him up another time.

When it was over, Greg had felt like an invisible block strapped to his chest had dropped off. It was the strangest thing. Before, he was reluctant to go to him, there were times when the Monsignor looked at you it was difficult to look back, but now there was just relief, he knew for sure everything had been absolved knowing not one stone had been left unturned, and to finally understand what was meant about 'God Strikes', in his case, those private happenings that only he and God knew about, to find the Monsignor knew about them too, or at least, he certainly knew what to say without ever having been told, an odd phrase someone in the family used, or a memory long forgotten then brought back as clear as day, perhaps one of those rambling conversations with Heaven he had during what was meant to be meditation time, wondering if God was really interested in the humdrum details of his day, then to hear snatches of this or that one-sided dialogue brought back and realize he was getting an answer to a few of his half-distracted prayerful musings directly from the Monsignor. It was a shock to the system to bring up past sins, true, but then, the *peace*. No wonder they all wanted to go to confession to him, you could get used to those training wheels, knowing your soul was safe in his hands, gently opening everything previously shut tight like a book, deftly turning the pages, helping to erase some of the ink blotches and correct the typos of the past quickly and mercifully without fear something was going to be left undone, renewing the courage to carry on with that newly turned leaf.

"You're well scrubbed now. A few more minutes rest, then it's back to work," Peter warned, giving a quick glance to his watch followed by a sidewise nod to the room next door. Greg reached for the water jug and poured them another cup. The sound of footsteps running up and down the hall accompanied by perturbed voices cut short their few minutes of reprieve: something was up.

Peter got up to check what was wrong and stopped a nurse.

"She's gone!"

"Gone? How?"

"I dunno! She was locked in! I opened the door to check in, and she's gone! We've gotta get security."

Peter let her go and then went to see for himself, Greg following. The door to the room left open, Peter looked at the empty bed, the manacles and belts holding her down were undone. He looked under the bed, then—up.

"Go get someone, and get the camera going."

Greg gasped.

Crouched on the high ceiling as though it were the floor, yet not hanging on to anything, she stared at them with those dead apertures that were more piercing than any clawed predator encountered in the deepest jungle.

"*Go.*"

He shot out of there to the room next door, griped in a primal panic induced by this unnatural sight, yet, instinctively he knew it was imperative to get this on film. No one would believe this, they needed to see it. The adrenalin pumping, he fumbled getting the cellophane off the new tape before running back and shoving it into the slot. The bed was still empty. He pointed the camera up. No, she hadn't moved.

"Did you find anyone," Peter asked quietly, still looking up.

"N ... no ... ."

"Nevermind, sounds like someone's coming."

Doctor Fareed entered breathless about to say a word, noticed where they were looking and glanced up.

"Allah! Have mercy!"

"*Allah? Allah* have mercy? You know you're worshipping *us*, don't you? We show mercy to no one!" She snarled at the doctor.

"Doctor, please close the door, you can let everyone in when they come back, except for Mrs. Fletcher, she might not be able to handle this."

What about *us*? Greg couldn't help think it. The camera shook with his hand. It was a wonder he could keep it together.

"*Wha..what shall we tell her?*" Shocked almost breathless, the doctor could barely form the words.

"Just say her niece is loose in the room, and in this unpredictable state, we don't want her to get hurt, which is the truth. We'll let her in when we can."

What about *us*? Greg couldn't help think it again, he had heard the possessed could attack. Peter, still calm but solemn as ever, kept watch. Making no unhurried movements, keeping his eyes trained up, he slowly made his way to the side table and took up his crucifix and holy water dispenser, patiently waiting for the rest of the staff. Then, a thought struck him: Peter went to the bed and blessed the manacles and straps used to tie her down. Another snarl was heard overhead.

"You're a smart black robe! Didn't think you'd figure *that* out!"

Greg's hair stood on end hearing that voice again, but what happened next electrified the atmosphere: she scampered from her position in the middle of the ceiling to the far corner and hunkered down like an animal expecting to be flushed out from its den. It was her movement that was terrifying, bolting across the ceiling with ease as if from a flip-sided parallel universe of earth, gravity non-existent. The sight screamed against all rational sense while the eyes simultaneously registered the scene was indeed real. The nurses scrambled for the door, it was difficult to keep panic from gaining mastery. Peter sprang into action before the rest of the staff lost the nerve to stay, quickly closing the door in case the patient tried to make an escape, then commanding her down with cross and holy water, sprinkling it upwards with powerful strokes of his arm, chasing her around from below when she bolted across the ceiling on all fours in a useless effort to avoid the burning spray of blessed water and his tormenting orders. After a lively hunt around the room with her making a few runs up and down the walls and back to the ceiling, he finally got her to come to heel and stop over the bed, she uttering hateful comments, sickening expletives and soul crushing blasphemies in response to his commands. One last imperative order from him followed by a shriek from her, and at last she obeyed. It would have been less terrifying if she had just fallen and landed on the bed, a natural cause and effect the senses could process, but she didn't. Hunkered down on her haunches coiled and ready to spring, her body remained in that fierce pose while she slowly, silently levitated still upside down, hardly seeming to move as she detached from the ceiling as though weightless in space and gradually returned to ground, her descent so excruciatingly deliberate it too induced a sense of panic. Reaching the bed, she turned at the same snailish, sluggish pace into an upright position before setting down, menacing in her hunkered state. Taking their cue from Peter's slight nod to them, the orderlies mustered up the courage to act and didn't wait for her to strike if that was the intent and pinned her down. She struggled but they eventually strapped her back into place amidst a heavy shower of verbal abuse.

"Okay, you can let Mrs. Fletcher in now, and the nurses if you can get them to come back."

Good chance that, Greg thought as he shakily snapped the camera back onto the tripod. He'd be long gone too if he had the option! Mrs. Fletcher resumed her post, not as unnerved as the rest as she hadn't seen the latest preternatural episode, but the nurses had to be coaxed back and doubly reassured the patient was restrained. Greg filled the aspergillum with more holy water for Peter then picked up the book. Round two, here we go.

Much to Greg's relief Peter read the Rite in English, this time for the benefit of the witnesses that they too could hear the prayers and grasp what was happening, but instead of going through it, he repeated certain passages several times before moving on, Greg noticed it was at the parts where she had turned the nastiest when first said in Latin, obviously the demons didn't like these particular commands and invocations. The girl howled as if multiple voices were articulating at once. Then, her body slowly began to bloat as though attached to an air pump. It was only a few minutes before the thin girl looked several hundred pounds overweight. The doctor tugged Peter's arm.

"Look! We'll have to undo the straps! Her circulation will cut off!"

Oh no, she could escape for the ceiling again Greg feared. Maybe that's what the plan was with this new trick, hoping the now blessed restraints would be undone. Peter guessed that too and said they could undo the arm bands, but only loosen the large straps around her chest and legs gradually to accommodate the abnormal physical change. In any case, Peter advised them to stand by and keep her from getting loose from those as they redid the straps.

"God, her skin has stretched too much," a nurse observed in horror, inducing a mental picture of the poor girl suddenly bursting at the seams. Greg wondered if that was possible, but Peter still seemed untroubled by this new manifestation.

"Don't worry, God won't permit her to be harmed. Enough! In the name of Jesus Christ, let the girl be, you will *not* do that again," Peter commanded, returning to attack mode, making the sign of the cross over her with his crucifix. The bloating reversed in the same deliberate pace as when she descended from the ceiling, obliging the orderlies to continually adjust the straps as she slowly returned to her normal size. Peter continued the prayers of deliverance as she struggled again, then, when it seemed she, 'it' or 'they' had wearied of struggling … .

"I command you, in the name of Christ, who are you? What are your names?"

"NoNoNo! Not telling!"

"By the merits of Christ's Passion, death and resurrection, you *will* give your names. Who are you?"

"Didn't we tell you already? Many! Many!"

"Not an answer. Speak!"

Peter flung more holy water.

"Ow! Ow! He torments us, but we cannot tell!"

"Why not?"

"They torment us, we like it here, we don't want to go … ."

"Who torments you?"

"We can't tell you, mustn't give away our secrets … !"

Peter took his container of blessed salt and managed to force a few grains inside her tightly clasped mouth.

"Why can't you give your names? Speak!"

"Poison! He forces us! We have to answer. No you cannot answer! Stay silent, you little pigs! No no no, we said nothing! He knows nothing! That's right! See to it he doesn't then!"

It seemed as if something *else* began to make the intruders squeal in pain, even the voice or voices changed between them denoting something else had briefly entered into the fray. Peter studied the girl for a moment. They were not ready to submit yet, the assault had to continue. He resumed the Rite, picking up where he left off and so did the round of sickening curses from the girl before returning to the abnormal growling. Hair-raising as it sounded, Greg could bear it, just no more upchucking please! He was already feeling drained again. She went quiet for a while, her lifeless eyes following the two of them intently. Those eyes bored right through, but unlike the Monsignor's pure penetrating glance, it was like malice had solidified, sharpened into a soul-piecing awl aimed straight and hard for the kill. No no no, *don't look!*

"All right! We'll give our names. Just put your book down and walk around the bed three times, and you'll have them."

Greg wasn't expecting that. The voice, still male-ish and guttural, had changed and sounded almost polite. Was that a sign the Monsignor had finally beaten them down? Walking around the bed was a simple enough thing to do … .

"Silence! We do not take orders from *you*. Christ compels you to answer. Speak! What are your names!"

"*No no, not yet! Not yet!* I told you he was too smart for that!"

She shrieked as Peter sprinkled her with more water.

It was a trick. Greg felt ashamed. He nearly fell for it. That's what they wanted, the Rite to be stopped, and to have them submit to their suggestions no matter how trivial or stupid the action.

He would have submitted to a devil.

That simple ruse nearly snared him. What had he gotten himself into? Was he cut out for this? The guilt surged. It was crushing.

"Told you, *juicy*. Easy meat. Naïve. Weak."

Greg could feel it, they were taunting him, again.

"Be silent! Unless you give your names, you are not to speak." Peter laid the crucifix on her head for a moment. She snarled. Greg though, was still weltering with the thought of his near slip up. Peter gave a quick glance over and seemed to sense his anguish.

"Peace, peace to all here." He paused to bless everyone with the sign of the cross, crucifix in hand. Instantly the guilty apprentice felt relieved. Never before had he literally felt the effect of a blessing. It was sobering as well as comforting. *And besides, giving blessings is our job, it's never a waste of time … .*

Resuming their work, this time it was hard to keep up with the Monsignor, he skipped around the Rite, returning to previous pages, picking up certain passages that caused her to grow in ferocity. Although the oppressive preternatural heat hadn't returned to the room this time, the Monsignor looked exhausted, hot, sapped, the sweat beading from his temples with exertion as if he had been hauling heavy loads. Greg too was feeling it. He had never known this type of strain with spiritual work alone. Usually one felt distracted or numbed from the repetition of certain rituals and prayers, a leeching tiredness that grew from complacent familiarity and human frailty, laziness even, but this was all-out participation, an exhaustion from expending active energy, their efforts felt like strenuous manual activity. The phrase *battling* the principalities and powers took on a whole new aspect, prayer becoming as physical as any piece of steel or iron they could wield against an enemy along with their holy water and crucifixes.

"God, Creator and defender of the human race, who made man in your own image, look down in pity on this your servant, Melissa, now in the toils of the unclean spirit, now caught up in the fearsome threats of man's ancient enemy, sworn foe of our race, who befuddles and stupefies the human mind, throws it into terror, overwhelms it with fear and panic … ."

Oh yes, the terror, the fear, the not knowing what to expect next. Greg knew the devil could only do what he was permitted, but still, *something* could happen, and that unknown factor of *something* was pervasive and infected the psyche like a chronic lingering ailment.

" … repel, O Lord, the devil's power, break asunder his snares and traps, put the unholy tempter to flight. By the sign of your name, let your servant be protected in mind and body … ."

Peter approached to make the sign of the cross on her forehead, then on her breast over her heart.

"No no no, she's *ours!* We'll see she rots in Hell forever! *Get AWAY!*"

The last phrase was said in a high shrieking pitch that jangled every nerve. Peter ignored the screech and repeated the blessings with the sign of the cross again and again, seeing the reaction it provoked. The bed began to jolt uncontrollably as though the only piece of furniture caught in the bucking tumult of an earthquake. Greg was full sure it was an attempt to shift the afflicted away from Peter's blessings, which didn't work. While everyone else including him instinctively jumped back from the bed, there was no stopping the Monsignor who persevered and managed to trace the necessary crosses on the unfortunate victim's head and over her heart.

The bed stopped jolting. Peter was about to draw back to continue the prayers, but received another manifestation of vomit, this time pus-green with black flecks projected straight down his front. Not again! Everyone jumped back or ducked, just in case it might be aimed at them, but it was Peter who was the number one target. He drew back to the farthest end of the room, but the distance didn't help, even in a flattened horizontal position, she could still aim directly at him by turning her head. Instinctively, he tried to shield his face with his arms, the force was unbelievable, but this had to be stuck out.

"GREG! Use the book, a tray, anything!"

The apprentice bolted into action, holding up the book, giving Peter a chance to make the sign of the cross, which abruptly stopped the latest episode that concluded with a tenebrous throaty laugh from the patient. Fareed opened the door for the clean-up crew, again. Peter mopped up his front and gave a swipe to his shoes with a fresh towel, while Greg wiped the book cover. If the sight of the floor's condition wasn't bad enough, one of the men on the cleaning crew let slip a choice cuss word, the dark flecks were not typical stomach matter—they were *squirming*. Peter examined the towel he was about to discard. Trapped in the thick mucus were insects of some kind, *uck*, they looked like cockroaches, *live ones* struggling to get loose. He quickly dropped it in the mop bucket. After the initial shock and repulsion surged then ebbed, the staff scurried into action, trying to clean the mess up before the vermin escaped. This time the doctor called for the nurses to hurry up and fetch ample containers, this needed to be tested. They need not have worried about haste, the bugs remained trapped in the noxious viscous matter, but that didn't make the job of cleaning up any easier on the nerves. At least the thunderstorm had moved away, that was something positive Greg thought as he threw towel after towel into the buckets that were rapidly filling up. After the doctor got the samples he wanted, bleach was poured into buckets and hauled them away, fresh supplies were brought in to slop up what was left of the aftermath while Peter finished the prayers and mercifully called it a day. He concluded his final 'amen' with a pat of the fingers on her forehead.

"*Enough.*"

The motion followed by this last command sent her into a deep but normal sleep. Her face softened, her breathing returned to normal, the eyelids did not seem as sunken in as before, she almost looked human again, just ill, dirty and dishevelled from all the struggling and torrential sickness.

The two priests quickly packed up as everyone exited the room, relieved to be getting out of that hell hole and into the hallway. The doctor offered the two bedraggled exorcists use of the hospital's shower facilities, which was greatly appreciated. Once they were presentable again, Mrs. Fletcher and the Doctor were eager to hear the Monsignor's prognosis.

"First of all, make sure Melissa gets rehydrated, fed, and plenty of rest. The devils can't harm her, but she might be tempted by them to go on a hunger strike and she could harm herself if she wilfully gives in."

"That we can deal with. It's the … unpredictable that has me worried."

"Understandable, but do your best. "

"In all my years of medical practise, I've never seen things like what happened today."

"Not many exorcists have either. This is an extreme case. Like I said, it will take time. We'll be back next week as arranged."

As the doctor showed them to the main entrance, the orderlies helping with the cases and bags of soiled clothing, Greg noticed the change in expressions they were getting from the staff. The gossip had travelled fast about what was happening in the isolation room, levitation, razor blades and live cockroaches were enough to show that this was no charlatan performance. They looked at them awestruck, in fear, or simply stared.

After she thanked them both, Peter had a few private words with Mrs. Fletcher while Greg finished packing up. The orderlies were still quiet, which was understandable. They had seen more than they had volunteered for. He thanked them for their work today, hopefully, they'd still be interested in volunteering next week. He wondered if he would be asking himself that next week. Man, it felt good to be outside again, doing something normal, even as mundane as sitting around in a parking lot, but how could he look at the world the same way again? The veil had been pulled back by what he had witnessed. He wouldn't ever forget, how *could* he? And as long as this case continued, he was going to see more of it. The scenes of the day continued to repeat in his mind as Peter buckled up.

All was quiet as they drove back to Greg's residence. Pensive, lost in thought, poor kid. Peter of all people understood the sensory and spiritual overload of the day needed to be processed, let some quiet time do its healing work. His apprentice was just beginning to grapple with this experience, coming face to face with the sombre realities of their ministry, that there was an entire unseen universe not any less real simply because it was invisible to mortal eyes most of the time. An ancient war was yet raging against enemies that never sleep, always plotting, continually ensnaring, sadistically feeding off destruction, despair and death, physical and eternal, glutted and glutting, never filled, never satisfied.

"It's *real*," the novice eventually muttered. "I mean, of course I believed there was a devil, things like that, but … this, you can really *see* … evil … and *hate!* I could literally feel it. It, they, wants us all destroyed. It wants *everything* destroyed."

"Yes. 'The Beast that is and is not'."

"'Is and is not', I never got that before, but … I mean, did you see her eyes? *Nothing.* There was something, but dead, nothing *alive.*" He paused, the scene was recalled, the feeling of being pierced through by a barren nothingness, darkness itself that was all hate and desired nothing but hate. "Man, the *suffering.* I could feel that too, Mrs. Fletcher, she had that look Mom had when my brother was in the hospital after he flipped on his bike … Melissa … can she really be freed from that?"

"If we go ahead with faith, confident, unwavering, yes, with God's help we will be the instruments used to deliver her."

"This is *way* different to what I thought I'd be doing. I wanted to help people, but this is so … deep," the novice admitted as Peter parked outside his house.

"Of course it is deep, or rather, high. Upon a pinnacle. Anyone can become a social worker or a volunteer, make sacrifices to feed the hungry, help the needy, everyone is called to do works of mercy like that, but no social worker can do the work put before us. Once the call is answered and God puts His hand on a man as priest, he has the authority to bless, heal, cast out demons in His name, even raise the dead if Heaven so desires and faith is strong, but first and foremost, he can absolve sin and bring Christ down upon our altars. By its very nature a vocation like this is immeasurable. It is the highest form of helping."

Yet, constantly under attack, persistently besieged by the enemy from within and without, the exorcism ministry sustaining the brunt of Hell's malice against religious these days. Over and above the sacrifices expected with their life, they were subjects of morbid curiosity, scorned, derided. Poor kid he would find out about that too. They were the sin-eaters, the sewer dredgers, the rat catchers, shunned and avoided until the pestilent vermin of the depths needed to be dealt with when the rational world could not find a rational explanation. Only then on such drastic occasions did the vital importance of this ministry come to the fore. They were a last resort, the only hope when everything else of and by the world had been tried, tested and failed. Sacrifice. Persecution. Spiritual martyrdom. For an exorcist, there was no other way.

෫ ❖ ෬

    "Okay, let's have it. What was it today?"

    "Nails. Lots of nails. Big ones too."

    "Mother of Mercy! You nearly have enough to build a house!"

    "Or at least a tool shed."

    "Just be thankful it wasn't bugs, Pete. I was full sure it was going to be bugs."

After a month of Peter's travelling to Trenton Psychiatric three times a week, what once was a shocker had become a common place 'how was your day' conversation piece at the rectory. Still intriguingly morbid, yes, but familiar enough by then that the Holy Bachelors couldn't help guessing amongst themselves what new addition might be going next into Pete's 'Believe It or Not' collection. It had steadily grown from the initial razor blades to shards of glass, pebbles, black ink, pennies, curled barbs from barbed wire, carpet tacks, lumps of wax, and plenty of organic matter such as flies, beetles, ticks and even fleas, (like the cockroaches Peter didn't take them home with him, they had to take his word for it). Jenkins wondered why he wanted to keep all those grisly mementos. If it were up to him he would have ditched the batch, but Peter insisted his macabre collection was rare evidence that demonic possessions were real, even if people still had to believe him about their provenance on say-so alone.

He handed over the jar of square headed nails for them to gawk at, wearily dragged the latest bags of soiled clothing to the laundry room and got the first load going, gone was the precaution over the 'dry-clean only' labels. Machine churning away, he hauled himself upstairs for another shower, his feet leaden with exhaustion. The reek was probably just in his head, but the quick shower he had at the hospital just wouldn't cut it this time, he could still feel the latest exorcism sessions clinging to him. *Uck*, the *stench*. No, better soak in the bath. Nothing short of pine all purpose cleaner would make him smell hygienic let alone clean. It was a joke, but at this point, it might be worth a shot. Plugging the tub, he spotted the almost forgotten purple tube of exotic shower gel hiding behind the other bottles. Speaking of jokes, now there's an idea. He never thought little Bro's gift of frankincense soap would come in handy, but he was sure glad of it tonight. Talk about Divine Providence. A good vegetative soak with fragrant steam to clear the head and he was ready for dinner, although after what he saw again today it would be easier on his stomach to stick to his fasting if it wasn't for the fact he really was hungry now. Starving to tell the truth.

"Hey there, you look better."

"Thanks, I feel better."

"And smell better. Like High Mass."

"Or Benediction."

Peter chuckled as he sat to the table. Maybe he used too much of the stuff.

Glad to see he was eating a little more tonight, that had to be a good sign, the conversation was lively among them, jokes flying as they shared the day's events, but relaxed as he was, Peter's thoughts were elsewhere, it was hard to not be rude and gaze distractingly into his plate as he ruminated over the month's progress, or lack thereof. As he kept reminding everyone this sort of thing takes time, but he wasn't getting anywhere close yet in pulling an identifying name from Melissa's tormentors. To anyone in the secular world it seemed a trivial thing, but there was a mystic significance in getting the demons to reveal themselves that was necessary to chip away at their possessive grip. There was authority attached to giving names. Adam was privileged to name the creatures of Creation, Joseph was given the honour of naming Christ and thereby assumed the full duties and responsibilities of a father, over the Messiah no less, and sure enough, doesn't every kid on earth jump to attention as though reacting to a war klaxon when their full name is called out? Names have meaning. Names have power. Names could make or break. Maybe it was still too soon, but he just *had* to get the devils to reveal their identities, drain them to a point, or rather bind them, weaken them. It would be a bonus if they were *known* devils, giving away what vices they are lords over, compel them to give away a weakness that can be used against them, torment them. Until he could weaken them, there would be no way he could demand the next thing necessary, an appointed time of release. Once weakened enough, they could be made to declare a sign by which an exorcist would know they had departed their victim, but obviously he was still way off from that yet. Names first, and right now he felt like he was spinning wheels. The one description he did get, 'Many', certainly not a good indicator. Legions were present, and to have so 'many' this resistant he had to be dealing with a pretty strong curse. Maybe the penance had to be doubled. Maybe? No. It *had* to. He was going to give himself one little treat by having dessert, but better skip that. Besides, he had letters to trawl through. That was worthy to offer up.

The housekeeper got bewildered by the mail delivery as five duffel bags were dropped off. That was just today. Yesterday it was three. It just kept coming. All she could do was lean them up against the wall. The troublesome part was, the mail for the other fellows was sometimes buried in the mix and *someone* had to sort the lot. The parish office was getting a bevy as well, keeping the secretaries busy. It was overwhelming. The fellows were about to chip in with the sorting, but Peter left them off tonight. After a couple of months of this, they needed a break too. He dragged a bag into what could be called the formal sitting room that was only ever used for the odd visitor or two and set to work, the piles of envelopes growing around him on the sofa, coffee table and chairs as he sifted through the contents.

Hundreds. Thousands maybe! In addition to the cries for help from spiritually depressed souls that had heard about him from as far away as Scotland, Australia, Hawaii, Bolivia, it was a surprise to see how far his name had trotted around the globe. Practically the last place left was Antarctica, and at this point it wouldn't surprise him if one arrived from there any day now. The downside was he received so many crank begging letters since wind got out he was from the dynastic Reinold family. Mercifully, his second sight wasn't denied him during this endless task of separating the bulk mail wheat from the chaff. Envelopes containing correspondence of spiritual importance emitted a golden glow, the light weak or strong depending on the urgency giving him an indication of which to attend to first, while the marauding begging letters pretending to be from people in need gave off a grey or black mist revealing the dishonesty of the sender and the level of duplicitous intent. There were times he received black flames. Curious, he opened one to see what the problem was to find he had been sent a poison pen missive from some malicious epistolary messenger who had a beef to pick with him, or rather the Church, someone wishing nothing but mayhem and needed a target to lash out against. He learned not to open those again, he tossed these darksome letters away without a thought, but not without a prayer for the sender. It was easy to separate the glowing letters from the not so glowing ones. Sometimes he could even tell the contents of a letter without having to read it, and got mail that didn't shimmer, an indicator the contents were not urgent in a spiritual nature leaving it was up to him if he wanted to answer or not, but usually the non-lighters were for the fellows. Of course, there were always the junk leaflets. Hmm, coupons. Hope there were any useful ones. Save $1.00 on Woolclean soap, nice timing. He was going through a ton of the stuff. That reminded him, got to get the next load in.

He stood up and stretched, tossed the misty letters into the garbage bag ready and waiting, then took another look at his handiwork piled neatly on the sofa. First bag sorted, not too many needed an immediate answer, their yellow glow was faint. That's good. He didn't have time to give long meticulous answers these days, just short liners and to the point. That reminded him, stamps, he needed a bucket load of stamps. His return letters may be short and sweet these days, but he had a lot of them to make. Okay, second mail bag next, just as soon as he tended to the wash. Hang on, one must have slipped under the sofa. There was a glow reflecting off his shoes.

Down on all fours, he fished the letter out. Uh oh. The light was strong with this one. Red and green edging, foreign airmail envelope, Italian stamps. Rome. Someone from his seminary? No, but close enough. Fr. Amaranth. He didn't need the light to alert him it was spiritually important. Peter sat for this one. His former teacher couldn't write in English, and trying to decipher his scrawling handwriting in Italian was a challenge, but he got the gist of the news. He too was in the midst of an exorcism, many actually, he had a load of cases as usual, the unfortunate thing was two of them were afflicted for ages, one young man under his care was possessed for fourteen years and no release from the demons yet in sight. Then, a word of warning. The demons he was exorcising let out they knew what was going on in the 'Great Babylon' overseas and boasted the 'Most Powerful Ones' were not leaving their host without a fight, that they would defeat his so-called best and bright-futured pupil. It didn't sound good. Fr. Amaranth reminded him this could be a lie, but on the off chance the demons were careless and revealed something, he didn't want him left unawares as he battled:

"My son, and brother priest in Christ, if you are up against the 'Most Powerful Ones', I think you know what that means. I have had an inspiration during prayers you were going to be asked much, very much. How willing are you to free this girl from the evil one? Please be strong. Fight courageously. Do the utmost sacrifices possible. It will take everything you can think of and are prepared to do. Courage!

God bless Fr. Amaranth, he really had a ton on his shoulders. Peter slipped the letter in his pocket, grateful for the news. Of course he would pray for him, his spiritual benefactor who now had given him the answer he was seeking, he was in his debt. 'Most Powerful Ones'. No, that did not sound good at all. True, the demons could have been lying, but after what he had seen this past month, no, there was something to that. Melissa was in the deepest, darkest grip ever, and that meant absolute suffering was necessary to counteract the evil she had gotten caught up in and was now holding her bound. More prayers. Sacrifices. Okay. Need to rethink.

He prayed for inspiration as he worked on the washing. What more could he do? He had asked everyone for additional prayers, check. Fasting, abstinence from food, he had been very careful, check. When he did eat, he picked stuff he hated for extra penance, check. Maybe it was time for a full black fast? Bread, water everyday except for Sundays. All right. Time for the next step. He could do that. What else? Curiosity. He had mortified that too. If he wanted to read something interesting, like yesterday's article about the Mets, he tossed it aside, also sacrificing the little lawful pleasures of life and offering them up. The TV was ignored now, including the news. Same with anything else that was of trivial concern, if not passed over outright as a sacrifice, he paused before giving himself any satisfaction in these little harmless pleasures. Same with his morning coffee, just let it sit there and go cold as a penance, or he would drink the dregs left in the bottom of the pot. If pebbles got caught in his shoe, he left them in. Cold showers. Done that, except when he really needed the hot water for grungy days. Every little mortification he heard about he had tried, even finding scraps of scratchy cloth and pinning them to the inside of his undershirt was another idea until he could actually find a place that still made the real hair shirts. Soon, those bits of irritating cloth weren't enough. Discovering a new package of scrubbing sponges in the utility room, he peeled off the green scouring side and added that too. He bound cords of itchy twine around his waist during the day. He picked up a chain at the hardware store, nothing too thick that could be spotted, something that could hang over his shoulders under his clothes unseen. He also bound twine on his arms. It was hard to think of things that wouldn't be seen by others. God only should see these mortifications. The little things done with love meant a lot to God but there had to be *more*.

Wait. He had to think on a larger scale. He was doing the small things right as far as he could tell, but *big* things were now asked of him. How willing are you to free this girl from the evil one? It will take everything you can think of and are prepared to do. He had been given much, much would be expected of him, after all—*he was warned he must be ready for the cutter's blades.*

Oh. Could that mean … ?

Peter wasn't prepared for this literally, not yet, but he always had a nagging disturbance in the back of his mind about it all right. Yes, maybe it was time to go *that* far. He was often grilled on how 'medieval' his ministry was, but after this he could be certified as demented. No, he had to make sure the fellows didn't know. This had to be his secret sacrifice or they'd never let him go through with it, and it had to be done. What to do though? He had to be quiet about it, nothing so draconian that could draw attention or be a danger, but enough … enough for … . Hanging up the second load of wash to drip dry on the line gave him an idea, for tonight … string … he needed more heavy string or twine. What else? A wire hanger. That will do until he could devise something better. He called it a day where the rest of the mail sorting was concerned and let the guys know he was off to bed early. Privacy was needed for this.

Looking through his jar collection lined up in the bottom of the wardrobe, he found the one he had in mind and filled it with antiseptic solution, closed the lid and gave its contents a few brisk shakes, letting them soak while he cut long lengths of twine, daubed them with antiseptic, gathered them into a bunch, then, bent the hanger into the desired handle shape, tying the fistful of twine strands at one end where he had twisted a loop. Opening the jar he fished out the finishing touch, the curled barbs, which he threaded onto the end of each string until they looked heavy enough, then secured the metal bits to the strings with a few knots. Yes, the barbs were heavy enough to do their job. His homespun flagellum was crude but small, easy to conceal when not in use, it would have to work. There was nothing left to do but test it. What a strange irony, to use the very things thrown up at him to become an instrument of deliverance! Getting down on his knees before his desktop crucifix and baring his back, he said a prayer of penitential offering and took up his scourging implement. If the patron saint of parish priests stained his bedroom wall with blood to save souls, he could do it too. Holding his breath, he braced himself for the first lash … .

Stop! Stop!

      The pressure of an unseen hand firmly grasped his wrist.

Who are you?

Your Friend.

      Can you not tell? The Lord isn't asking this of you.

If that's true, what was meant by the 'cutter's blades' then?

Truly? You who have studied theology do not know what it means?

Suffering? Much suffering. That I understand.

Yes. But not this.

      The unseen hand let go. He dropped the whip.

Not this, but still, much more!

I don't understand. This is confusing.

It shouldn't be! Don't you know you are called to be a spiritual martyr, not a physical one? The blades you will feel will be interior, the blood spilled will be spiritual, the cuts almost imperceptible to human eyes.

You waited to tell me? I nearly went through with this!

Yes. The Lord was pleased to see you were, but He wants to ask for a greater suffering.

Greater?

For her timely deliverance and also for those whom your benefactor is helping, are you willing to endure the worst suffering ever imaginable?

What's that?

You should know!

      Do you not preach about it?

        Have you not warned?

      What awaits for all those who do not repent?

His heart nearly froze.

      That could only mean … .

For how long?

Not long, directly for fifteen minutes, indirectly for a week after.

      Are you willing?

If the Lord asks, how can I say no? I've given my life to Him.

Good! Expect them soon.

'Them'.

      How soon?

Very soon, but do not be afraid. You will not see me, but you are not alone, I will not leave you, nor will your Mother. Courage!

      He waited. No other instructions.

The interior voice had finished. What else could his Friend say? He had accepted the suffering.

Nothing left now but to wait.

Buttoning up his top and putting on his robe, he retrieved his crude penance tool, placed it on the desk, then with quiet foreboding sat on his bed, back against the wall to wait. He now looked at his homemade multi-barbed whip with a conflicting sense of humour and dread: if the idea of scourging himself with that scrawny, scraggy thing was a gruesome prospect before, that would have been far, far easier to live with than what was coming.

How long was 'very soon' supposed to be?

Waiting. Waiting.

He checked his watch, half an hour had passed. It felt like five half hours. What are you doing? Don't be idle, waiting for the inevitable to come. Taking his beads in hand he began to pray. First Sorrowful Mystery, the Agony in the Garden. He should have started sooner, but it was almost impossible to concentrate, trying to abate the sense of terror that was steadily festering, chilling the atmosphere as he reached the prayers concluding the Second Sorrowful Mystery.

O, My Jesus, forgive us our sins ... save us from the fires of Hell ... lead all souls to Heaven ... .

You? YOU won't be saved, not this time—PRIEST!

Of your own free will you agreed to this!

An unseen hand ripped the beads out of his hands and shoved him roughly from the bed, sending him sprawling onto his stomach. He could feel the great heel of that something grind into his back, pinning him to the floor while the snapped string of beads scattered everywhere as they hit the wall opposite the bed, the crucifix falling in front of him. In terror, he couldn't cry out. His voice wouldn't work. The pain! Was his spine about to crack? It hurt to take a breath. The demon laughed. There was nothing so harrowing as that fiendish sadistic laugh revealing the entity taking gluttonous delight in causing him excruciating pain and fear.

That's it! Squirm! You filthy little maggot! There's no escape. We've got you now. Ha ha ha! You're OURS! Ite Missa est!

They were coming.

The confused tumult of a large rabble sounded in the distance, somewhere in front of him, yet, also from a great depth, rushing, growing louder, covering that great distance in rapid strides, shouting orders accompanied by shrieks of hate and malicious glee in the prize they were about to claim. From his constricted position he managed to turn and lift his head in the direction it seemed like they were at, the small dimensions of his room jarring with the sense of distance generated by the sound of the rabble. The walls of the room began to stretch, elasticize, expand outward until the space appeared to recede, melt, evaporate into that distance, the familiar elements of his bed, desk, wardrobe, the door fading into the emerging scene of an expansive, desolate scorched plain that stretched as far as the eye could see dotted with tall jagged rocks glowing a deep vermilion, yet, what seemed like the sky was oppressive, dark, pressured with a greasy putrid haze that made it more difficult to take a breath. He could see them, a black cloud of dust ripped up from the charred ground as they rushed upon him, dark ferocious shapes of varying height with claws, some with tattered wings, others with massive horns, but all bearing red hot chains.

He was about to be dragged into the Abyss.

"Well lads, that's it. I'm knackered."

"Off to bed then?"

"Better in bed than frozen to the chair. I've got enough cricks in me back as it is, don't want to add a few more in the morning."

"Smart man. Pleasant dreams then. We'll be up soon."

"See ye when the sun's back up."

Bed was a good idea, too bad it meant scaling all them stairs. Jeekers! Old age, what a gradual creeping shock it was. To O'Conner it seemed like only yesterday he was running with his hurley through the playing fields of Kerry cracking smashin' goals for the team, and now he was wondering if it was possible to whittle the thing down into a walking stick. Hullo. What's this? Pete's door open, light's on. Guess he can't fall asleep like he planned. Or, he's decided to tackle that growing heap of fan mail. Better remind him not to overdo it.

"Hey don't you think it's time you called it a … ?"

Huh. He wasn't there. He glanced down the hall. Nope, not a sight of him, and the bathroom door was open, the light off there. Mighty peculiar this. Maybe Pete's in the oratory again, but it's not like him to leave the door open, and have the light in his room burn away for nothin'. The crucifix on the floor caught his eye. Peter wouldn't leave a thing like that *there*. He lumbered in to pick it up, but stopped as he felt the scattered beads mash into the carpet under his feet. Puzzlement growing into concern, he noticed the bed was rumpled, the wardrobe left ajar. This didn't look good. Pete was always an example of tidiness. Then he saw what was on the desk, the makeshift flagellum laid beside the jar of unused barbs still soaking in antiseptic.

What the … ? I have to find him before he does a permanent mischief to himself! He's gone way too far! Drowsiness gone, O'Conner checked the oratory. He breathed a sigh of relief. Sakes alive. There he is. Prostrated on the floor as though renewing his vows, doing them vigils again, he's going to wear himself out. Time to talk to him about giving up them OTT penances, that whip certainly had to go. But leaving his room like that? Just not normal. He hoped Peter was okay.

"Pete?"

No answer. With a resigned sigh O'Conner got to his knees, with difficulty, and gave a gentle nudge.

"Come on lad, you're going way above and beyond the call of duty here."

No movement. With a start, O'Conner wondered if he had collapsed. He tried to turn him over, but he was as heavy as lead, and felt hot, like he was competing for the top spot in the Guinness World Records for the highest ever recorded fever. This time he gave him a good shake. Peter gasped heavily as though it was his first breath after a resuscitation attempt. *Thank God, he's breathing!* O'Conner tried to turn him over again, this time, he was back to his usual weight. He didn't know what to make of it, but that was not the end of it: he was the next to gasp when he saw that a swathe of Peter's hair starting from his forehead had turned white from root to tip. Sakes alive! He gave a few rigorous slaps to his cheeks to get him to come to. He was about to call for help, but Peter's fever suddenly disappeared. He opened his eyes, and they were filled with dread, confusion, disbelief as though not certain where he was, that he had been dropped off at a foreign destination, then recognition of his surroundings begin to creep in, but the look of fear didn't abate. At last, he grasped O'Conner's arm:

"Is it over?"

"What, lad? Is what over?"

"The time? Fifteen?"

"I don't rightly know what yeh … ."

"What … day is this?"

"Er, Monday."

"Monday … when?"

"When?" O'Conner showed him his watch. "Why, it's almost three hours since you went to bed."

Peter groaned.

"It really was only a quarter of an hour … . My God … my God … ."

"What's wrong lad? I think I'd better call … ."

"*No!* Please, don't call anyone. They can't help me … no one can help me … I still have a week to go … another week … another week … indirectly … indirectly … ."

"A week? A week for what? Oh laddie, how can I help if you don't *talk* to me?"

Peter didn't say anything, the harrowing look of despair still visible in his semi-glazed expression. At his wits end seeing Peter in this state, he did the only thing he could think of.

"As ye're confessor and spiritual director, I'm *ordering* you on the pain of obedience, what has happened?" He disliked pulling that, but the command worked. Peter's glazed expression changed, only his voice didn't, it was as bitter as any funeral lament:

"I've been among the damned, and … *I'm still there.*"

O'Conner was struck silent. Now he knew what had happened. Not the details, but he could easily fill in the blanks. Peter had offered himself as a victim soul for his ministry. Hopefully, not permanently!

"Heavens! Have mercy! What have ye done? Ye're a right worry you are! C'mon son, let's get ye to bed. We can't leave you here, victim or no victim."

Whatever he had done, he was in for another week of it, 'indirectly', whatever that meant!

It was a struggle getting him to his feet and supporting his weight, but the shock of seeing him in that condition gave him the extra push needed, the cricks of old age blocked out for the moment. He had heard stories like this from the Old Country, it abounded with blood curdling tales of ghosts, demon cats, divils, curses, and chilling things from the Other Side, but not all were just fairy *pishogues*. A cousin from Tipperary told him about the infamous 'Haunted Gatehouse' at one huge estate outside Clonmel on the Cashel road that nobody wanted to live in any more because it was too frightening. An exorcist was called in who decided to stay the night to see what was wrong. When he emerged from the building the next morning, his hair had turned the colour of snow. Nobody knew what he had encountered and if he managed to clear the place, but it was certainly a warning to the foolhardy who insisted the divil was invented by the clergy in order to scare everyone into obedience. All these strange stories kept running through his head, and to think Peter was now a witness and could be added to the bag! Eventually he got him to the bed and covered him up, robe and all. He looked in poor shape, having been through a mighty shock with a white wing and eyes still filled with terror to show for it. He knew he was telling the truth, it certainly looked like all of hell went through him for a short cut. Uh oh. Better not leave this thing sittin' around. O'Conner took the whip and locked it in the desk drawer of his own room then went back to Peter. He also took a gander inside the wardrobe and noticed the other jars, better get them blades and bits out of here too. In his rational mind Peter would never think of such a thing, but in his current condition he didn't know what he might do to himself. He settled into the chair. Best not leave him alone tonight.

The next morning, an exhausted O'Conner called up the parish office and informed Peter would be missing for the week due to illness, him as well. Poking his head out of Peter's bedroom, O'Conner stopped Jenkins and without letting him look in asked if he wouldn't mind helping to fill in their Mass slots.

"Er, sure. What's wrong? Is Pete sick?"

"Um, yes, he's doing pretty poorly. He's had a bad night, and he needs someone right now."

"Whoa, you've been here all night? Do you want me to take over?"

"No, I've got this."

"Er, if you're sure. Heck, I'm not surprised with all he's been doing these days. I was afraid he'd run himself into the ground. Should we take him to a doctor?"

"No, a doctor can't help with this, it has to, er, run its course."

"That sick? It must be that stupid stomach flu, there's a nasty outbreak going around lately."

"Nah, it's not that, but I can't explain right now. Ye'll just have to trust me on this."

That sounded rather iffy to Jenkins, especially as he refused to let him come in and see Peter, but since O'Conner insisted, he would have to go with it.

He and Mark grew more worried as the week wore on, not having an inkling from O'Conner what had happened the night Peter fell 'ill', and the old fellow insisted on not leaving him alone, also getting them to promise not to tell anyone about Peter being sick if they could help it, and that included any family and friends. That was really off, they protested to this promise, but they had never seen their old friend so adamant in wringing a promise from them. Well, Pete was barraged enough when he was healthy, so they agreed for the sake of him getting some much needed space. Cancelling Peter's appointments, parish and exorcism work, rescheduling Masses to be said, the old Irish guard dog also insisted on giving the housekeeper the week off, for when they were all out for the day, that's when Peter finally left his room, and even then, he hardly ate a thing. He skipped meals with them and refused all company, also ignored calls made to inquire about his health for his congregation was missing him at Old St. Patrick's as some had found out he wasn't 'feeling well'. Visitors shunned, Peter locked himself away in his room and would only see O'Conner. This strange behaviour was alarming, especially on Halloween, they could hear Peter sobbing and moaning in the middle of the night. That was it. Mark knocked on Peter's door. It opened slightly, O'Conner poked his head out. Jenkins was ready to force it all the way: if he wouldn't let them see Peter or tell them what was going on, it was time to call the Archbishop if not a doctor. And it was getting really impossible to fight the urge to call someone in his family. They couldn't let things continue like this.

"No need for that, I promise, ye'll see him tomorrow. Now, please *go away! Let* me handle this! I swear, ye'll find out tomorrow."

With that, he closed the door and locked it.

Dismayed, Jenkins threw up his hands and went away in frustration, Mark following. He had never seen his friend this persistent in telling him off.

"This doesn't look good, I think we should still call someone."

"All I can say is, it couldn't be life-threatening, he would have called an ambulance for Pete if it were."

"He said wait until tomorrow. He promised. We've gone this long, we can wait until the morning."

"Okay, but if he doesn't come out or let us in, we're calling His Eminence."

"Agreed."

Full sure that O'Conner had just said that to fob them off, they were actually surprised when he kept his word. Peter came down very early having showered, shaved, dressed, and seemingly ready for breakfast, but looking half the man he once was, certainly in body weight and hair colour.

"Geeze Pete, what's happened? You look like you've been through Hell!"

He looked up from his yet untouched coffee with a sombre look that nailed them to their seats. His glance then softened, tears welled in his eyes. Still, he remained silent. He looked back down into his cup to avoid their gaze. This worried them, it was as though he had lost all those dearest to him and had no hope of any happiness left on earth.

"Come on lad, they've been worried sick about ye. Don't leave them in the dark," O'Conner gently prodded at last.

He was right, they deserved to know, but what mortification! There were some private happenings in a soul that were difficult to reveal to a gawking world, even for the good of other souls. This was one of them. There were times these supernatural revelations and insights were granted when God wanted a soul to Himself, even in the frightening visions. He had ways of making someone feel like they were the only person in the world, it was a privilege to be let in on the Eternal secrets, it was a deep personal relationship, and to share that deep communion between his soul and its Creator to others who may not understand at all felt no different to letting himself be laid bare to prying eyes. Yet, Christ was stripped bare and raised up high on the cross, and so, one day these experiences will all be brought to light for the help of many. Yes, the fellows deserved to know.

"I saw souls falling into Hell as thick as hail during a thunderstorm. I didn't think there could be any people left on earth ... *and that was only for a quarter hour!*"

Mark's jaw dropped. Jenkins sat back and exhaled. If it was anyone but Peter, they would have called them a kook. There was no doubting his sincerity.

"Please tell us what's happened," Mark asked breathlessly, eventually breaking the stunned silence.

"And don't leave anything out," Jenkins added.

At long last Peter let them in on the secret mystical workings that he had been privileged to experience, beginning with the blessed vision of Light granted to him after his eyes had been anointed, then, what had happened to him that night they all thought he fell 'ill'. Yes, he had seen and experienced the Infernal Deep itself during a short minuscule wedge of time. Thrown from his bed and transported spiritually or physically to that burnt plain, he wasn't sure which, he was chained fast by the neck, ankles, arms and around the breast by the frightening black forms. They dragged him roughly through the freakish landscape, maliciously taking a course that would run him up against the few red hot jagged rocks jutting out of the ground, laughing as he cried out from pain, he thought he would be battered to pieces, but that wasn't Hell itself, not yet: that was just the ante-chamber, or so it seemed. His captors quickly covered ground until a small shape in the distance grew larger, it seemed like a solitary hill at first, like one of the rocks jutting out, only much bigger. By the time they reached it, he realised that this was no mere hill, it was one gigantic mountain scarred with fissures from which issued black smoke and ruddy flames that flashed green lurid sparks that were *lit*, but did not give any *light*. With horror he saw that he wasn't the only one being dragged or harried towards the black mountain, there were many prisoners being pulled to their doom as well. Many however, were running there themselves of their own accord, screaming, trying to get away from something or someone, rushing headlong in the direction he was being dragged. The terror only increased when he lifted his head enough to see that there was a huge entrance in the mountain, a gateway shaped like a ravenous monster waiting to swallow them whole. It was the Gates of Hell.

"Wait, why would the others *run* to them then? Surely, they knew they wouldn't escape their tormentors by doing that," Mark was eager to know.

"Shh! Don't interrupt! But now that he asked … ." Jenkins was curious too.

"Because when one is damned, you cannot feel the love of God any more, or have a flicker of hope or comfort, you literally cannot love or feel it, you can only feel the Almighty's wrath due to the sins committed, and you want to escape it, hide away, and the only place left for the soul to go, is Hell. The damned souls literally plunge into the depths to get away from the wrath of God and His All Seeing Divine Gaze that they have spurned, and only end up in torment themselves, free in the confining darkness to curse and blaspheme Him for the rest of eternity."

"But surely *you* weren't damned, Pete?" Mark was stunned.

"No, I couldn't pick out the transgressions that would have been damning for me in particular, but the rest of the souls did, they screamed and cursed themselves for the sins that brought them there."

Why other souls were bound and dragged, he didn't know, maybe as an extra punishment seeing the devilish jailers before they even get to Hell depending on the evil they did during their lives, (it certainly was an extra torment for him!) but while he was bound, he too suddenly felt what it was like to be damned: the ability to love gone, to care about anything or to feel any kindness, that was gone, gone, gone! One could no longer make an act of kindness either no matter how slight, not a thought, not a word. The thought of past joys of earth were torments now, there were no alleviations whatsoever, and he had not even entered the flames of Hell yet. He wanted to get up and run, run away from that Once Loving Gaze that now made him want to thrust himself away, that righteous Wrath for the outrages committed against His Infinite Majesty while the soul lived on earth. The terror of being stripped bare before that Wrath was searing, but so was the terror upon that first view of Hell, desperately, despairingly needing to throw oneself in even while knowing there was no escape from henceforth for all time. The sinner had rejected God, Who was all Goodness itself, anything that was, is, or would be good and beautific come from Him alone, there was no other goodness to be had, no other creators. The damned soul felt this keenly. To reject Him was to accept everything opposite to Him, and now, that opposite freely chosen by the soul during life was all that was left: evil, hate, rage, despair, no love or goodness, the rebels had to go to that place where everything opposed to the Creator was open to receive them. It was a conflicting agony to feel that panicked relentless urge to run towards your never-ending doom! It was a torture that could not be described.

Was he too damned? How he wanted to throw himself in! To get away from that harrowing feeling of having kindled God's just anger against him for all Eternity! He felt damned, damned damned! And that this would last for all eternity! No end, no end. Forever and ever. Ever! He still didn't know what he had done, he didn't have a dead conscience ripping him to pieces over unforgiven damning transgressions like the other unfortunate miserables being dragged or harried down the wide road with him. Wait ... fifteen minutes! He was promised only fifteen minutes, he would be released! But that didn't give any comfort. Was he lied to? Was he tricked, and he was *truly* damned? No no no! Wait! *He hadn't been judged yet.* No one went to Hell without being judged by God first ... but he couldn't feel a shred of hope or comfort in that knowledge. He realised he was being left to suffer the agony of a lost soul knowing it was damned and there was no hope, no reprieve, not one iota of relief. The only thing, he hadn't been judged, and there was nothing on his conscience accusing him like the other souls, but the sense of eternal banishment still clung to him, ripped him from the inside out.

Then, harried deep inside the maw, the path suddenly dropped, there was a cliff, a massive drop into a burning lake of souls. He was flung over the side into the abyss, the souls falling around him like water rushing in a torrent, the demons following them, prodding them along, submerging him into what looked like flames and molten lava. He looked back, and in the fleeting instant before he too was swallowed up in that seething mass, he saw with horror how rapidly he was plummeting, how the cascade of the lost that came before and after him didn't stop. Souls were also pushed through the fissures of the mountain above, making it seem like hail was falling everywhere, a hail of lost souls! So many, so many! Crushed and tossed in the mass, he was eventually pulled down and through that swirling cauldron, through the lava-like barrier into a lower domain that existed beneath, a compound of niches, a fiery honeycomb network of horizontal cells were souls were forced into and trapped for all time. His tormentors still dragged him along in the chains on what looked like a path through these tight walls and rows, until stopping at an empty filthy niche they roughly shoved him in.

The pain! He was tormented in flames as he was dragged, but now he was pressed in on all sides by walls of a darksome fire that flamed but strangely gave no light. Things could be seen in Hell, but it was yet all darkness, a complete separation from Divine Light. He was crushed, unable to move one tiny fraction, and that inability to move caused great torment. Knives seemed to rip from the inside out, leaving not one limb left untouched by pain. He thought his eyes would burst from their sockets from sheer agony. The putrid atmosphere was clogged with a stench that no words could frame: he thought he had smelled the scent of sin before, now, he was drowning in it, sulphur mixed with pitch, rot, decay, perpetual nausea was added to the torments. It was like he had landed in a demonic travesty of the Roman catacombs, but there, gloomy as the place was, there was *peace*, holiness exuded from the rock walls due to the martyrs, the dead laid there in peace, saved, martyrs, *saved forever*! But *here* ... just to think of that peace was a torment because it could no longer be felt. The remembrance of anything holy and having the odour of sanctity was agony. The thought of those saved forever while he was damned damned damned was torture!

Hate. All he wanted to do in a rage was hate, curse, blaspheme, it churned and bubbled within and wanted to pour out of his mouth, he felt the evil desire that all souls might be damned with him, suffer endless torments, the desire grew into a gluttonous frenzy that couldn't be satisfied. One was seized with the compulsive urge to spew profanity over and over and over. He wanted nothing other than to utter filth against anything and anyone in heaven, on earth and here too in hell, somehow, he was not able to say the dreadful things unlike the other damned souls ... they cursed their tormentors, they cursed their parents who bore them, other family members or teachers for giving them bad example and leading them to this place of eternal woe. Bad companions who gave bad example were cursed. Bad movies, dangerous books, lewd conversations and entertainments and unchecked thoughts, the inordinate desire for wealth, avarice, envy, hard-heartedness towards the poor and unfortunate, theft, coveting, murder, anything that led to serious sin and utter damnation received its share of abuse and curses. They cursed heaven, and blamed others, but then were forced to recognise that their damnation was caused by themselves by their own free will. They wailed knowing they had plenty of opportunities to reform their lives and repent, but they either lost the time and opportunities granted to them by letting earthly pleasure get in the way, or by deliberately dismissing them either through malice or slothful apathy, turning away from God, the scriptures, the warnings given by the saints, they had spurned all that, wasted time, refused to do penance, or, more atrocious yet, they had committed sacrileges, they were utterly deficient in the purpose of amendment while confessing that nullified the sacrament of confession, a situation that they didn't rectify, or they outright lied to the priest, purposely concealing a grave sin or purposely fluffed how many times they committed something mortal due to cowardice and shame, adding sin to sin, sacrilege to sacrilege, receiving Communion in that horrid state, purposely harbouring undisclosed sin, but now had to face their burning shame for all eternity when a proper, sincere confession lasting no more than a few minutes and a change of life would have saved them! Cowardice to face a few minutes of discomfort was now spread into an eternity of shame.

Shame, yes, great, revealing, stripping shame abounded. It was an appalling form of nakedness, undying guilt. He could feel it as though all his sins had been revealed to everyone there. Again, he could tell they weren't, but everyone else's were, and the damned took malicious sport in jabbing at each other with merciless taunts about the crimes and sins they committed that damned them there. The lost accused themselves bitterly before trying to curse and blame others again for their misfortune, then afflicted their fellow prisoners, a diabolical perpetual circle of bitter undying regret and blame. The anti-fellowship of the damned was another punishment in itself. The cacophony of screams, wails, groans, despair, it daggered the ears, the cries of pain and woe, the literal gnashing of teeth, it all ground down the sense of hearing. There was no alleviation to be found in any of the senses.

That also, all the senses were tormented depending on the sin, those who fell through pride and vain glory were tormented by the demons in particular, as they too had fallen through pride. The sight of these demonic creatures was a terror all of its own. Liars had their tongues ripped out over and over, murderers had their limbs torn apart, placed back on, then ripped off again. Impurity and lewdness, adultery, the flesh was torn, hot needles ran through the body, or devoured by worms and other vermin. Sins against charity, the chest was opened and molten lead was poured into the heart, a terrifying re-enactment of the gruesome exhibit he had seen in the allegorical trophy room so long ago. It never seemed to end, the different types and manner of tortures.

To make matters worse—if it could possibly be any worse—certain souls bore a mark, an interior sign letting the others know that they were a priest or a religious among them. He too could feel that mark, it was like that of Baptism and Confirmation, but this was something else, it was not possible to describe. The soul 'saw' it interiorly and felt its presence, so did the others. The torments were far worse for the likes of him, they, having left the world had been given all the extra graces and means for salvation and spiritual perfection, more so than souls who lived in the world, and yet, they had lost these great graces, misused them, wasted them. Disobedience to superiors, vicious murmuring, back biting against fellow religious, committing wilful infractions against the Holy Rule of their orders, having lived off the Mass stipends they received without saying the Masses, an atrocious theft, and worse yet, to have been chosen by God to save souls and yet had led them here by bad example, false teachings, scandals, sins, yes, even though he was not damned, he was recognised and tormented as if he were a fallen religious that had been a priest for himself but not for Christ. The devils particularly hated them, humans chosen and espoused by God! The lost religious were as so many Judases in which they took spiteful sadistic glee in throwing before the Divine Throne, showing they had snared another of His specially chosen ordained into His service.

Then, he was seen by someone whom he once knew on earth.

"Peter? Is that you? So, you are here with us then? My, my! Holier than thou! How does it feel to save others and not be able to save yourself, eh?"

The taunt whipped like a searing lash. He knew he wasn't damned, but if he were, that's the type of abuse he would be loaded with. He was allowed to turn and see who was mocking: it was someone he met during his days at the seminary. Oh, to see an acquaintance once known on earth in this place of no escape. What torture!

"Yes, Peter! I'm damned! Damned for all time! No escape!"

"Why?"

"I didn't listen to the Archbishop's warning and ignored all your good advice while we were studying together! I truly had a vocation, but I flippantly endangered it, then, refused to fight temptation! I lived a sinful life. Perhaps the torments would not be so bad if I remained in the secular world, but I took Holy Orders of my own free will, I refused to change or even repent on my deathbed when suddenly struck with pneumonia that inexplicably went septic. I could have at least done that! My sudden illness was my last warning! I could have been saved in those last few minutes, but now I am damned! I, who held God's Son in my hands like you, and now they, burn, *burn!*"

He lifted his hands, they were at a white heat intensity, he screamed in pain. Peter didn't seem to feel that pain … he looked, but no, his torment didn't go that far. Oh no, he then perceived why his former acquaintance was suffering this: sacrilegious Masses said while in the state of sin. It filled him with a disgust, and that was another torture, feeling the full force of sickening loathing by seeing and hearing about all the sins committed, the damned disgusting each other with the depths of their depravity. As the accusations were hurled everywhere, he saw other people he knew in life, infinite pain! They too were lost lost lost! People once famous in the world were also tormented, world leaders, celebrities as well as the thousands upon millions of unknown souls. Nothing was hidden here, except in his case. They couldn't see anything he did, and he couldn't accuse himself of anything either.

Mark took advantage of the pause at this point to ask who else he recognised, but Peter just shook his head.

"I could reveal them as a warning, but, in case I drive any of their living family members into despair should this get out, no, I'd better not."

"We won't tell anyone, not if you don't want. We promise, right guys," Jenkins affirmed, but Peter just shook his head again. He had already said too much about the seminarian he once knew. No point causing needless inconsolable pain. No, unless given the inspiration to, this had to stay quiet. It could be a sin against charity. He continued his story, for there was more.

"My Lord, Pete, how much did you see?"

"I was there for fifteen minutes, but enough for an eternity."

That was the thing, the *timelessness*, all sense of time was wiped out. If feeling sick or in pain made the passing of an hour drag to a wearying crawl on earth, it was thousands of times worse in the fiery pit. He was in a place of eternity too, so the sense was magnified unto a million times. The torments never seemed to end, stuck in that niche. Decades. Was it decades? And it would never end! Wait, what was that about 'fifteen'? *Minutes?* That promise seemed like a distant legend, a cruel myth let alone a memory. It must be well past that, by decades! As he was obsessing along these lines, a fearsome devil towered over him somehow, then lashed him with its whip made of incandescent lava cords.

"Fifteen? You've only been here eight minutes of your earth time, priest!"

No no no! *Just eight minutes? That's if the demon was telling the truth.* The demon laughed maliciously as it read his torment.

"All right, if you must know—*the real time is seven, not eight!*"

With another few lashes sent searing across him, the demon departed to torment other souls. There was no consolation, not one speck of respite or the tiniest pause, nothing!

He continued to suffer in this blasted cell for an age, until his jailers returned.

"Ha ha! He thinks this is it? Let's show him!"

He was roughly pulled out by the chains still binding him and was dragged along again. This time, he was shown that the blazing catacomb-like network was only one place in Hell. There were deeper dungeons with different tortures. One place featured a giant pit filled with blazing spikes on which souls were thrown, fished out with massive hooks, then thrown in again. Another featured a pit in which loathsome monsters and horrific unidentifiable beasts tore their victims to shreds, devoured them, then vomited them back up only to commit the same horrors again. There was one place where the souls ripped their own bodies apart, the pain of being damned for the nothings of the earth, mere sinful pleasures that had no comparison to the heavenly eternal joys that were now lost to them urged them to tear the flesh off themselves with their own teeth and nails then fling it at each other in despair, only to have it regenerate and repeat the never ending grisly ritual. Some souls were thrown in to molten lava pits over and over, the demons taking sadistic glee in their handiwork while they too suffered and burned within, the flames of Divine Justice tearing them apart. Abandon all hope, ye who enter here. Ha! Dante's *Inferno* with its circles, a poet's imaginary babble! That old epic was a child's whimsical rhyme compared to this place. He wondered if he too was going to suffer any of this, but his tormentors just stopped to show him the different levels, that was bad enough for the demons declared he hadn't seen all the levels! For now, there was one place in particular they were going to. They moved on, dragging him along.

Finally they came to a very dark place, deep, solitary. He then saw a glowing object as they approached the end of this desolate cavern. He wondered what it was, until he saw before him what looked like a narrow iron box smouldering and red from heat. It had a door, which they opened, it was filled with spikes, a hellish version of an Iron Maiden, but there wasn't a soul being tortured in there … .

"Of course not! Don't you know this is the place we have prepared just for you? *We're only waiting for you to fall! We prepare for everyone. If they will, it's up to them.*"

He screamed as they pushed him in and slammed the door shut, the spikes running through him, but he did not die, he couldn't! This was forever! The torments weren't done. The box jolted like it was being dropped into a hole, jarring the spikes right through. He had a sudden terror seize him, he was being buried, the sound of earth heavily thrown around him, but that was not all: an opening appeared at the top of the box, he suddenly understood they were going to slowly pour in molten material until he was finally submerged, drowning in liquid fire forever, buried for ever and ever and ever … no end … no end! The next thing he knew, he was surrounded in pitch blackness, then, found himself waking up in the oratory in O'Conner's arms.

Silence.

"Is there any hope for us, after hearing a story like that," Mark quietly wondered at last, the silence had grown almost unbearable.

"Oh, yes, of course." Peter quickly imparted an encouraging glance. "Don't lose heart. We have God's Mercy on our side too."

Now that he was back in the land of the living, he could see there were points of hope to be observed, he just couldn't feel it while he was there. There were times when the demons would suddenly fly into a rage that literally shook Hell like a violent earthquake, screaming and working themselves into a fury as they flew back to earth, spurring each other to devise new temptations to trick their escaping quarry: they were losing souls whom they thought had given themselves up to a life of sin, they were getting away. Someone was either praying for them, or making sacrifices and grace had been afforded to them which they did not ignore like the damned souls did that were now suffering intensely. Maybe a friend got through to a hardened heart with the right word and the right time, waking their conscience before they got any farther on the way to perdition, maybe it was a good sermon, or a close brush with death that made them wake up, but Mercy, hope in God's Mercy made many souls slip through the demons' grasp. Prayers, sacrifices made for sinners, repentance, trust in this Holy Mercy, there were conversions, there was always hope while a person yet lived and if repentance, amendment was earnestly willed and attempted no matter how many times a sinner fell and got up again. He was made to understand that clearly when the week was up.

"Oh right, what about that? You were only to be there fifteen minutes," Jenkins noted.

"Yes, directly. But the week was indirect."

He clarified that while he had indeed suffered a quarter hour of Hell in person, when he returned he no longer felt the fire or the physical tortures, (and even then it wasn't the full torments as they truly were!) but instead was to continue experiencing the worst pain there, the complete separation from God as he described it earlier, that full *knowledge* of having excited the Wrath of the Almighty and there was no possible way to feel love or kindness. He might as well have been thrown back into the flames, for this was still the worst psychological, emotional heart-rending torture imaginable. To feel you had become part of the Nothingness of evil! Awake but dead, existing but not! Cast off from God! The pain was magnified when this exile was manifested to him personally in not being able to see the Light at all, that gift was withdrawn from him. The emptiness was real, a cavernous chasm loomed black inside his very soul. He couldn't look at a holy picture or the little statues of the saints on his desk, they seemed angry at him too, their heavenly help withdrawn, he had to hide, cover up, it was agony simply to look at them because they were a reminder of what he had lost forever, grace, love, mercy, if he was truly damned of course. He still felt that frenzied urge to run away and hide from the wrath of God and all of Heaven as if he was being dragged to the Abyss. Say Mass? He didn't dare! He couldn't face His God! He could no longer look upon goodness or feel it, he was cut off forever! What agony! This went on for a whole week, that sensation of being damned for eternity, all sense of God and grace within the soul was completely cut off, there was no comfort for this type of affliction. He couldn't face the Bachelors either, it felt the same to face anyone living and who were therefore still open to God's Mercy. As his confessor, O'Conner was the only one. He could only bury himself in bed and let the emptiness and sense of despair eat him alive.

"And now?"

"I'm feeling better, don't worry Mark."

"You don't look it," Jenkins retorted.

"Why, of course he doesn't! What do yeh expect after seeing all them things? A ghost? He's seen a million of 'em!"

Peter certainly had changed. He looked like … well, it was hard to say. He now reminded Mark of the pictures of the little seers of Fatima although not as vexed as they, children who had old souls behind their solemn expressions uncharacteristic for their tender age, but they too had seen the Abyss after all.

"Are you sure you're okay, Peter? How do you feel now?"

"Like I'm in Purgatory."

Their faces dropped.

"That was figurative."

He observed their sudden relief. A flicker of a smile played at the corner of his mouth. Humour. To be able to feel that again! It was like a balm to his wounded soul, for wounded it felt, battered to have come through, but not damned, not damned thank God! Yet, outright hilarity in him was not possible right now, after what he had seen, there was too much at stake, the Four Last Things had been pressed hard into the spiritual fabric of his being: Death, Judgement, Hell or Heaven. There was no springing back right away from what he had experienced. The salvation of souls could not happen without wear and tear, as he knew all too well.

"The thing is, I don't feel the sense of damnation any more, but separation, the Light hasn't come back. Whether it will or not, I don't know. So, it is a Purgatory of sorts, not feeling damned, but still, cut off." The sense of this separation was cutting.

"Maybe yeh have to adjust back gradually. Ye're human, yeh can only take so much," O'Conner reasoned.

"How about you take another day to rest," Mark suggested.

"On All Saints? No, I'm not missing another Mass, no matter how I feel right now, especially today. And, thank you for picking up the slack for me, I really appreciate it. You don't know how much."

Gratitude. It was heaven to feel that again too.

"Aw, don't mention it," Jenkins replied with a wave of the hand. "We've got your back."

⊰ ❖ ⊱

Finishing the vesting ritual, Peter proceeded to the altar with his own jewelled chalice and paten for the feast day. Relief, gladness, then, shock, wonderment, whisperings among the crowd. It was bound to happen. He ignored it, this was not the first time he had caused a stirring, nor would it be the last the way things were going. Yes, the congregation was stunned. The poor Monsignor must have been really ill! The change in his dark hair and his deeper than usual expression showed the man had been through something beyond the normal run of things, but they were so glad he was back, and apart from the appearance of his white wing and thinner

711

physique, he seemed quite healthy. Speculations about what might have happened circled in their minds as well as their whisperings among the pews. Obviously, the evil one was not happy with their beloved Monsignor, he was doing too much good, and the devil always attacked such chosen souls through heavy illness along with the usual onslaught of temptations and earthly persecutions. It looked like he had been dragged through Hell.

Yes, but they had no idea, that also included his family, who had only just heard he had fallen sick. Katherine didn't attend service the day when it was announced he wouldn't be offering due to illness and only had found out much later. Without delay the news was passed on, so upon his return his Mass was also attended by a relieved yet frustrated family pride of lionesses headed up by his mother. Sophia, Lottie and Katherine were shocked like everyone else to see how he had grown gray in front. They wanted more answers than 'Peter was sick, but he's better now' when it was obvious something was seriously wrong. However, they couldn't see him until service was over and could only worry through the whole proceedings.

Talk about shocks, Peter on the contrary experienced a pleasant one: the Light came back, gradually, the gems and gold on his chalice simply glowed at first, but by the time of the Consecration, the grace had been fully restored to him. To witness such peaceful awe-inducing brilliance again after the Nothingness of the past week! What bliss! Perhaps this is what an ecstasy felt like. It was impossible not to linger around this sacred time and soak up the consoling reinvigorating sight after having experienced its exact harrowing opposite. It was so much greater than the evils Hell could ever throw at him. If only he could show everyone, and this was only a drop of the beauty of Heaven, a bare spark that reflected Divine Love. This was his mission, to bring everyone into the fullness of the Light for all Eternity. To love Love itself! How imperative it was to save souls! He had seen how many were taking the opposite path, if only he could stop the torrent heading to its never-ending destruction! Now he could understand more clearly the thirst of Christ to redeem, he recalled how He had revealed to a saint He would suffer His entire Passion for just one soul if that is all who turned to Him. Truly, there was no greater love than that. How he wanted to burn with that same desire!

As he genuflected before the Sacred Body and Blood blazing before him, he was gently interrupted by an Interior Voice and compelled to pause:

And you? Would you be willing to suffer Hell again for just one soul?

Of course Lord, you know it. I don't want another soul to be lost forever.

Alas, many will still choose the Abyss, but your willingness shall not go without its reward. So that all might believe, from this day forward, you shall be granted greater power over the demons. I shall make you a scourge to them, their resistance will be greatly diminished in your presence. They will be silent when you command them in My Name to be silent, and they shall speak when you compel them in My Name to speak. Deliverances will be numerous. But beware! Satan will try to spread his nets to snare you: the battle must continue for there can be no salvation without suffering. The Cross cannot be done away with, It is the truest test of Love. Embrace It, love It, and do not be afraid.

Thank you Lord, may I fulfil Your Will in this and always.

The congregation began to murmur as they noticed the long pause, raising their heads to see what might be happening. It was hard to tell as he was able to say the Latin Mass again, and this meant his back was to them. Still, there was always the thrilling hope that they might see *something* unusual. Nope, not this time. That was so disappointing! But what if he wasn't feeling well? He was sick for a week after all, and it really had to be bad for the Monsignor to miss his services. Eventually, the congregation regained some composure as he eventually rose to his feet and continued. Maybe it was nothing, just taking more time for adoration, he did that sometimes. Never mind, there was bound to be one of his unusual blessings, that was always interesting to see. Sure enough, the Monsignor turned, paused as he looked out into the congregation. He gave his additional blessing. A screech was heard this time, but nobody could tell what it was. Was it human or animal? Odd enough, it sounded like it came from outside, yet inside at the same time. Maybe it was a bus with screechy brakes and the sound had travelled in? No, it sounded like it came from something living … . There was some whispering, but the members of the congregation soon recollected themselves as they prepared to receive Communion.

When Mass had finished and Peter was leaving the altar in recollection with chalice and pall carefully in hand, worshippers rising to their feet and preparing to leave, the reverential atmosphere was shaken as a loud wailing cry rang out again in the church and reverberated around the arched ceiling. Peter stopped abruptly and peered out into the congregation as the gasps grew into a disturbed *sotto-voce* chatter. What was that all about? Nobody knew until a frenzied, dishevelled man rushed up the central aisle from the back of the church and stopped dead in the middle, clasping his head and staring down Peter with a look of pure terror and despair oblivious to the shocked and aghast expressions shot his way from the congregation. He cried out again in a wailing voice:

"Why did we torment you in Hell? We helped to give you more graces against us, you blasted priest!"

Peter drew closer to the steps without leaving the sanctuary to get a better view of the situation. A demon had given himself away. How to handle this though? He made the sign of the Cross in front of him with the chalice and pall.

"In the name of Jesus Christ, who are you?"

"One of the fallen!"

The congregation hushed up.

"What is your name, fallen one?"

"Bathin! Bathin! I hold this soul! Don't torment me!"

"In the name of Christ, on your knees!" Peter's commanding voice rang out. "You shall be silent and shall allow the soul you hold to speak!"

After another wail, 'Bathin' did as he was commanded in view of all, but slowly and grudgingly. Once on his knees, the man's harrowed look disappeared and transformed into one of surprise as though waking out of a dream and not knowing how he got there.

"Are you all right," Peter asked kindly this time. The congregation quickly turned from him to the tormented soul. The baffled victim found his voice.

"Praise be to God! I've been blacking out for five years, and this is the first time I can come near a church!"

"Can you come to the parish office to see me?"

"Yes! I ... I don't know ... sometimes I can't even get near a priest ... ."

"Oh, you will this time. Bathin!" The harrowed look on the victim instantly returned. "You are not to prevent his soul from coming to me. In the names of Jesus and Mary, you will obey!"

"*Nooooo!* But I must, I must! I'm compelled to! Favoured servant of the Son of David! What do you mean to do to us?" The screeching wail of a voice was terrible to hear.

"Silence! You shall not speak until we meet again." As soon as it appeared the victim had returned to human consciousness, Peter directed where to meet him, and suggested there be no delay.

"Thank you, thank you!"

The victim got up and rushed down the aisle and out the church as though he had taken the instruction 'no delay' as a strict condition of his spiritual release. Peter meanwhile calmly turned and left as if nothing had happened. The congregation erupted with a cacophony of mutterings and exclamations that continued even when shushed at by the ushers. If they hoped to see something unusual that morning, they got it. The family pride of lionesses however were the most surprised: they had never seen him in action like this before with someone who was obviously possessed, and the unexpected revelation made by the tormented man that alluded to Peter's recent 'illness' certainly renewed their worry for him. Katherine and Lottie decided they had better go and see him pronto, ask him what that was all about and find out for certain if he was okay, not to mention it was best they try and get away from the oogling congregation right now since quite a few people knew who they were and started to crush around to have a word, force an introduction or just catch a glimpse of the saintly Monsignor's family. Sophie eagerly agreed, on her way to see her son they could make a quick getaway through the sacristy. They caught up with him as he was about to lock away his precious chalice.

"Hello! Checking up on me, you worry pots?" He smiled as they gathered around him. "I'm sorry I can't stay long, as you just saw for yourselves, I've got an impromptu appointment to attend."

"Yes, we 'worry pots' worry about you," Lottie chided.

"And Peter! Your hair! Why didn't someone call us? Let me see," Sophia ordered in dismay. He lowered his head and submitted to the motherly inspection as she ran her hand through his new silver strands.

"I told the fellows not to, including Fr. O'Conner, they even kept it from the Archbishop at my request."

"But *why* Petey? We're *family!* You can tell us! You *should* have told us," Lottie exclaimed.

"Gerry's worried too. He's miffed at you, you know," Katherine noted, also in shock. It was hard not to take her eyes off his hair.

"I'm sorry, but I couldn't tell anyone, this was … no usual illness."

His mother dropped her hand. They exchanged a solemn glance. She seemed to know that the scene witnessed a few moments ago was indeed a revelation of what had happened. Why him? Why her Peter? God was asking too much of her son! It least that's how it felt to her, and knowing him, he would never say no. She was almost afraid to find out what had been demanded this time. No. No. She didn't want to know. It might break her heart. Peter was wise in not telling her.

"Wait until your father sees you like this! He's expecting a full report for the proverbial captain's log as you can imagine. We'll have to tell him … *something.*"

"Just say it's a price I had to pay for the wisdom I've gained."

"Now's not the time to be funny." Lottie pouted. She was used to his gentle teasing reminders of virtue whenever she worried about the day coming when a silver thread was bound to show up in her own brown locks, getting a Bible verse sent her way about wisdom displaying itself in grey hair. However, she didn't know there was more truth than a joke in his remark this time. "Being wise is one thing, Petey, but it makes you look old."

"We're supposed to grow older in wisdom."

"Yes, but do you have to *look* like it?"

"At least I don't have to look *at* it, except to comb it, and then only briefly."

"But everyone else does. O, elixir of youth, thy name is hair dye. Be kind to yourself. And us!"

"Vanity of vanities and all is vanity."

"Okay, that's enough you two." Mother lioness had spoken. "He can't stay chatting to us. You will be careful?" That encounter he just had looked positively frightening.

"Don't worry, just a spiritual client that needs healing."

"But what he said … what did he mean by that?" Katherine was curious to know. She like everyone else still couldn't stop herself from glancing beyond his face sussing out his new hair transformation.

"Maybe one day I'll tell you, but I can't now. As a consolation, want to take a look?"

"Huh?"

"Come on, I know you like beautiful things, now's your chance to get a close-up." He smiled as he indicated to the chalice. Katherine shyly smiled back. Busted. They realised he was jokingly trying to get her and them away from gawking at his white wing. Peter chuckled.

"You'll get used to it."

"If you say so, but now Kathy's got to get new photos of you all over again," Lottie observed.

"Huh? Oh! I forgot about the painting. How's it coming?"

"Still in the sketching phase, but Lottie's right! I'm going to have to do you over again!"

"Oh dear, you know I really do appreciate the thought, but at the same time, what was the Captain thinking? With everything you're busy with these days, to put another commission on your back? Remember, I won't hold you to it, dear," Sophia concluded turning to her.

"Don't worry, there're no time constraints, it's a 'do it when you can' thing," Katherine reminded. "Gosh, I do wish I could work this in though, it is beautiful," she continued, taking a closer look at the gold cup with its jewels and intricate designs. After giving her a few moments, Peter reminded them he had to run.

"Before we go, will you be out to see us soon? We all miss you," Sophia noted.

"No pressure." Katherine smiled. "But I can't wait to tell you what happened at my latest art show. Kevin and his nut cases! We had to call the loony truck to pick up the 'Palette Knife Prince'."

"That's right! I forgot about your latest art exhibit. That's the second one I've missed. I'm sorry, I know I've been tied up, but now I've got a lot of catching up to do in parish appointments. Maybe I can come to dinner next week? If not, maybe in a fortnight?"

"Thanksgiving will be almost upon us then … ."

"Oh right, I've lost track of time," Peter trailed. With all his work, not to mention what he had just seen, the approaching holiday had escaped him.

"Listen, if you can't come before then, we'll all just have to make do with Thanksgiving." His mother was pleased and relieved to announce that Gerry just received the all-clear to move into the penthouse after then, so they had something truly to celebrate.

"Wow, that is good news! Of course, I'll be there. However, if I can drop by earlier for a visit, I'll let you know."

"All right, give us a call."

"However, we're not going until we see you smile, Pete," Katherine insisted. His solemn look this morning troubled her. However, he couldn't help but to oblige her. "There! That's better."

After a quick group hug, he gave his lionesses another blessing, then had the sacristy to himself. He locked his chalice away. Whew. Secret still kept for the most part. Just a little longer Lord! Can't we keep this just between us? No answer. No, because he already knew what it was. He may be allowed to savour the intimacy of his experiences now, but not all these graces where meant just for him. They had to be shared. Eventually, the truth of what happened to him would come out, it was bound to one way or another. If the Holy Bachelors kept their promise and said nothing of his descent to the deep, by the very nature of the few public manifestations of his other spiritual gifts, he would most likely be ordered either by his spiritual director or the archbishop himself to write these things down, all of them, from his spiritual discernment to his Heavenly visitations plus his journey to the depths, to the interlocution he heard at the altar, and in obedience he would have to comply down to the last iota, which would also include turning over his dream journals with all their private mystic revelations. Mortifying! At least it wouldn't be a penance as bad as Hell itself, but just not yet, Lord! They already see too much of it all as it is! No time to reflect about it now, he had an emergency appointment. It was obvious that the 'many' deliverances that were promised his way had already begun.

He had never heard about anything like this before, the gift of speedy exorcisms, so he wasn't sure how it would all turn out when he got to his OR. Since no one had expected him back yet as he had only returned from his 'illness' that morning, there was no crowd waiting, just the poor unfortunate that had sought him out in the church. The dishevelled man rocked on the pew set out in the hallway, but stopped his motions and snapped into a stony state of leery attention as Peter entered the basement corridor.

"Curses on you, black robe! I'm forced to sit here!"

"Silence! In the name of Christ, you shall allow the victim to speak. You are to stay silent until I say so."

Peter made the sign of the cross over him and the frenzied look gave way to one of fear at the gesture of command, then relief as the controlling fiend was compelled to loosen its grip. Peter unlocked the door to the waiting room and let his new patient go in first, who looked very uncomfortable to be there. Peter offered him a seat and eventually coaxed his story out of him when he finally gave his name, Frank Silvio. Apparently, he had run with bad company, those who eventually made a joke of dabbling with a ouija board one night for a bit of fun, but he never felt the same after that. He couldn't put a finger on it, but he would black out and find himself in the strangest places. At first, he thought it was binge drinking, but it happened on nights he didn't drink too. Sometimes during the day, and he couldn't remember what happened, only that witnesses when there were any would later say he was like a completely different person, and a very nasty, ugly one at that. Bitterly sarcastic, fault finding, even disclosing hidden events and embarrassing secrets. His life soon fell apart, trying to hold a job was hard. He thought it was a medical issue, but doctors couldn't find anything wrong with him, including the shrink he was recommended. He was perfectly normal when he wasn't in a blackout, but they were becoming more frequent, and even his family started to shun him unless in dire charity they'd drop by on a rare occasion to see if he was all right and at least had food in the cupboards, bills paid, and something extra to help get him by. It wasn't until his sister said something like he was acting like a possessed person that he wondered if there wasn't something to it, but that sounded insane itself. He felt perfectly normal! Except, for when he passed a church, or someone mentioned God, he felt a deep repugnance, bitter, a smouldering hate even, and he didn't know why, he had never been anti-religious before eventhough he wasn't a regular practitioner for years. Still, unless he wanted to end up in a madhouse, he thought he had better talk to someone, a priest if he had to, but that's when things got really ugly, he'd black out at the mere suggestion. That's when he knew he really needed help, any help from a priest since he kept blacking out at the mere thought of it.

"Then, today I ended up outside Old St. Patrick's and thought I'd try one last time. In fact, I don't know why, but I was urged to go for a walk, and there I was! And I was able to go inside! It was at the end of your service, and this time I could feel myself blacking out, but you know the rest."

"Indeed."

"Can you help me?"

"Yes, I can help with your spiritual healing, but you will have to do much yourself."

"How?"

"What was that about hanging around bad companions? Binge drinking? A ouija board? Haven't been to church in awhile let alone confession? God is calling you back. You have to change your life for a complete cure, but it must be your decision."

Peter was very careful never to mention 'possession' or 'exorcism' in front of authentically obsessed or possessed patients until they were healed. Possession was not a sin, but to bring it up would only cripple the soul with additional guilt and cause more harm than good. Only the sins that may have been the gateway to the affliction could be touched upon at present.

"But can you help me now? What do I do *now*? What if I black out again? This is ruining my life!"

Peter studied his patient for a moment with compassion, he knew what it was like to be tormented by demons, and this poor fellow didn't fully know what was happening even if he was guessing it. Of course he had to start helping him now. Conversion would come bit by bit in the process.

"Yes, I can help, but I will need you to sign a consent form for the more powerful prayers of healing. And it may take some time, maybe more than a few sessions … ."

"All right, I'll sign anything, I just want this to stop! I don't care how often I have to come. It's a wonder I'm here at all … ."

Normally, Peter would have gone through the official process of sending a new patient to be evaluated by a certified psychoanalyst or psychiatrist first, but after all he had seen and heard this morning there was no need, this was definitely a real possession case. Curious, Peter flipped on his hidden vision, oh yes, there was a black flame hanging over the very heart of this poor soul. He turned off the Sight for now then went into his OR and took out the necessary form, Frank eagerly grabbed it from him when he returned, scrawled his name on it and quickly handed it back, no doubt afraid he might black out before he could put his John Hancock to the official paper. However, Peter wondered if it would be wise to start an exorcism alone without some assistants in case the patient got unruly?

Don't be afraid, you will be obeyed.

Encouraged by the interior Voice, he motioned for Frank to follow him into the OR. No sooner had he entered and locked the door when Bathin made another appearance, he could tell by the inhuman facial contortions and the strange abortive attempts to leap forward and strangle him. Naturally he was startled at first, but the victim wasn't permitted to touch him, he stopped only a few inches away as though hitting an invisible shield. Peter also noticed the spirit was forced to remain silent in obedience to his earlier instructions. That explained the fearsome voiceless expressions, but he was used to such grotesqueries by now, they were a spit in the bucket compared to his foray into the Inferno. Ordering Bathin into the chair and commanding him to stay put he went and got the video camera set up on its tripod and stationed at a safe distance from the work area before getting his other sacramentals ready, Bathin still displaying his silent rage while bucking around in the chair as though glued to it. Peter commanded him again to keep the chair down on all four legs, his feet planted on the floor, and the spirit was forced to comply, although he did try to slide it around awkwardly on the linoleum, gouging a few holes in the process, which Peter also commanded him to stop. For a moment, he couldn't help but pause and reflect. This was just *too* easy. For a demon to be *that* obedient? Yet, he also knew he could trust what he heard at the altar this morning, and therefore just had to go with what was happening. The demon certainly wasn't very happy about it, that was certain. Ah, maybe that was it, a weak case, only one spirit had manifested so far, perhaps that explained it.

Opening the book of rites he began on his new patient who squirmed every which way, but was obedience-bound to his sitting position. Peter was concerned there might be some vomiting episodes, which would be difficult to handle on his own, but Frank just bubbled out copious rivulets of drool which trailed down his face. Peter grabbed the box of tissues he had ready and ordered Bathin to clean up his mess. The patient forcefully grabbed a fistful, tearing the box in the process, and had to mop up after himself, rubbing his cheeks slowly and with deliberate force like a stubborn resentful child. The tissues balled up, in his rubbing he dropped bits all over his shirt. The demon's compliance was almost comical at this point if it wasn't for the fact Peter knew just how dangerous and conniving a demon could be that only desires to cause pain, suffering and the destruction of everything created.

Eventually Peter deemed it was time to loosen the demon's tongue and get some answers. Bathin uttered the expected curses and foul-mouthed blasphemies, but while he tried a few lies, they were too apparent and he was quickly obliged to truthfully answer Peter under the harrowing sight of the Crucifix placed before him. Were there any more demons present?

"NO! I wish there were, but I'm not permitted to call them! Curse you," Bathin concluded with a howl.

"How did you gain entry to possess this child of God?"

"'Child of God'?" Bathin sneered. "This maggot hasn't been acting like it for some time! The seance night got him, he finally threw the door open for me! It was I who gave answers on the board. You pathetic creatures are so easy!"

"What will be the sign of your departure?"

"*NO!*"

"Yes! In the name of Christ, you will give one!"

After some horrific howling, the demon was finally forced to give a sign.

"When the glass cracks! When the glass cracks! You will know!"

Peter only had an idea what that meant, but it was the answer he needed and decided to proceed with the remainder of the Rite in full as was the custom when treating a new patient. He didn't silence the trespasser this time, he needed to know what passages hurt him most. The demon was bellowing by the time he had finished the first session. He went straight into round two, this time repeating the passages that forced a response. He was about to go for round three despite how drained he felt when the demon shrieked, followed by an almighty *KRAC CRAC cric KRACK* resounding through the room. The small window had lightening shaped splinters running through it, the jars holding his blessed oils salt had also split, yet kept their shape and still were sound enough to hold their contents. Frank blinked back into consciousness while Peter checked the other room, sure enough, anything made of glass including the light bulbs in the lamps had also cracked, but were left unbroken. The sign had been given. Frank had been liberated. Peter quickly went to check on his patient. The black flame was gone, but there was a dark mist present. Still, it was a good sign.

"Welcome back! I think we may have gotten rid of your problem, but let me finish the last prayers to make sure."

This time Peter quietly said the rest under his breath to make them inaudible to Frank, he didn't want to frighten him. There was no demonic response only a confused man wondering why his face, shirt and face were all wet, his lap and the floor littered with balled up tissues, now just sitting and waiting to see if this was going to do anything for him, although he did look at the window with curiosity, it wasn't cracked like that when he first sat down in here … .

Yes, Bathin was gone. Peter quickly turned the pages to the prayers of Thanksgiving and had Frank repeat them with him.

"You think you've solved my problem then," he incredulously asked when they had finished. "I was in here no more than ten minutes, fifteen maybe."

"No, it's been more than two hours. Check your watch."

Frank was stunned as he checked the time, the glass on his watch also webbed, while Peter brought over the video camera, the lens had also cracked. Thankfully, the view screen didn't get more than a few hairlines as it was mostly plastic not glass, the image was still visible. Time for Frank to see what had been plaguing him for the last five years. Frank could only sit there stunned as Peter showed him the most significant parts of the tape.

"As you can see, a change of life is needed now to ensure this doesn't happen again."

"My God, I really was possessed," he noted quietly. "What do I do now? Will it come back?"

"Like I said, closing the last of the cracks will be up to you. Here, study this, calmly and no panic," Peter replied, handing him a booklet on how to examine the conscience and prepare for a full confession. "When you're ready, hopefully by tomorrow, come back and we'll see about scrubbing your soul, and try not to sin in the meantime, agreed?"

Frank simply nodded and took the booklet. Shakily getting to his feet, he offered his thanks and shook Peter's hand before he left still perplexed about the whole thing. True, Peter could read consciences and could have walked him through a thorough general confession, but the man wasn't ready yet, this morning was a lot to take in, and confession had to be done willingly. No need to worry though, something told him Frank would be back.

Tidying up his OR, he was about to close up when already he had a line waiting for him on the chairs and pew outside, news had spread he was back, but there was more than a few frightened faces after the bellowing they had just heard. My, my, looks like his afternoon was cut out for him! However, before he settled in to examining the next cases, he decided he'd better reschedule his regular sessions at Trenton. If anyone needed his increased spiritual gift, it was that poor girl confined in that solitary psych ward.

By now Mabel and Ethel had arrived for their shift and were manning the front desk of the parish office. Unnerved at the sounds bellowed by the patient he had just seen, they now had to get used to his unexpected change in appearance.

"Monsignor, are you all right?"

"Yes, I'm fine my good nurses, just some silver among the ebony. Sick leave over, it's back to work for me. Time to make some phone calls."

"Er, sure, the station is all yours," Mabel affirmed, indicating the phone. She was itching to ask him what happened to him all week, and what had he just done down there, but he was obviously in a rush to get caught up with missed appointments and didn't intrude with any more questions.

It didn't take too long to contact the parties involved. Fr. Greg was ready and waiting. He hoped he was all right, they heard he was sick, but Peter reassured him all was well again. While it was good to know he was better, to be honest, the doctor had called him and admitted the nurses and orderlies were glad for the break. After weeks of assisting at these hair-raising proceedings, their nerves were fraying. He might have to look for some more volunteers if the exorcism process was expected to continue much longer, it was bad enough he mentioned 'years'! Peter was not surprised, the extreme cases could be utterly sapping to the most seasoned exorcist let alone lukewarm laity and sceptical non-believers. Greg also had an intriguing bit of information, he had been told that the staff on the other floors hoped the exorcism sessions would be over soon because the minute the two of them appeared at the hospital, the necessity to drug the other patients suddenly increased, their very priestly presence in the hospital was costing the place a fortune in sedatives as a considerable number of the sick went all out crazy like there were a dozen full moons out. Peter had to agree that was intriguing, but in a sad way. It confirmed what he thought about the majority of mental illness cases. However, the staff might just get their wish. After this morning he hoped things might go more smoothly with Melissa than he had originally predicted. Only time would tell.

True to the Voice's promise, an uptick in possession and obsession cases were waiting at his door for the week. Mabel and the other nurses were stunned to see their once inside joke become what it truly was, an inner fear now come to pass. To hear the muffled shouts, and the odd roar or scream of the afflicted as they underwent their spiritual treatment behind the closed doors of the OR! They had to explain to newcomers at the office the cause of the waiting crowds and the scuffles down below, and to see their reactions was something else. Their own observations were not much different.

"Heavens! If I didn't know better, I'd swear he was murdering people right under our feet in broad daylight," Ethel exclaimed one morning as she opened the door to the basement to get a better ear on the situation. "Can you just imagine what's going on at Trenton?"

"I can, but let's not go there," Mabel replied as Ethel closed the door. "This place is enough for me, thank you!"

True, Peter still had a battle on his hands at the hospital, and yes, he was promised faster deliverances, but that could still mean months instead of years when driving out a bevy of hordes and legions, which was Melissa's dire condition. By now the staff at the hospital were used to seeing him and Fr. Greg. They opened up the doors and readily let him in with a nod and a wave as regulars to the place. The two priests had even earned a certain respect amongst the sceptics in the top ranking medical staff after all the stories that were now circulating, despite the cost in extra sedatives. Eventually Peter had allowed several of the doctors and other nurses watch the proceedings, and even they had to admit after seeing the preternatural manifestations this was way beyond what they could handle. However, Peter's first week back battling at Trenton after his reported 'illness' went almost the same as the last sessions. Apart from all the questions asking him how he was on the first day back and a few questioning glances at his hairline, Melissa was much the same, vomiting, shrieks, cursing and all, but the spirits present did obey quicker and for longer periods than when he first started praying over her. He hoped something might give way soon though, the staff that had helped him full-time up to now were at their breaking point with all the manifestations, the personal secrets revealed, and the sadistic psycho lies the spirits slipped out in their twisted game playing that would make any sane person question their mental state. He continually warned them not to pay attention to the prattle, but it was hard to do when the demons were leaving out veritable faults and moral failings of those present that nobody had known before, which made it easier to fool and convince them when threats and lies were spoken.

Then, at the end of the second week of November it looked like something was giving way. Peter and Greg, already battle-weary were let into the solitary confinement room to find Melissa fully conscious for the first time, unshackled, sitting on the edge of the bed and talking coherently with Dr. Fareed and Mrs. Fletcher as though nothing was wrong. Finally it would appear all his prayers and penances were having an effect, the demonic tormentors were giving her some freedom for the present.

"Here they are now, Missy, the priests who have been helping you," Mrs. Fletcher pointed out to her eagerly.

"Oh! I know you, I've seen you before!" The almost ecstatic expression was quite a welcome change.

"Technically, this is the first time we've met. Hello Melissa, I'm Monsignor Reinold, this is Fr. Simmons." Peter was kind, courteous as though nothing was the matter, for in fact the *girl* was fine despite her spiritual troubles, but he was on his guard without making it obvious. She timidly shook hands with them.

"Yeah, I know, but I've seen you, they are there in my dreams, and I saw you too, and they don't like you, they hate you."

"'They'.' Who or what are 'they'?"

"The voices, sometimes it's like I go into dream mode, I'm no longer in the room, but I see things then, I must be asleep or something. But … sometimes I see them … they're dark, beast-like creatures, sometimes like men, I can't see them directly, but they tell me horrible things! Like I'm gonna rot in Hell forever! Am I going to Hell?"

"Oh, no dear! There's always hope!" Her aunt was on the verge of tears.

"I wish I could believe that. God won't forgive what I've done, I can't look up," she whimpered again, Peter was troubled by this, she was in despair. He knew what that felt like.

"Nonsense," he gently replied. "You're aunt is right, while there's one breath of life left, there is always hope, and do you think God just sits around waiting to damn everyone? No. He just wants you to come back to Him."

"That's not what the voices say. They say I'm damned already, or they wouldn't be able to torment me like this."

"A lie, my dear. Even saints were tormented, sometimes as badly as you're being tormented now."

Melissa looked up at Peter but then down at her hands. She began to wring them in a nervous manner.

"Oh, but I'm no saint," she quietly trailed.

"After a good confession, you'll have taken your first step to becoming one. The voices may trouble you for a while yet until we get rid of them, but you won't be in danger of being damned, not once your soul is clean and kept clean. Your voices are cunning cheats. They don't want you to have what they can no longer have or feel: love. They despise you with a bitter envy because you have God and His love eventhough you can't feel it right now."

"Really? Even now?" She looked up at him.

"Yes, even now. We're here to help get those bad voices to stop plaguing you, but you have to help yourself too if our prayers are to work and have a lasting effect."

Peter answered her questioning look with the same advice he gave Frank Silvio, about how an All Powerful and Good God was waiting with open arms. All she had to do was choose the side of Light and Love, and reject the Darkness and Hate that was now tormenting her. He gently mentioned amendment, a firm desire to return to a proper spiritual life, and no more of anything 'dark', all that had to stay in the past.

"You know what I mean," he gently prompted. She looked at her hands again, downcast and ashamed, but slowly nodded in agreement. "Confession is the best way to make that first step on your journey back. Once you do that, God doesn't even remember what you've done wrong."

"Seriously? Are you for real?"

"Yes, absolutely." He smiled.

"And what about you? *You* won't forget. Not what *I* have to say."

"Oh, I forget a lot of what I hear, I hardly remember. In fact, I'd have to wrack my brain about what a specific person said after all the people who have come to me. You don't need to fear my hearing anything. I'm not here to judge, only heal and forgive. Believe me, you cannot shock me. And, I cannot tell a soul what you tell me, even if threatened with torture and death."

There was a long silence. Peter could see she was willing, but the uncertainty caused by shame of having to say out loud to another person what she had done was enough to choke her silent. Crippling shame, and the demonic trap of human respect, failing to do good for fear of what might be thought of you. Major hurdles. He would have to dispel that crippler, and fast.

"Do you want to happen to you what the voices say they will do to you?"

Her expression changed.

"I didn't think so. Isn't that far worse and more terrifying than having to tell me all your mistakes, which will only take a little bit of your time as opposed to torture for all Eternity? Get it all off your chest, live a good life, and you're on a fast track of getting rid of those horrific voices, not to mention getting out of this place."

"Okay then, but ... but I don't remember how to do it."

Mrs. Fletcher was on the verge of relief-filled tears.

"Don't worry, I'll help. It's not as bad as it sounds," Peter replied cheerfully. He had reason to be cheerful, 'okay' was a positive response. "Do you want to do it now?"

"Er, okay. How do we um, start?"

He motioned for Mrs. Fletcher, Greg and the staff to give them some privacy while he pulled over a chair, kissed his stole and sat down. After they had vacated the room, Peter suggested she kneel first, she could use the pillow for a cushion if the floor was too rough on the knees, make the sign of the cross, then try and remember to the best of her ability when she had last been to the sacrament.

As she was about to kneel, the girl was gone. Her face contorted, she leaped backwards onto the bed, crouching onto her haunches with a snort as she twisted the pillow as though intending to burst it open.

"Us *kneel*? Away with that! *Confession?* We won't let the little whore confess! She's ours!"

Her captors were back. So much for Melissa's first positive response. Peter also sprang into action, holding his crucifix ready.

"In the Name of Jesus Christ and the Blessed Virgin Mary, who are you? What are your names!"

"No no no! I don't want to give mine! But this time I must! Beleth! Beleth is my name! Blast you!"

At last. By her willingness to confess, she had helped to weaken them. Different breakthrough, but one all the same.

"Who else?"

"Many! I have my legion with me, but there are more! That's all I'm telling you!"

Peter commanded again, once one name had been given, the others were soon to follow. After much writhing to the point the girl's spine was bent backwards almost into a full circle, another presence came forward with reluctance, but admitted it was compelled to give its identity, Orias. Were there legions with him? No, but a band of two hundred. Good Lord, that meant anywhere from three to six thousand demons so far, plus the two hundred. Who else? Peter grabbed his holy water and doused the patient who immediately contorted back into an almost normal position and laid back down on the bed. The demon shrieked a howling wail, bringing everyone back to the door. Dr. Fareed looked through the pane, Peter motioned for him to come in.

"Yes yes yes! Bring all the worms back in," Orias spat.

The demons sneered, for many voices could be heard guffawing. There was a scramble to action. The video camera now set up, Melissa strapped to the bed with difficulty by five orderlies. Peter forced the demons to repeat their disclosures for the record before he continued with the name-pulling, for it was indeed like yanking teeth with some of the vulgarity and blasphemy-filled delays, but the names did come. Amdusias followed with his entourage of four legions, bringing the tally of spirits to a possible thirty-thousand. Bathin next made a surprise appearance, cursing him for casting him out of his victim in New York. Bathin then made a revelation: he was waiting for the time when some practitioner of the occult, be it witch, warlock, satanic priest or some gullible idiot fooling around with their Tarots and their boards to summon him back, even into another unwary person.

"You banish us to Hell, but we are always called back by our followers! There are so many ways to summon us! It will be like this until the End until we are forever banished! But now is our time, we have so many followers, both knowing and unknowing, the fools! It's never been so easy for us!"

Peter commanded Bathin to answer if he had also taken up possession of this girl. No, he was forced to give a message, that was all. He was going now: there were more powerful spirits present that claimed right of ownership, he had to give place to the 'greater ones'. Bathin had no sooner said this when he whimpered. From the sound of the yelp that followed, whoever had come had dismissed Bathin no different than a cruel master kicking a whelp out of his way.

"Out of here! Give way to your betters! So, you plan to thrust us out, do you, black robe? Even so, we've got other plans."

All attendants present were stunned to hear the various changes during the dialogue, voice tone, pitch and conversational style altered with each entity, but the laughing sneer and deep voice of the present demon sent chills down the spine. Peter dared to pump for more information.

"What is your name?"

"Yes, I think it's time we had this introduction. Moloch is who I am, also commander of legions, far more than you decrepit mortals can fathom."

"Do you have legions here possessing this girl?"

"What an asinine question coming from you! Of course! Six! Six of mine reside in this stinking little harlot! So is it with Astaroth! Yes, yes! Do your math, idiot! Thirty six more legions!"

"Who else is here? In the name of Christ, speak!"

"No one else!"

"Answer! In the name of Mary, the Immaculate Virgin, is that the lot of you?"

"No, because of *her* I have to answer, confound you! There's Stílitípota, but don't mind that wretch, he's nothing. He's only got six pesty imps with him, mute ones at that."

"Any more?"

"Well, there is one more, but we don't want to say … ."

"You will say!"

"No no! He will not be named!"

"Oh yes he will."

"Yes, yes, but not now … not until we go and he is the last."

"So you will be going then?"

"We don't want to!"

"Who is the one who doesn't want to be named now?"

"A great one! A defiant one!"

"Enough with your riddles! And he is the last? Speak!"

"Ah, more of your stupid cess water! Stop it! It sizzles us!"

"Speak!"

After several rounds of holy water, blessed salt, and not a small amount of howling in response, Peter was eventually convinced all the commanding demons had been hunted out and exposed except for the one who refused to be named. Apparently, he had to work at getting rid of all the others first. So what was it now? Two hundred and forty-six thousand! Yes, forty-one legions … a band of two hundred … six mute imps … .

"And a partridge in a pear tree," a demon sneered, guessing Peter's thoughts from his expression.

"You pride-bloated spirits dare mock a symbol of salvation, do you? You who have rejected heaven entirely? What a pitiful choice! How low you have fallen!"

This was a switch. Greg was stunned to see Peter retort back taunt for taunt, along with his liberal shaking of holy water, making the present demon shriek.

"No no no! Don't remind us! You torture us! We're lost! Forever lost! *And, yet, we would have it no other way!* We will not serve! We will drag as many of you down with us as we can!"

"Who's speaking now? Answer!"

"Astaroth!"

Peter handed the empty aspergillum to Greg to be refilled while he continued to question the arch demon.

"So, you want us all damned?"

"YES! We want nothing more than to snatch as many of His creatures from Him as possible. We cannot bear it that He wanted to be one of *you*, and especially through *Her*! How we hate *Her!*"

"She whose heel you dread?"

"Yes, yes, The Woman! Damn you, we have to admit it!"

"And yet, if you repented, she would not withhold her intercession. You would refuse her help?"

"It's true! She could secure the Divine Mercy for us, she has the power and grace to intercede, but we don't want it! HEAR THAT, PRIEST? *We refuse!* We would rather burn for all Eternity than submit to God let alone to the mercies of that human piece of ... ." Peter quickly prevented the blasphemy from being spoken with another sprinkling of water. "Stop that! It scorches!"

"Serves you right for your foul tongues. And so, while you fear being sent to Hell more than anything, you would rather go there than to serve God and be allowed back to Heaven?"

"YES, damn you!"

"And that is why you should never pity a demon or entertain the slightest hope it is possible for them to be saved," Peter stated unexpectedly, turning to the assistants present. "They grasp damnation and hang onto it with all their fallen angelic might because of their unrelenting pride and hatred of humility, especially God's humility in desiring to be made Man through Woman. Therefore in His Justice He has given Her whom they hate the honour to crush them with her heel, a fit punishment."

"Too true, pesty priest," the demon interrupted. "Too bad so many of you stupid imbeciles don't grasp this! Hate her, ignore her, and salvation is very sketchy for you! We work tirelessly to see her mocked and scorned! Cut you off from her, it's one of the surest ways to damnation! We want you to suffer everything we do!"

"Have no pity for the demons for they certainly have no pity for us. They have made their choice, and you don't want to be where they are. Take my word for it. So," Peter continued, turning back to the patient, or rather, the presence taking hold of her, "good to see you have to admit the truth."

"Yes! Bah! It torments us! You human excrement! We have to! We want to lie! We would like nothing better than to confound you, confuse you before you cast us out, but we cannot! Not to *you*! We're not allowed now! To think we helped give you that power over us! If only we could get you, what we wouldn't do to you, *eternally* this time!"

"No more of your threats! Now, what shall be the sign of your departure? All of you. Speak!"

"No no no no no! Don't tell him!" A roar followed by another group of infernal voices. "No no! We don't want to go! But *She* forces us! We despise Her! Yet we have to obey Her! The Queen we reject is still the Queen over the Universe, seen and unseen. We are compelled to obey! Great Lady! Great Lady! Ah, we tremble before her! We have to give him the sign! No we won't, we won't, but we must!"

"So? Spit it out! Name the sign!"

"Ah ha! Spit it! Spit it! All this time, and he didn't even see it, when he of all stupid mortals could have if he looked!"

What? Peter flipped on his 'dark' Sight to a greater intensity. As hinted there was something odd located in the area of the stomach, black all right, but a different 'black' from the flames and pitch mist surrounding the girl denoting the legions present. Of course—a sortilege. A cursed object that had been swallowed, usually part of an occult ritual. They could take many forms from food to inanimate objects. This particular one looked like … a balled up scrap of undigested paper, or was it cloth? It seemed like a pentagram with a skull was hovering over it, the image was a bit blurry with all the spiritual darkness present. Probably a spell was put on the cloth. As he had learned from Fr. Amaranth, the end of strong demonic possessions were sometimes signalled with the visible manifestation and removal of such items, but they were some of the hardest gateways to detect and eliminate. Of course, he should have thought of actually searching it out with his gifted vision, but it didn't strike him to *look* for the thing, especially as he didn't like turning on his 'dark vision' for this extreme possession case. Even so, the demons still had to name the sign themselves, which they just did.

"Yes, yes yes! Now, try to get her to spit it up, if you can!"

"She was possessed by you when she swallowed it?"

"No, not by all of us. Several of us were sent first through a curse, I came after, so did Moloch. She made it easy, I can tell you that! The rest came after that through the sortilege."

"Who cursed her?"

"The stepfather! He's also one of ours, you know! One of the fraternal brethren!"

"So, when she vomits the sortilege, is this the sign when the last of you will be gone?"

"Yes, to Hell with you!"

"And before then as the legions are driven out? What is the sign? Look upon the Cross and answer!"

"Put away your puppet stick! Blast it! You will see us leave! Everyone will!"

"You're saying the departures will be visible."

"Yes! Yes!"

Those attending the proceedings glanced nervously at each other.

"And when will you leave? Give a date and time."

"No no no! We like it here, we're quite comfortable! We're not going!"

"Let's make things uncomfortable and see how you like it!"

With that, Peter launched back into the Rite in Latin, causing the demons to shriek. Then, they started to weep, which was horrific in itself, to hear such piteous sobbing and wailing of a multitude of damned spirits, useless tears morphed into proliferating ashes of an empty sorrow that would eternally refuse to blossom and bear the fruit of sincere repentance.

"What pain! And you keep adding to it!"

"Yes, until you are weakened and driven out," Peter cut in, stopping the prayers. "You *will* give a time."

Showering the bed with blessed salt, the demons finally screamed they would be gone before the month was out, but not until then.

"You'll *all* be out before November ends? Including the unidentified one?"

"Yes, yes! Damn you!"

"And will the unknown one identify itself before then?"

"If he wants, it's up to him, isn't it?"

"No, it's up to God! Demon, whoever you are, you will be forced to obey!"

"Ow ow ow! Stop your putrid water! Yes, all right! He will name himself, but not now!"

"When?"

"When we're all gone first. Blast it! I didn't want to say that!"

"I bet you didn't. Let's get to it then!"

Now with their principle names revealed and the number of legions disclosed, the demons were in the weakening stage. Peter continued the Rite, skipping to and repeating the passages he found perturbed and hurt them the most. Shackled to the bed, the demons tried to levitate the whole thing. Peter commanded it down. This time they quickly obeyed, sending the bed down on its legs with a metallic crunch, but leaving the young woman unharmed. More screaming, and the vomit flow began, dark grey this time. Greg jumped into action, holding a thick piece of cardboard he had brought with him up behind the book, he thought it might give them some added protection, but their shoes couldn't escape it. Not again! One of the nurses groaned and got ready to mop while Peter commanded it to stop. The flow abruptly ended, faster than ever before. Yes, they were getting weaker. He continued to pummel them with the prayers, ignoring the crew trying to clean up around him and Greg. At this moment, he couldn't get distracted.

While he prayed, the orderlies kept an eye on the patient and cringed as a now familiar sound began. The patient wretched heavily. Her sunken eyes opened then rolled back into her head, then closed tight again. Her jaw dropped open, making her appear like a snake that was about to eat something bigger than its mouth, only … .

"Look out! Somethin's on the way up! What the … ?" The orderly grimaced.

She slowly disgorged a huge dead rat covered in mucous. Five more came, slowly, one after the other. This time the cleaning crew stood back along with the nurses. Bugs were bad enough, but no one wanted to handle *that*!

"What do you think of our little presents?" The demons laughed.

"Aw, you shouldn't have, it's not even my birthday," Peter calmly retorted.

"Ooow! He's got a tongue on him this one," one of the devils noted. "Hey, what are you doing … no no no! Let someone else pick them up!"

"But they were a gift for me, right?"

Greg was stunned to see Peter calmly put on a pair of the crew's rubber gloves and clean up the mess himself, by hand, picking up each dead rat and depositing them in a trash bag without flinching.

"Curses on you! You know exactly how to hurt us! Ow, he's using our tricks against us again!"

Man, that took a strong stomach … oh, right. Greg caught on. The Monsignor was keeping his cool and doing an extra bit of penance. Only, Greg had no idea how much of a penance it was for Peter who absolutely detested rats.

"Um, is that a sign they're leaving," one nurse dared to whisper.

"No," Peter replied, knotting the bag closed and dropping it into the waiting trash can, "just another sick manifestation like the ones before, but not a demonic departure. We'll know it when we see it." He took off the gloves and threw them into the can before the nervous cleaning crew scurried away with it. Might as well take a break, Greg and he could use a clean-up and a change.

"Running away so soon?" The mocking voice sneered.

"Don't you wish," Peter calmly retorted back. "Be silent, and lie still." Making the sign of the cross again, he motioned to everyone the time to take a break had arrived.

Twenty minuets later everyone was cleaned, rehydrated, and ready for the last bout of the day when an unexpected visitor arrived, Mr. Fletcher, who finally had a chance to leave work early and see what progress if any was made, but his wife wasn't sure what to say, she had seen so much. Where on earth could she begin, but taking them into their makeshift dressing-dash-recuperation room off to the side, Peter quickly filled him in.

"Names? Is that all?"

"Mr. Fletcher, that is a huge breakthrough. I also got the number of legions present. We're on our way to beating them down and out."

"*Legions?*"

"Quite a few in fact."

"Tom, dear, there's something else! Missy, she was awake today and was ready to confess to the Monsignor!" Mrs. Fletcher could see the breakthrough even if her husband couldn't understand yet. After all this time of Hell they had been through, he still couldn't get into his head that this would be over before the month was out, it just seemed too surreal, and the demons would then come and admit that? He hadn't seen everything that had happened over the few weeks, having been cooped up with work at the furniture factory, but Peter finally got to show him the video they had captured that day. Tom looked aghast as the last manifestation unfolded on film.

"Great scot … all that was *really* going on … ."

"Yes, I've seen practically everything." Margie nodded solemnly. "It's all true. Speaking of which, the Monsignor and Fr. Simmons were about to start again."

"Er, don't let me hold you up. I'll wait in here … ."

"Are you sure you don't want to come in," Margie prompted, but Tom wasn't about to get in the way of … whatever he could get in the way of.

"All right, let's go back in," Peter announced.

Unable to sit still for long, the muffled howling from the room and the sound of Peter's voice commanding obedience amidst the prayers finally nabbed Mr. Fletcher's curiosity and pulled him to the doorway to peer through the glass pane along with a few of the other nurses on duty in the next ward who couldn't resist the urge to slip away from their repetitive rounds to witness this rare occurrence. Caught between morbid fascination with the proceedings and disgust at the manifestations of preternatural spewing, he was suddenly struck with horror when everyone cried out and ducked with the exception of the Monsignor, and his niece strapped to the bed. The nurses at the door gasped too. No, he wasn't seeing things. The two pens in Dr. Fareed's front whitecoat pocket had jumped out and were whirling above everyone's heads like metallic angry hornets searching for someone to sting or puncture. Tom's knees went limp with the shock, but the sight of Margie cowering on the floor made him take action and he ordered the nurse beside him to open the door. Peter, the only one still standing, turned and forcefully shook his head as he put up his hand, the door must stay shut. The nurse was forced to obey, much to Mr. Fletcher's anxious frustration.

"My wife's in there! I've got to get her out!"

However, the Monsignor simply turned to the patient and doused her with holy water. Tom couldn't make out all the words through the door, but it sounded like a command. The pens dropped like lead, clattering slightly as they hit the floor. Everyone on their knees inside looked up warily, then with relief as they saw the new menace had been speedily dealt with. Tom however got the door unlocked and sprinted in to see if Margie was all right.

"I'm fine, just spooked. This isn't the first time I've seen things go in the air … ."

"Just to remind everyone, they can do this, but usually are not permitted to harm," Peter said aloud, turning to the witnesses. Still, it was only instinctive they all took cover.

"I forgot to leave the pens in my office," Dr. Fareed explained apologetically.

"And I forgot to remind you. I'm as much at fault. Come, let's keep going. Close the door, please."

Tom was now locked inside with them and dreaded what might come next, but he wasn't leaving Margie to face this without him again. They watched as Peter continued despite looking positively drained, the sweat running off his brow and temples, ignoring the screeches and bone-chilling threats made against him. How could Melissa look and sound like *that*? He had seen her in what looked like psychotic breaks, but *this*? That wasn't the girl he knew at all! Just when he thought his psyche couldn't bear it any longer, her sunken eyes shot open, lifeless seething holes of anger.

"Nooooo! I can't take it, he hurts us!"

The long drawn out wail of anguish grated the nerves, but that wasn't the last of it. She quickly shut her eyes and opened her mouth. Everyone in the room expected another appearance of some organic matter, either vomit, fauna or insect, but were rooted to the spot when small blackish green balls of fire issued instead and swirled up to the ceiling, then disappeared through leaving small scorch marks where they had passed. Everyone else except Peter felt on the verge of passing out or running away with the sight of those fireballs. He had the presence of mind to pay closer attention and count what came out, seven, one seemed a bit bigger than the rest. He turned to the patient and began demanding some answers.

"In the names of Jesus Christ and Mary, the Blessed Virgin, was that a departure?"

"Yessssss," a rasping voice answered.

"Who was it? Which of you? Speak!"

"Stílitípota, he would be the first to desert, damn himmmm and his cowardly lot! Nevermind, we are more powerfullll! You won't get us to leavvvvve!"

"God shall decide that. You will obey."

"Not now, not now. Later! Later!"

"Still, seven of you gone, we have reason to celebrate, a little victory party if you will."

While everyone else felt more like running away or passing out than making merry the demons began to howl and curse Peter as he commenced a prayer of thanksgiving for that first sign of departure, God triumphant over His enemies. As the demons wailed their first loss, one of the nurses outside the door quickly ran away, it wasn't long before news of the latest manifestation was making the rounds of the building along with the medication carts. Concluding his prayer, he leaned forward and as usual when ending the ceremony for the day, tapped the possessed on the forehead with his two fingers.

"Enough!"

The screaming stopped. Melissa blinked, looked around confused as she saw herself strapped down. Peter was satisfied, this was the first time she came back coherently rather than fall into a deep sleep.

"Oh … I blacked out again, didn't I? Did I confess?"

"No, I'm sorry, you were stopped. But it's all right, we'll try again next time." Peter motioned for her to be released from her bonds. Confused, she obviously didn't know what had happened. Peter motioned to Greg, it was time they gave the Fletchers some family time with their niece and call it a day.

ଔ ❖ ଵ

Wear and tear. Souls could not be helped nor saved but by wear and tear, but now the hard work, the sacrifices and the agony willingly endured were having an astounding effect, thanks be to God. True to the promise made by The Voice, the progress now experienced in Melissa's case was nothing short of miraculous. On Peter's next trip back to Trenton, she was again coherent and ready to confess again, this time not as downcast. She confided to Peter she felt a bit lighter since his previous visit, and now, was ready. Her tormentors threatened to make an appearance, but a simple command to keep silent was enough to tighten the screws on the occupiers and prevent them from holding her back. Of course, she was more willing this time to be free of her tormentors, her desire to fight this blackness holding her hostage was growing stronger, and that too made a big difference. Of course, there were many tears as she opened the book on the deeds of her past, how she had run away with Ashly, how they got mixed in with a really bad crowd that got them deeper into the occult, not to mention the multiple trips to the abortion mill when a 'problem' needed solving, then, to get dumped after all that, to find herself penniless and alone on the streets, and then, seemingly going insane … yes, there were many tears, but not a little astonishment at how Peter could actually read her right through, but the fact he simply let her talk between the tears, and only stopping to remind her of a forgotten incident, there was no condemnation or harsh rebukes, only … absolution! And, to begin a prayer life with only a few prayers each day for starters as a penance.

"Is … is that … *it*? After all that, that's … *it*? Don't I … need to be punished?"

He handed her more tissues.

"Do you expect me to hit you over the head? Besides, aren't you being harassed enough already? It's time to *heal*."

"Er, now what?"

"Time to begin the healing."

By that, he meant the next round of exorcisms. Unfortunately, the demons didn't let her stay in a coherent state for that, the screeching and the howling resumed. The battle was back on. However, with her conscience now clean, the next departure was almost immediate. A whirlwind of sparks left her mouth similar to what had been witnessed, this time they were purple, and there were more, hundreds, all heading to the ceiling and leaving little scorch marks in their sizzling wake. Peter demanded an answer from one the devils still present and discovered a commanding demon and his soldiers had been forced out. It was Orias and his company of two hundred. How the devils wailed when Peter began another prayer of thanksgiving! Amidst the din, this time it also sounded like they were giving a pep-rally to each other, stoking each other up, until an Arch Demon would make an appearance, striking terror among their own legions with threats of what they would do to them if they dared desert their post. Hell certainly was a kingdom of abject cruelty. The overlords of that realm not only tortured the damned, Peter had seen the demons insult and quarrel with each other to the point of striking blows over who held greater power or positions of command, there was no true fraternity or binding principle among them, save their sole desire to snatch souls and affront their Creator, that single purpose yoked them together and would continue to drive them on until the doomsday trumpets blared and heralded the time for them to be sealed away in their fiery prison for eternity.

Still, it was good to see they were displaying this diabolical morale boosting, it was a sign their hold on their victim was being pressured, sapped. The flip side was this sign of defeat only made them more desperate, compelling them to pull every trick they could at Peter, Greg and his assistants to make them cease and desist their attempts to free the prisoner.

Infestations.

Greg was perturbed by the sound of footsteps in the dead of night, always at three AM, and if it wasn't footsteps, it was the sound of dishes being moved in the kitchen, to find nothing had been touched, or, more disturbing yet, to hear what could only be a fist knocking above his bed, waking him up when he actually could get to sleep. The other assistants found themselves experiencing similar disturbances. A nurse disclosed to a friend that lights were turned on or off without anyone near the switches. Others felt a presence was constantly watching them to where they were starting to feel the effects of Persecution Syndrome, the sense of also having an 'unseen visitor' round the house was another phenomena. The fear was heightened when objects began disappearing in their homes, only to reappear in odd places without a rational explanation to account for it other than sudden onset dementia, or, 'it has to be the exorcisms', a final conclusion that defied all scientific logic and unnerved the once die-hard sceptics. Obsessive nightmares were now a common terror, one orderly was so rattled by the experience of having 'something' stand over him in the bed every night, that his wife finally demanded he stop volunteering. Peter was kept busy blessing holy water and handing out medals to everyone who had finally developed the good sense to take them.

No tactic was left untried. When the demons couldn't inflict terror, they induced frustration and stress over the draining of time and financial means to keep up with unnatural spates in breakages, repairs and replacements. One of the doctors at the hospital would find his clean shirts put away one day would be found the next covered in tiny rust stains or cut marks. That problem was solved by having a few drops of holy water added to each wash. A nurse had nothing but trouble with her car when it was perfectly fine only a week ago, or a bevy of equipment and domestic appliances would break down at once. Medals, blessed salt and little crucifixes were again handed out to be placed on everything that could go haywire. The problem seemed to abate, but the rectory wasn't completely spared despite Peter's vigilance, no doubt all the other exorcisms and the non-stop conversion confessions he was doing in the OR added to their assault: the hot water tank, the washing machine, the new stove oven *and* the fridge: all broke down or literally went *bang* within the space of two days.

"Sakes alive! At this time of year too, me arthritis won't be the better for it," O'Conner whinged, not happy at all, at all with this penitential turn of events.

"We can't even boil a pot for some hot water, but at least the heating is working, and we've got electricity," Mark noted, trying to stay positive.

"Shssssh! Not another word, or that'll be the next t'go!"

"You'd better hurry up Pete, or we'll be reduced to living in the wilderness like St. John the Baptist," Jenkins prodded.

"As long as we don't end up eating locusts, that would be the livin' end," O'Conner quipped, "I've had enough of them flies as it is."

They had been attacked by a freakish appearance of flies a few nights before just as they were about to sit to dinner, in the cold month of November no less, and they didn't seem like the typical big bluebottles that just buzzed around and went for the garbage or the few crumbs on the counter top. These were a particularly annoying species that were small, fast, and diabolically determined. They aimed for the dead centre of their plates and fell into the food, or right into the middle of their drinks and struggled as they drowned, an atypical situation as most flies they ever encountered normally went first for the edges of plates and glasses. Those that didn't kamikaze into their food buzzed into their faces, darting for the corners of their eyelids, their nostrils, and the edges of their mouths. Flapping at them didn't seem to bother them, they hovered around and instantly struck again. If they didn't go for the face they insisted on getting entangled and buzzed around in everyone's hair. The frustrating part, they were too fast and seemed to know what a swatter looked like. They took off the minute Mark was ready to slap them into the buggy netherworld. It reminded Jenkins of the film footage taken of drought ridden Ethiopia with malnourished children sitting motionless in their mother's arms while covered in flies that were left to pester them as it was a wasted effort in trying to brush them away. This was too much.

"That's it! I'm eating out, and so are you," Jenkins declared, throwing down his napkin and scraping back his chair. There was nothing for it but to leave everything on the table as is and simply walk out. After a calming dinner in their favourite greasy spoon all-night diner they sometimes went to the odd time they felt in the need of comfort food indulgence, they returned to find the flies had disappeared with the exception of those few that were floating belly up in their drinks. Of course, everything on the table had to be thrown out, and after Gertie had put together a nice dinner for them too! The waste galled them, but it couldn't be helped.

Yes, Peter wished he could 'hurry up' and end it all, but that was the stresser, this couldn't be hurried up. It had to run its course. Thankfully, he had his 'family banker' to turn to for emergency funding regarding the equipment malfunctions and little Bro was only happy to oblige. Gerry had a messenger quickly send them funds to cover the costs of the much needed appliances and then some with a note telling them to get a whole new furnace while they were at it since that thing probably hadn't been replaced in the last thirty years and due to blow up anyway, and if there was anything else the rectory was in need of, go for broke. Splurge. Peter couldn't help chuckle as he folded up Gerry's note. No, no splurging, just the necessities, but Gerry's cheerful liberality was much appreciated, the extra cash would come in handy if anything else went *whump* or *clank*. He gave him another call to thank him.

"Don't sweat it, Pete. I'm glad I can do something. It makes me feel less useless after all this sitting and lying around. I'll have Leroy drop by and see everything is handled all right." After just getting new appliances for the Holy Bachelors hardly a few months ago, he was worried now with this sudden turn, he wanted to make sure they weren't going too cheap and buying substandard models!

Sure enough, for Gerry's sake Leroy went to check up on them, especially as they were all still left wondering after Peter's 'illness', and enquired if everything had been delivered and in proper working order. As yancy as he was to be around a load of priests at one time, Lee felt better once he arrived, especially as he had promised O'Conner he wouldn't remain a stranger. It was nice to see him again and his old mentor was pleased to give him a tour around their pious abode. There was a bit of banter as they reached the door of their little oratory chapel.

"Oh ho ho! Trying to pull me through the pearly gates are we? Instead of saving me soul, the soles of me feet might blister if I step in there." Lee's voice was laced with mirth.

"Ah sure, you can't blame this old codger for try'n now."

"No, but ye've done you're duty like a man and dragged the horse to the trough. Speaking of which, I'm parched! I'd murder for a cup of tea."

"Ooh, I think it's a drop stronger and more sinful than tea ye're after, but tea is all *ye're* going to get here, you red-headed rake, you!" They both laughed.

Lee actually enjoyed himself that afternoon talking about the Old Country with O'Conner and the hurling legends of his time, the 'gee gees' and the grey hound racing, and a few wise cracks about settling down sometime and that it would be a grand idea having him visit the famed match-making town of Lisdoonvarna, all bantered over copious tea and bickies. O'Conner was sorry to see him go when Lee finally said he had to rush off, he had stayed way too long as it was.

"And remember! Don't stay a stranger."

"I won't. Hey listen, Mum's promised me some *ispini*, black and white puds, *and* a homemade barmbrack express airmail from Shannon sometime this week. How about I stop by and we can pick up where we left off over a bang-up meal? You guys haven't lived until you've eat'n an Irish breakfast."

"Puddin's n' barmbrack! You're on, laddie."

"And no, O King of Kerry, I won't forget the Kerrygold," Leroy promised. As he ran off down the street he gave a cheery-o wave over his shoulder.

"Ah, despite all his failings he's got a good heart that one, it's the hurt he's been through that's caused most of them. He's looking for comfort and acceptance in all the wrong ways and places," O'Conner wistfully noted to the others as he waved Lee off.

"I know. Isn't that why most fall astray," Peter reflected.

"Aye, that's true, but I'd give anythin' to see that one in particular straighten himself out, for good."

"There's always hope," Peter reminded him as they went back inside.

Repairs done, fly traps set everywhere along with medals and crucifixes, the frustrating manifestations could be tolerated, but the final threats came when the netherworld now tried to invisibly influence those with authority on earth to stop the proceedings at Trenton. The director of the hospital had a sudden change of mind to call a halt to the whole thing as the hospital was turning into a circus while all this was going on, but then was persuaded by Dr. Fareed to give the priests the few weeks they needed. By now the doctor was fully convinced this was not a case of mental insanity, but the director wasn't, at this point it was nothing but mass hallucinations to him and indignant Fareed would allow himself to get fooled despite the seeming evidence presented so far regarding the strange vomit samples and the charred ceiling. Why? Vomit is vomit, and didn't the priests use incense on occasion? No doubt the smoke from it had affected the chemical make up of the paint on the ceiling, that was all. The director ordered the ceiling to be repainted before the next session. Apparently, he hadn't seen all the tapes, maybe not at all, or he wouldn't be like this. Seeing Mr. Lieberman in this mood, Fareed approached the situation carefully: the patient's 'voices' had promised to end it soon, which was a good sign, and they did want to put the health of the patient first? Besides, if what the voices said didn't pan out, at least mass hallucinations could be proved then. At last, the director was forced to agree, the welfare of the patient was paramount, and while his tolerance was wearing thin, it would be worth seeing this to the end if nothing but for the satisfactory vindication in proving the priests frauds that had duped his staff with their macabre rituals and induced this mass hysteria.

The director wasn't the only one who wanted an end, some unknown troublemakers had called the local bishop and spread lies about how an invalid rite was taking place, which was immediately brought to the attention of Archbishop Morrison, who also was having second thoughts about having granted permission for Peter to go ahead with the Rite in the first place, but after an official summons to appear before him and explain what was happening along with the latest batch of tapes, the lies told against them were exposed. Even so, if what was revealed was true, they must finish with all of this, and the sooner the better. News was spreading and it was creating quite a stir, and he didn't want this added publicity.

Peter expected this trouble, but what worried him more was the extra time this all took, having to go clarify things with the Archbishop when he was already stretched thin as it was trying to keep up with his own parish work. He didn't doubt what the devils were forced to reveal about their departure, that was one truth they always had to reveal, but perhaps their departure could happen sooner rather than later. He prayed it might. He was getting exhausted! As it was, thankfully, the deliverances were still happening and in the same spectacular manner, not an exorcism session went by with Melissa without something being chased out. Amdusias and Moloch left with their legions in a dizzying whirlwind of green and black sparks, turning the ceiling almost black despite the new paint job. Astaroth and his armies were the next to battle, but they too were sent packing. The only difference in the last departure, while everyone else saw sparks Peter could see little flaming beasts and monsters of all descriptions, similar to what he had seen in the Abyss. They wailed or shook their fists at him as they were forced to flee under his command, the tables had been turned, a welcome change after the treatment they gave him not too long ago! However, one spark straggled behind and seemed to grow. A frightful creature with a long snout with boar tusks, sharp claws and a head sprouting crescent moon horns gave Peter a parting shot only he could see and hear:

"You may have gotten rid of us, you black robe son of a whore, but remember! This is a mighty one left, and he will not be gotten rid of so easily!"

Peter made the sign of the cross and the beast quickly went shrieking towards the ceiling like the rest.

Yes, how could he forget? There was one left still holding the patient bound through the sortilege embedded in her stomach, the last thing that had to be dispelled, once that was done, her deliverance would be complete, but before that could happen, the unnamed one had to be revealed.

The Showdown, that's what it quickly became known as whispers spread through the hospital halls. One demon left. The atmosphere was electric as everyone wondered when 'It' would name itself. This time, a few of the doctors who were not on duty elsewhere insisted on watching. While Peter was reticent, he didn't want to make waves in case they caused trouble for him now that he was nearing the final stretch, and at last said they could watch after he had given the usual warnings of what to expect. As Melissa was now coherent every time they arrived, she was permitted to remain sitting and untied like any of the harmless patients there until she displayed anything preternatural and required restraining, but that proved to be a costly lesson as she quickly flew into a rage the minute the priests entered. Trying to get at Peter but halted in her tracks, she managed to strike one of the doctors and gave him a bloody nose.

"My, my. Slipping up today, aren't you?"

The voice this time wasn't rasping guttural, or animalistic. It sounded androgynous yes, but clear, articulate, a cultured tone was audible, but haughty, dripping with disdain for all present, for Peter in particular as she turned her head askance and eyed him with a penetrating look.

He knew that voice, he knew who was speaking to him, he had hoped other wise, that it was another demon ... the flies, weren't they a clue? But no ... .

"No, not Beelzebub. I am *Magister caput! You out of all here know who I am*. All Hell shakes before me! I am the the real First, and for *you*, I have saved the best for last! *Hold fast your sight upon me and despair!*"

Peter's very soul began to freeze. This was one thing he had not yet told anyone whom he disclosed about his experience of Hell, the sight of the Beast, the fallen seraph himself. His presence was all pervasive in that realm of iniquity, looming, gigantic, titanic, seated on a flaming throne forged of lost souls from the hottest flames of hell, not one of the damned could escape the sight of him no matter the dungeon, niche or pit they were thrown into. The worst of all tortures, it was a terrorizing travesty, a demonic mimesis of the Eternal mystic vision of God in Heaven that could not be fully explained, and now, to hear that voice, to feel that harrowing presence again! It hit fast. No wonder! He saw the same punishing vision directly within the possessed, he was not able to turn the Darkness off as usual, he was forced to see this, and the memories flooded back, the sense of desolation, despair, the crushing emptiness ... it nearly paralysed him, sapped him of all courage were it not for the one simple prayer he quickly made, begging the Mother of God for help, for yes, he could still seek help! He was not cut off or damned as the Arch-Fiend would have him feel. Hope, he could still hope, and the will to love was not taken away. His courage was restored.

"Get thee behind me, Satan! Enough with your infectious poison! Drink it yourself!"

He dashed holy salt, causing the Fiend to roar. The very walls shook, several cried out in fright. Those present who held any religious belief couldn't help but utter prayerful exclamations of terror. However, the scene of the throne visible only to Peter disappeared. He now held the crucifix aloft.

"Enough with your tricks! You, who think you are so mighty have done the most stupid thing and have revealed yourself. Why, you could have hung on a few days extra at least pretending to be who I thought you were, but no, to get at me, you have only weakened yourself, and I hadn't even started the Rite yet. It's *you* who has slipped up."

"I have revealed myself only because I wanted to!"

"You *wanted* to slip up? What an answer! Again, not very bright, but we can't accuse anyone of throwing away eternal happiness of being intelligent."

"You dare burn me with that! Shut your mouth! And who are *you*, to come and fight with me? How dare you mock me, you swine? Ah! But *you* can dare, *you have been given much.* No no no! She's coming! The Great Lady! The Queen! All right! All right! I am forced to respect you and be more polite. But no matter, this wretched body is still mine, this little wretch gave herself to me! I will keep her!"

"She is no longer yours! Her soul is clean! She is a child of God, and you will not have her!"

"But I still have her right now. I am not afraid of you!"

"Nor I of you!"

Peter began the Rite and the Fiend stopped arguing, but the cadaverous crone-like appearance they had seen many times before now settled on the patient, making her frightful to look at. The room shook again. Peter ignored the phenomena, hitting the Fiend with all the prayers and commands at his disposal, repeating those that seemed to cause the girl pain, which was only a ruse, it was the demon that was feeling the spiritual blows. This time, instead of pushing for a name as he usually would, Peter demanded the sortilege be vomited up. Melissa would try to sit up and do as he commanded, but nothing would appear, only a long, dry wretching occurred. That was a welcome change after everything they had been bombarded with out of her mouth, but the sortilege had to come up, that would be the visible sign of departure, and so he continued the Rite when it looked like the Fiend wasn't about to relinquish the gateway just yet, hitting him further. Peter eventually stopped again to demand the demon to depart and throw up the sortilege.

"Ow, you know how to lash the whip! But no! I'm not leaving!"

"Look upon the Cross and leave!"

"Away with that! No, I've become too comfortable here."

"The Virgin Mary commands you to leave."

"Yes, but not yet! The moment isn't here yet. I may stay a little longer. I like making things difficult!"

"Of course you do, but you won't stay for long. You will be forced to leave."

"Maybe, and I must admit, you certainly know how to hit back, but I also know how to hit back. Remember that!"

"Enough of your idle threats."

"Oh, they aren't idle. As much as I am fond of idleness, this time I am not indulging in that pretty little vice. This cat wants to play with its prey!"

"Silence!"

No point dragging out the conversation and giving the Fiend any ammunition. He continued with the Rite. The battle continued with the Prince of Darkness making all manner of bestial sounds and compelling the girl to writhe in her restraints. Although sweat-soaked and exhausted, Peter refused to give in. Everyone was feeling the strain, the energy was also sapped out of them with the invisible soul-struggle, and at first they thought the stickiness they felt in the room was a result of the body heat of so many stressed out witnesses present, but soon realised this was no ordinary humidity, not when they began to wipe the sweat off their faces and temples to discover their tissues or sleeves were stained a deep, watery red.

Gasps of horror and cries of panic interrupted the proceedings as it quickly flashed across their minds some rapid, deadly viral outbreak could be the cause, a rational conclusion reached by those employed in the health profession and cooped up in a hospital for most of their waking hours, but the true horror began to sink in when the very air was humid with a vermilion mist that began to seep into and stain their clothes, condense on cold surfaces, steadily tickle down the walls and gradually puddle on the floor. Who knew what they were breathing in? There was an exodus for the door. The strange thing was Peter and Greg were left unaffected, nothing stained their white surplices, or dripped from their temples other than normal sweat. Farreed requested a surgical mask and went back inside. The religious articles and pictures the priests brought with them were also untouched and not dripping with the red condensation. This was definitely not anything natural. Fareed pulled himself together. After everything they had seen, this wasn't going to harm them, only frighten them. Whatever it was, it had succeeded there! Still, he played it safe and ordered those who had left to quarantine themselves into the other room until he collected a sample and had a nurse run it off to the nearest lab. He didn't want a complete chemical analysis right now, just please tell us it was something non-toxic, and hopefully, not from a living thing … . There was relief when the first observations came back: it wasn't blood, but definitely something once living … it looked like a species of plant, maybe an algae, at least from their first quick inspection under the microscope. Fareed collected a few more samples.

"Algae? Like Red Tide algae? Is it … poisonous?" Mr. Fletcher was afraid to say it as his wife quickly took off her jacket, the doctors, nurses and orderlies were hurriedly tugging off their lab coats and looking each other over to see where else it had seeped in.

"We won't know if it's a dangerous biological contaminant until the full report is in, but after everything we've been through, I doubt this will cause any harm, no matter how bad it looks. I have to … wait a minute." The doctor looked down at his clothes.

Everyone looked down, stunned to see the red had completely disappeared from their clothes and skin. Only the samples scraped up for the labs remained. Peter took a quick look inside the possessed patient's room, it was gone there too. Not a trace of the red remained anywhere. Clever trick. A new one for the books. The Fiend managed to stop the Rite with this new manifestation. After a much needed break, Peter was ready for the next round, although by now he had lost many of his curious extra witnesses. Eventhough they knew now it wasn't blood, their original impression was enough to shake them. They had seen enough and couldn't take it any more. He was back to the small band of old faithfuls save one or two new faces who were also determined to see it out. As the door to the patient's room was unlocked, they heard a growling in the hall. Turning to look, a huge black mastiff was standing near the end, baring its teeth.

"Ooooh! The Master's gonna get you all now!"

The patient a few doors down that often made faces or cursed at them was gleeful with the panic. He hopped up and down with vindictive excitement. Normally Peter would silence him with the sign of the cross, but at least he was locked away, this dog-thing wasn't. There was a scramble back into the other two rooms, someone knocked over the video camera in the panicked rush to close the doors. Just in time! The mastiff howled and ran at them, snapping at the heels of the nurse who nearly didn't make it, and bounded front paws up on the door to the room Peter had gone in, barking, howling, scratching at the door. Peter commanded it to stop with his crucifix in hand as he would with the demons of the possessed. The dog snarled but dropped back down to the ground on all fours, fell out of view. They could hear its nails *clickity, clickity, clickity, clickity* as it ran away.

"Whew! That was close! Quick! As much as I want to keep this door closed, we can't have that thing loose in the hospital," Dr. Fareed cried out.

Peter flung open the door and ran down the hall, catching sight of someone and asking where the dog went.

"Dog? What dog? I didn't see anything!"

"You must have," panted the doctor, running up behind Peter. "It went down this corridor and you couldn't possibly have missed it."

"But … but I didn't! All due respect, I don't know *what* you saw, there's no dog here."

Peter calmly placed his hand on the doctor's shoulder.

"Come, it was another trick."

"But we all saw it! It wasn't a hallucination!"

"No, but it probably wasn't any normal dog. Hopefully, that will be the last of it. Come, we have work to finish."

There was a low, vindictive laugh from the bed.

"How do you like my pet?"

"Do you expect me to pay a compliment? You won't get one."

Instead, The Rite was resumed, the last bout of the evening. Half an hour more of battling with the basic shrieking and roars, but enough to drain the last of his energy. Just as he was about to tap her forehead, the Fiend threw back the girl's head with a chilling laugh.

"You may be finished for the day, but I'm not finished with you! I never sleep! You are one of my worst enemies among the miserable humans on earth. My power is great! I will make you bleed!"

"You can only do what God permits, and as I wish to do His will, you cannot harm me but only make me more obedient to Him."

"Oh, but that's the beauty of it! I, the Great Satan, what don't I plan to do to you! I shall torment you and all you love and hold dear. I will prevent you for doing anything against me again! I will tear everything apart!"

"Silence! Enough!"

He tapped her on the forehead. Enough with the scaremongering for one day.

∛❖√

"Petey! Petey! Petey! Welcome aboard!"

"Hey Sinbad, it's good to see you too. Ready for Thanksgiving?"

"Yo ho *ho* and a bottle of *rum*!"

"That's the spirit, you little pirate. Just don't make the chair cushions part of the menu, okay?"

Peter smiled as he dropped his overnight case to give the family pet a few rubs on his feathery head. As usual, the steely grey parrot knew company was coming with all the fuss in the manor kitchen and was perched on the bannister post in the entrance hall waiting to see who would turn up. Peter was quickly greeted by someone else eager to see him.

"Peter! You're here! I'm so glad."

"Hi Mom! What's for dinner? Spaghetti!"

"Be quiet, you silly bird, I wasn't talking to you." Sophia sighed as she turned to Sinbad, who began bobbing his head. He certainly did know what was going on and had an answer for everything most of the time, even dragging up phrases heard years ago. To hear Gerry's ten year old voice again! Peter laughed. He forgot how much fun it was having the bird around. He gave his mother a hug, took off his coat and let the jabberer clamber onto his shoulder before they went in, but his brother heard the commotion and wheeled out to greet them.

"Pete! Long time no see! Whoa." Gerry stopped in his tracks as he looked up to see Peter's hair. His brother just ignored the reaction, he was used to it by now.

"Hi, Bro. Did you think I'd miss the gathering of the crew?"

"With your line of work these days, I wouldn't be surprised if you got held up. But c'mon, don't let *me* hold us up," Gerry continued, snapping out of his unintentional fit of staring. "We're having the big spread in the cozy comfort of the Rose Room."

"Is Mrs. Hunt coming?"

"No, her children came to visit, so she's decided to stay in and have dinner at her place, so you can rest easy, no unhitching paintings tonight."

Sophia smiled before continuing. "Lottie and Tom are on their way, but Kathy's staying with her family."

"How is she?"

"Worn to a frazzle! But she's so excited Gerry's been given the all clear to try apartment living again, so she was very busy getting whatever she needed to get done, done," Sophia filled in. "She's planning a house warning dinner, just for the few of us, with Mrs. Moritz's help of course."

Peter smiled to himself. Looked like Kathy got her sticky cherubs up on the ceiling at last. He couldn't say anything of course. A secret was a secret.

"We agreed she needed a break and insisted she should spend tonight with her family, it's really been good of her running down here as often as she has, it was time her family got to see a bit of her too."

"So, just us tonight."

"Yep, just us handful of scallywags. I must confess Bro, I'm going to sin. Gluttony to be exact. You know how I am about Mom's special walnut stuffing, and her pumpkin pie, she's made *three* of them," Gerry informed with a grin, wheeling the chair around and leading the way.

"Don't mind him Peter, not all of them are for tonight. One is for you to take to the Holy Bachelors," his mother explained as they followed along, but slowly pulling out of Gerry's earshot for a moment.

"How's he doing," Peter asked under his breath.

"Today is a good day, he's been looking forward to seeing you, and Thanksgiving of course. Other days … ." She turned her hand, just so-so.

"That bad?"

"It's touch and go, but come," she quickly changed subject, quickening their pace before he overheard them, "give us all your news," she said in a normal tone as they entered the room and found a comfy seat.

"Yeah, how are the Bachelors doing? Did Lee drop by?"

"Yes, he checked up on us, and then some."

Peter had to tell them about Leroy's recent visit. In fact, the promised care package from Ireland arrived, and he found out what real *ispíní* and Clonakilty puddings were supposed to taste like, for the blarney-brimming rogue had dropped by again to give them all that bang-up breakfast, or rather lunch as he seemed to have been informed about their customary Thanksgiving lunch, the only time the priests could celebrate together considering all their different schedules before getting pulled away by someone or something in the parish. Gerry laughed, confessed he told Lee about their yearly lunch, then nagged his big brother if he was going to fit in his dinner after Lee's hearty interruption to the day, knowing those breakfasts were practically the same in England, especially if it was the full mixed grill kind. Fried eggs, sausages, slices of back bacon, black and white puddings, which were larger slices of blood and white sausages, baked beans, a lamb chop or two, grilled mushrooms, a bit of liver for those who appreciate that sort of thing, two halves of a grilled tomato with a choice in the side serving of toast, scones, rock buns, or in this case Leroy's mother's home made barmbrack, a fruity loaf that was sliced, toasted and smathered with plenty of butter, all washed down with the obligatory pot or two of tea. Oh yes, all of that, Peter nodded, but not to worry, he told Lee not to give him much, Fr. O'Conner was happy to take what wasn't wanted or the others couldn't fit in. Gerry chuckled.

"I bet he was. How is he? By the way, I hope the Bachelors aren't on their own tonight."

"Oh no, Jenkins is staying with the vets at the VA hospital dinner. Mark on the other hand was invited by one of the kids from the youth group to go to his home, er, well, all the parents invited him, so he had to draw lots to see who to go with so he didn't upset them all and get accused of having any favourites among the kiddies. O'Conner got a ton of invites from his 'biddies' as he calls them, but decided to come with me."

"Where is he then? Did he change his mind? He knows he's more than welcome," Sophia replied.

"That was the plan until Lee insisted he joined him and his friends from Galway, so he couldn't refuse."

"Really? I know Leroy had his own plans with his friends, but to have a man of the collar around?" She was pleasantly surprised.

"You know how we all got on with him at school, he was a lot of fun," Gerry reminded her. "I think Lee's making an honoured exception in his case."

"That's okay then, as long as he's not on his own, that would be just awful, as bad as being left alone at Christmas."

"The thing is they don't celebrate Thanksgiving in Ireland, but Lee insisted on having a spread since he is also one hundred percent American as well as one hundred percent Irish, as he says. Although I can't help think they're going to end up freezing the turkey dinner," Peter noted, "because I heard O'Conner asking him as they left if there was any chance of having a few slices of pud with it, and maybe another sausage, and a piece of that, what was it? Barmbrack."

Gerry found that funny. It looked like Fr. O'Conner was going to get another breakfast for dinner. The real kicker was it would probably be the tamest dinner party Leroy ever had considering a priest was joining. That wasn't the end of Peter's news.

"You know, the Jersey mob boss kept his word and sent a turkey to the rectory. It's stuck in the freezer for now since we can't cook it yet. Might was well save it for Christmas, or give it to the sisters."

"You aren't the only one. Guess what's ending up on our table tonight. Kathy's family got a mob gobbler too." Gerry didn't know whether to look miffed or amused as his mother shot them both a quick 'don't-you-dare-let-your-father-know-anything' look.

"Sorry! Just finishing up an old stogie. No no, don't stand up," the Captain apologised as he entered smelling of cigars and giving Peter a welcoming pat on the back before taking a gander at his hairline. "Ho! Look at you! Now you're *really* starting to look like a chip off the old masthead! How long've you been here?"

"Hello! Hi! How are you!"

"Sinbad! Ow! Not in my ear. Hi Dad, only a few minutes. I was just telling everyone what the Bachelors are up to."

"Yo ho *ho* and a bottle of *rum*!"

"I don't think they were up to *that*, but the bird's got the right idea." The Captain chuckled. "I'd love a drink, and I'm sure you all would too."

The company was complete when Lottie and Tom arrived, apologising for being a little late, but they couldn't help it, they hit every red light in the city. They were relieved to see everyone was still enjoying the cocktail round and the first course hadn't been served yet. There was so much to catch up on and chat about, news from the offices to the latest doings at Kathy's gallery. Oh yes, Peter wanted to know how it was going since he had missed quite a bit there. Gerry said he wished he could have gone too, but the doctors wouldn't allow late night excursions for him like that at the time, but at least he had some pictures he could show him, thanks to Katherine's cousin. Gerry was wondering how the old bottle factory would work out as a modernistic addition, he was a bit worried to tell the truth, but he couldn't help but be surprised judging from the photos. Lottie jumped up to get them. Peter put down his glass to take a look.

"Oh yes, it's surprising, not a *drabby* modern, if you get what I mean," Lottie confirmed.

The only artistically grungy aspect of the new section were the bottling machines taking up most of the ground floor space, but it polished up nicely with a new paint job, the varnished floors, the interior brick walls painted out with crème and golden hues, the iron stair case painted a glossy forest green like its twin on the other side of the gallery complete with refurbished brass handrails, while Katherine's adjustable curtain wall idea featuring opulent silk brocades softened up the place immensely even with all the bottling contraptions and tied the décor in with her French setting next door. The fantastic part, instead of having potted ferns to liven the building, she had planters of full grown flowering vines ordered in specially that were trained up brass chains to the ceilings. The flowers on them were heavenly Lottie agreed, her favourites were the fluffy purple ones, and the trumpet blossoms, although how they were going to keep the creeping vines trimmed and out of the wiring was anyone's guess. Still, it was a sight. The only thing, the idea of studio lights as seen in movie shoots were a little too hot for the place. With the winter coming it wouldn't be too much of a problem, they would save on heating, but the summer would be another matter. She could guess that the climate control system would end up working overtime to keep the place at an even temperature, so Katherine admitted she may have to put in different lighting eventually, but it was one way to get the 'Harvey Dent' section ready in time and in an *avant garde* kind of way.

"Does she still have all the bottles?"

Lottie laughed.

"Oh Petey! Wait for it! Kathy never thought she'd see it happen, but Olivia had a plan for them suitable for an art gallery. She decided they would make great curiosity pieces to sell in the gift shop. The clear lemonade bottles have a small print of a famous masterpiece capped in them, but the way they're rolled up inside, you don't know what you're going to get until you buy one."

"That's a bright idea. What about the root beer ones?"

"I don't know if you'll approve, but they're the fortune cookie editions," Tom added. "Some have a wise quote or a fortune placed in them like 'Confucius says' or some old proverb."

"Also quotes by famous authors, that sort of thing, and don't worry, some Scripture quotes made it in too," Sophia quickly contributed with a smile.

Peter couldn't help but be amused by the cleverness of it. The funny part was his father pointed out that people's curiosity got the better of them and the bottles were flying off the shelves like hot cakes Katherine said, one would swear they held booze. The Gallery Gang was getting a kick about how successful their new bottling operation was running. Gerry shared in the buzz as he had asked Kathy to get him one of the lemonade bottles. What did he end up uncapping? *The Scream* by Edvard Munch.

"Ouch! You hate that series," Peter recalled.

"I know! With so many, she had to pick *that* one. Psycho bottle won out. Of all the luck!"

"Never mind, she left us a few more so we could have some fun tonight at dinner. You'll have another chance," the Captain told him.

"Talk about psycho, wait 'till you hear about her artist. Kathy will probably be miffed at us for telling it first, but," Lottie trailed.

"You mean the 'Palette Knife Prince'?"

"The very same. Here goes: Kevin, knowing the man has a screw loose, tried to slip him his medication in a drink, it didn't work, Denninger obviously left the drink somewhere while talking to someone. An hour later the man had a complete breakdown, thought the place was invaded by body-snatching lizard people who found out where he was and began running around like a lunatic trying to pull his artwork off the security tripwires in an effort to save them from the alien thieves! Kevin and the guards chased him and eventually got him cornered," Lottie related, wide eyed with the remembrance.

"Yep, it certainly made the evening, um, unforgettable," Tom continued. "Poor guy! Harmless enough, but definitely went off the reservation somewhere. Esther had to call for the cavalry, aka an ambulance."

"Is he all right," Peter wondered. "That must have been a shock for Kathy too! I hope the evening wasn't a failure."

"Apparently, Denninger is currently undergoing therapy, and his latest work was pronounced 'the créme-de-la créme of genius' by the house critic, a rare compliment coming from Horace the Horrible, with the result reserves have been placed on everything the Prince showed, so I guess it went all right. All's well that ends well as they say, although I'm glad the next artist sounds more down to earth," Gerry concluded.

"Yes, she's a vegetarian," Lottie added with a nod.

"Fifteen men on a dead man's chest, yo ho *ho* and a bottle of *rum*!"

"He hasn't sung that in ages, and now, he's been singing it all day. Sinbad, sush!" Sophia shook her head. "He's gone morbid."

"I think he found out you were stuffing a turkey," Gerry whispered over to her, "you know how he gets about that."

"Man overboard!"

"All right, that's it. While I and Lottie start getting the dishes up, could someone please put him in his play pen? We can't have him see the roast you know. Off to the brig he goes."

"Argh! Brig! No brig!" The feathered family member flap-jumped off Peter's shoulder and tried to make a fast waddling run for it along the back of the sofa, but Peter knew all his tricks and scooped him up.

"Sorry, to Purgatory you must be sent. But we'll leave you out for dessert."

"Sinbad, cookie?"

"Yeah, you can have a cookie, maybe two. It is Thanksgiving after all. I'll be back in a minute."

Peter took the captive to the 'brig', a window room that had been converted into a climate controlled aviary for the spoiled bird beside the great conservatory complete with branches, birdy treats and every parrot gnaw-toy money could buy. The way that featherball gave out about getting locked up everyone who didn't know better would swear he was getting thrown into a torture chamber, but being a people bird, it was the company he missed when getting sent to detention. Peter placed him up on the nearest branch and turned on the radio system they got just for him. He liked the classical station.

"Nice, they're playing *The Nutcracker*, one of your favourites."

Sinbad bobbed his head in time to the music.

"Cookie! Mmm!"

"I know, just give me a sec."

"Cookie! Yum yum! Cookie!"

"Avast matey! You need to learn the virtue of patience." Peter opened the cabinet where the seed was stored and retrieved Sinbad's favourite treat they had on hand in case they needed to bribe him into the brig, oatmeal raisin to be exact. "See? One, two, into the bowl they go."

Sure enough, the parrot still had the quirky habit of crumbling up the things just to get at the raisins. Holding a cookie in one claw, he proceeded to break it up and search for the dried fruit, which he chewed very very carefully, the pupils of his yellow eyes narrowing as he savoured the shrivelled delights hidden within. The funny part, if they gave him a dish piled full of raisins he wouldn't touch them. Having them served up all-you-can-eat fashion wasn't quite like wasting some perfectly good cookies. Maybe they just didn't taste the same without getting baked into sugary oatmeal. He stopped munching and dropped his treat.

"Oopsie! Man overboard!"

Peter picked it up for him, checking to make sure it didn't fall into anything unmentionable. Sinbad promptly dropped it again.

"Cookie! Fall down, go boom."

"That's your fault. You're loco, you know that?"

"Man overboard! Davy Jones' locker!"

"I rest my case. Unless, you're doing this just to keep me here, you sly, cookie crumbling Einstein. Okay, I gotta go. If you drop it this time, you'll have to fetch it yourself." Peter chuckled as he picked it up again. Sinbad took the treat with his beak and placed it in his claw.

"Bye bye. And don't drop it!"

Peter could hear the cookie go splat as he closed the brig door behind him. Peter shook his head. Sinbad was definitely in one of his weirdo moods.

On his way back to the family gathering the place suddenly erupted with the ringing of house phones. Uh oh, someone forgot to take one off the hook. As can happen with those who own a dynamic non-stop global business, the family never got a call at home unless there was something wrong and the Captain, or he and Gerry were needed to sort something out when they weren't working in the offices. For that reason nobody really liked answering the phones, especially this time of year. They could never forget the Christmas one of their cargo flagships got blown off course and sank during a major storm off the coast of Cornwall, whew! Thankfully, the crew where all rescued, but the cargo was practically a total loss save a few containers that washed up on shore and didn't get scavenged by the beach combers. Despite having full insurance, what a mess to sort out! The Captain was fuming for months. Hopefully, nothing that drastic was awaiting them on the line. It had to be someone calling to wish them all a happy Thanksgiving, but what bad timing, to call just as they were about to sit to dinner. The Captain was not going to be too happy about that either, especially if it turned out to be Aunt Penelope who was presently in Austria visiting their relatives. She was a dear, but she could be a proper do-as-I-say-don't-do-as-I-do terror when it came to the phone. If they called, she would promptly cut them short after ten minutes saying she had something to do, or they had caught her at a bad time, but when *she* decided to call, she just *had* to drop every tit-bit of news and gossip like an avalanche. She would never get off the phone no matter how many hints were let slip they had been talking for almost two hours well past the polite time of evening. If it was her, at least it would be a harmless enough call. Maybe she was dying to tell them all about the latest doings at cousin Heinrick's ski lodge, or some ball in Vienna. Peter suddenly got an odd inkling … . Lottie came flying out to find him.

"Petey! Quick! It's Leroy, he needs to talk to you! It's bad news!"

"Why? What's wrong?"

"Fr. O'Conner, he's just been taken to the hospital!"

Peter quickened his pace and picked up the phone in the hall, Gerry was on the line in the Rose Room, trying to calm down an upset Leroy.

"Pete, I'm glad I could get a hold of you! I'm sorry to trouble ye all, but it's urgent!"

"It's all right, Lee. Slow down, tell me what happened."

"We were havin' a grand old time, me friends brought their instruments, an' then we found out Father could play the fiddle and knew a jig or two, we were having a crackin' *ceili* session … he felt ill all of a sudden, complained of a thumpin' headache before slumping over," Leroy broke off. Gerry continued for him.

"They thought it was a heart attack at first, but the paramedics said it was a stroke." Gerry gave the name of the hospital.

"Yeah, I'm heading there now," Leroy cut back in.

"I'm on my way Lee, hang in there. I'll see you soon."

There was a quick gathering in the hallway as soon as the phones were hung up. Peter apologised to everyone, but he had to go, and fast.

"Don't worry about us, son, we know you're needed. Do you want us to come with you?"

"No, but thank you for offering. It's all right, please, try and eat your dinner. I'll call when I get some news."

After a quick hug for his mother and sister, he grabbed his coat while his father helped him out with his cases and a reminder that if he needed anything, to let them know. Thanking him again, he got in the car and sped down the driveway and out onto the road.

He mechanically went through the motions of keeping the car moving and manoeuvring it within its lane. His prayerfully distracted thoughts were duly disrupted by the red and blue flashing glare of the Sunoco Special behind him. Oh no. Holiday speed trap. He checked the speedometer. Stupid! Even if he was distracted and didn't deliberately speed, he was at fault. Still, he was in a desperate hurry, and now this! Peter pulled over. After all the times in the rigs racing Gerry cross country and never getting caught, and now tonight of all nights to get stopped within a few miles from the old homestead. The famous Ben Hur had just become a Blue Light Special and about to receive a driving award. Payback time, but what lousy timing it was. Patience. Just grit your teeth and take your punishment. He got out his documents, rolled down the window, put his hands on the steering wheel and waited for the officer to demand the expected.

"Well, well. Lookie here, all ready for me. So, I suppose I don't have to ask you if yah knew how fast you were going."

"Er, I didn't, but I do now."

"Wise guy, eh? I'll have a look at those, if you don't mind." Peter handed over the documents. "And what's here with all the get up? Costume party somewhere? Halloween's long over yah know," he jibed, having noticed his collar. "I sure hope you weren't drinkin' before you got behind that wheel."

Obviously, the cop was not in the best of moods having to work Thanksgiving night.

"Were you drinking?"

"Just a small glass of port, but I didn't get to finish it."

"Yeah, right. Bummer when that happens." The cop got out his officious-looking notebook. Uh oh, here it comes, on top of a driving award, he might end up having to take a breathalyser and walk the line to boot. The officer grimly looked over the documents. He went back to the squad car, then returned after the registration was checked.

"So, you *are* a minister. Explains the get up, I thought you were at a costume party."

"No, just about to have dinner and then got an emergency call, a hospital call in fact. I was in a hurry and didn't watch the speed."

"Uh huh. Wait a minute … you ain't from the same Reinolds who live about these parts now, are yah? The shipping family?"

"Yes. The very same."

"I'll be! I've heard plenty about you at the station! We have church-going boys on the force you know. You *are* the exorcist priest, right?"

"As it so happens … ."

"Shucks! Aw, you do know you were going well over the limit, but seeing it's an emergency an' all. Sick call you said?"

"That's right, a good friend of mine." Peter told him the hospital.

"Tonight of all nights too. Say no more, stick close behind me. Me an' my partner will get you there fast."

The officer quickly handed him his documents and jumped back into the squad car. Within seconds the cops drove by him in a red and blue flash with sirens blaring allowing Peter to officially floor it. What started as an embarrassing disaster was turning out in his favour. He not only escaped getting a driver's award, he had a police escort. Thank you Divine Providence! He was back in New York in record time, the officers clearing a path for him straight to the hospital doors.

"Thanks very much, your timely escort is greatly appreciated."

"Don't mention it! Now don't let us hold yah, after getting yah here."

Peter wished them a Happy Thanksgiving, he wished he could give them something, anything as a thank you, then remembered the bags of blessed miniature crucifixes and medals he had in his case. "For the guys in the station, you too if you want some."

"Er, gee thanks, the guys will appreciate this."

Peter was about to rush off, but was impelled to turn and say something: "By the way, congratulations! Don't worry, everything will be fine, Eggy will come safely through. Although it *is* high time you think about a few respectable names, and soon I might add. Excuse me, I have to go. God bless." Thanking them again, Peter quickly made his way inside the building.

"What the … ? Geeze, Marv. That's weird. Did you tell him?"

"No! Didn't say a thing! And you certainly didn't, you never left the car."

But how did he know? It was a prankish joke to call his expectant bundle of joy something ridiculous before he and the missus could decide on something more appropriate, they had no intention to doom the kid to a life of misery. Eventually, what started as something funny got his wife to obsessing they shouldn't make fun like this in case something could go wrong … .

With that, a call came in from dispatch alerting them that Marv's wife had just gone into labour: Eggbert was on his way, two weeks early! Holy … !

"Wait 'til the guys hear this!"

"I know, and, we're gonna be more popular than the doughnut shop tomorrow when they find out about these medal things, they're all gonna want one!"

"I'm glad we have them, they never woulda believed we almost ticketed the Monsignor of Manhattan."

"Good thing we didn't," Marv replied as they sped away. "He was on a mission from God."

After his experiences of running for sick calls and mercy missions, Peter knew his way around a number of the hospitals of the city and in all haste went to the Emergency Admissions desk where he was certain to find Leroy. His hunch was correct, Leroy was in the visitor's area, all fidgety, jigging his leg as he sat waiting for him to arrive.

"Pete! Ye must've been given wings! How did ye get here so fast?"

"Divine Providence and the Boys in Blue, I'll tell you in a minute. How is he?"

"I dunno yet, they're still working on him in there." Lee gave a quick nod to the emergency room. "Of course, they don't want to say much to me, not being family an' all that official coddology."

Peter gave him a reassuring pat on the back before he went to the desk to give asking for info a try, explaining to the staff he and Fr. O'Conner were together at the same rectory, so it was the closest thing he had to family right now. A couple of the nurses recognised 'The Monsignor of Manhattan' and gave a little sign to the desk troll he was okay.

"He's had a serious stroke, we're running several tests on him now to verify the extent of the damage, don't worry, he's comfortable. That's all I can say for now until we hear more," a doctor was kind enough to fill him in. Thanking her, Peter went back to relay the news to Lee, who looked worse for the hearing.

"Aw, hang in there, he's in good hands, I'm sure he'll be fine." Peter tried to sound comforting, when he himself was shaken by the news. "Sorry, I've got to start making some calls … ."

"Go ahead Pete, I'll be right here."

The Archbishop had to be informed right away, not to mention he had to hunt the Holy Bachelors down. Jenkins was easy enough to get a hold of, Mark however forgot to give them the number of the house he was invited to, and nobody thought to ask earlier anyway, never suspecting an emergency like this to happen. Naturally, there was shock as the news was broken, but it would not be long before the troops would be rallied. His Eminence and Jenkins were on their way. Peter called home next to tell his family the latest then returned to Lee who was looking like he was waiting for an execution to happen. Poor guy. Peter tried to make him feel better.

"I know, it must have been horrible to have been the first on the scene sort of thing." Peter knew what that was like, having to minister to the dying, not to mention this must be reminding Lee of all the other shocks they had been though. Peter was thinking back to the night of Gerry's accident, suddenly getting called to a hospital emergency ward conjured up in a flash all the stresses of that awful night. However, Lee was able to keep himself pulled together better then, in fact, he helped keep them all pulled together back then, and Gerry was in a lot worse condition than Fr. O'Conner was now. Something must be eating Leroy … yes, and it was obvious he was afraid to bring it up.

"Want to talk?"

"I've got a bad feeling, I can't help it."

"Come now, it can't be all … ." No, Lee was positively shook up. "Why? You can tell me."

"No, you'd only laugh, me an' me wives tales."

"Aw, after everything I've seen and heard, nothing would surprise me. Try me."

"Well," he begin tentatively, "remember the barmbrack we all had today? At lunch I mean?"

Sure he did, that home baked fruity tea loaf shipped from Ireland proved to be a grand source of hilarity when Jenkins found a dime store quality ring wrapped in baking paper in his slice, it had been purposely cooked into the thing. O'Conner was the first to quip a joke, asking him when they could all expect the wedding invitations. Eventually the two Irishmen let them in on the old tradition of baking items into the cake as a party game. A penny meant the person was about to get rich, a ring meant wedding bells were soon to peal, a bean or pea was a sign of a windfall or a time of prosperity but not necessarily through riches, while a rag indicated poverty was bound to come knocking. It was a silly game, rarely did anybody take it seriously. Nevertheless, nobody cooked the other items into the cake these days either, just the ring or maybe the penny for fun and tradition's sake as it became an unspoken understanding nobody wanted to wish the unlucky tokens on a person. However, O'Conner got ribbed next when he found a toothpick in his slice, a stick in the cake meant that person was going to get a beating from their husband or wife, or, it could indicate a walking stick, a sign a journey was about to be undertaken. That addition to their barmbarck must have been an accident, for Lee noted his Mum only put the ring in, she never did the rest, and if it *was* intentional, it would have been wrapped in greaseproof baking paper like the ring. Lee guessed she must've knocked over the toothpick cup she kept next to the flour in the overhead cupboard and never knew one had fallen into the mix, she usually being in a tear to get a million and one things done. It was past the traditional time for barmbracks, the Christmas cake, plum pudding and mince meat pie season was coming, so no doubt she had done this one on the fly for him since she knew he loved her home baking and her barmbracks were a favourite of his.

"Are you talking about the toothpick? But you said yourself, it must've been an accident."

"No, Pete, you don't understand!" Leroy gave a groan. "I didn't tell ye lads the whole thing. I didn't want to kill the buzz at our lunch, we were having such *craic* an' all. Never thought I'd have such a gas time with a household of priests." Lee gave a wistful grin before continuing. "There's an older tradition connected with that bit of stick. Being a Halloween cake an' all, some believe puttin' in a bit of wood means a coffin plank, not a walking stick. Everyone in our family goes with the coffin thing, another reason why I know Mum *never* stuck that thing in, it would put the heart in her crossways if she found out what happened."

"But Lee … ."

"Wait, I haven't gotten to the last of it. One of me old pictures fell only a few hours before the good Father arrived on the threshold for dinner tonight, the one with all of us at the annual school picnic. Nail still in the wall, the hooks an' string on the picture still in place an' as good as new? C'mon! What are the chances of all this happening? A million ta one! As ye keep saying, there're no coincidences."

True. Peter did not believe in coincidence, this had to be more than superstition at this stage. His patients in his exorcism OR had educated him about the seemingly natural but strange occurrences that let them know something odd or otherworldly was happening and they needed his advice or assistance. Mrs. Martinez and her black egg manifestations for one, pictures falling off the wall for no reason were another, an omen especially dreaded among the Irish. Fr. O'Conner said his whole family swore by it, so did his parishioners Irene and Fiona: never did a picture fall or get knocked over than it meant the passing of someone in some way connected to the picture was eminent. Once two pictures fell over in Irene's house and with a hushed awe she told him that not one but two cousins died within two months of it happening.

"See what I mean, Pete? You believe me now, don't you?"

They sat in silence, this was a hard realisation to take. If these were indeed meant to be little warnings to prepare for this sad event, Peter wondered how long did his old friend have?

Five days. Let both of them know. It is the grace he asked for.

A Voice, his guardian Friend this time.

Peter leaned forward in the chair, elbows on knees, instinctively clasping his hands in an attitude of prayer. What a heavy message, but still, what a blessing! Yes, it was a grace, not many were allowed to know in advance and be given time to prepare before they faced the Divine Tribunal, but still … .

"Pete, are you okay?"

"He has less than a week."

"Oh, Pete, no! Why did I have to be the bringer and getter of bad news?" Despite not wanting to get too netted up in all them religion things,

Leroy knew one thing was for certain: if anyone else other than Pete had said something like that … . Peter tried to be a source of comfort.

"I know Lee, it's hard. It's a sad day when it takes a tragedy to realize how precious a soul truly is."

Leroy started. He looked as if lightening had stuck him. If it was possible for him to turn any whiter, he would blend into the wall.

"Say … say what?"

"What did I say?"

"It's something Sr. Roberta said years ago," Leroy's voice was shaking. "You remember her? I thought she was off with the fairies, but now … ."

Peter's vision opened. He had hit upon a long forgotten memory, a gift of his discernment. In a twinkling, it was all made clear as crystal to him. He could see the prophetic message implanted by the pious Sister who taught at the Academy all those years ago slumbering deep within and now reawakened with his remark.

"No, she wasn't," Peter noted gently.

To his utter shock, Lee heard Peter repeating her strange message word for word: "How far you will wander, my dear child! Unfortunately it will take a tragedy before you realize how precious your soul truly is. A right arm and a leg."

Impossible! He was alone with Sister when she said that to him, Leroy was certain of it. Jeekers, he could remember it all now, but before Peter could say another thing, the doctor had found them sitting in the corner of the waiting room and approached them. At last, an update. The stroke was severe. The patient was stable for now, but completely paralysed down the right side. His speech was also severely impaired. However, it was good the paramedics were called for right away. Despite his age, with time and therapy, there was still a good chance of him regaining the ability to talk and a certain amount of mobility. Despite the positive outlook, the mystic and the rake knew better, but let the doctor finish with her report. They were grateful to be permitted to visit him. As much as they wanted to go make a visit right away, Leroy was unable to move. *Peter could literally read souls!* Everything Gran and Mum said about such priests were true, and that meant … *everything else was true.*

This wasn't the first time Peter had a distraught soul end up weeping on his shoulder. He let the returning prodigal quietly vent his inner grief as he too had to come to terms with what had happened. It felt like Sister Roberta's message to Leroy all those years ago also had something in it for him too. O'Conner did say he would give anything to see Lee change his life and didn't Irene warn him *whatever a priest said was held bound?* It was obvious his old mentor had offered up more than a prayer, he had offered himself, and the sacrifice was accepted. After lecturing him about going overboard with his fasting and medieval penances, the old Irish bulldog went and had done the ultimate. Peter was caught between sadness and joy knowing his friend could not have quit this earth in a more noble and predestined fashion. With a sense of pious spiritual envy, he had to admire the master had one trick left up his sleeve and had trumped the student. Now that the grace was dearly bought, he had better not waste it. He gingerly reached down and opened his case and felt around for his stole, the double length one reserved for his exorcism ministry was what came to hand. Nevermind. He kissed it and draped it over his shoulders, unavoidably getting Leroy draped with it too. Quietly Peter revealed one sorry transgression after another into his ear, and all Leroy could do was nod and confirm every misdeed. There was no struggle, all of it was true, it was the most heartfelt accusation against himself he had ever made with a simple 'yes' or nod of the head in affirmation, and it was made so easy for him. How softly it was all slipping out ... and now, slipping away ... so quietly and deftly did Peter handle it that with all the hubbub in the hospital, since that room was used to tears and distress, nobody knew a different kind of open heart surgery was taking place in that corner, save confessor and penitent.

"Three Hail Marys? Is that all ye're giv'n me?"

"Not quite. Lee, I know this will be difficult, but for this week you're to do an act of mercy, visit the sick, one patient in particular. You know who that is."

"Oh no! I've never been around a dying man before, I mean, know'n it for sure ... I ... I don't know if I can face it ... in a way, it's my fault!"

"Blessed fault to be a man's entrance ticket to Heaven."

And to think he got the honour of being the one to reel him in. That gave Peter an idea.

"He thinks an awful lot of you, Lee. Your visits will mean so much to him. Besides, I've never seen a nation more quick at finding joy in a sad situation than the Irish at a funeral. C'mon, let's cheer him up."

"How?" Leroy was intrigued. Peter took his lengthy stole and loosely tied one end around Lee's neck, giving the other end a playful shake.

"Let's go show him the latest catch, shall we?"

Leroy started chuckling amidst the last of his tears, wiped his eyes on his sleeves and ended up grinning with Peter.

"I'm game. Let's go."

"Wait! Absolution first," he reminded, taking back the stole for a moment, "then let's show off the big fish."

Surgery successfully concluded, the Monsignor lead the way still holding on to his stole with Lee reknotted on the other end and going along with making a holy show of himself as they bumped into the Archbishop and Jenkins, throwing fish-faces to Peter to their utter confusion. For such a sombre time as visiting a sick man, they had never seen Peter like this.

"Your Eminence, I've made a big haul tonight. Goldfish!"

"Nah, more like red herring," Lee returned.

"No, I've got it. Angel fish," Peter continued, opening the door.

"Oh ho! No that far, Pete! Ye've only just shorn this sheep. Clown fish is more like it."

The pantomime continued as they went into the room.

"Bless me, Father! Wait 'till I tell yah! Pete caught me hook, line, an' sinker he did!"

"By the gills. I've got a fine specimen on the end of my line, don't you think?" The fisherman led his catch right up to the bedside. He gave his stole a shake followed by a quick wink to the patient. "All de-scaled and cleaned, nothing left but the fillet."

O'Conner of course couldn't speak, his partially paralysed face was now supported by a specialised half-mask to prevent his features from sagging, but he heard and understood. The visible part of his face brightened up. What a sight! The two of them like this, acting the fool, with Lee making faces and oblivious to the presence of the Archbishop. Excitedly he motioned with his left hand to the pen and note pad on the table, he wanted to write something. Leroy brought them over. He slowly scrawled out in shaky letters :

a fine fish, but no chips & mushy peas?

"But of course! That must be them." Lee nodded over to Jenkins and his Eminence, then whispered in his ear, "I'll let you guess which of the pair is full of hot air." O'Conner tried to laugh again, then continued writing … .

youve got a slippery 1 pete

"Captain Birds Eye isn't letting this fishstick get away, that's a promise," Pete assured him.

The two-man act sobered up a bit so the other visitors could have the floor and spend some time with the patient, but Jenkins couldn't help throw a marvelling glance at Peter as he led Lee out of the room, stole still hooked around the fish. Once outside, he retrieved his stole. Leroy wondered what to do next.

"Are you going to tell him about, you know?"

"Yes, I must."

"Jeekers."

Leroy went silent for a spell and leaned against the wall. Peter noted he had to try and get a hold of Fr. Mark, maybe he was back at the rectory by now. Mark, always the last to find out what's happening. Leroy felt he should be doing something too and got an idea, promising to be back as soon as possible. Peter wondered what he had in mind as he watched him leave and fed some quarters into the public phone. He dialled and waited. Nope, Mark wasn't home yet. On his way back to the room, he met his Eminence on the way out. It seems like O'Conner was in fine form morale-wise despite the severity of the stroke and was comfortable for now, there was nothing more they could do for tonight. Had his family been called?

"No, not yet. As soon as I have the contacts, I'll get on it."

"Very well. Forgive me Peter, some paperwork needs handling here. It seems hospitals care more for their insurance files than they do for the patients these days. Tell him I'll be back to wish him good night before I go."

"Will do."

"He wants to see you," Jenkins informed as he went in, "I'll wait outside."

O'Conner was busy trying to write out left-handed a few spidery lines for him.

how did you hook Lee?

"It wasn't me, not completely. This was team effort. Along with the fisherman, sometimes big fish need big bait." His friend looked confused. "You said you would give anything to see Lee change his life … be prepared, you have a short time, five days." Fear passed his friend's face. "No! Don't be afraid! You're in the state of grace. Be at peace! You've brought a soul back. Greater love no man hath … ." Once the shock had passed, resignation set in. O'Conner started writing again.

it's true I did say anything as long as I know Lee's on the right track and you're with me

"Don't worry, I'll keep an eye on the fish stick, and yes, I'm with you. You know that."

just don't tell any1   only the bachelors 4 now

"I promise, just us. No sobbing biddies will be drowning you in the bed before your time." A big grin spread across the visible half of the patient's face. "But, they're going to find out you're here, expect some visitors and a lot of well-wishes sent your way," Peter warned.

That night it was just the Archbishop, Lee, who had returned from his place of gainful employment on Madison Avenue after rustling up a laptop for the bed-ridden *craitur* to type with, and finally Mark, once they got a hold of him. When his Eminence had left, Peter informed Jenkins and Mark of the news. It was a bitter blow, but they tried not to show it.

'SOrry lads i've wrecked yourt thanksgiving,' O'Conner slowly typed.

"I just *knew* I shouldn't have given you that last bit of pudding, too much of a good thing," Leroy quipped. "It did you in!"

Despite the situation, the patient thought that was very funny.

☙ ❖ ❧

True to Peter's word, once the news spread of Fr. O'Conner's stroke he was allowed some visitors, but besieged with get well cards, calls, bouquet deliveries and lots of balloons. He had made so many friends and acquaintances over the years in his parish work, not to mention all the students at the Academy who could never forget the sports-loving easygoing chaplain who helped to make school time memorable with games and witty helpful advice, a tidal wave of good wishes were sent his way. True to their promise, only Leroy and the Bachelors were in on the sad secret, with the exception of O'Conner's family as he didn't want them to be left in the dark at the last moment. It was a joy for him to see some of the cousins and his grand nephew had sprung for the air fare to come to visit all the way from

Ireland on such sort notice. However, Lee was the surprise of the lot, he adhered to the mercy mission set by Peter and never missed an hour of visiting time, cheering up the old priest as well as all the visitors with his silly antics, driving the doctors and nurses crazy during any free time from work he could get, no matter how hard it was for him, each visit quietly, silently gnawing into his conscience. Of course, once the visiting hours were over, the Bachelors had special permission from the staff to take turns with nightwatch duty, spending time with their friend, praying with him, and of course, performing the Last Rites as secretly as possible as O'Conner didn't want the word to get out if they could prevent it. Third night in the hospital they found he was able to swallow, so much to Peter's relief he was able to give him Viaticum, the last Eucharist in preparation for the soul's journey. O'Conner hoped he could be the one to give him the final Viaticum on his last day on earth, and of course Peter wanted to be with his friend as much as possible, for eventhough he knew his soul was prepared and ready, he wanted to ease his passage as far as it lay within his power and did not want him tortured at the last moments by fear of death. Despite his graced condition, already the last panic attacks felt by a soul knowing it is nearing the end were trying to set in: the sudden obsessive terrors he wasn't in God's grace despite the contrary, the plaguing memories of the past showing everything he wished he hadn't done, past regrets, failures, good deeds omitted, and now, time was fast slipping by, only a couple of days left to make it all right before the Almighty! He felt calm when Peter was around, not only did he remind him of trust in God's mercy, he more than anyone could assure him each night there was no fault left on his conscience. For his part, Peter quietly said prayers of protection under his breath after his friend had fallen asleep to dispel the final onslaught of fiendish tormentors that attempt to make a person despair of salvation despite the blessed condition they might be in.

Yet, O'Conner insisted they not spend all their time on him and tire themselves out, they still had their parish work to do, and of course, Peter was also at the final stretch of his punishing mission in Trenton. On top of all that was thrust upon him he still had a duty to accomplish, and since he was the only one who was predestined to deliver the possessed girl, he could not abandon her until all was done. On the morning of the promised date of the deliverance, Peter had time to make a quick stop at the hospital to see his friend, however, to his quiet dismay and the bafflement of the doctors, O'Conner had lost the ability to swallow again, he was unable to receive the Eucharist. This was his last day, and now unable to have the final Heavenly

Food for the journey! At least his friend was still in the state of grace, but this was hard to take. O'Conner started typing.

'maybe It was not meantfor me, bring It to the girl, she needs help mpre than I do. Now get to work youure needed You can see me again tonighht'

Even now, he was trying to comfort him and manfully remind him of his duty like a good spiritual director would. Silently, Peter blessed him with the pyx holding the Blessed Sacrament. O'Conner clasped his hand and tried to speak. It sounded like thank you for everything, don't forget me, his eye filled with tears.

"Forget you? Never. I'll be back, don't you worry."

That's if his mission at Trenton finished in time. The thought gnawed at him, but he could hope. Peter blessed him again, before tucking the sacred pyx close to his heart. It was difficult leaving, but he couldn't stay.

This was it.

The end of the month. The final battle.

There were many who wanted to see out of curiosity what would happen, the hallway to the room was lined with onlookers. Most of them knew the drill, they were warned anything could be revealed, but that did not stop them from wanting to witness this, including the director, Mr. Lieberman, who would be glad to see the end of this little farce for himself. It was he who had been the cause of this larger than normal audience, having granted *carte blanche* permission for any of the staff not on duty in addition to curious members of the board of directors to see this so they could observe with their clinical eye the dismal results the priest was bound to achieve with his hocus pocus delusions. Peter was not happy with that, it was a dangerous thing to do, having all those people about, but so be it. If they would not listen to his warnings, they would have to accept the consequences. To the astonishment of the psychiatric staff at Trenton, the building resounded with the shrieks and cries of many of the patients, those who were also suffering from the demonic unseen and who could tell a Mighty Presence was among the exorcists at this final stand-off. Today Peter took Greg aside and quietly informed him of the Hidden Guest he had next to his heart. Greg made a quick act of adoration towards the pyx. Considering the disturbance in the building, Peter quickly decided that Greg keep the pyx aside in the room reserved for them and keep guard over It. It was dangerous to have the Blessed Sacrament present at such a time lest It be profaned by those under the dark malice of evil. He reverently prepared a table for It with linens to be placed on repose, then took up his holy water and crucifix and went to cast out the enemy. The crowd made way for him to enter.

Already exhausted with his night watches and early morning parish work, fasting, penances, he knew this last session would take every last ounce of strength he had left, and he had to do this himself today. Gruelling. He wasn't given a minute's reprieve. No sooner had he started when the bed flipped onto its side and tried to slide up the wall. The onlookers gasped, screamed, someone fainted. A nurse tried to revive the stricken. Peter ignored the reactions and commanded the Demon to stop. The bed suddenly flipped back to its correct position and dropped to the floor. Peter continued. This time, the florescent light rods burst sending shattered glass all about the room. Doctor Fareed ordered everyone out. Those things were dangerous, with all the mercury dust scattering! Peter threw holy water around and the glass suddenly stopped in mid air, the dust along with it. Many onlookers gasped. Peter ordered the Demon to drop it in a corner far away from them all. To their amazement and fear, the clouds gathered as he commanded and slowly levitated over to the corner he indicated. He assured everyone they would not be harmed and continued with the Rite, the crowd inching its way back into the room and doorway to watch.

The girl howled, or rather, what was in her. This time the paint peeled and flaked off the walls and ceiling, revealing the scorch marks that had been hurriedly concealed a second time. The peeling strips crumbled into dust in mid air and sizzled into stinking grayish black cinders before forming a new particle cloud, swirling around like the fluid motion of a hellish flock of gnats, forming diabolical beasts or tortured faces in a seething rage that made everyone panic, forcing them to cower down in fear, the air rank with the chemical acrid reek of scorched paint. Once more the exorcist threw holy water into the air, the cloud tried to part and escape the watery bombardment but the particles were also compelled to banish themselves into the opposite corner away from the glass and mercury heap.

For a time, the girl writhed in her bonds and screeched, then howled again, the voice sounding like a roaring beast trapped deep within. A strange popping, cracking sound came next. The remaining witnesses who had dared to stay on looked with confusion to the ground: the floor tiles were slowly being pried up from the floor, standing up on edge, then one by one began to spin like tops or float in the air, the frightened onlookers didn't know where to stand, they could feel them trying to move under their feet! Horrified, they were caught between the conflicting instinct to run, or to keep their feet firmly planted on the tiles under them to prevent them from stirring. Tiles already up and about were scratching against their shins or threatening to hit them in the eye! Peter once more ordered the Demon to obey and stop his games, the tiles dropped to the floor with a clatter and lay scattered about. The walls shook with a fury like they had never felt before, the building itself seemed to be roaring, it felt like a massive earthquake, the place would be torn apart! There were cries and sobbing among the onlookers.

"Oh no you don't! No more of your parlour tricks this time, Old Scratch! No matter what you do, I'm not stopping the prayers, even to command you to cease!" The rumbling stopped.

"Is that so, priest? All right! Say your stupid prayers then, see if I care!"

As Peter continued the prayers, the Fallen One sounded hypnotic, slithery, mocking. The serpentine voice began to ridicule the onlookers, lies, fabrications, taunts, it unloaded its psycho-twisting tactics, insinuating to a doctor present his wife was cheating on him, right this minute in fact, shouldn't he better go home? And you, over there, you with the keys to the drug cabinet! Like helping yourself to get your highs, don't you? I wonder what everyone will think of you now that they know about your addiction! Oh and *you*, little nursy! I like you! What a little sadist you've become! I know what games you like to play! Getting cruel kicks with the patients, withholding pain meds, that's a lot of fun, isn't it? It wasn't true, the nurse shrieked it wasn't! But, all eyes were on her ... . Peter had to command silence over the Demon and sternly reminded them not to listen. Next came an even worse barrage, pointing out faults, sins, any transgressions of those who had a guilty conscience, not a few onlookers were either blushing, gasping, or tearing out of the room in shame. This time, even Liberman was not left unscathed, the demon showed a malicious glee tormenting him. Oh, I know about your comfy side business during your intern years! So easy to pimp out the unconscious patients unable to defend themselves! Not that you needed to pay for college, but some easy extra slush money is so satisfying, right? No, let's be modest, give credit where credit is due ... you do not think I exist, but who do you think gave you the idea? And you just ate up my suggestion like a ravenous dog in heat! The director bristled, turned almost grey. This time all eyes were on him, was it true or not? He quickly left the room.

Peter couldn't let this continue, the revealing of sins to the detriment of a soul's healing, no matter how grotesque the sin. He had to stop the prayers to command the Demon to be silent. Sneaky tactic! Every time he had to stop these braggart displays of power or malice, it meant the prayers had to be paused, but at least he was forced to show the Demon the value of humble obedience. Struggle, roar, flail as he might, the Devil was unable to refuse the command of a human whom he so despised! How he bellowed when humility was demanded of him! It went on and on, the mind games. However, when the usual time for a break came, Peter didn't stop. Not today, not the last day. This had to be seen out to the end. He repeated the Rite, the girl resuming her shrieking and howling. After he had struck enough with his arsenal of prayer, blessed salt, holy water and sacred oil, he demanded the sortliege to be thrown up. Nothing doing yet, Old Scratch was not about to give that, the sign of his defeat.

Hours. Peter was now drained, soaked with perspiration, feeling as if a ton was slowly being pressed down onto his shoulders, his energy was being leached right out of him, he could hardly hold up the crucifix, but he couldn't stop, he couldn't give in to the pressure. He took a breath and silently prayed for strength, then, continued on, starting the Rite from the beginning, again, stopping at key commands or adding prayers and lines from psalms that he discovered had hurt the Fiend the most.

“Humiliáre sub poténti manu Dei. Humiliáre! Humiliáre! *Humiliáre sub poténti manu Dei!*”

“Listen to me. You poor thing, give it up already.”

The serpentine voice became mesmerising, caressing, soothing.

“You're tired. You're only mortal. You're not meant for this. You know it.”

“Sancte Michaël Archángele, defénde nos in praelio, ut non pereámus in treméndo judicio … .”

“Why, you don't want to be here right now, do you? You're failing anyway you know, miserably I might add. You should never have been a priest. Sinner that you are! You have to know that's true.”

“Concússum est mare, et contrémuit terra, ubi Archangelus Michaël descenéndit de caelo … .”

“Even *you* know you are not worthy to receive the gifts you've been given. Now you're actually *throwing* them away.”

“Prótege, Dómine, plebum tuam per signum sanctae Crucis … .”

Be silent!

“You've messed up in something so simple as a case of priorities! And you think you can do *this* kind of work? You *shouldn't* be here. You know it. There's someone who needs you right now. How *could* you have left him? Alone. Dying. Afraid.”

Trickster! Get out of my head!

" … ab insídiis inimicórum ómnium: ut tibi gratam exhibeámus servitútem, et acceptáblile fiat sacrifícium nostrum … ."

"You've abandoned him, and he so much wants to see you right now, but where are you? He's so frightened right now … ."

Quiet!

"Per signum Crucis de inimicis nostris líbera nos, Deus noster … ."

"You see, we made him commit a sin only a few minutes ago, only you can give him peace … *and you're not there!*"

"Humiliáre sub poténti manu Dei!"

Silence, you liar!

"He called you friend, cherished you like a son, you know. And now … ?"

"In principio erat Verbum, et Verbum erat apud Deum, et Deus erat Verbum … "

"Of all the people to leave down! After all the help he gave you … ."

" … Hod erat in princípio apud Deum … "

"First you left your own father down … and now this … ."

Stop your infernal taunting!

"It won't be long, we've got him now, he'll be lost. And you could have saved him. His passing won't be easy either, it will be quite painful. You've helped many others, now, you can't help even him … ."

Shut up!

No, no, don't snap, don't lose it now … so close to the end … it can't be much longer!

The fight had taken a sinister turn, Peter now the brunt of the Demon's offensive tactics, his head and heart were being messed with, the Fiend hitting upon a sensitive spot he had discovered. Peter understood the Voice at the altar promised truthful answers would be given him … but wait! That was when he as exorcist demanded the answers, right? But *this?* This certainly couldn't have been part of the promise, no, not when the demons talked of their own accord, it couldn't be … the Devil was a liar from the beginning … a murderer from the beginning … there was no end to his subterfuges. Sick, twisted, sadistic … anything could be used as a point of attack, even the truth … but was it truth or lies this time … ? *No no, don't listen!* Don't bother to find out! Don't get sucked into that trap! That was the one thing that was imperative, don't listen to the Demon's whiles! Still, the pointed taunts reawakened those burning jeers that were thrown at him in Hell, it was hard not to relive the biting blows that seemed to twist like barbed daggers once they struck and then wrench back, ripping, gutting everything inside out. Hang in there … shut him out … don't pay attention … this last stretch, it was an endurance match, seeing who could last out, but to contend against a seraph, even a fallen one! If he relied on only himself, of course he would fail … .

Peter turned his thoughts to the One who had all power in Heaven and Earth given to Him, to the quiet, meek Hidden Presence waiting next door concealed in the humble appearance of bread … .

My God! My God! Don't abandon me!

"Deus, refúgium nostrum et virtus … ."

The walls shook again.

"Give it up, Reinold!"

" … pópulum ad Te clámántem propítius réspice … ."

"You're damned, Peter! You're lost! Remember the molten box! I'll have great pleasure throwing you in it myself!"

" … et intercendénte gloriósa et immaculáta Vírgine Dei Genitríce María … ."

"In fact, I might make it part of my throne. My footstool! Ah ha! All of Hell will see you crushed beneath my feet! However, if you stop now, I might be lenient. I too can be magnanimous."

"*Begone Satan! Depart, then, impious one, depart, accursed one, depart with all your deceits, for God has willed that man should be His temple. Why do you still linger here? Give honour to God the Father almighty!*"

"Depart? I'm taking you with me! Remember that! You're mine, Reinold!"

"*Begone, seducer! Your place is in solitude; your abode is in the nest of serpents; get down and crawl with them. This matter brooks no delay; for see, the Lord, the ruler comes quickly, kindling fire before Him, and it will run on ahead of Him and encompass His enemies in flames. You might delude man, but God you cannot mock. It is He who casts you out, from whose sight nothing is hidden … .*"

"Hear me? I will forever dog your steps! I never rest!"

"*The exalted Virgin Mary, Mother of Jesus, commands you, who in her lowliness crushed your proud head from the first moment of her Immaculate Conception!*"

"I will stop you, and you will forever be mine!"

"*Begone, Satan! Father and master of lies, enemy of man's welfare. Give place to Christ, in whom you have found none of your works!*"

"Damn you! The King and Queen of the Universe order me to obey! But I shall stop you! Destroy you! You, and all you hold dear! Remember what I said! You will be mine! Footstool! Footstool!"

The walls made one tremendous shake, Melissa started to choke, then vomited, nothing as forceful as before although still gruesome, she seemed to cough up blood, but with it came an object, the small balled up piece of cloth, it was the sortilege, the sign he had been waiting for. The hideous voice made one, last wailing cry that seemed to die away into the distance, then, all was still save the motion of people in the room, the witnesses wondering what might happen next. Expecting more horrors to come, no one dared approach the girl. Peter made a few more commands, demanded any spirit to show itself just in case this exit was a trick, but there was no answer, no reaction. The girl had already regained a human aspect, albeit pale and unconscious. He checked his watch—midnight. November was over, the sign had been given, the deliverance had been achieved. The nurses regained some composure and tentatively approached the girl to start cleaning up the blood from her mouth, tripping and sliding on a few of the loose floor tiles as they went, but Peter ordered they leave the sortilege for him to handle. He carefully teased open the cloth with a pair of tweezers, a satanic magic seal had been embroidered on it. Peter held it up for all to see. The cloth had been cursed with a powerful black spell. One of the doctors asked if they could keep it as a specimen? A proof of what they had seen?

"Absolutely not! Have you not seen? *Have you not heard enough?*"

Peter demanded a bowl be brought, he set the cloth on fire while dousing it was blessed salt and sacred oil as was his customary precaution, then swept up the ashes and submerged them in a jar of holy water. At last, he could say the concluding prayer reserved for the time of deliverance, a few lines so short, yet so eagerly awaited!

"Almighty God, we beg you to keep the evil spirit from further molesting this servant of yours, and to keep him far away, never to return. At your command, O Lord, may the goodness and peace of our Lord Jesus Christ, our Redeemer, take possession of this woman. May we no longer fear any evil since the Lord is with us; who lives and reigns with You, in the unity of the Holy Ghost, God, forever and ever. Amen!"

He made the sign of the cross.

"Look, Tom! Missy!" Mr. and Mrs. Fletcher quickly approached the bed to help the nurses. The girl had opened her eyes and looked about confused, then with sheer relief. They were gone! They were all truly gone! She was free!

"Get her out of those shackles," Peter kindly ordered. "She's been a prisoner long enough."

As uncle and aunt embraced their niece in a joyful scene of tears and a profusion of thanks, Peter wearily gathered his sacramentals in his case and made his way to the next room, the witnesses silently, respectfully parting to let him pass. Battle worn, he was not yet finished. Reverencing the Blessed Sacrament, he knelt besides Greg who was still on guard duty. The apprentice instinctively reached for Peter's arm and held him, he looked so exhausted and unsteady!

"Are you all right? Is it really finished?"

"Almost, we have one last thing to do here tonight."

Taking the pyx, he returned with all decorum to the liberated girl to give her the Bread of Angels. Greg motioned for everyone to kneel. No matter what faith or lack of faith existed among the bystanders, no one disobeyed or murmured. They readily got down and watched as the girl of her own volition went to her knees.

"May the Body of Our Lord Jesus Christ keep Thy soul unto life everlasting."

Her starved soul now received its first Divine nourishment in years. Overcome with emotion, she clasped Peter around the knees and buried her face in his surplice. Gently he placed his hand on her head. Poor child! Almost brought to destruction, now freed! After a few minutes, he gently raised her up.

"Today, your new life begins. My child, be good! Let Christ live in you from now on, and evil will never have a hold over you again."

Deeply moved by all they had seen, nobody wanted to get up. Eventually, Peter smiled and motioned everyone to stand.

"It's been a long day. I'm sure you all need to eat and get some rest."

Before they left for the night, Peter asked the staff if it would be all right to make an out of state call, it was rather urgent. Eagerly he was shown to an office and given some privacy. There was another soul on his mind tonight. Jenkins answered the line.

"Pete, there's no easy way to break this, but he's gone. He went into a seizure about twenty minutes before twelve … at least they tell us it was fast … he was asking for you, he wanted to tell you something … but he didn't … he didn't get a chance … ."

"I'll be there."

Replacing the receiver, he sank into the chair and prayed, prayed for his friend, prayed for him to be mercifully judged, that his soul find rest and peace. And he wept. It cut, how it cut! The splintered cross, how deep it can go! He knew he had done his duty, freed a soul from the bondage of the evil one, but he couldn't be there for his friend at his last moment. A life of sacrifices, painful ones. Victory only comes through wear and tear. Bleed, bleed chosen soul, since that is your vocation.

挃 ❖ 挂

According to Irish standards, it was a grand send off. The cathedral was filled with all who knew Father O'Conner, the casket respectfully laden with flowers and adorned with his picture and his priest's stole. The Archbishop doing the honours with the funeral Mass, the Bachelors along with a numerous amount of fellow priests all concelebrating with him. Not only did Leroy step forward for pall bearing duty along with some of their school mates from the Academy, he promised their old mentor would get a proper wake and asked permission from the Archbishop if he and a few of his old school mates could help make most of the arrangements, booking a reception room at stylish hotel, notifying come one, come all. Gerry had been given permission to leave Stonyvale a few days early so he could attend the services, and both he and Katherine along with the rest of the family were worried what wild ideas Lee might come up with, but were surprised how dignified the whole get-together went. Plenty of food and a crowd of family, friends, parishioners and acquaintances, it had practically turned into a school reunion, on the whole a good one at that, mostly happy and hilarious memories were shared. It turned into a celebration of the man's life and work, not a mournful tear-jerker, although there were fewer dry eyes in the house when Lee's Trad music pals from Galway played one of O'Conner's favourite exile songs, *The Fields of Athenry*. Soon, he would be returning to the old turf, for his family could only think of burying him in Ireland. He had given his life in service to the Good Shepherd overseas, now, it was time he could rest in peace in his beloved verdant Kerry hills.

Beautiful as the funeral was, the hardest part was left to Peter, who was made executor concerning his priestly personal effects, such as his belongings at the rectory, and what to do with his Mass bookings. It was a sad night packing up his things and preparing them for his family. He was somewhat amused and pained at the same time, finding his homemade whip

777

hidden amongst the belongings in an effort to keep it from him. Peter hid it back in his wardrobe again, not to be used, he was now bound on pain of obedience not to use it, one of O'Conner's last orders as a spiritual director to him, and so, it would be a good reminder of that holy virtue. Pain, pain in more ways than one, because it still lashed him with its barb without even being flung on his back, a reminder the night O'Conner literally saw him through Hell, and to think he couldn't be there for him on his last night on earth. Of course, Peter knew he had done the right thing, everyone knew he had a duty to accomplish, the departed soul was well attended and had all the necessary Rites and surely had died in God's favour, but still, the mind could play cruel, baseless guilt games.

O'Conner's grand nephew came by to pick up everything and kindly asked in addition to the In Memoriam cards if the Bachelors wanted the few bits and bobs that were left, his prayer books, some of his statues, they would make nice keepsakes to remember him by, he would certainly want them to have something. Not that they needed them for that, but Jenkins was grateful to be given his Rosary beads, Mark, a statue of the Christ Child of Prague, but Peter asked if he didn't mind giving him the little statue of St. Patrick. It wasn't for him, but for someone one else if that was all right. It was gladly given but surely, didn't he want to keep anything for himself? Peter refused, yet was forced to give in when he handed him his grand uncle's breviary explaining he didn't know who else who would use it, and he couldn't leave him without *something*, for which Peter was very grateful.

Down to three Bachelors at the rectory. Despite Old Scratch's mind-twisting attempts, Peter knew Fr. O'Conner had to be in a better place, no, he couldn't be lost. Still, it was now a glum household, one man down, Gertie accidentally setting out a fourth place for dinner a few nights, then, hurriedly putting the extra plate and cutlery away, the empty spot almost being worse than having an unused setting sitting out. It was good to keep busy with work then, no matter how fatigued he felt at the end of the day. The sorrow and toil was producing good fruit. Peter made additional trips to Trenton for some extra check-ups to ensure no relapse had occurred as was usual for so severe a possession case. True, his Sight let him know all was well with Melissa, but better be obedient and go by the book, and besides, after months of going through that arduous ceremony to be curt and unceremoniously drop her and everyone else now would have been uncharitably rude and just not like him. A few extra prayers of the Exorcism, said quietly this time so as not to alarm her, she was quiet, peaceful, respectful, no reaction. Old Scratch had left Melissa alone. She was free. She was perfectly normal to the amazement of the medical staff, although that did not surprise him. The best part, no longer was she kept in the isolation ward nor in any of the confined community areas. Her recovery, complete transformation more like it, got the doctors to agree they might try a probation period of observation and release her into the care of her uncle and aunt to see if she could adjust back into society. Fr. Greg faithfully brought her Communion in the meantime, and Peter had to smile at how enthusiastic his former apprentice had become when they got together for coffee. Greg found some of the Trenton staff sitting in the back of his church for Sunday services, taking it all in, including Dr. Fareed, who had signed up for the local RCIA course. Converts were in the making!

"You know, I had no idea how important this work is, frightening, but man, it's needed. We really *are* helping people."

"Yes, curing souls, bringing them back. So, how goes your parish?"

Since he followed his advice, consecrating his dwindling parish to the Immaculate Heart, there was a sudden upswing in attendance. Explosive even. Greg explained at his 'reformed' seminary, which he could now see was infected by errors, they were taught devotions like the Rosary and Benediction were deemed old and needed to give way to the New Spirit of the age. They even went so far as to say Confession wasn't needed that much any more, a sin was only if you thought it was! Now, he knew the opposite was true, that 'new spirit' was killing everything, it was all going to Hell. For this week he was about to start bringing back public Rosary recitations, Benediction for Friday nights. In the future, maybe he could turn one of the side chapels into a twenty-four hour adoration chapel, already he got a few requests for that! He was even considering asking permission from his bishop to see if he could offer a Latin Mass in his church at least once a month. In fact, he was thinking of returning to the seminary, a real one, to learn Latin so he might be able to do it himself eventually, since for now he'd have to find another priest who could. Good for you, Greg! Peter offered if he needed advice, he knew where to find him.

"You know, I don't get it. I was reading the documents of Trent. St. Pius V said the Latin Mass could be said for all time with no fear of penalty. Why does it feel like it's being kept from us? Why do we have to *beg* for what we have a right to? I feel like I've been robbed."

"Ah, you're just beginning to see what lies ahead. The smoke of Satan has entered the Church, which we must dispel as manfully as we would a demon. You have great plans Greg, but don't think they come from you! The road won't be easy, it will be laden with crosses, but when it is, then you know the work is good and true. Remain steadfast. So, do you plan to continue on as an exorcist?”

“Oh yeah, I've had a few consultation requests, I'll be starting this week. I hope you don't mind, but I made extra copies of all the video tapes as we went along, just in case I needed a refresher on everything. Is that okay?”

“I guess so, just don't let them get out. Melissa is healed, she has a right to privacy and a normal life.”

“Okay. Thanks, thanks for everything. I've really learned a lot.”

“You're welcome. Give me a call if you ever get stuck on something.”

“Will do.”

A parish reviving, gaining new life, that was good news to hear. Speaking of converts, Leroy was a gem. He was O'Conner's prize, but Peter couldn't help but be chuffed that the task of polishing up that diamond in the rough was left to him. Lee decided to drop by the rectory one evening and see how they were faring, and was invited to join them for Gertie's chicken-fried steak. After dinner, Peter took him into the parlour and gave him the statue of St. Patrick. Lee not only needed the spiritual moral support of the emerald green bishop right now, but would actually cherish it, a dear keepsake of an old friend who had helped see him through some of the difficult days of his childhood.

“And don't break this one, deal?”

Leroy gave a start, then smiled.

“Deal. Thanks, Pete.”

Pete's uncanny ability to see things obviously went into the past as well as into the soul. Leroy had broken the St. Patrick he received as a First Communion present from an aunt, it met its untimely demise along with other articles on his dresser by a careless practise swing of his hurley when attempting to impress his Irish-born cousins and teach them how to hit an American baseball with it. In a panic they tried to patch St. Patrick up with a dab of glue, but he was never quite the same, neither were they for awhile after Mum roared murder for swinging that hurley in the house!

“Hey Fishstick, do you want to help me label envelopes?”

Leroy laughed.

“Er, okay, sure.”

Why not? He was a bit lonesome at the moment, it was hard keeping that new leaf turned, he needed a bit of company to keep his good resolutions bolstered. Strange, eventhough Peter had seen everything, there was literally nothing left to hide, instead of feeling ashamed anymore, it felt good to be around him again, but quite different than when they were just old school pals. He always felt as close to him as much as Gerry his best friend, however now he felt *safe*. Lately he could see Pete's very glance *made* a person want to do better. Sometimes, grab your soul by the bootstraps. He didn't expect that. It was a different kind of feel-good factor, a distilled sense of well-being that didn't have anything to do with the illusory, evaporating, party-hardy happiness of the world that used to leave him sick or passed out somewhere and strangely empty when the thrill was gone. True, Pete used to unnerve him a bit, but now he understood. Why had he always been running away? That new leaf, new life, quiet, very quiet, but it had its attractions he just didn't see or feel until now. Peace. He could certainly feel that around Pete. Label envelopes, okay, anything to stick around for a bit. Sure looked like Pete needed help too, he saw the heaps of mail waiting for him the last few times he visited, to think he was that sought after, but then again, he understood. It was not often you came in contact with someone who obviously had a direct line of communication with Above.

"How do you plough through all this?"

"Oh, little by little. The fellows help when they can, but they've got their own work too. Um, sorry, here you go." Peter cleared a chair, sweeping up a pile of opened letters and placing them on the sofa. They settled in. "You see, I answer with a longer reply when I can, but for those I don't have time to do that but don't want to leave ignored, prayer requests, that sort of thing, I've printed out a card, which I sign, and send with a blessed holy picture I can fit in the envelope." He took one from the coffee table and handed it to Lee. *'Thank you for your letter, you are in my prayers. If it be God's will, may you receive the answer you seek.'* "I then put all their names into a special intention booklet and say a special Mass for them all once a month, considering the Mass load I've got, it's the best I can do. There's no way I can answer them all, and I can't save the whole world. Besides, I've got to leave something for the other priests to do!"

"Right you are!" Leroy chuckled. He took a look at the return addresses on some of the letters. Jeekers. They were coming in from all over the place. Some were addressed to Peter directly, other senders obviously didn't know his name but had heard of him and and wrote 'To the Exorcist Priest at St. John's Rectory', or better yet, the new title that was gaining in catchy popularity, 'The Monsignor of Manhattan, Exorcist'.

"Prayer requests, huh."

"Also a lot more than that, requests to give retreats, classes, interviews, people needing help, vocation counselling, marriage counselling, bereavements, marriage breakups and pleas for advice, tragic accidents, suicides, people seeking consolation, confirmation if they're loved ones are in Heaven or Purgatory, the list goes on. Sometimes I can only send comfort with that card, I can't see or advise on everything at will, mostly only what I'm shown."

There was a knock on the door, it was Gertie.

"Sorry to disturb you, but before I go, I forgot to tell you there are two more bags in the coat closet, they were delivered earlier, I had the mailman drop them there, since we're running out of space in here."

"Don't worry, we'll make space, I'll get them," Leroy offered, jumping up. Sakes alive! They were heavy! "Hey, Pete, you've got one big Agony Aunt fan club. You could get a hernia lifting these bloomin' things."

Peter looked over, dropped his pen, rushed up to help him with it, then almost like a kid who had been given permission to rifle a candy box, he excitedly fumbled undoing the knot keeping the huge duffle bag closed. Quick, quick!

"There are *big* flames coming out of this one, red and gold, white, royal blue!"

"Er, what?"

Leroy was amused and baffled as Peter began to dig down into the contents, letting the letters spill onto the floor.

"Don't worry, we can pick them up later."

Leroy then laughed when he saw Peter happily hold up a parcel meticulously wrapped in brown paper.

"Ha ha! So you get prezzies too! It's not all tears and begging letters in them bags."

"Quick, hand me the scissors, please!"

"Cheater! Aren't you going to wait until Christmas to open it?"

"No, not with this."

Inside was a carefully wrapped gilt display case that stood upon a pedestal, it wasn't empty. He had been sent a First Class relic of a saint, no, several saints, including the official papers certifying their provenance. St. Pius V, defender of the Latin Mass and the Faith, St. Benedict, patron saint of exorcists, St. Francis de Sales, gifted spiritual director and seer of souls, St. Margaret Mary, visionary of the Sacred Heart, the Curé of Ars, patron of parish priests, prisoner of the confessional.

"Wow Pete, looks like we're in grand company tonight."

"You said it! I wonder who sent this … ." It was as if the regal reliquary was tailored to be a light for his own apostolate. Why on earth would something like this be *given away*? Lee double-checked the box.

"French post marks, hmm. Wait, here it is, a card buried under the paper."

It was from his Eminence, the Cardinal Archbishop of Paris:

Greetings! Since our introduction and a few meetings in Rome at the College I've always had my mind on you, you have always been in my prayers! Now I know why – although you might wish it was otherwise, news of you is reaching us over here in France about the wonderful gifts entrusted to you. I know such gifts come with great trials. However, I beg you, please pray for me also when you can, and please, accept this reliquary for your altar. May it bring you graces and consolation. Your humble servant in Christ.

"What a dear old soul he is. To think of me, and to part with such a treasure! I must write to him, right now in fact," Peter noted while making the sign of the cross with the reliquary, then over Lee before gingerly placing it down on the coffee table.

"Okay, while you're busy there, what do I do then?"

"Right. See that pile of opened envelopes? They're the ones to be answered ... yeah, in the other chair. Next to them are all the signed and sealed cards, I just need them addressed and stamped. It will really help a lot."

"Right-o then. Uck! Stamp mouth. Let's see if I can't hunt up a sponge so I don't have to lick all them things."

"Try the kitchen, under the sink you should find a new pack."

Sponge discovered, Lee returned to addressing duty. Talk about working at the GPO. The Archbishop was right, quite a few from France, Rome, England, Mexico, a few from Ireland, anywhere and everywhere USA ... .

"Pete, you're going to need an assistant eventually. Tell you what, I'll be free these coming nights. I'll be glad to help out until then."

"Really? I don't want to hold you up. You sure?"

"Sure I'm sure! I don't have any major deadlines right now, a rarity. In fact, just finished up the latest ad project for *Harvey Jack's Smoky Mountain Pork and Beans.*"

"What? You mean the 'Best of the West' ads were yours?"

"Yeah! But not so honest, they're tinned in Massachusetts. The things you have to say to sell a tin of beans."

"Let me guess, canned somewhere near Bean Town, er, Boston."

"You got it, Pete. So, all done for now, I'm free, and besides, this is kinda a … safe house at the moment," he concluded quietly. He didn't have to say more, the office party season in the advert business held too many temptations considering his new delicate convert condition. Peter gave him an encouraging glance.

For the next few nights Leroy helped to cheer up the Bachelors, with that Irish accent and his zany expressions, it was like having a younger O'Conner around, albeit thinner, more energetic and with a shock of curly red hair. He was a good cook too, and bringing in the meat and potatoes, he gave Gertie a couple of extra nights off. Mark wondered if he could help on one occasion, while Jenkins started flashing Lee hand signs and facial signals behind the eager helper's back — no, no, no! Stop! Cease! Desist! Don't even think about it! Peter tried to keep a straight face as Lee politely declined Mark's offer, then had a good laugh later when Peter could take him aside and explain there wouldn't have been a spud left for the pot if Mark had gotten his hands on them, and they would have no idea what would have happened to the rest of the dinner either. Afterwards, Lee happily mucked in washing the dishes. For a former party-till-you-drop guy, he actually relished a bit of work and activity which revealed a down-to-earth serious side of him. He didn't like sitting still in an aimless fashion. Either work, be busy, or have a little fun and a joke or two, that seemed to be it with him. He did have a big heart as O'Conner had pointed out, and he just loved to help.

Quite content with his out-of-the-blue volunteer job, he addressed envelopes for Pete and got them ready to go out in the bags, chatting away with him as he did the signing and the blessing of the cards. A few times they were interrupted by an emergency visit, someone coming for confession, and only wanting to see Peter, another night it was an emergency, an accident, the Last Rites were needed. They only wanted Peter. Jenkins and Mark seemed left out, but they didn't mind he got most of the attention from the flock, only they wished Peter wouldn't overwork himself. Sometimes the person seeking help was finally persuaded to accept them instead, and good! Lee noticed that Peter never got much of a break. During the times Pete wasn't interrupted, he showed him some of the letters he was working on, good news of prayers having been answered, or thanks for the advice he had taken the time to write to them that had proved invaluable. Of, course being the time of year it was, he was bombarded with Christmas cards, they were propped up wherever he could find a space. Eventually, he had to just put them in a neat pile. However, Lee couldn't help notice Pete's uncanny abilities. There was a night he arrived to find Pete busy scribbling away in the dark without any light and able to write perfectly, then, he couldn't help notice he could sort things without ever having to open envelopes and wondered why he wouldn't open some of them but immediately got them ready for the trash.

"What's in this one," Lee eventually asked.

"Oh, don't mind it, a request for a good dollop of cash for a liver transplant for a dying relative, and it's bogus. A fake request."

"But ye haven't even touched it."

"Go ahead if you like, a request for a grandmother, whose been dead for two years."

Lee opened it, and sure enough, was gobsmacked to see it was a letter asking for exactly that. He couldn't say for sure about the grandmother being already planted in the ground, but of course a cadging con artist wouldn't put that in, and after getting the first part right, he could certainly take Pete's word for the rest! Leroy started to hold up other discarded envelopes … .

"Could I please donate to some video project to help the orphaned children of Bangladesh, but that's a fake too I'm afraid."

Lee wondered if he could … ?

"Yeah go ahead. Just so you know I'm not ditching people's letters for nothing."

Gobsmacked again.

"How do you do that? It's like being on the Johnny Carson Show with the envelope gag, only ye're getting it right!"

Pete playfully held an envelope to his forehead.

"It seems I am the lucky winner of the Clearing House Sweepstakes."

After a good laugh together, he placed the letter with the rest and went on with his sorting with a fatherly reminder to Lee this wasn't all a party game you know. This was a serious matter!

He didn't divulge any more unopened envelopes after that, but the whole thing fascinated Lee. He couldn't help watch him closely, wondering what was in a letter that was treated as if it contained poison, or within another that was looked upon like it was a pitiful thing before it was tossed, sometimes Pete looked pained, then, others were simply thrown away without too much of a reaction other than a sigh that seemed to say quietly, 'oh, another one'. One night Lee took note of some of these castaways that elicited a stronger response more than the others and couldn't help search for them as he went out back to dump these rejects into the trash. Never before would he do a thing like that, open someone else's post without permission, but it was too much of a pull to not find out what was going on, especially when the first one he took a gander at under the porch light was addressed in jagged bold letters: '*To the Scum-Sham Exorcist Who Thinks He's God*'. Jeekers. Lee furrowed his brow as he opened it and scanned the letter inside written in the same angry handwriting, the pen having gouged into the paper in places … .

> *I know your type, money-scamming, idolatrous boy-loving scum, hypocrite Catholic tyrants who think they speak for God! YOU'RE GOING TO HELL AND I HOPE YOU ROT THERE!!!*

It went on for several paragraphs. Disgusted, Lee crumpled it up and threw it into the garbage. There were some pretty messed up people out there, but whatever was wrong with them, they were taking all their ire out on a man they had never met, and of all men, the one who certainly didn't deserve such sick accusations levelled against him. What else did Pete have to put up with? He opened another. What the … ? Some mental case of a woman in Seattle claiming that her child was fathered by Peter through space and time via a cosmic union in the seventh sphere in the House of Aquarius and was demanding child support or she would reveal all to his church leaders. Definitely a basket case off with the fairies! Another crumpled paper ball was added to the pile in the trash. Okay, he got the picture, but it galled him.

Of course, he should've known Pete would be on to him. The first thing he did was give him a little shake of his head as he came through the door.

"I'm sorry Pete, I couldn't help me self."

"You're forgiven."

Still, forgiven and all, he felt like a heel. Opening another's letters *was* a pretty low class thing to do. If his mother saw what he did, she would have given him a right tongue lashing that would have knocked him into the next century. However, Lee got the distinct impression Peter wasn't angry, not even disappointed, just, hoping this could have been kept quiet, and more for the sake of sparing him from knowing about the demented waffle that came in the bags.

"No harm done, only, whatever seared your eyeballs. Aren't you glad you didn't go past two? I don't need to go preachy on you when you've already gotten an eyeful." Pete gave a wry smile. Lee was gobsmacked again, how did he ... but of course.

"Does this go on all the time?"

"Uh huh."

"Aw, Pete! Does your superior know?"

"Oh, his Eminence gets a pile of these about me too, so yes, he knows. It's to be expected. Try not to let it bother you."

How did he take it so quietly? How *could* he take it so quietly? Lee knew if this happened to him, his blood would be boiling. He couldn't help feel his respect for Peter deepen a hundredfold.

"Come, take your mind off it. Tell me, do you have plans this Christmas?" He was afraid Lee still had a holiday 'bash' in mind.

"Yeah. I sure do! It was hard to get the tickets, but someone cancelled their flight, so I'm off to see Mum in Galway. I've already got me bags packed."

"Hey! That's something to look forward to."

"Yeah! Except I'll be eating forty Christmas dinners."

Peter laughed, many of the Irish he met were certainly generous with their food, maybe too much so. He had to chuckle again when Lee explained what he meant in his case: on top of Mum and Gran's generous table, with the uncles, aunties, first cousins, and all those once, twice and thrice removed, each household will insist on cooking their Yank relative an Irish Christmas dinner, so everywhere he planned to visit he could expect nothing but turkey and ham, or the leftovers of the same, and, it might be two to three dinners of the same a day as he had to try and see everyone in the days off he had.

"I'll have turkey and Brussels sprouts shootin' out me ears morning, noon and night, but at least I'll be getting all the custard and sherry trifle I could ever want, if I have any room left that is."

No wonder he wanted to eat nothing but sausages for Thanksgiving before the next turkey glut struck. Who could blame him? Speaking of turkey gluts, they still had the Jersey mob gobbler in the rectory freezer, and, Vico just had another one dropped off for Christmas. It was an offer he couldn't refuse. Lee found that pretty funny.

❦

While Leroy was preparing to face Christmas with the clan, Peter had Katherine's house-warming dinner, which he looked forward to, and not only for the reason it gave everyone a change in dining fare before Christmas arrived. The two families were together again, the company was in good spirits to see Gerry out and about in his own home even if he did have to use the wheelchair on occasion, and what a home-maker Katherine had turned out to be. As she explained to them before, she hadn't the rest of the place fixed up yet, and true, they had seen what she had done with the old factory when converting it to a gallery and knew to expect excellence, but the formal combination of parlour-slash-dining room was elegantly impressive.

On first entering the eye was immediately drawn upward to the new ceiling of the seating area. Everyone oh'd and aw'd at the *trompe d'oeil* fresco featuring the playful cherubs they had heard so much about, the chubby babes amidst their billowing clouds and flower garlands, Katherine added the finishing touch by painting two cherubs over the new gleaming brass chandelier in such a way it appeared as though they were holding it overhead. Peter shot an amused glance at Katherine with a nod up. Which ones were the stickies? She suppressed the urge to laugh and quickly pointed out the culprits with a flick of an index finger while she thought no one else was looking, for the surroundings were admired by everyone next. A new Italianate fireplace had been installed that was built out three dimensional style into the room, the rectangular decorative setting consisting of polished crème granite, sandstone and marble with the chimney tapering upward into a triangular feature, the three sided-mantel adorned with a matching brass clock and candelabra set. Steves just *had* to quip the thing looked like a monument, but Jenny pucked his arm while Katherine simply ignored the teasing. They could tell he liked it. The walls were finished in an understated blend of golden creams with white mouldings, while the soft folds of the thick embossed deep rose and gold flecked draperies with a matching swag pelmet graced the windows. The seating arrangements were a stylish yet very comfortable mix of a leather sofas and wing chairs, the leather set in a creamy white, the other upholstered in similar material as the curtains in matching rose tones with

788

chair cushions, and, sporting brass casters. Aunt Martha looked around before choosing a seat. Katherine guessed she was looking for a missing item, the blue satin and pink rose cushy delight she had stitched for Gerry when he was in the hospital, so before there was war in the cabin, thought it best to let her know it was on Gerry's chair in the office, it matched the blue décor already there, (thank heavens). Everyone settled in with their drinks, and while Gramps usually loved leather chairs, this time he went to the upholstered sofa set and sank down into the luxury of it all.

"High up, yet, what comfort! It's like wallowing in a feather bed, by gum!"

Ordered from Italy were antique style oak and mahogany cabinets, side tables, the coffee table, the ornate bits and pieces, something to put the matching brass, china and polished stone lamps on, not to mention Gerry's collection of personal photo frames, and some of the petite samples of Classical Roman and Greek statuary he had collected which she had retrieved from the gallery. That wasn't all: she had also taken the Venetian *vedutti* scenes by Canaletto from the museum section, Gerry's and the one her father bought for her, placing them in their new home along with the picture of Rome she painted for Gerry now in pride of place among the venerable masters. Wishing to continue the angelic theme but lacking the time, she commissioned one of Gerry's infamous copy masters to recreate Bartolome Esteban Murillo's *The Assumption of the Virgin*, a legion of baby cherubs attending the Queen of Heaven, which Peter was pleased to see. The funny part was the original painting was by a Spanish artist, but nobody minded as it blended in quite beautifully. She had also found a bright watercolour featuring a text of Gerry's favourite poem about Italy where the lemon trees grow, and after adding that to their Italian themed art display, decided to do something quite quirky and ordered lemon trees, real ones with lemons, potted on either side of the double column archway opening into the dining area. That too had its own frescoed ceiling, not as large, but with the same theme, the cherubs artfully holding the matching brass chandelier overhead. Katherine had to admit to Peter a few 'stickies' had found their way up there too. The dining area also had a new large china cabinet and matching table for twelve, Italian classic reproductions that blended handsomely with the rest of the room. The final detail of the décor, the entire area was finished in Italian parquet marquetry with a flowering acanthus pattern in lighter wood tones bordering the outer edges of the floor along the wall allowing her to lay out the Turkish rug in the centre without compromising the artistic details of the ornate pattern. Peter took a quick look out on the balcony, which now had Roman benches and classical pots with box hedge plants carefully clipped to resemble miniature cypresses from the Mediterranean, the outdoor seating area matching the theme of the interior, which was made especially festive with the twinkling Christmas tree set by the blazing fireplace, the Nativity scene a model of Renaissance style figurines carefully arranged next to it, poinsettias and holly garlands adding the final holiday touch to the room. Nice, very nice. Formal, but with the warm colour scheme, the furnishings and soft lighting, it was cozy, comfortable, no unbearable starchiness notwithstanding all its elegance, it was a pleasant surprise to all.

"You don't mind I brought the painting you got for me here, are you Pops? I mean, you and Mom did want it for the gallery after all."

"No, Kathy dear, we got it for *you*. It wouldn't be much of a gift if you couldn't put it where you like," her mother pointed out, Pops nodding in agreement.

"You see, it was perfect for the Italian theme."

"Which is looking beautiful," Mrs. R added.

"Yes, it's just gorgeous," Lottie agreed.

"Thanks! But it's only one room so far, well, maybe two if you count the dining area. Wait until I get the whole thing done, the entertainment room is next, and Gerry's office, but that looks great already with his desk and the book collection, all it needs is some new blue draperies, same style to match here ... ."

"Yes, quite beautiful, although I *do* wish they would hang properly! Nobody knows how to hang a curtain these days." Aunt Martha got up and compulsively attempted to straighten out the soft folds into stiff pleats, contrary to her niece's original concept. Katherine got the distinct impression that living with the fiancé before the nuptials, even with separate bedrooms between them, was the real cause for Auntie's pickiness. Pops was a bit irked too, but was silent on the matter. Peter normally wouldn't have been happy either with such an arrangement, except this was the one very rare occasion he could actually trust them to do the right thing. From their confession sessions he knew Katherine still locked the door to her room each night to Gerry's amusement. Ger knew she did it as a running joke between them that he better not get any ideas beyond the 'croissants' and 'fudge cake' until they actually got to Italy, but even if she didn't turn the key on him, Peter could believe little Bro's resolution never to dare do anything to shake that trust he had arduously earned.

"Stop fussing with that, and come enjoy your drink with the rest of us," Helen ordered.

As Aunt Martha heard and obeyed her sister, still casting an eye at the curtains, Mr. R was dying to know which was the new artwork.

"I recognise all these pieces, Katie, but where's the new Fielding? You haven't shown that yet. I thought that would have pride of place."

"If it's any consolation Dad, I haven't seen it yet either. She has it all wrapped up too, bow and all," Gerry returned. "Can I open it now? Pretty please?"

"Nope, not until after dinner. I'm saving that for last. Be grateful I'm not making you wait until Christmas!"

"Awww, she's gong to keep us all jumpy like a bunch of tykes at a birthday party." Mr. R chuckled. "All right then, we can wait."

"Oh, I think Mrs. Moritz is ready to serve," Katherine announced, seeing her peek her head in through the doorway.

Moving to the dining area, there was a jovial crush as they figured out where they were all seated, the table for twelve having to be set for thirteen. Peter did the honours of saying grace before they settled in. As he finished with the sign of the cross … .

Pop!

Startled, they looked up.

"Hey, Pete. I think you just exorcised the light bulb!" Tom laughed, everyone joined in.

"Oh no! That's the second to go in less than a week! They must have brought a dud chandelier with a short. Don't tell me I'll have to get it replaced. How annoying!" Katherine was not impressed.

"Aw, don't worry pet, we can still see the table fine," Gramps assured her. There was plenty of candlelight, and the chandelier did have more than one bulb after all.

The two families exchanged their latest news in a chattering mish-mash over Mrs. Morritz's succulent beef roast with all the trimmings. Peter smiled, it sounded like Fiona's house with everyone trying to keep an ear on all and sundry, good thing he was getting well practised in the art of table talk tennis. Sophia had asked Helen and Aunt Martha if they wanted to try helping her with her historical society endeavours, if only for a change, since they were so kind to include her with their charity groups, and of course, they thought that was a great idea, especially if it meant getting a break from Cee's attentions now that she and Vico were unavoidably members of the Club. Then, maybe the gallery bug had gotten to them, getting in on fund raising for valuable museum collections seemed like such a *chic* thing to do. Speaking of galleries, Katherine was soon to get the first art arrivals from her lady vegetarian artist for her next showing that January. It sounded like she was going to be pretty busy as the collection had quite a number of paintings. Peter didn't have too much news since his schedule was now on a regular rhythm again with his parish work albeit it was quite packed, however, Steves tried to wrangle a few exorcism stories from him since he was getting a name in the city after all. Jenny, despite her scientific background as a molecular biology graduate couldn't help but listen in on the odd tale or two of things going bump in the night before Peter returned to parish news: Monsignor Inigo Hernandez was about to be transferred from St. Peter's to the cathedral, and since he requested somewhere closer to live, St. John's rectory was getting a new tenant. On the business side of the conversation, Walsingham Industries was working on the latest advancement in their asthma inhalers now in the initial trial phase, while Lottie with Gerry and Tom's help secured a shipping contract from Seoul, new cars to be exact. Steves then floored them with a sudden brain-storming idea he had been mulling over, but then decided to put it out on the table to see what everyone thought: since the two families were about to merge wedding-fashion, why not merge business-wise? Pops wondered what that was all about, Gramps also, along with the Reinolds. That got the ladies' attention too.

"I've been thinking," Steves began. "You've got your own packing plants alongside your air-freight centres at certain cargo hub airports, right?"

"Yeah, we've also got refrigerated warehouses, even banana ripening rooms, that sort of thing. However, with perishable goods, meat, veg, food products for restaurants too, all of that, it saves on delivery times with the planes practically right next door," Gerry informed everyone. "Why?"

"How about considering taking it up a notch?"

"Okay, what have you cooked up now," Pops wanted to know.

"You know those subsidiary companies I bought? Some are biological product developers, but they could be expanded, maybe on a massive scale. Bone grafts, spinal discs, tendons and ligaments, blood and haemoglobin, vaccinations, that kinda thing. Together we could work on medical grade packing and storage warehouses right next to the air freight centres, prepare and ship much needed biological material for surgery or research labs to anywhere in the country, not just a few states."

"Hmm, medical grade you say? A complete sterile environment not to mention specialized packaging would be needed," Mr. R mulled aloud.

"Sounds like a complicated endeavour," Tom noted.

"Yeah, I won't say it's like shipping crates of bananas, it won't be an overnight project either, we would be working with viable body part donations after all … ."

"Steven! That's *enough* if you please! We are trying to eat," Aunt Martha huffed.

However, even Pops seemed interested with the idea, and Gramps thought it amusing that after all these decades the family might be returning to some form of the packing trade, even if it did sound Frankensteinish, and therefore both agreed with Mr. R that they should all get together at a more appropriate venue to hear Steven out about the possibility of such a joint venture. Martha took the opportunity to bring up a less gory topic.

"Well, since we're on to 'weddings' and 'merging', when should we start preparing? Since Gerry is now out and about and back at work, not to mention Charlotte and Thomas here have to think about it, you can't leave us hanging forever you know. Plans have to be made! And, we've got to figure out who's going to the altar first, too."

Wow, Aunt Martha there you go again! Katherine wished she could learn to pick her times! Gerry was only back at work a few days a week, and then only half a day at most so he could readjust and not get over tired, he was in a lot of pain when the meds began to wear off, *and*, he was barely used to the bustle of life at home again. They had just gotten rid of the private nurse, *finally*. As much as she couldn't wait, Katherine knew throwing wedding plans at them *now* was not the best time, it might add to his stress and delay the last steps of his recovery, not to mention reminding Lottie and Tom were both stuck in a holding pattern too and hesitant to do anything until this could be sorted out was a bit cruel. Yes, who should be married first? Katherine didn't dare bring that up yet. Lottie and Tom by rights should have that honour since Lottie suffered the tragic loss of her previous fiancé and shouldn't have to wait any longer for her happy day, but Katherine knew Lottie hadn't said anything as she wouldn't want her brother to have to drag about after his own tragic delay either ... yet, her and Gerry, or Tom and Lottie ... *someone* might have to wait until the following year, or figure out *something*, maybe a winter wedding instead? Allow some space between the two? However, things would have to be started soon, they all knew that. Someone would get the summer slot, and the summer slots for the cathedral would be booked out if not attended to soon, nothing else could be started or decided upon until the first date was secured ... what a logistical nightmare! Did this *have* to be brought up now?

"Oh Martha, stop jumping the gun. We've got plenty of time. Let's enjoy the holidays first before we resume all that yet," Helen wisely advised.

That put the lid on the can of worms for the time being, but did nothing to alleviate the engaged couples of the quiet, silent agonizing torment of impatience, yearning to turn the new leaf over and begin the next chapter in their lives, yet wondering how to go about it considering the circumstances.

After Martha's suburb Paradise cake, (she refused to let Mrs. Mortiz bake one since it was her niece's dinner after all), Katherine finally brought out the eagerly awaited gift for Gerry to unwrap. Despite the long wait, he playfully tested the hefty weight of the box, trying to guess what object just might be in there, then opened the box and lifted the items out, surprised at the delicate intricacies of the colourful orbs as he unwrapped them from their tissue paper veils.

"Wow, they're beautiful, but … what are they?"

"You haven't finished opening it all!" Katherine laughed. "Keep going."

Gerry was further intrigued by the silver holders. With the exception of those mosaic pieces years ago, this was far different from Fielding's typical modern style. Whatever this was, he loved it already! When he opened the orb representing the world, and at last, the base with its representation of the outer cosmos with softly glowing galaxies and nebulas with five hollows waiting for the holders, it made sense.

"I get it now, the Four Seasons, they sit around the earth. Huh!"

Everyone commented on the elegant beauty of the spheres and the stunning base. How unique!

"How I envy you, son! Good thing Kathy spotted this first, or you never would have had a chance," the Captain chuckled.

Gerry passed the polished orbs around for everyone to view, carefully placing them in their positions when they made their way back to him. "Wow, this is beautiful and so thoughtful. Thank you so much, my dear."

"You like it?"

"Need you ask?"

After working so hard to turn his once stylish but lacking bachelor pad into a veritable palace let alone a home he was not only proud of now but loved, to see how attentive she was to the little details like this that she knew would surprise and please him … . He leaned over and delivered a croissant on the cheek of the gift-giver, still holding the soft rosy sphere of Summer for a moment while casting a longing 'I love you' to her, the love of his life. Like this extraordinary gift, good things come to those who wait. Italy, Italy! Oh, so near and yet so far. So far. It didn't seem fair, or right. In so many ways it seemed she was getting the worst end of the deal. He didn't deserve her, and she could do so much better than him.

☙ ❖ ❧

The Christmas season was always a hectic time of year: vigil Masses, the Christmas Day Mass, and, it could be three that day if he was scheduled in for concelebrated services in addition to his early morning Latin Mass slot, then there were the extra feast days such as the Epiphany coming up. Never mind, Peter wondered what the Luminescence would show him that season, and of course, was not disappointed. It was too beautiful to describe! It gave him the strength to keep going. A wonderful consolation as sadly he wouldn't be able to visit the family on Christmas Day with all his running, at least maybe not until the Epiphany when things might settle down, he had to get some sleep sometime, especially as his exorcism ministry tripled in work, new cases were driving in from out of state now, some even from out of the country as far as Canada, or flying in from Mexico. The rest of the Holy Bachelors were also on the run, Jenkins with his work at the hospitals not to mention the VA hospital holiday dinner, Mark was once again invited to spend the holiday with the parents of his youth group flock, another lot having to be drawn so one family wasn't favoured over the others.

That meant Peter was left alone Christmas evening with the new arrival, Monsignor Inigo Hernandez, who seemed dissatisfied with his new accommodations the moment he arrived. Perhaps he expected something grander, and yeah, the guys couldn't blame him there, but they did their best to make him feel welcome, although something told Jenkins and Mark he wouldn't appreciate the harmless pranks they usually played on a new room mate in the house and so, joking was politely laid aside. Their hunch seemed confirmed by the way their new tenant disapprovingly eyed with a tinge of disgust the coffee mug about recaffeinating in the confessional Peter let Jenkins have since he found the thing funny. Eventually to escape the stare, Jenkins stopped using it. In fact, Hernandez seemed rather stand-offish, he hardly spoke or thanked anyone for that matter, including Gertie for all her hard work cooking and cleaning for them. It was almost two weeks of that now. One night when they were alone before the Christmas vigil arrived, Jenkins couldn't help but admit it was not easy to like their new house mate, who seemed a smidgen arrogant.

795

"No, just pragmatic." Peter tried to explain. "It's his Hispanic culture. For instance, in Spain they don't believe in constantly thanking someone when the person does the job they're paid to do."

"Really? That's odd," Mark noted.

"Yeah, to them our northern habitual politeness in thanking everybody for everything seems illogically ridiculous. Basically you thank someone when they do you a favour, not an expected task."

"I don't know about Spain, but I was brought up to always thank the person who slaved over the stove to put a plate in front of me," Jenkins pointed out.

To his credit, Inigo did ask Peter to thank his mother for arranging their two-some Christmas Day supper. Knowing that the Bachelors wouldn't have time to put together a full traditional dinner together with their hectic schedules and Gertie enjoying her few days off, especially after hearing the fellows had nothing decent to prepare after donating the Jersey mob gobblers to the nuns' soup kitchen, Sophia began cooking early and had Reinold Express Delivery Services drop off at the rectory plenty of easy to reheat dishes the day before complete with stuffing and all the trimmings, a plum pudding too. It wasn't quite like getting it fresh on the day, but it was home cooking and much better than what she could imagine them eating on the hop without her timely assistance.

Just as the two priests had said grace and were about to sit, there was a telephone call. Inigo was gracious enough to let Peter sit and got it instead. He was back in a few seconds later.

"It's for you. It's the sacristan from St. Patrick's, the cathedral."

"All right, thanks. I'll be back in a minute, please, don't let your dinner go cold."

Good old Bill. Obviously he called to wish him a Merry Christmas, it was a while since they had seen each other since his transfer, and yes, that was *part* of it.

"You won't believe it, a bus load of people came for the evening service, but they were actually coming to see *you*."

"Oh?"

"Yeah! A whole pilgrim group, from Ireland! They even had their group scarves with the tour logo like you'd see in Rome or Lourdes. They must've thought you were still stationed here and not at the other church. What I'm getting at is someone at Mass gave them the rectory address instead of doing the smart thing and telling them to go to your Mass and office tomorrow, so … ."

Peter heard a rumble pull up outside, a screech and hiss of brakes, a chattering of voices … the doorbell rang.

"Thanks for the heads-up, Bill. I think my unexpected guests have arrived."

"I'd better leave you to it then. Bye, Monsignor."

Wow, this was a first. Hanging up the line, Peter opened the door. There was excited babble among the group getting off the bus. Yes, yes, that's him! They recognised him from the photographs … shoot. Peter couldn't stop the odd photographs that were taken during his Masses. Even when asked nicely before the services to please refrain from taking pictures, *someone* would take a bootleg snap. Only the Lord knew how many were now going around by now. It was going past photos too, he got caught on a few video and camcorders the few times he had to look out into the congregation, it was almost impossible to stop now. The inevitable was happening, but heavens, a whole group, here, *now?* He wasn't quite sure how to handle this, they didn't have enough room to accommodate over forty visiting guests at the rectory, certainly not with his mail bags taking up what little parlour they had!

"Monsignor Reinold, we're here on a three day trip, just to see you. I hope you don't mind, but we'd love to get your blessing, maybe hear some of our confessions?"

"Er … ." He looked over again. The group was excited, in awe of him, hoping he wouldn't turn them away … .

"You've come all the way from Ireland?"

"Yeah! I'm from Mayo!"

"We're from Athlone!"

"Wicklow here!"

Lee, and Fr. O'Conner too God rest him, had let him in on how the Irish were mad about travelling, a case of 'itchy feet'. When bit by the travelling bug they didn't think anything of saving up and taking a weekend jaunt to New York to do their Christmas shopping, and pilgrimage group tours were quite popular among the old faithfuls, but to come to *him?* Mortifying! Aw, well, after coming all this way, he couldn't have them standing out in the freezing cold. Duty called. The best he could do was tell them to get back on the bus to keep warm, then after he apologised to Inigo for leaving him in the lurch, he got on the bus after them, began their little get-together with a communal prayer and an announcement that if they wished to go to confession, he would have to take them one at a time, maybe it would be easier if they went by the order as they were seated on the bus, just come on up and ring the doorbell when their turn came. Peter couldn't keep each penitent long, he had to work fast and cut any talkative fluff short otherwise they would be up into the early hours of the morning. Still, the unexpected pilgrims were grateful and certainly got the experience they were hoping for, having seen the Monsignor personally, if only for a few minutes. Mark and Jenkins were certainly surprised to see this when they came home. By then Peter was halfway through the bus load. Noticing how late it was getting, Inigo wondered if they shouldn't help get through his confession load, if only to get some peace. The incessant doorbell rings and knocking every fifteen minutes or so was getting on his nerves. Peter welcomed the help, and returning to the bus, asked if some of them wouldn't mind going to his other colleagues … you, yes you, you … . Peter separated those that didn't really need his specialised assistance, they had come for the novelty of witnessing his spiritual discernment. Still, the disappointment was palpable when the selection process began, and Inigo couldn't help but feel it when those who went to him made it obvious he wasn't their first choice.

"We can absolve too, you know," he noted, joining the other Holy Bachelors in the kitchen after his stint with the unexpected visitors was finished.

"Er, well, it's him they all want to see, with good reason too," Mark tried to explain, but Inigo obviously was not able to comprehend how things worked once you lived in close proximity to the Monsignor, or didn't want to for that matter. From that moment on, things seemed to get rather stony regarding Inigo's aloof Iberian temperament, and most of it seemed directed at Peter. Mark and Jenkins couldn't help notice the subtle difference he treated their friend in comparison with them, slipping jokes that went beyond pulling a leg, such as remarks about the mail-room and how wonderful it must be to be allowed to shirk the virtue of humility for her shallow step-sister, celebrity. Other times if someone called for Peter, he said he would take a message, but never write anything down, and forget to tell him until much time had passed. It became blatantly obvious when Leroy finally came back from his trip three days into the New Year of '94 and dropped by to see how they were all doing … .

"Hi Father, you must be new. Is Peter in? Could you tell him I'm here?"

"I'm sorry, we're not expecting visitors now." Inigio nearly closed the door on him.

"Oh," Lee continued, sticking a toe in, "don't worry, I'm not ye're average visitor."

"Hey Lee! You're back! How was your vacation?"

"Oi! How are ye? Happy New Year! It was grand, but I don't think I want to see another turkey dinner for the next ten years."

Inigio let him in after hearing Mark's warm greeting. After they introduced him to their new house mate over a round of cake, tea and coffee, Lee opened up the bag he brought.

"I've got prezzies! I'm sorry it's way after Christmas, but better late than never."

"Aw, Lee, you didn't have to bring anything," Peter reminded. None of the Holy Bachelors went to too much trouble regarding holiday gifts since they had stipend budgets, usually didn't have time to look for gifts anyway, and, they got bombarded with loads of food and gifts from their parishioners, who needed more? As it was, it took them a while to get through the platters of food Peter's mother had sent them.

"Yeah I know, but still. Ma and Gran helped me find them," Lee continued. "I had no idea it would be hard getting these, but we found 'em! Hope they fit." Lee passed each an Aran wool cardigan in the hard-to-find black.

"Hey, nice," Jenkins pronounced. "Thanks!"

Mark put his on. "Wow, comfy and warm too," he pronounced.

Pete tried his on. "Thanks Lee, and thank your mother and grandmother for us."

"Sure will, Pete. Good! They fit. We had to guess the sizes, with me as the model."

"You got one too," Mark couldn't help but notice, Lee being the white sheep among all the black ones with his new woolly cable and honeycomb-patterned model just like theirs only in the traditional creamy colour, complete with the jaunty high collar and leather lattice buttons.

"Aw, I'm sorry Monsignor," Lee then noticed, "I would have one for you too, only I didn't know ye guys had a new flatmate."

"That's all right," Inigo replied.

"Nah, ye can't be the odd one out. I'll call Mum, see if she can't find us another. For now as a consolation prize, you get the choccies." He handed him a Milk Tray box of chocolates.

"Thank you."

Mark and Jenkins looked at each other. So, he *did* say thank you on occasion.

After a brief chat, Peter excused himself, time to hit the mailbags. Lee followed behind.

"Hey, you just got back. Are you sure you want to spend your evening sorting through this pile?"

"Sure Pete, by the looks of it, things have stacked up while I was gone."

True, he did get behind. "I've been up to my neck in it lately. The Christmas Mass schedule, parish work, you know how it is."

"Say no more, I'm ready and rarin' to go. Where're the stamps?"

Returning to his duty as assistant GPO manager, Lee settled in and told Pete about his trip back to the Emerald Isle. Mum sure got a surprise when he went to Midnight Mass with her, then a mighty shock when he went up for Communion. She *had* to find out what that was about! What's gotten into ye? You have to go to confession you know! Ah Lord, I hope you haven't committed a sacrilege?! After pesterin' and pokin' and proddin' and whinge'n, the whole story came out on the drive home, and that was that. The wild roving oat-sowing bucko was back in the fold. Ach, sakes alive! The days were unbearable after that! This kissin' and cuddlin' and, innumerable sappy faces of relief constantly thrown his way soon grew worse than the pokin' and proddin' for answers, not to mention all the questions asking what it was like to have confession with the Monsignor. Was it like the rumours said? Was he really able to see your soul? Finally the cousins decided to get him out of the house for a breather. What did they do but drive past the local pub and bring him on a long drive to Lisdoonvarna for New Year's, ribbing him all the while since he now had repented of the error of his ways, it was time to find a decent woman and settle down at last!

"Ah sure, it was all a lark to rile me up. It wasn't match makin' season, and now people go there just for the music and the *craic* rather than finding their match, but I couldn't get a moment's peace! See what ye've done to me, Pete!"

Peter laughed. "Oh, I think you'll live."

"I dunno, it's getting' kind of hard. I mean, let's face it, this temple has been run more like a carnival than a church for quite a spell. As much as I like the peace you an' the lads've got here, it's hard to stay away from the roller coaster ride, if you catch my meaning."

"Well, you weren't meant to be like us Lee, nor can your life be a perpetual roller coaster either. Have you ever thought of turning that carnival ground into a nice house and a picket fence with a wife and a few kids?"

"Ye're at me now. Settle down? There's a thought! Has the humour come upon me at last?" Leroy chuckled, then grew a bit thoughtful. "Aw, I dunno, the nice settling kind of girls aren't going to want a wild rover, even a reformed one, especially this soon after getting yoked back onto the straight and narrow."

"Don't knock yourself short. A man doing his best to stay on the straight and narrow is also attractive, maybe more so than the carnival ring leader. Just give it time, and prayer. You'll meet the right person."

"If *you* say so."

"So, have you seen anyone else since you've come back?"

"Oh yeah, I dropped by to see Ger and Kathy yesterday, it's good to see him out and about at last."

"It is, although I'm afraid I haven't seen them since their house warming dinner, and a few quick calls to wish them some holiday blessings and cheer. How are they," Peter enquired as he finished off sorting a pile of letters.

"They seemed grand, showing off the penthouse, and I could actually admire the end result. It sure is something! Oh, and guess what happened: Kathy said that Ger got stuck one morning with that freakin' Resident's Association woman, she had the gall to show up and poke about with a couple of engineers before I came, she demanded to see the latest upgrades and make sure all was according to building regulations. For flip's sake! Can you believe it?"

"Yeah, I can. It's not the first time Mrs. Beechwarz has done that. When Gerry got the place done the first time around, she was knocking on his door too."

"If it were me I'd kick 'em out on their ears! But, I dunno. I can't help get the feeling somethin's not quite right. Not the Beechworty woman, but that really would've got me boil'n! Maybe it's the stress of all they're trying to fit in, Kathy's got the next show coming up, or maybe, it's the newness of actually living together and real life hittin' them, but they don't seem like they're happy selves. Then, I could've waited, too much unexpected company. They just didn't need to see me, droppin' in right after the warty woman, and so close after the holidays too, but I didn't know when I'd get to see them after, I've got a lot of work coming up."

That didn't sound like them. Peter resolved to drop by, but in a few days, give them some space first. Maybe they just needed some quiet time. But, he couldn't shake the feeling of disquiet that this news brought. Yes, something seemed wrong, *off*, but what, he didn't know.

"Then again, there's other things," Lee continued, as he smoothed on another stamp, "it might just be a case of the post-holiday blues, they can be a mighty downer too, or they could just be plain worried. The new neighbours that moved next to Kathy's family have insisted they come to their place for dinner now that they've settled and finished fixing up their own home, and they were insistent on meet'n the man who got that prison education program goin', so, Kathy and Ger also got walked into an invite."

"You're not serious."

"Yeah, Ger's gonna meet Jersey's mobster ."

"When's the dinner?"

"Little Christmas, so yeah, that's three days from now. Kathy's family got out of a New Year's Day invite, but they couldn't wriggle out forever, not without finally admittin' why they don't want to be so closey closey and end up peeving them."

Uh oh, that really didn't sound good. If it was any consolation, at least Vico and Cee Becchino were appreciative of bro's charity work and had already made a good impression with them before they met. After their run-ins with the Mob families in New York trying to muscle in on their trucking and shipping for clandestine operations a few years back, they didn't need some added problems with the Jersey side of things. Yeah, that would definitely stress out Ger and Kathy. That had to be it. Peter could only pray that their dinner would work out all right and they didn't get walked into a few things they wished they could refuse.

☙ ❖ ❧

The line seemed to stretch forever, even for the Epiphany it seemed he was not going to get the hoped-for break away to the family today. That one bus load that appeared on his doorstep Christmas night seemed to have attracted seventy-seven times more since in those eleven days to his spiritual clinic, bringing hoards of curious pilgrims mixed among the troubled souls earnestly seeking his help. However Peter couldn't have his regular booked in exorcism patients left unattended for the novelty seekers, duty had to come first since he was the diocesan exorcist after all, and was driven to grab a few of his colleagues that he could find in the hallways of the parish office.

"Fr. Juan, are you free right now? I urgently need another confessor, if you could spare the time … ."

Gathering as many on the spot volunteers as he could muster, he set to work, sending everyone to them who did not need his particular confessional gifts. There were quite a few exorcism clients, sadly, one of

802

them was a new case, the first-time visit of a child who had been cursed before birth by some jealous member of the family who couldn't have children of their own. The parents were distraught seeing their young son who was only seven afflicted like this without the possession having been his fault, but thankfully, it was a weak curse with no sortilege present and the boy was innocent of any mortal sin. Although Peter could see and sense the demon present was desperate to hang on to this nursery catch, hoping it could get the boy at a later age, drive him to sin of his own accord, he assured them this should not be a difficult clearing. While the scene of the child experiencing the exorcism was frightening to the parents to witness, not to mention the waiting pilgrims who could hear the tumult out in the basement hallway, Peter was already well seasoned to the few bouts of screeching and the cussing, it wasn't anything like the battle he had faced in the Trenton psych ward. The other cases he currently had involved a few more devils, the clearings still drained him, the demons still tried to put on an unholy show, but as he was promised from Above the deliverances happened in less time. True to that heavenly promise, the demon holding the child before him grew livid that its time of casting out was already thrust upon him so fast, the imp was forced to reveal it would be cast out that very day when the clock struck twelve, however, before it left it delivered a parting threat: you think *Magister caput* has forgotten *his* promise? Just you wait, black robe! Everything you care about will crumble around you and *burn*! Ignoring the threat, Peter gave the final commands to depart as the clock hands pointed to noon, the demon shrieked off. It wasn't the first time he was threatened, it wouldn't be the last.

What a busy day! His exorcisms done, it was time to see to the many visitors hoping to receive confession from him, lunch as usual was skipped. He took only a few minute's break to call Stonyvale and give his regrets he wouldn't be making it home for dinner. Of course, his mother was disappointed, but understood completely. He had many, many children to take care of now. However, since she had him on the line, she asked him how it all was going.

"I'm getting overwhelmed. I may have to ask his Eminence for some assistants, maybe some new quarters, the office is getting inundated."

"I know, I just saw the afternoon news."

"What?"

"Yes, I'm afraid the bus loads of crowds emptying just to see the Monsignor of Manhattan have attracted a reporter or two, or three … ."

Uh no. He was definitely going to need more assistants.

"Have you eaten anything yet, dear?"

"Umm ... ."

"Oh Peter."

He reassured her he wouldn't skip dinner, whenever he got back to the rectory that was, and asked how everyone was doing. They were all fine, except as usual unpleasant news seemed to bombard them around the holidays, and the Epiphany was no exception. The Captain didn't like some of the reports about the west coast division, something wasn't running right. They were losing a lot of business in California the last three months, and so it looked like another globe trot to assess the situation was coming up, a domestic trip this time, but to hear this today after worrying how tonight was going to fare for Gerry and Kathy was all they needed. So far Ger had escaped meeting Vico the Mob Don, but now, there was no getting out of it.

"You know, Lottie dropped by yesterday to see them, and they didn't seem like themselves, so she told me. It has to be about tonight, they certainly don't need this stress. Say a prayer all will go well tonight, will you dear?"

She didn't need to ask, they were all in his prayers. Not wanting to hold him up any longer, she reluctantly left him go back to his work. Troubled by his mother's news, he wondered what was up with Ger and Kathy, but other than prayer, he couldn't do much for them at the moment, he was urgently needed back and forced himself to focus. He remained tapped into his spiritual intuition for so long, engrossed in trying to see as many of the eager visitors as possible that he forgot all sense of time until his mortal frame was sapped from the spiritual exertion not to mention hunger. It was nine at night when he finally realised he had to call it quits. Tomorrow was another day.

The Holy Bachelors had a plate of that night's supper ready for him to heat up in the oven when he came home, for which he was very grateful.

"Seriously, with all those buses, we didn't think you'd be back until midnight," Jenkins noted. "Tuck in."

"Hey! Quick! You guys gotta see this," Mark called from the community room. Peter picked up his plate and followed Jenkins, wondering what the hubbub was about. Mark pointed to the late evening news on the TV. "Isn't that your sister-in-law's neighbourhood in Jersey?"

It was. Peter nearly dropped his plate when the reporter announced that the home of Ludovico Becchino had been targeted by a drive-by shooter earlier that evening. What! Jenkins motioned for Mark to turn up the volume. Thank God, it appeared no one was hurt! A few shots through the front door and a rock through the window. Gerry! Kathy! The

Walsinghams! Were they okay? Peter abandoned his plate and headed for the phone. Helen answered his call.

"It's a miracle you got through! We haven't had a minute without the phone ringing!"

"I've just seen the late news. Are you all okay? What happened?"

No, no one was hurt, just shook up. The Becchino's dining room was at the side of the house near the back so it all missed them. Thank God it wasn't a barrage of bullet fire, just a few shots, however, that didn't make it any less frightening! To think a shooting happened at Oak Meadows, of all places! The police came, asked them questions, but there was not much to say. They certainly didn't know who could have done this. Considering who their dinner hosts were, they probably knew more about that then they did, and the police didn't have much to go on at the moment. Right now, they were all trying to repair their shattered nerves.

"Wait, here's your brother, let me put him on."

"Ger, are you all right?"

"Yeah, we've survived, no one's hurt. I've called Stonyvale, let them know we're okay. Poor Kathy, she's shook up though. Man, the questions we had to answer, and, to think we're now associated with the Jersey Mob! I wouldn't have minded if we could've snuck in for dinner and out, nobody would have known."

"Are you still going to stay the night?"

"As much as Kathy's parents want us to get away from the chaos, they don't want us driving out late either, and, the place outside is crawling with news crews, so yeah, we're still staying."

"Right, the media." Sure, wasn't he looking at the pandemonium outside Walsingham's house on the squawk box. Definitely the kind of publicity no one wanted.

"We'll try to venture out early. I hope we can keep as low a profile as possible. I saw you're having a time of it too. Your office has become a pilgrim destination."

"At least I'm stuck in the basement and out of sight. Well, since you've mentioned an early start in the morning, which I've also got, I won't keep you up. I'll drop by some evening to see you two. Tell everyone I was asking about them."

"Sure Pete, I will. Okay, I guess this is good night."

Peter returned to his cold dinner, setting up a TV tray to watch the news while he ate, a rare concession for him these days considering all his letters and workload. The Bachelors wondered how all was faring and were relieved to hear that despite how it looked on TV right now, all was okay.

Silently, Peter could only hope that all really *was* okay. His Mom was right, although Ger tried to sound like his usual self, something was eating at little Bro, but after tonight, of *course* he would sound out of sorts. Hopefully, the shock will have settled down by the time he visited them.

As Peter mused about the night's dramatic turn of events, something else on the TV distracted him. Huh, another scandal? He had given up TV as a penance most nights, however it didn't seem much of a penance any more, no wonder he didn't miss it that much when he heard reports of a troubled world that seemed to be getting worse by the day. What now? However, he sat up when he heard the arts and cultural segment of the news was agog with the latest report that three accusers had come forward with cases against Sir Conrad Elverton of the Elverton Gallery: he was now currently under arrest for one account of sexual assault and four accounts of sexual harassment, and that a request for extradition to face seven more charges of sexual assault made by five different victims in the United Kingdom had been issued the day before. *Elverton?* Him?

"Hey, Pete. You look like you've seen a ghost."

"Almost! He dropped into Kathy's gallery on occasion, and, was just about to open a second gallery not far from hers."

"Pete, you're not serious." Mark was stunned. "Whoa. Is she going to be freaked out when she hears this! Not to mention your brother."

"I know." Yes, without any spiritual gifts, Peter could predict that. He didn't say it just then, but Gerry mentioned a while back Elverton dared to get fresh with Katherine although she kept him in his place and didn't hang around too close when he was on the premises from what she told him. Obviously, her instincts had proved correct. Thank God if that man had any evil intentions towards her, he didn't get anywhere. "I'd better drop by to see them tomorrow."

Unfortunately, that promised visit didn't materialize. By the time he finished that day with his parishioners and hoards of visitors, it was too late to drop by and he had to settle for a phone call. Busy line. He tried three times. Okay, tomorrow then.

The following day, despite the ice, the snow and the cold, the crowds still came, long before now it was a common sight to see those who couldn't get into the church for his Mass spill outside onto the pavement. It was near impossible to get to the car when the service was over! Numerous requests for blessings and 'please could I have a word with you?' surrounded him. He stopped for a moment, but he couldn't stay, not with his schedule. He disliked his escape plan, but now there was nothing for it. He pulled out of his coat pocket a handful of blessed medals and passed them into the crowd, but that didn't give him much reprieve. Another group clustered around him. Suddenly, Peter saw Bill come through the crowd and clear a path for him.

"Quick Padre!"

Peter jumped into the car and motioned for Bill to sit in.

"Thanks Bill! What are you doing here today? Shouldn't you be at the cathedral?"

"Nah, I've given that up. I saw the news, you can't handle all this on your own. I thought you could use a permanent volunteer."

"Thanks, only, I do hope you know what you're letting yourself in for."

"Hey, no sweat. It's done already, I've quit at the cathedral. You'll have to put up with me now."

Peter chuckled.

"Er, well, I *do* need a consistent altar server who will show up in the mornings, not to mention someone who knows how to train the others, their Latin leaves a lot to be desired."

"Say no more, Padre. So, where do I begin?"

Bill was a God-send, keeping order in the basement hallway, attending to the growing line, sorting out the drop-ins from the scheduled appointments as Peter ministered to his patients. This was the first time he had seen the Padre at work as an exorcist, and wow, it *was* true. The strange howling and screeching that came behind the closed door of the OR was enough to set his hair on end, and to think, there were a surprising number coming to him for exorcisms. Good thing he didn't hear everything the Monsignor had to put up with. Peter often commanded the devils to be quiet and yes, the demons would obey, but often got a threat flung at him before then. Today the demon holding one of his patients let slip another taunt, this time, one that didn't make any sense: "Ha ha! You think she got away scot free? Burned! *Just like you got burned!*" Peter ordered the demon silent and didn't press for explanations. Although he knew he had the rare if not unique grace and privilege to demand truthful answers and get them from the devils, it was wise not to ask questions that didn't have anything to do with a particular exorcism underway, and his patients this morning were another boy and right now an older man, so he knew the demon wasn't talking about his current victims. The demons knew of his gift, so whatever answer they might give, even truthful ones, they might be used right now to get him to stop the proceedings. He continued the exorcism until noon, then reminded Bill to go to lunch.

"What about you?"

Peter said not to worry about him, he had another patient to see, he wouldn't be finished with them until after he came back. When Bill returned, sure enough, Peter was still in there, and the lines were also there patiently waiting for their turn. Peter eventually called Bill back when his penitent left and asked if he couldn't find some priests to help with the confessions. Bill did the best he could, no one seemed available today.

"That's all right. Just let me know when you want to go home."

Bill decided to stick around later than he planned. Wow, how did the Monsignor keep going? Nine at night! He went non stop all day without a break since early morning, and that would be from about six AM starting with his morning Mass. Even now there were desperate visitors trying to keep him from leaving, as tired as he looked. Bill had put a stop to it and reminded everyone to come back tomorrow.

"No, sorry Bill. Not this Sunday, after Mass I won't be here. I've got a few house clearings to do."

"Er, okay, make that the day after," Bill corrected. The late-night line groaned their disappointment. "You heard the Monsignor! Don't worry, he'll be here then. It's time to close up."

Peter gave them a blessing and decided he and Bill should give them all the quick slip through the secondary exit out the back that served as a fire escape. Thankfully, nobody outside expected him to leave that way and they made a clean getaway. Thanking Bill for his assistance, he dropped him off at his apartment. By then, it was too late to drive around to visit Ger and Kathy. He tried to call them again, but the phone was busy, or, off the hook. Something was definitely wrong. He could sense it. Tomorrow, you *have* to see them tomorrow.

The next day with his house clearing appointments, he was free of the crowds. At last he could make that promised visit when he was finished. Thing is, being Sunday, they were probably having dinner somewhere with either of the two families, maybe Stonyvale after what happened at Oak Meadows a few nights ago, but better check at the manor first. Lottie was there and answered the phone.

"Oh Petey! I'm so glad you called."

"What? What's wrong?"

"*Something* is. The Captain was talking about having to go see the west coast area of the company, you know the drill, but without much ado, Gerry said he would go."

"Heck, that's *way* to soon for him to make a trip like that. Have Tom talk him out of it, he can do the run instead."

"Too late! Gerry's already gone! He took the private jet yesterday. He's either in one of his bottle-up moods, or worse yet, he's finally burst and it's resulted in this crazy stunt! We've tried calling Kathy to see if she's all right, maybe have her come out for dinner, but she never went to the gallery yesterday we've discovered, and, we can't get through to her at the apartment. Something's gone very wrong."

"I'm a block from there. I'll see what's up."

"Oh good! I'd better let you go. Oh, I *do* hope everything is all right."

So did Peter. Why, *why* did you delay that visit? Whatever has happened, you might have been able to prevent it! But no, he had duties to accomplish too. His parish work had to come first, but how ironic. A shoemaker never has a new pair of shoes, a lawyer never has a will, a doctor often won't heal himself, and in his case, the Monsignor of Manhattan must help everyone else first before his own kin and kindred. He hoped whatever happened he was not too late to do something.

It was a distraught Katherine who opened the door to him.

"Oh Peter, he's called off the wedding."

"Called off the … ? What's happened?"

As they sat down Katherine tried to find the words, she wasn't sure what had gone wrong, she thought Gerry was happy to be in his own home at last, but then, she had to admit he seemed to grow quiet and withdrawn the whole month when not having to brave any company or go out in public, but then, she put it down to readjusting to life with the pain and the semi-immobility, and that seemed to be the reason all right. Obviously he was 'stewing' again, but yesterday the pot finally boiled over when he came home from the office and said they needed to have a serious talk before he left. Not only did he announce his sudden globe-trot, but went into a depressing speech he couldn't expect her to go through with the wedding now, roped to a crippled wreck for the rest of her life, and, he would be cruel to expect it when starting a family and having a normal life may not even be possible under his circumstances.

"He went into this 'you have your whole life ahead of you' spiel, he wouldn't give me a chance to talk him out of this frame of mind. And, what made it worse was the shooting the other night. It has to be, because he went on about me being in danger and all of that, considering what happened to him in the hit and run ordered by that Jade Cobra group, the fact that the guy who did it was still not caught, the same person could have done the shooting, he said in all likelihood it could happen again. He rambled on it was all for the best if I didn't stay with him."

"But they may not have been related at all!"

"I know, that's what I said. His accident and the other night couldn't have been related, but he said it had to be. He told me that he saw and overhead Vico near the dining room door muttering to his head bodyguard that it must've been the 'new chinks' moving in, because there was a note tied to the rock that went through the window that Vico quickly put in his pocket. Gerry didn't get much of a look, but on it was something that looked like an Asian style graphic the police in Jakarta showed him of a snake when he uncovered the gang's operations in their area of the dockyards, and of course, we all know what happened after *that*! Maybe it wasn't just the Mob Boss of Jersey getting a message, maybe two birds were meant to be hit at once with that stone. That's what he went on about."

Peter slowly exhaled.

"Did Gerry say anything to the police?"

"Maybe he did when the cops talked to everyone alone, I don't know, and I didn't ask him the other night. I was too busy trying to keep us patched together."

"Of course. What happened next?"

"I tried to tell him he was seeing too much into this, the papers were all on about a turf war between the crime syndicates these days, it had to be related to that, and I was about to pull the things out of the case as he packed, but he shut it so fast, it was best not to get in his way. I didn't know what to do! He was in such a mood! He was packed and gone before I knew it."

Peter was stunned. He knew something drastic must have happened to make Gerard snap if he could even think about giving up Katherine, but to keep her safe? Yes, he would do anything in that regard. Ger obviously used business across the country as an excuse to flee in order to keep her free from the enemies he had made, and in one leap, make the parting break between them fast and as far as he could in an attempt to make his sudden decision as painless as possible, albeit a blatantly futile plan with regards to the element of heartbreak.

"It's like he had it all figured out," she continued, the tears trickling down her cheeks. "He said when he came back we could sort out the practical matters of it all. I didn't have to leave, he insists I have the penthouse in recompense for breaking the engagement, especially after all the work I've put into it. It would be the proper thing to do he said, but oh so businesslike! Pete! What's gotten in to him? Doesn't he know I don't want this place if he's not in it?"

Peter handed her the box of tissues from the side table. By the few rumpled on the floor, it was obvious she had been busy at it before he arrived.

"At least he said he would come back. By then he will have seen what a rash and stupid thing he's done and come to his senses."

"I hope so, but then, in spite of what he told me, I still can't help feel *I'm* the one at fault and that he was using all of this as the excuse to call it off."

"Katherine, why would you think that? Of *course* you're not at fault. Come, what's really troubling you?" She couldn't look him in the eyes. "Oh. Is it confession-session time? Whatever's wrong, don't be afraid to tell me. You've never held back on me before. Besides, I can actually grant absolution you know."

She smiled wistfully. That was true, and for some reason it was always easy to open up to him, but now ... ?

Guilt covered Katherine like a shroud, guilt, and *fear*. Peter was used to diagnosing those cruel mind games that made one feel guilty over non-existent transgressions in addition to real sins. Strangling fear, and ... *shame*. It was as though she was drowning in it. He took the stole out of his pocket and slipped it on. The minute he made the sign of the cross he immediately saw there was no *sin* present, but shame was choking her silent, suffocating her. Oh Lord, what was *wrong*? He couldn't *see* anything, but he could sense ... an injury had happened. Yes, of course one would feel wounded having the one you love suddenly run out on you, but that wasn't completely it. This was much more deep, crushing. Katherine still couldn't look him in the eyes as she began, slowly, trying to find the words, bring them out ... .

Just before New Years she unavoidably had to stay late one night over some of the arrangements for the artwork now arriving for her next show and all the paperwork that was coming with it. She was busy alone at the desk in her office under the staircase, at first not paying attention to who just came in, the door shutting behind them. She thought perhaps Esther or Kevin had straggled late too, often a patron could hold them up, and now came to say goodnight before they left. When no one answered, she looked up. Elverton. What gall! She hadn't seen the creep in a few days, staying up and out of sight in the studio or making herself scarce when he appeared for his morning coffee and pastry, and lately when he came for his lunch, that was a new one. It seemed she was becoming a regular recluse in the upper floors of the gallery. With him in the neighbourhood, she never knew when she would bump into him. She stopped going to the framers and let

Dennis take over that job as the creep could be there too getting a framing job done, it seemed he would be there waiting just for her. On the few times he did manage to run into her, he refused to let her be, offers of lunch, dinner, come see the new building, anything to get her attention. A flat 'no' wasn't accepted and she had to abruptly break away with work as a valid pretext. What made these unpredictable encounters more uncomfortable, she had to watch him. He had a tendency not to keep his hands to himself, nothing compromising in public, a friendly pat or grip on the arm that was too touchy for someone she hardly knew, but since she kept face forward, thankfully he didn't try that friendly pat somewhere else, but the anxiety of not knowing if he would be brazen enough to try and hoping it would never go to that was always a plaguing thought, all the more reason to try and avoid him if only to spare herself the more uncomfortable prospect of the face-forward-get-away-from-him-as-soon-as-you-can occasions.   It had become an unsettling, cyclic, daily routine. The not knowing if she would successfully avoid him every time she drove up to the gallery, it was becoming an obsessive anxiety, breathing a sigh of relief at the end of the day when she did. It was getting to the point she was looking over her shoulder everywhere. It was like he was doing his best to make sure he would never leave her thoughts. At least the evenings were safe. Now he had the audacity to hunt her out in here, in her own office. She quickly stood up.

“Finally, we have some quality time together.”

“Who said you could come in here? You had better leave.”

“Still playing 'catch me if you can', are we?” He laughed, sneered more like it. “Or, just too loyal to have some excitement on the side, is that it? Touching, but how someone like *you* can stay with that crippled Kraut when you can have anyone is beyond me.”

“How dare you! Get out!”

He didn't. His expression changed. He turned the lock.

“No. No more playing hide and seek. It's time you know what it's like to have a *real* man. You should enjoy it.” Before she knew it he had her by the back of the neck and shoulder. He pulled her close, but she struggled, tried to get away from that noxious mouth. He paused. He sneered again. “I guess not. No matter, just lie back and think of England.” His grip tightened, he pulled her over.

“Katherine!”

“Oh no, Peter! He didn't get *that* far! But he shoved me onto the desk. I wanted to scream for help, but my voice wouldn't work. I grabbed for something, I got the phone, hit him across the head.”

"You little *bitch*," he spat after steadying himself, felt his head, then looked at the trickle of red in his hand, but having delivered a stunning broadside she was able to get out from under him. Still, he was blocking the door, he was about to come after her again but she reached for a control panel on the wall. He stopped. He knew she had the best security system, the whole neighbourhood did. Once in awhile the alarm got accidentally tripped and they could see what it was made of. Now, one push of a button, and she would have her security guards and half the Brooklyn police force on his back in ten seconds.

Furious, but sensing defeat, he glowered at her as he briskly tidied his jacket and tie then unlocked the door and left, but not without uttering a threat that if she ever said a word, he would see to it her gallery would be ruined. Katherine was now shaking, reliving it all. He didn't know the security panic button was on the other wall behind him. How she had the presence of mind to bluff with one of the circuit boxes to the climate control system was beyond her when she was not a good bluffer to begin with. Had he suspected otherwise … she was sick with that thought. No, he didn't do what he really wanted, but in those seconds to feel such a brutish … his breath, grasped … *the terror.* She felt soiled, dirty, used as if the worst had actually happened, but what was the wrenching part, the guilt of wondering *did she bring this on herself?* Did she encourage this? She was pretty sure she didn't, did she? She thought she had completely told him off. Maybe she should have never gone near his gallery at all the past summer, even to drop off those paintings, business or no business. Maybe she put the idea into his head … .

With a sickening knot in his stomach, Peter now realised the meaning of the strange phrase the devils had been taunting him with. God help them, they had both been burned, but unlike him who had been unexpectedly thrust into the most tantalizing temptation he had battled against his whole life to avoid in order to choose a greater spiritual good but nearly fell by the enticing beauty of it, Katherine suffered what every woman feared: to have one of the most intimate experiences corroded into a freakish and degrading nightmare. He escaped with a singeing after his first and only brief encounter with human passion, but she had been emotionally and psychologically scorched, and how long the healing would take, only time would tell.

"None of this is your fault! Don't blame yourself! That man is a sick, demonic predator. Didn't you see the news? Only evil could have obsessed a man to that level."

"I know, I did see, and I'm glad he's in jail! I should have gone home that night, I had the strangest feeling just to get home and not stay late, but I had so much to do … ."

"You haven't told anyone, have you."

"No! I can't! I can't!"

"What about the police? Don't you want to report this?"

"Oh no!"

How could she? If there was any consolation, he was already locked up, possibly going to be sent back to the UK for trial. She didn't really *have* to come forward to keep the public safe from him *now*, did she? Besides, she had no hard evidence to convict him: no cameras were in her office, it was her word against his. To report it in public when it wouldn't do any good? That dirty feeling clung notwithstanding her innocence in the matter. She just wanted to hide, not be seen, crawl away, not let anyone know what happened. She felt sick, disgusted. She could hear it now, that 'poor thing, you know what happened to her' among the gossipers, in the street, behind her back, that look that would be in their eyes. Their families were being dragged through the press enough as it was, they didn't need to be associated with that criminal and his string of sickening crimes too. It was hard enough going out in public. It felt as if the whole world already knew. *Why can't it just go away?*

"You can't go through this alone. What about your mother? And Gerry? You shouldn't hide this from him. When he comes back … ."

Katherine shook her head. No! No!

"How can I tell him?" She had no idea how he'd take it, she was on the verge of losing him already! What if this finally sent him over the edge? What if he could sense what had happened and now didn't want to be with her?

"Ger's not like that. He would never leave you over that. It's not your fault, and you're certainly not damaged goods, Katherine."

"But why do I *feel* it? Why do I feel as filthy and cheap as if I cheated behind his back?"

"Mind games. Dark, vicious ones. Don't let them play with you! Evil loves to subvert all blame onto the innocent. You'll have to fight this, and no, it won't be easy, but you can't let it win."

"How? I don't know how to do that. I can't get that night out of my head … or yesterday! But please, you won't tell anyone, will you? You promise? Please?"

"All right, I promise. If it will make you feel better."

"Thank you, Peter."

Although she did not need absolution, he had sworn to everlasting silence. He could only pray Katherine would not allow herself to succumb to the nightmare she went through. May she have the courage to tell someone else! God had the power to turn an evil event around, bring good out of it, but this time, Peter didn't see quite how that was possible. He had faith, but talk about *guilt*, Peter too felt burdened, responsible, the taunts from the Enemy still rung in his ears, Hell doing everything to stop him from continuing his work. Cease, and we'll leave you and those you care about alone. If not, *burn, burn, burn*!

∛❖√

Despite Peter and Katherine's sacrosanct pact, there was no hiding the other terrible news from the families and the Gallery Gang about Gerry's sudden change of mind regarding the wedding. She had to tell them. Within the next few days when she could face them all she broke it to them, what consternation that created. Surely Gerry wasn't serious? However, when the Captain heard about who could have done the shooting, yes, keeping Katherine safe and everyone safe was something to think about. He was about to order back his own team of bodyguards, but Lottie refused, she had just gotten rid of the 'Hulk' and was not about to take on another one. The Captain tried to talk Katherine into it at least, maybe if she was protected, it might persuade Gerry to change his mind. If it meant getting Gerry back, okay, she agreed. They tried to call him in San Diego hoping this would work, but if they tried to discuss anything other than business, the phone went dead. Maybe they shouldn't push him, give him space. In the meantime everyone commiserated with Katherine, tried their best to cheer her up. Maybe the business trip was what he needed, give him some space to get whatever was eating him off his chest. Everyone got a case of the jitters before the Big Day of vows and wedding bells arrived, Gerry was probably feeling it now. Once he had some time to himself and think it over, he'd be begging for forgiveness for suggesting such a thing. Yes, just give him time. He said he'd only be gone a few weeks, right? It'll have all blown over by then. For now, they all kept the sudden estrangement quiet, that's all they needed now, to see it in Beatrice Brandis' infamous gossip

815

column, which would only make matters worse and might wreck any chance of a reconciliation.

True, he said he would be back. Just a matter of weeks. Katherine now lived on this hope. At least Gerry sent in reports of his trip via faxes and in that way they knew he was alive, a check-in at the LA dock and depot yards then give the general manager of that sector a rat-a-tat-tat was next on his agenda, but he was not ready to talk about anything personal yet. Okay, matters like this were too serious for a long distance call. This was a face to face matter. Katherine decided not to be a pest and give him the space he desperately needed right now. Things would be different when he came back. She would sit him down and talk him out of this strange altruistic decision to liberate her from him and their engagement. Until then, work helped to keep her busy, mind-numbed, but she avoided the gallery office as much as possible. The memory of that sordid night was too raw. That space now felt violated. Mercifully she had a reliable team in Suzy, Esther and Kevin who could keep the book keeping end of things running and she didn't need to go in there too often. Plus, she had a show coming up with that vegetarian artist, the last major art event they had scheduled. So close to opening night, she couldn't cancel it now. The phrase proved correct, no matter what happens, the show must go on.

Reinold Enterprises also had to keep trucking, although the executive floor staff wondered why the Captain was suddenly more irritable of late and was ready to blow for the most trivial errors. Kells got a sharp bark or two for no reason at all. No doubt the Big Boss didn't want Mr. Gerard making such a trip so soon, it was an uncomfortable shock for the staff to see him in that wheelchair, and even more of a shock to see he needed canes when he did walk a few paces. That had to be it. Even Miss Reinold and Mr. Winthorne didn't look like their happy selves. Then, on top of a globe trot and all they had to manage, Mrs. Clarke called in sick. She rarely did that, but Kells or another personal assistant would just have to take the extra load for now, one or two days without her wouldn't kill them.

In truth, Lucinda didn't have the stomach bug that was going around, although she put on a good act as she wasn't feeling her tip top self lately, her husband believed it. She needed to be alone today. Geeze, would he stop fussing over her and get to work? Good. He's off. She waited until she was sure he was gone and then got washed and dressed. She had an appointment early that afternoon, what time was it? Better not mix it up with her work schedule. She had a lot on her mind these days. She got out her notebook to check. Yeah, okay. She had plenty of time to kill. What to do until then? New York was big but not that big. She couldn't leave the apartment until the last minute in case she was seen and word get back to her boss she was playing hookey. Sitting. Waiting. What are we waiting for, Lucy? There will never be a perfect time, honey. Shouldn't we try starting a family? We're not getting younger, you know. How Edward kept on about it! Her parents nagged her to death, now his were starting to get on their case. She did want a family, but not with him. However, she couldn't make a break, single, divorced, legal headaches and costs, not without first knowing there would be something, or rather, someone, waiting for her at the end of it all.

She unlocked the nightstand at her side of the bed. Inside she kept her box of hidden mementoes, but not of Edward. She quietly looked through them all again, the pictures, the articles. If only there was a sign! Nothing yet. No *isla bonita* was appearing on the horizon, but that didn't mean there wasn't one. It was there. She only had to wait for the currents to change favourably. Something might make them cross paths again. It happened before. For now she was stuck with Ed and his constant badgering about kids and how great it would be to have them. C'mon Lucy, you're skittish of the idea now, but won't be able to put that baby down once you have it. She hated being called Lucy! As much as she wanted to get rid of Ed, she just couldn't risk it right now. Okay, she hid the pills, but he caught her with them a few times, he began to wonder why she was still holding back on the idea. He knew she did want kids. Why did she tell him that before they got married? Now he was going to question her reluctance. It wouldn't be long before he'd start searching, her purse and elsewhere behind her back, either looking for more pills or some answers. She couldn't tell him any longer she wasn't ready yet, nor could she break up with him right now either. No, for the last several months she had to play happy family, it was not the time to break up, no, not yet, let him throw the pills down the drain. Fine then, there were other ways of taking care of that situation. She kept a stash in her desk at work, but once she got there sometimes she forgot with all the bustle that kept her running, it was hard to hide them there as well. Sometimes she missed taking them a few days. Then, sometimes they were known not to work too. This time it was hard to know what it was. How she hated Edward! Hated him for putting her through this! If only he would have left things alone! She couldn't be saddled with his brats. She *refused* to be saddled with them. To think this was the second time she had to go to the clinic on a sick-call pretence to solve the problem! However, *something* would have to give soon, she couldn't keep this up forever. Oh, to hell with it! She couldn't mope around this place. It felt too much like Edward. Stank of him actually. Quickly putting the box of trophies away under some books in the nightstand, she grabbed her coat, purse and keys. She had to get out.

As usual, there were a few places she just couldn't help going out of her way to drive past. His rectory, his church, his parish building, but these days there was no chance of getting close at all. His services were now filled to capacity and out into the street long before the hour they started, she could no longer get in let alone find some space in the back, and now, his parish office was that way too, not that she would venture in there, but hopefully catch a glimpse of him walking outside, anything. He had even made the afternoon news, this time not like the man of fortune on the cover image of Forbes, but as a priest! They showed a video someone had taken of him in church, the news crew obliviously paid for the clip. The church was packed like she had never seen a church packed, then, there was a quick view with him at the altar. Her heart stopped at the sight of him on the screen, to see a living image of him again after so many still pictures! But what had happened to him? He had turned white in front. What could have … ? Whatever it was, it was like he had been transformed. There was a compelling aura around him tinged with something she couldn't describe. Ecstasy, and wisdom born of acute pain that blended into a strange harmony. It was breathtaking. If only she had a recording of that clip! She was outside the parish office now. Oh yes, there they were, lines of people winding around the block. She drove on. She turned on the cassette player. *I fell in love with San Pedro … .*

In a few hours, it was over. It was never quite like they said it would be. Second time was not easier than the first. Her insides wrenched from the procedure, she left the clinic palliated with the idea that she had bought herself more time with Ed, and, hopefully had given the currents of change another opportunity to wend things in her direction. On that note, she couldn't resist the urge to drive by the parish office again, eyeing the waiting crowds, some were carrying their prayer beads and devotional icons. Lucinda noticed a few leaving the building obviously having seen the Monsignor of Manhattan and pleased with their visit. They were holding a statue. Lucinda knew what it was. The Madonna. This time She was depicted wearing all white with a blue sash around the waist, Her hands together in prayer as She gazed Heavenward. The sight perturbed Lucinda. She quickly drove away.

Her insides ached. It would be good to have another shower and lay down. She approached the apartment door, fumbled for the key. The door was open. Did she leave it like that? She did run out in a huff earlier, eager to get away. She never did that before, leave the place unlocked. That was stupid. They could have been robbed! Everything looked okay though, nothing in the sitting room was touched, the TV and stereo system were still there. Relieved, she dropped her purse on the counter, and went straight to the bedroom to get undressed. She gasped. The lamp on her side of the bed was on the floor, she couldn't see it but the light was on, shining up on the ceiling at a weird angle, her clothes were strewn everywhere, the closet was open, the light left on inside … maybe they *were* robbed! She started to panic, thought about calling the police. Stupid! You can't call. Edward would find out you weren't here all day. What to do? Anything taken? Wait a minute. Her clothes were there, *his* were missing. A suitcase was gone too. She went to her side of the bed where the lamp was smashed, the bulb still working, the nightstand was broken open … she swore. Her trophies of Peter were scattered everywhere on the carpet. Edward must have come home for lunch. He *never* did that before. She cussed again. Why now? She went through the rest of the apartment looking for clues. Her answer lay in the kitchen. In her hurry that morning she forgot to take her notebook, but it wasn't exactly where she left it. He must have looked. The clinic, the address, the phone number, it wasn't their family doctor, and, it wasn't the type of place you went to for the flu. Then, she could smell flowers. She looked around, nothing, searched under the sink. A bouquet was smashed into the garbage can. She took it out. Damn, Ed tried to surprise her, make her feel better. Then, to see there was a little slender box tied to it wrapped in teddy bear gift paper. Jewellery? She ripped it open. No. A testing kit. Seriously? He thought her stomach flu might be something else and in a cutesy way was going to suggest they find out. The irony! He wasn't wrong. She stared at the box, then – laughed. She couldn't stop, it gripped her, a compulsive, impelling laugh that refused to die in spite of the travesty of it all.

She was free of him. The currents of fate had finally swept in, showed her she had been going the wrong way about this. Peter was never going to come to her while she was still with Edward. She should have cut the chains long before now. Now, Ed with his walking in and finding out about everything, that took a load off. After seeing her notebook, guessing or finding out where she was, he wanted answers, broke into the nightstand … well, he got some. Let his imagination run with it. He was gone, it was only a matter of time before the divorce proceedings started, probably without too much delay. It was done. She finally stopped laughing and caught her breath. She was *free.* Might as well look up a good lawyer, after that much needed shower of course.

Her insides still churning after the day, she still didn't feel relieved. She tried to concentrate on the water, let its warmth relax her. Of course, idiot. *You* might be free soon, but if *he* wasn't, there was still no making it to that *isla bonita* just yet. He was still chained. Yes, look what was happening. The crowds. She could no longer get close to him, shoved out, kept away. Suddenly, she recalled the sight of that statue with its pristine white veil and little blue sash. The memory of it now seemed to mock her, irritate her. Of course. *She* was keeping her away. The Rival still had to be sorted out. Those waves of crowds, his beloved 'children', they too needed to be gotten rid of along with the Rival. But how? Why, you've still not seeing the solution, are you? What solution? Is there one? Oh, yes, there is always one, or rather, a plan of action. It will come at a price, and it might not work, but better to try than not try at all. Lucinda wondered what her thoughts were trying to tell her. They seemed more than thoughts, they seemed to have the answer. Don't you see? Like you were with Edward, Peter is chained into inaction, indecision, unable to make the break until it is made for him. I know that. What am I not seeing? Oh, it's quite simple. You waited for your *isla bonita* to sail into view, but you see that wasn't working. Why not *you* become the island, have him sail to *you*? A shipwrecked man will cling to an island you know, any island.

Of course. She thought of her favourite photo of him. Shipwreck. Peter needed to be shipwrecked. What better way to get rid of the Woman in his life than make him unfaithful? Mother Church was not so forgiving of a wayward son, even a hint of a mistress and any wife will doubt and then eventually reject her man. The thing in Peter's case, *it need not even be true.* Of all Women, Mother Church could be vicious, the crowds would leave … he would see himself abandoned, be shown how cruel his Bride could be. A plan began to coalesce, but, would he come to her after *that*? There had to be another way. But there was no other way that was convincing. For the anchor chains to be broken, it had to be convincing, and that would mean risk losing everything, the island of paradise along with the shipwrecked sailor … .

Even so, *do you want Her to have him*?

A seething irrational hatred grew, festered, metastasised.

No. No! Never!

I'll rip him from her.

If I can't have him, neither will *She!*

He'll either come to the island with me, or, we'll burn with it together!

The latest art show went without a hitch, but Katherine couldn't take pleasure in the success. It felt empty, stripped of all purpose and meaning. The three weeks after that, waiting, waiting, time itself seemed to become a lifeless haze. At the gallery she went through the motions, avoiding the office, but now was unable to paint, just staring at her canvases when she did uncover them only to daub a few spots of colour, then quietly cover them up again. Inspiration seemed to have forsaken her along with her motivation. The sight of Gerry's canvases left abandoned in the corner also made her depressed. Dennis and the Professor glanced at each other, but decided to let silence do its healing work. They of all people knew that despite the saying that tragedy brought out the best kind of art, it could not be forced when the heart was pierced beyond endurance by the tenebrous influence of melancholy, that strange, sombre muse. Esther and Suzy couldn't help but feel for her, Kevin was also worried, they had to get her interested in work at least. Eventually Kevin tentatively enquired if it was time for him to take a quick look through his books? Have something in the offering for the Spring season? Summer at least? Katherine didn't feel like it, but she had to pull herself together. He was right, the gallery needed to be kept relevant, popular, the place to be, basically just kept filled and running, however that happened. A show. Another one. All right. She also decided she couldn't leave the apartment in the state it was in, half-finished, she had to continue with the decorating. Nothing for it but to start in the entertainment room.

Productivity did help to bring her out of the doldrums to a point while she waited for the latest updates on Gerry's whereabouts. Like her, the Reinolds were on tenterhooks until this business trip was over and they could make a drastic attempt to get him to see reason. San Jose, back to LA, then on to San Francisco, it looked like he might have to extend it to Portland, the end of January was coming, he would be home soon. That hope too was dashed when he had a few more issues spring up in San Francisco, back he went. An additional few weeks were needed there. No matter. Surely he'd be home by St. Valentine's Day? She had a gift ready for him, an illustration from a medieval manuscript she found courtesy of his rare book dealer who was only too pleased to help her find a rare gem. No, the inspection trip was extended, again. Never mind. Katherine sent the gift using the family firm's priority shipping service to make sure it arrived on the day. The parcel was returned unopened. What made it worse: nothing. No call, no note, none of their signature bouquets, no word. What had happened for Gerry to act like this? Not even a call? Then to hang up on her when she tried?

He really meant it. He was breaking up with her.

Rejection. The blade lanced, sliced deep, straight to the core. The strange part was, she wasn't angry with him. Hurt, bleeding inside, but she just couldn't get angry. She had never known him to be cruel. Tease once in awhile in fun, yes, but never malicious or sadistic, and even now this was not deliberate malice on his part. She understood he thought he had to 'save' her from something, but this supreme attempt to cut her free still felt so much like rejection, and yet, she couldn't comprehend him or his drastic departure. Free? Free her from what? From *him?* Be 'free' to find someone else? *Impossible!* Her heart had made its choice, she was bound to him come what may. Why he thought he was no longer worthy of her just didn't make any sense. No, this couldn't be the end of them. No, not yet. She resolved to wait. Once he was home, they had a chance to resolve this, face to face.

A few days after the shock had subsided, Lottie dropped by the gallery during her lunch hour to give the latest report: he had leased a penthouse in San Francisco.

"What?"

"It's true, Kathy. That's not the worst part." Lottie hesitantly continued. "He says the west coast needs better management, someone from the top, and, he's insisting on taking over that division, personally."

"But ... but, what about his job here? Isn't he the International Manager of Distribution?"

"He says he's giving it up, that Tom or I should take over that position now, whatever is deemed best. He's ... he's not coming back, at least, not in the foreseeable future."

Katherine's world shattered.

She hardly heard the rest of Lottie's news, that he had given unlimited power of attorney to do whatever she wanted with the apartment, and, his art collection. He was leaving all that to her, literally all of it. The documents would arrive soon. Things! That's not what she wanted! *Things!*

Everybody was stunned when the latest development was disclosed. Her parents were at a loss for words with this unorthodox situation, so were the Reinolds and the Gallery Gang. At least she shouldn't be on her own.

Her mother had the presence of mind to suggest she come back to Oak Meadows for awhile, even if it meant a longer drive to the gallery in the mornings. She should be with family right now until they figured out what to do. Just to please them Katherine packed a bag, yes, maybe a few days back at home to clear her head was a good idea.

Strangely, this time they could not offer words of hope, that things would sort themselves out. They too seemed to sense things were at a break-up point. After a few days, it appeared they were taking Gerry's view on the situation. Obviously in an effort to get her to face the unpleasant prospect of reality. Yes, maybe it was for the best, he was letting her go before she became legally tied to a difficult life. He was doing the kind and selfless thing. It was hard to listen to. How do you stop loving someone? How *can* you? Even so, could this be it? If he insisted on this, was it really the end? Should she just accept it?

"Maybe it was meant to be, Kathy," Aunt Martha finally pointed out. "Look what could have happened if you were already married? You would have been stuck with an invalid in a wheelchair for the rest of your life! Just let him go dear, and move on. Look, now you can come back to your own church, with us, where you really belong!"

Something snapped.

Invalid? Gerry *in-valid*? *To be tossed aside like a worthless piece of garbage?*

Katherine packed her bag and returned to the apartment. *She* was not gong to leave, and he possibly couldn't stay away forever.

She could wait, she *would* wait.

Charlie arrived a few days later to the gallery with the unwanted legalities and wanted to speak to her alone. To the dreaded office it was then. She motioned him in and offered a seat.

"I'm so sorry to have to be the bearer of this, however as a member of their law firm as well as yours, I thought it best if I came. I wish I could do or say something."

She took the file with the power of attorney paperwork. This was surreal. Talk about a conflict of interests! To have a former suitor whom she had friend-zoned now offer consolation. She laid it on the desk unopened.

"I'm sorry Charlie. You know, I never meant to … I'm sorry for putting you through this, now … and then."

"Kathy, don't apologise again. Our situation was different. Not that I didn't go through the blues, but well, at least we never did get to the engagement part. We're still friends and have moved on. But this? I can't imagine what you're going through now. I said if he ever did anything to hurt you I'd punch him in the nose, but that doesn't seem to apply here.”

“No, no it doesn't. Even Olivia can't get mad at him for running away. Of all things, he thinks he's protecting me.”

“And, maybe he can't face himself either. Especially not in your eyes,” he continued. “He has his pride. You fell in love with him when he had life and the world by the tail, and now, in his condition, it's obvious he doesn't want to be pitied, feel you *have* to marry him as a charity case.”

“What I feel for him hasn't changed! So to a point yes, I *am* marrying him for charity, love, the *real* term. Although, I just wish he didn't suffer so much. I can't help him, not with the pain, the walking, that's what hurts me the most.”

“He doesn't want to put you through that. That's what he sees.”

“But it hurts *because* I care for him, not because I wish to be free of him!”

“You're gong to have to make him see that, somehow.”

How, that was the problem.

February passed and the wet, windy month of March roared in, the grey heavens and the drenching rain seemed determined to mirror Katharine's interior desolation. Despite her new-found hectic corporate career, Lottie once again dropped by for lunch at the gallery. Katherine guessed by her expression that the weather wasn't the cause of the long face and waited to hear what had happened now, dreading the worse.

“Well, Tom and I have been talking, and … um, this is a terrible timing to bring it up, but … oh, this sounds awful, but I don't think we can wait, we've discussed setting a date, but it wouldn't be right without letting you know first.”

Katherine breathed a sigh of relief.

“Is that all? I thought Gerry might have died or something!”

“Oh no! But, well, you know … .”

“Please, I'm not upset, not at all. Don't wait. You two go ahead, you can't put it off any longer, I know you need to book places.” Katherine's hope suddenly soared again as a thought struck her. “That's right! How can he miss his own sister's wedding? It just might bring him back.”

“Kathy, of course! But we were thinking of July. Four months, that's still going to be some time to wait.”

"Never mind! It's better than not having him back at all. Actually, he might wake up sooner before then with the prospect. Could you give Gerry a call? I've stopped trying, I can't bear him hanging up on me any more."

"Of course I will. I'm so sorry about that. It's not like him, despite his stewing habit. I don't know what's gotten into him. After I tell Tom and then my parents, I'll get in touch. I'll let you know how it goes."

It went worse than anyone expected. He wasn't answering the phone.

They waited three days, then called the offices in San Francisco, he hadn't been to work in the last two before then. Alarmed, the Captain asked for someone to go see if he was still at his penthouse. They got word back he was there, but not in a good mood. Basically they were told to leave him alone. He was fine, he just needed some space. Okay, maybe the pain in his legs had gotten to him, the winter weather didn't help his physical situation, and he needed a few days off. They had to consider that too and not push him. However, it became apparent he was in a severe stewing mode when another week passed without a word from him at all and no sign of him at any of the offices. Once more the Captain had someone go around and check up on him, but Gerry cussed the unfortunate messenger off. Leave me the hell alone! I'll come out when I'm damn well good and ready! The last part was left out when the news was relayed to Katherine, who by now was at a loss as to what to do, how to handle this. Gerry had put a whole country between them that felt as wide and yawning as an abyss, and was doing everything to keep the chasm gaping, cutting all lines, burning all bridges. To add the final insult to injury, Beatrice Brandis the gossip columnist spilled the ink on Tom and Lottie's wedding plans, that they were obviously going ahead because 'something else' must have been cancelled in the meantime, with the result the families were now pestered for comments by the press for more information. How on earth did that nasty woman get hold of the news before they had announced anything? Her and Gerry's engagement wasn't publicly broken off! The infamous house art critic Horace the Horrible could answer that and let Katherine in on a little secret: regrettably Beatrice the Beastie bug must have looked up the parish appointments at the cathedral and saw the wedding booking for Tom and Lottie and so conclusions were easily made. First the accident a year ago, now this. Her heartbreak was once again public fodder. This was unbearable. No longer could Katherine face the gallery, face people, face life. She wanted to hide, and sleep, sleep until the furore died down, sleep the hurt and rejection away, sleep until she felt better, whenever that would be, if it would ever happen.

ଔ ❖ ଈ

Not since his own mother passed away did the house feel this funereal. His wife and her sister were understandably distraught, but Harold had never seen his daughter like this no matter what had gone wrong, locking herself away, refusing company, keeping away from her gallery that she loved. Steven dropped by to see how she was, and could only say his sister was not ready to see anyone. A week passed with the place under a paradoxical state of mourning for the living. Eventhough he would never interfere in a relationship, he knew something had to be done. His father felt the same. Katherine would never give up on Gerard, they had to get him back. They privately discussed the matter in the den when the women were occupied in the kitchen also pouring out their concerns to each other.

"We can't leave her sit there, Har, pining away in that apartment. I swear she'll become like Miss Havisham that was jilted at the altar and let her estate crumble around her, frozen in time, never getting past her wedding day."

"I know. Although I can appreciate why he wants to let her go, at the same time, it's obvious he's just as devastated. Those two are inseparable, which is killing them. I can't see this continue."

"I know son, neither can I, but other than kidnap the fellow, I can't see how to bring him back."

"Definitely find some way to keep Katherine safe, that's one issue that perturbed him."

"One we can all agree on, even if a wedding isn't forthcoming." Gramps nodded.

The two men sat for a moment, lost in thought. Kidnap. That gave Harold an idea, a desperate one. His expression took on a look of deep resolve Gramps had not seen with his son in a long time. Harold then exhaled.

"God help me, I never thought I'd contemplate doing something like this, but for Katherine's sake … ."

Gramps sat up.

"What do you have in mind? I hope nothing illegal?"

"That depends. I'm going to visit the neighbours."

Gramps furrowed his brow, wondering what that was about until Harold told him what he had in mind.

"You're serious."

"I am. You don't approve."

"Hrumph. I didn't say that. Sure, it's loco, but the kind of loco that's genius. I'll go talk to him."

"No, I'll go. I'm her father, I must handle this."

"All right. When are you going?"

"The sooner the better, in fact, now. And this is just between us, don't tell anyone."

"Of course not, the less the women know the better. You just do what you have to do."

Harold got up and went for his coat. Gramps heard the front door close.

No, he didn't like Har's idea, it could get them mixed up in a lot of trouble, but if it helped Katie at this point it was worth whatever aftermath might befall them. It was true she was his favourite grandkid, he couldn't help it, but none of the other kids minded or were jealous, they understood. She looked so much like his own dear departed Amelia, down to the expressions and her quick tongue that could clip a hedge. Despite her fiery streak, she was also a kind soul. All these years without Amelia would have been unbearable if it weren't for Katherine, reminding them all that she still lived on, she was never truly gone. Gramps looked up at her picture on the wall now, feeling a bit heartsick. Seeing Katie in this state over Gerry only reminded him of what he was privileged to experience, the love of a woman who cared deeply enough to do anything for him.

He thought for a moment. Age and experience taught him that problems are like doors, you have to go through them to put them behind you. If you try and avoid them, be prepared to walk into a wall. What a predicament. If she was his Mell and he was off wallowing somewhere on the other side of the country, she wouldn't stop night or day to hunt him down and bring him back, not to mention give him a good word-whipping for putting her through that! But Katie? What was he missing? Maybe that's where she and Mell differed, or, Katie was so miserable over this first real heartbreak she had experienced couldn't see what needed to be done. Right now, both of them had hit a wall, but only she could talk sense into Gerry, heal whatever had broken in him, not to mention in her. How to get her to see that though? How could he help nudge her towards that proverbial door? He pondered for a moment, then hit upon a bright idea of his own. It was so depressing it just might work, and after all, like was known to cure like. He went to his bedroom, Jasper following, and began to pack a case. He looked through his stash of videos next, where is … ? Ah. There it is. He packed the cassette. Let's hope this does the trick.

Helen was looking for him.

"Where's Harold?"

"Gone out, he'll be back."

"And where might *you* be going?"

"I'm going to a slumber party," he huffed as he lumbered down the rest of the stairs, cane in one hand, case in the other. "Don't worry about me, and don't you ladies wait up. I'll see you in the morning, maybe the afternoon, depending."

Helen brightened up, helped him with his coat and let him go. Whatever he has in mind, please let it work.

He rang the bell again.

"Hullo Katie. It's only me. You're not going to leave your poor old Gramps out on the doorstep now, are you? Shall I have to leave? Drive out again in that cold, cruel city all on my lonesome?"

He waited, then heard the lock. The door opened.

It was as he surmised: days in the same robe, fuzzy jammies, slippers, uncombed hair, red eyes, a fistful of tissues, more stuffed in her pockets, and probably a bucket of ice cream with a spoon in it hiding somewhere on a couch no less, which may also have become a temporary bed.

"Gramps, what are you doing here?"

"What's it look like? Jasper and I are joining the pity parade. You gotta have more than one float for a parade, so here we are."

She wistfully smiled, but still, it was a smile.

"That's it. C'mon, I know you have another bucket of ice cream in here somewhere, and a bucket of popcorn wouldn't go awry either. I brought us a movie. Let's have a good cry over it all with the Gipper."

There was nothing for it but to let him in and make it a movie night, although she was not in the mood. After he had changed into his night attire, the popcorn was made, this time with real butter, accompanied by that second bucket of ice cream, rocky road to be precise, and plenty of soda pop. Comfort food ready, Gramps put on the tape and settled in with her on the new sofa that had just arrived for the entertainment room, another beauty from Italy, their feet up, wrapped in their robes, not minding they looked a frumpy sight. It had been awhile since she snuggled in to watch a good old black and white classic with Gramps, this time amidst ladders, paint buckets, plastic sheeting, for this room was not done, it almost felt like they were camping in a hodgepodge blanket fort. It felt strangely comforting. Okay, she could survive the sappy movie.

She hadn't seen this one in a long while and had forgotten much of the plot and the scenes, but then as they watched couldn't help wonder why out of all the movies on earth he had to pick this.

"Gee, thanks Gramps. This is depressing. Just what I needed."

"I know. Shh!"

He munched on another fistful of popcorn, throwing a few bits to Jasper who happily lapped them up.

She sighed resignedly, watching the story of Parris who falls in love with the curiously shy daughter of his mentor, a tormented girl, a shut-in overshadowed by her father. Despite Parris' proposal of marriage and the prospect of taking her away from whatever is troubling her, she is unable to break away from her restrictive paternal guard, afraid of him and yet cannot bring herself to leave him, a curious state of affairs that Parris doesn't understand. Her fear of starting a new life with Parris turns out to be a fatal decision, for she and her widower father both end up dead, a tragic murder-suicide event. Only then does Parris discover why she was so tormented in mind and spirit. If that wasn't enough, in a strange twist of fate, Parris finds her father has bequeathed to him all his worldly possessions. Unable to face the house left to him after the tragedy, Parris escapes to Europe to finish his medical studies in the new field of psychiatry, determined to dedicate his life helping those tortured in mind like his lost love.

It certainly wasn't the same situation. Katherine knew her Pops would never be like *that.* Protective, yes, but not on the psycho level. Why would Gramps bring her this of out of all the old videos he had? It was disturbing! Still, she found herself thinking of her life as it was that moment and comparing it to the similarities of Parris' heartbreaking experience, wondering what was truly tormenting her loved one, wanting more than anything for him to be whole again in mind and spirit, to come back to her, and yet, be left his apartment instead, to be left behind in this living death since he insisted on embracing his disability, offering her his earthly possessions as if that could give her any consolation.

The story didn't end there. The good old Gipper played the role of Parris' friend, a happy-go-lucky guy who tragically loses his legs, not on account of the crushing box-car accident he suffered at the railroad yards as he is led to believe, but due to the cruel whim of a doctor noted for his sadism who unnecessarily amputated them in revenge for dating his daughter then leaving her for another. Parris discovers the truth but is reluctant to tell his friend who is now depressed and unable to face life, afraid if he found out he needlessly lost his legs because of a vindictive man that hated him he would never recover from his interior downward spiral, that the truth would ultimately destroy him. However, truth can heal as well as destroy, but he wouldn't know until he tried. Despite his fears, Parris decides to tell him as his doctor, not as a friend, that his condition is not the result of a fluke nor the cruel whims of fate but brought about by an enemy who wished to destroy him. He is surprised to find upon receiving this revelation his friend makes an instant recovery. Revenge? He would show him! Living well is the best revenge. There was much more to him than a pair of old legs!

Katherine sat up. She felt the key around her neck still hanging there on its gold chain.

Parris.

Paris.

She jumped off the couch, ran to her room.

"Whoa! What's up?"

"Packing! I'm going to San Francisco."

"That's my girl."

He grabbed another fistful of popcorn.

❦€

The next morning with Pop's blessing Katherine had permission to take the family corporate jet. During the flight, she couldn't stop running it all through her head. Not just the plot of the movie, but the undercurrent that surged through it. Fear, fear holding everyone back, Parris' childhood girlfriend paralysed by it, afraid to leave, only to die by not facing that fear and leaving to start a new life, and Parris himself dreading to tell his other friend about his accident, only to find doing the thing he dreaded was the

830

healing antidote. What a strange paradox, humanity was always drawn to the unknown and mysterious, and yet when it comes to daily life, the unknown becomes a terror, fear, uncertainty crippling everything. In Gerry's case, he too had fears, but the depth and true nature of them didn't strike her until Gramps had the insight to simply bring her that movie. Gerry's one phobia about elevators ever since the Great Blackout came to mind, but recently when he returned home from the hospital he didn't make that little facial twitch when they entered an elevator car, or crack a wry joke about 'these waiting death traps'. Whatever had happened, she realised he was no longer afraid, more grim and resigned, the phobia was put to rest. Now she understood. What he truly feared was gone – because it had happened.

She recalled the story of how he and the Captain were rescued from the stuck elevator during the Great Blackout, pulled up and through the doors while the car was between two floors, then, horrified when the car suddenly moved as they were freed. The freakish incident occurred when he was young and therefore Gerry was forever stamped with the harrowing realisation they could have been crushed between the floors as the car descended, that thought of what might have been forever impressed into his memory and had wormed its way into his subconscious. And now, it had come true in the accident, the lower half of him crushed, disabled, maimed for life.

Fear of what might happen was gone with the reality.

It now made sense. Gerard was drawn inward into a nihilistic whirlpool of success by defeat: if the worst fear comes true, then it will no longer torment you. It was so simple. It was like the effective if somewhat dubious tactic of getting rid of a gnawing temptation by giving in to it. Not the morally best solution, but still, it worked.

If he loved her as much as he professed, then, he feared to lose her. That was it. Charlie made her see how Gerry didn't want to look in her eyes, maybe tormented she would no longer love him maimed and eventually become jaded in having to help care for him, feared she would leave him, forever agonising about it happening, wondering if it would happen, obsessing it would happen, *obsessing that it was inevitable.* It was a strange tortuous trick the mind could play, and so, best to get the pain and misery over with, cause the dreaded inevitable to come to pass, make the pain come now rather than later while he had the strength to do it, eradicate the fear and bring on the torment on his own terms.

And so, she must remind him that was never going to happen.

She was never going to leave. She loved him too much.

She had to remind him of Paris.

But, that meant facing her own fear, that despite what he felt, he may still turn his back on what they shared. Still, this was a risk she had to take. She would never know until she tried. She just had to convince him he would always be her Gerry, no matter what, but could she? The plane touched down. This was it. San Francisco. Despite the song, she prayed she wouldn't end up leaving her heart there. She intended to bring it home.

Getting off the plane and entering the arrivals area, she was surprised by someone calling her.

"Leroy! What are you doing here?"

"I had an advertising convention to attend, I've been here three days, but it's all over now. Pete got on to me in time and said you were on your way in a hurry, so here I am! I've managed to extend my visit. If it's a rescue we're about to do, you can use all the help ye can get. Here, let me get that." He took her bag. It was good to see a friendly face.

"Thank you Lee, you have no idea what this means. Have you tried to see Gerry?"

"Of course, but he's not seeing anyone, however, we'll get to that in a minute. Where are you staying?"

"Nowhere yet, I just packed and hoped for the best, but I'm sure I'll find a hotel."

"Now that the convention is over, you just might get that room. I'm at the Sheraton, we'll try our luck there. Best if we stay together. C'mon, lets grab a cab, my treat and no blithering about it."

She might have enjoyed the drive through the city, this being her first time in the hilly metropolis of cable cars and the Golden Gate bridge, were her mission there not so heart-consuming. She wasn't sure how to handle it now that she had arrived, all she could think about was just getting on that plane, but Leroy seemed to have things already worked out as he laid out their plan of action during the drive. First, see if they could get that room, then once she was settled in, call her folks to let them know she had touched down safely, next go out for something to eat, she must be famished. After that, she should rest, don't bother doing anything, just think about what you want to say to him, for tomorrow they were storming Gerry's apartment.

"I've already called everyone back home not to try and get through to him about your flight. We can't let him know you're here. The element of surprise might do wonders."

"But, do you think he'll let us in?"

"Don't worry about that part, I've been doin' some brainstorming too, got that all worked out." He tapped the side of his head before continuing, "I've got troops mustered."

During his attempted visit to Gerry yesterday and getting the royal cold shoulder, he did a little scouting afterwards through the building and enlisted the services of the concierge, the maintenance man and Gerry's housekeeper, who were only to happy to help in the next attempt to make the breach into the recluse's fort. At least he had a housekeeper! That was good news. He had some contact with the outside world and wasn't completely left alone. Katherine hoped the plan would work. They would find out in the morning.

Leroy got them up early, they had to get there while his housekeeper was in as she had morning shifts. Arriving at his building, the doorman and the concierge were pleased to meet the fiancée after Leroy had let them in on the story of their melancholic tenant upstairs. As planned, the janitor turned off the water mains to Gerry's apartment. It wasn't long before the phone at the desk began to ring.

"There's your cue. Jake's got the call. I won't hold you two Caped Crusaders up. Go save Howard Hughes."

"Right, thanks." Leroy gave him a tip.

They met Jake the maintenance man outside Gerry's door with his tool box in tow, but stayed hidden out of view behind him as the housekeeper opened the door. She gave them the 'all clear'.

"He's still asleep, so you needn't have gone to all the trouble," she whispered to them.

"Never mind, we didn't know what we were facing," Leroy whispered back. "How is he?"

"Pickled. He's going to kill himself if he keeps this up."

Katherine's face blanched.

"Okay, thank you both. You can turn the water back on. We've got it from here. Go have a night on the town, or something." Lee tipped them generously then softly closed the door behind them after the troops had left. "Stage one accomplished. We're in!"

Katherine wanted to go search for Gerry right away, but Lee stopped her, he put his finger to his lips. He motioned to his eye, then around the room. Katherine caught on, he wanted to do some recognizance work first, see the state of things and determine if they were stepping into a minefield. The main area of the place looked grand with a beautiful view of the bay, it certainly was a nice penthouse, Gerry always picked the best, nothing *seemed* amiss. Lee motioned to the kitchen and they carefully made their way. They looked in the fridge, fresh food was there, that was a good sign, but it was hard to tell if he had touched any or not. The garbage can was next for inspection and that told a darker tale with empty bourbon and painkiller bottles as the snitches.

"Jeenymac. This doesn't look good."

No, no it didn't. Especially when she realised what today was, it was March 15th — exactly one year since the accident. Gerry was trying to forget the worst day in his life, the day that he believed had doomed them to separation. She had arrived just in time. Leroy shook his head.

"Okay. Nothin' for it. We're going to have to do a rude awakening." Lee sprang out of stealth mode and took off his raincoat. "Stage two. Now, don't come with me, it's not going to be pretty. I've got to try and make him presentable." Katherine was about to protest, she so desperately wanted to see him after that gruesome discovery, but Lee insisted. "Look, you won't get through to him if he's as langer'd as I think he is. When I've gotten him to where he can show his face, next thing is to sober him up and put something solid in that stomach of his. You go make a pot of coffee as stiff as you can, if you can pave a road with it the better, and get some breakfast going. Cor, this brings back memories, except I'm usually the one at the receiving end of these things! Right, I'm off. Once more into the breech!" Without further ado he went and searched for the bedroom.

Flustered, Katherine set her purse down, took off her coat and tried to do what Lee suggested. Coffee was easy, but trying to think up and and organize a decent breakfast in a strange kitchen when she was such a hopeless cook was going to be interesting. Um, right. Toast, bacon and eggs. Scrambled eggs couldn't be too complicated, better than going for the plain fried variety, she wouldn't have to worry about trying not to break the yolks. Besides, she watched the cooks in her life do it a million times, how hard could it be? It was good to stay active right now too. As she rummaged around in the fridge and cupboards, trying to get herself sorted, a commotion broke out in the bedroom, snatches of it reverberated into the kitchen area. She nearly dropped the eggs.

"The hell? What are you doing here?"

"What do you think, you twat! This is an intervention! And just in the nick of time by the looks of it. Come on Ger, up and at 'em."

"Damn it, Lee! Let me go! Get out of here! Scram!"

"How do ye like them apples? There's a fine and mighty *cead millé failte* for ye! I'm not goin' anywhere, and neither is Kathy. She's here too you know. So stop yer swearin', we've got a lady in the house. C'mon. Let's get you showered."

Despite the yelling, Katherine breathed a sigh of relief.

He was alive.

She wasn't sure what was happening next, but it sounded like Lee had managed to drag him into the bathroom and got the shower going.

"Getttofff!!"

"Sit still, you blathering unchook! Kathy!"

Leaving her culinary endeavour, she came running. Lee put his arm out the bathroom door holding his sweater. His new Aran cardigan was soaked.

"Here, love. Would ye mind doin' something with this? Put it somewhere to dry? Thanks. I've got him propped up against the wall in the shower, can't leave him slip. Don't you worry, I'll have him scrubbed up in no time."

Uh, okay. She looked around. There was a service area off the kitchen complete with washer and dryer. That should do the trick. Later as Katherine was setting the dining room table, another roar issued from the bathroom.

"*Would you stop that?* I can shave myself!"

"If ye insist, Sweeny Todd."

Eventually, Leroy delivered a somewhat grim looking Gerry via the wheelchair to the head of the table, washed, dressed in clean pyjamas and navy robe, combed and smelling a lot better with a touch of cologne, although suffering from a mild case of shaver's chicken pox with bits of paper stuck over his chin line. Katherine brought his breakfast then sat beside him. Lee then took a look at Gerry's plate.

"What kind of brekkie do you call this?"

"I did my best. I eat Pop Tarts, remember?"

"The Novice Chef Special it is then. Eat at your own risk, Ger. Where's me jumper, Katie?"

"Huh? Oh. It's in the laundry room, in the kitchen." He went to retrieve his sweater, leaving them alone for a minute.

This was an awkward situation. They could only look at each other in silence. Gerry then glanced at the breakfast before him. The bacon looked over crisped, but decided to test the eggs. He took a bite, crunched on a shell. He next sipped at the black coffee, grimaced. Lee ran back in.

"Argh! Look what she's done! The dryer! She's shrunk me sheep! Look at the cut of it, will ya?" He held it up, the sleeves did look a tad shorter than they were before. "Can't cook, hasn't a clue about woollies, she's not domesticated at all, at all! I can see why you felt like cuttin' and runnin' Ger. They say beauty never boiled the pot, but having said that, do give her a chance. There's more to love than boiling a pot." Pausing, he gave a quick nod of the head. "Well, looks like I've done me duty, I can do no more here. The rest is up to you. You know where to find me." He picked up his coat and headed for the door.

Now, they were alone. They sat in silence for a moment. Eventually Gerry looked down at his plate, sighed, put down his fork, pushed the plate away.

"Katherine, you shouldn't have come."

No, not with him looking like this, still somewhat hammered from the night before, several nights in succession actually, the pain meds now starting to wear off, he was feeling irritable, and, despite his best and drastic efforts, here she was. Oh God, to have to turn her away again!

However, as he was tormenting himself, the long speech Katherine intended to say evaporated as she spotted the hint of gold on his wrist. No, he hadn't taken it off, the engagement bracelet she had given him, which meant … .

"Yes, I did have to come. Do you still have the chain? With the key?"

He instinctively felt around his neck.

She knew it! She held up the chain she also had around her neck.

His adamant expression softened. Truce had been declared. He was willing to hear what she had to say.

This was it. This was their make or break moment.

"Gerry, remember what Peter told us? That an engagement is just one step away from marriage, without the vows made yet of course, but under an engagement we already belong to each other, and we haven't truly broken up yet unless we both agree to it. Maybe *you* think you've broken it off, but I haven't agreed to it … no … wait, hear me out." She took off the golden chain around her neck with the key on the end, the key that bore his initial. "Here's your heart, Gerry. I will willingly give it back to you without a protest and will never bother you again, but on one condition: that you can look me directly in the eyes and say from the depths of what this key represents that you want to give me back mine, not because you thought of a hundred and one reasons why we shouldn't be together, but because you no longer *want* me. That you honestly *want* to give me up. In short, that you don't love me any more. I need to hear it from you, and it has to be true."

She took her chain and put it in his hand, closed his palm over it, then held out her hand, palm open, waiting ... waiting ... .

God no, he couldn't look her in the eyes. He couldn't tell her that. As much as he didn't want her shackled to him as a cripple, he couldn't say that and mean it. He couldn't lie about something like that, even in an attempt to save her from the painful life he could foresee. His expression said it all.

"Oh Gerry, then please come home! You also remember all that stuff I said? That even if with all the travelling you have to do and I could only have you for one month out of each year, if that was it, I would be happy? Gerry, I mean that in other ways too. I will always be with you, no matter what. I will always love you no matter what."

His eyes brightened for a moment, then, his expression darkened as conflicting thoughts broke in, invasive memories about experiences and past events that plagued him for weeks and seemed stuck on perpetual replay. How eager he had been to get out of the hospital and finally back home, only to find the world no longer saw him the same way. He was still the same man, or so he thought, but no, he wasn't in the same world any more. Once discharged to restart his life, he was abruptly made aware of the culture and taboos of the chair-bound. It felt odd, invasive even when someone would just hold the armrest of it during a friendly conversation, or even if one of the family members decided to grab the handles and wheel him somewhere without asking first. It was strange, but the chair had become an extension of himself, it was rather disturbing in fact, especially the expressions of shock or compassion from his old schoolmates at Fr. Conner's funeral when they beheld him in the contraption or using the canes, the same expressions at work when he returned for his first days back. He just gritted his teeth, it would wear off once they got used to him like this. It was inevitable. But then, he couldn't help see how the social unease would register or display itself, people trying too hard to act 'normal' around him, overcompensating in the effort to be inclusive to the disabled guy, that effort was so discomfiting to experience, sometimes going so far as the person bending down in order to talk to him when in the chair. Of course, he knew people with two sound healthy legs did it as a friendly gesture, an attempt to make polite direct eye-level contact on a one-to-one basis and not stand over him. He was guilty of it too when he was once whole, and now to have the tables turned, to see how condescending it actually felt, to have someone bend down as if you were a kid no older than five. Some people were on the verge of taking that tone of voice, the action triggering the corresponding association. They treated him as if he had regressed mentally along with his mobility. It didn't help what was left of his ego either when one day out at lunch he was suddenly made aware of his new social status. He had just sat to the table, this time deciding to take a booth, folding his chair and placing it aside for a moment, and got a few engaging smiles from a table across the way from two young women who had just arrived and were being seated, not that he would have ever cheated on Katherine, but simply took it as a compliment they smiled first, that he could still catch an eye, only to find those smiles suddenly fade as one girlfriend to another gave the quick 'uh oh' glance to his folded chair. What a shame. Broken goods. Their gaze was quickly diverted to their menus with a hint of embarrassment. They didn't look at him again. This sudden flip-side bought on a gamut of uncomfortable realisations that never struck him before until he was now experiencing them for himself. He once thought it was a polite thing to say to someone in his 'situation', that they 'inspired them' and how 'brave' they were, but then saw it was a slap in the face that was when it sounded more like 'thanks for showing me how blessed I am in comparison with your pathetic, restricted life'. Thanks for making me feel like that. I'm not really interested in inspiring *you*, I'm just trying to get on with things, but thank you again for making me feel abnormal. It was bad enough dealing with the pain. It was beginning to change him, make him irritable, short-tempered, it was bringing out a side to his nature he didn't like, reminding him too much of the explosive quirk his father had, that short fuse he always dreaded inheriting to discover it may have always been lurking beneath the surface. Yes, there were the pain meds to help with that, but that was another concern. He couldn't think clearly with them, and what happened when they no longer felt like they were working? Would he build up a resistance, end up taking more to get the same relief, then one day max out, unknowingly taking that one too many? In order not to fall into the drug dependency cycle, he knew that would mean taking less during the day, no matter how painful it felt, then, get what he needed in the evenings if only to get a decent night's rest if he could. It didn't feel like a life. His daytime temper suffered for it. The littlest things now made him irritable, his patience always at a low ebb. He felt like a ticking time bomb in more ways than one, no longer like himself, the man with Katherine in those black and white photos on his desk seemed like a stranger living in another age, another story.

It didn't seem fair or right that she would become tied to him now, staying with him, especially if it was out of pity. She deserved to live and have a full life. However, he felt selfish, unable to make the break or come to a decision, that is, until he received a visit one morning from the warty head of the Resident's Association with an architect and a building inspector in tow to see the latest upgrades to the apartment. He dreaded it might happen, was about to complain, but the two men with her looked sympathetically at him, they had been through this before too. One shared look let him know 'just get it done, please, we won't find anything, and we'll be out of your hair again'. Thankfully Katherine was out for the day. Using the crutches for exercise that morning, he just pointed them towards the rooms under development and painfully heaved himself to the kitchen. He didn't need this! Hadn't had his breakfast yet, but let's try not to be rude, at least not to the two council shmucks roped into Beechworz's inspections, but by the looks of it they might need a cup of morning Joe too. He was about to start the coffee machine and see if there were some muffins to offer when he heard sounds coming from elsewhere, from a place they shouldn't be in. He went down the hall, someone was in Katherine's room, and it wasn't the two inspectors. The Beechwart woman was satisfying her curiosity, but doing more than just scoping out the décor of the bedroom. Unaware he was at the door, he caught her spraying on liberal squirts of Katherine's perfume, then peek through her jewellery box, opening the lid and pulling out the little minuscule drawers. She wasn't touching anything inside, but still. How he blew at her! Threatened if he didn't find everything accounted for in that box when his fianceé came home, she would hear about it from the police! Startled she was busted, she closed the box and scurried from the room. And don't she dare ever again bother us about joining her blasted Resident's Association he yelled after her! The two inspectors also left in a hurry. He heard the front door close. What a start to the day! He took a breath, calmed himself down. The box had been moved, better put it back. He had never been past that door since Katherine moved in, but felt under the circumstances it was a permissible exception. He went to the dresser and reached over. A jolt of pain went through his leg and hip, with the shock he knocked the box over onto the floor instead. Damn it! Again, he forgot. How he had once taken movement for granted! He couldn't twist or reach a certain way any more, or put too much weight on the leg that suffered the malunion, or he'd yank that trapped nerve. Now slightly shorter than the other by a fraction, he needed custom made footwear to compensate for that too, and his other healed but still damaged hip wasn't too much better having to take the extra weight. He had to watch it, but now it just became easier to use the chair, walking was painful and laborious now. Even with his exercise routine, his legs were looking more lame and alien with the lack of usage, almost mutating before his eyes. He felt he was growing old way before his time, and seeing the bathrooms in the place fitted up with hospital grade safety bars didn't help his bruised ego either.

He sighed. The housekeeper wasn't in yet to help tidy this, so he had to painfully get down to pick everything up. He managed to get to his knees and began the clean-up, at least he had the pleasure of admiring some of the pieces he hadn't seen Kathy wear yet, and one was a bit comical, a bracelet hanging with a motley assortment of gold charms of every description. Okay, she liked collecting charms. That was a new thing he just learned. No wonder she didn't wear it, it weighed a ton and jangled like a bunch of jingle bells. Was that everything? He had better look under the furniture. He then noticed it among a few other glittering valuables that had rolled under the dresser: a diamond ring set between emeralds. He had seen it once before, and never in a million years did he ever expect to see it here, now. Katherine hadn't given it back to Charles. *Why?* Why didn't she give it back? He tidied up the rest of the jewels as best he could, put them in the box, then painfully got himself seated on the bed. Once the initial surprise and shock wore off with this find, he realised he wasn't terribly upset about it either. Although curious as to why she still had it, it didn't matter if she gave it back to him or not. True, he used to suffer jealousy over them, but no, not this time. Charles and Katherine were over, whatever there was between them never really went anywhere, and he also knew nothing was happening now, especially with Charlie getting married soon and actually looking quite happy about it. He had moved on. That was the crux of the matter. Maybe this was a sign telling him Katherine deserved that too, to be released from her engagement obligation and have her chance at finding love again with someone who could give her a normal life, not be tied to a deformed cripple who was becoming more drug dependant. It seemed that this was what she wanted too, for after he told her he had to go into her room and why, she became unsettled. Maybe it was because she knew he had seen the ring and had received the same idea herself but felt duty-bound to stay with him now. That hurt. The harrowing incident at the Becchinos only propelled his decision: if he was still on the hit-list of that Asian gang, it was best Katherine had nothing more to do with him. Perhaps she realised that too. She seemed to be pulling away from him lately, didn't want to get close. It reminded him of the incident in the restaurant. God, it was the hardest decision he ever had to make in his life, separate, but it had to be done quickly for both their sakes. The sudden inspection tour to the west coast was exactly what he needed.

And now, to hear this?

I will always love you no matter what.

"Katherine, you still actually want *me*? I don't know, but I got the distinct impression before I came here that what you're saying now isn't entirely true."

"What do you mean?"

"Let's just say you weren't terribly happy with the thought of a croissant or two," he noted with bitterness, hurt edging his voice. "If I didn't know better, I could have sworn you didn't want me to even touch you any more."

With a shock, Katherine realised what had happened. She had distanced herself from everything, she just didn't realise to what extent. But now, her worst fear had raised its ugly head sooner than expected, that she would have to tell him what had happened. Now he may not want her after hearing what she had to say, but, he had to know it wasn't him, it was that other ... she didn't want to think of that creep, but think of that night she must. She wanted to cry.

"Oh Gerry, it's not you, and yes, you're right, something is wrong, but not *you*, don't you dare ever think it's you ... but you're right, and you have a right to know."

Wondering at her sudden change and what she meant by that, the hurt and the stinging smart of betrayal left when she hesitantly bared her dreadful confession about Elverton's perverted advances that horrible night.

God, *no wonder she pulled away from him*. Knowing Katherine like he did, extremely shy, reticent about things of that nature thanks to past uncomfortable vulgar experiences she merely hinted about, and he, after all his efforts to win her confidence, never making her feel uncomfortable, never pushing beyond where she was willing to take things, in just a few minutes of freakish terror that no-good bastard had undone all the intimacy he and Kathy shared together, be it ever so simple as a kiss, nothing that would make her distrust him, but still heart-binding ones. Now, they had all been poisoned on her, all future ones had been poisoned.

"Why didn't you tell me? Why didn't you say something!"

How he wanted to strangle Elverton. Tear him limb from limb, smash him into a bloody pulp.

"I couldn't Gerry! Please don't be angry! You did say you didn't want me around him, and I can't help but feel it's my fault ... I know I didn't go to his gallery alone, but still ... did I ... encourage him?"

"Purposely? *You*? Oh, Katherine, of all people, not you." He cooled his sudden surge of anger, grabbed her hand, held it tight. "The way you can give the brush-off, my once upon a time ice queen? I was put through my paces to get noticed at all, remember?”

The tears were trickling down her face, but she couldn't help smiling a little. It was true, she did keep him in Lover's Limbo to where he did whatever it took until her heart finally let her know she couldn't run any longer.

“You were persistent, that's true.”

“But Katherine, we need to report him! Say something to the police!”

“Oh no, Gerry! No! I can't bring that out in public! Besides I've got no proof, nothing that would add to his sentence if he's convicted for the other charges. I would be branded with what he did, it will stick to me not him, and afterwards, no justice at the end of it all. But I'm also relieved you know, it's out in the open. I just wish we could put it behind us.”

It made him sick to think about it, but she was right. Without solid proof other than her word against that s.o.b.'s there was nothing they could do, and he certainly didn't want her dragged through the media with this. They already had enough hassle as it was with the press.

“All right. Don't think about him any more. We'll keep this between ourselves.” However he still wished to beat Elverton to a pulp. He hoped one day he might get the opportunity. “Did you tell anyone else?”

“Just Peter, I couldn't help it. He wanted me to tell you, but I was afraid to. I … I'm sorry for the times I pulled away, but it wasn't because of *you*, it's just … .”

“Katherine, look at me.” He gently held her chin, raised her face to meet his gaze. “You're not at fault or to blame. What you went through is unforgivable … but … did I ever make you feel that way?”

“Oh no, not you. You've always been the perfect gentleman.”

“Even when I did the unthinkable and stole our first kiss?”

She smiled on that one, he nearly rendered her comatose! In a very good kind of way.

“I'm glad you did, Mr. Persistence.” She held his hands. “You've got my heart now, that's not going to anyone else, you've won it fair and square, and I assume that's not going to anyone else either?” She nodded down to the key she had given him. He looked fondly at it for a moment.

“No, you're always had my heart the moment we met. However,” he grew slightly pensive, one confession deserved another. “It's only fair you should be aware of what you're getting in to now, I don't feel like the same man … .” She wondered what he meant until he began laying out the tumult that was going through his mind that led him to the decision to make that sudden break between them, but she didn't let him get to the end, gently telling him to 'sshh', laying a finger on his mouth.

"So that's the stew you were brewing? Gerry, as long as we love each other, that's all that matters. Besides, I'm used to the men in my life having short tempers, well, except for Gramps, he's really mellowed with age." He smiled. "What I'm saying is I understand. Completely. And stop tormenting yourself! You're the same man, you just can't move as fast, that's all."

"And I'll be grouchy."

"And you'll be grouchy, but you'll be *my* Mr. Grouchy."

"But what about keeping you safe? Look what happened at that dinner … ."

"Ger, life itself is dangerous! You can't protect me from every bad thing that could happen, and frankly, I can't live without you. I'd rather live happy with you and worried about what life might throw at us, rather than be miserable without you and still worried about what life might throw. And besides, you're always telling me to 'live dangerously', wouldn't you rather we do that together?"

"You're not going to ever let me go, are you?"

"No more than you can let me go. Try as you might, your heart isn't in it, this key is proof of that. I'll hunt you down across the world if that's what it takes. I'll become a right sticky burr."

He smiled. Did she know what that phrase once used to mean to him? Even if she did, in no way was she like 'The Burr', Katherine sticking to him until Kingdom Come was quite another matter. He gently shook out the chain she had put in his hand, placed it back around her neck. She took his hand and held it against her cheek. It felt so soft. How he had missed her.

"Let's get you packed. Time to go home."

He thought about it for a minute. Hesitated.

"Wait, Kathy. I'm so sorry. After all I've put you through these last few weeks … ."

"You're forgiven. It's water under the bridge. Come … ."

"No listen, give me a few days, then I'll contact you." She looked worried. Was he backing out? "We can't go yet, not like this, not until we've fixed things properly. It is your first time in San Francisco after all and … I've let myself go. Will you give me a few days to pull myself together?"

She was about to kiss him, but stopped. He understood too, obviously with what happened to her she wasn't ready for that yet … but, she *laughed.*

"Ugh! You're right. I'll wait for that until you dry up some more! Your mouthwash isn't cutting it this morning."

So that's what it was! He settled for a hug instead, and was very grateful for it.

"You'll hear from me. In the meantime, have Lee take you around, he knows this city pretty good. Try and have some fun."

"It won't be the same without you, but all right. You will call me, Gerry?"

"All in good time."

She recognised that look. Her intrepid knight was planning something. One last hug, she reluctantly picked up her purse and coat. She didn't want to leave him, but best to let him pull himself together like he asked. Lee was waiting for her in the lobby, playing a game of cards with the concierge. He slapped down his hand.

"Okay, pullin' the bluff on me? Beat that! I've got a full house, try and … hey! She's returned. Mission report. How did it go?" Her big smile told Leroy everything. "Aha! Mission accomplished. Howard Hughes is flying the coop! Where is he?"

Katherine explained the situation, adding that Gerry had now designated him her chaperone for the time being and that they were to see the sights.

"Here I am, running off with the fiancée again. Seriously though, I'd be happy to show you around and play tourist with ye. C'mon, let's get some decent food in us. Bye Bob, catch you later."

After that decent lunch, Lee knew just the place to go play tourist: Fisherman's Wharf. It was a bit chilly and foggy that day, but Katherine did have a lot of fun with him, going to the novelty museums, trying out the vintage seaside arcade games, taking a cruise around the bay under the famous bridges even if they couldn't see much of them with the mist, then feed the colony of sea lions that had taken up residence on Pier 39. Katherine was amused when Lee started giving out to the barking creatures, they weren't touching the fish they were giving them, the ingrates! The fish-seller told them what the problem was: they got a taste for salmon that morning, and so they weren't having any of the other stuff after that. Okay, he could cut the creatures a break, he was partial to smoked salmon himself. Of course, since this was the Wharf, what better way to finish the day after all that ice cream and cotton candy than with the best-ever seafood dinner?

She wondered what he planned for the next day and got her answer as they drank their morning coffee in the elegant atrium ambiance of the Garden Room with its champagne-hued marble pillars and glittering chandeliers.

"Mass first, it is St. Paddy's Day after all, and then on to Chinatown. The one here is the best ever. You can't say you've been to the Bay Area and not have visited Chinatown, not to mention take a ride on a cable car."

"And miss the St. Patrick's Day parade? Don't you want to watch it?"

"Ye've seen one parade, ye've seen them all. Speaking of which, you forgot a piece of green. Do you want to get pinched all day?" He gave her his scarf with the green shamrock border. "The funny part is, they don't do that in Ireland, and, they don't eat corned beef either."

"Thanks Lee, and not just for the scarf. Thanks for staying the few extra days."

"No need to thank me, you think I'd leave ye two in the lurch? Besides, I'm having a grand time meself now that you and Ger have made up. I needed a few days of larkin' about."

They certainly had fun larkin' about Chinatown, sight-seeing the exotic butcher shops and food stores, antique dealers and curiosity nooks, not to mention browsing through all the knock off stores. In one of the authentic stores that sold the real stuff, Katherine was unable to resist the urge to buy Chinese lanterns, she had no idea where she was going to put them, but they simply fascinated her. The little satin slippers with the chrysanthemum blossoms were lovely too, and, look at that! Delicate dioramas of lace-like miniatures of Far Eastern palaces carved out of cork and set in black lacquered wood frames caught her eye, she had to have a few of those too! These were all nice gifts to bring back. Oh! And see all those mother-of-pearl inlay things, her two mothers and Lottie would like some of them, but she definitely had to get that gold Imperial dragon charm for her bracelet.

"Here Lee, help me pick something out for Gerry, something he might use or like."

Lee looked stuck on that one, but Katherine eventually found a black satin quilted robe with traditional Chinese patterns in gold thread, it looked like an Imperial design. He was going to look dashing in that. However, there were so many beautiful colours it was apparent to Lee that everyone else back home was getting one of them too. Maybe he shouldn't have suggested Chinatown. Along with his new role as chaperone, he was now the official shopping bag carrier, but still, he was enjoying himself.

Enough shopping, there was a lot to see, and besides, they couldn't hold on to any more bags. Despite her abhorrence of the ivory trade, she couldn't help but be awed by one shop featuring nothing but antique ivory tusks carved in the most intricate shell-thin designs similar to the little palace miniatures she discovered, hanging gardens, terraced palaces, elephants, tigers, Imperial soldiers and horses in battle array, princesses and emperors, the work was breathtaking. Eventually it was time to stop, she had walked the feet off Lee, but before they left they were in for a treat when they chanced upon a traditional dragon dance street performance.

Back at the hotel a message was waiting for Katherine at the front desk, it was from Gerry: although the day might be a bit boring, he hoped she wouldn't mind sticking close to the hotel tomorrow, a package would be arriving. Inside she would find a clue as to what the plans for the next night would be. Signed, Sir Suspense, Master of Riddles.

"Brilliant! He's made contact, and, by the looks of it is making things right between ye two in grand style."

Katherine wondered what he had planned and could hardly wait.

As requested she didn't go out to play tourist the next day. After having breakfast with Lee and a short walk around the area together, went back to her room and amused herself by watching the local channels, curious to see what they broadcast on this side of the country, and was constantly getting calls to her room from Lee wondering if whatever it was had arrived yet.

"Not yet! I'll call you when it has."

Eventually she was surprised by the arrival of a high priority delivery from Reinold 24-7 Air Express all the way from New York. It was a decent sized box too. Oh my. Inside was her royal blue satin opera gown with her matching shoes, elbow length white gloves, clutch purse, beaded hair clip, and also her formal velvet evening coat. There was also a note from her mother:

> *"Dear Kathy, Gerry called us out of the blue and asked us to put this together and fast, I hope you don't mind, it meant I had to go searching through your things, but if this means what I think it means, I hope I'm forgiven. Enjoy your evening. Come home soon. Love, Mom."*

Yes, she was quite happily forgiven for Katherine now knew what Gerry was up to, he was starting afresh by recreating a very special night. Not long after, there was another knock on the door.

"Delivery for a Miss Walsingham?"

She checked through the peep hole and opened immediately. He had sent her a massive bouquet of red roses and yellow sunflowers. Laying it on the dressing table, she eagerly read the little greeting card attached – the carriage would be arriving for an early supper, then, on to the entertainment. She checked her watch. This all came just in the nick of time! Better get ready, but not until she called Lee and finally let him in on the delivery.

"Aha! Ger always does things in style. I shall leave you two love birds alone tonight. Have a good time."

Wonder where we're heading tonight? Obviously somewhere very formal. She looked at her ensemble in the mirror once she was ready, hair up, French style, gloves on, oh. What a pity Mom didn't think to pack her matching diamond-drop necklace and earrings that went with this, but never mind, she had to get this together fast, her little gold chain was still pretty, and of course, she had her chain with the key. That was never coming off. Last minute prep work, smoothing out creases, tidying up a loose strand of hair, she was ready. It was time. She entered the lobby to find her dashing man in black waiting for her. As she anticipated, there he was, dressed in his fetching caped coat and formal evening attire, standing as tall as possible with both his canes in one hand, another bouquet with red and yellow roses in the crook of his other arm. Just like that other special night, they took each other's breath away.

"Hello, my prince."

"Hello, my princess. I'd gallantly take your hand and kiss it, but my own hands are a bit full at the moment."

With a smile she held up her hand to his mouth instead, and he happily fulfilled his gallant desire. She then noticed the wheelchair was nowhere in sight. He let her know it was there, just around the corner.

"I swore I'm standing up to greet my beloved in all her finery tonight, even if it meant I'd have to be propped up against the wall to do it."

She couldn't help but smile again. He handed her the bouquet, then told her to look under his arm. Hidden under the folds of his cape was a sizeable flat velvet box.

"Quick, take that would you? I can't move until you do."

She hurriedly took the box from under his arm, and he was able to place the other cane back in his hand and reposition his weight.

"Whew! Thank you, dear."

"Will I go get the … ?"

"Nope, we're not done yet. Go on, open it. You know you want to."

Now she understood why her mother didn't send her the matching accessories for the evening dress. Inside were jewels truly fit for a princess, a large diamond and sapphire necklace with matching drop earrings and bracelet shone up at her. She gasped. A few passing guests staying at the hotel took a double-take, some ladies also gasped.

"Gerry! You didn't!" She shyly looked around, a bit bashful the scene this was creating. I hope this is just a rental."

"What?"

"You know, like the celebrities do for big events you see on TV? They don't own *all* that stuff!"

"Hey! I have serious making-up to do, and you think I'd go rental on you?" He laughed then grew thoughtful. "No, my dear. Custom made, one of a kind, and all for you. You're already gorgeous, but come, let's get you shimmering for the night."

He took his canes and hooked them on his arm for a moment and stood on his own, gritting his teeth, but he was bound and determined to have the honour of clasping her new treasure around her neck after she had removed her everyday chain, but not the one with the key, that was never coming off she whispered to him. He smiled.

"I've only discovered lately that you like emeralds, but I hope these blue beauties are also acceptable."

He watched as she laid down her bouquet for a moment to put the earrings on, next the bracelet, which he also helped with. She looked stunning. He was breathless again.

"Acceptable? Gerry! Thank you, thank you so much, they are so beautiful! But it's too much! Why do you spoil me like this?"

"Because you can't be spoiled. And, because I love you."

"Oh Gerry, I love you too, but you don't have to buy me the world to show it."

"Why not? You did."

She looked puzzled, then laughed. *The Four Seasons.*

"The artist would beg to differ if he heard me, but that wasn't quite like this! And all this is a make-up gift?"

"Ah, let's not get into quibbles now. We're going to be late for supper. However, I do have a confession to make," he continued as she went to retrieve the hidden wheelchair, "this was meant to be your wedding present, but I figured you deserved it now after ... well, I do have serious making-up to do. Thing is, I'm going to have to find you a new wedding gift."

"Enough with the gifts! I just want you." She leaned over and gave him a kiss on the cheek.

"Oh, I like that. But come! We're going to be late."

"I thought you liked to be fashionably late."

"Not tonight. We don't want to miss the opening curtain now, do we? And, we have dinner to eat first you know."

Outside a sleek black stretch limo was waiting to take them to the Westin St. Francis hotel where a sumptuous five course dining experience was waiting for them at one of the most exclusive restaurants in town. Situated on the thirty-second floor Victor's could boast of having the most beautiful views of the city. Accessed by elevator, Katherine asked Gerry if he was ready to get into the 'contraption', but it was she who had a surprise coming when the lights dimmed, the gold tinted glass behind melted away revealing the city buildings swiftly dwindling outside as they ascended into the skyline. She jumped closer to the sliding doors. He laughed.

"That's usually my reaction."

"I wasn't expecting that! It's beautiful! Wow, look how fast we're going." Once the initial shock had subsided, she admired the stunning view.

"The St. Francis is famous for its glass elevators, they have five in all. I never had the nerve to get in one in my last trips here, that is, until tonight," he admitted. The car slowed, the lights came back on, the glass regained its opacity, the city skyline disappeared.

"Oh no, that was too fast. I want to go again!"

Gerry chuckled as she pressed the ground floor button, then the top number button. Katherine watched his reaction as they were given a volant vertical tour of the city, he actually enjoyed that as much as she did, especially when she began reciting the poem he first taught her when they made a similar ascent in an elevator and his nerves were not as strong. Finally, they arrived at the restaurant and were seated to their table. She admired the views again overlooking the city, the Coit Tower and the Golden and Bay bridges visible in the distance. This reminded her of another very special night they shared, which he had also done his very best to recreate on such short notice: they could never forget Paris.

Once they had ordered, Gerry asked what she and Lee had been up to while he had been busy pulling himself together arranging this special evening. He was amused when she told him where Lee had taken her the last few days, then didn't know whether to laugh or be concerned when she confessed where they accidentally ended up for lunch in Chinatown. There was this tiny little café style place, the aroma was too good to pass, she decided they were stopping there. Lee wasn't too sure, but okay, if that's where she wanted to go. It wasn't fancy, in fact it was more basic than most eating establishments, no frills whatsoever, however, they couldn't walk out now after they had walked in, that would have been too embarrassing, especially as they were pointed towards a table, so they went with it. The food kept coming, and it was very good, and reasonable too. In fact, it was way too reasonable. They didn't know how the owners could make a living on their 'all you can eat' line of business until Lee noticed the odd comings and goings from the back area near the kitchen, there was too much foot traffic with hardly anyone staying to eat and tumbled to the fact this could actually be a front for a different kind of business the general population didn't know about.

“You mean you two ended up in a house of ill repute?”

“Lee figured it could be an opium den, but um, yeah. Well, how was I supposed to know? And we were hungry. Had to stop somewhere.”

“Of all the places you could have picked. It's not safe to leave you off!” Gerry laughed. “Maybe they thought you were cops and were happy to give you all you could eat just to make sure you didn't go inspecting the place.”

“Maybe! We certainly got a story out of it, but this certainly is another experience,” she noted as the tuxedo dressed waiters deftly attended to their table and served the sorbet course. “May I ask now? What else have you got planned for tonight?”

“I shall reveal in good time. Or rather, our destination itself shall do the revealing.”

After a superb main course, followed by an equally magnificent dessert, Katherine decided to try the white chocolate 'Supreme' cake this time, it was on to the show, but not before they took another quick skyline tour on the glass elevator.

“Yes, I do believe you're cured.”

“What?”

“Elevator? A glass one? And, you didn't flinch, not once. You're enjoying this too,” she noted.

“Oh. Right.” He chuckled. She was correct, his stomach hadn't knotted at all. “But, how could I not enjoy this? We're having Paris again.”

“So true, although we're going to have another treat tonight, we only had dinner in Paris.”

"Ah, but now we're continuing on to the night we should have had a year ago."

She didn't know what he meant until the limo drove up to the opera house and saw what tonight's performance was: *Sleeping Beauty*. To her amazement, it was the same ballet company they missed seeing. They were currently on tour, and to think Gerry got tickets so fast! He never ceased to surprise her. Three nights now combined into one, two of the most memorable times, and now, a sign it was time to heal and move on together.

"The fact it was the same company surprised me too," he admitted. "I'm so glad I could arrange this for today," he noted as they settled into their box, "a very important date in the calendar you know," he said with an appreciative little nod.

"Really? What's today?"

"Seriously? After all my rush to make sure we had our special make-up date on this day of all days?"

He began to sing quietly into her ear: "*You'll know when it happens … .*"

Her eyes brightened. Her hands flew to her mouth. March 18th.

"Aha. She remembers! I can't believe it. You mean the hubby and not the woman of the house is going to remember the anniversaries in this relationship? There's a switch."

"Oh Gerry, what's the matter with me? And you remembered that!"

"The day my Ice Queen melted and spring arrived? Of *course* I did."

She laughed. How she loved him! She gave him a warm kiss on the cheek. He retuned the gesture with a kiss on her hands.

"I love it when you sing."

"Then I solemnly promise I shall serenade you more often."

"I shall hold you to that, your highness."

He actually started to hum the the rest of the melody for her, but had to cut his performance short, the lights dimmed, the ballet was about to begin. Hand and hand laced together in the dark as Tchaikovsky's melodies weaved around them. Katherine thought of all they had experienced, all they had been through, and now, how far they had come in just a few days with the realisation of how deeply in love they were after the harrowing discovery of what it felt like to be on the brink of losing each other, how they were now determined that they were never going to allow that ever happen again. She nestled a little closer to him and happily closed her eyes, soaking in the music, blissful they were together once more, never to part.

"Uh oh. I thought taking you to a ballet would be safer than an opera," he whispered in her ear.

"Huh?"

"You don't have any tonsil torpedoes to annoy you this time, and yet, you're closing your eyes. Is my princess about to go snoozing?"

"No," she whispered back.

"I dunno. No more silly juice. It's back to the ginger ale for you."

"I'm fine! Can't you tell I'm just enjoying the the whole thing?"

"Quietly basking in my company, are you?"

"If you must know, yes! Now shh! Be quiet, or they'll boot us out." Of all times to try and fluster her up, but she couldn't help but smile and cuddle against him again. Yes, it felt good just to be together, she knew he was feeling the same about her. She leaned over and gave him a quick kiss, and not on the cheek.

"Whoa. This is my lucky night! I actually got my first kiss in a public place," he whispered. "Hmm, maybe that doesn't count, it is a bit dark in here, nobody saw that … we'll have to do it again."

"Shhhh! "

He chuckled. She was probably blushing right now. He shushed up, allowing her to nestle against him in peace. With each passing note of music, the ballet drew closer to the end faster than they would have liked. The curtain fell, the last note played, the applause thundered. The ballet may be over, but determined to make this night last a little longer, he instructed the chauffeur to drive around for a bit.

"That was beautiful. I enjoyed the performance, and your company of course."

"Me too, my dear," however, he grew quiet.

"What's on your mind, Lancelot?" Maybe the meds were starting to wear off.

"Oh, I don't mean to throw a dampener on the end of a wonderful night. It's just that after watching that, I wish for our wedding day I could have danced with my beautiful bride, but well, you know."

That was a difficult thing to face for both of them. Gerry liked to dance, and had cured her of her own phobia for doing anything like that in public. True, she would have given anything to waltz with him again. Suddenly, a thought struck her.

"Nothing for it. We'll just have to go back to Plan B," she replied matter-of-factly. He looked puzzled until she recalled to mind: "We can always play 'Pin the Tail on the Donkey'.

Of all the things he said when they first met, she remembered that!

He laughed. It sounded so good to hear him laugh.

The next few days were spent busily wrapping up business at Reinold Enterprises in California and getting Gerry packed up for home. He had fun telling her that not only he but probably the regional manager was glad she came, no doubt they were all terrified at the idea of having the Boss there on a permanent basis and were all relieved he was heading back to the east coast. Katherine was certainly happy he was coming home, and so were their families. Still, he had to face the music in that he had run off and left them all in shock too, but if they were upset with him at the time, they didn't show it now, except for Aunt Martha who was not going to let him get off the hook that easily after he had abandoned her niece like that.

"We're ever so glad you're home, but don't you dare ever do that to us again, young man, or you'll be sorry!"

Katherine thought that was a bit rich when Auntie viewed Gerry's gallant self-sacrificing act of 'abandonment' as the perfect opportunity to try and get her back to her childhood home, however, he meekly took the rebuke, and the big suffocating bear hug Auntie gave him. There was a more difficult reminder to face of what he had done when they were alone together. Katherine was able at last to present him with his Valentine's Day gift, which he had unceremoniously returned while he was caught in his depressed state of mind on the other side of the country.

"It's not anything as grand as the crown jewels you just gave me, but I think you'll still like it."

He looked at the sealed box with regret.

"I'm sorry, I didn't even get you anything for that day."

"Gerry! Our make-up date made up for that big time, and I'm not talking about the jewels. No more apologies. We're home now, and together again." She gave him a kiss on the forehead, then eagerly prodded, "Go on! Open it."

Inside he found a folio sheet from a medieval manuscript set in a special frame, an intricate illuminated page featuring a pair of courtly young lovers exchanging a heart they held in their hands with each other as they sat together under a bountiful fruit tree in a flowering garden filled with a myriad of creatures, including a unicorn and a lion. It meant so much more now than if he had opened it on the day it was intended.

"Like the tapestries. It's exquisite, my dear. Thank you so much. I love it." He gave her a kiss. "I know the perfect place for it."

Upon his arrival home he noticed a new addition among the artwork in their elegant Italianate parlour, the rare unicorn folio set he had given her when he was desperate to catch her attention. The frame was hung a little lower then usual, leaving a conspicuous place above on the wall. In fact the hook was ready and waiting. It was one of the first things he noticed when he came home, wondered what she had in mind for the space, now he knew. There was no mistaking this is where she wanted him to put his new gift. He insisted on standing and hanging it up himself. It was the crowning glory, to receive such a beautiful confirmation that he had won her heart. He added the finishing touch by placing the orbs of the *Four Seasons* on the table underneath. The seasons may come and go, but their love would endure, they meant the world to each other.

∛❖√

Hectic days followed the happy homecoming. Gerry had to return to business, reporting on his latest inspection and catching up at the main office, while Katherine had to work out some well deserved break time for the Gallery Gang, especially Suzy who also had her own wedding to plan, part of which was one major hurdle her friend was facing that earned her deepest sympathies: Suzy's parents were coming from Iowa that Easter to meet Charlie's folks for the first time, and she was all jitters wondering how it would turn out. It was an awkward situation for Katherine as well, she having once been the centre of Charlie's affections, and Gerry accidentally witnessing his botched proposal, the memory of which was the bane of Charlie's mother who had been eager to see her son make an agreeable match with her, and now was making Suzy feel her ire that it all went awry. Katherine didn't quite escape either the night everyone got together for dinner since Suzy asked her to be one of her bridesmaids. She received an undisguised smuggish look from Mrs. Kraylor after she gave a pitying one to Gerry in his chair. She quickly deciphered those pointed glances: 'Hmph! you got what you deserved for dumping my son, now look what you're stuck with'. It was an insult intended for her, but had thoughtlessly spread like a cluster bomb to other targets. She hoped Gerry didn't see that. Katherine understood what he was facing from the ignorant and the cruel who could only see the chair and not the man. For his sake she was livid. How she wanted to slap that woman senseless! But they were in public, and, she was raised a lady. She could quip her a retaliatory tongue dart

854

instead, but then there was Suzy and Charlie to think about, let's not make a scene. Count to ten, count to ten, count to ten … . One thing was for certain, she was eternally grateful Mrs. Kraylor was not going to be her mother-in-law.

The meeting of the parents went off without too much of a hitch after that, the air was filled with excitement as Charlie and Suzy revealed they decided on a May date, and, wanted to go back to her home town church for the ceremony. Tom and Lottie were also beginning to consider what to do about their own plans set for July. Katherine and Gerry were happy for everyone, but were now in a tight spot wondering when they should reschedule their wedding: too close to Tom and Lottie's date seemed a bit manic to manage, they might have to wait, again. Besides, all the summer dates were already booked out at the cathedral. Maybe a slot would open up if a cancellation happened, maybe they could go to another church. No, late fall and winter was what they had to work with. Katherine didn't mind if it couldn't be summer, officially having Gerry declared hers and she his before the whole world never to put asunder was what was important. She had her prince, he his princess, who cared if they couldn't get the 'perfect day' she pointed out? They would have their whole lives to share. Gerry loved that consolation speech and the woman who made it even more, but quietly wished Italy could happen a little sooner.

Everyone felt for them. It wasn't long before the two mothers got together and decided enough was enough, Katherine and Gerry needed their day of happiness too, which had been postponed long enough. A big family pow-wow was convened at Stonyvale, with the two matriarchs of the Reinold and Walsingham clans sitting Tom, Lottie, Gerry and Katherine down in the Rose Room while the rest of the men had their chin-wag and after dinner drinks in the Red Room with the Captain.

"Look, we've discussed it, and Kathy's mother also agrees with me on this, but you four have to decide: would you consider having a double-wedding?"

Sophia and Helen watched their reactions as the solution sunk in.

"Oh! Everybody would be here! They'd practically all be on your guest list too again, right guys? And we were going to have our reception here too at the manor so … what do you think Kathy? I know you wanted your own day … but," Lottie broke off.

"Hey, you wouldn't mind sharing yours? Don't you want your own day too?"

"Not at all! Sure, we're *family*!"

"Wow! I don't mind if you don't. You really don't?" Lottie shook her head. Katherine was thrilled. "Then I'm happy. Imagine getting married with your sister Gerry, with your brother marrying us all! Not many people have that happen. I think it's fantastic!"

"Ohhhhh think of it! The summer event of the decade! It's not often you get a double wedding like this! Thank heavens you suggested this before we got the invitations made out," Lottie realised.

The mothers gave each other a little satisfactory nod. Mission accomplished.

Katherine then thought of another serendipitous aspect: what a way to get back at the nasty columnist that assumed it was all over between her and Gerry. They will think this was planned all along, a secret double wedding until the news broke.

"Yes! You're right Kathy! Serves Beatrice the Bug right!"

While their ladies were elated with the idea, Gerry looked over at Tom who looked stunned with the simplicity of it.

"Well Ger, I'm willing, if you are."

"Fine by me, if the women are happy, what more could we want?"

Gerry smiled. The summer honeymoon in Italy was back on.

The excitement! It was almost impossible trying to carry on with normal life while everyone had their wedding arrangements, Katherine managing the gallery and working on the rest of the decorations in the apartment, meeting up with Lottie when she could carve out free time to start considering colour themes with the Matriarchs, then, wondering how on earth she was going to finish her portrait commissions in the midst of all this, while Gerry was doing his best to manage the offices after Steve's new business proposal that would merge the Walsingham's medical biotech enterprise with theirs. It was a cutting edge idea. However, it was hard to keep up with it all with his own medical conditions. Some days were tougher than others, especially when he was determined not to become dependant on the heavier medications and decided to go with plain aspirin management during the daytime, saving the heavier stuff for night so he could get some rest. Some nights were fine, others not so good to where he could not find any relief in bed. Katherine found him in the mornings in his favourite leather recliner in the library, wrapped up in his blanket finally fast asleep with the headphones still on and his sketchbook beside him after trying to block out the pain with his favourite music and some artful distraction. Some days were more depressing than others when he just had to go in during the afternoons, or in the worse case scenario call in sick, there was no way he could leave the house. The rainy weather must be making that trapped nerve worse. However, he was glad Katherine was with him, even if she did tend to hover a bit, wrap him up tighter in his blanket, run and fetch whatever he needed, make sure a thousand times he was okay and didn't need anything else before she had to head out to the gallery. Trying so hard to make sure he was okay and getting very protective of him were all signs she cared, loved him deeply, he had to remember that.

Despite her own worry for him, she knew how to cheer him up when he felt stuck in a rut. One evening he had a bad time blocking out the jabbing aches and trying not to let the resulting grouchiness affect everything, but asked how the decorating in the entertainment room was coming when she poked her head in to see if he was okay, he couldn't figure out how she could paint the cherubs so fast, it took him ages to get anything looking that good on regular canvas, and here she was, painting them on the ceiling no less. Laughing, at last she confessed about the sticky-wicky cherubs that were the imposters among the painted ones. As a patron of the con artists whose famous forgeries he also collected, he should appreciate her methods she playfully told him. Touché! You conniving little cheat, he retorted! Now I'll be craning my head at the ceiling the whole time trying to find the fakes! But he found that very funny. Before she returned to work on their Sistine Chapel, she gave him a longed-for croissant, a quick one, she had a lot to do! Maybe she was covering, she was still having a hard time overcoming what had happened to her, so he waited until she initiated a hug or a croissant, letting her decide when to pull back, letting her determine the healing pace she needed to take, although some days he got desperate enough to ask for a kiss, at least she wouldn't refuse. God help her, she was trying for his sake not to let an evil memory fester what they had together.

Sometimes, that was hard to take too, loving her so much and feeling helpless at the same time. He should be the one looking out for her, he couldn't protect her from that slithering no-good pervert, and now, on the bad days to feel like a outright invalid unable to do much at all when he also had a lot of work waiting for him. Then, to have a constant sense of anxiety under the surface, eating at the back of his mind after that unnerving dinner at the Becchino's house, wondering if that shooting was also meant for him. Some days his concern morphed into a quiet anger, seething at whoever had done this to him and to Kathy too, having to put up with him like this, especially on the really bad days. He felt like beating that jerk into a pulp along with the pervert. The frightening part, something like his 'accident' could happen again. There was nothing in the news these last few weeks but a swathe of arrests were made, a considerable number of the Jade Cobra gang was mentioned, their grip on the underworld element of the city was starting to slip the last couple of weeks, which was a relief to discover, but what about the guy who actually did this to him? Over a year since his non-accidental accident and nothing yet. No leads. His case had gone cold. How could he rest knowing that criminal was still on the loose? Of course, Katherine could sense him stewing, he didn't want her to worry. He tried to cheer up for her sake. When he could work, that was a help, keeping him productive kept him from getting too morose, and thank heavens planning the double-wedding was a good if somewhat chaotic distraction.

At first, he thought what was a simple solution that the mothers proposed would eventually go south with not one but two brides trying to plan the thing, he was certain disagreements would break out and the hair would fly. The Rampage of the Bridezillas! There was a B movie title for you. Strange enough, the opposite was happening. One bride to be didn't want to leave the other out by making all the decisions without giving the other their chance to consider too. This was a nice state of affairs actually, but it had its drawback he and Tom were discovering. The brides were being so agreeable with each other they couldn't agree on anything. Case in point: they finally had decided to go with Kathy's original colour scheme, pink with white and mint green accents, but Lottie wanted to make sure they were happy with the final shadings, and since Katherine didn't want Lottie stuck with a colour scheme she chose without having a say, went along with it. However, unable to make up their minds, Tom was suddenly thrust into the whirlwind when Lottie dropped a table linen sampler book on him with their narrowed-down choices, asking he and Gerry to decide, they were getting married too and should have the opportunity to pick something. Tom wandered into Gerry's office with the sampler book in hand looking utterly perplexed.

“Geeze Ger, I can't tell the difference. 'Summer Sighs'? 'Cotton Candy Dreams'? 'Dawn's Delight?' 'Rose Heaven'? Heck, they're all pink to me.”

Gerry chuckled.

“When it comes to a wedding, all women are artists and the least shading out of synch with their creative thought can make or break their magnum opus. It makes it worse when one of them is actually an artist.”

“Can we stall?”

“Nope. If we don't pick something once in awhile and just let them do it, they don't believe we're happy with what makes them happy. They'll mistake our willingness to go along with anything they decide the wrong way, a.k.a. 'I don't care what you do'.”

“So that's it, huh? Okay then, this looks good.” He laughed, landing his finger on a shade eeny meeny miny moe fashion. Rose Heaven won out. “But this is just the table cloths, you should see all the other books waiting for us to skim through.”

“Been there, done that, doing it again. Honestly though, I'm thankful for this double-wedding idea, it has saved me from having to relive another ordeal.”

Tom wondered what that could be until Gerry explained the matter of Aunt Martha's wedding etiquette book. She couldn't barge in with that this time, not since she couldn't dictate how Lottie should get married too. Auntie was looking like a right sour-puss over it, but settled for a compromise in that Lottie was willing to consider Katherine's input, which she made diligently sure to influence behind the scenes as much as possible.

“You have it easy Tom, look what I'm marrying in to.”

Tom laughed again.

“It's a good thing we love our women, or this would drive us insane.”

In order to cut through the insanity of the wedding planning, he and Tom hit upon a scheme of their own: when any more sampler books arrived, to make a big show over picking things, but quietly do the eenmy meeny bit between themselves. Everything looked good to them, so they couldn't go wrong. If they did and the girls protested their choice, just keep picking until their faces lit up and they agreed. Anything for peace.

“So, have you decided on a honeymoon destination yet?”

“Lottie says she'd love to see Prague, so that's settled.”

That reminded Gerry while he had some time he'd better get a hoof on it and sort out Italy. This was one thing he didn't mind doing twice. He insisted he and Katherine still have a whole month together and had a grand plan laid out, private villas to book and classic cars to take them there, although he felt like switching things around this time, maybe Rome first, oh yeah! Then on to Florence, Venice, Milan … that sounded like the perfect itinerary. Tom decided he'd better let him at it, he'd see him later to discuss the latest reports from Ohio regarding their airfreight shipping warehouses and the estimates to upgrade them to A-grade medical standards. Gerry reached to pick up the phone, but had to put his honeymoon planning on hold when an unexpected call came.

"Mr. Gerard, there's a Detective Davenport on the line for you. Will I put him through?"

Davenport. He knew of only one reason why he'd be calling.

"Yes, certainly."

"Good afternoon, Mr. Reinold. I know, you've waited a long time to hear this, and yeah, I've got good news for you, we've got the suspect."

Just like that. Gerry was stunned.

"Seriously? When did this happen?"

"Like, an hour ago. This is the strange thing, we didn't make the arrest, he was turned in."

"I don't care how he was caught, you've got him, that's the main thing."

"Right, but that's not all. We found out he's North Korean, with no political asylum status granted. He's here illegally. Maybe a member of the Syndicate, but you can guess Uncle Sam is going to think he's a spy. This could become an international incident! He can speak some English. Eventhough we've got evidence that will nail him, he says he's willing to confess to the whole deal, literally spill the beans on what he knows, but he's insisting you're here too. We've already got Feds crawling the place here and so they've taken this one. They've tried to get him to open up if he's ready to confess, but it's obvious they'd be able to break in and riffle Kim Il-sung's palace faster than getting that confession out of him unless you're witness to it. Since we were first on this case, they've allowed us to call you. Would you be willing to come to the station?"

"You bet your badge I'm willing. I'll be right there."

"I thought you might be. See you then."

North Korean? Whatever. He had tried to kill him. At long last, he would finally see that s.o.b. squirm in the hot seat, then, watch him get thrown into the slammer, or deported, whatever came, even if it was back to North Korea. An end to the not knowing. Justice, finally. How satisfying, not to mention the relief hearing he was caught and couldn't harm Katherine as collateral damage. After instructing Clarke to put all afternoon business on hold and tell everyone he was out, he grabbed his jacket off the back of his office chair and set himself back into the wheeled contraption, ready to hit the road. There was a knock at the door.

"Hi Gerry! Oh good, I caught you in time. I thought I would surprise you and we could have lunch together today. Not to mention to ask if you guys have decided on a colour yet … ."

"You've succeeded! I'm surprised, my dear. Serendipitous timing, but not for lunch."

"Oh?" Katherine gave him a quick kiss on the cheek, wondering what he meant.

"You won't believe the news I just got. As for the colour, Tom picked 'Rose Heaven', and I like it. Good name too."

"That must be a sign! We liked that, but now that you've picked it as well, that's another thing decided. However, I'm dying to know, what's the news?"

She was floored when he told her.

"I'm coming with you. You can't go alone, not for that."

"No, Kathy, I don't want you in the station, this is something I have to handle."

"Look, we have to get lunch anyway. I'll sit outside in the car and wait if you like, but you're not going alone."

Okay, he finally had to agree to that, and so they were off, he insisting on driving. That was one thing he could still do on a good day thanks to automatic gear shifts in his brand new Merc.

Katherine went not just to give him moral support, but also to try and curb the mounting temper of his. She understood he was angry for what had happened to him, but also knew he would never be at peace until he accepted his situation. Maybe seeing the guy turned in would help, but she worried for Gerry. Thanks to Peter and his spiritual exercises, it was a long time ago since she had practised the virtue of forgiveness and cooled her own temper, but Gerry wasn't there yet, and she didn't know how she could help him. She was afraid what his anger might do to him in the long run, change him, and not for the better.

As they pulled up outside the station, she watched as cops dragged cuffed suspects in, the scene looked ominous, not to mention she would be walking into a rather gritty environment, and then, she had forgotten he had also made enemies among the corrupt members of the force awhile back, dirty cops in on the take regarding robbed and fenced shipments. She thought the Reinolds had succeeded in getting them exposed and put away, but were there other dirty cops still there? Bad blood still at the station? She could see why he wanted her not to go in. However, the detectives they knew seemed okay, and he had made friends too considering the generous donations Reinold Enterprises made to the force's Retirement Fund as a reward to the good cops who helped to clear the station and the Reinold name.

"Will you be all right here?"

"I'll be fine. And Gerry," she took his hand for a moment after helping to unfold the wheelchair, "do what you have to do, but justice is one thing, vengeance is another. Don't let the two get mixed up. Please, don't let this turn you into someone you don't want to be. Someone I won't recognise."

He looked taken aback for a moment, then bit his lip.

"I just want this over with, see him get what's coming to him. I won't rest until I do."

He turned and wheeled himself into the station, Katherine watching after him. The place looked unbelievably busy today, apparently lots of arrests were being made. He announced himself at the reception desk and was soon escorted to Detective Davenport's private office.

"Hello Mr. Reinold, sorry about the ruckus. It's been crazy lately."

"I see that. What's up? If you can tell me."

"I don't know what's happened, it seems like a turf war has exploded. Not just here, but also Jersey. Now, you didn't hear this from me, and I'll deny I ever told yah, but sometimes we let them at it, they're doing the job faster than we can. Let the trash take out the trash, yah get my drift? The funny part is, this usually ends up with a lot more bodies, but they're all getting turned in, like a bunch of vigilantes went haywire or something."

"So, that's what happened to the guy who tried to do me in?"

Before Davenport could answer, there was a knock on the door. It was another familiar face, Detective Shumaker.

"Hey! Long time, no see. How are you Mr. Reinold?" They shook hands. "How's the repair work on your art collection coming?"

"Pretty good, the paintings are almost restored, the tapestry is going to take some time, but all's good. How about you?"

"I've been moved on to old murder investigations, cold cases. Sometimes I'm assigned the still warm ones that have lost leads, but I didn't have much to do with solving this. Davy, did you tell him the news yet?"

"Not all of it. You give him the rest."

Shumaker drew up a chair. The fingerprints found in the truck that hit him matched the detainee. The photo in the phony ID the detainee had at the time also matched. The odd part was, similar to the blitz in arrests being made thanks to the upsurge in tips and leads getting called in, the guy who tried to kill him was literally dropped off tied-up. They didn't catch who was in the car or the plates, they sped away. A rather gutsy thing to do in the middle of the day with the station as busy as it was.

"Maybe he was meant as a wedding present for you, who knows? Whoever is at this, frankly, they're doin' such a good job I almost want to applaud them. As much as I detest the Mob, that Jade Cobra Syndicate was worse, bad news."

Gerry was intrigued, so were the detectives.

They had no idea that back near the Ides of March a desperate father helped to start this clean-up of the city by some rather questionable means for the sake of his daughter and his soon to be son-in law. The night Harold went to visit his neighbour, the bodyguards left him in when the master of the house eagerly told him to sally on through to the kitchen where he found him garbed in a chef's apron, messing around with dinner as Cee was having a girls night out.

"Benvenuto! It's good to see you! Frankly, I wouldn't blame yous if yah never came back after what happened. I got the urge for some steak pizzaiola, want some?"

"Looks good, but no thanks."

"Ah here, give it a go at least." Vico cut him a piece of steak and handed it to him on a clean fork. "Uh huh. Good, eh? I knew yah'd like it. Here, have a plate, I got plenty. So, what brings yah here? I got a feeling this is more than a social how do yah do."

"You're correct," Harold confirmed as he politely accepted a plate of steak at the island counter and settled on one of the breakfast chairs, knowing both the spicy sauce and what he had to say was going to murder his ulcers.

When they first met, he offered his help regarding information on the man who had attacked Gerry—was that offer still on the table?

"Sure! I like Gerry, swell guy. It's not many who give a thought to cons in the slammer. He's such a do-gooder. Awful what happened to him. How are they? I'm sorry about the other night, they must have been shook bad."

Harold gave the news at that time, Gerry on the other side of the country attempting to break off the engagement in an effort to spare her considering his injuries, while Katherine had locked herself away in the Manhattan apartment waiting for him to come home, refusing to give him up, both devastated. True, the shooting at the dinner didn't help either.

"Geeze, that's terrible. They looked like a swell couple. I feel bad for them."

"The thing is, Mr. Becchino … ."

"Vico, Vico! Go on."

"Well, apart from Gerry's condition, he's afraid for my daughter too. Is there any way you can get more than just information?"

"Uh humh." Vico wiped his mouth and put down his napkin. This was business talk. "I got kids, I know how you feel. Family is everything. What kind of, um, services, were yous thinking of?"

"You see, there's a chance if he's out of the picture Gerry might not break off the wedding, but we need to get one thing straight: I would like things done, er, the hard way. Above board and legal, you understand. I was hoping for something that wouldn't get either of us in trouble and keep us out of a scrape, like perhaps keeping the guy alive?"

"Despite what you think yah know about me, I can appreciate that. Straight and above board, huh? I'll see what I can do. I can't make any promises, but if I find out who did that to Gerry, he'll get the legal treatment. Although I wouldn't suggest it, he might get off if one of our, um, well, friendly neighbourhood judges isn't assigned the case. There's a risk of that. There's only one sure way tah keep him out of your hair … ."

"No! Alive, or we don't go through with this at all. However, I understand 'payment' might be in order. What might I expect for, er, your services?"

"Nah, we're good. After all you've done for us, and especially after that other night, I'm the one who owes you. Call it even. Although free prescriptions now and again would be appreciated, yah know? Your stuff works!"

"Done. However, there won't be any unexpected blow back from this? When 'business' is done, it's done between us?"

"Hey, I owe you remember? I'm ticked off about what happened here too, might've helped cause this break up with your kiddos. When Vico Becchino gives his word, he gives his word. Don't worry, we'll get the guy, no strings attached. Finito."

"All right then. We're agreed." They shook hands. "Also, Gerard and Katherine must never know of this, nor anybody else."

"No need to tell me. C'mon! Eat up! There's more where that came from."

Vico found it very intriguing that Mr. Walsingham would come to him for assistance, and just at some rather unusual timing. He and the other Families were getting it heavy from the Jade Cobra Syndicate moving in, shoot outs, territory stepped on. Even the Chinese mob and the black drug crews were not happy with this new crowd making trouble, stirring the pot. It was getting ugly in both New York and Jersey. This new crime syndicate, like some of the eastern European mob bosses who were also a problem, had no sense of the Old Ways, no sense of honour, no respect. With him, girls were never forced to turn tricks, it was a voluntary thing. Vico always believed customers were usually happier with a girl who was willing anyway. If they became snitches and ratted on their business, well, punishment was coming to them then, but Vico believed in upholding the voluntary code: if a girl wanted to leave, go live a normal if somewhat poorer tax-ridden life, fine, as long as she didn't become a rat, then he believed in respecting that, but now these new slime balls were bringing in girls from poor countries, tricked into thinking they were going to a modelling school or would be given a good paying job in the States, kidnapped, victims of human trafficking, drugged up, forced into the racket, then when they were too sick to work, or had managed to escape, they were hunted down like dogs, their bodies dumped or buried not to be found for a long time. The Syndicate was also snaring their own home-grown country girls in backwater hick towns with the promises of a glamorous theatre career, bright city lights, anything to make them fall into the trap. If that wasn't bad enough, they were also harassing his working girls, who told him what was going on. There were rumours of underground slave auctions, girls being sold off to high bidders. Some of his girls who found out ended up dead. These guys were getting too big for their boots. Something had to be done. Vico had just put the word out and issued a mutual truce summons: it was a long time since the Old Families were called for a formal meeting, a gathering of the clans. The meeting was to be held two nights after Mr Walsingham showed up in his kitchen. But going all legal? Not a bad idea. It would be a feather in his cap if he could get the rest of the Families to consider less bloody tactics with their retaliations against the gang, for he also had his own reasons for going a bit soft. Like he said to Mr. Walsingham, he too had kids.

Times were changing. The old rackets were no longer enough. He could see organisations like the Syndicate could not be kept from moving in, things were going to get uglier for the next generation. Before, there was the usual way of doing things, don't step into my business, and I won't step into yours, there was a certain respect among the Families, but this new crowd was another thing. It was a virus. He was hoping his sons would not have to deal with that. Even with the 'Old Understanding', rarely did loyal members of a Family live long enough or escape a feud or the slammer to become the next head of the business, the respect given and taken between them was fragile, there was always the possibility of a greedy subordinate wanting to step out on their own, breaking old loyalties and end up starting something that resulted with mayhem let loose. But now?

The threat of war would always be eminent with these new ones in town. It was one of the reasons he insisted his boys get a decent eduction, hopefully they might be interested in having an honest to goodness career, ween them off the family business, or perhaps make all their fronts go legit for real. In any case, they had enough dough to set them up for life. Unfortunately his eldest son Paulo was already too heavily invested in the running of things as they were, but Gio still had a chance despite all his kicking and screaming about going to college. Hopefully if it wasn't Paulo, then maybe Gio could one day not have to look over his shoulder. This was one of the reasons he moved to Oak Meadows in the first place, make a stab at settling in a real classy place for Gio's sake where a prosperous normal life was possible with new connections, nothing from the underworld. It was tough seeing how their reputation had already soured things, the initial cold reception, the new neighbours shunning them, that is until he got the Walsingham's welcome invitation. Maybe they didn't know who they had invited at first, but despite the stiffness, he certainly did his best to be friendly. Then, to be asked to the Country Club, the openings at the gallery, that was really nice of them. He could still see the trepidation, but they gave his family a chance. Cee was certainly enjoying the new change and the household seemed happier of late because of it. He respected the Walsinghams for that, so yes, as much as it would have been something to keep strings tied to them to pull on when needed, this time, no. He would keep his word. He did owe them in more ways than Harold anticipated, not to mention he also respected Gerry's brother too, quite a number of the other Families did as well. The whole city was talking about the 'Monsignor of Manhattan'. To touch a priest or those belonged to him was bad news. It would be a wise thing to make sure he and those around him were protected, got help if and when they needed it. Yeah, Har's idea was not bad at all: if he could get some payback on the Cobra Syndicate legally, it would help keep the heat of the law off all the Families and give the next generation a better chance at making that escape into a less risky future should they choose.

No, he didn't reveal this particular motive to the Families when they eventually convened in an exclusive yet secret location for the gathering, but he did manage to convince them that an all out blood war with bodies showing up in dumpsters or littering the bottom of the river was not the way to go. True, it was usually a point of dishonour with them to turn anyone in to the law, but this Syndicate was different, they had no respect and therefore did not deserve any, and in any case, they needed to be dealt with. It was time to form an alliance for their mutual benefit: they might get some peace from the clean-nosed cops if they helped turn in and clear out the Syndicate by legal means behind the scenes. Plus, the cops and judges on the take would have to go along with these orders on their say-so, and it wouldn't do them any harm to go legit too once in awhile, keep their cover good and secure. In all, this could help restore the balance of things. Keep the cops so busy with stake outs, sting operations, arrests and dealing with the Feds that the Families could be left undisturbed to reorganise, regroup. They could try it.

At first, there was noticeable hesitation around the table. They were used to bumping off troublesome enemies, and, going legit seemed the yellow-livered thing to do, and someone had to protest, but despite the disgruntled objection, the Don from 'Little Italy' suddenly spoke up. Vico was right. There was enough blood spilled, wars often made business suffer. Vico had a sound head on his shoulders, what he said made sense, now was not the time to get hot and lose sight of things. This had nothing to do about going legit forever, just a change of tactics, and things were getting to the point it was time to try a change. If they handled things in their usual way, sure, they would send a message, but that wouldn't weaken the newcomers to the point of dealing a serious death blow. War would be imminent. The Syndicate had international tentacles, and it would take the government to stop their smuggling pipelines and all their other activities. Doing it Vico's way had possibilities. Once they had exposed the Syndicate, the governments could take care of their international rackets that the Families couldn't reach. For the respect he held for him, not to mention his father whose memory had not been forgotten, also a man of his word, he was willing to implement Vico's suggestions, but it would take all of them for it to work. One by one, the rest of the Godfathers looked around. There was always a chance for an uneasy peace, but an all-out alliance? Yes, it would mean putting aside any old feuds from the past too and pool resources, but eventually, they agreed. Truce had been declared between them, the Great Clean-up had begun.

No, Gerry and the detectives were still in the dark about Katherine's father making that deal with Vico, and in the process unintentionally helped to unite the Mob families, but they could see the end result, the Feds also getting in on the cleaning frenzy. There were quite a few unsolved cases on their books too, and all these tip-offs and turn-ins were helping them crack quite a number of international smuggling and trafficking operations.

"I can't stand them here, but there's enough cases for everyone to go around at the moment," Davenport declared as he eyed two Feds passing by the office window, also willing to call a truce when wrangling over who had what jurisdiction. Although he didn't say it, Davenport was glad this case was permitted to continue as a joint operation and they weren't cut out of it since they had gotten to know Gerry and wanted him to get some justice after what had happened to him. The Feds entered the office and introduced themselves, Agents Gillan and Lindmann. Gerry politely shook hands.

"Thank you for coming Mr. Reinold. Have you been briefed on what's happened," Gillan dutifully enquired.

"Yes. I don't know why he wants me here other than to gloat, but if I can help at all by listening. Fine."

"We appreciate this. The detainee could have valuable intel we need." He was interrupted as the phone on his desk buzzed: he was now in Interrogation Room Two. They could proceed. "Well, Mr. Reinold, this is it. We've got a translator here, just in case."

As they escorted him, they met up with the translator.

"Okay, in here please."

They didn't lead him to the detainee directly, the agents and detectives gave Gerry a chance to take a good look first through the mirror in the adjoining room, get used to the prospect of facing the man who tried to kill him. So, at last. This was him. Real name Chin-Hae Jeong. Gerry could only stare. He expected a hardened man of the streets, but this thin, drained figure with the demeanour of someone utterly defeated as he looked at his cuffed, folded hands on the table in front of him didn't match the mental picture he had of the guy. Still, no doubt he wanted to make this face to face confession to rub in what he had done to him before he was sent to prison. That had to be it.

"Are you ready?"

"Yeah. Let's get this over with."

Davenport led the way with the agents, Gerry following, Shumaker and the translator the last to enter.

As soon as the detainee saw his victim, he stood up. The guard watching over him in the background tried to get him to sit, but Gillan gave a sign to let him be.

With an expression filled with shame and remorse, he made a profound bow to Gerry and begged his forgiveness for the crime he committed against him, adding that for this misdeed he deserved all the shame, disgrace and public dishonour that was due him.

Gerry wasn't expecting that.

Gillan motioned for the guard to help sit the detainee back down. He meekly obeyed, head still bowed, unable to look Gerry in the face, but as promised, he gave his confession, lapsing into his Koren dialect with the translator assisting when he was unsure or ignorant of the correct expressions in English, the detectives and agents grimly listened.

The man before him slowly began. After watching his wife die from lack of medical attention, then his two youngest children die of malnutrition, decided to save what was left of his family, his eight year old daughter, from the unbearable conditions of his home country that had designated him among the 'hostile class' in the Songbun, a political caste system where position in North Korean society is determined according to loyalty, and therefore he received the least amount of help with regards to everything from the meagre job assignments to life's basic necessities were meted out. How he got designated to hostile class, he wasn't sure, maybe a neighbour or a loyal citizen thought they saw him do something suspicious and reported on him. At that point, he had to get out. A fisherman who had succeeded in smuggling people across the border to China via a sea route agreed to take them, there was a tense moment as coast guard patrols were spotted in the distance, but they made it through.

It wasn't over though. Life as a refugee was just as bad. A stranger in a strange land, opportunities were practically non-existent, especially when there was a language barrier. He quickly had to pick up a smattering of Chinese. They eventually ended up in Shanghai where he managed to scrape some money together doing odd jobs, hopefully he would one day save enough to get them resettled in South Korea. Then, good fortune seemed to smile on him when he was offered a job at the docks only to discover he had a run in with a member of the Jade Cobra Syndicate. He was threatened if he didn't do everything they told him to do, they would hurt him and his daughter. When they let him go and he returned to their one-room excuse for a home he found one of their gang tags stuck into the wall with a knife. They knew where he lived. He had no choice but to be their errand boy, frightened of what they might do to his little Jin Ae, he didn't care about himself if she was all right. This went on for several months, doing their running, picking up and dropping off packages or messages until one day he was ordered into the cargo hold of a fishing trawler, he was 'taking a little trip'. Hidden in a cramped, stinking nook that was carefully concealed by the smugglers, he spent a week crammed up, hardly given any food or time to walk to stretch his legs. He was then put on another ship, a cargo one, he had no idea where they were, it was in the middle of the night, and they were out on the ocean with no land in sight when he was put on this new vessel. There were other smaller vessels pulling up alongside, unloading human cargo from their dank holes. He and the rest of the new arrivals were herded into an empty container and locked in. Crammed, no light, hardly any food or water, and only two buckets to take care of the necessities of nature, it was worse than the smuggler's hole in the fishing boat, he thought he would never make it, but he did. To his astonishment, this 'little trip' had taken him to the United States. Only later when he overheard talk among the smugglers and Syndicate henchmen as he and a group of other unfortunates were bundled into the back of a mercantile truck he had landed in the port of Long Beach. Why was he brought here? He soon found out when they told him they had a job for him to do: if he was successful, they would bring his daughter to him. If not, they left her fate to his imagination. He was even given proof of life via a telephone call. He was barely allowed to ask her if she was all right and if they had hurt her or not before the line went dead. They had her. He had no choice.

He wondered what manner of job they had in mind for him now. It had to be something big if they had taken the trouble to smuggle him this far, but they didn't tell him what it was this time, not for a long while. He was held prisoner with the group of illegal immigrants he was bundled up with who were also under the thumb of the Cobras, they were hidden in some kind of windowless basement for what seemed like a week, then shifted around to different locations, an abandoned factory, an old barn out in the country another time. It was disorientating, they were hauled around in cargo trucks or containers, they could never see where they were going. However, his one thought was to try and get his daughter back. Maybe it was only a ruse to get him to do their bidding, maybe they would never keep their word, maybe now she was already ... no he couldn't think that. He had to cling to the hope she was alive and they would be reunited. Maybe they could escape and start a new life here, seek political asylum. It was the only thing that kept him going, for the gang were relentless in training him up for his new job, whatever it was. He was given a crash course in English, western customs and geography of the United States, also driving lessons that included how to handle every kind of vehicle. It was apparent they wanted him to blend in. As soon as he could speak, read and write tolerably well, he was surprised when they took his photo. He found out what that was for when they handed him a package of documents several days later, forged he could easily assume, a New York driving licence, anything and everything that would allow him to live like a legal immigrant. Considering all the driving and geography lessons, he guessed they wanted him to be their mule again, this time for bigger cargo, not simply package drop-offs from the back of a motorbike like in Shanghai. Again he had assumed correctly, but it wasn't for anything illegal, which was another surprise, for they had managed to get him hired at a trucking firm.

"Reinold Enterprises," Gerry cut in.

The detainee nodded, before continuing.

To make sure he continued to do their bidding, he was allowed another proof of life call, his Jin Ae was still alive, and from the background noise, he could tell she was in the States too, it sounded like a TV was playing in the background, local news, English, and the accent was American. He also heard a rumble, it sounded like a city train. She was still alive, and she was *here*! Somewhere in the States. He had to continue to do what they wanted. Only then did he realise with all the moving they had smuggled him to the other side of the country, which was confirmed when he was finally allowed out to start his new job. Strange enough, the Syndicate didn't ask anything illegal of him yet, or it didn't look like it. Just be a truck driver at the new job. Maybe they were sneaking things through the business? He didn't know. They had even given him a dirty studio apartment, no doubt to help him blend in, or he would be still stuck in a basement with a guard over him, but by now it was apparent they knew holding his daughter captive was enough incentive not to run or go to the authorities. He was allowed to keep enough of his pay to get food and the bare necessities to look like a normal city dweller, the rest the Syndicate took for rent, but it was more than he had ever had before. In a few weeks, just when he thought this was all he was expected to do, he got an assignment: he was handed photos of a black Jaguar and told to memorise it and the license plates along with a picture of his intended target.

He stopped.

Gerry knew the rest. The Syndicate were sending a message after he had accidentally uncovered one of their main trafficking routes during one of his inspection trips in the Far East. He also had a sickening hunch they didn't let the girl go either after he was forced to do their dirty work. His hunch was confirmed when Chin-Hae continued his story, she was not released, and he was made to do more of the sweat work in hiding as his cover was blown. He needed all those documents to keep that trucking job, but now that it was over they took those documents away. He was set up in hidden factories and labs packing drugs, counting money, washing counterfeit currencies at other times, whatever he could do hidden from sight. Also, since his face was now on the most wanted list, he couldn't go back to the apartment either. He was locked up each night when his work was done with the rest of the kidnapped illegals. They didn't say anything about his daughter after that, he had no idea where she was, or if she was still alive. At this point he could only hope she was dead: alive, her future in the hands of this Syndicate would be far worse than the grave.

Chin-Hae laid his head down on his arms on the table and wept.

The man was speaking the truth. Gerry was appalled. He didn't know the meaning of suffering.

"I swear, I'll do everything in my power to help find your little girl." Chin-Hae looked up at Gerry when the translator finished. "And I'll also do my best to get you through this and see you both get political asylum."

Dazed at first, he couldn't understand what he had heard. Gerry nodded. He meant it. Chin-Hae uttered his profuse thanks amid his still flowing tears.

The agents motioned they should go outside.

"Agent Gillan, is there any way to drop the charges," Gerry enquired once they were alone.

"He's wanted for attempted murder among other things, but considering you don't want to press for that, and after what we've heard today, if his story pans out, then it will look good for him. He's a victim too in all this."

"Whatever legal help he needs, I'll provide. I also know a few people in Washington. He's seen the worst side of our country, he should also see the best it can do. I want this man's life turned around, his daughter found."

"So do we, Mr. Reinold."

After asking if he would be willing to help in their investigations should anything turn up regarding the illegal smuggling operations, considering they seemed to be using shipping trucks and ports. Gerry readily agreed, if any of those snakes were using their cargo ships and rigs, he wanted them hunted down and crushed. For now, one of their priorities was concentrating on what they heard about the hideouts coming from some other suspects, see if they could find that man's daughter. No doubt if they found her, they were going to end up rescuing many others. Gerry wished them luck, and if possible to please keep him updated on their case, to which they promised.

Sunlight. It was so good to get out into the street after that.

He was then surprised and a little alarmed to see the car surrounded by a few cops, but they seemed in a good mood.

"Officers, this is my fiancé," Katherine announced as Gerry drew close.

"Hey! It's an honour to meet you," one officer heartily greeted, holding out his hand. They all followed suit. "I never thought I'd get to meet the Monsignor of Manhattan's family."

Oh, so that's what this was about. Gerry smiled. "For a minute I thought you were making an arrest and the car was getting impounded." The officers laughed.

"Nah, we just saw the lady sitting here on her lonesome and wondered if she was okay, only to get talkin' and finding out why yer here. So, you're really the Monsignor's brother, huh?"

Gerry nodded.

"Man, you won't believe what's happened. One of the guys on patrol a few months back got some medals from a friend in another precinct who said he caught your brother speeding, but it was an emergency, so he left him go. Some of them were passed around here too, Joey my partner got one he always wears it under his shirt. One night two weeks ago a suspect we were chasing took aim an' fired point blank, he didn't get hit, but we found the bullet hole behind in the wall, point blank, I'm telling yah. I saw it with my own eyes. It has to be the medal." Joey nodded and pulled out the chain and medal from under his shirt.

That wasn't all, they had a hunch that this sudden serendipitous upturn in catching criminals had something to do with the good Monsignor's medals and little crucifixes circulating among the guys too. They were sure of it. Gerry didn't know what to make of that. Katherine could only smile as she heard the story again. When it came to Peter, nothing would surprise her.

"Well, we've got to go. Nice to meet you Miss Walsingham, Mr. Reinold."

"Likewise. Stay safe out there."

Alone again with Katherine, Gerry sat for a moment in the car, not saying anything. It was kind of funny hearing about Pete getting out of a speeding ticket with his holy medals, but still, to see the effect he was having, his pious influence literally spreading through the city, it was too much to comprehend sometimes. And then, after hearing Chin-Hae's account, this whole afternoon was a lot to take in. All he could think about was the suffering the man and his little girl had gone through, not to mention the other victims of the Cobra group he had found hidden in the cargo containers awhile back. Katherine didn't press for answers, but something was different, something had changed. It was hard to read his expression.

"Gerry?"

"I'd do it again," he found himself saying aloud.

"What?" That sounded ominous. "See that man get locked away?"

"No. If somehow I knew beforehand that finding those people in Jakarta and helping to stop the Syndicate would mean ending up the way I am now, I'd do it again."

Their terror, the dreadful conditions they were found in, their similar tales of trying to escape poverty or some other drastic hardship only to find themselves in the clutches of that gang that knew no pity or mercy. He then gave a short synopsis of what he heard this afternoon, two more lives shattered, enslaved. Damn right he'd do it again. The wheelchair was a small price to pay to stop this.

Katherine suddenly but gently interrupted him, held his face in her hands, turned it towards her. Whoa. It was a long time since they had kissed like that.

"What was that for?"

"*There* he is. *There's* the man I fell in love with. There's the rest of him."

∛❖√

Lucinda settled in at her desk, looked around. There was a palpable difference today, a giddy charge in the atmosphere. Everyone seemed agog about something. She asked Kells what had happened. What? She of all people hadn't heard the news? The invitations for the wedding were out and so were the Reinolds' secret: a double-wedding. It was in all the morning papers. Seriously? Lucinda couldn't believe she didn't catch it, not with Miss Charlotte and Miss Walsingham thick as two thieves these days with their sample books, pestering Mr Gerard and Winthorne. Then again, she had assumed Mr Gerard's fiancé was just helping out as the bridesmaid. She grabbed the newspapers from Kells before he dropped them off to the intended destinations and did a quick flip through. Hell! Bad enough there were two weddings in the works, now it was a double-wedding, and, it was predicted to be the event of not just the year, but the decade.

"I suppose we'll be kept on the go. Who else is going to help the Captain run the place while most of the senior staff are away on their

874

honeymoons," Kells joked. "I wonder if we might get a raise after all the extra work."

"You could try asking, since they're in such a good mood." Lucinda handed him back the papers.

"True. It's worth a shot, right?" Kells smiled again. He obviously didn't catch the curtness in her voice. "Gotta run. I've got a ton of stuff to go through."

Yep. Back to work. She unpacked her valise, her mind prey to a pensive whirlwind.

The fact Mr. Gerard and Miss Walsingham had reconciled, whatever had happened, nettled her. How come *they* could get back together, while her own battered hopes were constantly dashed in her face? All there seemed to be this day was talk of brides walking down aisles, it was only a few days since Mr. Gerard had come back from Mr. Kraylor Jr.'s wedding in Iowa with his fiancée's best friend, now, a double wedding was rubbed in her face. After that, she never felt more like just dropping it all and taking a day off. To the devil with duty. She was sick of it! She slapped down a folder heavy with documents, put her hand to her forehead for a moment, ignoring the quick look of surprise she elicited from some passers-by heading to their own tasks. Day in, day out, always punctual, prompt, making herself indispensable, it had all turned on her. Just being within the dynastic family's domain used to give her that satisfactory consolation of being connected to *him*. Now, it was no longer enough. That feeling of emptiness continued to gnaw, living in a shadow, eclipsed, unseen, taken for granted. She would never enjoy the same closeness of connection as a family member like Mr. Winthorne or Miss Walsingham. She was the office aid, the hired help, the pleb, the commoner. And, what was it all for? He was no longer there. What was the good of just hanging in for sentiment's sake? Everything about this place made her churn inside.

It was the last tie. Already her own divorce came through painless enough, she made sure of that. No bickering, easy division of personal property, she didn't want anything from him anyway. Papers signed. The make-do husband was at last gone from her life.

I fell in love with San Pedro ... only San Pedro wasn't free yet.

She had expected to hear something by now. Surely that letter she had sent to his archbishop would have caused a stir in the ant heap? Get him pulled from active service? What she put in that missive should have done the trick, but no, no reaction whatsoever.

To her disbelief and frustration she saw the adoring crowds around his church and parish office had not diminished, he was still at work. She couldn't hear any gossip of scandal about him either, eavesdropping among the crowds outside the church early one morning. Her letter hadn't made a ripple at all!

Absolutely nothing.

Seriously? Did you honestly think that would be enough?

Why? What had she missed?

They hide indiscretions like that. Sweep any taboo-breaking sons under the rug, ship them off to other countries if they have to.

Right, she hadn't really thought of that, and considering his reputation not to mention his family being acquainted with the Archbishop for years, of *course* they'd make sure there would be no scandal aired. Her letter had probably been thrown to the trash heap the minute it was opened.

Exactly.

It made something inside of her seethe with quiet fury. The phone blipped. In a foul mood, she gruffly answered it.

"Good morning, Mr. Gerard Reinold's office." The new art shipment was in. It seemed Mr. Gerard had finally found something to fill the blank places on the walls. "All right, I'll be down in a minute."

She went to the lobby to sign for the consignment, bring it back up to his office. Yes, two pictures. She wondered what they were, especially as this time he was going to risk having the originals in the office, no putting these in the vault and passing off a couple of fake masterpieces for the sake of insurance precautions. Blast. She was hoping she would have a pretext to visit the vault again, but no matter. She learned later that afternoon what the pictures were when Mr. Gerard finally arrived to open them.

"Aha! I knew they would look good in here," he beamed. Rome. Oil paintings of Rome. The sight of the city in one of them with the Vatican in the horizon line taking precedence unnerved her even more, especially when the little grim statue of the apostle clutching the keys to the kingdom that *he* had left behind for his brother on the desk seemed to stare her down, read her inner turmoil. It unnerved her further. Made her seethe.

Isn't it about time you face it at last? Peter is never going to leave that kingdom.

It made her boil inside.

And, why bother staying with this domain? *Why should they all be happy? They don't even know you exist.*

Well then! Make them feel it! They need me more than I need them … .

The way she had made herself indispensable, there was a certain ring of truth to that … .

She testily went back to her desk, tried to be composed as she answered the blipping phone. Blast it, another reporter wanting info about the weddings, if Mr. Reinold, Miss Reinold, or perhaps Mr. Winthorne were available for an interview or were willing to provide any juicy tit-bits for their readers.

"No, I'm sorry, no interviews or comments."

Enough with those damned weddings!

You could stop it all you know, or at least, make it the not-so-happy day they all anticipate … .

The thoughts cascaded.

What?

You know exactly what to do. *Put an end to it.*

A strange, thrilling sense of destructive satisfaction took hold.

Yes. That's it. Now's your chance. Cut yourself free.

Burn the bridges. Scuttle the ship.

Yes, maybe it was time to light the torches.

"Wait a minute, I'm sorry. Did you say you're Beatrice Brandis?"

"Yes, that's correct, from the *Manhattan Daily Post*. Would you be willing to share some exclusive information about the wedding? My paper would be willing to offer some compensation for your trouble."

"Mr. Reinold and Mr. Winthorne aren't giving interviews, and I personally don't have any new information about it."

"Oh, that's a shame … thanks anyway … ."

"But," Lucinda broke in, "how about an exclusive that would have all New York talking, and not just for a week?"

"Is it a scandal we've got here? About the Reinolds? Now *that* I and my faithful readers might be interested in."

"One of them, but still, hot enough to make your paper cut a cheque."

At this point she didn't care about the compensation, but she wasn't stupid either, a little extra to feather the nest wouldn't do any harm after what she was burning to do next.

"All right, now we're talking. Can you meet me somewhere discreet this afternoon?"

Sure she could. It was arranged. As soon as she hung up the phone, she stood up, and with a sense of liberating venom burst in on Mr. Gerard in the midst of his typing.

"*I quit.*"

She marched out, slamming the door and grabbing her jacket and valise as she stormed past her desk, leaving them all gaping in her wake.

"What in blue blazes was that all about?" The Captain came out of the his office, checking to see where the squall had blown in from.

"Heck if I know," replied a stunned Gerry as he wheeled out. He looked around. No, she was already gone. Wow, that was fast. Whoa. What had he done? She left no opportunity to talk her out of her sudden resignation. "She just walked in and quit!"

Thomas was now out of his office, looking just as shocked as they overheard what had happened. Lottie came down the hall, Mrs. Clarke had nearly knocked her over!

"She couldn't have quit over nothing," the Captain grumbled.

"*Quit?* She quit? Oh no!" Lottie gasped. "What happened?"

"Nothing as far as I know," Gerry returned.

"Well, maybe it's just her, she just survived a divorce after all," Lottie pointed out. "That can make a person do weird things, so I've been told."

"Right, I didn't think of that," the Captain conceded. "And what a time to do it too! As we haven't got enough … okay, back to your stations! Don't you have any work to do," he bellowed at the office gawkers, who hurriedly scurried away about their work.

Tom suggested they give Clarke a few days then call her, see if she could be persuaded to rethink her hasty decision. Gerry agreed, although something told him by the way she inexplicably glowered that persuade all he might, that was not going to happen.

೮❖ೞ

"Okay everyone, I know our department isn't the high and mighty investigative reporting squad, we aren't going to be breaking with the next Watergate, but c'mon people! Artsy section and all, you can do better than this!"

Christopher 'Horace the Horrible' Smith slapped down the latest proofs on his desk. Man, how he hated to play the heavy copy editor, but to have drivel like this dropped on him before the weekend run was enough to

878

kill a guy. Scheduling for the TV section all wrong, the latest movie opening reviews sounded flat, and then there were the articles.

"What about the Whitmore's charity art gala yesterday? Yo, Gary, I thought you were to do that?"

Gary showed him his piece. He quickly scanned through it.

"Yawn! Boring! It's like reading a bowl of slewy oatmeal. What's up with you?" The obituaries appeared like the Tony Awards in comparison! Gary was usually better than this. "Try and jazz it up a bit, will you?" Maybe his own article from the 'Horrible Horace' side of things would liven it up, a double perspective.

"Where's Beatrice?" As much as he hated her trashy gossip column, he could always count on her to pull the section through should everyone else hit a rutty slump.

"I haven't seen her the last few days, I think she's got a new juicy scandal to follow," Gary informed. Okay, just as long as she had her article ready by tonight, he could overlook her missing the meeting.

"All right, all right." Chris sat back and ruffled his hair. "See if you guys can fix this before we run tonight." They could all feel the crushing print deadline. There was an exodus for the door. The industrious cacophony of telephones blipping, copiers whining and clickity snipity tapping of keyboards in the general office area outside muffled down as the door closed, leaving him alone to his own work. He had his own acidic articles to brush up too. There was a knock. He looked up from his furious typing.

"Hey, tiger. Here're the shots you wanted."

"Whew! Thanks, Steph." He quickly flipped through them. "Nice, as always."

"I'm guessing the latest round-up didn't go so well," she noted looking over his shoulder at the monitor to see how his own articles were progressing while wrapping her arms around him, giving a quick hug from behind.

"That obvious, huh?"

"Yeah, judging from the scowls I saw out there. Aw, cut 'em some slack. It's one thing being cooped up in the winter, an introvert's environment, it's a writer's element, but with summer almost here? The first week of June's arrived, the sun's out, their minds are telling them it's time to go outside and play. They've all got beach brain and weekend brain rolled into one."

True. And, having the air conditioning on the fritz this week didn't help. He sighed.

"Yeah, I know, but the paper stops for no season or brain fog, and we've got a deadline to meet. You with your magazine and portfolio deadlines know better."

"Ha ha, too true. So, I guess I'd better leave you to it then. Shall I pick you up for dinner?"

"Okay, I'll give a call if we have a 'stop the presses' alert and I can't make it."

"Sure thing."

He gave her a quick kiss before she left. However, just before she closed the door, a coiffured, buxom figure with file in hand darting across the cubicled office floor caught his eye through the door pane. Beatrice was back from wherever she had been snooping, but what? Going already? Avoiding me, huh. What are you up to? Christopher left off a choice word or two under his breath. She was leaving the floor, heading for the elevator, he was in no doubt she was slinking off to the Editor, and she only did that when she had something she knew he would refuse to print and would have the authority to pull from their section of the rag, unless the Chief ruled otherwise. What slop did she have now? However, he had to be smart about it this time, already he was accused by the Boss of going too soft. He picked up the phone, dialled Accounting.

"Hi Cheryl, it's Horace the Gnarly ... yeah, I know, listen, could you do us a favour? Has the Chief given his OK for a cheque lately? One for Beastie's snitches? ... Uh, huh, I guessed so ... yeah, she's gone over my head again. ... Seriously? *That* much? ... No, the name doesn't ring a bell. ... Okay, thanks, I owe you one."

He hung up. Hmm. That was something. The last time the paper cut someone a scoop cheque that big was when a call girl revealed some of her big wig clientèle and their dope parties, which included the DA and a Jersey senator. He got up, opened the door.

"Hey, Lance. Does a 'Lucinda Clarke' mean anything to you?"

Lance, who was on the run with his hands full of something important, shook his head.

"Nah, sorry."

Okay, looked like it was time to make another call. He picked up the phone, dialled the Investigative floor. He knew one unscrupulous reporter that had acquired a neat trick along the way in the line of his career, he had learned to lip read and didn't think anything of lipdropping in on the Chief's office when the blinds were up, or when he was close enough in their own work area to where he could get a good look at the conversation. He was making quite a tidy wad of money and some perks on the side tipping off his colleagues letting them know what was going on in the building, if the Chief was pleased or ready to blow a gasket. A lot of requests came in regarding job security and if they were the next to be axed. He also picked up on a piece of gossip or two.

"Hi, Horace."

"Hey Ozzie, how did you know it was me?"

" 'Cause I just saw the Wildebeest pass by on her way to the Chief. She was here yesterday too. Gone over your head again, huh?" Christopher groaned. "Okay, just 'cause I like yah, and I can't stand the witch, this one's on the house."

"Gee thanks, but nah, I owe yah. You're running quite a risk you know, if the Chief ever finds out … ."

"Forgedda 'bout it. But if you happen to get some freebies to something decent on Broadway or invites to some swanky do the wife would die for, spare us a thought, will yah?"

"You got it. So, what happened yesterday?"

"There's this broad who says she's got something big for the column, she's Mr. Reinold's personal aid, or was. Apparently she quit her job."

Something on the Reinolds! No wonder the Beast skipped right by him.

"Was it about Gerard Reinold?"

"Nope, his brother, the priest."

Christopher laughed on that one.

"Him? A scandal? New York's own resident holy man? The Beastie is really trying to staple together a hit piece this time. What could she possibly have on him?"

"That's just it. It seems the dame has got something on him, something that's good enough to make some ragged headlines if proved true, enough to where the Chief has given the Beastie the all clear to stir up the suspicions in her dirt corner."

"To the point of raking up a libel suit?"

"Yeah, at least that's what I could read when they didn't turn their backs."

Holy cow.

"Thanks Ozzie, if you find out anything more, you'll let me know?"

"Yep, let me see what she's gonna say today, hopefully something before we go to print."

Now all he could do was wait, see what Dick Tracy came up with. He didn't have to wait too long. Ozzie called back with a truly vile report.

"Looks like I read right, that chick says she had an affair with him, then he made her get rid of something … couldn't quite catch it. Whatever it is, she gave the Beastie copies, she showed them to the Chief. I guess it's proof of what he wanted her to get rid of."

Oh hell no! It couldn't be true. Christopher didn't know Peter very well, but enough to sense something stank.

"Thanks."

"Sure, no sweat."

He sat back, whistled with disbelief. The few times he had bumped into him at Katherine's gallery a while back, he didn't seem the type at all, but then, did anyone really know a person? No, don't jump to conclusions, the man could be innocent. Considering what the city was saying about him, how could he hide such a thing anyway? Katherine said he was always mobbed, never alone. Better confront the Wildebeest about this, see what she actually had to print. He thought it might have to be a showdown in front of the Chief, but no, he caught her as she was coming out of the elevator. He took her by the arm and led her back in, pulled her was more like it. He closed the doors and hit the emergency stop button, jamming the elevator shut.

"Hey! Paws off!" She yanked her arm free. "What's this all about?"

"Don't play stupid. So, you didn't even have the guts to show me your piece this time before sneaking off upstairs."

"Oh. That." She sneered. "Here, I was just coming to show it to you. No point trying to stop it now, the Chief wants it in."

He testily snatched the file from her hand, before opening it he gave her a look that could have pinned her to the steel wall. Geeze, Ozzie had read right, this Clarke woman was accusing the Monsignor of having an affair with her, that he had talked her into getting two abortions to cover it all up. That was the 'something' that was to be gotten rid of.

"And, the copies of the clinic appointments are there," the Beastie smugly continued. "I found out that sham saint wasn't too long back in his parish after helping out at the family firm when the first one was done, so, they had enough time to have a last whirlwind goodbye before he left the office, which means there has to be truth to the second."

It looked very bad, but then again … .

"That's pushing it a bit, don't you think? Too loose a time structure. And besides, how do you know it was *his* kids that were offed? Did you catch them in the act during that 'whirlwind goodbye' as you put it? They could have been anyone's! And now that they're gone, a paternity test is out of the question. She could be taking some grudge out on her former employers. Or, that it's not all about the money? Let's face it, her ploy to take down the Monsignor of Manhattan has just made her a pretty penny from the paper.”

“So what? I don't know what her motives are, and I don't care. That part is none of my business. If what she says is false and she wants to go down in flames, it's up to her, she came to *me* with this. These documents are enough to show something's behind her story, and that's the beauty of it! As the city's most astute gossip crafter, I can allege 'this' and 'that' happened all I want. It's her word against his, and hers is looking pretty good right now.”

He of all people knew how this part of the rag worked. Since this was for a chatter column and not an investigative piece, it didn't matter if the story was true or not as long as there was enough circumstantial evidence to make something look the way she wanted it to look. Either way, it would all turn out in the best interests of the paper. If true, they would be the first to break a major scandal and the investigative boys upstairs would have a field day later. If not, an apology and a retraction would be given for spreading rumours on scanty evidence, and by the time that happened the Chief wouldn't be too bothered about it, he would have sold enough papers in the following weeks depending on how big the scandal was to cover any compensation backlash should it be demanded. More headaches when it did, but sometimes bad publicity didn't cost that much more than the legitimate advertising kind. But in this case, even if it was retracted … .

“This could destroy the man, not to mention the rest of his family, drag them all through the mud! This isn't some sleazy corrupt city official we're talking about here,” he retorted, sickened by her lack of ethics when it came to dropping a smear exclusive.

“But there is enough talk though. I've done my digging, she's been seen hanging around the places he works, and, I have a couple of sources who used to work there who say they seemed pretty close years ago before he ditched everything and scampered off to Rome.”

“So? Even if something did happen back then, he wasn't in the priesthood. There is such a thing as two consenting adults you know. And, that still doesn't prove what he's being accused of *now*.”

“But where there's smoke there's fire. I have enough conjectural puff that will do just dandy.”

“At least wait.” Christopher tried to reason with her. Surely she had an atom of a conscience left let alone a heart somewhere! “He's to marry his brother and sister. Once this gets out, he may not be allowed. It could ruin their big day, maybe even force them to call it off.”

"All the more material for me." He looked at her with disgust. She laughed. "My, Horace really has gone a bit mushy! Honestly, we'd be doing them a favour, letting them know what sort of man their brother really is. After this, they may be glad to keep him from officiating."

"And if it's not true? You're not even going to try and get his side of the story? Guilty as charged? You really enjoy this, don't you. Playing judge, jury and executioner," Christopher icily returned. "You really are some piece of work. No wonder you can't keep a man around for long. Third marriage on the rocks already?"

"Get out of my way, or I'll tell the Chief you've been making things difficult for me around here. Very difficult," she growled. "I'd love a raise, not to mention a promotion. The *Manhattan Daily Post* could do with a real copy editor on this floor that knows how to get the readers turning to the cultural section. It would be a sorry thing if Horace's poor, sick granny has one less source of dough coming in, wouldn't it?"

Dammit, that was underhanded. He could give and take a dig, but that was real low, even for her. She sure knew where to stab. Even if his secret job as C.S. Turris the nocturnal artist was starting to bring in returns, he couldn't afford to lose this job. He could only cuss at her as she jabbed at the button, set the doors working and pushed past him, storming by the group that had gathered around the stalled elevator to get a glimpse of what was happening when they emerged. They speedily went back to work when Horace slapped the file in hand against the open doors.

"Deadline people! C'mon! Move it, move it, move it!"

Fuming, he stormed back to his office, slammed the door shut. He slumped into the chair, his mood aggravated by the mounting stress as his own half polished article stared him down from the screen, the cursor blink, blink, blinking for him to finish. He was really getting to hate this place. Still, ugly as it was, playing Horace the Art Attacker was not as bad, not compared with what Brandis loved doing, that was beyond the pale. To think he would be forced to oversee the thing and make sure it was print ready! He picked up the phone, took a breath, calmed down so he could talk. No, he couldn't stop her piece, blast it, but at least he could warn those who were going to be affected. Kathy was a good friend, and after all she had done for him, he owed her big time. He never would have had all those art gala exclusives, or a new start with his art career that he thought was gone and now kept him from going insane with this rotten day job, not to mention he probably would never have met her cousin Steph if he hadn't gotten to know her first let alone pluck up the courage to make a real go of it.

"Kathy? Hi, yeah it's me. I'm glad I caught you before you left, well, sort of."

"Oh? What's up? You sound like you've just critiqued a funeral."

"Not too far from it. I hope you're sitting, and if not, you'd better brace yourself: Brandis is up to her old tricks, but this time flinging dirt is not enough. She's going in for the kill." She was dumbstruck when he had finished. "Um, Kathy, are you still there?"

"Er, yes ... oh my God. If it was anyone other than Peter, I might believe it, but *him*? Oh no, that woman is making up some horrible lie! I know it!"

"Maybe you could get some proof of innocence before we go to press that I can run? Get his side of the story?" He might be able to pull her column out if there was proof of it being a pack of lies.

"I don't know! I gotta run! Ill see if I can do something! I've got to warn him."

Christopher let her go. Hung up the phone. He did his best. Maybe she could get something in time. Blink. Blink. Blink. All right! All right! Another nasty column awaited him. Horace had to get back to work.

She had to see him. This couldn't be said over the phone. Katherine was so flustered she hardly realised how she made it to the rectory. During the distracted drive, all she could do was think out the terrible consequences if that sordid lie was made public. She knew it wasn't true, but if they couldn't prove it ... . She rang the doorbell a few times, desperate to see it open.

"Hello, Kathy! Whoa, what's wrong? Where's the fire?"

"Leroy! You won't believe what I've just heard! But what are you doing here?"

"Oh, right, I didn't tell ye guys, I've been helping Pete out. But come in."

"Helping out? Why? With what?"

"You'll see in a minute. I hope I can find you a space." He led her to the front parlour.

"Wow." She had never seen so many letters before. Surprised with her sudden appearance, Peter rose from the clutter to give her a hug as Leroy cleared a chair for her among the mail piles, but grew concerned when he read her expression.

"Oh my, what's wrong? Gerry hasn't broken off the engagement again, has he?"

"No. Worse! My friend at the paper just gave me a head's up about the Beastie Bug's trash column for the Sunday morning run, and it concerns you.

"Me? Well, it wouldn't be the first time I've made the papers."

"But not like this."

Lee couldn't contain his annoyance when Katherine mentioned an affair, and who was accusing Peter. How dare that woman! Still, it was just the trash column after all.

"Ha! What a load of rubbish! I wouldn't worry, pet. I hate to say it, but this isn't the first time our Pete has gotten threats like that, but it went nowhere. No proof, just accusations, and much of it complete nonsense."

"Even so, Clarke is not just stopping there." Katherine told them the rest of the details. "Why would she do such a thing to you? After working for your family for years, and now this," she blurted out.

"Easy.   It's either fame, money or revenge, maybe a bit of everything," Lee reasoned, disgusted by what he had heard. "Jeenymac! If it was anyone else, but *you* Pete? You to condone an abortion? *Two* of them? No one's going to believe it."

"They will when the Beastie is finished. She's got clinic documents and enough hearsay to make it look bad enough," Katherine was dismayed to report.

"My God." Leroy was thunderstruck.

"Er, Peter, aren't you going to say something?" Katherine couldn't believe how calm he was. Pained, but calm. "Do you have any proof of your innocence? Horace the Unusually Nice says he'll try and stop the article tonight before they go to print if you do, or at least print something in your defence, but we'd have to hurry. If you don't, the matter is out of his hands, he can't do much."

Peter shook his head. No, he had no evidence, not conclusive at least.

What were they going to do? Katherine and Leroy were busy trying to come up with a plan. Maybe they could call the Archbishop? Could he put a stop to it? They would certainly have to warn everyone, it would be a horrible thing to be surprised by hearing it first in the media over their morning coffee. Peter held up his hand.

"Let's not get over anxious. Yes, we'd better warn the family, just in case."

"Then what," Lee wondered.

"Nothing. I'll say my Mass tomorrow, do my parish work. Do it again the day after that. I will not change anything of my schedule unless ordered to."

"You can't go out there to face those crowds, not when this breaks!" Katherine had a feeling things could get ugly, she just wanted to shelter him away.

"At least my early Mass will be over by the time the paper is out, we'll just have to see what happens after that. Maybe nothing at all since like you say it is just the tattle column."

"But that's just it! The Beastie is not just any gossip columnist. Since a number of the nasty rumours she spreads usually end up true, people believe what she writes. People are going to think you're guilty!" Katherine was desperate to do something.

Peter remained steady. "Listen, calm down, panic won't help now. We'll warn everybody, but that's all we can do. If the worst comes to the worst, we'll have to brace ourselves. I can't run from what's coming, but I do thank you for trying to help."

Peter noted Lee needed a break too, enough mail sorting for the night. He gave them a blessing before they reluctantly left him. After calling Stonyvale to pass on the warning, there was only one other thing left – pray. He went to the chapel, knelt before the altar, begged for the strength to withstand the coming storm, his cross was about to become much heavier. The devil's threats at last made sense. Accusations against a priest regarding his vow of celibacy had consequences, but even more so for an exorcist. The spiritual stamina required to cast out evil required that he be of exceptional moral and spiritual character, especially as the devils threw explicit concupiscent temptations at an exorcist who was expected to withstand the onslaught. Any public knowledge of indulging in a carnal weakness would immediately rule a priest out for that ministry, but to be charged with the grave sin of supporting abortion, an automatic case of excommunication, let alone forcing a woman to do it twice? One who claimed she was a lover no less? Not only would his exorcism ministry be withdrawn from him, he could forget any notion he had of founding an order. Worst yet, he could be withdrawn from priestly service altogether, and, in obedience, he would have to comply until his innocence could be proved, if ever. Now, he understood the term cutter's blades. His reputation was about to be torn to shreds. But didn't the Lord suffer that too? If he as a priest was to represent Christ, he had to suffer everything He did. Wear and tear. There was no other way.

My life, my adherence to my vows, God Himself, these must be my defence. I've been faithful to the utmost of my ability. *No, He won't abandon me.*

There was nothing they could do. Richard was sickened by what his son was accused of, it was all lies! The late hours of the night and early morning were spent in making desperate phone calls to the management and at last the majority stock holder of the *Manhattan Daily Post*, but this time, his entreaties to hold back went unheeded. They told him flat out that unless he had proof of innocence, there was no way they were going to stop the story. He was nearly tempted to bribe them to pull it, but he knew he couldn't resort to such tactics, should the bribe become public, it would appear to be a sign of guilt corroborating the rumours. He threatened to sue, but no, even that wouldn't phase them, not until they had proof to the contrary since it was just gossip, Brandis wasn't writing an investigative piece after all. He slammed the phone down. Reaching out to the paper didn't work. There was nothing for it but to go directly to the Archbishop's residence.

"Richard! What's happened? You usually don't call on me at this hour of the night."

"I know James, but an emergency has just come up which you had better know about, privately."

This sounded serious. They went to his study. He was offered a drink, Richard refused, he was not in the mood for one. After laying out what Beatrice Brandis was about to publish tomorrow, he wondered if there was anything that could be done in the way of damage control.

"Can't you at least prepare a statement? That you have full confidence there is no truth behind these allegations?"

"That's the thing, I'm afraid that may not help now," his Eminence hesitantly replied. He had received a letter from Mrs. Clarke listing the same accusations. He didn't take it seriously, not with all the poison pen letters he was used to getting about Peter already. He showed him the letter, along with the others he had received. Richard was aghast as he scanned them, whipping through one page after another. None of this was true! Richard angrily looked up.

"But considering she worked for us, you should have realised there would be trouble with this one, even if it is a lie. You should have handled it then and there! If an official investigation was necessary, this could have been dealt with quietly. Now she's gone public with her accusations! This could destroy him!" Richard knew what was to happen next: with a scandal of this nature, Peter would have to go through the indignity of an official examination into his character, and, could be pulled from all active ministry while that was carried out. That alone after such a public report would add to the false impression of guilt.

"I know. This grieves me no end. Certainly, I'll prepare a statement for the morning press should the Archdiocese office be called for any comments, however, if Peter can come up with evidence displaying his innocence, all the better. If not … ."

"I know, I know. I'm sorry. You know what my temper is like. Is there anything else we can do?"

The Archbishop shook his head. No, this had to run its course now. Wait and see what reaction the article might drag up. If nothing came of it, then they could easily pass it off as a rumour, just ignore the whole thing. If not, then he might have to start an investigation. At worst, it could go to a canonical trial, but Peter's innocence could be proved during that too … .

True. There was nothing for it, but to wait tomorrow out.

ೞ ❖ ೦

As he had predicted, nothing happened at Mass since no one at his morning time slot had a chance to get copies of the early edition papers yet. Peter went to his packed basement as usual to begin his gruelling work which continued into the evening. Nothing seemed amiss, that is, until his ministry was over for the day. The moment he stepped out he was berated by members of the crowd who were still gathered outside the parish office along with his faithfuls. Those who had not heard the news yet were aghast and cried down the belligerent mockers who had arrived demanding he be thrown out of the priesthood, but when they saw the newspapers thrust in their faces, their shock grew. Was it true? No! It was a lie! An accusation! Anything to tarnish the Monsignor! I don't know, where there's smoke, there's fire. She was his secretary? Uh oh, you know what they say about office love affairs. I don't believe it! Not the *Monsignor*! Hey, didn't you hear the news? The Archbishop has full confidence that the truth will come out about this, we shouldn't presume he's guilty! The scandal spread rapidly among the crowd, but by then, Peter was in the car and gone. He soon discovered the Bachelors had not been spared either. They were questioned all day as soon as the news broke if it was true or not and what they thought about the whole thing to give no comment, then to come home and have no peace at the rectory which had been inundated with calls, another round of what they had run through all day: reporters asking for interviews, comments, angry parishioners giving their two-cents worth of what they thought, along with those who called to give him moral support, not believing the lies.

If they thought that Sunday was rough, it continued for the next few days. Angry shouts could be heard outside Old St. Patrick's during Mass, scuffles were breaking out among protesters and supporters waiting outside the parish office for the 'baby killing priest' to appear. By Tuesday, protesters tried to disrupt the Mass itself, they had to be dragged out by the ushers. The rectory was inundated with more calls, vicious letters, the Bachelors also feeling the heat simply by being in close proximity. They had only just started telling him about their latest chaotic day when a loud *thump, thump, thump* was heard. Fr. Jenkins opened the front door to find eggs splattered about, the new cars Peter's father had donated were covered in slimy glop. At least it wasn't rocks. He quickly ran for the hose, they washed off the mess before it could damage the paintwork. They then turned around. Oh no. They were confronted by obscene graffiti on the wall. That would have to be washed off with something stronger. Fr. Mark ran to see if they had any white spirits in the laundry room, Peter hunted for more towels, sponges and brushes. He splashed paint thinner about and scrubbed with the wire barbecue brush, the others joining in with what they had, hoping if the spray paint wouldn't wash off that they could at least blur the awful images down to an unrecognisable smear. One mercy, it was dark now, the images couldn't be seen as easily, even if it did make for harder cleaning. Turning on the outdoor lights didn't help much either. Eventually the street lamps glowed into action.

"Oh man, after today, now this," Jenkins then added wearily as he scrubbed. "Of course, we tried to say none of it was true, but will anyone listen to us?"

It had begun.

Whatever the world thought of him, Peter wished everyone else could be spared the backlash, but he knew that was not going to happen. However, this was nothing. He could only imagine what was to come next, although he didn't expect the next phase to happen so soon. The Archbishop unexpectedly appeared for an emergency visit.

"Your Eminence!" Monsignor Hernandez quickly jumped to attention, dropping his sponge. Peter looked up from his scrubbing, reeking of paint thinner.

"I see you've all had a time of it too."

Peter wiped off his hands in an old towel, and showed him in to the TV room after giving him a glimpse as to why the parlour was not available for his company as would usually be the case.

"My! And I thought I had it rough. I heard you received a lot of correspondence, but not anything like this," he noted, settling into a chair. Peter left for a moment to wash his hands, then asked if he could get him anything.

"No, I'm fine. Better sit down. As you can guess, this isn't exactly a social call, but I am also here to check that you're okay." Peter did as he was asked, sat down, nodded he understood. "Please, is there anything you can say in your own defence right now before I have to go all official?"

"Other than my word, it's not true, but my word will not be enough. It is now down to a case of hard evidence."

"I'm sorry, Pete. Well, I have to let you know what's going to happen next."

"A canonical trial."

"Not right away. I do, however, have to assign some instigators from the Archdiocese Metropolitan Tribunal to see if there truly is enough evidence for that. Also, you have the right to have your reputation protected, innocent until proven guilty and all of that, which means your ability to stay in active ministry should continue."

Peter heard a 'but' coming.

"However, we have a problem in your case. Usually, a quiet transfer to another parish would work until something like this was cleared up or blew over, but since you're already too well known … ."

"I know." Peter sighed. "My very presence is creating a disturbance and the Mass must not be disturbed. There's nothing for it but a sabbatical." He would have to stay hidden, out of sight to where he would not draw any more attention. He would not have minded being hidden, a solitary life, but this was different. "No public Masses, no public meeting with parishioners. What about confessions?"

"Like I said, your ministry has to continue, you're not being defrocked yet! Innocence before proven guilty! Still, you do have to keep a low profile. You may hear confessions, and, you can try and get through all those letters if you can, but please keep your ministry discreet. However, for the time being, this also means no more exorcisms."

Peter nodded. He may not be defrocked, but close enough to it.

"Again, I'm awfully sorry. I would have had you remain here, or maybe situate you at another rectory, but from what I saw outside, that's also out of the question. You're going to need somewhere away from this place. Yet, I'll need you to stay close by for the investigation of course, so maybe you could go home for a spell? Yes, that might be best. The sooner, the better. You'll have security and privacy at the manor, and, it would do you good to see your family. Think of it as a retreat if it would help. Besides, you look like you could use a break anyway. I hear your ministry has been tough lately."

"I must ask, what about tomorrow?"

"I'll have it taken care of. Make the announcements of your sabbatical, try and find someone willing to be exorcist for a while, etcetera."

"And, the wedding?"

His Eminence looked pained on that reminder.

"Well, like I said, your ministry should continue, but the way the crowds are … ."

Peter nodded again with quiet resignation. Not with a scandal of this magnitude, despite the whole innocent until proven guilty thing. His presence could create a scene and cast a black cloud over what was supposed to be a joyous occasion. The thing was, their happy day would be ruined without him too, but there was nothing he could do. Where he was concerned, it was now a matter of damage control.

"I'm sorry it has come to this, especially as I feel responsible. I should never have permitted you to go back to the family company."

"No, please, don't blame yourself. It was an act of charity you asked me to perform after all, and it did allow me to give a proper goodbye and help heal old ruptures."

"Ah yes. That's something to be grateful for. About those 'old ruptures', is that why you tore out of the business in the first place?"

"Yes, to a point. I knew for a long time before then I had a vocation, but … ."

"I know, your father would not have approved then."

"No he wouldn't have. It was hard to find some way to tell him the news, a case of dragging feet."

"Well, I must say, old bygones are certainly that, bygones. It sure was a switch to see your father come to your defence with cannons blazing." Peter looked slightly surprised. "Oh yes. He came to see me. He went to the paper too, did everything he could. Like him, I wish there was something I could do. Listen, is there anything, *anything* at all you can say that would put my mind at rest about the whole thing? I'd like to hear your side. Even if it won't clear the matter right now."

"I understand, but I must admit the ironic appearance of a sudden temptation in the office actually helped me make the break and follow my vocation."

"Really?" His Eminence sat forward. Uh oh, maybe he could use a drink after all. Just a small one, he had to drive. Peter took out a bottle of Irish whisky from the cabinet on which the TV sat, a birthday gift that a parishioner had given to Fr. O'Conner, which they still had. He went for some ice, poured Foley one on the rocks. Just a small one.

"Thanks. Wow, this is good stuff. So, there is something to this office romance rumour? I'm sorry to have to ask, unless this is something that pertains to the confessional, then you don't need to tell me, but please, if it has any bearing on the current accusations … ."

"To a point it does since the paper mentioned it and it may come up again, but it's all exaggerated. I admit I was attracted, I almost got snagged by that attraction, but I've never known a woman in the Biblical sense. And, I did hit the brakes, let her know exactly what my future plans were, that is until she tried to take things into her own hands."

Foley wondered what he meant by that. Peter explained the 'ambush' Clarke pulled on him. Is that all? Heavens! A kiss wasn't damnable material! There would be no hope at all for the human race if that were the case. And, he wasn't even ordained then.

"Let me guess, that was the mighty temptation. Here, you'd better have one too." He indicated towards the bottle.

"No, thank you."

"Do I have to give a command as your superior? Come on, don't let me finish this glass on my own. Even O'Conner would agree you could use one."

"True, he would."

"For him then."

Peter relented and poured one small glass of whiskey, watered it down.

"So, what happened after this temptation of yours?"

"I literally ran from the office the moment it happened, knew it was time to make a choice. Fr. O'Conner was my angel of mercy, reminded me of where I belonged. That day, I arrived on your doorstep and I finally ran away from home. I haven't looked back since."

"A blessed escape. And, did anything happen when you went back to help out?"

"No, nothing, not on my part anyway. I was very careful not to get caught in any compromising situation."

"So, it looks like this Lucinda is completely stuck on you. Hasn't been able to give you up."   "No, I'm afraid she hasn't. Wait," Peter suddenly though of something. "If it might help, I kept my old agenda book."

Foley sat up with interest.

"Please, fetch it, it could help the investigators."

Peter excused himself, went to his room and retrieved his planner from 1993. He also took out the months from January to May of the current year as well. Wow. When he said Peter was thorough, he had no idea. Nearly every action of the day was jotted down.

"Ah, of course. You got the lecture on 'Madame Georgette', didn't you?" The Archbishop of Paris always gave that famous little speech every time he visited the seminarians in Rome. He was quite famous for it. Peter definitely took notes that day! Peter gave a little smile.

Foley thought for a moment. Maybe, maybe Peter's precautions would help. Speaking of Fr. O'Conner, rest his soul, Foley was tempted with a terrible, sacrilegious thought. May God forgive him, but he wished in this one instance Peter's spiritual director was still alive and it was permissible to ask him to break the seal of confession and testify to Peter's virginal innocence, even it meant revealing something that was a virtue. But, the seal could not be broken under any circumstances and bring the sacrament into scandal and discredit. O'Conner would have been an excellent character witness to back up Peter's side of things, but his testimony in that regard could not have been done without incurring the risk of excommunication, even if he did try not to mention sins confessed, they *could* accidentally have come out, if Peter had any real sins to confess! He wasn't the only man to be tempted to not follow through with a vocation, and the way he bolted off and ran to it instead, that was nothing short of heroic! No use thinking about it, O'Conner had gone to his Eternal reward now anyway. Foley finished off his whiskey, dispirited by the lack of viable solutions to this disaster.

"I don't know what I can do now, other than go through the investigative process. Thank God you kept that book." In Heaven's name Foley wondered how he could possibly have had an affair in the midst of all that! "I'm sure something will turn up that will corroborate your notes and will knock all these allegations clear out the window. I pray long before the wedding takes place. I shall assign the best investigators we have at the

Tribunal office, make sure they make getting to the bottom of this their top priority."

"Thank you."

Maybe he was trying to cheer him up before he left, but Peter knew such accusations didn't disappear that easily. After he was thanked for the drink, he politely saw the Archbishop to his car. Mark and Jenkins were waiting to hear the worst when he came back in. Not only did he have to leave, but it looked like he would have to pack that very night, slip away before they got hit with more crowds in the morning, the angry protesting type that would camp it out, see him publicly humiliated. For their sake, he had to go now. They were inconsolable as the scenario they feared came true. They didn't want to leave him alone on a night like this, so he unavoidably had a small good-bye audience by his bedroom door as he packed his suitcase with the few things he owned. If there was anything else he forgot, he could send for it later. About the mailbags, maybe if Lee dropped by, they could ask him to tidy up the letters, stuff them in the bags and have everything ready for when he could arrange to have a shipping truck pick it all up, drop it off at the manor. Wasn't it time they could finally see the parlour again?

"How can you joke, Pete?" Mark couldn't believe this was happening. It felt like he was losing a family member who was emigrating to a far off continent.

"Now, don't look so glum, you know it was getting crazy around here with all the visitors and late night calls, you could use a break as much as me," Peter found himself saying, now trying to cheer them up.

"Not under these circumstances," Jenkins replied quietly.

"No, but it can't be helped."

"Is there anything we can do," Mark pleaded.

"Just keep me in your prayers. Hmm, I'm packed, I don't have anything else. I guess this is it." They helped with his cases, saw him to the car, Monsignor Hernandez joined them at last. "If anything comes up, or you just want to say 'hi' you know where to find me, and you have my number. God bless, and take care." Mark and Jenkins gave him a quick embrace and pat on the back. Hernandez stonily shook his hand goodbye before he sat in the car. Mark and Jenkins quietly watched him drive off, turn the corner. He was gone, forced to slink away like a thief in the night. It was crushing.

"Come now, you must have known *something* like this was bound to happen sooner or later," Hernandez suddenly piped up. True, that brought to mind the Curé of Ars was wrongfully accused of fathering a child, not the only saint that happened to. Then, there was Padre Pio who was ordered into solitary seclusion for ten years, unable to say Mass publicly, or even keep in touch with his spiritual children by letter. Chosen souls were often tested with such spirit-grinding trials. However, they soon found out that's not what Hernandez meant. "Mistress Celebrity is a master courtesan and good friends with Lady Lust," he continued. "I had a feeling he wouldn't last too long. Pride comes before a fall." He then strode inside.

Jenkins gritted his teeth as he watched him leave.

"Mark, will you hear my confession?"

"Of course, but … you just confessed yesterday."

"I know, but after what just came to mind right now about a certain high and mighty housemate of ours, I'm not fit to say Mass until I've 'fessed up," he admitted, eyeing the back of Fr. Inigo.

∛❖√

The shock was palpable as the announcement for Monsignor Reinold's necessary sabbatical was made during the morning service, the gasps and chatter echoing in the church despite the clarification in the announcement that the Monsignor's removal from Old St. Patrick's was not a declaration of guilt, but simply a temporary procedure until the matter could be settled. The service was still packed that day with those who refused to believe the article in addition to those who hadn't heard yet not being paper readers. Now, the worst fears of those who knew were realised, and those who were previously in the dark about the scandal were stunned as the gravity of the situation sunk in. True, it was all part of the formal procedure, even if he was innocent as many of them believed, but to have him pulled from public service still looked like an admission of guilt. It was a blow to hear, and to be witness to how fast he was removed was also a sharp jolt. The Seer of Souls was taken from them, and now who was going to help them? The man who made Heaven feel like only a step away was now snatched and silenced. Calls of support rang throughout the day in the archdiocesan office, anyone who knew the Monsignor could see this was all a diabolical smear campaign! Surely, his Eminence didn't believe such stories? He was framed, a set-up job, that's what it was! The striking amount of well-wishers were a consolation to Foley, a sign Peter had brought in a bountiful spiritual harvest, the amount of which he had no idea until then, the fruit of his labours was a good testimony, but there were other calls as well, many of them, angry, abusive ones with messages of venom, cries for the hypocrite womanising priest to be defrocked, removed from the priesthood altogether. The scandal also ignited a whole other tinder pile, the liberals once again had something they could use as convincing evidence justifying their argument that a celibate priesthood was not possible in this day and age and that the Church needed to consider allowing married clergy if only to avoid repeats of such débâcles. On top of it all, the effects of Brandis' original article continued to ripple out with the consequence that news of Peter's sudden removal from service soon made the next gossip column, rekindling the fire of the previous days.

Reinold Enterprises was blindsided by a spate of shipping and contract cancellations in the New York and New Jersey area as the conflagration spread and new business leads suddenly dried up. Was the hatred *that* bad? It was a bitter reversal to stomach, but still, this was something they could weather Richard stoically reminded his downcast family.   The business taking a hit was one thing, they always had contingency plans for downturns anyway.   Besides, this had happened before, and at least this wasn't anything like the discrimination the family endured during the wars when the public took a hostile view of their German-sounding name, forgetting or unaware they were of Austrian extraction and harboured no sympathy for the Nazis. It had taken awhile, but they recovered. They would live through this too. If anything, their recent merger with the Walsingham's medical enterprise was looking good. Cheer up!

Still, pep talk and all, which Richard made for himself as well as the others, the hardest thing to bear was Peter's hands were tied when it came to marry his own brother and sister and had to remain hidden away in Stonyvale as though he was a disgraced criminal. The worst part was seeing the steady arrival of the wedding presents to the manor, which only added to the sense of travesty. At least he had permission to keep the Blessed Sacrament reserved at the manor and say his Mass there. He was given a large room in the east wing for that purpose for however long his stay would be. A suitable home altar was set up with his picture of Our Lady of Good Success that he had sent to him as one of the main centre piece along with his personal chalice and paten, also an antique Spanish Baroque crucifix with matching candlesticks in gold that was part of the family's heirloom collection. His mother's rare roses also contributed to the sacred setting. Peter was about to send to the local church for some vestments they could spare until his mother decided they both needed some cheering up, he needed some presents too.

"Honestly, with all the spaces, halls and nooks the ancestors decided to add to the homestead over the years, they never thought of a chapel. Never mind, I think you can make do with these."

Sophia brought out several flat garment boxes, a special birthday surprise she had ready for him, but might as well give them now, a whole set of liturgical garments handmade with silk brocades from Lyon embellished with embroidery work made of gold, silver, and coloured silk threads in a cloistered convent in France. They had already been blessed too. No wonder the growing pile of boxes looked like it was on fire!

"I wish they could all see your face! But they will when they get here later. Besides, you need these right now."

"How did you manage to order these? In French?"

"Oh, it wasn't easy," his mother noted. "Gerry told me about some of your pipe dreams, and so he also helped with this. We had the regional managers of Reinold Enterprises over there search for a convent who still did this kind of work, and the district manager of Nantes found one. They normally just make these for the priests in their own order, but when they heard it was for you, they made an exception and told him what they had already or were just finishing work on. The poor man had to try and describe everything to us over the phone. Yes, we knew you or Archbishop Foley could have blessed them, but we thought it would be nice to have a bishop there do it. The Archbishop of Paris was most obliging."

"Seriously? You two went to an awful lot of trouble!"

"Well worth it, hmm? We know you probably wanted to pick your own … ."

"These are wonderful, I couldn't have picked better myself."

She smiled as she saw his expression as he carefully went through them. They were exquisite, the sacred images and symbols matching the colours for the various feast days. White with gold fleur-de-lys, red with the Dove of the Holy Spirit, the violet one featured a hand embroidered representation of Christ on the cross. A special golden chasuble with an acanthus pattern and the Lamb of God standing on the book of the Seven Seals embroidered on the back was in another box, along with a Rose Sunday vestment, the Cross adorned with pink roses. There was of course a green vestment, this one had a large cross in gold and silver threads, but with an added touch of shamrocks around the border, O' Conner would have loved this one, there was no way he would wear this and not think of him. As it turned out, it was the product of another rare concession, an order for an Irish priest in Chicago, but the order was suddenly cancelled. Even a funeral vestment was included among the lot to make sure the set was complete, a black velvet chasuble with the cross worked in with gold thread embroidery featuring the instruments of the Passion. Another box showed they had not forgotten a new amice, and also a long enough alb to fit him with hand made lace bordering the hem, also maniples, palls and burses that matched each vestment. Another few boxes held matching copes, just in case he was ever going to preside at a procession.

"All of this for my birthday? You thought of everything, haven't you?"

"I'm your mother, it's my job to think of everything my children need, but the nuns knew what to send too."

There was an added surprise when he found another white vestment with gold work and a representation for the Sacred Heart. She couldn't decide what to get when she heard about all that the nuns had available, they had just finished that one, so she took that too. To be given this now! Just in time! The feast of the Sacred Heart was tomorrow. True, another reason why she wanted him to open his present early. He graciously thanked her for all of this, brand new vestments, something that was so dear to his own heart. He gave her a hug, then a blessing. Gerry was going to get his share of thanks too when he stopped by. It was such a pity that these beautiful things should come to him now under these circumstances, but nevertheless, they were indeed a mighty consolation amidst this dark time of trial.

At least he had Mass and now was properly attired for the August Sacrifice, but it was a heartbreak to see him in this strange, almost prison-like sentence, offering a quiet service to a small handful present, walking through the gardens with his breviary or along their private beach with the rosary beads quietly slipping through his fingers, all alone in the midst of his prayers, silent, solitary, not uttering a complaint, undergoing a white martyrdom that they could do nothing about except be there for him if only in the background. When he wasn't praying, saying Mass, writing letters, or catching up on spiritual reading, he decided not to be idle with regards to active work either. If this was going to be a retreat of sorts imposed on him, at least he could make it something bordering the monastic life with a healthy balance of contemplation, prayer and manual labour along the order of *pax, ora et labora*, the motto of one of his favourite saints. He helped Victor polish the silver and dust the furniture with the house staff, then helped the cook prepare meals and scrub the floor in the kitchen, another day he mucked around with the gardeners pulling weeds, spraying the aphids, and picking off yellow leaf. The staff were somewhat abashed at his humility, the eldest son who by rights deserved to be served was now assuming the role of a servant in his own house, and his parents were grieved to see him reduced to this, catching a glimpse of what rectory life must have been like for him and the Bachelors until they got the housekeeper, but they let him at it. At least if he was busy, it was something positive, no matter how humble the task. Even the house mascot sensed something was amiss seeing Peter like this and thought he needed cheering up, the grey feather ball clung to his shoulder for as long as he could during the day when permitted, constantly bopping him on the cheek for rubs on the ear or on the neck, once in awhile yelling a few "Yo ho ho's!" with the suggestion he have a bottle of rum.

The rest of the family certainly felt like having a few bottles anyway, with all the hate mail and other unpleasantness they were experiencing. Peter's mail still got delivered to him, and it seemed he got a lot more that needed to be burned in the trash cans out back than opened and answered. Leroy drove out to the manor every night he was not needed after hours at work to help him go through it. Katharine's gallery also got inundated with calls from reporters plaguing them for comments, if the Monsignor was still presiding at her wedding, if it was going to be called off, if she knew about the Monsignor's illicit affairs. So it was 'affairs' now?   They were automatically assuming more than one? Was he a radical in supporting the Pro-Choice agenda?   Did she know anything about that? The last straw dropped when one caller accused him of being a baby killer. The Gallery Gang were well seasoned by the importunities of the pesky press and just mumbled off 'no comment' and hung up the phone. That was not the end of it: the gallery was now awash with curious visitors who came to the place simply because of the scandal. It galled them to see once more how 'business was good' thanks to gossip-loving crowds rather than coming for art's sake. Seasoned as they were, it was hard to take, none of the Gang believed the lies. Mrs Hunt dropped by to give her commiserations, but her way of cheering them up was by having them unhitch all the paintings and taking them to the ground floor, which didn't help matters. At least it kept them busy. When they didn't have unhitching to do, Katherine ended up hiding in the studio again when she could, too many people were gawking at her as well. Anyway, she was in the odd holding pattern where the wedding plans were done and was now just waiting for it all to fall into place. She had no appointments she needed to be at to put those plans into action. Might as well work on a painting. She needed to calm down.

Alone with the Professor, quietly brushing away, she heard footsteps on the stairs.

"Kathy? Are you up there? It's me."

She recognised the house critic's voice through the door.

"Hey Horace, you know the studio is off limits if you're here to critique! The resident artists will never forgive me if I let you in. I'll come down," she called out.

"Oh, that's just it. I'm not Horace any more."

Huh?

She put down her brush, wiped her hands. She opened the door.

"Whoa. What's wrong?"

"Like I said, I'm not Horace any more. I've been canned, dropped, fired, kaput."

Uh oh! She let him in and fired up the coffee pot.

"It's okay, only the Professor's up here today. What happened?"

The leading stockholders of the rag he worked for were not very impressed with getting late night calls from the CEO and majority shareholder of Reinold Enterprises. He got a tip from his investigative friend near the Editor's office that the Bosses knew only one person near Brandis that was close enough to give a tip-off to anyone connected with the Reinolds, aka, him. They couldn't trust anyone on their floor who gave off any leaks, and so, he knew the sack was coming. It did. That morning.

"Oh gosh, I'm so sorry!" She gave him a hug. "Listen, it's not the end of the world. Does Stephie know yet?"

"No, but she will tonight. Argh!"

"Never mind, at least you'll get to spend more time together."

"Well, it looks that way. There's a plus out of all this."

"That's the spirit."

"I've got a suggestion," the Professor suddenly piped up in his quiet way, looking around his canvas, "maybe C.S. Turris will now consider taking up a space here full time?"

"What? How did you know I ... ."

"Easy my boy. For awhile 'Horace' had one big diatribe after another to vent over Mr. Turris and his 'nocturnal abominations' that methinks 'Horace' protesteth too much while Turris was suddenly becoming a great success. Not to mention we seem to get a batch of new 'abominations' every time 'Horace' made a visit. Don't look so worried, your secret is safe with me, and the rest of us." The Professor smiled as he looked over his glasses, then returned to work.

"Yeah! In fact, another two of those 'abominations' went this morning. That should help tide you over until you figure out what to do, go artist full time or look for another job if you want, but for now, welcome to the Gallery Gang, the studio is yours. At least you have some time for daylight scenes, Mr. Bruce Wane," Katherine noted. "They should be a hit."

Christopher Smith 'Turris' chuckled. Yeah, maybe they would.

"Besides, you hated that job anyway, right? Relax, breathe. Go paint."

Yeah, it was good to be out from under that seedy grit mill. He hadn't felt this free in a long time. He took off his trench coat, set up an easel, Katherine pointed to where the canvases, paints and extra work clothes were, go help yourself.

She was about to sit down when one set of calls came through she was glad to receive, her friends Martin, Justine, Maurice and Theresa from Paris who had to give their commiserations—Justine and Martin were particularly upset. The Monsignor appeared out of the blue when they were in a very dark point in their lives and saw them through, the very least they could do was to call and ask if there was anything they could do?

"I'm afraid prayer is all we have. He's under investigation now, we can only hope for the best. The wedding is still going ahead. It's just upsetting he may not be the one to marry us."

"Kathy, I don't know what to say! Not him of all people, we just can't believe it! You will tell him we were asking about him?"

"I will, and of course, you'll still get to see him when you're here. Listen don't worry. How is the little one?"

"Oh! Pierre is a terror! Some days he is a quiet little lamb, other days we think he's going to grow up to be a mountain climber, and guess what? He is going to have another permanent playmate."

"You mean … oh! That's wonderful! Congratulations! When is it due?"

"About seven months, so I can still travel. No problems, although, I might be a little plump, which is another reason why I'm calling. I hope the dress has some material to let out, if not, you may have to find another bridesmaid."

"Don't worry! You're still our bridesmaid, and you'll look beautiful too. Our dressmaker is a miracle worker, my cousin accidentally ripped the sleeve getting out of hers during the fitting yesterday, she's not much of a frills girl, but she repaired it in no time. I think she can handle your happy bump. We'll worry about that when you all get here."

" 'Happy bump'. Oh, how adorable! I like that! What expressions you Americans come up with!" Katherine heard a baby crying in the background, that had to be Pierre. "Oh *mon ami*, he may be a lamb, but not today! He can scream like a siren when he wants to! I'd better go. We'll be seeing each other soon. I know you don't feel like it right now, please concentrate on the happy time this is too, your Peter would want that."

"I know, thank you Justine. Thank you for calling. We can't wait to see you."

By then, the approaching wedding date was truly starting to sink in when the rest of the preparations went into full swing. Presents were still being delivered, some accidentally to the wrong house or to the gallery, so there were madcap runs to get them all out to the manor. Both Oak Meadows and Stonyvale had the full works regarding a late spring cleaning job done, their many rooms prepared for all the guests that would be staying, not to mention the reception preparations. The tables and chairs, also the linens and the table settings were arriving and had to be stored in the ballroom until it was time to set up the marquis tents in the garden for the day itself, the ballroom could then be made presentable for the evening celebrations once they could get the tables set up. Andre and his caterer friends both came another time to check out the kitchen and see what they had to work with and was not surprised to see the manor could handle a wedding party of that magnitude, which was also a relief. Some things were working out! Other plans weren't going to work as well. Sophia's famous roses had bloomed a bit early, and the last crop of her Firepearls would never make it to the July date with the result there was a manic extra order sent in to the florist to make sure the brides and bridesmaids had bouquets ready, and the grooms and the grooms men their boutonnières. That was another issue, trying to get the men all together for a final fitting of their new morning suits with work and all still needing to be done, but at last they made it. Thankfully, no alterations were needed.

However, the mounting tension of making sure everything was perfect for the Big Day wasn't helped by the fact they couldn't make one thing perfect, Peter couldn't preside, and, he was reluctant to even attend the church service lest news of his presence there might get out and cause a scene.

"You will come to the reception at least? You aren't going to stay up in your bedroom, are you?" Katherine was devastated it had come to this.

"No, I can come to the festivities, this is the family home, that is, if you don't mind."

"Of course we don't mind, you goof! I'm glad! But it won't be the same," Lottie added. Katherine shook her head. No, it wouldn't.

"Listen, I'm not completely removed from ministry altogether. Maybe it would be possible to get permission that before the party starts, you all renew your vows here where I say Mass? By church law you'd have to be married in church, but since that would have been done, renewing your vows might be a different matter. We could keep it nice and private just for you and the immediate family."

That was something! Sophia ordered the Captain to call the Archbishop's office right away, see if that could be done, while Gerry took Peter aside, he had something more personal to ask him away from earshot of the others.

"This reminds me, the Archdiocese investigators are coming tomorrow to the office, Dad has given orders that all assistance is to be given to them, and has given anyone a free day who wants to come and give depositions if they so wish, but we're going to get questioned too. What shall I tell them?"

"Gerry, don't worry. Just tell them the truth."

"Everything? I need to know, since you told me to be quiet and all, can I say nothing happened between you and Clarke? I mean, even the early days when even I suspected something different?"

"Ah, that. Well, it's out now, so you have no need to worry about secrecy there. I told Archbishop Foley already, that people's imaginations have exaggerated the whole thing. And, whatever you say, the investigators will keep it private among themselves and the Archbishop."

Gerry looked visibly relieved. Thank God. At least he could say something now in his brother's defence.

"Look Ger, don't worry, this is all in God's hands. We must accept whatever comes."

That was just it, the wedding was coming. While Peter hit upon the next best thing by his brilliant suggestion of renewing their vows, it just didn't feel the same. They all hoped something could be resolved soon before then, but that was asking for a miracle.

೮ ❖ ೪

While everyone was praying for a miracle, for now, they got Fr. Hugh MacIllan, a burly Scot with silver hair and dark bushy eyebrows, an expert in canon law battle-hardened by all the disturbing cases he had to investigate in recent years, and a layperson, Jeannine Fraser, a happily married woman. Jeannine once worked in the annulment branch of the office and had a sixth sense when it came to uncovering dishonest applicants with the result she was asked if she was willing to join the investigators and help out with the serious cases in the Tribunal. It was soon discovered she had a gift for inspiring trust and could tread softly. Victims and accused alike often opened up easier to her when it came time to discuss matters of an intimate nature. However, like Fr. MacIllan, she left no stone unturned, and together they were a formidable team when it came to gathering facts. Since they were ordered to make the accusations brought against Monsignor Reinold their top priority, they wasted no time in getting started.

The first thing they did was to call Mrs. Clarke, or rather, Ms Andrews as she had returned to using her maiden name the last few days. Archdiocesan Tribunal? Was the Monsignor going to trial? No, this was just the investigative period to see if there was enough evidence to begin one they explained. What happens if there is one and he's found guilty? Will he be removed from the priesthood? If moral certitude is reached that a delict, that is, a crime in the eyes of the Church has been committed then, yes, it was possible. Would she be willing to come to the Tribunal office, or perhaps, feel more comfortable in a neutral setting to give her statements? She thought about it. All right, she would come to the Tribunal office, give her testimony.

Lucinda felt rather smug walking in to the Tribunal place on First Avenue, ready to get him away from *Her* if at all possible, and on *Her* territory too. She eyed a picture of the Madonna on the wall as she waited to be called in. I've got him now, he'll be booted out after I'm finished here! She was shown into an office, introduced to the investigators, asked if she wanted anything first before they began. No, thanks. Let's get this started.

Before the inquiry began, Fr. MacIllan let her know that these proceedings would be confidential and anything she said would be told only to those who were involved with the case, although the accused had a right to hear what he was accused of, however, she would in all likelihood not have to face him unless it went to trial. Also, she was not being judged. She could speak freely. Today's meeting was just to gather facts, confirm dates, exclude rumours, especially as the press had become involved.

The questions began. They asked when the affair started.

Perhaps it would explain matters if she told them they were actually seeing each other before he was ordained she wondered?

"Well, what happened before the Monsignor's ordination is a different matter," Fr. MacIllan informed her, folding his hands. He was a free man in the world then, no vows taken. This was an enquiry to ascertain if he had violated them now, with a married woman, and, if he had actually encouraged or condoned her terminations. That was the pressing issue.

"Oh, but you see, we couldn't help ourselves, not when he came back," Lucinda continued, they couldn't ignore what they had once. Of course she played that one up. Yes, they were pretty steady then, she thought marriage would come of it, but he suddenly announced he was leaving for Rome, and that was that. It broke her heart, but she had to let him go. When they saw each other again … . Jeannine typed away. Fr. MacIllan jotted down some notes.

That part was easy. Now they had to ask some personal questions, but it had to be done. Lucinda agreed, she was ready.

Okay, when the Monsignor came back to the company to help out after his brother's accident, when did the affair start? Was it only a few times, or, something that was more involved?

Lucinda knew to be careful, as much as she wanted to drag him through the mud right now to break *him* completely free, or simply break him, she knew there was no way Peter could have seen her if she said it was more involved, not with the different workloads they had back then. Best to keep it to a simple fling, a few nights on which they couldn't help themselves.

How many times? Just two times, were there more?

No, er yes, three.

Did anybody see them?

She had to be careful here too. No, they weren't seen, not that she was aware of.

Where did those few nights happen? At the office, at a pre-arranged rendezvous?

"I'm sorry, I know this is personal, but we need to know," Jeannine added. "We have to determine if this was simply a heat of the moment thing, or a steady affair."

Lucinda wanted to swear. She couldn't say where they would have met! The office, yes, it had to be there. If she said a hotel, or some other place, than that would have contradicted her claim of a momentary weakness, arraigning a place was too ordered, structured, preplanned, evidence of something more serious.

"So," Fr. MacIllan continued, going through the copy of Brandis' article, "these few times of, shall we say, passion, ended up with a child being conceived on two occasions, and, the two pregnancies terminated."

"Yes. When he found out, he pleaded with me to 'do something about it', said he would even cover the costs."

"Okay, the first termination took place in the last week of September of last year, on the 29th. Am I correct," Fr. MacIllan checked.

Lucinda nodded.

"About how long were you? Eight weeks? Twelve weeks," Jeannine asked.

"Eight, maybe nine."

"So, the last week in July then?"

"Yes, about then."

"Can you give us the exact date?"

"Um, on the 30th, no, the 31st."

"All right. When was the second child conceived?" Jeannine waited.

Lucinda now knew there were going to ask that, however, she couldn't give the real time ... that would have given her away! Wait? What about October? That might work.

"Last week of October you say? Can you remember the date?"

"I can't say ... ." Lucinda tried to think.

"All right, and the termination happened in, January of this year, Friday the fifth?"

Lucinda confirmed the date.

"You say you met at the office on all occasions, are we correct here," Fr. MacIllan checked again.

"Um." Uh oh. She had to think fast. It was hard to think clearly, the large medal the priest had around his neck was annoying her, a large one of *Her*. Come on! Think!

"Well, er, yes, we had to see each other, we couldn't help it."

"So, you were together three times, was this second pregnancy a result of the second or third time you met?"

"Er, well, it could have been either or ... ." They looked at her, waiting for her to clarify. Hell! They were insistent! "We saw each other within a month that time, so ... ."

"I see, so, you also met in early October then, or was it sometime the end of November?"

Before she realized it she blurted out the time she actually got pregnant: the weekend after Thanksgiving. Why did she do that? No matter, maybe she could squeak by with it. The investigators appeared like they had all the preliminary information they needed for now, but they read out her testimony, made her verify first.

"Okay, the first time you had the affair was Saturday, July the 30th?"

"No."

What?

"The 30th was on a Friday, and we met on the 31st, which was Saturday."

"Are you sure?"

"Yes, his going away party at the office was a Saturday. He was returning to his parish work the next day."

They took notes.

"So, it was the night of this party you met." She nodded. "And are you sure you cannot remember more specific dates the last two times you were together?"

"October, um, 30th and November 28th, that was it."

"Just to make sure, Friday the 30th of October, and November, Saturday, the 28th," Fr. MacIllan, repeated, tapping his notebook with his pencil.

"No, in November it was Sunday. October, was, um, yes, er, a Saturday."

There was a pause. Fr. MacIllan then asked.

"Why have you decided to come forward now?"

"Excuse me?"

"You went so far as to cover for him, going to the clinic. Why come forward now?"

Lucinda wasn't expecting that. Why she didn't think they would ask that was a stupid assumption. However, she had a good alibi.

"Simply put, we knew it couldn't go on, it was not going to last, and we couldn't expect anything out of it. We moved on. However, my husband found out. Why should my life fall apart now while he gets to continue on, no consequences for his actions? It takes two to have an affair you know."

"All right, thank you Ms. Andrews. If we need to ask anything else, we'll give you a call," Fr. MacIllan declared, ending the meeting. "Good afternoon."

Rising from the table they politely saw her to the door, although Jeannine couldn't help feel sickened by it all. She was glad when the door closed and she could relax a bit.

"Well, Father, what do you think?"

"I dunno yet, something seems fishy to me. If they 'couldn't help themselves', and nothing was pre-planned, then how or why did they meet in October and November? He was back in his parish work in August and out of the office then."

"I know, that sounds pre-planned and contradicts her statements. She was seen hanging around the church and parish office, maybe she chased him down and he couldn't refuse? No, that doesn't make sense either, not if all their meetings were in the office, and they had moved on like she claims," Jeannine reflected aloud.

"True," Fr. MacIllan noted, sitting back, chewing on his pen cap for a moment, "we can't make any final judgement yet. We'll have to keep digging, gather all the facts."

For the moment, they took out the copy of Peter's yearly planner and went through his meticulous notes. So, according to Ms. Andrews, they met on July 31th last year ... wow, look at this? Jeannine was an astute planner, a wife and working mother had to be, but even she didn't take notes like this! Still, this party would have been the perfect distraction, and everyone was not stupid about what could happen at office parties. They would have to check that out.

"Was it me, or did she seem hesitant about giving out dates too? She wasn't sure if it was two or three times they were together." Jeannine thought for a moment. "I mean, forgive me Father for saying, but I've had two kids, when they happen it's a pretty special time. I wouldn't mix up stuff like that, especially as she says they met so few times. You'd remember something like that, especially if it was a deeply forbidden affair like this."

"You may have something there. I did try and trip her up on the days," Fr. MacIllan admitted, sitting back again, thinking for a moment. "Hmm, she was pretty sure about November, but October sounded like she was fishing. I sense something a wee bit off there ... oh. Come to think of it, it would be easy to remember the 30th was a Saturday because Halloween fell on a Sunday last year. Something for the memory to latch on to. So, if she is lying, me trying to catch her out there didn't work either."

Jeannine looked through the months in Peter's planner, checked if anything correlated. Okay, first time, Ms. Andrews did say eight or nine weeks and she was right there, she would have been eight and a half weeks along into the first trimester.

And the second time? Well, it would be hard to say on that one, they were supposedly together October 30th and November 28th, uh oh. MacIllan saw Jeannine's reaction, took a closer look. A whole week of parish appointments had been cancelled the end of October.

"Mass too? That is very odd, mighty peculiar." Father had to agree. They would have to look into that. "What about the November date?"

"I see 'hospital' and 'sick runs' marked down, oh, right, Fr. O'Conner, he fell ill then," Jeannine recalled. "They were good friends. He was the Monsignor's spiritual director too."

"Ah right, God rest him."

Jeannine's face fell. "There's 'sleep-over' marked after 'hospital' on a few occasions, one on the 28th, that doesn't sound good."

MacIllan looked at the book again. "Hmm, to have a secret tryst right then? With his friend in the hospital? But if so, that would have sounded pre-planned, which Ms. Andrews claimed wasn't. Frankly, what strange timing. If it was pre-planned, I would have called it off with that kind of an emergency. Too risky to go ahead, and, to go ahead with the rendezvous sounds pretty cold. Too cold for a 'heat of the moment' thing. Something sounds off, but I can't put my finger on it."

"You know what gets me? The way she says he should also face 'the consequences'. It sounded vindictive. I don't think it's justice she's after."

"Facts, Jeannine, facts. We have to stick to facts, or enough reliable testimony to give us moral certitude of what has or hasn't happened," MacIllan wearily reminded, wishing for once he could actually go on feelings and gut instinct.

"I know, we need to find out more, especially about this October week. See if there isn't some explanation."

The next task was to bring the accusations to the accused and to hear his side of the story.   They arranged to meet him at the manor the next morning. They arrived in the midst of a delivery hubbub for the wedding reception, Mrs. Reinold doing her best to get the delivery men not to bang the boxes about, they held the crystal candelabras for the tables.

"Please, forgive the chaos at the moment, this arrived earlier than expected. Come, he's just finished Mass, and he's waiting for you." She showed them into the Violet Room away from the noise and bustle. Peter stood up and greeted them.

"Fr. MacIllan, good morning. When his Eminence said he was putting his best investigators on this, he wasn't kidding." They shook hands.

"Good morning, it's been awhile, Peter. I wish this visit was under better circumstances. This is Jeannine Fraser, but I believe you've met."

"A few times, yes. Please, sit down."

Peter ordered for coffee to be sent in, and once delivered, Fr. MacIllan decided it was best if they began immediately. He read out

Lucinda's accusations. Peter bit his lip. To think she would go this far, and she had those medical receipts, he was grieved to think she could go to such a place. What had she done?

"Laddie, I'm sorry we have to go through this, but we have to start at the beginning, did you see each other, before you became a priest?"

Peter told them the truth of what happened, openly, no holding back. Was he tempted? Yes, but not with a *laison*: the temptation was a choice between what he knew was his vocation, and another that would have been all right if he wasn't called to the priesthood. Yes, when he was out in the world marriage would have been lawful for him then, but to ignore an obvious calling from God was dangerous in its own right. He had to get away, he ran from the spot, his brother remembers the day too, he nearly ploughed him over as he left. Fr. MacIllan couldn't help nodding at that, he understood. To be tempted with another lawful good was a difficult thing to overcome, especially if the other calling required much more sacrifice.

"We appreciate your candour. So, forgive me, you're um … ? Never … ?"

"I've stayed chaste all my life."

"Well, maybe you could help us out with these then," Jeannine asked, showing him his planner.

Uh oh, the October week. Peter was a bit mortified, he didn't want them to know what had happened then, why he was 'indisposed'. He hoped they would simply accept he was ill.

"Ill? Okay, the thing is, she says you were together on the 30th. Were you?"

Peter shook his head, took a sip of coffee before answering.

"I hadn't left the rectory all that week, I was almost in bed the whole time. Fr. O'Conner was with me all week too."

"That bad? He stayed with you all week? Didn't you go to or call a doctor?"

"Um, no."

"Oh? Why not?"

"It … wasn't that kind of illness."

"Okay, forgive me for being blunt my son, innocence until proven guilty, but right now, it's not looking too good. If you want to save your priesthood, you had better open up that haggis, so to speak, or we can't help you."

He meant well, but had no idea what he was about to hear next. By the time Peter was finished, Jeannine was lost for words. Was that true? *Has he seen Hell itself?* They had heard stories about Peter, but this?

Fr. MacIllan, however, sat back, bowed his head for a moment. Something had also happened to him he dared not tell anyone, it had disturbed him too much. He had always been concerned for a certain priest, someone he himself had encouraged to enter the seminary, but was later shocked and terribly disappointed to hear of rumours of his hidden life, he was about to be brought before his local diocesan Tribunal too, then, his sudden death. To die as he did, and so young! Pneumonia, then sepsis that was resistant to every antibiotic. He worried for him, decided to offer Mass for the repose of his soul, but a terrible thing happened when he approached the altar. He felt an invisible hand stop him for a brief second, and a voice in his ear whispered – *it is too late! Offer It for someone who will profit from It.* It terrified him, he had never experienced anything like that, despite all the mystical history he had studied over the years. Did it mean what he thought it meant? He didn't know, not until now, to his grief. He now knew Peter was telling the truth, about *everything*. It was hard to continue after this revelation. The bad part was that even with his own experience at the altar that confirmed Peter's story, it was not good enough, a private mystical occurrence with only his word as evidence.

"I believe you. Honestly, I do. But, I hate to tell you, what you saw might not help keep this from going to a canonical trial. We're going to need proof of some kind you were home all week, and God rest him, O' Conner can't confirm your whereabouts now," Fr. MacIllan was finally able to say.

"I know, but maybe the others can, there were there too, well, most of the time, when not on duty," Peter noted.

"Also," Jeannine added, finally able to say something after hearing all of that, "what does 'hospital - sleepover' mean?" They had the November date to clear up too.

"Oh, we took turns staying with Fr. O'Conner all night, those were the nights I stayed."

"You didn't leave the hospital at all?"

"No, knowing that … ," Peter stopped himself short.

"Knowing what?" MacIllan gently prodded. Peter sighed.

"He wasn't going to live more than a week. I was warned. I told the others too. They'll confirm, we all took night shifts with him."

"Okay. And the July date, you had house blessings?"

"Yes, after work, and I also went home to the rectory straight afterwards each time. I also kept the addresses of the homes I visited, the parishioners might also confirm how long I was there."

Okay, that was something, the other priests at the rectory could vouch for him. They knew where to go investigating next.

"Oh, one more thing, she says these three times of, indiscretion, happened at the office."

"That would have been quite impossible. I loaded her with work, kept her at a safe distance, and, whenever I was at the office, I left my door open, except for private meetings with clients or when the staff started coming for confession. I allowed us no privacy together. The only places would have been the records area, the archive office, but I never went there, also the company vault, and I was not there the time I went back to help. The security code logs should help verify that, not to mention the CCTV cameras would not have given us any privacy. Also, only a handful of people have the code. If she was in the vault, it was not during the times I was at the office anyway, I'm pretty sure of it. Not to mention I always told everyone where I was at all times. They knew where to find me in the building."

Fr. MacIllan actually started to chuckle. This kind of precaution could only have been the result of … .

"Let me guess, you got the 'Madame Georgette' lecture, didn't you?"

Peter gave a little shrug.

Well, it looked like there was nothing else to ask for the moment. They read back his statement, however, leaving his account of visiting Hell out. Peter understood, and was relieved about that part.

As they drove off, MacIllan told Jeannine what had happened to him, why he believed the Monsignor's account, and thank God. He was sick, sick and weary of finding priests guilty due to a lapse in human weakness, others prey to some very sick, depraved disorders, this time it was a relief to discover someone was innocent, especially Peter Reinold. If *he* had fallen, he would have lost faith in everything then, but it was obvious this was a case of persecution to the point of utter destruction. Yes, he knew the man was innocent, he vowed he was going to get to the bottom of this. However, as he warned, Peter's account of Hell would not be enough, it might not be believed, and on top of it open up a whole other can of worms that they did not need right now. What they had to get was witness testimony of Peter's whereabouts. They needed enough to where the accusations could be dismissed. They cancelled whatever other engagements they had for other cases that afternoon and arranged a meeting with Fr Jenkins and Fr. Mark. Fr. Mark was questioned first.

"Oh yes, Fr. O'Conner was with Peter that whole week in October, we nearly didn't recognise him when he came out on All Saints Day, he was a different man, and no, he didn't leave the rectory at night."

"Are you sure?" Fr. MacIllan checked. "How do you know he didn't sneak out?"

"Peter? No, not him. Anyway, I would have known. Once you've had kids, you never sleep again. You're up the minute you hear someone else is up." Jeannine smiled at that. How true that was. "No, I would have heard him up and about. And, he never leaves without telling someone where he's going. Never."

About the November date, no way in God's blue heaven would he have dreamed of sneaking off then! They all knewg O'Conner had not long left to live, Peter told them. No, he was positive Peter would never had done such a thing, used that tragedy as a cover to see some woman on the side. That would be pretty sleazy. If you knew Peter, you would know the idea was crazy! Not to mention Peter was flat out on the run with his exorcism case in Trenton the end of November. The time they were supposed to meet in July was all bogus too! He could remember because Peter was about to go back to parish work full time that August 1st, and Mark admitted it was easy for him to remember those three last days in July because a new battery had been put in the smoke detector and he set the thing off with the roast beef he had tried to cook on the Thursday. The fellows ribbed him all the night and the next morning, the couldn't wait for Peter's cooking the next night, which turned out to be a salmon dinner, he gave them a treat. He felt sorry for Peter, after getting supper ready on that Friday, he couldn't enjoy it much and ate in a hurry, he remembered that, because he was out again, he went to bless a house, but was home by about ten-ish. He didn't leave again. Peter often stayed up to pray, or, catch up on letters, get about five hours sleep, sometimes only four, then head off to his early Mass. Okay, yeah, he went to the party the next night on the Saturday, but could he see Peter meeting up and … no, no way, no matter how bad it looked, it just wasn't *Peter.*

Fr. Jenkins was next to give his statement: he said pretty much the same thing. Being an army base chaplain, not to mention the late night sick calls, he explained you learn to sleep light, and, the way the stairs creaked at the rectory, there was no way anyone was getting past him in the night. Yes, Peter was home all week during his 'October illness' there was no doubt about that, and with O'Conner's stroke, no he was definitely not seeing this Mrs Clarke, or Andrews, or whatever she was calling herself now.

"And July? Um, no, no way. Peter was home, and yes, the only time he was late was on the 31ˢᵗ, but that was for a surprise party they threw for him at the office."

Fr. MacIllan and Jeannine looked at each other. This party kept coming up.

"So, he was at the office, late."

"Oh, no! It wasn't like that! Look, Peter's whole family was there, there was no way he could have been alone to do anything like that, not with it being his party and all. I know, Mark and I were there."

They took a note. They would have to rule out that night too if they could. In any case, it looked like the two priests' accounts added up, and they had been questioned separately.

Back in the car, they compared their impressions again.

"Hmm, I don't know. Okay, this party *may* have given them an opportunity, but she couldn't remember the 30 or 31 for the July liaison, it's like she couldn't pick what to say," Jeannine reflected.

"Yeah, I got that feeling too. Either something happened at the party, or this is another convenient date she could remember, one with the perfect frame-up setting."

"Something tells me we need to question Ms Andrews' ex too, see if he knew where she could have been at those times. We have to check that out," Jeannine noted.

"You're right, let's see if we can find him."

That took a few weeks to hunt down his new address and arrange a time to meet with them, in the meantime, they had to catch-up on other cases they were working on. Also, they had to set up a day to make a visit to Reinold Enterprises, the day Gerry and all the family was dreading, but it also gave them a chance to defend Peter. To everyone's surprise, many of the office staff lined up outside the boardroom, which had been set aside for the investigation process. All wanted to say something in his defence. However, the investigators began with those who would have been closest to him in the senior staff section, starting with Mr. Reinold. They commenced with her accusations, that the office was their place of rendezvous, but Richard guffawed on that.

"No way. First off, he was only here in the afternoons, rarely late at night, and when he was here, he was always with someone … oh yeah, he constantly left the door open. Made sure we all left it open if we had to go in to see him, unless he had an important call to make or had a meeting. I always wondered how he could work like that, but now I see the wisdom in it.”

“And, just to clarify, did you hear anything about them being a couple before he left for the priesthood?”

“Oh yeah, I did, and frankly, I was glad at the time. He was always on his own as a kid, showed no interest in girls, or if he did, I and his mother never knew. So when the rumours were circulating, well, it seemed a good sign that he had finally found someone, and about time! Hmph! I can see why he ran now. He belonged elsewhere, although I was so angry, leaving us like that, I couldn't see it. Obviously he was stopping something before it got any farther, since it's clear as daylight that by bolting off he had other plans and was not going to let anyone get in the way, including me.”

“One more thing, the night of the party, was he on his own at any time?”

“Hardly! Just five maybe ten minutes to pack his things, which weren't much, but we were right behind him, his mother and I. We had a few good night drinks in my office, he left with us. If Clarke was still there, we didn't see her.”

The investigators didn't like the sound of that, MacIllan knew Peter was innocent, but those few minutes alone on the top floor still sounded bad. Still, for a couple that was supposed to be passionate, that was *too* much of a quick fling, and, for a man who kept himself away from women as a precaution, and, others noted that heightened sense of precaution … hmm.

Gerry was interviewed next. Of course, he was in the hospital, so he couldn't verify Peter's whereabouts in the office building, but he did tell him how purposely busy he kept Mrs Clarke, er, Ms Andrews. Peter knew he had a problem on his hands. Heck, he tried to give Peter extra ideas on how to keep her occupied. They would have to ask Thomas and Charlotte about his workday at the office. Peter did help train Lottie after all.

“Oh, and you can forget this office affair crud, if not our offices or the board room, where could they have met? CCTV cameras, too many people everywhere, and you can forget the copy room, which is not really a room, so forgive me for saying but it's not exactly a lover's nook. No doors. The staff room is right next to it, that's also open.”

“All right then. So, there was no opportunity for them to be together here,” Jeannine confirmed.

“Well, I'll give you a tour, you can see for yourself. Unless you consider the underground parking garage, but we have cameras all over there too, they would have been spotted. If it was happening, and they didn't want to be seen, it would have been stupid to try something with security watching."

True, MacIllan knew even a tryst in the lot would have been planned, while the office would have been spur of the moment, which is what she claimed.

"Peter did mention the vault, if only to help us rule it out," MacIllan added.

"The vault?" Gerry nearly laughed at the absurdity of it, but okay. "That's all wired up with cameras too. And, only seven people have the code apart from Security: my father and I, my brother, Charlotte, and Thomas, and Kells, my father's personal assistant, and yes, Lucinda had the code. She was in there the most often since she took care of the art consignments when they came in. We trusted her. At the time."

Gerry called for Kells, instructed him to fetch a printout of the log for the vault starting as far back as March of last year. While they waited, Gerry wheeled around, took them on a tour of where Peter would have spent most of his time. The investigators saw he was right, there would have been no opportunity except for one of the senior staff offices or the boardroom, and that would have been pretty risky. They went back to the boardroom.

"My father likes to spread out his paperwork in here if there are no meetings planned, and I know he likes to have lunch delivered here sometimes. Tom and Lottie do too, if they have something to go through, it all gets lined up on the table, so, they probably did that when Peter was still here. Peter and Lucinda try and … ? Well, they would be pretty foolhardy, taking the risk of someone walking in on them, especially family. The whole idea of them having a fling is just … pfft!" Peter just wasn't like that! The idea was insane. There was a knock on the door. The printout had arrived. "Thank you Kells."

Gerry took a pen, looked for 'Clarke', underlined all the pertinent lines. None of the dates she was in the vault matched the times she gave, nor did any of the other log-ins Fr. MacIllan was relieved to see, ruling out the possibility someone else's keycard could have been swiped and used, but then, that would have been pre-planning again. So, if an unplanned moment of passion happened at all, it would have needed some serious planning in this place! However, Gerry noted something else … .

"Huh."

"Is something wrong?"

"Well, something my father should check out, we had no art deliveries this May as far as I know, Dad would have told me, he loves showing off his latest art acquisitions to me, we're kinda in competition there." He thought to himself. Hmm, his new paintings of Rome came the first week of June, and nothing for the vault that time either. Gerry wondered why Clarke would go to the vault? He would have to ask his father about this. Anyway, the investigators didn't think this was important so far, the vault opened last month had nothing to do with the dates given them. "Is there anything else I can help you with?"

"Maybe send in Mr. Winthorne and your sister?"

"Sure thing."

They too verified what Mr. Reinold and his son said: Peter was busy trying to keep things running and train Miss Reinold in the meantime, Thomas helping him. He was just too occupied.

Since their security had been upgraded, there were hardly any places left unobserved. Mr. Reinold was insistent the place be fitted with cameras, including the records and archive rooms. And, Peter always said where he was going, even if it was the executive rest room.

"Yes, my brother was that careful. We always knew where to find him," Lottie confirmed. "I thought he was a bit over the top, but I get it now."

"All right, I think that's it for now, we'll see some of the staff who are waiting outside, and please, could you inform them we need to speak to only those who worked with the Monsignor, while he was here, or can verify his presence in the building or elsewhere at work?" Fr. MacIllan couldn't waste the precious time they had hearing anything that didn't help, only that which would be of use.

"Of course," Thomas replied, closing the door and relaying the announcement outside. A few people left, but those who stayed behind were some who went to the Monsignor for confession before his father put a stop to it since it was interfering with work. After interviewing them, MacIllan and Jeannine had a very interesting picture pieced together. The Monsignor always had the door open, except when confession began, and then it was only him and the penitent, Mrs. Clarke was not there or always outside. Also, anyone who worked in the building couldn't believe the accusations made against him, not him, a man who could see your very soul! In fact, if something was happening, it would have been very hard to hide here, and, the rumours would have been circulating like crazy if anything was suspected at all, just like the first time, but this time, no. When he first came back, okay, among the office chatter there were bets wondering if some illicit flare-up was going to happen, but soon the wager that started as some crude spicy joke around the coffee pot station to lighten the dull work day died pretty fast when his 'abilities' became noticeable, it was seen in very poor taste to suggest such a thing again, even in jest. No way. People got mighty protective of him, just wished they could be around him more when they did get to see him. Everyone admired him. Then, to see the amount of faithful that believed in him crowded around the parish office on the news, yes, it was easy to be in awe of him in fact. To think Clarke would say anything *now*? No, no one believed it.

It looked like there was no more information they could get here for now. However, Fr. MacIllan noticed the cameras in the outer hallway. There was one pointed in the area where the senior offices and aides desks were situated. Was it possible to get the footage from them? Thomas put a call through to security. Yes, but not for the times Peter was in the office. They only kept the tapes for up to six months. It was eleven months since he was last here. Oh no. Evidence gone. What a shame, no tapes to confirm all the testimony they received, but the fact there was so much said in his defence … it was something positive. However, it could look like they were all covering for Peter. If only they had something concrete proving the claims made against him were baseless, or at least a bigger mountain of circumstantial evidence in his favour that would outweigh hers, enough to dismiss the case. Fr. MacIllan and Jeannine were determined to find that something, however, as with all the situations they were presented with like this, finding it was going to be very difficult, and then to try and find it within a couple of weeks before the wedding? Fr. MacIllan could sense it. The Serpent was trying its best to choke the Monsignor in its coils. There was One who was given the grace to put that Serpent under heel. Instinctively he held the medal around his neck for a moment, which he often did when faced with an insurmountable difficulty.

Mother of God, you have to help us.

It was a tough day that Sunday. Fr. Greg had seen three exorcism cases and was tired after it all. Strange enough, he wasn't completely sapped, but of course, these three cases weren't anything like the one he helped out with in Trenton. He had screeching and convulsions to deal with, but not anything as intense. Of course, the Monsignor told him their Trenton case was an exceptional situation.

Greg set his dinner in the microwave, leftovers from the night before. He felt like his dinner looked, and not just because of the exorcisms. It was hard to believe the news these past few weeks, that Peter was guilty of such a thing. His parish buzzed with it. Those who were curious enough approached and asked if he thought any of it was true, but he evaded their probing and said it was up to the Church authorities to look into it. He personally didn't believe a word of it, it was all a horrible lie, it had to be. If only he knew of some way to help the Monsignor other than prayer! He owed him so much, and not just for his lessons on exorcisms, he truly knew what it meant to have a spiritual life after being with him, even for such a short space of time. He missed his company, that quiet strength one felt when he was around. Him have an affair? Tell a woman to kill his own children if he did father them? Never!

After his dinner and his evening prayers, Greg felt in the need of seeing the videos, the copies he had made of the Trenton case. Why, he didn't know, especially after the day he had, but he took out the first tape, put it in the player. Man, to think they went through that! Wow. He was about to turn it off when something he heard made him stop. What? He hit rewind and played that bit again.

Holy smokes!

Greg spent the night replaying every tape he had, taking notes at certain spots, taking down the times. The next morning, exhausted as he was, he called Archbishop Foley's office. Is his Eminence in? Please, this is urgent!

"Good morning, this is Fr. Simmons calling. I helped Monsignor Reinold with his exorcism in Trenton. I've got something important you need to see."

The investigators in the meantime were with Mr. Clarke who came to the Tribunal office that Monday morning. His testimony was anything but encouraging.

"An affair with him? Not surprised! Not now! I suspected she was pregnant in January, came home to surprise her, found her gone but she had left her notebook behind. Did she want me to find out? It sure looked like it! I saw the appointment for a clinic that wasn't our usual one. I called the number to confirm exactly what 'appointment' it was. Did I get an earful!"

"Forgive me, how do you know the child was the Monsignor's," duty obliged Fr. MacIllan to ask, his heart knotting with this disagreeable turn of events.

"I didn't until I wondered why after telling me she wanted kids before we married that she suddenly didn't want to have any right away. I caught her with pills, and now this! An abortion appointment? So, I did some searching, and discovered her dirty little secret. Her nightstand was full of him! Articles, photos, pens from the office, copies of company letters in his handwriting, it was quite a little shrine, I can tell you that! I packed and got out. If that's who she wanted, fine, I was out of there. I was finished. Her statement to that gossip reporter later only confirmed my worst nightmare."

"All right. Forgive me, but I have to ask, do you know were she was on the last two days of July?"

"Oh yeah, hard to forget. The 30th is, was, our anniversary, the next night was the party she helped plan, for him."

"Your anniversary? She was with you the night before?"

"Oh yeah, she was with me, definitely was 'with' me," he said with bitter finality. "We finally had a romantic night together with all the office work she was bringing home that week, and preparing for his party too and all."

"So, she was home with you all that week," Fr. MacIllan checked.

"Yeah, although she came home late the night of his party, but I didn't think anything of it then, stupid idiot that I was. I was invited, but I couldn't go, I had an emergency show up at my own place of work."

"Excuse me for getting more personal, but when you said you had a romantic night together for your anniversary," Jeannine trailed.

"Yeah, exactly what you think."

Jeannine then asked about his ex wife's whereabouts for Thanksgiving weekend, and the last week of October, if he could remember.

"She was with me then, we spent the night at my parents' place for Thanksgiving, and she was home for dinner that weekend, because I remember the leftovers my parents insisted we bring home, it took us the weekend to finish them. I also remember that because she griped about my Mom's cooking the whole time. October? Oh yeah, she was home too, her parents came for Halloween being Sunday and all, she was busy trying to get the place straightened up, she hated her mother nagging her how she kept the place, and she had the dinner planned the few days before, she yeah, she was home."

"Do you have a romantic time of it then those two occasions," Jeannine gently pressed.

"Excuse me, why do you need to know? It's *their* love-life you should be … ."

He stopped short.

"When … when did you say she had the first abortion?"

Jeannine gave him the date again. Yes, he had seen the second date in Lucinda's book for January, but not the first date in September. He knew nothing of that.

Oh my God. July was *his* kid, and November's too, October was when he had discovered she was taking the pills, so nothing could have happened then at all. Even if the Monsignor was involved too … she couldn't have gotten pregnant then.

"Oh geeze, that woman, is sick. *Sick*! She needs some help."

"Mr. Clarke? Are you all right," Jeannine asked.

"No. I'm not! Don't you get it? They were not *his* kids. They were mine. They had to be!"

It made sense now. Yes she wanted children—but not his! Not those of Mr. Second Choice, the passable lookalike. If it was Peter Reinold she really wanted, and she actually had *his* kids, why get rid of them? She could have easily slipped them under the radar, used their marriage as the perfect cover and raise the kids of the man she really wanted, and, shut him and their parents up too while she was at it. They had bugged her enough it was time to think about having kids … it would have been the perfect set up for her. But no, they weren't the kids she wanted. The way she didn't protest the divorce, just signed the papers, geeze, she didn't even bother to squabble over their personal belongings like most wives would do. Fight over what? What for? There was no question what she felt. She wanted out. She didn't want him or anything from him, boring Eddy Clarke the accountant, and that included his kids. Edward was sickened by this revelation.

"You are positive about this," Fr. MacIllan quietly asked him to confirm.

"Oh yeah. I'll make a statement for you too, if that's what you want."

"I'm so sorry. You've just discovered some horrible news. We know someone who can help you through this bereavement," Jeannine began. Edward looked up. "Yes, bereavement. You've lost your wife, and, your children in the most horrible way imaginable. This is not going to be easy," she continued.

"Listen, I need to know. Was there anything between them? Before me, like the papers say?"

"Well, I shouldn't say, but, from what we heard, it almost did, but never got a chance. She knew he wanted to be a priest, tried to keep him from leaving. That's his statement."

"Oh! She tried to trap him? Didn't she? Sure sounds like her all right! The b ... sorry. Man, he dumped her flat! Good, he escaped from what I walked into, someone who really didn't give a damn about anyone but herself."

After he checked his testimony, he asked if he could go. He just had a very upsetting morning. They left him go. The two investigators sat alone for a moment, took a deep breath. At last, the pieces were starting to fit.

Maybe Ms. Andrews fell in love with Peter, or, maybe she was only just fascinated by him to the point of obsession, mistaking it for the real thing. Her stalking tendencies hadn't gone unnoticed, and to collect trophies from the office? Hide them in her nightstand? And yes, the times she claimed she was with Peter, she was actually with her husband, which explained why she was so certain of the dates to the point she couldn't be tricked, and yet so hesitant. She *was* with someone, her husband, but could she pin those nights on Peter? Make the clinic dates line up to trap him. Unrequited love or impassioned obsession left unnoticed can make people do vindictive things. Mr. Clarke had tumbled to it, and he of all people would know her. When she couldn't have a lost love or even his children, she descended into a very dark place, was prepared to destroy what she couldn't have. They were pretty sure they now had enough that even the Archdiocesan therapist who usually checked out the exorcism cases for verifiable metal illnesses when called upon might agree with their findings if her opinion was needed.

The phone buzzed.

"Father, the Archbishop and a Fr. Simmons are waiting to see you. Will I show them in?"

"The Archbishop? Now? Of course." They rose to meet the sudden arrivals. The Archbishop introduced Greg to them, who was a bit nervous, but eager to show what he had. He and the Archbishop wheeled in a TV and video player.

"Forgive us for just jumping in like this, but, Fr. Simmons has something important you need to see. It's convinced me."

"Um, I wanted to show you the exorcism case I helped the Monsignor with. Normally, we can't pay attention to what demons say since they lie so much," Fr. Greg hesitantly began, "but listen to this first. This happened in September, Saturday the 25th."

The investigators were glued to their seats. They had never seen an exorcism case of this magnitude before. It nearly went over their heads what Greg was trying to show them.

"Listen! They're taunting Peter, taunting him he's a virgin. The demons usually lie, but they can also take a virtue, make it sound like something bad, to be ashamed of, twist it. They're telling the truth here. It's not the only time."

Greg pulled out the tape, put in another, and another. Not only where the demons taunting Peter, but upset they couldn't make him fall 'there', but they would get him in 'other ways'.

"Also, get this: we know Our Lady was there, she was helping us. The demons admitted that, they weren't permitted to lie when she was there, even said they were forced to tell the Monsignor the truth, they tried mocking him again, angry about not having fallen to the 'temptation in the office'. Listen!"

Fr. MacIllan held his medal for a moment. Yes, there was truth to that. The Mother of God could force a truthful answer from the demons during exorcisms. His prayer had been answered.

"And, Fr. Greg continued, "they were forced to say they always had to be truthful to him now, that he got a huge grace somehow, so they say, I don't know what it was, but they were so angry when it happened. Let's see, when he came back after he was sick in the end of October, they were really mad at him then, but, the clearings started to happen. The evidence is all here. The Monsignor could not have had that affair! Even the demons were forced to admit he's as pure as the driven snow! But, they're out to destroy him. That's what this is all about. It has to be." Fr. Greg played the last of Satan's taunts, the threat he would get Peter by his very obedience. "How else do you take a priest and exorcist down and out of action? Destroy his reputation. In obedience, he would have to stop his ministry, maybe for years, maybe once and for all. Doesn't that make sense?"

"Yes, yes it does. Thank you for coming to us with this. Not only was it the most astounding thing I've seen in my life," Fr. MacIllan admitted, and to have seen it all on the feast of St. Benedict no less, "it proves the conclusion we have just come to this morning, there are no grounds for a canonical trial. Monsignor Reinold is innocent."

At that moment, as Peter was finishing up his Mass honouring Pope Pius I, the Gospel passage for the day seemed more than coincidental, " ... thou art Peter, and upon this rock I shall build My Church ... the gates of Hell shall not prevail against it ... and I will give to thee the keys of the kingdom of Heaven." He suddenly felt liberated, loosened, like he too had been freed from a heavy burden. A new light from his picture of Our Lady of Good Success caught his eye, She looked radiant today with her keys, like she had scored a hard but relished victory.

The day has been won, but not without wear and tear, right?

She seemed to give a little smile.

؃❖؅

The Archdiocesan office wasted no time preparing and issuing the next set of statements. The accusations against Monsignor Reinold were fabricated and that he would be returning to his full parish duties within two weeks. The Archbishop privately deciding after the trials they had faced, Peter and the family needed to recover and enjoy some extra time together before the big festivities. Richard Reinold also wasted no time having Kraylor and Kraylor Associates officially threaten the *Manhattan Daily Post* with a libel suit complete with a copy of Mr. Clarke's statement affirming Peter's innocence given with his and the Archdiocese's blessing. It was one of the rare times the paper quickly issued a retraction and a gushy apology in a prominent section of the paper, not stuck in some ignored corner near the classified ads. Satisfied, Richard dropped the suit, no point having this disagreeable situation dragged out any longer, not when the wedding day was fast approaching. It was disagreeable enough he solved the riddle of why Lucinda went to the vault in May. After Gerry showed him the printout of the vault log, he went to inspect the place. One of the crates was not sealed properly, and on taking a closer look, discovered the painting inside was gone. As it happened, it was Peter's favourite seascape in the corporate collection by Vlieger. It had been unstapled from its canvas supports that were placed back in the frame, which was then returned to the crate. Richard ordered the security footage for the vault. Well, well! Look at that! The hussy had no shame taking out the picture! Maybe she thought only outside the vault was under security surveillance and had no idea there was another camera hidden inside. He along with Gerry, Tom and Lottie watched with a mixture of surprise and disgust as the recording of the vault interior showed her pulling out the staples, then rolling up the canvas and putting it in a poster tube, which she slipped into her valise.

925

Okay, that's how she got it out of the vault, but how did she get away with it? True, security didn't often check the bags of the workers *leaving* the building, they were more preoccupied with trying to keep any scoundrels from coming in. Richard ordered for the other tapes showing where she went to after that. The mail room? She took the tube from her valise, placed it in the outgoing mail cart. If that wasn't smart! Where the heck did she mail it to? Pausing the video, they tried zooming in on the frozen image, but the fine print was too blurred to make out the address. Wherever it went, she just made off with a masterpiece! Gerry was about to call the detectives at the station when his father stopped him.

"Don't get too hot and bothered, son. Like your new pictures of Rome, I got tired of being surrounded by fakes and thought it was time to enjoy the real things for a change. She has no idea she actually took off with the repro."

"What? Are you serious?"

"Yeah! See the few times I checked into the vault in April? I made a couple of switches. Good thing too! That fake is worth only a few hundred, maybe a thousand at most."

"Wow. That was a lucky break. Still, she's not only a liar, but a thief! After what she did to Pete, not to mention us, she deserves to rot in jail." Gerry went to pick up the phone again, but Lottie stopped him.

"Aw, let it go. Let her keep if it she wanted it that bad. I have a feeling her future is not going to be much to look forward to. Let that be it's own punishment."

Lottie had a point. Lucinda had tried to destroy Peter, but had ended up destroying herself. Never again would she have a decent job, for they certainly weren't going to give her references! And, what could they say? Great worker, no complaints there, just make sure she stays away from the boss's son, and don't leave any valuables around. Gerry let out a breath as he put the phone down. Enough with her anyway. They had their own future to look forward to. Yes, there was another matter he would rather see to right now, however, a very important call beat him to his next project. It was Detective Davenport.

"Mr. Reinold, we've got some more good news for you, we found Mr. Jeong's little girl."

"What? Seriously? Is she okay? Where is she?"

"Yes to all the above, and, she's at the paediatric hospital right now, but so far, other than the terror of what she's gone through, she seems to be all right, just slightly undernourished, which she is making up for, double time. The staff have found out she loves grilled cheese sandwiches, and lots of them. They don't know where she's putting them. The nurses are spoiling her."

"This is good news. How did you find her?"

"Another tip off. Last night's sting operation just uncovered a few sweat shops, and they had the kids working. It's going to be a nightmare trying to see if we can find parents, and all of that, but still, it's a good day."

"Now what?"

"Well, Mr. Jeong's testimony has proven invaluable, he's been a great help. So, they'll be put into witness protection, granted asylum, maybe get fast-tracked with green cards, so they would like to say goodbye before that happens. Which is going to be pretty soon I figure."

"Can we meet them today? I'd like Katherine to come too, if she can make it."

"Sure thing, you can meet us at the hospital if you like."

Gerry quickly hunted down Katherine, who was with the Matriarchs at the manor helping to figure out the seating arrangements for the reception to fit in a few extra guests that decided to invite themselves, some very, very, very distant cousins that they hadn't heard from in an age, but oh well. The family wasn't going to get upset now that everything was feeling so festive, they could find room for the unexpected blow-ins. They quickly let her go when they heard the good news.

"Yes, we've got this. Go!"

It meant a drive back into town, but Katherine didn't want to miss this. She found Gerry waiting for her in the lobby of the hospital with a cheerful assortment of stuffed animals, dolls, candy, crayons and colouring books piled in a basket having raided the gift shop of practically everything it had to offer. Katherine kissed him on the cheek. Good thinking! The detectives showed them to the room guarded by an agent. They gently knocked on the door and let the two visitors enter. Mr. Jeong stood up when he saw who had just arrived, uttering profuse thank yous for helping to find his little Jin Ae whom he thought was gone forever. Gerry was somewhat bashful with all the praise.

"Oh, I didn't really do anything. Please, this is my fianceé. She wanted to meet you too."

Katherine received a profound bow, and congratulations on their coming nuptials, Mr. Jeong wished them many years of prosperity on their house.

"We wish the same for you too. You're safe now," Gerry returned.

"So, you're Jin Ae, you're very pretty." Katherine smiled. The little girl looked timidly at the new faces, then back at her father, who explained in her native language they had helped them get away from the bad people. She brightened up.

"There's a smile! Look, we brought this for you." Gerry held up the basket.

"All? For, me," she asked in a broken accent.

"She's learning English already!" Katherine was surprised. "She's adorable."

"Yep, all for you," Gerry replied. Katherine carefully helped him place it on her bed.

"Thank, you, very, much!"

"And, I have a gift for you too," Gerry continued, taking out a fat envelope from his inside jacket pocket, deftly handing it to a shocked Mr. Jeong.

"Please, what is this?"

"A little something to help set you up."

"Little?"

Gerry smiled.

"I know you will be under witness protection and we most likely won't be permitted to see each other again, but still, if for some reason you ever need our help, you can always come to us. Welcome to America, and I hope you and your daughter have a very happy life here."

They shook hands, Mr. Jeong bowed profusely. Before they left, it was a touching sight to see Jin Ae show her father all the amazing things she had just been given, a windfall the like of which she had never had dropped on her before as though she had been visited by a magic fairy that could grant every desire.

"It did my heart good to see that," Katherine noted as they went to the car.

"Yeah, mine too."

"You know, that reminds me of something I've been wanting to talk to you about."

"Uh oh. That sounds serious."

It was. She wanted to discuss her wedding present.

"Ah! At last! Have you thought of something?"

"That's just it. Yes, I've got you your present, but me, I don't want or need anything else, Gerry, so don't spend your money on me. Instead, I've been thinking. We have each other, we couldn't want better presents, right? *We're* our wedding presents! Instead of buying more stuff for us we really don't need, we have so much already, way too much, I think we should do something to help others for a change. Look at how happy you've just made that man and his little girl. They've been through some of the worst things imaginable that anyone could ever experience, and now, they've suddenly got hope and a reason to live. I want to do that! Frankly, we should be doing more, don't you think? Giving today without expecting anything back except to see lives changed for the better certainly made us happier than if we received.”

She was right.

“What do you have in mind?”

“That's just it, I don't know yet, but you've made a really good start with your art and education program at the prison, things like that. I mean, yes, America is the land of opportunity, but how many of its own citizens get what this land promises? For instance, I caught Andre loading food into a van a few nights ago, and I wondered what that was about. He was donating all he had in the restaurant that was still good but couldn't serve because of some health code. He didn't want to throw it out, so whatever the help doesn't want, he gives it to the local shelters.”

“That's good of him.”

“I know, the shelter keeps getting compliments it has the best food in the area Andre told me. Anyway, I then hear Pete talking about the nuns and their soup kitchen. It got me thinking about all the homeless we have on our streets, but I want to do more than just feed them. That doesn't help stop the depressing cycle because they can't get a foot up with a decent address, training or a job. Then, what about the elderly homeless with no family and are too old to try and get back on their feet? We could start a home for them, or something. Maybe we could set up a charity or a foundation, I don't know yet. I do know the mothers would love to help, they're so good at running charity events, they have a lot of experience. Instead of running things for others, maybe they'd like to get involved with something that the family has started.”

“Not only me, but Pete would be so proud of you. It's exactly what he wanted me to do too. And the two of you are correct, we really don't need more stuff. I have to say, I also promised Pete if his idea for a new religious order ever gets off the ground, I'd help.”

“Oh, that's a given.”

“All righty then! It's settled. The Princess has spoken. Your wish is my command. We can get into the nuts and bolts of it all when we come back from Italy. Although I shall continue to reserve the right to spoil you with a few flowers and chocolates.”

“Oh, okay.”

“And a night out on the town, just now and again.”

"All right."
"And, maybe, just maybe, a trinket or two."
"Don't push it, bub."
He laughed.

☙ ❖ ❧

The excitement was building, guests were arriving, and despite the many rooms at Oak Meadows and Stonyvale, hotels in the city were getting a share of their guests. Katherine's friends from Paris had arrived thanks to her family's private jet, making things a lot easier for them to bring all their accoutrements, Martin and Justice not only hauling the little one, diaper bags and bottles, but also their latest collections to be shown at the gallery, while Maurice had his 'cello to play some of the music at the ceremony, his personal contribution to the happy event. Theresa was thankful for the jet too because at least she was spared the moaning of the musician of the artistic clique who dreaded to bring his 'baby' on long haul travel through public airlines since he could never trust the luggage handlers. Honestly! Sometimes it seemed he cared more for that hollow piece of wood and strings than her, one of those situations that had become a running joke between them all. The friends also brought special traditional gifts from France for the bridal couples, two silver *coupe de marriage* goblets intended to become heirlooms, and, Justine's father wanted to do something special for Katherine and Charlotte by hand carving for each of them a trousseau chest, Justine explained she remembered how Kathy and Gerry had admired these things at their own wedding, and so, it seemed like the perfect gifts to bring. Although it was a week early, they wanted them to have them come before the truly hectic days took over, for there were a few fittings left to do, Justine and Martin being the last of the wedding party to check that their outfits were all right, not to mention the rehearsal was coming up, the rehearsal dinner, and, the hen night and stag party.

"So much to fit in, and now, Gerry has disappeared, *again*," Aunt Martha huffed, wondering what extra work he could be doing that he was missing some of the get togethers with the families, especially as relatives had taken the trouble to travel from all over for the happy event. "I hope he'll be at the rehearsal at least."

930

"And the bachelor party," Steves had to chip in, to the further flusteration of Martha.

True. Where was he? Katherine was wondering where he was off to late at night as well, especially now as it was all starting to come down to the final days and they could have used his help, it didn't make much sense, until Steves did some sleuthing.

"Don't worry, I followed him after work tonight," he reported. "It's not what you think. He's actually planning a surprise."

Now Katherine was really curious, especially as she told him there was no need to go all crazy spending on her.

"Can you give me a hint?"

"No, Kats. You're just going to have to wait until your wedding day."

Sir Lancelot was at it again! Him and his surprises! Nevermind. She had a surprise for him too, he'd have to wait a little later for his. Only now, the curiosity was really getting at her.

Whatever Gerry had planned, he did make it to the rehearsal at the cathedral, which had its fair share of glitches. Blip number one happened when ring boy aka Pierre the little mountain climber from France didn't want to carry the practise pillow up the aisle. He ran half way screeching, then attempted to throw the cushion the rest of the way before running back where he came from. Mortified Justine zipped after him while everyone tried to stop laughing.

"Aw shucks, look at the length of the aisle, probably scared the little guy half to death walking up that. We should know, we're next," Gerry whispered to Katherine, who caught a case of the giggles over it. Well, if Pierre was not up to it on the day, Leroy would have to assume his full best man duties and bring the rings himself, he dare not lose them Aunt Martha warned! Next it was time for the grooms and groomsmen to take their places, Gerry escorting his mother up the aisle to her seat walking beside his chair, Tom and Helen next. After them, the fathers with the brides to be, the Captain and Charlotte going first, with Harold and Katherine following behind, the bridesmaids also practising with them.

"Stately pace! Stately pace, nice and easy. It's a regal march, not an Olympic sprint," Aunt Martha called out!

"Auntie, I think they've got this," cousin Stephie called back while Katherine and Pops cracked a smile. Happy as tonight felt, it was only a rehearsal, it quickly struck them they would be doing this for real in a couple of days. Nerves were starting to kick in once everyone who was meant to be at the altar waited for Peter's instructions.

"Okay, I start by welcoming everyone and giving my long-winded, dearly-beloved-we-are-gathered-here-today-to-see-these-couples-tie-the-knot-and-be-doomed-forever wedding spiel ... ." Everyone chuckled. "But seriously, after the greeting, I next ask 'who gives these women?' Peter reminded the fathers, "then you both say 'I do', or maybe 'we do' would work just as nicely."

" 'We do', sounds good," the Captain agreed.

"That's sorted. All right. We then start the vows, but, I'm not doing them *now*, or you'd actually get married tonight! So, you're practising saying each other's names instead."

"Okay Pete, easy peasy." Gerry smiled.

Thomas had no trouble saying Charotte Anne Joan Reinold, and while Charlotte was terrified she'd slip up on Thomas James Bartholomew Winthorne, but made it.

"I did it! I did it! Yes! Whoops!" She clapped her hands over her mouth. She was in church after all! Gerry next proudly called out 'I take thee, Katherine Amelia Bernadette Walsingham', too bad this was just the practise run, while thank heavens this was just the practise run when Katherine got tongue tied. Gerry burst out laughing, she kept tripping up on Gerard Johannes Thomas Reinold, which made everyone else fall into infectious peals of laughter.

"It's *Johannes*, not Your Highness! I just knew you'd blooper this one."

"I know, I know! Shoot! I can't think of your name without wanting to say that!"

Their joke was now coming back to haunt them! Eventually she stopped laughing, took a breath and nailed it.

"Finally! She succeeds! It only took three tries." Peter chuckled. "Okay, once the vows are made, Mass will begin. A word to our Protestant friends here tonight, the Mass will be in the traditional Latin form as the couples have requested, but you will all have your wedding programs with the English translation, they arrived today and are over there in the boxes, so don't worry, you will be able to follow along. Also, his Eminence has given permission for Reverend Dobbson to do the first reading before I read the Gospel in English to the congregation, then you all get preached at again. Just saying." Laughter was heard. "After Mass, the happy couples then sign the registry. You'll officially be man and wife, er, men and wives. I guess that's it. When the Big Day finally comes, may we all make it to the church on time."

"Amen," Gramps heartily called out.

While everyone else was leaving to go to the rehearsal dinner, Leroy took Peter aside for a moment.

"I need some help! I'm the best man for the two of them, and while I used to be the go-to guy for a stag night, you more than anyone know that's all changed now! I can't think of a traditional 'bachelor party' that won't get me thrown back into your confessional, and them two are not going to want to do anything to where they can't face you or their women either on their wedding day, so I'm stuck! All this time, and I've got nothing planned, and this is practically their last night of freedom! What am I gonna do? I gotta think of something before the other frat boys find out and beat me to it, and you know what they might do. I wouldn't be surprised if they got Gerry blithered and he woke up with his eyebrows shaved off, or something."

"Bachelor night, huh? Why not hang out with a bunch of bachelors then? You seemed to have enjoyed it so far."

"You mean you'll help?"

"Yeah, sure. We men in collars are allowed a bit of fun too. Besides, someone needs to keep an eye on you when it comes to parties, I'm the best man for that job."

Leroy found that funny.

Sure enough, the Holy Bachelors were eager to join, it was so good knowing they were going to have Pete back soon they too wanted to celebrate. Peter joked with Gerry, hoping he didn't mind slumming with him and the fellows for the night, but he, Tom, and the groomsmen were game for it, although do come dressed Peter advised. Dressed to go slumming? They didn't know what that was about, but okay. Peter surprised them by saying they were going to a club. Gerry wondered what on earth Peter was up to, *Peter* now taking them to a club? True, Peter would never dream of going to any kind of night club and cause a scandal, but for the sake of charity in keeping the grooms in check, he made sure they went to a respectable place to where he could keep an eye on them while giving them a good time. They drove up outside one exclusive jazz joint, Gerry's favourite, which he hadn't been to in an age.

"Slumming? You had us there! Hey, this is great! No wonder you wanted us dressed. Are you up for some jazz, Tom?"

"Yeah! I didn't think there were still places like this," he noted.

It was a lively classy dinner and music joint, one of the last authentics that hadn't been touched with the exception of a restoration job, returning its vintage décor to its former glory, with shaded lamps on linen draped tables, the waiters in tuxedoes, the waitresses dressed in classic dinner dresses, and, toe-tapping Jazz, not the confused modern jumble with melodies that didn't quite know where they were ending up. It was also the best place for good 'ole swing and croon tunes. The real deal. It was easy to imagine some of the greats singing or playing here with all the tribute singers taking their place tonight. Boy, that guy really sounds like old Blue Eyes! Some of the patrons were surprised to see a bunch of priests in with a bachelor party, it was hilarious, but the waitresses soon spread the word they were chaperoning the guys about to get hitched, which was a first. When the news got back to the management, the owner then came out to greet them, it had been a long time since he'd seen Gerry and wanted to wish him and his soon-to-be brother-in-law congratulations. Peter also had some thanks to give, that they could squeeze them in on such short notice, but hey, anything for Gerry and the Monsignor of Manhattan! They were then treated to the best champagne, on the house. Despite having the drink intake watched by Big Brother, they were all having a great time, although Monsignor Ingio looked like a cat dropped into a bathtub. Apparently, he didn't think jazz was something worth listening to.

"Yo Ger, what do you think the girls are up to tonight," Leroy wondered loudly over the swing number that just started.

"Kats do anything wild? Nah! I think you can relax. I wouldn't be surprised if she made Steph organise a quilting bee." Steves laughed.

True enough, Gerry or Tom didn't have to worry, the girls had decided on a slumber party in the penthouse, no stress or fuss, just a fun night of gaggle talk, all wrapped up in robes, painting each other's toenails and trying the latest strawberry beauty peel masks that the cosmetic branch of Walsingham industries had just released all the while binging on junk food, finally caving in after the torturous dieting they had endured the last few months to ensure they fit into their dresses on the Big Day. Enjoyable as it was, Stephie was the only one who thought things were a bit too tame.

"Geeze Kathy, I'm supposed to give you a rip roaring party before you're tied down forever, and you won't let me take us to one Chippendale show!"

"No way! You can do what you want for your hen night when it comes, I'm enjoying myself quite nicely, thank you. Besides, I promised Uncle Tim to give a full report on what we thought of these new beauty masks."

Stephie shook her head. Imagine turning her hen night into a product review club!

In the end they were all glad they didn't go too party hardy, for the next day began the real countdown, and with it, a lot of rushing around.

There were the final flower deliveries to check, and she was driving back to New Jersey to spend the last night of freedom at Oak Meadows since her dress was there, ready and waiting, and, it was bad luck for the groom to catch a glimpse of the bride before the day anyway. Gerry, however, disappeared again, this time for the whole day, and Steves refused to divulge his secret except to the Mothers, who quickly forgave him.

"What is he up to," Katherine tried to wheedle from them, but with no success. She would have to find out tomorrow.

Tomorrow!

It came with a panicked rude awakening.

"Kathy, wake up! The hairdresser! He's arrived early!"

"Wha? Oh no!"

Somewhat dazed as she was so excited the night before she couldn't get much sleep, she sipped at the coffee mug thrust in her face while she tried to pull on her robe.

So, this is it! How the nerves kicked in! They didn't blend well with caffeine, or perhaps too well.

In a few minutes she was wide awake, the master hair artist along with the professional make-up beautician set to work, while Aunt Barbara ran with Helen to get ready, Aunt Martha stayed to eye every detail, giving a little nod of approval. Katherine certainly didn't have any complaints, her hair styled up with white rose buds to match her dress. Next, her mother and her aunt now dressed helped her put on her own gown, then, stood back to admire their handiwork. The final touch, the sapphire set Gerry had given her, then the bridal veil edged in lace. Katherine did not recognise herself as she stood before the full length mirror. She also took someone else's breath away.

"May we come in?"

"Good morning! Oh! Don't you two look handsome." Her father and grandfather were quite regal in their morning suits, waistcoats and boutonnières.

"Thankee Katie, but I believe all the compliments belong to you today." Gramps was thunderstruck, she looked so much like Amelia on a very special day oh so long ago and yet felt like only a few minutes.

"True, today, you really are a princess. Come, as much as I don't want to see you grow up, we can't keep your prince waiting," Pops noted, holding out his arm to escort her to the limo.

Elsewhere on Long Island a similar scene was happening, Lottie's mother helping her to dress, her proud father coming to say his last goodbyes as her paternal guardian, trying to steel himself to the idea he was giving her away, eventhough he totally approved of Thomas.

Both limos made it to the cathedral on schedule, and for a jittery moment the brides couldn't stop complimenting each other until they heard the organ strike up, it was time. The mothers were escorted in, the grooms were waiting. Quick girls, to our places the fathers reminded while the bridesmaids hurriedly smoothed out their trains. Justine watched nervously through the door, uh oh, was Pierre going to stop up the aisle? He turned, looked back for mama. Was her little lamb going to go rogue on them? Charlotte hooshed Justine in through the doors, so what if they were down a bridesmaid? We'll survive! Hurry! Before he throws the thing at Petey again! Chuckles could be heard inside as Justine quickly but elegantly went in and swept up the reluctant ring-bearer and carried him up the rest of the aisle, handing Leroy the ring cushion before taking her place earlier than the brides with Pierre in her arms. Nobody minded and thought it was rather cute.

The organ music changed, the march began. A rumbling echo could be heard as everyone turned and stood to attention in honour of the brides.

Charlotte gave a nervous little smile as she and the Captain went in first, arm in arm, then, Katherine and her father following behind. It was beautiful and surreal, to see what they all had waited for so long, the cathedral filled with flowers, the pews decorated with matching floral arrangements and packed with family and guests to witness this momentous milestone in their lives, Peter dressed in his new white vestments waiting to receive them at the altar along with the Archbishop who was serving his Mass. Although this was all so exquisite, Katherine knew one memory she would hold the most dear, seeing Gerry's expression as she walked down the aisle, her heart giving a little leap then melting at the sight of him waiting for her, he looked so handsome dressed to the nines, insisting on standing despite her slow, steady march. The emotive atmosphere was overwhelming, Aunt Martha was already weeping as the fathers stood waiting to give away their treasures to others for safekeeping, next Peter almost at a loss for words, another rarity! It truly was an honour and a grace to preside at his own brother and sister's wedding, on the same day no less, but also to think he was marrying his best friends, who were now joining his family. Despite the emotion of it, he did give his opening speech, reminding the happy couples of the sanctity of the calling they were now about to enter, love bound in a holy lifelong vocation, to accompany one another their whole lives through, bringing new life into the world, and, to also help one another in a way so many people often forget, to assist each other in reaching the happiest of all places, Heaven.

Next, the vows. Despite the nerves, no mistake was made, names were properly spoken, the gold wedding bands gently slipped on, at long last, each couple were pronounced man and wife, Peter adding one traditional touch, taking his stole and wrapping it around the couples' joined hands with the solemn pronouncement:

"What God has joined together, let no man put asunder."

The cathedral thundered with applause. It was difficult remaining dutifully attentive to the High Nuptial Mass in Latin after that, Katherine just wanted to smile at Gerry and had to be content holding his hand, gently turning the ring and giving him a smile once in awhile, and he was not about to let go of her hand either. After signing the registry, photos taken of the records being officiated, the nerves began to finally subside, it all went okay! Peter gave the brides a kiss on the cheek and the grooms a brotherly embrace. The Archbishop also congratulated the happy couples, then announced to the witnesses present they should all give them a few minutes alone in the sacristy before they once more faced the gaze of the crowd and not get a moment's peace for the rest of the day.

"Thomas, aren't our ladies beautiful," Gerry could finally say at last, still awed by the whole proceedings.

"Stunning! I couldn't believe it when you walked down the aisle," Tom complimented Lottie.

"I'm so glad you're happy, you know we dressed not just for us, but for you too," Katherine reminded the grooms, who also looked quite debonair.

"I can't believe it, yet here we are! I'm so happy," Charlotte exclaimed.

No more words, Gerry couldn't wait any longer for a kiss from his bride, neither could Tom.

At last they emerged from the sacristy, the newly married couples started laughing when they saw what Lee, Steves and the guys had done to Gerry's wheelchair in those few minutes they were in there, all tied up with lace, satin bows and bells, a few cans dangling on strings with a 'Just Married!' sign tagged on the back. Lee said the vintage Rolls-Royces were waiting for them got the same treatment. However, before they left the church, Peter asked if the brides wouldn't mind that instead of tossing their bouquets at the reception they complete another old tradition and honour Our Lady by giving them to Her instead, a gift with a request She watch over them and grant Her maternal protection on this new chapter in their lives. That sounded beautiful. They readily agreed, the curious guests watched as the brides went to place their bouquets at Her shrine in the Lady Chapel.

Photo time again! Since Stephanie couldn't take photos of everything while she was accomplishing her duties as Matron of Honour, she had hired one of the most sought after professionals to complete the job, and he was not about to let one imperfect snap deface his film! The man raced everywhere, making sure he didn't miss a thing. As beautiful as they knew the interior scenes would be, at the same time everyone couldn't wait to see how the shot in front of the cathedral turned out with the guests all tossing confetti at the newly weds.

However as they reached their waiting vehicles, Katherine and Gerry were accosted by one individual they weren't expecting that had detached from the crowd of spectators clapping outside the cathedral, Beatrice Brandis who wanted a few comments from the happy bride and groom before she joined them at the manor since Katherine promised all exclusives to the *Manhattan Daily Post* after all. How dare she, after all she had done to them! Gerry was about to intervene when Katherine calmly placed her hand on his arm.

“Oh, but it's to Robert Horace that I promised all my exclusives, not the *Manhattan Daily Post*,” she clarified ever so politely. “Too bad he's been fired. Since *he's* invited to the wedding reception, he could have given such a wonderful write-up of it all. I'm afraid that's now out of the question. However, if the editor considers giving him his job back, with a decent pay rise, your paper still might get an exclusive on the wedding party after all. So if you're interested, you might want to hurry and let them know. Good day.”

Surprised and somewhat intrigued Gerry studied his bride as they settled beside each other in the car.

“Wow. You put her in her place and as cool as a cucumber too! I pray I never get stuck in your bad books!”

“Not a chance of that, your Highness!” Gerry cracked a smile on that. “Anyway, that woman needed to be brought down a peg or two. Too bad I couldn’t drop a really good rumour that Horace has become engaged to Stephie, the next most eligible heiress in town. Boy how that would have stomached her!”

“Who knows, that might still be in the works,” he noted as he caught Stephie give Christopher a quick kiss before they drove off. “Anyway, I overheard Stephie at the rehearsal ask him if he would be willing to be manager of her studio, and now I hope your cool as a cucumber comeback has given him some options. Think of it. He could have the sweet satisfaction of ditching the paper but good-oh should they come crawling back to give him his job."

"Good! After what happened to him too, I hope he does! He deserves things to go his way at last."

"And us too," he noted as he took her left hand and kissed it, taking a moment to appreciate the circle of gold gracing it.

"Our silver ships have come in at last."

"Yes they have."

That gave Katherine an idea, she finally knew how to arrange the family portrait, it was only right the silver ships were included, and therefore a happy gathering of both their families at the Stonyvale manor dining room table seemed just the right scene. Gerry loved the idea and knew his mother would too. Until she could get to it, for the present another happy scene awaited them.

The manor had not been witness to a reception of this felicitous magnificence in an age. The bridal couples arriving just in time to greet their guests, family members and cherished friends, members of the boards of their business empires, city and state dignitaries, business associates, it was rather exciting to see the crowd that had come, the United Nations Gerry had humorously but aptly described their guest list, the families doing their bit to introduce all their relatives and associates to each other. The guests were wowed by the elegant garden buffet in the terraced garden overlooking the sea presided over by Andre, who had baked a stunning multi tiered cake decorated with swans and roses as his gift for the occasion. The afternoon was filled with laughter, speeches and toasts, and as the sun began to set, the chandelier lights glinting through the tall windows from the ballroom beckoned. It was time to open the entertainment with the traditional father and daughter dance, after which Katherine had fully expected to sit down with Gerry at the head table since he couldn't join this part of the festivities, but was surprised when she saw him approach with Thomas to the centre of the dance floor and toss his canes back to Lee with panache who caught them with a smile and a nod. The guests gasped.

Gerry was standing, not very straight, but he was standing.

As Thomas took Charlotte to begin the waltz, Gerry revealed to Katherine as he also took her hand, posed for the next dance:

"As fun as it would have been to see the World Expo play Pin the Tail on the Donkey tonight, I was determined not to let that happen. We were dancing at our wedding, even if only once."

At last, the surprise was out. He could manage a carefully paced waltz step thanks to his physiotherapist and Lady Zamara and her dance studio, who helped him to work out some kinks with the aid of leg braces. That's where he had disappeared to those last few nights. Braces, meds and all, this must still be painful, to be up on his feet, and all for her. How she loved him! They danced close, cheek to cheek, she was so proud of him right now.

After that, they were happy just sitting together and watching their guests enjoy themselves for the rest of the evening. Steves and Lee asked Kathy if she'd dance with them, and Gerry insisted she not sit out of her own wedding party, but she refused.

"No, after that lovely surprise, I'm not dancing with anyone else, like I promised, I only have twinkle toes for you. There's no place I'd rather be now than sitting right here."

At last, the mothers reminded them the helicopter would be coming soon to take them to the airport, they had better get changed. In the meantime, Lee came up with an unorthodox way to make up for the brides not having their bouquets to toss, why not switch the tradition for once? The grooms were game and took off their boutonnières and chucked them at the men among the guests whom Steves had rounded up willing to go along with the fun. It almost felt like dodge ball. To Christopher Smith's surprise, Stephie jumped in and deftly caught Gerry's boutonnière with a laugh, while Lee jumped back as Tom's rose bounced off him and landed at his feet, to everyone's amusement.

"Pick it up, Lee! You never know, besides, it was your idea," Peter jovially called out.

"Must I? Ohh, okay." Feeling the happiness tonight, maybe he might meet someone, a real keeper this time, someone who thought the same way about him. If he could experience only a smidgeon of what he saw Gerry and Kathy had, that would be doing all right.

Reappearing in their going away outfits, there was one last emotive goodbye with the parents before the newly weds waved to the crowd and boarded the chopper that had nosily landed on the beach to take them to the airport where the private jets awaited them, their flight plans set for Prague and Rome. Once again, Aunt Martha had her tissues out. In a few minutes, the chopper lifted, they were gone.

"So, what is this surprise you keep telling me about," Gerry playfully badgered as they enjoyed a glass of wine together on the plane.

"It's waiting for us when we get there."

"You aren't going to tell me?"

She shook her head. Okay, he would just have to wait. She yawned.

"Excuse me!"

"I know, exhausting day, and too much silly juice. A lethal combination, especially for you."

Now that they could relax and had several hours of flight time ahead, they could take a snooze. A rest would freshen them up. She was already nodding off before he could finish his suggestion. He chuckled, took the glass out of her hand, covering her up. He studied her relaxed features, she was so beautiful. He didn't realise he had dozed off too until the pilot announced they were landing in Rome.

"I'm sorry Gerry, I didn't want to wake you, but we're here!"

Katherine was excited, her first time in Italy. However, as they were on their way to their exclusive residence, the driver made a turn and ended up at another place, exquisite, historic, but not where he had rented for their honeymoon. Gerry recognised the property as they drove up the driveway lined with Roman statuary and cypresses, but then wondered what was going on.

"I didn't pick here."

"No, but you did once. I hope you like it."

"Well, yeah, this was the villa I was thinking of buying awhile back."

"I know, and I know you said you had too much to think of at the time and decided despite your plans, you didn't want more property, but I hope you like it." She handed him the keys. "It's yours."

So this was the surprise!

"What? You mean you bought it?"

"And all the parents, they wanted to get you something you'd really appreciate, but didn't know what."

"Us you mean! But how did you know about this? This particular one?"

"Educated guess. When I was decorating the apartment and needed some ideas, I noticed all the Italian real estate brochures you had, this one was the most crinkled, and it had a check mark in the corner with a big circle around it, also the word 'bingo' in your handwriting. So, there."

"And what was that about us not buying each other more stuff," he queried, intrigued by her once again.   She had sleuthed him out to perfection.

"Well, this was purchased long before then, we didn't have that serious discussion then, so this doesn't count."

"Fair enough," he looked around as they got out of the car, the historic villa of his dreams. "Thank you so much, I am literally blown away. We have our own place, in *Italy*! *Ours*! This is fantastic."

He gave her one very appreciative croissant before the staff came out to greet them. It felt so good to see him this happy.

"Wait! Hang on a minute. This may not be the most elegant way of doing it, but I've gotta do this. It's tradition you know."

He opened the front entrance to its full width, leaned up against the door jam. Okay, one, two, three! He swept her up, held her close, looked long into her eyes, then pivoted her over, balancing his weight.

"That worked!"

She gave him another kiss.

"Before they did anything else, they realised they had better call everyone and announce they had arrived safe and sound. Katherine got a kick telling them she wondered if the new place had a shovel somewhere, because she needed to scrape Gerry's jaw off the floor, yeah, he's still in shock. Overhearing the conversation, he laughed. Here, let me talk to them for a minute, yes, they both loved it! He didn't what to say, 'thank you' wasn't hardly enough, but he said it profusely. After the family gave them the news that Tom and Lottie had arrived safely in Prague, Peter was the last one that got on the line to say hello, and to give one little reminder … .

"Don't forget it's Sunday you two."

"Pete's right! We forgot! We can't miss Mass!" Katherine gasped.

"Wait a minute, we've just been through one of the longest Masses I've even been to in my life, a wedding one no less, and still that's not enough," Gerry had to quip. Peter laughed.

"*Morning* Mass on a Saturday does not fulfil the vigil obligation. Besides, you're in Rome, you should have no trouble finding a church."

"Right, no excuses," Katheine added, who had her ear to the receiver.

"True. So, I guess this is goodbye, God bless, see you two in a month. Love you both."

"Love ya too, Bro." Gerry looked like a petulant child as he hung up the receiver. "Aw, we just got here, and now we have to head out the door!"

"This place has been here a few hundred years, it'll be waiting for us when we come back. Besides, we don't want to mess up now, do we? Just offer it up as Pete says."

"So, barely married a day and already you're taking your duties seriously." Katherine looked puzzled. "It's a conspiracy! Between the two of you, you're going to drag me kicking and screaming to the pearly gates if that's what it takes."

She laughed. The staff looked puzzled as the couple got straight back into the car. Sunday duty accomplished, they enjoyed a stupendous lunch, a walk together in the glorious afternoon sun, then with great pleasure explored the villa upon their return. As to be expected of a residence that once housed aristocracy, no luxury was spared, furnished with all original antiques, marble floors, tall ceilings with frescoes illuminated with chandeliers, a sweeping marble staircase, the grounds were extensive and featured fountains, rose gardens, arbours, trellises, swimming and reflection pools, niches, all arranged in the classical Roman style. It literally was a dream come true. Looking at the stairs, Gerry regretted he couldn't push his limits any farther and sweep his beloved off her feet to take her on a tour above, but Katherine noticed where he was gazing and had to remind him that it didn't matter.

"Dearest, everyday you sweep me off my feet. You don't need the staircase. You never did."

God, how he loved her! In any case, they did not need to go up there for now. The villa had a grand master bedroom on the ground floor overlooking the swimming pool and featured separate dressing rooms for him and her, a full *en suite*, and a sitting room. Katherine felt overindulged as she unpacked and set out her things in her own private area, then took another look at the bedroom with its canopied bed already turned down for the evening and adorned with a white rose. Her gaze shyly went to the floor when Gerry entered.

"Come, let's sit outside and watch the sun set."

She followed him through the large doors leading out onto the garden. He got out of his chair, joined her on the Roman bench. She leaned against his shoulder, yes, this was beautiful, listening to the southern birds whose warbling songs sounded foreign yet familiar, watching the azure sky dress for the evening, changing to peach and violet hues before the deep twilight descended. Shall we? Quietly she followed his lead. He exchanged a searching glance before they went to their separate dressing rooms. She changed into something she had saved and knew he would like, the aquamarine silk kimono with the peach blossom trees he had brought for her from Japan. She felt a chill. Her hands started to tremble. She unpinned and combed her hair, letting her tresses gently fall around her shoulders. No! Tonight was not going to be like that. She took a breath. She had tried to run from him before, she was not going to run now. She loved him. It was time to show it.

Gerry was not in the bedroom, she timidly knocked on his dressing room door. No answer. She found him in the adjoining sitting room seated in the leather wing chair staring into the empty fireplace, the clock ticking on the mantelpiece, he didn't hear or see her there. Lost in thought, he absent-mindedly twisted one of his canes into the floor. For a moment she studied him, dressed in the black satin robe she had given him, he looked so handsome waiting for her, she wanted to keep this picture in her mind forever. Yet, the master of the house seemed like he harboured some deep trouble he dared not or feared to share. That too was strangely captivating. She then realised he also had his anxieties about tonight. She gently knocked on the side of the door. He looked up. His expression matched that when he waited for her at the altar.

Beautiful seemed so banal a word to describe the scene before him, Katherine standing in the doorway in the gift he had given her, that flowing robe shimmering in the lamplight, her brown hair let down and left to gently frame her face, then approaching with a timid smile, pulling over the footstool to sit beside his chair for a moment. Yes, he was anxious about tonight, he hadn't felt like this in a long time, now, inadequate, injured, and, he wanted tonight to be special, nothing for her to be afraid of, he was afraid of rushing her. Yet, here she was, waiting for him. She took his hand kissed it, laid it against her cheek. She loved doing that. They looked into each other's eyes, immersed in their expressions. She then stood up, still holding his hand, finding her voice at last.

"After all the croissants, don't you think it's about time for wedding cake?"

It was an invitation he couldn't refuse.

Contrary to their original plans, they didn't get to see much of Italy.

Nearly a year later when they had settled into life's daily rhythm, and, despite their promise not to go overboard changing gifts, Gerry arrived at the breakfast table one morning to find a gift-wrapped box beside his plate topped with a cheery pop-pom bow. It wasn't a birthday, an anniversary, or at least, not a special date that he knew of. Practically still newly weds, did he forget one already? Amused, Katherine watched his

trepidation set in. She urged him to open it. When he saw what was inside
he wanted to jump and shout yet was happily at a loss for words as he held
up a pair of miniature knitted booties with pink and blue ribbons. He
couldn't believe it, but she nodded. Yes, it's true. He hugged her, held her
tight, whispered how much he loved her. No, he hadn't forgotten the date,
it was just he was never the occasion of its celebration before—Father's Day.

Did you like *Vocation of a Gadfly*?

Share your thoughts, write a review!